EVELYN WAUGH

EVELYN WAUGH
EVELYN WAUGH
EVELYN WAUGH
EVELYN WAUGH
EVELYN WAUGH
EVELYN WAUGH
EVELYN WAUGH
EVELYN WAUGH
EVELYN WAUGH
EVELYN WAUGH

EVELYN
WAUGH

EVELYN WAUGH

Decline and Fall
Black Mischief
A Handful of Dust
Scoop
Put Out More Flags
Brideshead Revisited

Heinemann/Octopus

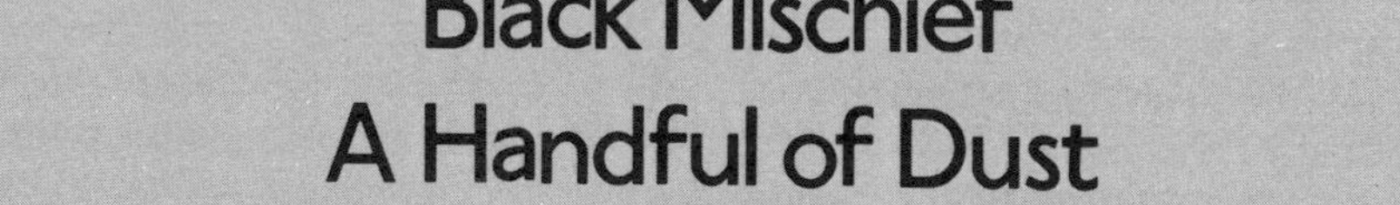

Decline and Fall first published in Great Britain in 1928 by Chapman & Hall Ltd.
Black Mischief first published in Great Britain in 1932 by Chapman & Hall Ltd.
A Handful of Dust first published in Great Britain in 1934 by Chapman & Hall Ltd.
Scoop first published in Great Britain in 1938 by Chapman & Hall Ltd.
Put Out More Flags first published in Great Britain in 1942 by Chapman & Hall Ltd.
Brideshead Revisited first published in Great Britain in 1945 by Chapman & Hall Ltd.

This edition first published
jointly in 1977 by

William Heinemann Limited,
15–16 Queen Street,
London W1

Martin Secker & Warburg Limited,
14 Carlisle Street,
London W1

and

Octopus Books Limited,
59 Grosvenor Street,
London W1

ISBN 0 905712 15 3

Printed in Great Britain by
Jarrold & Sons Ltd., Norwich

EVELYN WAUGH

Decline and Fall

EVELYN WAUGH

DECLINE AND FALL

To Harold Acton
in homage and affection

PRELUDE

ALMA MATER

Mr Sniggs, the Junior Dean, and Mr Postlethwaite, the Domestic Bursar, sat alone in Mr Sniggs' room overlooking the garden quad at Scone College. From the rooms of Sir Alastair Digby-Vaine-Trumpington, two staircases away, came a confused roaring and breaking of glass. They alone of the senior members of Scone were at home that evening, for it was the night of the annual dinner of the Bollinger Club. The others were all scattered over Boar's Hill and North Oxford at gay, contentious little parties, or at other senior common-rooms, or at the meetings of learned societies, for the annual Bollinger dinner is a difficult time for those in authority.

It is not accurate to call this an annual event, because quite often the club is suspended for some years after each meeting. There is tradition behind the Bollinger; it numbers reigning kings among its past members. At the last dinner, three years ago, a fox had been brought in in a cage and stoned to death with champagne bottles. What an evening that had been! This was the first meeting since then, and from all over Europe old members had rallied for the occasion. For two days they had been pouring into Oxford: epileptic royalty from their villas of exile; uncouth peers from crumbling country seats; smooth young men of uncertain tastes from embassies and legations; illiterate lairds from wet granite hovels in the Highlands; ambitious young barristers and Conservative candidates torn from the London season and the indelicate advances of debutantes; all that was most sonorous of name and title was there for the beano.

'The fines!' said Mr Sniggs, gently rubbing his pipe along the side of his nose. 'Oh, my! the fines there'll be after this evening!'

There is some very particular port in the senior common-room cellars that is only brought up when the College fines have reached £50.

'We shall have a week of it at least,' said Mr Postlethwaite, 'a week of Founder's port.'

A shriller note could now be heard rising from Sir Alastair's rooms; any who have heard that sound will shrink at the recollection of it; it is the sound of the English county families baying for broken glass. Soon they would all be tumbling out into the quad, crimson and roaring in their bottle-green evening coats, for the real romp of the evening.

'Don't you think it might be wiser if we turned out the light?' said Mr Sniggs.

In darkness the two dons crept to the window. The quad below was a kaleidoscope of dimly discernible faces.

'There must be fifty of them at least,' said Mr Postlethwaite. 'If only they were all members of the College! Fifty of them at ten pounds each. Oh my!'

'It'll be more if they attack the Chapel,' said Mr Sniggs. 'Oh, please God, make them attack the Chapel.'

'It reminds me of the communist rising in Budapest when I was on the debt commission.'

'I know,' said Mr Postlethwaite. Mr Sniggs' Hungarian reminiscences were well known in Scone College.

'I wonder who the unpopular undergraduates are this term. They always attack their rooms. I hope they have been wise enough to go out for the evening.'

'I think Partridge will be one; he possesses a painting by Matisse or some such name.'

'And I'm told he has black sheets in his bed.'

'And Sanders went to dinner with Ramsay MacDonald once.'

'And Rending can afford to hunt, but collects china instead.'

'And smokes cigars in the garden after breakfast.'

'Austen has a grand piano.'

'They'll enjoy smashing that.'

'There'll be a heavy bill for tonight; just you see! But I confess I should feel easier if the Dean or the Master were in. They can't see us from here, can they?'

It was a lovely evening. They broke up Mr Austen's grand piano, and stamped Lord Rending's cigars into his carpet, and smashed his china, and tore up Mr Partridge's sheets, and threw the Matisse into his lavatory; Mr Sanders had nothing to break except his windows, but they found the manuscript at which he had been working for the Newdigate Prize Poem, and had great fun with that. Sir Alastair Digby-Vaine-Trumpington felt quite ill with excitement, and was supported to bed by Lumsden of Strathdrummond. It was half-past eleven. Soon the evening would come to an end. But there was still a treat to come.

Paul Pennyfeather was reading for the Church. It was his second year of uneventful residence at Scone. He had come there after a creditable career at a small public school of ecclesiastical temper on the South Downs, where he had edited the magazine, been President of the Debating Society, and had, as his report said, 'exercised a wholesome influence for good' in the House of which he was head boy. At home he lived in Onslow Square with his guardian, a prosperous solicitor who was proud of his progress and abysmally bored by his company. Both his parent had died in India at the time when he won the essay prize at his preparatory school. For two years he had lived within his allowance, aided by two valuable scholarships. He smoked three ounces of tobacco a week–John Cotton, Medium–and drank a pint and a half of beer a day, the half at luncheon and the pint at dinner, a meal he invariably ate in Hall. He had four friends, three of whom had been at school with him. None of the Bollinger Club had ever heard of Paul Pennyfeather, and he, oddly enough, had not heard of them.

Little suspecting the incalculable consequences that the evening was to have for him, he bicycled happily back from a meeting of the League of Nations Union. There had been a most interesting paper about plebiscites in Poland. He thought of smoking a pipe and reading another chapter of the *Forsyte Saga* before going to bed. He knocked at the gate, was admitted, put away his bicycle, and diffidently, as always, made his way across the quad towards his rooms. What a lot of people there seemed to be about! Paul had no particular objection to drunkenness–he had read rather a daring paper to the Thomas More Society on the subject–but he was consumedly shy of drunkards.

Out of the night Lumsden of Strathdrummond swayed across his path like a druidical rocking-stone. Paul tried to pass.

Now it so happened that the tie of Paul's old school bore a marked resemblance to the pale blue and white of the Bollinger Club. The difference of a quarter of an inch in the width of the stripes was not one that Lumsden of Strathdrummond was likely to appreciate.

'Here's an awful man wearing the Boller tie,' said the Laird. It is not for nothing that since pre-Christian times his family has exercised chieftainship over unchartered miles of barren moorland.

Mr Sniggs was looking rather apprehensively at Mr Postlethwaite.

'They appear to have caught somebody,' he said. 'I hope they don't do him any serious harm.'

'They appear to be tearing off his clothes.'

'Dear me, can it be Lord Rending? I think I ought to intervene.'

'No, Sniggs,' said Mr Postlethwaite, laying a hand on his impetuous colleague's arm. 'No, no, no. It would be unwise. We have the prestige of the senior common-room to consider. In their present state they might not prove amenable to discipline. We must at all costs avoid an *outrage*.'

The crowd parted, and Mr Sniggs gave a sigh of relief.

'But it's quite all right. It isn't Rending. It's Pennyfeather–someone of no importance.'

'Well, that saves a great deal of trouble. I am glad, Sniggs; I am, really. What a lot of clothes the young man appears to have lost!'

Next morning there was a lovely College meeting. 'Two hundred and thirty pounds,' murmured the Domestic Bursar ecstatically, '*not* counting the damage! That means five evenings, with what we have already collected. Five evenings of Founder's port!'

'The case of Pennyfeather,' the Master was saying, 'seems to be quite a different matter altogether. He ran the whole length of the quadrangle, you say, *without his trousers. That* is indecency. It is *not* the conduct we expect of a scholar.'

'Perhaps if we fined him really heavily?' suggested the Junior Dean.

'I very much doubt whether he could pay. I understand he is not well off. *Without trousers*, indeed! And at that time of night! I think we should do far better to get rid of him altogether. That sort of young man does the College no good.'

Two hours later, while Paul was packing his three suits in his little leather trunk, the Domestic Bursar sent a message that he wished to see him.

'Ah, Mr Pennyfeather,' he said, 'I have examined your rooms and notice two slight burns, one on the window-sill and the other on the chimney-piece, no doubt from cigarette ends. I am charging you five and sixpence for each of them on your battels. That is all, thank you.'

As he crossed the quad Paul met Mr Sniggs.

'Just off?' said the Junior Dean brightly.

'Yes, sir,' said Paul.

And a little further on he met the Chaplain.

'Oh, Pennyfeather, before you go, surely you have my copy of Dean Stanley's *Eastern Church*?'

'Yes. I left it on your table.'

'Thank you. Well, goodbye, my dear boy. I suppose that after that reprehensible affair last night you will have to think of some other profession. Well, you may congratulate yourself that you discovered your unfitness for the priesthood before it was too late. If a parson does a thing of that sort, you know, all the world knows. And so many do, alas! What do you propose doing?'

'I don't really know yet.'

'There is always commerce, of course. Perhaps you may be able to bring to the great world of business some of the ideals you have learned at Scone. But it won't be easy, you know. It is a thing to be lived down with courage. What did Dr Johnson say about fortitude? . . . Dear, dear! *no trousers*!'

At the gates Paul tipped the porter.

'Well, goodbye, Blackall,' he said. 'I don't suppose I shall see you again for some time.'

'No, sir, and very sorry I am to hear about it. I expect you'll be becoming a schoolmaster, sir. That's what most of the gentlemen does, sir, that gets sent down for indecent behaviour.'

'God damn and blast them all to hell,' said Paul meekly to himself as he drove to the station, and then he felt rather ashamed, because he rarely swore.

PART I

I

VOCATION

'Send down for indecent behaviour, eh?' said Paul Pennyfeather's guardian. 'Well, thank God your poor father has been spared this disgrace. That's all I can say.'

There was a hush in Onslow Square, unbroken except by Paul's guardian's daughter's gramophone playing Gilbert and Sullivan in her little pink boudoir at the top of the stairs.

'My daughter must know nothing of this,' continued Paul's guardian.

There was another pause.

'Well,' he resumed, 'you know the terms of your father's will. He left the sum of five thousand pounds, the interest of which was to be devoted to your education and the sum to be absolutely yours on your twenty-first birthday. That, if I am right, falls in eleven months' time. In the event of your education being finished before that time, he left me with complete discretion to withold this allowance should I not consider your course of life satisfactory. I do not think that I should be fulfilling the trust which your poor father placed in me if, in the present circumstances, I continued any allowance. Moreover, you will be the first to realize how impossible it would be for me to ask you to share the same home with my daughter.'

'But what is to happen to me?' said Paul.

'I think you ought to find some work,' said his guardian thoughtfully. 'Nothing like it for taking the mind off nasty subjects.'

'But what kind of work?'

'Just work, good healthy toil. You have led too sheltered a life, Paul. Perhaps I am to blame. It will do you the world of good to face facts for a bit–look at life in the raw, you know. See things steadily and see them whole, eh?' And Paul's guardian lit another cigar.

'Have I no legal right to any money at all?' asked Paul.

'None whatever, my dear boy,' said his guardian quite cheerfully. . . .

That spring Paul's guardian's daughter had two new evening frocks and, thus glorified, became engaged to a well-conducted young man in the Office of Works.

'Sent down for indecent behaviour, eh?' said Mr Levy, of Church and Gargoyle, scholastic agents. 'Well, I don't think we'll say anything about that.

In fact, officially, mind, you haven't told me. We call that sort of thing "Education discontinued for personal reasons", you understand.' He picked up the telephone. 'Mr Samson, have we any "education discontinued" posts, male, on hand? . . . Right! . . . Bring it up, will you? I think,' he added, turning again to Paul, 'we have just the thing for you.'

A young man brought in a slip of paper.

'What about that?'

Paul read it:

> Private and Confidential Notice of Vacancy.
>
> Augustus Fagan, Esquire, Ph.D., Llanabba Castle, N. Wales, requires immediately junior assistant master to teach Classics and English to University Standard with subsidiary Mathematics, German and French. Experience essential; first-class games essential.
>
> STATUS OF SCHOOL: School.
>
> SALARY OFFERED: £120 resident post.
>
> Reply promptly but carefully to Dr Fagan ('Esq., Ph.D.', on envelope), enclosing copies of testimonials and photograph, if considered advisable, mentioning that you have heard of the vacancy through us.

'Might have been made for you,' said Mr Levy.

'But I don't know a word of German, I've had no experience, I've got no testimonials, and I can't play cricket.'

'It doesn't do to be too modest,' said Mr Levy. 'It's wonderful what one can teach when one tries. Why, only last term we sent a man who had never been in a laboratory in his life as senior Science Master to one of our leading public schools. He came wanting to do private coaching in music. He's doing very well, I believe. Besides, Dr Fagan can't expect *all* that for the salary he's offering. Between ourselves, Llanabba hasn't a good name in the profession. We class schools, you see, into four grades: Leading School, First-rate School, Good School, and School. Frankly,' said Mr Levy, 'School is pretty bad. I think you'll find it a very suitable post. So far as I know, there are only two other candidates, and one of them is totally deaf, poor fellow.'

Next day Paul went to Church and Gargoyle to interview Dr Fagan. He had not long to wait. Dr Fagan was already there interviewing the other candidates. After a few minutes Mr Levy led Paul into the room, introduced him, and left them together.

'A most exhaustive interview,' said Dr Fagan. 'I am sure he was a very nice young man, but I could not make him understand a word I said. Can *you* hear me quite clearly?'

'Perfectly, thank you.'

'Good; then let us get to business.'

Paul eyed him shyly across the table. He was very tall and very old and very well dressed; he had sunken eyes and rather long, white hair over jet black eyebrows. His head was very long, and swayed lightly as he spoke; his voice had a thousand modulations, as though at some remote time he had taken lessons in elocution; the backs of his hands were hairy, and his fingers were crooked like claws.

'I understand you have had no previous experience?'

'No, sir, I am afraid not.'

'Well, of course, that is in many ways an advantage. One too easily acquires the professional tone and loses vision. But of course we must be practical. I am offering a salary of one hundred and twenty pounds, but only to a man with experience. I have a letter here from a young man who holds a diploma in forestry. He wants an extra ten pounds a year on the strength of it, but it is vision I need, Mr Pennyfeather, not diplomas. I understand, too, that you left your University rather suddenly. Now–why was that?'

This was the question that Paul had been dreading, and, true to his training, he had resolved upon honesty.

'I was sent down, sir, for indecent behaviour.'

'Indeed, indeed? Well, I shall not ask for details. I have been in the scholastic profession long enough to know that nobody enters it unless he has some very good reason which he is anxious to conceal. But, again to be practical, Mr Pennyfeather, I can hardly pay one hundred and twenty pounds to anyone who has been sent down for indecent behaviour. Suppose that we fix your salary at ninety pounds a year to begin with? I have to return to Llanabba tonight. There are six more weeks of term, you see, and I have lost a master rather suddenly. I shall expect you tomorrow evening. There is an excellent train from Euston that leaves at about ten. I think you will like your work,' he continued dreamily; 'you will find that my school is built upon an ideal–an ideal of service and fellowship. Many of the boys come from the very best families. Little Lord Tangent has come to us this term, the Earl of Circumference's son, you know. Such a nice little chap, erratic, of course, like all his family, but he has *tone*.' Dr Fagan gave a long sigh. 'I wish I could say the same for my staff. Between ourselves, Pennyfeather, I think I shall have to get rid of Grimes fairly soon. He is *not* out of the top drawer, and boys notice these things. Now, your predecessor was a thoroughly agreeable young man. I was sorry to lose him. But he used to wake up my daughters coming back on his motor bicycle at all hours of the night. He used to borrow money from the boys, too, quite large sums, and the parents objected. I had to get rid of him. . . . Still, I was very sorry. *He* had tone.'

Dr Fagan rose, put on his hat at a jaunty angle, and drew on a glove.

'Goodbye, my dear Pennyfeather. I think, in fact I know, that we are going to work well together. I can always tell these things.'

'Goodbye, sir,' said Paul. . . .

'Five per cent. of ninety pounds is four pounds ten shillings,' said Mr Levy cheerfully. 'You can pay now or on receipt of your first term's salary. If you pay now there is a reduction of fifteen per cent. That would be three pounds sixteen shillings and sixpence.'

'I'll pay when I get my wages,' said Paul.

'Just as you please,' said Mr Levy. 'Only too glad to have been of use to you.'

2

LLANABBA CASTLE

Llanabba Castle presents two quite different aspects, according as you approach it from the Bangor or the coast road. From the back it looks very much like any other large country house, with a great many windows and a terrace, and a chain of glass houses and the roofs of innumerable nondescript kitchen buildings disappearing into the trees. But from the front–and that is how it is approached from Llanabba station–it is formidably feudal; one drives past at least a mile of machicolated wall before reaching the gates; these are towered and turreted and decorated with heraldic animals and a workable portcullis. Beyond them at the end of the avenue stands the Castle, a model of medieval impregnability.

The explanation of this rather striking contrast is simple enough. At the time of the cotton famine in the 'sixties Llanabba House was the property of a prosperous Lancashire mill-owner. His wife could not bear to think of their men starving; in fact, she and her daughters organized a little bazaar in their aid, though without very substantial results. Her husband had read the Liberal economists and could not think of paying without due return. Accordingly 'enlightened self-interest' found a way. An encampment of mill hands was settled in the park, and they were put to work walling the grounds and facing the house with great blocks of stone from a neighbouring quarry. At the end of the American war they returned to their mills, and Llanabba House became Llanabba Castle after a great deal of work had been done very cheaply.

Driving up from the station in a little closed taxi, Paul saw little of all this. It was almost dark in the avenue and quite dark inside the house.

'I am Mr Pennyfeather,' he said to the butler. 'I have come here as a master.'

'Yes,' said the butler, 'I know all about you. This way.'

They went down a number of passages, unlit and smelling obscurely of all the ghastly smells of school, until they reached a brightly lighted door.

'In there. That's the Common Room.' Without more ado, the butler made off into the darkness.

Paul looked round. It was not a very big room. Even he felt that, and all his life he had been accustomed to living in constricted spaces.

'I wonder how many people live here,' he thought, and with a sick thrust of apprehension counted sixteen pipes in a rack at the side of the chimney-piece. Two gowns hung on a hook behind the door. In a corner were some golf clubs, a walking stick, an umbrella and two miniature rifles. Over the chimney-piece was a green baize notice-board covered with lists; there was a typewriter on the table. In a bookcase were a number of very old text-books and some new exercise-books. There were also a bicycle-pump, two armchairs, a straight chair, half a bottle of invalid port, a boxing glove, a bowler hat, yesterday's *Daily News* and a packet of pipe-cleaners.

Paul sat down disconsolately on the straight chair.

Presently there was a knock at the door, and a small boy came in.

'Oh!' he said, looking at Paul intently.

'Hullo!' said Paul.

'I was looking for Captain Grimes,' said the little boy.

'Oh!' said Paul.

The child continued to look at Paul with a penetrating, impersonal interest.

'I suppose you're the new master?' he said.

'Yes,' said Paul. 'I'm called Pennyfeather.'

The little boy gave a shrill laugh. 'I think that's terribly funny,' he said, and went away.

Presently the door opened again, and two more boys looked in. They stood and giggled for a time and then made off.

In the course of the next half-hour six or seven boys appeared on various pretexts and stared at Paul.

Then a bell rang, and there was a terrific noise of whistling and scampering. The door opened, and a very short man of about thirty came into the Common Room. He had made a great deal of noise in coming because he had an artificial leg. He had a short red moustache, and was slightly bald.

'Hullo!' he said.

'Hullo!' said Paul.

'Come in, you,' he said to someone outside.

Another boy came in.

'What do you mean,' he said, 'by whistling when I told you to stop?'

'Everyone else was whistling,' said the boy.

'What's that got to do with it?' he said.

'I should think it had a lot to do with it,' said the boy.

'Well, just you do a hundred lines, and next time, remember, I shall beat you,' he said, 'with this,' he said, waving the walking stick.

'That wouldn't hurt much,' said the boy, and went out.

'There's no discipline in the place,' said the master, and then he went out too.

'I wonder whether I'm going to enjoy being a schoolmaster,' thought Paul.

Quite soon another and older man came into the room.

'Hullo!' he said to Paul.

'Hullo!' said Paul.

'Have some port?' he said.

'Thank you, I'd love to.'

'Well, there's only one glass.'

'Oh, well, it doesn't matter, then.'

'You might get your tooth-glass from your bedroom.'

'I don't know where that is.'

'Oh, well, never mind; we'll have some another night. I suppose you're the new master?'

'Yes.'

'You'll hate it here. I know. I've been here ten years. Grimes only came this term. He hates it already. Have you seen Grimes?'

'Yes, I think so.'

'He isn't a gentleman. Do you smoke?'

'Yes.'

'A pipe, I mean.'

'Yes.'

'Those are my pipes. Remind me to show them to you after dinner.'

At this moment the butler appeared with a message that Dr Fagan wished to see Mr Pennyfeather.

Dr Fagan's part of the Castle was more palatial. He stood at the end of a long room with his back to a rococo marble chimney-piece; he wore a velvet dinner-jacket.

'Settling in?' he asked.

'Yes,' said Paul.

Sitting before the fire, with a glass bottle of sweets in her lap, was a brightly dressed woman in early middle age.

'That,' said Dr Fagan with some disgust, 'is my daughter.'

'Pleased to meet you,' said Miss Fagan. 'Now what I always tell the young chaps as comes here is, "Don't let the Dad overwork you." He's a regular Tartar is Dad, but then you know what scholars are–inhuman. Ain't you,' said Miss Fagan, turning on her father with sudden ferocity–'ain't you inhuman?'

'At times, my dear, I am grateful for what little detachment I have achieved. But here,' he added, 'is my other daughter.'

Silently, except for a scarcely perceptible jingling of keys, another woman had entered the room. She was younger than her sister, but far less gay.

'How do you do?' she said. 'I do hope you have brought some soap with you. I asked my father to tell you, but he so often forgets these things. Masters are not supplied with soap or with boot polish or with washing over two shillings and sixpence weekly. Do you take sugar in your tea?'

'Yes, usually.'

'I will make a note of that and have two extra lumps put out for you. Don't let the boys get them, though.'

'I have put you in charge of the fifth form for the rest of this term,' said Dr Fagan. 'You will find them delightful boys, quite delightful. Clutterbuck wants watching, a very delicate little chap. I have also put you in charge of the games, the carpentering class and the fire drill. And I forget, do you teach music?'

'No, I'm afraid not.'

'Unfortunate, most unfortunate. I understood from Mr Levy that you did. I have arranged for you to take Beste-Chetwynde in organ lessons twice a week. Well, you must do the best you can. There goes the bell for dinner. I won't detain you. Oh, one other thing. Not a word to the boys, please, about the reasons for your leaving Oxford! We schoolmasters must temper discretion with deceit. There, I fancy I have said something for you to think about. Good night.'

'Tootle-oo,' said the elder Miss Fagan.

3

CAPTAIN GRIMES' STORY

Paul had very little difficulty in finding the dining-hall. He was guided there by the smell of cooking and the sound of voices. It was a large, panelled room, far from disagreeable, with fifty or sixty boys of ages ranging from ten to eighteen settled along four long tables.

He was led to a place at the head of one of the tables. The boys on either side of him stood up very politely until he sat down. One of them was the boy who had whistled at Captain Grimes. Paul thought he rather liked him.

'I'm called Beste-Chetwynde,' he said.

'I've got to teach you the organ, I believe.'

'Yes, it's great fun: we play in the village church. Do you play terribly well?'

Paul felt this was not a moment for candour, and so, 'tempering discretion with deceit,' he said, 'Yes, remarkably well.'

'I say, do you really, or are you rotting?'

'Indeed, I'm not. I used to give lessons to the Master of Scone.'

'Well, you won't be able to teach me much,' said Beste-Chetwynde cheerfully. 'I only do it to get off gym. I say, they haven't given you a table-napkin. These servants are too awful. Philbrick' he shouted to the butler 'why haven't you given Mr Pennyfeather a napkin?'

'Forgot,' said Philbrick, 'and it's too late now because Miss Fagan's locked the linen up.'

'Nonsense!' said Beste-Chetwynde; 'go and get one at once. That man's all right, really,' he added, 'only he wants watching.'

In a few minutes Philbrick returned with the napkin.

'It seems to me that you're a remarkably intelligent boy,' said Paul.

'Captain Grimes doesn't think so. He says I'm half-witted. I'm glad you're not like Captain Grimes. He's so common, don't you think?'

'You mustn't talk about the other masters like that in front of me.'

'Well, that's what we all think about him, anyway. What's more, he wears combinations. I saw it in his washing-book one day when I was fetching him his hat. I think combinations are rather awful, don't you?'

There was a commotion at the end of the hall.

'I expect that's Clutterbuck being sick,' said Beste-Chetwynde. 'He's usually sick when we have mutton.'

The boy on Paul's other side now spoke for the first time.

'Mr Prendergast wears a wig,' he said, and then became very confused and subsided into a giggle.

'That's Briggs,' said Beste-Chetwynde, 'only everyone calls him Brolly, because of the shop, you know.'

'They're silly rotters,' said Briggs.

All this was a great deal easier than Paul had expected; it didn't seem so very hard to get on with boys, after all.

After a time they all stood up, and amid considerable noise Mr Prendergast said grace. Someone called out 'Prendy!' very loudly just by Paul's ear.

'*. . . per Christum Dominum nostrum. Amen*,' said Mr Prendergast. 'Beste-Chetwynde, was that you who made that noise?'

'Me, sir? No, sir.'

'Pennyfeather, did Beste-Chetwynde make that noise?'

'No, I don't think so,' said Paul, and Beste-Chetwynde gave him a friendly look, because, as a matter of fact, he had.

Captain Grimes linked arms with him outside the dining-hall.

'Filthy meal, isn't it, old boy?' he said.

'Pretty bad,' said Paul.

'Prendy's on duty tonight. I'm off to the pub. How about you?'

'All right,' said Paul.

'Prendy's not so bad in his way,' said Grimes, 'but he can't keep order. Of course, you know he wears a wig. Very hard for a man with a wig to keep order. I've got a false leg, but that's different. Boys respect that. Think I lost it in the war. Actually,' said the Captain, 'and strictly between ourselves, mind, I was run over by a tram in Stoke-on-Trent when I was one-over-the-eight. Still, it doesn't do to let that out to everyone. Funny thing, but I feel I can trust you. I think we're going to be pals.'

'I hope so,' said Paul.

'I've been feeling the need of a pal for some time. The bloke before you wasn't bad–a bit stand-offish, though. He had a motor-bike, you see. The daughters of the house didn't care for him. Have you met Miss Fagan?'

'I've met two.'

'They're both bitches,' said Grimes, and added moodily, 'I'm engaged to be married to Flossie.'

'Good God! Which is she?'

'The elder. The boys call them Flossie and Dingy. We haven't told the old boy yet. I'm wating till I land in the soup again. Then I shall play that as my last card. I generally get into the soup sooner or later. Here's the pub. Not such a bad little place in its way. Clutterbuck's father makes all the beer round here. Not bad stuff, either. Two pints, please, Mrs Roberts!'

In the further corner sat Philbrick, talking volubly in Welsh to a shady-looking old man.

'Damned cheek his coming in here!' said Grimes.

Mrs Roberts brought them their beer. Grimes took a long draught and sighed happily.

'This looks like being the first end of term I've seen for two years,' he said dreamily. 'Funny thing, I can always get on all right for about six weeks, and then I land in the soup. I don't believe I was ever meant by Nature to be a schoolmaster. Temperament,' said Grimes, with a far-away look in his eyes–'that's been my trouble, temperament and sex.'

'Is it quite easy to get another job after–after you've been in the soup?' asked Paul.

'Not at first, it isn't, but there are ways. Besides, you see, I'm a public school man. That means everything. There's a blessed equity in the English social system,' said Grimes, 'that ensures the public school man against starvation.

One goes through four or five years of perfect hell at an age when life is bound to be hell anyway, and after that the social system never lets one down.

'Not that I stood four or five years of it, mind; I left soon after my sixteenth birthday. But my house-master was a public school man. He knew the system. "Grimes," he said, "I can't keep you in the House after what has happened. I have the other boys to consider. But I don't want to be too hard on you. I want you to start again." So he sat down there and then and wrote me a letter of recommendation to any future employer, a corking good letter, too. I've got it still. It's been very useful at one time or another. That's the public school system all over. They may kick you out, but they never let you down.

'I subscribed a guinea to the War Memorial Fund. I felt I owed it to them. I was really sorry,' said Grimes, 'that that cheque never got through.

'After that I went into business. Uncle of mine had a brush factory at Edmonton. Doing pretty well before the war. That put the lid on the brush trade for me. You're too young to have been in the war, I suppose? Those were days, old boy. We shan't see the like of them again. I don't suppose I was really sober for more than a few hours for the whole of that war. Then I got into the soup again, pretty badly that time. Happened over in France. They said, "Now, Grimes, you've got to behave like a gentleman. We don't want a court-martial in this regiment. We're going to leave you alone for half an hour. There's your revolver. You know what to do. Goodbye, old man," they said quite affectionately.

'Well, I sat there for some time looking at that revolver. I put it up to my head twice, but each time I brought it down again. "Public school men don't end like this," I said to myself. It was a long half-hour, but luckily they had left a decanter of whisky in there with me. They'd all had a few, I think. That's what made them all so solemn. There wasn't much whisky left when they came back, and, what with that and the strain of the situation, I could only laugh when they came in. Silly thing to do, but they looked so surprised, seeing me there alive and drunk.

'"The man's a cad," said the colonel, but even then I couldn't stop laughing, so they put me under arrest and called a court-martial.

'I must say I felt pretty low next day. A major came over from another battalion to try my case. He came to see me first, and bless me if it wasn't a cove I'd known at school!

'"God bless my soul," he said, "if it isn't Grimes of Podger's! What's all this nonsense about a court-martial?" So I told him. "H'm," he said, "pretty bad. Still it's out of the question to shoot an old Harrovian. I'll see what I can do about it." And next day I was sent to Ireland on a pretty cushy job connected with postal service. That saw me out as far as the war was concerned. You can't get into the soup in Ireland, do what you like. I don't know if all this bores you?'

'Not at all,' said Paul. 'I think it's most encouraging.'

'I've been in the soup pretty often since then, but never quite so badly. Someone always turns up and says, "I can't see a public school man down and out. Let me put you on your feet again." I should think,' said Grimes, 'I've been put on my feet more often than any living man.'

Philbrick came across the bar parlour towards them.

'I've been talking to the station-master here,' he said, 'and if either of you ever wants a woman, his sister–'

'Certainly not,' said Paul.

'Oh, all right,' said Philbrick, making off.

'Women are an enigma,' said Grimes, 'as far as Grimes is concerned.'

4

MR PRENDERGAST'S STORY

Paul was awakened next morning by a loud bang on his door, and Beste-Chetwynde looked in. He was wearing a very expensive-looking Charvet dressing-gown.

'Good morning, sir,' he said. 'I thought I'd come and tell you, as you wouldn't know: there's only one bathroom for the masters. If you want to get there before Mr Prendergast, you ought to go now. Captain Grimes doesn't wash much,' he added, and then disappeared.

Paul went to the bath and was rewarded some minutes later by hearing the shuffling of slippers down the passage and the door furiously rattled.

As he was dressing Philbrick appeared.

'Oh, I forgot to call you. Breakfast is in ten minutes.'

After breakfast Paul went up to the Common Room. Mr Prendergast was there polishing his pipes, one by one, with a chamois leather. He looked reproachfully at Paul.

'We must come to some arrangement about the bathroom,' he said. 'Grimes very rarely has a bath. I have one before breakfast.'

'So do I,' said Paul defiantly.

'Then I suppose I shall have to find some other time,' said Mr Prendergast, and he gave a deep sigh as he returned his attention to his pipes. 'After ten years, too,' he added, 'but everything's like that. I might have known you'd want the bath. It was so easy when there was only Grimes and that other young man. He was never down in time for breakfast. Oh dear! oh dear! I can see that things are going to be very difficult.'

'But surely we could both have one?'

'No, no, that's out of the question. It's all part of the same thing. Everything has been like this since I left the ministry.'

Paul made no answer, and Mr Prendergast went on breathing and rubbing.

'I expect you wonder how I came to be here?'

'No, no,' said Paul soothingly. 'I think it's very natural.'

'It's not natural at all; it's most unnatural. If things had happened a little differently I should be a rector with my own house and bathroom. I might even have been a rural dean, only'–and Mr Prendergast dropped his voice to a whisper–'only I had *Doubts*.

'I don't know why I'm telling you all this; nobody else knows. I somehow feel you'll understand.

'Ten years ago I was a clergyman of the Church of England. I had just been presented to a living in Worthing. It was such an attractive church, not old, but *very* beautifully decorated, six candles on the altar, Reservation in the Lady Chapel, and an excellent heating apparatus which burned coke in a little shed by the sacristy door; no graveyard, just a hedge of golden privet between the church and the rectory.

'As soon as I moved in my mother came to keep house for me. She bought some chintz, out of her own money, for the drawing-room curtains. She used to be "at home" once a week to the ladies of the congregation. One of them, the dentist's wife, gave me a set of the *Encyclopaedia Britannica* for my study. It was all very pleasant until my *Doubts* began.'

'Were they as bad as all that?' asked Paul.

'They were insuperable,' said Mr Prendergast; 'that is why I am here now. But I expect I am boring you?'

'No, do go on. That's to say, unless you find it painful to think about.'

'I think about it all the time. It happened like this, quite suddenly. We had been there about three months, and my mother had made great friends with some people called Bundle–rather a curious name. I think he was an insurance agent until he retired. Mrs Bundle used very kindly to ask us in to supper on Sundays after Evensong. They were pleasant, informal gatherings, and I used quite to look forward to them. I can see them now as they sat there on this particular evening; there was my mother and Mr and Mrs Bundle, and their son, rather a spotty boy, I remember, who used to go in to Brighton College by train every day, and Mrs Bundle's mother, a Mrs Round, rather deaf, but a very good Churchwoman, and Mrs Abel–that was the name of the dentist's wife who gave me the *Encyclopaedia Britannica*–and old Major Ending, the people's warden. I had preached two sermons that day besides taking the children's Bible-class in the afternoon, and I had rather dropped out of the conversation. They were all talking away quite happily about the preparations that were being made on the pier for the summer season, when suddenly, for no reason at all, my *Doubts* began.' He paused, and Paul felt constrained to offer some expression of sympathy.

'What a terrible thing!' he said.

'Yes, I've not known an hour's real happiness since. You see, it wasn't the ordinary sort of Doubt about Cain's wife or the Old Testament miracles or the consecration of Archbishop Parker. I'd been taught how to explain all those while I was at college. No, it was something deeper than all that. *I couldn't understand why God had made the world at all.* There was my mother and the Bundles and Mrs Round talking away quite unconcernedly while I sat there wrestling with this sudden assault of doubt. You see how fundamental that is. Once granted the first step, I can see that everything else follows–Tower of Babel, Babylonion captivity, Incarnation, Church, bishops, incense, everything–but what I couldn't see, and what I can't see now, is, *why* did it all begin?

'I asked my bishop; he didn't know. He said that he didn't think the point really arose as far as my practical duties as a parish priest were concerned. I discussed it with my mother. At first she was inclined to regard it as a passing phase. But it didn't pass, so finally she agreed with me that the only honourable thing to do was to resign my living; she never really recovered from the shock, poor old lady! It was a great blow after she had bought the chintz and got so friendly with the Bundles.'

A bell began ringing down a distant passage.

'Well, well, we must go to prayers, and I haven't finished my pipes.' He took his gown from the peg behind the door and slipped it over his shoulders.

'Perhaps one day I shall see Light,' he said, 'and then I shall go back to the ministry. Meanwhile –'

Clutterbuck ran past the door, whistling hideously.

'That's a nasty little boy,' said Mr Prendergast, 'if ever there was one.'

5

DISCIPLINE

Prayers were held downstairs in the main hall of the Castle. The boys stood ranged along the panelled walls, each holding in his hands a little pile of books. Grimes sat on one of the chairs beside the baronial chimney-piece.

''Morning,' he said to Paul; 'only just down, I'm afraid. Do I smell of drink?'

'Yes,' said Paul.

'Comes of missing breakfast. Prendy been telling you about his Doubts?'

'Yes,' said Paul.

'Funny thing,' said Grimes, 'but I've never been worried in that way. I don't pretend to be a particularly pious sort of chap, but I've never had any Doubts. When you've been in the soup as often as I have, it gives you a sort of feeling that everything's for the best, really. You know, God's in His heaven; all's right with the world. I can't quite explain it, but I don't believe one can ever be unhappy for long provided one does just exactly what one wants to and when one wants to. The last chap who put me on my feet said I was "singularly in harmony with the primitive promptings of humanity". I've remembered that phrase because somehow it seemed to fit me. Here comes the old man. This is where we stand up.'

As the bell stopped ringing Dr Fagan swept into the hall, the robes of a Doctor of Philosophy swelling and billowing about him. He wore an orchid in his button-hole.

'Good morning, gentlemen,' he said.

'Good morning, sir,' chorused the boys.

The Doctor advanced to the table at the end of the room, picked up a Bible, and opening it at random, read a chapter of blood-curdling military history without any evident relish. From that he plunged into the Lord's Prayer, which the boys took up in a quiet chatter. Mr Prendergast's voice led them in tones that testified to his ecclesiastical past.

Then the Doctor glanced at a sheet of notes he held in his hand. 'Boys,' he said, 'I have some announcements to make. The Fagan cross-country running challenge cup will not be competed for this year on account of the floods.'

'I expect the old boy has popped it,' said Grimes in Paul's ear.

'Nor will the Llanabba Essay Prize.'

'On account of the floods,' said Grimes.

'I have received my account for the telephone,' proceeded Dr Fagan, 'and I find that during the past quarter there have been no less than twenty-three trunk calls to London, none of which was sent by me or by members of my family. I look to the prefects to stop this, unless of course they are themselves responsible, in which case I must urge them in my own interests to make use of the village post-office, to which they have access.

'I think that is everything, isn't it, Mr Prendergast?'

'*Cigars*,' said Mr Prendergast in a stage whisper.

'Ah, yes, cigars. Boys, I have been deeply distressed to learn that several cigar ends have been found–where have they been found?'

'Downstair lavatory.'

'In the downstair lavatory. I regard this as reprehensible. What boy has been smoking cigars in the downstair lavatory?'

There was a prolonged silence, during which the Doctor's eye travelled down the line of boys.

'I will give the culprit until luncheon to give himself up. If I do not hear from him by then the whole school will be heavily punished.'

'Damn!' said Grimes. 'I gave those cigars to Clutterbuck. I hope the little beast has the sense to keep quiet.'

'Go to your classes,' said the Doctor.

The boys filed out.

'I should think, by the look of them, they were exceedingly cheap cigars,' added Mr Prendergast sadly. 'They were a pale yellow colour.'

'That makes it worse,' said the Doctor. 'To think of any boy under my charge smoking pale yellow cigars in a lavatory! It is *not* a gentlemanly fault.'

The masters went upstairs.

'That's your little mob in there,' said Grimes; 'you let them out at eleven.'

'But what am I to teach them?' said Paul in sudden panic.

'Oh, I shouldn't try to *teach* them anything, not just yet, anyway. Just keep them quiet.'

'Now that's a thing I've never learned to do,' sighed Mr Prendergast.

Paul watched him amble into his class-room at the end of the passage, where a burst of applause greeted his arrival. Dumb with terror, he went into his own class-room.

Ten boys sat before him, their hands folded, their eyes bright with expectation.

'Good morning, sir,' said the one nearest him.

'Good morning,' said Paul.

'Good morning, sir,' said the next.

'Good morning,' said Paul.

'Good morning, sir', said the next.

'Oh, shut up,' said Paul.

At this the boy took out a handkerchief and began to cry quietly.

'Oh, sir,' came a chorus of reproach, 'you've hurt his feelings. He's very sensitive; it's his Welsh blood, you know: it makes people very emotional. Say "Good morning" to him, sir, or he won't be happy all day. After all, it is a good morning, isn't it, sir?'

'Silence!' shouted Paul above the uproar, and for a few moments things were quieter.

'Please, sir,' said a small voice–Paul turned and saw a grave-looking youth holding up his hand–'please, sir, perhaps he's been smoking cigars and doesn't feel well.'

'Silence!' said Paul again.

The ten boys stopped talking and sat perfectly still, staring at him. He felt himself getting hot and red under their scrutiny.

'I suppose the first thing I ought to do is to get your names clear. What is your name?' he asked, turning to the first boy.

'Tangent, sir.'

'And yours?'

'Tangent, sir,' said the next boy. Paul's heart sank.

'But you can't both be called Tangent.'

'No, sir, *I'm* Tangent. He's just trying to be funny.'

'I like that. *Me* trying to be funny! Please, sir, I'm Tangent, sir; really I am.'

'If it comes to that,' said Clutterbuck from the back of the room 'there is only one Tangent here, and that is me. Anyone else can jolly well go to blazes.'

Paul felt desperate.

'Well, is there anyone who isn't Tangent?'

Four or five voices instantly arose.

'I'm not, sir; I'm not Tangent. I wouldn't be called Tangent, not on the end of a barge-pole.'

In a few seconds the room had become divided into two parties: those who were Tangent and those who were not. Blows were already being exchanged, when the door opened and Grimes came in. There was a slight hush.

'I thought you might want this,' he said, handing Paul a walking stick. 'And if you take my advice, you'll set them something to do.'

He went out; and Paul, firmly grasping the walking stick, faced his form.

'Listen,' he said. 'I don't care a damn what any of you are called, but if there's another word from anyone I shall keep you all in this afternoon.'

'You can't keep me in,' said Clutterbuck; 'I'm going for a walk with Captain Grimes.'

'Then I shall very nearly kill you with this stick. Meanwhile you will all write an essay on "Self-indulgence". There will be a prize of half a crown for the longest essay, irrespective of any possible merit.'

From then onwards all was silence until break. Paul, still holding the stick, gazed despondently out of the window. Now and then there rose from below the shrill voices of the servants scolding each other in Welsh. By the time the bell rang Clutterbuck had covered sixteen pages, and was awarded the half-crown.

'Did you find those boys difficult to manage?' asked Mr Prendergast, filling his pipe.

'Not at all,' said Paul.

'Ah, you're lucky. I find all boys utterly intractable. I don't know why it is. Of course my wig has a lot to do with it. Have you noticed that I wear a wig?'

'No, no, of course not.'

'Well, the boys did as soon as they saw it. It was a great mistake my ever getting one. I thought when I left Worthing that I looked too old to get a job easily. I was only forty-one. It was very expensive, even though I chose the cheapest quality. Perhaps that's why it looks so like a wig. I don't know. I knew from the first that it was a mistake, but once they had seen it, it was too late to go back. They make all sorts of jokes about it.'

'I expect they'd laugh at something else if it wasn't that.'

'Yes, no doubt they would. I dare say it's a good thing to localize their ridicule as far as possible. Oh dear! oh dear! If it wasn't for my pipes, I don't know how I should manage to keep on. What made you come here?'

'I was sent down from Scone for indecent behaviour.'

'Oh, yes, like Grimes?'

'No,' said Paul firmly, 'not like Grimes.'

'Oh, well, it's all much the same really. And there's the bell. Oh dear! oh dear! I believe that loathsome little man's taken my gown.'

Two days later Beste-Chetwynde pulled out the *vox humana* and played *Pop goes the Weasel.*

'D'you know, sir, you've made rather a hit with the fifth form?'

He and Paul were seated in the organ-loft of the village church. It was their second music lesson.

'For goodness' sake, leave the organ alone. How d'you mean "hit"?'

'Well, Clutterbuck was in the matron's room this morning. He'd just got a tin of pine-apple chunks Captain Grimes had given him. Tangent said, "Are you going to take that into Hall?" and he said, "No, I'm going to eat them in Mr Pennyfeather's hour." "Oh, no, you're not," said Tangent. "Sweets and biscuits are one thing, but pine-apple chunks are going too far. It's little stinkers like you," he said, "who turn decent masters savage."'

'Do you think that's so very complimentary?'

'I think it's one of the most complimentary things I ever heard said about a master,' said Beste-Chetwynde; 'would you like me to try that hymn again?'

'No,' said Paul decisively.

'Well, then, I'll tell you another thing,' said Beste-Chetwynde. 'Have you ever wondered what happens to Dingy on Thursday evenings?'

'Good heavens, no.'

'Well, she's always out.'

'That doesn't seem very important. I only wish she'd go out more often.'

'Yes, but Thursday is Philbrick's evening out.'

'You don't mean to suggest . . .'

'Well just you see. It's my opinion and Brolly's that Dingy and Philbrick are having an intrigue.'

'It's not a bad idea,' said Paul.

'But Brolly thinks Philbrick has a wife in Australia.'

'Has Philbrick ever been to Australia?'

'That's what Brolly's not sure of but he says he looks as though he had and he once gave Tangent some Australian stamps. I'll tell you another thing. You know all those trunk calls the Doctor was talking about. It was Philbrick made them. That man never leaves the telephone day or night. If you ask me, there's something fishy about Philbrick.'

'I can well believe that.'

'And now I *am* going to play the organ,' said Beste-Chetwynde. 'After all, my mother does pay five guineas a term extra for me to learn.'

6

CONDUCT

Sitting over the Common Room fire that afternoon waiting for the bell for tea, Paul found himself reflecting that on the whole the last week had not been quite as awful as he had expected. As Beste-Chetwynde had told him, he was a distinct success with his form; after the first day an understanding had been established between them. It was tacitly agreed that when Paul wished to read or to write letters he was allowed to do so undisturbed while he left them to employ the time as they thought best; when Paul took it upon him to talk to them about their lessons they remained silent, and when he set them work to do some of it was done. It had rained steadily, so that there had been no games. No punishments, no reprisals, no exertion, and in the evenings the confessions of Grimes, any one of which would have glowed with outstanding shamelessness from the appendix to a treatise in sexual psychology.

Mr Prendergast came in with the post.

'A letter for you, two for Grimes, nothing for me,' he said. 'No one ever writes to me. There was a time when I used to get five or six letters a day, not counting circulars. My mother used to file them for me to answer–one heap of charity appeals, another for personal letters, another for marriages and funerals, another for baptisms and churchings and another for anonymous abuse. I wonder why it is the clergy always get so many letters of that sort, sometimes from quite educated people. I remember my father had great trouble in that way once, and he was forced to call in the police because they became so threatening. And, do you know, it was the curate's wife who had sent them–such a quiet little woman. There's your letter. Grimes's look like bills. I can't think why shops give that man credit at all.'

'I always pay cash,' said Paul.

'Yes, so do I, or at least I should if I ever bought anything. But d'you know that except for my tobacco and the *Daily News* and occasionally a little port when it's very cold, I don't think I've bought anything for two years. The last thing I bought was that walking stick. I got it at Shanklin, and Grimes uses it for beating the boys with. I hadn't really meant to buy one, but I was there for the day–two years this August–and I went into the tobacconist's to buy some tobacco. He hadn't the sort I wanted, and I felt I couldn't go without getting something, so I bought that. It cost one and six,' he added wistfully, 'so I had no tea.'

Paul took his letter. It had been forwarded from Onslow Square. On the flap were embossed the arms of Scone College. It was from one of his four friends.

Scone College, J.C.R.
Oxford

My Dear Pennyfeather (*it ran*),

I need hardly tell you how distressed I was when I heard of your disastrous misfortune. It seems to me that a real injustice has been done to you. I have not heard the full facts of the case, but I was confirmed in my opinion by a very curious incident last evening. I was just going to bed when Digby-Vaine-Trumpington came into my rooms without knocking. He was smoking a cigar. I had never spoken to him before, as you know, and was very much surprised at his visit. He said: 'I'm told you are a friend of Pennyfeather's.' I said I was, and he said: 'Well, I gather I've rather got him into a mess.' I said: 'Yes,' and he said: 'Well, will you apologize to him for me when you write?' I said I would. Then he said: 'Look here, I'm told he's rather poor. I thought of sending him some money–£20 for sort of damages you know. It's all I can spare at the moment. Wouldn't it be a useful thing to do?' I fairly let him have it, I can tell you, and told him just what I thought of him for making such an insulting suggestion. I asked him how he dared treat a gentleman like that just because he wasn't in his awful set. He seemed rather taken aback and said: 'Well, all *my* friends spend all their time trying to get money out of me,' and went off.

I bicycled over to St Magnus's at Little Beckley and took some rubbings of the brasses there. I wished you had been with me.

Yours,
Arthur Potts

P.S.–I understand you are thinking of taking up educational work. It seems to me that the great problem of education is to train the moral perceptions, not merely to discipline the appetites. I cannot help thinking that it is in greater fastidiousness rather than in greater self-control that the future progress of the race lies. I shall be interested to hear what your experience has been over the matter. The chaplain does not agree with me in this. He says great sensibility usually leads to enervation of will. Let me know what you think.

'What do you think about that?' asked Paul, handing Mr Prendergast the letter.

'Well,' he said after studying it carefully, 'I think your friend is wrong about sensibility. It doesn't do to rely on one's own feelings, does it, not in anything?'

'No, I mean about the money.'

'Good gracious, Pennyfeather! I hope you are in no doubt about that. Accept it at once, of course.'

'It's a temptation.'

'My dear boy, it would be a sin to refuse. Twenty pounds! Why, it takes me half a term to earn that.'

The bell rang for tea. In the dining-hall Paul gave the letter to Grimes.

'Shall I take that twenty pounds?' he asked.

'Take it? My God! I should think you would.'

'Well, I'm not sure,' said Paul.

He thought about it all through afternoon school, all the time he was dressing for dinner, and all through dinner. It was a severe struggle, but his early training was victorious.

'If I take that money,' he said to himself, 'I shall never know whether I have acted rightly or not. It would always be on my mind. If I refuse, I shall be sure of having done right. I shall look back upon my self-denial with exquisite self-approval. By refusing I can convince myself that, in spite of the unbelievable things that have been happening to me during the last ten days, I am still the same Paul Pennyfeather I have respected so long. It is a test-case of the durability of my ideals.'

He tried to explain something of what he felt to Grimes as they sat in Mrs

Roberts' bar parlour that evening.

'I'm afraid you'll find my attitude rather difficult to understand,' he said. 'I suppose it's largely a matter of upbringing. There is every reason why I should take this money. Digby-Vaine-Trumpington is exceedingly rich; and if he keeps it, it will undoubtedly be spent on betting or on some deplorable debauch. Owing to his party I have suffered irreparable harm. My whole future is shattered, and I have directly lost one hundred and twenty pounds a year in scholarships and two hundred and fifty pounds a year allowance from my guardian. By any ordinary process of thought, the money is justly mine. But,' said Paul Pennyfeather, 'there is my honour. For generations the British bourgeoisie have spoken of themselves as gentlemen, and by that they have meant, among other things, a self-respecting scorn of irregular perquisites. It is the quality that distinguishes the gentleman from both the artist and the aristocrat. Now I am a gentleman. I can't help it: it's born in me. I just can't take that money.'

'Well, I'm a gentleman too, old boy,' said Grimes, 'and I was afraid you might feel like that, so I did my best for you and saved you from yourself.'

'What d'you mean by that?'

'Dear old boy, don't be angry, but immediately after tea I sent off a wire to your friend Potts: *Tell Trumpington send money quick*, and signed it "*Pennyfeather*". I don't mind lending you the bob till it comes, either.'

'Grimes, you wretch!' said Paul, but, in spite of himself, he felt a great wave of satisfaction surge up within him. 'We must have another drink on that.'

'Good for you,' said Grimes, 'and it's on me this round.'

'To the durability of ideals!' said Paul as he got his pint.

'My word, what a mouthful!' said Grimes; 'I can't say that. Cheerioh!'

Two days later came another letter from Arthur Potts:

> Dear Pennyfeather,
>
> I enclose Trumpington's cheque for £20. I am glad that my dealings with him are at an end. I cannot pretend to understand your attitude in this matter, but no doubt you are the best judge.
>
> Stiggins is reading a paper to the O.S.C.U. on 'Sex Repression and Religious Experience'. Everyone expects rather a row, because you know how keen Walton is on the mystical element, which I think Stiggins is inclined to discount.
>
> Yours,
>
> Arthur Potts
>
> There is a most interesting article in the *Educational Review* on the new methods that are being tried at the Innesborough High School to induce co-ordination of the senses. They put small objects into the children's mouths and make them draw the shapes in red chalk. Have you tried this with your boys? I must say I envy you your opportunities. Are your colleagues enlightened?

'This same Potts,' said Grimes as he read the letter, 'would appear to be something of a stinker. Still, we've got the doings. How about a binge?'

'Yes,' said Paul, 'I think we ought to do something about one. I should like to ask Prendy too.'

'Why, of course. It's just what Prendy needs. He's been looking awfully down in the mouth lately. Why shouldn't we all go over to the Metropole at

Cwmpryddyg for dinner one night? We shall have to wait until the old boy goes away, otherwise he'll notice that there's no one on duty.'

Later in the day Paul suggested the plan to Mr Prendergast.

'Really, Pennyfeather,' he said, 'I think that's uncommonly kind of you. I hardly know what to say. Of course, I should love it. I can't remember when I dined at an hotel last. Certainly not since the War. It *will* be a treat. My dear boy, I'm quite overcome.'

And, much to Paul's embarrassment, a tear welled up in each of Mr Prendergast's eyes, and coursed down his cheeks.

7

PHILBRICK

That morning just before luncheon the weather began to show signs of clearing, and by half-past one the sun was shining. The Doctor made one of his rare visits to the school dining-hall. At his entry everybody stopped eating and laid down his knife and fork.

'Boys,' said the Doctor, regarding them benignly, 'I have an announcement to make. Clutterbuck, will you kindly stop eating while I am addressing the school. The boys' manners need correcting, Mr Prendergast. I look to the prefects to see to this. Boys, the chief sporting event of the year will take place in the playing-fields tomorrow. I refer to the Annual School Sports, unfortunately postponed last year owing to the General Strike. Mr Pennyfeather, who, as you know, is himself a distinguished athlete, will be in charge of all arrangements. The preliminary heats will be run off today. All boys must compete in all events. The Countess of Circumference has kindly consented to present the prizes. Mr Prendergast will act as referee, and Captain Grimes as time-keeper. I shall myself be present tomorrow to watch the final competitions. That is all, thank you. Mr Pennyfeather, perhaps you will favour me with an interview when you have finished your luncheon?'

'Good God!' murmured Paul.

'I won the long jump at the last sports,' said Briggs, 'but everyone said that it was because I had spiked shoes. Do you wear spiked shoes, sir?'

'Invariably,' said Paul.

'Everyone said it was taking an unfair advantage. You see, we never know beforehand when there's going to be sports, so we don't have time to get ready.'

'My mamma's coming down to see me tomorrow,' said Beste-Chetwynde; 'just my luck! Now I shall have to stay here all the afternoon.'

After luncheon Paul went to the morning-room, where he found the Doctor pacing up and down in evident high excitement.

'Ah, come in, Pennyfeather! I am just making the arrangements for tomorrow's fête. Florence, will you get on to the Clutterbucks on the telephone and ask them to come over, and the Hope-Brownes. I think the Warringtons are too far away, but you might ask them, and of course the Vicar and old Major Sidebotham. The more guests the better, Florence!

'And, Diana, you must arrange the tea. Sandwiches, *foie gras* sandwiches–last time, you remember, the liver sausage you bought made Lady Bunyan ill–and cakes, plenty of cakes, with coloured sugar! You had better take the car into Llandudno and get them there.

'Philbrick, there must be champagne-cup, and will you help the men putting up the marquee? And flags, Diana! There should be flags left over from last time.'

'I made them into dusters,' said Dingy.

'Well, we must buy more. No expense must be spared. Pennyfeather, I want you to get the results of the first heats out by four o'clock. Then you can telephone them to the printers, and we shall have the programmes by tomorrow. Tell them that fifty will be enough; they must be decorated with the school colours and crest in gold. And there must be flowers, Diana, banks of flowers,' said the Doctor, with an expansive gesture. 'The prizes shall stand among banks of flowers. Do you think there ought to be a bouquet for Lady Circumference?'

'No,' said Dingy.

'Nonsense!' said the Doctor. 'Of course there must be a bouquet. It is rarely that the scholarly calm of Llanabba gives place to festival, but when it does taste and dignity shall go unhampered. It shall be an enormous bouquet, redolent of hospitality. You are to procure the most expensive bouquet that Wales can offer; do you understand? Flowers, youth, wisdom, the glitter of jewels, music,' said the Doctor, his imagination soaring to dizzy heights under the stimulus of the words; 'music! There must be a band.'

'I never heard of such a thing,' said Dingy. 'A band, indeed! You'll be having fireworks next.'

'*And fireworks*,' said the Doctor, 'and do you think it would be a good thing to buy Mr Prendergast a new tie? I noticed how shabby he looked this morning.'

'No,' said Dingy with finality, 'that is going too far. Flowers and fireworks are one thing, but I insist on drawing a line somewhere. It would be sinful to buy Mr Prendergast a tie.'

'Perhaps you are right,' said the Doctor. 'But there shall be music. I understand that the Llanabba Silver Band was third at the North Wales Eisteddfod last month. Will you get on to them, Florence? I think Mr Davies at the station is the bandmaster. Can the Clutterbucks come?'

'Yes,' said Flossie, 'six of them.'

'Admirable! And then there is the Press. We must ring up the *Flint and Denbigh Herald* and get them to send a photographer. That means whisky. Will you see to that, Philbrick? I remember at one of our sports I omitted to offer whisky to the Press, and the result was a *most* unfortunate photograph. Boys do get into such indelicate positions during the obstacle race, don't they?

'Then there are the prizes. I think you had better take Grimes into Llandudno with you to help with the prizes. I don't think there is any need for undue extravagance with the prizes. It gives boys a wrong idea of sport. I wonder whether Lady Circumference would think it odd if we asked her to present parsley crowns. Perhaps she would. Utility, economy and apparent durability are the qualities to be sought for, I think.

'And, Pennyfeather, I hope you will see that they are distributed fairly evenly about the school. It doesn't do to let any boy win more than two events; I leave you to arrange that. I think it would be only right if little Lord Tangent won something, and Beste-Chetwynde–yes, his mother is coming down, too.

'I am afraid all this has been thrown upon your shoulders rather suddenly. I only learned this morning that Lady Circumference proposed to visit us, and as Mrs Beste-Chetwynde was coming too, it seemed too good an opportunity to be missed. It is not often that the visits of two such important parents coincide. She is the Honourable Mrs Beste-Chetwynde, you know–sister-in-law of Lord Pastmaster–a very wealthy woman, South American. They always say that she poisoned her husband, but of course little Beste-Chetwynde doesn't know that. It never came into court, but there was a great deal of talk about it at the time. Perhaps you remember the case?'

'No,' said Paul.

'Powdered glass,' said Flossie shrilly, 'in his coffee.'

'Turkish coffee,' said Dingy.

'To work!' said the Doctor; 'we have a lot to see to.'

It was raining again by the time that Paul and Mr Prendergast reached the playing-fields. The boys were waiting for them in bleak little groups, shivering at the unaccustomed austerity of bare knees and open necks. Clutterbuck had fallen down in the mud and was crying quietly behind a tree.

'How shall we divide them?' said Paul.

'I don't know,' said Mr Prendergast. 'Frankly, I deplore the whole business.'

Philbrick appeared in an overcoat and a bowler hat.

'Miss Fagan says she's very sorry, but she's burnt the hurdles and the jumping posts for firewood. She thinks she can hire some in Llandudno for tomorrow. The Doctor says you must do the best you can till then. I've got to help the gardeners put up the blasted tent.'

'I think that, if anything, sports are rather worse than concerts,' said Mr Prendergast. 'They at least happen indoors. Oh dear! oh dear! How wet I am getting. I should have got my boots mended if I'd known this was going to happen.'

'Please sir,' said Beste-Chetwynde, 'we're all getting rather cold. Can we start?'

'Yes, I suppose so,' said Paul. 'What do you want to do?'

'Well, we ought to divide up into heats and then run a race.'

'All right! Get into four groups.'

This took some time. They tried to induce Mr Prendergast to run too.

'The first race will be a mile. Prendy, will you look after them? I want to see if Philbrick and I can fix up anything for the jumping.'

'But what am I to do? said Mr Prendergast.

'Just make each group run to the Castle and back and take the names of the first two in each heat. It's quite simple.'

'I'll try,' he said sadly.

Paul and Philbrick went into the pavilion together.

'Me, a butler,' said Philbrick, 'made to put up tents like a blinking Arab!'

'Well, it's a change,' said Paul.

'It's a change for me to be a butler,' said Philbrick. 'I wasn't made to be anyone's servant.'

'No, I suppose not.'

'I expect you wonder how it is that I come to be here?' said Philbrick.

'No,' said Paul firmly, 'nothing of the kind. I don't in the least want to know anything about you; d'you hear?'

'I'll tell you,' said Philbrick; 'it was like this–'

'I don't want to hear your loathsome confessions; can't you understand?'

'It isn't a loathsome confession,' said Philbrick. 'It's a story of love. I think it is without exception the most beautiful story I know.

'I dare say you may have heard of Sir Solomon Philbrick?'

'No,' said Paul.

'What, never heard of old Solly Philbrick?'

'No; why?'

'Because that's me. And I can tell you this. It's a pretty well-known name across the river. You've only to say Solly Philbrick, of the "Lamb and Flag", anywhere south of Waterloo Bridge to see what fame is. Try it.'

'I will one day.'

'Mind you, when I say *Sir* Solomon Philbrick, that's only a bit of fun, see? That's what the boys call me. Plain Mr Solomon Philbrick I am, really, just like you or him,' with a jerk of the thumb towards the playing-fields, from which Mr Prendergast's voice could be heard crying weakly: 'Oh, do get into line, you beastly boys,' 'but *Sir* Solomon's what they call me. Out of respect, see?'

'When I say, "Are you ready? Go!" I want you to go,' Mr Prendergast could be heard saying. 'Are you ready? Go! Oh, why *don't* you go?' and his voice became drowned in shrill cries of protest.

'Mind you,' went on Philbrick, 'I haven't always been in the position that I am now. I was brought up rough, damned rough. Ever heard speak of "Chick" Philbrick?

'No, I suppose he was before your time. Useful little boxer, though. Not first-class, on account of his drinking so much *and* being short in the arm. Still, he used to earn five pound a night at the Lambeth Stadium. Always popular with the boys, he was, even when he was so full, he couldn't hardly fight. He was my dad, a good-hearted sort of fellow but rough, as I was telling you; he used to knock my poor mother about something awful. Got jugged for it twice, but my! he took it out of her when he got out. There aren't many left like him nowadays, what with education and whisky the price it is.

'"Chick" was all for getting me on in the sporting world, and before I left school I was earning a few shillings a week holding the sponge at the Stadium on Saturday nights. It was there I met Toby Cruttwell. Perhaps you ain't never heard of him, neither?'

'No, I am terribly afraid I haven't. I'm not very well up in sporting characters.'

'Sporting! What, Toby Cruttwell a sporting character! You make me laugh. Toby Cruttwell,' said Philbrick with renewed emphasis, 'what brought off the Buller diamond robbery of 1912, and the Amalgamated Steel Trust robbery of 1910, and the Isle of Wight burglaries in 1914! He wasn't no sporting character, Toby wasn't. Sporting character! D'you know what he done to Alf Larrigan, what tried to put it over on one of his girls? I'll tell you. Toby had a doctor in tow at the time, name of Peterfield; lives in Harley Street, with a swell lot of patients. Well, Toby knew a thing about him. He'd done in one of Toby's girls what went to him because she was going to have a kid. Well, Toby knew that, so he had to do what Toby told him, see?

'Toby didn't kill Alf; that wasn't his way. Toby never killed no one except a lot of blinking Turks the time they gave him the V.C. But he got hold of him and took him to Dr Peterfield, and–' Philbrick's voice sank to a whisper.

'Second heat, get ready. Now, if you don't go when I say "Go", I shall disqualify you all; d'you hear? Are you ready? *Go!*'

'. . . He hadn't no use for girls after that. Ha, ha, ha! Sporting character's good. Well, me and Toby worked together for five years. I was with him in the Steel Trust and the Buller diamonds, and we cleared a nice little profit. Toby took seventy-five per cent., him being the older man, but even with that I did pretty well. Just before the war we split. He stuck to safe-cracking, and I settled down comfortable at the "Lamb and Flag", Camberwell Green. A very fine house that was before the war, and it's the best in the locality now, though I says it. Things aren't quite so easy as they was, but I can't complain. I've got the Picture House next to it, too. Just mention my name there any day you like to have a free seat.'

'That's very kind of you.'

'You're welcome. Well, then, there was the war. Toby got the V.C. in the Dardanelles and turned respectable. He's in Parliament now–Major Cruttwell, M.P., Conservative member for some potty town on the South Coast. My old woman ran the pub for me. Didn't tell you I was married, did I? Pretty enough bit of goods when we was spliced, but she ran to fat. Women do in the public-house business. After the war things were a bit slow, and then my old woman kicked the bucket. I didn't think I'd mind much, her having got so fat and all, nor I didn't not at first, but after a time, when the excitement of the funeral had died down and things were going on just the same as usual, I began to get restless. You know how things get, and I took to reading the papers. Before that my old woman used to read out the bits she'd like, and sometimes I'd listen and sometimes I wouldn't, but anyhow they weren't the things that interested me. She never took no interest in crime, not unless it was a murder. But I took to reading the police news, and I took to dropping in at the pictures whenever they sent me a crook film. I didn't sleep so well, neither, and I used to lie awake thinking of old times. Of course I could have married again: in my position I could have married pretty well who I liked; but it wasn't that I wanted.

'Then one Saturday night I came into the bar. I generally drop in on Saturday evenings and smoke a cigar and stand a round of drinks. It sets the right tone. I wear a button-hole in the summer, too, and a diamond ring. Well, I was in the saloon when who did I see in the corner but Jimmy Drage–cove I used to know when I was working with Toby Cruttwell. I never see a man look more discouraged.

'"Hullo, Jimmy!" I says. "We don't see each other as often as we used. How are things with you?" I says it cordial, but careful like, because I didn't know what Jimmy was up to.

'"Pretty bad," says Jimmy. "Just fooled a job."

'"What sort of job?" I says. "Nobbling," he says, meaning kidnapping.

'"It was like this," he says. "You know a toff called Lord Utteridge?"

'"The bloke what had them electric burglar alarms," I says, "Utteridge House, Belgrave Square?"

'"That's the blinking bastard. Well, he's got a son–nasty little kid about twelve, just going off to college for the first time. I'd had my eye on him," Jimmy said, "for a long time, him being the only son and his father so rich, so when I'd finished the last job I was on I had a go at him. Everything went as easy as drinking," Jimmy said. There was a garage just round the corner behind Belgrave Square where he used to go every morning to watch them messing about with the cars. Crazy about cars the kid was. Jimmy comes in one day with his motor bike and side-car and asks for some petrol. He comes up and looks at it in the way he had.

'"That bike's no good," he says. "No good?" says Jimmy. "I wouldn't sell it not for a hundred quid, I wouldn't. This bike," he says, "won the Grand Prix at Boulogne." "Nonsense!" the kid says: "it wouldn't do thirty, not downhill." "Well, just you see," Jimmy says. "Come for a run? I bet you I'll do eighty on the road." In he got, and away they went till they got to a place Jimmy knew. Then Jimmy shuts him up safe and writes to the father. The kid was happy as blazes taking down the engine of Jimmy's bike. It's never been the same since, Jimmy told me, but then it wasn't much to talk of before. Everything had gone through splendid till Jimmy got his answer from Lord Utteridge. Would you believe it, that unnatural father wouldn't stump up, him that owns ships and coal-mines enough to buy the blinking Bank of England. Said he was much obliged to Jimmy for the trouble he had taken, that the dearest wish of his life had been gratified and the one barrier to his complete happiness removed, but that, as the matter had been taken up without his instructions, he did not feel called upon to make any payment in respect of it, and remained his sincerely, Utteridge.

'That was a nasty one for Jimmy. He wrote once or twice after that, but got no answer, so by the time the kid had spread bits of the bike all over the room Jimmy let him go.

'"Did you try pulling out 'is teeth and sending them to his pa?" I asks.

'"No," says Jimmy. "I didn't do that."

'"Did you make the kid write pathetic, asking to be let out?"

'"No," says Jimmy, "I didn't do that."

'"Did you cut off one of his fingers and put it in the letter-box?"

'"No," he says.

'"Well, man alive," I says, "you don't deserve to succeed. You just don't know your job."

'"Oh, cut that out," he says; "it's easy to talk. You've been out of the business ten years. You don't know what things are like nowadays."

'Well, that rather set me thinking. As I say, I'd been getting restless doing nothing but just pottering round the pub all day. "Look here," I says, "I bet you I can bring off a job like that any day with any kid you like to mention." "Done!" says Jimmy. So he opens a newspaper. "The first toff we find what's got a only son," he says. "Right!" says I. Well, about the first thing we found was a picture of Lady Circumference with her only son, Lord Tangent, at Warwick Races. "There's your man," says Jimmy. And that's what brought me here.'

'But, good gracious,' said Paul, 'why have you told me this monstrous story? I shall certainly inform the police. I never heard of such a thing.'

'That's all right,' said Philbrick. 'The job's off. Jimmy's won his bet. All this was before I met Dina, see?'

'Dina?'

'Miss Diana. Dina I calls her, after a song I heard. The moment I saw that girl I knew the game was up. My heart just stood still. There's a song about that, too. That girl,' said Philbrick, 'could bring a man up from the depths of hell itself.'

'You feel as strongly as that about her?'

'I'd go through fire and water for that girl. She's not happy here. I don't think her dad treats her proper. Sometimes,' said Philbrick, 'I think she's only marrying me to get away from here.'

'Good heavens! Are you going to get married?'

'We fixed it up last Thursday. We've been going together for some time. It's bad for a girl being shut away like that, never seeing a man. She was in a state she'd have gone with anybody until I come along, just housekeeping day in, day out. The only pleasure she ever got was cutting down the bills and dismissing the servants. Most of them leave before their month is up, anyway, they're that hungry. She's got a head on her shoulders, she has. Real business woman, just what I need at the "Lamb".

'Then she heard me on the 'phone one day giving instructions to our manager at the Picture Theatre. That made her think a bit. A prince in disguise, as you might say. It was she who actually suggested our getting married. I shouldn't have had the face to, not while I was butler. What I'd meant to do was to hire a car one day and come down with my diamond ring and button-hole and pop the question. But there wasn't any need for that. Love's a wonderful thing.'

Philbrick stopped speaking and was evidently deeply moved by his recital. The door of the pavilion opened, and Mr Prendergast came in.

'Well,' asked Paul, 'how are the sports going?'

'Not very well,' said Mr Prendergast; 'in fact, they've gone.'

'All over?'

'Yes. You see, none of the boys came back from the first race. They just disappeared behind the trees at the top of the drive. I expect they've gone to change. I don't blame them, I'm sure. It's terribly cold. Still, it was discouraging launching heat after heat and none coming back. Like sending troops into battle, you know.'

'The best thing for us to do is to go back and change too.'

'Yes, I suppose so. Oh, what a day!'

Grimes was in the Common Room.

'Just back from the gay metropolis of Llandudno,' he said. 'Shopping with Dingy is not a seemly occupation for a public school man. How did the heats go?'

'There weren't any,' said Paul.

'Quite right,' said Grimes; 'you leave this to me. I've been in the trade some time. These things are best done over the fire. We can make out the results in peace. We'd better hurry. The old boy wants them sent to be printed this evening.'

And taking a sheet of paper and a small stub of pencil, Grimes made out the programme.

'How about that?' he said.

'Clutterbuck seems to have done pretty well,' said Paul.

'Yes, he's a splendid little athlete,' said Grimes. 'Now just you telephone that through to the printers, and they'll get it done tonight. I wonder if we ought to have a hurdle race?'

'No,' said Mr Prendergast.

8

THE SPORTS

Happily enough, it did not rain next day, and after morning school everybody dressed up to the nines. Dr Fagan appeared in a pale grey morning coat and sponge-bag trousers, looking more than ever *jeune premier*; there was a spring in his step and a pronounced sprightliness of bearing that Paul had not observed before. Flossie wore a violet frock of knitted wool made for her during the preceding autumn by her sister. It was the colour of indelible ink on blotting paper, and was ornamented at the waist with flowers of emerald green and pink. Her hat, also home-made, was the outcome of many winter evenings of ungrudged labour. All the trimmings of all her previous hats had gone to its adornment. Dingy wore a little steel brooch made in the shape of a bull-dog. Grimes wore a stiff evening collar of celluloid.

'Had to do something to celebrate the occasion,' he said, 'so I put on a "choker". Phew, though, it's tight. Have you seen my fiancée's latest creation? Ascot ain't in it. Let's get down to Mrs Roberts for a quick one before the happy throng rolls up.'

'I wish I could, but I've got to go round the ground with the Doctor.'

'Righto, old boy! See you later. Here comes Prendy in his coat of many colours.'

Mr Prendergast wore a blazer of faded stripes, which smelt strongly of camphor.

'I think Dr Fagan encourages a certain amount of display on these occasions,' he said. 'I used to keep wicket for my college, you know, but I was too short-sighted to be much good. Still, I am entitled to the blazer,' he said with a note of defiance in his voice, 'and it is more appropriate to a sporting occasion than a stiff collar.'

'Good old Prendy!' said Grimes. 'Nothing like a change of clothes to bring out latent pep. I felt like that my first week in khaki. Well, so long. Me for Mrs Roberts. Why don't you come too, Prendy?'

'D'you know,' said Mr Prendergast, 'I think I will.'

Paul watched them disappear down the drive in amazement. Then he went off to find the Doctor.

'Frankly,' said the Doctor, 'I am at a loss to understand my own emotions. I can think of no entertainment that fills me with greater detestation than a display of competitive athletics, none–except possibly folk dancing. If there are two women in the world whose company I abominate–and there are very many more than two–they are Mrs Beste-Chetwynde and Lady Circumference. I have, moreover, had an extremely difficult encounter with my butler, who–will you believe it?–waited at luncheon in a mustard-coloured suit of plus-fours and a diamond tie-pin, and when I reprimanded him, attempted to tell me some ridiculous story about his being the proprietor of a circus or swimming-bath or some such concern. And yet,' said the Doctor, 'I am filled with a wholly delightful exhilaration. I can't understand it. It is not as though this was the first occasion of the kind. During the fourteen years that I have been at Llanabba there have been six sports days and two concerts, all of them, in one way or another, utterly disastrous. Once Lady Bunyan was taken ill; another time it was the matter of the Press photographers and the obstacle race; another time some quite unimportant parents brought a dog with them which bit two of the boys very severely and one of the masters, who swore terribly in front of everyone. I could hardly blame him, but of course he had to go. Then there was the concert when the boys refused to sing "God save the King" because of the pudding they had had for luncheon. One way and another, I have been consistently unfortunate in my efforts at festivity. And yet I look forward to each new fiasco with the utmost relish. Perhaps, Pennyfeather, you will bring luck to Llanabba; in fact, I feel confident you have already done so. Look at the sun!'

Picking their way carefully among the dry patches in the water-logged drive, they reached the playing-fields. Here the haphazard organization of the last twenty-four hours seemed to have been fairly successful. A large marquee was already in position, and Philbrick–still in plus-fours–and three gardeners were at work putting up a smaller tent.

'That's for the Llanabba Silver Band,' said the Doctor. 'Philbrick, I required you to take off those loathsome garments.'

'They were new when I bought them,' said Philbrick, 'and they cost eight pounds fifteen. Anyhow I can't do two things at once, can I? If I go back to change, who's going to manage all this, I'd like to know?'

'All right! Finish what you are doing first. Let us just review the arrangements. The marquee is for the visitors' tea. That is Diana's province. I expect we shall find her at work.'

Sure enough, there was Dingy helping two servants to arrange plates of highly coloured cakes down a trestle-table. Two other servants in the background were cutting sandwiches. Dingy, too, was obviously enjoying herself.

'Jane, Emily, remember that that butter has to do for three loaves. Spread it thoroughly, but don't waste it, and cut the crusts as thin as possible. Father, will you see to it that the boys who come in with their parents come in *alone*? You remember last time how Briggs brought in four boys with him, and they ate all the jam sandwiches before Colonel Loder had had any. Mr Pennyfeather, the champagne-cup is *not* for the masters. In fact, I expect you will find yourselves too much occupied helping the visitors to have any tea until they have left the tent. You had better tell Captain Grimes that, too. I am sure Mr Prendergast would not think of pushing himself forward.'

Outside the marquee were assembled several seats and tubs of palms and flowering shrubs. 'All this must be set in order,' said the Doctor; 'our guests may arrive in less than an hour.' He passed on. 'The cars shall turn aside from the drive here and come right into the ground. It will give a pleasant background to the photographs, and, Pennyfeather, if you would with tact direct the photographer so that more prominence was given to Mrs Beste-

Chetwynde's Hispano Suiza than to Lady Circumference's little motor-car, I think it would be all to the good. All these things count, you know.'

'Nothing seems to have been done about marking out the ground,' said Paul.

'No,' said the Doctor, turning his attention to the field for the first time, 'nothing. Well, you must do the best you can. They can't do everything.'

'I wonder if any hurdles have come?'

'They were ordered,' said the Doctor. 'I am certain of it. Philbrick, have any hurdles come?'

'Yes,' said Philbrick with a low chuckle.

'Why, pray, do you laugh at the mention of hurdles?'

'Just you look at them!' said Philbrick. 'They're behind the tea-house there.'

Paul and the Doctor went to look and found a pile of spiked iron railings in sections heaped up at the back of the marquee. They were each about five feet high and were painted green with gilt spikes.

'It seems to me that they have sent the wrong sort,' said the Doctor.

'Yes.'

'Well, we must do the best we can. What other things ought there to be?'

'Weight, hammer, javelin, long-jump pit, high-jump posts, low hurdles, eggs, spoons and greasy pole,' said Philbrick.

'Previously competed for,' said the Doctor imperturbably. 'What else?'

'Somewhere to run,' suggested Paul.

'Why, God bless my soul, they've got the whole park! How did you manage yesterday for the heats?'

'We judged the distance by eye.'

'Then that is what we shall have to do today. Really, my dear Pennyfeather, it is quite unlike you to fabricate difficulties in this way. I am afraid you are getting unnerved. Let them go on racing until it is time for tea; and remember,' he added sagely, 'the longer the race the more time it takes. I leave the details to you. I am concerned with *style*. I wish, for instance, we had a starting pistol.'

'Would this be any use?' said Philbrick, producing an enormous service revolver. 'Only take care; it's loaded.'

'The very thing,' said the Doctor. 'Only fire into the ground, mind. We must do everything we can to avoid an accident. Do you always carry that about with you?'

'Only when I'm wearing my diamonds,' said Philbrick.

'Well, I hope that is not often. Good gracious! Who are these extraordinary-looking people?'

Ten men of revolting appearance were approaching from the drive. They were low of brow, crafty of eye and crooked of limb. They advanced huddled together with the loping tread of wolves, peering about them furtively as they came, as though in constant terror of ambush; they slavered at their mouths, which hung loosely over their receding chins, while each clutched under his ape-like arm a burden of curious and unaccountable shape. On seeing the Doctor they halted and edged back, those behind squinting and mouthing over their companions' shoulders.

'Crikey!' said Philbrick. 'Loonies! This is where I shoot.'

'I refuse to believe the evidence of my eyes,' said the Doctor. 'These creatures simply do not exist.'

After brief preliminary shuffling and nudging, an elderly man emerged from the back of the group. He had a rough black beard and wore on his uneven shoulders a druidical wreath of brass mistletoe-berries.

'Why, it's my friend the station-master!' said Philbrick.

'We are the silver band the Lord bless and keep you,' said the station-master in one breath, 'the band that no one could beat whatever but two indeed in the Eisteddfod that for all North Wales was look you.'

'I see,' said the Doctor; 'I see. That's splendid. Well, will you please go into your tent, the little tent over there.'

'To march about you would not like us?' suggested the station-master; 'we have a fine yellow flag look you that embroidered for us was in silks.'

'No, no. Into the tent!'

The station-master went back to consult with his fellow-musicians. There was a baying and growling and yapping as of the jungle at moonrise, and presently he came forward again with an obsequious, sidelong shuffle.

'Three pounds you pay us would you said indeed to at the sports play.'

'Yes, yes, that's right, three pounds. Into the tent!'

'Nothing whatever we can play without the money first,' said the station-master firmly.

'How would it be,' said Philbrick, 'if I gave him a clout on the ear?'

'No, no, I beg you to do nothing of the kind. You have not lived in Wales as long as I have.' He took a note-case from his pocket, the sight of which seemed to galvanize the musicians into life; they crowded round, twitching and chattering. The Doctor took out three pound notes and gave them to the station-master. 'There you are, Davies!' he said. 'Now take your men into the tent. They are on no account to emerge until after tea; do you understand?'

The band slunk away, and Paul and the Doctor turned back towards the Castle.

'The Welsh character is an interesting study,' said Dr Fagan. 'I have often considered writing a little monograph on the subject, but I was afraid it might make me unpopular in the village. The ignorant speak of them as Celts, which is of course wholly erroneous. They are of pure Iberian stock – the aboriginal inhabitants of Europe who survive only in Portugal and the Basque district. Celts readily inter-marry with their neighbours and absorb them. From the earliest times the Welsh have been looked upon as an unclean people. It is thus that they have preserved their racial integrity. Their sons and daughters mate freely with the sheep but not with human kind except their own blood relations. In Wales there was no need for legislation to prevent the conquering people intermarrying with the conquered. In Ireland that was necessary, for there intermarriage was a political matter. In Wales it was moral. I hope, by the way, you have no Welsh blood?'

'None whatever,' said Paul.

'I was sure you had not, but one cannot be too careful. I once spoke of this subject to the sixth form and learned later that one of them had a Welsh grandmother. I am afraid it hurt his feelings terribly, poor little chap. She came from Pembrokeshire, too, which is of course quite a different matter. I often think,' he continued, 'that we can trace almost all the disasters of English history to the influence of Wales. Think of Edward of Carnarvon, the first Prince of Wales, a perverse life, Pennyfeather, and an unseemly death, then the Tudors and the dissolution of the Church, then Lloyd George, the temperance movement, Nonconformity and lust stalking hand in hand through the country, wasting and ravaging. But perhaps you think I exaggerate? I have a certain rhetorical tendency, I admit.'

'No, no,' said Paul.

'The Welsh,' said the Doctor, 'are the only nation in the world that has produced no graphic or plastic art, no architecture, no drama. They just sing,' he said with disgust, 'sing and blow down wind instruments of plated silver. They are deceitful because they cannot discern truth from falsehood, depraved because they cannot discern the consequences of their indulgence. Let us consider,' he continued, 'the etymological derivations of the Welsh language. . . .'

But here he was interrupted by a breathless little boy who panted down the drive to meet them. 'Please, sir, Lord and Lady Circumference have arrived, sir. They're in the library with Miss Florence. She asked me to tell you.'

'The sports will start in ten minutes,' said the Doctor. 'Run and tell the other boys to change and go at once to the playing-fields. I will talk to you about the Welsh again. It is a matter to which I have given some thought, and I can see that you are sincerely interested. Come in with me and see the Circumferences.'

Flossie was talking to them in the library.

'Yes, isn't it a sweet colour?' she was saying. 'I do like something bright myself. Diana made it for me; she does knit a treat, does Diana, but of course I chose the colour, you know, because, you see, Diana's taste is all for wishy-washy greys and browns. Mournful, you know. Well, here's the dad. Lady Circumference was just saying how much she likes my frock what you said was vulgar, so there!'

A stout elderly woman dressed in a tweed coat and skirt and jaunty Tyrolean hat advanced to the Doctor. 'Hullo!' she said in a deep bass voice, 'how are you? Sorry if we're late, Circumference ran over a fool of a boy. I've just been chaffing your daughter here about her frock. Wish I was young enough to wear that kind of thing. Older I get the more I like colour. We're both pretty long in the tooth, eh?' She gave Dr Fagan a hearty shake of the hand, that obviously caused him acute pain. Then she turned to Paul.

'So you're the Doctor's hired assassin, eh? Well, I hope you keep a firm hand on my toad of a son. How's he doin'?'

'Quite well,' said Paul.

'Nonsense!' said Lady Circumference. 'The boy's a dunderhead. If he wasn't he wouldn't be here. He wants beatin' and hittin' and knockin' about generally, and then he'll be no good. That grass is shockin' bad on the terrace, Doctor; you ought to sand it down and resow it, but you'll have to take that cedar down if ever you want it to grow properly at the side. I hate cuttin' down a tree–like losin' a tooth–but you have to choose, tree or grass; you can't keep 'em both. What d'you pay your head man?'

As she was talking Lord Circumference emerged from the shadows and shook Paul's hand. He had a long fair moustache and large watery eyes which reminded Paul a little of Mr Prendergast.

'How do you do?' he said.

'How do you do?' said Paul.

'Fond of sport, eh?' he said. 'I mean these sort of sports?'

'Oh, yes,' said Paul. 'I think they're so good for the boys.'

'Do you? Do you think that?' said Lord Circumference very earnestly; 'you think they're good for the boys?'

'Yes,' said Paul; 'don't you?'

'Me? Yes, oh, yes. I think so, too. Very good for the boys.'

'So useful in case of a war or anything,' said Paul.

'D'you think so? D'you really and truly think so? That there's going to be another war, I mean?'

'Yes, I'm sure of it; aren't you?'

'Yes, of course, I'm sure of it too. And that awful bread, and people coming on to one's own land and telling one what one's to do with one's own butter and milk, and commandeering one's horses! Oh yes, all over again! My wife shot her hunters rather than let them go to the army. And girls in breeches on all the farms! All over again! Who do you think it will be this time?'

'The Americans,' said Paul stoutly.

'No, indeed, I hope not. We had German prisoners on two of the farms. That wasn't so bad, but if they start putting Americans on my land, I'll just refuse to stand it. My daughter brought an American down to luncheon the other day, and, do you know . . . ?'

'Dig it and dung it,' said Lady Circumference. 'Only it's got to be dug deep, mind. Now how did your calceolarias do last year?'

'I really have no idea,' said the Doctor. 'Flossie, how did our calceolarias do?'

'Lovely,' said Flossie.

'I don't believe a word of it,' said Lady Circumference. 'Nobody's calceolarias did well last year.'

'Shall we adjourn to the playing-fields?' said the Doctor. 'I expect they are all waiting for us.'

Talking cheerfully, the party crossed the hall and went down the steps.

'Your drive's awful wet,' said Lady Circumference. 'I expect there's a blocked pipe somewhere. Sure it ain't sewage?'

'I was never any use at short distances,' Lord Circumference was saying. 'I was always a slow starter, but I was once eighteenth in the Crick at Rugby. We didn't take sports so seriously at the 'Varsity when I was up; everybody rode. What college were you at?'

'Scone.'

'Scone, were you? Ever come across a young nephew of my wife's called Alastair Digby-Vaine-Trumpington?'

'I just met him,' said Paul.

'That's very interesting. Greta, Mr Pennyfoot knows Alastair.'

'Does he? Well, that boy's doing no good for himself. Got fined twenty pounds the other day, his mother told me. Seemed proud of it. If my brother had been alive he'd have licked all that out of the young cub. It takes a man to bring up a man.'

'Yes,' said Lord Circumference meekly.

'Who else do you know at Oxford? Do you know Freddy French-Wise?'

'No.'

'Or Tom Obblethwaite or that youngest Castleton boy?'

'No, I'm afraid not. I had a great friend called Potts.'

'*Potts!*' said Lady Circumference, and left it at that.

All the school and several local visitors were assembled in the field. Grimes stood by himself, looking depressed. Mr Prendergast, flushed and unusually vivacious, was talking to the Vicar. As the headmaster's party came into sight the Llanabba Silver Band struck up *Men of Harlech*.

'Shockin' noise,' commented Lady Circumference graciously.

The head prefect came forward and presented her with a programme, beribboned and embossed in gold. Another prefect set a chair for her. She sat down with the Doctor next to her and Lord Circumference on the other side of him.

'Pennyfeather,' cried the Doctor above the band, 'start them racing.'

Philbrick gave Paul a megaphone. 'I found this in the pavilion.' he said. 'I thought it might be useful.'

'Who's that extraordinary man?' asked Lady Circumference.

'He is the boxing coach and swimming professional,' said the Doctor. 'A finely developed figure, don't you think?'

'First race,' said Paul through the megaphone, 'under sixteen, Quarter-mile!' He read out Grimes's list of starters.

'What's Tangent doin' in this race?' said Lady Circumference. 'The boy can't run an inch.'

The silver band stopped playing.

'The course,' said Paul, 'starts from the pavilion, goes round that clump of elms . . .'

'Beeches,' corrected Lady Circumference loudly.

'. . . and ends in front of the band-stand. Starter, Mr Prendergast; timekeeper, Captain Grimes.'

'I shall say, "Are you ready? one, two, three!" and then fire,' said Mr Prendergast. 'Are you ready? One'–there was a terrific report. 'Oh dear! I'm sorry'–but the race had begun. Clearly Tangent was not going to win; he was sitting on the grass crying because he had been wounded in the foot by Mr Prendergast's bullet. Philbrick carried him, wailing dismally into the refreshment tent, where Dingy helped him off with his shoe. His heel was slightly grazed. Dingy gave him a large slice of cake, and he hobbled out surrounded by a sympathetic crowd.

'That won't hurt him,' said Lady Circumference, 'but I think some one ought to remove the pistol from that old man before he does anything serious.'

'I knew that was going to happen,' said Lord Circumference.

'A most unfortunate beginning,' said the Doctor.

'Am I going to die?' said Tangent, his mouth full of cake.

'For God's sake, look after Prendy,' said Grimes in Paul's ear. 'The man's as tight as a lord, whisky.'

'First blood to me!' said Mr Prendergast gleefully.

'The last race will be run again,' said Paul down the megaphone. 'Starter, Mr Philbrick; timekeeper, Mr Prendergast.'

'On your marks! Get set.' Bang went the pistol, this time without disaster. The six little boys scampered off through the mud, disappeared behind the beeches and returned rather more slowly. Captain Grimes and Mr Prendergast held up a piece of tape.

'Well run, sir!' shouted Colonel Sidebotham. 'Jolly good race.'

'Capital,' said Mr Prendergast, and dropping his end of the tape, he sauntered over to the Colonel. 'I can see you are a fine judge of a race, sir. So was I once. So's Grimes. A capital fellow, Grimes; a bounder, you know, but a capital fellow. Bounders can be capital fellows; don't you agree, Colonel Slidebottom? In fact, I'd go further and say that capital fellows *are* bounders. What d'you say to that? I wish you'd stop pulling at my arm, Pennyfeather. Colonel Shybotham and I are just having a most interesting conversation about bounders.'

The silver band struck up again, and Mr Prendergast began a little jig, saying: 'Capital fellow! capital fellow!' and snapping his fingers. Paul led him to the refreshment tent.

'Dingy wants you to help her in there,' he said firmly, 'and, for God's sake, don't come out until you feel better.'

'I never felt better in my life,' said Mr Prendergast indignantly. 'Capital fellow! capital fellow!'

'It is not my affair, of course,' said Colonel Sidebotham, 'but if you ask me I should say that man had been drinking.'

'He was talking very excitedly to me,' said the Vicar, 'about some apparatus for warming a church in Worthing and about the Apostolic Claims of the Church of Abyssinia. I confess I could not follow him clearly. He seems deeply interested in Church matters. Are you quite sure he is right in the head? I have noticed again and again since I have been in the Church that lay interest in ecclesiastical matters is often a prelude to insanity.'

'Drink, pure and simple,' said the Colonel. 'I wonder where he got it? I could do with a spot of whisky.'

'Quarter-mile Open!' said Paul through his megaphone.

Presently the Clutterbucks arrived. Both the parents were stout. They brought with them two small children, a governess, and an elder son. They debouched from the car one by one, stretching their limbs in evident relief.

'This is Sam,' said Mr Clutterbuck, 'just down from Cambridge. He's joined me in the business, and we've brought the nippers along for a treat. Don't mind, do you, Doc? And last, but not least, my wife.'

Dr Fagan greeted them with genial condescension and found them seats.

'I am afraid you have missed all the jumping-events,' he said. 'But I have a list of the results here. You will see that Percy has done extremely well.'

'Didn't know the little beggar had it in him. See that, Martha? Percy's won the high-jump and the long-jump and the hurdles. How's your young hopeful been doing, Lady Circumference?'

'My boy has been injured in the foot,' said Lady Circumference coldly.

'Dear me! Not badly, I hope? Did he twist his ankle in the jumping?'

'No,' said Lady Circumference, 'he was shot at by one of the assistant masters. But it is kind of you to inquire.'

'Three Miles Open!' announced Paul. 'The course of six laps will be run as before.'

'On your marks! Get set.' Bang went Philbrick's revolver. Off trotted the boys on another race.

Father,' said Flossie,'don't you think it's time for the tea interval?'

'Nothing can be done before Mrs Beste-Chetwynde arrives,' said the Doctor.

Round and round the muddy track trotted the athletes while the silver band played sacred music unceasingly.

'Last Lap!' announced Paul.

The school and the visitors crowded about the tape to cheer the winner. Amid loud applause Clutterbuck breasted the tape well ahead of the others.

'Well run! Oh, good, jolly good, sir!' cried Colonel Sidebotham.

'Good old Percy! That's the stuff,' said Mr Clutterbuck.

'Well run, Percy!' chorused the two little Clutterbucks, prompted by their governess.

'That boy cheated,' said Lady Circumference. 'He only went round five times. I counted.'

'I think unpleasantness so mars the afternoon,' said the Vicar.

'How dare you suggest such a thing?' asked Mrs Clutterbuck. 'I appeal to the referee. Percy ran the full course, didn't he?'

'Clutterbuck wins,' said Captain Grimes.

'Fiddlesticks!' said Lady Circumference. 'He deliberately lagged behind and joined the others as they went behind the beeches. The little toad!'

'Really, Greta,' said Lord Circumference, 'I think we ought to abide by the referee's decision.'

'Well, they can't expect me to give away the prizes, then. Nothing would induce me to give that boy a prize.'

'Do you understand, madam, that you are bringing a serious accusation against my son's honour?'

'Serious accusation, fiddlesticks! What he wants is a jolly good hidin'.'

'No doubt you judge other people's sons by your own. Let me tell you, Lady Circumference . . .'

'Don't attempt to browbeat me, sir. I know a cheat when I see one.'

At this stage of the discussion the Doctor left Mrs Hope-Browne's side, where he had been remarking upon her son's progress in geometry, and joined the group round the winning post.

'If there is a disputed decision,' he said genially, 'they shall race again.'

'Percy has won already,' said Mr Clutterbuck. 'He has been adjudged the winner.'

'Splendid! splendid! A promising little athlete. I congratulate you, Clutterbuck.'

'But he only ran five laps,' said Lady Circumference.

'Then clearly he has won the five furlongs race, a very exacting length.'

'But the other boys,' said Lady Circumference, almost beside herself with rage, 'have run six lengths.'

'Then they,' said the Doctor imperturbably, 'are first, second, third, fourth and fifth respectively in the Three Miles. Clearly there has been some confusion. Diana, I think we might now serve tea.'

Things were not easy, but there was fortunately a distraction, for as he spoke an enormous limousine of dove-grey and silver stole soundlessly onto the field.

'But what could be more opportune? Here is Mrs Beste-Chetwynde.'

Three light skips brought him to the side of the car, but the footman was there before him. The door opened, and from the cushions within emerged a tall young man in a clinging dove-grey overcoat. After him, like the first breath of spring in the Champs-Elysées, came Mrs Beste-Chetwynde – two lizard-skin feet, silk legs, chinchilla body, a tight little black hat, pinned with platinum and diamonds, and the high invariable voice that may be heard in any Ritz Hotel from New York to Buda-Pest.

'I hope you don't mind my bringing Chokey, Dr Fagan?' she said. 'He's just crazy about sport.'

'I sure am that,' said Chokey.

'Dear Mrs Beste-Chetwynde!' said Dr Fagan; 'dear, dear, Mrs Beste-Chetwynde!' He pressed her glove, and for the moment was at a loss for words of welcome, for 'Chokey', though graceful of bearing and irreproachably dressed, was coal black.

9

THE SPORTS–CONTINUED

The refreshment tent looked very nice. The long table across the centre was covered with a white cloth. Bowls of flowers were ranged down it at regular intervals, and between them plates of sandwiches and cakes and jugs of lemonade and champagne-cup. Behind it against a background of palms stood the four Welsh housemaids in clean caps and aprons, pouring out tea. Behind them again sat Mr Prendergast, a glass of champagne-cup in his hand, his wig slightly awry. He rose unsteadily to his feet at the approach of the guests, made a little bow, and then sat down again rather suddenly.

'Will you take round the *foie gras* sandwiches, Mr Pennyfeather?' said Dingy. 'They are not for the boys or Captain Grimes.'

'One for little me!' said Flossie as he passed her.

Philbrick, evidently regarding himself as one of the guests, was engaged in a heated discussion on greyhound-racing with Sam Clutterbuck.

'What price the coon?' he asked as Paul gave him a sandwich.

'It does my heart good to see old Prendy enjoying himself,' said Grimes. 'Pity he shot that kid, though.'

'There's not much the matter with him to see the way he's eating his tea. I say, this is rather a poor afternoon, isn't it?'

'Circulate, old boy, circulate. Things aren't going too smoothly.'

Nor indeed were they. The sudden ebullition of ill-feeling over the Three-mile race, though checked by the arrival of Mrs Beste-Chetwynde, was by no means forgotten. There were two distinctly hostile camps in the tea-tent. On one side stood the Circumferences, Tangent, the Vicar, Colonel Sidebotham and the Hope-Brownes, on the other the seven Clutterbucks, Philbrick, Flossie and two or three parents who had been snubbed already that afternoon by Lady Circumference. No one spoke of the race, but outraged sportsmanship glinted perilously in every eye. Several parents, intent on their tea, crowded round Dingy and the table. Eminently aloof from all these stood Chokey and Mrs Beste-Chetwynde. Clearly the social balance was delicately poised, and the issue depended upon them. With or without her nigger, Mrs Beste-Chetwynde was a woman of vital importance.

'Why, Dr Fagan,' she was saying, 'it is too disappointing that we've missed the sports. We had just the slowest journey, stopping all the time to see the churches. You can't move Chokey once he's seen an old church. He's just crazy about culture, aren't you, darling?'

'I sure am that,' said Chokey.

'Are you interested in music?' said the Doctor tactfully.

'Well, just you hear that, Baby,' said Chokey; 'am *I* interested in music? I should say I am.'

'He plays just too divinely,' said Mrs Beste-Chetwynde.

'Has he heard my new records, would you say?'

'No, darling, I don't expect he has.'

'Well, just you hear *them*, sir, and then you'll know–am I interested in music.'

'Now, darling, don't get discouraged. I'll take you over and introduce you to Lady Circumference. It's his inferiority-complex, the angel. He's just crazy to meet the aristocracy, aren't you, my sweet?'

'I sure am that,' said Chokey.

'I think it's an insult bringing a nigger here,' said Mrs Clutterbuck. 'It's an insult to our own women.'

'Niggers are all right,' said Philbrick. 'Where I draw a line is a Chink, nasty inhuman things. I had a pal bumped off by a Chink once. Throat cut horrible, it was, from ear to ear.'

'Good gracious!' said the Clutterbuck governess; 'was that in the Boxer rising?'

'No,' said Philbrick cheerfully. 'Saturday night in the Edgware Road. Might have happened to any of us.'

'What did the gentleman say?' asked the children.

'Never you mind, my dears. Run and have some more of the green cake.'

They ran off obediently, but the little boy was later heard whispering to his sister as she knelt at prayers, 'cut horrible from ear to ear', so that until quite late in her life Miss Clutterbuck would feel a little faint when she saw a 'bus that was going to the Edgware Road.

'I've got a friend lives in Savannah,' said Sam, 'and he's told me a thing or two about niggers. Of course it's hardly a thing to talk about before the ladies, but, to put it bluntly, *they have uncontrollable passions*. See what I mean?'

'What a terrible thing!' said Grimes.

'You can't blame 'em, mind: it's just their nature. Animal, you know. Still, what I do say is, since they're like that, the less we see of them the better.'

'Quite,' said Mr Clutterbuck.

'I had such a curious conversation just now,' Lord Circumference was saying to Paul, 'with your bandmaster over there. He asked me whether I should like to meet his sister; and when I said, "Yes, I should be delighted to," he said that it would cost a pound normally, but that he'd let me have special terms. What *can* he have meant, Mr Pennyfoot?'

''Pon my soul,' Colonel Sidebotham was saying to the Vicar, 'I don't like the look of that nigger. I saw enough of Fuzzy-Wuzzy in the Soudan–devilish good enemy and devilish bad friend. I'm going across to talk to Mrs Clutterbuck. Between ourselves, I think Lady C. went a bit far. I didn't see the race myself, but there are limits. . . .'

'Rain ain't doin' the turnip crop any good,' Lady Circumference was saying.

'No, indeed,' said Mrs Beste-Chetwynde. 'Are you in England for long?'

'Why, I live in England, of course,' said Lady Circumference.

'My dear, how divine! But don't you find it just too expensive?'

This was one of Lady Circumference's favourite topics, but somehow she did not feel disposed to enlarge on it to Mrs Beste-Chetwynde with the same gusto as when she was talking to Mrs Sidebotham and the Vicar's wife. She never felt quite at ease with people richer than herself.

'Well, we all feel the wind a bit since the war,' she said briefly. 'How's Bobby Pastmaster?'

'Dotty,' said Mrs Beste-Chetwynde, 'terribly dotty, and he and Chokey don't get on. You'll like Chokey. He's just crazy about England, too. We've been round all the cathedrals, and now we're going to start on the country houses. We were thinking of running over to see you at Castle Tangent one afternoon.'

'That would be delightful, but I'm afraid we are in London at present. Which did you like best of the cathedrals, Mr Chokey?'

'Chokey's not really his name, you know. The angel's called "Mr Sebastian Cholmondley".'

'Well,' said Mr Cholmondley, 'they were all fine, just fine. When I saw the cathedrals my heart just rose up and sang within me. I sure am crazy about culture. You folk think because we're coloured we don't care about nothing but jazz. Why, I'd give all the jazz in the world for just one little stone from one of your cathedrals.'

'It's quite true. He would.'

'Well, that's most interesting, Mr Cholmondley. I used to live just outside Salisbury when I was a girl, but, little as I like jazz, I never felt quite as strongly as that about it.'

'Salisbury is full of historical interest, Lady Circumference, but in my opinion York Minster is the more refined.'

'Oh, you angel!' said Mrs Beste-Chetwynde. 'I could eat you up every bit.'

'And is this your first visit to an English school?' asked the Doctor.

'I should say not. Will you tell the Doctor the schools I've seen?'

'He's been to them all, even the quite new ones. In fact, he liked the new ones best.'

'They were more spacious. Have you ever seen Oxford?'

'Yes; in fact, I was educated there.'

'Were you, now? I've seen Oxford and Cambridge and Eton and Harrow. That's me all over. That's what I like, see? *I* appreciate art. There's plenty coloured people come over here and don't see nothing but a few night clubs. I read Shakespeare,' said Chokey, '*Hamlet*, *Macbeth*, *King Lear*. Ever read them?'

'Yes,' said the Doctor; 'as a matter of fact, I have.'

'My race,' said Chokey, 'is essentially an artistic race. We have the child's love of song and colour and the child's natural good taste. All you white folks despise the poor coloured man. . . .'

'No, no,' said the Doctor.

'Let him say his piece, the darling,' said Mrs Beste-Chetwynde. 'Isn't he divine?'

'You folks all think the coloured man hasn't got a soul. Anything's good enough for the poor coloured man. Beat him; put him in chains; load him with burdens. . . .' Here Paul observed a responsive glitter in Lady Circumference's eye. 'But all the time that poor coloured man has a soul same as you have. Don't he breathe the same as you? Don't he eat and drink? Don't he love Shakespeare and cathedrals and the paintings of the old masters same as you? Isn't he just asking for your love and help to raise him from the servitude into which your forefathers plunged him? Oh, say, white folks, why don't you stretch out a helping hand to the poor coloured man, that's as good as you are, if you'll only let him be?'

'My sweet,' said Mrs Beste-Chetwynde, 'you mustn't get discouraged. They're all friends here.'

'Is that so?' said Chokey' 'Should I sing them a song?'

'No, don't do that, darling. Have some tea.'

'I had a friend in Paris,' said the Clutterbuck governess, 'whose sister knew a girl who married one of the black soldiers during the war, and you wouldn't believe what he did to her. Joan and Peter, run and see if Daddy wants some more tea. He tied her up with a razor strop and left her on the stone floor for the night without food or covering. And then it was over a year before she could get a divorce.'

'Used to cut the tent ropes,' Colonel Sidebotham was saying, 'and then knife the poor beggars through the canvas.'

'You can see 'em in Shaftesbury Avenue and Charing Cross Road any night of the week,' Sam Clutterbuck was saying. 'The women just hanging on to 'em.'

'The mistake was ever giving them their freedom,' said the Vicar. 'They were far happier and better looked after before.'

'It's queer,' said Flossie, 'that a woman with as much money as Mrs Beste-Chetwynde sshould wear such *ddull* clothes.'

'That ring didn't cost less than five hundred,' said Philbrick.

'Let's go and talk to the Vicar about God,' said Mrs Beste-Chetwynde. 'Chokey thinks religion is just divine.'

'My race is a very spiritual one,' said Chokey.

'The band has been playing *Men of Harlech* for over half an hour,' said the Doctor. 'Diana, do go and tell them to try something else.'

'I sometimes think I'm getting rather bored with coloured people,' Mrs Beste-Chetwynde said to Lady Circumference. 'Are you?'

'I have never had the opportunity.'

'I dare say you'd be good with them. They take a lot of living up to; they *are* so earnest. Who's that dear, dim, drunk little man?'

'That is the person who shot my son.'

'My dear, how too shattering for you. Not dead, I hope? Chokey shot a man at a party the other night. He gets gay at times, you know. It's only when he's on his best behaviour that he's so class-conscious. I must go and rescue the Vicar.'

The station-master came into the tent, crab-like and obsequious.

'Well, my good man?' said the Doctor.

'The young lady I have been telling that no other tunes can we play whatever with the lady smoking at her cigarette look you.'

'God bless my soul! Why not?'

'The other tunes are all holy tunes look you. Blasphemy, it would be to play the songs of Sion while the lady at a cigarette smokes whatever. *Men of Harlech* is good music look you.'

'This is most unfortunate. I can hardly ask Mrs Beste-Chetwynde to stop smoking. Frankly, I regard this as impertinence.'

'But no man can you ask against his Maker to blaspheme whatever unless him to pay more you were. Three pounds for the music is good and one for the blasphemy look you.'

Dr Fagan gave him another pound. The station-master retired, and in a few minutes the silver band began a singularly emotional rendering of *In Thy courts no more are needed Sun by day and Moon by night*.

10

POST MORTEM

As the last car drove away the Doctor and his daughters and Paul and Grimes walked up the drive together towards the Castle.

'Frankly the day has been rather a disappointment to me,' said the Doctor. 'Nothing seemed to go quite right in spite of all our preparations.'

'And expense,' said Dingy.

'I am sorry, too, that Mr Prendergast should have had that unfortunate disagreement with Mrs Beste-Chetwynde's coloured friend. In all the ten years during which we have worked together I have never known Mr Prendergast so self-assertive. It was *not* becoming of him. Nor was it Philbrick's place to join in. I was seriously alarmed. They seemed so angry, and all about some minor point of ecclesiastical architecture.'

'Mr Cholmondley was very sensitive,' said Flossie.

'Yes, he seemed to think that Mr Prendergast's insistence on the late development of the rood-screen was in some way connected with colour-prejudice. I wonder why that was? To my mind it showed a very confused line of thought. Still, it would have been more seemly if Mr Prendergast had let the matter drop, and what would Philbrick know of the matter?'

'Philbrick is not an ordinary butler,' said Dingy.

'No, indeed not,' said the Doctor. 'I heartily deplore his jewellery.'

'I didn't like Lady Circumference's speech,' said Flossie. 'Did you?'

'I did not,' said the Doctor; 'nor, I think, did Mrs Clutterbuck. I thought her reference to the Five Furlong race positively brutal. I was glad Clutterbuck had done so well in the jumping yesterday.'

'She rather wanders from the point, doesn't she?' said Dingy. 'All that about hunting, I mean.'

'I don't think Lady Circumference is conscious of any definite divisions in the various branches of sport. I have often observed in women of her type a tendency to regard all athletics as inferior forms of fox-hunting. It is *not* logical. Besides, she was nettled at some remark of Mr Cholmondley's about cruelty to animals. As you say, it was irrelevant and rather unfortunate. I also resented the references to the Liberal party. Mr Clutterbuck has stood three times, you know. Taken as a whole, it was *not* a happy speech. I was quite glad when I saw her drive away.'

'What a pretty car Mrs Beste-Chetwynde has got!' said Flossie, 'but how ostentatious of her to bring a footman.'

'I can forgive the footman,' said Dingy, 'but I can't forgive Mr Cholmondley. He asked me whether I had ever heard of a writer called Thomas Hardy.'

'He asked *me* to go to Reigate with him for the weekend,' said Flossie, '. . . in rather a sweet way, too.'

'Florence, I trust you refused?'

'Oh yes,' said Flossie sadly, 'I refused.'

They went on up the drive in silence. Presently Dingy asked: 'What are we going to do about those fireworks you insisted on buying? Everyone has gone away.'

'I don't feel in a mood for fireworks,' said the Doctor. 'Perhaps another time, but not now.'

Back in the Common Room, Paul and Grimes subsided moodily into the two easy-chairs. The fire, unattended since luncheon, had sunk to a handful of warm ashes.

'Well, old boy,' said Grimes, 'so that's over.'

'Yes,' said Paul.

'All the gay throng melted away?'

'Yes,' said Paul.

'Back to the daily round and cloistral calm?'

'Yes,' said Paul.

'As a beano,' said Grimes, 'I have known better.'

'Yes,' said Paul.

'Lady C.'s hardly what you might call bonhomous.'

'Hardly.'

'Old Prendy made rather an ass of himself?'

'Yes.'

'Hullo, old boy! You sound a bit flat. Feeling the strain of the social vortex, a bit giddy after the gay whirl, eh?'

'I say, Grimes,' said Paul, 'what d'you suppose the relationship is between Mrs Beste-Chetwynde and that nigger?'

'Well, I don't suppose she trots round with him just for the uplift of his conversation; do you?'

'No, I suppose not.'

'In fact, I don't mind diagnosing a simple case of good old sex.'

'Yes, I suppose you're right.'

'I'm sure of it. Great Scott, what's that noise?'

It was Mr Prendergast.

'Prendy, old man,' said Grimes, 'you've let down the morale of the Common Room a pretty good wallop.'

'Damn the Common Room!' said Mr Prendergast. 'What does the Common Room know about rood-screens?'

'That's all right, old boy. We're all friends here. What you say about rood-screens goes.'

'They'll be questioning the efficacy of infant baptism next. The Church has never countenanced lay opinion on spiritual matters. Now if it were a question of food and drink,' said Mr Prendergast, 'if it were a question of drink–But not infant baptism. Just drink.' And he sat down.

'A sad case, brother,' said Grimes, 'truly a sad case. Prendy, do you realize that in two minutes the bell will go for Prep. and you're on duty?'

'Ding, dong, dell! Pussy's in the well.'

'Prendy, that's irrelevant.'

'I know several songs about bells. Funeral bells, wedding bells, sacring bells, sheep-bells, door-bells, dumb-bells and just plain bells.'

Paul and Grimes looked at each other sadly.

'It seems to me,' said Paul, 'that one of us will have to take Prep. for him tonight.'

'No, no, old boy; that'll be all right,' said Grimes. 'You and I are off to Mrs Roberts'. Prendy gives me a thirst.'

'But we can't leave him like this.'

'He'll be all right. The little beasts can't make any more noise than they do usually.'

'You don't think the old man will find him?'

'Not a chance.'

The bell rang. Mr Prendergast jumped to his feet, straightened his wig and steadied himself gravely against the chimney-piece.

'There's a good chap,' said Grimes gently. 'Just you trot down the passage to the little boys and have a good nap.'

Singing quietly to himself, Mr Prendergast sauntered down the passage.

'I hope he's none the worse for this,' said Grimes. 'You know, I feel quite fatherly towards old Prendy. He did give it to that blackamoor about Church architecture, bless him.'

Arm in arm they went down the main avenue towards the inn.

'Mrs Beste-Chetwynde asked me to call on her in London,' said Paul.

'Did she? Well, just you go. I've never been much of a one for society and the smart set myself, but if you like that sort of thing, Mrs Beste-Chetwynde is the goods all right. Never open a paper but there's a photograph of her at some place or other.'

'Does she photograph well?' asked Paul. 'I should rather think that she would.'

Grimes looked at him narrowly. 'Fair to middling. Why the sudden interest?'

'Oh, I don't know. I was just wondering.'

At Mrs Roberts' they found the Llanabba Silver Band chattering acrimoniously over the division of the spoils.

'All the afternoon the band I have led in *Men of Harlech* and sacred music too look you and they will not give me a penny more than themselves whatever. The college gentleman whatever if it is right I ask,' said the station-master, 'me with a sister to support too look you.'

'Now don't bother, old boy,' said Grimes, 'because, if you do, I'll tell your pals about the extra pound you got out of the Doctor.'

The discussion was resumed in Welsh, but it was clear that the station-master was slowly giving way.

'That's settled him all right. Take my tip, old boy: never get mixed up in a Welsh wrangle. It doesn't end in blows, like an Irish one, but goes on for ever. They'll still be discussing that three pounds at the end of term; just you see.'

'Has Mr Beste-Chetwynde been dead long?' asked Paul.

'I shouldn't say so; why?'

'I was just wondering.'

They sat for some time smoking in silence.

'If Beste-Chetwynde is fifteen,' said Paul, 'that doesn't necessarily make her more than thirty-three, does it?'

'Old boy,' said Grimes, 'you're in love.'

'Nonsense!'

'Smitten?' said Grimes.

'No, no.'

'The tender passion?'

'No.'

'Cupid's jolly little darts?'

'No.'

'Spring fancies, love's young dream?'

'Nonsense!'

'Not even a quickening of the pulse?'

'No.'

'A sweet despair?'

'Certainly not.'

'A trembling hope?'

'No.'

'A *frisson?* a *Je ne sais quoi?*'

'Nothing of the sort.'

'Liar!' said Grimes.

There was another long pause. 'Grimes,' said Paul at length, 'I wonder if you can be right?'

'Sure of it, old boy. Just you go in and win. Here's to the happy pair! May all your troubles be little ones.'

In a state of mind totally new to him, Paul accompanied Grimes back to the Castle. Prep. was over. Mr Prendergast was leaning against the fire-place with a contented smile on his face.

'Hullo, Prendy, old wine-skin! How are things with you?'

'Admirable,' said Mr Prendergast. 'I have never known them better. I have just caned twenty-three boys.'

II

PHILBRICK–CONTINUED

Next day Mr Prendergast's self-confidence had evaporated.

'Head hurting?' asked Grimes.

'Well, as a matter of fact, it is rather.'

'Eyes tired? Thirsty?'

'Yes, a little.'

'Poor old Prendy! Don't I know? Still, it was worth it, wasn't it?'

'I don't remember very clearly all that happened, but I walked back to the Castle with Philbrick, and he told me all about his life. It appears he is really a rich man and not a butler at all.'

'I know,' said Paul and Grimes simultaneously.

'You both knew? Well, it came as a great surprise to me, although I must admit I had noticed a certain superiority in his manner. But I find almost everyone like that. Did he tell you his whole story–about his shooting the Portuguese Count and everything?'

'No, he didn't tell me *that*,' said Paul.

'Shooting a Portuguese count? Are you sure you've got hold of the right end of the stick, old boy?'

'Yes, yes, I'm sure of it. It impressed me very much. You see Philbrick is really Sir Solomon Philbrick, the shipowner.'

'The novelist, you mean,' said Grimes.

'The retired burglar,' said Paul.

The three masters looked at each other.

'Old boys, it seems to me someone's been pulling our legs.'

'Well, this is the story that he told me,' continued Mr Prendergast. 'It all started from our argument about Church architecture with the black man. Apparently Philbrick has a large house in Carlton House Terrace.'

'Camberwell Green.'

'Cheyne Walk.'

'Well, I'm telling you what he told me. He has a house in Carlton House Terrace. I remember the address well because a sister of Mrs Round's was once governess in a house in the same row, and he used to live there with an actress who, I regret to say, was not his wife. I forget her name, but I know it is a particularly famous one. He was sitting in the Athenaeum Club one day when the Archbishop of Canterbury approached him and said that the Government were anxious to make him a peer, but that it was impossible while he lived a life of such open irregularity. Philbrick turned down the offer. He is a Roman Catholic, I forgot to tell you. But all that doesn't really explain why he is here. It only shows how important he is. His ships weigh *hundreds* and *hundreds* of tons, he told me.

'Well, one evening he and this play-actress were giving a party, and they were playing baccarat. There was a Portuguese count there–a very dark man from the Legation, Philbrick said. The game rapidly became a personal contest between these two. Philbrick won over and over again until the Count had no more money left and had signed many I.O.U.'s. Finally, very late in the night he took from the Countess's hand–she was sitting beside him with haggard eyes watching him play–an enormous emerald. As big as a golf ball, Philbrick said.

'"This has been an heirloom of my family since the first Crusade," said the Portuguese Count. "It is the one thing which I had hoped to leave to my poor, poor little son." And he tossed in on to the table.

'"I will wager against it my new four-funnel, turbine-driven liner called *The Queen of Arcady*," said Philbrick.

'"That's not enough," said the Portuguese Countess.

'"And my steam-yacht *Swallow* and four tugs and a coaling-barge," said Philbrick. All the party rose to applaud his reckless bid.

'The hand was played. Philbrick had won. With a low bow he returned the emerald to the Portuguese Countess. "For your son!" he said. Again the guests applauded, but the Portuguese Count was livid with rage. "You have insulted my honour," he said. "In Portugal we have only one way of dealing with such an occurrence."

'There and then they went out into Hyde Park, which was quite close. They faced each other and fired: it was just dawn. At the feet of the Achilles statue Philbrick shot the Portuguese Count dead. They left him with his smoking revolver in his hand. The Portuguese Countess kissed Philbrick's hand as she entered her car. "No one will ever know," she said. "It will be taken for suicide. It is a secret between us."

'But Philbrick was a changed man. The actress was driven from his house. He fell into a melancholy and paced up and down his deserted home at night, overpowered by his sense of guilt. The Portuguese Countess rang him up, but he told her it was the wrong number. Finally he went to a priest and confessed. He was told that for three years he must give up his house and wealth and live among the lowest of the low. That,' said Mr Prendergast simply, 'is why he is here. Wasn't that the story he told you?'

'No, it wasn't,' said Paul.

'Not the shade of a likeness,' said Grimes. 'He told me all about himself one evening at Mrs Roberts'. It was like this:

'Mr Philbrick, senior, was a slightly eccentric sort of a cove. He made a big pile out of diamond mines while he was quite young and settled in the country and devoted his declining years to literature. He had two kids: Philbrick and a daughter called Gracie. From the start Philbrick was the apple of the old chap's eye, while he couldn't stick Miss Gracie at any price. Philbrick could spout Shakespeare and *Hamlet* and things by the yard before Gracie could read "The cat sat on the mat". When he was eight he had a sonnet printed in the local paper. After that Gracie wasn't in it anywhere. She lived with the servants like Cinderella, Philbrick said, while he, sensible little beggar, had the best of everything and quoted classics and flowery language to the old boy upstairs. After he left Cambridge he settled down in London and wrote away like blazes. The old man just loved that; he had all Philbrick's books bound in blue leather and put in a separate bookcase with a bust of Philbrick on top. Poor old Gracie found things a bit thin, so she ran off with a young chap in the motor-trade who didn't know one end of a book from the other, or of a car for that matter, as it turned out. When the old boy popped off he left Philbrick everything, except a few books to Gracie. The young man had only married her because he thought the old boy was bound to leave her something, so he hopped it. That didn't worry Philbrick. He lived for his art, he said. He just moved into a bigger house, and went on writing away fifteen to the dozen. Gracie tried to get some money out of him more than once, but he was so busy writing books, he couldn't bother about her. At last she became a cook in a house at Southgate. Next year she died. That didn't worry Philbrick at first. Then after a week or so he noticed an odd thing. There was always a smell of cooking all over the house, in his study, in his bedroom, everywhere. He had an architect in who said he couldn't notice any smell, and rebuilt the kitchen and put in all sorts of ventilators. Still, the smell got worse. It used to hang about his clothes so that he didn't dare go out, a horrible fatty smell. He tried going abroad, but the whole of Paris reeked of English cooking. That was bad enough, but after a time plates began rattling round his bed when he tried to sleep at nights and behind his chair as he wrote his books. He used to wake up in the night and hear the frizzling of fried fish and the singing of kettles. Then he knew what it was: it was Gracie haunting him. He went to the Society for Psychical Research, and they got through a conversation to Gracie. He asked how he could make reparation. She said that he must live among servants for a year and write a book about them that would improve their lot. He tried to go the whole hog at first and started as *chef*, but of course that wasn't really in his line, and the family he was with got so ill, he had to leave. So he came here. He says the book is most moving, and that he'll read me bits of it some day. Not quite the same story as Prendy's.'

'No, it's not. By the way, did he say anything about marrying Dingy?'

'Not a word. He said that as soon as the smell of cooking wore off he was going to be the happiest man in the world. Apparently he's engaged to a female poet in Chelsea. He's not the sort of cove I'd have chosen for a brother-in-law. But then Flossie isn't really the sort of wife I'd have chosen. These things happen, old boy.'

Paul told them about the 'Lamb and Flag' at Camberwell Green and about Toby Cruttwell. 'D'you think that story is true, or yours, or Prendy's?' he asked.

'No,' said Mr Prendergast.

12

THE AGONY OF CAPTAIN GRIMES

Two days later Beste-Chetwynde and Paul were in the organ-loft of the Llanabba parish church.

'I don't think I played that terribly well, do you, sir?'

'No.'

'Shall I stop for a bit?'

'I wish you would.'

'Tangent's foot has swollen up and turned black,' said Beste-Chetwynde with relish.

'Poor little brute!' said Paul.

'I had a letter from my mamma this morning,' Beste-Chetwynde went on. 'There's a message for you in it. Shall I read you what she says?'

He took out a letter written on the thickest possible paper. 'The first part is all about racing and a row she's had with Chokey. Apparently he doesn't like the way she's rebuilt our house in the country. I think it was time she dropped that man, don't you?'

'What does she say about me?' asked Paul.

'She says: "By the way, dear boy, I must tell you that the spelling in your last letters has been *just too shattering* for words. You know how terribly anxious I am for you to get on and go to Oxford, and everything, and I have been thinking don't you think it might be a good thing if we were to have a tutor next holidays? Would you think it *too* boring? Some one young who would fit in? I thought, would that good-looking young master you said you liked care to come? How much ought I to pay him? I never know these things. I don't mean the drunk one, tho' he was sweet too." I think that must be you, don't you?' said Beste-Chetwynde; 'it can hardly be Captain Grimes.'

'Well, I must think that over,' said Paul. 'It sounds rather a good idea.'

'Well, yes,' said Beste-Chetwynde doubtfully, 'it might be all right, only there mustn't be too much of the schoolmaster about it. That man Prendergast beat me the other evening.'

'And there shall be no organ lessons,' said Paul.

Grimes did not receive the news as enthusiastically as Paul had hoped; he was sitting over the Common Room fire despondently biting his nails.

'Good, old boy! That's splendid,' he said abstractedly. 'I'm glad; I am really.'

'Well, you don't sound exactly gay.'

'No, I'm not. Fact is, I'm in the soup again.'

'Badly?'

'Up to the neck.'

'My dear chap, I *am* sorry. What are you going to do about it?'

'I've done the only thing: I've announced my engagement.'

'That'll please Flossie.'

'Oh yes, she's as pleased as hell about it all, damn her nasty little eyes.'

'What did the old man say?'

'Baffled him a bit, old boy. He's just thinking things out at the moment. Well, I expect everything 'll be all right.'

'I don't see why it shouldn't be.'

'Well, there *is* a reason. I don't think I told you before, but fact is, I'm married already.'

That evening Paul received a summons from the Doctor. He wore a double-breasted dinner-jacket, which he smoothed uneasily over his hips at Paul's approach. He looked worried and old.

'Pennyfeather,' he said, 'I have this morning received a severe shock, two shocks in fact. The first was disagreeable, but not wholly unexpected. Your colleague, Captain Grimes, has been convicted before me, on evidence that leaves no possibility of his innocence, of a crime–I might almost call it a course of action–which I can neither understand nor excuse. I dare say I need not particularize. I discerned Captain Grimes's weakness early in our acquaintance and a man of your intelligence and sensibility living at close quarters with him can scarcely have done otherwise also. But I had hoped, I had fondly hoped, that I might be spared the unpleasantness of a public denunciation. However, that is all a minor question. I have quite frequently met with similar cases during a long experience in our profession. But what has disturbed and grieved me more than I can moderately express is the information that he is engaged to be married to my elder daughter. That, Pennyfeather, I had not expected. In the circumstances it seemed a humiliation I might reasonably have been spared. I tell you all this, Pennyfeather, because in our brief acquaintance I have learned to trust and respect you.'

The Doctor sighed, drew from his pocket a handkerchief of *crêpe de chine*, blew his nose with every accent of emotion, and resumed:

'He is *not* the son-in-law I should readily have chosen. I could have forgiven him his wooden leg, his slavish poverty, his moral turpitude, and his abominable features; I could even have forgiven him his incredible vocabulary, if only he had been a *gentleman*. I hope you do not think me a snob. You may have discerned in me a certain prejudice against the lower orders. It is quite true. I *do* feel deeply on the subject. You see, I married one of them. But that, fortunately, is neither here nor there. What I really wished to say to you was this: I have spoken to the unhappy young woman my daughter, and find that she has no particular inclination towards Grimes. Indeed, I do not think that any daughter of mine could fall as low as that. But she is, for some reason, uncontrollably anxious to be married to somebody fairly soon. Now, I should be quite prepared to offer a partnership in Llanabba to a son-in-law of whom I approved. The income of the school is normally not less than three thousand a year–that is with the help of dear Diana's housekeeping–and my junior partner would start at an income of a thousand and of course succeed to a larger share upon my death. It is a prospect that many young men would find inviting. And I was wondering, Pennyfeather, whether by any chance, looking at the matter from a businesslike point of view, without prejudice, you understand, fair and square, taking things as they are for what they are worth, facing facts, whether possibly *you* . . . I wonder if I make myself plain?'

'No,' said Paul. 'No, sir, I'm afraid it would be impossible. I hope I don't appear rude, but–no, really, I'm afraid . . .'

'That's all right, my dear boy. Not another word! I quite understand. I was afraid that would be your answer. Well, it must be Grimes, then. I don't think it would be any use approaching Mr Prendergast.'

'It was very kind of you to suggest it, sir.'

'Not at all, not at all. The wedding shall take place a week today. You might tell Grimes that if you see him. I don't want to have more to do with him than I can help. I wonder whether it would be a good thing to give a small party?' For a moment a light sprang up in Dr Fagan's eyes and then died out. 'No, no, there will be no party. The sports were not encouraging. Poor little Lord Tangent is still laid up, I hear.'

Paul returned to the Common Room with the Doctor's message.

'Hell!' said Grimes. 'I still hoped it might fall through.'

'What d'you want for a wedding present?' Paul asked.

Grimes brightened. 'What about that binge you promised me and Prendy?'

'All right! said Paul. 'We'll have it tomorrow.'

The Hotel Metropole, Cwmpryddyg, is by far the grandest hotel in the north of Wales. It is situated on a high and healthy eminence overlooking the strip of water that railway companies have gallantly compared to the Bay of Naples. It was built in the ample days preceding the war, with a lavish expenditure on looking-glass and marble. Today it shows signs of wear, for it has never been quite as popular as its pioneers hoped. There are cracks in the cement on the main terrace, the winter garden is draughty, and one comes disconcertingly upon derelict bath-chairs in the Moorish Court. Besides this, none of the fountains ever plays, the string band that used to perform nightly in the ballroom has given place to a very expensive wireless set which one of the waiters knows how to operate, there is never any note-paper in the writing-room, and the sheets are not long enough for the beds. Philbrick pointed out these defects to Paul as he sat with Grimes and Mr Prendergast drinking cocktails in the Palm Court before dinner.

'And it isn't as though it was really cheap', he said. Philbrick had become quite genial during the last few days. 'Still, one can't expect much in Wales, and it is something. I can't live without some kind of luxury for long. I'm not staying this evening, or I'd ask you fellows to dine with me.'

'Philbrick, old boy,' said Grimes, 'me and my pals here have been wanting a word with you for some time. How about those yarns you spun about your being a shipowner and a novelist and a burglar?'

'Since you mention it,' said Philbrick with dignity, 'they were untrue. One day you shall know my full story. It is stranger than any fiction. Meanwhile I have to be back at the Castle. Good night.'

'He certainly seems quite a swell here,' said Grimes as they watched him disappear into the night escorted with every obsequy by the manager and the head-waiter. 'I dare say he *could* tell a story if he wanted to.'

'I believe it's their keys,' said Mr Prendergast suddenly. It was the first time that he had spoken. For twenty minutes he had been sitting very upright in his gilt chair and very alert, his eyes unusually bright, darting this way and that in his eagerness to miss nothing of the gay scene about him.

'What's their keys, Prendy?'

'Why, the things they get given at the counter. I thought for a long time it was money.'

'Is that what's been worrying you? Bless your heart, I thought it was the young lady in the office you were after.'

'Oh, Grimes!' said Mr Prendergast, and he blushed warmly and gave a little giggle.

Paul led his guests into the dining-room.

'I haven't taught French for nothing all these years,' said Grimes, studying the menu. 'I'll start with some jolly old *huitres*.'

Mr Prendergast ate a grape-fruit with some difficulty. 'What a big orange!' he said when he had finished it. 'They do things on a large scale here.'

The soup came in little aluminium bowls. 'What price the ancestral silver?' said Grimes. The Manchester merchants on the spree who sat all round them began to look a little askance at Paul's table.

'Someone's doing himself well on bubbly,' said Grimes as a waiter advanced staggering under the weight of an ice-pail from which emerged a Jeroboam of champagne. 'Good egg! It's coming to us.'

'With Sir Solomon Philbrick's compliments to Captain Grimes and congratulations on his approaching marriage, sir.'

Grimes took the waiter by the sleeve. 'See here, old boy, this Sir Solomon Philbrick–know him well?'

'He's here quite frequently, sir.'

'Spends a lot of money, eh?'

'He doesn't entertain at all, but he always has the best of everything himself, sir.'

'Does he pay his bill?'

'I really couldn't say, I'm afraid, sir. Would you be requiring anything else?'

'All right, old boy! Don't get sniffy. Only he's a pal of mine, see?'

'Really, Grimes,' said Mr Prendergast, 'I am afraid you made him quite annoyed with your questions, and that stout man over there is staring at us in the most marked way.'

'I've got a toast to propose. Prendy, fill up your glass. Here's to Trumpington, whoever he is, who gave us the money for this binge!'

'And here's to Philbrick,' said Paul, 'whoever *he* is!'

'And here's to Miss Fagan,' said Mr Prendergast, 'with our warmest hopes for her future happiness!'

'Amen,' said Grimes.

After the soup the worst sort of sole. Mr Prendergast made a little joke about soles and souls. Clearly the dinner-party was being a great success.

'You know,' said Grimes, 'look at it how you will, marriage is rather a grim thought.'

'The three reasons for it given in the Prayer-book have always seemed to me quite inadequate,' agreed Mr Prendergast. 'I have never had the smallest difficulty about the avoidance of fornication, and the other two advantages seem to me nothing short of disastrous.'

'My first marriage,' said Grimes, 'didn't make much odds either way. It was in Ireland. I was tight at the time, and so was the chaplain. God knows what became of Mrs Grimes. It seems to me, though, that with Flossie I'm in for a pretty solemn solemnization. It's not what I should have chosen for myself, not by a long chalk. Still, as things are, I suppose it's the best thing that could have happened. I think I've about run through the schoolmastering profession. I don't mind telling you I might have found it pretty hard to get another job. There are limits. Now I'm set up for life, and no more worry about testimonials. That's something. In fact, that's all there is to be said. But there have been moments in the last twenty-four hours, I don't mind telling you, when I've gone cold all over at the thought of what I was in for.'

'I don't want to say anything discouraging,' said Mr Prendergast, 'but I've known Flossie for nearly ten years now, and–'

'There isn't anything you can tell me about Flossie that I don't know already. I almost wish it was Dingy. I suppose it's too late now to change. Oh, dear!' said Grimes despondently, gazing into his glass. 'Oh, Lord! oh, Lord! That I should come to this!'

'Cheer up, Grimes. It isn't like you to be as depressed as this,' said Paul.

'Old friends,' said Grimes–and his voice was charged with emotion–'you see a man standing face to face with retribution. Respect him even if you cannot understand. Those that live by the flesh shall perish by the flesh. I am a very sinful man, and I am past my first youth. Who shall pity me in that dark declivity to which my steps inevitably seem to tend? I have boasted in my youth and held my head high and gone on my way careless of consequence, but ever behind me, unseen, stood stark Justice with his two-edged sword.'

More food was brought them. Mr Prendergast ate with a hearty appetite.

'Oh, why did nobody warn me?' cried Grimes in his agony. 'I should have been told. They should have told me in so many words. They should have warned me about Flossie, not about the fires of hell. I've risked them, and I don't mind risking them again, but they should have told me about marriage. They should have told me that at the end of that gay journey and flower-strewn path were the hideous lights of home and the voices of children. I should have been warned of the great lavender-scented bed that was laid out for me, of the wistaria at the windows, of all the intimacy and confidence of family life. But I dare say I shouldn't have listened. Our life is lived between two homes. We emerge for a little into the light, and then the front door closes. The chintz curtains shut out the sun, and the hearth glows with the fire of home, while upstairs, above our heads, are enacted again the awful accidents of adolescence. There's a home and family waiting for every one of us. We can't escape, try how we may. It's the seed of life we carry about with us like our skeletons, each one of us unconsciously pregnant with desirable villa residences. There's no escape. As individuals we simply do not exist. We are just potential home-builders, beavers and ants. How do we come into being? What is birth?'

'I've often wondered,' said Mr Prendergast.

'What is this impulse of two people to build their beastly home? It's you and me, unborn, asserting our presence. All we are is a manifestation of the impulse to family life, and if by chance we have escaped the itch ourselves, Nature forces it upon us another way. Flossie's got that itch enough for two. I just haven't. I'm one of the blind alleys off the main road of procreation, but it doesn't matter. Nature always wins. Oh, Lord! oh, Lord! Why didn't I die in that first awful home? Why did I ever hope I could escape?'

Captain Grimes continued his lament for some time in deep bitterness of heart. Presently he became silent and stared at his glass.

'I wonder,' said Mr Prendergast, 'I wonder whether I could have just a little more of this very excellent pheasant?'

'Anyway,' said Grimes, 'there shan't be any children; I'll see to that.'

'It has always been a mystery to me why people marry,' said Mr Prendergast. 'I can't see the smallest reason for it. Quite happy, normal people. Now I can understand it in Grimes's case. He has everything to gain by the arrangement, but what does Flossie expect to gain? And yet she seems more enthusiastic about it than Grimes. It has been the tragedy of my life that whenever I start thinking about any quite simple subject I invariably feel myself confronted by some flat contradiction of this sort. Have you ever thought about marriage–in the abstract, I mean, of course?'

'Not very much, I'm afraid.'

'I don't believe,' said Mr Prendergast, 'that people would ever fall in love or want to be married if they hadn't been told about it. It's like abroad: no one would want to go there if they hadn't been told it existed. Don't you agree?'

'I don't think you can be quite right,' said Paul; 'you see, animals fall in love quite a lot, don't they?'

'Do they?' said Prendergast. 'I didn't know that. What an extraordinary thing! But then I had an aunt whose cat used to put its paw up to its mouth when it yawned. It's wonderful what animals can be taught. There is a sea-lion at the circus, I saw in the paper, who juggles with an umbrella and two oranges.'

'I know what I'll do,' said Grimes. 'I'll get a motor-bicycle.'

This seemed to cheer him up a little. He took another glass of wine and smiled wanly. 'I'm afraid I've not been following all you chaps have said. I was thinking. What were we talking about?'

'Prendy was telling me about a sea-lion who juggled with an umbrella and two oranges.'

'Why, that's nothing. I can juggle with a whacking great bottle and a lump of ice and two knives. Look!'

'Grimes, don't! Everyone is looking at you.'

The head-waiter came over to remonstrate. 'Please remember where you are, sir,' he said.

'I know where I am well enough,' said Grimes. 'I'm in the hotel my pal Sir Solomon Philbrick is talking of buying, and I tell you this, old boy: if he does, the first person to lose his job will be you. See?'

Nevertheless he stopped juggling, and Mr Prendergast ate two *pêches Melba* undisturbed.

'The black cloud has passed,' said Grimes. 'Grimes is now going to enjoy his evening.'

13

THE PASSING OF A PUBLIC SCHOOL MAN

Six days later the school was given a half-holiday, and soon after luncheon the bigamous union of Captain Edgar Grimes and Miss Florence Selina Fagan was celebrated at the Llanabba Parish Church. A slight injury to his hand prevented Paul from playing the organ. He walked down the church with Mr Prendergast, who, greatly to his dismay, had been instructed by Dr Fagan to give away the bride.

'I do not intend to be present,' said the Doctor. 'The whole business is exceedingly painful to me.' Everybody else, however, was there except little Lord Tangent, whose foot was being amputated at a local nursing home. The boys for the most part welcomed the event as a pleasant variation to the rather irregular routine of their day. Clutterbuck alone seemed disposed to sulk.

'I don't suppose that their children will be terribly attractive,' said Beste-Chetwynde.

There were few wedding presents. The boys had subscribed a shilling each and had bought at a shop in Llandudno a silver-plated teapot, coyly suggestive of *art nouveau*. The Doctor gave them a cheque for twenty-five pounds. Mr Prendergast gave Grimes a walking stick–'because he was always borrowing mine'–and Dingy, rather generously, two photograph frames, a calendar, and a tray of Benares brassware. Paul was the best man.

The service passed off without a hitch, for Grimes's Irish wife did not turn up to forbid the banns. Flossie wore a frock of a rather noticeable velveteen and a hat with two pink feathers to match.

'I was so pleased when I found he didn't want me to wear white,' she said, 'though, of course, it might have been dyed afterwards.'

Both bride and bridegroom spoke up well in the responses, and afterwards the Vicar delivered a very moving address on the subject of Home and Conjugal Love.

'How beautiful it is,' he said, 'to see two young people in the hope of youth setting out with the Church's blessing to face life together; how much more beautiful to see them when they have grown to full manhood and womanhood coming together and saying "Our experience of life has taught us that *one* is not enough."'

The boys lined the path from the church door to the lych-gate, and the head prefect said: 'Three cheers for Captain and Mrs Grimes!'

Then they returned to the Castle. The honeymoon had been postponed until the end of term, ten days later, and the arrangements for the first days of their married life were a little meagre. 'You must do the best you can,' the Doctor had said. 'I suppose you will wish to share the same bedroom. I think there would be no objection to your both moving into the large room in the West Tower. It is a little damp, but I dare say Diana will arrange for a fire to be lighted there. You may use the morning-room in the evenings, and Captain Grimes will, of course, have his meals at my table in the dining-room, not with the boys. I do not wish to find him sitting about in the drawing-room, nor, of course, in my library. He had better keep his books and gown in the Common Room, as before. Next term I will consider some other arrangement. Perhaps I could hand over one of the lodges to you or fit up some sort of sitting-room in the tower. I was not prepared for a domestic upheaval.'

Diana, who was really coming out of the business rather creditably, put a bowl of flowers in their bedroom, and lit a fire of reckless proportions, in which she consumed the remains of a desk and two of the boys' play-boxes.

That evening, while Mr Prendergast was taking 'Prep.' at the end of the passage, Grimes visited Paul in the Common Room. He looked rather uncomfortable in his evening clothes.

'Well, dinner's over,' he said. 'The old man does himself pretty well.'

'How are you feeling?'

'Not too well, old boy. The first days are always a strain, they say, even in the most romantic marriages. My father-in-law is *not* what you might call easy. Needs thawing gently, you know. I suppose as a married man I oughtn't to go down to Mrs Roberts?'

'I think it might seem odd on the first evening, don't you?'

'Flossie's playing the piano; Dingy's making up the accounts; the old man's gone off to the library. Don't you think we've time for a quick one?'

Arm in arm they went down the familiar road.

'Drinks are on me tonight,' said Grimes.

The silver band were still sitting with their heads together discussing the division of their earnings.

'They tell me that married this afternoon you were?' said the station-master.

'That's right,' said Grimes.

'And my sister never at all you would meet whatever,' he continued reproachfully, 'because that women you do not like look you.'

'Look here, old boy,' said Grimes, 'just you shut up. You're not being tactful. See? Just you keep quiet, and I'll give you all some nice beer.'

When Mrs Roberts shut her doors for the night, Paul and Grimes turned back up the hill. A light was burning in the West Tower.

'There she is, waiting for me,' said Grimes. 'Now it might be a very romantic sight to some chaps, a light burning in a tower window. I knew a poem about a thing like that once. Forgot it now, though. I was no end of a one for poetry when I was a kid–love and all that. Castle towers came in quite a lot. Funny how one grows out of that sort of thing.'

Inside the Castle he turned off down the main corridor.

'Well, so long, old boy! This is the way I go now. See you in the morning.' The baize door swung to behind him, and Paul went up to bed.

Paul saw little of Grimes during the next few days. They met at prayers and on the way to and from their classrooms, but the baize door that separated the school from the Doctor's wing was also separating them. Mr Prendergast, now in unchallenged possession of the other easy chair, was smoking away one evening when he suddenly said:

'You know, I miss Grimes. I didn't think I should, but I do. With all his faults, he was a very cheery person. I think I was beginning to get on better with him.'

'He doesn't look as cheery as he did,' said Paul. 'I don't believe that life "above stairs" is suiting him very well.'

As it happened, Grimes chose that evening to visit them.

'D'you chaps mind if I come in for a bit?' he asked with unwonted diffidence. They rose to welcome him. 'Sure you don't mind? I won't stay long.'

'My dear man, we were just saying how much we missed you. Come and sit down.'

'Won't you have some of my tobacco?' said Prendergast.

'Thanks, Prendy! I just had to come in and have a chat. I've been feeling pretty fed up lately. Married life is *not* all beer and skittles, I don't mind telling you. It's not Flossie, mind; she's been hardly any trouble at all. In a way I've got quite to like her. She likes me, anyway, and that's the great thing. The Doctor's my trouble. He never lets me alone, that man. It gets on my nerves. Always laughing at me in a nasty kind of way and making me feel small. You know the way Lady Circumference talks to the Clutterbucks–like that. I tell you I simply dread going into meals in that dining-room. He's got a sort of air as though he always knew exactly what I was going to say before I said it, and as if it was always a little worse than he'd expected. Flossie says he treats *her* that way sometimes. He does it to me the whole time, damn him.'

'I don't expect he means it,' said Paul, 'and anyway I shouldn't bother about it.'

'That's the point. I'm beginning to feel he's quite right. I suppose I am a pretty coarse sort of chap. I don't know anything about art, and I haven't met any grand people, and I don't go to a good tailor, and all that. I'm not what he calls "out of the top drawer". I never pretended I was, but the thing is that up till now it hasn't worried me. I don't think I was a conceited sort of chap, but I felt just as good as anyone else, and I didn't care what people thought as long as I had my fun. And I *did* have fun, too, and, what's more, I enjoyed it. But now I've lived with that man for a week, I feel quite different. I feel half ashamed of myself all the time. And I've come to recognize that supercilious look he gives me in other people's eyes as well.'

'Ah, how well I know that feeling!' sighed Mr Prendergast.

'I used to think I was popular among the boys, but you know I'm not, and at Mrs Roberts' they only pretended to like me in the hope I'd stand 'em drinks. I did too, but they never gave me one back. I thought it was just because they were Welsh, but I see now it was because they despised me. I don't blame them. God knows I despise myself. You know, I used to use French phrases a certain amount–things like *savoir faire* and *Je ne sais quoi*. I never thought about it, but I suppose I haven't got much of an accent. How could I? I've never been in France except for that war. Well, every time I say one of them now the Doctor gives a sort of wince as if he's bitten on a bad tooth. I have to think the whole time now before I say anything, to see if there's any French in it or any of the expressions he doesn't think refined. Then when I do say anything my voice sounds so funny that I get in a muddle and he winces again. Old boy, it's been hell this last week, and it's worrying me. I'm getting an inferiority-complex. Dingy's like that. She just never speaks now. He's always making little jokes about Flossie's clothes, too, but I don't think the old girl sees what's he's driving at. That man'll have me crazy before the term's over.'

'Well, there's only a week more,' was all that Paul could say to comfort him.

Next morning at prayers Grimes handed Paul a letter. 'Irony,' he said.

Paul opened it and read:

John Clutterbuck & Sons
Wholesale Brewers and Wine Merchants

My Dear Grimes,

The other day at the sports you asked whether there was by any chance a job open for you at the brewery. I don't know if you were serious in this, but if you were a post has just fallen vacant which I feel might suit you. I should be glad to offer it to any friend who has been so kind to Percy. We employ a certain number of travellers to go round to various inns and hotels to sample the beer and see that it has not been diluted or in any way adulterated. Our junior traveller, who was a friend of mine from Cambridge, has just developed D.T.'s and has had to be suspended. The salary is two hundred a year with car and travelling expenses. Would this attract you at all? If so, will you let me know during the next few days.

Yours sincerely,
Sam Clutterbuck

'Just look at that,' said Grimes. 'God's own job, and mine for the asking! If that had come ten days ago my whole life might have been different.'

'You don't think of taking it now?'

'Too late, old boy, too late. The saddest words in the English language.'

In 'break' Grimes said to Paul: 'Look here, I've decided to take Sam Clutterbuck's job, and be damned to the Fagans!' His eyes shone with excitement. 'I shan't say a word to them. I shall just go off. They can do what they like about it. I don't care.'

'Splendid!' said Paul. 'It's much the best thing you can do.'

'I'm going this very afternoon,' said Grimes.

An hour later, at the end of morning-school, they met again. 'I've been thinking over that letter,' said Grimes. 'I see it all now. It's just a joke.'

'Nonsense!' said Paul. 'I'm sure it isn't. Go and see the Clutterbucks right away.'

'No, no, they don't mean it seriously. They've heard about my marriage from Percy, and they're just pulling my leg. It was too good to be true. Why should they offer *me* a job like that, even if such a wonderful job exists?'

'My dear Grimes, I'm perfectly certain it was a genuine offer. Anyway, there's nothing to lose by going to see them.'

'No, no, it's too late, old boy. Things like that don't happen.' And he disappeared beyond the baize door.

Next day there was fresh trouble at Llanabba. Two men in stout boots, bowler hats and thick grey overcoats presented themselves at the Castle with a warrant for Philbrick's arrest. Search was made for him, but it was suddenly discovered that he had already left by the morning train for Holyhead. The boys crowded round the detectives with interest and a good deal of disappointment. They were not, they thought, particularly impressive figures as they stood in the hall fingering their hats and drinking whisky and calling Dingy 'miss'.

'We've been after 'im for some time now,' said the first detective. 'Ain't we, Bill?'

'Pretty near six months. It's too bad, his getting away like this. They're getting rather restless at H.Q. about our travelling expenses.'

'Is it a very serious case?' asked Mr Prendergast. The entire school were by this time assembled in the hall. 'Not shooting or anything like that?'

'No, there ain't been no bloodshed up to date, sir. I oughtn't to tell about it, really, but seeing as you've all been mixed up in it to some extent, I don't mind telling you that I think he'll get off on a plea of insanity. Loopy, you know.'

'What's he been up to?'

'False pretences and impersonation, sir. There's five charges against him in different parts of the country, mostly at hotels. He represents himself as a rich man, stays there for some time living like a lord, cashes a big cheque and then goes off. Calls 'isself Sir Solomon Philbrick. Funny thing is, I think he really believes his tale 'isself. I've come across several cases like that one time or another. There was a bloke in Somerset what thought 'e was Bishop of Bath and Wells, and confirmed a whole lot of kids–very reverent, too.'

'Well, anyway,' said Dingy, 'he went without his wages from here.'

'I always felt there was something untrustworthy about that man,' said Mr Prendergast.

'Lucky devil!' said Grimes despondently.

'I'm worried about Grimes,' said Mr Prendergast that evening. 'I never saw a man more changed. He used to be so self-confident and self-assertive. He came in here quite timidly just now and asked me whether I believed that Divine retribution took place in this world or the next. I began to talk to him about it, but I could see he wasn't listening. He sighed once or twice and then went out without a word while I was still speaking.'

'Beste-Chetwynde tells me he has kept in the whole of the third form because the blackboard fell down in his class-room this morning. He was convinced they had arranged it on purpose.'

'Yes, they often do.'

'But in this case they hadn't. Beste-Chetwynde said they were quite frightened at the way he spoke to them. Just like an actor, Beste-Chetwynde said.'

'Poor Grimes! I think he is seriously unnerved. It will be a relief when the holidays come.'

But Captain Grimes' holiday came sooner than Mr Prendergast expected, and in a way which few people could have foreseen. Three days later he did not appear at morning prayers, and Flossie, red-eyed, admitted that he had not come in from the village the night before. Mr Davies, the station-master, confessed to seeing him earlier in the evening in a state of depression. Just before luncheon a youth presented himself at the Castle with a little pile of clothes he had found on the sea-shore. They were identified without difficulty as having belonged to the Captain. In the breast pocket of the jacket was an envelope addressed to the Doctor, and in it a slip of paper inscribed with the words: THOSE THAT LIVE BY THE FLESH SHALL PERISH BY THE FLESH.

As far as was possible this intelligence was kept from the boys.

Flossie, though severely shocked at this untimely curtailment of her married life, was firm in her resolution not to wear mourning. 'I don't think my husband would have expected it of me,' she said.

In these distressing circumstances the boys began packing their boxes to go away for the Easter holidays.

PART II

I

KING'S THURSDAY

Margot Beste-Chetwynde had two houses in England–one in London and the other in Hampshire. Her London house, built in the reign of William and Mary, was, by universal consent, the most beautiful building between Bond Street and Park Lane, but opinion was divided on the subject of her country house. This was very new indeed; in fact, it was scarcely finished when Paul went to stay there at the beginning of the Easter holidays. No single act in Mrs Beste-Chetwynde's eventful and in many ways disgraceful career had excited quite so much hostile comment as the building, or rather the rebuilding, of this remarkable house.

It was called King's Thursday, and stood on the place which since the reign of Bloody Mary had been the seat of the Earls of Pastmaster. For three centuries the poverty and inertia of this noble family had preserved its home unmodified by any of the succeeding fashions that fell upon domestic architecture. No wing had been added, no window filled in; no portico, façade, terrace, orangery, tower or battlement marred its timbered front. In the craze for coal-gas and indoor sanitation, King's Thursday had slept unscathed by plumber or engineer. The estate-carpenter, an office hereditary in the family of the original joiner who had panelled the halls and carved the great staircase, did such restorations as became necessary from time to time for the maintenance of the fabric, working with the same tools and with the traditional methods, so that in a few years his work became indistinguishable from that of his grandsires. Rush-lights still flickered in the bedrooms long after all Lord Pastmaster's neighbours were blazing away electricity, and in the last fifty years Hampshire had gradually become proud of King's Thursday. From having been considered rather a blot on the progressive county, King's Thursday gradually became the Mecca of week-end parties. 'I thought we might go over to tea at the Pastmasters',' hostesses would say after luncheon on Sundays. 'You really must see their house. Quite unspoilt, my dear. Professor Franks, who was here last week, said it was recognized as the finest piece of domestic Tudor in England.'

It was impossible to ring the Pastmasters up, but they were always at home and unaffectedly delighted to see their neighbours, and after tea Lord Pastmaster would lead the new-comers on a tour round the house, along the great galleries and into the bedrooms, and would point out the priest-hole and the closet where the third Earl imprisoned his wife for wishing to rebuild a smoking chimney. 'That chimney still smokes when the wind's in the east,' he would say, 'but we haven't rebuilt it yet.'

Later they would drive away in their big motor-cars to their modernized manors, and as they sat in their hot baths before dinner the more impressionable visitors might reflect how they seemed to have been privileged to step for an hour and a half out of their own century into the leisurely, prosaic life of the English Renaissance, and how they had talked at tea of field-sports and the reform of the Prayer-Book just as the very-great-grandparents of their host might have talked in the same chairs and before the same fire three hundred years before, when their own ancestors, perhaps, slept on straw or among the aromatic merchandize of some Hanse ghetto.

But the time came when King's Thursday had to be sold. It had been built in an age when twenty servants were not an unduly extravagant establishment, and it was scarcely possible to live there with fewer. But servants, the Beste-Chetwyndes found, were less responsive than their masters to the charms of Tudor simplicity; the bedrooms originally ordained for them among the maze of rafters that supported the arches of uneven stone roof were unsuited to modern requirements, and only the dirtiest and most tipsy of cooks could be induced to inhabit the enormous stone-flagged kitchen or turn the spits at the open fire. Housemaids tended to melt away under the recurring strain of trotting in the bleak hour before breakfast up and down the narrow servants' staircases and along the interminable passages with jugs of warm water for the morning baths. Modern democracy called for lifts and labour-saving devices, for hot-water taps and cold-water taps and (horrible invention!) drinking-water taps, for gas-rings and electric ovens.

With rather less reluctance than might have been expected, Lord Pastmaster made up his mind to sell the house; to tell the truth, he could never quite see what all the fuss was about; he supposed it was very historic, and all that, but his own taste lay towards the green shutters and semi-tropical vegetation of a villa on the French Riviera, in which, if his critics had only realized it, he was fulfilling the traditional character of his family far better than by struggling on at King's Thursday. But the county was slow to observe this, and something very like consternation was felt, not only in the Great Houses, but in the bungalows and the villas for miles about, while in the neighbouring rectories antiquarian clergymen devised folk-tales of the disasters that should come to crops and herds when there was no longer a Beste-Chetwynde at King's Thursday. Mr Jack Spire in the *London Hercules* wrote eloquently on the 'Save King's Thursday Fund', urging that it should be preserved for the nation, but only a very small amount was collected of the very large sum which Lord Pastmaster was sensible enough to demand, and the theory that it was to be transplanted and re-erected in Cincinnati found wide acceptance.

Thus the news that Lord Pastmaster's rich sister-in-law had bought the family seat was received with the utmost delight by her new neighbours and by Mr Jack Spire, and all sections of the London Press which noticed the sale. *Teneat Bene Beste-Chetwynde*, the motto carved over the chimney-piece in the great hall, was quoted exultantly on all sides, for very little was known about Margot Beste-Chetwynde in Hampshire, and the illustrated papers were always pleased to take any occasion to embellish their pages with her latest portrait; the reporter to whom she remarked: 'I can't think of anything more bourgeois and awful than timbered Tudor architecture,' did not take in what she meant or include the statement in his 'story'.

King's Thursday had been empty for two years when Margot Beste-Chetwynde bought it. She had been there once before, during her engagement.

'It's worse than I thought, far worse,' she said as she drove up the main avenue which the loyal villagers had decorated with the flags of the sometime allied nations in honour of her arrival. 'Liberty's new building cannot be compared with it,' she said, and stirred impatiently in the car, as she remembered, many years ago, the romantic young heiress, who had walked entranced among the cut yews, and had been wooed, how phlegmatically, in the odour of honeysuckle.

Mr Jack Spire was busily saving St Sepulchre's, Egg Street (where Dr Johnson is said once to have attended Matins), when Margot Beste-Chetwynde's decision to rebuild King's Thursday became public. He said, very seriously: 'Well, we did what we could,' and thought no more about it.

Not so the neighbours, who, as the work of demolition proceeded, with the aid of all that was most pulverizing in modern machinery, became increasingly enraged, and, in their eagerness to preserve for the county a little of the great manor, even resorted to predatory expeditions, from which they would return with lumps of carved stone-work for their rock-gardens, until the contractors were forced to maintain an extra watchman at night. The panelling went to South Kensington, where it has come in for a great deal of admiration from the Indian students. Within nine months of Mrs Beste-Chetwynde's taking possession the new architect was at work on his plans.

It was Otto Friedrich Silenus's first important commission. 'Something clean and square', had been Mrs Beste-Chetwynde's instructions, and then she had disappeared on one of her mysterious world-tours, saying as she left: 'Please see that it is finished by the spring.'

Professor Silenus–for that was the title by which this extraordinary young man chose to be called–was a 'find' of Mrs Beste-Chetwynde's. He was not yet very famous anywhere, though all who met him carried away deep and diverse impressions of his genius. He had first attracted Mrs Beste-Chetwynde's attention with the rejected design for a chewing-gum factory which had been reproduced in a progressive Hungarian quarterly. His only other completed work was the *décor* for a cinema-film of great length and complexity of plot–a complexity rendered the more inextricable by the producer's austere elimination of all human characters, a fact which had proved fatal to its commercial success. He was starving resignedly in a bed-sitting-room in Bloomsbury, despite the untiring efforts of his parents to find him–they were very rich in Hamburg–when he was offered the commission of rebuilding King's Thursday. 'Something clean and square'–he pondered for three hungry days upon the aesthetic implications of these instructions, and then began his designs.

'The problem of architecture as I see it,' he told a journalist who had come to report on the progress of his surprising creation of ferro-concrete and aluminium, 'is the problem of all art–the elimination of the human element from the consideration of form. The only perfect building must be the factory, because that is built to house machines, not men. I do not think it is possible for domestic architecture to be beautiful, but I am doing my best. All ill comes from man,' he said gloomily; 'please tell your readers that. Man is never beautiful; he is never happy except when he becomes the channel for the distribution of mechanical forces.'

The journalist looked doubtful. 'Now, Professor,' he said, 'tell me this. About how much do you reckon to make out of this job, if you don't mind my asking?'

'Fuel,' said Professor Silenus. 'While the work is being done, the machine must be fed. After that let it stand idle or be set to other work. Why should I receive fuel when I am not working?'

'Peer's Sister's-in-Law Mansion Builder refuses fee,' thought the journalist happily. 'Will machines live in houses? Amazing forecast of Professor-Architect.'

Professor Silenus watched the reporter disappear down the drive and then, taking a biscuit from his pocket, began to munch.

'I suppose there ought to be a staircase,' he said gloomily. 'Why can't the creatures stay in one place? Up and down, in and out, round and round! Why can't they sit still and work? Do dynamos require staircases? Do monkeys require houses? What an immature, self-destructive, antiquated mischief is man! How obscure and gross his prancing and chattering on his little stage of evolution! How loathsome and beyond words boring all the thoughts and self-approval of this biological by-product! This half-formed, ill-conditioned body! this erratic maladjusted mechanism of his soul: on one side the harmonious instincts and balanced responses of the animal, on the other the inflexible purpose of the engine, and between them man, equally alien from the *being* of Nature and the *doing* of the machine, the vile *becoming*!'

Two hours later the foreman in charge of the concrete-mixer came to consult with the Professor. He had not moved from where the journalist had left him; his fawn-like eyes were fixed and inexpressive, and the hand which had held the biscuit still rose and fell to and from his mouth with a regular motion, while his empty jaws champed rhythmically; otherwise he was wholly immobile.

2

INTERLUDE IN BELGRAVIA

Arthur Potts knew all about King's Thursday and Professor Silenus.

On the day of Paul's arrival in London he rang up his old friend and arranged to dine with him at the Queen's Restaurant in Sloane Square. It seemed quite natural that they should be again seated at the table where they had discussed so many subjects of public importance, Budgets and birth control and Byzantine mosaics. For the first time since the disturbing evening of the Bollinger dinner he felt at ease. Llanabba Castle, with its sham castellations and preposterous inhabitants, had sunk into the oblivion that waits upon even the most lurid of nightmares. Here were sweet corn and pimentoes, and white Burgundy, and the grave eyes of Arthur Potts, and there on the peg over his head hung the black hat he had bought in St James' that afternoon. For an evening at least the shadow that has flitted about this narrative under the name of Paul Pennyfeather materialized into the solid figure of an intelligent, well-educated, well-conducted young man, a man who could be trusted to use his vote at a general election with discretion and proper detachment, whose opinion on a *ballet* or a critical essay was rather better than most people's, who could order a dinner without embarrassment and in a creditable French accent, who could be trusted to see to luggage at foreign railway-stations and might be expected to acquit himself with decision and decorum in all the emergencies of civilized life. This was the Paul Pennyfeather who had been developing in the placid years which preceded this story. In fact, the whole of this book is really an account of the mysterious disappearance of Paul Pennyfeather, so that readers must not complain if the shadow which took his name does not amply fill the important part of hero for which he was originally cast.

'I saw some of Otto Silenus' work at Munich,' said Potts. 'I think that he's a man worth watching. He was in Moscow at one time and in the Bauhaus at Dessau. He can't be more than twenty-five now. There were some photographs of King's Thursday in a paper the other day. It looked extraordinarily interesting. It's said to be the only really *imaginative* building since the French Revolution. He's got right away from Corbusier, anyway.'

'If people only realized,' said Paul, 'Corbusier is a pure nineteenth-century, Manchester school utilitarian, and that's why they like him.'

Then Paul told Potts about the death of Grimes and the doubts of Mr Prendergast, and Potts told Paul about rather an interesting job he had got under the League of Nations and how he had decided not to take his Schools in consequence and of the unenlightened attitude adopted in the matter by Potts' father.

For an evening Paul became a real person again, but next day he woke up leaving himself disembodied somewhere between Sloane Square and Onslow Square. He had to meet Beste-Chetwynde and catch a morning train to King's Thursday, and there his extraordinary adventures began anew. From the point of view of this story Paul's second disappearance is necessary, because, as the reader will probably have discerned already, Paul Pennyfeather would never have made a hero, and the only interest about him arises from the unusual series of events of which his shadow was witness.

3

PERVIGILIUM VENERIS

'I'm looking forward to seeing our new house,' said Beste-Chetwynde as they drove out from the station. 'Mamma says it may be rather a surprise.'

The lodges and gates had been left undisturbed, and the lodge-keeper's wife, white-aproned as Mrs Noah, bobbed at the car as it turned into the avenue. The temperate April sunlight fell through the budding chestnuts and revealed between their trunks green glimpses of parkland and the distant radiance of a lake. 'English spring,' thought Paul. 'In the dreaming ancestral beauty of the English country.' Surely, he thought, these great chestnuts in the morning sun stood for something enduring and serene in a world that had lost its reason and would so stand when the chaos and confusion were forgotten? And surely it was the spirit of William Morris that whispered to him in Margot Beste-Chetwynde's motor-car about seed-time and harvest, the superb succession of the seasons, the harmonious inter-dependence of rich and poor, of dignity, innocence and tradition? But at a turn in the drive the cadence of his thoughts was abruptly transected. They had come into sight of the house.

'Golly!' said Beste-Chetwynde. 'Mamma has done herself proud this time.'

The car stopped. Paul and Beste-Chetwynde got out, stretched themselves, and were led across a floor of bottle-green glass into the dining-room, where Mrs Beste-Chetwynde was already seated at the vulcanite table beginning her luncheon.

'My dears,' she cried, extending a hand to each of them, 'how divine to see you! I have been waiting for this to go straight to bed.'

She was a thousand times more beautiful than all Paul's feverish recollections of her. He watched her, transported.

'Darling boy, how are you?' she said. 'Do you know, you're beginning to look rather lovely in a coltish kind of way. Don't you think so, Otto?'

Paul had noticed nothing in the room except Mrs Beste-Chetwynde; he now saw that there was a young man sitting beside her, with very fair hair and large glasses, behind which his eyes lay like slim fish in an aquarium; they woke from their slumber, flashed iridescent in the light, and darted towards little Beste-Chetwynde.

'His head is too big, and his hands are too small,' said Professor Silenus. 'But his skin is pretty.'

'How would it be if I made Mr Pennyfeather a cocktail?' Beste-Chetwynde asked.

'Yes, Peter, dear, do. He makes them rather well. You can't think what a week I've had, moving in and taking the neighbours round the house and the Press photographers. Otto's house doesn't seem to be a great success with the county, does it, Otto? What was it Lady Vanbrugh said?'

'Was that the woman like Napoleon the Great?'

'Yes, darling.'

'She said she understood that the drains were satisfactory, but that, of course, they were underground. I asked her if she wished to make use of them, and said that I did, and went away. But, as a matter of fact, she was quite right. They are the only tolerable part of the house. How glad I shall be when the mosaics are finished, and I can go!'

'Don't you like it?' asked Peter Beste-Chetwynde over the cocktail shaker. 'I think it's so good. It was rather Chokey's taste before.'

'I hate and detest every bit of it,' said Professor Silenus gravely. 'Nothing I have ever done has caused me so much disgust.' With a deep sigh he rose from the table and walked from the room, the fork with which he had been eating still held in his hand.

'Otto has real genius,' said Mrs Beste-Chetwynde. 'You must be sweet to him, Peter. There's a whole lot of people coming down tomorrow for the week-end, and, my dear, that Maltravers has invited himself again. You wouldn't like him for a stepfather, would you, darling?'

'No,' said Peter. 'If you must marry again, do choose someone young and quiet.'

'Peter, you're an angel. I will. But now I'm going to bed. I had to wait to see you both. Show Mr Pennyfeather the way about, darling.'

The aluminium lift shot up, and Paul came down to earth.

'That's an odd thing to ask me in a totally strange house,' said Peter Beste-Chetwynde. 'Anyway, let's have some luncheon.'

It was three days before Paul next saw Mrs Beste-Chetwynde.

'Don't you think that she's the most wonderful woman in the world?' said Paul.

'Wonderful? In what way?'

He and Professor Silenus were standing on the terrace after dinner. The half-finished mosaics at their feet were covered with planks and sacking; the great colonnade of black glass pillars shone in the moonlight; beyond the polished aluminium balustrade the park stretched silent and illimitable.

'The most beautiful and the most free. She almost seems like the creature of a different species. Don't you feel that?'

'No,' said the Professor after a few moments' consideration. 'I can't say that I do. If you compare her with other women of her age you will see that the particulars in which she differs from them are infinitesimal compared with the points of similarity. A few millimetres here and a few millimetres there, such variations are inevitable in the human reproductive system; but in all her essential functions–her digestion, for example–she conforms to type.'

'You might say that about anybody.'

'Yes, I do. But it's Margot's variations that I dislike so much. They are small, but obtrusive, like the teeth of a saw. Otherwise I might marry her.'

'Why do you think she would marry you?'

'Because, as I said, all her essential functions are normal. Anyway, she asked me to twice. The first time I said I would think it over, and the second time I refused. I'm sure I was right. She would interrupt me terribly. Besides, she's getting old. In ten years she will be almost worn out.'

Professor Silenus looked at his watch–a platinum disc from Cartier, the gift of Mrs Beste-Chetwynde. 'Quarter to ten,' he said. 'I must go to bed.' He threw the end of his cigar clear of the terrace in a glowing parabola. 'What do you take to make you sleep?'

'I sleep quite easily,' said Paul, 'except on trains.'

'You're lucky. Margot takes veronal. I haven't been to sleep for over a year. That's why I go to bed early. One needs more rest if one doesn't sleep.'

That night as Paul marked his place in *The Golden Bough*, and, switching off his light, turned over to sleep, he thought of the young man a few bedrooms away, lying motionless in the darkness, his hands at his sides, his legs stretched out, his eyes closed and his brain turning and turning regularly all the night through, drawing in more and more power, storing it away like honey in its intricate cells and galleries, till the atmosphere about it became exhausted and vitiated and only the brain remained turning and turning in the darkness.

So Margot Beste-Chetwynde wanted to marry Otto Silenus, and in another corner of this extraordinary house she lay in a drugged trance, her lovely body cool and fragrant and scarcely stirring beneath the bedclothes; and outside in the park a thousand creatures were asleep; and beyond that, again, were Arthur Potts, and Mr Prendergast, and the Llanabba station-master. Quite soon Paul fell asleep. Downstairs Peter Beste-Chetwynde mixed himself another brandy and soda and turned a page in Havelock Ellis, which, next to *The Wind in the Willows*, was his favourite book.

The aluminium blinds shot up, and the sun poured in through the vita-glass, filling the room with beneficent rays. Another day had begun at King's Thursday.

From his bathroom-window Paul looked down on to the terrace. The coverings had been removed, revealing the half-finished pavement of silver and scarlet. Professor Silenus was already out there directing two workmen with the aid of a chart.

The week-end party arrived at various times in the course of the day, but Mrs Beste-Chetwynde kept to her room while Peter received them in the prettiest way possible. Paul never learned all their names, nor was he ever sure how many of them there were. He supposed about eight or nine, but as they all wore so many different clothes of identically the same kind, and spoke in the same voice, and appeared so irregularly at meals, there may have been several more or several less.

The first to come were The Hon. Miles Malpractice and David Lennox, the photographer. They emerged with little shrieks from an Edwardian electric brougham and made straight for the nearest looking-glass.

In a minute the panatrope was playing, David and Miles were dancing, and Peter was making cocktails. The party had begun. Throughout the afternoon new guests arrived, drifting in vaguely or running in with cries of welcome just as they thought suited them best.

Pamela Popham, square-jawed and resolute as a big-game huntress, stared round the room through her spectacles, drank three cocktails, said: 'My God!' twice, cut two or three of her friends, and stalked off to bed.

'Tell Olivia I've arrived when she comes,' she said to Peter.

After dinner they went to a whist drive and dance in the village hall. By half-past two the house was quiet; at half-past three Lord Parakeet arrived, slightly drunk and in evening clothes, having 'just escaped less than one second ago' from Alastair Trumpington's twenty-first birthday party in London.

'Alastair was with me some of the way,' he said, 'but I think he must have fallen out.'

The party, or some of it, reassembled in pyjamas to welcome him. Parakeet walked round birdlike and gay, pointing his thin white nose and making rude little jokes at everyone in turn in a shrill, emasculate voice. At four the house was again at rest.

Only one of the guests appeared to be at all ill at ease: Sir Humphrey Maltravers, the Minister of Transportation. He arrived early in the day with a very large car and two very small suit-cases, and from the first showed himself as a discordant element in the gay little party by noticing the absence of their hostess.

'Margot? No, I haven't seen her at all. I don't believe she's terribly well,' said one of them, 'or perhaps she's lost somewhere in the house. Peter will know.'

Paul found him seated alone in the garden after luncheon, smoking a large cigar, his big red hands folded before him, a soft hat tilted over his eyes, his big red face both defiant and disconsolate. He bore a preternatural resemblance to his caricatures in the evening papers, Paul thought.

'Hullo, young man!' he said. 'Where's everybody?'

'I think Peter's taking them on a tour round the house. It's much more elaborate than it looks from outside. Would you care to join them?'

'No, thank you, not for me. I came here for a rest. These young people tire me. I have enough of the House during the week.' Paul laughed politely. 'It's the devil of a session. You keen on politics at all?'

'Hardly at all,' Paul said.

'Sensible fellow! I can't think why I keep on at it. It's a dog's life, and there's no money in it, either. If I'd stayed at the Bar I'd have been a rich man by now.

'Rest, rest and riches,' he said–'it's only after forty one begins to value things of that kind. And half one's life, perhaps, is lived after forty. Solemn thought that. Bear it in mind, young man, and it will save you from most of the worst mistakes. If everyone at twenty realized that half his life was to be lived after forty ...

'Mrs Beste-Chetwynde's cooking and Mrs Beste-Chetwynde's garden,' said Sir Humphrey meditatively. 'What could be desired more except our fair hostess herself? Have you known her long?'

'Only a few weeks,' Paul said.

'There's no one like her,' said Sir Humphrey. He drew a deep breath of smoke. Beyond the yew hedges the panatrope could be faintly heard. 'What did she want to build this house for?' he asked. 'It all comes of this set she's got into. It's not doing her any good. Damned awkward position to be in–a rich woman without a husband! Bound to get herself talked about. What Margot ought to do is to marry–someone who would stabilize her position, someone,' said Sir Humphrey, 'with a position in public life.'

And then, without any apparent connection of thought, he began talking about himself. '"Aim high" has been my motto,' said Sir Humphrey, 'all through my life. You probably won't get what you want, but you may get something; aim low, and you get nothing at all. It's like throwing a stone at a cat. When I was a kid that used to be great sport in our yard; I dare say you were throwing cricket-balls when you were that age, but it's the same thing. If you throw straight at it, you fall short; aim above, and with luck you score. Every kid knows that. I'll tell you the story of my life.'

Why was it, Paul wondered, that everyone he met seemed to specialize in this form of autobiography? He supposed he must have a sympathetic air. Sir Humphrey told of his early life: of a family of nine living in two rooms, of a father who drank and a mother who had fits, of a sister who went on the streets, of a brother who went to prison, of another brother who was born deaf-mute. He told of scholarships and polytechnics, of rebuffs and encouragements, of a University career of brilliant success and unexampled privations.

'I used to do proof-reading for the Holywell Press,' he said; 'then I learned shorthand and took down the University sermons for the local papers.'

As he spoke the clipped yews seemed to grow grey with the soot of the slums, and the panatrope in the distance took on the gay regularity of a barrel-organ heard up a tenement-staircase.

'We were a pretty hot lot at Scone in my time,' he said, naming several high officers of state with easy familiarity, 'but none of them had so far to go as I had.'

Paul listened patiently, as was his habit. Sir Humphrey's words flowed easily, because, as a matter of fact, he was rehearsing a series of articles he had dictated the evening before for publication in a Sunday newspaper. He told Paul about his first briefs and his first general election, the historic Liberal campaign of 1906, and of the strenuous days just before the formation of the Coalition.

'I've nothing to be ashamed of,' said Sir Humphrey. 'I've gone further than most people. I suppose that, if I keep on, I may one day lead the party. But all this winter I've been feeling that I've got as far as I shall ever get. I've got to the time when I should like to go into the other House and give up work and perhaps keep a race-horse or two'–and his eyes took on the far-away look of a popular actress describing the cottage of her dreams–'and a yacht and a villa at Monte. The others can do that when they like, and they know it. It's not till you get to my age that you really feel the disadvantage of having been born poor.'

On Sunday evening Sir Humphrey suggested a 'hand of cards'. The idea was received without enthusiasm.

'Wouldn't that be rather *fast*?' said Miles. 'It *is* Sunday. I think cards are divine, particularly the kings. Such *naughty* old faces! But if I start playing for money I always lose my temper and cry. Ask Pamela; she's so brave and manly.'

'Let's all play billiards and make a Real House Party of it,' said David, 'or shall we have a Country House Rag?'

'Oh, I do feel such a *rip*,' said Miles when he was at last persuaded to play. Sir Humphrey won. Parakeet lost thirty pounds, and opening his pocket-book, paid him in ten-pound notes.

'How he did cheat!' said Olivia on the way to bed.

'Did he, darling? Well, let's *jolly well* not pay him,' said Miles.

'It never occurred to me to do such a thing. Why, I couldn't afford to possibly.'

Peter tossed Sir Humphrey double or quits, and won.

'After all, I am host,' he explained.

'When I was your age,' said Sir Humphrey to Miles, 'we used to sit up all night sometimes playing poker. Heavy money, too.'

'Oh, you wicked old thing!' said Miles.

Early on Monday morning the Minister of Transportation's Daimler disappeared down the drive. 'I rather think he expected to see mamma,' said Peter. 'I told him what was the matter with her.'

'You shouldn't have done that,' said Paul.

'No, it didn't go down awfully well. He said that he didn't know what things were coming to and that even in the slums such things were not spoken about by children of my age. What a lot he ate! I did my best to make him feel at home, too, by talking about trains.'

'I thought he was a very sensible old man,' said Professor Silenus. 'He was the only person who didn't think it necessary to say something polite about the house. Besides, he told me about a new method of concrete construction they're trying at one of the Government Superannuation Homes.'

Peter and Paul went back to their cylindrical study and began another spelling-lesson.

As the last of the guests departed Mrs Beste-Chetwynde reappeared from her little bout of veronal, fresh and exquisite as a seventeenth-century lyric. The meadow of green glass seemed to burst into flower under her feet as she passed from the lift to the cocktail table.

'You poor angels!' she said. 'Did you have the hell of a time with Maltravers? And all those people? I quite forget who asked to come this week-end. I gave up inviting people long ago,' she said, turning to Paul, 'but it didn't make bit of difference.' She gazed into the opalescent depths of her *absinthe frappé*. 'More and more I feel the need of a husband, but Peter is horribly fastidious.'

'Well, your men are so awful,' said Peter, 'and tend to get flirtatious with me.'

'I sometimes think of marrying old Maltravers,' said Mrs Beste-Chetwynde, 'just to get my own back, only "Margot Maltravers" does sound a little too much, don't you think? And if they give him a peerage, he's bound to choose something quite awful. . . .'

In the whole of Paul's life no one had ever been quite so sweet to him as was Margot Beste-Chetwynde during the next few days. Up and down the shining lift shafts, in and out of the rooms and along the labyrinthine corridors of the great house he moved in a golden mist. Each morning as he dressed a bird seemed to be singing in his heart, and as he lay down to sleep he would pillow his head against a hand about which still hung a delicate fragrance of Margot Beste-Chetwynde's almost unprocurable scent.

'Paul, dear,' she said one day as hand in hand, after a rather fearful encounter with a swan, they reached the shelter of the lake house, 'I can't bear to think of you going back to that awful school. Do, please, write and tell Dr Fagan that you won't.'

The lake house was an eighteenth-century pavilion, built on a little mound above the water. They stood there for a full minute still hand in hand on the crumbling steps.

'I don't quite see what else I could do,' said Paul.

'Darling, *I* could find you a job.'

'What sort of job, Margot?' Paul's eyes followed the swan gliding serenely across the lake; he did not dare to look at her.

'Well, Paul, you might stay and protect me from swans, mightn't you?' Margot paused and then, releasing her hand, took a cigarette-case from her pocket. Paul struck a match. 'My dear, what an unsteady hand! I'm afraid you're drinking too many of Peter's cocktails' That child has a lot to learn yet about the use of vodka. But seriously, I'm sure I can find you a better job. It's absurd your going back to Wales. I still manage a great deal of my father's business, you know, or perhaps you didn't. It was mostly in South America in–in places of entertainment, cabarets and hotels and theatres, you know, and things like that. I'm sure I could find you a job helping in that, if you think you'd like it.'

Paul thought of this gravely. 'Oughtn't I to know Spanish?' he said. It seemed quite a sensible question, but Margot threw away her cigarette with a little laugh and said: 'It's time to go and change. You are being difficult this evening, aren't you?'

Paul thought about this conversation as he lay in his bath–a sunk bath of malachite–and all the time while he dressed and as he tied his tie he trembled from head to foot like one of the wire toys which street vendors dangle from trays.

At dinner Margot talked about matters of daily interest, about some jewels she was having reset, and how they had come back all wrong; and how all the wiring of her London house was being overhauled because of the fear of fire; and how the man she had left in charge of her villa at Cannes had a made a fortune at the Casino and given her notice, and she was afraid she might have to go out there to arrange about it; and how the Society for the Preservation of Ancient Buildings was demanding a guarantee that she would not demolish her castle in Ireland; and how her cook seemed to be going off his head that night, the dinner was so dull; and how Bobby Pastmaster was trying to borrow money from her again, on the grounds that she had misled him when she bought his house and that if he had known she was going to pull it down he would have made her pay more. 'Which is not logical of Bobby,' she said. 'The less I valued his house, the less I ought to have paid, surely? Still, I'd better send him something, otherwise he'll go and marry, and I think it may be nice for Peter to have the title when he grows up.'

Later, when they were alone, she said: 'People talk a great deal of nonsense about being rich. Of course it is a bore in some ways, and it means endless work, but I wouldn't be poor, or even moderately well-off, for all the ease in the world. Would you be happy if you were rich, do you think?'

'Well, it depends how I got the money,' said Paul.

'I don't see how that comes in.'

'No, I don't quite mean that. What I mean is that I think there's only one thing that could make me really happy, and if I got that I should be rich too, but it wouldn't matter being rich, you see, because, however rich I was, and I hadn't got what would make me happy, I shouldn't be happy, you see.'

'My precious, that's rather obscure,' said Margot, 'but I think it may mean something rather sweet.' He looked up at her, and her eyes met his unfalteringly. 'If it does, I'm glad,' she added.

'Margot, darling, beloved, please, will you marry me?' Paul was on his knees by her chair, his hands on hers.

'Well, that's rather what I've been wanting to discuss with you all day.' But surely there was a tremor in her voice?

'Does that mean that possibly you might, Margot? Is there a chance that you will?'

'I don't see why not. Of course we must ask Peter about it, and there are other things we ought to discuss first,' and then, quite suddenly, 'Paul, dear, dear creature, come here.'

They found Peter in the dining-room eating a peach at the sideboard.

'Hallo, you two!' he said.

'Peter, we've something to tell you,' said Margot. 'Paul says he wants me to marry him.'

'Splendid!' said Peter. 'I *am* glad. Is that what you've been doing in the library?'

'Then you don't mind?' said Paul.

'Mind? It's what I've been trying to arrange all this week. As a matter of fact, that's why I brought you here at all. I think it's altogether admirable,' he said, taking another peach.

'You're the first man he's said that about, Paul. I think it's rather a good omen.'

'Oh, Margot, let's get married at once.'

'My dear, I haven't said that I'm going to yet. I'll tell you in the morning.'

'No, tell me now, Margot. You do like me a little, don't you? Please marry me just terribly soon.'

'I'll tell you in the morning. There're several things I must think about first. let's go back to the library.'

That night Paul found it unusually difficult to sleep. Long after he had shut his book and turned out the light he lay awake, his eyes open, his thoughts racing uncontrollably. As in the first night of his visit, he felt the sleepless, involved genius of the house heavy about his head. He and Margot and Peter and Sir Humphrey Maltravers were just insignificant incidents in the life of the house: this new-born monster to whose birth ageless and forgotten cultures had been in travail. For half an hour he lay looking into the darkness until gradually his thoughts began to separate themselves from himself, and he knew he was falling asleep. Suddenly he was roused to consciousness by the sound of his door opening gently. He could see nothing, but he heard the rustle of silk as someone came into the room. Then the door shut again.

'Paul, are you asleep?'

'Margot!'

'Hush, dear! Don't turn on the light. Where are you?' The silk rustled again as though falling to the ground. 'It's best to make sure, isn't it, darling, before we decide anything? It may be just an idea of yours that you're in love with me. And, you see, Paul, I like you so very much, it would be a pity to make a mistake, wouldn't it?'

But happily there was no mistake, and next day Paul and Margot announced their engagement.

4

RESURRECTION

Crossing the hall one afternoon a few days later, Paul met a short man with a long red beard stumping along behind the footman towards Margot's study.

'Good lord!' he said.

'Not a word, old boy!' said the bearded man as he passed on.

A few minutes later Paul was joined by Peter. 'I say, Paul,' he said, 'who do you think's talking to Mamma?'

'I know,' said Paul. 'It's a very curious thing.'

'I somehow never felt he was dead,' said Peter. 'I told Clutterbuck that to try and cheer him up.'

'Did it?'

'Not very much,' Peter admitted. 'My argument was that if he'd really gone out to sea he would have left his wooden leg behind with his clothes, but Clutterbuck said he was very sensitive about his leg. I wonder what he's come to see Mamma about?'

A little later they ambushed him in the drive, and Grimes told them. 'Forgive the beaver,' he said, 'but it's rather important at the moment.'

'In the soup again?' asked Paul.

'Well, not exactly, but things have been rather low lately. The police are after me. That suicide didn't go down well. I was afraid it wouldn't. They began to fuss a bit about no body being found and about my game leg. And then my other wife turned up, and that set them thinking. Hence the vegetation. Clever of you two to spot me.'

They led him back to the house, and Peter mixed him a formidable cocktail, the principal ingredients of which were absinthe and vodka.

'It's the old story,' said Grimes. 'Grimes has fallen on his feet again. By the way, old boy, I have to congratulate you, haven't I? You've done pretty well for yourself, too.' His eye travelled appreciatively over the glass floor, and the pneumatic rubber furniture, and the porcelain ceiling, and the leather-hung walls. 'It's not everyone's taste,' he said, 'but I think you'll be comfortable. Funny thing, I never expected to see you when I came down here.'

'What we want to know,' said Peter, 'is what brought you down to see Mamma at all.'

'Just good fortune,' said Grimes. 'It was like this. After I left Llanabba I was rather at a loose end. I'd borrowed a fiver from Philbrick just before he left, and that got me to London, but for a week or so things were rather thin. I was sitting in a pub one day in Shaftesbury Avenue, feeling my beard rather warm and knowing I only had about five bob left in the world, when I noticed a chap staring at me pretty hard in the other corner of the bar. He came over after a bit and said: "Captain Grimes, I think?" That rather put the wind up me. "No, no, old boy," I said, "quite wrong, rotten shot. Poor old Grimes is dead, drowned. Davy Jones' locker, old boy!" And I made to leave. Of course it wasn't a very sensible thing to say, because, if I hadn't been Grimes, it was a hundred to one against my knowing Grimes was dead, if you see what I mean. "Pity," he said, "because I heard old Grimes was down on his luck, and I had a job I thought might suit him. Have a drink, anyway." Then I realized who he was. He was an awful stout fellow called Bill, who'd been quartered with me in Ireland. "Bill," I said, "I thought you were a bobby." "That's all right, old boy," said Bill. Well, it appeared that this Bill had gone off to the Argentine after the war and had got taken on as manager of a . . .'–Grimes stopped as though suddenly reminded of something–'a place of entertainment. Sort of night club, you know. Well, he'd done rather well in that job, and had been put in charge of a whole chain of places of entertainment all along the coast. They're a syndicate owned in England. He'd come back on leave to look for a couple of chaps to go out with him and help. "The Dagos are no use at the job," he said, "not dispassionate enough." Had to be chaps who could control themselves where women were concerned. That's what made him think of me. But it was a pure act of God, our meeting.

'Well, apparently the syndicate was first founded by young Beste-Chetwynde's grandpapa, and Mrs Beste-Chetwynde still takes an interest in it, so I was sent down to interview her and see if she agreed to the appointment. It never occurred to me it was the same Mrs Beste-Chetwynde who came down to the sports the day Prendy got so tight. Only shows how small the world is, doesn't it?'

'Did Mamma give you the job?' asked Peter.

'She did, and fifty pounds advance on my wages, and some jolly sound advice. It's been a good day for Grimes. Heard from the old man lately, by the way?'

'Yes,' said Paul, 'I got a letter this morning,' and he showed it to Grimes:

Llanabba Castle
North Wales

My Dear Pennyfeather,

Thank you for your letter and for the enclosed cheque! I need hardly tell you that it is a real disappointment to me to hear that you are not returning to us next term. I had looked forward to a long and mutually profitable connection. However, my daughters and I join in wishing you every happiness in your married life. I hope you will use your new influence to keep Peter at the school. He is a boy for whom I have great hopes. I look to him as one of my prefects in the future.

The holidays so far have afforded me little rest. My daughters and I have been much worried by the insistence of a young Irish woman of most disagreeable appearance and bearing who claims to be the widow of poor Captain Grimes. She has got hold of some papers which seem to support her claim. The police, too, are continually here asking impertinent questions about the number of suits of clothes my unfortunate son-in-law possessed.

Besides this, I have had a letter from Mr Prendergast stating that he too wishes to resign his post. Apparently he has been reading a series of articles by a popular bishop and has discovered that there is a species of person called a 'Modern Churchman' who draws the full salary of a beneficed clergymen and need not commit himself to any religious belief. This seems to be a comfort to him, but it adds greatly to my own inconvenience.

Indeed, I hardly think that I have the heart to keep on at Llanabba. I have had an offer from a cinema company, the managing director of which, oddly enough, is called Sir Solomon Philbrick, who wish to buy the Castle. They say that it's combination of mediaeval and Georgian architecture is a unique advantage. My daughter Diana is anxious to start a nursing-home or an hotel. So you see that things are not easy.

Yours sincerely,
Augustus Fagan

There was another surprise in store for Paul that day. Hardly had Grimes left the house when a tall young man with a black hat and thoughtful eyes presented himself at the front door and asked for Mr Pennyfeather. It was Potts.

'My dear fellow,' said Paul, 'I am glad to see you.'

'I saw your engagement in *The Times*,' said Potts, 'and, as I was in the neighbourhood, I wondered if you'd let me see the house.'

Paul and Peter led him all over it and explained its intricacies. He admired the luminous ceiling in Mrs Beste-Chetwynde's study and the india-rubber fungi in the recessed conservatory and the little drawing-room, of which the floor was a large kaleidoscope, set in motion by an electric button. They took him up in the lift to the top of the great pyramidical tower, from which he could look down on the roofs and domes of glass and aluminium which glittered like Chanel diamonds in the afternoon sun. But it was not this that he had come to see. As soon as he and Paul were alone he said, as though casually: 'Who was that little man I met coming down the drive?'

'I think he was something to do with the Society for the Preservation of Ancient Buildings,' said Paul. 'Why?'

'Are you sure?' asked Potts in evident disappointment. 'How maddening! I've been on a false scent again.'

'Are you doing Divorce Court shadowings, Potts?'

'No, no, it's all to do with the League of Nations,' said Potts, vaguely, and he called attention to the tank of octopuses which was so prominent a feature of the room in which they were standing.

Margot invited Potts to stay to dinner. He tried hard to make a good impression on Professor Silenus, but in this he was not successful. In fact, it was probably Potts' visit which finally drove the Professor from the house. At any rate, he left early the next morning without troubling to pack or remove his luggage. Two days later, when they were all out, he arrived in a car and took away his mathematical instruments, and some time after that again appeared to fetch two clean handkerchiefs and a change of underclothes. That was the last time he was seen at King's Thursday. When Margot and Paul went up to London, they had his luggage packed and left downstairs for him in case he should come again, but there it stayed, none of the male servants finding anything in it that he would care to wear. Long afterwards Margot saw the head gardener's son going to church in a *batik* tie of Professor Silenus' period. It was the last relic of a great genius, for before that King's Thursday had been again rebuilt.

5

THE LATIN-AMERICAN ENTERTAINMENT CO. LTD

At the end of April Peter returned to Llanabba, Dr Fagan having announced that the sale of the Castle had not been effected, and Margot and Paul went up to London to make arrangements for the wedding, which, contrary to all reasonable expectation, Margot decided was to take place in church with all the barbaric concomitants of bridesmaids, Mendelssohn and Mumm. But before the wedding she had a good deal of South American business to see to.

'My first honeymoon was rather a bore,' she said, 'so I'm not taking any chances with this one. I must get everything settled before we start, and then we're going to have the three best months of your life.'

The work seemed to consist chiefly of interviewing young women for jobs in cabarets and as dancing partners. With some reluctance Margot allowed Paul to be present one morning as she saw a new batch. The room in which she conducted her business was the Sports Room, which had been decorated for her, in her absence, by little Davy Lennox, the society photographer. Two stuffed buffaloes stood one on each side of the door. The carpet was of grass-green marked out with white lines, and the walls were hung with netting. The lights were in glass footballs, and the furniture was ingeniously designed of bats and polo-sticks and golf-clubs. Athletic groups of the early 'nineties and a painting of a prize ram hung on the walls.

'It's terribly common,' said Margot, 'but it rather impresses the young ladies, which is a good thing. Some of them tend to be rather mannery if they aren't kept in order.'

Paul sat in the corner–on a chair made in the shape of an inflated Channel swimmer–enraptured at her business ability. All her vagueness had left her; she sat upright at the table, which was covered with Balmoral tartan, her pen poised over an inkpot, which was set in a stuffed grouse, the very embodiment of the Feminist movement. One by one the girls were shown in.

'Name?' said Margot.

'Pompilia de la Conradine.'

Margot wrote it down.

'Real name?'

'Bessy Brown.'

'Age?'

'Twenty-two.'

'Real age?'

'Twenty-two.'

'Experience?'

'I was at Mrs Rosenbaum's, in Jermyn Street, for two years, mum.'

'Well, Bessy, I'll see what I can do for you. Why did you leave Mrs Rosenbaum's?'

'She said the gentlemen liked a change.'

'I'll just ask her.' Margot took up the telephone, which was held by a boxing glove. 'Is that Mrs Rosenbaum? This is Latin-American Entertainments, Ltd, speaking. Can you tell me about Miss de la Conradine? . . . Oh, that was the reason she left you? Thank you so much! I rather thought that might be it.' She rang off. 'Sorry, Bessy; nothing for you until you're well again.'

She pressed the bell, which was in the eye of a salmon trout, and another young lady was shown in.

'Name?'

'Jane Grimes.'

'Who sent you to me?'

'The gentleman at Cardiff. He gave me this to give you.' She produced a crumpled envelope and handed it across the table. Margot read the note. 'Yes, I see. So you're new to the business, Jane?'

'Like a babe unborn, mum.'

'But you married?'

'Yes, mum, but nothing happened. It was in the war, and he was very drunk.'

'Where's your husband?'

'Dead, so they do say.'

'That's excellent, Jane. You're just the sort we want. How soon can you sail?'

'How soon would you be wanting me to?'

'Well, there's a vacancy in Rio I'm filling at the end of the week. I'm sending out two very nice girls. Would you like to be going with them?'

'Yes, mum, very pleased, I'm sure.'

'D'you want any money in advance?'

'Well, I could do with a bit to send my dad if you could spare it.'

Margot took some notes from a drawer, counted them, and made out the receipt.

'Sign this, will you? I've got your address. I'll send you your tickets in a day or so. How are you off for clothes?'

'Well, I've got a fine silk dress, but it's at Cardiff with the other things. The gentleman said I'd be getting some new clothes, perhaps.'

'Yes, quite right. I'll make a note of that. The arrangement we generally make is that our agent chooses the clothes and you pay for them out of your salary in instalments.'

Mrs Grimes went out, and another girl took her place.

By luncheon time Margot Beste-Chetwynde was tired. 'Thank heavens, that's the last of them,' she said. 'Were you terribly bored, my angel?'

'Margot, you're wonderful. You ought to have been an empress.'

'Don't say that you were a Christian slave, dearest.'

'It never occurred to me,' said Paul.

'There's a young man just like your friend Potts on the other side of the street,' said Margot at the window. 'And, my dear, he's picked up the last of those poor girls, the one who wanted to take her children and her brother with her.'

'Then it can't be Potts,' said Paul lazily. 'I say, Margot, there was one thing I couldn't understand. Why was it that the less experience those chorus-girls had, the more you seemed to want them? You offered much higher wages to the ones who said they'd never had a job before.'

'Did I, darling? I expect it was because I feel so absurdly happy.'

At the time this seemed quite a reasonable explanation, but, thinking the matter over, Paul had to admit to himself that there had been nothing noticeably light-hearted in Margot's conduct of her business.

'Let's have luncheon out today,' said Margot. 'I'm tired of this house.'

They walked across Berkeley Square together in the sunshine. A footman in livery stood on the steps of one of the houses. A hatter's van, emblazoned with the royal arms, trotted past them on Hay Hill, two cockaded figures upright upon the box. A very great lady, bolstered up in an old-fashioned landaulette, bowed to Margot with an inclination she had surely learned in the Court of the Prince Consort. All Mayfair seemed to throb with the heart of Mr Arlen.

Philbrick sat at the next table at the *Maison Basque* eating the bitter little strawberries which are so cheap in Provence and so very expensive in Dover Street.

'Do come and see me some time,' he said. 'I'm living up the street at Batts'.'

'I hear you're buying Llanabba,' said Paul.

'Well, I thought of it,' said Philbrick. 'But I'm afraid it's too far away, really.'

'The police came for you soon after you left,' said Paul.

'They're bound to get me some time,' said Philbrick. 'But thanks for the tip all the same! By the way, you might warn your fiancée that they'll be after her soon, if she's not careful. That League of Nations Committee is getting busy at last.'

'I haven't the least idea what you mean,' said Paul, and returned to his table.

'Obviously the poor man's dotty,' said Margot when he told her of the conversation.

6

A HITCH IN THE WEDDING PREPARATIONS

Meanwhile half the shops in London were engaged on the wedding preparations. Paul asked Potts to be his best man, but a letter from Geneva declined the invitation. In other circumstances this might have caused him embarrassment, but during the past fortnight Paul had received so many letters and invitations from people he barely remembered meeting that his only difficulty in filling his place was the fear of offending any of his affectionate new friends. Eventually he chose Sir Alastair Digby-Vaine-Trumpington, because he felt that, however indirectly, he owed him a great deal of his present good fortune. Sir Alastair readily accepted; at the same time borrowing the money for a new tall hat, his only one having come to grief a few nights earlier.

A letter from Onslow Square, which Paul left unanswered, plainly intimated that Paul's guardian's daughter would take it as a personal slight, and as a severe blow to her social advancement, if she were not chosen as one of the bridesmaids.

For some reason or other Paul's marriage seemed to inspire the public as being particularly romantic. Perhaps they admired the enterprise and gallantry with which Margot, after ten years of widowhood, voluntarily exposed herself to a repetition of the hundred and one horrors of a fashionable wedding, or perhaps Paul's sudden elevation from schoolmaster to millionaire struck a still vibrant chord of optimism in each of them, so that they said to themselves over their ledgers and typewriters: 'It may be me next time.' Whatever the reason, the wedding was certainly an unparalleled success among the lower orders. Inflamed by the popular Press, a large crowd assembled outside St Margaret's on the eve of the ceremony equipped, as for a first night, with collapsible chairs, sandwiches and spirit stoves, while by half-past two, in spite of heavy rain, it had swollen to such dimensions that the police were forced to make several baton charges, and many guests were crushed almost to death in their attempts to reach the doors, and the route down which Margot had to drive was lined as for a funeral with weeping and hysterical women.

Society was less certain in its approval, and Lady Circumference, for one, sighed for the early nineties, when Edward Prince of Wales, at the head of *ton*, might have given authoritative condemnation to this ostentatious second marriage.

'It's maddenin' Tangent having died just at this time,' she said. 'People may think that that's my reason for refusin'. I can't imagine that *anyone* will go.'

'I hear your nephew Alastair Trumpington is the best man,' said Lady Vanbrugh.

'You seem to be as well informed as my chiropodist,' said Lady Circumference with unusual felicity, and all Lowndes Square shook at her departure.

In the unconverted mewses of Mayfair and the upper rooms of Shepherd's Market and North Audley Street, where fashionable bachelors lurk disconsolately on their evenings at home, there was open lamentation at the prey that had been allowed to slip through their elegantly gloved fingers, while more than one popular dancing man inquired anxiously at his bank to learn whether his month's remittance had been paid in as usual. But Margot remained loyal to all her old obligations, and invitations to her wedding reception were accepted by whole bevies of young men who made it their boast that they never went out except to a square meal, while little Davy Lennox, who for three years had never been known to give any one a 'complimentary sitting', took two eloquent photographs of the back of her head and one of the reflection of her hands in a bowl of ink.

Ten days before the wedding Paul moved into rooms at the Ritz, and Margot devoted herself seriously to shopping. Five or six times a day messengers appeared at his suite bringing little by-products of her activity–now a platinum cigarette-case, now a dressing-gown, now a tie-pin or a pair of links–while Paul, with unaccustomed prodigality, bought two new ties, three pairs of shoes, an umbrella and a set of Proust. Margot had fixed his personal allowance at two thousand a year.

Far away in the Adriatic feverish preparations were being made to make Mrs Beste-Chetwynde's villa at Corfu ready for the first weeks of her honeymoon, and the great bed, carved with pine-apples, that had once belonged to Napoleon III, was laid out for her reception with fragrant linen and pillows of unexampled softness. All this the newspapers retailed with uncontrolled profusion, and many a young reporter was handsomely commended for the luxuriance of his adjectives.

However, there was a hitch.

Three days before the date fixed for the wedding Paul was sitting in the Ritz opening his morning's post, when Margot rang him up.

'Darling, rather a tiresome thing's happened,' she said. 'You know those girls we sent off to Rio the other day? Well, they're stuck at Marseilles for some reason or other. I can't quite make out why. I think it's something to do with their passports. I've just had a very odd cable from my agent there. He's giving up the job. It's such a bore all this happening just now. I do so want to get everything fixed before Thursday. I wonder if you could be an angel and go over and see to it for me? It's probably only a matter of giving the right man a few hundred francs. If you fly you'll be back in plenty of time. I'd go myself, only you know, don't you, darling, I simply haven't one minute to spare.'

Paul did not have to travel alone. Potts was at Croydon, enveloped in an ulster and carrying in his hand a little attaché-case.

'League of Nations business,' he said, and was twice sick during the flight.

At Paris Paul was obliged to charter a special aeroplane. Potts saw him off.

'Why are you going to Marseilles?' he asked. 'I thought you were going to be married.'

'I'm only going there for an hour or two, to see some people on business,' said Paul.

How like Potts, he thought, to suppose that a little journey like this was going to upset his marriage. Paul was beginning to feel cosmopolitan–the Ritz today, Marseilles tomorrow, Corfu next day, and afterwards the whole world stood open to him like one great hotel, his way lined for him with bows and orchids. How pathetically insular poor Potts was, he thought, for all his talk of internationalism.

It was late evening when Paul arrived at Marseilles. He dined at Basso's in the covered balcony off bouillabaisse and Meursault at a table from which he could see a thousand lights reflected in the still water. Paul felt very much a man of the world as he paid his bill, calculated the correct tip and sat back in the open cab on his way to the old part of the town.

'They'll probably be at *Alice's*, in the Rue de Reynarde,' Margot had said. 'Anyway, you oughtn't to have any difficulty in finding them if you mention my name.'

At the corner of the Rue Ventomargy the carriage stopped. The way was too narrow and two crowded for traffic. Paul paid the driver. '*Merci, Monsieur! Gardez bien votre chapeau*,' he said as he drove off. Wondering what the expression could mean, Paul set off with less certain steps down the cobbled alley. The houses overhung perilously on each side, gaily alight from cellar to garret; between them swung lanterns; a shallow gutter ran down the centre of the path. The scene could scarcely have been more sinister had it been built at Hollywood itself for some orgiastic incident of the Reign of Terror. Such a street in England, Paul reflected, would have been saved long ago by Mr Spire and preserved under a public trust for the sale of brass toasting forks, picture post cards and 'Devonshire teas'. Here the trade was of a different sort. It did not require very much worldly wisdom to inform him of the character of the quarter he was now in. Had he not, guide-book in hand, traversed the forsaken streets of Pompeii?

No wonder, Paul reflected, that Margot had been so anxious to rescue her protégées from this place of temptation and danger.

A negro sailor, hideously drunk, addressed Paul in no language known to man, and invited him to have a drink. He hurried on. How typical of Margot that, in all her whirl of luxury, she should still have time to care for the poor girls she had unwittingly exposed to such perils.

Deaf to the polyglot invitations that arose on all sides, Paul pressed on his way. A young lady snatched his hat from his head; he caught a glimpse of her bare leg in a lighted doorway; then she appeared at a window, beckoning him to come in and retrieve it.

All the street seemed to be laughing at him. He hesitated; and then, forsaking, in a moment of panic, both his black hat and his self-possession, he turned and fled for the broad streets and the tram lines where, he knew at heart, was his spiritual home.

By daylight the old town had lost most of its terrors. Washing hung out between the houses, the gutters ran with fresh water and the streets were crowded with old women carrying baskets of fish. *Chez Alice* showed no sign of life, and Paul was forced to ring and ring before a tousled old concierge presented himself.

'*Avez-vous les jeunes filles de Madame Beste-Chetwynde?*' Paul asked, acutely conscious of the absurdity of the question.

'Sure, step right along, Mister,' said the concierge; 'she wired us you was coming.'

Mrs Grimes and her two friends were not yet dressed, but they received Paul with enthusiasm in dressing-gowns which might have satisfied the taste for colour of the elder Miss Fagan. They explained the difficulty of the passports, which, Paul thought, was clearly due to some misapprehension by the authorities of their jobs in Rio. They didn't know any French, and of course they had explained things wrong.

He spent an arduous morning at consulates and police bureaux. Things were more difficult than he had thought, and the officials received him either with marked coldness or with incomprehensible winks and innuendo.

Things had been easier six months ago, they said, but now, with the League of Nations–And they shrugged their shoulders despairingly. Perhaps it might be arranged once more, but Madame Beste-Chetwynde must really understand that there were forms that must be respected. Eventually the young ladies were signed on as stewardesses.

'And if they should not go further with me than Rio,' said the captain, 'well, I have a sufficient staff already. You say there are posts waiting for them there? No doubt their employers will be able to arrange things there with the authorities.'

But it cost Paul several thousand francs to complete the arrangements. 'What an absurd thing the League of Nations seems to be!' said Paul. 'They seem to make it harder to get about instead of easier.' And this, to his surprise, the officials took to be a capital joke.

Paul saw the young ladies to their ship, and all three kissed him goodbye. As he walked back along the quay he met Potts.

'Just arrived by the morning train,' he said. Paul felt strongly inclined to tell him his opinion of the League of Nations, but remembering Potts' prolixity in argument and the urgency of his own departure, he decided to leave his criticisms for another time. He stopped long enough in Marseilles to cable to Margot, 'Everything arranged satisfactorily. Returning this afternoon. All my love' and then left for Paris by air, feeling that at last he had done something to help.

At ten o'clock on his wedding morning Paul returned to the Ritz. It was raining hard, and he felt tired, unshaven and generally woebegone. A number of newspaper reporters were waiting for him outside his suite, but he told them that he could see no one. Inside he found Peter Beste-Chetwynde, incredibly smart in his first morning-coat.

'They've let me come up from Llanabba for the day,' he said. 'To tell you the truth, I'm rather pleased with myself in these clothes. I bought you a button-hole in case you'd forgotten. I say, Paul, you're looking tired.'

'I am, rather. Turn on the bath for me like an angel.'

When he had had his bath and shaved he felt better. Peter had ordered a bottle of champagne and was a little tipsy. He walked round the room, glass in hand, talking gaily, and every now and then pausing to look at himself in the mirror. 'Pretty smart,' he said, 'particularly the tie; don't you think so, Paul? I think I shall go back to the school like this. That would make them see what a superior person I am. I hope you notice that I gave you the grander button-hole? I can't tell you what Llanabba is like this term, Paul. Do try and persuade Mamma to take me away. Clutterbuck has left, and Tangent is dead, and the three new masters are quite awful. One is like your friend Potts, only he stutters, and Brolly says he's got a glass eye. He's called Mr Makepeace. Then there's another one with red hair who keeps beating every one all the time, and the other's rather sweet, really, only he has fits. I don't think the Doctor cares for any of them much. Flossie's been looking rather discouraged all the time. I wonder if Mamma could get her a job in South America? I'm glad you're wearing a waistcoat like that. I nearly did, but I thought perhaps I was a bit young. What do you think? We had a reporter down at the school the other day wanting to know particulars about you. Brolly told a splendid story about how you used to go out swimming in the evenings and swim for hours and hours in the dark composing elegiac verses, and then he spoilt it by saying you had webbed feet and a prehensile tail, which made the chap think he was having his leg pulled. I say, am I terribly in the way?'

As Paul dressed his feeling of well-being began to return. He could not help feeling that he too looked rather smart. Presently Alastair Digby-Vaine-Trumpington came in, and drank some champagne.

'This wedding of ours is about the most advertised thing that's happened for a generation,' he said. 'D'you know, the *Sunday Mail* has given me fifty pounds to put my name to an article describing my sensations as best man. I'm afraid everyone will know it's not me, though; it's too jolly well written. I've had a marvellous letter from Aunt Greta about it, too. Have you seen the presents? The Argentine Chargé d'Affaires has given you the works of Longfellow bound in padded green leather, and the Master of Scone has sent those pewter plates he used to have in his hall.'

Paul fastened the gardenia in his button-hole, and they went down to luncheon. There were several people in the restaurant obviously dressed for a wedding, and it gave Paul some satisfaction to notice that he was the centre of interest of the whole room. The *maître d'hôtel* offered his graceful good wishes as he led them to their table. Peter, earlier in the morning, had ordered the luncheon.

'I doubt if we shall have time to eat it all,' he said, 'but fortunately the best things all come at the beginning.'

As he was peeling his second plover's egg Paul was called away to the telephone.

'Darling,' said Margot's voice, 'how are you? I've been so anxious all the time you were away. I had an awful feeling something was going to stop you coming back. Are you all right, dearest? Yes, I'm terribly well. I'm at home having luncheon in my bedroom and feeling, my dear, I can't tell you how virginal, really and truly completely debutante. I hope you'll like my frock. It's Boulanger, darling; do you mind? Goodbye, my sweet. Don't let Peter get too drunk, will you?'

Paul went back to the dining-room.

'I've eaten your eggs,' said Peter. 'I just couldn't help it.'

By two o'clock they had finished their luncheon. Mrs Beste-Chetwynde's second-best Hispano Suiza was waiting in Arlington Street.

'You must just have one more drink with me before you go,' said the best man; 'there's heaps of time.'

'I think perhaps it would be a mistake if I did,' said Peter.

Paul and his best man refilled their glasses with brandy.

'It is a funny thing,' said Alastair Digby-Vaine-Trumpington. 'No one could have guessed that when I had the Boller blind in my rooms it was going to end like this.'

Paul turned the liqueur round in his glass, inhaled its rich bouquet for a second, and then held it before him.

'To Fortune,' he said, 'a much-maligned lady!'

'Which of you gentlemen is Mr Paul Pennyfeather?'

Paul put down his glass and turned to find an elderly man of military appearance standing beside him.

'I am,' he said. 'But I'm afraid that, if you're from the Press, I really haven't time . . .'

'I'm Inspector Bruce, of Scotland Yard,' said the stranger. 'Will you be so good as to speak to me for a minute outside?'

'Really, officer,' said Paul, 'I'm in a great hurry. I suppose it's about the men to guard the presents. You should have come to me earlier.'

'It's not about presents, and I couldn't have come earlier. The warrant for your arrest has only this minute been issued.'

'Look here,' said Alastair Digby-Vaine-Trumpington, 'don't be an ass. You've got the wrong man. They'll laugh at you like blazes over this at Scotland Yard. This is the Mr Pennyfeather who's being married today.'

'I don't know anything about that,' said Inspector Bruce. 'All I know is, there's a warrant out for his arrest, and that anything he says may be used as evidence against him. And as for you, young man, I shouldn't attempt to obstruct an officer of the law, not if I was you.'

'It's all some ghastly mistake,' said Paul. 'I suppose I must go with this man. Try and get on to Margot and explain to her.'

Sir Alastair's amiable pink face gaped blank astonishment. 'Good God,' he said, 'how damned funny! At least it would be at any other time.' But Peter, deadly white, had left the restaurant.

PART III

I

STONE WALLS DO NOT A PRISON MAKE

Paul's trial, which took place some weeks later at the Old Bailey, was a bitter disappointment to the public, the news editors and the jury and counsel concerned. The arrest at the Ritz, the announcement at St Margaret's that the wedding was postponed, Margot's flight to Corfu, the refusal of bail, the meals sent in to Paul on covered dishes from Boulestin's, had been 'front-page stories' every day. After all this, Paul's conviction and sentence were a lame conclusion. At first he pleaded guilty on all charges, despite the entreaties of his counsel, but eventually he was galvanized into some show of defence by the warning of the presiding judge that the law allowed punishment with the cat-o'-nine-tails for offences of this sort. Even then things were very flat. Potts as chief witness for the prosecution was unshakable, and was later warmly commended by the court; no evidence, except of previous good conduct, was offered by the defence; Margot Beste-Chetwynde's name was not mentioned, though the judge in passing sentence remarked that 'no one could be ignorant of the callous insolence with which, on the very eve of arrest for this most infamous of crimes, the accused had been preparing to join his name with one honoured in his country's history, and to drag down to his own pitiable depths of depravity a lady of beauty, rank and stainless reputation. The just censure of society,' remarked the judge, 'is accorded to those so inconstant and intemperate that they must take their pleasures in the unholy market of humanity that still sullies the fame of our civilization; but for the traders themselves, these human vampires who prey upon the degradation of their species, society had reserved the right of ruthless suppression.' So Paul was sent off to prison, and the papers headed the column they reserve for home events of minor importance with PRISON FOR EX-SOCIETY BRIDEGROOM. JUDGE ON HUMAN VAMPIRES, and there, as far as the public were concerned, the matter ended.

Before this happened, however, a conversation took place which deserves the attention of all interested in the confused series of events of which Paul had become a part. One day, while he was waiting for trial, he was visited in his cell by Peter Beste-Chetwynde.

'Hullo!' he said.

'Hullo, Paul!' said Peter. 'Mamma asked me to come in to see you. She wants to know if you are getting the food all right she's ordered for you. I hope you like it, because I chose most of it myself. I thought you wouldn't want anything very heavy.'

'It's splendid,' said Paul. 'How's Margot?'

'Well, that's rather what I've come to tell you, Paul. Margot's gone away.'

'Where to?'

'She's gone off alone to Corfu. I made her, though she wanted to stay and see your trial. You can imagine what a time we've had with reporters and people. You don't think it awful of her, do you? And listen, there's something else. Can that policeman hear? It's this. You remember that awful old man Maltravers. Well, you've probably seen he's Home Secretary now. He's been round to Mamma in the most impossible Oppenheim kind of way, and said that if she'd marry him he could get you out. Of course he's obviously been reading books. But Mamma thinks it's probably true, and she wants to know how you feel about it. She rather feels the whole thing's her fault, really, and, short of going to prison herself, she'll do anything to help. You can't imagine Mamma in prison, can you? Well, would you rather get out now and her marry Maltravers, or wait until you do get out and marry her yourself? She was rather definite about it.'

Paul thought of Professor Silenus' 'In ten years she will be worn out', but he said:

'I'd rather she waited if you think she possibly can.'

'I thought you'd say that, Paul. I'm so glad. Mamma said: "I won't say I don't know how I shall ever be able to make up to him for all this, because I think he knows I can." Those were her words. I don't suppose you'll get more than a year or so, will you?'

'Good Lord, I hope not,' said Paul.

His sentence of seven years' penal servitude was rather a blow. 'In ten years she will be worn out,' he thought as he drove in the prison-van to Blackstone Gaol.

On his first day there Paul met quite a number of people, some of whom he knew already. The first person was a warder with a low brow and distinctly menacing manner. He wrote Paul's name in the 'Body Receipt Book' with some difficulty and then conducted him to a cell. He had evidently been reading the papers.

'Rather different from the Ritz Hotel, eh?' he said. 'We don't like your kind 'ere, see? And we knows 'ow to treat 'em. You won't find nothing like the Ritz 'ere, you dirty White Slaver.'

But there he was wrong, because the next person Paul met was Philbrick. His prison clothes were ill-fitting, and his chin was unshaven, but he still bore an indefinable air of the grand manner.

'Thought I'd be seeing you soon,' he said. 'They've put me on to reception bath cleaner, me being an old hand. I've been saving the best suit I can find for you. Not a louse on it, hardly.' He threw a little pile of clothes, stamped with the broad arrow, on to the bench.

The warder returned with another, apparently his superior officer. Together they made a careful inventory of all Paul's possessions.

'Shoes, brown, one pair; socks, fancy, one pair; suspenders, black silk, one pair,' read out the warder in a sing-song voice. 'Never saw a bloke with so much clothes.'

There were several checks due to difficulties of spelling, and it was some time before the list was finished.

'Cigarette case, white metal, containing two cigarettes; watch, white metal; tie-pin, fancy'–it had cost Margot considerably more than the warder earned in a year, had he only known–'studs, bone, one pair; cuff links, fancy, one pair.' The officers looked doubtfully at Paul's gold cigar piercer, the gift of the best man. 'What's this 'ere?'

'It's for cigars,' said Paul.

'Not so much lip!' said the warder, banging him on the top of his head with the pair of shoes he happened to be holding. 'Put it down as "instrument". That's the lot,' he said, 'unless you've got false teeth. You're allowed to keep them, only we must make a note of it.'

'No,' said Paul.

'Truss or other surgical appliance?'

'No,' said Paul.

'All right! You can go to the bath.'

Paul sat for the regulation ten minutes in the regulation nine inches of warm water–which smelt reassuringly of disinfectant–and then put on his prison-clothes. The loss of his personal possessions gave him a curiously agreeable sense of irresponsibility.

'You look a treat,' said Philbrick.

Next he saw the Medical Officer, who sat at a table covered with official forms.

'Name?' said the Doctor.

'Pennyfeather.'

'Have you at any time been detained in a mental home or similar institution? If so, give particulars.'

'I was at Scone College, Oxford,' said Paul.

The Doctor looked up for the first time. 'Don't you dare to make jokes here, my man,' he said, 'or I'll soon have you in the straight-jacket in less than no time.'

'Sorry,' said Paul.

'Don't speak to the Medical Officer unless to answer a question,' said the warder at his elbow.

'Sorry,' said Paul unconsciously, and was banged on the head.

'Suffering from consumption, V.D., or any contagious disease?' asked the M.O.

'Not that I know of,' said Paul.

'That's all,' said the Doctor. 'I have certified you as capable of undergoing the usual descriptions of punishment as specified below, to wit, restraint of handcuffs, leg-chains, cross-irons, body-belt, canvas dress, close confinement, No. 1 diet, No. 2 diet, birch-rod and cat-o'-nine-tails. Any complaints?'

'But must I have all these at once?' asked Paul, rather dismayed.

'You will if you ask impertinent questions. Look after that man, officer; he's obviously a troublesome character.'

'Come 'ere, you,' said the warder. They went up a passage and down two flights of iron steps. Long galleries with iron railings stretched out in each direction, giving access to innumerable doors. Wire netting was stretched between the landings. 'So don't you try no monkey-tricks. Suicide isn't allowed in this prison. See?' said the warder. 'This is your cell. Keep it clean, or you'll know the reason why, and this is your number.' He buttoned a yellow badge on to Paul's coat.

'Like a flag-day,' said Paul.

'Shut up, you—,' remarked the warder, and locked the door.

'I suppose I shall learn to respect these people in time,' thought Paul. 'They all seem so much less awe-inspiring than anyone I ever met.'

His next visit was from the Schoolmaster. The door was unlocked, and a seedy-looking young man in a tweed suit came into the cell.

'Can you read and write, D.4.12?' asked the newcomer.

'Yes,' said Paul.

'Public or secondary education?'

'Public,' said Paul. His school had been rather sensitive on this subject.

'What was your standard when you left school?'

'Well, I don't quite know. I don't think we had standards.'

The Schoolmaster marked him down as 'Memory defective' on a form, and went out. Presently he returned with a book.

'You must do your best with that for the next four weeks,' he said. 'I'll try and get you into one of the morning classes. You won't find it difficult, if you can read fairly easily. You see, it begins there,' he said helpfully, showing Paul the first page.

It was an English Grammar published in 1872.

'*A syllable is a single sound made by one simple effort of the voice*,' Paul read.

'Thank you,' he said; 'I'm sure I shall find it useful.'

'You can change it after four weeks if you can't get on with it,' said the Schoolmaster. 'But I should stick to it, if you can.'

Again the door was locked.

Next came the Chaplain. 'Here is your Bible and a book of devotion. The Bible stays in the cell always. You can change the book of devotion any week if you wish to. Are you Church of England? Services are voluntary–that is to say, you must either attend all or none.' The Chaplain spoke in a nervous and hurried manner. He was new to his job, and he had already visited fifty prisoners that day, one of whom had delayed him for a long time with descriptions of a vision he had seen the night before.

'Hallo, Prendy!' said Paul.

Mr Prendergast looked at him anxiously. 'I didn't recognize you,' he said. 'People look so much alike in those clothes. This is most disturbing, Pennyfeather. As soon as I saw that you'd been convicted I was afraid they might send you here. Oh dear! oh dear! It makes everything still more difficult.'

'What's the matter, Prendy? Doubts again?'

'No, no, discipline, my old trouble. I've only been at the job a week. I was very lucky to get it. My bishop said he thought there was more opening for a Modern Churchman in this kind of work than in the parishes. The Governor is very modern too. But criminals are just as bad as boys, I find. They pretend to make confessions and tell me the most dreadful things just to see what I'll say, and in chapel they laugh so much that the warders spend all their time correcting them. It makes the services seem so irreverent. Several of them got put on No. 1 diet this morning for singing the wrong words to one of the hymns, and of course that only makes me more unpopular. Please, Pennyfeather, if you don't mind, you mustn't call me Prendy, and if anyone passes the cell will you stand up when you're talking to me. You're supposed to, you see, and the Chief Warder has said some very severe things to me about maintaining discipline.'

At this moment the face of the warder appeared at the peep-hole in the door.

'I trust you realize the enormity of your offence and the justice of your punishment?' said Mr Prendergast in a loud voice. 'Pray for penitence.'

A warder came into the cell.

'Sorry to disturb you, sir, but I've got to take this one to see the Governor. There's D.4.18 down the way been asking for you for days. I said I'd tell you, only, if you'll forgive my saying so, I shouldn't be too soft with 'im, sir. We know 'im of old. 'E's a sly old devil, begging your pardon, sir, and 'e's only religious when 'e thinks it'll pay.'

'I think that I am the person to decide that, officer,' said Mr Prendergast with some dignity. 'You may take D.4.12 to the Governor.'

Sir Wilfred Lucas-Dockery had not been intended by nature or education for the Governor of a prison; his appointment was the idea of a Labour Home Secretary who had been impressed by an appendix on the theory of penology which he had contributed to a report on the treatment of 'Conscientious Objectors'. Up to that time Sir Wilfred had held the Chair of Sociology at a Midland university; only his intimate friends and a few specially favoured pupils knew that behind his mild and professional exterior he concealed an ardent ambition to serve in the public life of his generation. He stood twice for Parliament, but so diffidently that his candidature passed almost unnoticed. Colonel MacAdder, his predecessor in office, a veteran of numberless unrecorded campaigns on the Afghan frontier, had said to him on his retirement: 'Good luck, Sir Wilfred! If I may give you a piece of advice, it's this. Don't bother about the lower warders or the prisoners. Give hell to the man immediately below you, and you can rely on him to pass it on with interest. If you make prison bad enough, people'll take jolly good care to keep out of it. That's been my policy all through, and I'm proud of it' (a policy which soon became quite famous in the society of Cheltenham Spa).

Sir Wilfred, however, had his own ideas. 'You must understand,' he said to Paul, 'that it is my aim to establish personal contact with each of the men under my care. I want you to take a pride in your prison and in your work here. So far as possible, I like the prisoners to carry on with their avocations in civilized life. What was this man's profession, officer?'

'White Slave traffic, sir.'

'Ah, yes. Well, I'm afraid you won't have much opportunity for that here. What else have you done?'

'I was nearly a clergyman once,' said Paul.

'Indeed? Well, I hope in time, if I find enough men with the same intention, to get together a theological class. You've no doubt met the Chaplain, a very broad-minded man. Still, for the present we are only at the beginning. The Government regulations are rather uncompromising. For the first four weeks you will have to observe the solitary confinement ordained by law. After that we will find you something more creative. We don't want you to feel that your personality is being stamped out. Have you any experience of art leather work?'

'No, sir.'

'Well, I might put you into the Arts and Crafts Workshop. I came to the conclusion many years ago that almost all crime is due to the repressed desire for aesthetic expression. At last we have the opportunity for testing it. Are you an extravert or an introvert?'

'I'm afraid I'm not sure, sir.'

'So few people are. I'm trying to induce the Home Office to instal an official psycho-analyst. Do you read the *New Nation*, I wonder? There is rather a flattering article this week about our prison called *The Lucas-Dockery Experiments*. I like the prisoners to know these things. It gives them corporate pride. I may give you one small example of the work we are doing that affects your own case. Up till now all offences connected with prostitution have been put into the sexual category. Now I hold that an offence of your kind is essentially acquisitive and shall grade it accordingly. It does not, of course, make any difference as far as your conditions of imprisonment are concerned–the routine of penal servitude is prescribed by Standing Orders–but you see what a difference it makes to the annual statistics.'

'The human touch,' said Sir Wilfred after Paul had been led from the room, 'I'm sure it makes all the difference. You could see with that unfortunate man just now what a difference it made to him to think that, far from being a mere nameless slave, he has now become part of a great revolution in statistics.'

'Yes, sir,' said the Chief Warder; 'and, by the way, there are two more attempted suicides being brought up tomorrow. You must really be more strict with them, sir. Those sharp tools you've issued to the Arts and Crafts School is just putting temptation in the men's way.'

Paul was once more locked in, and for the first time had the opportunity of examining his cell. There was little to interest him. Besides his Bible, his book of devotion–*Prayers on Various Occasions of Illness, Uncertainty and Loss, by the Rev. Septimus Bead, M.A., Edinburgh, 1863*–and his English Grammar, there were a little glazed pint pot, a knife and spoon, a slate and slate-pencil, a salt-jar, a metal water-can, two earthenware vessels, some cleaning materials, a plank bed upright against the wall, a roll of bedding, a stool and a table. A printed notice informed him that he was not permitted to look out of the window. Three printed cards on the wall contained a list of other punishable offences, which seemed to include every human activity, some Church of England prayers, and an explanation of the 'system of progressive stages'. There was also a typewritten 'Thought for the Day', one of Sir Wilfred Lucas-Dockery's little innovations. The message for the first day of Paul's imprisonment was: SENSE OF SIN IS SENSE OF WASTE, *the Editor of the 'Sunday Express'*. Paul studied the system of progressive stages with interest. After four weeks, he read, he would be allowed to join in associated labour, to take half an hour's exercise on Sundays, to wear a stripe on his arm, if illiterate to have school instruction, to take one work of fiction from the library weekly, and, if special application were made to the Governor, to exhibit four photographs of his relatives or of approved friends; after eight weeks, provided that his conduct was perfectly satisfactory, he might receive a visit of twenty minutes' duration and write and receive a letter. Six weeks later he might receive another visit and another letter and another library book weekly.

Would Davy Lennox's picture of the back of Margot's head be accepted as the photograph of an approved friend, he wondered?

After a time his door was unlocked again and opened a few inches. A hand thrust in a tin, and a voice said: 'Pint pot quick!' Paul's mug was filled with cocoa, and the door was again locked. The tin contained bread, bacon and beans. That was the last interruption for fourteen hours. Paul fell into a reverie. It was the first time he had been really alone for months. How very refreshing it was, he reflected.

The next four weeks of solitary confinement were among the happiest of Paul's life. The physical comforts were certainly meagre, but at the Ritz Paul had learned to appreciate the inadequacy of purely physical comfort. It was so exhilarating, he found, never to have to make any decision on any subject, to be wholly relieved from the smallest consideration of time, meals or clothes, to have no anxiety ever about what kind of impression he was making; in fact, to be free. At some rather chilly time in the early morning a bell would ring, and the warder would say: 'Slops outside!'; he would rise, roll up his bedding, and dress; there was no need to shave, no hesitation about what tie he should wear, none of the fidgeting with studs and collars and links that so distracts the waking moments of civilized man. He felt like the happy people in the advertisements for shaving soap who seem to have achieved very simply that peace of mind so distant and so desirable in the early morning. For about an hour he stitched away at a mail-bag, until his door was again unlocked to admit a hand with a lump of bread and a large ladle of porridge. After breakfast he gave a cursory polish to the furniture and crockery of his cell and did some more sewing until the bell rang for chapel. For a quarter of an hour or twenty minutes he heard Mr Prendergast blaspheming against the beauties of sixteenth-century diction. This was certainly a bore, and so was the next hour, during which he had to march round the prison square, where between concentric paths of worn asphalt a few melancholy cabbages showed their heads. Some of the men during this period used to fall out under the pretence of tying a shoe-lace and take furtive bites at the leaves of the vegetables. If observed they were severely punished. Paul never felt any temptation to do this. After that the day was unbroken save for luncheon, supper and the Governor's inspection. The heap of sacking which every day he was to turn into mail-bags was supposed by law to keep him busy for nine hours. The prisoners in the cells on either side of him, who were not quite in their right minds, the warder told Paul, found some difficulty in finishing their task before lights out. Paul found that with the least exertion he had finished long before supper, and spent the evenings in meditation and in writing up on his slate the thoughts which had occurred to him during the day.

2

THE LUCAS-DOCKERY EXPERIMENTS

Sir Wilfred Lucas-Dockery, as has already been suggested, combined ambition, scholarship and genuine optimism in a degree rarely found in his office. He looked forward to a time when the Lucas-Dockery experiments should be recognized as the beginning of a new epoch in penology, and he rehearsed in his mind sentences from the social histories of the future which would contain such verdicts as '*One of the few important events of this Labour Government's brief tenure of power was the appointment as Governor of Blackstone Jail of Sir Wilfred Lucas-Dockery. The administration of this intrepid and far-seeing official is justly regarded as the foundation of the present system of criminal treatment. In fact, it may safely be said that no single man occupies so high a place in the history of the social reform of his century, etc.*' His eminent qualities, however, did not keep him from many severe differences of opinion with the Chief Warder. He was sitting in his study one day working at a memorandum for the Prison Commissioners–one of the neglected series of memoranda whose publication after his retirement indicated Sir Wilfred's claim to be the pioneer of artificial sunlight in prisons–when the Chief Warder interrupted him.

'A bad report from the Bookbinding Shop, sir. The instructor says that a practice is growing among the men of eating the paste issued to them for their work. They say it is preferable to their porridge. We shall either have to put on another warder to supervise the bookbinding or introduce something into the paste which will make it unpalatable.'

'Has the paste any nutritive value?' asked Sir Wilfred.

'I couldn't say, sir.'

'Weigh the men in the Bookbinding Shop, and then report to me any increase in weight. How many times must I ask you to ascertain *all* the facts before reporting on any case?'

'Very good sir! And there's a petition from D.4.12. He's finished his four months' solitary, and he wants to know if he can keep at it for another four.'

'I disapprove of cellular labour. It makes a man introvert. Who is D.4.12?'

'Long sentence, sir, waiting transference to Egdon.'

'I'll see D.4.12 myself.'

'Very good, sir!'

Paul was led in.

'I understand you wish to continue cellular labour instead of availing yourself of the privilege of working in association. Why is that?'

'I find it so much more interesting, sir,' said Paul.

'It's a most irregular suggestion,' said the Chief Warder. 'Privileges can only be forfeited by a breach of the regulations witnessed and attested by two officers. Standing Orders are most emphatic on the subject.'

'I wonder whether you have narcissistic tendencies?' said the Governor. 'The Home Office has not as yet come to any decision about my application for a staff psycho-analyst.'

'Put him in the observation cell,' said the Chief Warder. 'That brings out any insanity. I've known several cases of men you could hardly have told were mad–just eccentric, you know–who've been put on observation, and after a few days they've been raving lunatics. Colonel MacAdder was a great believer in the observation cells.'

'Did you lead a very lonely life before conviction? Perhaps you were a shepherd or a lighthouse-keeper, or something of the kind?'

'No, sir.'

'Most curious. Well, I will consider your case and give you my answer later.'

Paul was led back to his cell, and next day was again summoned before the Governor.

'I have considered your application,' said Sir Wilfred, 'with the most minute care. In fact, I have decided to include it in my forthcoming work on the criminal mind. Perhaps you would like to hear what I have written about you?'

'*Case R.*', he read:

'A young man of respectable family and some education. No previous criminal record. Committed to seven years' penal servitude for traffic in prostitution. Upon completing his first four months R. petitioned for extension of cellular labour. Treatment as prescribed by Standing Orders: either (a) *detention in observation cell for the Medical Officer to satisfy himself about the state of prisoner's mind or* (b) *compulsory work in association with other prisoners unless privilege forfeited by misdemeanour.*

'Treatment by Sir Wilfred Lucas-Dockery–I decided that R. was suffering from misanthropic tendencies induced by a sense of his own inferiority in the presence of others. R.'s crime was the result of an attempt to assert individuality at the expense of community. (Cp. *Cases D, G and I.*) *Accordingly I attempted to break down his social inhibitions by a series of progressive steps. In the first stage he exercised daily for half an hour in the company of one other prisoner. Conversation was allowed during this period upon approved topics, history, philosophy, public events, etc., the prisoners being chosen among those whose crimes would tend as little as possible to aggravate and encourage R.'s.*

'I have not yet thought of the other stages of your treatment,' said Sir Wilfred, 'but you can see that individual attention is being paid to your reclamation. It may cause you some gratification to realize that, thanks to my report, you may in time become a case of scientific interest throughout the world. Sir Wilfred Lucas-Dockery's treatment of Case R. may haply become a precedent for generations yet unborn. That is something to lift you above the soul-destroying monotony of routine, is it not?'

Paul was led away.

'The men in the kitchen have lodged a complaint that they cannot work with C.2.9,' said the Chief Warder. 'They say he has an infectious skin disease all over his hands.'

'I can't be worried with things like that,' said the Governor irritably. 'I am trying to decide upon Case R.'s–I mean D.4.12's–third stage of reclamation.'

Case R. of the Lucas-Dockery experiments began on the new régime that afternoon.

'Come out,' said the warder, unlocking his cell, 'and bring your 'at.'

The parade ground, empty of its revolving squads, looked particularly desolate.

'Stand there and don't move till I come back,' said the warder.

Presently he returned with a little bony figure in prison dress.

'This 'ere's your pal,' he said; 'this 'ere's the path you've got to walk on. Neither of you is to touch the other or any part of 'is clothing. Nothing is to be passed from one to the other. You are to keep at a distance of one yard and talk of 'istory, philosophy or kindred subjects. When I rings the bell you stops talking, see? Your pace is to be neither quicker nor slower than average walking-pace. Them's the Governor's instructions, and Gawd 'elp yer if yer does anything wrong. Now walk.'

'This is a silly dodge,' said the little man. 'I've been in six prisons, and I never seen nothing to touch it. Most irregular. You doesn't know where you are these days. This blinking prison is going to the dogs. Look at the Chaplain. Wears a wig!'

'Are you here for long?' asked Paul politely.

'Not this time. They couldn't get a proper charge against me. "Six months for loitering with intent." They'd been watching me for weeks, but I wasn't going to let them have a chance this time. Now six months is a very decent little sentence, if you take my meaning. One picks up with old friends, and you like it all the more when you comes out. I never minds six months. What's more, I'm known here, so I always gets made "landing-cleaner". I expect you've seen my hand often enough coming round with the grub. The warders know me, see, so they always keeps the job open for me if they hears I'm coming back. If you're nice to 'em the first two or three times you're 'ere, they'll probably do the same for you.'

'Is it a very good job?'

'Well, not as jobs go, but it's a nice start. The best job of all is Reception-cleaner. One doesn't get that for years, unless you've special recommendations. You see, you has all the people coming in fresh from outside, and you hears all the news and gets tobacco sometimes and racing tips. Did you see the cleaner when you came in? Know who he is?'

'Yes,' said Paul, 'as a matter of fact, I do. He's called Philbrick.'

'No, no, old man, you've got the wrong chap. I mean a big stout man. Talks a lot about hotels and restaurants.'

'Yes, that's the man I mean.'

'Why, don't you know who that is? That's the Governor's brother: Sir Solomon Lucas-Dockery. Told me so hisself. 'Ere for arson. Burnt a castle in Wales. You can see he's a toff.'

3

THE DEATH OF A MODERN CHURCHMAN

Some days later Paul entered on another phase of his reclamation. When he came into the prison-square for his afternoon exercise he found that his companion's place had been taken by a burly man of formidable aspect. He had red hair and beard, and red-rimmed eyes, and vast red hands which twirled convulsively at his sides. He turned his ox-like eyes on Paul and gave him a slight snarl of welcome.

'Your new pal,' said the warder. 'Get on with it.'

'How do you do?' said Paul politely. 'Are you here for long?'

'Life,' said the other. 'But it doesn't matter much. I look daily for the Second Coming.'

They marched on in silence.

'Do you think that this is a good plan of the Governor's?' asked Paul.

'Yes,' said his companion. They walked on in silence, once round, twice round, three times round.

'Talk, you two,' shouted the warder. 'That's your instructions. Talk.'

'It makes a change,' said the big man.

'What are you here for?' asked Paul. 'You don't mind my asking, do you?'

'It's all the Bible,' said the big man. 'You should read about it there. Figuratively, you know,' he added. 'It wouldn't be plain to you, I don't suppose, not like it is to me.'

'It's not an easy book to understand, is it?'

'It's not understanding that's needed. It's visions. Do you ever have visions?'

'No, I'm afraid I don't.'

'Nor does the Chaplain. He's no Christian. It was a vision brought me here, an angel clothed in flame, with a crown of flame on his head, crying "Kill and spare not. The kingdom is at hand." Would you like to hear about it? I'll tell you. I'm a carpenter by profession, or at least I was, you understand.' He spoke a curious blend of cockney and Biblical English. 'Not a joiner–a cabinet-maker. Well, one day I was just sweeping out the shop before shutting up when the angel of the Lord came in. I didn't know who it was at first. "Just in time," I said. "What can I do for you?" Then I noticed that all about him there was a red flame and a circle of flame over his head, same as I've been telling you. Then he told me how the Lord had numbered His elect and the day of tribulation was at hand. "Kill and spare not," he says. I'd not been sleeping well for some time before this. I'd been worrying about my soul and whether I was saved. Well, all that night I thought of what the angel had told me. I didn't see his meaning, not at first, same as you wouldn't. Then it all came to me in a flash. Unworthy that I am, I am the Lord's appointed,' said the carpenter, 'I am the sword of Israel; I am the lion of the Lord's elect.'

'And did you kill anybody?' asked Paul.

'Unworthy that I am, I smote the Philistine; in the name of the Lord of hosts, I struck off his head. It was for a sign in Israel. And now I am gone into captivity, and the mirth is turned into weeping, but the Lord shall deliver me in His appointed time. Woe unto the Philistine in that day! woe unto the uncircumcised! It were better that a stone were hanged about his neck and he were cast into the depths of the sea.'

The warder rang his bell. 'Inside, you two!' he shouted.

'Any complaints?' asked the Governor on his rounds.

'Yes, sir,' said Paul.

The Governor looked at him intently. 'Are you the man I put under special treatment?'

'Yes, sir.'

'Then it's ridiculous to complain. What is it?'

'I have reason to believe that the man I have to take exercise with is a dangerous lunatic.'

'Complaints by one prisoner about another can only be considered when substantiated by the evidence of a warder or of two other prisoners,' said the Chief Warder.

'Quite right,' said the Governor. 'I never heard a more ridiculous complaint.

All crime is a form of insanity. I myself chose the prisoner with whom you exercise. I chose him for his peculiar suitability. Let me hear no more on this subject, please.'

That afternoon Paul spent another disquieting half-hour on the square.

'I've had another vision,' said the mystical homicide. 'But I don't yet know quite what it portends. No doubt I shall be told.'

'Was it a very beautiful vision?' asked Paul.

'No words can describe the splendour of it. It was all crimson and wet like blood. I saw the whole prison as if it were carved of ruby, hard and glittering, and the warders and the prisoners creeping in and out like little red ladybirds. And then as I watched all the ruby became soft and wet, like a great sponge soaked in wine, and it was dripping and melting into a great lake of scarlet. Then I woke up. I don't know the meaning of it yet, but I feel that the hand of the Lord is hanging over this prison. D'you ever feel like that, as though it were built in the jaws of a beast? I sometimes dream of a great red tunnel like the throat of a beast and men running down it, sometimes one by one and sometimes in great crowds, running down the throat of the beast, and the breath of the beast is like the blast of a furnace. D'you ever feel like that?'

'I'm afraid not,' said Paul. 'Have they given you an interesting library book?'

'*Lady Almina's Secret*,' said the lion of the Lord's elect. 'Pretty soft stuff, old-fashioned too. But I keep reading the Bible. There's a lot of killing in that.'

'Dear me, you seem to think about killing a great deal.'

'I do. It's my mission, you see,' said the big man simply.

Sir Wilfred Lucas-Dockery felt very much like Solomon at ten o'clock every morning of the week except Sunday. It was then that he sat in judgment upon the cases of misconduct among the prisoners that were brought to his notice. From this chair Colonel MacAdder had delivered sentence in undeviating accordance with the spirit and the letter of the Standing Orders Concerning the Government of His Majesty's Prisons, dispensing automatic justice like a slot machine: in went the offence; out came the punishment. Not so Sir Wilfred Lucas-Dockery. Never, he felt, was his mind more alert or resourceful or his vast accumulation of knowledge more available than at his little court of summary justice. 'No one knows what to expect,' complained warders and prisoners alike.

'Justice,' said Sir Wilfred, 'is the capacity for regarding each case as an entirely new problem.' After a few months of his administration, Sir Wilfred was able to point with some pride to a marked diminution in the number of cases brought before him.

One morning, soon after Paul began on his special régime of reclamation, his companion was called up before the Governor.

'God bless my soul!' said Sir Wilfred; 'that's the man I put on special treatment. What is he here for?'

'I was on night duty last night between the hours of 8 p.m. and 4 a.m.,' testified the warder in a sing-song voice, 'when my attention was attracted by sounds of agitation coming from the prisoner's cell. Upon going to the observation hole I observed the prisoner pacing up and down his cell in a state of high excitement. In one hand he held his Bible, and in the other a piece of wood which he had broken from his stool. His eyes were staring; he was breathing heavily, and at times muttering verses of the Bible. I remonstrated with the prisoner, when he addressed me in terms prejudicial to good discipline.'

'What are the words complained of?' asked the Chief Warder.

'He called me a Moabite, an abomination of Moab, a wash-pot, an unclean thing, an uncircumcised Moabite, an idolator, and a whore of Babylon, sir.'

'I see. What do you advise, officer?'

'A clear case of insubordination, sir,' said the Chief Warder. 'Try him on No. 1 diet for a bit.'

But when he asked the Chief Warder's opinion Sir Wilfred was not really seeking advice. He liked to emphasize in his own mind, and perhaps that of the prisoners, the difference between the official view and his own.

'What would you say was the most significant part of the evidence?' he asked.

The Chief Warder considered. 'I think whore of Babylon, on the whole, sir.'

Sir Wilfred smiled as a conjurer may who has forced the right card.

'Now I,' he said, 'am of a different opinion. It may surprise you, but I should say that the *significant* thing about this case was the fact that the prisoner held a piece of the stool.'

'Destruction of prison property,' said the Chief Warder. 'Yes, that's pretty bad.'

'Now what was your profession before conviction?' asked the Governor, turning to the prisoner.

'Carpenter, sir.'

'*I knew it*,' said the Governor triumphantly. 'We have another case of the frustrated creative urge. Now listen, my man. It is very wrong of you to insult the officer, who is clearly none of the things you mentioned. He symbolizes the just disapproval of society and is, like all the prison staff, a member of the Church of England. But I understand your difficulty. You have been used to creative craftsmanship, have you not, and you find prison life deprives you of the means of self-expression, and your energies find vent in these foolish outbursts? I will see to it that a bench and a set of carpenter's tools are provided for you. The first thing you shall do is to mend the piece of furniture you so wantonly destroyed. After that we will find other work for you in your old trade. You may go. Get to the cause of the trouble,' Sir Wilfred added when the prisoner was led away; 'your Standing Orders may repress the symptoms; they do not probe to the underlying cause.'

Two days later the prison was in a state of intense excitement. Something had happened. Paul woke as the bell rang at the usual time, but it was nearly half an hour before the doors were unlocked. He heard the warder's 'Slops outside!' getting nearer and nearer, interjected with an occasional 'Don't ask questions.' 'Mind your own business,' or a sinister 'You'll know soon enough,' in reply to the prisoner's questions. They, too, had sensed something unusual. Perhaps it was an outbreak of some disease–spotted fever, Paul thought, or a national disaster in the world outside–a war or revolution. In their enforced silence the nerves of all the men were tightened to an acuteness of perception. Paul read wholesale massacres in the warder's face.

'Anything wrong?' he asked.

'I should bleeding well say there was,' said the warder, 'and the next man as asks me a question is going to cop it hot.'

Paul began scrubbing out his cell. Dissatisfied curiosity contended in his thoughts with irritation at this interruption of routine. Two warders passed his door talking.

'I don't say I'm not sorry for the poor bird. All I says is, it was time the Governor had a lesson.'

'It might have been one of us,' said the other warder in a hushed voice.

Breakfast arrived. As the hand appeared at his door Paul whispered: 'What's happened?'

'Why, ain't you 'eard? There's been a murder, shocking bloodthirsty.'

'Get on there,' roared the warder in charge of the landing.

So the Governor had been murdered, thought Paul; he had been a mischievous old bore. Still, it was very disturbing, for the news of a murder which was barely noticed in the gay world of trams and tubes and boxing-matches caused an electric terror in this community of silent men. The interval between breakfast and chapel seemed interminable. At last the bell went. The doors were opened again. They marched in silence to the chapel. As it happened, Philbrick was in the next seat to Paul. The warders sat on raised seats, watchful for any attempt at conversation. The hymn was the recognized time for the exchange of gossip. Paul waited for it impatiently. Clearly it was not the Governor who had been murdered. He stood on the chancel steps, Prayer-book in hand. Mr Prendergast was nowhere to be seen. The Governor conducted the service. The Medical Officer read the lessons, stumbling heavily over the longer words. Where was Mr Prendergast?

At last the hymn was announced. The organ struck up, played with great feeling by a prisoner who until his conviction had been assistant organist at a Welsh cathedral. All over the chapel the men filled their chests for a burst of conversation.

'O God, our help in ages past,' sang Paul.
'Where's Prendergast today?'
'What, ain't you 'eard? 'e's been done in.'
'And our eternal home.'

'Old Prendy went to see a chap
What said he'd seen a ghost;
Well, he was dippy, and he'd got
A mallet and a saw.'

'Who let the madman have the things?'
'The Governor; who d'you think?
He asked to be a carpenter,
He sawed off Prendy's head.

'A pal of mine what lives next door,
'E 'eard it 'appening;
The warder must 'ave 'eard it too,
'E didn't interfere.'

'Time, like an ever-rolling stream,
Bears all its sons away.'
'Poor Prendy 'ollered fit to kill
For nearly 'alf an hour.

'Damned lucky it was Prendergast,
Might 'ave been you or me!
The warder says–and I agree–
It serves the Governor right.'

'Amen.'

From all points of view it was lucky that the madman had chosen Mr Prendergast for attack. Some people even suggested that the choice had been made in a more responsible quarter. The death of a prisoner or warder would have called for a Home Office inquiry which might seriously have discouraged the Lucas-Dockery reforms, and also reflected some discredit upon the administration of the Chief Warder. Mr Prendergast's death passed almost unnoticed. His assassin was removed to Broadmoor, and the life of the prison went on smoothly. It was observed, however, that the Chief Warder seemed to have more influence with his superior than he had had before. Sir Wilfred concentrated his attention upon the statistics, and the life of the prison was equitably conducted under the Standing Orders. It was quite like it had been in old MacAdder's day, the warders observed. But Paul did not reap the benefits of this happy reversion to tradition, because some few days later he was removed with a band of others to the Convict Settlement at Egdon Heath.

4

NOR IRON BARS A CAGE

The granite walls of Egdon Heath Penal Settlement are visible, when there is no mist, from the main road, and it is not uncommon for cars to stop there a few moments while the occupants stand up and stare happily about them. They are looking for convicts, and as often as not they are rewarded by seeing move across the heath before them a black group of men chained together and uniformly dressed, with a mounted and armed warder riding at their side. They give an appearance of industry which on investigation is quite illusionary, for so much of the day at Egdon is taken up with marching to and from the quarries, in issuing and counting tools, in guarding and chaining and releasing the workmen, that there is very little work done. But there is usually something to be seen from the road, enough, anyway, to be imagined from the very aspect of the building to send the trippers off to their teas with their consciences agreeably unquiet at the memory of small dishonesties in railway trains, inaccurate income-tax returns, and the hundred and one minor infractions of law that are inevitable in civilized life.

Paul arrived from Blackstone late one afternoon in early autumn with two warders and six other long-sentence prisoners. The journey had been spent in an ordinary third-class railway carriage, where the two warders smoked black tobacco in cheap little wooden pipes and were inclined towards conversation.

'You'll find a lot of improvements since you were here last,' said one of them. 'There's two coloured-glass windows in the chapel, presented by the last Governor's widow. Lovely they are, St Peter and St Paul in prison being released by an angel. Some of the Low Church prisoners don't like them, though.

'We had a lecture last week, too, but it wasn't very popular–"The Work of the League of Nations", given by a young chap of the name of Potts. Still, it makes a change. I hear you've been having a lot of changes at Blackstone.'

'I should just about think we have,' said one of the convicts, and proceeded to give a somewhat exaggerated account of the death of Mr Prendergast.

Presently one of the warders, observing that Paul seemed shy of joining in the conversation, handed him a daily paper. 'Like to look at this, sonny?' he said. 'It's the last you'll see for some time.'

There was very little in it to interest Paul, whose only information from the outside world during the last six weeks had come from Sir Wilfred Lucas-Dockery's weekly bulletins (for one of the first discoveries of his captivity was that interest in 'news' does not spring from genuine curiosity, but from the desire for completeness. During his long years of freedom he had scarcely allowed a day to pass without reading fairly fully from at least two newspapers, always pressing on with a series of events which never came to an end. Once the series was broken, he had little desire to resume it), but he was deeply moved to discover on one of the middle pages an obscure but recognizable photograph of Margot and Peter. 'The Honourable Mrs Beste-Chetwynde', it said below, 'and her son Peter, who succeeds his uncle as Earl of Pastmaster.' In the next column was an announcement of the death of Lord Pastmaster and a brief survey of his uneventful life. At the end it said, 'It is understood that Mrs Beste-Chetwynde and the young Earl, who have been spending the last few months at their villa in Corfu, will return to England in a few days. Mrs Beste-Chetwynde has for many years been a prominent hostess in the fashionable world and is regarded as one of the most beautiful women in Society. Her son's succession to the earldom recalls the sensation caused in May of this year by the announcement of her engagement to Mr Paul Pennyfeather and the dramatic arrest of the bridegroom at a leading West End hotel a few hours before the wedding ceremony. The new Lord Pastmaster is sixteen years old, and has up till now been educated privately.'

Paul sat back in the carriage for a long time looking at the photograph, while his companions played several hands of poker in reckless disregard of Standing Orders. In his six weeks of solitude and grave consideration he had failed to make up his mind about Margot Beste-Chetwynde; it was torn and distracted by two conflicting methods of thought. On one side was the dead weight of precept, inherited from generations of schoolmasters and divines. According to these, the problem was difficult but not insoluble. He had 'done the right thing' in shielding the woman: so much was clear, but Margot had not quite filled the place assigned to her, for in this case, she was grossly culpable, and he was shielding her, not from misfortune nor injustice, but from the consequence of her crimes; he felt a flush about his knees as Boy Scout honour whispered that

Margot had got him into a row and ought jolly well to own up and face the music. As he sat over his post-bags he had wrestled with this argument without achieving any satisfactory result except a growing conviction that there was something radically inapplicable about this whole code of ready-made honour that is the still small voice, trained to command, of the Englishman all the world over. On the other hand was the undeniable cogency of Peter Beste-Chetwynde's 'You can't see Mamma in prison, can you?' The more Paul considered this, the more he perceived it to be the statement of a natural law. He appreciated the assumption of comprehension with which Peter had delivered it. As he studied Margot's photograph, dubiously transmitted as it was, he was strengthened in his belief that there was, in fact, and should be, one law for her and another for himself, and that the raw little exertions of nineteenth-century Radicals were essentially base and trivial and misdirected. It was not simply that Margot had been very rich or that he had been in love with her. It was just that he *saw* the *impossibility* of Margot in prison; the bare connection of vocables associating the ideas was obscene. Margot dressed in prison uniform, hustled down corridors by wardresses–all like the younger Miss Fagan–visited by philanthropic old ladies with devotional pamphlets, set to work in the laundry washing the other prisoners' clothes–these things were *impossible*, and if the preposterous processes of law had condemned her, then the woman that they actually caught and pinned down would not have been Margot, but some quite other person of the same name and somewhat similar appearance. It was impossible to imprison the Margot who had committed the crime. If someone had to suffer that the public might be discouraged from providing poor Mrs Grimes with the only employment for which civilization had prepared her, then it had better be Paul than that other woman with Margot's name, for anyone who has been to an English public school will always feel comparatively at home in prison. It is the people brought up in the gay intimacy of the slums, Paul learned, who find prison so soul-destroying.

How lovely Margot was, Paul reflected, even in this absurd photograph, this grey-and-black smudge of ink! Even the most hardened criminal there–he was serving his third sentence for blackmail–laid down his cards for a moment and remarked upon how the whole carriage seemed to be flooded with the delectable savour of the Champs-Elysées in early June. 'Funny,' he said. 'I thought I smelt scent.'

And that set them off talking about women.

Paul found another old friend at Egdon Heath Prison: a short, thick-set, cheerful figure who stumped along in front of him on the way to chapel, making a good deal of noise with an artificial leg. 'Here we are again, old boy!' he remarked during one of the responses. 'I'm in the soup as per usual.'

'Didn't you like the job?' Paul asked.

'Top hole,' said Grimes, 'but the hell of a thing happened. Tell you later.'

That morning, complete with pickaxes, field-telephone and two armed and mounted warders, Paul and a little squad of fellow-criminals were led to the quarries. Grimes was in the party.

'I've been here a fortnight,' said Grimes as soon as they got an opportunity of talking, 'and it seems too long already. I've always been a sociable chap, and I don't like it. Three years is too long, old boy. Still, we'll have God's own beano when I get out. I've been thinking about that day and night.'

'I suppose it was bigamy?' said Paul.

'The same. I ought to have stayed abroad. I was arrested as soon as I landed. You see, Mrs Grimes turned up at the shop, so off Grimes went. There are various sorts of hell, but that young woman can beat up a pretty lively one of her own.'

A warder passed them by, and they moved apart, banging industriously at the sandstone cliff before them.

'I'm not sure it wasn't worth it, though,' said Grimes, 'to see poor old Flossie in the box and my sometime father-in-law. I hear the old man's shut down the school. Grimes gave the place a bad name. See anything of old Prendy ever?'

'He was murdered the other day.'

'Poor old Prendy! He wasn't cut out for the happy life, was he? D'you know, I think I shall give up schoolmastering for good when I get out. It doesn't lead anywhere.'

'It seems to have led us both to the same place.'

'Yes. Rather a coincidence, isn't it? Damn, here's that policeman again.'

Soon they were marched back to the prison. Except for the work in the quarries, life at Egdon was almost the same as at Blackstone.

'Slops outside', chapel, privacy.

After a week, however, Paul became conscious of an alien influence at work. His first intimation of this came from the Chaplain.

'Your library books,' he said one day, popping cheerfully into Paul's cell and handing him two new novels, still in their wrappers, and bearing inside them the label of a Piccadilly bookseller. 'If you don't like them I have several for you to choose from.' He showed him rather coyly the pile of gaily-bound volumes he carried under his arm. 'I thought you'd like the new Virginia Woolf. It's only been out two days.'

'Thank you, sir,' said Paul politely. Clearly the library of his new prison was run on a much more enterprising and extravagant plan than at Blackstone.

'Or there's this book on Theatrical Design,' said the Chaplain, showing him a large illustrated volume that could hardly have cost less than three guineas. 'Perhaps we might stretch a point and give you that as well as your "educational work".'

'Thank you, sir,' said Paul.

'Let me know if you want a change,' said the Chaplain. 'And, by the way, you're allowed to write a letter now, you know. If, by any chance, you're writing to Mrs Beste-Chetwynde, do mention that you think the library good. She's presenting a new pulpit to the chapel in carved alabaster,' he added irrelevantly, and popped out again to give Grimes a copy of Smiles' *Self-Help*, out of which some unreceptive reader in the remote past had torn the last hundred and eight pages.

'People may think as they like about well-thumbed favourites,' thought Paul, 'but there is something incomparably thrilling in first opening a brand-new book. Why should the Chaplain want me to mention the library to Margot?' he wondered.

That evening at supper Paul noticed without surprise that there were several small pieces of coal in his dripping: that kind of thing did happen now and then;

but he was somewhat disconcerted, when he attempted to scrape them out, to find that they were quite soft. Prison food was often rather odd; it was a mistake to complain; but still. . . . He examined his dripping more closely. It had a pinkish tinge that should not have been there and was unusually firm and sticky under his knife. He tasted it dubiously. It was *pâté de foie gras*.

From then onwards there was seldom a day on which some small meteorite of this kind did not mysteriously fall from the outside world. One day he returned from the heath to find his cell heavy with scent in the half-dark, for the lights were rarely lit until some time after sundown, and the window was very small. His table was filled with a large bunch of winter roses, which had cost three shillings each that morning in Bond Street. (Prisoners at Egdon are allowed to keep flowers in their cells, and often risk severe reprimand by stooping to pick pimpernels and periwinkles on their way from work.)

On another occasion the prison-doctor, trotting on his daily round of inspection, paused at Paul's cell, examined his name on the card hanging inside his door, looked hard at him and said, 'You need a tonic.' He trotted on without more ado, but next day a huge medicine-bottle was placed in Paul's cell. 'You're to take two glasses with each meal,' said the warder, 'and I hopes you like it.' Paul could not quite decide whether the warder's tone was friendly or not, but he liked the medicine, for it was brown sherry.

On another occasion great indignation was aroused in the cell next door to him, whose occupant–an aged burglar–was inadvertently given Paul's ration of caviare. He was speedily appeased by the substitution for it of an unusually large lump of cold bacon, but not before the warder in charge had suffered considerable alarm at the possibility of a complaint to the Governor.

'I'm not one to make a fuss usually,' said the old burglar, 'but I will be treated fair. Why, you only had to look at the stuff they give me to see it was bad, let alone taste it. And on bacon night, too! You take my tip,' he said to Paul as they found themselves alone in the quarries one day, 'and keep your eyes open. You're a new one, and they might easily try and put a thing like that over on you. Don't eat it; that's putting you in the wrong. Keep it and show it to the Governor. They ain't got no right to try on a thing like that, and they knows it.'

Presently a letter came from Margot. It was not a long one.

Darling Paul (*it said*),

It is so difficult writing to you because, you know, I never can write letters, and it's so particularly hard with you because the policemen read it and cross it all out if they don't like it, and I can't really think of anything they will like. Peter and I are back at King's Thursday. It was divine at Corfu, except for an English doctor who was a bore and would call so often. Do you know, I don't really like this house terribly, and I'm having it redone. Do you mind? Peter has become an earl–did you know?–and is rather sweet about it, and very self-conscious, which you wouldn't expect, really, would you, knowing Peter? I'm going to come and see you some time–may I?–when I can get away, but Bobby P.'s death has made such a lot of things to see to. I do hope you're getting enough food and books and things, or will they cross that out? Love, Margot. I was cut by Lady Circumference, my dear, at Newmarket, a real point-blank Tranby Croft cut. Poor Maltravers says if I'm not careful I shall find myself socially ostracized. Don't you think that will be marvellous? I may be wrong, but, d'you know, I rather believe poor little Alastair Trumpington's going to fall in love with me. What shall I do?

Eventually Margot came herself.

It was the first time they had met since the morning in June when she had sent him off to rescue her distressed protégées in Marseilles. The meeting took place in a small room set aside for visitors. Margot sat at one end of the table, Paul at the other, with a warder between them.

'I must ask you both to put your hands on the table in front of you,' said the warder.

'Like Up Jenkins,' said Margot faintly, laying her exquisitely manicured hands with the gloves beside her bag. Paul for the first time noticed how coarse and ill-kept his hands had become. For a moment neither spoke.

'Do I look awful?' Paul said at last. 'I haven't seen a looking-glass for some time.'

'Well, perhaps just a little *mal soigné*, darling. Don't they let you shave at all?'

'No discussion of the prison régime is permitted. Prisoners are allowed to make a plain statement of their state of health, but must on no account make complaints or comments upon their general condition.'

'Oh dear!' said Margot; 'this is going to be very difficult. What are we to say to each other? I'm almost sorry I came. You are glad I came, aren't you?'

'Don't mind me, mum, if you wants to talk personal,' said the warder kindly. 'I only has to stop conspiracy. Nothing I hears ever goes any further, and I hears a good deal, I can tell you. They carry on awful, some of the women, what with crying and fainting and hysterics generally. Why, one of them,' he said with relish, 'had an epileptic fit not long ago.'

'I think it's more than likely I shall have a fit,' said Margot. 'I've never felt so shy in my life. Paul, *do* say something, please.'

'How's Alastair?' said Paul.

'Rather sweet, really. He's always at King's Thursday now. I like him.'

Another pause.

'Do you know,' said Margot, 'it's an odd thing, but I do believe that after all these years I'm beginning to be regarded as no longer a respectable woman. I told you when I wrote, didn't I, that Lady Circumference cut me the other day? Of course she's just a thoroughly bad-mannered old woman, but there have been a whole lot of things rather like that lately. Don't you think it's rather awful?'

'You won't mind much, will you?' said Paul. 'They're awful old bores, anyway.'

'Yes, but I don't like *them* dropping *me*. Of course, I don't mind, really, but I think it's a pity, particularly for Peter. It's not just Lady Circumference, but Lady Vanbrugh and Fanny Simpleforth and the Stayles and all those people. It's a pity it should happen just when Peter's beginning to be a little class-conscious, anyway. It'll give him all the wrong ideas, don't you think?'

'How's business?' asked Paul abruptly.

'Paul, you mustn't be nasty to me,' said Margot in a low voice. 'I don't think you'd say that if you knew quite how I was feeling.'

'I'm sorry, Margot. As a matter of fact, I just wanted to know.'

'I'm selling out. A Swiss firm was making things difficult. But I don't think that business has anything to do with the–the ostracism, as Maltravers would say. I believe it's all because I'm beginning to grow old.'

'I never heard anything so ridiculous. Why, all those people are about eighty, and anyway you aren't at all.'

'I was afraid you wouldn't understand,' said Margot, and there was another pause.

'Ten minutes more,' said the warder.

'Things haven't turned out quite as we expected them to, have they?' said Margot.

They talked about some parties Margot had been to and the books Paul was reading. At last Margot said: 'Paul, I'm going. I simply can't stand another moment of this.'

'It was nice of you to come,' said Paul.

'I've decided something rather important,' said Margot, 'just this minute. I am going to be married quite soon to Maltravers. I'm sorry, but I am.'

'I suppose it's because I look so awful?' said Paul.

'No, it's just everything. It's that, too, in a way, but not the way you mean, Paul. It's simply something that's going to happen. Do you understand at all, dear? It may help you, too, in a way, but I don't want you to think that that's the reason, either. It's just how things are going to happen. Oh dear! How difficult it is to say anything.'

'If you should want to kiss goodbye,' said the gaoler, 'not being husband and wife, it's not usual. Still, I don't mind stretching a point for once. . . .'

'Oh, God!' said Margot, and left the room without looking back.

Paul returned to his cell. His supper had already been served out to him, a small pie from which protruded the feet of two pigeons; there was even a table-napkin wrapped round it. But Paul had very little appetite, for he was greatly pained at how little he was pained by the events of the afternoon.

5

THE PASSING OF A PUBLIC SCHOOL MAN

A day or two later Paul again found himself next to Grimes in the quarry. When the warder was out of earshot Grimes said: 'Old boy, I can't stand this much longer. It just ain't good enough.'

'I don't see any way out,' said Paul. 'Anyway, it's quite bearable. I'd as soon be here as at Llanabba.'

'Not so Grimes,' said Grimes. 'He just languishes in captivity, like the lark. It's all right for you–you like reading and thinking, and all that. Well, I'm different, you know. I like drink and a bit of fun, and chatting now and then to my pals. I'm a sociable chap. It's turning me into a giddy machine, this life, and there's an awful chaplain, who gives me the pip, who keeps butting in in a breezy kind of way and asking if I feel I'm "right with God". Of course I'm not, and I tell him so. I can stand most sorts of misfortune, old boy, but I can't stand repression. That was what broke me up at Llanabba, and it's what's going to break me up here, if I don't look out for myself. It seems to me it's time Grimes flitted off to another clime.'

'No one has ever succeeded in escaping from this prison,' said Paul.

'Well, just you watch Grimes next time there's a fog!'

As luck would have it, there was a fog next day, a heavy impenetrable white mist which came up quite suddenly while they were at work, enveloping men and quarry in the way that mists do on Egdon Heath.

'Close up there,' said the warder in charge. 'Stop work and close up. Look out there, you idiot!' for Grimes had stumbled over the field-telephone. 'If you've broken it you'll come up before the Governor tomorrow.'

'Hold this horse,' said the other warder, handing the reins to Grimes.

He stooped and began to collect the chains on which the men were strung for their march home. Grimes seemed to be having some difficulty with the horse, which was plunging and rearing further away from the squad. 'Can't you even hold a horse?' said the warder. Suddenly Grimes, with remarkable agility considering his leg, was seen to be in the saddle riding away into the heath.

'Come back,' roared the warder, 'come back, or I'll fire.' He put his rifle to his shoulder and fired into the fog. 'He'll come back all right,' he said. 'No one ever gets away for long. He'll get solitary confinement and No. 1 diet for this, poor fish.'

No one seemed to be much disturbed by the incident, even when it was found that the field-telephone was disconnected.

'He hasn't a hope,' said the warder. 'They often do that, just put down their tools sudden and cut and run. But they can't get away in those clothes and with no money. We shall warn all the farms tonight. Sometimes they stays out hiding for several days, but back they comes when they're hungry, or else they get arrested the moment they shows up in a village. I reckon it's just nerves makes them try it.'

That evening the horse came back, but there was no sign of Grimes. Special patrols were sent out with bloodhounds straining at their leashes; the farms and villages on the heath were warned, and the anxious inhabitants barred their doors closely and more pertinently forbade their children to leave the house on any pretext whatever; the roads were watched for miles, and all cars were stopped and searched, to the intense annoyance of many law-abiding citizens. But Grimes did not turn up. Bets were slyly made among the prisoners as to the day of his recovery; but days passed, and rations of bread changed hands, but still there was no Grimes.

A week later at morning service the Chaplain prayed for his soul: the Governor crossed his name off the Body Receipt Book and notified the Home Secretary, the Right Honourable Sir Humphrey Maltravers, that Grimes was dead.

'I'm afraid it was a terrible end,' said the Chaplain to Paul.

'Did they find the body?'

'No, that is the worst thing about it. The hounds followed his scent as far as Egdon Mire; there it ended. A shepherd who knows the paths through the bog found his hat floating on the surface at the most treacherous part. I'm afraid there is no doubt that he died a very horrible death.'

'Poor old Grimes!' said Paul. 'And he was an old Harrovian, too.'

But later, thinking things over as he ate peacefully, one by one, the oysters that had been provided as a 'relish' for his supper, Paul knew that Grimes was not dead. Lord Tangent was dead; Mr Prendergast was dead; the time would even come for Paul Pennyfeather; but Grimes, Paul at last realized, was of the immortals. He was a life force. Sentenced to death in Flanders, he popped up in

Wales; drowned in Wales, he emerged in South America; engulfed in the dark mystery of Egdon Mire, he would rise again somewhere at some time, shaking from his limbs the musty integuments of the tomb. Surely he had followed in the Bacchic train of distant Arcady, and played on the reeds of myth by forgotten streams, and taught the childish satyrs the art of love? Had he not suffered unscathed the fearful dooms of all the offended gods of all the histories–fire, brimstone and yawning earthquakes, plague and pestilence? Had he not stood, like the Pompeian sentry, while the Citadels of the Plain fell to ruin about his ears? Had he not, like some grease-caked Channel-swimmer, breasted the waves of the Deluge? Had he not moved unseen when darkness covered the waters?

'I often wonder whether I am blameless in the matter,' said the Chaplain. 'It is awful to think of someone under my care having come to so terrible an end. I tried to console him and reconcile him with his life, but things are so difficult; there are so many men to see. Poor fellow! To think of him alone out there in the bog, with no one to help him!'

6

THE PASSING OF PAUL PENNYFEATHER

A few days later Paul was summoned to the Governor's room.

'I have an order here from the Home Secretary granting leave for you to go into a private nursing home for the removal of your appendix. You will start under escort, in plain clothes, this morning.'

'But, sir,' said Paul, 'I don't want to have my appendix removed. In fact, it was done years ago when I was still at school.'

'Nonsense!' said the Governor. 'I've got an order here from the Home Secretary especially requiring that it shall be done. Officer, take this man away and give him his clothes for the journey.'

Paul was led away. The clothes in which he had been tried had been sent with him from Blackstone. The warder took them out of a locker, unfolded them and handed them to Paul. 'Shoes, socks, trousers, waistcoat, coat, shirt, collar, tie and hat,' he said. 'Will you sign for them? The jewellery stays here.' He collected the watch, links, tie-pin, note-case and the other odds and ends that had been in Paul's pockets and put them back in the locker. 'We can't do anything about your hair,' said the warder, 'but you're allowed a shave.'

Half an hour later Paul emerged from his cell, looking for all the world like a normal civilized man, such as you might see daily in any tube-railway.

'Feels funny, don't it?' said the warder who let him out. 'Here's your escort.'

Another normal civilized man, such as you might see daily in any tube-railway, confronted Paul.

'Time we started, if you're quite ready,' he said. Robbed of their uniforms, it seemed natural that they should treat each other with normal consideration. Indeed, Paul thought he detected a certain deference in the man's tone.

'It's very odd,' said Paul in the van that took them to the station; 'it's no good arguing with the Governor, but he's made some ridiculous mistake.

I've had my appendix out already.'

'Not half,' said the warder with a wink, 'but don't go talking about it so loud. The driver's not in on this.'

A first-class carriage had been reserved for them in the train. As they drew out of Egdon Station the warder said: 'Well, that's the last you'll see of the old place for some time. Solemn thought, death, ain't it?' And he gave another shattering wink.

They had luncheon in their carriage, Paul feeling a little too shy of his closely-cropped head to venture hatless into the restaurant car. After luncheon they smoked cigars. The warder paid from a fat note-case. 'Oh, I nearly forgot,' he said. 'Here's your will for you to sign, in case anything should happen.' He produced a long blue paper and handed it to Paul. *The Last Will and Testament of Paul Pennyfeather* was handsomely engraved at the top. Below, it was stated, with the usual legal periphrases, that he left all he possessed to Margot Beste-Chetwynde. Two witnesses had already signed below the vacant space. 'I'm sure this is all very irregular,' said Paul, signing; 'I wish you'd tell me what all this means.'

'I don't know nothing,' said the warder. 'The young gentleman give me the will.'

'What young gentleman?'

'How should I know!' said the warder. 'The young gentleman what's arranged everything. Very sensible to make a will. You never know with an operation what may happen, do you? I had an aunt died having gall-stones taken out, and she hadn't made a will. Very awkward it was, her not being married properly, you see. Fine, healthy woman, too, to look at her. Don't you get worried, Mr Pennyfeather; everything will be done strictly according to regulations.'

'Where are we going? At least you must know that.'

For answer the warder took a printed card from his pocket.

Cliff Place, Worthing, he read. *High-class Nursing and Private Sanatorium. Electrical thermal treatment under medical supervision. Augustus Fagan, M.D., Proprietor*. 'Approved by the Home Secretary,' said the warder. 'Nothing to complain of.'

Late in the afternoon they arrived. A car was waiting to take them to Cliff Place.

'This ends my responsibility,' said the warder. 'From now on the doctor's in charge.'

Like all Dr Fagan's enterprises, Cliff Place was conceived on a large scale. The house stood alone on the sea-shore some miles from the town, and was approached by a long drive. In detail, however, it showed some signs of neglect. The veranda was deep in driven leaves; two of the windows were broken. Paul's escort rang the bell at the front door, and Dingy, dressed as a nurse, opened it to them.

'The servants have all gone,' she said. 'I suppose this is the appendicitis case. Come in.' She showed no signs of recognizing Paul as she led him upstairs. 'This is your room. The Home Office regulations insisted that it should be on an upper story with barred windows. We have had to put the bars in specially. They will be charged for in the bill. The surgeon will be here in a few minutes.'

As she went out she locked the door. Paul sat down on the bed and waited. Below his window the sea beat on the shingle. A small steam-yacht lay at anchor some distance out to sea. The grey horizon faded indistinctly into the grey sky.

Presently steps approached, and his door opened. In came Dr Fagan, Sir Alastair Digby-Vaine-Trumpington, and an elderly little man with a drooping red moustache, evidently much the worse for drink.

'Sorry we're late,' said Sir Alastair, 'but I've had an awful day with this man trying to keep him sober. He gave me the slip just as we were starting. I was afraid at first that he was too tight to be moved, but I think he can just carry on. Have you got the papers made out?'

No one paid much attention to Paul.

'Here they are,' said Dr Fagan. 'This is the statement you are to forward to the Home Secretary, and a duplicate for the Governor of the prison. Shall I read them to you?'

''Sh'all right!' said the surgeon.

'They merely state that you operated on the patient for appendicitis, but that he died under the anaesthetic without regaining consciousness.'

'Poor ole chap!' said the surgeon. 'Poor, poor l'il girl!' And two tears of sympathy welled up in his eyes. 'I dare say the world had been very hard on her. It's a hard world for women.'

'That's all right,' said Sir Alastair. 'Don't worry. You did all that was humanly possible.'

'That's the truth,' said the surgeon, 'and I don't care who knows it.'

'This is the ordinary certificate of death,' said Dr Fagan. 'Will you be so good as to sign it there?'

'Oh, death, where is thy sting-a-ling-a-ling?' said the surgeon, and with these words and a laboured effort of the pen he terminated the legal life of Paul Pennyfeather.

'Splendid!' said Sir Alastair. 'Now here's your money. If I were you I should run off and have a drink while the pubs are still open.'

'D'you know, I think I will,' said the surgeon, and left the sanatorium.

There was a hush for nearly a minute after he had left the room. The presence of death, even in its coldest and most legal form, seemed to cause an air of solemnity. It was broken by the arrival of Flossie, splendidly attired in magenta and green.

'Why, here you all are!' she said with genuine delight. 'And Mr Pennyfeather too, to be sure! Quite a little party!'

She had said the right thing. The word 'party' seemed to strike a responsive note in Dr Fagan.

'Let us go down to supper,' he said. 'I'm sure we all have a great deal to be thankful for.'

After supper Dr Fagan made a little speech. 'I think this an important evening for most of us,' he said, 'most of all for my dear friend and some-time colleague Paul Pennyfeather, in whose death tonight we are all to some extent participants. For myself as well as for him it is the beginning of a new phase of life. Frankly, this nursing home has not been a success. A time must come to every man when he begins to doubt his vocation. You may think me almost an old man, but I do not feel too old to start light-heartedly on a new manner of life. This evening's events have made this possible for me. I think,' he said, glancing at his daughters, 'that it is time I was alone. But this is not the hour to review the plans of my future. When you get to my age, if you have been at all observant of the people you have met and the accidents which have happened to you, you cannot help being struck with an amazing cohesiveness of events. How promiscuously we who are here this evening have been thrown together! How enduring and endearing the memories that from now onwards will unite us! I think we should drink a toast–to Fortune, a much-maligned lady.'

Once before Paul had drunk the same toast. This time there was no calamity. They drank silently, and Alastair rose from the table.

'It's time Paul and I were going,' he said.

They walked down to the beach together. A boat was waiting for them.

'That's Margot's yacht,' said Alastair. 'It's to take you to her house at Corfu until you've decided about things. Goodbye. Good luck!'

'Aren't you coming any further?' asked Paul.

'No, I've got to drive back to King's Thursday. Margot will be anxious to know how things have gone off.'

Paul got into the boat and was rowed away. Sir Alastair, like Sir Bedivere, watched him out of sight.

7

RESURRECTION

Three weeks later Paul sat on the veranda of Margot's villa, with his evening *aperitif* before him, watching the sunset on the Albanian hills across the water change, with the crude brilliance of a German picture-postcard, from green to violet. He looked at his watch, which had that morning arrived from England. It was half-past six.

Below him in the harbour a ship had come in from Greece and was unloading her cargo. The little boats hung round her like flies, plying their trade of olive-wood souvenirs and forged francs. There were two hours before dinner. Paul rose and descended the arcaded street into the square, drawing his scarf tight about his throat; the evenings began to get cold about this time. It was odd being dead. That morning Margot had sent him a bunch of Press cuttings about himself, most of them headed WEDDING SENSATION ECHO or DEATH OF SOCIETY BRIDEGROOM CONVICT. With them were his tie-pin and the rest of his possessions which had been sent to her from Egdon. He felt the need of the bustle of the cafés and the quay-side to convince him fully of his existence. He stopped at a stall and bought some Turkish delight. It was odd being dead.

Suddenly he was aware of a familiar figure approaching him across the square.

'Hullo!' said Paul.

'Hullo!' said Otto Silenus. He was carrying on his shoulder a shapeless knapsack of canvas.

'Why don't you give that to one of the boys? They'll take it for a few drachmas.'

'I have no money. Will you pay him?'

'Yes.'

'All right! Then that will be best. I suppose you are staying with Margot?'

'I'm staying at her house. She's in England.'

'That's a pity. I hoped I should find her here. Still I will stay for a little, I think. Will there be room for me?'

'I suppose so. I'm all alone here.'

'I have changed my mind. I think, after all, I will marry Margot.'

'I'm afraid it's too late.'

'Too late?'

'Yes, she's married someone else.'

'I never thought of that. Oh well, it doesn't matter really. Whom did she marry? That sensible Maltravers?'

'Yes, he's changed his name now. He's called Viscount Metroland.'

'What a funny name!'

They walked up the hill together. 'I've just been to Greece to see the buildings there,' said Professor Silenus.

'Did you like them?'

'They are unspeakably ugly. But there were some nice goats. I thought they sent you to prison.'

'Yes, they did, but I got out.'

'Yes, you must have, I suppose. Wasn't it nice?'

'Not terribly.'

'Funny! I thought it would suit you so well. You never can tell with people, can you, what's going to suit them?'

Margot's servants did not seem surprised at the arrival of another guest.

'I think I shall stay here a long time,' said Professor Silenus after dinner. 'I have no money left. Are you going soon?'

'Yes, I'm going back to Oxford again to learn theology.'

'That will be a good thing. You used not to have a moustache, used you?' he asked after a time.

'No,' said Paul. 'I'm just growing one now. I don't want people to recognize me when I go back to England.'

'I think it's uglier,' said Professor Silenus. 'Well, I must go to bed.'

'Have you slept any better lately?'

'Twice since I saw you. It's about my average. Good night.'

Ten minutes later he came back on to the terrace, wearing silk pyjamas and a tattered old canvas dressing-gown.

'Can you lend me a nail file?' he asked.

'There's one on my dressing table.'

'Thank you.' But he did not go. Instead he walked to the parapet and leant out, looking across the sea. 'It's a good thing for you to be a clergyman,' he said at last. 'People get ideas about a thing they call life. It sets them all wrong. I think it's poets that are responsible chiefly. Shall I tell you about life?'

'Yes, do,' said Paul politely.

'Well, it's like the big wheel at Luna Park. Have you seen the big wheel?'

'No, I'm afraid not.'

'You pay five francs and go into a room with tiers of seats all round, and in the centre the floor is made of a great disc of polished wood that revolves quickly.

At first you sit down and watch the others. They are all trying to sit in the wheel, and they keep getting flung off, and that makes them laugh, and you laugh too. It's great fun.'

'I don't think that sounds very much like life,' said Paul rather sadly.

'Oh, but it is, though. You see, the nearer you can get to the hub of the wheel the slower it is moving and the easier it is to stay on. There's generally someone in the centre who stands up and sometimes does a sort of dance. Often he's paid by the management, though, or, at any rate, he's allowed in free. Of course at the very centre there's a point completely at rest, if one could only find it. I'm not sure I am not very near that point myself. Of course the professional men get in the way. Lots of people just enjoy scrambling on and being whisked off and scrambling on again. How they all shriek and giggle! Then there are others, like Margot, who sit as far out as they can and hold on for dear life and enjoy that. But the whole point about the wheel is that you needn't get on it at all, if you don't want to. People get hold of ideas about life, and that makes them think they've got to join in the game, even if they don't enjoy it. It doesn't suit every one.

'People don't see that when they say "life" they mean two different things. They can mean simply existence, with its physiological implications of growth and organic change. They can't escape that–even by death, but because that's inevitable they think the other idea of life is too–the scrambling and excitement and bumps and the effort to get to the middle. And when we do get to the middle, it's just as if we never started. It's so odd.

'Now you're a person who was clearly meant to stay in the seats and sit still and if you get bored watch the others. Somehow you got on to the wheel, and you got thrown off again at once with a hard bump. It's all right for Margot, who can cling on, and for me, at the centre, but you're static. Instead of this absurd division into sexes they ought to class people as static and dynamic. There's a real distinction there, though I can't tell you how it comes. I think we're probably two quite different species spiritually.

'I used that idea of the wheel in a cinema film once. I think it rather sounds like it, don't you? What was it I came back for?'

'A nail file.'

'Oh, yes, of course. I know of no more utterly boring and futile occupation than generalizing about life. Did you take in what I was saying?'

'Yes, I think so.'

'I think I shall have my meals alone in future. Will you tell the servants? It makes me feel quite ill to talk so much. Good night.'

'Good night,' said Paul.

Some months later Paul returned to Scone College after the absence of little more than a year. His death, though depriving him of his certificates, left him his knowledge. He sat successfully for Smalls and Matriculation and entered his old college once more, wearing a commoner's gown and a heavy cavalry moustache. This and his natural diffidence formed a complete disguise. Nobody recognized him. After much doubt and deliberation he retained the name of Pennyfeather, explaining to the Chaplain that he had, he believed, had a distant cousin at Scone a short time ago.

'He came to a very sad end,' said the Chaplain, 'a wild young man.'

'He was a *very* distant cousin,' said Paul hastily.

'Yes, yes, I am sure he was. There is no resemblance between you. He was a thoroughly degenerate type, I am afraid.'

Paul's scout also remembered the name.

'There used to be another Mr Pennyfeather on this staircase once,' he said, 'a very queer gentleman indeed. Would you believe it, sir, he used to take off all his clothes and go out and dance in the quad at night. Nice quiet gentleman, too, he was, except for his dancing. He must have been a little queer in his head, I suppose. I don't know what became of him. They say he died in prison.' Then he proceeded to tell Paul about an Annamese student who had attempted to buy one of the Senior Tutor's daughters.

On the second Sunday of term the Chaplain asked Paul to breakfast. 'It's a sad thing,' he said, 'the way that the 'Varsity breakfast–"brekker" we used to call it in my day–is dying out. People haven't time for it. Always off to lectures at nine o'clock, except on Sundays. Have another kidney, won't you?'

There was another don present, called Mr Sniggs, who addressed the Chaplain rather superciliously, Paul thought, as 'Padre'.

There was also an undergraduate from another college, a theological student called Stubbs, a grave young man with a quiet voice and with carefully formed opinions. He had a little argument with Mr Sniggs about the plans for rebuilding the Bodleian. Paul supported him.

Next day Paul found Stubbs' card on his table, the corner turned up. Paul went to Hertford to call on Stubbs, but found him out. He left his card, the corner turned up. Two days later a little note came from Hertford:

> Dear Pennyfeather,
> I wonder if you would care to come to tea next Tuesday, to meet the College Secretary of the League of Nations Union and the Chaplain of the Oxford prison. It would be so nice if you could.

Paul went and ate honey buns and anchovy toast. He liked the ugly, subdued little College, and he liked Stubbs.

As term went on Paul and Stubbs took to going for walks together, over Mesopotamia to Old Marston and Beckley. One afternoon, quite light-hearted at the fresh weather, and their long walk, and their tea, Stubbs signed *Randal Cantuar* in the visitors' book.

Paul rejoined the League of Nations Union and the O.S.C.U. On one occasion he and Stubbs and some other friends went to the prison to visit the criminals there and sing part-songs to them.

'It opens the mind,' said Stubbs, 'to see all sides of life. How those unfortunate men appreciated our singing!'

One day in Blackwell's bookshop Paul found a stout volume, which, the assistant told him, was rapidly becoming a best-seller. It was called *Mother Wales*, by Augustus Fagan. Paul bought it and took it back with him. Stubbs had already read it.

'Most illuminating,' he said. 'The Hospital statistics are terrible. Do you think it would be a good idea to organize a joint debate with Jesus on the subject?' The book was dedicated '*To my wife, a wedding present*'. It was eloquently written. When he had read it Paul put it on his shelves next to Dean Stanley's *Eastern Church*.

One other incident recalled momentarily Paul's past life.

One day, at the beginning of his second year, as Paul and Stubbs were bicycling down the High as from one lecture to another, they nearly ran into an open Rolls-Royce that swung out of Oriel Street at a dangerous speed. In the back, a heavy fur rug over his knees, sat Philbrick. He turned round as he passed and waved a gloved hand to Paul over the hood.

'Hullo!' he said; 'hullo! How are you? Come and look me up one day. I'm living on the river–Skindle's.'

Then the car disappeared down the High Street, and Paul went on to his lecture.

'Who was your opulent friend?' asked Stubbs, rather impressed.

'Arnold Bennett,' said Paul.

'I thought I knew his face,' said Stubbs.

Then the lecturer came in, arranged his papers and began a lucid exposition of the heresies of the second century. There was a bishop in Bithynia, Paul learned, who had denied the Divinity of Christ, the immortality of the soul, the existence of good, the legality of marriage, and the validity of the Sacrament of Extreme Unction! How right they had been to condemn him!

EPILOGUE

It was Paul's third year of uneventful residence at Scone.

Stubbs finished his cocoa, knocked out his pipe and rose to go. 'I must be off to my digs,' he said. 'You're lucky staying in college. It's a long ride back to Walton Street on a night like this.'

'D'you want to take Von Hugel?' asked Paul.

'No, not tonight. May I leave it till tomorrow?'

Stubbs picked up his scholar's gown and wrapped it round his shoulders. 'That was an interesting paper tonight about the Polish plebiscites.'

'Yes, wasn't it?' said Paul.

Outside there was a confused roaring and breaking of glass.

'The Bollinger seem to be enjoying themselves,' said Paul. 'Whose rooms are they in this time?'

'Pastmaster's, I think. That young man seems to be going a bit fast for his age.'

'Well, I hope he enjoys it,' said Paul. 'Good night.'

'Good night, Paul,' said Stubbs.

Paul put the chocolate biscuits back in the cupboard, refilled his pipe, and settled down in his chair.

Presently he heard footsteps and a knock at his door.

'Come in,' he said, looking round.

Peter Pastmaster came into the room. He was dressed in the bottle-green and white evening coat of the Bollinger Club. His face was flushed and his dark hair slightly disordered.

'May I come in?'

'Yes, do.'

'Have you got a drink?'

'You seem to have had a good many already.'

'I've had the Boller in my rooms. Noisy lot. Oh, hell! I must have a drink.'

'There's some whisky in the cupboard. You're drinking rather a lot these days, aren't you, Peter?'

Peter said nothing, but helped himself to some whisky and soda.

'Feeling a bit ill,' he said. Then, after a pause, 'Paul, why have you been cutting me all this time?'

'I don't know. I didn't think there was much to be gained by our knowing each other.'

'Not angry about anything?'

'No, why should I be?'

'Oh, I don't know.' Peter turned his glass in his hand, staring at it intently. 'I've been rather angry with you, you know.'

'Why?'

'Oh, I don't know–about Margot and the man Maltravers and everything.'

'I don't think I was much to blame.'

'No, I suppose not, only you were part of it all.'

'How's Margot?'

'She's all right–*Margot Metroland*. D'you mind if I take another drink?'

'I suppose not.'

'Viscountess Metroland,' said Peter. 'What a name. What a man! Still, she's got Alastair all the time. Metroland doesn't mind. He's got what he wanted. I don't see much of them really. What do you do all the time, Paul?'

'I'm going to be ordained soon.'

'Wish I didn't feel so damned ill. What were we saying? Oh yes, about Metroland. You know, Paul, I think it was a mistake you ever got mixed up with us; don't you? We're different somehow. Don't quite know how. Don't think that's rude, do you, Paul?'

'No, I know exactly what you mean. You're dynamic, and I'm static.'

'Is that it? Expect you're right. Funny thing you used to teach me once; d'you remember? Llanabba–Latin sentences, *Quominus* and *Quin*, and the organ; d'you remember?'

'Yes, I remember,' said Paul.

'Funny how things happen. You used to teach me the organ; d'you remember?'

'Yes, I remember,' said Paul.

'And then Margot Metroland wanted to marry you; d'you remember?'

'Yes,' said Paul.

'And then you went to prison, and Alastair–that's Margot Metroland's young man–and Metroland–that's her husband–got you out; d'you remember?'

'Yes,' said Paul, 'I remember.'

'And here we are talking to one another like this, up here, after all that! Funny, isn't it?'

'Yes, it is rather.'

'Paul, do you remember a thing you said once at the Ritz–Alastair was there–that's Margot Metroland's young man, you know–d'you remember? I was rather tight then too. You said, "Fortune, a much-maligned lady". D'you remember that?'

'Yes,' said Paul, 'I remember.'

'Good old Paul! I knew you would. Let's drink to that now; shall we? How did it go? Damn, I've forgotten it. Never mind. I wish I didn't feel so ill.'

'You drink too much, Peter.'

'Oh, damn, what else is there to do? You going to be a clergyman, Paul?'

'Yes.'

'Damned funny that. You know you ought never to have got mixed up with me and Metroland. May I have another drink?'

'Time you went to bed, Peter, don't you think?'

'Yes, I suppose it is. Didn't mind my coming in, did you? After all, you used to teach me the organ; d'you remember? Thanks for the whisky!'

So Peter went out, and Paul settled down again in his chair. So the ascetic Ebionites used to turn towards Jerusalem when they prayed. Paul made a note of it. Quite right to suppress them. Then he turned out the light and went into his bedroom to sleep.

Black Mischief

EVELYN WAUGH

BLACK MISCHIEF

To Mary and Dorothy Lygon
with love

I

'*We, Seth, Emperor of Azania, Chief of the Chiefs of Sakuyu, Lord of Wanda and Tyrant of the Seas, Bachelor of the Arts of Oxford University, being in this the twenty-fourth year of our life, summoned by the wisdom of Almight God and the unanimous voice of our people to the throne of our ancestors, do hereby proclaim . . .*' Seth paused in his dictation and gazed out across the harbour where in the fresh breeze of early morning the last dhow was setting sail for the open sea. 'Rats,' he said; 'stinking curs. They are all running away.'

The Indian secretary sat attentive, his fountain pen poised over the pad of writing paper, his eyes blinking gravely behind rimless pince-nez.

'Is there still no news from the hills?'

'None of unquestionable veracity, your majesty.'

'I gave orders that the wireless was to be mended. Where is Marx? I told him to see to it.'

'He evacuated the town late yesterday evening.'

'He evacuated the town?'

'In your majesty's motor-boat. There was a large company of them–the stationmaster, the chief of police, the Armenian Archbishop, the Editor of the *Azanian Courier*, the American vice-consul. All the most distinguished gentlemen in Matodi.'

'I wonder you weren't with them yourself, Ali.'

'There was not room. I suppose that with so many distinguished gentlemen there was danger of submersion.'

'Your loyalty shall be rewarded. Where had I got to?'

'The last eight words in reproof of the fugitives were an interpolation?'

'Yes, yes, of course.'

'I will make the erasion. Your majesty's last words were "*do hereby proclaim*".'

'*Do hereby proclaim amnesty and free pardon to all those of our subjects recently seduced from their loyalty, who shall during the eight days subsequent to this date return to their lawful allegiance. Furthermore . . .*'

They were in the upper story of the old fort at Matodi. Here, three hundred years before, a Portuguese garrison had withstood eight months' siege from the Omani Arabs; at this window they had watched for the sails of the relieving fleet, which came ten days too late.

Over the main door traces of an effaced escutcheon were still discernible, an idolatrous work repugnant to the prejudice of the conquerors.

For two centuries the Arabs remained masters of the coast. Behind them in the hills the native Sakuyu, black, naked, anthropophagous, had lived their own tribal life among their herds–emaciated, puny cattle with rickety shanks and elaborately branded hide. Farther away still lay the territory of the Wanda–Galla immigrants from the mainland who, long before the coming of the Arabs, had settled in the north of the island and cultivated it in irregular communal holdings. The Arabs held aloof from the affairs of both these people; war drums could often be heard inland and sometimes the whole hillside would be aflame with burning villages. On the coast a prosperous town arose: great houses of Arab merchants with intricate latticed windows and brass-studded doors, courtyards planted with dense mango trees, streets heavy with the reek of cloves and pineapple, so narrow that two mules could not pass without altercation between their drivers; a bazaar where the money changers, squatting over their scales, weighed out the coinage of a world-wide trade, Austrian thalers, rough stamped Mahratta gold, Spanish and Portuguese guineas. From Matodi the dhows sailed to the mainland, to Tanga, Dar-es-Salaam, Malindi and Kismayu, to meet the caravans coming down from the great lakes with ivory and slaves. Splendidly dressed Arab gentlemen paraded the water-front hand in hand and gossiped in the coffee houses. In early spring when the monsoon was blowing from the north-east, fleets came down from the Persian Gulf bringing to market a people of fairer skin who spoke a pure Arabic barely intelligible to the islanders, for with the passage of years their language had become full of alien words–Bantu from the mainland, Sakuyu and Galla from the interior–and the slave markets had infused a richer and darker strain into their Semitic blood; instincts of swamp and forest mingled with the austere tradition of the desert.

In one of these Muscat trading fleets came Seth's grandfather, Amurath, a man wholly unlike his companions, a slave's son, sturdy, bow-legged, three-quarters Negro. He had received education of a kind from Nestorian monks near Basra. At Matodi he sold his dhow and entered the Sultan's service.

It was a critical time in local history. The white men were returning. From Bombay they had fastened on Aden. They were in Zanzibar and the Sudan. They were pushing up round the Cape and down through the Canal. Their warships were cruising the Red Sea and the Indian Ocean intercepting slavers; the caravans from Tabora were finding difficulty in getting through to the coast. Trade in Matodi was almost at a standstill and a new listlessness became apparent in the leisured life of the merchants; they spent their days in the town moodily chewing khat. They could no longer afford to keep up their villas round the bay. Gardens ran wild and roofs fell into disrepair. The grass huts of the Sakuyu began to appear on the more remote estates. Groups of Wanda and Sakuyu came into town and swaggered insolently about the bazaars; an Arab party returning from one of the country villas was ambushed and murdered within a mile of the walls. There were rumours of a general massacre, planned in the hills. The European powers watched their opportunity to proclaim a Protectorate.

In this uncertain decade there suddenly appeared the figure of Amurath; first as commander-in-chief of the Sultan's forces, then as general of an independent army; finally as Emperor Amurath the Great. He armed the Wanda and at their head inflicted defeat after defeat on the Sakuyu, driving off their cattle, devastating their villages and hunting them down in the remote valleys of the island. Then he turned his conquering army against his old allies on the coast. In three years he proclaimed the island a single territory and himself its ruler. He changed its name. Until now it had been scored on the maps as Sakuyu Island; Amurath renamed it the Empire of Azania. He founded a new capital at Debra Dowa, two hundred miles inland on the borders of the Wanda and Sakuyu territories. It was the site of his last camp, a small village, partially burnt out. There was no road to the coast, only a faltering bush path which an experienced scout could follow. Here he set up his standard.

Presently there was a railway from Matodi to Debra Dowa. Three European companies held the concession in turn and failed; at the side of the line were the graves of two French engineers who went down with blackwater, and of numerous Indian coolies. The Sakuyu would wrench up the steel sleepers to forge spear heads and pull down lengths of copper telegraph wire to adorn their women. Lions came into the labour lines at night and carried off workmen; there were mosquitoes, snakes, tsetse fly, spirillum ticks; there were deep water courses to be bridged which for a few days in the year bore a great torrent down from the hills, bundling with it timber and boulders and an occasional corpse; there was a lava field to be crossed, a great waste of pumice five miles broad; in the hot season the metal blistered the hands of workmen; during the rains landslides and washouts would obliterate the work of months. Reluctantly, step by step, barbarism retreated; the seeds of progress took root and, after years of slow growth, burst finally into flower in the single, narrow-gauge track of the Grand Chemin de Fer Impérial d'Azanie. In the sixteenth year of his reign Amurath travelled in the first train from Matodi to Debra Dowa. With him sat delegates from France, Great Britain, Italy and the United States, his daughter and heir, her husband, while, in a cattle truck behind, rode a dozen or so illegitimate children; in another coach sat the hierarchies of the various Churches of Azania; in another the Arab sheiks from the coast, the paramount chief of the Wanda, and a shrivelled, scared old Negro, with one eye, who represented the Sakuyu. The train was decked with bunting, feathers and flowers; it whistled continuously from coast to capital; levies of irregular troops lined the way; a Jewish nihilist from Berlin threw a bomb which failed to explode; sparks from the engine started several serious bush fires; at Debra Dowa Amurath received the congratulations of the civilized world and created the French contractor a Marquess in the Azanian peerage.

The first few trains caused numerous deaths among the inhabitants, who for some time did not appreciate the speed or strength of this new thing that had come to their country. Presently they became more cautious and the service less frequent. Amurath had drawn up an elaborate time-table of express trains, local trains, goods trains, boat trains, schemes for cheap return tickets and excursions; he had printed a map showing the future developments of the line in a close mesh all over the island. But the railway was the last great achievement of his life; soon after its opening he lapsed into a coma from which he never recovered consciousness; he had a wide reputation for immortality; it was three years before his ministers, in response to insistent rumours, ventured to announce his death to the people. In the succeeding years the Grand Chemin de Fer Impérial d'Azanie failed to develop on the lines adumbrated by its founder. When Seth came down from Oxford there was a weekly service; a goods train at the back of which was hitched a single shabby saloon car, upholstered in threadbare plush. It took two days to accomplish the journey, resting the night at Lumo, where a Greek hotel proprietor had proposed a contract profitable to the president of the line; the delay was officially attributed to the erratic efficacy of the engine lights and the persistence of the Sakuyu in their depredations of the permanent way.

Amurath instituted other changes, less sensational than the railway, but nevertheless noteworthy. He proclaimed the abolition of slavery and was warmly applauded in the European Press; the law was posted up prominently in the capital in English, French and Italian where every foreigner might read it; it was never promulgated in the provinces nor translated into any of the native languages; the ancient system continued unhampered but European intervention had been anticipated. His Nestorian upbringing had strengthened his hand throughout in his dealings with the white men. Now he declared Christianity the official religion of the Empire, reserving complete freedom of conscience to his Mohammedan and pagan subjects. He allowed and encouraged an influx of missionaries. There were soon three Bishops in Debra Dowa–Anglican, Catholic and Nestorian–and three substantial cathedrals. There were also Quaker, Moravian, American-Baptist, Mormon and Swedish-Lutheran missions handsomely supported by foreign subscribers. All this brought money into the new capital and enhanced his reputation abroad. But his chief safeguard against European intrusion was a force of ten thousand soldiers, maintained under arms. These he had trained by Prussian officers. Their brass bands, goosestep and elaborate uniforms were at first the object of mild amusement. Then there was an international incident. A foreign commercial agent was knifed in a disorderly house on the coast. Amurath hanged the culprits publicly in the square before the Anglican Cathedral–and with them two or three witnesses whose evidence was held to be unsatisfactory–but there was a talk of indemnities. A punitive force was landed, composed half of European, half of mainland native troops. Amurath marched out against them with his new army and drove them in hopeless rout to the seashore where they were massacred under the guns of their own fleet. Six European officers of field rank surrendered and were hanged on the battlefield. On his triumphal return to the capital Amurath offered the White Fathers a silver altar to Our Lady of Victories.

Throughout the highlands his prestige became superhuman. 'I swear by Amurath' was a bond of inviolable sanctity. Only the Arabs remained unimpressed. He ennobled them, creating the heads of the chief families Earls, Viscounts and Marquesses, but these grave, impoverished men whose genealogies extended to the time of the Prophet preferred their original names. He married his daughter into the house of the old Sultan–but the young man accepted the elevation and his compulsory baptism into the National Church without enthusiasm. The marriage was considered a great disgrace by the Arabs. Their fathers would not have ridden a horse with so obscure a pedigree. Indians came in great numbers and slowly absorbed the business of the country. The large houses of Matodi were turned into tenements, hotels or offices. Soon the maze of mean streets behind the bazaar became designated as the 'Arab quarter'.

Very few of them migrated to the new capital, which was spreading out round the palace in a haphazard jumble of shops, missions, barracks, legations, bungalows and native huts. The palace itself, which occupied many acres enclosed by an irregular fortified stockade, was far from orderly or harmonious.

Its nucleus was a large stucco villa of French design; all round this were scattered sheds of various sizes which served as kitchens, servants' quarters and stables; there was a wooden guard-house and a great thatched barn which was used for state banquets; a domed, octagonal chapel and the large rubble and timber residence of the Princess and her consort. The ground between and about the buildings was uneven and untidy; stacks of fuel, kitchen refuse, derelict carriages, cannon and ammunition lay in prominent places; sometimes there would be a flyblown carcase of a donkey or camel, and after the rains pools of stagnant water; gangs of prisoners, chained neck to neck, could often be seen shovelling as though some project were on hand of levelling or draining, but except for the planting of a circle of eucalyptus trees, nothing was done in the old Emperor's time to dignify his surroundings.

Many of Amurath's soldiers settled round him in the new capital; in the first few years they were reinforced by a trickle of detribalized natives, drawn from their traditional grounds by the glamour of city life; the main population, however, was always cosmopolitan, and as the country's reputation as a land of opportunity spread through the less successful classes of the outside world Debra Dowa gradually lost all evidence of national character. Indians and Armenians came first and continued to come in yearly increasing numbers. Goans, Jews and Greeks followed, and later a race of partially respectable immigrants from the greater powers, mining engineers, prospectors, planters and contractors, on their world-wide pilgrimage in quest of cheap concessions. A few were lucky and got out of the country with modest fortunes; most were disappointed and became permanent residents, hanging round the bars and bemoaning over their cups the futility of expecting justice in a land run by a pack of niggers.

When Amurath died, and the courtiers at last could devise no further explanation of his prolonged seclusion, his daughter reigned as Empress. The funeral was a great occasion in East African history. A Nestorian patriarch came from Iraq to say the Mass; delegates from the European powers rode in the procession and as the bugles of the Imperial guard sounded the last post over the empty sarcophagus, vast crowds of Wanda and Sakuyu burst into wailing and lamentation, daubed their bodies with chalk and charcoal, stamped their feet, swayed and clapped in frantic, personal grief at the loss of their master.

Now the Empress was dead and Seth had returned from Europe to claim his Empire.

Noon in Matodi. The harbour lay still as a photograph, empty save for a few fishing boats moored motionless against the sea wall. No breeze stirred the royal standard that hung over the old fort. No traffic moved on the water-front. The offices were locked and shuttered. The tables had been cleared from the hotel terrace. In the shade of a mango the two sentries lay curled asleep, their rifles in the dust beside them.

'From Seth, Emperor of Azania, Chief of the Chiefs of Sakuyu, Lord of Wanda and Tyrant of the Seas, Bachelor of the Arts of Oxford University, to His Majesty of the King of England, Greeting. May this reach you. Peace be to your house . . .'

He had been dictating since dawn. Letters of greeting, Patents of Nobility, Pardons, Decrees of Attainder, Army Ordinances, police regulations, orders to

European firms for motor-cars, uniforms, furniture, electric plant, invitations to the Coronation, proclamations of a public holiday in honour of his victory, lay neatly clipped together on the secretary's table.

'Still no news from the hills. We should have heard of the victory by now.' The secretary recorded these words, considered them with his head cocked slightly to one side and then drew a line through them. 'We should have heard, shouldn't we, Ali?'

'We should have heard.'

'What has happened? Why don't you answer me? Why have we heard nothing?'

'Who am I? I know nothing. I only hear what the ignorant people are saying in the bazaar, since the public men evacuated the city. The ignorant people say that your majesty's army has not gained the victory you predict.'

'Fools, what do they know? What can they understand? I am Seth, grandson of Amurath. Defeat is impossible. I have been to Europe. I know. We have the Tank. This is not a war of Seth against Seyid but of Progress against Barbarism. And Progress must prevail. I have seen the great tattoo of Aldershot, the Paris Exhibition, the Oxford Union. I have read modern books–Shaw, Arlen, Priestley. What do the gossips in the bazaars know of all this? The whole might of Evolution rides behind him; at my stirrups run woman's suffrage, vaccination and vivisection. I am the New Age. I am the Future.'

'I know nothing of these things,' said Ali. 'But the ignorant men in the bazaars say that your majesty's guards have joined Prince Seyid. You will remember my pointing out that they had received no wages for several months?'

'They shall be paid. I have said it. As soon as the war is over they shall be paid. Besides I raised them in rank. Every man in the brigade is now a full corporal. I issued the edict myself. Ungrateful curs. Old-fashioned fools. Soon we will have no more soldiers. Tanks and aeroplanes. That is modern. I have seen it. That reminds me. Have you sent off instructions for the medals?'

Ali turned over the file of correspondence.

'Your majesty has ordered five hundred Grand Cross of Azania, first class; five hundred second; and seven hundred third; also designs for the Star of Seth, silver gilt and enamel with parti-coloured ribbon . . .'

'No, no. I mean the Victory Medal.'

'I have received no instructions concerning the Victory Medal.'

'Then take this down.'

'The invitation to the King of England?'

'The King of England can wait. Take down the instructions for the Victory Medal. Obverse, the head of Seth–that is to be copied from the photograph taken in Oxford. You understand–it is to be modern, European–top hat, spectacles, evening dress collar and tie. Inscription SETH IMPERATOR IMMORTALIS. The whole to be simple and in good taste. Many of my grandfather's medals were florid. Reverse. The figure of Progress. She holds in one hand an aeroplane, in the other some small object symbolic of improved education. I will give you the detail of that later. The idea will come to me . . . a telephone might do . . . I will see. Meanwhile begin the letter:

'*From Seth, Emperor of Azania, Chief of the Chiefs of Sakuyu, Lord of*

Wanda and Tyrant of the Seas, Bachelor of the Arts of Oxford University, to Messrs Mappin and Webb of London, Greeting. May this reach you. Peace be to your house . . .'

Evening and a small stir of life. Muezzin in the minaret. Allah is great. There is no Allah but Allah and Mohammed is his prophet. Angelus from the mission church. *Ecce ancilla Domini: fiat mihi secundum verbum tuum.* Mr Youkoumian behind the bar of the Amurath Café and Universal Stores mixed himself a sundowner of mastika and water.

'What I want to know is do I get paid for the petrol?'

'You know I am doing all I can for you, Mr Youkoumian. I'm your friend. You know that. But the Emperor's busy today. I've only just got off. Been on all day. I'll try and get your money for you.'

'I've done a lot for you, Ali.'

'I know you have, Mr Youkoumian, and I hope I am not ungrateful. If I could get you your money just by asking for it you should have it this evening.'

'But I must have it this evening. I'm going.'

'Going?'

'I've made my arrangements. Well, I don't mind telling you, Ali, since you're a friend.' Mr Youkoumian glanced furtively round the empty bar–they were speaking in Sakuyu–'I've got a launch beached outside the harbour, behind the trees near the old sugar mill in the bay. What's more, there's room in it for another passenger. I wouldn't tell this to anyone but you. Matodi's not going to be a healthy place for the next week or two. Seth's beaten. We know that. I'm going to my brother on the mainland. Only I want my money for the petrol before I go.'

'Yes, Mr Youkoumian, I appreciate your offer. But you know it's very difficult. You can hardly expect the Emperor to pay for having his own motor-boat stolen.'

'I don't known anything about that. All I know is that yesterday evening Mr Marx came into my store and said he wanted the Emperor's motor-boat filled up with petrol. Eighty rupees' worth. I've served Mr Marx with petrol before for the Emperor. How was I to know he wanted to steal the Emperor's motor-boat? Should I have given it to him if I did?'

Mr Youkoumian spread his hands in the traditional gesture of his race. 'I am a poor man. Is it right that I should suffer in this way? Is it fair? Now, Ali, I know you. You're a just man. I've done a lot for you in the past. Get me my eighty rupees and I will take you to stay with my brother in Malindi. Then when the troubles are over, we can come back or stay or go somewhere else, just as we like. You don't want your throat cut by the Arabs. I'll look after you.'

'Well, I appreciate your offer, Mr Youkoumian, and I'll do what I can. I can't say more than that.'

'I know you, Ali. I trust you as I'd trust my own father. Not a word to anyone about the launch, eh?'

'Not a word, Mr Youkoumian, and I'll see you later this evening.'

'That's a good fellow. Au revoir and remember, not a word to anyone about the launch.'

When Ali had left the Amurath Café, Youkoumian's wife emerged from the curtain behind which she had been listening to the conversation.

'What's all this you've been arranging? We can't take that Indian to Malindi.'

'I want my eighty rupees. My dear, you must leave these business matters to me.'

'But there isn't room for anyone else in the launch. We're overloaded already. You know that.'

'I know that.'

'Are you mad, Krikor? Do you want to drown us all?'

'You must leave these things to me, my flower. There is no need to worry. Ali is not coming with us. All I want is my eighty rupees for Mr Marx's petrol. Have you finished your packing? We start as soon as Ali returns with the money.'

'Krikor, you wouldn't . . . you aren't going to leave me behind, are you?'

'I should not hesitate to do so if I thought it necessary. Finish your packing, girl. Don't cry. Finish your packing. You are coming to Malindi. I have said it. Finish your packing. I am a just man and a peaceful man. You know that. But in time of war one must look after oneself and one's own family. Yes, one's family, do you hear me? Ali will bring us the money. We shall not take him to Malindi. Do you understand? If he is a trouble I shall hit him with my stick. Don't stand there like a fool. Finish your packing.'

The sun had now set. As Ali walked back to the fort through the dark lane he was aware of new excitement in the people around him. Groups were hurrying to the water-front, others stood in their doorways chattering eagerly. He heard the words 'Seyid', 'Victory' and 'Army'. In the open space before the harbour he found a large crowd collected with their backs to the water, gazing inland over the town. He joined them and in the brief twilight saw the whole dark face of the hills alight with little points of fire. Then he left the crowd and went to the old fort. Major Joab, the officer of the guard, stood in the court studying the hills through field-glasses.

'You have seen the fires inland, secretary?'

'I have seen them.'

'I think there is an army encamped there.'

'It is the victorious army, major.'

'Praise God. It is what we have waited to see.'

'Certainly. We should praise God whether in prosperity or adversity,' said Ali, piously; he had accepted Christianity on entering Seth's service. 'But I bring orders from the Emperor. You are to take a picket and go with them to the Amurath Bar. There you will find the Armenian Youkoumian, a little fat man wearing a black skull cap. You know him? Very well. He is to be put under arrest and taken a little outside the town. It does not matter where, but take him some distance from the people. There you are to hang him. Those are the Emperor's orders. When it is done, report to me personally. There is no need to mention the matter directly to His Majesty. You understand?'

'I understand, secretary.'

Upstairs, Seth was deep in a catalogue of wireless apparatus.

'Oh, Ali, I have decided on the Tudor model in fumed oak. Remind me tomorrow to write for it. Is there still no news?'

Ali busied himself in arranging the papers on the table and fitting the typewriter into its case.

'Is there no news?'

'There is news of a kind, Majesty. I opine that there is an army bivouacked in the hills. Their fires are visible. If your majesty will come outside, you will see them. No doubt they will march into the city tomorrow.'

Seth sprang gaily from his chair and ran to the window.

'But this is magnificent news. The best you could have brought. Ali, I will make you a Viscount tomorrow. The army back again. It is what we have been longing for the last six weeks, eh, Viscount?'

'Your majesty is very kind. I said *an* army. There is no means of knowing which one it may be. If, as you surmise, it is General Connolly, is it not curious that no runner has come to salute your majesty with news of the victory?'

'Yes, he should have sent word.'

'Majesty, you are defeated and betrayed. Everyone in Matodi knows it except yourself.'

For the first time since the beginning of the campaign, Ali saw that there was uncertainty in his master's mind. 'If I am defeated,' said Seth, 'the barbarians will know where to find me.'

'Majesty, it is not too late to escape. Only this evening I heard of a man in the town who has a launch hidden outside the harbour. He means to leave in it himself, for the mainland, but he would sell it at a price. There are ways for a small man to escape where a great man like your majesty would be trapped. For two thousand rupees he will sell this boat. He told me so, in so many words. He named the price. It is not much for the life of an Emperor. Give me the money, Majesty, and the boat shall be here before midnight. And in the morning Seyid's troops will march into the town and find it empty.'

Ali looked hopefully across the table, but before he had finished speaking he realized that Seth's mood of uncertainty was past.

'Seyid's troops will not march into the town. You forget that I have the Tank. Ali, you are talking treasonable nonsense. Tomorrow I shall be here to receive my victorious general.'

'Tomorrow will show, Majesty.'

'Tomorrow will show.'

'Listen,' said Ali, 'my friend is very loyal to your majesty and a most devoted man. Perhaps if I were to use my influence he might reduce his price.'

'I shall be here in the morning to receive my army.'

'Suppose he would accept eighteen hundred rupees?'

'I have spoken.'

Without further discussion Ali picked up his typewriter and left the room. As he opened the doors his ears caught the inevitable shuffle of bare feet, as a spy slipped away down the dark passage. It was a sound to which they had grown accustomed during the past months.

In his own quarters Ali poured out a glass of whisky and lit a cheroot. Then he drew out a fibre trunk from beneath the bed and began a methodical arrangement of his possessions preparatory to packing them. Presently there was a knock at the door and Major Joab came in.

'Good evening, secretary.'

'Good evening, major. The Armenian is dead?'

'He is dead. Heavens, how he squealed. You have whisky there.'

'Will you help yourself?'

'Thank you, secretary . . . you seem to be preparing for a journey.'

'It is well to be prepared–to have one's things in good order.'

'I think there is an army in the hills.'

'It is what they are saying.'

'I think it is the army of Seyid.'

'That, too, is being said.'

'As you say, secretary, it is well to be prepared.'

'Will you take a cheroot, major? I expect that there are many people in Matodi who would be glad to leave. The army will be here tomorrow.'

'It is not far away. And yet there is no way of leaving the town. The boats are all gone. The railway is broken. The road leads straight to the encampment.'

Ali folded a white drill suit and bent over the trunk, carefully arranging the sleeves. He did not look up as he said: 'I heard of a man who had a boat. It was spoken of in the bazaar, I forget by whom. An ignorant fellow no doubt. But this man, whoever it was, spoke of a boat concealed outside the harbour. He was going to the mainland tonight. There was room for two others, so they said. Do you think a man would find passengers to the mainland at five hundred rupees each? That is what he asked.'

'It is a great price for a journey to the mainland.'

'It is not much for a man's life. Do you think such a man, supposing there is any truth in the tale, would find passengers?'

'Perhaps. Who can tell? A man of affairs who can take his wisdom with him–a foreigner with no stock but a typewriter and his clothes. I do not think a soldier would go.'

'A soldier might pay three hundred?'

'It is not likely. What life would there be for him in a foreign country? And among his own people he would be dishonoured.'

'But he would not hinder others from going. A man who would pay five hundred rupees for his passage money, would not grudge another hundred to the guard who allowed him to pass?'

'Who can say? Some soldiers might hold that a small price for their honour.'

'But two hundred.'

'I think soldiers are for the most part poor men. It is seldom they earn two hundred rupees. . . . Well, I must bid you good night, secretary. I must return to my men.'

'How late do you stay on guard, major?'

'Till after midnight. Perhaps I shall see you again.'

'Who can say? . . . Oh, major, you have forgotten your papers.'

'So I have. Thank you, secretary. And good night.'

The major counted the little pile of notes which Ali had placed on the dressing-table. Two hundred exactly. He buttoned them into his tunic pocket and returned to the guard house.

Here, in the inner room, sat Mr Youkoumian talking to the captain. Half an hour before the little Armenian had been very near death, and awe of the experience still overcast his normally open and loquacious manner. It was not until the rope was actually round his neck that he had been inspired to mention the existence of his launch. His face was damp and his voice jerky and subdued.

'What did the Indian dog say?'

'He wanted to sell me a place in the boat for five hundred rupees. Does he know where it is hidden?'

'Fool that I was, I told him.'

'It is of little consequence. He gave me two hundred rupees to let him past the guard, also some whisky and a cheroot. There is no need for us to worry about Ali. When do we start?'

'There is one point, officers . . . my wife. There is not room for her in the boat. She must not know of our departure. Where was she when you–when we left the café together?'

'She was making a noise. One of the corporals locked her in the loft.'

'She will get out of there.'

'You leave all that to us.'

'Very well, major. I am a just man and a peaceable man. You know that. I only want to be sure that everything will be agreeable for everyone.'

Ali finished his packing and sat down to wait. 'What's Major Joab up to?' he wondered. 'It is curious his refusing to leave the town. I suppose he thinks he will get a price for Seth in the morning.'

Night and the fear of darkness. In his room at the top of the old fort Seth lay awake and alone, his eyes wild with the inherited terror of the jungle, desperate with the acquired loneliness of civilization. Night was alive with beasts and devils and the spirits of dead enemies; before its power Seth's ancestors had receded, slid away from its attack, abandoning in retreat all the baggage of Individuality; they had lain six or seven in a hut; between them and night only a wall of mud and a ceiling of thatched grass; warm, naked bodies breathing in the darkness an arm's reach apart, indivisibly unified so that they ceased to be six or seven scared blacks and became one person of more than human stature, less vulnerable to the peril that walked near them. Seth could not expand to meet the onset of fear. He was alone, dwarfed by the magnitude of the darkness, insulated from his fellows, strapped down to mean dimensions.

The darkness pulsed with the drumming of the unknown conquerors. In the narrow streets of the city the people were awake–active and apprehensive. Dark figures sped to and fro on furtive errands, hiding from each other in doorways till the way was empty. In the houses they were packing away bundles in secret places, little hoards of coins and jewellery, pictures and books, ancestral sword hilts of fine workmanship, shoddy trinkets from Birmingham and Bombay, silk shawls, scent bottles, anything that might attract attention next morning when the city was given over to loot. Huddled groups of women and children were being herded to refuge in the cellars of the old houses or into the open country beyond the walls; goats, sheep, donkeys, livestock and poultry of all kinds jostled with them for precedence in the city gates. Mme Youkoumian, trussed like a chicken on the floor of her own bedroom, dribbled through her gag and helplessly writhed her bruised limbs.

Ali, marching back to the fort under arrest between two soldiers, protested angrily to the captain of the guard.

'You are making a great mistake, captain. I have made all arrangements with the major for my departure.'

'It is the Emperor's orders that no one leaves the city.'

'When we see the major he will explain everything.'

The captain made no reply. The little party marched on; in front between two other soldiers shambled Ali's servant, bearing his master's trunk on his head.

When they reached the guard-room, the captain reported. 'Two prisoners, major, arrested at the South Gate attempting to leave the city.'

'You know me, major; the captain has made a mistake. Tell him it is all right for me to go.'

'I know you, secretary; captain, report the arrests to His Majesty.'

'But, major, only this evening I gave you two hundred rupees. Do you hear, captain, I gave him two hundred rupees. You can't treat me like this. I shall tell His Majesty everything.'

'We had better search his luggage.'

The trunk was opened and the contents spread over the floor. The two officers turned them over with interest and appropriated the few articles of value it contained. The minor possessions were tossed to the corporals. At the bottom, wrapped in a grubby nightshirt, were two heavy objects which, on investigation, proved to be the massive gold crown of the Azanian Empire and an elegant ivory sceptre presented to Amurath by the President of the French Republic. Major Joab and the captain considered this discovery for some time in silence. Then the major answered the question that was in both their minds. 'No,' he said, 'I think we had better show these to Seth.'

'Both of them?'

'Well, at any rate, the sceptre. It would not be so easy to dispose of. Two hundred rupees,' said the major bitterly, turning on Ali, 'two hundred rupees and you proposed to walk off with the Imperial regalia.'

From the inner room Mr Youkoumian listened to this conversation in a mood of sublime contentment; the sergeant had given him a cigarette out of a box lifted from the shop at the time of his arrest; the captain had given him brandy–similarly acquired–of his own distillation; a fiery, comforting spirit. The terrors of the gallows were far behind him. And now Ali had been caught red-handed with the crown jewels. Nothing was required to complete Mr Youkoumian's happiness, except a calm sea for their crossing to the mainland; and the gentle night air gave promise that this, too, would be vouchsafed him.

It was only a matter of a few words for Major Joab to report the circumstances of Ali's arrest. The damning evidence of the sceptre and the soiled nightshirt was laid before Seth on the table. The prisoner stood between his captors without visible interest or emotion. When the charge had been made, Seth said, 'Well, Ali.'

Until now they had spoken in Sakuyu. Ali answered, as he always spoke to his master, in English. 'It is regrettable that this should have happened. These ignorant men have greatly disturbed the preparations for your majesty's departure.'

'For *my* departure?'

'For whom else would I prepare a boat? What other reason could I have for supervising the safe conduct of your majesty's sceptre, and of the crown which the officers have omitted to bring from the guard-room?'

'I don't believe you, Ali.'

'Your majesty wrongs himself. You are a distinguished man, educated in Europe–not like these low soldiers. Would you have trusted me had I been unworthy? Could I, a poor Indian, hope to deceive a distinguished gentleman educated in Europe? Send these low men out and I will explain everything to you.'

The officers of the guard had listened uneasily to these alien sentences; now at Seth's command they withdrew their men. 'Shall I make preparations for the execution, Majesty?'

'Yes . . . no . . . I will tell you when. Stand by for further orders below, Major.'

The two officers saluted and left the room. When they had gone Ali sat down opposite his master and proceeded at his ease. There was no accusation or reproach in the Emperor's countenance, no justice or decision, trust or forgiveness; one emotion only was apparent in the dark young face before him, blank terror. Ali saw this and knew that his case was won. 'Majesty, I will tell you why the officers have arrested me. It is to prevent your escape. They are plotting to sell you to the enemy. I know it. I have heard it all from one of the corporals who is loyal to us. It was for this reason that I prepared the boat. When all was ready I would have come to you, told you of their treachery and brought you away safely.'

'But, Ali, you say they would hand me over to the enemy. Am I then really beaten?'

'Majesty, all the world knows. The British General Connolly has joined Prince Seyid. They are there on the hills together now. Tomorrow they will be in Matodi.'

'But the Tank?'

'Majesty, Mr Marx, the distinguished mechanic who made the tank, fled last night, as you well know.'

'Connolly too. Why should he betray me? I trusted him. Why does everyone betray me? Connolly was my friend.'

'Majesty, consider the distinguished general's position. What would he do? He might conquer Seyid and your majesty would reward him, or he might be defeated, If he joins Seyid, Seyid will reward him, and no one can defeat him. How would you expect a distinguished gentleman, educated in Europe, should choose?'

'They are all against me. All traitors. There is no one I can trust.'

'Except me, Majesty.'

'I do not trust you. You, least of all.'

'But you must trust me. Don't you understand? If you do not trust me there will be no one. You will be alone, quite alone.'

'I am alone. There is no one.'

'Then since all are traitors, trust a traitor. Trust me. You must trust me. Listen. It is not too late to escape. No one but I knows of the boat. The Armenian Youkoumian is dead. Do you understand, Majesty? Give the order to the guards to let me pass. I will go to where the boat is hidden. In an hour I will have it here, under the sea wall. Then when the guard is changed you will join me. Don't you understand? It is the only chance. You must trust me. Otherwise you will be alone.'

The Emperor stood up. 'I do not know if I can trust you. I do not think there is anyone I can trust. I am alone. But you shall go. Why should I hang you? What is one life more or less when all are traitors. Go in peace.'

'Your majesty's faithful servant.'

Seth opened the door; again the scamper of the retreating spy.

'Major.'

'Majesty.'

'Ali is to go free, He may leave the fort.'

'The execution is cancelled?'

'Ali may leave the fort.'

'As your majesty commands.' Major Joab saluted. As Ali left the lighted room he turned back and addressed the Emperor.

'Your majesty does well to trust me.'

'I trust no one . . . I am alone.'

The Emperor was alone. Faintly on the night air he heard the throbbing of drums from the encamped army. Quarter-past two. Darkness for nearly four hours more.

Suddenly the calm was splintered by a single, shrill cry–a jet of sound, spurting up from below, breaking in spray over the fort, then ceasing. Expressive of nothing, followed by nothing; no footsteps; no voices; silence and the distant beat of the tomtoms.

Seth ran to the door. 'Hullo! Who is there? What is that? Major! Officer of the guard!' No answer. Only the inevitable scuffle of the retreating spy. He went to the window. 'Who is there? What has happened? Is there no one on guard?'

A long silence.

Then a quiet voice from below. 'Majesty?'

'Who is that?'

'Major Joab of the Imperial Infantry at your majesty's service.'

'What was that?'

'Majesty?'

'What was that cry?'

'It was a mistake, your majesty. There is no cause for alarm.'

'What has happened?'

'The sentry made a mistake. That is all.'

'What has he done?'

'It is only the Indian, Majesty. The sentry did not understand his orders. I will see to it that he is punished.'

'What has happened to Ali? Is he hurt?'

'He is dead, your majesty. It is a mistake of the sentry's. I am sorry your majesty was disturbed.'

Presently Major Joab, the captain of the guard, and Mr Youkoumian, accompanied by three heavily burdened corporals, left the fort by a side door and made their way out of the town along the coast path towards the disused sugar mills.

And Seth was alone.

Another dawn. With slow feet Mr Youkoumian trudged into Matodi. There was no one about in the streets. All who could had left the city during the darkness; those who remained lurked behind barred doors and barricaded windows; from the cracks of shutters and through keyholes a few curious eyes observed the weary little figure dragging down the lane to the Amurath Café and Universal Stores.

Mme Youkoumian lay across the bedroom doorstep. During the night she had bitten through her gag and rolled some yards across the floor; that far her strength had taken her. Then, too exhausted to cry out or wrestle any further with the ropes that bound her, she had lapsed into intermittent coma, disturbed by nightmares, acute spasms of cramp and the scampering of rats on the earthen floor. In the green and silver light of dawn this bruised, swollen and dusty figure presented a spectacle radically repugnant to Mr Youkoumian's most sensitive feelings.

'Krikor, Krikor. Oh praise God you've come . . . I thought I should never see you again. . . . Blessed Mary and Joseph. . . . Where have you been? . . . What has happened to you? . . . Oh, Krikor, my own husband, praise God and his angels who have brought you back to me.'

Mr Youkoumian sat down heavily on the bed and pulled off his elastic-sided button boots. 'I'm tired,' he said. 'God, how tired I am. I could sleep for a week.' He took a bottle from the shelf and poured out a drink. 'I have had one of the most disagreeable nights of my life. First I am nearly hanged. Will you believe it? The noose was actually round my neck. Then I am made to walk out as far as the sugar mills, then the next thing I know I am alone, lying on the beach. My luggage is gone, my boat is gone, the damned soldiers are gone and I have a lump on the back on my head the size of an egg. Just you feel it.'

'I'm tied up, Krikor. Cut the string and let me help you. Oh, my poor husband.'

'How it aches. What a walk back. And my boat gone. I could have got fifteen hundred rupees for that boat yesterday. Oh my head. Fifteen hundred rupees. My feet ache too. I must go to bed.'

'Let me loose, Krikor, and I will attend to you, my poor husband.'

'No, it doesn't matter, my flower. I'll go to bed. I could sleep for a week.'

'Krikor, let me loose.'

'Don't worry. I shall be all right when I have had a sleep. Why, I ache all over.' He tossed off the drink and with a little grunt of relief drew his feet up on to the bed and rolled over with his face to the wall.

'Krikor, please . . . you must let me loose . . . don't you see? I've been like this all night. I'm in such pain . . .'

'You stay where you are. I can't attend to you now. You're always thinking of yourself. What about me? I'm tired. Don't you hear me?'

'But, Krikor—'

'Be quiet, you slut.'

And in less than a minute Mr Youkoumian found consolation for the diverse fortunes of the night in profound and prolonged sleep.

He was awakened some hours later by the entry into Matodi of the victorious army. Drums banging, pipes whistling, the soldiers of Progress and the New Age passed under his window. Mr Youkoumian rolled off the bed, rubbing his eyes, and peeped through the chink of the shutters.

'God save my soul,' he remarked. 'Seth's won after all.' Then with a chuckle. 'What a pair of fools Major Joab and the captain turn out to be.'

Mme Youkoumian looked up from the floor with piteous appeal in her dark eyes. He gave her a friendly little prod in the middle with his stockinged foot. 'Stay there, that's a good girl, and don't make a noise. I'll come and see to you in a minute or two.' Then he lay down on the bed, nuzzled into the bolster, and after a few preliminary grunts and wriggles, relapsed into slumber.

It was a remarkable procession. First in tattered, field grey uniforms came the brass band of the Imperial Guard, playing *John Brown's Body*.

Mine eyes have seen the glory of the coming of the Lord;
He is trampling out the vintage where the grapes of wrath are stored;
He has loosed the mighty lightning of his terrible swift sword;
His truth is marching on.

Behind them came the infantry; hard, bare feet rhythmically kicking up the dust, threadbare uniforms, puttees wound up anyhow, caps at all angles, Lee-Enfield rifles with fixed bayonets slung on their shoulders; fuzzy heads, jolly nigger-minstrel faces, black chests shining through buttonless tunics, pockets bulging with loot. Dividing these guardsmen from the irregular troops rode General Connolly on a tall, grey mule, with his staff officers beside him. He was a stocky Irishman in early middle age who had seen varied service in the Black and Tans, the South African Police and the Kenya Game Reserves before enlisting under the Emperor's colours. But on this morning his appearance was rather that of a lost explorer than a conquering commander-in-chief. He had a week's growth of reddish beard below his cavalry moustaches; irregular slashes had converted his breeches into shorts; open shirt and weather-worn white topee took the place of tunic and cap. Field glasses, map case, sword and revolver holster hung incongruously round him. He was smoking a pipe of rank local tobacco.

On their heels came the hordes of Wanda and Sakuyu warriors. In the hills these had followed in a diffuse rabble. Little units of six or a dozen trotted round the stirrups of the headmen; before them they drove geese and goats pillaged from surrounding farms. Sometimes they squatted down to rest; sometimes they ran to catch up. The big chiefs had bands of their own–mounted drummers thumping great bowls of cowhide and wood, pipers blowing down six-foot chanters of bamboo. Here and there a camel swayed above the heads of the mob. They were armed with weapons of every kind: antiquated rifles, furnished with bandoliers of brass cartridges and empty cartridge cases; short hunting spears, swords and knives; the great, seven-foot broad-bladed spear of the Wanda; behind one chief a slave carried a machine-gun under a velvet veil; a few had short bows and iron-wood maces of immemorial design.

The Sakuyu wore their hair in a dense fuzz, their chests and arms were embossed with ornamental scars; the Wanda had their teeth filed into sharp points, their hair braided into dozens of mud-caked pigtails. In accordance with their unseemly usage, any who could wore strung round his neck the members of a slain enemy.

As this great host swept down on the city and surged through the gates, it broke into a dozen divergent streams, spurting and trickling on all sides like water from a rotten hose-pipe, forcing out jets of men, mounts and livestock into the by-ways and back streets, eddying down the blind alleys and into enclosed courts. Solitary musicians, separated from their bands, drummed and piped among the straggling crowds; groups split away from the mêlée and began dancing in the alleys; the doors of the liquor shops were broken in and a new and nastier element appeared in the carnival, as drink-crazed warriors began to re-enact their deeds of heroism, bloodily laying about their former comrades-in-arms with knives and clubs.

'God,' said Connolly, 'I shall be glad when I've got this menagerie off my hands. I wonder if his nibs has really bolted. Anything is possible in this abandoned country.'

No one appeared in the streets. Only rows of furtive eyes behind the shuttered windows watched the victors' slow progress through the city. In the main square the General halted the guards and such of the irregular troops as were still amenable to discipline; they squatted on the ground, chewing at bits of sugar cane, crunching nuts and polishing their teeth with little lengths of stick, while above the drone of confused revelling which rose from the side streets, Connolly from the saddle of his mule in classical form exhorted his legions.

'Guards,' he said loudly, 'Chiefs and tribesmen of the Azanian Empire. Hear me. You are good men. You have fought valiantly for your Emperor. The slaughter was very splendid. It is a thing for which your children and your children's children will hold you in honour. It was said in the camp that the Emperor had gone over the sea. I do not know if that is true. If he has, it is to prepare a reward for you in the great lands. But it is sufficient reward to a soldier to have slain his enemy.

'Guards, Chiefs and tribesmen of the Azanian Empire. The war is over. It is fitting that you should rest and rejoice. Two things only I charge you are forbidden. The white men, their houses, cattle, goods or women you must not take. Nor must you burn anything or any of the houses nor pour out the petrol in the streets. If any man do this he shall be killed. I have spoken. Long live the Emperor.

'Go on, you lucky bastards,' he added in English. 'Go and make whoopee. I must get a brush up and some food before I do anything else.'

He rode across to the Grand Azanian Hotel. It was shut and barred. His two servants forced the door and he went in. At the best of times, even when the fortnightly Messageries liner was in and gay European sightseers paraded every corner of the city, the Grand Azanian Hotel had a gloomy and unwelcoming air. On this morning a chill of utter desolation struck through General Connolly as he passed through its empty and darkened rooms. Every movable object had been stripped from walls and floor and stowed away subterraneously during the preceding night. But the single bath at least was a fixture. Connolly set his servants to work pumping water and unpacking his uniform cases. Eventually an hour later he emerged, profoundly low in spirits, but clean, shaved and very fairly dressed. Then he rode towards the fort where the Emperor's colours hung limp in the sultry air. No sign of life came from the houses; no welcome; no resistance. Marauding bands of his own people skulked from corner to corner; once a terrified Indian rocketed up from the gutter and shot across his path like a rabbit. It was not until he reached the White Fathers' mission that he heard news of the Emperor. Here he encountered a vast Canadian priest with white habit and sun-hat and spreading crimson beard, who was at that moment occupied in shaking almost to death the brigade sergeant-major of the Imperial Guard. At the General's approach the reverend father released his victim with one hand–keeping a firm grip in his woollen hair with the other–removed the cheroot from his mouth and waved it cordially.

'Hullo, General, back from the wars, eh? They've been very anxious about you in the city. Is this creature part of the victorious army?'

'Looks like one of my chaps. What's he been up to?'

'Up to? I came in from Mass and found him eating my breakfast.' A tremendous buffet on the side of his head sent the sergeant-major dizzily across the road. 'Don't you let me find any more of your fellows hanging round the mission today or there'll be trouble. It's always the same when you have troops in a town. I remember in Duke Japheth's rebellion, the wretched creatures were all over the place. They frightened the sisters terribly over at the fever hospital.'

'Father, is it true that the Emperor's cut and run?'

'If he hasn't he's about the only person. I had that old fraud of an Armenian Archbishop in here the other night, trying to make me join him in a motor-boat. I told him I'd sooner have my throat cut on dry land than face that crossing in an open boat. I'll bet he was sick.'

'But you don't know where the Emperor is?'

'He might be over in the fort. He was the other day. Silly young ass, pasting up proclamations all over the town. I've got other things to bother about than young Seth. And mind you keep your miserable savages from my mission or they'll know the reason why. I've got a lot of our people camped in here so as to be out of harm's way, and I am not going to have them disturbed. Good morning to you, General.'

General Connolly rode on. At the fort he found no sentry on guard. The courtyard was empty save for the body of Ali, which lay on its face in the dust, the cord which had strangled him still tightly twined round his neck. Connolly turned it over with his boot but failed to recognize the swollen and darkened face.

'So His Imperial Majesty *has* shot the moon.'

He looked into the deserted guard-house and the lower rooms of the fort; then he climbed the spiral stone staircase which led to Seth's room, and here, lying across the camp bed in spotted silk pyjamas recently purchased in the Place Vendôme, utterly exhausted by the horror and insecurity of the preceding night, lay the Emperor of Azania fast asleep.

From his bed Seth would only hear the first, rudimentary statement of his victory. Then he dismissed his commander-in-chief and with remarkable self-restraint insisted on performing a complete and fairly elaborate toilet before giving his mind to the details of the situation. When, eventually, he came downstairs dressed in the full and untarnished uniform of the Imperial Horse Guards, he was in a state of some elation. 'You see, Connolly,' he cried, clasping his general's hand with warm emotion, 'I was right. I knew that it was impossible for us to fail.'

'We came damn near it once or twice,' said Connolly.

'Nonsense, my dear fellow. We are Progress and the New Age. Nothing can stand in our way. *Don't you see?* The world is already ours; it is our world now, because we are of the Present. Seyid and his ramshackle band of brigands were the Past. Dark barbarism. A cobweb in a garret; dead wood; a whisper echoing in a sunless cave. We are Light and Speed and Strength, Steel and Steam, Youth, Today and Tomorrow. Don't you see? Our little war was won on other fields five centuries back.' The young darky stood there transfigured; his eyes shining; his head thrown back; tipsy with words. The white man knocked out his pipe on the heel of his riding boot and felt for a pouch in his tunic pocket.

'All right, Seth, say it your way. All I know is that *my* little war was won the day before yesterday and by two very ancient weapons–lies and the long spear.'

'But my tank? Was it not that which gave us the victory?'

'Marx's tin can? A fat lot of use that was. I told you you were wasting money, but you would have the thing. The best thing you can do is to present it to Debra Dowa as a war memorial, only you couldn't get it so far. My dear boy, you can't take a machine like that over this country under this sun. The whole thing was red hot after five miles. The two poor devils of Greeks who had to drive it nearly went off their heads. It came in handy in the end though. We used it as a punishment cell. It was the one thing these black bastards would really take notice of. It's all right getting on a high horse about progress now that everything's over. It doesn't hurt anyone. But if you want to know, you were as near as nothing to losing the whole bag of tricks at the end of last week. Do you know what that clever devil Seyid had done? Got hold of a photograph of you taken at Oxford in cap and gown. He had several thousand printed and circulated among the guards. Told them you'd deserted the Church in England and that there you were in the robes of an English Mohammedan. All the mission boys fell for it. It was no good telling them. They were going over to the enemy in hundreds every night. I was all in. There didn't seem a damned thing to do. Then I got an idea. You know what the name of Amurath means among the tribesmen. Well, I called a shari of all the Wanda and Sakuya chiefs and spun them the yarn. Told them that Amurath never died–which they believed already most of them–but that he had crossed the sea to commune with the spirits of his ancestors; that you were Amurath, himself, come back in another form. It went down from the word go. I wish you could have seen their faces. The moment they'd heard the news they were mad to be at Seyid there and then. It was all I could do to keep them back until I had him where I wanted him. What's more, the story got through to the other side and in two days we had a couple of thousand of Seyid's boys coming over to us. Double what we'd lost on the Mohammedan story and real fighters–not dressed-up mission boys. Well, I kept them back as best I could for three days. We were on the crest of the hills all the time and Seyid was down in the valley, kicking up the devil burning villages, trying to make us come down to him. He was getting worried about the desertions. Well, on the third day I sent half a company of guards down with a band and a whole lot of mules and told them to make themselves as conspicuous as they could straight in front of him in the Ukaka pass. Trust the guards to do that. He did just what I expected; thought it was the whole army and spread out on both sides trying to surround them. Then I let the tribesmen in on his rear. My word, I've never seen such a massacre. Didn't they enjoy themselves, bless them. Half of them haven't come back yet; they're still chasing the poor devils all over the hills.'

'And the usurper Seyid, did he surrender?'

'Yes, he surrendered all right. But, look here, Seth, I hope you aren't going to mind about this, but you see how it was, well, you see, Seyid surrendered and . . .'

'You don't mean you've let him escape?'

'Oh no, nothing like that, but the fact is, he surrendered to a party of

Wanda . . . and, well, you know what the Wanda are.'

'You mean . . .'

'Yes, I'm afraid so, I wouldn't have had it happen for anything. I didn't hear about it until afterwards.'

'They should not have eaten him–after all, he was my father . . . It is so . . . so barbarous.'

'I knew you'd feel that way about it, Seth, and I'm sorry. I gave the headmen twelve hours in the tank for it.'

'I am afraid that as yet the Wanda are totally out of touch with modern thought. They need education. We must start some schools and a university for them when we get things straight.'

'That's it, Seth, you can't blame them. It's want of education. That's all it is.'

'We might start them on Montessori methods,' said Seth dreamily. 'You can't blame them.' Then rousing himself: 'Connolly, I shall make you a Duke.'

'That's nice of you, Seth. I don't mind so much for myself, but Black Bitch will be pleased as Punch about it.'

'And, Connolly.'

'Yes.'

'Don't you think that when she is a Duchess, it might be more suitable if you were to try and call your wife by another name? You see, there will probably be a great influx of distinguished Europeans for my coronation. We wish to break down colour barriers as far as possible. Your name for Mrs Connolly, though suitable as a term of endearment in the home, seems to emphasize the racial distinction between you in a way which might prove disconcerting.'

'I dare say you're right, Seth. I'll try and remember when we're in company. But I shall always think of her as Black Bitch, somehow. By the way, what has become of Ali?'

'Ali? Yes, I had forgotten. He was murdered by Major Joab yesterday evening. And that reminds me of something else. I must order a new crown.'

2

'Lovey dovey, cat's eyes.'

'You got that out of a book.'

'Well, yes. How did you know?'

'I read it too. It's been all round the compound.'

'Anyway, I said it as a quotation. We have to find new things to say somehow sometimes, don't we?'

William and Prudence rolled apart and lay on their backs, sun hats tilted over their noses, shading their eyes from the brilliant equatorial sun. They were on the crest of the little hills above Debra Dowa; it was cool there, eight thousand feet up. Behind them in a stockade of euphorbia trees stood a thatched Nestorian shrine. At its door the priest's youngest child lay sunning his naked belly, gazing serenely into the heavens, indifferent to the flies which settled on the corners of his mouth and sauntered across his eyeballs. Below them the tin roofs of Debra Dowa and a few thin columns of smoke were visible among the blue gums. At a distance the Legation syce sat in charge of the ponies.

'William, darling, there's something so extraordinary on your neck. I believe it's two of them.'

'Well, I think you might knock it off.'

'I believe it's that kind which sting worst.'

'Beast.'

'Oh, it's gone now. It *was* two.'

'I can feel it walking about.'

'No, darling, that's me. I think you might *look* sometimes when I'm being sweet to you. I've invented a new way of kissing. You do it with your eyelashes.'

'I've known that for years. It's called a butterfly kiss.'

'Well you needn't be so high up about it. I only do these things for your benefit.'

'It was very nice, darling. I only said it wasn't very new.'

'I don't believe you liked it at all.'

'It was so like the stinging thing.'

'Oh, how maddening it is to have no one to make love with except you.'

'Sophisticated voice.'

'That's not sophisticated. It's my gramophone record voice. My sophisticated voice is quite different. It's like this.'

'I call that American.'

'Shall I do my vibrant-with-passion voice?'

'No.'

'Oh dear, men are hard to keep amused.' Prudence sat up and lit a cigarette. 'I think you're effeminate and under-sexed,' she said, 'and I hate you.'

'That's because you're too young to arouse serious emotion. You might give me a cigarette.'

'I hoped you'd say that. It happens to be the last. Not only the last in my pocket but the last in Debra Dowa. I got it out of the Envoy Extraordinary's bedroom this morning.'

'Oh Lord, when will this idiotic war be over? We haven't had a bag for six weeks. I've run out of hair-wash and detective stories and now no cigarettes. I think you might give me some of that.'

'I hope you go bald. Still, I'll let you have the cigarette.'

'Pru, how sweet of you. I never thought you would.'

'I'm that kind of girl.'

'I think I'll give you a kiss.'

'No, try the new way with eyelashes.'

'Is that right?'

'Delicious. Do it some more.'

Presently they remounted and rode back to the Legation. On the way William said:

'I hope it doesn't give one a twitch.'

'What doesn't, darling?'

'That way with the eyelashes. I've seen people with twitches. I dare say that's how they got it. There was once a man who got run in for winking at girls in the street. So he said it was a permanent affliction and he winked all through his trial and got off. But the sad thing is that now he can't stop and he's been winking ever since.'

'I will say one thing for you,' said Prudence. 'You do know a lovely lot of stories. I dare say that's why I like you.'

Three Powers–Great Britain, France and the United States–maintained permanent diplomatic representatives at Debra Dowa. It was not an important appointment. Mr Schonbaum, the doyen, had adopted diplomacy late in life. Indeed the more formative years of his career had already passed before he made up his mind, in view of the uncertainty of Central European exchanges, to become a citizen of the republic he represented. From the age of ten until the age of forty he had lived an active life variously engaged in journalism, electrical engineering, real estate, cotton broking, hotel management, shipping and theatrical promotion. At the outbreak of the European war he had retired first to the United States, and then, on its entry into the war, to Mexico. Soon after the declaration of peace he became an American citizen and amused himself in politics. Having subscribed largely to a successful Presidential campaign, he was offered his choice of several public preferments, of which the ministry at Debra Dowa was by far the least prominent or lucrative. His European upbringing, however, had invested diplomacy with a glamour which his later acquaintance with the great world had never completely dimmed; he had made all the money he needed; the climate at Debra Dowa was reputed to be healthy and the environment romantic. Accordingly he had chosen that post and had not regretted it, enjoying during the last eight years a popularity and prestige which he would hardly have attained among his own people.

The French Minister, M. Ballon, was a Freemason.

His Britannic Majesty's minister, Sir Samson Courteney, was a man of singular personal charm and wide culture whose comparative ill-success in diplomatic life was attributable rather to inattention than to incapacity. As a very young man he had great things predicted of him. He had passed his examinations with a series of papers of outstanding brilliance; he had powerful family connections in the Foreign Office; but almost from the outset of his career it became apparent that he would disappoint expectations. As third secretary at Peking he devoted himself, to the exclusion of all other interests, to the construction of a cardboard model of the Summer Palace; transferred to Washington he conceived a sudden enthusiasm for bicycling and would disappear for days at a time to return dusty but triumphant with reports of some broken record for speed or endurance; the scandal caused by this hobby culminated in the discovery that he had entered his name for an international long-distance championship. His uncles at the Foreign Office hastily shifted him to Copenhagen, marrying him, on his way through London, to the highly suitable daughter of a Liberal cabinet minister. It was in Sweden that his career was finally doomed. For some time past he had been noticeably silent at the dinner table when foreign languages were being spoken; now the shocking truth became apparent that he was losing his mastery even of French; many ageing diplomats, at loss for a word, could twist the conversation and suit their opinions to their vocabulary; Sir Samson recklessly improvised or lapsed into a kind of pidgin English. The uncles were loyal. He was recalled to London and established in a department of the Foreign Office. Finally, at the age of fifty, when his daughter Prudence was thirteen years old, he was created a Knight of

St Michael and St George and relegated to Azania. The appointment caused him the keenest delight. It would have astonished him to learn that anyone considered him unsuccessful or that he was known throughout the service as the 'Envoy Extraordinary'.

The Legation lay seven miles out of the capital; a miniature garden city in a stockaded compound, garrisoned by a troop of Indian cavalry. There was wireless communication with Aden and a telephone service, of capricious activity, to the town. The road, however, was outrageous. For a great part of the year it was furrowed by water-courses, encumbered with boulders, landslides and fallen trees, and ambushed by cut-throats. On this matter Sir Samson's predecessor had addressed numerous remonstrances to the Azanian government with the result that several wayfarers were hanged under suspicion of brigandage; nothing, however, was done about the track; the correspondence continued and its conclusion was the most nearly successful achievement of Sir Samson's career. Stirred by his appointment and zealous for his personal comfort, the Envoy Extraordinary had, for the first time in his life, thrown himself wholeheartedly into a question of public policy. He had read through the entire file bearing on the subject and within a week of presenting his papers, re-opened the question in a personal interview with the Prince Consort. Month after month he pressed forward the interchange of memoranda between Palace, Legation, Foreign Office and Office of Works (the posts of Lord Chamberlain, Foreign Secretary and Minister of Works were all, as it happened at that time, occupied by the Nestorian Metropolitan), until one memorable day Prudence returned from her ride to say that a caravan of oxen, a load of stones and three chain-gangs of convicts had appeared on the road. Here, however, Sir Samson suffered a setback. The American commercial attaché acted, in his ample spare time, as agents for a manufacturer of tractors, agricultural machinery and steam-rollers. At his representation the convicts were withdrawn and the Empress and her circle settled down to the choice of a steam-roller. She had always had a weakness for illustrated catalogues and after several weeks' discussion had ordered a threshing machine, a lawn mower and a mechanical saw. About the steam-roller she could not make up her mind. The Metropolitan Archbishop (who was working with the American attaché on a half-commission basis) supported a very magnificent engine named Pennsylvania Monarch; the Prince Consort, whose personal allowance was compromised by any public extravagance, headed a party in favour of the more modest Kentucky Midget. Meanwhile guests to the British Legation were still in most seasons of the year obliged to ride out to dinner on mule-back, preceded by armed Askaris and a boy with a lantern. It was widely believed that a decision was imminent, when the Empress's death and the subsequent civil war postponed all immediate hope of improvement. The Envoy Extraordinary bore the reverse with composure but real pain. He had taken the matter to heart and he felt hurt and disillusioned. The heap of stones at the roadside remained for him as a continual reproach, the monument to his single ineffective excursion into statesmanship.

In its isolation, life in the compound was placid and domestic. Lady Courteney devoted herself to gardening. The bags came out from London laden with bulbs and cuttings and soon there sprang up round the Legation a luxuriant English garden; lilac and lavender, privet and box, grass walks and croquet lawn, rockeries and wildernesses, herbaceous borders, bowers of rambler roses, puddles of water-lilies and an immature maze.

William Bland, the honorary attaché, lived with the Courteneys. The rest of the staff were married. The Second Secretary had clock golf and the Consul two tennis courts. They called each other by their Christian names, pottered in and out of each others' bungalows and knew the details of each others' housekeeping. The Oriental Secretary, Captain Walsh, alone maintained certain reserves. He suffered from recurrent malaria and was known to ill-treat his wife. But since he was the only member of the Legation who understood Sakuyu, he was a man of importance, being in frequent demand as arbiter in disputes between the domestic servants.

The unofficial British population of Debra Dowa was small and rather shady. There was the manager of the bank and his wife (who was popularly believed to have an infection of Indian blood); two subordinate bank clerks; a shipper of hides who described himself as President of the Azanian Trading Association; a mechanic on the railway who was openly married to two Azanians; the Anglican Bishop of Debra Dowa and a shifting community of canons and curates; the manager of the Eastern Exchange Telegraph Company; and General Connolly. Intercourse between them and the Legation was now limited to luncheon on Christmas Day, to which all the more respectable were invited, and an annual garden party on the King's Birthday which was attended by everyone in the town, from the Georgian Prince who managed the Perroquet Night Club to the Mormon Missionary. This aloofness from the affairs of the town was traditional to the Legation, being dictated partly by the difficulties of the road and partly by their inherent disinclination to mix with social inferiors. On Lady Courteney's first arrival in Debra Dowa she had attempted to break down these distinctions, saying that they were absurd in so small a community. General Connolly had dined twice at the Legation and a friendship seemed to be in bud when its flowering was abruptly averted by an informal call paid on him by Lady Courteney in his own quarters. She had been lunching with the Empress and turned aside on her way home to deliver an invitation to croquet. Sentries presented arms in the courtyard, a finely uniformed servant opened the door, but this dignified passage was interrupted by a resolute little Negress in a magenta tea-gown who darted across the hall and barred her way to the drawing-room.

'I am Black Bitch,' she had explained simply. 'What do you want in my house?'

'I am Lady Courteney. I came to see General Connolly.'

'The General is drunk today and he doesn't want any more ladies.'

After that Connolly was not asked even to Christmas luncheon.

Other less dramatic incidents occurred with most of the English community until now, after six years, the Bishop was the only resident who ever came to play croquet on the Legation lawn. Even his Lordship's visits had become less welcome lately. His strength did not enable him to accomplish both journeys in the same day, so that an invitation to luncheon involved also an invitation for the night and, usually, to luncheon next day as well. More than this, the Envoy Extraordinary found these incursions from the outside world increasingly disturbing and exhausting as his momentary interest in Azania began to subside. The Bishop would insist on talking about Problems and Policy,

Welfare, Education and Finance. He knew all about native law and customs and the relative importance of the various factions at court. He had what Sir Samson considered an ostentatious habit of referring by name to members of the royal household and to provincial governors, whom Sir Samson was content to remember as 'the old black fellow who drank so much Kummel' or 'that what-do-you-call-him Prudence said was like Aunt Sarah' or 'the one with glasses and gold teeth'.

Besides, the Bishop's croquet was not nearly up to Legation standards.

As it happened, however, they found him at table when, twenty minutes late for luncheon, Prudence and William returned from their ride.

'Do you know,' said Lady Courteney, 'I thought for once you *had* been massacred. It would have pleased Monsieur Ballon so much. He is always warning me of the danger of allowing you to go out alone during the crisis. He was on the telephone this morning asking what steps we had taken to fortify the Legation. Madame Ballon had made sandbags and put them all round the windows. He told me he was keeping his last cartridge for Madame Ballon.'

'Everyone is in a great state of alarm in the town,' said the Bishop. 'There are so many rumours. Tell me, Sir Samson, you do not think really, seriously, there is any danger of a massacre?'

The Envoy Extraordinary said: 'We seem to have tinned asparagus for luncheon every day . . . I can't think why . . . I'm so sorry–you were talking about the massacre. Well, I hardly know. I haven't really thought about it . . . Yes, I suppose there might be one. I don't see what's to stop them, if the fellows take it into their heads. Still I dare say it'll all blow over, you know. Doesn't do to get worried . . . I should have thought we could have grown it ourselves. Much better than spending so much time on that Dutch garden. So like being on board ship, eating tinned asparagus.'

For some minutes Lady Courteney and Sir Samson discussed the relative advantages of tulips and asparagus. Presently the Bishop said: 'One of the things which brought me here this morning was to find out if there was any News. If I could take back something certain to the town . . . You cannot imagine the distress everyone is in . . . It is the silence for so many weeks and the rumours. Up here you must at least know what is going on.

'News,' said the Envoy Extraordinary. 'News. Well, we've generally got quite a lot going on. Let's see, when were you here last? You knew that the Anstruthers have decided to enter David for Uppingham? Very sensible of them, I think. And Percy Legge's sister in England is going to be married–the one who was out here staying with them last year–you remember her? Betty Anstruther got run away with and had a nasty fall the other morning. I thought that pony was too strong for the child. What else is there to tell the Bishop, my dear?'

'The Legges' Frigidaire is broken and they can't get it mended until after the war. Poor Captain Walsh has been laid up with fever again. Prudence began another novel the other day . . . or wasn't I to tell about that, darling?'

'You certainly were not to. And anyway it isn't a novel. It's a Panorama of Life. Oh, I've got some news for all of you. Percy scored twelve-hundred-and-eighty at bagatelle this morning.'

'No, I say,' said Sir Samson, 'did he really?'

'Oh, but that was on the chancery table,' said William. 'I don't count that.

We've all made colossal scores there. The pins are bent. I still call my eleven-hundred-and-sixty-five at the Anstruthers' a record.'

For some minutes they discussed the demerits of the chancery bagatelle table. Presently the Bishop said:

'But is there no news about the war?'

'No, I don't think so. Can't remember anything particularly. I leave all that to Walsh, you know, and he's down with fever at the moment. I dare say when he comes back we shall hear something. He keeps in touch with all these local affairs . . . There were some cables the other day, now I come to think of it. Was there anything about the war in them, William, d'you know?'

'I can't really say, sir. The truth is we've lost the cipher book again.'

'Awful fellow, William, he's always losing things. What would you say if you had a chaplain like that, Bishop? Well, as soon as it turns up, get them deciphered, will you? There might be something wanting an answer.'

'Yes, sir.'

'Oh, and William–I think you ought to get those pins put straight on the chancery bagatelle board. It's an awful waste of time playing if it doesn't run true.'

'Golly,' said William to Prudence when they were alone. 'Wasn't the Enoy on a high horse at luncheon. Telling me off right and left. First about the cipher book and then about the bagatelle. Too humiliating.'

'Poor sweet, he was only showing off to the Bishop. He's probably frightfully ashamed of himself already.'

'That's all very well, but why should I be made to look a fool just so as he can impress the Bishop?'

'Sweet, sweet William, please don't be in a rage. It isn't my fault if I have a martinet for a father, is it, darling? Listen, I've got a whole lot of new ideas for us to try.'

The Legges and the Anstruthers came across to tea: cucumber sandwiches, gentleman's relish, hot scones and seed-cake.

'How's Betty after her fall?'

'Rather shaken, poor mite. Arthur wants her to start riding again as soon as she can. He's afraid she may lose her nerve permanently.'

'But not on Majesty.'

'No, we hope Percy will lend her Jumbo for a bit. She can't really manage Majesty yet, you know.'

'More tea, Bishop? How is everyone at the Mission?'

'Oh dear, how bare the garden is looking. It really is heart-breaking. This is just the time it should be at its best. But all the antirrhinums are in the bag, heaven knows where.'

'This war is too exasperating. 'I've been expecting the wool for baby's jacket for six weeks. I can't get on with it at all and there are only the sleeves to finish. Do you think it would look too absurd if I put in the sleeves in another colour?'

'It might look rather sweet.'

'More tea, Bishop? I want to hear *all* about the infant school some time.'

'I've found the cipher book, sir.'

'Good boy, where was it?'

'In my collar drawer. I'd been decoding some telegrams in bed last week.'

'Splendid. It doesn't matter as long as it's safe, but you know how particular the F.O. are about things like that.'

'Poor Monsieur Ballon. He's been trying to get an aeroplane from Algiers.'

'Mrs Schonbaum told me that the reason we're all so short of supplies is that the French Legation have been buying up everything and storing it in their cellars.'

'I wonder if they'd like to buy my marmalade. It's been rather a failure this year.'

'More tea, Bishop? I want to talk to you some time about David's confirmation. He's getting such an independent mind, I'm sometimes quite frightened what he'll say next.'

'I wonder if you know anything about this cable. I can't make head or tail of it. It isn't in any of the usual codes. *Kt to QR3 CH.*'

'Yes, they're all right. It's a move in the chess game Percy's playing with Babbit at the F.O. He was wondering what had become of it.'

'Poor Mrs Walsh. Looking quite done up. I'm sure the altitude isn't good for her.'

'I'm sure Uppingham is just the place for David.'

'More tea, Bishop? I'm sure you must be tired after your ride.'

Sixty miles southward in the Ukaka pass bloody bands of Sakuyu warriors played hide-and-seek among the rocks, chivvying the last fugitives of the army of Seyid, while behind them down the gorge, from cave villages of incalculable antiquity, the women crept out to rob the dead.

After tea the Consul looked in and invited Prudence and William over to play tennis.

'I'm afraid the balls are pretty well worn out. We've had some on order for two months. Confound this war.'

When it was too dark to play, they dropped in on the Legges for cocktails, overstayed their time and ran back to the Legation to change for dinner. They tossed for first bath. Prudence won but William took it. He finished her bath salts and they were both very late for dinner. The Bishop, as had been feared, stayed the night. After dinner a log fire was lit in the hall; the evenings were cold in the hills. Sir Samson settled down to his knitting. Anstruther and Legge came in to make up the bridge table with Lady Courteney and the Bishop.

Legation bridge was played in a friendly way.

'I'll go one small heart.'

'One no-trump, and I hope you remember what that means, partner.'

'How you two do cheat.'

'No.'

'I say, can't you do better than that?'

'What did you call?'

'A heart.'

'Oh, well, I'll go two hearts.'

'That's better.'

'Damn, I've forgotten what a no-trump call means. I shall have to pass.'

'No. I'm thinking of riding Vizier with a gag. He's getting heavy in the mouth.'

'No. Then it's you to play, Bishop. It's hopeless using a steel bit out here.'

'I say, what a rotten dummy; is that the best you can do, partner?'

'Well, you wanted me to put you up. If you can make the syces water the bit before bridling it's all right.'

Prudence played the gramophone to William, who lay on his back in front of the hearth smoking one of the very few remaining cigars. 'Oh dear,' he said, 'when will the new records come?'

'I say, Prudence, do come and look at the jumper. I'm starting on the sleeves.'

'Envoy, you *are* clever.'

'Well, it's very exciting . . .'

'Pretty tune that. I say, is it my turn?'

'Percy, *do* attend to the game.'

'Sorry, anyway I've taken the trick.'

'It was ours already.'

'No, I say, was it? Put on the other side, Prudence–the one about Sex Appeal Sarah.'

'*Percy*, it's you to play again. Now trump it this time.'

'Sorry, no trumps left. Good that about "*start off with cocktails and end up with Eno's*".'

A few miles away at the French Legation the minister and the first secretary were discussing the report of the British movements which was brought to them every evening by Sir Samson's butler.

'Bishop Goodchild is there again.'

'*Clericalism.*'

'That is how they keep in touch with the town. He is an old fox, Sir Courteney.'

'It is quite true that they have made no attempt to fortify the Legation. I have confirmed it.'

'No doubt they have made their preparations in another quarter. Sir Courteney has been financing Seth.'

'Without doubt.'

'I think he is behind the fluctuations of the currency.'

'They are using a new code. Here is a copy of today's telegram. It means nothing to me. Yesterday there was one the same.'

'*Kt to QR3 CH*. No, that is not one of the ordinary codes. You must work on that all night. Pierre will help.'

'I should not be surprised if Sir Samson were in the pay of the Italians.'

'It is more than likely. The guard has been set?'

'They have orders to shoot at sight.'

'Have the alarms been tested?'

'All are in order.'

'Excellent. Then I will wish you good night.'

M. Ballon ascended the stairs to bed. In his room he first tested the steel shutters, then the lock of the door. Then he went across to the bed where his wife was already asleep and examined the mosquito curtains. He squirted a little Flit round the windows and door, sprayed his throat with antiseptic and rapidly divested himself of all except his woollen cummerbund. He slipped on his pyjamas, examined the magazine of his revolver and laid it on the chair at his bedside; next to it he placed his watch, electric torch and a bottel of Vittel. He slipped another revolver under his pillow. He tiptoed to the window and called down softly: 'Sergeant.'

There was a click of heels in the darkness. 'Excellence.'

'Is all well?'

'All well, Excellence.'

M. Ballon moved softly across to the electric switches, and before extinguishing the main lamp switched on a small electric night-light which shed a faint blue radiance throughout the room. Then he cautiously lifted the mosquito curtain, flashed his torch round to make sure that there were no insects there, and finally, with a little grunt, lay down to sleep. Before losing consciousness his hand felt, found and grasped a small carved nut which he kept under his bolster in the belief that it would bring him good luck.

Next morning by eleven o'clock the Bishop had been seen off the premises and the British legation had settled down to its normal routine. Lady Courteney was in the potting-shed; Sir Samson was in the bath; William, Legge and Anstruther were throwing poker dice in the chancery; Prudence was at work on the third chapter of the *Panorama of Life*. *Sex,* she wrote in round, irregular characters, *is the crying out of the Soul for Completion*. Presently she crossed out '*Soul*' and substituted '*Spirit*'; then she inserted '*of man*', changed it to '*manhood*' and substituted '*humanity*'. Then she took a new sheet of paper and copied out the whole sentence. Then she wrote a letter. *Sweet William. You looked so lovely at breakfast you know all half awake and I wanted to pinch you only didn't. Why did you go away at once? Saying 'decode'. You know you hadn't got to. I suppose it was the Bishop. Darling, he's gone now so come back and I will show you something lovely. The Panorama of Life is rather a trial to-day. Very literary and abstruse but it won't get any* LONGER. *Oh dear. Prudence. XXXX.* She folded this letter very carefully into a three-cornered hat, addressed it *The Honble William Bland, Attaché Honoraire, près La Legation du Grande Bretagne*, and sent it down to the chancery, with instructions to the boy to wait for an answer. William scribbled, *So sorry darling desperately busy today see you at luncheon. Longing to read Panorama. W.*, and threw four kings in two.

Prudence disconsolately abandoned her fountain pen and went out to watch her mother thinning the michaelmas daisies.

Prudence and William had left an inflated india-rubber sea-serpent behind them in the bathroom. Sir Samson sat in the warm water engrossed with it. He swished it down the water and caught it in his toes; he made waves for it; he blew it along; he sat on it and let it shoot up suddenly to the surface between his thighs; he squeezed some of the air out of it and made bubbles. Chance treats of this kind made or marred the happiness of the Envoy's day. Soon he was rapt in daydream about the pleistocene age, where among mists and vast, unpeopled crags schools of deep-sea monsters splashed and sported; oh happy fifth day of creation, thought the Envoy Extraordinary, oh radiant infant sun, newly weaned from the breasts of darkness, oh rich steam of the soggy continents, oh jolly whales and sea-serpents frisking in new brine . . . Knocks at the door. William's voice outside.

'Walker's just ridden over, sir. Can you see him?'

Crude disillusionment.

Sir Samson returned abruptly to the twentieth century, to a stale and crowded world; to a bath grown tepid and an india-rubber toy. 'Walker? never heard of him.'

'Yes, sir, you know him. The American secretary.'

'Oh, yes, to be sure. Extraordinary time to call. What on earth does the fellow want? If he tries to borrow the tennis marker again, tell him it's broken.'

'He's just got information about the war. Apparently there's been a decisive battle at last.'

'Oh, well, I'm glad to hear that. Which side won, do you know?'

'He did tell me, but I've forgotten.'

'Doesn't matter. I'll hear all about it from him. Tell him I'll be down directly. Give him a putter and let him play clock golf. And you'd better let them know he'll be staying to luncheon.'

Half an hour later Sir Samson came downstairs and greeted Mr Walker.

'My dear fellow, how good of you to come. I couldn't get out before; the morning is always rather busy here. I hope they've been looking after you properly. I think it's about time for a cocktail, William.'

'The Minister thought that you'd like to have news of the battle. We got it on the wireless from Matodi. We tried to ring you up yesterday evening but couldn't get through.'

'No, I always have the telephone disconnected after dinner. Must keep some part of the day for oneself, you know.'

'Of course, we haven't got any full details yet.'

'Of course not. Still, the war's over, William tells me, and I, for one, am glad. It's been on too long. Very upsetting to everything. Let me see, which of them won it?'

'Seth.'

'Ah yes, to be sure. Seth. I'm very glad. He was . . . now let me see . . . which was he?'

'He's the old Empress's son.'

'Yes, yes, now I've got him. And the Empress, what's become of her?'

'She died last year.'

'I'm glad. It's very disagreeable for an old lady of her age to get involved in all these disturbances. And What's-his-name, you know the chap she was married to? He dead, too?'

'Seyid? There's no news of him. I think we may take it that we've seen the last of him.'

'Pity. Nice fellow. Always liked him. By the by, hadn't one of the fellows been to school in England?'

'Yes, that's Seth.'

'Is it, by Jove. Then he speaks English?'

'Perfectly.'

'That'll be one in the eye for Ballon, after all the trouble he took to learn Sakuyu, Here's William with the cocktails.'

'I'm afraid they won't be up to much this morning, sir. We've run out of Peach Brandy.'

'Well, never mind. It won't be long now before we get everything straight again. You must tell us all your news at luncheon. I hear Mrs Schonbaum's mare is in foal. I'll be interested to see how she does. We've never had any luck breeding. I don't believe the native syces understand bloodstock.'

At the French Legation, also, news of Seth's victory had arrived. 'Ah,' said M. Ballon, 'so the English and the Italians have triumphed. But the game is not over yet. Old Ballon is not outwitted yet. There is a trick or two still to be won. Sir Samson must look to his laurels.'

While at that moment the Envoy was saying: 'Of course, it's all a question of the altitude. I've not heard of anyone growing asparagus up here but I can't see why it shouldn't do. We get the most delicious green peas.'

3

Two days later news of the battle of Ukaka was published in Europe. It made very little impression on the million or so Londoners who glanced down the columns of their papers that evening.

'Any news in the paper tonight, dear?'

'No, dear, nothing of interest.'

'Azania? That's part of Africa, ain't it?'

'Ask Lil, she was at school last.'

'Lil, where's Azania?'

'I don't know, father.'

'What do they teach you at school, I'd like to know.'

'Only niggers.'

'It came in a cross-word quite lately. *Independent native principality*. You would have it it was Turkey.'

'Azania? It sounds like a Cunarder to me.'

'But, my dear, surely you remember that *madly* attractive blackamoor at Balliol.'

'Run up and see if you can find the atlas, deary . . . Yes, where it always is, behind the stand in father's study.'

'Things look quieter in East Africa. That Azanian business cleared up at last.'

'Care to see the evening paper? There's nothing in it.'

In Fleet Street, in the offices of the daily papers: 'Randall, there might be a story in the Azanian cable. The new bloke was at Oxford. See what there is to it.'

Mr Randall typed: *His Majesty B.A. . . . ex-undergrad among the cannibals . . . scholar emperor's desperate bid for throne . . . barbaric splendour . . . conquering hordes . . . ivory . . . elephants . . . east meets west . . .*

'Sanders. Kill that Azanian story in the London edition.'

'Anything in the paper this morning?'

'No, dear, nothing of interest.'

Late in the afternoon Basil Seal read the news on the Imperial and Foreign page of *The Times* as he stopped at his club on the way to Lady Metroland's to cash a bad cheque.

For the last four days Basil had been on a racket. He had woken up an hour ago on the sofa of a totally strange flat. There was a gramophone playing. A lady in a dressing jacket sat in an armchair by the gas-fire, eating sardines from the tin with a shoe-horn. An unknown man in shirtsleeves was shaving, the glass propped on the chimneypiece.

The man had said: 'Now you're awake you'd better go.'

The woman: 'Quite thought you were dead.'

Basil: 'I can't think why I'm here.'

'I can't think why you don't go.'

'Isn't London hell?'

'Did I have a hat?'

'That's what caused half the trouble.'

'What trouble?'

'Oh, why don't you go?'

So Basil had gone down the stairs, which were covered in worn linoleum, and emerged through the side door of a shop into a busy street which proved to be King's Road, Chelsea.

Incidents of this kind constantly occurred when Basil was on a racket.

At the club he found a very old member sitting before the fire with tea and hot muffins. He opened *The Times* and sat on the leather-topped fender.

'You see the news from Azania?'

The elderly member was startled by the suddenness of his address. 'No . . . no . . . I am afraid I can't really say that I have.'

'Seth has won the war.'

'Indeed . . . well, to tell you the truth I haven't been following the affair very closely.'

'Very interesting.'

'No doubt.'

'I never thought things would turn out quite in this way, did you?'

'I can't say I've given the matter any thought.'

'Well, fundamentally it is an issue between the Arabs and the christianized Sakuyu.'

'I see.'

'I think the mistake we made was to underestimate the prestige of the dynasty.'

'Oh.'

'As a matter of fact, I've never been satisfied in my mind about the legitimacy of the old Empress.'

'My dear young man, no doubt you have some particular interest in the affairs of this place. Pray understand that I know nothing at all about it and that I feel it is too late in the day for me to start improving my knowledge.'

The old man shifted himself in his chair away from Basil's scrutiny and began reading his book. A page came in with the message: 'No reply from either of those numbers, sir.'

'Don't you hate London?'

'Eh?'

'Don't you hate London?'

'No, I do not. Lived here all my life. Never get tired of it. Fellow who's tired of London is tired of life.'

'Don't you believe it,' said Basil.

'I'm going away for some time,' he told the hall-porter as he left the club.

'Very good, sir. What shall I do about correspondence?'

'Destroy it.'

'Very good, sir.' Mr Seal was a puzzle to him. He never could forget Mr Seal's father. He had been a member of the club. Such a different gentleman. So spick and span, never without silk hat and an orchid in his buttonhole. Chief Conservative Whip for twenty-five years. Who would have thought of him having a son like Mr Seal? *Out of town until further notice. No letters forwarded* he entered against Basil's name in his ledger. Presently the old gentleman emerged from the smoking-room.

'Arthur, is that young man a member here?'

'Mr Seal, sir? Oh yes, sir.'

'What d'you say his name is?'

'Mr Basil Seal.'

'Basil Seal, eh? Basil Seal. Not Christopher Seal's son?'

'Yes, sir.'

'Is he now? Poor old Seal. 'Pon my soul, what a sad thing. Who'd have thought of that? Seal of all people . . .' and he shuffled back into the smoking-room, to the fire and his muffins, full of the comfort that glows in the hearts of old men when they contemplate the misfortunes of their contemporaries.

Basil walked across Piccadilly and up to Curzon Street. Lady Metroland was giving a cocktail party.

'Basil,' she said, 'you had no business to come. I particularly didn't ask you.'

'I know. I only heard you had a party quite indirectly. What I've really come for is to see if my sister is here.'

'Barbara? She may be. She said she was coming. How horrible you look.'

'Dirty?'

'Yes.'

'Not shaven?'

'No.'

'Well, I've only just woken up. I haven't been home yet.' He looked round the room. 'All the same people. You don't make many new friends, Margot.'

'I hear you've given up your constituency?'

'Yes, in a way. It wasn't worth while. I told the P.M. I wasn't prepared to fight on the tariff issue. He had a chance to hold over the bill but the Outrage section were too strong so I threw in my hand. Besides, I want to go abroad. I've been in England too long.'

'Cocktail, sir.'

'No, bring me a Pernod and water will you? . . . there isn't any? Oh well, whisky. Bring it into the study. I want to go and telephone. I'll be back soon, Margot.'

'God, what I feel about that young man,' said Lady Metroland.

Two girls were talking about him.

'Such a lovely person.'

'Where?'

'Just gone out.'

'You don't mean Basil Seal?'

'Do I?'

'Horrible clothes, black hair over his face.'

'Yes, tell me about him.'

'My dear, he's enchanting . . . Barbara Sothill's brother, you know. He's been in hot water lately. He'd been adopted as candidate somewhere in the West. Father says he was bound to get in at the next election. Angela Lyne was paying his expenses. But they had trouble over something. You know how careful Angela is. I never thought Basil was really her tea. They never quite made sense, I mean, did they? So that's all over.'

'It's nice his being so dirty.'

Other people discussed him.

'No, the truth about Basil is just that he's a *bore*. No one minds him being rude, but he's so *teaching*. I had him next to me at dinner once and he would talk all the time about Indian dialects. Well, what *was* one to say? And I asked afterwards and apparently he doesn't know anything about them either.'

'He's done all kinds of odd things.'

'Well, yes, and I think that's so boring too. Always in revolutions and murders and things, I mean, what is one to say? Poor Angela is *literally* off her head with him. I was there yesterday and she could talk of nothing else but the row he's had with his committee in his constituency. He does seem to have behaved rather oddly at the Conservative ball and then he and Alastair Trumpington and Peter Pastmaster and some others had a five-day party up there and left a lot of bad cheques behind and had a motor accident and one of them got run in–you know what Basil's parties are. I mean, that sort of thing is all right in London, but you know what provincial towns are. So what with one thing and another they've asked him to stand down. The trouble is that poor Angela still fancies him rather.'

'What's going to happen to him?'

'I *know*. That's the *point*. Barbara says she won't do another thing for him.'

Someone else was saying, 'I've given up trying to be nice to Basil. He either cuts me or corners me with an interminable lecture about Asiatic politics. It's odd Margot having him here–particularly after the way he's always getting Peter involved.'

Presently Basil came back from telephoning. He stood in the doorway, a glass of whisky in one hand, looking insolently round the room, his head back, chin forward, shoulders rounded, dark hair over his forehead, contemptuous grey eyes over grey pouches, a proud, rather childish mouth, a scar on one cheek.

'My word, he is a corker,' remarked one of the girls.

His glance travelled round the room. 'I'll tell you who I want to see, Margot. Is Rex Monomark here?'

'He's over there somewhere, but, Basil, I absolutely forbid you to tease him.'

'I won't tease him.'

Lord Monomark, owner of many newspapers, stood at the far end of the drawing-room discussing diet. Round him in a haze of cigar smoke were ranged his ladies and gentlemen in attendance: three almost freakish beauties, austerely smart, their exquisite, irregular features eloquent of respect; two gross men of the world, wheezing appreciation; a dapper elderly secretary, with pink, bald pate and in his eyes that glazed, gin-fogged look that is common to sailors and the secretaries of the great, and comes from too short sleep.

'Two raw onions and a plate of oatmeal porridge,' said Lord Monomark. 'That's all I've taken for luncheon in the last eight months. And I feel two hundred per cent better–physically, intellectually and ethically.'

The group was slightly isolated from the rest of the party. It was very rarely that Lord Monomark consented to leave his own house and appear as a guest. The few close friends whom he honoured in this way observed certain strict conventions in the matter: new people were not to be introduced to him except at his own command; politicians were to be kept at a distance; his cronies of the moment were to be invited with him; provision had to be made for whatever health system he happened to be following. In these conditions he liked now and then to appear in society–an undisguised Haroun al-Rashid among his townspeople–to survey the shadow-play of fashion, and occasionally to indulge the caprice of singling out one of these bodiless phantoms and translating her or him into the robust reality of his own world. His fellow guests, meanwhile, flitted in and out as though unconscious of his presence, avoiding any appearance of impinging on the integrity of this glittering circle.

'If I had my way,' said Lord Monomark, 'I'd make it compulsory throughout the country. I've had a notice drafted and sent round the office recommending the system. Half the fellows think nothing of spending one and six or two shillings on lunch every day–that's out of eight or nine pounds a week.'

'Rex, you're wonderful.'

'Read it out to Lady Everyman, Sanders.'

'*Lord Monomark wishes forcibly to bring to the attention of his staff the advantages to be derived from a carefully chosen diet . . .*' Basil genially intruded himself into the party.

'Well, Rex, I thought I'd find you here. It's all stuff about that onion and porridge diet, you know. Griffenbach exploded that when I was in Vienna three years ago. But that's not really what I came to talk about.'

'Oh, Seal, isn't it? I've not seen you for a long time. I remember now you wrote to me some time ago. What was it about, Sanders?'

'Afghanistan.'

'Yes, of course. I turned it over to one of my editors to answer. I hope he explained.'

Once, when Basil had been a young man of promise, Lord Monomark had considered taking him up and invited him for a cruise in the Mediterranean.

Basil at first refused and then, after they had sailed, announced by wireless his intention of joining the yacht at Barcelona; Lord Monomark's party had waited there for two sultry days without hearing news and then sailed without him. When they next met in London Basil explained rather inadequately that he had found at the last minute he couldn't manage it after all. Countless incidents of this kind had contributed to Basil's present depreciated popularity.

'Look here, Rex,' he said, 'what I want to know is what you're going to do about Seth.'

'Seth?' Lord Monomark turned an inquiring glance on Sanders. 'What am I doing about Seth?'

'Seth?'

'It seems to me there's an extremely tricky political situation developing there. You've seen the news from Ukaka. It doesn't tell one a thing. I want to get some first-hand information. I'm probably sailing almost at once. It occurred to me that I might cover it for you in the *Excess*.'

Towards the end of this speech, Lord Monomark's bewilderment was suddenly illumined. This was nothing unusual after all. It was simply someone after a job. 'Oh,' he said, 'I'm afraid I don't interfere with the minor personnel of the paper. You'd better go and see one of the editors about it. But I don't think you'll find him anxious to take on new staff at the moment.'

'I'll tell them you sent me.'

'No, no, I never interfere. You must just approach them through the normal channels.'

'All right. I'll come up and see you after I've fixed it up. Oh, and I'll send you Griffenbach's report on the onion and porridge diet if I can find it. There's my sister. I've got to go and talk to her now, I'm afraid. See you before I sail.'

Barbara Sothill no longer regarded her brother with the hero-worship which had coloured the first twenty years of her life.

'Basil,' she said. 'What on earth have you been doing? I was lunching at mother's today and she was wild about you. She's got one of her dinner parties and you promised to be in. She said you hadn't been home all night and she didn't know whether to get another man or not.'

'I was on a racket. We began at Lottie Crump's. I rather forget what happened except that Allan got beaten up by some chaps.'

'And she's just heard about the committee.'

'Oh *that*. I meant to give up the constituency anyhow. It's no catch being in the Commons now. I'm thinking of going to Azania.'

'Oh, were you?–and what'll you do there?'

'Well, Rex Monomark wants me to represent the *Excess*, but I think as a matter of fact I shall be better off if I keep a perfectly free hand. The only thing is I shall need some money. D'you think our mother will fork out five hundred pounds?'

'I'm sure she won't.'

'Well, someone'll have to. To tell you the truth I can't very well stay on in England at the moment. Things have got into rather a crisis. I suppose you wouldn't like to give me some money.'

'Oh, Basil, what's the good? You know I can't do it except by getting it from Freddy and he was furious last time.'

'I can't think why. He's got packets.'

'Yes, but might try and be a little polite to him sometimes–just in public I mean.'

'Oh, of course if he thinks that by lending me a few pounds he's setting himself up for life as a good fellow . . .'

In the days when Sir Christopher was Chief Whip, Lady Seal had entertained frequently and with relish. Now, in her widowhood, with Barbara successfully married and her sons dispersed, she limited herself to four or five dinner parties every year. There was nothing elastic or informal about these occasions. Lady Metroland was a comparatively rich woman and it was her habit when she was tired to say casually to her butler at cocktail time, 'I am not going out tonight. There will be about twenty to dinner,' and then to sit down to the telephone and invite her guests, saying to each, 'Oh, but you *must* chuck them tonight. I'm all alone and feeling like death.' Not so Lady Seal, who dispatched engraved cards of invitation a month in advance, supplied defections from a secondary list one week later, fidgeted with place cards and a leather board as soon as the acceptances began to arrive, borrowed her sister's chef and her daughter's footmen and on the morning of the party exhausted herself utterly by trotting all over her house in Lowndes Square arranging flowers. Then at half-past five when she was satisfied that all was ready she would retire to bed and doze for two hours in her darkened room; her maid would call her with cachet Faivre and clear China tea; a touch of ammonia in the bath; a touch of rouge on the cheeks; lavender water behind the ears; half an hour before the glass, fiddling with her jewel case while her hair was being done; final conference with the butler; then a happy smile in the drawing-room for all who were less than twenty minutes late. The menu always included lobster cream, saddle of mutton and brown-bread ice, and there were silver-gilt dishes ranged down the table holding a special kind of bonbon supplied to Lady Seal for twenty years by a little French shop whose name she would sometimes coyly disclose.

Basil arrived among the first guests. There was carpet on the steps; the doors opened with unusual promptness; the hall seemed full of chrysanthemums and footmen.

'Hullo, her ladyship got a party? I forgot all about it. I'd better change.'

'Frank couldn't find your evening clothes, Mr Basil. I don't think you can have brought them back last time you went away. I don't think her Ladyship is expecting you to dinner.'

'Anyone asked for me?'

'There *were* two persons, sir.'

'Duns?'

'I couldn't say, sir. I told them that we had no information about your whereabouts.'

'Quite right.'

'Mrs Lyne rang up fifteen times, sir. She left no message.'

'If anyone else wants me, tell them I've gone to Azania.'

'Sir?'

'Azania.'

'Abroad?'

'Yes, if you like.'

'Excuse me, Mr Basil. . . .'

The Duke and Duchess of Stayle had arrived. The Duchess said, 'So you are not dining with us tonight. You young men are all so busy nowadays. No time for going out. I hear things are going very well up in your constituency.' She was often behindhand with her news. As they went up the Duke said, 'Clever young fellow that. Wonder if he'll ever come to anything though.'

Basil went into the dark little study next to the front door and rang up the Trumpingtons.

'Sonia, are you and Alastair doing anything tonight?'

'We're at home. Basil, what have you been doing to Alastair? I'm furious with you. I think he's going to die.'

'We had rather a racket. Shall I come to dinner?'

'Yes, do. We're in bed.'

He drove to Montagu Square and was shown up to their room. They lay in a vast, low bed, with a backgammon board between them. Each had a separate telephone, on the tables at the side, and by the telephone a goblet of 'black velvet'. A bull terrier and chow flirted on their feet. There were other people in the room: one playing the gramophone, one reading, one trying Sonia's face things at the dressing-table. Sonia said, 'It's such a waste not going out after dark. We have to stay in all day because of duns.'

Alastair said, 'We can't have dinner with these infernal dogs all over the place.'

Sonia: 'You're a cheerful chap to be in bed with, aren't you?' and to the dog, 'Was oo called infernal woggie by owid man? Oh God, he's made a mess again.'

Alastair: 'Are those chaps staying to dinner?'

'We asked one.'

'Which?'

'Basil.'

'Don't mind him, but all those others.'

'I do hope not.'

They said: 'Afraid we'll have to. It's so late to go anywhere else.'

Basil: 'How dirty the bed is, Sonia.'

'I know. It's Alastair's dog. Anyway, you're a nice one to talk about dirt.'

'Isn't London hell?'

Alastair: 'I don't, anyway, see why those chaps shouldn't have dinner downstairs.'

They said: 'It *would* be more comfortable.'

'What are their names?'

'One we picked up last night. The other has been staying here for days.'

'It's not only the expense I mind. They're boring.'

They said: 'We wouldn't stay a moment if we had anywhere else to go.'

'Ring for dinner, sweet. I forget what there is, but I know it's rather good. I ordered it myself.'

There was whitebait, grilled kidneys and toasted cheese. Basil sat between them on the bed and they ate from their knees. Sonia threw a kidney to the dogs and they began a fight.

Alastair: 'It's no good. I can't eat anything.'

Sonia's maid brought in the trays. She asked her: 'How are the gentlemen getting on downstairs?'

'They asked for champagne.'

'I suppose they'd better have it. It's very bad.'

Alastair: 'It's very good.'

'Well it tasted awful to me. Basil, sweety, what's your news?'

'I'm going to Azania.'

'Can't say I know much about that. Is it far?'

'Yes.'

'Fun?'

'Yes.'

'Oh, Alastair, why not us too?'

'Hell, now those dogs have upset everything again.'

'How pompous you're being.'

After dinner they all played happy families. 'Have you got Miss Chips the Carpenter's daughter?'

'*Not at home* but have *you* got Mr Chips the Carpenter? *Thank you and* Mrs Chips the Carpenter's wife? *Thank you* and Basil have *you* got Miss Chips? *Thank you*. That's the Chips family.'

Basil left early so as to see his mother before she went to bed.

Sonia said, 'Good-bye, darling. Write to me from wherever it is. Only I don't expect we'll be living here much longer.'

One of the young men said: 'Could you lend me a fiver? I've a date at the Café de Paris.'

'No, you'd better ask Sonia.'

'But it's so boring. I'm *always* borrowing money from *her*.'

In the course of the evening Lady Seal had found time to touch her old friend Sir Joseph Mannering on the sleeve and say, 'Don't go at once, Jo. I'd like to talk to you afterwards.' As the last guests left he came across to the fireplace, hands behind his coat-tails and on his face an expression of wisdom, discretion, sympathy, experience and contentment. He was a self-assured old booby who in the easy and dignified role of family friend was invoked to aggravate most of the awkward situations that occurred in the lives of his circle.

'A delightful evening, Cynthia, typically delightful. I sometimes think that yours is the only house in London nowadays where I can be sure both of the claret and the company. But you wanted to consult me. Not, I hope, that little trouble of Barbara's.'

'No, it's nothing about Barbara. What's the child been doing?'

'Nothing, nothing. It was just some idle bit of gossip I heard. I'm glad it isn't worrying you. I suppose Basil's been up to some mischief again.'

'Exactly, Jo. I'm at my wit's end with the boy. But what was it about Barbara?'

'Come, come, we can't fuss about too many things. I *did* hear Basil had been up to something. Of course there's plenty of good in the boy. It only wants bringing out.'

'I sometimes doubt it.'

'Now, Cynthia, you're overwrought. Tell me exactly what has been happening.'

It took Lady Seal some time to deliver herself of the tale of Basil's misdemeanours. '. . . if his father were alive . . . spent all the money his Aunt left him on that idiotic expedition to Afghanistan . . . give him a very handsome allowance . . . all and more than all that I can afford . . . paid his debts again and again . . . no gratitude . . . no self-control . . . no longer a child, twenty-eight this year . . . his father . . . the post kind Sir William secured him in the bank in Brazil . . . great opening and such interesting work . . . never went to the office once . . . never know where or whom he is with . . . most undesirable friends, Sonia Trumpington, Peter Pastmaster, all sorts of people whose names I've never even heard . . . of course I couldn't really *approve* of his going about so much with Mrs Lyne–though I dare say there was nothing *wrong* in it–but at least I hoped she might steady him a little . . . stand for Parliament . . . his father . . . behaved in the most irresponsible way in the heart of his constituency . . . Prime Minister . . . Central Office . . . Sonia Trumpington threw it at the mayor . . . Conservative ball . . . one of them actually arrested . . . come to the end, Jo . . . I've made up my mind. I won't do another thing for him–it's not fair on Tony that I should spend all the money on Basil that should go to them equally . . . marry and settle down . . . if his father were alive . . . it isn't even as though he were the kind of man who would do in Kenya,' she concluded hopelessly.

Throughout the narration Sir Joseph maintained his air of wisdom, discretion, sympathy, experience and contentment; at suitable moments he nodded and uttered little grunts of comprehension. At length he said: 'My dear Cynthia. I had no idea it was as bad as that. What a terrible time you have had and how brave you have been. But you mustn't let yourself worry. I dare say even this disagreeable incident may turn to good. It may very likely be the turning-point in the boy's life . . . Learned his lesson. I shouldn't wonder if the reason he hasn't come home is that he's ashamed to face you. I tell you what, I think I'd better have a talk to him. Send him round as soon as you get into touch with him. I'll take him to lunch at the club. He'll probably take advice from a man he might resent from a woman. Didn't he begin reading for the Bar once? Well, let's set him going at that. Keep him at home. Don't give him enough money to go about. Let him bring his friends here. Then he'll only be able to have friend's he's willing to introduce to you. We'll try and get him into a different set. He didn't go to any dances all last summer, I remember you telling me. Heaps of jolly girls coming out he hasn't had the chance of meeting yet. Keep him to his work. The boy's got brains, bound to find it interesting. Then when you're convinced he's steadied up a bit, let him have chambers of his own in one of the Inns of Court. Let him feel you trust him. I'm sure he'll respond . . .'

For nearly half an hour they planned Basil's future, punctually rewarding each stage of his moral recuperation. Presently Lady Seal said: 'Oh Jo, what a help you are. I don't know what I should do without you.'

'Dear Cynthia, it is one of the privileges of maturity to bring new strength and beauty to old friendships.'

'I shan't forget how wonderful you've been tonight, Jo.'

The old boy bounced back in his taxi-cab to St James's and Lady Seal slowly ascended the stairs to her room; both warm at heart and aglow from their fire-lit, nursery game of 'let's pretend'. She sat before her bedroom fire, slipped off her dress and rang the bell beside the chimney-piece.

'I'll have my milk now, Bradshawe, and then go straight to bed.'

The maid lifted the jug from the fender where it had been keeping warm and deftly held back the skin with a silver apostle-spoon as she poured the hot milk into a glass. Then she brought the jewel case and held it while wearily, one by one, the rings, bracelet, necklace and earrings were slipped off and tumbled in. Then she began taking the pins from her mistress's hair. Lady Seal held the glass in both hands and sipped.

'Don't trouble to brush it very long tonight, I'm tired.'

'I hope the party was a success, my lady.'

'I suppose so. Yes, I'm sure it was. Captain Cruttwell is very silly, but it was kind of him to come at all at such short notice.'

'It's the first time Her Grace's youngest daughter has been to dinner?'

'Yes, I think it is. The child looked very well, I thought, and talked all the time.'

Lady Seal sipped the hot milk, her thoughts still wandering innocently in the soft places where Sir Joseph had set them. She saw Basil hurrying to work in the morning, by bus at first, later–when he had proved his sincerity–he should have a two-seater car; he would be soberly but smartly dressed and carry some kind of business-like attaché-case or leather satchel with him. He would generally have papers to go through before changing for dinner. They would dine together and afterwards often go out to the theatre or cinema. He would eat with good appetite, having lunched quickly and economically at some place near his work. Quite often she would entertain for him, small young people's parties of six or eight–intelligent, presentable men of his own age, pretty, well-bred girls. During the season he would go to two dances a week, and leave them early . . . 'Bradshawe, where is the spoon? It's forming a skin again.' . . . Later she went to tea with him in his rooms in Lincoln's Inn. He lifted a pile of books from the armchair before she sat down. 'I've brought you a looking-glass.' 'Oh, Mother, how sweet of you.' 'I saw it in Helena's shop this morning and thought it just the thing to go over your fire. It will lighten the room. It's got a piece chipped off in one place but it is a good one.' 'I *must* try it at once.' 'It's down in the car, dear. Tell Andrews to bring it up . . .'

A knock at the door.

'What can they want at this time? See who it is, Bradshawe.'

'Mr Basil, my lady.'

'Oh, dear.'

Basil came in, so unlike the barrister of her dream that it required an effort to recognize him.

'I'll ring for you in a few minutes, Bradshawe . . . Basil, I really can't talk to you now. I have a great deal to say and I am very tired. Where have you been?'

'Different places.'

'You might have let me know. I expected you at dinner.'

'Had to go and dine with Alastair and Sonia. Was the party a success?'

'Yes, I think so, so far as can be expected. I had to ask poor Toby Cruttwell. Who else *was* there I *could* ask at the last moment? I do wish you wouldn't fiddle with things. Shut the jewel case like a good boy.'

'By the way, I've given up politics; did you know?'

'Yes, I am most distressed about the whole business–vexed and distressed, but I can't discuss it now. I'm so tired. It's all arranged. You are to lunch with Sir Joseph Mannering at his club and he will explain everything. You are to meet some new girls and later have tea–I mean rooms–in Lincoln's Inn. You'll like that, won't you, dear? Only you mustn't ask about it now.'

'What I came to say is that I'm just off to Azania.'

'No, no, dear boy. You are to lunch with Jo at The Travellers'.'

'And I shall need some money.'

'It's all decided.'

'You see I'm fed up with London and English politics. I want to get away. Azania is the obvious place. I had the Emperor to lunch once at Oxford. Amusing chap. The thing is this,' said Basil, scratching in his pipe with a delicate pair of gold manicure scissors from the dressing-table. 'Every year or so there's *one* place in the globe worth going to where things are happening. The secret is to find out where and be on the spot in time.'

'Basil dear, *not* with the scissors.'

'History doesn't happen everywhere at once. Azania is going to be terrific. Anyway, I'm off there to-morrow. Flying to Marseilles and catching the Messageries ship. Only I must raise at least five hundred before I start. Barbara wanted to give it to me but I thought the simplest thing was to compound for my year's allowance. There may be a few debts that'll want settling while I'm away. I thought of giving you a power of attorney . . .'

'Dear boy, you are talking nonsense. When you've had luncheon with Sir Joseph you'll understand. We'll get into touch with him first thing in the morning. Meanwhile run along and get a good night's sleep. You aren't looking at all well, you know.'

'I must have at least three hundred.'

'There. I've rung for Bradshawe. You'll forget all about this place in the morning. Good night, darling boy. The servants have gone up. Don't leave the lights burning downstairs, will you?'

So Lady Seal undressed and sank at last luxuriously into bed. Bradshawe softly paddled round the room performing the last offices; she picked up the evening gown, the underclothes, and the stockings, and carried them outside to her workroom; she straightened the things on the dressing-table, shut the drawers, wiped the points of the nail scissors with a wad of cotton; she opened the windows four inches at the top, banked up the fire with a shovelful of small coal, hitched on the wire guard, set a bottle of Vichy water and a glass on the chamber cupboard beside the bed and stood at the door, one hand holding the milk tray, the other on the electric switch.

'Is that everything for the night, my lady?'

'That's all, Bradshawe. I'll ring in the morning. Good night.'

'Good night, my lady.'

Basil went back to the telephone and called Mrs Lyne. A soft, slightly impatient voice answered him. 'Yes, who is it?'

'Basil.'

A pause.

'Hullo, are you there, Angela? Basil speaking.'

'Yes, darling, I heard. Only I didn't quite know what to say . . . I've just got in . . . Such a dull evening . . . I rang you up today . . . couldn't get on to you.'

'How odd you sound.'

'Well, yes . . . why did you ring up? It's late.'

'I'm coming round to see you.'

'My dear, you can't possibly.'

'I was going to say good-bye–I'm going away for some time.'

'Yes, I suppose that's a good thing.'

'Well, don't you want me to come?'

'You'll have to be sweet to me. You see I've been in rather a muddle lately. You will be sweet, darling, won't you? I don't think I could bear it if you weren't.'

And later, as they lay on their backs smoking, her foot just touching his under the sheets, Angela interrupted him to say: 'How would it be if, just for a little, we didn't talk about this island? . . . I'm going to find things different when you've gone.'

'I'm mad for it.'

'I know,' said Angela. 'I'm not kidding myself.'

'You're a grand girl.'

'It's time you went away . . . shall I tell you something?'

'What?'

'I'm going to give you some money.'

'Well, that is nice.'

'You see, when you rang up I knew that was what you wanted. And you've been sweet tonight really, though you were boring about that island. So I thought that just for tonight I'd like to have you not asking for money. Before, I've enjoyed making it awkward for you. Did you know? Well I had to have *some* fun, hadn't I?–and I think I used to embarrass even you sometimes. And I used to watch you steering the conversation round. I knew that anxious look in your eye so well . . . I had to have something to cheer me up all these weeks, hadn't I? You don't do much for a girl. But tonight I thought it would be a treat just to let you be nice and no bother and I've enjoyed myself. I made out a cheque before you came . . . on the dressing-table. It's for rather a lot.'

'You're a grand girl.'

'When d'you start?'

'Tomorrow.'

'I'll miss you. Have a good time.'

Next morning at twenty to ten Lady Seal rang her bell. Bradshawe drew the curtains and shut the windows, brought in the orange juice, the letters and the daily papers.

'Thank you, Bradshawe. I had a very good night. I only woke up once and then was asleep again almost directly. Is it raining?'

'I'm afraid so, my lady.'

'I shall want to see Mr Basil before he goes out.'

'Mr Basil has gone already.'

'So early. Did he say where?'

'He did say, my lady, but I am not sure of the name. Somewhere in Africa.'

'How very provoking. I know there was something I wanted him to do today.'

At eleven o'clock a box of flowers arrived from Sir Joseph Mannering and at twelve Lady Seal attended a committee meeting; it was four days before she discovered the loss of her emerald bracelet and by that time Basil was on the sea.

Croydon, Le Bourget, Lyons, Marseilles; colourless, gusty weather, cloud-spray dripping and trickling on the windows; late in the afternoon, stillness from the roar of the propellers; sodden turf; the road from the aerodrome to the harbour heavily scented with damp shrub; wind-swept sheds on the quay; an Annamite boy swabbing the decks; a surly steward, the ship does not sail until tomorrow, the commissaire knows of the allotment of the cabins, he is on shore, it is not known when he will return, there is nowhere to leave the baggage, the baggage-room is shut and the commissaire has the key, any-one might take it if it were left on deck–twenty francs–the luggage could go in one of the cabins, it will be safe there, the steward has the key, he will see to it. Dinner at the restaurant de Verdun. Basil alone with a bottle of fine burgundy.

Next afternoon they sailed. She was an ugly old ship snatched from Germany after the war as part of the reparations; at most hours of the day two little men in alpaca coats played a fiddle and piano in the deck bar; luncheon at twelve, dinner at seven; red Algerian wine; shrivelled, blotchy dessert; a small saloon full of children; a smoking-room full of French officials and planters playing cards. The big ships do not stop at Matodi. Basil at table talking excellent French ceaselessly, in the evenings paying attention to a woman of mixed blood from Madagascar, getting bored with her and with the ship, sitting sulkily at meals with a book, complaining to the captain about the inadequacy of the wireless bulletins, lying alone in his bunk for hours at a time, smoking cheroots and gazing blankly at the pipes on the ceiling.

At Port Said he sent lewd postcards to Sonia, disposed of his mother's bracelet at a fifth of its value to an Indian jeweller, made friends with a Welsh engineer in the bar of the Eastern Exchange, got drunk with him, fought him, to the embarrassment of the Egyptian policeman, and returned to the ship next morning a few minutes before the companion-way was raised, much refreshed by his racket.

A breathless day in the canal; the woman from Madagascar exhausted with invitation. The Red Sea, the third-class passengers limp as corpses on the lower deck; fiddle and piano indefatigable; dirty ice swimming in the dregs of lemon juice; Basil in his bunk sullenly consuming cheroots, undeterred by the distress of his cabin-companion. Jibuti; portholes closed to keep out the dust, coolies jogging up the planks with baskets of coal; contemptuous savages in the streets scraping their teeth with twigs; an Abyssinian noble-woman in a green veil shopping at the French Emporium; an ill-intentioned black monkey in an acacia tree near the post office. Basil took up with a Dutch South African; they dined on the pavement of the hotel and drove later in a horse-cab to the Somali quarter where in a lamplit mud hut Basil began to talk of the monetary systems of the world until the Boer fell asleep on a couch of plaited hide and the four dancing girls huddled together in the corner like chimpanzees and chattered resentfully among themselves.

The ship was sailing for Azania at midnight. She lay far out in the bay, three lines of lights reflected in the still water; the sound of fiddle and piano was borne through the darkness, harshly broken by her siren intermittently warning passengers to embark. Basil sat in the stern of the little boat, one hand trailing in the sea; half-way to the ship the boatmen shipped their oars and tried to sell him a basket of limes; they argued for a little in broken French, then splashed on irregularly towards the liner; an oil lantern bobbed in the bows. Basil climbed up the companion-way and went below; his companion was asleep and turned over angrily as the light went up; the porthole had been shut all day and the air was gross, Basil lit a cheroot and lay for some time reading. Presently the old ship began to vibrate and later, as she drew clear of the bay, to pitch very slightly in the Indian Ocean. Basil turned out the light and lay happily smoking in the darkness.

In London Lady Metroland was giving a party. Sonia said: 'No one asks us to parties now except Margot. Perhaps there aren't any others.'

'The boring thing about parties is that it's far too much effort to meet new people, and if it's just all the ordinary people one knows already one might just as well stay at home and ring them up instead of having all the business of remembering the right day,'

'I wonder why Basil isn't here. I thought he was bound to be.'

'Didn't he go abroad?'

'I don't think so. Don't you remember, he had dinner with us the other evening?'

'Did he? When?'

'Darling, how *can* I remember that? . . . there's Angela–she'll know.'

'Angela, has Basil gone away?'

'Yes, somewhere quite extraordinary.'

'My dear, is that rather heaven for you?'

'Well, in a way . . .'

Basil was awakened by the clank and rattle of steel cable as the anchor was lowered. He went up on deck in pyjamas. The whole sky was aflame with green and silver dawn. Half-covered figures of other passengers sprawled asleep on benches and chairs. The sailors paddled between them on bare feet, clearing the hatches; a junior officer on the bridge shouting orders to the men at the winch. Two lighters were already alongside preparing to take off cargo. A dozen small boats clustered round them, loaded with fruit.

Quarter of a mile distant lay the low sea-front of Matodi; the minaret, the Portuguese ramparts, the mission church, a few warehouses taller than the rest, the Grand Hotel de l'Empereur Amurath stood out from the white-and-dun cluster of roofs; behind and on either side stretched the meadowland and green plantations of the Azanian coast-line, groves of tufted palm at the water's edge. Beyond and still obscured by mist rose the great crests of the Sakuyu mountains, the Ukaka pass and the road to Debra Dowa.

The purser joined Basil at the rail.

'You disembark here, Mr Seal, do you not?'

'Yes.'

'You are the only passenger. We sail again at noon.'

'I shall be ready to go ashore as soon as I am dressed.'

'You are making a long stay in Azania?'

'Possibly.'

'On business? I have heard it is an interesting country.'

But for once Basil was disinclined to be instructive. 'Purely for pleasure,' he said. Then he went below, dressed and fastened his bags. His cabin companion looked at his watch, scowled and turned his face to the wall; later he missed his shaving soap, bedroom slippers and the fine topee he had bought a few days earlier at Port Said.

4

The Matodi terminus of the Grand Chemin de Fer d'Azanie lay half a mile inland from the town. A broad avenue led to it, red earth scarred by deep ruts and potholes; on either side grew irregular lines of acacia trees. Between the trees were strings of different-coloured flags. A gang of convicts, chained neck to neck, were struggling to shift a rusty motor-car which lay on its side blocking the road. It had come to grief there six months previously, having been driven recklessly into some cattle by an Arab driver. He was now doing time in prison in default of damages. White ants had devoured the tyres; various pieces of mechanism had been removed from time to time to repair other engines. A Sakuyu family had set up house in the back, enclosing the space between the wheels with an intricate structure of rags, tin, mud and grass.

That was in the good times when the Emperor was in the hills. Now he was back again and the town was overrun with soldiers and government officials. It was by his orders that this motor-car was being removed. Everything had been like that for three weeks, bustle everywhere, proclamations posted up on every wall, troops drilling, buglings, hangings, the whole town kept awake all day; in the Arab Club feeling ran high against the new régime.

Mahmud el Khali bin Sai-ud, frail descendant of the oldest family in Matodi, sat among his kinsmen, moodily browsing over his lapful of khat. The sunlight streamed in through the lattice shutters, throwing a diaper of light over the worn carpets and divan; two of the amber mouthpieces of the hubble-bubble were missing; the rocking-chair in the corner was no longer safe, the veneer was splitting and peeling off the rosewood table. These poor remnants were all that remained of the decent people of Matodi; the fine cavaliers had been scattered and cut down in battle. Here were six old men and two dissipated youngsters, one of whom was liable to fits of epilepsy. There was no room for a gentleman in Matodi nowadays, they remarked. You could not recount an anecdote in the streets or pause on the waterfront to discuss with full propriety the sale of land or the pedigree of a stallion, but you were jostled against the wall by black men or Indians, dirty fellows with foreskins; unbelievers, descendants of slaves; judges from up-country, upstarts, jack-in-office, giving decisions against you in the courts . . . Jews foreclosing on mortgages . . . taxation . . . vulgar display . . . no respect of leisure, hanging up wretched little flags everywhere, clearing up the streets, moving derelict motor-cars while their owners were not in a position to defend them. Today there was an ordinance forbidding the use of Arab dress. Were they, at their time of life, to start decking themselves out in coat and trousers and topee like a lot of half-caste bank clerks? . . . besides, the prices tailors charged . . . it was a put-up job . . . you might as well be in a British colony.

Meanwhile, with much overseeing and shouting and banging of behinds, preparations were in progress on the route to the railway station; the first train since the troubles was due to leave that afternoon.

It had taken a long time to get a train together. On the eve of the battle of Ukaka the stationmaster and all the more responsible members of his staff had left for the mainland. In the week that followed Seth's victory they had returned one by one with various explanations of their absence. Then there had been the tedious business of repairing the line which both armies had ruined at several places; they had had to collect wood fuel for the engine and wire for the telegraph lines. This had been the longest delay, for no sooner was it procured from the mainland than it was stolen by General Connolly's disbanded soldiers to decorate the arms and legs of their women. Finally, when everything had been prepared, it was decided to delay the train a few days until the arrival of the mail ship from Europe. It thus happened that Basil Seal's arrival in Matodi coincided with the date fixed for Seth's triumphal return to Debra Dowa.

Arrangements for his departure had been made with great care by the Emperor himself, and the chief features embodied in a proclamation in Sakuyu, Arabic and French, which was posted prominently among the many pronouncements which heralded the advent of Progress and the New Age.

ORDER FOR THE DAY OF THE EMPEROR'S DEPARTURE

(1) The Emperor will proceed to Matodi railway station at 14.30 hours (8.30 Mohammedan time). He will be attended by his personal suite, the Commander-in-Chief and the General Staff. The guard of honour will be composed of the first battalion of the Imperial Life Guards. Full dress uniform (boots for officers), will be worn by all ranks. Civilian gentlemen will wear jackets and orders. Ball ammunition will not be issued to the troops.

(2) The Emperor will be received at the foot of the station steps by the stationmaster who will conduct him to his carriage. The public will not be admitted to the platforms, or to any of the station buildings with the exception of the following, in the following order of precedence. Consular representatives of foreign powers, the Nestorian Metropolitan of Matodi, the Vicar Apostolic, the Mormon elder, officers of H.I.M. forces, directors of the Grand Chemin de Fer d'Azanie, peers of the Azanian Empire, representatives of the Press. No person, irrespective of rank, will be admitted to the platform improperly dressed or under the influence of alcohol.

(3) The public will be permitted to line the route to the station. The police will prevent the discharge of firearms by the public.

(4) The sale of alcoholic liquor is forbidden from midnight until the departure of the Imperial train.

(5) One coach will be available for the use of the unofficial travellers to Debra Dowa. Applications should be made to the stationmaster. No passenger will be admitted to the platform after 14.00.

(6) Any infringement of the following regulations renders the offender liable to a penalty not exceeding ten years' imprisonment, or confiscation of property and loss of rights, or both.

Basil read this at the railway station, where he drove in a horse-cab as soon as he landed. He went to the booking-office and bought a first-class ticket to Debra

Dowa. It cost two hundred rupees.

'Will you please reserve me a seat on this afternoon's train?'

'That is impossible. There is only one carriage. The places have been booked many days.'

'When is the next train?'

'Who can say? Perhaps next week. The engine must come back from Debra Dowa. The others are broken and the mechanic is busy on the tank.'

'I must speak to the stationmaster.'

'I am the stationmaster.'

'Well, listen, it is very urgent that I go to Debra Dowa today.'

'You should have made your arrangements sooner. You must understand, monsieur, that you are no longer in Europe.'

As Basil turned to go, a small man who had been sitting fanning himself on a heap of packing-cases, scrambled down and came across the booking-hall towards him. He was dressed in alpaca and skull cap; he had a cheerful, round, greasy, yellowish face and 'Charlie Chaplin' moustache.

''Ullo Englishmans, you want something.'

'I want to go to Debra Dowa.'

'O.K. I fix it.'

'That's very nice of you.'

'Honour to fix it. You know who I am. Look here.' He handed Basil a card on which was printed: *M. Krikor Youkoumian, Grand Hotel et Bar Amurath Matodi, grand Hotel Café Epicerie, et Bibliothèque Empereur Seyid Debra Dowa. Tous les renseignements*. The name Seyid had been obliterated in purple ink and *Seth* substituted for it.

'You keep that,' said Mr Youkoumian. 'You come to Debra Dowa. You come to me. I fix everything. What's your name, sir?'

'Seal.'

'Well look, Mr Seal. You want to come to Debra Dowa. I got two seats. You pay me two hundred rupees, I put Mme Youkoumian in the mule truck. 'Ow's that, eh?'

'I'm not going to pay anything like that, I'm afraid.'

'Now listen, Mr Seal. I fix it for you. You don't know this country. Stinking place. You miss this train, you stay in Matodi one, two, three, perhaps six weeks. How much you pay then? I like Englishmens. They are my favourite gentlemen. Look, you give me hundred and fifty rupees I put Mme Youkoumian with the mules. You don't understand what that will be like. They are the General's mules. Very savage stinking animals. All day they will stamp at her. No air in the truck. 'Orrible, unhealthy place. Very like she die or is kicked. She is good wife, work 'ard, very loving. If you are not Englishmans I would not put Mme Youkoumian with the mules for less than five hundred. I fix it for you, O.K.?'

'O.K.,' said Basil. 'You know, you seem to me a good chap.'

'Look, 'ow about you give me money now. Then I take you to my café. Dirty little place, not like London. But you see. I got fine brandy. Very fresh, I made him myself Sunday.'

Basil and Mr Youkoumian took their seats in the train at two o'clock and settled down to wait for the arrival of the imperial party. There were six other occupants of the carriage–a Greek who offered them oranges and soon fell asleep, four Indians who discussed their racial grievances in an eager undertone, and an Azanian nobleman with his wife who shared a large pie of spiced mutton, lifting the slices between pieces of newspaper and eating silently and almost continuously throughout the afternoon. Mr Youkoumian's personal luggage was very small, but he had several crates of merchandise for his Debra Dowa establishment: by a distribution of minute tips he had managed to get these into the mail van. Mme Youkoumian squatted disconsolately in a corner of the van clutching a little jar of preserved cherries which her husband had given her to compensate for the change of accommodation; a few feet from her in the darkness came occasional nervous brays and whinnies and a continuous fretful stamping of the straw.

In spite of Seth's proclamation the police were at some difficulty in keeping the platform clear of the public; twenty or thirty of them prosecuted a vigorous defence with long bamboo staves, whacking the woolly heads as they appeared above the corrugated iron fence. Even so, large numbers of unauthorized spectators were established out of reach on the station roof. The Indian who supplied pictures of local colour to an International Press Agency was busily taking snapshots of the notables. These had not observed the Emperor's instructions to the letter. The Nestorian Metropolitan swayed on the arm of his chaplain, unquestionably drunk; the representative of the *Courier d'Azanie* wore an open shirt, a battered topee, crumpled white trousers and canvas shoes; the Levantine shipping agent who acted as vice-consul for Great Britain, the Netherlands, Sweden, Portugal and Latvia had put on a light waterproof over his pyjamas and come to the function straight from bed; the Eurasian bank manager who acted as vice-consul for Soviet Russia, France and Italy was still asleep; the general merchant of inscrutable ancestry who represented the other great powers was at the moment employed on the mainland making final arrangements for the trans-shipment from Alexandria of a long-awaited consignment of hashish. Some Azanian dignitaries in national costume sat in a row on the carpets their slaves had spread for them, placidly scratching the soles of their bare feet and conversing intermittently on questions of sex. The stationmaster's livestock–two goats and a few small turkeys–had been expelled in honour of the occasion from their normal quarters in the ladies' waiting-room, and wandered at will about the platform gobbling at fragments of refuse.

It was more than an hour after the appointed time when the drums and fifes of the Imperial guard announced the Emperor's arrival. They had been held up by the derelict motor-car which had all the morning resisted the efforts of the convicts to move it. The Civil Governor, on whom rested the ultimate responsibility for the mishap, was soundly thrashed and degraded from the rank of Viscount to that of Baronet before the procession could be resumed. It was necessary for the Emperor to leave his car and complete the journey on mule back, his luggage bobbing behind him on the heads of a dozen suddenly conscripted spectators.

He arrived in a bad temper, scowled at the stationmaster and the two vice-consuls, ignored the native nobility and the tipsy Bishop, and bestowed only the most sour of smiles on the press photographers. The guard presented arms, the interlopers on the roof set up an uncertain cheer and he strode across to the carriage prepared for him. General Connolly and the rest of the royal entourage bundled into their places. The stationmaster stood hat in hand waiting for orders.

'His Majesty is now ready to start.'

The stationmaster waved his hat to the engine-driver; the guard once more presented their arms. The drums and fifes struck up the national anthem. The two daughters of the director of the line scattered rose petals round the steps of the carriage. The engine whistled, Seth continued to smile . . . nothing happened. At the end of the verse the band music died away; the soldiers stood irresolutely at the present; the Nestorian Metropolitan continued to beat the time of some interior melody; the goats and turkeys wandered in an out among the embarrassed spectators. Then, when all seemed frozen in silence, the engine gave a great wrench, shaking the train coach by coach from the tender to the mule boxes, and suddenly, to the immense delight of the darkies on the roof, shot off by itself into the country.

'The Emperor has given no orders for a delay.'

'It is a thing I did not foresee,' said the stationmaster. 'Our only engine has gone away alone. I think I shall be disgraced for this affair.'

But Seth made no comment. The other passengers came out on to the platform, smoking and making jokes. He did not look out at them. This gross incident had bruised his most vulnerable feelings. He had been made ridiculous at a moment of dignity and triumph; he had been disappointed in plans he had made eagerly; his own superiority was compromised by contact with such service. Basil passed his window and caught a glimpse of a gloomy but very purposeful black face under a white sun helmet. And at that moment the Emperor was resolving. 'My people are a worthless people. I give orders; there is none to obey me. I am like a great musician without an instrument. A wrecked car broadside across the line of my procession . . . a royal train without an engine . . . goats on the platform . . . I can do nothing with these people. The Metropolitan is drunk. Those old land-owners giggled when the engine broke away; I must find a man of culture, a modern man . . . a representative of Progress and the New Age.' And Basil again passed the window; this time in conversation with General Connolly.

Presently, amid cheers, the runaway engine puffed backwards into the station.

Mechanics ran out to repair the coupling.

At last they started.

Basil began the journey in a cheerful temper. He had got on very well with the general and had accepted an invitation to 'Pop in for a spot any time' when they reached the capital.

The train which brought the Emperor to Debra Dowa also brought the mail. It was a great day at the British Legation. The bags were brought into the dining-room and they all sat round dealing out the letters and parcels, identifying the handwritings and reading over each other's shoulders . . . 'Peter's heard from Flora.' 'Do let me read Anthony's letter after you, Mabel.' 'Here's a page to go on with.' 'Does anyone want Jack's letter from Sybil?' 'Yes, I do, but I haven't finished Mabel's from Agnes yet.' 'What a lot of money William owes. Here's a bill for eighty-two pounds from his tailor.' 'And twelve from his book-shop.' 'Who's this from, Prudence? I don't know the writing . . .'

'Awful lot of official stuff,' complained Sir Samson. 'Can't bother about that now. You might take charge of it, Peter, and have a look through it when you get time.'

'It won't be for a day or two, I'm afraid, sir. We're simply snowed under with work in the chancery over this gymkhana.'

'Yes, yes, my boy, of course, all in good time. Always stick to the job in hand. I dare say there's nothing that needs an answer, and anyway there's no knowing when the next mail will go . . . I say, though, here's something interesting, my word it is. Can't make head or tail of the thing. It says, "*Good luck. Copy this letter out nine times and send it to nine different friends*" . . . What an extraordinary idea.'

'Envoy dear, do be quiet. I want to try the new records.'

'No, but Prudence, do listen. It was started by an American officer in France. If one breaks the chain one gets bad luck, and if one sends it on, good luck. There was one woman lost her husband and another one who made a fortune at roulette–all through doing it and not doing it . . . you know I should never have believed that possible . . .'

Prudence played the new records. It was a solemn thought to the circle that they would hear these eight tunes daily, week after week, without release, until that unpredictable day when another mail should arrive from Europe. In their bungalows, in their compound, in their rare, brief excursions into the outer world, these words would run in their heads . . . Meanwhile they opened their letters and unrolled their newspapers.

'Envoy, what *have* you got there?'

'My dear, another most extraordinary thing. Look here. It's all about the Great Pyramid. You see it's all a "cosmic allegory". It depends on the "Displacement factor". Listen, "*The combined length of the two tribulation passages is precisely 153 Pyramid inches–153 being the number symbolic of the Elect in Our Lord's mystical enactment of the draught of 153 great fishes*". I say, I must go into this. It sounds frightfully interesting! I can't think who sends me these things. Jolly decent of them whoever it is.'

Eleven *Punches*, eleven *Graphics*, fifty-nine copies of *The Times*, two *Vogues* and a mixed collection of *New Yorkers*, *Week End Reviews*, *St James's Gazettes*, *Horses and Hounds*, *Journals of Oriental Studies*, were unrolled and distributed. Then came novels from Mudie's, cigars, soda-water sparklets.

'We ought to have a Christmas tree next time the bag comes in.'

Several Foreign Office dispatches were swept up and incinerated among the litter of envelopes and wrappings.

'Apparently inside the Pyramid there is a chamber of the Triple Veil of Ancient Egyptian Prophecy . . . the east wall of the Antechamber symbolizes Truce in Chaos . . .'

'There is a card announcing a gala night at the Perroquet tomorrow, Envoy. Don't you think we might go?'

'. . . *Four limestone blocks representing the Final Tribulation in 1936* . . .'

'*Envoy*.'

'Eh . . . I'm so sorry. Yes, we'll certainly go. Haven't been out for weeks.'

'By the way,' said William, 'we had a caller in today.'

'Not the Bishop?'

'No, someone new. He wrote his name in the book. Basil Seal.'

'What does *he* want, I wonder? Know anything about him?'

'I seem to have heard his name. I don't quite know where.'

'Ought we to ask him to stay? He didn't bring any letters?'

'No.'

'Thank God. Well, we'll ask him to luncheon one day. I expect he'll find it too hot to come out often.'

'Oh,' said Prudence, 'somebody *new*. That's more than one could have hoped for. Perhaps he'll be able to teach us backgammon.'

That evening M. Ballon received a disquieting report.

'Mr Basil Seal, British politician travelling under private title, has arrived in Debra Dowa, and is staying in M. Youkoumian's house. He is avoiding all open association with the Legation. This evening he called, but presented no credentials. He is obviously expected. He has been seen in conversation with General Connolly, the new Duke of Ukaka.'

'I do not like the look of this Mr Seal. The old fox, Sir Courteney, is playing a deep game–but old Ballon will outwit him yet.'

The Victory Ball at the Perroquet exceeded all its promoter's highest expectations in splendour and gaiety. Every side of Azanian life was liberally represented. The court circle and diplomatic corps, the army and government services, the Church, commerce, the native nobility and the cosmopolitan set.

A gross of assorted novelties–false noses, paper caps, trumpets and dolls–had arrived by the mail from Europe, but demands exceeded the supply. Turbans and tarbooshes bobbed round the dancing floor; there were men in Azanian state robes, white jackets, uniforms, and reach-me-down tail coats; women of all complexions in recently fashionable gowns, immense imitation jewels and lumpy ornaments of solid gold. There was Mme 'Fifi' Fatim Bey, the town courtesan, and her present protector Viscount Boaz, the Minister of the Interior; there was the Nestorian Patriarch and his favourite deacon; there was the Duke and Duchess of Ukaka; there was the manager, Prince Fyodor Krononin, elegant and saturnine, reviewing the late arrivals at the door; there was Basil Seal and Mr Youkoumian, who had been hard at work all that day, making champagne for the party. At a long table near the back were the British Legation in full force.

'Envoy, you *can't* wear a false nose.'

'I don't at all see why not. I think it's very amusing.'

'I don't think that you ought really to be here at all.'

'Why? M. Ballon is.'

'Yes, but *he* doesn't look as if he were enjoying himself.'

'I say, shall I send him one of those chain letters?'

'Yes, I don't see why you shouldn't do that.'

'It will puzzle him terribly.'

'Envoy, who's that young man? I'm sure he's English.'

Basil had gone across to Connolly's table.

'Hullo, old boy. Take a pew. This is Black Bitch.'

'How do you do.' The little Negress put down her trumpet, bowed with grave dignity and held out her hand. 'Not Black Bitch any more. Duchess of Ukaka now.'

'My word, hasn't she got an ugly mug?' said the Duke. 'But she's a good little thing.'

Black Bitch flashed a great, white grin of pleasure at the compliment. It was a glorious night for her; it would have been rapture enough to have her man back from the wars; but to be made a Duchess and taken to supper among all the white ladies . . . all in the same day . . .

'You see,' said M. Ballon to his first secretary. '*That is* the man, over there with Connolly. You are having him watched?'

'Ceaselessly.'

'You have instructed the waiter to attend carefully to the conversation at the English table?'

'He reported to me just now in the cloakroom. It is impossible to understand. Sir Samson speaks all the time of the dimensions of the Great Pyramid.'

'A trap, doubtless.'

The Emperor had signified his intention of making an appearance some time during the evening. At the end of the ballroom a box had been improvised for him with bunting, pots of palm, and gilt cardboard. Soon after midnight he came. At a sign from Prince Fyodor the band stopped in the middle of the tune and struck up the national anthem. The dancing couples scuttled to the side of the ballroom; the guests at supper rose awkwardly to their feet, pushing their tables forward with a rattle of knives and glass; there was a furtive self-conscious straightening of ties and removing of paper caps. Sir Samson Courteney alone absent-mindedly retained his false nose. The royal entourage in frogged uniforms advanced down the polished floor; in their centre, half a pace ahead, looking neither to right nor left, strode the Emperor in evening dress, white kid gloves, heavily starched linen, neat pearl studs and jet black face.

'Got up just as though he were going to sing Spirituals at a party,' said Lady Courteney.

Prince Fyodor glided in front and ushered him to his table. He sat down alone. The suite ranged themselves behind his chair. He gave a slight nod to Prince Fyodor. The band resumed the dance music. The Emperor watched impassively as the company began to settle down to a state of enjoyment.

Presently, by means of an agency, he invited the wife of the American minister to dance with him. The other couples fell back. With gravity and grace he led Mrs Schonbaum into the centre, danced with her twice round the room, led her back to her table, bowed and returned to his box.

'Why, he dances beautifully,' reported Mrs Schonbaum. 'I often wonder what they would say back home to see me dancing with a man of colour.'

'I do pray he comes and dances with Mum,' said Prudence. 'Do you think it's any use me trying to vamp him, or does he only go for wives?'

The evening went on.

The *maître d'hôtel* approached Prince Fyodor in some distress.

'Highness, they are complaining about the champagne.'

'Who are?'

'The French Legation.'

'Tell them we will make a special price for them.'

'. . .Highness, more complaints of the champagne.'

'Who this time?'

'The Duke of Ukaka.'

'Take away the bottle, pour in a tumbler of brandy and bring it back.'

'. . . Highness, is it proper to serve the Minister of the Interior with more wine? He is pouring it in his lady's lap.'

'It is proper. You ask questions like an idiot.'

The English party began to play consequences on the menu cards. They were of the simplest sort: *The amorous Duke of Ukaka met the intoxicated Mme Ballon in the Palace w.c. He said to her 'Floreat Azania'* . . .

'Envoy, if you laugh so much we'll have to stop playing.'

'Upon my soul, though, that's funny.'

'Mum, do you think that young man with the Connollys is the one who called?'

'I dare say. We must ask him to something some time. Perhaps he'll be here for the Christmas luncheon . . . but he seems to have plenty of friends already.'

'Mum, don't be snobbish–particularly now Connolly's a Duke. Do let's have him to everything always . . .'

Basil said, 'I've been trying to catch the Emperor's eye. I don't believe he remembers me.'

'The old boy's on rather a high horse now the war's over. He'll come down a peg when the bills start coming in. They've brought us a better bottle of fizz this time. Like Fyodor's impudence trying to palm off that other stuff on us.'

'I wonder if it would be possible to arrange an audience.'

'Look here, old boy, have you come here to enjoy yourself or have you not? I've been in camp with that Emperor off and on for the last six months and I want to forget him. Give Black Bitch some bubbly and help yourself and for the love of Mike talk smut.'

'Monsieur Jean, something terrible has come to my knowledge,' said the French second secretary.

'Tell me,' said the first secretary.

'I can scarcely bring myself to do so. It affects the honour of the Minister's wife.'

'Incredible. Tell me at once. It is your duty to France.'

'For France then . . . when affected by wine she made an assignation with the Duke of Ukaka. He loves her.'

'Who would have thought it possible? Where?'

'In the toilette at the Palace.'

'But there is no toilette at the Palace.'

'Sir Samson Courteney has written evidence to that effect. The paper has been folded into a narrow strip. No doubt it was conveyed to him by one of his spies. Perhaps in a roll of bread.'

'Extraordinary. We will keep this from the Minister. We will watch, ourselves. It is a secret between us. No good can come of it. Alas, poor Monsieur Ballon. He trusted her. We must prevent this thing.'

'For France.'

'For France and Monsieur Ballon.'

'. . . I have never observed Madame Ballon the worse for drink . . .'

Paper caps were resumed: bonnets of liberty, conical dunce's hats, jockey caps, Napoleonic casques, hats for pierrots and harlequins, postmen, highlanders, old Mothers Hubbard and little Misses Muffet over faces of every complexion, brown as boots, chalk white, dun and the fresh boiled pink of Northern Europe. False noses again: brilliant sheaths of pigmented cardboard attached to noses of every anthropological type, the high arch of the Semite, freckled Nordic snouts, broad black nostrils from swamp villages of the mainland, the pulpy inflamed flesh of the alcoholic, and unlovely syphilitic voids. Ribbons of coloured papers tangled and snapped about the dancers' feet; coloured balls volleyed from table to table. One, erratically thrown by Madame Fifi, bounced close to the royal box; the Minister of the Interior facetiously applauded her aim. Prince Fyodor glanced anxiously about him. His patrons were beginning to enjoy themselves. If only the Emperor would soon leave; an *incident* might occur at any moment.

But Seth sat alone among the palms and garlands, apparently deep in thought, his fingers fidgeted with the stem of his wine glass; sometimes, without raising his head, he half furtively surveyed the room. The equerries behind his chair despaired of permission to dance. If only His Majesty would go home, they could slip back before the fun was all over . . .

'Old boy, your pal the Great Panjandrum is something of a damper on this happy throng. Why can't the silly mutt go off home and leave us to have a jolly up?'

'Can't conceive why young Seth doesn't move. Can't be enjoying himself.'

But the Emperor sat tight. This was the celebration of his Victory. This was the society of Debra Dowa. There was the British Minister happy as a parent at a children's party. There was the Minister of the Interior, behaving hideously. There was the Commander-in-Chief of the Azanian army. And with him was Basil Seal. Seth recognized him in his first grave survey of the restaurant and suddenly, on this triumphal night in his own capital, he was overcome by shyness. It was nearly three years since they last met and Seth recalled the light drizzle of rain in the Oxford quadrangle, a scout carrying a tray of dirty plates, a group of undergraduates in tweeds lounging about among bicycles in the porch. He had been an undergraduate of no account in his College, amiably classed among Bengali babus, Siamese, and grammar school scholars as one of the remote and praiseworthy people who had come a long way to the University. Basil had enjoyed a reputation of peculiar brilliance among his contemporaries. On the rare occasions when evangelically minded undergraduates asked Seth to tea or coffee, his name occurred in the conversation with awed disapproval. He played poker for high stakes. His luncheon parties lasted until dusk, his dinner parties dispersed in riot. Lovely young women visited him from London in high-powered cars. He went away for week-ends without leave and climbed into College over the tiles at night. He had travelled all over Europe, spoke six languages, called dons by their Christian names and discussed their books with them.

Seth had met him at breakfast with the Master of the College. Basil had talked to him about Azanian topography, the Nestorian Church, Sakuyu dialects, the idiosyncrasies of the chief diplomats in Debra Dowa. Two days later he invited him to luncheon. There had been two peers present and the President of the Union, the editor of a new undergraduate paper and a young don. Seth had sat silent and entranced throughout the afternoon. Later, after long consultation with his scout, he had returned the invitation. Basil accepted and at the last moment made his excuses for not coming. There the acquaintance had ended. Three years had intervened, during which Seth had become Emperor, but Basil still stood for him as the personification of all that glittering, intangible Western culture to which he aspired. And there he was, unaccountably, at the Connollys' table. What must he be thinking? If only the Minister for the Interior were more sober . . .

The *maître d'hôtel* again approached Prince Fyodor.

'Highness, there is someone at the door who I do not think should be admitted.'

'I will see him.'

But as he turned to the door, the newcomer appeared. He was a towering Negro in full gala dress: on his head a lion's-mane busby; on his shoulders a shapeless fur mantle; a red satin skirt; brass bangles and a necklace of lion's teeth; a long, ornamental sword hung at his side; two bandoliers of brass cartridges circled his great girth; he had small blood-shot eyes and a tousle of black wool over his cheeks and chin. Behind him stood six unsteady slaves carrying antiquated rifles.

It was one of the backwoods peers, the Earl of Ngumo, feudal overlord of some five hundred square miles of impenetrable highland territory. He had occupied himself throughout the civil war in an attempt to mobilize his tribesmen. The battle of Ukaka occurring before the levy was complete, saved him the embarrassment of declaring himself for either combatant. He had therefore left his men in the hills and marched down with a few hundred personal attendants to pay his respects to the victorious side. His celebrations had lasted for some days already and had left some mark upon even his rugged constitution.

Prince Fyodor hurried forward. 'The tables are all engaged. I regret very much that there is no room. We are full up.'

The Earl blinked dully and said, 'I will have a table, some gin and some women and some raw camel's meat for my men outside.'

'But there is no table free.'

'Do not be put out. That is a simple matter. I have some soldiers with me who will quickly find room.'

The band had stopped playing and a hush fell on the crowded restaurant; scared faces under the paper hats and false noses.

'Under the table, Black Bitch,' said Connolly. 'There's going to be a rough house.'

Mr Youkoumian's plump back disappeared through the service door.

'*Now* what's happening?' said the British Minister. 'Someone's up to something, I'll be bound.'

But at that moment the Earl's bovine gaze, moving up the rows of scared faces to its natural focus among the palms and bunting, reached the Emperor. His hand fell to the jewelled hilt of his sword–and twenty hands in various parts of the room felt for pistols and bottle necks–a yard of tarnished damascene flashed into the light and with a roar of homage he sank to his knees in the centre of the polished floor.

Seth rose and folded his hands in the traditional gesture of welcome.

'Peace be upon your house, Earl.'

The vassal rose and Prince Fyodor's perplexities were solved by the departure of the royal party.

'I will have that table,' said the Earl, pointing to the vacated box.

And soon, quite unconscious of the alarm he had caused, with a bottle of M. Youkoumian's gin before him, and a vast black cheroot between his teeth, the magnate was pacifically winking at the ladies as they danced past him.

Outside the royal chauffeur was asleep and only with difficulty could be awakened. The sky was ablaze with stars; dust hung in the cool air, fragrant as crushed herbs; from the Ngumo camp, out of sight below the eucalyptus trees, came the thin smoke of burning dung and the pulse and throb of the hand drummers. Seth drove back alone to the black litter of palace buildings.

'Insupportable barbarians,' he thought. 'I am sure that the English lords do not behave in that way before their King. Even my loyalest officers are ruffians and buffoons. If I had *one* man by me whom I could trust . . . a man of progress and culture . . .'

Six weeks passed. The victorious army slowly demobilized and dispersed over the hills in a hundred ragged companies; livestock and women in front, warriors behind laden with alarm clocks and nondescript hardware looted in the bazaars; soldiers of progress and the new age homeward bound to the villages.

The bustle subsided and the streets of Matodi resumed their accustomed calm: copra, cloves, mangoes and khat; azan and angelus; old women with obdurate donkeys; trays of pastry black with flies; shrill voices in the mission school reciting the catechism; lepers and pedlars, and Arab gentlemen with shabby gamps decently parading the water-front at the close of day. In the derelict van outside the railway station, a patient black family repaired the ravages of invasion with a careful architecture of mud, twigs, rag and flattened petrol tins.

Two mail ships outward bound from Marseilles, three on the home journey from Madagascar and Indo-China paused for their normal six hours in the little bay. Four times the train puffed up from Matodi and Debra Dowa; palm belt, lava fields, bush and upland; thin cattle scattered over the sparse fields; shallow furrows in the brittle earth; white-gowned Azanian ploughboys scratching up furrows with wooden ploughs; conical grass roofs in stockades of euphorbia and cactus; columns of smoke from the tukal fires, pencil-drawn against the clear sky.

Vernacular hymns in the tin-roofed missions, ancient liturgy in the murky Nestorian sanctuaries; tonsure and turban, hand drums and innumerable jingling bells of debased silver. And beyond the hills on the low Wanda coast where no liners called and the jungle stretched unbroken to the sea, other more ancient rites and another knowledge furtively encompassed; green, sunless paths; forbidden ways unguarded save for a wisp of grass plaited between two stumps, ways of death and initiation, the forbidden places of juju and the masked dancers; the drums of the Wanda throbbing in sunless, forbidden places.

Fanfare and sennet; tattoo of kettle drums; tricolour bunting strung from window to window across the Boulevard Amurath, from Levantine café to Hindu drugstore; Seth in his Citroën drove to lay the foundation stone of the Imperial Institutes of Hygiene; brass band of the Imperial army raised the dust of the main street. Floreat Azania.

5

On the south side of the Palace Compound, between the kitchen and the stockade, lay a large irregular space where the oxen were slaughtered for the public banquets. A minor gallows stood there which was used for such trivial, domestic executions as now and then became necessary within the royal household. The place was deserted now except for the small cluster of puzzled blacks who were usually congregated round the headquarters of the One Year Plan and a single dog who gnawed her hindquarters in the patch of shadow cast by two corpses, which rotated slowly face to face, half circle East, half circle West, ten foot high in the limpid morning sunlight.

The Ministry of Modernization occupied what had formerly been the old Empress's oratory; a circular building of concrete and corrugated iron, its outer wall enriched with posters from all parts of Europe and the United States advertising machinery, fashion and foreign travel. The display was rarely without attendance and today the customary loafers were reinforced by five or six gentlemen in the blue cotton cloaks which the official class of Debra Dowa assumed in times of bereavement. These were mourners for the two criminals–peculators and perjurers both–who had come to give a dutiful tug at their relatives' heels in case life might not yet be extinct, and had stayed to gape, entranced by the manifestations of Progress and the New Age.

On the door was a board painted in Arabic, Sakuyu and French with the inscription:

MINISTRY OF MODERNIZATION
HIGH COMMISSIONER & COMPTROLLER GENERAL:
MR BASIL SEAL
FINANCIAL SECRETARY: MR KRIKOR YOUKOUMIAN

A vague smell of incense and candle-grease still possessed the interior; in all other ways it had been completely transformed. Two partitions divided it into unequal portions. The largest was Basil's office, which contained nothing except some chairs, a table littered with maps and memoranda, and a telephone. Next door Mr Youkoumian had induced a more homely note: his work was economically confined to two or three penny exercise-books filled with figures and indecipherable jottings, but his personality extended itself and pervaded the room, finding concrete expression in the seedy red plush sofa that he had scavenged from one of the state apartments, the scraps of clothing hitched negligently about the furniture, the Parisian photographs pinned to the walls, the vestiges of food on enamelled tin plates, the scent spray, cigarette ends, spittoon and the little spirit-stove over which perpetually simmered a brass pan of coffee. It was his idiosyncrasy to prefer working in stockinged feet, so that when he was at his post a pair of patent leather, elastic-sided boots proclaimed his presence from the window-ledge.

In the vestibule sat a row of native runners with whose services the modernizing party were as yet unable to dispense.

At nine in the morning both Basil and Mr Youkoumian were at their desks. Instituted a month previously by royal proclamation, the Ministry of Modernization was already a going concern. Just how far it was going, indeed, was appreciated by very few outside its circular placarded walls. Its function as defined in Seth's decree was '*to promote the adoption of modern organization and habits of life throughout the Azanian Empire*' which, liberally interpreted, comprised the right of interference in most of the public and private affairs of the nation. As Basil glanced through the correspondence that awaited him and the rough agenda for the day, he felt ready to admit that anyone but himself and Mr Youkoumian would have bitten off more than he could chew. Reports from eight provincial viceroys on a questionnaire concerning the economic resources and population of their territory–documents full of ponderous expressions of politeness and the minimum of trustworthy information; detailed recommendations from the railway authorities at Matodi; applications for concessions from European prospectors; inquiries from tourist bureaux about the possibilities of big-game hunting, surf bathing and mountaineering; applications for public appointments; protests from missions and legations; estimates for building; details of court etiquette and precedence–everything seemed to find its way to Basil's table. The other ministers of the crown had not yet begun to feel uneasy about their own positions. They regarded Basil's arrival as a direct intervention of heaven on their behalf. Here was an Englishman who was willing to leave them their titles and emoluments and take all the work off their hands. Each was issued with the rubber stamp REFER TO BUREAU OF MODERNIZATION, and in a very few days the Minister of the Interior, the Lord Chamberlain, the Justiciar, the City Governor, and even Seth himself, acquired the habit of relegating all decisions to Basil with one firm stab of indelible ink. Two officials alone, the Nestorian patriarch and the Commander-in-Chief of the army, failed to avail themselves of the convenient new institution, but continued to muddle through the routine of their departments in the same capricious, dilatory but independent manner as before the establishment of the new régime.

Basil had been up very late the night before working with the Emperor on a codification of the criminal law, but the volume of business before him left him undismayed.

'Youkoumian.'

''Ullo. Mr Seal?'

The financial secretary padded in from the next room.

'Connolly won't have boots.'

'Won't 'ave boots? But, Mr Seal, he got to 'ave boots. I bought them from Cape Town. They come next ship. I bought them, you understand, as a personal enterprise, out of my own pocket. What in 'ell can I do with a thousand pair of boots if Connolly won't take them?'

'You ought to have waited.'

'Waited? And then when the order is out and everyone knows Guards to 'ave boots, what'll 'appen then? Some pig wanting to make money will go to the Emperor and say I get you boots damned cheaper than Youkoumian. Where am I then? They might as well go barefoot all same as they do now like the dirty niggers they are. No, Mr Seal, that is not business. I fix it so that one morning the Army Order says Guards must have boots. Everyone say, but where are boots? No one got enough boots in this stinking hole. Someone say, I get you boots in three weeks, month, five weeks, so long. I come up and say, *I* got boots, How many pairs you want? Thousand? O.K. I fix it. That is business. What does the General say?'

Basil handed him the letter. It was emphatic and almost ungenerously terse, coming as it did in answer to a carefully drafted recommendation beginning, '*The Minister of Modernization presents his compliments to the Commander-in-Chief of the Imperial Army and in pursuance of the powers granted him by royal decree begs to advise . . .*'

It consisted of a single scrap of lined paper torn from a note-book across which Connolly had scrawled in pencil: *The Minister of Damn All can go to blazes. My men couldn't move a yard in boots. Try and sell Seth top hats next time. Ukaka C. in C.*

'Well,' said Mr Youkoumian doubtfully, 'I *could* get top 'ats.'

'That is one of Connolly's jokes, I'm afraid.'

'Jokes, is it? And 'ere am I with a thousand pair black boots on my 'ands. Ha. Ha. Like 'ell it's a joke. There isn't a thousand people in the whole country that wears boots. Besides these aren't the kind of boots people buys for themselves. Government stuff. Damn rotten. See what I mean?'

'Don't you worry,' Basil said. 'We'll find a use for them. We might have them served out to the clergy.' He took back the General's note, glanced through it frowning and clipped it into the file of correspondence; when he raised his head his eyes were clouded in an expression characteristic to him, insolent, sulky and curiously childish. 'But as a matter of fact,' he added, 'I shouldn't mind a show-down with Connolly. It's nearly time for one.'

'They are saying that the General is in love with Madame Ballon.'

'I don't believe it.'

'I am convinced,' said Mr Youkoumian. 'It was told me on very 'igh authority by the barber who visits the French Legation. Everyone in the town is speaking of it. Even Madame Youkoumian has heard. I tell you 'ow it is,' he added complacently. 'Madame Ballon drinks. That is 'ow Connolly first 'ad 'er.'

Quarter of an hour later both Basil and Mr Youkoumian were engaged in what seemed more important business.

A morning's routine at the Ministry of Modernization.

'Now, look, Mister, I tell you exactly how we are fixed. We have His Majesty's interests to safeguard. See what I mean? You think there is tin in the

Ngumo mountains in workable quantities. So do we. So do other companies. They want concession too. Only today two gentlemen come to ask me to fix it for them. What do I do? I say, we can only give concession to company we have confidence in. Look. How about if on your board of directors you had a man of financial status in the country; someone who His Majesty trusts . . . see what I mean? . . . someone with a fair little block of share allocated to him. He would protect His Majesty's interests and interests of company too . . . see?'

'That's all very well, Mr Youkoumian, but it isn't so easy to find anyone like that. I can't think of anyone at the moment.'

'No, can't you? Can't you think?'

'Unless, of course, you yourself? But I can hardly suggest that. You are far too busy.'

'Mister, I have learned how to be busy and still have time for things that please me . . .'

Next door: Basil and the American commercial attaché: 'The situation is this, Walker. I'm–the Emperor is spending a quarter of a million sterling on road construction this year. It can't come out of the ordinary revenue. I'm floating a loan to raise the money. You're acting over here for Cosmopolitan Oil Trust and for Stetson cars. Every mile of road we make is worth five hundred cars a year and God knows how many gallons of oil. If your companies like to take up the loan I'm prepared to give them a ten-years' monopoly . . .'

Later, the editor of the *Courier d'Azanie*.

M. Bertrand did not look a man of any importance–nor, in fact, was he. The *Courier* consisted of a single sheet, folded quarto, which was issued weekly to rather less than a thousand subscribers in Debra Dowa and Matodi. It retailed in French the chief local events of the week–the diplomatic entertainments, official appointments, court circular, the programmes of the cinemas and such few items of foreign news as came through on the wireless. It occupied one day a week of M. Bertrand's time, the remainder of which was employed in printing menus, invitation cards, funeral and wedding announcements, in acting as local correspondent for a European news-agency and in selling stationery over the counter of his little office. It was in the hope of a fat order for crested note-paper that he presented himself in answer to Basil's invitation at the offices of the new Ministry.

'Good morning, Monsieur Bertrand. It's good of you to come. We may as well get to business at once. I want to buy your paper.'

'Why, certainly, Monsieur Seal. I have a very nice cream-laid line suitable for office use or a slightly more expensive quality azure-tinted with a linen surface. I suppose you would want the name of the Ministry embossed at the head?'

'I don't think you understand me. I mean the *Courier d'Azanie*.'

M. Bertrand's face showed disappointment and some vexation. It was really unpardonably high-handed of this young man to demand a personal call from the proprietor and editor-in-chief whenever he bought a copy of his journal.

'I will tell my clerk. You wish to subscribe regularly?'

'No, no, you don't understand. I wish to become the proprietor–to own the entire concern. What is your price?'

Slowly the idea took root, budded and blossomed; then M. Bertrand said:

'Oh no, that would be quite impossible. I don't want to sell.'

'Come, come. It can't be worth much to you and I am willing to pay a generous price.'

'It is not that, sir; it is a question of prestige, you understand,' he spoke very earnestly. 'You see, as the proprietor and editor of the *Courier* I am *someone*. Twice a year Madame Bertrand and I dine at the French Legation; once we go to the garden party, we go to the Court and the polo club. That is something. But if I become Bertrand, job-printer, who will regard me then? Madame Bertrand would not forgive it.'

'I see,' said Basil. To be someone in Debra Dowa . . . it seemed a modest ambition; it would be a shame to deprive M. Bertrand. 'I see. Well, suppose that you retained the position of editor and were nominally proprietor. That would fulfil my purpose. You see I am anxious to enlarge the scope of your paper. I wish it to publish leading articles explaining the political changes. Listen . . .' and for a quarter of an hour Basil outlined his intentions for the *Courier*'s development . . . three sheets, advertisements of European firms and government services to meet increased cost of production; enlarged circulation; features in Sakuyu and Arabic; intelligent support of government policy . . . At the end of the interview M. Bertrand left, slightly bewildered, carrying with him a fair-sized cheque and the notes for a leading article forecasting possible changes in the penal code . . . convict settlements to replace local prisons. . . . What extraordinary subjects to mention in the *Courier*!

At eleven the Anglican Bishop came to protest against the introduction of State Lotteries.

At a quarter past William came from Sir Samson Courteney to discuss the possibility of making a road out to the Legation. William and Basil did not like each other.

At half-past the Lord Chamberlain came to consult about cookery. A banquet was due to some Wanda notables next week. Seth had forbidden raw beef. What was he to give them? 'Raw beef,' said Basil. 'Call it steak tartare.'

'That is in accordance with modern thought?'

'Perfectly.'

At noon Basil went to see the Emperor.

The heat, rarely intolerable in the hills, was at this time of day penetrating and devitalizing. The palace roofs glared and shimmered. A hot breeze lifted the dust and powdered the bodies of the dangling courtiers and carried across the yard a few waste shreds of paper, baked crisp and brittle as dead leaves. Basil sauntered with half-shut eyes to the main entrance.

Soldiers stood up and saluted clumsily; the captain of the guard trotted after him and plucked at his sleeve.

'Good morning, captain.'

'Good morning, Excellency. You are on your way to the Emperor?'

'As usual.'

'There is a small matter. If I could interest your excellency . . . It is about the two gentlemen who were hanged. One was my cousin.'

'Yes?'

'His post has not yet been filled. It has always been held by my family. My uncle has made a petition to His Majesty . . .'

'Yes, yes. I will speak on his behalf.'

'But that is exactly what you must not do. My uncle is a wicked man, Excellency. It was he who poisoned my father. I am sure of it. He wanted my mother. It would be most unjust for him to have the post. There is my little brother–a man of supreme ability and devotion . . .'

'Very well, captain, I'll do what I can.'

'The angels preserve your excellency.'

The Emperor's study was strewn with European papers and catalogues; his immediate concern was a large plan of Debra Dowa on which he was working with ruler and pencil.

'Come in, Seal, I'm just rebuilding the city. The Anglican Cathedral will have to go, I think, and all the South quarter. Look, here is Seth Square with the avenues radiating from it. I'm calling this, Boulevard Basil Seal.'

'Good of you, Seth.'

'And this, Avenue Connolly.'

'Ah, I wanted to talk about him.' Basil sat down and approached his subject discreetly. 'I wouldn't say anything against him. I know you like him and in his rough-and-tumble way he's a decent soldier. But d'you ever feel that he's *not quite modern?*'

'He never made full use of our tank.'

'Exactly. He's opposed to progress throughout. He wants to keep the army under *his* control. Now there's the question of boots. I don't think we told you, but the matter came before the Ministry and we sent in a recommendation that the Guards should be issued with boots. It would increase their efficiency a hundred per cent. Half the sick list is due to hook-worm which as you know comes from going about barefooted. Besides, you know, there's the question of prestige. There's not a single Guards regiment in Europe without boots. You've seen them for yourself at Buckingham Palace. You'll never get the full respect of the powers until you give your troops boots.'

'Yes, yes, by all means. They shall have boots at once.'

'I was sure you'd see it that way. But the trouble is that Connolly's standing out against it. Now we've no power at present to issue an army ordinance. That has to come through him–or through you as commander-in-chief of the army.'

'I'll make out an order today. Of course they must have boots. I'll hang any man I see barefooted.'

'Fine. I thought you'd stand by us, Seth. You know,' he added reflectively, 'we've got a much easier job now than we should have had fifty years ago. If we'd had to modernize a country then it would have meant constitutional monarchy, bi-cameral legislature, proportional representation, women's suffrage, independent judicature, freedom of the Press, referendums . . .'

'What is all that?' asked the Emperor.

'Just a few ideas that have ceased to be modern.'

Then they settled down to the business of the day.

'The British Legation are complaining again about their road.'

'That is an old question. I am tired of it. Besides, you will see from the plan I have orientated all the roads leading out of the capital; they go by the points of the compass. I cannot upset my arrangements.'

'The Minister feels very strongly about it.'

"'Well, another time . . . no, I tell you what I will do. Look, we will name this street after him. Then he will be satisfied.'

The Emperor took up his indiarubber and erased Connolly's name from the new metropolis. *Avenue Sir Samson Courteney* he wrote in its place.

'I wish we had a tube railway,' he said. 'Do you think it would pay?'

'No.'

'So I feared. But one day we will have one. Listen. You can tell Sir Samson that. When there is a tube railway he shall have a private station in the Legation compound. Now listen; I have had a letter from the Society for the Prevention of Cruelty to Animals. They want to send out a Commission to investigate Wanda methods of hunting. Is it cruel to spear lions, do you think?'

'No.'

'No. However, here is the letter. From Dame Mildred Porch. Do you know her?'

'I've heard of her. An intolerable old gas-bag.'

'What is gas-bag? An orator?'

'Yes, in a way.'

'Well, she is returning from South Africa and wishes to spend a week here. I will say yes?'

'I shouldn't.'

'I will say yes . . . And another thing. I have been reading in my papers about something very modern called Birth Control. What is it?'

Basil explained.

'I must have a lot of that. You will see to it, Perhaps it is not a matter for an ordinance, what do you think? We must popularize it by propaganda–educate the people in sterility. We might have a little pageant in its honour . . .'

Sir Samson accepted the rebuff to his plans with characteristic calm. 'Well, well, I don't suppose young Seth will keep his job long. There's bound to be another revolution soon. The boy's head over heels in debt, they tell me. I dare say the next government, whoever they are, will be able to afford something. And anyway, you may laugh at me, Prudence, but I think it's uncommonly decent of the young fellow to name that avenue after me. I've always liked him. You never know. Debra Dowa may become a big city one day. I like to think of all the black johnnies in a hundred years' time driving up and down in their motor-cars and going to the shops and saying "Number a hundred Samson Courteney" and wondering who I was. Like, like . . .'

'Like the Avenue Victor Hugo, Envoy.'

'*Exactly, or St James's Square.*'

But the question of the boots was less easily settled.

On the afternoon of the day when the new ordinance was issued, Basil and Mr Youkoumian were in conference. A major difficulty had arisen with regard to the plans for the new guest house at the Palace. The Emperor had been captivated by some photographs he had discovered in a German architectural magazine and had decided to have the new building constructed of steel and vita-glass. Basil had spent half the morning in a vain attempt to persuade the royal mind that this was not a style at all suitable to his tropical climate and he was now at work with his financial secretary on a memorandum of the prohibitive extravagance of the new plans, when the door was pushed noisily open and the Duke of Ukaka strode into the room.

'Clear out, Youkoumian,' he said. 'I want to talk to your boss.'

'O.K., General. I'll 'op off. No offence.'

'Nonsense. Mr Youkoumian is financial secretary of the Ministry. I should like him to be present at our interview.'

'What, me, Mr Seal? I got nothing to say to the General.'

'I wish you to stay.'

'Quick,' said the Duke, making a menacing motion towards him.

'Very sorry, gentlemen,' said Mr Youkoumian and shot through the door into his own office.

First trick to Connolly.

'I notice even that little dago has the sense to take off his boots.'

Second trick to Connolly.

But in the subsequent interview Basil held his own. The General began: 'Sorry to have to sling that fellow out. Can't stand his smell. Now let's talk. What's all this infernal nonsense about boots?'

'His Majesty's ordinance seemed perfectly explicit to me.'

'*His Majesty's trousers*. For the Lord's sake come off the high horse, old boy, and listen to me. I don't give a hoot in hell about your modernization. It's none of my business. You can set every damn coon in the place doing crossword puzzles for all I care. But I'm not going to have any monkeying about with my men. You'll lame the whole army in a day if you try to make 'em wear boots. Now look here, there's no reason why we should scrap over this. I've been in the country long enough to see through Youkoumian's game. Selling junk to government has been the staple industry of Debra Dowa as long as I can remember it. I'd as soon you got the boodle as anyone else. Listen. If I tip the wink to the people on the line I can have the whole consignment of boots carried off by Sakuyu. You'll get compensation, the ordinance will be forgotten and no one will be any the worse off. What do you say? Is it a deal?'

For an appreciable time Basil hesitated in a decision of greater importance than either of them realized. The General sat jauntily on the edge of the table bending his riding-cane over his knee; his expression was one of cordiality and of persuasive good sense. Basil hesitated. Was it some atavistic sense of a caste, an instinct of superiority, that held him aloof? Or was it vexed megalomania because Mr Youkoumian had trotted so obediently from the room in his stockinged feet?

'You should have made your representations before,' he said. 'The tone of your first note made discussion impossible. The boots will be issued to the war department next week.'

'Bloody young fool,' said Connolly and took his leave.

As the door opened Mr Youkoumian hastily stepped back from the keyhole. The General pushed past him and left the Ministry.

'Oh, Mr Seal, why the 'ell do you want a bust-up with 'im for? Look, how about I go after 'im and fix it, eh, Mr Seal?'

'You won't do anything of the sort. We'll carry right on with the plans for the pageant of contraception.'

'Oh dear, oh dear, Mr Seal, there ain't no sense at all in 'aving bust-ups.'

News of the rupture spread like plague through the town. It was first-class gossip. The twenty or so spies permanently maintained by various interests in the Imperial Household carried tidings of the split through the Legations and commercial houses; runners informed the Earl of Ngumo; Black Bitch told her hairdresser; a Eurasion bank clerk told his manager and the bank manager told the Bishop; Mr Youkoumian recounted the whole incident in graphic gesture over the bar of the Empereur Seth; Connolly swore hideously about it at the Perroquet to Prince Fyodor; the Minister of the Interior roared out a fantastically distorted version to the assembled young ladies of the leading *maison de société*. That evening there was no dinner table of any importance in Debra Dowa where the subject was not discussed in detail.

'Pity,' remarked Sir Samson Courteney. 'I suppose this'll mean that young Seal will be coming up here more than ever. Sorry, Prudence, I dare say he's all right, but the truth is I can never find much to say to the chap . . . interested in different things . . . always going on about local politics . . . Damn fool thing to quarrel about, anyway. Why shouldn't he wear boots if he wants to?'

'That wasn't quite the point, Envoy.'

'Well, it was something of the kind, I know.'

'Ha! Ha! said Monsieur Ballon. 'Here is a thing Sir Samson did *not* foresee. Where is his fine web now, eh? Gossamer in the wind. Connolly is our man.'

'Alas, blind, trusting husband, if he only knew,' murmured the first to the second secretary.

'The Seal-Courteney faction and their puppet emperor have lost the allegiance of the army. We must consolidate our party.'

It was in this way it happened that next morning there occurred an event unique in Black Bitch's experience. She was in the yard in front of her house laundering some of the General's socks (for she could not bear another woman to touch her man's clothes), chewing nut and meditatively spitting the dark juice into the soap-suds, when a lancer dismounted before her in the crimson and green uniform of the French Legation.

'Her Grace the Duchess of Ukaka.'

She lifted her dress, so as not to soil it, and wiped her hands on her knickers. 'Me,' she said.

The man saluted, handed her a large envelope, saluted again, mounted and rode away.

The Duchess was left alone with her large envelope; she squatted on her heels and examined it, turning it this way and that, holding it up to her ear and shaking it, her head sagely cocked on one side. Then she rose, padded into the house and across the hall to her bedroom; there, after circumspection, she raised a loose corner of the fibre matting and slipped the letter beneath it.

Two or three times during the next hour she left her wash-tub to see if her treasure was safe. At noon the General returned to luncheon and she handed it over to him, to await his verdict.

'Hullo, Black Bitch, what do you suppose this is? Madame Ballon wants us to dine at the French Legation tomorrow.'

'You go?'

'But it's for both of us, old girl. The invitation is addressed to you. What d'you think of that?'

'Oh, my! Me dine with Madame Ballon! Oh my, that's good!'

The Duchess could not contain her excitement; she threw back her head, rolled her eyes, and emitting deep gurgles of pleasure began spinning about the room like a teetotum.

'Good for the old geeser,' said the Duke, and later when the acceptance was written and dispatched by the hand of the Imperial Guard's most inspiring sergeant-major, and Connolly had answered numerous questions about the proper conduct of knife, fork, glass and gloves, and the Duchess had gone bustling off to Mr Youkoumian's store for ribbon and gold braid and artificial peonies to embellish her party frock, he went back to barracks with unusual warmth at heart towards the French Legation, remarking again, 'Good for the old geeser. He's the first person who's troubled to ask Black Bitch to anything in eight years. And wasn't she pleased as Punch about it too, bless her black heart?'

As the time approached Black Bitch's excitement became almost alarming and her questions on etiquette so searching that the General was obliged to thump her soundly on the head and lock her in a cupboard for some hours before she could be reduced to a condition sufficiently subdued for diplomatic society. The dinner party, however, was a great success. The French Legation were there in full force, the director of the railway with his wife and daughters, and Lord Boaz, the Minister for the Interior. Black Bitch as Duchess of Ukaka took precedence and sat beside M. Ballon, who spoke to her in English in praise of her husband's military skill, influence and discretion. Any small errors in deportment which she may have committed were completely eclipsed by the Minister for the Interior who complained of the food, drank far too much, pinched the ladies on either side of him, pocketed a dozen cigars and a silver pepper mill which happened to take his fancy, and later in the drawing-room insisted on dancing by himself to the gramophone until his slaves appeared to hoist him into his car and carry him back to Mme 'Fifi', of whose charms he had been loudly boasting throughout the evening with a splendour of anatomical detail which was, fortunately, unintelligible to many of the people present.

In the dining-room when the succession of wines finally ended with the few ceremonial spoonfuls of sweet champagne and the men were left alone–the Minister for the Interior being restrained with difficulty from too precipitately following the ladies–M. Ballon signalled for a bottle of eau de vie and, moving round to the General's side, filled his glass and prompted him to some frank criticism of the Emperor and the present régime.

In the drawing-room the French ladies crowded about their new friend, and before the evening was out several of them, including Madame Ballon, had dropped the 'Duchess' and were on terms of calling her 'Black Bitch'. They asked her to come and see their gardens and children, they offered to teach her tennis and piquet, they advised her about an Armenian dressmaker in the town and a Hindu fortune-teller; they were eager to lend her the patterns of their pyjamas; they spoke seriously of pills; best of all they invited her to sit on the committee which was being organized in the French colony to decorate a car for the forthcoming Birth-Control Gala. There was no doubt about it: the Connollys had made the French set.

Ten days later the boots arrived at Debra Dowa; there were some formalities to be observed, but these were rendered simple by the fact that the departments involved were now under the control of the Ministry of Modernization. Mr Youkoumian drew up an application to himself from the Ministry of War for the delivery of the boots; he made out a chit from the War Office to the Ministry of Supplies; passed it on to the Treasury, examined and countersigned it, drew himself a cheque and in the name of the Customs and Excise Department allowed his own claim to rebate of duty on the importation of articles of 'national necessity'. The whole thing took ten minutes. A few hours later a thousand pairs of black boots had been dumped in the square of the Guards barracks, where a crowd of soldiers rapidly collected and studied them throughout the entire afternoon with vivid but nervous interest.

That evening there was a special feast in honour of the boots. Cook-pots steaming over the wood fires; hand drums beating; bare feet shuffling unforgotten tribal rhythms; a thousand darkies crooning and swaying on their haunches, white teeth flashing in the fire-light.

They were still at it when Connolly returned from dinner at the French consulate.

'What in hell are the boys making whoopee for tonight? It's not one of their days, is it?'

'Yes, General, very big day,' said the sentry. 'Boots day.'

The singing reached Basil as he sat at his writing-table at the Ministry, working long after midnight at the penal code.

'What's going on at the barracks?' he asked the servant.

'Boots.'

'They like 'em, eh?'

'They like 'em fine.'

'That's one in the eye for Connolly,' he said, and next day, meeting the General in the Palace yard, he could not forbear to mention it. 'So the boots went down all right with your men after all, Connolly.'

'They went down.'

'No cases of lameness yet, I hope?'

The General leant over in his saddle and smiled pleasantly. 'No cases of lameness,' he replied. 'One or two of bellyache, though. I'm just writing a report on the matter to the Commissioner of Supplies–that's our friend Youkoumian, isn't it? You see, my adjutant made rather a silly mistake. He hadn't had much truck with boots before and the silly fellow thought they were extra rations. My men ate the whole bag of tricks last night.'

Dust in the air; a light wind rattling the leaves in the eucalyptus trees. Prudence sat over the Panorama of Life gazing through the window across the arid Legation croquet lawn; dun grass rubbed bare between the hoops, a few sapless stalks in the beds beyond. She drew little arabesques in the corners of the page and thought about love.

It was the dry season before the rains, when the cattle on the hills strayed miles from their accustomed pastures and herdsmen came to blows over the brackish dregs of the drinking holes; when, preceded by a scutter of children, lions would sometimes appear, parading the streets of the town in search of water; when Lady Courteney remarked that her herbaceous borders were a positive eye-sore.

How out of tune with Nature is the spirit of man! wrote Prudence in her sprawling, schoolroom characters. *When the earth proclaims its fertility, in running brooks, bursting seed, mating of birds and frisking of lambs, then the thoughts of man turn to athletics and horticulture, water-colour painting and amateur theatricals. Now in the arid season when Nature seems all dead under the cold earth, there is nothing to think about except sex.* She bit her pen and read it through, substituting *hot soil* for *cold earth.* 'I am sure I've got something wrong in the first part,' she thought, and called to Lady Courteney who, watering-can in hand, was gloomily surveying a withered rose tree. 'Mum, how soon after the birds mate are the lambs born?'

'Eggs, dear, not lambs,' said her mother and pottered off towards some azalea roots which were desperately in need of water.

'Damn the panorama of life,' said Prudence, and she began drawing a series of highly stylized profiles which by an emphasis of the chin and disordering of the hair had ceased during the last six weeks to be portraits of William and had come to represent Basil Seal. 'To think that I wanted to be in love so much,' she thought, 'that I even practised on William.'

'Luncheon,' said her mother, repassing the window. 'And I shall be late again. Do go in and be bright to your father.'

But when Lady Courteney joined them in the dining-room she found father, daughter and William sitting in moody silence.

'Tinned asparagus,' said Sir Samson. 'And a letter from the Bishop.'

'He's not coming out to dinner again?'

'No, no, it isn't as bad as that. But apparently Seth wants to pull down his Cathedral for some reason. What does he expect *me* to do about it I should like to know? Shocking ugly building, anyhow. I wish, Prudence and William, you'd take the ponies out this afternoon. They haven't had any proper exercise for days.'

'Too hot,' said Prudence.

'Too busy,' said William.

'Oh, well,' said Sir Samson Courteney. And later he remarked to his wife: 'I say, there isn't any trouble between those two, is there? They used to be such pals.'

'I've been meaning to mention it for some time, Sam, only I was so worried about the antirrhinums. I don't think Prudence is at all herself. D'you think it's good for a girl of her age living at this height all the year round? It might be an idea to send her back to England for a few months. Harriet could put her up in Belgrave Place. I'm not sure it wouldn't be a good thing for her to go out in London for a season and meet some people of her own age. What d'you think?'

'I dare say you're right. All that What-d'you-call-it of Life she keeps working away at . . . Only you must write to Harriet. I'm far too busy at the moment. Got to think of something to say to the Bishop.'

But next day Prudence and William went out with the ponies. She had an assignation with Basil.

'Listen, William, you're to go out of the city by the lane behind the Baptist school and the Jewish abattoirs, then past the Parsee death-house and the fever hospital.'

'Not exactly the prettiest ride.'

'Darling, don't be troublesome. You might get seen the other way. Once you're clear of the Arab cemetery you can go where you like. And you're to fetch me at Youkoumian's at five.'

'Jolly afternoon for me leading Mischief all the time.'

'Now, William, you know you manage him perfectly. You're the only person

I'd trust to take him. I can't leave him outside Youkoumian's, can I, because of *discretion*.'

'What you don't seem to see is that it's pretty dim for me, floundering about half the day, I mean, in a dust heap with two ponies while you neck with the chap who's cut me out.'

'*William*, don't be *coarse*. And anyway, "cut you out" nothing. You had me all to yourself for six months and weren't you just bored blue with it?'

'Well, I dare say he'll be bored soon.'

'Cad.'

Basil still lived in the large room over Mr Youkoumian's store. There was a verandah, facing on to a yard littered with scrap iron and general junk, accessible by an outside staircase. Prudence passed through the shop, out and up. The atmosphere of the room was rank with tobacco smoke. Basil, in shirt-sleeves, rose from the deck-chair to greet her. He threw the butt of his Burma cheroot into the tin hip-bath which stood unemptied at the side of the bed; it sizzled and went out and floated throughout the afternoon, slowly unfurling in the soapy water. He bolted the door. It was half dark in the room. Dusty parallels of light struck through the shutters on to the floor-boards and the few shabby mats. Prudence stood isolated, waiting for him, her hat in her hand. At first neither spoke. Presently she said, 'You might have shaved,' and then 'Please help with my boots.'

Below, in the yard, Madame Youkoumian upbraided a goat. Strips of sunlight traversed the floor as an hour passed. In the bath water, the soggy stub of tobacco emanated a brown blot of juice.

Banging on the door.

'Heavens,' said Prudence, 'that can't be William already.'

'Mr Seal, Mr Seal.'

'Well, what is it? I'm resting.'

'Well, you got to stop,' said Mr Youkoumian. 'They're looking for you all over the town. Damn fine rest I've had this afternoon, like 'ell I 'aven't.'

'What is it?'

'Emperor must see you at once. 'E's got a new idea. Very modern and important. Some damn fool nonsense about Swedish drill.'

Basil hurried to the Palace to find his master in a state of high excitement.

'I have been reading a German book. We must draft a decree at once . . . Communal physical exercises. The whole population, every morning, you understand. And we must get instructors from Europe. Cable for them. Quarter of an hour's exercise a morning. And community singing. That is very important. The health of the nation depends on it. I have been thinking it over. Why is there no cholera in Europe? Because of community singing and physical jerks . . . and bubonic plague . . . and leprosy.'

Back in her room Prudence reopened the Panorama of Life and began writing: *a woman in love . . .*

'A woman,' said Mr Youkoumian. 'That's what Seth needs to keep 'im quiet. Always sticking 'is nose in too much everywhere. You listen to me, Mr Seal if we can fix Seth with a woman our modernization will get along damn fine.'

'There's always Fifi.'

'Oh Mr Seal, 'e 'ad 'er when 'e was a little boy. Don't you worry. I'll fix it O.K.'

Royal interruptions of the routine of the Ministry were becoming distressingly frequent in the last few days as the Emperor assimilated the various books that had arrived for him by the last mail. Worst of all, the pageant of birth control was proving altogether more trouble than it was worth; in spite of repeated remonstrances, however, it continued to occupy the mind of the Emperor in precedence of all other interests. He had already renamed the site of the Anglican Cathedral, Place Marie Stopes.

'Heaven knows what will happen if he ever discovers psycho-analysis,' remarked Basil, gloomily foreseeing a Boulevard Kraft-Ebing, and Avenue Oedipus and a pageant of coprophagists.

'He'll discover every damn modern thing,' said Mr Youkoumian, 'if we don't find him a woman damn quick . . . 'ere's another letter from the Vicar Apostolic. If I 'adn't ordered all that stuff from Cairo I'd drop the whole pageant. But you can't use it for nothing else but what it's for–so far as I can see, not like boots what they can eat.'

The opposition to the pageant was firm and widespread. The Conservative Party rallied under the leadership of the Earl of Ngumo. This nobleman, himself one of a family of forty-eight (most of whom he had been obliged to assassinate on his succession to the title), was the father of over sixty sons and uncounted daughters. This progeny was a favourite boast of his; in fact, he maintained a concert party of seven minstrels for no other purpose than to sing at table about this topic when he entertained friends. Now in ripe age, with his triumphs behind him, he found himself like some scarred war veteran surrounded by pacifists, his prestige assailed and his proudest achievements held up to vile detraction. The new proposals struck at the very roots of sport and decency and he expressed the general feeling of the landed gentry when he threatened amid loud grunts of approval to dismember any man on his estates whom he found using the new-fangled and impious appliances.

The smart set, composed (under the leadership of Lord Boaz) of cosmopolitan blacks, courtiers, younger sons and a few of the decayed Arab intelligentsia, though not actively antagonistic, were tepid in their support; they discussed the question languidly in Fifi's salon and, for the most part, adopted a sophisticated attitude maintaining that of course *they* had always known about these things, but why invite trouble by all this publicity; at best it would only make contraception middle-class. In any case this circle was always suspect to the popular mind and their allegiance was unlikely to influence public opinion in the Emperor's favour.

The Churches came out strong on the subject. No one could reasonably accuse the Nestorian Patriarch of fanatical moral inflexibility–indeed there had been incidents in his Beatitude's career when all but grave scandal had been caused to the faithful–but whatever his personal indulgence, his theology had always been unimpeachable. Whenever a firm lead was wanted on a question of opinion, the Patriarch had been willing to forsake his pleasures and pronounce freely and intransigently for the tradition he had inherited. There had been the ugly affair of the Metropolitan of Matodi who had proclaimed himself fourth member of the Trinity; there was the parish priest who was unsound about the Dual Will; there was the ridiculous heresy that sprang up in the province of

Mhomala that the prophet Esaias had wings and lived in a tree; there was the painful case of the human sacrifices at the Bishop of Popo's consecration–on all these and other uncertain topics the Patriarch had given proof of a sturdy orthodoxy.

Now, on the question of Birth Control, his Beatitude left the faithful in no doubt as to where their duty lay. As head of the Established Church he called a conference which was attended by the Chief Rabbi, the Mormon Elder and the chief representatives of all the creeds of the Empire; only the Anglican Bishop excused himself, remarking in a courteous letter of refusal, that his work lay exclusively among the British community who, since they were already fully informed and equipped in the matter, could scarcely be injured in any way by the Emperor's new policy; he wished his Beatitude every success in the gallant stand he was making for the decencies of family life, solicited his prayers and remarked that he was himself too deeply embroiled with the progressive party, who were threatening the demolition of his Cathedral, to confuse the issue with any other cause, however laudable it might be in itself.

As a result of the conference, the Patriarch composed an encyclical in rich, oratorical style and dispatched copies of it by runners to all parts of the island. Had the influence of the Established Church on the popular mind been more weighty, the gala should have been doomed, but, as has already been mentioned, the Christianizing of the country was still so far incomplete that the greater part of the Empire retained with a minimum of disguise their older and grosser beliefs, and it was, in fact, from the least expected quarter, the tribesmen and villagers, that the real support of Seth's policy suddenly appeared.

This development was due directly and solely to the power of advertisement. In the dark days when the prejudice of his people compassed him on every side and even Basil spoke unsympathetically of the wisdom of postponing the gala, the Emperor found among the books that were mailed to him monthly from Europe a collection of highly inspiring Soviet posters. At first the difficulties of imitation appeared to be insuperable. The *Courier* office had no machinery for reproducing pictures. Seth was contemplating the wild expedient of employing slave labour to copy his design when Mr Youkoumian discovered that some years ago an enterprising philanthropist had by bequest introduced lithography into the curriculum of the American Baptist school. The apparatus survived the failure of the attempt. Mr Youkoumian purchased it from the pastor and resold it at a fine profit to the Department of Fine Arts in the Ministry of Modernization. An artist was next found in the Armenian colony who, on Mr Youkoumian's introduction, was willing to elaborate Seth's sketches. Finally there resulted a large, highly coloured poster well calculated to convey to the illiterate the benefits of birth control. It was in many ways the highest triumph of the new Ministry and Mr Youkoumian was the hero. Copies were placarded all over Debra Dowa; they were sent down the line to every station latrine, capital and coast; they were sent into the interior to vice-regal lodges and headmen's huts, hung up at prisons, barracks, gallows and juju trees, and wherever the poster was hung there assembled a cluster of inquisitive, entranced Azanians.

It portrayed two contrasted scenes. On one side a native hut of hideous squalor, overrun with children of every age, suffering from every physical incapacity–crippled, deformed, blind, spotted and insane; the father prematurely aged with paternity squatted by an empty cook-pot; through the door could be seen his wife, withered and bowed with child-bearing, desperately hoeing at their inadequate crop. On the other side a bright parlour furnished with chairs and table; the mother, young and beautiful, sat at her ease eating a huge slice of raw meat; her husband smoked a long Arab hubble-bubble (still a caste mark of leisure throughout the land), while a single healthy child sat between them reading a newspaper. Inset between the two pictures was a detailed drawing of some up-to-date contraceptive apparatus and the words in Sakuyu: WHICH HOME DO YOU CHOOSE?

Interest in the pictures was unbounded; all over the island woolly heads were nodding, black hands pointing, tongues clicking against filed teeth in unsyntactical dialects. Nowhere was there any doubt about the meaning of the beautiful new pictures.

See: on right hand: there is rich man: smoke pipe like big chief: but his wife she no good; sit eating meat: and rich man no good: he only one son.

See: on left hand: poor man: not much to eat: but his wife she very good, work hard in field: man he good too: eleven children: one very mad, very holy. And in the middle: Emperor's juju. Make you like that good man with eleven children.

And as a result, despite admonitions from squire and vicar, the peasantry began pouring into town for the gala, eagerly awaiting initiation to the fine new magic of virility and fecundity.

Once more, wrote Basil Seal, in a leading article in the *Courier*, *the people of the Empire have overridden the opposition of a prejudiced and interested minority, and with no uncertain voice have followed the Emperor's lead in the cause of Progress and the New Age.*

So brisk was the demand for the Emperor's juju that some time before the day of the carnival Mr Youkoumian was frantically cabling to Cairo for fresh supplies.

Meanwhile the Nestorian Patriarch became a very frequent guest at the French Legation.

'We have the army, we have the Church,' said M. Ballon. 'All we need now is a new candidate for the throne.'

'If you ask me,' said Basil, one morning soon after the distribution of the poster, 'loyalty to the throne is one of the hardest parts of our job.'

'Oh, gosh, Mr Seal, don't you ever say a thing like that. I seen gentlemen poisoned dead for less. What's 'e done now?'

'Only this.' He handed Mr Youkoumian a chit which had just arrived from the Palace: *For your information and necessary action, I have decided to abolish the following:*

Death penalty.

Marriage.

The Sakuyu language and all native dialects.

Infant mortality.

Totemism.

Inhuman butchery.

Mortgages.

Emigration.

Please see to this. Also organize system of reservoirs for city's water supply and draft syllabus for competitive examination for public services. Suggest compulsory Esperanto. Seth.

''E's been reading books again, Mr Seal, that's what it is. You won't get no peace from 'im not till you fix 'im with a woman. Why can't 'e drink or something?'

In fact, the Ministry's triumph in the matter of Birth Control was having highly embarrassing consequences. If before, Basil and Mr Youkoumian had cause to lament their master's tenacity and singleness of purpose, they were now harassed from the opposite extreme of temperament. It was as though Seth's imagination like a volcanic lake had in the moment of success become suddenly swollen by the irruption of unsuspected subterranean streams until it darkened and seethed and overflowed its margins in a thousand turbulent cascades. The earnest and rather puzzled young man became suddenly capricious and volatile; ideas bubbled up within him, bearing to the surface a confused sediment of phrase and theory, scraps of learning half understood and fantastically translated.

'It's going to be awkward for us if the Emperor goes off his rocker.'

'Oh my, Mr Seal, you do say the most damned dangerous things.'

That afternoon Basil called at the Palace to discuss the new proposals, only to find that since his luncheon the Emperor's interests had veered suddenly towards archaeology.

'Yes, yes, the abolitions. I sent you a list this morning, I think. It is a mere matter of routine. I leave the details to the Ministry. Only you must be quick, please ... it is not that which I want to discuss with you now. It is our Museum.'

'Museum?'

'Yes, of course we must have a Museum. I have made a few notes to guide you. The only serious difficulty is accommodation. You see, it must be inaugurated before the arrival of the Cruelty to Animals Commission at the beginning of next month. There is hardly time to build a house for it. The best thing will to be confiscate one of the town palaces. Ngumo's or Boaz's would do after some slight adjustments. But that is a matter for the Ministry to decide. On the ground floor will be the natural history section. You will collect examples of all the flora and fauna of the Empire–lions, butterflies, birds' eggs, specimens of woods, everything. That should easily fill the ground floor. I have been reading,' he added earnestly, 'about ventilation. That is very important. The air in the cases must be continually renewed–a cubic metre an hour is about the right draught–otherwise the specimens suffer. You will make a careful note of that. Then on the first floor will be the anthropological and historical section–examples of native craft, Portuguese and Arab work, a small library. Then in the Central Hall, the relics of the Royal House. I have some of the medals of Amurath upstairs under one of the beds in a box–photographs of myself, some of my uniforms, the cap and gown I wore at Oxford, the model of the Eiffel Tower which I brought back from Paris. I will lend some pages of manuscript in my own hand to be exhibited. It will be most interesting.'

For some days Mr Youkoumian busied himself with the collection of specimens. Word went round that there was a market for objects of interest at the Ministry of Modernization and the work of the office was completely paralysed by the hawkers of all races who assembled in and around it, peddling brass pots and necklaces of carved nut, snakes in baskets and monkeys in cages, cloth of beaten bark and Japanese cotton, sacramental vessels pouched by Nestorian deacons, iron-wood clubs, homely household deities, tanned human scalps, cauls and navel strings and wonder-working fragments of meteorite, amulets to ward off the evil eye from camels, M. Ballon's masonic apron purloined by the Legation butler, and a vast, monolithic phallus borne by three oxen from a shrine in the interior. Mr Youkoumian bargained briskly and bought almost everything he was offered, reselling them later to the Ministry of Fine Arts of which Basil had created him the director. But when, at a subsequent interview, Basil mentioned their progress to the Emperor he merely nodded a listless approval, and even while he unscrewed the cap of his fountain pen to sign the order evicting the Earl of Ngumo from his town house, began to speak of the wonders of astronomy.

'Do you realize the magnitude of the fixed stars? They are immense. I have read a book which says that the mind boggles at their distances. I did not know that word, boggles. I am immediately founding an Institute for Astronomical Research. I must have Professors. Cable for them to Europe. Get me tiptop professors, the best procurable.'

But next day he was absorbed in ectogenesis. 'I have read here,' he said, tapping a volume of speculative biology, 'that there is to be no more birth. The ovum is fertilized in the laboratory and then the foetus is matured in bottles. It is a splendid idea. Get me some of those bottles . . . and no boggling.'

Even while discussing the topic that immediately interested him, he would often break off in the middle of a sentence, with an irrelevant question. 'How much are autogyros?' or 'Tell me exactly, please, what is Surrealism?' or 'Are you convinced of Dreyfus's innocence?' and then, without pausing for the reply, would resume his adumbrations of the New Age.

The days passed rapturously for Mr Youkoumian who had found, in the stocking of the Museum, work for which early training and all his natural instincts richly equipped him; he negotiated endlessly between the Earl of Ngumo and Viscount Boaz, armed with orders for the dispossession of the lowest bidder; he bought and resold, haggled, flattered and depreciated, and ate and slept in a clutter of dubious antiques. But on Basil the strain of modernity began to leave its traces. Brief rides with Prudence through the tinder-dry countryside, assignations furtively kept and interrupted at a moment's notice by some peremptory, crazy summons to the Palace, alone broke the unquiet routine of his day.

'I believe that odious Emperor is slowly poisoning you. It's a thing he does do,' said Prudence. 'And I never saw anyone look so ill.'

'You know it sounds absurd, but I miss Connolly. It's rather a business living all the time between Seth and Youkoumian.'

'Of course, you wouldn't remember that there's me too, would you?' said Prudence. 'Not just to cheer me up, you wouldn't.'

'You're a grand girl, Prudence. What Seth calls tiptop. But I'm so tired I could die.'

And a short distance away the Legation syce moodily flicked with his whip at a train of ants while the ponies shifted restlessly among the stones and shelving earth of a dry watercourse.

Two mornings later the Ministry of Modernization received its sharpest blow. Work was going on as usual. Mr Youkoumian was interviewing a coast Arab who claimed to possess some 'very old, very genuine' Portuguese manuscripts; Basil, pipe in his mouth, was considering how best to deal with the Emperor's latest memorandum, *Kindly insist straw hats and gloves compulsory peerage*, when he received an unexpected and disturbing call from Mr Jagger, the contractor in charge of the demolition of the Anglican Cathedral; a stocky, good-hearted little Britisher who after a succession of quite honourable bankruptcies in Cape Town, Mombasa, Dar-es-Salaam and Aden had found his way to Debra Dowa where he had remained ever since, occupied with minor operations in the harbour and along the railway line. He threaded his way through the antiquities which had lately begun to encroach on Basil's office, removed a seedy-looking caged vulture from the chair and sat down; his manner was uncertain and defiant.

'It's not playing the game, Mr Seal,' he said. 'I tell you that fair and square and I don't mind who knows it, not if it's the Emperor himself.'

'Mr Jagger,' said Basil impressively, 'you should have been long enough in this country to know that that is a very rash thing to say. Men have been poisoned for less. What is your trouble?'

'This here's my trouble,' said Mr Jagger, producing a piece of paper from a pocket full of pencils and foot rules and laying it on the table next to the mosaic portrait of the late Empress recently acquired by the Director of Fine Arts. 'What is it, eh, that's what I want to know?'

'What indeed?' said Basil. He picked it up and examined it closely.

In size, shape and texture it resembled an English five-pound note and was printed on both sides with intricate engraved devices of green and red. There was an Azanian eagle, a map of the Empire, a soldier in the uniform of the Imperial Guard, an aeroplane and a classical figure bearing a cornucopia, but the most prominent place was taken by a large medallion portrait of Seth in top hat and European tail coat. The words *Five Pounds* lay in flourished script across the middle; above them THE IMPERIAL BANK OF AZANIA and below them a facsimile of Seth's signature.

The normal currency of the capital and the railway was in Indian rupees, although East African shillings, French and Belgian colonial francs and Maria Theresa thalers circulated with equal freedom; in the interior the mediums of exchange were rock-salt and cartridges.

'This is a new one on me,' said Basil. 'I wonder if the Treasury know anything about it. Mr Youkoumian, come in here a minute, will you?'

The Director of Fine Arts and First Lord of the Treasury trotted through the partition door in his black cotton socks; he carried a model dhow he had just acquired.

'No, Mr Seal,' he pronounced, 'I ain't never seen a thing like that before. Where did the gentleman get it?'

'The Emperor's just given me a whole packet of them for the week's wages bill. What is the Imperial Bank of Azania, anyway? I never see such a thing all the time I been in the country. There's something here that's not on the square. You must understand, Mr Seal, that it's not anyone's job breaking up that Cathedral. Solid granite shipped all the way from Aberdeen. Why, Lord love you, the pulpit alone weighs seven and a half ton. I had two boys hurt only this morning through the font swinging loose as they were hoisting it into a lorry. Smashed up double one of them was. The Emperor ain't got no right to try putting that phoney stuff across me.'

'You may be quite confident,' said Basil with dignity, 'that in all your dealings with His Majesty you will encounter nothing but the highest generosity and integrity. However, I will institute inquiries on your behalf.'

'No offence meant, I'm sure,' said Mr Jagger.

Basil watched him across the yard and then snatched up his topee from a fossilized tree-fern. 'What's that black lunatic been up to this time?' he asked, starting off towards the Palace.

'Oh, Mr Seal, you'll get into trouble one day with the things you say.'

The Emperor rose to greet him with the utmost cordiality.

'Come in, come in. I'm very glad you've come. I'm in some perplexity about Nacktkultur. Here have I spent four weeks trying to enforce the edict prescribing trousers for the official classes, and now I read that it is more modern not to wear any at all.'

'Seth, what's the Imperial Bank of Azania?'

The Emperor looked embarrassed.

'I thought you might ask . . . Well, actually it is not quite a bank at all. It is a little thing I did myself. I will show you.'

He led Basil to a high cupboard which occupied half the wall on one side of the library, and opening it showed him a dozen or so shelves stacked with what might have been packets of writing paper.

'What is that?'

'Just under three million pounds,' said the Emperor proudly. 'A little surprise. I had them done in Europe.'

'But you can't possibly do this.'

'Oh, yes, I assure you. It was easy. All these on this shelf are for a thousand pounds each, and now that the plates have been made, it is quite inexpensive to print as many more as we require. You see there were a great many things which needed doing and I had not a great many rupees. Don't look angry, Seal. Look, I'll give you some.' He pressed a bundle of fivers into Basil's hand. 'And take some for Mr Youkoumian, too. Pretty fine picture of me, eh? I wondered about the hat. You will see that in the fifty-pound notes I wear a crown.'

For some minutes Basil attempted to remonstrate; then quite suddenly he abandoned the argument.

'I knew you would understand,' said the Emperor. 'It is so simple. As soon as these are used up we will send for some more. And tomorrow you will explain to me about Nacktkultur, eh?'

Basil returned to his office very tired.

'There's only one thing to hope for now. That's a fire in the Palace to get rid of the whole lot.'

'We must change these quick,' said Mr Youkoumian. 'I know a damn fool Chinaman might do it. Anyway, the Ministry of Fine Arts can take one at par for the historical section.'

It was on that afternoon that Basil at last lost his confidence in the permanence of the One Year Plan.

6

FROM DAME MILDRED PORCH TO HER HUSBAND

S.S. Le Président Carnot
Matodi
March 8th

My Dear Stanley,

I am writing this before disembarking. It will be posted at Marseilles and should reach you as nearly as I can calculate on 17th of the month. As I wrote to you from Durban, Sarah and I decided to break our return journey in Azania. The English boat did not stop here. So we had to change at Aden into this outward-bound French ship. Very dirty and *unseamanlike*. I have heard very disagreeable accounts of the hunting here. Apparently the natives dig deep pits into which the poor animals fall; they are often left in these traps for several days without food or water (imagine what that means in the heat of the jungle) and are then mercilessly butchered in cold blood. Of course the poor ignorant people know no better. But the young Emperor is by all accounts a comparatively enlightened and well-educated person and I am sure he will do all he can to introduce more humane methods if it is really necessary to kill these fine beasts at all–as I very much doubt. I expect to resume our journey in about a fortnight. I enclose cheque for another month's household expenses. The coal bill seemed surprisingly heavy in your last accounts. I hope that you are not letting the servants become extravagant in my absence. There is no need for the dining-room fire to be lit before luncheon at this time of year.

Yours affec.
Mildred

March 8th

Disembarked Matodi 12.45. Quaint and smelly. Condition of mules and dogs *appalling*, also children. In spite of radio message British consul was not there to meet us. Quite civil native led us to his office. Tip five annas. Seemed satisfied. Consul not English at all. Some sort of Greek. Very unhelpful (probably drinks). Unable or unwilling to say when train starts for Debra Dowa, whether possible engage sleeper. Wired Legation. Went to Amurath Hotel. Positive pot-house. Men sitting about drinking all over terrace. Complained. Large bedroom overlooking harbour apparently clean. Sarah one of her headaches. Complained of her room over street. Told her very decent little room.

March 9th

No news of train. Sarah disagreeable about her room. Saw Roman Missionary. Unhelpful. Typical dago attitude towards animals. Later saw American Baptists. Middle-class and unhelpful because unable talk native languages. No answer Legation. Wired again.

March 10th

No news train. Wired legation again. Unhelpful answer. Fed doggies in market-place. Children tried to take food from doggies. Greedy little wretches. Sarah still headache.

March 11th

Hotel manager suddenly announced train due to leave at noon. Apparently has been here all the time. Sarah very slow packing. Outrageous bill. Road to station blocked brown motor lorry. Natives living in it. Also two goats. Seemed well but cannot be healthy for them so near natives. Had to walk last quarter-mile. Afraid would miss train. Arrived with five minutes to spare. Got tickets, no sleepers. Just in time. V. hot and exhausted. Train did not start until three o'clock. Arrived dinnertime Lumo station where apparently we have to spend night. Shower bath and changed underclothes. Bed *v. doubtful.* Luckily remembered Keatings Durban. Interesting French hotel manager about local conditions. Apparently there was quite civil war last summer. How little the papers tell us. New Emperor v. goahead. English adviser named Seal. Any relation Cynthia Seal? Hotel man seemed to doubt government's financial stability. Says natives are *complete savages* but no white slave traffic–or so he says.

March 12th

Awful night. Bitten all over. Bill outrageous. Thought manager decent person too. Explained provisions hard to get. Humbug. Train left at seven in morning. Sarah nearly missed it. Two natives in carriage. I must say quite civil but v. uncomfortable as no corridor and had left so early. Tiring journey. Country seemed dry. Due in Debra Dowa some time this afternoon. Must say shall be thankful.

Dame Mildred Porch and Miss Sarah Tin were in no way related to each other, but constant companionship and a similarity of interests had so characterized them that a stranger might easily have taken them to be sisters as they stepped from the train on to the platform at Debra Dowa. Dame Mildred was rather stout and Miss Tin rather spare. Each wore a khaki sun-hat in an oilcloth cover, each wore a serviceable washable frock, and thick shoes and stockings, each had smoked spectacles and a firm mouth. Each carried an attaché-case containing her most inalienable possessions–washing things and writing things, disinfectant and insecticide, books, passport, letters of credit–and held firmly to her burden in defiance of an eager succession of porters who attempted in turn to wrest it from her.

William pushed his way forward and greeted them amiably. 'Dame Mildred Porch? Miss Tin? How are you? So glad you got here all right. I'm from the Legation. The Minister couldn't come himself. He's very busy just now, but he asked me to come along and see if you were all right. Any luggage? I've got a car outside and can run you up to the Hotel.'

'Hotel? But I thought we should be expected at the Legation. I wired from Durban.'

'Yes, the Minister asked me to explain. You see, we're some way out of the town. No proper road. Awful business getting in and out. The Minister thought you'd be much more comfortable in the town itself. Nearer the animals and everything. But he particularly said he hoped you'd come over to tea one day if you ever have the time.'

Dame Mildred and Miss Tin exchanged that look of slighted citizenship which William had seen in the eyes of every visitor he had ever greeted at Debra Dowa. 'I'll tell you what,' he said. 'I'll go and look for the luggage. I dare say it's got stolen on the way. Often is, you know. And I'll get our mail out at the same time. No King's messengers or anything here. If there's no European travelling it's put in charge of the guard. We thought of wiring to you to look after it and then we thought probably you had the devil of a lot of luggage yourselves.'

By the time that the two-seater car had been loaded with the Legation bags and the two ladies there was very little room left for their luggage. 'I say, d'you mind awfully,' said William. 'I'm afraid we'll have to leave this trunk behind. The hotel'll fetch it up for you in no time.'

'Young man, did you come to meet us or your own mail?'

'Now, you know,' said William, 'that simply isn't a fair question. Off we go.' And the overladen little car began jolting up the broad avenue into the town.

'Is *this* where we are to stay?' asked Miss Tin as they drew up opposite the *Grand Café et Hotel Restaurant de l'Empereur Seth.*

'It doesn't look terribly smart,' admitted William, 'but you'll find it a mine of solid comfort.'

He led them into the murky interior, dispersing a turkey and her brood from the Reception Hall. 'Anyone in?' There was a bell on the counter which he rang.

''Ullo,' said a voice from upstairs. 'One minute,' and presently Mr Youkoumian descended, buttoning up his trousers. 'Why, it's Mr Bland. 'Ullo, sir, 'ow are you? I 'ad the Minister's letter about the road this afternoon and the answer I am afraid is nothing doing. Very occupied, the Emperor . . .'

'I've brought you two guests. They are English ladies of great importance. You are to make them comfortable.'

'I fix them O.K.' said Mr Youkoumian.

'I'm sure you'll find everything comfortable here,' said William. 'And I hope we shall see you soon at the Legation.'

'One minute, young man, there are a number of things I want to know.'

'I fix you O.K.,' said Mr Youkoumian again.

'Yes, you ask Mr Youkoumian here. He'll tell you everything far better than I could. Can't keep them waiting for the mail, you know.'

'Impudent young puppy,' said Dame Mildred as the car drove away. 'I'll report him to the Foreign Office as soon as I get home. Stanley shall ask a question about him in the House.'

Mail day at the British Legation. Sir Samson and Lady Courteney, Prudence and William, Mr Legge and Mrs Legge, Mr and Mrs Anstruther, sitting round the fireplace opening the bags. Bills, provisions, family news, official dispatches, gramophone records, newspapers scattered on the carpet. presently William said, 'I say, d'you know who I ran into on the platform? Those two cruelty-to-animals women who kept telegraphing.'

'How very annoying. What *have* you done with them?'

'I shot them into Youkoumian's. They wanted to come and stay here.'

'Heaven forbid. I do hope they won't stay long. Ought we to ask them to tea or anything?'

'Well, I *did* say that perhaps you'd like to see them some time.'

'Hang it, William, that's a bit thick.'

'Oh, I don't suppose they thought I meant it.'

'I sincerely hope not.'

March 12th (continued)

Arrived Debra Dowa late in afternoon. Discourteous cub from Legation met us and left Sarah's trunk at station. Brought us to *frightful* hotel. But Armenian proprietor v. obliging. Saved me visit to bank by changing money for us into local currency. Quaint bank-notes with portrait of Emperor in European evening dress. Mr Seal came in after dinner. He is Cynthia's son. V. young and ill-looking. Off-hand manner. V. tired, going to bed early.

That evening M. Ballon's report included the entry. *Two British ladies arrived, suspects. Met at station by Mr Bland. Proceeded Youkoumian*'s.

'They are being watched?'

'Without respite.'

'Their luggage?'

'A trunk was left at the station. It has been searched but nothing incriminating was found. Their papers are in two small bags which never leave their hands.'

'Ah, they are old stagers. Sir Samson is calling out his last reserves.'

March 13th Sunday

No news Sarah's trunk. Went to Anglican Cathedral but found it was being pulled down. Service in Bishop's drawing-room. Poor congregation. V. silly sermon. Spoke to Bishop later about cruelty to animals. Unhelpful. Old humbug. Later went to write name in book at Palace. Sarah in bed. Town very crowded, apparently preparing for some local feast or carnival. Asked Bishop about it but he could not tell me. Seemed unaccountably embarrassed. Asked Mr Youkoumian. Either he cannot have understood my question or I cannot have understood what I thought him to say. Did not press point. He did not speak English at all well but is an obliging man.

March 14th

Hideous night. Mosquito in net and v. large brown bugs in bed. Up and dressed at dawn and went for long walk in hills. Met quaint caravan–drums, spears, etc. No news Sarah's trunk.

Other people besides Dame Mildred were interested in the little cavalcade which had slipped unobtrusively out of the city at dawn that day. Unobtrusively, in this connection, is a relative term. A dozen running slaves had preceded the procession, followed by a train of pack mules; then ten couples of mounted spearmen, a platoon of uniformed Imperial Guardsmen and a mounted band, blowing down reed flutes eight feet long and beating hand drums of hide and wood. In the centre on a mule loaded with silver and velvet trappings, had ridden a stout figure, heavily muffled in silk shawls. It was the Earl of Ngumo travelling incognito on a mission of great delicacy.

'Ngumo left town today. I wonder what he's after.'

'I think the Earl's pretty fed up, Mr Seal. I take his 'ouse Saturday for the Museum. 'E's gone back to 'is estates, I expect.'

'Estates, nothing. He's left five hundred men in camp behind him. Besides, he left on the Popo road. That's not his way home.'

'Oh gosh, Mr Seal, I 'ope there ain't going to be no bust-up.'

Only three people in Debra Dowa knew the reason for the Earl's departure. They were M. Ballon, General Connolly and the Nestorian Patriarch. They had dined together on Saturday night at the French Legation, and after dinner, when Mme Ballon and Black Bitch had withdrawn to the salon to discuss their hats and physical disorders, and the sweet champagne frothed in the shallow glasses, the Patriarch had with considerable solemnity revealed his carefully guarded secret of State.

'It happened in the time of Gorgias, my predecessor, of evil memory,' said his Beatitude, 'and the intelligence was delivered to me on my assumption of office, under a seal so holy that only extreme personal vexation induces me to break it. It concerns poor little Achon. I say "poor little" although he must now, if he survives at all, be a man at least ninety years of age, greatly my own senior. He, as you know, was the son of the Great Amurath and it is popularly supposed that a lioness devoured him while hunting with his sister's husband, Seyid, in the Ngumo mountains. My Lords, nothing of the kind happened. By order of his sister and the Patriarch Gorgias the wretched boy was taken while under the influence of liquor to the monastery of St Mark the Evangelist and incarcerated there.'

'But this is a matter of vital importance,' cried M. Ballon. 'Is the man still alive?'

'Who can say? To tell you the truth I have not visited the Monastery of St Mark the Evangelist. The Abbot is inclined to the lamentable heresy that the souls in hell marry and beget hobgoblins. He is pertinacious in error. I sent the Bishop of Popo there to reason with him and they drove the good man out with stones.'

'Would they accept an order of release over your signature?'

'It is painful to me to admit it, but I am afraid they would not. It will be a question of hard cash or nothing.'

'The Abbot may name his own price. I must have Achon here in the capital. Then we shall be ready to strike.'

The bottle circulated and before they left for the drawing-room M. Ballon reminded them of the gravity of the occasion. 'Gentlemen. This is an important evening in the history of East Africa. The future of the country and perhaps our own lives depend on the maintenance of absolute secrecy in regard to the Earl of Ngumo's expedition on Monday. All inside this room are sworn to inviolable silence.'

As soon as his guests were gone he assembled his subordinates and explained the latest developments; before dawn the news was in Paris. On the way home in the car Connolly told Black Bitch about it. 'But it's supposed to be secret for a little, so keep your silly mouth shut, see.'

March 14th (continued)

As Keatings obviously deteriorated, went to store attached hotel to buy some more. Met native Duchess who spoke English. V. helpful re bugs. Went with her to her home where she gave me insecticide of her own preparation. Gave me tea and biscuits. V. interesting conversation. She told me that it has just been discovered that Emperor is not real heir to the throne. Elderly uncle in prison. They have gone to get him out. Most romantic, but hope new Emperor equally enlightened re animals.

March 15th

Better night. Native Duchess's insecticide v. helpful though nasty smell. Received invitation dine Palace tonight. Short notice but thought it best accept for us both. Sarah says nothing to wear unless trunk turns up.

It was the first time since Seth's accession that European visitors had been entertained at the Palace. The Ministry of Modernization was called in early that morning to supervise the invitations and the menu.

'It shall be an entirely Azanian party. I want the English ladies to see how refined we are. I was doubtful about asking Viscount Boaz. What do you think? Will he be sober? . . . and there is the question of food. I have been reading that now it is called Vitamins. I am having the menu printed like this. It is good, modern, European dinner, eh?'

Basil looked at the card. A month ago he might have suggested emendations. Today he was tired.

'That's fine, Seth, go ahead like that.'

'You see,' said the Emperor proudly, 'already we Azanians can do much for ourselves. Soon we shall not need a Minister of Modernization. No, I do not mean that, Basil. Always you are my friend and adviser.'

So the menu for Seth's first dinner party went to the *Courier* office to be printed and came back a packet of handsome gilt-edged cards, laced with silk ribbons in the Azanian colours and embossed with a gold crown.

'It is so English,' explained Seth. 'From courtesy to your great Empire.'

MARCH 15TH

Imperial Banquet for Welcoming the English Cruelty to Animals

MENU OF FOODS

VITAMIN A *Tin Sardines*	VITAMIN E *Spiced Turkey*
VITAMIN B *Roasted Beef*	VITAMIN F *Sweet Puddings*
VITAMIN C *Small Roasted Sucking Porks*	VITAMIN G *Coffee*
VITAMIN D *Hot Sheep and Onions*	VITAMIN H *Jam*

At eight o'clock that evening Dame Mildred and Miss Tin arrived at the Palace for the banquet. The electric-light plant was working that evening and a string of coloured bulbs shone with Christmas welcome over the main doorway. A strip of bright linoleum had been spread on the steps and as the taxi drew up a dozen or so servants ran down to conduct the guests into the hall. They were in mixed attire; some in uniforms of a kind, tunic frogged with gold braid discarded or purloined in the past from the wardrobes of visiting diplomats; some in native costume of striped silk. As the two ladies stepped from the car a platoon of Guards lounging on the Terrace alarmed them with a ragged volley of welcome.

There was a slight delay as the driver of the taxi refused to accept the new pound note which Dame Mildred tendered him in payment, but the captain of the Guard, hurrying up with a jingle of spurs, curtailed further discussion by putting the man under arrest and signified in a few graphic gestures his sorrow for the interruption and his intention of hanging the troublesome fellow without delay.

The chief saloon was brilliantly lighted and already well filled with the flower of Azanian native society. One of the first acts of the new reign had been an ordinance commanding the use of European evening dress. This evening was the first occasion for it to be worn and all round the room stood sombre but important figures completely fitted up by Mr Youkoumian with tail coats, white gloves, starched linen and enamelled studs; only in a few cases were shoes and socks lacking; the unaccustomed attire lent a certain dignified rigidity to their deportment. The ladies had for the most part allowed their choice to fix upon frocks of rather startling colour; aniline greens and violets with elaborations of ostrich feather and sequin. Viscountess Boaz wore a backless frock newly arrived from Cairo combined with the full weight of her ancestral jewellery; the Duchess of Mhomala carried on her woolly head a three-pound tiara of gold and garnets; Baroness Batulle exposed shoulders and back magnificently tattooed and cicatrized with arabesques.

Beside all this finery the guests of honour looked definitely dowdy as the Lord Chamberlain conducted them round the room and performed the introductions in French scarcely more comfortable than Dame Mildred's own.

Two slaves circulated among them carrying trays of brandy. The English ladies refused. The Lord Chamberlain expressed his concern. Would they have preferred whisky; no doubt some could be produced? Or beer?

'*Mon bon homme*,' said Dame Mildred severely, '*il vous faut comprendre que nous ne buvons rien de tout, jamais*'; an announcement which considerably raised their prestige among the company; they were not much to look at, certainly, but at least they knew a thing or two which the Azanians did not. A useful sort of woman to take on a journey, reflected the Lord Chamberlain, and inquired with polite interest whether the horses and camels in their country were as conveniently endowed.

Further conversation was silenced by the arrival of the Emperor, who at this moment entered the hall from the far end and took his seat on the raised throne which had stood conspicuously on the dais throughout the preliminary presentations. Court etiquette was still in a formative stage. There was a moment of indecision during which the company stood in embarrassed silence waiting for a lead. Seth said something to his equerry, who now advanced down the room and led forward the guests of honour. They curtseyed and stood on one side, while the other guests filed past in strict precedence. Most of them bowed low in the Oriental manner, raising the hand to forehead and breast. The curtsey, however, had been closely observed and found several imitators among both sexes. One elderly peer, a stickler for old-world manners, prostrated himself fully and went through the mimic action of covering his head with dust. When all had saluted him in their various ways, Seth led the party in to dinner, fresh confusion over the places and some ill-natured elbowing; Dame Mildred and Miss Tin sat on either side the of the Emperor; soon everyone was eating and drinking at a great pace.

March 15th (continued)

Dinner at Palace. Food v. nasty. Course after course different kinds of meat, overseasoned and swimming in grease. Tried to manage some of it from politeness. Sarah ate nothing. Emperor asked great number of questions, some of which I was unable to answer. How many suits of clothes had the King of England? Did he take his bath before or after his breakfast? Which was the more civilized? What was the best shop to buy an artesian well? etc. Sarah v. silent. Told Emperor about co-education and 'free-discipline'. Showed great interest.

Dame Mildred's neighbour on her other side was the punctilious man who had prostrated himself in the drawing-room; he seemed engrossed in his eating. In point of fact he was rehearsing in his mind and steeling his nerve to enunciate some English conversation in which he had painfully schooled himself during that day; at last it came up suddenly.

''Ow many ox 'ave you?' he demanded, lifting up sideways from his plate a great bearded face, ''ow many sons? 'ow many daughters? 'ow many brothers? 'ow many sisters? My father is dead fighting.'

Dame Mildred turned to him a somewhat startled scrutiny. There were crumbs and scraps of food in various parts of his beard. 'I beg your pardon?' she said.

But the old gentleman had shot his bolt; he felt that he had said all and more than all that good breeding required, and to tell the truth was more than a little taken aback by his own fluency. He gave her a nervous smile and resumed his dinner without again venturing to address her.

'Which of the white ladies would you like to have?'

'The fat one. But both are ugly.'

'Yes. It must be very sad for the English gentlemen to marry English ladies.'

Presently, when the last vitamin had been guzzled, Viscount Boaz rose to propose the health of the guests of honour. His speech was greeted by loud applause and was then done into English by the Court Interpreter.

'Your Majesty, Lords and Ladies. It is my privilege and delight this evening to welcome with open arms of brotherly love to our city Dame Mildred Porch and Miss Tin, two ladies renowned throughout the famous country of Europe for their great cruelty to animals. We Azanians are a proud and ancient nation but we have much to learn from the white people of the West and North. We too, in our small way, are cruel to our animals'–and here the Minister for the Interior digressed at some length to recount with hideous detail what he had himself once done with a woodman's axe to a wild boar–'but it is to the great nations of the West and North, especially to their worthy representatives that are with us tonight, that we look as our natural leaders on the road of progress. Ladies and gentlemen, we must be Modern, we must be refined in our Cruelty to Animals. That is the message of the new Age brought to us by our guests this evening. May I, in conclusion, raise my glass and ask you to join with me in wishing them old age and prolonged fecundity.'

The toast was drunk and the company sat down. Boaz's neighbours congratulated him on his speech. There seemed no need for a reply and, indeed, Dame Mildred, rarely at a loss for telling phrases, would on this occasion have been hard put to it to acknowledge the welcome in suitable terms. Seth appeared not to have heard either version of the speech. He sat inattentive, his mind occupied with remote speculation. Dame Mildred attempted two or three conversations.

'A very kind meant speech, but he seems to misunderstand our mission . . . It is so interesting to see your people in their own milieu. Do tell me who is who . . . Have they entirely abandoned native costume? . . .'

But she received only abstracted answers.

Finally she said, 'I was so interested to learn about your Uncle Achon.' The Emperor nodded. 'I do hope they get him out of the monastery. Such a useless life, I always think, and so selfish. It makes people introspective to think all the time about their own souls, don't you think? So sensible of that Earl of wherever it is to go and look for him.'

But Seth had not heard a word.

March 16th

Could not sleep late after party. Attempted to telephone legation. No reply. Attempted to see Mr Seal. Said he was too busy. No sign of Sarah's trunk. She keeps borrowing my things. Tried to *pin* down Emperor last night, no result. Went for walk in town. V. crowded, no one working. Apparently some trouble about currency. Saw man strike camel, would have reported him but no policeman about. Begin to feel I am wasting my time here.

The Monastery of St Mark the Evangelist, though infected of late with the taint of heresy, was the centre of Azanian spiritual life. Here in remote times Nestorian missionaries from Mesopotamia had set up a church, and here, when the great Amurath proclaimed Christianity the official creed of the Empire, the old foundations had been unearthed and a native community installed. A well-substantiated tradition affirmed that the little river watering the estate was, in fact, the brook Kedron conveyed there subterraneously; its waters were in continual requisition for the relief of skin diseases and stubborn boils. Here too were preserved, among other relics of less certain authenticity, David's stone prised out of the forehead of Goliath (a boulder of astonishing dimensions), a leaf from the Barren Fig Tree, the rib from which Eve had been created and a wooden cross which had fallen from heaven quite unexpectedly during Good Friday luncheon some years back. Architecturally, however, there was nothing very remarkable: no cloister or ambulatory, library, gallery, chapter house or groined refectory. A cluster of mud huts around a larger hut; a single stone building, the Church dedicated to St Mark by Amurath the Great. It could be descried from miles around, perched on a site of supreme beauty, a shelf of the great escarpment that overlooked the Wanda lowlands, and through it the brook Kedron, narrowed at this season to a single thread of silver, broke into innumerable iridescent cascades as it fell to join the sluggish Izol five thousand feet below. Great rocks of volcanic origin littered the fields. The hillside was full of unexplored caverns whence hyenas sallied out at night to exhume the corpses which it was a pious practice to transport from all over the empire to await the last trump on that holy ground.

The Earl of Ngumo had made good time. The road lay through the Sakuyu cattle country, high plains covered with brown slippery grass. At first the way led along the caravan route to the royal cities of the north; a clearly defined track well frequented. They exchanged greetings with mule trains coming into market and unusual bands of travellers, loping along on foot, drawn to the capital by the name of the great Gala and the magnetic excitement which all the last weeks had travelled on the ether, radiating in thrilling waves to bazaar, farm and jungle, gossiped about over camp fires, tapped out on hollow tree trunks in the swamplands, sniffed, as it were, on the breeze, sensed by subhuman faculties that something was afoot.

Later they diverged into open country; only the heaps of stones bridging the water-courses and an occasional wooden culvert told them they were still on the right road. On the first night they camped among shepherds. The simple men recognized a great nobleman and brought him their children to touch.

'We hear of changes in the great city.'

'There are changes.'

On the second night they reached a little town. The head-man had been forewarned of their approach. He came out to meet them, prostrating himself and covering his head with dust.

'Peace be upon your house.'

'You come from the great city of changes. What is your purpose among my people?'

'I wish well to your people. It is not suitable for the low to babble of what the high ones do.'

They slept in and around the headman's hut; in the morning he brought them honey and eggs, a trussed chicken, dark beer in a jug and a basket of flat bread: they gave him salt in bars, and continued their journey.

The third night they slept in the open; there was a picket of royal Guards somewhere in that country. Late on the fourth day they reached the Monastery of St Mark the Evangelist.

A monk watching on the hilltop sighted them and fired a single musket shot into the still air; a troop of baboons scattered frightened into the rocks. In the church below the great bell was rung to summon the community. The Abbot under his yellow sunshade stood in the enclosure to greet them; he wore steel-rimmed spectacles. A little deacon beside him plied a horsehair fly whisk.

Obeisance and benediction. The Earl presented the Patriarch's letter of commendation, which was slipped un-opened into the folds of the Abbot's bosom, for it is not etiquette to show any immediate curiosity about such documents. Official reception in the twilit hut; the Earl seated on a chair hastily covered with carpet. The chief men of the monastery stood round the wall with folded hands. The Abbot opened the letter of introduction, spat and read it aloud amid grunts of approval; it was all preamble and titles of honour; no word of business. A visit to the shrine of the Barren Fig Tree; the Earl kissed the lintel of the door three times, laid his forehead against the steps of the sanctuary and made a present of a small bag of silver. Dinner in the Abbot's lodging; it was one of the numerous fast days of the Nestorian Church; vegetable mashes in wooden bowls, one of bananas, one of beans; earthenware jugs and brown vessels of rough beer. Ponderous leave-takings for the night. The Earl's tent meanwhile had been pitched in the open space within the enclosure; his men squatted on guard; they had made a fire; two or three monks joined them; soon they began singing, wholly secular words in monotonous cadence. Inside the tent a single small lamp with floating wick. The Earl squatted among his rugs waiting for the Abbot who, he knew, would come that night. Presently through the flap of the tent appeared the bulky white turban and straggling beard of the prelate. The two great men squatted opposite each other, on either side of the little lamp; outside the guards singing at the camp fire; beyond the stockade the hyenas and a hundred hunting sounds among the rocks. Grave courtesies: 'Our little convent resounds with the fame of the great Earl . . . his prowess in battle and in bed . . . the thousand enemies slain by his hand . . . the lions he has speared . . . his countless progeny . . .'

'All my life I have counted the days wasted until I saluted the Abbot . . . his learning and sanctity . . . his dauntless fidelity to the faith, his chastity . . . the austerities of his spiritual practices . . .'

Slowly by a multitude of delicately graded steps the conversation was led to a more practical level. Was there any particular object in the Earl's visit, other than the infinite joy afforded to all by his presence?

What object could be more compelling that the universal ambition to pay respect to the Abbot and the glorious shrine of the Barren Fig Tree? But there was, as it so happened, a little matter, a thing scarcely worth a thought, which since he were here, the Earl might mention if it would not be tedious to his host.

Every word of the Earl's was a jewel, valued beyond human computation; what was this little matter?

It was an old story . . . in the days of His Beatitude Gorgias of evil memory . . . a prisoner, brought to the convent; now an old man . . . One of whom only high ones might speak . . . supposing that this man were alive . . .

'Oh, Earl, you speak of that towards which my lips and ears are sealed. There are things which are not suitable.'

'Abbot, once there comes a time for everything when it must be spoken of.'

'What should a simple monk know of these high affairs? But I have indeed heard it said that in the times of His Beatitude Gorgias of evil memory, there was such a prisoner.'

'Does he still live?'

'The monks of St Mark the Evangelist guard their treasures well.'

After this all-important admission they sat for some time in silence; then the Abbot rose and with ample formalities left his guest to sleep. Both parties felt that the discussion had progressed almost too quickly. There were decencies to be observed.

Negotiations were resumed after Mass next morning and occupied most of the day; before they parted for the night Earl and Abbot had reduced their differences to a monetary basis. Next morning the price was decided and Achon, son of Amurath, legitimate Emperor of Azania, Chief of the Chiefs of Sakuyu, Lord of Wanda and Tyrant of the Seas, was set at liberty.

The event took place without ceremony. After a heavy breakfast of boiled goat's-meat, cheese, olives, smoked mutton, goose and mead–it was one of the numerous feast days of the Nestorian Church–the Earl and the Abbot set out for the hillside unaccompanied except by a handful of slaves. A short climb from the compound brought them to the mouth of a small cave.

'We will wait here. The air is not good.'

Instead they sent in a boy with lantern and hammer. From the depths they heard a few muffled words and then a series of blows as a staple was splintered from the rock. Within five minutes the slave had returned leading Achon by a chain attached to his ankle. The prince was completely naked, bowed and shrivelled, stained white hair hung down his shoulders, a stained white beard over his chest; he was blind, toothless and able to walk only with the utmost uncertainty.

The Earl had considered a few words of homage and congratulation. Instead he turned to the Abbot. 'He won't be able to ride.'

'That was hardly to be expected.'

Another night's delay while a litter was constructed; then on the fifth morning the caravan set out again for Debra Dowa. Achon swung between the shoulders of four slaves, heavily curtained from curious eyes. Part of the time he slept; at others he crooned quietly to himself, now and then breaking into little moans of alarm at the sudden jolts and lurches in his passage. On the eighth day, under cover of darkness, the little procession slipped by side roads and unfrequented lanes into the city, and, having delivered his charge to the Patriarch, the Earl hurried out to the French Legation to report to M. Ballon the successful performance of his mission.

Meanwhile Dame Mildred was not enjoying herself at all. Everyone seemed to conspire to be unhelpful and disobliging. First there was the intolerable impudence of that wretched boy at the Legation. She had attempted to ring them up every morning and afternoon; at last when she had almost despaired of effecting connection Mme Youkoumian had announced that she was through. But it had been a most unsatisfactory conversation. After some minutes with an obtuse native butler ('probably drinks' Dame Mildred had decided) the voice had changed to a pleasant, slightly languid English tone.

'I am Dame Mildred Porch. I wish to speak to the Minister.'

'Oh, I don't suppose you can do that, you know. Can *I* do anything for you?'

'Who are you?'

'I'm William.'

'Well, I wish to speak to you in particular . . . it's about Miss Tin's trunk.'

'Drunk?'

'Miss Sarah Tin, the organizing secretary of the overseas department of the League of Dumb Chums. She has lost her trunk.

'Ah.'

There was a long pause. Dame Mildred could hear a gramophone being played at the other end of the line.

'Hullo . . . Hullo . . . Are you there?'

Then William's gentle drawl said: 'You know the trouble about the local telephone is that one's always getting cut off.'

There had been a click and the dance music suddenly ceased. 'Hullo . . . Hullo.' She rattled the machine but there was no answer. 'I'm convinced he did it on purpose,' she told Miss Tin. 'If we could only prove it.'

Then there was trouble about her money. The twenty or so pounds which she had changed into Bank of Azania currency on her first afternoon seemed to be quite worthless. Even Mr Youkoumian, from whom she had first received them, was unable to help, remarking that it was a question of politics; he could not accept the notes himself in settlement of the weekly hotel bill or in payment for the numerous articles of clothing which Miss Tin was obliged to purchase from day to day at his store.

Then there was the Emperor's prolonged neglect of the cause of animals. The banquet, so far from being the prelude to more practical association, seemed to be regarded as the end of her visit. Her daily attempts to obtain an audience were met with consistent refusal. At times she fell into a fever of frustration; there, all over the country, were dumb chums being mercilessly snared and speared, and here was she, impotent to help them; throughout those restless Azanian nights Dame Mildred was continually haunted by the appealing reproachful eyes, limpid as spaniel puppies', of murdered lions and the pathetic patient whinnying of trapped baboons. Consciousness of guilt subdued her usually confident manner. Who was she to complain–betrayer that she was of mandril, hyena and wild pig, wart hog and porcupine–if Mr Youkoumian overcharged her bill or mislaid her laundry?

'Mildred, I don't think you're looking at all well. I don't believe this place agrees with you.'

'No, Sarah, I'm not sure that it does. Oh, do let's go away. I don't like the people or the way they look or anything and we aren't doing any good.'

'Basil, Mum wants me to go home–back to England, I mean.'

'I shan't like that.'

'Do you mean it? Oh, lovely Basil, I don't want to go a bit.'

'We may all have to go soon. Things seem breaking up here . . . only I'm not so sure about going to England . . . Can't we go somewhere else?'

'Darling, what's the good of talking . . . we'll see each other again, whatever happens. You do promise that, don't you?'

'You're a grand girl, Prudence, and I'd like to eat you.'

'So you shall, my sweet . . . anything you want.'

Strips of sunlight through the shutters; below in the yard a native boy hammering at the engine of a broken motor-car.

'I am sending Mme Ballon and the other ladies of the Legation down to the coast. I do not anticipate serious trouble. The whole thing will pass off without a shot being fired. Still, it is safer so. Monsieur Floreau will accompany them. He will have the delicate work of destroying the Lumo bridge. That is necessary because Seth has three regiments at Matodi who might prove loyal. The train leaves on the day before the Gala. I suggest that we advise Mr and Mrs Schonbaum a few hours before it starts. It would compromise the *coup d'état* if there were an international incident. The British must fend for themselves.'

'What is the feeling in the army, General?'

'I called a meeting of the Staff today and told them of Prince Achon's arrival in Debra Dowa. They know what is expected of them. Yesterday their salaries were paid in the new notes.'

'And the Prince, your Beatitude?'

'He is no worse.'

'But content?'

'Who can say? He has been sleeping most of the day. He does not speak. He is all the time searching for something on the floor, near his foot. I think he misses his chain. He eats well.'

'Mr Seal, I think I go down to Matodi day after tomorrow. Got things to fix there, see? How about you come too?'

'No good this week, Youkoumian. I shall have to wait and see poor Seth's gala.'

'Mr Seal, you take my tip and come to Matodi. I hear things. You don't want to get into no bust-up.'

'I've been hearing things too. I want to stay and see the racket.'

'Damn foolishness.'

It was not often that the Oriental Secretary called on the Minister. He came that evening after dinner. They were playing animal snap.

'Come in, Walsh. Nice to see you. You can settle a dispute for us. Prudence insists that a giraffe neighs like a horse. Now, does it?'

Later he got the Minister alone.

'Look here, sir. I don't know how closely you've followed local affairs, but I thought I ought to come and tell you. There's likely to be trouble on Tuesday on the day of this Birth Control Gala.'

'Trouble? I should think so. I think the whole thing perfectly disgusting. None of us are going.'

'Well, I don't exactly know what sort of trouble. But there's *something* up. I've just heard this evening that the French and Americans are going down to the coast *en bloc* by the Monday train. I thought you ought to know.'

'Pooh, another of these native disturbances. I remember that last civil war was just the same. Ballon thought he was going to be attacked the whole time. I'd sooner risk being bombed up here than bitten by mosquitoes at the coast. Still, jolly nice of you to tell me.'

'You wouldn't mind, sir, if my wife and myself went down on the train.'

'Not a bit, not a bit. Jolly glad. You can take charge of the bags. Can't say I envy you, but I hope you have a jolly trip.'

On the morning preceding the gala, Basil went as usual to his office. He found Mr Youkoumian busily packing a canvas grip with the few portable objects of value that had been collected for the museum. 'I better take care of these in case anything 'appens,' he explained. 'Catching train eleven o'clock. Very much crowded train. I think many wise men will be aboard. You better come too, Mr Seal. I fix it O.K.'

'What *is* going to happen?'

'I don't know nothing, Mr Seal. I don't ask questions. All I think that if there is a bust-up I will better be at the coast. They were preaching in all the Churches Sunday against the Emperor's Birth Control. Madame Youkoumian told me which is a very pious and churchgoing woman. But I think there is more than that going to happen. I think General Connolly knows something. You better come to the coast, Mr Seal. No?'

There was nothing to do that morning; no letters to answer; no chits from the Palace; the work of the Ministry seemed suddenly over. Basil locked his office door, pocketed the key and strode across the yard to see Seth. Two officers at the gate-house hushed their conversation as Basil passed them.

He found Seth, in an elegant grey suit and pale-coloured shoes, moodily poring over the map of the new city.

'They have stopped work on the Boulevard Seth. Jagger has dismissed his men. Why is this?'

'He hadn't been paid for three weeks. He didn't like the new bank-notes.'

'Traitor. I will have him shot. I sent for Connolly an hour ago. Where is he?'

'A great number of Europeans left for the coast by this morning's train–but I don't think Connolly was with them.'

'Europeans leaving? What do I care? The city is full of my people. I have watched them from the tower with my field-glasses. All day they come streaming in by the four roads . . . But the work must go on. The Anglican Cathedral for example; it should be down by now. I'll have it down if I have to work with my own hands. You see, it is right in the way of the great northern thoroughfare. Look at it on the plan–so straight . . .'

'Seth, there's a lot of talk going about. They say there may be trouble tomorrow.'

'God, have I not had trouble today and yesterday? Why should I worry about tomorrow?'

That evening Dame Mildred and Miss Tin saw a very curious sight. They had been to tea with the Bishop and, leaving him, made a slight detour, in order to take advantage of the singular sweetness of the evening air. As they passed the Anglican Cathedral they noticed a young man working alone. He wore light grey and parti-coloured shoes and he was engaged in battering at the granite archway at the West End with an energy very rare among Azanian navvies.

'How like the Emperor.'

'Don't be absurd, Sarah.'

They left the grey figure chipping diligently in the twilight, and returned to their hotel where the Youkoumians' departure had utterly disorganized the service.

'Just when we had begun to make them understand how we liked things . . .' complained Dame Mildred.

Next morning the ladies were up early. They had been awakened before dawn by the traffic under their windows, mules and ponies, chatter and scuffling, cars hooting for passage. Dame Mildren opened the shutters and looked down into the crowded street. Miss Tin joined her.

'I've been ringing for twenty minutes. There doesn't seem to be a soul in the hotel.'

Nor was there; the servants had gone out last night after dinner and had not returned. Fortunately Dame Mildred had the spirit stove, without which she never ventured abroad, some biscuits and cubes of bouillon. They breakfasted in this way upstairs while the crowd outside grew every moment in volume and variety, as the sun, brilliant and piercing as on other less notable mornings, mounted over the city. Dust rose from the crowded street and hung sparkling in the air.

'So nice for the Emperor to have a good day for his Pageant. Not at all like any of the pageants I can remember in England. Do you remember the girl guides' rally when there was that terrible hail storm–in August too? *How* the Brownies cried.'

The route of the procession lay past the Hotel de l'Empereur Seth. Shop fronts had been boarded up and several of the householders had erected stands and temporary balconies outside their windows. Some weeks earlier, when the Pageant had first been announced. Mr Youkoumian had advertised accommodation of this kind and sold a number of tickets to prospective sightseers. In the subsequent uncertainty he had abandoned this among other of his projects. Now, however, two or three Indians, a Greek and four or five Azanians in gala clothes presented themselves at the hotel to claim their seats in the stand. They explored the deserted vestibule and dining-room, climbed the stairs and finally reached the bedrooms of the English ladies. Hardened by the long exposure to rebuffs and injustice, the Indians paid no attention to Dame Mildred's protests. Instead, they pulled up the bed across the window, seated themselves in positions of excellent advantage and then, producing small bags of betel nuts from their pockets, settled down to wait, patiently chewing and spitting. Encouraged by this example the other intruders took possession of the other windows. The Greek politely offered Miss Tin a place in their midst and accepted her refusal with somewhat puzzled concern. The two ladies of the Azanian party wandered round the room, picking up and examining the articles on the washstand and dressing-table, and chattering with simple pleasure over the contents of the chest-of-drawers.

'This is an intolerable outrage. But I don't see what we can do about it at the moment. Sir Samson will have to lodge a complaint.'

'We can't possibly remain here. We can't possibly go out into the street. There is only one place for us–the roof.'

This position was easily accessible by means of a ladder and trap-door. Hastily equipping themselves with rugs, pillows, sunshades, two light novels, cameras and the remains of the biscuits, the resolute ladies climbed up into the blazing sunlight. Dame Mildred handed up their provisions to Miss Tin, then followed her. The trap-door could not be bolted from above, but fortunately the tin roof was weighted in many places by rock boulders, placed there to strengthen it in times of high wind. One of these they rolled into place, then, sliding down the hot corrugations to the low cement parapet, they made their nest in a mood of temporary tranquillity.

'We shall see very well from here, Sarah. There will be plenty of time to have those natives punished tomorrow.'

Indeed, from where they sat the whole city lay very conveniently exposed to their view. They could see the irregular roofs of the palace buildings in their grove of sapling blue gums and before them the still unfinished royal box from which the Emperor proposed to review the procession; small black figures could be observed working on it, tacking up coloured flags, spreading carpets and bobbing up the path with pots of palm and fern. They could see the main street of the city diverge, to the barracks on one side and the Christian quarter on the other. They could see the several domes and spires of the Catholic, Orthodox, Armenian, Anglican, Nestorian, American Baptist and Mormon places of worship; the minaret of the mosque, the Synagogue and the flat white roof of the Hindu snake temple. Miss Tin took a series of snapshots.

'Don't use all the films, there are bound to be some interesting things later.'

The sun rose high in the heavens; the corrugated iron radiated a fierce heat. Propped on their pillows under green parasols the two ladies became drowsy and inattentive to the passage of time.

The procession was due to start at eleven, but it must have been past noon before Dame Mildred, coming to with a jerk and snort, said, 'Sarah, I think something is beginning to happen.'

A little dizzily, for the heat was now scarcely bearable, the ladies leant over the parapet. The crowd was halloing loudly and the women gave out their peculiar throbbing whistle; there seemed to be a general stir towards the royal box, a quarter of a mile down the road.

'That must be the Emperor arriving.'

A dozen lancers were cantering down the street, forcing the crowds back into the side alleys and courtyards, only to surge out again behind them.

'The procession will come up from the direction of the railway station. Look, here they are.'

Fresh swelling and tumult in the crowded street. But it was only the lancers returning towards the Palace.

Presently Miss Tin said, 'You know, this may take all day. How hungry we shall be.'

'I've been thinking of that for some time. I am going to go down and forage.'

'Mildred, you can't. *Anything* might happen to you.'

'Nonsense, we can't live on this roof all day with four petit-beurre biscuits.'

She rolled back the stone and carefully, rung by rung, descended the ladder. The bedroom doors were open, and as she passed she saw that quite a large party was now assembled at the windows. She reached the ground floor, crossed the dining-room and opened the door at the far end where, she had been informed by many penetrating smells during the past weeks, lay the kitchen quarters. Countless flies rose with humming alarm as she opened the larder door. Uncovered plates of horrible substances lay on the shelves; she drew back instinctively; then faced them again. There were some black olives in an earthenware basin and half a yard of brick-dry bread. Armed with these and breathing heavily she again climbed to the trap-door.

'Sarah, open it at once.' The rock was withdrawn. 'How could you be so selfish as to shut it? Supposing I had been pursued.'

'I'm sorry, Mildred. Indeed I am, but you were so long and I grew nervous. And, my dear, you have been missing such a lot. All kinds of things have been happening.'

'What things?'

'Well, I don't know exactly, but look.'

Indeed, below, the crowds seemed to be in a state of extreme agitation, jostling and swaying without apparent direction around a wedge-shaped phalanx of police who were forcing a way with long bamboo staves; in their centre was an elderly man under arrest.

'Surely, those are clothes of the native priests? What can the old man have been up to?'

'Almost anything. I have never had any belief in the clergy after that curate we liked so much who was Chaplain of the Dumb Chums and spoke so feelingly and then . . .'

'Look, here *is* the procession.'

Rising strains of the Azanian anthem; the brass band of the Imperial Guards swung into sight, drowning the sounds of conflict. The Azanians loved a band and their Patriarch's arrest was immediately forgotten. Behind the soldiers drove Viscount and Viscountess Boaz, who had eventually consented to act as patrons. Then, marching four abreast in brand-new pinafores, came the girls of the Amurath Memorial High School, an institution founded by the old Empress to care for the orphans of murdered officials. They bore, somewhat unsteadily, a banner whose construction had occupied the embroidery and dressmaking class for several weeks. It was emblazoned in letters of appliquéd silk with the motto: WOMEN OF TOMORROW DEMAND AN EMPTY CRADLE. Slowly the mites filed by, singing sturdily.

'Very sensible and pretty,' said Miss Tin. 'Dear Mildred, what very stale bread you have brought.'

'The olives are excellent.'

'I never liked olives. Good gracious, look at this.'

The first of the triumphal cars had come into sight. At first an attempt had been made to induce ladies of rank to take part in the tableaux; a few had wavered, but Azanian society still retained certain standards; the peerage were not going to have their wives and daughters exhibiting themselves in aid of charity; the idea had to be dropped and the actresses recruited less ambitiously from the demi-monde. This first car, drawn by oxen, represented the place of women in the modern world. Enthroned under a canopy of coloured cotton sat Mlle 'Fifi' Fatim Bey; in one hand a hunting-crop to symbolize sport, in the other a newspaper to symbolize learning; round her were grouped a court of Azanian beauties with typewriters, tennis rackets, motor-bicycling goggles, telephones, hitch-hiking outfits and other patents of modernity inspired by the European illustrated papers. An orange-and-green appliquéd standard bore the challenging motto: THROUGH STERILITY TO CULTURE.

Enthusiastic applause greeted this pretty invention. Another car came into sight down the road, bobbing decoratively above the black pates; other banners.

Suddenly there was a check in the progress and a new note in the voice of the crowd.

'Has there been an accident? I do hope none of the poor oxen are hurt.'

The trouble seemed to be coming from the front of the procession, where bodies of men had pushed through from the side streets and were endeavouring to head the procession back. The brass band stopped, faltered and broke off, scattering before the assault and feebly defending their heads with trombones and kettle drums.

'Quick, Sarah, your camera. I don't know what in the world is happening, but I must get a snap of it. Of course the sun *would* be in the wrong place.'

'Try with the very small stop.'

'I do pray they come out; I had such bad luck with those very interesting films of Cape Town that the wretched man ruined on the boat. You know it looks like quite a serious riot. Where are the police?'

The attackers, having swept the band out of the road and underfoot, were making easy work of the High School Orphans; they were serious young men armed with clubs, the athletic group, as the ladies learned later, of Nestorian Catholic Action, muscular Christians who for many weeks now had been impatiently biding their time to have a whack at the modernists and Jews who were behind the new movement.

Down went the embroidered banner as the girls in their pinafores ran for safety between the legs of the onlookers.

The main focus of the assault was now the triumphal car immediately in front of the Hotel de l'Empereur Seth. At the first sign of disturbance the members of the tableau had abandoned their poses and huddled together in alarm; now without hesitation they forsook their properties and bundled out of the wagon into the street. The Christian party swarmed on to it and one of them began addressing the crowd. Dame Mildred snapped him happily as he turned in their direction, arms spread, mouth wide open, in all the fervour of democratic leadership.

Hitherto, except for a few jabs with trumpets and drumsticks, the attackers had met with no opposition. Now, however, the crowd began to take sides, individual scuffles broke out among them and a party of tribesmen from up-country, happily welcoming this new diversion in a crowded day, began a concerted charge to the triumphal car, round which there was soon raging a contest of I'm-king-of-the-castle game. The Nestorian orator was thrown overboard and a fine savage in lion skins began doing a jig in his place. The patient oxen stood unmoved by the tumult.

'Quick, Sarah, another roll of films. What *can* the police be thinking of?'

Then authority asserted itself.

From the direction of the royal box flashed out a ragged volley of rifle shots. A bullet struck the parapet with a burst of splintered concrete and ricocheted, droning, over the ladies' heads. Another volley and something slapped on to the iron roof a few yards from where they sat. Half comprehending, Dame Mildred picked up and examined the irregular disc of hot lead. Shrill wails of terror rose from the street below and then a clattering of horses and oxen. Without a word spoken Dame Mildred and Miss Tin rolled to cover.

The parapet was a low one and the ladies were obliged to lie full length in positions of extreme discomfort. Dame Mildred slid out her arm for a cushion and hastily withdrew it as a third burst of firing broke out as though on purpose to frustrate her action. Presently silence fell, more frightening than the tumult. Dame Mildred spoke in an awed whisper.

'Sarah, that was a *bullet*.'

'I know. Do be quiet or they'll start again.'

For twenty minutes by Miss Tin's wrist-watch the two ladies lay in the gutter, their faces almost touching the hot tarnished iron of the roof. Dame Mildred shifted on to her side.

'Oh, *what is it*, Mildred?'

'Pins and needles in my left leg. I don't care if I am shot.'

Dim recollections of some scouting game played peaceably in somewhat different circumstances among Girl Guides in the bracken of Epping prompted Dame Mildred to remove her topee and, holding it at arm's length, expose it over the edge of their rampart. The silence of the stricken field was unbroken. Slowly, with infinite caution, she raised her head.

'For heaven's sake, take care, Mildred. *Snipers*.'

But everything was quiet. At length she sat up and looked over. From end to end the street was silent and utterly deserted. The strings of flags hung limp in the afternoon heat. The banner of the Amurath High School lay spread across the way, dishevelled and dusty from a thousand footsteps but still flaunting its message bravely to the heavens, WOMEN OF TOMORROW DEMAND AN EMPTY CRADLE. The other banner lay crumpled in the gutter. Only one word was visible in the empty street. STERILITY pleaded in orange-and-green silk to an unseeing people.

'I think it is all over.'

The ladies sat up and stretched their cramped legs, dusted themselves a little, straightened their hats and breathed deeply of the fresh air. Dame Mildred retrieved her camera and wound on the film. Miss Tin shook out the pillows and looked for food. The olives were dry and dull-skinned, the bread crisp as biscuit and gritted with dust.

'*Now* what are we going to do? I'm thirsty and I think one of my headaches is coming on.'

Regular steps of marching troops in the street below.

'Look out. They're coming again.'

The two ladies slid back under cover. They heard the grounding of rifle butts, some unintelligible orders, marching steps proceeding down the street. Inch by inch they emerged again.

'Some of them are still there. But I think it's all right.'

A picket of Guards squatted round a machine-gun on the pavement opposite.

'I'm going down to find something to drink.'

They rolled back the stone from the trap-door and descended into the silent hotel. The sightseers had left their bedrooms. There was no one about on either floor.

'I wonder where they keep the Evian.'

They went into the bar. Alcohol everywhere, but no water. In a corner of the kitchen they found a dozen or so bottles bearing the labels of various mineral waters–Evian, St Galmiet, Vichy, Malvern–all empty. It was Mr Youkoumian's practice to replenish them, when required, from the foetid well at the back of the house.

'I must get something to drink or I shall die. I'm going out.'

'*Mildred.*'

'I don't care, I am.'

She strode through the twilit vestibule into the street. the officer in charge of the machine-gun section waved her back. She walked on, making pacific gestures. He spoke to her rapidly and loudly, first in Sakuyu, then in Arabic. Dame Mildred replied in English and French.

'*Taisez-vous, officer. Je désire de l'eau. Où peut-on trouver ça, s'il vous plait.*'

The soldier showed her the hotel, then the machine-gun.

'British subject. Me. British subject. No savvy? Oh, don't any of you speak a word of English?'

The soldiers grinned and nodded, pointing her back to the hotel.

'It's no good. They won't let us out. We must wait.'

'Mildred, I'm going to drink wine.'

'Well, let's take it up to the roof–it seems the only safe place.'

Armed with a bottle of Mr Youkoumian's Koniak they strode back up the ladder.

'Oh dear, it's very strong.'

'I think it may help my headache.'

The afternoon wore on. The burning sun dipped towards the edge of the mountains. The ladies sipped raw brandy on the iron roof.

At length there was a fresh movement in the street. An officer on mule-back galloped up, shouting an order to the picket. They dismantled their machine-gun, hoisted it on to their shoulders, fell in, and marched away towards the

Palace. Other patrols tramped past the hotel. From their eminence they could see bodies of troops converging from all sides on the Palace square.

'They're calling in the guard. It must be all right now. But I feel too sleepy to move.'

Presently, as the soldiers withdrew, little bodies of civilians emerged from hiding. A marauding band of Christians swung confidently into view.

'I believe they're coming here.'

Splintering of glass and drunken, boastful laughter came from the bar below. Another party broke in the shutters of the drapers opposite and decked themselves with lengths of bright stuff. But oblivious of the excursions below them, worn out by the heat and anxiety of the day, and slightly drugged by Mr Youkoumian's spirit, the two ladies slept.

It was after seven when they awoke. The sun had set and there was a sharp chill in the air. Miss Tin shivered and sneezed.

'My head's splitting. I'm very hungry again,' she said, 'and thirstier than ever.'

The windows were all dark. Blackness encircled them save for a line of light which streamed across the street from the door of the bar and a dull red glow along the roof-tops of the South quarter, in which the Indian and Armenian merchants had their warehouses.

'That can't be sunset at this time. Sarah, I believe the town is on fire.'

'*What* are we to do? We can't stay here all night.'

A sound of tipsy singing rose from below and a small knot of Azanians came into sight, swaying together with arms across each other's shoulders; two or three of them carried torches and lanterns. A party sallied out from the bar below; there was a confused scuffling. One of the lamps was dropped in a burst of yellow flame. The tussle broke up, leaving a little pool of burning oil in the centre of the road.

'We can't possibly go down.'

Two hours dragged by; the red glow behind the rooftops died, revived and died again; once there was a short outbreak of firing some distance away. The beleaguered ladies sat and shuddered in the darkness. Then the lights of a car appeared and stopped outside the hotel. A few topers emerged from the bar and clustered round it. There were some words spoken in Sakuyu and then a clear English drawl rose to them.

'Well, the old girls don't seem to be here. These chaps say they haven't seen anyone.'

And another answered: 'I dare say they've been raped.'

'I hope so. Let's try the Mission.'

'Stop,' shrieked Dame Mildred. 'Hi! Stop.'

The motor-car door clicked to; the engine started up.

'Stop,' cried Miss Tin. 'We're up here.'

Then, in a moment of inspiration, untaught in the Girl Guides, Dame Mildred threw down the half-empty bottle of brandy. William's head popped out of the car window and shouted a few words of easily acquired abuse in Sakuyu; then a pillow followed the bottle on to the roadway.

'I believe there's someone up there. Be an angel and go and see, Percy. I'll stick in here if there's going to be any bottle-throwing.'

The second secretary advanced with caution and had reached only the foot of the stairs when the two ladies greeted him.

'Thank God you've come,' said Miss Tin.

'Well,' he said, a little confused by this sudden cordiality; 'jolly nice of you to put it like that. All I mean is, we just dropped in to see that you were all right. Minister said we'd better. Not scared or anything, I mean.'

'*All right?* We've had the most terrible day of our lives.'

'Oh I say, not as bad as that, I hope. We heard at the Legation that there'd been some kind of a disturbance. Well, you'll be right as rain now, you know. Everything pretty quiet except for a few drunks. If there's anything we can do, just let us know.'

'Young man, do you intend leaving us here all night?'

'Well . . . I suppose it sounds inhospitable, but there's nothing else for it. Full up at the Legation, you know. The Bishop arrived unexpectedly and two or three of the commercial fellows took fright and came over for some reason. Jolly awkward . . . You see how it is, don't you?'

'Do you realize that the town is on fire?'

'Yes, rare old blaze. We passed quite near it. It looks awfully jolly from the Legation.'

'Young man, Miss Tin and myself are coming with you now.'

'Oh, look here, I say, you know . . .'

'Sarah, get in the car. I will bring down a few things for the night.'

The discussion had brought them to the street. William and Anstruther exchanged glances of despair. Sir Samson's instructions had been: 'Just see that those tiresome old women are safe, but on no account bring them back here. The place is a bear garden already.' (This with a scowl towards the Bishop who was very quietly playing Peggity with Prudence in a corner of the drawing-room.)

Dame Mildred, putting little trust in Miss Tin's ability to restrain the diplomats from starting without her, took few pains with the packing. In less than a minute she was down again with an armful of night clothes and washing materials. At last, with a squeeze and a grunt, she sank into the back seat.

'Tell me,' asked William with some admiration, as he turned the car round. 'Do you always throw bottles at people when you want a lift?'

7

Sir Samson Courteney arose next morning in a mood of high displeasure, which became the more intense as with every minute of his leisurely toilet he recalled in detail the atrocious disorders of the preceding evening.

'Never known anything like it,' he reflected on the way to the bathroom. 'These wretched people don't seem to realize that a Legation is a place of business. How can I be expected to get through the day's work, with my whole house over-run with uninvited guests?'

First there had been the Bishop, who arrived during tea with two breathless curates and an absurd story about another revolution and shooting in the streets. Well, why not? You couldn't expect the calm of *Barchester Towers* in a place like Azania. Missionary work was known to involve some physical work. Nincompoops. Sir Samson lashed the bath water in his contempt and vexation. Then, when they were half-way through dinner, who should turn up but the Bank Manager and a scrubby little chap named Jagger. Never heard of him. More wild talk about murder, loot and fire. Dinner started all over again, with the result that the duck was ruined. And then the most damnable treachery of all: his wife of all people, infected with the general panic, had begun to ask about Dame Mildred and Miss Tin. Had they gone down to the coast when the other English people left? Should not something be done about them? The Minister poohpoohed the suggestion for some time, but at length so far yielded to popular appeal as to allow William and Percy to take the car and go out, just to see that the old women had come to no harm. That was the explicit limit of their instructions. And what did they do but bring *them* along too? Here, in fact, was the entire English population of Debra Dowa taking refuge under his roof. 'They'll have to clear out today,' decided the Minister as he lathered his chin, 'every man jack of them. It's an intolerable imposition.'

Accommodation in the compound had eventually been found for all the newcomers. The Bishop slept in the Legation, the curates with the Anstruthers, who, in the most sporting manner, moved the children into their own room for the night, Dame Mildred and Miss Tin at the Legges and the Bank Manager and Mr Jagger alone in the bungalow vacated by the Walshes. By the time Sir Samson came down to breakfast, however, they were all together again, chattering uproariously on the croquet lawn.

'. . . my back quite sore . . . not really accustomed to riding.' 'Poor Mr Raith.' 'The Church party started it. The priests had been haranguing them for days against birth-control. The police learned that an attempt would be made to break up the procession so they arrested the Patriarch just before it was due to start . . .' 'Troops cleared the streets . . . fired over their heads . . . no damage done . . .' '. . . a bullet within a few inches, literally *inches* of my head . . .' 'Seth went back to the Palace as soon as it was clear the procession couldn't take place. My word, he looked angry . . .' 'Young Seal with him . . .' '. . . it wasn't so bad when the beast was going uphill. It was that terrible *sliding* feeling . . .' 'Poor Mr Raith . . .' 'Then the patrols were all withdrawn and concentrated in front of the Palace. Jagger and I were quite close and saw the whole thing. They had the whole army drawn up in the square and gradually when they realized the shooting was over the crowd began to come back, little knots of sixes and sevens creeping out from the side alleys and then creeping in round the soldiers. This was about half-past five . . .' '. . . and not having proper breeches my knees got so *rubbed* . . .' 'Poor Mr Raith . . .' 'Everyone thought Seth was going to appear. The royal box was still there, shoddy sort of affair, but it provided a platform. Everyone kept looking in that direction. Suddenly who should climb up but the Patriarch, who had been released from prison by the rioters, and after him Connolly and old Ngumo and one or two others of the notables. Well, the crowd cheered like mad for the Patriarch and Ngumo and the soldiers cheered for Connolly and started firing off their rifles again into the air and for a quarter of an hour the place was in an uproar . . .' '. . . and two bruises on the lower part of my shin where the stirrups came . . .' 'Poor Mr Raith . . .' 'Then came the big surprise of the day. The Patriarch made a speech, don't suppose half the people heard it. Announced that Seth had abdicated and that Achon, Amurath's son who's supposed to have been dead for fifty years, was still alive and would be crowned Emperor today. The fellows near started cheering and the others took it up–they didn't know why–and soon they had a regular party going. Meanwhile the Christians had been making hay in the Indian and Jewish quarters, breaking up the shops and setting half the place on fire. That's when Jagger and I made our get-away . . .' '. . . very stiff and chafed . . .' '. . . poor, poor Mr Raith.'

'All talking shop as usual,' said Sir Samson, as these voices floated in to him through the dining-room windows. 'And eating me out of house and home,' he added sourly as he noted that there was a shortage of kedgeree that morning.

'But what about Basil Seal?' Prudence asked.

'He went off with Seth, I believe,' said the Bank Manager, 'wherever that may be.'

Lady Courteney appeared among her guests, wearing gum-boots and pushing a barrow and spade. Emperors might come and go, but there was heavy digging to be done in the lily-pond.

'Good morning,' she said. 'I do hope you all slept well after your adventures and found enough breakfast. I'm afraid this is a very topsy-turvy house party. Prudence, child, I want you to help with the mud-puddle this morning. Mr Raith, I'm sure you're tired after your ride. Take an easy morning like a sensible man. The Bishop will show you the best parts of the garden. Take some deck chairs. You'll find them in the porch. Dame Mildred and Miss Tin, *how* are you both? I hope my maid found you all you needed. Do please all make yourselves at home. Mr Jagger, perhaps you play croquet.'

The Envoy Extraordinary finished his second cup of coffee, filled and lit his pipe, and, avoiding the social life of the lawn, pottered round by the back way to the Chancery. Here at least there survived an atmosphere of normal tranquillity. Anstruther, Legge and William were playing cut-throat bridge.

'Sorry to disturb you fellows. I just wanted to know whether any of you knew anything about this revolution.'

'Not much, I'm afraid. Care to take a hand, sir?'

'No, thanks very much. I think I'll have a talk with the Bishop about his Cathedral. Save writing that letter. Dare say everything'll be all right now that Seth's left–I suppose I shall have to write a report of this business. No one will read it. But one of you might pop down into town sometimes and see exactly what's happened, will you?'

'That's going to be a bore,' said William, as the Minister left them. 'God, what a mean dummy.'

An hour later he visited them again.

'I say, I've just got a letter asking me to this coronation. I suppose someone from here ought to go? It means putting on uniform and mine's got so infernally tight. William, be a good fellow and represent me, will you?'

The Nestorian Cathedral, like the whole of the city, was of quite recent construction, but its darkness and stuffiness endowed it with an air of some antiquity. It was an octagonal, domed building, consisting of a concentric ambulatory round an inner sanctuary. The walls were painted in primitive simplicity with saints and angels, battle scenes from the Old Testament history and portraits of Amurath the Great, faintly visible in the murky light of a dozen or so branch candlesticks. Three choirs had been singing since dawn. There was an office of enormous length to be got through before the coronation Mass–psalms, prophecies, lections and many minor but prolix rites of purification. Three aged lectors recited Leviticus from manuscript rolls while a band of deacons played a low rhythm on hand drums and a silver gong. The Church party were in the ascendant at the moment and were not disposed to forgo a single liturgical luxury.

Meanwhile chairs and carpets were being arranged in the outer aisle and an awning improvised through which, after the Mass, the new Emperor was to be led to take the final vows in the presence of the populace. All roads to the Cathedral were heavily policed and the square was lined with Guardsmen. At eleven M. Ballon arrived and took his place in the seats set aside for the diplomatic corps. The Americans had all left the town, so that he was now in the position of doyen. The native nobility had already assembled. The Duke of Ukaka found a place next to the Earl of Ngumo.

'Where's Achon now?'

'Inside with the priests.'

'How is he?'

'He passed a good night. I think he finds the robes uncomfortable.'

Presently the Office ended and the Mass began, said behind closed doors by the Patriarch himself, with all the complex ritual of his church. An occasional silver tinkle from inside informed the worshippers of the progress of the ceremony, while a choir of deacons maintained a solemn chant somewhere out of sight in the gloom. M. Ballon stirred uneasily, moved by tiny, uncontrollable shudders of shocked atheism. Presently William arrived, carrying cocked hat, white gloves, very elegant in gold braid. He smiled pleasantly at M. Ballon and sat beside him.

'I say, have they started?'

M. Ballon nodded but did not reply.

A long time passed and the diplomat shifted from buttock to buttock in his gilt chair. It was no longer a matter of anti-clericalism but of acute physical discomfort.

William twiddled his gloves and dropped his hat and gaped miserably at the frescoed ceiling. Once, absent-mindedly, he took out his cigarette-case, tapped a cigarette on the toe of his shoe and was about to light when he caught a glance from M. Ballon which caused him hastily to return it to his pocket.

But eventually an end came. The doors of the inner sanctuary were thrown open; the trumpeters on the Cathedral steps sounded a fanfare; the band in the square recognized their signal and struck up the Azanian Anthem. The procession emerged into the open. First came the choir of deacons, the priests, Bishops and the Patriarch. Then a canopy of brocade supported on poles at each corner by the four premier peers of the Empire. Under it shuffled the new Monarch in the robes of state. It was not clear from his manner that he understood the nature of the proceedings. He wriggled his shoulders irritably under the unaccustomed burden of silk and jewellery, scratched his ribs and kept feeling disconsolately towards his right foot and shaking it sideways as he walked, worried at missing his familiar chain. Some drops of the holy oil with which he had been recently anointed trickled over the bridge of his nose and, drop by drop, down his white beard. Now and then he faltered and halted in his pace and was only moved on by a respectful dig in the ribs from one of his attendant peers. M. Ballon, William and the native nobility fell in behind him, and with slow steps proceeded to the dais for the final ceremonies.

A great shout rose from the concourse as the Imperial party mounted the steps and Achon was led to the throne prepared for him. Here, one by one, he was invested with the royal regalia. First, holding the sword of state, the Patriarch addressed him:

'Achon, I give you this sword of the Empire of Azania. Do you swear to fight in the cause of Justice and Faith for the protection of your people and the glory of your race?'

The Emperor grunted and the ornate weapon was laid across his lap and one of his listless hands placed upon its hilt while cannonades of applause rose from his assembled subjects.

Then the gold spur.

'Achon, I give you this spur. Do you swear to ride in the cause of Justice and Faith for the protection of your people and the glory of your race?'

The Emperor gave a low whimper and turned away his face; the Earl of Ngumo buckled the spur about the foot that had so lately borne a graver weight. Huzzas and halloing in the crowded square.

Finally the crown.

'Achon, I give you this crown. Do you swear to use it in the cause of Justice and Faith for the protection of your people and the glory of your race?'

The Emperor remained silent and the Patriarch advanced towards him with the massive gold tiara of Amurath the Great. With great gentleness he placed it over the wrinkled brow and straggle of white hairs; but Achon's head lolled forward under its weight and the bauble was pitched back into the Patriarch's hands.

Nobles and prelates clustered about the old man and then dismay spread among them and a babble of scared undertones. The people, seeing that something was amiss, broke off short in their cheering and huddled forward towards the dais.

'Tcha!' exclaimed M. Ballon. 'This is something infinitely vexatious. It was not to be foreseen.'

For Achon was dead.

'Well,' said Sir Samson, when, rather late for luncheon, William brought back news of the coronation, 'I can't for the life of me see how they think they're any better off. They'll have to get Seth back now, I suppose, and we've all been disturbed for nothing. It'll look infernally silly when we send in a report of this to the F.O. Not sure we hadn't better keep quiet about the whole business.'

'By the way,' said William, 'I heard something else in the town. The bridge is down at Lumo, so there'll be no more trains to the coast for weeks.'

'One thing after another.'

They were all there, cramped at the elbows, round the dining-room table. Bishop and curates, Bank Manager and Mr Jagger, Dame Mildred and Miss Tin, and they all began asking William questions about the state of the town. Was the fire completely put out? Was there looting in the shops? Did the life of the place seem to be going on normally? Were there troops patrolling the streets? Where was Seth? Where was Seal? Where was Boaz?

'I don't think it at all fair to tease William,' said Prudence, 'particularly when he looks so nice in his uniform.'

'But if, as you say, this bridge is demolished,' demanded Dame Mildred, 'how can one get to Matodi?'

'There isn't any other way, unless you like to ride down on a camel with one of the caravans.'

'D'you mean to say we must stay here until the bridge is rebuilt?'

'Not here,' interposed Sir Samson involuntarily, 'not here.'

'I think the whole thing is *scandalous*,' said Miss Tin.

At last, before coffee was served, the Minister left the table.

'Got to get back to work,' he said cheerfully, 'and I shall be at it all the afternoon, so I'd better say good-bye now. I expect you'll all be gone before I get through with it.'

And he left in the dining-room seven silent guests whose faces were eloquent of consternation. Later they assembled furtively in a corner of the garden to discuss their circumstances.

'I must admit,' said the Bishop, 'that it seems to me unreasonable and inconsiderate of the Minister to expect us to return to the town until we have more reassuring information about the conditions.'

'As British subjects we have the right to be protected by our flag,' said Dame Mildred, 'and I for one intend to stay here whether Sir Samson likes it or not.'

'That's right,' said Mr Jagger.

And after further mutual reassurances, the Bishop was sent to inform their host of their decision to remain. He found him peacefully dozing in a hammock under the mango trees.

'You put me in a very difficult position,' he said when the situation had been explained to him. 'I wish that nothing of the sort had occurred at all. I am sure you would all be much more comfortable and equally safe in the town, but since you wish to remain, pray consider yourselves my guests for as long as it takes to relieve your apprehensions,' and feeling that affairs had got completely outside his control, the Envoy relapsed into sleep.

Later that afternoon, when Lady Courteney had contrived to find occupation for all her guests, some at the bagatelle board, others with Peggity, photograph albums, cards or croquet, the party suffered a further and far from welcome addition; a dusty figure in native costume who propped a rifle against the fireplace before coming forward to shake her hand.

'Oh dear, oh dear,' she said, 'have *you* come to stay with us too?'

'Only for tonight,' said Basil. 'I've got to be off first thing tomorrow. Where can I put up my camels?'

'Good gracious, I don't think we've ever had such a thing here before. Have you more than one?'

'Ten. I'm passing as a Sakuyu merchant. They're outside with the boys. I dare say they'll find a place for them. They're vicious beasts though. D'you think I could have some whisky?'

'Yes, no doubt the butler can find you some, and would you like William to lend you some clothes?'

'No, I'll stay in these, thanks. Got to get used to moving about in them. It's the only way I can hope to get through. They had two shots at bumping me off yesterday.'

The company forsook their pastimes and crowded round the newcomer.

'How are things in the city?'

'As bad as they can be. The army feel they've been sold a pup and won't leave barracks. Connolly's gone off with most of his staff to try and find Seth. The Patriarch's in hiding somewhere in the town. Ngumo's men have had a big dust-up with the police and are pretty well on top at the moment. They've got into the liquor saloons which Connolly closed yesterday. As soon as it's dark they'll start looting again.'

'*There*,' said Dame Mildred, 'and the Minister expected us to leave today.'

'Oh, I shouldn't count on being too safe here. There's a gang breaking up the American Legation now. Ballon's ordered an aeroplane from the mainland. I expect you'll get a raid tonight or tomorrow. Your sowars don't look up to much serious work.'

'And where are you going?'

'After Seth and Boaz. We've a rendezvous five days' ride out of town at a farm of Boaz's on the edge of the Wanda country. There's just a chance of getting the boy back if he plays his cards properly. But there's bound to be serious fighting, whatever happens.'

Shivers of half-pleasant alarm went through his listeners.

'Mr Seal,' Lady Courteney benignly interposed at last. 'I think it's very mischievous of you saying all this. I'm sure that things are not nearly as bad as you make out. You're just *talking*. Now go and get yourself some whisky and talk to Prudence, and I think you might put that dirty gun outside in the lobby.'

'Oh, Basil, what *is* going to happen? I can't bear your going off like this and everything being so messy.'

'Don't you worry, Prudence, everything'll be all right. We'll meet again, I promise you.'

'But you said it was dangerous.'

'I was just piling it on to scare the old women.'

'Basil, I don't believe you were.'

'I should think they'll take you off by air from Khormaksar. You've got Walsh down at Matodi. He's a sound-enough fellow. As soon as he learns what's happened he'll get through to Aden and arrange everything. You'll be all right, just you see.'

'But it's you I'm worring about.'

'Don't you do that, Prudence. It's one of the things there's no sense in at all. People are always doing it and it doesn't get them anywhere.'

'Anyway, you look lovely in those clothes.'

Basil talked a great deal at dinner; the same large party was assembled, but he kept them all silent with tales of Sakuyu savagery, partly invented, partly remembered from the days of Connolly's confidence. '. . . shaved all the hair off her head and covered it with butter. White ants ate straight through into her skull . . . You still find blind old Europeans working with the slaves on some of the farms in the interior; they're prisoners of war that were conveniently forgotten about when peace was made . . . the Arab word for Sakuyu means Man-without-mercy . . . when they get drink in them they go completely insane. They can stay like that for days at a time, utterly unconscious of fatigue. They'd think nothing of the road out here if they thought they'd find alcohol when they got here. May I have another glass of whisky? . . .'

When the men were left together at the table, the Minister said, 'My boy, I don't know how much truth there is in all you've been saying, but I think you might not have talked like that before the ladies. If there *is* any danger, and I for one don't for a moment believe there is, the ladies should be kept in ignorance of the fact.'

'Oh, I like to see them scared,' said Basil. 'Pass the decanter, will you, Jagger, and now, sir, what arrangements are we making for defence?'

'Arrangements for defence?'

'Yes, of course you can't possibly have everyone separated in the different bungalows. They could all have their throats cut one at a time and none of us any the wiser. The compound is far too big to form a defensible unit. You'd better get everyone up here, arrange for shifts of guard and put a picket of your sowars with horses half a mile down the road to the town to bring the alarm if a raiding party comes into sight. You run in and talk to the women. I'll arrange it all for you.'

And the Envoy Extraordinary could find nothing to say. The day had been too much for him. Everyone was stark crazy and damned bad-mannered too. They could do what they liked. He was going to smoke a cigar, alone, in his study.

Basil took command. In half an hour the Legges and the Anstruthers, bearing children wrapped in blankets and their meagre supply of firearms, arrived in the drawing-room.

'I suppose that this is necessary,' said Lady Courteney, 'but I'm afraid that you'll none of you be at all comfortable.'

An attempt to deceive the children that nothing unusual was afoot proved unsuccessful; it was not long before they were found in a corner of the hall enacting with tremendous gusto the death agonies of the Italian lady whose scalp was eaten by termites.

'The gentleman in the funny clothes told us,' the explained. 'Coo, mummy, it must have hurt.'

The grown-ups moved restlessy about.

'Anything we can do to help?'

'Yes, count the cartridges out into equal piles . . . it might be a good thing to prepare some bandages too . . . Legge, the hinges of this shutter aren't too good. See if you can find a screwdriver.'

It was about ten o'clock when it was discovered that the native servants, who had been massed in the Legation kitchens from the surrounding households, had silently taken their leave. Only Basil's camel boys remained in possession. They had compounded for themselves a vast stew of incongruous elements and were sodden with eating.

'Other boys going home. No want cutting off heads. They much no good boys. We like it fine living here.'

News of the desertion made havoc among the nerves in the drawing-room. Sir Samson merely voiced the feelings of all his guests when, turning petulantly from the table, he remarked: 'It's no good. My heart is *not* in halma this evening.'

But the night passed and no assault was made. The men of the party watched, three hours on, three hours off, at the various vulnerable points. Each slept with a weapon beside him, revolver, rook rifle, shot-gun or meat chopper. Continuous low chattering in the rooms upstairs, rustle of dressing-gowns, patter of slippers and frequent shrill cries from the youngest Anstruther child in nightmare, told that the ladies were sleeping little. At dawn they assembled again with pale faces and strained eyes. Lady Courteney's English maid and the Goanese butler went to the kitchen and, circumventing with difficulty the recumbent camel boys, made hot coffee. Spirits rose a little; they abandoned the undertones which had become habitual during the last ten hours and spoke in normal voices; they began to yawn. Basil said, 'One night over. Of course your real danger will come when supplies begin running short in the town.'

That discouraged them from any genuine cheerfulness.

They went out on to the lawn. Smoke lay low over the town.

'Something still burning.'

Presently Anstruther said, 'I say, though, look over there. Aren't those clouds?'

'It's a week early for the rains.'

'Still, you never know.'

'That's rain all right,' said Basil. 'I was counting on it today or tomorrow. They got it last week in Kenya. It'll delay the repairs on the Lumo bridge pretty considerably.'

'Then I must get those bulbs in this morning,' said Lady Courteney. 'It'll be a relief to have something sensible to do after tearing up sheets for bandages and sewing sand-bags. You might have told me before, Mr Seal.'

'If I were you,' said Basil, 'I should start checking your stores and making out a scheme of rations. I should think my boys must have eaten a good week's provisions last night.'

The party split up and attempted to occupy themselves in useful jobs about the house; soon, however, there came a sound which brought them out helter-skelter, all together again, chattering on the lawn; the drone of an approaching aeroplane.

'That'll be Ballon,' said Basil, 'making his get-away.'

But as the machine came into sight it became clear that it was making for the Legation; it flew low, circling over the compound and driving the ponies to frenzy in their stables. They could see the pilot's head looking at them over the side. A weighted flag fluttered from it to the ground, then the machine mounted again and soared off in the direction of the coast. The Anstruther children ran, crowing with delight, to retrieve the message from the rose garden and bring it to the Minister. It was a brief pencil note, signed by the squadron-leader at Aden. *Am bringing two troop carriers, three bombers. Be prepared to evacuate whole British population from Legation in one hour from receiving this. Can carry official archives and bare personal necessities only.*

'That's Walsh's doing. Clever chap, always said so. But I say, though, what a rush.'

For the next hour the Legation was in a ferment as a growing pile of luggage assembled on the lawn.

'*Official archives*, indeed. There may be some papers about somewhere, William. See if any of them seem at all interesting.'

'We'll have to put the ponies out to grass and hope for the best.'

'Lock all doors and take the keys away. Not that it's likely to make any difference.'

'Envoy, you can't bring *all* the pictures.'

'How about passports?'

The visitors from the town, having nothing to pack, did what they could to help the others.

'I've never been up before. I'm told it often makes people unwell.'

'Poor Mr Raith.'

Basil, suddenly reduced to unimportance, stood by and watched the preparations, a solitary figure in his white Sakuyu robes leaning over his rifle like a sentinel.

Prudence joined him and they walked together to the edge of the compound, out of sight behind some rhododendrons. She was wearing a red beret jauntily on one side of her head.

'Basil, give up this absurd Emperor, darling, and come with us.'

'Can't do that.'

'*Please.*'

'No, Prudence, everything's going to be all right. Don't you worry. We'll meet again somewhere.'

Rain clouds on the horizon grew and spread across the bright sky.

'It seems so much *more* going away when it's in an aeroplane, if you see what I mean.'

'I see what you mean.'

'*Prudence, Prudence*,' from Lady Courteney beyond the rhododendrons. 'You really can't take so many boxes.'

In Basil's arms Prudence said, 'But the clothes smell odd.'

'I got them second-hand from a Sakuyu. He'd just stolen an evening suit from an Indian.'

'*Prudence.*'

'All right, mum, *coming* . . . sweet Basil, I can't really bear it.'

And she ran back to help eliminate her less serviceable hats.

Quite soon, before anyone was ready for them, the five aeroplanes came into sight, roaring over the hills in strictly maintained formation. They landed and came to rest in the compound. Air Force officers trotted forward and saluted, treating Sir Samson with a respect which somewhat surprised his household.

'We ought to start as soon as we can, sir. There's a storm coming up.'

With very little confusion the party embarked. The Indian troopers and the Goan butler in one troop carrier, the children, clergy and senior members in the other. Mr Jagger, William and Prudence took their places in the cockpits of the three bombers. Just as they were about to start, Prudence remembered something and clambered down. She raced back to the Legation, a swift, gay figure under her red beret, and returned panting with a loose sheaf of papers.

'Nearly left the *Panorama of Life* behind,' she explained.

The engines started up with immense din; the machines taxied forward and took off, mounted steadily, circled about in a neat arrow-head, dwindled and disappeared. Silence fell on the compound. It had all taken less than twenty minutes.

Basil turned back alone to look for his camels.

Prudence crouched in the cockpit, clutching her beret to her head. The air shrieked past her ears while the landscape rolled away below in a leisurely fashion; the straggling city, half shrouded in smoke, disappeared behind them; open pasture dotted with cattle and little clusters of huts; presently the green lowlands and jungle country. She knew without particular regret that she was leaving Debra Dowa for good.

'Anyway,' she reflected, 'I ought to get some new ideas for the *Panorama*,' and already she seemed to be emerging into the new life which her mother had planned for her, and spoken of not long ago seated on Prudence's bed as she came to wish her good night. Aunt Harriet's house in Belgrave Place; girls, luncheons, dances and young men, week-ends in country houses, tennis and hunting; all the easy circumstances of English life which she had read about often but never experienced. She would resume the acquaintance of friends she had known at school, 'and shan't I be able to show off to them? They'll all seem so young and innocent . . .' English cold and fog and rain, grey twilight among isolated, bare trees and dripping coverts; London streets when the shops were closing and the pavements crowded with people going to Tube stations with evening papers; empty streets, late at night after dances, revealing unsuspected slopes, sluiced by men in almost mediaeval overalls . . . an English girl returning to claim her natural heritage . . .

The aeroplane dipped suddenly, recalling her to the affairs of the moment. The pilot shouted back to her something which was lost on the wind. They were the extremity of one of the arms of the V. A goggled face from the machine in front looked back and down at them as they dropped below him, but her pilot signalled him on. Green undergrowth swam up towards them; the machine tilted a little and circled about, looking for a place to land.

'Hold tight and don't worry,' was borne back to her on the wind. An open space appeared among the trees and bush. They circled again and dropped precisely into place, lurched for a moment as though about to overturn, righted themselves and stopped dead within a few feet of danger.

'Wizard show that,' remarked the pilot.

'Has anything awful happened?'

'Nothing to worry about. Engine trouble. I can put it right in two shakes. Stay where you are. We'll catch them up before they reach Aden.'

Rain broke late that afternoon with torrential tropic force. The smouldering warehouses of the city sizzled and steamed and the fire ended in thin black mud. Great pools collected in the streets; water eddied in the gutters, clogging the few drains with its burden of refuse. The tin roofs rang with the falling drops. Sodden rioters waded down the lanes to shelter; troops left their posts and returned to barracks huddled under cover in a stench of wet cloth. The surviving decorations from the pageant of birth control clung limply round the posts or, grown suddenly too heavy, snapped their strings and splashed into the mud below. Darkness descended upon a subdued city.

For six confused days Basil floundered on towards the lowlands. For nine hours out of the twenty-four the rain fell regularly and unremittingly so that it usurped the sun's place as the measure of time and the caravan drove on through the darkness, striving hopelessly to recover the hours wasted under cover during the daylight.

On their second day's journey Basil's boys brought a runner to him, who was carrying a sodden letter in the end of a cleft staff.

'A great chief will not suffer his messengers to be robbed.'

'There is a time,' said Basil, 'when all things must be suffered.'

They took the message. It read:

> From Viscount Boaz, Minister of the Interior of the Azanian Empire, to the Earl of Ngumo, Greeting. May this reach you. Peace be upon your house. Salute, in my name and in the name of my family, Achon whom some style Emperor of Azania, Chief of the Chiefs of Sakuyu, Lord of Wanda and Tyrant of the Seas. May his days be many and his progeny uncounted. I, Boaz, no mean man in the Empire, am now at Gulu on the Wanda marches; with me is Seth whom some style Emperor. I tell you this so that Achon may know me for what I am, a loyal subject of the crown. I fear for Seth's health and await word from your Lordship as to how best he may be relieved of what troubles him. Boaz.

'Go on in front of us,' Basil ordered the man, 'and tell Lord Boaz that Achon is dead.'

'How can I return to my Lord, having lost the letter he gave me? Is my life a small thing?'

'Go back to your Lord. Your life is a small thing beside the life of the Emperor.'

Later two beasts lost their footing in the bed of a swollen water-course and were washed down and tumbled among the boulders; during the third night march five of the hindermost deserted their leaders. The boys mutinied, first for more money; later they refused every inducement to proceed. For two days Basil rode on alone, swaying and slipping towards his rendezvous.

Confusion dominated the soggy lanes of Matodi. Major Walsh, the French secretaries and Mr Schonbaum daily dispatched conflicting messages by wireless and cable. First that Seth was dead and that Achon was Emperor, then that Achon was dead and Seth was Emperor.

'Doubtless Mme Ballon could tell us where General Connolly is to be found.'

'Alas, M. Jean, she will not speak.'

'Do you suspect she knows more?'

'M. Ballon's wife should be above suspicion.'

The officials and soldiers loafed in the dry intervals about barracks and offices; they had no instructions and no money; no news from the capital. Destroyers of four nations lurked in the bay standing by to defend their nationals. The town governor made secret preparations for an early escape to the mainland. Mr Youkoumian, behind the bar at the Amurath Hotel, nervously decocted his fierce spirits.

'There ain't no sense in 'aving bust-ups. 'Ere we are, no Emperor, no railway, and those low niggers making 'ell with my property at Debra Dowa. And just you see, in less than no time the civilized nations will start a bombardment. *Gosh.*'

In the dingy calm of the Arab club the six senior members munched their khat in peace and spoke gravely of a very old error of litigation.

Amidst mud and liquid ash at Debra Dowa a leaderless people abandoned their normal avocations and squatted at home, occupying themselves with domestic bickerings; some of the rural immigrants drifted back to their villages, others found temporary accommodation in the saloons of the deserted palace, expecting something to happen.

Among the dry clinkers of Aden, Sir Samson and Lady Courteney waited for news of the missing aeroplane. They were staying at the Residency, where everything was done that hospitality and tact could do to relieve the strain of their anxiety; newspaper agents and sympathetic compatriots were kept from them. Dame Mildred and Miss Tin were shipped to Southampton by the first P. & O. Mr Jagger made preparations to leave a settlement he had little reason to like. Sir Samson and Lady Courteney walked alone on the cliff paths, waiting for news. Air patrols crossed to Azania, flying low over the impenetrable country where Prudence's machine was last observed, returned to refuel, set out again and at the end of the week had seen nothing to report. The military authorities discussed and despaired of the practicability of landing a search party.

In the dry spell between noon and sunset, Basil reached Seth's encampment at Gulu. His men had taken possession of a small village. A dozen or so of them, in ragged uniforms, sat on their haunches in the clearing, silently polishing their teeth with pieces of stick.

His camel lurched down on to its knees and Basil dismounted. None of the Guardsmen rose to salute him; no sign of greeting from inside the mud huts. The squatting men looked into the steaming forest beyond him.

He asked: 'Where is the Emperor?' But no one answered.

'Where is Boaz?'

'In the great house. He is resting.'

They indicated the headman's hut which stood on the far side of the compound, distinguished from the others by its superior size and a narrow verandah, floored with beaten mud and shaded by thatch.

'Why is the Emperor not in the great house?'

They did not answer. Instead, they scoured their teeth and gazed abstractedly into the forest, where a few monkeys swung in the steaming air, shaking the water from bough to bough.

Basil crossed through them to the headman's hut. It was windowless and for a short time his eyes could distinguish nothing in the gloom. Only his ears were aware of a heavily breathing figure somewhere not far distant in the dark interior. Then he gradually descried a jumble of household furniture, camp equipment and the remains of a meal; and Boaz asleep. The great dandy lay on his back in a heap of rugs and sacking; his head pitched forward into his blue-black curly beard. There was a rifle across his middle. He wore a pair of mud-splashed riding breeches, too tight to button to the top, which Basil recognized as the Emperor's. A Wanda girl sat at his head. She explained: 'The Lord has been asleep for some time. For the last days it has been like this. He wakes only to drink from the square bottle. Then he is asleep again.'

'Bring me word when he wakes.'

Basil approached the oafish fellows in the clearing.

'Show me a house where I can sleep.'

They pointed one out to him without rising to accompany him to its door. Water still dripped through its leaky thatch, there was a large puddle of thin mud made during the rain. Basil lay down on the dry side and waited for Boaz to wake.

They called him an hour after sunset. The men had lit a fire, but only a small one, because they knew that at midnight the rain would begin again and dowse it. There was a light in the headman's hut–a fine brass lamp with wick and chimney. Boaz had put out two glasses and two bottles of whisky. Basil's first words were, 'Where is Seth?'

'He is not here. He has gone away.'

'Where?'

'How shall I know? Look, I have filled your glass.'

'I sent a messenger to him, with the news that Achon was dead.'

'Seth had already gone when the messenger came.'

'And where is the messenger?'

'He brought bad tidings. He is dead. Turn the light higher. It is bad to sit in the dark.'

He gulped down a glass of spirit and refilled his glass. They sat in silence.

Presently Boaz said, 'Seth is dead.'

'I knew. How?'

'The sickness of the jungle. His legs and his arms swelled. He turned up his eyes and died. I have seen others die in just that way.'

Later he said, 'So now there is no Emperor. It is a pity that your messenger did not come a day sooner. I hanged him because he was late.'

'Boaz, the sickness of the jungle does not wait on good or bad news.'

'That is true. Seth died in another way. By his own hand. With a gun raised to his mouth and his great toe crooked round the trigger. That is how Seth died.'

'It is not what I should have expected.'

'Men die that way. I have heard of it often. His body lies outside. The men will not bury it. They say it must be taken down to Moshu to the Wanda people to be burned in their own fashion. Seth was their chief.'

'We will do that tomorrow.'

Outside round the fire, inevitably, they had started singing. The drums pulsed. In the sodden depths of the forest the wild beasts hunted, shunning the light.

'I will go and see Seth's body.'

'The women are sewing him up. They made a bag for him out of pieces of skin. It is the custom when the chief dies. They put grain in with him and several spices. Only the women know what. If they can get it they put in a lion's paw, I have been told.'

'We will go and look at him.'

'It is not the custom of the people.'

'I will carry the lamp.'

'You must not leave me in the dark. I will come with you.'

Past the camp fire and the singing Guardsmen to another hut: here by the light of a little lamp four or five women were at work stitching. Seth's body lay on the floor half covered by a blanket. Boaz leant tipsily in the doorway while Basil went forward, lamp in hand. The eldest of the women tried to bar his entrance, but he pushed her aside and approached the dead Emperor.

His head lay inclined to one side, the lips agape, the eyes open and dull. He wore his Guards tunic, buttoned tight at the throat, the epaulettes awry and bedraggled. There was no wound visible. Basil drew the blanket higher and rejoined the Minister.

'The Emperor did not shoot himself.'

'No.'

'There is no wound to be seen.'

'Did I say he was shot? That is a mistake. He took poison. That is how it happened . . . it has happened before in that way to other great men. It was a draught given him by a wise man in these parts. When he despaired he took some of it . . . a large cupful and drank it . . . there in the hut. I was with him. He made a wry face and said that the draught was bitter. Then he stood still a little until his knees gave. On the floor he rolled up and down several times. He could not breathe. Then his legs shot straight out and he arched his back. That is how he lay until yesterday when the body became limp again. That was how he died . . . The messenger was late in coming.'

They left the women to their work. Boaz stumbled several times as he returned to the headman's hut and his bottle of whisky. Basil left him with the lamp and returned in the firelit night to his hut.

A man was waiting for him in the shadows. 'Boaz is still drunk.'

'Yes. Who are you?'

'Major Joab of the Imperial Infantry, at your service.'

'Well, major?'

'It has been like this since the Emperor's death.'

'Boaz?'

'Yes.'

'Did you see the Emperor die?'

'I am a soldier. It is not for me to meddle with high politics. I am a soldier without a master.'

'There is duty due to a master, even when he is dead.'

'Do I understand you?'

'Tomorrow we take down the body of Seth to be burned at Moshu among his people. He should rejoin the great Amurath and the spirits of his fathers like a king and a fine man. Can he meet them unashamed if his servants forget their duty while his body is still with them?'

'I understand you.'

After midnight the rain fell. The men round the fire carried a burning brand into one of the huts and lit a fire there. Great drops sizzled and spat among the deserted embers; they changed from yellow to red and then to black.

Heavy patter of rain on the thatched roofs, quickening to an even blurr of sound.

A piercing, womanish cry, that mounted, soared shivering, quavered and merged in the splash and gurgle of the water.

'Major Joab of the Imperial Infantry at your service. Boaz is dead.'

'Peace be on your house.'

Next day they carried the body of the Emperor to Moshu. Basil rode at the head of the procession. The others followed on foot. The body, sewn in skins, was strapped to a pole and carried on the shoulders of two Guardsmen. Twice during the journey they slipped and their burden fell in the soft mud of the jungle path. Basil sent on a runner to the Chief, saying: 'Assemble your people, kill your best meat and prepare a feast in the manner of your people. I am bringing a great chief among you.'

But the news preceded him and tribesmen came out to greet them on the way and conduct them with music to Moshu. The wise men of the surrounding villages danced in the mud in front of Basil's camel, wearing livery of the highest solemnity, leopards' feet and snake-skins, necklets of lions' teeth, shrivelled bodies of toads and bats, and towering masks of painted leather and wood. The women daubed their hair with ochre and clay in the fashion of the people.

Moshu was a royal city; the chief market and government centre of the Wanda country. It was ditched round and enclosed by high ramparts. Arab slavers had settled there a century ago and built streets of two-storied, lightless houses; square, with flat roofs on rubble walls washed over with lime and red earth. Among them stood circular Wanda huts of mud and thatched grass. A permanent artisan population lived there, blacksmiths, jewellers, leather workers, ministering to the needs of the scattered jungle people. There were several merchants in a good way of business with barns storing grain, oil, spices and salt, and a few Indians trading in hardware and coloured cottons, products of the looms of Europe and Japan.

A pyre had been heaped up, of dry logs and straw, six foot high, in the market-place. A large crowd was already assembled there and in another quarter a communal kitchen had been improvised where great cook-pots rested over crackling sticks. Earthenware jars of fermented coconut sap stood ready to be broached when the proper moment arrived.

The feast began late in the afternoon. Basil and Joab sat among the chiefs and headmen. The wise men danced round the pyre, shaking their strings of charms and amulets, wagging their tufted rumps and uttering cries of ecstasy. They carried little knives and cut themselves as they capered round. Meanwhile Seth's body was bundled on to the faggots and a tin of oil sluiced over it.

'It is usual for the highest man present to speak some praise of the dead.'

Basil nodded and in the circle of fuzzy heads rose to declaim Seth's funeral oration. It was no more candid than most royal obituaries. It was what was required. 'Chiefs and tribesmen of the Wanda,' he said, speaking with confident fluency in the Wanda tongue, of which he had acquired a fair knowledge during his stay in Azania. 'Peace be among you. I bring the body of the Great Chief, who has gone to rejoin Amurath and the spirits of his glorious ancestors. It is right for us to remember Seth. He was a great Emperor and all the peoples of the world vied with each other to do him homage. In his own island, among the people of Sakuyu and the Arabs, across the great waters to the mainland, far beyond in the cold lands of the North, Seth's name was a name of terror. Seyid rose against him and is no more. Achon also. They are gone before him to prepare suitable lodging among the fields of his ancestors. Thousands fell by his right hand. The words of his mouth were like thunder in the hills. Weep, women of Azania, for your royal lover is torn from your arms.

His virility was inexhaustible, his progeny numerous beyond human computation. His staff was a grown palm tree. Weep, warriors of Azania. When he led you to battle there was no retreating. In council the most guileful, in justice the most terrible, Seth the magnificent is dead.'

The bards caught phrases from the lament and sang them. The wise men ran whooping among the spectators carrying torches. Soon the pyre was enveloped in towering flames. The people took up the song and swayed on their haunches, chanting. The bundle on the crest bubbled and spluttered like fresh pine until the skin cerements burst open and revealed briefly in the heart of the furnace the incandescent corpse of the Emperor. Then there was a subsidence among the timbers and it disappeared from view.

Soon after sunset the flames declined and it was necessary to refuel them. Many of the tribesmen had joined the dance of the witches. With hands on each other's hips they made a chain round the pyre, shuffling their feet and heaving their shoulders, spasmodically throwing back their heads and baying like wild beasts.

The chiefs gave the sign for the feast to begin.

The company split up into groups, each round a cookpot. Basil and Joab sat with the chiefs. They ate flat bread and meat, stewed to pulp among peppers and aromatic roots. Each dipped into the pot in rotation, plunging with his hands for the best scraps. A bowl of toddy circulated from lap to lap and great drops of sweat broke out on the brows of the mourners.

Dancing was resumed, faster this time and more clearly oblivious of fatigue. In emulation of the witch doctors, the tribesmen began slashing themselves on chest and arms with their hunting knives; blood and sweat mingled in shining rivulets over their dark skins. Now and then one of them would pitch forward on to his face and lie panting or roll stiff in a nervous seizure. Women joined in the dance, making another chain, circling in the reverse way to the men. They were dazed with drink, stamping themselves into ecstasy. The two chains jostled and combined. They shuffled together interlocked.

Basil drew back a little from the heat of the fire, his senses dazed by the crude spirit and the insistence of the music. In the shadows, in the extremities of the market-place, black figures sprawled and grunted, alone and in couples. Near him an elderly woman stamped and shuffled; suddenly she threw up her arms and fell to the ground in ecstasy. The hand-drums throbbed and pulsed; the flames leapt and showered the night with sparks.

The headman of Moshu sat where they had dined, nursing the bowl of toddy. He wore an Azanian white robe, splashed with gravy and spirit. His scalp was closely shaven; he nodded down to the lip of the bowl and drank. Then he clumsily offered it to Basil. Basil refused; he gaped and offered it again. Then took another draught himself. Then he nodded again and drew something from his bosom and put it on his head. 'Look,' he said. 'Pretty.'

It was a beret of pillar-box red. Through the stupor that was slowly mounting and encompassing his mind Basil recognized it. Prudence had worn it jauntily on the side of her head, running across the Legation lawn with the *Panorama of Life* under her arm. He shook the old fellow roughly by the shoulder.

'Where did you get that?'

'Pretty.'

'Where did you get it?'

'Pretty hat. It came in the great bird. The white woman wore it. On her head like this.' He giggled weakly and pulled it askew over his glistening pate.

'But the white woman. Where is she?'

But the headman was lapsing into coma. He said 'Pretty' again and turned up sightless eyes.

Basil shook him violently. 'Speak, you old fool. Where is the white woman?'

The headman grunted and stirred; then a flicker of consciousness revived in him. He raised his head. 'The white woman? Why, here,' he patted his distended paunch. 'You and I and the big chiefs–we have just eaten her.'

Then he fell forward into a sound sleep.

Round and round circled the dancers, ochre and blood and sweat glistening in the firelight; the wise men's headgear swayed high above them, leopards' feet and snake skins, amulets and necklaces, lion's teeth and the shrivelled bodies of bats and toads, jigging and spinning. Tireless hands drumming out the rhythm; glistening backs heaving and shivering in the shadows.

Later, a little after midnight, it began to rain.

8

When the telephone bell rang Alastair said: 'You answer it. I don't think I can stand up,' so Sonia crossed to the window where it stood and said: 'Yes, who is it? . . . *Basil* . . . well, who'd have thought of that? Where *can* you be?'

'I'm at Barbara's. I thought of coming round to see you and Alastair.'

'Darling, do . . . how did you know where we lived?'

'It was in the telephone book. Is it nice?'

'Lousy. You'll see when you come. Alastair thought it would be cheaper, but it isn't really. You'll never find the door. It's painted red and it's next to a pretty shady sort of chemist.'

'I'll be along.'

Ten minutes later he was there. Sonia opened the door. 'We haven't any servants. We got very poor suddenly. How long have you been back?'

'Landed last night. What's been happening?'

'Almost nothing. Everyone's got very poor and it makes them duller. It's more than a year since we saw you. How are things at Barbara's?'

'Well, Freddy doesn't know I'm here yet. That's why I'm dining out. Barbara's going to tell him gently. I gather my mamma is sore with me about something. How's Angela?'

'Just the same. She's the only one who doesn't seem to have lost money. Margot's shut up her house and is spending the winter in America. There was a general election and a crisis–something about gold standard.'

'I know. It's amusing to be back.'

'We've missed you. As I say, people have gone serious lately, while you've just been loafing about the tropics. Alastair found something about Azania in the papers once. I forget what. Some revolution and a minister's daughter who disappeared. I suppose you were in on all that.'

'Yes.'

'Can't think what you see in revolutions. They said there was going to be one here, only nothing came of it. I suppose you ran the whole country.'

'As a matter of fact, I did.'

'And fell madly in love.'

'Yes.'

'And intrigued and had a court official's throat cut.'

'Yes.'

'And went to a cannibal banquet. Darling, I just don't want to hear about it, d'you mind? I'm sure it's all very fine and grand, but it doesn't make much sense to a stay-at-home like me.'

'That's the way to deal with him,' said Alastair from his armchair. 'Keep a stopper on the far-flung stuff.'

'Or write a book about it, sweety. Then we can buy it and leave it about where you'll see and then you'll think we know . . . What are you going to do now you're back?'

'No plans. I think I've had enough of barbarism for a bit. I might stay in London or Berlin or somewhere like that.'

'That'll be nice. Make it London. We'll have some parties like the old ones.'

'D'you know, I'm not sure I shouldn't find them a bit flat after the real thing. I went to a party at a place called Moshu . . .'

'*Basil*. Once and for all, we don't want to hear travel experiences. Do try and remember.'

So they played Happy Families till ten, when Alastair said, 'Have we had dinner?' and Sonia said, 'No, let's.' Then they went out to a new cocktail club which Alastair had heard was cheap, and had lager beer and liver sandwiches; they proved to be very expensive.

Later Basil went round to see Angela Lyne, and Sonia as she undressed said to Alastair, 'D'you know, deep down in my heart I've got a tiny fear that Basil is going to turn serious on us too!'

Evening in Matodi. Two Arab gentlemen, hand in hand, sauntered by the sea-wall.

Among the dhows and nondescript craft in the harbour lay two smart launches manned by British and French sailors, for Azania had lately been mandated by the League of Nations as a joint protectorate.

'They are always at work polishing the brass.'

'It must be very expensive. And they are building a new customs house.'

'And a police station and a fever hospital, a European club.'

'There are many new bungalows on the hills.'

'They are making a big field to play games in.'

'Every week they wash the streets with water. They take the children in the schools and scratch their arms to rub in poison. It makes them very ill.'

'They put a man in prison for overburdening his camel.'

'There is a Frenchman in charge at the post office. He is always hot and in a great hurry.'

'They are building a black road through the hills to Debra Dowa. The railway is to be removed.'

'Mr Youkoumian has bought the rails and what was left of the engines. He hopes to sell them in Eritrea.'

'Things were better in the time of Seth. It is no longer a gentleman's country.'

The muezzin in the tower turned north towards Mekka and called azan over the city. The Arabs paused reverently and stood in silence . . . God is great . . . There is no God but God . . . Mohammed is the apostle of God . . .

A two-seater car whizzed by, driven by Mr Reppington, the district magistrate. Mrs Reppington sat beside him.

'The little bus took that nicely.'

Angelus from the mission church . . . *gratia plena; dominus tecum; Benedicta tu in mulieribus* . . .

The car left town and mounted towards the hills.

'Phew. It's a relief to get out into the fresh air.'

'Awful road. It ought to be finished by now. I get quite afraid for her back axle.'

'I said we'd drop into the Brethertons for a sundowner.'

'Right you are. Only we can't stay long. We're dining with the Lepperidges.'

A mile above the town they stopped at the second of six identical bungalows. Each had a verandah and a garden path; a slotted box on the gate-post for calling cards. The Brethertons were on the verandah.

'Cheerio, Mrs Reppington. Cocktail?'

'Please.'

'And you, Reppington?'

'Chota peg.'

Bretherton was sanitary inspector and consequently of slightly inferior station to Reppington, but that year he would sit for his Arabic exam.; if he brought it off it would make them level on the salary list.

'What sort of day?'

'Oh, the usual. Just tooled round condemning native houses. How are things at the Fort?'

'Not so dusty. We settled that case I told you about. You know, the one of the natives who built a house in a broken lorry in the middle of the road.'

'Oh, ah. Who won it?'

'Oh, we gave it to the chap in possession on both counts. The Arab who originally owned the car was suing him. So were the Works Department–wanted to evict him because he blocked the traffic. They'll have to make a new road round him now. They're pretty fed up, I can tell you. So are the Frenchies.'

'Good show.'

'Yes, give the natives respect for British justice. Can't make your Frenchy see that . . . Why, it's later than I thought. We must be pushing along, old girl. You're not dining with the Lepperidges by any chance?'

'No.'

The Brethertons were not on dining terms with the Lepperidges. He was O.C. of the native levy, seconded from India and a very considerable man in Matodi. He always referred to Bretherton as the 'latrine wallah'.

So the Reppingtons went to dress in their bungalow (fifth of the row), she in black lace, he in white mess-jacket. Punctually at 8.15 they stepped across to the Lepperidges'. There were five courses at dinner, mostly from tins, and a glass dish in the centre of the table held floating flower heads. Mr and Mrs Grainger were there; Mr Grainger was immigration officer. He said: 'We've had rather a shari this afternoon about that fellow Connolly. You see, strictly speaking, he can claim Azanian nationality. He seems to have been quite a big bug under the Emperor. Ran the army for him. Got made a Duke or something. Last sort of fellow one wants hanging about.'

'Quite.'

'Jungly Wallah. They say in the old days he had an affair with the wife of the French Minister. That made the Frenchies anxious to get rid of him.'

'Quite. It helps if one can oblige them now and then in small things.'

'Besides, you know, he's married to a wog. Well, I mean to say . . .'

'Quite.'

'But I think we're going to get rid of him all right. Deport him D.B.S. He lost all his money in the revolution.'

'And the woman in the case?'

'Well, that's no business of ours once we clear him out of here. They seem struck on each other all right. He'll find it pretty awkward. Aren't many places would have him. Abyssinia might. It was different when this place was independent.'

'Quite.'

'Jolly good tinned fruit salad, if you don't mind my saying so, Mrs Lepperidge.'

'So glad you like it. I got it from Youkoumian's.'

'Useful little fellow Youkoumian. I use him a lot. He's getting me boots for the levy. Came to me himself with the idea. Said they pick up hookworm through going barefoot.'

'Good show.'

'Quite.'

Night over Matodi. English and French police patrolling the water-front. Gilbert and Sullivan played by gramophone in the Portuguese Fort.

Three little maids from school are we,
Pert as a schoolgirl well can be,
Filled to the brim with girlish glee–
Three little maids from school.

The melody and the clear voices floated out over the harbour and the water lapping very gently on the sea-wall. Two British policemen marched abreast through the involved ways of the native quarter. The dogs had long ago been rounded up and painlessly put away. The streets were empty save for an occasional muffled figure slipping by them silently with a lantern. The blank walls of the Arab tenements gave no sign of life.

On a tree by a river a little tom tit
Sang Willow, tit-willow, tit-willow.
And I said to him 'Dicky bird, why do you sit
Singing Willow, tit-willow, tit-willow?'

Mr Youkoumian tactfully ejected his last customer and fastened the shutters of the café. 'Very sorry,' he said. 'New regulation. No drinking after ten-thirty. I don't want no bust-ups.'

'Is it weakness of intellect, birdie?' I cried,
'Or a rather tough worm in your little inside?'
With a shake of his poor little head, he replied,
'Oh willow, tit-willow, tit-willow.'

The song rang clear over the dark city and the soft, barely perceptible lapping of the water along the sea-wall.

A Handful of Dust

EVELYN WAUGH

A HANDFUL OF DUST

'. . . I will show you something different from either
Your shadow at morning striding behind you
Or your shadow at evening rising to meet you;
I will show you fear in a handful of dust.'

I

DU CÔTÉ DE CHEZ BEAVER

'Was anyone hurt?'

'No one, I am thankful to say,' said Mrs Beaver, 'except two housemaids who lost their heads and jumped through a glass roof into the paved court. They were in no danger. The fire never reached the bedrooms, I am afraid. Still, they are bound to need doing up, everything black with smoke and drenched in water, and luckily they had that old-fashioned sort of extinguisher that ruins *everything*. One really cannot complain. The chief rooms were *completely* gutted and everything was insured. Sylvia Newport knows the people. I must get on to them this morning before that ghoul Mrs Shutter snaps them up.'

Mrs Beaver stood with her back to the fire, eating her morning yoghourt. She held the carton close under her chin and gobbled with a spoon.

'Heavens, how nasty this stuff is. I wish you'd take to it, John. You're looking so tired lately. I don't know how I should get through my day without it.'

'But, mumsy, I haven't as much to do as you have.'

'That's true, my son.'

John Beaver lived with his mother at the house in Sussex Gardens where they had moved after his father's death. There was little in it to suggest the austerely elegant interiors which Mrs Beaver planned for her customers. It was crowded with the unsaleable furniture of two larger houses, without pretension to any period, least of all to the present. The best pieces and those which had sentimental interest for Mrs Beaver were in the L-shaped drawing room upstairs.

Beaver had a dark little sitting room (on the ground floor, behind the dining room) and his own telephone. The elderly parlourmaid looked after his clothes. She also dusted, polished and maintained in symmetrical order on his dressing table and on the top of his chest of drawers the collection of sombre and bulky objects that had stood in his father's dressing room: indestructible presents for his wedding and twenty-first birthday, ivory, brass bound, covered in pigskin, crested and gold mounted, suggestive of expensive Edwardian masculinity–racing flasks and hunting flasks, cigar cases, tobacco jars, jockeys, elaborate meerschaum pipes, button hooks and hat brushes.

There were four servants, all female and all, save one, elderly.

When anyone asked Beaver why he stayed there instead of setting up on his own, he sometimes said that he thought his mother liked having him there (in spite of her business she was lonely); sometimes that it saved him at least five pounds a week.

His total income varied around six pounds a week, so this was an important saving.

He was twenty-five years old. From leaving Oxford until the beginning of the slump he had worked in an advertising agency. Since then no one had been able to find anything for him to do. So he got up late and sat near his telephone most of the day, hoping to be rung up.

Whenever it was possible, Mrs Beaver took an hour off in the middle of the morning. She was always at her shop punctually at nine, and by half past eleven she needed a break. Then, if no important customer was imminent, she would get into her two-seater and drive home to Sussex Gardens. Beaver was usually dressed by then and she had grown to value their morning interchange of gossip.

'What was your evening?'

'Audrey rang up at eight and asked me to dinner. Ten of us at the Embassy, rather dreary. Afterwards we all went on to a party given by a woman called de Trommet.'

'I know who you mean. American. She hasn't paid for the toile-de-Jouy chaircovers we made her last April. I had a dull time too; didn't hold a card all the evening and came away four pounds ten to the bad.'

'Poor mumsy.'

'I'm lunching at Viola Chasm's. What are you doing? I didn't order anything here, I'm afraid.'

'Nothing so far. I can always go round to Brat's.'

'But that's so expensive. I'm sure if we ask Chambers she'll be able to get you something in. I thought you were certain to be out.'

'Well, I still may be. It isn't twelve yet.'

(Most of Beaver's invitations came to him at the last moment; occasionally even later, when he had already begun to eat a solitary meal from a tray . . . 'John, darling, there's been a muddle and Sonia has arrived without Reggie. Could you be an angel and help me out? Only be quick, because we're going in now' . . . Then he would go headlong for a taxi and arrive, with apologies, after the first course . . . One of his few recent quarrels with his mother had occurred when he left a luncheon party of hers in this way.)

'Where are you going for the week-end?'

'Hetton.'

'Who's that? I forget.'

'Tony Last.'

'Yes, of course. She's lovely, he's rather a stick. I didn't know you knew them.'

'Well, I don't really. Tony asked me in Brat's the other night. He may have forgotten.'

'Send a telegram and remind them. It is far better than ringing up. It gives them less chance to make excuses. Send it tomorrow just before you start. They owe me for a table.'

'What's their dossier?'

'I used to see her quite a lot before she married. She was Brenda Rex, Lord St Cloud's daughter, very fair, underwater look. People used to be mad about her when she was a girl. Everyone thought she would marry Jock Grant-Menzies at one time. Wasted on Tony Last, he's a prig. I should say it was time she began to be bored. They've been married five or six years. Quite well off but everything goes in keeping up the house. I've never seen it but I've an idea it's huge and quite hideous. They've got one child at least, perhaps more.'

'Mumsy, you are wonderful. I believe you know about everyone.'

'It's a great help. All a matter of paying attention while people are talking.'

Mrs Beaver smoked a cigarette and then drove back to her shop. An American woman bought two patchwork quilts at thirty guineas each, Lady Metroland telephoned about a bathroom ceiling, an unknown young man paid cash for a cushion; in the intervals between these events, Mrs Beaver was able to descend to the basement where two dispirited girls were packing lampshades. It was cold down there in spite of a little oil stove, and the walls were always damp. The girls were becoming quite deft, she noticed with pleasure, particularly the shorter one who was handling the crates like a man.

'That's the way,' she said, 'you are doing very nicely, Joyce. I'll soon get you on to something more interesting.'

'Thank you, Mrs Beaver.'

They had better stay in the packing department for a bit, Mrs Beaver decided; as long as they would stand it. They had neither of them enough chic to work upstairs. Both had paid good premiums to learn Mrs Beaver's art.

Beaver sat on beside his telephone. Once it rang and a voice said, 'Mr Beaver? Will you please hold the line, sir, Mrs Tipping would like to speak to you.'

The intervening silence was full of pleasant expectation. Mrs Tipping had a luncheon party that day, he knew; they had spent some time together the evening before and he had been particularly successful with her. Someone had chucked . . .

'Oh, Mr Beaver, I *am* so sorry to trouble you. I was wondering, could you *possibly* tell me the name of the young man you introduced to me last night at Madam de Trommet's? The one with the reddish moustache. I think he was in Parliament.'

'I expect you mean Jock Grant-Menzies.'

'Yes, that's the name. You don't by any chance know where I can find him, do you?'

'He's in the book, but I don't suppose he'll be at home now. You might be able to get him at Brat's at about one. He's almost always there.'

'Jock Grant-Menzies, Brat's Club. Thank you so *very* much. It *is* kind of you. I hope you will come and see me some day. *Good*-bye.'

After that the telephone was silent.

At one o'clock Beaver despaired. He put on his overcoat, his gloves, his bowler hat and with neatly rolled umbrella set off to his club, taking a penny bus as far as the corner of Bond Street.

The air of antiquity pervading Brat's, derived from its elegant Georgian façade, and finely panelled rooms, was entirely spurious, for it was a club of recent origin, founded in the burst of bonhomie immediately after the war. It was intended for young men, to be a place where they could straddle across the fire and be jolly in the card room without incurring scowls from older members. But now these founders were themselves passing into middle age; they were heavier, balder and redder in the face than when they had been demobilized, but their joviality persisted and it was their turn now to embarrass their successors, deploring their lack of manly and gentlemanly qualities.

Six broad backs shut Beaver from the bar. He settled in one of the armchairs in the outer room and turned over the pages of the *New Yorker*, waiting until someone he knew should turn up.

Jock Grant-Menzies came upstairs. The men at the bar greeted him, saying, 'Hullo, Jock old boy, what are you drinking?' or, more simply, 'Well, old boy?' He was too young to have fought in the war but these men thought he was all right; they liked him far more than they did Beaver, who, they thought, ought never to have got into the club at all. But Jock stopped to talk to Beaver. 'Well, old boy?' he said. 'What are you drinking?'

'Nothing so far.' Beaver looked at his watch. 'But I think it's time I had one. Brandy and ginger ale.'

Jock called to the barman and then said:

'Who was the old girl you wished on me at that party last night?'

'She's called Mrs Tipping.'

'I thought she might be. That explains it. They gave me a message downstairs that someone with a name like that wanted me to lunch with her.'

'Are you going?'

'No, I'm no good at lunch parties. Besides I decided when I got up that I'd have oysters here.'

The barman came with the drinks.

'Mr Beaver, sir, there's ten shillings against you in my books for last month.'

'Ah, thank you, Macdougal, remind me sometime, will you?'

'Very good, sir.'

Beaver said, 'I'm going to Hetton tomorrow.'

'Are you now? Give Tony and Brenda my love.'

'What's the form?'

'Very quiet and enjoyable.'

'No paper games?'

'Oh no, nothing like that. A certain amount of bridge and backgammon and low poker with the neighbours.'

'Comfortable?'

'Not bad. Plenty to drink. Rather a shortage of bathrooms. You can stay in bed all the morning.'

'I've never met Brenda.'

'You'll like her, she's a grand girl. I often think Tony Last's one of the happiest men I know. He's got just enough money, loves the place, one son he's crazy about, devoted wife, not a worry in the world.'

'Most enviable. You don't know anyone else who's going, do you? I was wondering if I could get a lift down there.'

'I don't, I'm afraid. It's quite easy by train.'

'Yes, but it's more pleasant by road.'

'And cheaper.'

'Yes, and cheaper, I suppose . . . well, I'm going down to lunch. You won't have another?'

Beaver rose to go.

'Yes, I think I will.'

'Oh, all right, Macdougal. Two more, please.'

Macdougal said, 'Shall I book them to you, sir?'

'Yes, if you will.'

Later, at the bar, Jock said, 'I made Beaver pay for a drink.'

'He can't have liked that.'

'He nearly died of it. Know anything about pigs?'

'No. Why?'

'Only that they keep writing to me about them from my constituency.'

Beaver went downstairs but before going into the dining room he told the porter to ring up his home and see if there was any message for him.

'Mrs Tipping rang up a few minutes ago and asked whether you could come to luncheon with her today.'

'Will you ring her up and say that I shall be delighted to, but that I may be a few minutes late?'

It was just after half past one when he left Brat's and walked at a good pace towards Hill Street.

2

ENGLISH GOTHIC–I

I

Between the villages of Hetton and Compton Last lies the extensive park of Hetton Abbey. This, formerly one of the notable houses of the county, was entirely rebuilt in 1864 in the Gothic style and is now devoid of interest. The grounds are open to the public daily until sunset and the house may be viewed on application by writing. It contains some good portraits and furniture. The terrace commands a fine view.

This passage from the county Guide Book did not cause Tony Last any serious annoyance. Unkinder things had been said. His aunt Frances, embittered by an upbringing of unremitting severity, remarked that the plans of the house must have been adapted by Mr Pecksniff from one of his pupils' designs for an orphanage. But there was not a glazed brick or encaustic tile that was not dear to Tony's heart. In some ways, he knew, it was not convenient to run, but what big house was? It was not altogether amenable to modern ideas of comfort; he had many small improvements in mind, which would be put into effect as soon as the death duties were paid off. But the general aspect and atmosphere of the place; the line of its battlements against the sky; the central clock tower where quarterly chimes disturbed all but the heaviest sleepers; the ecclesiastical gloom of the great hall, its ceiling groined and painted in diapers of red and gold, supported on shafts of polished granite with vine-wreathed capitals, half-lit by day through lancet windows of armorial stained glass, at night by a vast gasolier of brass and wrought iron, wired now and fitted with twenty electric bulbs; the blasts of hot air that rose suddenly at one's feet, through grills of cast-iron trefoils from the antiquated heating apparatus below; the cavernous chill of the more remote corridors where, economizing in coke, he had had the pipes shut off; the dining hall with its hammer-beam roof and pitch-pine minstrels' gallery; the bedrooms with their brass bedsteads, each with a frieze of Gothic text, each named from Malory, Yseult, Elaine, Mordred and Merlin, Gawaine and Bedivere, Lancelot, Perceval Tristram, Galahad, his own dressing room, Morgan le Fay, and Brenda's Guinevere, where the bed stood on a dais, the walls hung with tapestry, the fireplace like a tomb of the thirteenth century, from whose bay window one could count, on days of exceptional clearness, the spires of six churches–all these things with which he had grown up were a source of constant delight and exultation to Tony: things of tender memory and proud possession.

They were not in the fashion, he fully realized. Twenty years ago people had liked half timber and old pewter; now it was urns and colonnades; but the time would come, perhaps in John Andrew's day, when opinion would reinstate Hetton in its proper place. Already it was referred to as 'amusing', and a very civil young man had asked permission to photograph it for an architectural review.

The ceiling of Morgan le Fay was not in perfect repair. In order to make an appearance of coffered wood, moulded slats had been nailed in a chequer across the plaster. They were painted in chevrons of blue and gold. The squares between were decorated alternately with Tudor roses and fleurs-de-lys. But damp had penetrated into one corner, leaving a large patch where the gilt had tarnished and the colour flaked away; in another place the wooden laths had become warped and separated from the plaster. Lying in bed, in the grave ten minutes between waking and ringing, Tony studied these defects and resolved anew to have them put right. He wondered whether it would be easy, nowadays, to find craftsmen capable of such delicate work.

Morgan le Fay had been in his room since he left the night nursery. He had been put there so that he would be within calling distance of his parents (inseparable in Guinevere), for until quite late in his life he was subject to nightmares. He had taken nothing from the room since he had slept there, but every year added to its contents, so that it now formed a gallery representative of every phase of his adolescence–the framed picture of a dreadnought (a coloured supplement from *Chums*), all its guns spouting flame and smoke; a photographic group of his private school; a cabinet called 'the Museum', filled with the fruits of a dozen desultory hobbies, eggs, butterflies, fossils, coins; his parents, in the leather diptych which had stood by his bed at school; Brenda, eight years ago when he had been trying to get engaged to her; Brenda with John, taken just after the christening; an aquatint of Hetton, as it had stood until his great-grandfather demolished it; some shelves of books, *Bevis, Woodwork at Home, Conjuring for All, The Young Visitors, The Law of Landlord and Tenant, Farewell to Arms.*

All over England people were waking up, queasy and despondent. Tony lay for ten minutes very happily planning the renovation of his ceiling. Then he rang the bell.

'Has her ladyship been called yet?'

'About quarter of an hour ago, sir.'

'Then I'll have breakfast in her room.'

He put on his dressing gown and slippers and went through into Guinevere. Brenda lay on the dais.

She had insisted on a modern bed. Her tray was beside her and the quilt was littered with envelopes, letters and the daily papers. Her head was propped against a very small blue pillow; clean of make-up, her face was almost colourless, rose-pearl, scarcely deeper in tone than her arms and neck.

'Well?' said Tony.

'Kiss.'

He sat by the tray at the head of the bed; she lent forward to him (a nereid emerging from fathomless depths of clear water). She turned her lips away and rubbed against his cheek like a cat. It was a way she had.

'Anything interesting?'

He picked up some of the letters.

'No. Mama wants nanny to send John's measurements. She's knitting him something for Christmas. And the mayor wants me to open something next month. I needn't, need I?.

'I think you'd better, we haven't done anything for him for a long time.'

'Well, you must write the speech. I'm getting too old for the girlish one I used to give them all. And Angela says, will we stay for the New Year?'

'That's easy. Not on her life, we won't.'

'I guessed not . . . though it sounds an amusing party.'

'You go if you like. I can't possibly get away.'

'That's all right. I knew it would be "no" before I opened the letter.'

'Well, what sort of pleasure can there be in going all the way to Yorkshire in the middle of winter?'

'Darling, don't be cross. I know we aren't going. I'm not making a thing about it. I just thought it might be fun to eat someone else's food for a bit.'

Then Brenda's maid brought in the other tray. He had it put by the window seat, and began opening his letters. He looked out of the window. Only four of the six church towers were visible that morning. Presently he said, 'As a matter of fact I probably *can* manage to get away that week-end.'

'Darling, are you sure you wouldn't hate it?'

'I daresay not.'

While he ate his breakfast Brenda read to him from the papers. 'Reggie's been making another speech . . . There's such an extraordinary picture of Babe and Jock . . . a woman in America has had twins by two different husbands. Would you have thought possible? . . . Two more chaps in gas ovens . . . a little girl has been strangled in a cemetery with a bootlace . . . that play we went to about a farm is coming off.' Then she read him the serial. He lit his pipe. 'I don't believe you're listening. Why doesn't Sylvia want Rupert to get the letter?'

'Eh? Oh well, you see, she doesn't really trust Rupert.'

'I *knew* it. There's no such character as Rupert in the story. I shall never read to you again.'

'Well, to tell you the truth I was just thinking.'

'Oh.'

'I was thinking how delightful it is, that it's Saturday morning and we haven't got anyone coming for the week-end.'

'Oh, you thought that?'

'Don't you?'

'Well, it sometimes seems to me rather pointless keeping up a house this size if we don't now and then ask some other people to stay in it.'

'*Pointless?* I can't think what you mean. I don't keep up this house to be a hostel for a lot of bores to come and gossip in. We've always lived here and I hope John will be able to keep it on after me. One has a duty towards one's employees, and towards the place, too. It's a definite part of English life which would be a serious loss if . . .' Then Tony stopped short in his speech and looked at the bed. Brenda had turned on her face and only the top of her head appeared above the sheets.

'Oh God,' she said into the pillow. 'What have I done?'

'I say, am I being pompous again?'

She turned sideways so that her nose and one eye emerged. 'Oh no, darling, not *pompous*. You wouldn't know how.'

'Sorry.'

Brenda sat up. 'And, please, I didn't mean it. I'm jolly glad, too, that no one's coming.'

(These scenes of domestic playfulness had been more or less continuous in Tony and Brenda's life for seven years.)

Outside, it was soft English weather; mist in the hollows and pale sunshine on the hills; the coverts had ceased dripping, for there were no leaves to hold the recent rains, but the undergrowth was wet, dark in the shadows, iridescent where the sun caught it; the lanes were soggy and there was water running in the ditches.

John Andrew sat his pony, solemn and stiff as a Life Guard, while Ben fixed the jump. Thunderclap had been a present on his sixth birthday from Uncle Reggie. It was John who had named her, after lengthy consultation. Originally she had been called Christabelle which, as Ben said, was more the name for a hound than a horse. Ben had known a strawberry roan called Thunderclap who killed two riders and won the local point-to-point four years running. He had been a lovely little horse, said Ben, till he staked himself in the guts, hunting, and had to be shot. Ben knew stories about a great many different horses. There was one called Zero on whom he had won five Jimmy-o-goblins at ten to three at Chester one year. And there was a mule he had known during the war, called Peppermint, who had died of drinking the company's rum ration. But John was not going to name his pony after a drunken mule. So in the end they had decided on Thunderclap, in spite of her imperturbable disposition.

She was a dark bay, with long tail and mane. Ben had left her legs shaggy. She cropped the grass, resisting John's attempts to keep her head up.

Before her arrival riding had been a very different thing. He had jogged round the paddock on a little Shetland pony called Bunny, with his nurse panting at the bridle. Now it was a man's business. Nanny sat at a distance, crocheting, on her camp stool; out of earshot. There had been a corresponding promotion in Ben's position. From being the hand who looked after the farm horses, he was now, perceptibly, assuming the air of a stud groom. The handkerchief round his neck gave place to a stock with fox-head pin. He was a man of varied experience in other parts of the country.

Neither Tony nor Brenda hunted but they were anxious that John should like it. Ben foresaw the time when the stables would be full and himself in authority; it would not be like Mr Last to get anyone in from outside.

Ben had got two posts bored for iron pegs, and a white-washed rail. With these he erected a two-foot jump in the middle of the field.

'Now take it quite easy. Canter up slow and when she takes off lean forward in the saddle and you'll be over like a bird. Keep her head straight at it.'

Thunderclap trotted forwards, cantered two paces, thought better of it and, just before the jump, fell into a trot again and swerved round the obstacle. John recovered his balance by dropping the reins and gripping the mane with both hands; he looked guiltily at Ben, who said, 'What d'you suppose your bloody legs are for? Here, take this and just give her a tap when you get up to it.' He handed John a switch.

Nanny sat by the gate re-reading a letter from her sister.

John took Thunderclap back and tried the jump again. This time they made straight for the rail.

Ben shouted, 'Legs!', and John kicked sturdily, losing his stirrups. Ben raised his arms as if scaring crows. Thunderclap jumped; John rose from the saddle and landed on his back in the grass.

Nanny rose in alarm, 'Oh, what's happened, Mr Hacket, is he hurt?'

'He's all right,' said Ben.

'I'm all right,' said John. 'I think she put in a short step.'

'Short step my grandmother. You just opened your bloody legs and took an arser. Keep hold on to the reins next time. You can lose a hunt that way.'

At the third attempt John got over and found himself, breathless and insecure, one stirrup swinging loose and one hand grabbing its old support in the mane, but still in the saddle.

'There, how did that feel? You just skimmed over like a swallow. Try it again?'

Twice more John and Thunderclap went over the little rail, then nanny called that it was time to go indoors for his milk. They walked the pony back to the stable. Nanny said, 'Oh dear, look at all the mud on your coat.'

Ben said, 'We'll have you riding the winner at Aintree soon.'

'Good morning, Mr Hacket.'

'Good morning, miss.'

'Goodbye, Ben, may I come and see you doing the farm horses this evening?'

'That's not for me to say. You must ask nanny. Tell you what though, the grey carthorse has got worms. Would you like to see me give him a pill?'

'Oh yes; please, nanny, may I?'

'You must ask mother. Come along now, you've had quite enough of horses for one day.'

'Can't have enough of horses,' said John, 'ever.' On the way back to the house he said, 'Can I have my milk in mummy's room?'

'That depends.'

Nanny's replies were always evasive, like that–'We'll see' or 'That's asking' or 'Those that ask no questions hear no lies'–altogether unlike Ben's decisive and pungent judgments.

'What does it depend on?'

'Lots of things.'

'Tell me one of them.'

'On your not asking a lot of silly questions.'

'Silly old tart.'

'*John!* How dare you? What do you mean?'

Delighted by the effect of this sally, John broke away from her hand and danced in front of her, saying, 'Silly old tart, silly old tart' all the way to the side entrance. When they entered the porch his nurse silently took off his leggings; he was sobered a little by her grimness.

'Go straight up to the nursery,' she said. 'I am going to speak to your mother about you.'

'Please, nanny. I don't know what it means, but I didn't mean it.'

'Go straight to the nursery.'

Brenda was doing her face.

'It's been the same ever since Ben Hacket started teaching him to ride, my lady, there's been no doing anything with him.'

Brenda spat in the eye black. 'But, nanny, what exactly did he say?'

'Oh, I couldn't repeat it, my lady.'

'Nonsense, you must tell me. Otherwise I shall be thinking it something far worse that it was.'

'It couldn't have been worse . . . he called me a silly old tart, my lady.'

Brenda choked slightly into her face towel. 'He said *that*?'

'Repeatedly. He danced in front of me all the way up the drive, *singing* it.'

'I see . . . well, you were quite right to tell me.'

'Thank you, my lady, and since we are talking about it I think I ought to say that it seems to me that Ben Hacket is making the child go ahead far too quickly with his riding. It's very dangerous. He had what might have been a serious fall this morning.'

'All right, nanny, I'll speak to Mr Last about it.'

She spoke to Tony. They both laughed about it a great deal. 'Darling,' she said, '*you* must speak to him. You're so much better at being serious than I am.'

'I should have thought it was very nice to be called a tart.' John argued, 'and anyway it's a word Ben often uses about people.'

'Well, he's got no business to.'

'I like Ben more than anyone in the world. And I should think he's cleverer, too.'

'Now you know you don't like him more than your mother.'

'Yes I do. *Far* more.'

Tony felt that the time had come to cut out the cross talk and deliver the homily he had been preparing. 'Now listen, John. It was very wrong of you to call nanny a silly old tart. First, because it was unkind to her. Think of all the things she does for you every day.'

'She's paid to.'

'Be quiet. And secondly, because you were using a word which people of your age and class do not use. Poor people use certain expressions which gentlemen do not. You are a gentleman. When you grow up all this house and lots of other things besides will belong to you. You must learn to speak like someone who is going to have these things and to be considerate to people less fortunate than you, particularly women. Do you understand?'

'Is Ben less fortunate than me?'

'That has nothing to do with it. Now you are to go upstairs and say you are sorry to nanny and promise never to use that word about anyone again.'

'All right.'

'And because you have been so naughty today you are not to ride tomorrow.'

'Tomorrow's Sunday.'

'Well, next day then.'

'But you said "tomorrow". It's isn't fair to change now.'

'John, don't argue. If you are not careful I shall send Thunderclap back to Uncle Reggie and say that I find you are not a good enough boy to keep it. You wouldn't like that, would you?'

'What would Uncle Reggie do with her? She couldn't carry him. Besides, he's usually abroad.'

'He'd give it to some other little boy. Anyway, that's got nothing to do with it. Now run off and say you're sorry to nanny.'

At the door John said, 'It's all right about riding on Monday, isn't it? You did *say* "tomorrow".'

'Yes, I suppose so.'

'Hooray. Thunderclap went very well today. We jumped a big post and rail. She refused first time but went like a bird after that.'

'Didn't you come off?'

'Yes, once. It wasn't Thunderclap's fault. I just opened my bloody legs and cut an arser.'

'How did the lecture go?' Brenda asked.

'Bad. Rotten bad.'

'The trouble is that nanny's jealous of Ben.'

'I'm not sure we shan't both be soon.'

They lunched at a small, round table in the centre of the dining hall. There seemed no way of securing an even temperature in that room; even when one side was painfully roasting in the direct blaze of the open hearth, the other was numbed by a dozen converging draughts. Brenda had tried numerous experiments with screens and a portable electric radiator, but with little success. Even today, mild elsewhere, it was bitterly cold in the dining hall.

Although they were both in good health and of unexceptional figure, Tony and Brenda were on a diet. It gave an interest to their meals and saved them from the two uncivilized extremes of which solitary diners are in danger–absorbing gluttony or an irregular régime of scrambled eggs and raw beef sandwiches. Under their present system they denied themselves the combination of protein and starch at the same meal. They had a printed catalogue telling them which foods contained protein and which starch. Most normal dishes seemed to be compact of both, so that it was fun for Tony and Brenda to choose the menu. Usually it ended by their declaring some food 'joker'.

'I'm sure it does me a great deal of good.'

'Yes, darling, and when we get tired of it we might try an alphabetical diet, having things beginning with a different letter every day. J would be hungry, nothing but jam and jellied eels . . . What are your plans for the afternoon?'

'Nothing much. Carter's coming up at five to go over a few things. I may go to Pigstanton after luncheon. I think we've got a tenant for Lowater Farm, but it's been empty some time and I ought to see how much needs doing to it.'

'I wouldn't say "no" to going in to the "movies".'

'All right. I can easily leave Lowater till Monday.'

'And we might go to Woolworth's afterwards, eh?'

What with Brenda's pretty ways and Tony's good sense, it was not surprising that their friends pointed to them as a pair who were pre-eminently successful in solving the problem of getting along well together.

The pudding, without protein, was unattractive.

Five minutes afterwards a telegram was brought in. Tony opened it and said, 'Hell'.

'Badders?'

'Something too horrible has happened. Look at this.'

Brenda read, *Arriving 3.18 so looking forward visit. Beaver.* And asked, 'What's Beaver?'

'It's a young man.'

'That sounds all right.'

'Oh no, it's not. Wait till you see him.'

'What's he coming here for? Did you ask him to stay?'

'I suppose I did in a vague kind of way. I went to Brat's one evening and he was the only chap there so we had some drinks and he said something about wanting to see the house . . .'

'I suppose you were tight.'

'Not really, but I never thought he'd hold it against me.'

'Well, it jolly well serves you right. That's what comes of going up to London on business and leaving me alone here . . . Who is he anyway?'

'Just a young man. His mother keeps that shop.'

'I used to know her. She's hell. Come to think of it we owe her some money.'

'Look here, we must put a call through and say we're ill.'

'Too late, he's in the train now, recklessly mixing starch and protein in the Great Western three and sixpenny lunch. . . . Anyway he can go into Galahad. No one who sleeps there ever comes again–the bed's agony, I believe.'

'What on earth are we going to do with him? It's too late to get anyone else.'

'You go over to Pigstanton. I'll look after him. It's easier alone. We can take him to the movies tonight, and tomorrow he can see over the house. If we're lucky he may go up by the evening train. Does he have to work on Monday morning?'

'I shouldn't know.'

Three-eighteen was far from being the most convenient time for arrival. One reached the house at about a quarter to four and if, like Beaver, one was a stranger, there was an awkward time until tea; but without Tony there to make her self-conscious, Brenda could carry these things off quite gracefully and Beaver was so seldom wholly welcome anywhere that he was not sensitive to the slight constraint of his reception.

She met him in what was still called the smoking room; it was in some ways the least gloomy place in the house. She said, 'It is nice that you were able to come. I must break it to you at once that we haven't got a party. I'm afraid you'll be terribly bored . . . Tony had to go out but he'll be in soon . . . was the train crowded? It often is on Saturdays . . . would you like to come outside? It'll be dark soon and we might get some of the sun while we can . . .' and so on. If Tony had been there it would have been difficult, for she would have caught his eye and her manner as châtelaine would have collapsed. Beaver was well used to making conversation, so they went out together through the French windows on to the terrace, down the steps, into the Dutch garden, and back round the orangery without suffering a moment's real embarrassment. She even heard herself telling Beaver that his mother was one of her oldest friends.

Tony returned in time for tea. He apologized for not being at home to greet his guest and almost immediately went out again to interview the agent in his study.

Brenda asked about London and what parties there were. Beaver was particularly knowledgeable.

'Polly Cockpurse is having one soon.'

'Yes, I know.'

'Are you coming up for it?'

'I don't expect so. We never go anywhere nowadays.'

The jokes that had been going round for six weeks were all new to Brenda; they had become polished and perfected with repetition and Beaver was able to bring them out with good effect. He told her of numerous changes of alliance among her friends.

'What's happening to Mary and Simon?'

'Oh, didn't you know? That's broken up.'

'When?'

'It began in Austria this summer . . .'

'And Billy Angmering?'

'He's having a terrific walk out with a girl called Sheila Shrub.'

'And the Helm-Hubbards?'

'That marriage isn't going too well either. . . . Daisy has started a new restaurant. It's going very well . . . and there's a new night club called the Warren . . .'

'Dear me,' Brenda said at last. 'What fun everyone seems to be having.'

After tea John Andrew was brought in and quickly usurped the conversation. 'How do you do?' he said. 'I didn't know you were coming. Daddy said he had a week-end to himself for once. Do you hunt?'

'Not for a long time.'

'Ben says it stands to reason everyone ought to hunt who can afford to, for the good of the country.'

'Perhaps I can't afford to.'

'Are you poor?'

'Please, Mr Beaver, you mustn't let him bore you.'

'Yes, very poor.'

'Poor enough to call people tarts?'

'Yes, quite poor enough.'

'How did you get poor?'

'I always have been.'

'Oh.' John lost interest in this topic. 'The grey horse at the farm has got worms.'

'How do you know?'

'Ben says so. Besides you've only got to look at his dung.'

'Oh dear,' said Brenda, 'what would nanny say if she heard you talking like that?'

'How old are you?'

'Twenty-five. How old are you?'

'What do you do?'

'Nothing much.'

'Well, if I was you, I'd do something and earn some money. Then you'd be able to hunt.'

'But I shouldn't be able to call people tarts.'

'I don't see any point in that anyway.'

(Later, in the nursery, while he was having his supper, John said, 'I think Mr Beaver's a very silly man, don't you?'

'I'm sure I don't know,' said nanny.

'I think he's the silliest man who's ever been here.'

'Comparisons are odious.'

'There just isn't anything nice about him. He's got a silly voice and a silly face, silly eyes and silly nose,' John's voice fell into a liturgical sing-song, 'silly feet and silly toes, silly head and silly clothes . . .'

'Now you eat up your supper,' said nanny.)

That evening before dinner Tony came up behind Brenda as she sat at her dressing table and made a face over her shoulder in the glass.

'I feel rather guilty about Beaver–going off and leaving you like that. You were heavenly to him.'

She said, 'Oh, it wasn't bad really. He's rather pathetic.'

Further down the passage Beaver examined his room with the care of an experienced guest. There was no reading lamp. The inkpot was dry. The fire had been lit but had gone out. The bathroom, he had already discovered, was a great distance away, up a flight of turret steps. He did not at all like the look or feel of the bed; the springs were broken in the centre and it creaked ominously when he lay down to try it. The return ticket, third class, had been eighteen shillings. Then there would be tips.

Owing to Tony's feeling of guilt they had champagne for dinner, which neither he nor Brenda particularly liked. Nor, as it happened, did Beaver, but he was glad that it was there. It was decanted into a tall jug and was carried round the little table, between the three of them as a pledge of hospitality. Afterwards they drove into Pigstanton to the Picturedrome, where there was a film Beaver had seen some months before. When they got back there was a grog tray and some sandwiches in the smoking room. They talked about the film but Beaver did not let on that he had seen it. Tony took him to the door of Galahad.

'I hope you sleep well.'

'I'm sure I shall.'

'D'you like to be called in the morning?'

'May I ring?'

'Certainly. Got everything you want?'

'Yes, thanks. Goodnight.'

'Goodnight.'

But when he got back, he said, 'You know, I feel awful about Beaver.'

'Oh, Beaver's all right,' said Brenda.

But he was far from being comfortable and as he rolled patiently about the bed in quest of a position in which it was possible to go to sleep, he reflected that, since he had no intention of coming to the house again, he would give the butler nothing and only five shillings to the footman who was looking after him. Presently he adapted himself to the rugged topography of the mattress and dozed, fitfully, until morning. But the new day began dismally with the information that all the Sunday papers had already gone to her ladyship's room.

Tony invariably wore a dark suit on Sundays and a stiff white collar. He went to church, where he sat in a large pitch-pine pew, put in by his great-grandfather at the time of rebuilding the house, furnished with very high crimson hassocks and a fireplace, complete with iron grate and a little poker which his father used to rattle when any point in the sermon excited his disapproval. Since his father's day a fire had not been laid there; Tony had it in mind to revive the practice next winter. On Christmas Day and Harvest Thanksgiving Tony read the lessons from the back of the brass eagle.

When the service was over he stood for a few minutes at the porch chatting affably with the vicar's sister and the people from the village. Then he returned home by a path across the fields which led to a side door in the walled garden; he visited the hothouses and picked himself a button-hole, stopped by the gardener's cottages for a few words (the smell of Sunday dinner rising warm and overpowering from the little doorways) and then, rather solemnly, drank a glass of sherry in the library. That was the simple, mildly ceremonious order of his Sunday morning, which had evolved more or less spontaneously from the more severe practices of his parents; he adhered to it with great satisfaction. Brenda teased him whenever she caught him posing as an upright God-fearing gentleman of the old school, and Tony saw the joke, but this did not at all diminish the pleasure he derived from his weekly routine, or his annoyance when the presence of guests suspended it.

For this reason his heart sank when, emerging from his study into the great hall at quarter to eleven, he met Beaver already dressed and prepared to be entertained; it was only a momentary vexation, however, for while he wished him good morning he noticed that his guest had an *A.B.C.* in his hands and was clearly looking out a train.

'I hope you slept all right?'

'Beautifully,' said Beaver, though his wan expression did not confirm the word.

'I'm so glad. I always sleep well here myself. I say, I don't like the look of that train guide. I hope you weren't thinking of leaving us yet?'

'Alas, I've got to get up tonight, I'm afraid.'

'Too bad. I've hardly seen you. The trains aren't very good on Sundays. The best leaves at five-forty-five and gets up about nine. It stops a lot and there's no restaurant car.'

'That'll do fine.'

'Sure you can't stay until tomorrow?'

'Quite sure.'

The church bells were ringing across the park.

'Well, I'm just off to church. I don't suppose you'd care to come.'

Beaver always did what was expected of him when he was staying away, even on a visit as unsatisfactory as the present one. 'Oh yes, I should like to very much.'

'No, really, I shouldn't if I were you. You wouldn't enjoy it. I only go because I more or less have to. You stay here. Brenda will be down directly. Ring for a drink when you feel like it.'

'Oh, all right.'

'See you later then.' Tony took his hat and stick from the lobby and let himself out. 'Now I've behaved inhospitably to that young man again,' he reflected.

The bells were clear and clamorous in the drive and Tony walked briskly towards them. Presently they ceased and gave place to a single note, warning the village that there was only five minutes to go before the organist started the first hymn.

He caught up nanny and John, also on their way to church. John was in one of his rare, confidential moods; he put his small gloved hand into Tony's and, without introduction, embarked upon a story which lasted them all the way to the church door; it dealt with the mule Peppermint who had drunk the company's rum ration, near Wipers in 1917; it was told breathlessly, as John trotted to keep pace with his father. At the end, Tony said, 'How very sad.'

'Well, *I* thought it was sad, too, but it isn't. Ben said it made him laugh fit to bust his pants.'

The bell had stopped and the organist was watching from behind his curtain for Tony's arrival. He walked ahead up the aisle, nanny and John following. In the pew he occupied one of the armchairs; they sat on the bench at his back. He leant forward for half a minute with his forehead on his hand, and, as he sat back, the organist played the first bars of the hymn, 'Enter not into judgment with Thy servant, O Lord. . . .' The service followed its course. As Tony inhaled the agreeable, slightly musty atmosphere and performed the familiar motions of sitting, standing and leaning forward, his thoughts drifted from subject to subject, among the events of the past week and his plans for the future. Occasionally some arresting phrase in the liturgy would recall him to his surroundings, but for the most part that morning he occupied himself with the question of bathrooms and lavatories, and of how more of them could best be introduced without disturbing the character of his house.

The village postmaster took round the collecting bag. Tony put in his half-crown; John and nanny their pennies.

The vicar climbed, with some effort, into the pulpit. He was an elderly man who had served in India most of his life. Tony's father had given him the living at the instance of his dentist. He had a noble and sonorous voice and was reckoned the best preacher for many miles around.

His sermons had been composed in his more active days for delivery at the garrison chapel; he had done nothing to adapt them to the changed conditions of his ministry and they mostly concluded with some reference to homes and dear ones far away. The villagers did not find this in any way surprising. Few of the things said in church seemed to have any particular reference to themselves. They enjoyed their vicar's sermons very much and they knew that when he began about their distant homes, it was time to be dusting their knees and feeling for their umbrellas.

'. . . And so as we stand here bareheaded at this solemn hour of the week,' he read, his powerful old voice swelling up for the peroration, 'let us remember our Gracious Queen Empress in whose service we are here, and pray that she may long be spared to send us at her bidding to do our duty in the uttermost parts of the earth; and let us think of our dear ones far away and the homes we have left in her name, and remember that though miles of barren continent and leagues of ocean divide us, we are never so near to them as on these Sunday mornings, united with them across dune and mountain in our loyalty to our sovereign and thanksgiving for her welfare; one with them as proud subjects of her sceptre and crown.'

('The Reverend Tendril 'e do speak uncommon 'igh of the Queen,' a gardener's wife had once remarked to Tony.)

After the choir had filed out, during the last hymn, the congregation crouched silently for a few seconds and then made for the door. There was no sign of recognition until they were outside among the graves; then there was an exchange of greetings, solicitous, cordial, garrulous.

Tony spoke to the vet's wife and Mr Partridge from the shop; then he was joined by the vicar.

'Lady Brenda is not ill, I hope?'

'No, nothing serious.' This was the invariable formula when he appeared at church without her. 'A most interesting sermon, vicar.'

'My dear boy, I'm delighted to hear you say so. It is one of my favourites. But have you never heard it before?'

'No, I assure you.'

'I haven't used it here lately. When I am asked to supply elsewhere it is the one I invariably choose. Let me see now, I always make a note of the times I use it.' The old clergyman opened the manuscript book he was carrying. It had a limp black cover and the pages were yellow with age. 'Ah yes, here we are. I preached it first in Jellalabad when the Coldstream Guards were there; then I used it in the Red Sea coming home from my fourth leave; then at Sidmouth ... Mentone ... Winchester ... to the Girl Guides at their summer rally in 1921 ... the Church Stage Guild at Leicester ... twice at Bournemouth during the winter of 1926 when poor Ada was so ill ... No, I don't seem to have used it here since 1911 when you would have been too young to enjoy it. ...'

The vicar's sister had engaged John in conversation. He was telling her the story of Peppermint: '... he'd have been all right, Ben says, if he had been able to cat the rum up, but mules can't cat, neither can horses ...'

Nanny grasped him firmly and hurried him towards home. 'How many times have I told you not to go repeating whatever Ben Hacket tells you? Miss Tendril didn't want to hear about Peppermint. And don't ever use that rude word "cat" again.'

'It only means to be sick.'

'Well, Miss Tendril isn't interested in being sick ...'

As the gathering between porch and lychgate began to disperse, Tony set off towards the gardens. There was a good choice of buttonholes in the hothouses; he picked lemon carnations with crinkled, crimson edges for himself and Beaver and a camellia for his wife.

Shafts of November sunshine streamed down from lancet and oriel, tinctured in green and gold, gules and azure by the emblazoned coats, broken by the leaded devices into countless points and patches of coloured light.

Brenda descended the great staircase step by step through alternations of dusk and rainbow. Both hands were occupied, holding to her breast a bag, a small hat, a half-finished panel of petit-point embroidery and a vast, disordered sheaf of Sunday newspapers, above which only her eyes and forehead appeared as though over a yashmak. Beaver emerged from the shadows below and stood at the foot of the stairs looking up at her.

'I say, can't I carry something?'

'No thanks, I've got everything safe. How did you sleep?'

'Beautifully.'

'I bet you didn't.'

'Well, I'm not a very good sleeper.'

'Next time you come you shall have a different room. But I daresay you won't ever come again. People so seldom do. It is very sad because it's such fun for us having them and we never make any new friends living down here.'

'Tony's gone to church.'

'Yes, he likes that. He'll be back soon. Let's go out for a minute or two, it looks lovely.'

When Tony came back they were sitting in the library. Beaver was telling Brenda's fortune with cards. '. . . Now cut to me again,' he was saying, 'and I'll see if it's any clearer. . . . Oh yes . . . there is going to be a sudden death which will cause you great pleasure and profit. In fact you are going to kill someone. I can't tell if it's a man or a woman . . . yes, a woman . . . then you are going to go on a long journey across the sea, marry six dark men and have eleven children, grow a beard and die.'

'Beast. And all this time I've been thinking it was serious. Hullo, Tony, jolly church?'

'Most enjoyable; how about some sherry?'

When they were alone together, just before luncheon, he said, 'Darling, you're being heroic with Beaver.'

'Oh, I quite enjoy coping–in fact I'm bitching him rather.'

'So I saw. Well, I'll look after him this afternoon and he's going this evening.'

'Is he? I'll be quite sorry. You know that's a difference between us, that when someone's awful you just run away and hide, while I actually enjoy it–making up to them and showing off to myself how well I can do it. Besides, Beaver isn't so bad. He's quite like us in some ways.'

'He's not like me,' said Tony.

After luncheon Tony said, 'Well, if it would really amuse you, we might go over the house. I know it isn't fashionable to like this sort of architecture now–my Aunt Frances says it is an authentic Pecksniff–but I think it's good of its kind.'

It took them two hours. Beaver was well practised in the art of being shown over houses; he had been brought up to it in fact, ever since he had begun to accompany his mother, whose hobby it had always been, and later, with changing circumstances, profession. He made apt and appreciative comments and greatly enhanced the pleasure Tony always took in exposing his treasures.

They saw it all: the shuttered drawing-room, like a school speech-hall, the cloistral passages, the dark inner courtyard, the chapel where, until Tony's succession, family prayers had been daily read to the assembled household, the plate room and estate office, the bedrooms and attics, the water-tank concealed among the battlements. They climbed the spiral staircase into the works of the clock and waited to see it strike half-past three. Thence they descended with ringing ears to the collections–enamel, ivories, seals, snuff boxes, china, ormolu, cloisonné; they paused before each picture in the oak gallery and discussed its associations; they took out the more remarkable folios in the library and examined prints of the original buildings, manuscript account books of the old Abbey, travel journals of Tony's ancestors. At intervals Beaver would say, 'The So-and-so's have got one rather like that at Such-and-such a place,' and Tony would say, 'Yes, I've seen it but I think mine is the earlier.'

Eventually they came back to the smoking room and Tony left Beaver to Brenda.

She was stitching away at the petit point, hunched in an armchair. 'Well,' she asked, without looking up from her needlework, 'what did you think of it?'

'Magnificent.'

'You don't have to say that to me, you know.'

'Well, a lot of the things are very fine.'

'Yes, the *things* are all right I suppose.'

'But don't you like the house?'

'Me? I *detest* it . . . at least I don't mean that really, but I do wish sometimes that it wasn't *all*, every bit of it, so appallingly ugly. Only I'd die rather than say that to Tony. We could never live anywhere else, of course. He's crazy about the place . . . It's funny. None of us minded very much when my brother Reggie sold *our* house–and that was built by Vanbrugh, you know . . . I suppose we're lucky to be able to afford to keep it up at all. Do you know how much it costs just to live here? We should be quite rich if it wasn't for that. As it is we support fifteen servants indoors, besides gardeners and carpenters and a night watchman and all the people at the farm and odd little men constantly popping in to wind the clocks and cook the accounts and clean the moat, while Tony and I have to fuss about whether it's cheaper to take a car up to London for the night or buy an excursion ticket . . . I shouldn't feel so badly about it if it were a really lovely house–like my home for instance–but of course Tony's been brought up here and sees it all differently . . .'

Tony joined them for tea. 'I don't want to seem inhospitable, but if you're going to catch that train, you ought really to be getting ready.'

'That's all right. I've persuaded him to stay on till tomorrow.'

'If you're sure you don't . . .'

'Splendid. I *am* glad. It's beastly going up at this time, particularly by that train.'

When John came in he said, 'I thought Mr Beaver was going.'

'Not till tomorrow.'

'Oh.'

After dinner Tony sat and read the papers. Brenda and Beaver were on the sofa playing games together. They did a cross-word. Beaver said, 'I've thought of something,' and Brenda asked him questions to find what it was. He was thinking of the rum Peppermint drank. John had told him the story at tea. Brenda guessed it quite soon. Then they played 'Analogies' about their friends and finally about each other.

They said goodbye that night because Beaver was catching the 9.10.

'Do let me know when you come to London.'

'I may be up this week.'

Next morning Beaver tipped both butler and footman ten shillings each. Tony, still feeling rather guilty in spite of Brenda's heroic coping, came down to breakfast to see his guest off. Afterwards he went back to Guinevere.

'Well, that's the last of *him*. You were superb, darling. I'm sure he's gone back thinking that you're mad about him.'

'Oh, he wasn't too awful.'

'No. I must say he took a very intelligent interest when we went round the house.'

Mrs Beaver was eating her yoghourt when Beaver reached home. 'Who was there?'

'No one.'

'No one?' My poor boy.'

'They weren't expecting me. It was awful at first but got better. They were just as you said. She's very charming. He scarcely spoke.'

'I wish I saw her sometimes.'

'She talked of taking a flat in London.'

'*Did* she?' The conversion of stables and garages was an important part of Mrs Beaver's business. 'What does she want?'

'Something quite simple. Two rooms and a bath. But it's all quite vague. She hasn't said anything to Tony yet.'

'I am sure I shall be able to find her something.'

II

If Brenda had to go to London for a day's shopping, hair-cutting, or bone-setting (a recreation she particularly enjoyed), she went on Wednesday, because the tickets on that day were half the usual price. She left at eight in the morning and got home soon after ten at night. She travelled third class and the carriages were often full, because other wives on the line took advantage of the cheap fare. She usually spent the day with her younger sister Marjorie, who was married to the prospective Conservative candidate for a South London constituency of strong Labour sympathies. She was more solid than Brenda. The newspapers used always to refer to them as 'the lovely Rex sisters'. Marjorie and Allan were hard up and popular; they could not afford a baby; they lived in a little house in the neighbourhood of Portman Square, very convenient for Paddington Station. They had a Pekingese dog named Djinn.

Brenda had come on impulse, leaving the butler to ring up and tell Marjorie of her arrival. She emerged from the train, after two hours and a quarter in a carriage crowded five a side, looking as fresh and fragile as if she had that moment left a circle of masseuses, chiropodists, manicurists and coiffeuses in an hotel suite. It was an aptitude she had, never to look half finished; when she was really exhausted, as she often was on her return to Hetton after these days in London, she went completely to pieces quite suddenly and became a waif; then she would sit over the fire with a cup of bread and milk, hardly alive, until

Tony took her up to bed.

Marjorie had her hat on and was sitting at her writing table puzzling over her cheque book and a sheaf of bills.

'Darling, what *does* the country do to you? You look like a thousand pounds. Where *did* you get that suit?'

'I don't know. Some shop.'

'What's the news at Hetton?'

'All the same. Tony madly feudal. John Andrew cursing like a stable boy.'

'And you?'

'Me? Oh, I'm all right.'

'Who's been to stay?'

'No one. We had a friend of Tony's called Mr Beaver last week-end.'

'John Beaver? . . . How very odd. I shouldn't have thought he was at all Tony's ticket.'

'He wasn't . . . What's he like?'

'I hardly know him. I see him at Margot's sometimes. He's a great one for going everywhere.'

'I thought he was rather pathetic.'

'Oh, he's *pathetic* all right. D'you fancy him?'

'Heavens, no.'

They took Djinn for a walk in the Park. He was a very unrepaying dog who never looked about him and had to be dragged along by his harness; they took him to Watt's *Physical Energy*; when loosed he stood perfectly still, gazing moodily at the asphalt until they turned towards home; only once did he show any sign of emotion, when he snapped at a small child who attempted to stroke him; later he got lost and was found a few yards away, sitting under a chair and staring at a shred of waste paper. He was quite colourless, with pink nose and lips and pink circles of bald flesh round his eyes. 'I don't believe he has a spark of human feeling,' said Marjorie.

They talked about Mr Cruttwell, their bone-setter, and Marjorie's new treatment. 'He's never done that to me,' said Brenda enviously; presently, 'What do you suppose is Mr Beaver's sex-life?'

'I shouldn't know. Pretty dim, I imagine . . . You *do* fancy him?'

'Oh well,' said Brenda, 'I don't see such a lot of young men . . .'

They left the dog at home and did some shopping–towels for the nursery, pickled peaches, a clock for one of the lodge-keepers who was celebrating his sixtieth year of service at Hetton, a pot of Morecambe Bay shrimps as a surprise for Tony; they made an appointment with Mr Cruttwell for that afternoon. They talked about Polly Cockpurse's party. 'Do come up for it. It's certain to be amusing.'

'I might . . . if I can find someone to take me. Tony doesn't like her . . . I can't go to parties alone at my age.'

They went out to luncheon, to a new restaurant in Albemarle Street which a friend of theirs named Daisy had recently opened. 'You're in luck,' said Marjorie, as soon as they got inside the door, 'there's your Mr Beaver's mother.'

She was entertaining a party of eight at a large round table in the centre of the room; she was being paid to do so by Daisy, whose restaurant was not doing all she expected of it–that is to say, the luncheon was free and Mrs Beaver was getting the order, should the restaurant still be open, for its Spring redecorations. It was, transparently, a made-up party, the guests being chosen for no mutual bond–least of all affection for Mrs Beaver or for each other–except that their names were in current use–an accessible but not wholly renegade Duke, an unmarried girl of experience, a dancer and a novelist and a scene designer, a shamefaced junior minister who had not realized what he was in for until too late, and Lady Cockpurse. 'God, what a party,' said Marjorie, waving brightly to them all.

'You're both coming to my party, darlings?' Polly Cockpurse's strident tones rang across the restaurant. 'Only don't tell anyone about it. It's just a very small, secret party. The house will only hold a few people–just old friends.'

'It would be wonderful to see what Polly's *real* old friends were like,' said Marjorie. 'She hasn't known anyone more than five years.'

'I wish Tony could see her point.'

(Although Polly's fortune was derived from men, her popularity was chiefly among women, who admired her clothes and bought them from her second-hand at bargain prices; her first steps to eminence had been in circles so obscure that they had made her no enemies in the world to which she aspired; some time ago she had married a good-natured Earl, whom nobody else happened to want at the time; since then she had scaled all but the highest peaks of every social mountain.)

After luncheon Mrs Beaver came across to their table. 'I *must* come and speak to you, though I'm in a great hurry. It's *so* long since we met and John has been telling me about a *delightful* week-end he had with you.'

'It was very quiet.'

'That's just what he *loves*. Poor boy, he gets rushed off his feet in London. Tell me, Lady Brenda, is it true you are looking for a flat, because I think I've got just the place for you? It's being done up now and will be ready well before Christmas.' She looked at her watch. 'Oh dear, I must fly. You couldn't possibly come in for a cocktail, this evening? Then you could hear all about it.'

'I *could* . . .' said Brenda doubtfully.

'Then *do*. I'll expect you about six. I daresay you don't know where I live?' She told her and left the table.

'What's all this about a flat?' Marjorie asked.

'Oh, just something I thought of . . .'

That afternoon, as she lay luxuriously on the osteopath's table, and her vertebræ, under his strong fingers, snapped like patent fasteners, Brenda wondered whether Beaver would be at home that evening. 'Probably not, if he's so keen on going about,' she thought, 'and, anyhow, what's the sense? . . .'

But he was there, in spite of two other invitations.

She heard all about the maisonette. Mrs Beaver knew her job. What people wanted, she said, was somewhere to dress and telephone. She was subdividing a small house in Belgravia into six flats at three pounds a week, of one room each and a bath; the bathrooms were going to be slap-up, with limitless hot water and every transatlantic refinement; the other room would have a large built-in wardrobe with electric light inside, and space for a bed. It would fill a long-felt need, Mrs Beaver said.

'I'll ask my husband and let you know.'

'You *will* let me know soon, won't you, because *everyone* will be wanting one.'

'I'll let you know very soon.'

When she had to go, Beaver came with her to the station. She usually ate some chocolate and buns in her carriage; they bought them together at the buffet. There was plenty of time before the train left and the carriage was not yet full. Beaver came in and sat with her.

'I'm sure you want to go away.'

'No, really.'

'I've got lots to read.'

'I *want* to stay.'

'It's very sweet of you.' Presently she said, rather timidly, for she was not used to asking for that sort of thing, 'I suppose you wouldn't like to take me to Polly's party, would you?'

Beaver hesitated. There would be several dinner parties that evening and he was almost certain to be invited to one or other of them . . . if he took Brenda out it would mean the Embassy or some smart restaurant . . . three pounds at least . . . and he would be responsible for her and have to see her home . . . and if, as she said, she really did not know many people nowadays (why indeed should she have asked him if that were not true?) it might mean tying himself up for the whole evening . . . 'I wish I could,' he said, 'but I've promised to dine out for it.'

Brenda had observed his hesitation. 'I was afraid you would have.'

'But we'll meet there.'

'Yes, if I go.'

'I wish I could have taken you.'

'It's quite all right . . . I just wondered.'

The gaiety with which they had bought the buns was all gone now. They were silent for a minute. Then Beaver said, 'Well, I think perhaps I'll leave you now.'

'Yes, run along. Thank you for coming.'

He went off down the platform. There were still eight minutes to go. The carriage suddenly filled up and Brenda felt tired out. 'Why *should* he want to take me, poor boy?' she thought. 'Only he might have done it better.'

'Barnardo case?'

Brenda nodded. 'Down and out,' she said, 'sunk, right under.' She sat nursing her bread and milk, stirring it listlessly. Every bit of her felt good for nothing.

'Good day?'

She nodded. 'Saw Marjorie and her filthy dog. Bought some things. Lunched at Daisy's new joint. Bone-setter. That's all.'

'You know I wish you'd give up these day trips to London. They're far too much for you.'

'Me? Oh, I'm all right. Wish I was dead, that's all . . . and please, please, darling Tony, don't say anything about bed, because I can't move.'

Next day a telegram came from Beaver. *Have got out of dinner 16th. Are you still free.*

She replied: *Delighted. Second thoughts always best. Brenda.*

Up till then they had avoided Christian names.

'You seem in wonderful spirits today,' Tony remarked.

'I feel big. I think it's Mr Cruttwell. He puts all one's nerves right and one's circulation and everything.'

III

'Where's mummy gone?'

'London.'

'Why?'

'Someone called Lady Cockpurse is giving a party.'

'Is she nice?'

'Mummy thinks so. I don't.'

'Why?'

'Because she looks like a monkey.'

'I should love to see her. Does she live in a cage? Has she got a tail? Ben saw a woman who looked like a fish, with scales all over instead of skin. It was in a circus in Cairo. Smelt like a fish too, Ben says.'

They were having tea together on the afternoon of Brenda's departure. 'Daddy, what does Lady Cockpurse eat?'

'Oh, nuts and things.'

'Nuts and what things?'

'Different kinds of nuts.'

For days to come the image of this hairy, mischievous Countess occupied John Andrew's mind. She became one of the inhabitants of his world, like Peppermint, the mule who died of rum. When kindly people spoke to him in the village he would tell them about her and how she swung head down from a tree throwing nutshells at passers-by.

'You mustn't say things like that about real people,' said nanny. 'Whatever would Lady Cockpurse do if she heard about it?'

'She'd gibber and chatter and lash round with her tail, and then I expect she'd catch some nice, big juicy fleas and forget all about it.'

Brenda was staying at Marjorie's for the night. She was dressed first and came into her sister's room. 'Lovely, darling. New?'

'Fairly.'

Marjorie was rung up by the woman at whose house she was dining. ('Look here, are you absolutely sure you can't make Allan come tonight?' 'Absolutely. He's got a meeting in Camberwell. He may not even come to Polly's.' 'Is there *any* man you can bring?' 'Can't think of anybody.' 'Well, we shall have to be one short, that's all. I can't think what's happened tonight. I rang up John Beaver but even *he* won't come.')

'You know,' said Marjorie putting down the telephone, 'you're causing a great deal of trouble. You've taken London's only spare man.'

'Oh dear, I didn't realize . . .'

Beaver arrived at quarter to nine in a state of high self-approval; he had refused two invitations to dinner while dressing that evening; he had cashed a cheque for ten pounds at his club; he had booked a divan table at Espinosa's. It was almost the first time in his life that he had taken anyone out to dinner, but he knew perfectly well how it was done.'

'I must see your Mr Beaver properly,' said Marjorie. 'Let's make him take off his coat and drink something.'

The two sisters were a little shy as they came downstairs, but Beaver was perfectly at his ease. He looked very elegant and rather more than his age.

'Oh, he's not so bad, your Mr Beaver,' Marjorie's look seemed to say, 'not by any means,' and he, seeing the two women together, who were both beautiful, though in a manner so different that, although it was apparent that they were sisters, they might have belonged each to a separate race, began to understand what had perplexed him all the week; why, contrary to all habit and principle, he had telegraphed to Brenda asking her to dine.

'Mrs Jimmy Deane's very upset that she couldn't get you for tonight. I didn't give away what you were doing.'

'Give her my love,' said Beaver. 'Anyway, we'll all meet at Polly's.'

'I must go, we're dining at nine.'

'Stay a bit,' said Brenda. 'She's sure to be late.'

Now that it was inevitable, she did not want to be left alone with Beaver.

'No, I must go. Enjoy yourselves, bless you both.' She felt as though she were the elder sister, seeing Brenda timid and expectant at the beginning of an adventure.

They were awkward when Marjorie left, for in the week that they had been apart, they had, in thought, grown more intimate with the other than any actual occurrence warranted. Had Beaver been more experienced, he might have crossed to where Brenda was sitting on the arm of a chair, and made love to her at once; and probably he would have got away with it. Instead he remarked in an easy manner, 'I suppose we ought to be going, too.'

'Yes, where?'

'I thought Espinosa's.'

'Yes, lovely. Only listen. I want you to understand right away that it's *my* dinner.'

'Of course not . . . nothing of the sort.'

'Yes it is. I'm a year older than you and an old married woman and quite rich, so, please, I'm going to pay.'

Beaver continued protesting to the taxi door.

But there was still a constraint between them and Beaver began to wonder, 'Does she expect me to pounce?' So, as they waited in a traffic block by the Marble Arch, he leaned forward to kiss her; when he was quite near, she drew back. He said, '*Please*, Brenda,' but she turned away and looked out of the window, shaking her head several times quickly. Then, her eyes still fixed on the window, she put out her hand to his and they sat in silence till they reached the restaurant.

Beaver was thoroughly puzzled.

Once they were in public again, his confidence returned. Espinosa led them to their table; it was the one by itself on the right of the door, the only table in the restaurant at which one's conversation was not overheard. Brenda handed him the card. 'You choose. Very little for me, but it must only have starch, no protein.'

The bill at Espinosa's was, as a rule, roughly the same whatever one ate, but Brenda would not know this, so, since it was now understood that she was paying, Beaver felt constrained from ordering anything that looked obviously expensive. However, she insisted on champagne, and later a balloon of liqueur brandy for him. 'You can't think how exciting it is for me to take a young man out. I've never done it before.'

They stayed at Espinosa's until it was time to go to the party, dancing once or twice, but most of the time sitting at the table, talking. Their interest in each other had so far outdistanced their knowledge that there was a great deal to say.

Presently Beaver said, 'I'm sorry I was an ass in the taxi just now.'

'Eh?'

He changed it and said, 'Did you mind when I tried to kiss you just now?'

'Me? No, not particularly.'

'Then why wouldn't you let me?'

'Oh dear, you've got a lot to learn.'

'How d'you mean?'

'You mustn't ever ask questions like that. Will you try and remember?'

Then he was sulky. 'You talk to me as if I was an undergraduate having his first walk out.'

'Oh, is this a walk out?'

'Not as far as I am concerned.'

There was a pause in which Brenda said, 'I am not sure it hasn't been a mistake, taking you out to dinner. Let's ask for the bill and go to Polly's.'

But they took ten minutes to bring the bill, and in that time Beaver and Brenda had to say something, so he said he was sorry.

'You've got to *learn* to be nicer,' she said soberly. 'I don't believe you'd find it impossible.' When the bill eventually came, she said, 'How much do I tip him?' and Beaver showed her. 'Are you sure that's enough? I should have given twice as much.'

'It's exactly right,' said Beaver, feeling older again, just as Brenda had meant him to feel.

When they sat in the taxi Beaver knew at once that Brenda wished him to make love to her. But he decided it was time she took the lead. So he sat at a distance from her and commented on an old house that was being demolished to make way for a block of flats.

'Shut up,' said Brenda. 'Come here.'

When he had kissed her, she rubbed against his cheek in the way she had.

Polly's party was exactly what she wished it to be, an accurate replica of all the best parties she had been to in the last year; the same band, the same supper and, above all, the same guests. Hers was not the ambition to create a sensation, to have the party talked about in months to come for any unusual feature, to hunt out shy celebrities or introduce exotic strangers. She wanted a perfectly straight, smart party and she had got it. Practically everyone she asked had come. If there were other, more remote worlds upon which she did not impinge, Polly did not know about them. These were the people she was after, and here they were. And looking round on her guests, with Lord Cockpurse, who was for the evening loyally putting in one of his rare appearances, at her side, she was able to congratulate herself that there were very few people present whom she did not want. In other years people had taken her hospitality more casually and brought on with them anyone with whom they happened to have been dining. This year, without any conscious effort on her part, there had been more formality. Those who wanted to bring friends had rung up in the morning and asked whether they might do so, and on the whole they had been cautious of even so much presumption. People who, only eighteen months before, would have pretended to be ignorant of her existence were now crowding up her stairs. She had got herself in line with the other married women of her world.

As they started to go up, Brenda said, 'You're not to leave me, please. I'm not going to know anybody,' and Beaver again saw himself as the dominant male.

They went straight through to the band and began dancing, not talking much except to greet other couples whom they knew. They danced for half an hour and then she said, 'All right, I'll give you a rest. Only don't let me get left.'

She danced with Jock Grant-Menzies and two or three old friends and did not see Beaver again until she came on him alone in the bar. He had been there a long time, talking sometimes to the couples who came in and out, but always ending up alone. He was not enjoying the evening and he told himself rather resentfully that it was because of Brenda; if he had come there in a large party it would have been different.

Brenda saw he was out of temper and said, 'Time for supper.'

It was early, and the tables were mostly empty except for earnest couples sitting alone. There was a large round table between the windows, with no one at it; they sat there.

'I don't propose to move for a long time, d'you mind?' She wanted to make him feel important again, so she asked him about the other people in the room.

Presently their table filled up. These were Brenda's old friends, among whom she used to live when she came out and in the first two years of her marriage, before Tony's father died; men in their early thirties, married women of her own age, none of whom knew Beaver or liked him. It was by far the gayest table in the room. Brenda thought 'How my poor young man must be hating this'; it did not occur to her that, from Beaver's point of view, these old friends of hers were quite the most desirable people at the party, and that he was delighted to be seen at their table. 'Are you dying of it?' she whispered.

'No, indeed, never happier.'

'Well, I am. Let's go and dance.'

But the band was taking a rest and there was no one in the ballroom except the earnest couples who had migrated there away from the crowd and were sitting huddled in solitude round the walls, lost in conversation. 'Oh dear,' said Brenda, 'now we're done.' We can't go back to the table . . . it almost looks as though we should have to go home.'

'It's not two.'

'That's late for me. Look here, don't you come. Stay and enjoy yourself.'

'Of course I'll come,' said Beaver.

It was a cold, clear night. Brenda shivered and he put his arm round her in the taxi. They did not say much.

'There already?'

They sat for a few seconds without moving. Then Brenda slipped free and Beaver got out.

'I am afraid I can't ask you in for a drink. You see it isn't my house and I shouldn't know where to find anything.'

'No, of course not.'

'Well, goodnight, my dear. Thank you a thousand times for looking after me. I'm afraid I rather bitched your evening.'

'No, of course not,' said Beaver.

'Will you ring me in the morning . . . promise?' She touched her hand to her lips and then turned to the keyhole.

Beaver hesitated a minute whether he should go back to the party, but decided not to. He was near home, and everyone at Polly's would have settled down by now; so he gave his address in Sussex Gardens, and went up to bed.

Just as he was undressed he heard the telephone ringing downstairs. It was his telephone. He went down, two flights in the cold. It was Brenda's voice.

'Darling, I was just going to ring off. I thought you must have gone back to Polly's. Is the telephone not by your bed?'

'No, it's on the ground floor.'

'Oh dear, then it wasn't a very good idea to ring up, was it?'

'Oh, I don't know. What is it?'

'Just to say "goodnight".'

'Oh, I see, well–goodnight.'

'And you'll ring me in the morning?'

'Yes.'

'Early, before you've made any plans.'

'Yes.'

'Then goodnight, bless you.'

Beaver went up the two flights of stairs again and got into bed.

'. . . going away in the middle of the party.'

'I can't tell you how innocent it was. He didn't even come in.'

'No one is going to know that.'

'And he was furious when I rang him up.'

'What does he think of you?'

'Simply can't make me out at all . . . terribly puzzled, and rather bored in bits.'

'Are you going to go on with it?'

'I shouldn't know.' The telephone rang. 'Perhaps that's him.'

But it was not.

Brenda had come into Marjorie's room and they were having breakfast in bed. Marjorie was more than ever like an elder sister that morning. 'But, really, Brenda, he's such a *dreary* young man.'

'I know it all. He's second rate and a snob and, I should think, as cold as a fish, but I happen to have a fancy for him, that's all . . . besides I'm not sure he's *altogether* awful . . . he's got that odious mother whom he adores . . . and he's always been very poor. I don't think he's had a fair deal. I heard all about it last night. He got engaged once but they couldn't get married because of money and since then he's never had a proper affair with anyone decent . . . he's got to be taught a whole lot of things. That's part of his attraction.'

'Oh dear, I see you're very serious.'

The telephone rang.

'Perhaps *that's* him.'

But a familiar voice rang out from the instrument so that Brenda could hear it, 'Good-morning, darling, what's the dirt today?'

'Oh, Polly, what a good party last night.'

'Not so bad for the old girl, was it? I say, what about your sister and Mr Beaver?'

'What about them?'

'How long has *that* been on?'

'There's nothing doing there, Polly.'

'Don't you tell me. They were well away last night. How's the boy managed it? That's what I want to know. He must have something we didn't know about . . .'

'So Polly's on to your story. She'll be telling everyone in London at this moment.'

'How I wish there was anything to tell! The cub hasn't even rung me up . . . Well, I'll leave him in peace. If he doesn't do anything about me, I'll go down to Hetton this afternoon. Perhaps that's him.' But it was only Allan from the Conservative Central Office, to say how sorry he had been not to get to the party the night before. 'I hear Brenda disgraced herself,' he said.

'Goodness,' said Brenda. 'People do think that young men are easily come by.'

'I scarcely saw you at Polly's last night,' said Mrs Beaver. 'What became of you?'

'We went early. Brenda Last was tired.'

'She was looking lovely. I am so glad you've made friends with her. When are you going to see her again?'

'I said I'd ring up.'

'Well, why don't you?'

'Oh, mumsy, what's the use? I can't afford to start taking about women like Brenda Last. If I ring up she'll say, what are you doing, and I shall have to ask her to something, and it will be the same thing every day. I simply haven't the money.'

'I know, my son. It's very difficult for you . . . and you're wonderful about money. I ought to be grateful that I haven't a son always coming to me with debts. Still, it doesn't do to deny yourself *everything*, you know. You're getting to be an old bachelor already at twenty-five. I could see Brenda liked you, that evening she came here.'

'Oh, she likes me all right.'

'I hope she makes up her mind about that flat. They're going like hot cakes. I shall have to look about for another suitable house to split up. You'd be surprised who've been taking them–quite a number of people with houses in London already . . . Well, I must be getting back to work. I'm away for two nights by the way. See that Chambers looks after you properly. There are some Australians Sylvia Newport discovered who want to take a house in the country, so I'm driving them round to one or two that might do for them. Where are you lunching?'

'Margot's.'

By one o'clock, when they came back from taking Djinn to the Park, Beaver had not rung up. 'So that's that,' said Brenda, 'I daresay I'm glad really.' She sent a telegram to Tony to expect her by the afternoon train and, in a small voice, ordered her things to be packed. 'I don't seem to have anywhere to lunch,' she said.

'Why don't you come to Margot's? I know she'd love it.'

'Well, ring up and ask her.'

So she met Beaver again.

He was sitting some way from her and they did not speak to each other until everyone was going. 'I kept trying to get through to you this morning,' he said, 'but the line was always engaged.'

'Oh come on,' said Brenda, 'I'll sock you a movie.'

Later she wired to Tony: *Staying with Marjorie another day or two all love to you both.*

IV

'Is mummy coming back today?'

'I hope so.'

'That monkey-woman's party has lasted a long time. Can I come in to the station and meet her?'

'Yes, we'll both go.'

'She hasn't seen Thunderclap for four days. She hasn't seen me jump the new post and rail, has she, daddy?'

She was coming by the 3.18. Tony and John Andrew were there early. They wandered about the station looking at things, and bought some chocolate from a slot machine. The stationmaster came out to talk to them. 'Her ladyship coming back today?' He was an old friend of Tony's.

'I've been expecting her every day. You know what it is when ladies get to London.'

'Sam Brace's wife went to London and he couldn't get her back. Had to go up and fetch her himself. And then she gave him a hiding.'

Presently the train came in and Brenda emerged exquisitely from her third class carriage. 'You've *both* come. What angels you are. I don't at all deserve it.'

'Oh mummy, have you brought the monkey-lady?'

'What *does* the child mean?'

'He's got it into his head that your chum Polly has a tail.'

'Come to think of it, I shouldn't be surprised if she had.'

Two little cases held all her luggage. The chauffeur strapped them on behind the car, and they drove to Hetton.

'What's all the news?'

'Ben's put the rail up ever so high and Thunderclap and I jumped it six times yesterday and six times again today and two more of the fish in the little pond are dead, floating upside down all swollen and nanny burnt her finger on the kettle yesterday and daddy and I saw a fox just as near as anything and he sat quite still and then went away into the wood and I began drawing a picture of a battle only I couldn't finish it because the paints weren't right and the grey carthorse the one that had worms is quite well again.'

'Nothing much has happened,' said Tony. 'We've missed you. What did you find to do in London all this time?'

'Me? Oh I've been behaving rather badly to tell you the truth.'

'Buying things?'

'Worse. I've been carrying on madly with young men and I've spent heaps of money and I've enjoyed it very much indeed. But there's one awful thing.'

'What's that?'

'No, I think it had better keep. It's something you won't like at all.'

'You've bought a Pekingese.'

'Worse, far worse. Only I haven't done it yet. But I *want* to dreadfully.'

'Go on.'

'Tony, I've found a flat.'

'Well, you'd better lose it again, quick.'

'All right. I'll attack you about it again later. Meanwhile try not to brood about it.'

'I shan't give it another thought.'

'What's a flat, daddy?'

Brenda wore pyjamas at dinner, and afterwards sat close to Tony on the sofa and ate some sugar out of his coffee cup.

'I suppose all this means that you're going to start again about your flat?'

'Mmmm.'

'You haven't signed any papers yet, have you?'

'Oh, no.' Brenda shook her head emphatically.

'Then no great harm's done.' Tony began to fill his pipe.

Brenda knelt on the sofa, sitting back on her heels. 'Listen, you haven't been brooding?'

'No.'

'Because, you see, when you say "flat" you're thinking of something quite different to me. *You* mean by a flat, a lift and a man in uniform, and a big front door with knobs, and an entrance hall and doors open in all directions, with kitchens and sculleries and dining rooms and drawing rooms and servants' bedrooms . . . don't you, Tony?'

'More or less.'

'*Exactly*. Now *I* mean just a bedroom and a bath and a telephone. You see the difference? Now a woman I know—'

'Who?'

'Just a woman–has fixed up a whole house like that off Belgrave Square and they are three pounds a week, no rates and taxes, constant hot water and central heating, woman comes in to make the bed when required, what d'you think of that?'

'I see.'

'Now this is how I look at it. What's three pounds a week? Less than nine bob a night. Where could one stay for less than nine bob a night with all those advantages? You're always going to the club, and that costs more, and I can't stay often with Marjorie because it's hell for her having me, and anyway she's got that dog, and you're always saying when I come back in the evenings after shopping, "Why didn't you stay the night," you say, "instead of killing yourself?" Time and again you say it. I'm sure we spend much more than three pounds a week through not having a flat. Tell you what, I'll give up Mr Cruttwell. How's that?'

'D'you really want this thing.'

'Mmm.'

'Well, I'll have to see. We *might* manage it, but it'll mean putting off the improvements down here.'

'I don't really deserve it,' she said, clinching the matter. 'I've been carrying on *anyhow* this week.'

Brenda's stay at Hetton lasted only for three nights. Then she returned to London, saying that she had to see about the flat. It did not, however, require very great attention. There was only the colour of the paint to choose and some few articles of furniture. Mrs. Beaver had them ready for her inspection, a bed, a carpet, a dressing table and chair–there was not room for more. Mrs Beaver tried to sell her a set of needlework pictures for the walls, but these she refused, also an electric bed warmer, a miniature weighing machine for the bathroom, a frigidaire, an antique grandfather clock, a backgammon set of looking-glass and synthetic ivory, a set of prettily bound French eighteenth-century poets, a massage apparatus, and a wireless set fitted in a case of Regency lacquer, all of which had been grouped in the shop for her as a 'suggestion'. Mrs Beaver bore Brenda no ill will for the modesty of her requirements; she was doing very well on the floor above with a Canadian lady who was having her walls covered with chromium plating at immense expense.

Meanwhile Brenda stayed with Marjorie, on terms which gradually became acrimonious. 'I'm sorry to be pompous,' she said one morning, 'but I just don't want your Mr Beaver hanging about the house all day and calling me Marjorie.'

'Oh well, the flat won't be long now.'

'And I shall go on saying that I think you're making a ridiculous mistake.'

'It's just that you don't like Mr Beaver.'

'It isn't only that. I think it's hard cheese on Tony.'

'Oh, Tony's all right.'

'And if there's a row—'

'There won't be a row.'

'You never know. If there is, I don't want Allan to think I've been helping to arrange things.'

'I wasn't so disagreeable to you about Robin Beaseley.'

'There was never much in that,' said Marjorie.

But with the exception of her sister's, opinion was greatly in favour of Brenda's adventure. The morning telephone buzzed with news of her; even people with whom she had the barest acquaintance were delighted to relate that they had seen her and Beaver the evening before at a restaurant or cinema. It had been an autumn of vary sparse and meagre romance; only the most obvious people had parted or come together, and Brenda was filling a want long felt by those whose simple, vicarious pleasure it was to discuss the subject in bed over the telephone. For them her circumstances shed peculiar glamour; for five years she had been a legendary, almost ghostly name, the imprisoned princess of fairy story, and now that she had emerged there was more enchantment in the occurrence than in the mere change of habit of any other circumspect wife. Her very choice of partner gave the affair an appropriate touch of fantasy;

Beaver, the joke figure they had all known and despised, suddenly caught up to her among the luminous clouds of deity. If, after seven years looking neither to right nor left, she had at last broken away with Jock Grant-Menzies or Robin Beaseley or any other young buck with whom nearly everyone had had a crack one time or another, it would have been thrilling no doubt, but straighforward, drawing-room comedy. The choice of Beaver raised the whole escapade into a realm of poetry for Polly and Daisy and Angela and all the gang of gossips.

Mrs Beaver made no bones about her delight. 'Of course the subject has not been mentioned between John and myself, but if what I hear is true, I think it will do the boy a world of good. Of course he's always been very much in demand and had a great number of friends, but *that isn't the same thing*. I've felt for a long time a Lack of Something in him, and I think that a charming and experienced woman like Brenda Last is just the person to help him. He's got a *very* affectionate nature, but he's so sensitive that he hardly ever lets it appear . . . to tell you the truth I felt something of the kind was in the air last week, so I made an excuse to go away for a few days. If I had been there things might never have come to anything. He's very shy and reserved even to me. I'll have the chess-men done up and sent round to you this afternoon. Thank you so much.'

And Beaver, for the first time in his life, found himself a person of interest and, almost, of consequence. Women studied him with a new scrutiny, wondering what they had missed in him; men treated him as an equal, even as a successful fellow competitor. 'How on earth has *he* got away with it?' they may have asked themselves, but now, when he came into Brat's, they made room for him at the bar and said, 'Well, old boy, how about one?'

Brenda rang up Tony every morning and evening. Sometimes John Andrew spoke to her, too, as shrill as Polly Cockpurse; quite unable to hear her replies. She went to Hetton for the week-end, and then back to London, this time to the flat where the paint was already dry, though the hot water was not yet in perfect working order; everything smelt very new–walls, sheets, curtains–and the new radiators gave off a less agreeable reek of hot iron.

That evening as usual she telephoned to Hetton. 'I'm talking from the flat.'

'Oh ah.'

'*Darling*, do try to sound interested. It's very exciting for me.'

'What's it like?'

'Well, there are a good many smells at present and the bath makes odd sounds and when you turn on the hot tap there's just a rush of air and that's all, and the cold tap keeps dripping and the water is rather brown and the cupboard doors are jammed and the curtains won't pull right across so that the street lamp shines in all night . . . but it's *lovely*.'

'You don't say so.'

'Tony, you must be nice about it. It's all so exciting–front door and a latch key and all . . . And someone sent me a lot of flowers today–so many that there's hardly room for them and I have to put them in the basin on account of having no pots. It wasn't you, was it?'

'Yes . . . as a matter of fact.'

'Darling, I did so hope it was . . . how like you.'

'Three minutes please.'

'Must stop now.'

'When are you coming back?'

'Almost at once. Goodnight, my sweet.'

'What a lot of talk,' said Beaver.

All the time that she was speaking, she had been kept busy with one hand warding him off the telephone, which he threatened playfully to disconnect.

'Wasn't it sweet of Tony to send those flowers?'

'I'm not awfully fond of Tony.'

'Don't let that worry you, my beauty, he doesn't like you *at all.*'

'*Doesn't* he? Why not?'

'No one does except me. You must get that clear . . . it's very good that *I* should.'

Beaver and his mother were going to Ireland for Christmas, to stay with cousins. Tony and Brenda had a family party at Hetton: Marjorie and Allan, Brenda's mother, Tony's Aunt Frances and two families of impoverished Lasts, humble and uncomplaining victims of primogeniture, to whom Hetton meant as much as it did to Tony. There was a little Christmas tree in the nursery for John Andrew and a big one downstairs in the central hall which was decorated by the impoverished Lasts and lit up for half an hour after tea (two footmen standing by with wet sponges on the end of poles, to extinguish the candles which turned turtle and threatened to start a fire). There were presents for all the servants, of value strictly graded according to their rank, and for all the guests (cheques for the impoverished Lasts). Allan always brought a large croûte of foie gras, a delicacy of which he was particularly fond. Everyone ate a great deal and became slightly torpid towards Boxing-day evening; silver ladles of burning brandy went round the table, crackers were pulled and opened; paper hats, indoor fireworks, mottoes. This year, everything happened in its accustomed way; nothing seemed to menace the peace and stability of the house. The choir came up and sang carols in the pitch pine gallery, and later devoured hot punch and sweet biscuits. The vicar preached his usual Christmas sermon. It was one to which his parishioners were greatly attached.

'How difficult it is for us,' he began, blandly surveying his congregation, who coughed into their mufflers and chafed their chilblains under their woollen gloves, 'to realize that this is indeed Christmas. Instead of the glowing log fire and windows tight shuttered against the drifting snow, we have only the harsh glare of an alien sun; instead of the happy circle of loved faces, of home and family; we have the uncomprehending stares of the subjugated, though no doubt grateful, heathen. Instead of the placid ox and ass of Bethlehem,' said the vicar, slightly losing the thread of his comparison, 'we have for companions the ravening tiger and the exotic camel, the furtive jackal and the ponderous elephant . . .' And so on, through the pages of faded manuscript. The words had temporarily touched the heart of many an obdurate trooper, and hearing them again, as he had heard them year after year since Mr Tendril had come to the parish, Tony and most of Tony's guests felt that it was an integral part of their Christmas festivities; one with which they would find it very hard to dispense. 'The ravening tiger and exotic camel' had long been bywords in the family, of frequent recurrence in all their games.

These games were the hardest part for Brenda. They did not amuse her and she still could not see Tony dressed up for charades without a feeling of shyness. Moreover, she was tortured by the fear that any lack of gusto on her part might be construed by the poor Lasts as superiority. These scruples, had she known it, were quite superfluous, for it never occurred to her husband's relatives to look on her with anything but cousinly cordiality and certain tolerance, for, as Lasts, they considered they had far more right in Hetton than herself. Aunt Frances, with acid mind, quickly discerned the trouble and attempted to reassure her, saying, 'Dear child, all these feelings of delicacy are valueless; only the rich realize the gulf that separates them from the poor,' but the uneasiness persisted, and night after night she found herself being sent out of the room, asking or answering questions, performing actions in uncouth manners, paying forfeits, drawing pictures, writing verses, dressing herself up and even being chased about the house, and secluded in cupboards, at the will of her relatives. Christmas was on a Friday that year, so the party was a long one, from Thursday until Monday.

She had forbidden Beaver to sent her a present or to write to her; in self protection, for she knew that whatever he said would hurt her by its poverty, but in spite of this she awaited the posts nervously, hoping that he might have disobeyed her. She had sent him to Ireland a ring of three interlocked hoops of gold and platinum. An hour after ordering it she regretted her choice. On Tuesday a letter came from him thanking her. *Darling Brenda,* he wrote. *Thank you so very much for the charming Christmas present. You can imagine my delight when I saw the pink leather case and my surprise at opening it. It really was* sweet *of you to send me such a charming present. Thank you again very much for it. I hope your party is being a success. It is rather dull here. The others went hunting yesterday. I went to the meet. They did not have a good day. Mother is here too and sends her love. We shall be leaving tomorrow or the day after. Mother has got rather a cold.*

It ended there at the bottom of a page. Beaver had been writing it before dinner and later had put it in the envelope without remembering to finish it.

He wrote a large, schoolgirlish hand with wide spaces between the lines.

Brenda felt a little sick when she read this letter but she showed it to Marjorie, saying, 'I can't complain, he's never pretended to like me much. And anyway it was a damned silly present.'

Tony had become fretful about his visit to Angela's. He always hated staying away.

'Don't come, darling. I'll make it all right with them.'

'No, I'll come. I haven't seen so much of you in the last three weeks.'

They had the whole of Wednesday alone together. Brenda exerted herself and Tony's fretfulness subsided. She was particularly tender to him at this time and scarcely teased him at all.

On Thursday they went North to Yorkshire. Beaver was there. Tony discovered him in the first half hour and brought the news to Brenda upstairs.

'I'll tell you something very odd,' he said. 'Who do you think is here?'

'Who?'

'Our old friend Beaver.'

'Why's that odd particularly?'

'Oh, I don't know. I'd forgotten all about him, hadn't you? D'you think he sent Angela a telegram as he did to us?'

'I daresay.'

Tony supposed Beaver must be fairly lonely and took pains to be agreeable to him. He said, 'All kinds of changes since we saw you last. Brenda's taken a flat in London.'

'Yes, I know.'

'How?'

'Well, my mother let it to her, you know.'

Tony was greatly surprised and taxed Brenda with this. 'You never told me who was behind your flat. I might not have been so amiable if I'd known.'

'No, darling, that's why.'

Half the house party wondered why Beaver was there; the other half knew. As a result of this he and Brenda saw each other very little, less than if they had been casual acquaintances, so that Angela remarked to her husband, 'I daresay it was a mistake to ask him. It's so hard to know.'

Brenda never started the subject of the half finished letter, but she noticed that Beaver was wearing his ring, and had already acquired a trick of twisting it as he talked.

On New Year's Eve there was a party at a neighbouring house. Tony went home early and Beaver and Brenda returned together in the back of a car. Next morning, while they were having breakfast, she said to Tony, 'I've made a New Year resolution.'

'Anything to do with spending more time at home?'

'Oh no, *quite* the reverse. Listen, Tony, it's serious. I think I'll take a course of something.'

'Not bone-setters again? I thought that was over.'

'No, something like economics. You see, I've been thinking. I don't really *do* anything at all at present. The house runs itself. It seems to me time I *took* to something. Now you're always talking about going into Parliament. Well, if I had done a course of economics I could be some use canvassing and writing speeches and things–you know, the way Marjorie did when Allan was standing on the Clydeside. There are all sorts of lectures in London to do with the University, where girls go. Don't you think it's rather a good idea?'

'It's one better than the bone-setters,' Tony admitted.

That was how the New Year began.

3

HARD CHEESE ON TONY

I

It is not uncommon at Brat's Club, between nine and ten in the evening, to find men in white ties and tail coats sitting by themselves and eating, in evident low spirits, large and extravagant dinners. They are those who have been abandoned at the last minute by their women. For twenty minutes or so they have sat in the foyer of some restaurant, gazing expectantly towards the revolving doors and alternatively taking out their watches and ordering cocktails, until at length a telephone message has been brought them that their guests are unable to come. Then they go to Brat's, half hoping to find friends but, more often than not, taking a melancholy satisfaction in finding the club deserted or peopled by strangers. So they sit there, round the walls, morosely regarding the mahogany tables before them, and eating and drinking heavily.

It was in this mood and for this reason that, one evening towards the middle of February, Jock Grant-Menzies arrived at the club.

'Anyone here?'

'Very quiet tonight, sir. Mr Last is in the dining-room.'

Jock found him seated in a corner; he was in day clothes; the table and the chair at his side were littered with papers and magazines; one was propped up in front of him. He was half-way through dinner and three-quarters of the way through a bottle of Burgundy. 'Hullo,' he said. 'Chucked? Come and join me.'

It was some time since Jock had seen Tony; the meeting embarrassed him slightly, for like all his friends, he was wondering how Tony felt and how much he knew about Brenda and John Beaver. However, he sat down at Tony's table.

'Been chucked?' asked Tony again.

'Yes, it's the last time I ask that bitch out.'

'Better have a drink. I've been drinking a whole lot. Much the best thing.'

They took what was left of the Burgundy and ordered another bottle.

'Just come up for the night,' said Tony. 'Staying here.'

'You've got a flat now, haven't you?'

'Well, Brenda has. There isn't really room for two . . . we tried it once and it wasn't a success.'

'What's she doing tonight?'

'Out somewhere. I didn't let her know I was coming . . . silly not to, but you see I got fed up with being alone at Hetton and thought I'd like to see Brenda, so I came up suddenly on the spur of the moment, just like that. Damned silly thing to do. Might have known she'd be going out somewhere . . . she's very high-principled about chucking . . . so there it is. She's going to ring me up here later, if she can get away.'

They drank a lot.

Tony did most of the talking. 'Extraordinary idea of hers, taking up economics,' he said. 'I never thought it would last, but she seems really keen on it . . . I suppose it's a good plan. You know there wasn't really much for her to do all the time at Hetton. Of course she'd rather die than admit it, but I believe she got a bit bored there sometimes. I've been thinking it over and that's the conclusion I came to. Brenda must have been bored . . . Dare say she'll get bored with economics some time . . . Anyway she seems cheerful enough now. We've had parties every week-end lately . . . I wish you'd come down sometimes, Jock. I don't seem to get on with Brenda's new friends.'

'People from the school of economics?'

'No, but ones I don't know. I believe I bore them. Thinking it over that's the conclusion I've come to. I bore them. They talk about me as "the old boy". John heard them.'

'Well, that's friendly enough.'

'Yes, that's friendly.'

They finished the Burgundy and drank some port. Presently Tony said, 'I say, come next week-end, will you?'

'I think I'd love to.'

'Wish you would. I don't see many old friends . . . Sure to be lots of people in the house, but you won't mind that, will you? . . . sociable chap, Jock . . . doesn't mind people about. *I* mind it like hell.' They drank some more port. Tony said, 'Not enough bathrooms, you know . . . but of course you know. You've been there before, often. Not like the new friends who think me a bore. You don't think I'm a bore, do you?'

'No, old boy.'

'Not even when I'm tight, like this? . . . There would have been bathrooms. I had the plans out. Four new ones. A chap down there made the plans . . . but then Brenda wanted the flat so I had to postpone them as an economy . . . I say, that's funny. We had to economize because of Brenda's economics.'

'Yes, that's funny. Let's have some port.'

Tony said, 'You seem pretty low tonight.'

'I am rather. Worried about the Pig Scheme. Constituents keep writing.'

'*I* felt low, *bloody* low, but I'm all right again now. The best thing is to get tight. That's what I did and I don't feel low any more . . . discouraging to come to London and find you're not wanted. Funny thing, *you* feel low because your girl's chucked, and *I* feel low because mine won't chuck.'

'Yes, that's funny.'

'But you know I've felt low for weeks now . . . bloody low . . . how about some brandy?'

'Yes, why not? After all there are other things in life besides women and pigs.'

They had some brandy and after a time Jock began to cheer up.

Presently a page came to their table to say, 'A message from Lady Brenda, sir.'

'Good, I'll go and speak to her.'

'It's not her ladyship speaking. Someone was sending a message.'

'I'll come and speak to her.'

He went to the telephone in the lobby outside. 'Darling,' he said.

'Is that Mr Last? I've got a message here, from Lady Brenda.'

'Right, put me through to her.'

'She can't speak herself, but she asked me to give you this message, that she's very sorry but she cannot join you tonight. She's very tired and has gone home to bed.'

'Tell her I want to speak to her.'

'I can't I'm afraid, she's gone to bed. She's very tired.'

'She's very tired and she's gone to bed?'

'That's right.'

'Well, I want to speak to her.'

'Goodnight,' said the voice.

'The old boy's plastered,' said Beaver as he rang off.

'Oh, dear. I feel rather awful about him. But what *can* he expect, coming up suddenly like this? He's got to be taught not to make surprise visits.'

'Is he often like that?'

'No, it's quite new.'

The telephone bell rang. 'Do you suppose that's him again? I'd better answer it.'

'I want to speak to Lady Brenda Last.'

'Tony darling, this *is* me, Brenda.'

'Some damn fool said I couldn't speak to you.'

'I left a message from where I was dining. Are you having a lovely evening?'

'Hellish. I'm with Jock. He's worried about the Pig Scheme. Shall we come round and see you?'

'No, not now, darling, I'm terribly tired and just going to bed.'

'We'll come and see you.'

'Tony, are you a tiny bit tight?'

'Stinking. Jock and I'll come and see you.'

'*Tony*, you're *not* to. D'you hear? I can't have you making a brawl. The flats are getting a bad name anyhow.'

'Their name'll be mud when Jock and I come.'

'Tony, listen, will you please not come, not tonight. Be a good boy and stay at the club. Will you *please* not?'

'Shan't be long.' He rang off.

'Oh God,' said Brenda. 'This isn't the least like Tony. Ring up Brat's and get on to Jock. He'll have more sense.'

'That was Brenda.'

'So I gathered.'

'She's at the flat. I said that we'd go round.'

'Splendid. Haven't seen her for weeks. Very fond of Brenda.'

'So am I. Grand girl.'

'Grand girl.'

'A lady on the telephone for you, Mr Grant-Menzies.'

'Who?'

'She didn't give a name.'

'All right. I'll come.'

Brenda said to him, 'Jock, what *have* you been doing to my husband?'

'He's a bit tight, that's all.'

'He's roaring. Look here, he threatens to come round. I simply can't face him tonight in that mood, I'm tired out. You understand, don't you?'

'Yes, I understand.'

'So will you, *please*, keep him away? Are you tight too?'

'A little bit.'

'Oh dear, can I trust you?'

'I'll try.'

'Well, it doesn't sound too good. Goodbye' . . . 'John, you've got to go. Those hooligans may turn up at any moment. Have you got your taxi fare? You'll find some change in my bag.'

'Was that your girl?'

'Yes.'

'Made it up?'

'Not exactly.'

'Far better to make it up. Shall we have some more brandy or go round to Brenda straight away?'

'Let's have some more brandy.'

'Jock, you aren't still feeling low, are you? Doesn't do to feel low. *I'm* not feeling low. I *was*, but I'm not any more.'

'No, I'm not feeling low.'

'Then we'll have some brandy and then go to Brenda's.'

'All right.'

Half an hour later they got into Jock's car. 'Tell you what, I shouldn't drive if I were you.'

'Not drive?'

'No, I shouldn't drive. They'd say you were drunk.'

'Who would?'

'Anyone you ran over. They'd say you were drunk.'

'Well, so I am.'

'Then I shouldn't drive.'

'Too far to walk.'

'We'll take a taxi.'

'Oh hell, I can drive.'

'Or let's not go to Brenda's at all.'

'We'd better go to Brenda's,' said Jock. 'She's expecting us.'

'Well, I can't walk all that way. Besides, I don't think she really wanted us to come.'

'She'll be pleased when she sees us.'

'Yes, but it's a long way. Let's go some other place.'

'I'd like to see Brenda,' said Jock. 'I'm very fond of Brenda.'

'She's a grand girl.'

'She's a grand girl.'

'Well, let's take a taxi to Brenda's.'

But half way Jock said, 'Don't let's go there. Let's go some other place. Let's go to some low joint.'

'All the same to me. Tell him to go to some lousy joint.'

'Go to some lousy joint,' said Jock, putting his head through the window.

The cab wheeled round and made towards Regent Street.

'We can always ring Brenda from the lousy joint.'

'Yes, I think we ought to do that. She's a grand girl.'

'Grand girl.'

The cab turned into Golden Square and then down Sink Street, a dingy little place inhabited for the most part by Asiatics.

'D'you know, I believe he's taking us to the Old Hundredth.'

'Can't still be open? Thought they closed it down years ago.'

But the door was brightly illuminated and a seedy figure in peaked cap and braided overcoat stepped out to open the taxi for them.

The Old Hundredth has never been shut. For a generation, while other night clubs have sprung into being, with various names and managers, and various pretensions to respectability, have enjoyed a precarious and brief existence, and come to grief at the hands either of police or creditors, the Old Hundredth has maintained a solid front against all adversity. It has not been immune from persecution; far from it. Times out of number, magistrates have struck it off, cancelled its licence, condemned its premises; the staff and proprietor have been constantly in and out of prison; there have been questions in the House and committees of enquiry, but whatever Home Secretaries and Commissioners of Police have risen into eminence and retired discredited, the doors of the Old Hundredth have always been open from nine in the evening until four at night, and inside there has been an unimpeded flow of dubious, alcoholic preparations. A kindly young lady admitted Tony and Jock to the ramshackle building.

'D'you mind signing on?' Tony and Jock inscribed fictitious names at the foot of a form which stated, *I have been invited to a Bottle Party at 100 Sink Street given by Captain Weybridge.* 'That's five bob each, please.'

It is not an expensive club to run, because none of the staff, except the band, receive any wages; they make what they can by going through the overcoat pockets and giving the wrong change to drunks. The young ladies get in free but they have to see to it that their patrons spend money.

'Last time I was here, Tony, was the bachelor party before your wedding.'

'Tight that night.'

'Stinking.'

'I'll tell you who else was tight that night–Reggie. Broke a fruit-gum machine.'

'Reggie was stinking.'

'I say, you don't still feel low about that girl?'

'I don't feel low.'

'Come on, we'll go downstairs.'

The dance-room was fairly full. An elderly man had joined the band and was trying to conduct it. 'I like this joint.' said Jock. 'What'll we drink?'

'Brandy.'

They had to buy the bottle. They filled in an order form to the Montmorency Wine Company and paid two pounds. When it came there was a label saying *Very Old Liqueur Fine Champagne. Imported by the Montmorency Wine Co.* The waiter brought ginger ale and four glasses. Two young ladies came and sat with them. They were called Milly and Babs. Milly said, 'Are you in town for long?' Babs said, 'Have you got such a thing as a cigarette?'

Tony danced with Babs. She said, 'Are you fond of dancing?'

'No, are you?'

'So-so.'

'Well, let's sit down.'

The waiter said, 'Will you buy a ticket in a raffle for a box of chocolates?'

'No.'

'Buy one for me,' said Babs.

Jock began to describe the specifications of the Basic Pig.

Milly said, 'You're married, aren't you?'

'No,' said Jock.

'Oh, I can always tell,' said Milly. 'You friend is too.'

'Yes, *he* is.'

'You'd be surprised how many gentlemen come here just to talk about their wives.'

'He hasn't.'

Tony was leaning across the table and saying to Babs, 'You see the trouble is my wife is studious. She's taking a course in economics.'

Babs said. 'I think it's nice for a girl to be interested in things.'

The waiter said, 'What will you be taking for supper?'

'Why, we've only just had dinner.'

'How about a nice haddock?'

'I tell you what I must do, is to telephone. Where is it?'

'D'you mean really the telephone or the gentlemen's?' Milly asked.

'No, the telephone.'

'Upstairs in the office.'

Tony rang up Brenda. It was some time before she answered, then, 'Yes, who is it?'

'I have a message here from Mr Anthony Last and Mr Jocelyn Grant-Menzies.'

'Oh it's you, Tony. Well, what do you want?'

'You recognized my voice?'

'I did.'

'Well, I only wanted to give a message but as I am speaking to you I can give it myself, can't I?'

'Yes.'

'Well, Jock and I are terribly sorry but we can't come round this evening after all.'

'Oh.'

'You don't think it very rude, I hope, but we have a lot to attend to.'

'That's all right, Tony.'

'Did I wake you up by any chance?'

'That's all right, Tony.'

'Well, goodnight.'

Tony went down to the table. 'I've been talking to Brenda. She sounded rather annoyed. D'you think we *ought* to go round there?'

'We promised we would,' said Jock.

'You should never disappoint a lady,' said Milly.

'Oh, it's too late now.'

Babs said, 'You two are officers, aren't you?'

'No, why?'

'I thought you were.'

Milly said, 'I like business gentlemen best, myself. They've more to say.'

'What d'you do?'

'I design postmen's hats,' said Jock.

'Oh, go on.'

'And my friend here trains sea lions.'

'Tell us another.'

Babs said, 'I've got a gentleman friend who works on a newspaper.'

After a time Jock said, 'I say, ought we to do something about Brenda?'

'I told her we weren't coming, didn't I?'

'Yes . . . but she might still be *hoping*.'

'I tell you what, you go and ring her up and find out if she really wants us.'

'All right.' He came back ten minutes later, '*I* thought she sounded rather annoyed,' he reported. 'But I said in the end we wouldn't come.'

'She may be tired,' said Tony. 'Has to get up early to do economics. Now I come to think of it someone *did* say she was tired, earlier on in the evening.'

'I say, what's this frightful piece of fish?'

'The waiter said you ordered it.'

'Perhaps I did.'

'I'll give it to the club cat,' said Babs, 'she's a dear called Blackberry.'

They danced once or twice. Then Jock said, 'D'you think we ought to ring up Brenda again?'

'Perhaps we ought. She sounded annoyed with us.'

'Let's go now and ring her up on the way out.'

'Aren't you coming home with us?' said Babs.

'Not tonight, I'm afraid.'

'Be a sport,' said Milly.

'No, we can't, really.'

'All right. Well, how about a little present? We're professional dancing partners, you know,' said Babs.

'Oh yes, sorry, how much?'

'Oh, we leave that to the gentlemen.'

Tony gave them a pound. 'You might make it a bit more,' said Babs. 'We've sat with you two hours.'

Jock gave another pound. 'Come and see us again one evening when you've got more time,' said Milly.

'I'm feeling rather ill,' said Tony on the way upstairs. 'Don't think I shall bother to ring up Brenda.'

'Send a message.'

'That's a good idea . . . Look here,' he said to the seedy commissionaire. 'Will you ring up this Sloane number and speak to her ladyship and say Mr Grant-Menzies and Mr Last are very sorry but they cannot call this evening? Got that?' He gave the man half a crown and they sauntered out into Sink Street. 'Brenda can't expect us to do more than that,' he said.

'I tell you what I'll do. I go almost past her door, so I'll ring the bell a bit just in case she's awake and still waiting up for us.'

'Yes, you do that. What a good friend you are, Jock.'

'Oh, I'm fond of Brenda . . . a grand girl.'

'Grand girl . . . I wish I didn't feel ill.'

Tony was awake at eight next morning, miserably articulating in his mind the fragmentary memories of the preceding night. The more he remembered, the baser his conduct appeared to him. At nine he had his bath and some tea. At ten he was wondering whether he should ring Brenda up when the difficulty was solved by her ringing him.

'Well, Tony, how do you feel?'

'Awful. I *was* tight.'

'You were.'

'I'm feeling pretty guilty, too.'

'I'm not surprised.'

'I don't remember everything very clearly but I have the impression that Jock and I were rather bores.'

'You were.'

'Are you in a rage?'

'Well, I was last night. What made you do it, Tony, grown up men like you two?'

'We felt low.'

'I bet you feel lower this morning . . . A box of white roses has just arrived from Jock.'

'I wish I'd thought of that.'

'You're such infants, both of you.'

'You aren't really in a rage?'

'Of course I'm not, darling. Now just you go straight back to the country. You'll feel all right again tomorrow.'

'Am I not going to see you?'

'Not today, I'm afraid. I've got lectures all the morning and I'm lunching out. But I'll be coming down on Friday evening or anyway Saturday morning.'

'I see. You couldn't possibly chuck lunch or one of the lectures?'

'Not possibly, darling.'

'I see. You are an angel to be so sweet about last night.'

'Nothing could have been more fortunate,' Brenda said. 'If I know Tony, he'll be tortured with guilt for weeks to come. It was maddening last night but it was worth it. He's put himself so much in the wrong now that he won't dare to *feel* resentful, let alone say anything, whatever I do. And he hasn't really enjoyed himself at all, the poor sweet, so *that's* a good thing too. He had to learn not to make surprise visits.'

'You are one for making people learn things,' said Beaver.

Tony emerged from the 3.18 feeling cold, tired, and heavy with guilt. John Andrew had come in the car to meet him. 'Hallo, daddy, had a good time in London? You didn't mind me coming to the station, did you? I *made* nanny let me.'

'Very pleased to see you, John.'

'How was mummy?'

'She sounded very well. I didn't see her.'

'But you *said* you were going to see her.'

'Yes, I thought I was, but I turned out to be wrong. I talked to her several times on the telephone.'

'But you can telephone her from here, can't you, daddy? Why did you go all the way to London to telephone her? . . . *Why*, daddy?'

'It would take too long to explain.'

'Well tell me some of it . . . *Why*, daddy?'

'Look here, I'm tired. If you don't stop asking questions I shan't let you ever come and meet the train again.'

John Andrew's face began to pucker. 'I thought you'd *like* me to come and meet you.'

'If you cry I shall put you in front with Dawson. It's absurd to cry at your age.'

'I'd *sooner* go in front with Dawson,' said John Andrew between his tears.

Tony picked up the speaking tube to tell the chauffeur to stop, but he could not make him hear. So he hitched the mouthpiece back on its hook and they drove on in silence, John Andrew leaning against the window and snivelling slightly. When they got to the house, he said, 'Nanny, I don't want John to come to the station in future unless her ladyship or I specially say he can.'

'No, sir, I wouldn't have let him go today, only he went on so. Come along now, John, and take off your coat. Goodness, child, where's your handkerchief?'

Tony went and sat alone in front of the library fire. 'Two men of thirty,' he said to himself, 'behaving as if they were up for the night from Sandhurst–getting drunk and ringing people up and dancing with tarts at the Old Hundredth . . . And it makes it all the worse that Brenda was so nice about it.' He dozed a little; then he went up to change. At dinner he said, 'Ambrose, when I'm alone I think in future I'll have dinner in the library.' Afterwards he sat with a book in front of the fire but he was unable to read. At ten o'clock he scattered the logs in the fireplace before going upstairs. He fastened the library windows and turned out the lights. That night he went into Brenda's empty room to sleep.

II

That was Wednesday; on Thursday Tony felt well again. He had a meeting of the county council in the morning. In the afternoon he went down to the home farm and discussed a new kind of tractor with his agent. From then onwards he was able to say to himself, 'This time tomorrow Brenda and Jock will be here.' He dined in front of the fire in the library. He had given up the diet some weeks ago. ('Ambrose, when I'm alone I don't really need a long dinner. In future I'll just have two courses.') He looked over some accounts his agent had left for him and then went to bed, saying to himself, 'When I wake up it will be the week-end.'

But there was a telegram for him next morning from Jock, saying, *Week-end impossible have to go to constituency how about one after next*. He wired back, *Delighted any time always here*. 'I suppose he's made it up with that girl,' Tony reflected.

There was also a note from Brenda, written in pencil:

> Coming Sat. with Polly and a friend of Polly's called Veronica in P.'s car. Perhaps Daisy. Maids and luggage on 3.18. Will you tell Ambrose and Mrs Mossop. We had better open Lyonesse for Polly you know what she is about comfort. Veronica can go anywhere–not Galahad. Polly says she's v. amusing. Also Mrs Beaver coming please don't mind it is only on business, she thinks she can do something to morning-room. Polly bringing chauffeur. By the way I'm leaving Grimshawe at Hetton next week tell Mrs Mossop. It's a bore and expense boarding her out in London. In fact I think I might do without her altogether what do you think; except she's useful for sewing. Longing to see John again. All going back Sunday evening. Keep *sober* darling. *Try*. x x x x x x
>
> B.

Tony found very little to occupy his time on Friday. His letters were all finished by ten o'clock. He went down to the farm but they had no business for him there. The duties which before had seemed so multifarious, now took up a very small part of his day; he had not realized how many hours he used to waste with Brenda. He watched John riding in the paddock. The boy clearly bore him ill will for their quarrel on Wednesday; when he applauded a jump, John said, 'She usually does better than this.' Later, 'When's mummy coming down?'

'Not till tomorrow.'

'Oh.'

'I've got to go over to Little Bayton this afternoon. Would you like to come too and perhaps we could see the kennels?'

John had for weeks past been praying for this expedition. 'No, thank you,' he said. 'I want to finish a picture I'm painting.'

'You can do that any time.'

'I want to do it this afternoon.'

When Tony had left them, Ben said, 'Whatever made you speak to your dad like that for? You've been going on about seeing the kennels since Christmas.'

'Not with *him*,' said John.

'You ungrateful little bastard, that's a lousy way to speak of your dad.'

'And you ought not to say bastard or lousy in front of me, nanny says not.'

So Tony went over alone to Little Bayton where he had some business to discuss with Colonel Brink. He hoped they would ask him to stay on, but the Colonel and his wife were themselves going out to tea, so he drove back in the dusk to Hetton.

A thin mist lay breast high over the park; the turrets and battlements of the abbey stood grey and flat; the boiler man was hauling down the flag on the main tower.

'My poor Brenda, it's an appalling room,' said Mrs Beaver.

'It's not one we use a great deal,' said Tony very coldly.

'I should think not,' said the one they called Veronica.

'I can't see much wrong with it,' said Polly, 'except it's a bit mouldy.'

'You see,' Brenda explained, not looking at Tony. 'What I thought was that I must have one *habitable* room downstairs. At present there's only the smoking-room and the library. The drawing-room is vast and quite out of the question. I thought what I needed was a small sitting-room more or less to myself. Don't you think it has possibilities?'

'But, my angel, the *shape's* all wrong,' said Daisy, 'and that chimney piece–what is it made of, pink granite, and all the plaster work and the dado. *Everything's* horrible. It's so *dark*.'

'I know exactly what Brenda wants,' said Mrs Beaver more moderately. 'I don't think it will be impossible. I must think about it. As Veronica says, the structure does rather limit one . . . you know I think the only thing to do would be to disregard it altogether and find some treatment so definite that it *carried* the room, if you see what I mean . . . supposing we covered the walls with white chromium plating and had natural sheepskin carpet . . . I wonder if that would be running you in for more than you meant to spend?'

'I'd blow the whole thing sky-high,' said Veronica.

Tony left them to their discussion.

'D'you really want Mrs Beaver to do up the morning-room?'

'Not if you don't, sweet.'

'But can you imagine it–white chromium plating?'

'Oh, that was just an idea.'

Tony walked in and out between Morgan le Fay and Guinevere as he always did while they were dressing. 'I say,' he said, returning with his waistcoat. 'You aren't going away tomorrow, too, are you?'

'Must.'

He went back to Morgan le Fay for his tie and bringing it to Brenda's room again, sat by her side at the dressing-table to fasten it.

'By the way,' said Brenda, 'what did you think about keeping on Grimshawe? – it seems rather a waste.'

'You used always to say you couldn't get on without her.'

'Yes, but now I'm living at the flat everything's so simple.'

'*Living?* Darling, you talk as though you had settled there for good.'

'D'you mind moving a second, sweet? I can't see properly.'

'Brenda, how long are you going on with this course of economics?'

'Me? I don't know.'

'But you must have some idea?'

'Oh, it's surprising what a lot there is to learn . . . I was so backward when I started . . .'

'Brenda . . .'

'Now run and put on your coat. They'll all be downstairs waiting for us.'

That evening Polly and Mrs Beaver played backgammon. Brenda and Veronica sat together on the sofa sewing and talking about their needlework; occasionally there were bursts of general conversation between the women; they had the habit of lapsing into a jargon of their own which Tony did not understand; it was a thieves' slang, by which the syllables of each word were transposed. Tony sat just outside the circle reading under another lamp.

That night when they went upstairs, the guests came to sit in Brenda's room and talk to her while she went to bed. Tony could hear their low laughter through the dressing-room door. They had boiled water in an electric kettle and were drinking Sedobrol together.

Presently, still laughing, they left, and Tony went into Brenda's room. It was in darkness, but hearing him come and seeing the square of light in the doorway she turned on the little lamp by the bedside.

'Why, Tony,' she said.

She was lying on the dais with her head deep back in the pillows; her face was shining with the grease she used for cleaning it; one bare arm on the quilted eiderdown, left there from turning the switch. 'Why, Tony,' she said, 'I was almost asleep.'

'Very tired?'

'Mm.'

'Want to be left alone?'

'So tired . . . and I've just drunk a lot of that stuff of Polly's.'

'I see . . . well, goodnight.'

'Goodnight . . . don't mind, do you? . . . so tired.'

He crossed to the bed and kissed her; she lay quite still, with closed eyes. Then he turned out the light and went back to the dressing-room.

'Lady Brenda not ill, I hope?'

'No, nothing serious, thank you very much. She gets rather done up in London, you know, during the week, and likes to take Sunday quietly.'

'And how are the great studies progressing?'

'Very well, I gather. She seems keen on it still.'

'Splendid. We shall all be coming to her soon to solve our economic problems. But I daresay you and John miss her?'

'Yes, we do rather.'

'Well, please give her my kindest regards.'

'I will indeed. Thank you so much.'

Tony left the church porch and made his accustomed way to the hot houses; a gardenia for himself; some almost black carnations for the ladies. When he reached the room where they were sitting there was a burst of laughter. He paused on the threshold, rather bewildered.

'Come in, darling, it isn't anything. It's only we had a bet on what coloured buttonhole you'd be wearing and none of us won.'

They still giggled a little as they pinned on the flowers he had brought them; all except Mrs Beaver, who said, 'Any time you are buying cuttings or seeds do get them through me. I've made quite a little business of it, perhaps you didn't know . . . all kinds of rather unusual flowers. I do everything like that for Sylvia Newport and all sorts of people.'

'You must talk to my head man about it.'

'Well, to tell you the truth I *have*–this morning while you were in church. He seems quite to understand.'

They left early, so as to reach London in time for dinner. In the car Daisy said, 'Golly, what a house.'

'Now you can see what I've been through all these years.'

'My poor Brenda,' said Veronica, unpinning her carnation and throwing it from the window into the side of the road.

'You know,' Brenda confided next day, 'I'm not *absolutely* happy about Tony.'

'What's the old boy been up to?' asked Polly.

'Nothing much yet, but I do see it's pretty boring for him at Hetton all this time.'

'I shouldn't worry.'

'Oh, I'm not *worrying*. It's only, supposing he took to drink or something. It would make everything very difficult.'

'I shouldn't have said that was his thing . . . We must get him interested in a girl.'

'If only we could . . . Who is there?'

'There's always old Sybil.'

'Darling, he's known her all his life.'

'Or Souki de Foucauld-Esterhazy.'

'He isn't his best with Americans.'

'Well, we'll find him someone.'

'The trouble is that I've become such a habit with him–he won't take easily to a new one . . . ought she to be like me, or quite different?'

'I'd say different, but it's hard to tell.'

They discussed this problem in all its aspects.

III

Brenda wrote:

Darling Tony,

Sorry not to have written or rung up but I've had such a busy time with bimetallism. V. complicated.

Coming down Saturday with Polly again. Good her coming twice—Lyonesse can't be as beastly as most of the rooms, can it.

Also charming girl I have taken up with who I want us to be kind to. She's had a *terrible* life and she lives in one of these flats, called Jenny Abdul Akbar. Not black but married one. Get her to tell you. She'll come by train 3.18 I expect. Must stop now and go to lecture.

Keep away from the Demon Rum. x x x x x x

Brenda

Saw Jock last night at Café de Paris with shameless blonde. Who?

Gin. No. Djin–how?–has rheumatism and Marjorie is v. put out about it. She thinks his pelvis is out of place and Cruttwell won't do him which is pretty mean considering all the people she has brought there.

'Are you *certain* Jenny will be Tony's tea?'

'You can't ever be certain,' said Polly. 'She bores my pants off, but she's a good trier.'

'Is mummy coming down today, daddy?'

'Yes.'

'Who else?'

'Someone called Jenny Abdul Akbar.'

'What a silly name. Is she foreign?'

'I don't know.'

'Sounds foreign, doesn't she, daddy? D'you think she won't be able to talk any English? Is she black?'

'Mummy says not.'

'Oh . . . who else?'

'Lady Cockpurse.'

'The monkey woman. You know she wasn't a bit like a monkey except perhaps her face and I don't think she had a tail because I looked as close as anything . . . unless perhaps she has it rolled up between her legs. D'you think she has, daddy?'

'I shouldn't be surprised.'

'*Very uncomfortable.*'

Tony and John were friends again; but it had been a leaden week.

It was part of Polly Cockpurse's plan to arrive late at Hetton. 'Give the girl a chance to get down to it,' she said. So she and Brenda did not leave London until Jenny was already on her way from the station. It was a day of bitter cold and occasional rain. The resolute little figure huddled herself in the rugs until she reached the gates. Then she opened her bag, tucked up her veil, shook out her powder-puff and put her face to rights. She licked the rouge from her finger with a sharp red tongue.

Tony was in the smoking-room when she was announced; the library was now too noisy during the daytime, for there were men at work on the walls of the morning-room next door, tearing down the plaster tracery.

'Princess Abdul Akbar.'

He rose to greet her. She was preceded by a heavy odour of musk.

'Oh, Mr Last,' she said, 'what a sweet old place this is.'

'I'm afraid its been restored a great deal,' said Tony.

'Ah, but its *atmosphere*. I always think that's what counts in a house. Such dignity, and repose. But of course you're used to it. When you've been very unhappy as I have, you appreciate these things.'

Tony said, 'I'm afraid Brenda hasn't arrived yet. She's coming by car with Lady Cockpurse.'

'Brenda's been *such* a friend to me.' The Princess took off her furs and sat down on the stool before the fire, looking up at Tony. 'D'you mind if I take off my hat?'

'No, no . . . of course.'

She threw it on to the sofa and shook out her hair, which was dead black and curled. 'D'you know, Mr Last, I'm going to call you Teddy right away. You don't think that very fresh of me? And you must call me Jenny. "Princess" is so formal, isn't it, and suggests tight trousers and gold braid . . . Of course,' she went on, stretching out her hands to the fire and letting her hair fall forwards a little across her face, 'my husband was not called "Prince" in Morocco; his title was Moulay–but there's no proper equivalent for a woman, so I've always called myself Princess in Europe . . . Moulay is *far* higher really . . . my husband was a descendant of the Prophet. Are you interested in the East?'

'No . . . yes. I mean I know very little about it.'

'It has an uncanny fascination for me. You must go there, Teddy. I know you'd like it. I've been saying the same to Brenda.'

'I expect you'd like to see your room,' said Tony. 'They'll bring tea soon.'

'No, I'll stay here. I like just to curl up like a cat in front of the fire, and if you're nice to me I'll purr, and if you're cruel I shall pretend not to notice–just like a cat . . . Shall I purr, Teddy?'

'Er . . . yes . . . do, please, if that's what you like doing.'

'Englishmen are so gentle and considerate. It's wonderful to be back among them . . . mine own people. Sometimes when I look back at my life, especially at times like this among lovely old English things and kind people, I think the whole thing must be a frightful nightmare . . . then I remember my *scars* . . .'

'Brenda tells me you've taken one of the flats in the same house as hers. They must be very convenient.'

'How English you are, Teddy–so shy of talking about personal things, intimate things . . . I like you for that, you know. I love everything that's solid and homely and *good* after . . . after all I've been through.'

'You're not studying economics too, are you, like Brenda?'

'No; is Brenda? She never told me. What a wonderful person she is. When *does* she find the time?'

'Ah, here comes tea at last,' said Tony. 'I hope you allow yourself to eat muffins. So many of our guests nowadays are on a diet. I think muffins one of the few things that make the English winter endurable.'

'Muffins stand for so much,' said Jenny.

She ate heartily; often she ran her tongue over her lips, collecting crumbs that had become embedded there and melted butter from the muffin. One drop of butter fell on her chin and glittered there unobserved except by Tony. It was a relief to him when John Andrew was brought in.

'Come and be introduced to Princess Abdul Akbar.'

John Andrew had never before seen a Princess; he gazed at her fascinated.

'Aren't you going to give me a kiss?'

He walked over to her and she kissed him on the mouth.

'Oh,' he said, recoiling and rubbing away the taste of the lipstick; and then, 'What a beautiful smell.'

'It's my last link with the East,' she said.

'You've got butter on your chin.'

She reached for her bag, laughing. 'Why, so I have. Teddy, you *might* have told me.'

'Why do you call daddy Teddy?'

'Because I hope we are going to be great friends.'

'What a funny reason.'

John stayed with them for an hour, and all the time watched fascinated. 'Have you got a crown?' he asked. 'How did you learn to speak English? What is that big ring made of? Did it cost much? Why are your nails that colour? Can you ride?'

She answered all his questions, sometimes enigmatically with an eye on Tony. She took out a little heavily scented handkerchief and showed John the monogram. 'That is my only crown . . . now,' she said. She told him about the horses she used to have–glossy black, with arched necks; foam round their silver bits; plumes tossing on their foreheads; silver studs on the harness, crimson saddle cloths. 'On the Moulay's birthday—'

'What's the Moulay?'

'A beautiful and very bad man,' she said gravely, 'and on his birthday all his horsemen used to assemble round a great square, with all their finest clothes and trappings and jewels, with long swords in their hands. The Moulay used to sit on a throne under a great crimson canopy.'

'What's a canopy?'

'Like a tent,' she said more sharply, and then, resuming her soft voice, 'and all the horsemen used to gallop across the plain, in a great cloud of dust, waving their swords, straight towards the Moulay. And everyone used to hold their breath, thinking the horsemen were bound to ride right on top of the Moulay, but when they were a few feet away, as near as I am to you, galloping at full speed, they used to rein their horses back, up on to their hind legs and salute—'

'Oh, but they *shouldn't*,' said John. 'It's *very* bad horsemanship indeed. Ben says so.'

'They're the most wonderful horsemen in the world. Everyone knows that.'

'Oh, no, they can't be, if they do *that*. It's one of the *worst* things. Were they natives?'

'Yes, of course.'

'Ben says natives aren't humans at all really.'

'Ah, but he's thinking of negroes, I expect. These are pure Semitic type.'

'What's that?'

'The same as Jews.'

'Ben says Jews are worse than natives.'

'Oh dear, what a very severe boy you are. I was like that once. Life teaches one to be tolerant.'

'It hasn't taught Ben,' said John. 'When's mummy coming? I thought she'd be here, otherwise I wouldn't have stopped painting my picture.'

But when nanny came to fetch him, John, without invitation, went over and kissed Jenny goodnight. 'Goodnight, Johnny-boy,' she said.

'What did you call me?'

'Johnny-boy.'

'You are funny with names.'

Upstairs, meditatively splashing his spoon in the bread and milk, he said, 'Nanny, I do think that Princess is beautiful, don't you?'

Nanny sniffed. 'It would be a dull world if we all thought alike,' she said.

'She's more beautiful than Miss Tendril, even. I think she's the most beautiful lady I've ever seen . . . D'you think she'd like to watch me have my bath?'

Downstairs, Jenny said, 'What a heavenly child . . . I love children. That has been my great tragedy. It was when he found I couldn't have children that the Moulay first showed the Other Side of his Nature. It wasn't my fault . . . you see my womb is out of place . . . I don't know why I'm telling you all this, but I feel you'll understand. It's such a *waste of time*, isn't it, when one knows one is going to like someone and one goes on *pretending* . . . I know at once if someone is going to be a real friend . . .'

Polly and Brenda arrived just before seven. Brenda went straight up to the nursery. 'Oh mummy,' said John, 'there's such a beautiful lady downstairs. Do ask her to come and say goodnight. Nanny doesn't think she'd want to.'

'Did daddy seem to like her?'

'He didn't talk much . . . She doesn't know anything about horses or natives but she *is* beautiful. Please tell her to come up.'

Brenda went downstairs and found Jenny with Polly and Tony in the smoking-room. 'You've made a wild success with John Andrew. He won't go to sleep until he's seen you again.'

They went up together, and Jenny said, 'They're both such dears.'

'Did you and Tony get on? I was so sorry not to be here when you arrived.'

'He was *so* sympathetic and gentle . . . and so wistful.'

They sat on John's small bed in the night-nursery. He threw the clothes back and crawled out, nestling against Jenny. 'Back to bed,' she said, 'or I shall spank you.'

'Would you do it hard? I shouldn't mind.'

'Oh dear,' said Brenda, 'what a terrible effect you seem to have. He's never like this as a rule.'

When they had gone nanny threw open another window. 'Poof!' she said, 'making the whole place stink.'

'Don't you like it? *I* think it's lovely.'

Brenda took Polly up to Lyonesse. It was a large suite, fitted up with satinwood for King Edward when, as Prince of Wales, he was once expected at a shooting party; he never came.

'How's it going?' she asked anxiously.

'Too soon to tell. I'm sure it will be all right.'

'She's got the wrong chap. John Andrew's mad about her . . . quite embarrassing.'

'I should say Tony was a slow starter. It's a pity she's got his name wrong. Ought we to tell her?'

'No, let's leave it.'

When they were dressing, Tony said, 'Brenda, who *is* this joke-woman?'

'Darling, don't you like her?'

The disappointment and distress in her tone were so clear that Tony was touched. 'I don't know about not liking her exactly. She's just a joke, isn't she?'

'Is she . . . oh, dear . . . She's had a terrible life, you know.'

'So I gathered.'

'Be nice to her, Tony, please.'

'Oh, I'll be nice to her. Is she a Jewess?'

'I don't know. I never thought. Perhaps she is.'

Soon after dinner Polly said she was tired and asked Brenda to come with her while she undressed. 'Leave the young couple to it,' she whispered outside the door.

'My dear, I don't believe it's going to be any good . . . the poor old boy's got *some* taste you know, and a sense of humour.'

'She didn't show up too well at dinner, did she?'

'She will *go on* so . . . and after all, Tony's been used to me for seven years. It's rather a sudden change.'

'Tired?'

'Mmm. Little bit.'

'You gave me a pretty long bout of Abdul Akbar.'

'I know. I'm sorry, darling, but Polly takes so long to get to bed . . . Was it awful? I wish you liked her more.'

'She's awful.'

'One has to make allowances . . . she's got the most terrible scars.'

'So she told me.'

'I've seen them.'

'Besides I hoped to see something of you.'

'Oh.'

'Brenda, you aren't angry still about my getting tight that night and waking you up?'

'No, sweet, do I seem angry?'

'. . . I don't know. You do rather . . . Has it been an amusing week?'

'Not amusing, very hard work. Bimetallism, you know.'

'Oh, yes . . . well, I suppose you want to go to sleep.'

'Mm . . . so tired. Goodnight, darling.'

'Goodnight.'

'Can I go and say good-morning to the Princess, mummy?'

'I don't expect she's awake yet.'

'Please, mummy, may I go and see? I'll just peep and, if she's asleep, go away.'

'I don't know what room she's in.'

'Galahad, my lady,' said Grimshawe, who was putting out her clothes.

'Oh dear, why was she put there?'

'It was Mr Last's orders, my lady.'

'Well, she's probably awake, then.'

John slipped out of the room and trotted down the passage to Galahad. 'May I come in?'

'Hullo, Johnny-boy. Come in.'

He swung on the handles of the door, half in, half out of the room. 'Have you had breakfast? Mummy said you wouldn't be awake.'

'I've been awake a long time. You see I was once very badly hurt, and now I don't always sleep well. Even the softest beds are too hard for me now.'

'Ooh. What did you do? Was it a motor-car accident?'

'Not an accident, Johnny-boy, not an accident . . . but come in. It's cold with the door open. Look, there are some grapes here. Would you like to eat them?'

Johnny climbed on to the bed. 'What are you going to do today?'

'I don't know yet. I haven't been told.'

'Well, I'll tell you. We'll go to church in the morning because I have to and then we'll go and look at Thunderclap and I'll show you the place we jump and then you can come with me while I have dinner because I have it early and afterwards we can go down to Bruton Wood and we needn't take nanny because it makes her so muddy and you can see where they dug out a fox in the drain just outside the wood, he nearly got away, and then you can come and have tea in the nursery and I've got a little gramophone Uncle Reggie gave me for Christmas and it plays "When Father Papered the Parlour", do you know that song? Ben can sing it and I've got some books to show you and a picture I did of the battle of Marston Moor.'

'I think that sounds a lovely day. But don't you think I ought to spend some time with daddy and mummy and Lady Cockpurse?'

'Oh, *them* . . . besides it's all my foot about Lady Cockpurse having a tail. Please you *will* spend the day with me?'

'Well, we'll see.'

'She's gone to church with him. That's a good sign, isn't it?'

'Well, not really, Polly. He likes going alone, or with me. It's the time he gossips to the village.'

'She won't stop him.'

'I'm afraid you don't understand the old boy altogether. He's much odder than you'd think.'

'I could see from your sermon that you knew the East, Rector.'

'Yes, yes, most of my life.'

'It has an uncanny fascination, hasn't it?'

'Oh, come on,' said John, pulling at her coat. 'We must go and see Thunderclap.'

So Tony returned alone with the buttonholes.

After luncheon Brenda said, 'Why don't you show Jenny the house?'

'Oh yes, *do*.'

When they reached the morning-room he said, 'Brenda's having it done up.'

There were planks and ladders and heaps of plaster about.

'Oh Teddy, what a shame. I do hate seeing things modernized.'

'It isn't a room we used very much.'

'No, but still . . .' She stirred the mouldings of fleurs-de-lys that littered the floor, fragments of tarnished gilding and dusty stencil-work. 'You know, Brenda's been a wonderful friend to me. I wouldn't say anything against her . . . but ever since I came here I've been wondering whether she really understands this beautiful place and all it means to you.'

'Tell me more about your terrible life,' said Tony, leading her back to the central hall.

'You *are* shy of talking about yourself, aren't you, Teddy? It's a mistake, you know, to keep things bottled up. I've been very unhappy, too.'

Tony looked about him desperately in search of help; and help came. 'Oh there you are,' said a firm, child's voice. 'Come on. We're going down to the woods now. We must hurry, otherwise it will be dark.'

'Oh Johnny-boy, must I really? I was just talking to daddy.'

'*Come on*. It's all arranged. And afterwards you're to be allowed to have tea with me upstairs.'

Tony crept into the library, habitable today, since the workmen were at rest. Brenda found him there two hours later. '*Tony*, here all alone? We thought you were with Jenny. What have you done with her?'

'John took her off . . . just in time before I said something rude.'

'Oh dear . . . well there's only me and Polly in the smoking-room. Come and have some tea. You look all funny–have you been asleep?'

'We must write it down a failure, definitely.'

'What *does* the old boy expect? It isn't as though he was everybody's money.'

'I daresay it would have been all right, if she hadn't got his name wrong.'

'Anyway, this lets *you* out. You've done far more than most wives would to cheer the old boy up.'

'Yes, that's certainly true,' said Brenda.

IV

Another five days; then Brenda came to Hetton again. 'I shan't be here next week-end,' she said, 'I'm going to stay with Veronica.'

'Am I asked?'

'Well, you *were*, of course, but I refused for you. You know you always hate staying away.'

'I wouldn't mind coming.'

'Oh, darling, I wish I'd known. Veronica would have loved it so . . . but I'm afraid it will be too late now. She's only got a tiny house . . . to tell you the truth I didn't think you liked her much.'

'I hated her like hell.'

'Well then . . .?'

'Oh, it doesn't matter. I suppose you must go back on Monday? The hounds are meeting here on Wednesday, you know.'

'Are we giving them a lawner?'

'Yes, darling, you know we do every year.'

'So we do.'

'You couldn't stay down till then?'

'Not possibly, darling. You see if I miss one lecture I get right behind and can't follow the next. Besides I am not mad keen to see the hounds.'

'Ben was asking if we'd let John go out.'

'Oh, he's far too young.'

'Not to hunt. But I thought he might bring his pony to the meet and ride with them to the first covert. He'd love it so.'

'Is it quite safe?'

'Oh, yes, surely?'

'Bless his heart, I wish I could be here to see him.'

'Do change your mind.'

'Oh no, that's quite out of the question. Don't make a thing about it, Tony.'

That was when she first arrived; later everything got better. Jock was there that week-end, also Allan and Marjorie and another married couple whom Tony had known all his life. Brenda had arranged the party for him and he enjoyed it. He and Allan went out with rook rifles and shot rabbits in the twilight; after dinner the four men played billiard fives while one wife watched. 'The old boy's happy as a lark,' said Brenda to Marjorie. 'He's settling down wonderfully to the new regime.'

They came in breathless and rather flushed for whisky and soda.

'Tony nearly had one through the window,' said Jock.

That night Tony slept in Guinevere.

'Everything *is* all right, isn't it?' he said once.

'Yes, of course, darling.'

'I get depressed down here all alone and imagine things.'

'You aren't to *brood*, Tony. You know that's one of the things that aren't allowed.'

'I won't brood any more,' said Tony.

Next day Brenda came to church with him. She had decided to devote the week-end wholly to him; it would be the last for some time.

'And how are the abstruse sciences, Lady Brenda?'

'Absorbing.'

'We shall all be coming to you for advice about our overdrafts.'

'Ha, ha.'

'And how's Thunderclap?' asked Miss Tendril.

'I'm taking her out hunting on Wednesday,' said John. He had forgotten Princess Abdul Akbar in the excitement of the coming meet. 'Please God make there be a good scent. Please God make me see the kill. Please God don't let me do anything wrong. God bless Ben and Thunderclap. Please God make me jump an enormous great oxer,' he had kept repeating throughout the service.

Brenda did the round with Tony of cottages and hot houses; she helped him choose his buttonhole.

Tony was in high spirits at luncheon. Brenda had begun to forget how amusing he could be. Afterwards he changed into other clothes and went with Jock to play golf. They stayed some time at the club house. Tony said, 'We've got the hounds meeting at Hetton on Wednesday. Couldn't you stay down till then.'

'Must be back. There's going to be a debate on the Pig Scheme.'

'I wish you'd stay. Look here, why don't you ask that girl down? Everyone goes tomorrow. You could ring her up, couldn't you?'

'I *could*.'

'Would she hate it? She could have Lyonesse–Polly slept there two week-ends running, so it can't be too uncomfortable.'

'She'd probably love it. I'll ring up and ask her.'

'Why don't you hunt too? There's a chap called Brinkwell who's got some quite decent hirelings, I believe.'

'Yes, I might.'

'Jock's staying on. He's having the shameless blonde down. You don't mind?'

'Me? Of course not?'

'This *has* been a jolly week-end.'

'I thought you were enjoying it.'

'Just like old times–before the economics began.'

Marjorie said to Jock, 'D'you think Tony knows about Mr Beaver?'

'Not a thing.'

'I haven't mentioned it to Allan. D'you suppose he knows?'

'I doubt it.'

'Oh Jock, how d'you think it'll end?'

'She'll get bored with Beaver soon enough.'

'The trouble is that he doesn't care for her in the least. If he did, it would soon be over . . . What an ass she is being.'

'I should say she was managing it unusually well, if you ask me.'

The other married couple said to each other, 'D'you think Marjorie and Allan know about Brenda?'

'I'm sure they don't.'

Brenda said to Allan, 'Tony's as happy as a sandboy, isn't he?'

'Full of beans.'

'I was getting worried about him . . . You don't think he's got any idea about my goings on?'

'Lord, no. It's the last thing that would come into his head.'

Brenda said, 'I don't want him to be unhappy, you know . . . Marjorie's been frightfully governessy about the whole thing.'

'Has she? I haven't discussed it with her.'

'How did *you* hear?'

'My dear girl, until this minute I didn't know you had any goings on. And I'm not asking any questions about them now.'

'Oh . . . I thought everyone knew.'

'That's always the trouble with people when they start walking out. They either think no one knows, or everybody. The truth is that a few people like Polly and Sybil make a point of finding out about everyone's private life; the rest of us aren't interested.'

'Oh.'

Later he said to Marjorie, 'Brenda tried to be confidential about Beaver this evening.'

'I didn't know you knew.'

'Oh, I knew all right. But I wasn't going to let her feel important by talking about it.'

'I couldn't disapprove more of the whole thing. Do you know Beaver?'

'I've seen him about. Anyway, it's her business and Tony's, not ours.'

V

Jock's blonde was called Mrs Rattery. Tony had conceived an idea of her from what he overheard of Polly's gossip and from various fragments of information let fall by Jock. She was a little over thirty. Somewhere in the Cottesmore country there lived a long-legged, slightly discredited Major Rattery, to whom she had once been married. She was an American by origin, now totally denationalized, rich, without property or possessions, except those that would pack in five vast trunks. Jock had had his eye on her last summer at Biarritz and had fallen in with her again in London where she played big bridge, very ably, for six or seven hours a day and changed her hotel, on an average, once every three weeks. Periodically she was liable to bouts of morphine; then she gave up her bridge and remained for several days at a time alone in her hotel suite, refreshed at intervals with glasses of cold milk.

She arrived by air on Monday afternoon. It was the first time that a guest had come in this fashion, and the household was appreciably excited. Under Jock's direction the boiler man and one of the gardeners pegged out a dust sheet in the park to mark a landing for her and lit a bonfire of damp leaves to show the direction of the wind. The five trunks arrived in the ordinary way by train, with an elderly, irreproachable maid. She brought her own sheets with her in one of the trunks; they were neither silk nor coloured, without lace or ornament of any kind, except small, plain monograms.

Tony, Jock and John went out to watch her land. She climbed out of the cockpit, stretched, unbuttoned the flaps of her leather helmet, and came to meet them. 'Forty-two minutes,' she said, 'not at all bad with the wind against me.'

She was tall and erect, almost austere in helmet and overalls; not at all as Tony had imagined her. Vaguely, at the back of his mind, he had secreted the slightly absurd expectation of a chorus girl, in silk shorts and brassiere, popping out of an immense beribboned Easter egg with a cry of 'Whoopee, boys.' Mrs Rattery's greetings were deft and impersonal.

'Are you going to hunt on Wednesday?' asked John. 'They're meeting here, you know.'

'I might go out for half the day, if I can find a horse. It'll be the first time this year.'

'It's my first time, too.'

'We shall both be terribly stiff.' She spoke to him exactly as though he were a man of her own age. 'You'll have to show me the country.'

'I expect they'll draw Bruton Wood first. There's a big fox there, daddy and I saw him.'

When they were alone together, Jock said, 'It's delightful your coming down. What d'you think of Tony?'

'Is he married to that rather lovely woman we saw at the Café de Paris?'

'Yes.'

'The one you said was in love with that young man?'

'Yes.'

'Funny of her . . . What's this one's name again?'

'Tony Last. It's a pretty ghastly house, isn't it?'

'Is it? I never notice houses much.'

She was an easy guest to entertain. After dinner on Monday she produced four packs of cards and laid out for herself on the smoking-room table a very elaborate patience, which kept her engrossed all the evening. 'Don't wait up for me,' she said. 'I shall stay here until it comes out. It often takes several hours.'

They showed her where to put the lights out and left her to it.

Next day Jock said, 'Have you got any pigs at the farm?'

'Yes.'

'Would you mind if I went to see them?'

'Not in the least–but why?'

'And is there a man who looks after them, who will be able to explain about them?'

'Yes.'

'Well, I think I'll spend the morning with him. I've got to make a speech about pigs, fairly soon.'

They did not see Mrs Rattery until luncheon. Tony assumed she was asleep until she appeared in overalls from the morning-room. 'I was down early,' she explained, 'and found the men at work stripping the ceiling. I couldn't resist joining in. I hope you don't mind.'

In the afternoon they went to a neighbouring livery stables to look for hirelings. After tea Tony wrote to Brenda; he had taken to writing letters in the past few weeks.

> How enjoyable the week-end was, *he wrote*. Thank you a thousand times for all your sweetness. I wish you were coming down next week-end, or that you had been able to stay on a little, but I quite understand.
>
> The Shameless Blonde is not the least what we expected–very serene and distant. Not at all like Jock's usual taste. I am sure she hasn't any idea where she is or what my name is.
>
> The work in the morning-room is going on well. The foreman told me today he thought he would begin on the chromium plating by the end of the week. You know what I think about that.
>
> John can talk of nothing except his hunting tomorrow. I hope he doesn't break his neck. Jock and his S.B. are going out too.

Hetton lay near the boundary of three packs; the Pigstanton, who hunted it, had, in the division of territory, come off with the worst country and they cherished a permanent resentment about some woods near Bayton. They were a somewhat ill-tempered lot, contemptuous of each other's performance, hostile to strangers, torn by internal rancour, united only in their dislike of the Master. In the case of Colonel Inch this unpopularity, traditional to the hunt, was quite undeserved; he was a timid, inconspicuous man who provided the neighbourhood with sport of a kind at great personal expense. He himself was seldom in sight of hounds and could often be found in another part of the country morosely nibbling ginger nut biscuits in a lane, or towards the end of the day cantering heavily across country, quite lost, a lonely scarlet figure against the ploughed land, staring about him in the deepening twilight and shouting at yokels for information. The only pleasure he gained from his position, but that a substantial one, was in referring to it casually at Board Meetings of the various companies he directed.

The Pigstanton met twice a week. There was seldom a large field on Wednesday, but the Hetton meet was popular; it lay in their best country and the prospect of stirrup cups had drawn many leathery old ladies from the neighbouring packs. There were also followers on foot and in every kind of vehicle, some hanging back diffidently, others, more or less known to Tony, crowding round the refreshment table. Mr Tendril had a niece staying with him, who appeared on a motor bicycle.

John stood beside Thunderclap, solemn with excitement. Ben had secured a powerful, square-headed mare from a neighbouring farmer; he hoped to have a hunt after John had been taken home; at John's earnest entreaty nanny was confined indoors, among the housemaids whose heads obtruded at the upper windows; it was not her day. She had been out of temper while dressing him. 'If I'm in at the death I expect Colonel Inch will blood me.'

'You won't see any death,' said nanny.

Now she stood with her eyes at an arrow slit gazing rather resentfully at the animated scene below. 'It's all a lot of nonsense of Ben Hacket's,' she thought. She deplored it all, hounds, Master, field, huntsmen and whippers-in. Mr Tendril's niece in her mackintosh, Jock in a rat-catcher, Mrs Rattery in tall hat and cutaway coat, oblivious of the suspicious glances of the subscribers, Tony smiling and chatting to his guests, the crazy old man with the terriers, the Press photographer, pretty Miss Ripon in difficulties with a young horse, titupping sideways over the lawn, the grooms and second horses, the humble, unknown followers in the background–it was all a lot of nonsense of Ben Hacket's. 'It was after eleven before the child got to sleep last night,' she reflected, 'he was that over-excited.'

Presently they moved off towards Bruton Wood. The way lay down the south drive through Compton Last, along the main road for half a mile, and then through fields. 'He can ride with them as far as the covert,' Tony had said.

'Yes, sir, and there'd be no harm in his staying a bit to see hounds working, would there?'

'No, I suppose not.'

'And if he breaks away towards home, there'd be no harm in our following a bit, if we keeps to the lanes and gates, would there, sir?'

'No, but he's not stay out more than an hour.'

'You wouldn't have me take him home with hounds running, would you, sir?'

'Well, he's got to be in before one.'

'I'll see to that, sir.' 'Don't you worry, my beauty,' he said to John, 'you'll get a hunt right enough.'

They waited until the end of the line of horses and then trotted soberly behind them. Close at their heels followed the motor-cars, at low gear, in a fog of exhaust. John was breathless and slightly dizzy. Thunderclap was tossing her head and worrying at her snaffle. Twice while the field was moving off, she had tried to get away and had taken John round in a little circle, so that Ben had said, 'Hold on to her, son,' and had come up close beside him so as to be able to catch the reins if she looked like bolting. Once, boring forwards with her head, she took John by surprise and pulled him forwards out of his balance; he caught hold of the front of the saddle to steady himself and looked guiltily at Ben. 'I'm afraid I'm riding very badly today. D'you think anyone has noticed?'

'That's all right, son. You can't keep riding-school manners when you're hunting.'

Jock and Mrs Rattery trotted side by side. 'I rather like this absurd horse,' she said. She rode astride and it was evident from the moment she mounted that she rode extremely well.

The members of the Pigstanton noted this with ill-concealed resentment, for it disturbed their fixed opinion according to which, while all fellow members of the hunt were clowns and poltroons, strangers were, without exception, mannerless lunatics, and a serious menace to anyone within a quarter of a mile of them.

Halfway through the village Miss Ripon had difficulties in getting past a stationary baker's van. Her horse plunged and reared, trembling all over, turning about, and slipping frantically over the tarmac. They rode round her, giving his heels the widest berth, scowling ominously and grumbling about her. They all knew that horse. Miss Ripon's father had been trying to sell him all the season, and had lately come down to eighty pounds. He was a good jumper on occasions but a beast of a horse to ride. Did Miss Ripon's father really imagine he was improving his chances of a sale by letting Miss Ripon make an exhibition of herself? It was like that skinflint, Miss Ripon's father, to risk Miss Ripon's neck for eighty pounds. And, anyway, Miss Ripon had no business out on *any* horse . . .

Presently she shot past them at a gallop; she was flushed in the face and her bun was askew; she leant back, pulling with all her weight. 'That girl will come to no good,' said Jock.

They encountered her later at the covert. Her horse was sweating and lathered at the bridle but temporarily at rest cropping the tufts of sedge that lay round the woods. Miss Ripon was much out of breath, and her hands shook as she fiddled with veil, bun and bowler. John rode up to Jock's side.

'What's happening, Mr Grant-Menzies?'

'Hounds are drawing the covert.'

'Oh.'

'Are you enjoying yourself?'

'Oh yes. Thunderclap's terribly fresh. I've never known her like this.'

There was a long wait as the horn sounded in the heart of the wood. Everyone stood in the corner of the big field, near a gate. Everyone, that is to say, except Miss Ripon, who some minutes ago had disappeared suddenly, indeed in the middle of a sentence, at full gallop towards Hetton Hills. After half an hour Jock said, 'They're calling hounds off.'

'Does that mean it's a blank?'

'I'm afraid so.'

'I hate this happening in *our* woods,' said Ben. 'Looks bad.'

Indeed the Pigstanton were already beginning to forget their hospitality and to ask each other what did one expect when Last did not hunt himself, and to circulate dark reports of how one of the keepers had been observed last week burying Something late in the evening.

They moved off again, away from Hetton. Ben began to feel his responsibility. 'D'you think I ought to take the young gentleman home, sir?'

'What did Mr Last say?'

'He said he could go as far as the covert. He didn't say which, sir.'

'I'm afraid it sounds as if he ought to go.'

'*Oh, Mr Menzies!*'

'Yes, come along, Master John. You've had enough for today.'

'But I haven't had *any*.'

'If you come back in good time today your dad will be all the more willing to let you come out another day.'

'But there mayn't *be* another day. The world may come to an end. *Please*, Ben. *Please*, Mr Menzies.'

'It is a shame they shouldn't have found,' said Ben. 'He's been looking forward to it.'

'Still, I think Mr Last would want him to go back,' said Jock.

So John's fate was decided; hounds went in one direction, he and Ben in another. John was very near tears as they reached the main road.

'Look,' said Ben, to encourage him. 'Here comes Miss Ripon on that nappy bay. Seems as if she's going in, too. Had a fall by the looks of her.'

Miss Ripon's hat and back were covered with mud and moss. She had had a bad twenty minutes after her disappearance. 'I'm taking him away,' she said. 'I can't do anything with him this morning.' She jogged along beside them towards the village. 'I thought perhaps Mr Last would let me come up to the house and telephone for the car. I don't feel like hacking him home in his present state. I can't think what's come over him,' she added loyally. 'He was out on Saturday. I've never known him like this before.'

'He wants a man up,' said Ben.

'Oh, he's no better with the groom, and daddy won't go near him,' said Miss Ripon, stung to indiscretion. 'At least . . . I mean . . . I don't think that they'd be any better with him in this state.'

He was quiet enough at that moment, keeping pace with the other horses. They rode abreast, she on the outside with John's pony between her and Ben.

Then this happened: they reached a turn in the road and came face to face with one of the single-decker country buses that covered that neighbourhood. It was not going fast and, seeing the horses, the driver slowed down still further and drew into the side. Mr Tendril's niece, who had also despaired of the day's sport, was following behind them at a short distance on her motor bicycle; she too slowed down and, observing that Miss Ripon's horse was likely to be difficult, stopped.

Ben said, 'Let me go first, Miss. He'll follow. Don't hold too hard on his mouth and just give him a tap.'

Miss Ripon did as she was told; everyone in fact behaved with complete good-sense.

They drew abreast of the omnibus. Miss Ripon's horse did not like it, but it seemed as though he would get by. The passengers watched with amusement. At that moment the motor bicycle, running gently in neutral gear, fired back into the cylinder with a sharp detonation.

For a second Miss Ripon's horse stood rigid with alarm; then, menaced in front and behind, he did what was natural to him and shied sideways, cannoning violently into the pony at his side. John was knocked from the saddle and fell on the road while Miss Ripon's bay, rearing and skidding, continued to plunge away from the bus.

'Take a hold of him, Miss. Use your whip,' shouted Ben. 'The boy's down.'

She hit him and the horse collected himself and bolted up the road into the village, but before he went one of his heels struck out and sent John into the ditch, where he lay bent double, perfectly still.

Everyone agreed that it was nobody's fault.

It was nearly an hour before the news reached Jock and Mrs Rattery where they were waiting beside another blank covert. Colonel Inch stopped hunting for the day and sent the hounds back to the kennels. The voices were hushed which, five minutes before, had been proclaiming that they knew it for a fact, Last had given orders to shoot every fox on the place. Later, after their baths, they made up for it in criticism of Miss Ripon's father, but at the moment everyone was shocked and silent. Someone lent Jock and Mrs Rattery a car to get home in, and a groom to see to the hirelings.

'It's the most appalling thing,' said Jock in the borrowed car. 'What on earth are we going to say to Tony?'

'I'm the last person to have about on an occasion like this,' said Mrs Rattery.

They passed the scene of the accident; there were still people hanging about, talking.

There were people hanging about, talking in the hall at the house. The doctor was buttoning up his coat, just going.

'Killed instantly,' he said. 'Took it full on the base of the skull. Very sad, awfully fond of the kid. No one to blame though.'

Nanny was there in tears, also Mr Tendril and his niece; a policeman and Ben and two men who had helped bring up the body were in the servants' hall. 'It wasn't the kid's fault,' said Ben.

'It wasn't anyone's fault,' they said.

'He'd had a lousy day too, poor little bastard,' said Ben.

'If it was anyone's fault it was Mr Grant-Menzies making him go in.'

'It wasn't anyone's fault,' they said.

Tony was alone in the library. The first thing he said, when Jock came in was, 'We've got to tell Brenda.'

'D'you know where to get her?'

'She's probably at that school . . . But we can't tell her over the telephone . . . Anyway Ambrose has tried there and the flat but he can't get through . . . What on earth are we going to say to her?'

Jock was silent. He stood in the fireplace with his hands in the pockets of his breeches, with his back to Tony. Presently Tony said, 'You weren't anywhere near, were you?'

'No, we'd gone on to another covert.'

'That niece of Mr Tendril's told me first . . . then we met them coming up, and Ben told me all that happened. . . . It's awful for the girl.'

'Miss Ripon?'

'Yes, she's just left . . . she had a nasty fall too, just after. Her horse slipped up in the village . . . she was in a terrible state, poor child, what with that and . . . John. She didn't know she'd hurt him until quite a time afterwards . . . she was in the chemist's shop having a bandage put on her head, when they told her. She cut it falling. She was in a terrible state. I sent her back in the car . . . it wasn't her fault.'

'No, it wasn't anybody's fault. It just happened.'

'That's it,' said Tony. 'It just happened . . . how are we going to tell Brenda?'

'One of us will have to go up.'

'Yes . . . I think I shall have to stay here. I don't know why really, but there will be things to see to. It's an awful thing to ask anyone to do . . .'

'I'll go,' said Jock.

'There'll be things to see to there . . . there's got to be an inquest the doctor says. It's purely formal of course, but it will be ghastly for that Ripon girl. She'll have to give evidence . . . she was in a terrible state. I hope I was all right to her. They'd just brought John in and I was rather muddled. She looked awful. I believe her father's bloody to her . . . I wish Brenda had been here. She's so good with everyone. I get in a muddle.'

The two men stood in silence. Tony said, 'Can you really face going up and seeing Brenda?'

'Yes, I'll go,' said Jock.

Presently Mrs Rattery came in. 'Colonel Inch has been here,' she said. 'I talked to him. He wanted to give you his sympathy.'

'Is he still here?'

'No, I told him you'd probably prefer to be left alone. He thought you'd be glad to hear he stopped the hunt.'

'Nice of him to come . . . Were you having a good day?'

'No.'

'I'm sorry. We saw a fox in Bruton Wood last week, John and I . . . Jock's going up to London to fetch Brenda.'

'I'll take him in the aeroplane. It'll be quicker.'

'Yes, that will be quicker.'

'I'll go and change now. I won't be ten minutes.'

'I'll change too,' said Jock.

When he was alone Tony rang the bell. A young footman answered; he was quite young and had not been long at Hetton.

'Will you tell Mr Ambrose that Mrs Rattery is leaving today. She is flying up with Mr Grant-Menzies. Her ladyship will probably be coming by the evening train.'

'Very good, sir.'

'They had better have some luncheon before they go. I will have it with them . . . And will you put a call through to Colonel Inch and thank him for coming? Say I will write. And to Mr Ripon's to enquire how Miss Ripon is? And to the vicarage and ask Mr Tendril if I can see him this evening? He's not here still?'

'No, sir, he left a few minutes ago.'

'Tell him I shall have to discuss arrangements with him.'

'Very good, sir.'

Mr Last was very matter of fact about everything, the footman reported later.

It was perfectly quiet in the library, for the workmen in the morning-room had laid aside their tools for the day.

Mrs Rattery was ready first.

'They're just getting luncheon.'

'We shan't want any,' she said. 'You forget we were going hunting.'

'Better have something,' said Tony, and then, 'It's awful for Jock, having to tell Brenda. I wonder how long it will be before she arrives.'

There was something in Tony's voice as he said this which made Mrs Rattery ask, 'What are you going to do while you're waiting?'

'I don't know. I suppose there will be things to see to.'

'Look here,' said Mrs Rattery, 'Jock had better go up by car. I'll stay here until Lady Brenda comes.'

'It would be awful for you.'

'No, I'll stay.'

Tony said, 'I suppose it's ridiculous of me, but I wish you would . . . I mean, won't it be awful for you? I am all in a muddle. It's so hard to believe yet, that it really happened.'

'It happened all right.'

The footman came to say that Mr Tendril would call after tea that day; that Miss Ripon had gone straight to bed and was asleep.

'Mr Grant-Menzies is going up in his car. He may be back tonight,' said Tony. 'Mrs Rattery is waiting until her ladyship arrives.'

'Very good, sir. And Colonel Inch wanted to know whether you would care to have the huntsman blow "Gone to ground" at the funeral.'

'Say that I'll write to him,' and, when the footman had left the room, Tony said, 'An atrocious suggestion.'

'Oh, I don't know. He's very anxious to be helpful.'

'They don't like him much as Master.'

Jock left soon after half past two. Tony and Mrs Rattery had coffee in the library.

'I'm afraid this is a very difficult situation,' said Tony. 'After all we scarcely know each other.'

'You don't have to think about me.'

'But it must be awful for you.'

'And you must stop thinking that.'

'I'll try . . . the absurd thing is that I'm not thinking it, just saying it . . . I keep thinking of other things all the time.'

'I know. You don't have to say anything.'

Presently Tony said, 'It's going to be so much worse for Brenda. You see she'd got nothing else, much, except John. I've got her, and I love the house . . . but with Brenda John always came first . . . naturally . . . And then you know she's seen so little of John lately. She's been in London such a lot. I'm afraid that's going to hurt her.'

'You can't ever tell what's going to hurt people.'

'But, you see, I know Brenda so well.'

VI

The library windows were open and the clock, striking the hour, high overhead among its crockets and finials, was clearly audible in the quiet room. It was some time since they had spoken. Mrs Rattery sat with her back to Tony; she had spread out her intricate four pack patience on a card table; he was in front of the fire, in the chair he had taken after lunch.

'Only four o'clock?' he said.

'I thought you were asleep.'

'No, just thinking . . . Jock will be more than half way there by now, about Aylesbury or Tring.'

'It's a slow way to travel.'

'It's less than four hours ago that it happened . . . it's odd to think that this is the same day; that it's only five hours ago they were all here at the meet having drinks.' There was a pause, in which Mrs Rattery swept up the cards and began to deal them again. 'It was twenty-eight minutes past twelve when I heard. I looked at my watch . . . It was ten to one when they brought John in . . . just over three hours ago . . . It's almost incredible, isn't it, everything becoming absolutely different, suddenly like that?'

'It's always that way,' said Mrs Rattery.

'Brenda will hear in an hour now . . . if Jock finds her in. Of course she may very likely be out. He won't know where to find her, because there's no one else in the flat. She leaves it locked up, empty, when she goes out . . . and she's out half the day. I know because I sometimes ring up and can't get an answer. He may not find her for hours . . . It may be as long again as the time since it happened. That would only make it eight o'clock. It's quite likely she won't come in until eight . . . Think of it, all the time between now and when it happened, before Brenda hears. It's scarcely credible, is it? And then she's got to get down here. There's a train that leaves at nine something. She might get that. I wonder if I ought to have gone up too . . . I didn't like to leave John.'

(Mrs Rattery sat intent over her game, moving little groups of cards adroitly backwards and forwards about the table like shuttles across a loom; under her fingers order grew out of chaos; she established sequence and precedence; the symbols before her became coherent, interrelated.)

'. . . Of course she may be at home when he arrives. In that case she can get the evening train she used always to come by, when she went to London for the day, before she got the flat . . . I'm trying to see it all, as it's going to happen,

Jock coming and her surprise at seeing him, and then his telling her . . . It's awful for Jock . . . She may know at half past five or a bit earlier.'

'It's a pity you don't play patience,' said Mrs Rattery.

'In a way I shall feel happier when she knows . . . it feels all wrong as it is at present, having it as a secret that Brenda doesn't know . . . I'm not sure how she fits in her day. I suppose her last lecture is over at about five . . . I wonder if she goes home first to change if she's going out to tea or cocktails. She can't sit about much in the flat, it's so small.'

Mrs Rattery brooded over her chequer of cards and then drew them towards her into a heap, haphazard once more and without meaning; it had nearly come to a solution that time, but for a six of diamonds out of place, and a stubbornly congested patch at one corner, where nothing could be made to move. 'It's a heart-breaking game,' she said.

The clock struck again.

'Is that only quarter past? . . . You know I think I should have gone off my head if I were alone. It's nice of you to stay with me.'

'Do you play bezique?'

'I'm afraid not.'

'Or piquet?'

'No. I've never been able to learn any card game except animal snap.'

'Pity.'

'There's Marjorie and several people I ought to wire to, but I'd better wait until I know that Jock has seen Brenda. Suppose she was with Marjorie when the telegram arrived.'

'You've got to try and stop thinking about things. Can you throw craps?'

'No.'

'That's easy; I'll show you. There'll be some dice in the backgammon board.'

'I'm all right, really. I'd sooner not play.'

'You get the dice and sit up here at the table. We've got six hours to get through.'

She showed him how to throw craps. He said, 'I've seen it on the cinema–pullman porters and taxi men.'

'Of course you have, it's easy . . . there, you see, you've won, you take all.'

Presently Tony said, 'I've just thought of something.'

'Don't you ever take a rest from thinking?'

'Suppose the evening papers have got hold of it already. Brenda may see it on a placard, or just pick up a paper casually and there it will be . . . perhaps with a photograph.'

'Yes, I thought of that just now, when you were talking about telegraphing.'

'But it's quite likely, isn't it? They get hold of everything so quickly. What can we do about it?'

'There isn't anything we can do. We've just got to wait . . . Come on, boy, throw up.'

'I don't want to play any more. I'm worried.'

'I know you're worried. You don't have to tell me . . . you aren't going to give up playing just when the luck's running your way?'

'I'm sorry . . . it isn't any good.'

He walked about the room, first to the window, then to the fireplace. He began to fill his pipe. 'At least we can find out whether the evening papers have got it in. We can ring up and ask the hall porter at my club.'

'That's not going to prevent your wife reading it. We've just got to wait. What was the game you said you knew? Animal something?'

'Snap.'

'I'll buy it.'

'It's just a child's game. It would be ridiculous with two.'

'Show me.'

'Well, each of us chooses an animal.'

'All right, I'm a dog and you're a hen. Now what?'

Tony explained.

'I'd say it was one of those games that you have to feel pretty good first, before you can enjoy them,' said Mrs Rattery. 'But I'll try anything.'

They each took a pack and began dealing. Soon a pair of eights appeared. 'Bow-wow,' said Mrs Rattery, scooping in the cards.

Another pair. 'Bow-wow,' said Mrs Rattery. 'You know you aren't putting your heart into this.'

'Oh,' said Tony. 'Coop-coop-coop.'

Presently he said again, 'Coop-coop-coop.'

'Don't be dumb,' said Mrs Rattery, 'that isn't a pair . . .'

They were still playing when Albert came in to draw the curtains. Tony had only two cards left which he turned over regularly; Mrs Rattery was obliged to divide hers, they were too many to hold. They stopped playing when they found that Albert was in the room.

'What must that man have thought?' said Tony, when he had gone out.

('Sitting there clucking like a 'en,' Albert reported, 'and the little fellow lying dead upstairs.')

'We'd better stop.'

'It wasn't a very good game. And to think it's the only one you know.'

She collected the cards and began to deal them into their proper packs. Ambrose and Albert brought in tea. Tony looked at his watch. 'Five o'clock. Now that the shutters are up we shan't hear the chimes. Jock must be in London by now.'

Mrs Rattery said, 'I'd rather like some whisky.'

Jock had not seen Brenda's flat. It was in a large, featureless house, typical of the district. Mrs Beaver deplored the space wasted by the well staircase and empty, paved hall. There was no porter; a woman came three mornings a week with bucket and mop. A board painted with the names of the tenants informed Jock that Brenda was IN. But he put little reliance on this information, knowing that Brenda was not one to remember, as she came in and out, to change the indicator. He found her front door on the second floor. After the first flight the staircase changed from marble to a faded carpet that had been there before Mrs Beaver undertook the reconstruction. Jock pressed the bell and heard it ringing just inside the door. Nobody came to open it. It was past five, and he had not expected to find Brenda at home. He had decided on the road up that after trying the flat, he would go to his club and ring up various friends of Brenda's who might know where she was. He rang again, from habit, and waited a little; then turned to go. But at that moment the door next to Brenda's opened and a dark lady in a dress of crimson velvet looked out at him; she wore very large earrings of oriental filigree, set with bosses of opaque, valueless stone.

'Are you looking for Lady Brenda Last?'

'I am. Is she a friend of yours?'

'Oh, *such* a friend,' said Princess Abdul Akbar.

'Then perhaps you can tell me where I can find her?'

'I think she's bound to be at Lady Cockpurse's. I'm just going there myself. Can I give her any message?'

'I had better come and see her.'

'Well, wait five minutes and you can go with me. Come inside.'

The Princess's single room was furnished promiscuously and with truly Eastern disregard of the right properties of things; swords meant to adorn the state robes of a moorish caid were swung from the picture rail; mats made for prayer were strewn on the divan; the carpet on the floor had been made in Bokhara as a wall covering; while over the dressing-table was draped a shawl made in Yokohama for sale to cruise-passengers; an octagonal table from Port Said held a Thibetan Buddha of pale soapstone; six ivory elephants from Bombay stood along the top of the radiator. Other cultures, too, were represented by a set of Lalique bottles and powder boxes, a phallic fetish from Senegal, a Dutch copper bowl, a waste-paper basket made of varnished aquatint, a golliwog presented at the gala dinner of a seaside hotel, a dozen or so framed photographs of the Princess, a garden scene ingeniously constructed in pieces of coloured wood, and a radio set in fumed oak, Tudor style. In so small a room the effect was distracting. The princess sat at the looking glass, Jock behind her on the divan.

'What's your name?' she asked over her shoulder. He told her. 'Oh, yes, I've heard them mention you. I was at Hetton the week-end before last . . . such a quaint old place.'

'I'd better tell you. There's been a frightful accident there this morning.'

Jenny Abdul Akbar spun round on the leather stool; her eyes were wide with alarm, her hand pressed to her heart.

'Quick,' she whispered. '*Tell me*. I can't bear it. Is it *death*?'

John nodded. 'Their little boy . . . kicked by a horse.'

'*Little Jimmy*.'

'John.'

'John . . . *dead*. It's *too* horrible.'

'It wasn't anybody's fault.'

'Oh yes,' said Jenny. 'It was. It was *my* fault. I ought never to have gone there . . . a terrible curse hangs over me. Wherever I go I bring nothing but sorrow . . . if only it was *I* that was dead . . . I shall never be able to face them again. I feel like a murderess . . . that brave little life snuffed out.'

'I say, you know, really, I shouldn't take that line about it.'

'It isn't the first time it's happened . . . always, anywhere, I am hunted down . . . without remorse. O God,' said Jenny Abdul Akbar. 'What have I done to deserve it?'

She rose to leave him; there was nowhere she could go except the bathroom. Jock said, through the door, 'Well, I must go along to Polly's and see Brenda.'

'Wait a minute and I'll come too.' She had brightened a little when she emerged. 'Have you got a car here,' she asked, 'or shall I ring up a taxi?'

After tea Mr Tendril called. Tony saw him in his study and was away half an hour. When he returned he went to the tray, which, on Mrs Rattery's instructions, had been left in the library, and poured himself out whisky and ginger ale. Mrs Rattery had resumed her patience. 'Bad interview?' she asked, without looking up.

'Awful.' He drank the whisky quickly and poured out some more.

'Bring me one too, will you?'

Tony said, 'I only wanted to see him about arrangements. He tried to be comforting. It was very painful . . . after all the last thing one wants to talk about at a time like this is religion.'

'Some like it,' said Mrs Rattery.

'Of course,' Tony began, after a pause, 'when you haven't got children yourself–'

'I've got two sons,' said Mrs Rattery.

'Have you? I'm sorry. I didn't realize . . . we know each other so little. How very impertinent of me.'

'That's all right. People are always surprised. I don't see them often. They're at school somewhere. I took them to the cinema last summer. They're getting quite big. One's going to be good-looking, I think. His father is.'

'Quarter past six,' said Tony. 'He's bound to have told her by now.'

There was a little party at Lady Cockpurse's, Veronica and Daisy and Sybil, Souki de Foucauld-Esterhazy, and four or five others, all women. They were there to consult a new fortune-teller called Mrs Northcote. Mrs Beaver had discovered her and for every five guineas that she earned at her introduction Mrs Beaver took a commission of two pounds twelve and sixpence. She told fortunes in a new way, by reading the soles of the feet. They waited their turn impatiently. 'What a time she is taking over Daisy.'

'She is very thorough,' said Polly, 'and it tickles rather.'

Presently Daisy emerged. 'What was she like?' they asked.

'I mustn't tell or it spoils it all,' said Daisy.

They had dealt cards for precedence. It was Brenda's turn now. She went next door to Mrs Northcote, who was sitting at a stool beside an armchair. She was a dowdy, middle-aged woman with a slightly genteel accent. Brenda sat down and took off her shoe and stocking. Mrs Northcote laid the foot on her knee and gazed at it with great solemnity; then she picked it up and began tracing the small creases of the sole with the point of a silver pencil case. Brenda wriggled her toes luxuriously and settled down to listen.

Next door they said, 'Where's Mr Beaver today?'

'He's flown over to France with his mother to see some new wall papers. She's been worrying all day thinking he's had an accident.'

'It's all very touching, isn't it? Though I can't see his point myself . . .'

'You must never do anything on Thursdays,' said Mrs Northcote.

'Nothing?'

'Nothing important. You are intellectual, imaginative, sympathetic, easily led by others, impulsive, affectionate. You are highly artistic and are not giving full scope to your capabilities.'

'Isn't there anything about love?'

'I am coming to love. All these lines from the great toe to the instep represent lovers.'

'Yes, go on some more about that . . .'

Princess Abdul Akbar was announced. 'Where's Brenda?' she said. 'I thought she'd be here.'

'Mrs Northcote's doing her now.'

'Jock Menzies wants to see her. He's downstairs.'

'Darling Jock . . . Why on earth didn't you bring him up?'

'No, it's something terribly important. He's got to see Brenda alone.'

'My dear, how mysterious. Well, she won't be long now. We can't disturb them. It would upset Mrs Northcote.'

Jenny told them her news.

On the other side of the door, Brenda's leg was beginning to feel slightly chilly. 'Four men dominate your fate,' Mrs Northcote was saying, 'one is loyal and tender but he has not yet disclosed his love, one is passionate and overpowering, you are a little afraid of him.'

'Dear me,' said Brenda. 'How very exciting. Who *can* they be?'

'One you must avoid; he bodes no good for you, he is steely hearted and rapacious.'

'I bet that's my Mr Beaver, bless him.'

Downstairs Jock was waiting in the small front room where Polly's guests usually assembled before luncheon. It was five past six.

Soon Brenda pulled on her stocking, stepped into her shoe, and joined the ladies. '*Most* enjoyable,' she pronounced. 'Why, how odd you all look.'

'Jock Grant-Menzies wants to see you downstairs.'

'Jock? How very extraordinary. It isn't anything awful, is it?'

'You'd better go and see him.'

Suddenly Brenda became frightened by the strange air of the room and the unfamiliar expression in her friends' faces. She ran downstairs to the room where Jock was waiting.

'What is it, Jock? Tell me quickly, I'm scared. It's nothing awful, is it?'

'I'm afraid it is. There's been a very serious accident.'

'John?'

'Yes.'

'Dead?'

He nodded.

She sat down on a hard little Empire chair against the wall, perfectly still with her hands folded in her lap, like a small well-brought up child introduced into a room full of grown-ups. She said, 'Tell me what happened. Why do you know about it first?'

'I've been down at Hetton since the week-end.'

'Hetton?'

'Don't you remember? John was going hunting today.'

She frowned, not at once taking in what he was saying. 'John . . . John Andrew . . . I . . . oh, thank God . . .' Then she burst into tears.

She wept helplessly, turning round in the chair and pressing her forehead against its gilt back.

Upstairs Mrs Northcote had Souki Foucauld-Esterhazy by the foot and was saying, 'There are four men dominating your fate. One is loyal and tender but has not yet disclosed his love . . .'

In the silence of Hetton, the telephone rang near the housekeeper's room and was switched through to the library. Tony answered it.

'This is Jock speaking. I've just seen Brenda. She's coming down by the seven o'clock train.'

'Is she terribly upset?'

'Yes, naturally.'

'Where is she now?'

'She's with me. I'm speaking from Polly's.'

'Shall I talk to her?'

'Better not.'

'All right . . . I'll meet that train. Are you coming too?'

'No.'

'Well, you've been wonderful. I don't know what I should have done without you and Mrs Rattery.'

'Oh, that's all right. I'll see Brenda off.'

She had stopped crying and sat crouched in the chair. She did not look up while Jock telephoned. Then she said, 'Yes, I'll go by that train.'

'We ought to start. I suppose you will have to get some things from the flat.'

'My bag . . . upstairs. You get it. I can't go in there again.'

She did not speak on her way to her flat. She sat beside Jock as he drove, looking straight ahead. When they arrived she unlocked her door and led him in. The room was extremely empty of furniture. She sat down in the only chair. 'There's plenty of time really. Tell me exactly what happened.'

Jock told her.

'Poor little boy,' she said. 'Poor little boy.'

Then she opened her cupboard and began to put a few things into a suit case; she went in and out from the bathroom once or twice. 'That's everything,' she said. 'There's still too much time.'

'Would you like anything to eat?'

'Oh no, nothing to eat.' She sat down again and looked at herself in the glass. She did not attempt to do anything to her face. 'When you first told me,' she said, 'I didn't understand. I didn't know what I was saying.'

'I know.'

'I didn't say anything, did I?'

'You know what you said.'

'Yes, I know . . . I didn't mean . . . I don't think it's any good trying to explain.'

Jock said, 'Are you sure you've got everything?'

'Yes, that's everything,' she nodded towards the little case on the bed. She looked quite hopeless.

'Well, we'd better go to the station.'

'All right. It's early. But it doesn't matter.'

Jock took her to the train. As it was Wednesday the carriages were full of women returning after their day's shopping.

'Why not go first class?'

'No, no. I always go third.'

She sat in the middle of a row. The women on either side looked at her curiously wondering if she were ill.

'Don't you want anything to read?'

'Nothing to read.'

'Or eat?'

'Or eat.'

'Then I'll say goodbye.'

'Goodbye.'

Another woman pushed past Jock into the carriage, laden with light parcels.

When the news became known Marjorie said to Allan, 'Well, anyway, this will mean the end of Mr Beaver.'

But Polly Cockpurse said to Veronica, 'That's the end of Tony so far as Brenda is concerned.'

The impoverished Lasts were stunned by the telegram. They lived on an extensive but unprofitable chicken farm near Princes Risborough. It did not enter the heads of any of them that now, if anything happened, they were the heirs to Hetton. Had it done so, their grief would have been just as keen.

Jock drove from Paddington to Brat's. One of the men by the bar said, 'Ghastly thing about Tony Last's boy.'

'Yes, I was there.'

'No, were you? What a ghastly thing.'

Later a telephone message came: 'Princess Abdul Akbar wishes to know whether you are in the club.'

'No, no, tell her I'm not here,' said Jock.

VII

The inquest was held at eleven o'clock next morning; it was soon over. The doctor, the bus-driver, Ben and Miss Ripon gave evidence. Miss Ripon was allowed to remain seated. She was very white and spoke in a trembling voice; her father glared at her from a nearby seat; under her hat was a small bare patch, where they had shaved off the hair to clean her cut. In his summary the coroner remarked that it was clear from the evidence that nobody was in any way to blame for the misadventure; it only remained to express their deep sympathy of the court to Mr Last and Lady Brenda in their terrible loss. The people fell back to allow Tony and Brenda to leave the room. Colonel Inch and the hunt secretary were both present. Everything was done with delicacy and to show respect for their sorrow.

Brenda said, 'Wait a minute. I must just speak to that poor Ripon girl.'

She did it charmingly. When everyone had gone, Tony said, 'I wish you had been here yesterday. There were so many people about and I didn't know what to say to them.'

'What did you do all day?'

'There was the shameless blonde ... we played animal snap some of the time.'

'Animal snap? Was that any good?'

'Not much . . . It's odd to think that yesterday this time it hadn't happened.'

'Poor little boy,' said Brenda.

They had scarcely spoken to each other since Brenda's arrival. Tony had driven to the station to meet her; by the time they reached the house Mrs Rattery had gone to bed; that morning she left in her aeroplane without seeing either of them. They heard the machine pass over the house, Brenda in her bath, Tony downstairs in his study attending to the correspondence that had become necessary.

A day of fitful sunshine and blustering wind; white and grey clouds were scarcely moving, high overhead, but the bare trees round the house swayed and shook and there were swift whirlpools of straw in the stable yard. Ben changed from the Sunday suit he had worn at the inquest and went about his duties. Thunderclap, too, had been kicked yesterday and was very slightly lame in the off fore.

Brenda took off her hat and threw it down on a chair in the hall. 'Nothing to say, is there?'

'There's no need to talk.'

'No. I suppose there'll have to be a funeral.'

'Well, of course.'

'Yes; tomorrow?'

She looked into the morning-room. 'They've done quite a lot, haven't they?'

All Brenda's movements were slower than usual and her voice was flat and expressionless. She sank down into one of the armchairs in the centre of the hall, which nobody ever used. She sat there doing nothing. Tony put his hand on her shoulder but she said 'Don't,' not impatiently or nervously but without any expression. Tony said, 'I'll go and finish those letters.'

'Yes.'

'See you at luncheon.'

'Yes.'

She rose, looked round listlessly for her hat, found it and went very slowly upstairs, the sunlight through the stained glass windows glowing and sparkling all about her.

In her room she sat on the window seat, looking out across the meadows and dun ploughland, the naked tossing trees, the church towers, the maelstroms of dust and leaf which eddied about the terrace below; she still held her hat and fidgeted with her fingers on the brooch which was clipped to one side of it.

Nanny knocked at the door and came in, red-eyed. 'If you please, my lady, I've been going through John's things. There's this handkerchief doesn't belong to him.'

The heavy scent and crowned cypher at the corner proclaimed its origin.

'I know whose it is. I'll send it back to her.'

'Can't think how it came to be there,' said nanny.

'Poor little boy. Poor little boy,' said Brenda to herself, when nanny had left her, and gazed out across the troubled landscape.

'I was thinking about the pony, sir.'

'Oh yes, Ben?'

'Will you want to be keeping her now?'

'I hadn't thought . . . no, I suppose not.'

'Mr Westmacott over at Restall was asking about her. He thought she might do for his little girl.'

'Yes.'

'How much shall we be asking?'

'Oh, I don't know . . . whatever you think is right.'

'She's a good little pony and she's always been treated well. I don't think she ought to go under twenty-five quid, sir.'

'All right, Ben, you see about it.'

'I'll ask thirty, shall I, sir, and come down a bit?'

'Do just what you think best.'

'Very good, sir.'

At luncheon Tony said, 'Jock rang up. He wanted to know if there was anything he could do.'

'How sweet of him. Why don't you have him down for the week-end?'

'Would you like that?'

'I shan't be here. I'm going to Veronica's.'

'You're going to Veronica's?'

'Yes, don't you remember?'

There were servants in the room so that they said nothing more until later, when they were alone in the library. Then, 'Are you really going away?'

'Yes. I can't stay here. You understand that, don't you?'

'Yes, of course. I was thinking we might both go away, abroad somewhere.'

Brenda did not answer him but continued in her own line. 'I couldn't stay here. It's all over, don't you see, our life down here.'

'Darling, what *do* you mean?'

'Don't ask me to explain . . . not just now.'

'But Brenda, sweet, I don't understand. We're both young. Of course, we can never forget John. He'll always be our eldest son but . . .'

'Don't go on, Tony, please don't go on.'

So Tony stopped and after a time said, 'So you're going to Veronica's tomorrow?'

'Mmmm.'

'I think I will ask Jock to come.'

'Yes, I should.'

'And we can think about plans later when we've got more used to things.'

'Yes, later.'

Next morning.

'A sweet letter from mother,' said Brenda, handing it across. Lady St Cloud had written:

> . . . I shall not come down to Hetton for the funeral, but I shall be thinking of you both all the time and of my dear grandson. I shall think of you as I saw you all three, together, at Christmas. Dear children, at a time like this only yourselves can be any help to each other. Love is the only thing that is stronger than sorrow . . .

'I got a telegram from Jock,' said Tony, 'he *can* come.'

'It's really rather embarrassing for us all, Brenda coming,' said Veronica. 'I do think she might have chucked. I shan't in the least know what to say to her.'

Tony said to Jock, as they sat alone after dinner, 'I've been trying to understand, and I think I do now. It's not how I feel myself but Brenda and I are quite different in lots of ways. It's *because* they were strangers and didn't know John, and were never in our life here, that she wants to be with them. That's it, don't you think? She wants to be absolutely alone and away from everything that reminds her of what has happened . . . all the same, I feel awful about letting her go. I can't tell you what she was like here . . . quite mechanical. It's so much worse for her than it is for me. I see that. It's so terrible not being able to do anything to help.'

Jock did not answer.

Beaver was staying at Veronica's. Brenda said to him, 'Until Wednesday, when I thought something had happened to you, I had no idea that I loved you.'

'Well you've said it often enough.'

'I'm going to make you understand,' said Brenda. 'You clod.'

On Monday morning Tony found this letter on his breakfast tray.

> Darling Tony,
>
> I am not coming back to Hetton. Grimshawe can pack everything and bring it to the flat. Then I shan't want her any more.
>
> You must have realized for some time that things were going wrong.
>
> I am in love with John Beaver and I want to have a divorce and marry him. If John Andrew had not died things might not have happened like this. I can't tell. As it is, I simply can't begin over again. Please do not mind too much. I suppose we shan't be allowed to meet while the case is on but I hope afterwards we shall be *great* friends. Anyway I shall always look on you as one whatever you think of me.
>
> Best love from
>
> Brenda

When Tony read this his first thought was that Brenda had lost her reason. 'She's only seen Beaver twice to my knowledge,' he said.

But later he showed the letter to Jock, who said, 'I'm sorry it should have happened like this.'

'But it's not true, is it?'

'Yes, I'm afraid it is. Everyone has known for some time.'

But it was several days before Tony fully realized what it meant. He had got into a habit of loving and trusting Brenda.

4

ENGLISH GOTHIC–II

I

'How's the old boy taking it?'

'Not so well. It makes me feel rather a beast,' said Brenda. 'I'm afraid he minds a lot.'

'Well, you wouldn't like it if he didn't,' said Polly to console her.

'No, I suppose not.'

'I shall stick by you whatever happens,' said Jenny Abdul Akbar.

'Oh, everything is going quite smoothly now,' said Brenda. 'There was a certain amount of *gêne* with relatives.'

Tony had been living with Jock for the last three weeks. Mrs Rattery had gone to California and he was grateful for company. They dined together most evenings. They had given up going to Brat's; so had Beaver; they were afraid of meeting each other. Instead Tony and Jock went to Brown's, where Beaver was not a member. Beaver was continually with Brenda nowadays, at one of half a dozen houses.

Mrs Beaver did not like the turn things had taken; her workmen had been sent back from Hetton with their job unfinished.

In the first week Tony had had several distasteful interviews. Allan had attempted to act as peacemaker.

'You just wait a few weeks,' he had said. 'Brenda will come back. She'll soon get sick of Beaver.'

'But I don't want her back.'

'I know just how you feel, but it doesn't do to be medieval about it. If Brenda hadn't been upset at John's death this need never have come to a crisis. Why last year Marjorie was going everywhere with that ass Robin Beaseley. She was mad about him at the time, but I pretended not to notice and it all blew over. If I were you I should refuse to recognize that anything has happened.'

Marjorie had said, 'Of *course* Brenda doesn't love Beaver. How could she? . . . And if she thinks she does at the moment, I think it's your duty to prevent her making a fool of herself. You must refuse to be divorced–anyway until she has found someone more reasonable.'

Lady St Cloud had said, 'Brenda has been very, very foolish. She always was an excitable girl, but I am sure there was never anything *wrong*, quite sure. *That* wouldn't be like Brenda at all. I haven't met Mr Beaver and I do not wish to. I understand he is unsuitable in every way. Brenda would never want to marry anyone like that. I will tell you exactly how it happened, Tony. Brenda must have felt a tiny bit neglected–people often do at that stage of marriage; I have known countless cases–and it was naturally flattering to find a young man to beg and carry for her. That's all it was, nothing *wrong*. And then the terrible shock of little John's accident unsettled her and she didn't know what she was saying or writing. You'll both laugh over this fracas in years to come.'

Tony had not set eyes on Brenda since the afternoon of the funeral. Once he spoke to her over the telephone.

It was during the second week when he was feeling most lonely and bewildered by various counsels. Allan had been with him urging a reconciliation. 'I've been talking to Brenda,' he had said. 'She's sick of Beaver already. The one thing she wants is to go back to Hetton and settle down with you again.'

While Allan was there, Tony resolutely refused to listen, but later the words, and the picture they evoked, would not leave his mind. So he rang her up and she answered him calmly and gravely.

'Brenda, this is Tony.'

'Hullo, Tony, what is it?'

'I've been talking to Allan. He's just told me about your change of mind.'

'I'm not sure I know what you mean.'

'That you want to leave Beaver and come back to Hetton.'

'Did Allan say that?'

'Yes; isn't it true?'

'I'm afraid it's not. Allan is an interfering ass. I had him here this afternoon. He told me that you didn't want a divorce but that you were willing to let me stay on alone in London and do as I liked provided there was no public scandal. It seemed a good idea and I was going to ring you up about it. But I suppose that's just his diplomacy, too. Anyway I'm afraid there's no prospect of my coming back to Hetton just at present.'

'Oh I see. I didn't think it was likely . . . I just rang you up.'

'That's all right. How are you, Tony?'

'All right, thanks.'

'Good, so am I. Goodbye.'

That was all he had heard of her. Both avoided places where there was a likelihood of their meeting.

It was thought convenient that Brenda should appear as the plaintiff. Tony did not employ the family solicitors in the matter but another less reputable firm who specialized in divorce. He had steeled himself to expect a certain professional gusto, even levity, but found them instead disposed to melancholy and suspicion.

'I gather Lady Brenda is being far from discreet. It is quite likely that the King's Proctor may intervene . . . Moreover there is the question of money. You understand that by the present arrangement, since she is the innocent and injured party, she will be entitled to claim substantial alimony from the courts?'

'Oh that's all right,' said Tony. 'I've been into all that with her brother-in-law and have decided to make a settlement of five hundred a year. She has four hundred of her own and I understand Mr Beaver has something.'

'It's a pity we can't put it in writing,' said the solicitor, 'but that might constitute Conspiracy.'

'Lady Brenda's word is quite good enough,' said Tony.

'We like to protect our clients against even the most remote contingencies,' said the lawyer with an air of piety, for he had not had Tony's opportunities to contract the habit of loving and trusting Brenda.

The fourth week-end after Brenda's departure from Hetton was fixed for Tony's infidelity. A suite was engaged at a seaside hotel ('We always send our clients there. The servants are well accustomed to giving evidence') and private detectives were notified. 'It only remains to select a partner,' said the solicitor; no hint of naughtiness lightened his gloom. 'We have on occasions been instrumental in accommodating our clients but there have been frequent complaints, so we find it best to leave the choice to them. Lately we had a particularly delicate case involving a man of very rigid morality and a certain diffidence. In the end his own wife consented to go with him and supply the evidence. She wore a red wig. It was quite successful.'

'I don't think that would do in this case.'

'No. Exactly. I was merely quoting it as a matter of interest.'

'I expect I shall be able to find someone,' said Tony.

'I have no doubt of it,' said the solicitor, bowing politely.

But when he came to discuss the question later with Jock, it did not seem so easy. 'It's not a thing one can ask every girl to do,' he said, 'whichever way you put it. If you say it is merely a legal form it is rather insulting, and if you suggest going the whole hog it's rather fresh–suddenly, I mean, if you've never paid any particular attention to her before and don't propose to carry on with it afterwards . . . Of course there's always old Sybil.'

But even Sybil refused. 'I'd do it like a shot any other time,' she said, 'but just at the moment it wouldn't suit my book. There's a certain person who might hear about it and take it wrong . . . There's an awfully pretty girl called Jenny Abdul Akbar. I wonder if you've met her.'

'Yes, I've met her.'

'Well, won't she do?'

'No.'

'Oh dear, I don't know who to suggest.'

'We'd better go and study the market at the Old Hundredth,' said Jock.

They dined at Jock's house. Lately they had found it a little gloomy at Brown's for people tended to avoid anyone they knew to be unhappy. Though they drank a magnum of champagne they could not recapture the lighthearted mood in which they had last visited Sink Street. And then Tony said, 'Is it any good going there yet?'

'We may as well try. After all we aren't going there for enjoyment.'

'No, indeed.'

The doors were open at a Hundred Sink Street and the band was playing to an empty ballroom. The waiters were eating at a little table in the corner. Two or three girls were clustered round the Jack-pot machine, losing shillings hard and complaining about the cold. They ordered a bottle of the Montmorency Wine Company's brand and sat down to wait.

'Any of those do?' asked Jock.

'I don't much care.'

'Better get someone you like. You've got to put in a lot of time with her.'

Presently Milly and Babs came downstairs.

'How are the postman's hats?' said Milly.

They could not recognize the allusion.

'You are the two boys who were here last month, aren't you?'

'Yes. I'm afraid we were rather tight.'

'You don't say?' It was very seldom that Milly and Babs met anyone who was quite sober during their business hours.

'Well, come and sit down. How are you both?'

'I think I'm starting a cold,' said Babs. 'I feel awful. Why can't they heat this hole, the mean hounds?'

Milly was more cheerful and swayed in her chair to the music. 'Care to dance?' she said, and she and Tony began to shuffle across the empty floor.

'My friend is looking for a lady to take to the seaside,' said Jock.

'What, this weather? That'll be a nice treat for a lonely girl.' Babs sniffed into a little ball of handkerchief.

'It's for a divorce.'

'Oh, I see. Well, why doesn't he take Milly? She doesn't catch cold easy. Besides, she knows how to behave at an hotel. Lots of the girls here are all right to have a lark with in town, but you have to have a *lady* for a divorce.'

'D'you often get asked to do that?'

'Now and then. It's a nice rest–but it means so much *talking* and the gentlemen will always go on so about their wives.'

While they were dancing Tony came straight to business. 'I suppose you wouldn't care to come away for the week-end?' he asked.

'Shouldn't mind,' said Milly. 'Where?'

'I thought of Brighton.'

'Oh . . . Is it for a divorce?'

'Yes.'

'You wouldn't mind if I brought my little girl with us? She wouldn't be any trouble.'

'Yes.'

'You mean you wouldn't mind?'

'I mean I should mind.'

'Oh . . . You wouldn't think I had a little girl of eight, would you?'

'No.'

'She's called Winnie. I was only sixteen when I had her. I was the youngest of the family and our stepfather wouldn't leave any of us girls alone. That's why I have to work. She lives with a lady at Finchley. Twenty-eight bob a week it costs me, not counting her clothes. She does like the seaside.'

'No,' said Tony. 'I'm sorry but it would be quite impossible. We'll get a lovely present for you to take back to her.'

'All right . . . One gentleman gave her a fairy cycle for Christmas. She fell off and cut her knee . . . When do we start?'

'Would you like to go by train or car?'

'Oh, train. Winnie's sick if she goes in a car.'

'Winnie's not coming.'

'No, but let's go by train anyway.'

So it was decided that they should meet at Victoria on Saturday afternoon.

Jock gave Babs ten shillings and he and Tony went home. Tony had not slept much lately. He could not prevent himself, when alone, from rehearsing over and over in his mind all that had happened since Beaver's visit to Hetton; searching for clues he had missed at the time; wondering where something he had said or done might have changed the course of events; going back further to his earliest acquaintance with Brenda to find indications that should have made him more ready to understand the change that had come over her; reliving scene after scene in the last eight years of his life. All this kept him awake.

II

There was a general rendezvous at the first-class booking office. The detectives were there earliest, ten minutes before their time. They had been pointed out to Tony at the solicitor's office so that he should not lose them. They were cheerful middle-aged men in soft hats and heavy overcoats. They were looking forward to their week-end, for most of their daily work consisted in standing about at street corners watching front doors and a job of this kind was eagerly competed for in the office. In more modest divorces the solicitors were content to rely on the evidence of the hotel servants. The detectives were a luxury and proposed to treat themselves as such.

There was a slight fog in London that day. The station lamps were alight prematurely.

Tony came next, with Jock at his side, loyally there to see him off. They bought the tickets and waited. The detectives, sticklers for professional etiquette, made an attempt at self effacement, studying the posters on the walls and peering from behind a pillar.

'This is going to be hell,' said Tony.

It was ten minutes before Milly came. She emerged from the gloom with a porter in front carrying her suitcase and a child dragging back on her arm behind her. Milly's wardrobe consisted mainly of evening dresses, for during the day she usually spent her time sitting before a gas-fire in her dressing gown. She made an insignificant and rather respectable appearance. 'Sorry if I'm late,' she said. 'Winnie here couldn't find her shoes. I brought her along too. I knew you wouldn't mind really. She travels on a half ticket.'

Winnie was a plain child with large gold-rimmed spectacles. When she spoke she revealed that two of her front teeth were missing.

'I hope you don't imagine she's coming with us.'

'Yes, that's the idea,' said Milly. 'She won't be any trouble–she's got her puzzle.'

Tony bent down to speak to the little girl. 'Listen,' he said. 'You don't want to come to a nasty big hotel. You go with this kind gentleman here. He'll take you to a shop and let you choose the biggest doll you can find and then he'll drive you back in his motor to your home. You'll like that, won't you?'

'No,' said Winnie. 'I want to go to the seaside. I won't go with that man. I don't want a doll. I want to go to the seaside with my mummy.'

Several people besides the detectives were beginning to take notice of the oddly assorted group.

'Oh God!' said Tony. 'I suppose she's got to come.'

The detectives followed at a distance down the platform. Tony settled his companions in a pullman car. 'Look,' said Milly, 'we're travelling first class. Isn't that fun? We can have tea.'

'Can I have an ice?'

'I don't expect they've got an ice. But you can have some nice tea.'

'But I want an ice.'

'You shall have an ice when you get to Brighton. Now be a good girl and play with your puzzle or mother won't take you to the seaside again.'

'The Awful Child of popular fiction,' said Jock as he left Tony.

Winnie sustained the part throughout the journey to Brighton. She was not inventive but she knew the classic routine thoroughly, even to such commonplace but alarming devices as breathing heavily, grunting and complaining of nausea.

Rooms at the hotel had been engaged for Tony by the solicitors. It was therefore a surprise to the reception clerk when Winnie arrived. 'We have reserved in your name double and single communicating rooms, bathroom and sitting-room,' he said. 'We did not understand you were bringing your daughter. Will you require a further room?'

'Oh, Winnie can come in with me,' said Milly.

The two detectives who were standing nearby at the counter exchanged glances of disapproval.

Tony wrote *Mr and Mrs Last* in the Visitors' Book.

'And daughter,' said the clerk with his fingers on the place.

Tony hesitated. 'She is my niece,' he said, and inscribed her name on another line, as *Miss Smith.*

The detective, registering below, remarked to his colleague, 'He got out of that all right. Quite smart. But I don't like the look of this case. Most irregular. Sets a nasty, respectable note bringing a kid into it. We've got the firm to consider. It doesn't do them any good to get mixed up with the King's Proctor.'

'How about a quick one?' said his colleague indifferently.

Upstairs, Winnie said, 'Where's the sea?'

'Just there across the street.'

'I want to go and see it.'

'But it's dark now, pet. You shall see it tomorrow.'

'I want to see it tonight.'

'You take her to see it now,' said Tony.

'Sure you won't be lonely?'

'Quite sure.'

'We won't be long.'

'That's all right. You let her see it properly.'

Tony went down to the bar where he was pleased to find the two detectives. He felt the need of male company. 'Good evening,' he said.

They looked at him askance. Everything in this case seemed to be happening as though with deliberate design to shock their professional feelings. 'Good evening,' said the senior detective. 'Nasty, raw evening.'

'Have a drink.'

Since Tony was paying their expenses in any case, the offer seemed superfluous but the junior detective brightened instinctively and said, 'Don't mind if I do.'

'Come and sit down. I feel rather lonely.'

They took their drinks to a table out of hearing of the barman. 'Mr Last, sir, this is all *wrong*,' said the senior detective. 'You haven't no business to recognize us at all. I don't know what they'd say at the office.'

'Best respects,' said the junior detective.

'This is Mr James, my colleague,' said the senior detective. 'My name is Blenkinsop. James is new to this kind of work.'

'So am I,' said Tony.

'A pity we've such a nasty week-end for the job,' said Blenkinsop, 'very damp and blowy. Gets me in the joints.'

'Tell me,' said Tony. 'Is it usual to bring children on an expedition of this kind?'

'It is *not*.'

'I thought it couldn't be.'

'Since you ask me, Mr Last, I regard it as most irregular and injudicious. It looks wrong, and cases of this kind depend very much on making the right impression. Of course as far as James and me are concerned, the matter is O.K. There won't be a word about it in our evidence. But you can't trust the servants. You might very likely happen to strike one who was new to the courts, who'd blurt it out, and then where would we be? I don't like it, Mr Last, and that's the truth.'

'You can't feel more strongly about it than I do.'

'Fond of kids myself,' said James, who was new to this kind of work. 'How about one with us?'

'Tell me,' said Tony, when they had been at their table some little time. 'You must have observed numerous couples in your time, qualifying for a divorce; tell me, how do they get through their day?'

'It's easier in the summer,' said Blenkinsop, 'the young ladies usually bathe and the gentlemen read the papers on the esplanade; some goes for motor drives and some just hangs around the bar. They're mostly glad when Monday comes.'

Milly and her child were in the sitting-room when Tony came up.

'I've ordered an ice,' said Milly.

'Quite right.'

'I want late dinner. I want late dinner.'

'No, dear, not late dinner. You have an ice up here.'

Tony returned to the bar. 'Mr James,' he said. 'Did I understand you to say you were fond of children?'

'Yes, in their right place.'

'You wouldn't, I suppose, consider dining tonight with the little girl who has accompanied me? I should take it as a great kindness.'

'Oh no, sir, hardly that.'

'You would not find me ungrateful.'

'Well, sir, I don't want to appear unobliging, but it's not part of my duties.'

He seemed to be wavering but Blenkinsop interposed. 'Quite out of the question, sir.'

When Tony left them Blenkinsop spoke from the depth of his experience; it was the first job that he and James had been on together, and he felt under some obligation to put his junior wise. 'Our trouble is always the same–to make the clients realize that divorce is a serious matter.'

Eventually extravagant promises for the morrow, two or three ices and the slight depression induced by them, persuaded Winnie to go to bed.

'How are we going to sleep?' asked Milly.

'Oh, just as you like.'

'Just as *you* like.'

'Well, perhaps Winnie would be happier with you . . . she'll have to go into the other room tomorrow morning when they bring in breakfast, of course.'

So she was tucked up in a corner of the double bed and to Tony's surprise was asleep before they went down to dinner.

A change of clothes brought to both Tony and Milly a change of temper. She, in her best evening frock, backless and vermilion, her face newly done and her bleached curls brushed out, her feet in high red shoes, some bracelets on her wrist, a dab of scent behind the large sham pearls in her ears, shook off the cares of domesticity and was once more in uniform, reporting for duty, a legionary ordered for active service after the enervating restraints of a winter in barracks; and Tony, filling his cigar case before the mirror, and slipping it into the pocket of his dinner jacket, reminded himself that phantasmagoric, and even gruesome as the situation might seem to him, he was nevertheless a host, so that he knocked at the communicating door and passed with a calm manner into his guest's room; for a month now he had lived in a world suddenly bereft of order; it was as though the whole reasonable and decent constitution of things, the sum of all he had experienced or learned to expect, were an inconspicuous, inconsiderable object mislaid somewhere on the dressing table; no outrageous circumstances in which he found himself, no new, mad thing brought to his notice, could add a jot to the all-encompassing chaos that shrieked about his ears. He smiled at Milly from the doorway. 'Charming,' he said, 'perfectly charming. Shall we go down to dinner?'

Their rooms were on the first floor. Step by step, with her hand on his arm, they descended the staircase into the bright hall below.

'Cheer up,' said Milly. 'You have a tongue sandwich. That'll make you talk.'

'Sorry, am I being a bore?'

'I was only joking. You are a serious boy, aren't you?'

In spite of the savage weather the hotel seemed full of week-end visitors. More were arriving through the swing doors, their eyes moist and their cheeks rigid from the icy cold outside.

'Yids,' exclaimed Milly superfluously. 'Still it's nice to get a change from the club once in a while.'

One of the new arrivals was a friend of Milly's. He was supervising the collection of his luggage. Anywhere else he would have been a noticeable figure, for he wore a large fur coat and a béret; under the coat appeared tartan stockings and black and white shoes. 'Take em up and get em unpacked and quick about it,' he said. He was a stout little young man. His companion, also in furs, was staring resentfully at one of the showcases that embellished the hall.

'Oh, for Christ's sake,' she said.

Milly and the young man greeted each other. 'This is Dan,' she said.

'Well, well, well,' said Dan, 'what next?'

'Do I get a drink?' said Dan's girl.

'Baby, you do, if I have to get it myself. Won't you two join us, or are we de trop?'

They went together into the glittering lounge. 'I'm cold like hell,' said Baby.

Dan had taken off his great-coat and revealed a suit of smooth, purplish plus fours and a silk shirt of a pattern Tony might have chosen for pyjamas. 'We'll soon warm you up,' he said.

'This place stinks of yids,' said Baby.

'I always think that's the sign of a good hotel, don't you?' said Tony.

'Like hell,' said Baby.

'You mustn't mind Baby, she's cold,' Dan explained.

'Who wouldn't be, in your lousy car?'

They had some cocktails. Then Dan and Baby went to their room; they must doll up, they explained, as they were going to a party given by a friend of

Dan's, at a place of his near there. Tony and Milly went in to dinner. 'He's a very nice boy,' she said, 'and comes to the club a lot. We get all sorts there, but Dan's one of the decent ones. I was going to have gone abroad with him once but in the end he couldn't get away.'

'His girl didn't seem to like us much.'

'Oh, she was cold.'

Tony did not find conversation easy at dinner. At first he commented on their neighbours as he would have done if he had been dining with Brenda at Espinosa's. 'That's a pretty girl in the corner.'

'I wonder you don't go and join her, dear,' said Milly testily.

'Look at that woman's diamonds. Do you think they can be real?'

'Why don't you ask her, if you're so interested?'

'That's an interesting type–the dark woman dancing.'

'I'm sure she'd be delighted to hear it.'

Presently Tony realized that it was not etiquette in Milly's world to express interest in women, other than the one you were with.

They drank champagne. So also, noticed Tony with displeasure, did the two detectives. He would have something to say about that when their bill for expenses came in. It was not as though they had been accommodating in the matter of Winnie. All the time, at the back of his mind, he was worrying with the problem of what they could possibly do after dinner, but it was solved for him, just as he was lighting his cigar, by the appearance of Dan from the other side of the dining-room. 'Look here,' he said, 'if you two aren't doing anything special, why don't you join up with us and come to the party at my friend's place. You'll like it. He always gives one the best of everything.'

'Oh, do let's,' said Milly.

Dan's evening clothes were made of blue cloth that was supposed to appear black in artificial light; for some reason, however, they remained very blue.

So Milly and Tony went to Dan's friend's place and had the best of everything. There was a party of twenty or thirty people, all more or less like Dan. Dan's friend was most hospitable. When he was not fiddling with the wireless, which gave trouble off and on throughout the evening, he was sauntering among his guests refilling their glasses. 'This stuff's all right,' he said, showing the label, 'it won't hurt you. It's the right stuff.'

They had a lot of the right stuff.

Quite often Dan's friend noticed that Tony seemed to be out of the party. Then he would come across and put his hand on Tony's shoulder. 'I'm so glad Dan brought you,' he would say. 'Hope you're getting all you want. Delighted to see you. Come again when there isn't a crowd and see over the place. Interested in roses?'

'Yes, I like them very much.'

'Come when the roses are out. You'd like that if you're interested in roses. Damn that radio, it's going wonky again.'

Tony wondered whether he was as amiable when people he did not know were brought over unexpectedly to Hetton.

At one stage in the evening he found himself sitting on a sofa with Dan, who said, 'Nice kid, Milly.'

'Yes.'

'I'll tell you a thing I've noticed about her. She attracts quite a different type from the other girls. People like you and me.'

'Yes.'

'You wouldn't think she had a daughter of eight, would you?'

'No, it's very surprising.'

'I didn't know for ages. Then I was taking her to Dieppe for the week-end and she wanted to bring the child along too. Of course that put the kybosh on it, but I've always liked Milly just the same. You can trust her to behave anywhere.' He said this with a sour glance towards Baby, who was full of the right stuff and showing it.

It was after three before the party broke up. Dan's friend renewed his invitation to come again when the roses were out. 'I doubt if you'll find a better show of roses anywhere in the south of England,' he said.

Dan drove them back to the hotel. Baby sat beside him in front, disposed to be quarrelsome. 'Where were you?' she kept asking. 'Never saw you all the evening. Where did you get to? Where were you hiding? I call it a lousy way to take a girl out.'

Tony and Milly sat at the back. From habit and exhaustion she put her head on his shoulder and her hand in his. When they reached their rooms, however, she said, 'Go quietly. We don't want to wake Winnie.'

For an hour or so Tony lay in the warm little bedroom, reviewing over and over again the incidents of the last three months; then he too fell asleep.

He was awakened by Winnie. 'Mother's still asleep,' she said.

Tony looked at his watch. 'So I should think,' he said. It was a quarter past seven. 'Go back to bed.'

'No, I'm dressed. Let's go out.'

She went to the window and pulled back the curtains, filling the room with glacial, morning light. 'It's hardly raining at all,' she said.

'What do you want to do?'

'I want to go on the pier.'

'It won't be open yet.'

'Well, I want to go down to the sea. Come on.'

Tony knew that he would not get to sleep again that morning. 'All right. You go and wait while I dress.'

'I'll wait here. Mother snores so.'

Twenty minutes later they went downstairs into the hall where aproned waiters were piling up the furniture and brushing the carpets. A keen wind met them as they emerged from the swing door. The asphalt promenade was wet with spray and rain. Two or three female figures were scudding along, bowed to the wind, prayer books clutched in their gloved hands. Four or five rugged old men were hobbling down to bathe, hissing like ostlers. 'Oh, come on,' said Winnie.

They went down to the beach and stumbled painfully across the shingle to the margin of the sea. Winnie threw some stones. The bathers were in the water now; some of them had dogs who swam snorting beside them.

'Why don't you bathe?' asked Winnie.

'Far too cold.'

'But *they're* bathing. I want to.'

'You must ask your mother.'

'I believe you're afraid. Can you swim?'

'Yes.'

'Well, why don't you? Bet you can't.'

'All right. I can't.'

'Then why did you say you could. Fibber.'

They walked along the shingle. Winnie slithered about astride a backwater. 'Now my knickers are wet,' she said.

'Better come back and change.'

'It feels horrible. Let's go and have breakfast.'

The hotel did not, as a rule, cater for guests who breakfasted downstairs at eight o'clock on Sunday morning. It took a long time before anything could be got ready. There were no ices, much to Winnie's annoyance. She ate grapefruit and kippers and scrambled eggs on toast, complaining fitfully about her wet clothing. After breakfast Tony sent her upstairs to change and himself smoked a pipe in the lounge and glanced over the Sunday papers. Here at nine o'clock he was interrupted by the arrival of Blenkinsop. 'We missed you last night,' he said.

'We went to a party.'

'You shouldn't have done that–not strictly, but I daresay no harm will come of it. Have you had your breakfast?'

'Yes, in the dining-room with Winnie.'

'But Mr Last, what are you thinking of? You've got to get evidence from the hotel servants.'

'Well, I didn't like to wake Milly.'

'She's paid for it, isn't she? Come, come, Mr Last, this won't do at all. You'll never get your divorce if you don't give your mind to it more.'

'All right,' said Tony. 'I'll have breakfast again.'

'In bed, mind.'

'In bed.' And he went wearily upstairs to his rooms.

Winnie had drawn the curtains but her mother was still asleep. 'She woke up once and then turned over. Do get her to come out. I want to go on the pier.'

'Milly,' said Tony firmly. 'Milly.'

'Oh,' she said. 'What time is it?'

'We've got to have breakfast.'

'Don't want any breakfast. I think I'll sleep a little.'

'You've had breakfast,' said Winnie.

'Come on,' said Tony. 'Plenty of time to sleep afterwards. This is what we came for.'

Milly sat up in bed. 'O.K.,' she said. 'Winnie darling, give mother her jacket off the chair.' She was a conscientious girl ready to go through with her job, however unattractive it might seem. 'But it's early.'

Tony went into his room and took off his shoes, collar and tie, coat and waistcoat, and put on a dressing gown.

'You are greedy,' said Winnie, 'eating two breakfasts.'

'When you're a little older you'll understand these things. It's the Law. Now I want you to stay in the sitting-room for quarter of an hour very quietly. Promise? And afterwards you can do exactly what you like.'

'Can I bathe?'

'Yes certainly, if you're quiet now.'

Tony got into bed beside Milly and pulled the dressing gown tight round his throat. 'Does that look all right?'

'Love's young dream,' said Milly.

'All right then. I'll ring the bell.'

When the tray had been brought Tony got out of bed and put on his things. 'So much for my infidelity,' he said. 'It is curious to reflect that this will be described in the papers as "intimacy".'

'Can I bathe now?'

'Certainly.'

Milly turned over to sleep again. Tony took Winnie to the beach. The wind had got up and a heavy sea was pounding on the shingle.

'This little girl would like to bathe,' said Tony.

'No bathing for children today,' said the beach attendant.

'The very idea,' said various onlookers. 'Does he want to drown the child?' 'He's no business to be trusted with children.' '*Unnatural beast.*'

'But I *want* to bathe,' said Winnie. 'You said I could bathe if you had two breakfasts.'

The people who had clustered round to witness Tony's discomfort looked at one another askance. 'Two breakfasts? Wanting to let the child bathe? The man's balmy.'

'Never mind,' said Tony. 'We'll go on the pier.'

Several of the crowd followed them round the slots, curious to see what new enormity this mad father might attempt. 'There's a man who's eaten two breakfasts and tries to drown his little girl,' they informed other spectators, sceptically observing his attempts to amuse Winnie with skee-ball. Tony's conduct confirmed the view of human nature derived from the weekly newspapers which they had all been reading that morning.

'Well,' said Brenda's solicitor. 'We have our case now, all quite regular and complete. I don't think it can come on until next term–there's a great rush at the moment–but there's no harm in having your own evidence ready. I've got it typed out for you. You'd better keep it by you and get it clear in your mind.'

'. . . *My marriage was an ideally happy one*', she read, '*until shortly before Christmas last year when I began to suspect that my husband's attitude had changed towards me. He always remained in the country when my studies took me to London. I realized that he no longer cared for me as he used to. He began to drink heavily and on one occasion made a disturbance at our flat in London, constantly ringing up when drunk and sending a drunken friend round to knock on the door.* Is that necessary?'

'Not strictly, but it is advisable to put it in. A great deal depends on psychological impression. Judges in their more lucid moments sometimes wonder why perfectly respectable, happily married men, go off for week-ends to the seaside with women they do not know. It is always helpful to offer evidence of general degeneracy.'

'I see,' said Brenda. '*From then onwards I had him watched by private agents and as a result of what they told me, I left my husband's house on April 5th.* Yes, that all seems quite clear.'

III

Lady St Cloud preserved an atavistic faith in the authority and preternatural good judgment of the Head of the Family; accordingly, her first act, on learning from Marjorie of Brenda's wayward behaviour, was to cable for Reggie's return from Tunisia, where he was occupied in desecrating some tombs. His departure, like all his movements, was leisurely. He did not take the first available boat or the second, but eventually he arrived in London on the Monday after Tony's visit to Brighton. He held a family conclave in his library, consisting of his mother, Brenda, Marjorie, Allan and the solicitor; later he discussed the question fully with each of them severally; he took Beaver out to luncheon; he dined with Jock; he even called on Tony's Aunt Frances. Finally on Thursday evening he arranged to meet Tony for dinner at Brown's.

He was eight years older than Brenda; very occasionally a fugitive, indefinable likeness was detectable between him and Marjorie, but both in character and appearance he was as different from Brenda as it was possible to imagine. He was prematurely, unnaturally stout, and he carried his burden of flesh as though he were not yet used to it; as though it had been buckled on to him that morning for the first time and he was still experimenting for its better adjustment; there was an instability in his gait and in his eyes a furtive look as though he were at any moment liable to ambush and realized that he was unfairly handicapped for flight. This impression, however, was due solely to his physical appearance; it was the deep bed of fat in which his eyes lay, that gave them this look of suspicion; the caution of his movements resulted from the exertion of keeping his balance and not from any embarrassment at his own clumsiness, for it had never occurred to him that he looked at all unusual.

Rather more than half Reggie St Cloud's time and income was spent abroad in modest archaeological expeditions. His house in London was full of their fruit–fragmentary amphoras, corroded bronze axe-heads, little splinters of bone and charred stick, a Graeco-Roman head in marble, its features obliterated and ground smooth with time. He had written two little monographs about his work, privately printed and both dedicated to members of the royal family. When he came to London he was regular in attendance at the House of Lords; all his friends were well over forty and for some years now he had established himself as a member of their generation; few mothers still regarded him as a possible son-in-law.

'This whole business of Brenda is *very* unfortunate,' said Reggie St Cloud.

Tony agreed.

'My mother is extremely upset about it, naturally. I'm upset myself. I don't mind admitting, perfectly frankly, that I think she has behaved very foolishly, foolishly and wrongly. I can quite understand your being upset about it too.'

'Yes,' said Tony.

'But all the same, making every allowance for your feelings, I do think that you are behaving rather vindictively in the matter.'

'I'm doing exactly what Brenda wanted.'

'My dear fellow, she doesn't know what she wants. I saw this chap Beaver yesterday. I didn't like him *at all*. Do you?'

'I hardly know him.'

'Well, I can assure you I didn't like him. Now you're just throwing Brenda into his arms. That's what it amounts to, as I see it, and I call it vindictive. Of course at the moment Brenda's got the idea that she's in love with him. But it won't last. It couldn't with a chap like Beaver. She'll want to come back in a year, just you see. Allan says the same.'

'I've told Allan. I don't want her back.'

'Well, that's vindictive.'

'No, I just couldn't feel the same about her again.'

'Well, why feel *the same*? One has to change as one gets older. Why, ten years ago I couldn't be interested in anything later than the Sumerian age and I assure you that now I find even the Christian era full of significance.'

For some time he spoke about some *tabulae execrationum* that he had lately unearthed. 'Almost every grave had them,' he said, 'mostly referring to the circus factions, scratched on lead. They used to be dropped in through a funnel. We had found forty-three up to date, before this wretched business happened, and I had to come back. Naturally I'm upset.'

He sat for a little eating silently. This last observation had brought the conversation back to its point of departure. He clearly had more to say on the subject and was meditating the most convenient approach. He ate in a ruthless manner, champing his food (it was his habit, often, without noticing it, to consume things that others usually left on their plates, the heads and tails of whiting, whole mouthfuls of chicken bone, peach stones and apple cores, cheese rinds and the fibrous parts of the artichoke). 'Besides, you know,' he said, 'it isn't as though it was all Brenda's fault.'

'I haven't been thinking particularly whose fault it is.'

'Well, that's all very well, but you seem rather to be taking the line of the injured husband–saying you can't feel the same again, and all that. I mean to say, it takes two to make a quarrel and I gather things had been going wrong for some time. For instance you'd been drinking a lot–have some more burgundy, by the way.'

'Did Brenda say that?'

'Yes. And then you'd been going round a bit with other girls yourself. There was some woman with a Moorish name you had to stay at Hetton while Brenda was there. Well, that's a bit thick, you know. I'm all for people going their own way, but if they do they can't blame others, if you see what I mean.'

'Did Brenda say that?'

'Yes. Don't think I'm trying to lecture you or anything, but all I feel is that you haven't any right to be vindictive to Brenda, as things are.'

'She said I drank and was having an affair with the woman with a Moorish name?'

'Well, I don't know she actually said that, but she said you'd been getting tight lately and that you were certainly interested in that girl.'

The fat young man opposite Tony ordered prunes and cream. Tony said he had finished dinner.

He had imagined during the preceding week-end that nothing could now surprise him.

'So that really explains what I want to say,' continued Reggie blandly. 'It's about money. I understand that when Brenda was in a very agitated state just after the death of her child, she consented to some verbal arrangement with you about settlements.'

'Yes, I'm allowing her five hundred a year.'

'Well, you know, I don't think that you have any right to take advantage of her generosity in that way. It was most imprudent of her to consider your proposal–she admits now that she was not really herself when she did so.'

'What does she suggest instead?'

'Let's go outside and have coffee.'

When they were settled in front of the fire in the empty smoking-room, he answered, 'Well, I've discussed it with the lawyers and with the family and we decided that the sum should be increased to two thousand.'

'That's quite out of the question. I couldn't begin to afford it.'

'Well, you know, I have to consider Brenda's interests. She has very little of her own and there will be no more coming to her. My mother's income is an allowance which I pay under my father's will. I shan't be able to give her anything. I am trying to raise everything I can for an expedition to one of the oases in the Libyan desert. This chap Beaver has got practically nothing and doesn't look like earning any. So you see—'

'But, my dear Reggie, you know as well as I do that it's out of the question.'

'It's rather less than a third of your income.'

'Yes, but almost every penny goes straight back to the estate. Do you realize that Brenda and I together haven't spent half that amount a year on our personal expenses? It's all I can do to keep things going as it is.'

'I didn't expect you to take this line, Tony. I think it's extremely unreasonable of you. After all, it's absurd to pretend in these days that a single man can't be perfectly comfortable on four thousand a year. It's as much as I've ever had.'

'It would mean giving up Hetton.'

'Well, I gave up Brakeleigh, and I assure you my, dear fellow, I never regret it. It was a nasty wrench at the time of course, of association and everything like that, but I can tell you this, that when the sale was finally through I felt a different man, free to go where I liked . . .'

'But I don't happen to want to go anywhere else except Hetton.'

'There's a lot in what these Labour fellows say, you know. Big houses are a thing of the past in England.'

'Tell me, did Brenda realize when she agreed to this proposal that it meant my leaving Hetton?'

'Yes, it was mentioned, I think. I daresay you'll find it quite easy to sell to a school or something like that. I remember the agent said when I was trying to get rid of Brakeleigh that it was a pity it wasn't Gothic, because schools and convents always go for Gothic. I daresay you'll get a very comfortable price and find yourself better off in the end than you are now.'

'No. It's impossible,' said Tony.

'You're making things extremely awkward for everyone,' said Reggie. 'I can't understand why you are taking up this attitude.'

'What is more, I don't believe that Brenda ever expected or wanted me to agree.'

'Oh yes, she did, my dear fellow. I assure you of that.'

'It's inconceivable.'

'Well,' said Reggie, puffing at his cigar, 'there's more to it than just money. Perhaps I'd better tell you everything. I hadn't meant to. The truth is that Beaver is cutting up nasty. He says he can't marry Brenda unless she's properly provided for. Not fair on her, he says. I quite see his point in a way.'

'Yes, I see his point,' said Tony. 'So what your proposal really amounts to, is that I should give up Hetton in order to buy Beaver for Brenda.'

'It's not how I should have put it,' said Reggie.

'Well, I'm not going to and that's the end of it. If that's all you wanted to say, I may as well leave you.'

'No, it isn't quite all I wanted to say. In fact I think I must have put things rather badly. It comes from trying to respect people's feelings too much. You see I wasn't so much asking you to agree to anything as explaining what our side propose to do. I've tried to keep everything on a friendly basis but I see it's not possible. Brenda will ask for alimony of two thousand a year from the Court and on our evidence we shall get it. I'm sorry you oblige me to put it so bluntly.'

'I hadn't thought of that.'

'No, nor had we, to be quite frank. It was Beaver's idea.'

'You seem to have got me in a fairly hopeless position,'

'It's not how I should have put it.'

'I should like to make absolutely sure that Brenda is in on this. D'you mind if I ring her up?'

'Not at all, my dear fellow. I happen to know she's at Marjorie's tonight.'

'Brenda, this is Tony . . . I've just been dining with Reggie.'

'Yes, he said something about it.'

'He tells me that you are going to sue for alimony. Is that so?'

'Tony, don't be so bullying. The lawyers are doing everything. It's no use coming to me.'

'But did you know that they proposed to ask for two thousand?'

'Yes. They did say that. I know it sounds a lot but . . .'

'And you know exactly how my money stands, don't you? You know it means selling Hetton, don't you? . . . hullo, are you still there?'

'Yes, I'm here.'

'You know it means that?'

'Tony, don't make me feel a beast. Everything has been so difficult.'

'You do know just what you are asking?'

'Yes . . . I suppose so.'

'All right, that's all I wanted to know.'

'Tony, how odd you sound . . . don't ring off.'

He hung up the receiver and went back to the smoking-room. His mind had suddenly become clearer on many points that had puzzled him. A whole Gothic world had come to grief . . . there was now no armour glittering through the forest glades, no embroidered feet on the green sward; the cream and dappled unicorns had fled . . .

Reggie sat expanded in his chair. 'Well?'

'I got on to her. You were quite right. I'm sorry I didn't believe you. It seemed so unlikely at first.'

'That's all right, my dear fellow.'

'I've decided exactly what's going to happen.'

'Good.'

'Brenda is not going to get her divorce. The evidence I provided at Brighton isn't worth anything. There happens to have been a child there all the time. She slept both nights in the room I am supposed to have occupied. If you care to bring the case I shall defend it and win, but I think when you have seen my evidence you will drop it. I am going away for six months or so. When I come back, if she wishes it, I shall divorce Brenda without settlements of any kind. Is that clear?'

'But look here, my dear fellow.'

'Goodnight. Thank you for the dinner. Good luck to the excavations.'

On his way out of the club he noticed that John Beaver of Brat's Club was up for election.

'Who on earth would have expected the old boy to turn up like that?' asked Polly Cockpurse.

'Now I understand why they keep going on in the papers about divorce law reform,' said Veronica. 'It's *too* monstrous that he should be allowed to get away with it.'

'The mistake they made was in telling him first,' said Souki.

'It's so like Brenda to trust everyone,' said Jenny Abdul Akbar.

'I do think Tony comes out of this pretty poorly,' said Marjorie.

'Oh I don't know,' said Allan. 'I expect your ass of a brother put the things wrong.'

5

IN SEARCH OF A CITY

I

'Any idea how many times round the deck make a mile?'

'None, I'm afraid,' said Tony. 'But I should think you must have walked a great distance.'

'Twenty-two times. One soon gets out of sorts at sea if you're used to an active life. She's not much of a boat. Travel with this line often?'

'Never before.'

'Ah. Thought you might have been in business in the islands. Not many tourists going out this time of year. Just the other way about. All coming home, if you see what I mean. Going far?'

'Demerara.'

'Ah. Looking for minerals perhaps?'

'No, to tell you the truth I am looking for a city.'

The genial passenger was surprised and then laughed. 'Sounded just like you said you were looking for a city.'

'Yes.'

'That *was* what you said?'

'Yes.'

'I thought it sounded like that . . . well, so long. I must do another few rounds before dinner.'

He paced off up the deck, straddling slightly in order to keep his balance and occasionally putting out a hand to the rail for support.

Regularly every three minutes for the last hour or so, this man had come by. At first Tony had looked up at his approach and then turned away again, out to sea. Presently the man had taken to nodding, then to saying 'Hullo' or 'Bit choppy' or 'Here we are again'; finally he had stopped and began a conversation.

Tony went aft to break this rather embarrassing sequence. He descended the companionway which led to the lower deck. Here, in crates lashed to the side, was a variety of livestock–some stud bulls, a heavily blanketed race-horse, a couple of beagles, being exported to various West Indian islands. Tony threaded a way between them and the hatches to the stern, where he sat against a winch watching the horizon mount above the funnels, then fall until they stood out black against the darkening sky. The pitch was more sensible here than it had been amidships; the animals shifted restlessly in their cramped quarters; the beagles whined intermittently. A lascar took down from a line some washing which had been flapping there all day.

The wash of the ship was quickly lost in the high waves. They were steaming westward down the Channel. As it grew to be night, lighthouses appeared flashing from the French coast. Presently a steward walked round the bright upper deck, striking chimes on a gong of brass cylinders, and the genial passenger went below to prepare himself for dinner in hot sea water which splashed from side to side of the bath and dissolved the soap in a thin, sticky scum. He was the only man to dress that evening. Tony sat in the mustering darkness until the second bell. Then he left his great-coat in the cabin and went down to dinner.

It was the first evening at sea.

Tony sat at the captain's table, but the captain was on the bridge. There were empty chairs on either side of him. It was not rough enough for the fiddles to be out, but the stewards had removed the flower vases and damped the table-cloth to make it adhesive. A coloured archdeacon sat facing him. He ate with great refinement but his black hands looked immense on the wet, whitish cloth. 'I'm afraid our table is not showing up very well tonight,' he said. 'I see you are not a sufferer. My wife is in her cabin. *She* is a sufferer.'

He was returning from a Congress, he told Tony.

At the top of the stairs was a lounge named the Music and Writing Room. The light here was always subdued, in the day by the stained glass of the windows, at night by pink silk shades which hid the electric candles. Here the passengers assembled for their coffee, sitting on bulky, tapestry-covered chesterfields or on swivel chairs irremovably fastened before the writing tables. Here too the steward for an hour every day presided over the cupboardful of novels which constituted the ship's library.

'It's not much of a boat,' said the genial passenger, sitting himself beside Tony. 'But I expect things will look brighter when we get into the sun.'

Tony lit a cigar and was told by a steward that he must not smoke in this room. 'That's all right,' said the genial passenger, 'we're just going down to the bar. You know,' he said a few minutes later, 'I feel I owe you an apology. I thought you were potty just now before dinner. Honestly I did, when you said you were going to Demerara to look for a city. Well, it sounded pretty potty. Then the purser–I'm at his table; always get the cheeriest crowd at the purser's table *and* the best attention–the purser told me about you. You're the explorer, aren't you?'

'Yes, come to think of it, I suppose I am,' said Tony.

It did not come easily to him to realize that he was an explorer. It was barely a fortnight ago that he had become one. Even the presence in the hold of two vast crates, bearing his name and labelled *NOT WANTED ON THE VOYAGE*–crates containing such new and unfamiliar possessions as a medicine chest, an automatic shot gun, camping equipment, pack saddles, a cinema camera, dynamite, disinfectants, a collapsible canoe, filters, tinned butter and, strangest of all, an assortment of what Dr Messinger called 'trade goods'–failed to convince him fully of the serious nature of his expedition. Dr Messinger had arranged everything. It was he who chose the musical boxes and mechanical mice, the mirrors, combs, perfumery, pills, fish hooks, axe-heads, coloured rockets, and rolls of artificial silk, which were packed in the box of 'trade goods'. And Dr Messinger himself was a new acquaintance who, prostrate now in his bunk with what the negro clergyman would have called 'suffering', that day, for the first time since Tony had met him, seemed entirely human.

Tony had spent very little of his life abroad. At the age of eighteen, before going to the University, he had been boarded for the summer with an elderly gentleman near Tours, with the intention that he should learn the language. (. . . a grey stone house surrounded by vines. There was a stuffed spaniel in the bathroom. The old man had called it 'Stop' because it was chic at that time to give dogs an English name. Tony had bicycled along straight, white roads to visit the chateaux; he carried rolls of bread and cold veal tied to the back of the machine, and the soft dust seeped into them through the paper and gritted against his teeth. There were two other English boys there, so he had learned little French. One of them fell in love and the other got drunk for the first time on sparkling Vouvray at a fair that had been held in the town. That evening Tony won a live pigeon at a tombola; he set it free and later saw it being recaptured by the proprietor of the stall with a butterfly net . . .) Later he had gone to Central Europe for a few weeks with a friend from Balliol. (They had found themselves suddenly rich with the falling mark and had lived in unaccustomed grandeur in the largest hotel suites. Tony had bought a fur for a few shillings and given it to a girl in Munich who spoke no English.) Later still his honeymoon with Brenda in a villa, lent to them, on the Italian Riviera. (. . . cypress and olive trees, a domed church half way down the hill, between the villa and the harbour, a café where they sat out in the evening, watching the fishing boats and the lights reflected in the quiet water, waiting for the sudden agitation of sound and motion as the speed boat came in. It had been owned by a dashing young official, who called it *JAZZ GIRL*. He seemed to spend twenty hours a day running in and out of the little harbour . . .) Once Brenda and he had gone to Le Touquet with Brat's golf team. That was all. After his father died he had not left England. They could not easily afford it; it was one of the things they postponed until death duties were paid off; besides that, he was never happy away from Hetton, and Brenda did not like leaving John Andrew.

Thus Tony had no very ambitious ideas about travel, and when he decided to go abroad his first act was to call at a tourist agency and come away laden with a sheaf of brightly coloured prospectuses, which advertised commodious cruises among palm trees, negresses and ruined arches. He was going away because it seemed to be the conduct expected of a husband in his circumstances, because the associations of Hetton were for the time poisoned for him, because he wanted to live for a few months away from people who would know him or Brenda, in places where there was no expectation of meeting her or Beaver or Reggie St Cloud at every corner he frequented, and with this feeling of evasion dominant in his mind, he took the prospectuses to read at the Greville Club. He had been a member there for some years, but rarely used it; his resignation was only postponed by his recurrent omission to cancel the banker's order for his subscription. Now that Brat's and Brown's were distasteful to him he felt thankful that he had kept on with the Greville. It was a club of intellectual flavour, composed of dons, a few writers and the officials of museums and learned societies. It had a tradition of garrulity, so that he was not surprised when, seated in an armchair and surrounded with his illustrated folders, he was addressed by a member unknown to him who asked if he were thinking of going away. He was more surprised when he looked up and studied the questioner.

Dr Messinger, though quite young, was bearded, and Tony knew few young men with beards. He was also very small, very sun-burned and prematurely bald; the ruddy brown of his face ended abruptly along the line of his forehead, which rose in a pale dome; he wore steel-rimmed spectacles and there was something about his blue serge suit which suggested that the wearer found it uncomfortable.

Tony admitted that he was considering taking a cruise.

'I am going away shortly,' said Dr Messinger, 'to Brazil. At least it may be Brazil or Dutch Guiana. One cannot tell. The frontier has never been demarcated. I ought to have started last week, only my plans were upset. Do you by any chance know a Nicaraguan calling himself alternately Ponsonby and FitzClarence?'

'No, I don't think I do.'

'You are fortunate. That man has just robbed me of two hundred pounds and some machine guns.'

'Machine guns?'

'Yes, I travel with one or two mostly for show you know, or for trade, and they are not easy to buy nowadays. Have you ever tried?'

'No,'

'Well you can take it from me that it's not easy. You can't just walk into a shop and order machine guns.'

'No, I suppose not.'

'Still, at a pinch I can do without them. But I can't do without two hundred pounds.'

Tony had, open on his knee, a photograph of the harbour at Agadir. Dr Messinger looked over his shoulder at it. 'Ah yes,' he said, 'interesting little place. I expect you know Zingermaun there?'

'No, I've not been there yet.'

'You'd like him–a very straight fellow. He used to do quite a lot, selling ammunition to the Atlas caids before the pacification. Of course it was easy money with the capitulations, but he did it better than most of them. I believe he's running a restaurant now in Mogador.' Then he continued dreamily, 'The pity is I can't let the R.G.S. in on this expedition. I've got to find the money privately.'

It was one o'clock and the room was beginning to fill up; an Egyptologist was exhibiting a handkerchief full of scarabs to the editor of a church weekly.

'We'd better go up and lunch,' said Dr Messinger.

Tony had not intended to lunch at the Greville but there was something compelling about the invitation; moreover, he had no other engagement.

Dr Messinger lunched off apples and a rice pudding. ('I have to be very careful what I eat,' he said.) Tony ate cold steak and kidney pie. They sat at a window in the big dining-room upstairs. The places round them were soon filled with members, who even carried the tradition of general conversation so far as to lean back in their chairs and chat over their shoulders from table to table–a practice which greatly hindered the already imperfect service. But Tony remained oblivious to all that was said, absorbed in what Dr Messinger was telling him.

'. . . You see there had been a continuous tradition about the City since the first explorers of the sixteenth century. It has been variously allocated, sometimes down in Matto Grosso, sometimes on the upper Orinoco in what is now Venezuela. I myself used to think it lay somewhere on the Uraricuera. I was out there last year and it was then that I established contact with the Pie-wie Indians; no white man had ever visited them and got out alive. And it was from the Pie-wies that I learned where to look. None of them had ever visited the City, of course, but they *knew about it*. Every Indian between Ciudad Bolivar and Para knows about it. But they won't talk. Queer people. But I became blood-brother with a Pie-wie–interesting ceremony. They buried me up to the neck in mud and all the women of the tribe spat on my head. Then we ate a toad and a snake and a beetle and after that I was a blood brother–well, he told me that the City lies between the head waters of the Courantyne and the Takutu. There's a vast track of unexplored country there. I've often thought of visiting it.

'I've been looking up the historical side, too, and I more or less know how the City got there. It was the result of a migration from Peru at the beginning of the fifteenth century when the Incas were at the height of their power. It is mentioned in all the early Spanish documents as a popular legend. One of the younger princes rebelled and led his people off into the forest. Most of the tribes had a tradition in one form or another, of a strange race passing through their territory.'

'But what do you suppose this city will be like?'

'Impossible to say. Every tribe has a different word for it. The Pie-wies call it the "Shining" or "Glittering", the Arekuna the "Man Watered", the Patamonas the "Bright Feathered", the Warau, oddly enough, use the same word for it that they use for a kind of aromatic jam they make. Of course one can't tell how a civilization may have developed or degenerated in five hundred years of isolation. . . .'

Before Tony left the Greville that day, he tore up his sheaf of cruise prospectuses, for he had arranged to join Dr Messinger in his expedition.

'Done much of that kind of thing?'

'No, to tell you the truth it is the first time.'

'Ah. Well, I daresay it's more interesting than it sounds,' conceded the genial passenger, 'else people wouldn't do it so much.'

The ship, so far as any consideration of comfort had contributed to her design, was planned for the tropics. It was slightly colder in the smoking-room than on deck. Tony went to his cabin and retrieved his cap and great-coat; then he went aft again, to the place where he had sat before dinner. It was a starless night and nothing was visible beyond the small luminous area round the ship, save for a single lighthouse that flashed short-long, short-long, far away on the port bow. The crests of the waves caught the reflection from the promenade deck and shone for a moment before plunging away into the black depths behind. The beagles were awake, whining.

For some days now, Tony had been thoughtless about the events of the immediate past. His mind was occupied with the City, the Shining, the Many Watered, the Bright Feathered, the Aromatic Jam. He had a clear picture of it in his mind. It was Gothic in character, all vanes and pinnacles, gargoyles, battlements, groining and tracery, pavilions and terraces, a transfigured Hetton, pennons and banners floating on the sweet breeze, everything luminous and translucent; a coral citadel crowning a green hill top sown with daisies, among groves and streams; a tapestry landscape filled with heraldic and fabulous animals and symmetrical, disproportionate blossom.

The ship tossed and tunnelled through the dark waters towards this radiant sanctuary.

'I wonder if anyone is doing anything about those dogs,' said the genial passenger, arriving at his elbow. 'I'll ask the purser tomorrow. We might exercise them a bit. Kind of mournful the way they go on.'

Next day they were in the Atlantic. Ponderous waves rising over murky, opaque depths. Dappled with foam at the crests, like downland where on the high, exposed places, snow has survived the thaw. Lead-grey and slate in the sun, olive, field blue and khaki like the uniforms of a battlefield; the sky overhead was neutral and steely with swollen clouds scudding across it, affording rare half hours of sunlight. The masts swung slowly across this sky and the bows heaved and wallowed below the horizon. The man who had made friends with Tony paraded the deck with the two beagles. They strained at the end of their chains, sniffing the scuppers; the man lurched behind them unsteadily. He wore a pair of race glasses with which he occasionally surveyed the seas; he offered them to Tony whenever they passed each other.

'Been talking to the wireless operator,' he said. 'We ought to pass quite near the *Yarmouth Castle* at about eleven.'

Few of the passengers were on their feet. Those who had come on deck lay in long chairs on the sheltered side, pensive, wrapped in tartan rugs. Dr Messinger kept to his cabin. Tony went to see him and found him torpid, for he was taking large doses of chloral. Towards evening the wind freshened and by dinner time was blowing hard; portholes were screwed up and all destructible objects disposed on the cabin floors; a sudden roll broke a dozen coffee cups in the music- and reading-room. That night there was little sleep for anyone on board; the plating creaked, luggage shifted from wall to wall. Tony wedged himself firm in his bunk with the lifebelt and thought of the City.

. . . Carpet and canopy, tapestry and velvet, portcullis and bastion, water fowl on the moat and kingcups along its margin, peacocks trailing their finery across the lawns; high overhead in a sky of sapphire and swansdown silver bells chiming in a turret of alabaster.

Days of shadow and exhaustion, salt wind and wet mist, foghorn and the constant groan and creak of straining metal. Then they were clear of it, after the Azores. Awnings were out and passengers moved their chairs to windward. High noon and an even keel; the blue water lapping against the sides of the ship, rippling away behind her to the horizon; gramophones and deck tennis; bright arcs of flying fish ('Look, Ernie, come quick, there's a shark.' 'That's not a shark, it's a dolphin.' 'Mr Brink said it was a porpoise.' 'There he is again. Oh, if I had my camera.'); clear, tranquil water and the regular turn and tread of the screw; there were many hands to caress the beagles as they went loping by. Mr Brink amid laughter suggested that he should exercise the race-horse, or, with a further burst of invention, the bull. Mr Brink sat at the purser's table with the cheery crowd.

Dr Messinger left his cabin and appeared on deck and in the dining saloon. So did the wife of the archdeacon; she was very much whiter than her husband. On Tony's other side at table sat a girl named Thérèse de Vitré. He had noticed her once or twice during the grey days, a forlorn figure almost lost among furs and cushions and rugs; a colourless little face with wide dark eyes. She said, 'The last days have been terrible. I saw you walking about. How I envied you.'

'It ought to be calm all the way now,' and inevitably, 'Are you going far?'

'Trinidad. That is my home . . . I tried to decide who you were from the passenger list.'

'Who was I?'

'Well . . . someone called Colonel Strapper.'

'Do I look so old?'

'Are colonels old? I didn't know. It's not a thing we have much in Trinidad. Now I know who you are because I asked the head steward. Do tell me about your exploring.'

'You'd better ask Doctor Messinger. He knows more about it than I do.'

'No, *you* tell me.'

She was eighteen years old; small and dark, with a face that disappeared in a soft pointed chin, so that attention was drawn to the grave eyes and the high forehead; she had not long outgrown her schoolgirl plumpness and she moved with an air of exultance, as though she had lately shed an encumbrance and was not yet fatigued by the other burdens that would succeed it. For two years she had been at school in Paris.

'. . . Some of us used to keep lipstick and rouge secretly in our bedrooms and try it on at night. One girl called Antoinette came to Mass on Sunday wearing it. There was a terrible row with Madame de Supplice and she left after that term. It was awfully brave. We all envied her . . . But she was an ugly girl, always eating chocolates . . .

'. . . Now I am coming home to be married . . . No, I am not yet engaged, but you see there are so few young men I can marry. They must be Catholic and of an island family. It would not do to marry an official and go back to live in England. But it will be easy, because I have no brothers or sisters and my father has one of the best houses in Trinidad. You must come and see it. It is a stone house, outside the town. My family came to Trinidad in the French Revolution. There are two or three other rich families and I shall marry into one of them. Our son will have the house. It will be easy . . .'

She wore a little coat, of the kind that was then fashionable, and no ornament except a string of pearls. '. . . There was an American girl at Madame de Supplice's who was engaged. She had a ring with a big diamond, but she could never wear it except in bed. Then, one day she had a letter from her young man, saying he was going to marry another girl. How she cried. We all read the letter and most of us cried too . . . But in Trinidad it will be quite easy.'

Tony told her about the expedition; of the Peruvian emigrants in the middle ages and their long caravan working through the mountains and forests, llamas packed with works of intricate craftsmanship; of the continual rumours percolating to the coast and luring adventurers up into the forests; of the route they would take up the rivers, then cutting through the bush along Indian trails and across untravelled country; of the stream they might strike higher up and how, Dr Messinger said, they would make woodskin canoes and take to the water again; how finally they would arrive under the walls of the city like the Vikings at Byzantium. 'But of course,' he added, 'there may be nothing in it. It ought to be an interesting journey in any case.'

'How I wish I was a man,' said Thérèse de Vitré.

After dinner they danced to the music of an amplified gramophone and the girl drank lemon squash on the bench outside the deck bar, sucking it through two straws.

A week of blue water that grew clearer and more tranquil daily, of sun that grew warmer, radiating the ship and her passengers, filling them with good humour and ease; blue water that caught the sun in a thousand brilliant points, dazzling the eyes as they searched for porpoises and flying fish; clear blue water in the shallows revealing its bed of silver sand and smooth pebble, fathoms down; soft warm shade on deck under the awnings; the ship moved amid unbroken horizons on a vast blue disc of blue, sparkling with sunlight.

Tony and Miss de Vitré played quoits and shuffle-board; they threw rope rings into a bucket from a short distance. ('We'll go in a small boat,' Dr Messinger had said, 'so as to escape all that hideous nonsense of deck games.') Twice consecutively Tony won the sweep-stake on the ship's run; the prize was eighteen shillings. He bought Miss de Vitré a woollen rabbit at the barber's shop.

It was unusual for Tony to use 'Miss' in talking to anyone. Except Miss Tendril he could think of no one he addressed in that way. But it was Thérèse who first called him 'Tony', seeing it engraved in Brenda's handwriting in his cigarette case. 'How funny,' she said, 'that was the name of the man who didn't marry the American girl at Madame de Supplice's; and after that they used each other's Christian names to the great satisfaction of the other passengers who had little to interest them on board except the flowering of this romance.

'I can't believe this is the same ship as in those cold, rough days,' said Thérèse.

They reached the first of the islands; a green belt of palm trees with wooded hills rising beyond them and a small town heaped up along the shores of a bay. Thérèse and Tony went ashore and bathed. Thérèse swam badly with her head ridiculously erect out of the water. There was practically no bathing in Trinidad, she explained. They lay for some time on the firm, silver beach; then drove back into the town in the shaky, two-horse carriage he had hired, past ramshackle cabins from which little black boys ran out to beg or swing behind on the axle, in the white dust. There was nowhere in the town to dine so they returned to the ship at sundown. She lay out at some distance but from where they stood after dinner, leaning over the rail, they could just hear in the intervals when the winch was not working, the chatter and singing in the streets. Thérèse put her arm through Tony's, but the decks were full of passengers and agents and swarthy little men with lists of cargo. There was no dancing that night. They went above on to the boat deck and Tony kissed her.

Dr Messinger came on board by the last launch. He had met an acquaintance in the town. He had observed the growing friendship between Tony and Thérèse with the strongest disapproval and told him of a friend of his who had been knifed in a back street of Smyrna, as a warning of what happened if one got mixed up with women.

In the islands the life of the ship disintegrated. There were changes of passengers; the black archdeacon left after shaking hands with everyone on board; on their last morning his wife took round a collecting box in aid of an organ that needed repairs. The captain never appeared at meals in the dining saloon. Even Tony's first friend no longer changed for dinner; the cabins were stuffy from being kept locked all day.

Tony and Thérèse bathed again at Barbados and drove round the island visiting castellated churches. They dined at an hotel high up out of town and ate flying fish.

'You must come to my home and see what real creole cooking is like,' said Thérèse. 'We have a lot of old recipes that the planters used to use. You must meet my father and mother.'

They could see the lights of the ship from the terrace where they were dining; the bright decks with figures moving about and the double line of portholes.

'Trinidad the day after tomorrow,' said Tony.

They talked of the expedition and she said it was sure to be dangerous. 'I don't like Doctor Messinger at all,' she said. 'Not anything about him.'

'And you will have to choose your husband.'

'Yes. There are seven of them. There was one called Honoré I liked, but of course I haven't seem him for two years. He was studying to be an engineer. There's one called Mendoza who's very rich but he isn't really a Trinidadian. His grandfather came from Dominica and they say he has coloured blood. I expect it will be Honoré. Mother always brought in his name when she wrote to me and he sent me things at Christmas and on my fête. Rather silly things because the shops aren't good in Port of Spain.'

Later she said, 'You'll be coming back by Trinidad, won't you? So I shall see you then. Will you be a long time in the bush?'

'I expect you'll be married by then.'

'Tony, why haven't you ever got married?'

'But I am.'

'Married?'

'Yes.'

'You're teasing me.'

'No, honestly I am. At least I was.'

'Oh.'

'Are you surprised?'

'I don't know. Somehow I didn't think you were. Where is she?'

'In England. We had a row.'

'Oh . . . What's the time?'

'Quite early.'

'Let's go back.'

'D'you want to?'

'Yes, please. It's been a delightful day.'

'You said that as if you were saying goodbye.'

'Did I? I don't know.'

The negro chauffeur drove them at great speed into the town. Then they sat in a rowing boat and bobbed slowly out to the ship. Earlier in the day, in good spirits, they had bought a stuffed fish. Thérèse found she had left it behind at the hotel. 'It doesn't matter,' she said.

Blue water came to an end after Barbados. Round Trinidad the sea was opaque and colourless, full of the mud which the Orinoco brought down from the mainland. Thérèse spent all that day in her cabin, doing her packing.

Next day she said goodbye to Tony in a hurry. Her father had come out to meet her in the tender. He was a wiry bronzed man with a long grey moustache. He wore a panama hat and smart silk clothes, and smoked a cheroot; the complete slave-owner of the last century. Thérèse did not introduce him to Tony. 'He was someone on the ship,' she explained, obviously.

Tony saw her once next day in the town, driving with a lady who was obviously her mother. She waved but did not stop. 'Reserved lot, these real old creoles,' remarked the passenger who had first made friends with Tony and had now attached himself again. 'Poor as church mice most of them but stinking proud. Time and again I've palled up with them on board and when we got to port it's been goodbye. Do they ever so much as ask you to their houses? Not they.'

Tony spent the two days with his first friend who had business connections in the place. On the second day it rained heavily and they could not leave the terrace of the hotel. Dr Messinger was engaged on some technical enquiries at the Agricultural Institute.

Muddy sea between Trinidad and Georgetown; and the ship lightened of cargo rolled heavily in the swell. Dr Messinger took to his cabin once more. Rain fell continuously and a slight mist enclosed them so that they seemed to move in a small puddle of brown water; the foghorn sounded regularly through the rain.

Scarcely a dozen passengers remained on board and Tony prowled disconsolately about the deserted decks or sat alone in the music-room, his mind straying back along the path he had forbidden it, to the tall elm avenue at Hetton and the budding copses.

Next day they arrived at the mouth of the Demerara. The customs sheds were heavy with the reek of sugar and loud with the buzzing of bees. There were lengthy formalities in disembarking their stores. Dr Messinger saw to it while Tony lit a cigar and strayed out on to the quay. Small shipping of all kinds lay round them; on the further bank a low, green fringe of mangrove; behind, the tin roofs of the town were visible among feathery palm trees; everything steamed from the recent rain. Black stevedores grunted rhythmically at their work; East Indians trotted busily to and fro with invoices and bills of lading. Presently Dr Messinger pronounced that everything was in order and that they could go into the town to their hotel.

II

The storm lantern stood on the ground between the two hammocks, which, in their white sheaths of mosquito net, looked like the cocoons of gigantic silk worms. It was eight o'clock, two hours after sundown; river and forest were already deep in night. The howler monkeys were silent but tree frogs near at hand set up a continuous, hoarse chorus; birds were awake, calling and whistling, and far in the depths about them came the occasional rending and reverberation of dead wood falling among the trees.

The six black boys who manned the boat squatted at a distance round their fire. They had collected some cobs of maize, three days back in a part of the bush, deserted now, choked and overrun with wild growth, that had once been a farm. (The rank second growth at that place had been full of alien plants, fruit and cereals, all gross now, and reverting to earlier type.) The boys were roasting their cobs in the embers.

Fire and storm lantern together shed little light; enough only to suggest the dilapidated roof over their heads, the heap of stores, disembarked and overrun by ants and beyond, the undergrowth that had invaded the clearing and the vast columns of tree-trunks that rose above it, disappearing out of sight in the darkness.

Bats like blighted fruit hung in clusters from the thatch and great spiders rode across it astride their shadows. This place had once been a balata station. It was the furthest point of commercial penetration from the coast. Dr Messinger marked it on his map with a triangle and named it in red 'First Base Camp'.

The first stage of the journey was over. For ten days they had been chugging upstream in a broad, shallow boat. Once or twice they had passed rapids (there the outboard engine had been reinforced by paddles; the men strained in time to the captain's count; the bo'sun stood in the bows with a long pole warding them off the rocks). They had camped at sundown on patches of sandbank or in clearings cut from the surrounding bush. Once or twice they came to a 'house' left behind by balata bleeders or gold washers.

All day Tony and Dr Messinger sprawled amidships among their stores, under an improvised canopy of palm thatch; sometimes in the hot hours of the early afternoon they fell asleep. They ate in the boat, out of tins, and drank rum mixed with the water of the river which was mahogany brown but quite clear. The nights seemed interminable to Tony; twelve hours of darkness, noisier than a city square with the squealing and croaking and trumpeting of the bush denizens. Dr Messinger could tell the hours by the succession of sounds. It was not possible to read by the light of the storm lantern. Sleep was irregular and brief after the days of lassitude and torpor. There was little to talk about; everything had been said during the day, in the warm shade among the stores. Tony lay awake, scratching.

Since they had left Georgetown there had not been any part of his body that was ever wholly at ease. His face and neck were burned by the sun reflected from the water; the skin was flaking off them so that he was unable to shave. The stiff growth of beard pricked him between chin and throat. Every exposed part of his skin was bitten by cabouri fly. They had found a way into the buttonholes of his shirt and the laces of his breeches; mosquitoes had got him at the ankles when he changed into slacks for the evening. He had picked up bêtes rouges in the bush and they were crawling and burrowing under his skin; the bitter oil which Dr Messinger had given him as protection, had set up a rash of its own wherever he had applied it. Every evening after washing he had burned off a few ticks with a cigarette end but they had left irritable little scars behind them; so had the djiggas which one of the black boys had dug out from under his toe nails and the horny skin on his heels and the balls of his feet. A marabunta had left a painful swelling on his left hand.

As Tony scratched he shook the framework from which the hammocks hung. Dr Messinger turned over and said, 'Oh, for God's sake.' He tried not to scratch; then he tried to scratch quietly; then in a frenzy he scratched as hard as he could, breaking the skin in a dozen places. 'Oh, for God's sake,' said Dr Messinger.

'Half past eight,' thought Tony. 'In London they are just beginning to collect for dinner.' It was the time of year in London when there were parties every night. (Once, when he was trying to get engaged to Brenda, he had gone to them all. If they had dined in different houses, he would search the crowd for Brenda and hang about the stairs waiting for her to arrive. Later he would hang about to take her home. Lady St Cloud had done everything to make it easy for him. Later, after they were married, in the two years they had spent in London before Tony's father died, they had been to fewer parties, one or two a week at the most, except for one very gay month, when Brenda was well again, after John Andrew's birth.) Tony began to imagine a dinner party assembling at that moment in London, with Brenda there and the surprised look with which she greeted each new arrival. If there was a fire she would be as near it as she could get. Would there be a fire at the end of May? He could not remember. There were nearly always fires at Hetton in the evening, whatever the season.

Then, after another bout of scratching, it occurred to Tony that it was not half past eight in England. There was five hours' difference in time. They had altered their watches daily on the voyage out. Which way? It ought to be easy to work out. The sun rose in the east. England was east of America, so he and Dr Messinger got the sun later. It came to them at second hand and slightly soiled after Polly Cockpurse and Mrs Beaver and Princess Abdul Akbar had finished with it . . . Like Polly's dresses which Brenda used to buy for ten or fifteen pounds each . . . he fell asleep.

He woke an hour later to hear Dr Messinger cursing, and to see him sitting astride his hammock working with bandages and iodine at his great toe.

'A vampire bat got it. I must have gone to sleep with my foot against the netting. God knows how long he had been at it, before I woke up. That lamp ought to keep them off but it doesn't seem to.'

The black boys were still awake, munching over the fire. 'Vampires plenty bad this side, Chief,' they said. 'Dat for why us no leave de fire.'

'It's just the way to get sick, blast it,' said Dr Messinger. 'I may have lost pints of blood.'

Brenda and Jock were dancing together at Anchorage House. It was late, the party was thinning, and now for the first time that evening, it was possible to dance with pleasure. The ballroom was hung with tapestry and lit by candles. Lady Anchorage had lately curtsied her farewell to the last royalty.

'How I hate staying up late,' Brenda said, 'but it seems a shame to take my Mr Beaver away. He's so thrilled to be here, bless him, and it was a great effort to get him asked . . . Come to think of it,' she added later, 'I suppose that this is the last year *I* shall be able to go to this kind of party.'

'You're going through with the divorce?'

'I don't know, Jock. It doesn't really depend on me. It's all a matter of holding down Mr Beaver. He's getting very restive. I have to feed him a bit of high life every week or so, and I suppose that'll all stop if there's a divorce. Any news of Tony?'

'Not for some time now. I got a cable when he landed. He's gone off on some expedition with a crook doctor.'

'Is it *absolutely* safe?'

'Oh, I imagine so. The whole world is civilized now, isn't it–charabancs and Cook's offices everywhere.'

'Yes, I suppose it is . . . I hope he's not *brooding*. I shouldn't like to think of him being unhappy.'

'I expect he's getting used to things.'

'I do hope so. I'm very fond of Tony, you know, in spite of the monstrous way he behaved.'

There was an Indian village a mile or two distant from the camp. It was here that Tony and Dr Messinger proposed to recruit porters for the two-hundred-mile march that lay between them and the Pie-wie country. The niggers were river men and could not be taken into Indian territory. They would go back with the boat.

At dawn Tony and Dr Messinger drank a mug each of hot cocoa and ate some biscuits and what was left over from the bully beef opened the night before. Then they set out for the village. One of the blacks went in front with a cutlass to clear the trail. Dr Messinger and Tony followed, one behind the other; another black came behind them carrying samples of trade goods–a twenty-dollar Belgian gun, some rolls of printed cotton, hand-mirrors in coloured celluloid frames, some bottles of highly scented pomade.

It was a rough, unfrequented trail, encumbered by numerous fallen trunks; they waded knee deep through two streams that ran to feed the big river; underfoot there was sometimes a hard network of bare root, sometimes damp and slippery leaf mould.

Presently they reached the village. They came into sight of it quite suddenly, emerging from the bush into a wide clearing. There were eight or nine circular huts of mud and palm thatch. No one was visible, but two or three columns of smoke, rising straight and thin into the morning air, told them that the place was inhabited.

'Dey people all afeared,' said the black boy.

'Go and find someone to speak to us,' said Dr Messinger.

The nigger went to the low door of the nearest house and peered in.

'Dere ain't no one but women dere,' he reported. 'Dey dressing deirselves. Come on out dere,' he shouted into the gloom. 'De chief want talk to you.'

At last, very shyly, a little old woman emerged, clad in the filthy calico gown that was kept for use in the presence of strangers. She waddled towards them on bandy legs. Her ankles were tightly bound with blue beads. Her hair was lank and ragged; her eyes were fixed on the earthenware bowl of liquid which she carried. When she was a few feet from Tony and Dr Messinger she set the bowl on the ground, and still with downcast eyes, shook hands with them. Then she stopped, picked up the bowl once more and held it to Dr Messinger.

'Cassiri,' he explained, 'the local drink made of fermented cassava.'

He drank some and handed the bowl to Tony. It contained a thick, purplish liquid. When Tony had drunk a little, Dr Messinger explained, 'It is made in an interesting way. The women chew the root up and spit it into a hollow tree trunk.'

He then addressed the woman in Wapishiana. She looked at him for the first time. Her brown, mongol face was perfectly blank, devoid alike of comprehension and curiosity. Dr Messinger repeated and amplified his question. The woman took the bowl from Tony and set it on the ground.

Meanwhile other faces were appearing at the doors of the huts. Only one woman ventured out. She was very stout and she smiled confidently at the visitors.

'Good morning,' she said. 'How do you do? I am Rosa. I speak English good. I live bottom-side two years with Mr Forbes. You give me cigarette.'

'Why doesn't this woman answer?'

'She no speak English.'

'But I was speaking Wapishiana.'

'She Macushi woman. All these people Macushi people.'

'Oh. I didn't know. Where are the men?'

'Men all go hunting three days.'

'When will they be back?'

'They go after bush pig.'

'When will they back?'

'No, bush pig. Plenty bush pig. Men all go hunting. You give me cigarette.'

'Listen, Rosa. I want to go to the Pie-wie country.'

'No, this Macushi. All the people Macushi.'

'But we want to go Pie-wie.'

'No, *all* Macushi. You give me cigarette.'

'It's hopeless,' said Dr Messinger. 'We shall have to wait till the men come back.' He took a packet of cigarettes from his pocket. 'Look,' he said, 'cigarettes.'

'Give me.'

'When men come back from hunting you come to river and tell me. Understand?'

'No, men hunting bush pig. You give me cigarettes.'

Dr Messinger gave her the cigarettes.

'What else you got?' she said.

Dr Messinger pointed to the load which the second nigger had laid on the ground.

'Give me,' she said.

'When men come back, I give you plenty things if men come with me to Pie-wies.'

'No, *all* Macushi here.'

'We aren't doing any good,' said Dr Messinger. 'We'd better go back to camp and wait. The men have been away three days. It's not likely they will be much longer . . . I wish I could speak Macushi.'

They turned about, the four of them, and left the village. It was ten o'clock by Tony's wristwatch when they reached their camp.

Ten o'clock on the river Waurupang was question time at Westminster. For a long time now Jock had had a question which his constituents wanted him to ask. It came up that afternoon.

'Number twenty,' he said.

A few members turned to the order paper.

No. 20.

To ask the Minister of Agriculture whether in view of the dumping in this country of Japanese pork pies, the right honourable member is prepared to consider a modification of the eight-and-a-half score basic pig from two and a half inches of thickness round the belly as originally specified, to two inches.

Replying for the Minister, the under-secretary said, 'The matter is receiving the closest attention. As the honourable member is no doubt aware, the question of the importation of pork pies is a matter for the Board of Trade, not for the Board of Agriculture. With regard to the specification of the basic pig, I must remind the honourable member that, as he is doubtless aware, the eight-and-a-half-score pig is modelled on the requirements of the bacon curers and has no direct relation to pig meat for sale in pies. That is being dealt with by a separate committee who have not yet made their report.'

'Would the honourable member consider an increase of the specified maximum of fatness on the shoulders?'

'I must have notice of that question.'

Jock left the House that afternoon with the comfortable feeling that he had at last done something tangible in the interest of his constituents.

Two days later the Indians returned from hunting. It was tedious waiting. Dr Messinger put in some hours daily in checking the stores. Tony went into the bush with his gun, but the game had all migrated from that part of the river bank. One of the black boys was badly injured in the foot and calf by a sting-ray;

after that they stopped bathing and washed in a zinc pail. When the news of the Indians' return reached camp, Tony and Dr Messinger went to the village to see them, but a feast had already started and everyone in the place was drunk. The men lay in their hammocks and the women trotted between them carrying calabashes of cassiri. Everything reeked of roast pork.

'It will take them a week to get sober,' said Dr Messinger.

All that week the black boys lounged in camp; sometimes they washed their clothes and hung them out on the gunwales of the boat to dry in the sun; sometimes they went fishing and came back with a massive catch, speared on a stick (the flesh was tasteless and rubbery); usually in the evenings they sang songs round the fire. The fellow who had been stung kept to his hammock, groaning loudly and constantly asking for medicine.

On the sixth day the Indians began to appear. They shook hands all round and then retired to the margin of the bush where they stood gazing at the camp equipment. Tony tried to photograph them but they ran away giggling like schoolgirls. Dr Messinger spread out on the ground the goods he had brought for barter.

They retired at sundown but on the seventh day they came again, greatly reinforced. The entire population of the village was there. Rosa sat down on Tony's hammock under the thatch roof.

'Give me cigarettes,' she said.

'You tell them I want men to go Pie-wie country,' said Dr Messinger.

'Pie-wie bad people. Macushi people no go with Pie-wie people.'

'You say I want ten men. I give them guns.'

'You give me cigarettes . . .'

Negotiations lasted for two days. Eventually twelve men agreed to come; seven of them insisted on bringing their wives with them. One of these was Rosa. When everything was arranged there was a party in the village and all the Indians got drunk again. This time, however, it was a shorter business as the women had not had time to prepare much cassiri. In three days the caravan was able to set out.

One of the men had a long, single-barrelled, muzzle-loading gun; several others carried bows and arrows; they were naked except for red cotton cloths round their loins. The women wore grubby calico dresses–they had been issued to them years back by an itinerant preacher and kept for occasions of this kind; they had wicker panniers on their shoulders, supported by a band across the forehead. All the heaviest luggage was carried by the women in these panniers, including the rations for themselves and their men. Rosa had, in addition, an umbrella with a dented, silver crook, a relic of her association with Mr Forbes.

The negroes returned downstream to the coast. A dump of provisions, in substantial tin casing, was left in the ruinous shelter by the bank.

'There's no one to touch it. We can send back for it in case of emergency from the Pie-wie country,' said Dr Messinger.

Tony and Dr Messinger walked immediately behind the man with the gun who was acting as guide; behind them the file straggled out for half a mile or more through the forest.

'From now onwards the map is valueless to us,' said Dr Messinger with relish.

(Roll up the map–you will not need it again for how many years, said William Pitt . . . memories of Tony's private school came back to him at Dr Messinger's words, of inky little desks and a coloured picture of a Viking raid, of Mr Trotter who had taught him history and wore very vivid ties.)

III

'Mummy, Brenda wants a job.'

'Why?'

'Just like everybody else, short of money and nothing to do. She wondered if she could be any use to you at the shop.'

'Well . . . It's hard to say. At any other time she is exactly the kind of saleswoman I am always looking for . . . but I don't know. *As things are* I'm not sure it would be wise.'

'I said I'd ask you, that's all.'

'John, you never tell me *anything* and I don't like to seem interfering; but what *is* going to happen between you and Brenda?'

'I don't know.'

'You never tell me *anything*,' repeated Mrs Beaver. 'And there are so many rumours going round. Is there going to be a divorce?'

'I don't know.'

Mrs Beaver sighed. 'Well, I must get back to work. Where are you lunching?'

'Brat's.'

'Poor John. By the way, I thought you were joining Brown's.'

'I haven't heard anything from them. I don't know whether they've had an election yet.'

'Your father was a member.'

'I've an idea I shan't get it . . . anyway, I couldn't really afford it.'

'I'm not happy about you, John. I'm not sure that things are working out as well as I hoped about Christmas time.'

'There's my telephone. Perhaps it's Margot. She hasn't asked me to anything for weeks.'

But it was only Brenda.

'I'm afraid mother's got nothing for you at the shop,' he said.

'Oh well. I expect something will turn up. I could do with a little good luck just at the moment.'

'So could I. Have you asked Allan about Brown's?'

'Yes, I did. He says they elected about ten chaps last week.'

'Oh, does that mean I've been black-balled?'

'I shouldn't know. Gentlemen are so odd about their clubs.'

'I thought that you were going to make Allan and Reggie support me.'

'I asked them. What does it matter, anyway? D'you want to come to Veronica's for the week-end?'

'I'm not sure that I do.'

'*I'd* like it.'

'It's a beastly little house–and I don't think Veronica likes me. Who'll be there?'

'I shall be.'

'Yes . . . well, I'll let you know.'

'Am I seeing you this evening?'

'I'll let you know.'

'Oh dear,' said Brenda as she rang off. 'Now he's taken against me. It isn't my fault he can't get into Brown's. As a matter of fact I believe Reggie *did* try to help.'

Jenny Abdul Akbar was in the room with her. She came across every morning now in her dressing gown and they read the newspapers together. Her dressing gown was of striped Berber silk.

'Let's go and have a cosy lunch at the Ritz,' she said.

'The Ritz isn't cosy at lunch time and it costs eight and six. I daren't cash a cheque for three weeks, Jenny. The lawyers are so disagreeable. I've never been like this before.'

'What wouldn't I do to Tony? Leaving you stranded like this.'

'Oh, what's the good of knocking Tony? I don't suppose he's having a packet of fun himself in Brazil or wherever it is.'

'I hear they are putting in bathrooms at Hetton–while you are practically starving. And he hasn't even gone to Mrs Beaver for them.'

'Yes, I *do* think that was mean?

Presently Jenny went back to dress. Brenda telephoned to a delicatessen store round the corner for some sandwiches. She would spend that day in bed, as she spent two or three days a week at this time. Perhaps, if Allan was making a speech somewhere, as he usually was, Marjorie would have her to dinner. The Helm-Hubbards had a supper party that night but Beaver had not been asked. 'If I went there without him it would be a major bust-up . . . Come to think of it, Marjorie's probably going. Well, I can always have sandwiches for dinner there. They make all kinds. Thank God for the little shop round the corner.' She was reading a biography of Nelson that had lately appeared; it was very long and would keep her going well into the night.

At one o'clock Jenny came in to say goodbye (she had a latch key of Brenda's), dressed for a cosy lunch. 'I got Polly and Souki,' she said. 'We're going to Daisy's joint. I *wish* you were coming.'

'Me? Oh, I'm all right,' said Brenda and she thought, 'It might occur to her to sock a girl a meal once in a way.'

They walked for a fortnight, averaging about fifteen miles a day. Sometimes they would do much more and sometimes much less; the Indian who went in front decided the camping places; they depended on water and evil spirits.

Dr Messinger made a compass traverse of their route. It gave him something to think about. He took readings every hour from an aneroid. In the evening, if they had halted early enough, he employed the last hours of daylight in elaborating a chart. '*Dry watercourse, three deserted huts, stony ground . . .*'

'We are now in the Amazon system of rivers,' he announced with satisfaction one day. 'You see, the water is running South.' But almost immediately they crossed a stream flowing in the opposite direction. 'Very curious,' said Dr Messinger. 'A discovery of genuine scientific value.'

Next day they waded through four streams at intervals of two miles, running alternately North and South. The chart began to have a mythical appearance.

'Is there a name for any of these streams?' he asked Rosa.

'Macushi people called him Waurupang.'

'No, not river where we first camped. *These rivers.*'

'Yes, Waurupang.'

'*This river here.*'

'Macushi people call him all Waurupang.'

'It's hopeless,' said Dr Messinger.

When they were near water they forced their way through blind bush; the trail there was grown over and barred by timber; only Indian eyes and Indian memory could trace its course; sometimes they crossed little patches of dry savannah, dun grass growing in tufts from the baked earth; thousands of lizards scampered and darted before their feet and the grass rustled like newspaper; it was burning hot in these enclosed spaces. Sometimes they climbed up into the wind, over loose red pebbles that bruised their feet; after these painful ascents they would lie in the wind till their wet clothes grew cold against their bodies: from these low eminences they could see other hill tops and the belts of bush through which they had travelled, and the file of porters trailing behind them. As each man and woman arrived he sank on to the dry grass and rested against his load; when the last of them came up with the party Dr Messinger would give the word and they would start off again, descending into the green heart of the forest before them.

Tony and Dr Messinger seldom spoke to one another, either when they were marching or at the halts, for they were constantly strained and exhausted. In the evenings, after they had washed and changed into dry shirts and flannel trousers, they talked a little, mostly about the number of miles they had done that day, their probable position and the state of their feet. They drank rum and water after their bath; for supper there was usually bully beef stewed with rice and flour dumplings. The Indians ate farine, smoked hog and occasional delicacies picked up by the way–armadillo, iguana, fat white grubs from the palm trees. The women had some dried fish with them that lasted for eight days; the smell grew stronger every day until the stuff was eaten; then it still hung about them and the stores, but grew fainter until it merged into the general, indefinable smell of the camp.

There were no Indians living in this country. In the last five days of the march they suffered from lack of water. The streams they came to were mostly dry; they had to reconnoitre up and down their beds in search of tepid, stagnant puddles. But after two weeks they came to a river once more, flowing deep and swift to the South East. This was the border of the Pie-wie country and Dr Messinger marked the place where they stopped, Second Base Camp. The cabouri fly infested this stream in clouds.

'John, I think it's time you had a holiday.'

'A holiday what from, mumsy?'

'A change . . . I'm going to California in July. To the Fischbaums–Mrs Arnold Fischbaum, not the one who lives in Paris. I think it would do you good to come with me.'

'Yes, mumsy.'

'You *would* like it, wouldn't you?'

'Me? Yes, I'd like it.'

'You've picked up that way of talking from Brenda. It sounds ridiculous in a man.'

'Sorry, mumsy.'

'All right then, that's settled.'

At sunset the cabouri fly disappeared. Until then, through the day, it was necessary to keep covered; they settled on any exposed flesh like house flies upon jam; it was only when they were gorged that their bite was perceptible; they left behind a crimson, smarting circle with a black dot at its centre. Tony and Dr Messinger wore cotton gloves which they had brought for the purpose, and muslin veils, hanging down under their hats. Later they employed two women to squat beside their hammocks and fan them with leafy boughs; the slightest breeze was enough to disperse the flies, but as soon as Tony and Dr Messinger dozed the women would lay aside their work, and they woke instantly, stung in a hundred places. The Indians bore the insects as cows bear horse-flies; passively with occasional fretful outbursts when they would slap their shoulders and thighs.

After dark there was some relief, for there were few mosquitoes at this camp, but they could hear the vampire bats all night long nuzzling and flapping against their netting.

The Indians would not go hunting in this forest. They said there was no game, but Dr Messinger said it was because they were afraid of the evil spirits of the Pie-wie people. Provisions were not lasting as well as Dr Messinger had calculated. During the march it had been difficult to keep a proper guard over the stores. They were short of a bag of farine, half a bag of sugar and a bag of rice. Dr Messinger instituted careful rationing; he served them himself, measuring everything strictly in an enamel cup; even so the women managed to get to the sugar behind his back. He and Tony finished the rum, except for one bottle which was kept in case of emergency.

'We can't go on breaking into tinned stores,' said Dr Messinger peevishly. 'The men must go out and shoot something.'

But they received the orders with expressionless, downcast faces and remained in camp.

'No birds, no animals here,' explained Rosa. 'All gone. May be they get some fish.'

But the Indians could not be persuaded to exert themselves. They could see the sack and bales of food heaped on the bank; it would be plenty of time to start hunting and fishing when that had been exhausted.

Meanwhile there were canoes to be built.

'This is clearly Amazon water,' said Dr Messinger. 'It probably flows into the Rio Branco of the Rio Negro. The Pie-wies live along the bank, and the City, from all accounts, must be downstream of us, up one of the tributaries. When we reach the first Pie-wie village we will be able to get guides.'

The canoes were made of woodskin. Three days were spent in finding trees of suitable age and straightness and in felling them. They cut four trees and worked on them where they lay, clearing the bush for a few feet round them. They stripped the bark with their broad-bladed knives; that took another week. They worked patiently but clumsily; one woodskin was split in getting it off the trunk. There was nothing Tony and Dr Messinger could do to help. They spent that week guarding the sugar from the women. As the men moved about the camp and the surrounding bush, their steps were soundless; their bare feet seemed never to disturb the fallen leaves, their bare shoulders made no rustle in that tangled undergrowth; their speech was brief and scarcely audible, they never joined in the chatter and laughter of their women; sometimes they gave little grunts as they worked; only once they were merry, when one of them let his knife slip as he was working on the tree-trunk and cut deeply into the ball of his thumb. Dr Messinger dressed the wound with iodine, lint and bandages. After that the women constantly solicited him, showing him little scratches on their arms and legs and asking for iodine.

Two of the trees were finished on one day, then another the next day (that was the one which split) and the fourth two days after that; it was a larger tree than the others. When the last fibre was severed four men got round the trunk and lifted the skin clear. It curled up again at once making a hollow cylinder, which the men carried down to the water-side and set afloat, fastening it to a tree with a loop of vine-rope.

When all the woodskins were ready it was an easy matter to make canoes of them. Four men held them open while two others fixed the struts. The ends were left open, and curled up slightly so as to lift them clear (when the craft was fully laden it drew only an inch or two of water). Then the men set about fashioning some single-bladed paddles; that, too, was an easy matter.

Every day Dr Messinger asked Rosa. 'When will the boats be ready? Ask the men,' and she replied, 'Just now.'

'How many days–four?–five?–how many?'

'No, not many. Boats finished just now.'

At last when it was clear that the work was nearly complete, Dr Messinger busied himself with arrangements. He sorted out the stores, dividing the necessary freight into two groups; he and Tony were to sit in separate boats and each had with him a rifle and ammunition, a camera, tinned rations, trade goods and his own luggage. The third canoe which would be manned solely by Indians was to hold the flour and rice, sugar and farine, and the rations for the men. The canoes would not hold all the stores and an 'emergency dump' was made a little way up the bank.

'We shall take eight men with us. Four can stay behind with the women to guard the camp. Once we are among the Pie-wies everything will be easy. These Macushis can go home then. I don't think they will rob the stores. There is nothing here that would be much use to them.'

'Hadn't we better keep Rosa with us to act as interpreter with the Macushis?'

'Yes, perhaps we had. I will tell her.'

That evening everything was finished except the paddles. In the first exhilarating hour of darkness, when Tony and Dr Messinger were able to discard the gloves and veils that had been irking them all day, they called Rosa across to the part of the camp where they ate and slept.

'Rosa, we have decided to take you down the river with us. We need you to help us talk to the men. Understand?'

Rosa said nothing; her face was perfectly blank, lit from below by the storm lantern that stood on a box between them; the shadow of her high cheek bones hid her eyes; lank, ragged hair, a tenuous straggle of tattooing along forehead and lip, rotund body in its filthy cotton gown, bandy brown legs.

'Understand?'

But still she said nothing; she seemed to be looking over their heads into the dark forest, but her eyes were lost in shadow.

'Listen Rosa, all women and four men stay here in camp. Eight men come in boats to Pie-wie village. You come with boats. When we reach Pie-wie village, you and eight men and boats go back to camp to other women and men. Then back to Macushi country. Understand?'

At last Rosa spoke. 'Macushi peoples no go with Pie-wie peoples.'

'I am not asking you to *go with* Pie-wie people. You and the men take us as far as Pie-wies, then you go back to Macushi people. Understand?'

Rosa raised her arm in an embracing circle which covered the camp and the road they had travelled and the broad savannahs behind them. 'Macushi peoples there,' she said. Then she raised the other arm and waved it downstream towards the hidden country. 'Pie-wie peoples there,' she said. 'Macushi peoples no go with Pie-wie peoples.'

'Now listen, Rosa. You are sensible, civilized woman. You lived two years with black gentleman, Mr Forbes. You like cigarettes—'

'Yes, give me cigarettes.'

'You come with men in boats, I give you plenty, plenty cigarettes.'

Rosa looked stolidly ahead of her and said nothing.

'Listen. You will have your men and seven others to protect you. How can we talk with men without you?'

'Men no go,' said Rosa.

'Of course the men will go. The only question is, will you come too?'

'Macushi peoples no go with Pie-wie peoples,' said Rosa.

'Oh God,' said Dr Messinger wearily. 'All right, we'll talk about it in the morning.'

'You give me cigarette . . .'

'It's going to be awkward if that woman doesn't come.'

'It's going to be much more awkward if none of them come,' said Tony.

Next day the boats were ready. By noon they were launched and tied in to the bank. The Indians went silently about the business of preparing their dinner. Tony and Dr Messinger ate tongue, boiled rice and some tinned peaches.

'We're all right for stores,' said Dr Messinger. 'There's enough for three weeks at the shortest and we are bound to come across the Pie-wies in a day or two. We will start tomorrow.'

The Indians' wages, in rifles, fish hooks and rolls of cotton, had been left behind for them at their village. There were still half a dozen boxes of 'trade' for use during the later stages of the journey. A leg of bush pig was worth a handful of shot or twenty gun caps in that currency; a fat game bird cost a necklace.

When dinner was over, at about one o'clock, Dr Messinger called Rosa over to them. 'We start tomorrow,' he said.

'Yes, just now.'

'Tell the men what I told you last night. Eight men to come in boats, others wait here. You come in boats. All these stores stay here. All these stores go in boats. You tell men that.'

Rosa said nothing.

'Understand?'

'No peoples go in boats,' she said. 'All peoples go this way,' and she extended her arm towards the trail that they had lately followed. 'Tomorrow or next day all people go back to village.'

There was a long pause; at last Dr Messinger said, 'You tell the men to come here . . . It's no use threatening them,' he remarked to Tony when Rosa had waddled back to the fireside. 'They are a queer, timid lot. If you threaten them they take fright and disappear, leaving you stranded. Don't worry, I shall be able to persuade them.'

They could see Rosa talking at the fireside but none of the group moved. Presently, having delivered her message, she was silent and squatted down among them with the head of one of the women between her knees. She had been searching it for lice when Dr Messinger's summons had interrupted her.

'We'd better go across and talk to them.'

Some of the Indians were in hammocks. The others were squatting on their heels; they had scraped earth over the fire and extinguished it. They gazed at Tony and Dr Messinger with slit, pig eyes. Only Rosa seemed incurious; her head was averted; all her attention went to her busy fingers as she picked and crunched the lice from her friend's hair.

'What's the matter?' asked Dr Messinger, 'I told you to bring the men here.'

Rosa said nothing.

'So Macushi people are cowards. They are afraid of Pie-wie people.'

'It is the cassava field,' said Rosa. 'We must go back to dig the cassava. Otherwise it will be bad.'

'Listen. I want the men for one, two weeks. No more. After that, all finish. They can go home.'

'It is the time to dig the cassava. Macushi people dig cassava before the big rains. All people go home just now.'

'It's pure blackmail,' said Dr Messinger. 'Let's get out some trade goods.'

He and Tony together prised open one of the cases and began to spread out the contents on a blanket. They had chosen these things together at a cheap store in Oxford Street. The Indians watched the display in unbroken silence. There were bottles of scent and pills, bright celluloid combs set with glass jewels, mirrors, pocket knives with embossed aluminium handles, ribbons and necklaces and barter of more solid worth in the form of axe-heads, brass cartridge cases and flat, red flasks of gunpowder.

'You give me this,' said Rosa picking out a pale blue rosette, that had been made as a boatrace favour. 'Give me this,' she repeated, rubbing some drops of scent into the palm of her hands and inhaling deeply.

'Each man can choose three things from this box if he comes in the boats.'

But Rosa replied monotonously, 'Macushi peoples dig cassava field just now.'

'It's no good,' said Dr Messinger after half an hour's fruitless negotiation. 'We shall have to try with the mice. I wanted to keep them till we reached the Pie-wies. It's a pity. But they'll fall for the mice, you see. I *know* the Indian mind.'

These mice were comparatively expensive articles; they had cost three and sixpence each, and Tony remembered vividly the embarrassment with which he had witnessed their demonstration on the floor of the toy department.

They were of German manufacture; the size of large rats but conspicuously painted in spots of green and white; they had large glass eyes, stiff whiskers and green-and-white-ringed tails; they ran on hidden wheels, and inside them were little bells that jingled as they moved. Dr Messinger took one out of their box, unwrapped the tissue paper and held it up to general scrutiny. There was no doubt that he had captured his audience's interest. Then he wound it up. The Indians stirred apprehensively at the sound.

The ground where they were camping was hard mud, inundated at flood time. Dr Messinger put the toy down at his feet and set it going; tinkling merrily it ran towards the group of Indians. For a moment, Tony was afraid that it would turn over or become stuck against a root but the mechanism was unimpaired and by good chance there was a clear course. The effect exceeded anything that he had expected. There was a loud intake of breath, a series of horrified, small grunts, a high wail of terror from the women, and a sudden stampede; a faint patter of bare brown feet among the fallen leaves, bare limbs, quiet as bats, pushed through the undergrowth, ragged cotton gowns caught and tore in the thorn bushes. Before the toy had run down, it had jingled its way to the place where the nearest Indian had been squatting and the camp was empty.

'Well, I'm damned,' said Dr Messinger, 'that's better than I expected.'

'More than you expected anyway.'

'Oh it's all right. They'll come back. I know them.'

But by sundown there was still no sign. Throughout the hot afternoon Tony and Dr Messinger, shrouded from cabouri fly, sprawled in their hammocks. The empty canoes lay in the river; the mechanical mouse had been put away. At sundown Dr Messinger said, 'We'd better make a fire. They'll come back when it is dark.'

They brushed the earth away from the old embers, brought new wood and made a fire; they lit the storm lantern.

'We'd better get some supper,' said Tony.

They boiled water and made some cocoa, opened a tin of salmon and finished the peaches that were left over from mid-day. They lit their pipes and drew the sheaths of mosquito netting across their hammocks. Most of this time they were silent. Presently they decided to go to sleep.

'We shall find them all here in the morning,' said Dr Messinger. 'They're an odd bunch.'

All round them the voice of the bush whistled and croaked changing with the hours as the night wore on to morning.

Dawn broke in London, clear and sweet, dove grey and honey, with promise of good weather; the lamps in the streets paled and disappeared; the empty streets ran with water, and the rising sun caught it as it bubbled round the hydrants; the men in overalls swung the nozzles of their hoses from side to side and the water jetted and cascaded in a sparkle of light.

'Let's have the window open,' said Brenda. 'It's stuffy in here.'

The waiter drew back the curtains, opened the windows.

'It's quite light,' she added.

'After five. Oughtn't we to go to bed?'

'Yes.'

'Only another week and then all the parties will be over,' said Beaver.

'Yes.'

'Well, let's go.'

'All right. Can you pay? I just haven't any money.'

They had come on after the party, for breakfast at a club Daisy had opened. Beaver paid for the kippers and tea. 'Eight shillings,' he said. 'How does Daisy expect to make a success of the place when she charges prices like that?'

'It does seem a lot . . . So you really *are* going to America?'

'I must. Mother has taken the tickets.'

'Nothing I've said tonight makes any difference?'

'Darling, don't go on. We've been through all that. You know it's the only thing that *can* happen. Why spoil the last week?'

'You *have* enjoyed the summer, haven't you?'

'Of course . . . well, shall we go?'

'Yes. You needn't bother to see me home.'

'Sure you don't mind? It *is* miles out of the way and it's late.'

'There's no knowing what I mind.'

'Brenda, darling, for heaven's sake . . . It isn't like you to go on like this.'

'I never was one for making myself expensive.'

The Indians returned during the night, while Tony and Dr Messinger were asleep; without a word spoken the little people crept out of hiding; the women had removed their clothes and left them at a distance so that no twig should betray their movements; their naked bodies moved soundlessly through the undergrowth; the glowing embers of the fire and the storm lantern twenty yards away were their only light; there was no moon. They collected their wicker baskets and their rations of farine, their bows and arrows, the gun and their broad-bladed knives; they rolled up their hammocks into compact cylinders. They took nothing with them that was not theirs. Then they crept back through the shadows into the darkness.

When Tony and Dr Messinger awoke it was clear to them what had happened.

'The situation is grave,' said Dr Messinger. 'But not desperate.'

IV

For four days Tony and Dr Messinger paddled downstream. They sat, balancing themselves precariously, at the two ends of the canoe; between them they had piled the most essential of their stores; the remainder, with the other canoes, had been left at the camp, to be called for when they had recruited help from the Pie-wies. Even the minimum which Dr Messinger had selected overweighted the craft so that it was dangerously low; any movement brought the water to the lip of the gunwale and threatened disaster; it was heavy to steer and they made slow progess, contenting themselves for the most part, with keeping end on, and drifting with the current.

Twice they came to stretches of cataract, and here they drew in to the bank, unloaded, and waded beside the boat, sometimes plunging waist deep, sometimes clambering over the rocks, guiding it by hand until they reached clear water again. Then they tied up to the bank and carried their cargo down to it through the bush. For the rest of the way the river was broad and smooth; a dark surface which reflected in fine detail the walls of forest on either side, towering up from the undergrowth to their blossoming crown a hundred or more feet above them. Sometimes they came to a stretch of water scattered with fallen petals and floated among them, moving scarcely less slowly than they, as though resting in a flowering meadow. At night they spread their tarpaulin on stretches of dry beach, or hung their hammocks in the bush. Only the cabouri fly and rare, immobile alligators menaced the peace of their days.

They kept a constant scrutiny of the banks but saw no sign of human life.

Then Tony developed fever. It came on him quite suddenly, during the fourth afternoon. At their mid-day halt he was in complete health and shot a small deer that came down to drink on the opposite bank; an hour later he was shivering so violently that he had to lay down his paddle; his head was flaming with heat, his body and limbs frigid; by sunset he was slightly delirious.

Dr Messinger took his temperature and found that it was a hundred and four degrees, Fahrenheit. He gave him twenty-five grains of quinine and lit a fire so close to his hammock that by morning it was singed and blacked with smoke. He told Tony to keep wrapped up in his blanket, but at intervals throughout that night he woke from sleep to find himself running with sweat; he was consumed with thirst and drank mug after mug of river water. Neither that evening nor next morning was he able to eat anything.

But next morning his temperature was down again. He felt weak and exhausted but he was able to keep steady in his place and paddle a little.

'It was just a passing attack, wasn't it?' he said. 'I shall be perfectly fit tomorrow, shan't I?'

'I hope so,' said Dr Messinger.

At mid-day Tony drank some cocoa and ate a cupful of rice. 'I feel grand,' he said.

'Good.'

That night the fever came on again. They were camping on a sand bank. Dr Messinger heated stones and put them under Tony's feet and in the small of his back. He was awake most of the night fuelling the fire and refilling Tony's mug with water. At dawn Tony slept for an hour and woke feeling slightly better; he was taking frequent doses of quinine and his ears were filled with a muffled sound as though he were holding those shells to them in which, he had been told in childhood, one could hear the beat of the sea.

'We've got to go on,' said Dr Messinger. 'We can't be far from a village now.'

'I feel awful. Wouldn't it be better to wait a day till I am perfectly fit again?'

'It's no good waiting. We've got to get on. D'you think you can manage to get into the canoe?'

Dr Messinger knew that Tony was in for a long bout.

For the first few hours of that day Tony lay limp in the bows. They had shifted the stores so that he could lie full length. Then the fever came on again and his teeth chattered. He sat up and crouched with his head in his knees, shaking all over; only his forehead and cheeks were burning hot under the noon sun. There was still no sign of a village.

It was late in the afternoon when he first saw Brenda. For some time he had been staring intently at the odd shape amidships where the stores had been piled; then he realized that it was a human being.

'So the Indians came back?' he said.

'Yes.'

'I knew they would. Silly of them to be scared by a toy. I suppose the others are following.'

'Yes, I expect so. Try and sit still.'

'Damned fool, being frightened of a toy mouse,' Tony said derisively to the woman amidships. Then he saw that it was Brenda. 'I'm sorry,' he said. 'I didn't see it was you. *You* wouldn't be frightened of a toy mouse.'

But she did not answer him. She sat as she used often to sit when she came back from London, huddled over her bowl of bread and milk.

Dr Messinger steered the boat in to the side. They nearly capsized as he helped Tony out. Brenda got ashore without assistance. She stepped out in her delicate, competent way, keeping the balance of the boat.

'That's what poise means,' said Tony. 'D'you know, I once saw a questionnaire that people had to fill in when they applied for a job in an American firm, and one of the things they had to answer was "Have you poise?"'

Brenda was at the top of the bank waiting for him. 'What was so absurd about the question was that they only had the applicant's word for it,' he explained laboriously. 'I mean–is it a sign of poise to think you have it?'

'Just sit quiet here while I sling your hammock.'

'Yes, I'll sit here with Brenda. I am so glad she could come. She must have caught the three-eighteen.'

She was with him all that night and all the next day. He talked to her ceaselessly but her replies were rare and enigmatic. On the succeeding evening he had another fit of sweating. Dr Messinger kept a large fire burning by the hammock and wrapped Tony in his own blanket. An hour before dawn Tony fell asleep and when he awoke Brenda had gone.

'You're down to normal again.'

'Thank God. I've been pretty ill, haven't I? I can't remember much.'

Dr Messinger had made something of a camp. He had chopped a square clear of undergrowth, the size of a small room. Their two hammocks hung on opposite sides of it. The stores were all ashore, arranged in an orderly pile on the tarpaulin.

'How d'you feel?'

'Grand,' said Tony, but when he got out of his hammock he found he could not stand without help. 'Of course, I haven't eaten anything. I expect it will be a day or two before I'm really well.'

Dr Messinger said nothing, but strained the tea clear of leaves by pouring it slowly from one mug into another; he stirred into it a large spoonful of condensed milk.

'See if you can drink this.'

Tony drank it with pleasure and ate some biscuits.

'Are we going on today?' he asked.

'We'll think about it.' He took the mugs down to the bank and washed them in the river. When he came back he said, 'I think I'd better explain things. It's no use your thinking you are cured because you are out of fever for one day.

That's the way it goes. One day fever and one day normal. It may take a week or it may take much longer. That's a thing we've got to face. I can't risk taking you in the canoe. You nearly upset us several times the day before yesterday.'

'I thought there was someone there I knew.'

'You thought a lot of things. It'll go on like that. Meanwhile we've provisions for about ten days. There's no immediate anxiety there, but it's a thing to remember. Besides, what you need is a roof over your head and constant nursing. If only we were at a village . . .'

'I'm afraid I'm being a great nuisance.'

'That's not the point. The thing is to find what is best for us to do.'

But Tony felt too tired to think; he dozed for an hour or so. When he awoke, Dr Messinger was cutting back the bush further. 'I'm going to fix up the tarpaulin as a roof.'

(He had marked this place on his map *Temporary Emergency Base Camp*.)

Tony watched him listlessly. Presently he said, 'Look here, why don't you leave me here and go down the river for help?'

'I thought of that. It's too big a risk.'

That afternoon Brenda was back at Tony's side and he was shivering and tossing in his hammock.

When he was next able to observe things, Tony noted that there was a tarpaulin over his head, slung to the tree-trunks. He asked, 'How long have we been here?'

'Only three days.'

'What time is it now?'

'Getting on for ten in the morning.'

'I feel awful.'

Dr Messinger gave him some soup. 'I am going downstream for the day,' he said, 'to see if there's any sign of a village. I hate leaving you but it's a chance worth taking. I shall be able to get a long way in the canoe now it's empty. Lie quiet. Don't move from the hammock. I shall be back before night, I hope with some Indians to help.'

'All right,' said Tony and fell asleep.

Dr Messinger went down to the river's edge and untied the canoe; he brought with him a rifle, a drinking cup and a day's provisions. He sat in the stern and pushed out from the bank; the current carried the bows down and in a few strokes of the paddle he was in midstream.

The sun was high and its reflection in the water dazzled and scorched him; he paddled on with regular, leisurely strokes; he was travelling fast. For a mile's stretch the river narrowed and the water raced so that all he had to do was to trail the paddle as a rudder; then the walls of forest on either side of him fell back and he drifted into a great open lake, where he had to work heavily to keep in motion; all the time he watched keenly to right and left for the column of smoke, the thatched dome, the sly brown figure in the undergrowth, the drinking cattle, that would disclose the village he sought. But there was no sign. In the open water he took up his field glasses and studied the whole wooded margin. But there was no sign.

Later the river narrowed once more and the canoe shot forward in the swift current. Ahead of him the surface was broken by rapids; the smooth water seethed and eddied; a low monotone warned him that beyond the rapids was a fall. Dr Messinger began to steer for the bank. The current was running strongly and he exerted his full strength; ten yards from the beginning of the rapids his bows ran in under the bank. There was a dense growth of thorn here, overhanging the river, the canoe slid under them and bit into the beach; very cautiously Dr Messinger knelt forward in his place and stretched up to a bough over his head. It was at that moment he came to grief; the stern swung out downstream and as he snatched at the paddle, the craft was swept broadside into the troubled waters; there it adopted an eccentric course, spinning and tumbling to the falls. Dr Messinger was tipped into the water; it was quite shallow in places and he caught at the rocks but they were worn smooth as ivory and afforded no hold for his hands; he rolled over twice, found himself in deep water and attempted to swim, found himself among boulders again and attempted to grapple with them. Then he reached the falls.

They were unspectacular as falls go in that country–a drop of ten feet or less–but they were enough for Dr Messinger. At their foot the foam subsided into a great pool, almost still, and strewn with blossom from the forest trees that encircled it. Dr Messinger's hat floated very slowly towards the Amazon and the water closed over his bald head.

Brenda went to see the family solicitors.

'Mr Graceful,' she said, 'I've got to have some more money.'

Mr Graceful looked at her sadly. 'I should have thought that was really a question for your bank manager. I understand that your securities are in your own name and that the dividends are paid into your account.'

'They never seem to pay dividends nowadays. Besides, it's really very difficult to live on so little.'

'No doubt. No doubt.'

'Mr Last left you with power of attorney, didn't he?'

'With strictly limited powers, Lady Brenda. I am instructed to pay the wage bill at Hetton and all expenses connected with the upkeep of the estate–he is putting in new bathrooms and restoring some decorations in the morning-room which had been demolished. But I am afraid that I have no authority to draw on Mr Last's account for other charges.'

'But Mr Graceful, I am sure he didn't intend to stay abroad so long. He can't possibly have meant to leave me stranded like this, can he? . . . Can he?'

Mr Graceful paused and fidgeted a little. 'To be quite frank, Lady Brenda, I fear that *was* his intention. I raised this particular point shortly before his departure. He was quite resolved on the subject.'

'But is he *allowed* to do that? I mean, haven't I got any rights under the marriage settlement or anything?'

'Nothing which you can claim without application to the courts. You *might* find solicitors who would advise you to take action. I cannot say that I should be one of them. Mr Last would oppose any such order to the utmost and I think that, in the present circumstances, the courts would undoubtedly find for him. In any case it would be a prolonged, costly and slightly undignified proceeding.'

'Oh, I see . . . well, that's that, isn't it?'

'It certainly looks as though it were.'

Brenda rose to go. It was high summer and through the open windows she could see the sun-bathed gardens of Lincoln's Inn.

'There's one thing. Do you know, I mean, can you tell me whether Mr Last made another will?'

'I'm afraid that is a thing I cannot discuss.'

'No, I suppose not. I'm sorry if it was wrong to ask. I just wanted to know how I am with him.'

She still stood between the door and the table, looking lost, in her bright summer clothes. 'Perhaps I can say as much as this to guide you. The heirs presumptive to Hetton are now his cousins, the Richard Lasts at Princes Risborough. I think that your knowledge of Mr Last's character and opinions will tell you that he would always wish his fortune to go with the estate, in order that it may be preserved in what he holds to be its right condition.'

'Yes,' said Brenda, 'I ought to have thought of that. Well, goodbye.'

And she went out alone into the sunshine.

All that day Tony lay alone, fitfully oblivious of the passage of time. He slept a little; once or twice he left his hammock and found himself weak and dizzy. He tried to eat some of the food which Dr Messinger had left out for him, but without success. It was not until it grew dark that he realized the day was over. He lit the lantern and began to collect wood for the fire, but the sticks kept slipping from his fingers and each time that he stooped he felt giddy, so that after a few fretful efforts he left them where they had fallen and returned to his hammock. And lying there, wrapped in his blanket, he began to cry.

After some hours of darkness the lamp began to burn low; he leant painfully over, and shook it. It needed refilling. He knew where the oil was kept, crept to it, supporting himself first on the hammock rope and then on a pile of boxes. He found the keg, pulled out the bung and began to refill the lamp, but his hand trembled and the oil spilled over the ground, then his head began to swim again so that he shut his eyes; the keg rolled over on its side and emptied itself with slow gurglings. When he realized what had happened he began to cry again. He lay down in his hammock and in a few minutes the light sank, flickered and went out. There was a reek of kerosene on his hands and on the sodden earth. He lay awake in the darkness crying.

Just before dawn the fever returned and a constant company of phantoms perplexed his senses.

Brenda awoke in the lowest possible spirits. The evening before she had spent alone at a cinema. Afterwards she felt hungry–she had had no proper meal that day–but she had not the strength to go alone into any of the supper restaurants. She bought a meat pie at a coffee stall and took it home. It looked delicious but, when she came to eat, she found that she had lost her appetite. The remains of that pie lay on the dressing table when she awoke.

It was August and she was entirely alone. Beaver was that day landing in New York. (He had cabled her from mid-ocean that the crossing was excellent.) It was for her the last of Beaver. Parliament was over and Jock Grant-Menzies was paying his annual visit to his elder brother in Scotland; Marjorie and Allan at the last moment had made Lord Monomark's yacht and were drifting luxuriously down the coast of Spain attending bull-fights (they had even asked her to look after Djinn). Her mother was at the chalet Lady Anchorage always lent her on the Lake of Geneva. Polly was everywhere. Even Jenny Abdul Akbar was cruising in the Baltic.

Brenda opened her newspaper and read an article by a young man who said that the London Season was a thing of the past; that everyone was too busy in those days to keep up the pre-war routine; that there were no more formal dances but a constant round of more modest entertaining; that August in London was the gayest time of all (he rewrote this annually in slightly different words). It did not console Brenda to read that article.

For weeks past she had attempted to keep a fair mind towards Tony and his treatment of her; now at last she broke down and turning over buried her face in the pillow, in an agony of resentment and self-pity.

In Brazil she wore a ragged cotton gown of the same pattern as Rosa's. It was not unbecoming. Tony watched her for some time before he spoke. 'Why are you dressed like that?'

'Don't you like it? I got it from Polly.'

'It looks so dirty.'

'Well, Polly travels about a lot. You must get up now to go to the County Council meeting.'

'But it isn't Wednesday?'

'No, but time is different in Brazil; surely you remember?'

'I can't get as far as Pigstanton. I've got to stay here until Messinger comes back. I'm ill. He told me to be quiet. He's coming this evening.'

'But all the County Council are here. The Shameless Blonde brought them in her aeroplane.'

Sure enough they were all there. Reggie St Cloud was chairman. He said, 'I strongly object to Milly being on the committee. She is a woman of low repute.'

Tony protested. 'She has a daughter. She has as much right here as Lady Cockpurse.'

'Order,' said the Mayor. 'I must ask you gentlemen to confine your remarks to the subject under discussion. We have to decide about the widening of the Bayton–Pigstanton road. There have been several complaints that it's impossible for the Green Line buses to turn the corner safely at Hetton Cross.'

'Green Line *rats*.'

'I said Green Line rats. Mechanical green line rats. Many of the villagers have been scared by them and have evacuated their cottages.'

'I evacuated,' said Reggie St Cloud. 'I was driven out of my house by mechanical green rats.'

'Order,' said Polly Cockpurse. 'I move that Mr Last address the meeting.'

'Hear, hear.'

'Ladies and gentlemen,' said Tony. 'I beg you to understand that I am ill and must not move from the hammock. Dr Messinger has given the clearest instructions.'

'Winnie wants to bathe.'

'No bathing in Brazil. No bathing in Brazil.' The meeting took up the cry. 'No bathing in Brazil.'

'But you had two breakfasts.'

'Order,' said the Mayor. 'Lord St Cloud, I suggest you put the question to the vote.'

'The question is whether the contract for the widening of the corner of Hetton Cross shall be given to Mrs Beaver. Of the tenders submitted, hers was by far the most expensive but I understand that her plans include a chromium plated wall on the south side of the village . . .'

'. . . and two breakfasts,' prompted Winnie.

'. . . and two breakfasts for the men engaged on the work. Those in favour of the motion will make a clucking sound in imitation of hens, those against will say bow-wow.'

'A most improper proceeding,' said Reggie. 'What will the servants think?'

'We have got to do something until Brenda has been told.'

'. . . Me? I'm all right.'

'Then I take it the motion is carried.'

'Oh, I *am* glad Mrs Beaver got the job,' said Brenda. 'You see I'm in love with John Beaver, I'm in love with John Beaver, I'm in love with John Beaver.'

'Is that the decision of the committee?'

'Yes, she is in love with John Beaver.'

'Then that is carried unanimously.'

'No,' said Winnie. 'He ate two breakfasts.'

'. . . by an overwhelming majority.'

'Why are you all changing your clothes?' asked Tony, for they were putting on hunting coats.

'For the lawn meet. Hounds are meeting here today.'

'But you can't hunt in summer.'

'Time is different in Brazil and there is no bathing.'

'I saw a fox yesterday in Bruton Wood. A mechanical green fox with a bell inside him that jingled as he ran. It frightened them so much that they ran away and the whole beach was deserted and there was no bathing except for Beaver. He can bathe every day, for the time is different in Brazil.'

'I'm in love with John Beaver,' said Ambrose.

'Why, I didn't know you were here.'

'I came to remind you that you were ill, sir. You must on no account leave your hammock.'

'But how can I reach the City if I stay here?'

'I will serve it directly, Sir, in the library.'

'Yes, in the library. There is no point in using the dining hall now that her Ladyship has gone to live in Brazil.'

'I will send the order to the stables, Sir.'

'But I don't want the pony. I told Ben to sell her.'

'You will have to ride to the smoking-room, Sir. Dr Messinger has taken the canoe.'

'Very well, Ambrose.'

'Thank you, Sir.'

The committee had moved off down the avenue; all except Colonel Inch who had taken the other drive and was trotting towards Compton Last. Tony and Mrs Rattery were all alone.

'Bow-wow,' she said, scooping in the cards. 'That carries the motion.'

Looking up from the card table, Tony saw beyond the trees the ramparts and battlements of the City; it was quite near him. From the turret of the gatehouse a heraldic banner floated in the tropic breeze. He struggled into an upright position and threw aside his blankets. He was stronger and steadier when the fever was on him. He picked his way through the surrounding thorn-scrub; the sound of music rose from the glittering walls; some procession or pageant was passing along them. He lurched into tree-trunks and became caught up in roots and hanging tendrils of bush-vine; but he pressed forward unconscious of pain and fatigue.

At last he came into the open. The gates were before him and trumpets were sounding along the walls, saluting his arrival; from bastion to bastion the message ran to the four points of the compass; petals of almond and apple blossom were in the air; they carpeted the way, as, after a summer storm, they lay in the orchards at Hetton. Gilded cupolas and spires of alabaster shone in the sunlight.

Ambrose announced, 'The City is served.'

6

DU CÔTÉ DE CHEZ TODD

Although Mr Todd had lived in Amazonas for nearly sixty years, no one except a few families of Pie-wie Indians was aware of his existence. His house stood in a small savannah, one of those little patches of sand and grass that crop up occasionally in that neighbourhood, three miles or so across, bounded on all sides by forest.

The stream which watered it was not marked on any map; it ran through rapids, always dangerous and at most seasons of the year impassable, to join the upper waters of the river where Dr Messinger had come to grief. None of the inhabitants of the district, except Mr Todd, had ever heard of the governments of Brazil or Dutch Guiana, both of which from time to time claimed its possession.

Mr Todd's house was larger than those of his neighbours, but similar in character–a palm thatch roof, breast-high walls of mud and wattle, and a mud floor. He owned the dozen or so head of puny cattle which grazed in the savannah, a plantation of cassava, some banana and mango trees, a dog and, unique in the neighbourhood, a single-barrelled, breech-loading shot gun. The few commodities which he employed from the outside world, came to him through a long succession of traders, passed from hand to hand, bartered for in a dozen languages at the extreme end of one of the longest threads in the web of commerce that spreads from Manáos into the remote vastness of the forest.

One day while Mr Todd was engaged in filling some cartridges, a Pie-wie came to him with the news that a white man was approaching through the forest, alone and very sick. He closed the cartridge and loaded his gun with it, put those that were finished into his pocket and set out in the direction indicated.

The man was already clear of the bush when Mr Todd reached him, sitting on the ground, clearly in a very bad way. He was without hat or boots, and his clothes were so torn that it was only by the dampness of his body that they adhered to it; his feet were cut and grossly swollen; every exposed surface of skin was scarred by insect and bat bites; his eyes were wild with fever. He was talking to himself in delirium but stopped when Todd approached and addressed him in English.

'You're the first person who's spoken to me for days,' said Tony. 'The others won't stop. They keep bicycling by . . . I'm tired . . . Brenda was with me at first but she was frightened by a mechanical mouse, so she took the canoe and went off. She said she would come back that evening but she didn't. I expect she's staying with one of her new friends in Brazil . . . You haven't seen her, have you?'

'You are the first stranger I have seen for a very long time.'

'She was wearing a top hat when she left. You can't miss her.' Then he began talking to someone at Mr Todd's side, who was not there.

'Do you see that house over there? Do you think you can manage to walk to it? If not, I can send some Indians to carry you.'

Tony squinted across the savannah at Mr Todd's hut.

'Architecture harmonizing with local character,' he said, 'indigenous material employed throughout. Don't let Mrs Beaver see it or she will cover it with chromium plating.'

'Try and walk.' Mr Todd hoisted Tony to his feet and supported him with a stout arm.

'I'll ride your bicycle. It *was* you I passed just now on a bicycle, wasn't it? . . . except that your beard is a different colour. His was green . . . green as mice.'

Mr Todd led Tony across the hummocks of grass towards the house.

'It is a very short way. When we get there I will give you something to make you better.'

'Very kind of you . . . rotten thing for a man to have his wife go away in a canoe. That was a long time ago. Nothing to eat since.' Presently he said, 'I say, you're English. I'm English too. My name is Last.'

'Well, Mr Last, you aren't to bother about anything more. You're ill and you've had a rough journey. I'll take care of you.'

Tony looked round him. 'Are you all English?'

'Yes, all of us.'

'That dark girl married a Moor . . . It's very lucky I met you all. I suppose you're some kind of cycling club?'

'Yes.'

'Well, I feel too tired for bicycling . . . never liked it much . . . you fellows ought to get motor bicycles, you know, much faster and noisier . . . Let's stop here.'

'No, you must come as far as the house. It's not very much farther.'

'All right . . . I suppose you would have some difficulty getting petrol here.'

They went very slowly, but at length reached the house.

'Lie there in the hammock.'

'That's what Messinger said. He's in love with John Beaver.'

'I will get something for you.'

'Very good of you. Just my usual morning tray–coffee, toast, fruit. And the morning papers. If her Ladyship has been called I will have it with her . . .'

Mr Todd went into the back room of the house and dragged a tin canister from under a heap of skins. It was full of a mixture of dried leaf and bark. He took a handful and went outside to the fire. When he returned, his guest was bolt upright astride the hammock, talking angrily.

'. . . You would hear better and it would be more polite if you stood still when I addressed you instead of walking round in a circle. It is for your own good that I am telling you . . . I know you are friends of my wife and that is why you will not listen to me. But be careful. She will say nothing cruel, she will not raise her voice, there will be no hard words. She hopes you will be great friends afterwards as before. But she will leave you. She will go away quietly during the night. She will take her hammock and her rations of farine . . . Listen to me. I know I am not clever but that is no reason why we should forget all courtesy. Let us kill in the gentlest manner. I will tell you what I have learned in the forest, where time is different. There is no City. Mrs Beaver has covered it with chromium plating and converted it into flats. Three guineas a week, each with a separate bathroom. Very suitable for base love. And Polly will be there. She and Mrs Beaver under the fallen battlements . . .'

Mr Todd put a hand behind Tony's head and held up the concoction of herbs in the calabash. Tony sipped and turned away his head.

'Nasty medicine,' he said, and began to cry.

Mr Todd stood by him holding the calabash. Presently Tony drank some more, screwing up his face and shuddering slightly at the bitterness. Mr Todd stood beside him until the draught was finished; then he threw out the dregs on to the mud floor. Tony lay back in the hammock sobbing quietly. Soon he fell into a deep sleep.

Tony's recovery was slow. At first, days of lucidity alternated with delirium; then his temperature dropped and he was conscious even when most ill. The days of fever grew less frequent, finally occurring in the normal system of the tropics, between long periods of comparative health. Mr Todd dosed him regularly with herbal remedies.

'It's very nasty,' said Tony, 'but it does do good.'

'There is medicine for everything in the forest,' said Mr Todd; 'to make you well and to make you ill. My mother was an Indian and she taught me many of them. I have learned others from time to time from my wives. There are plants to cure you and give you fever, to kill you and send you mad, to keep away snakes, to intoxicate fish so that you can pick them out of the water with your hands like fruit from a tree. There are medicines even I do not know. They say that it is possible to bring dead people to life after they have begun to stink, but I have not seen it done.'

'But surely you are English?'

'My father was–at least a Barbadian. He came to Guiana as a missionary. He was married to a white woman but he left her in Guiana to look for gold. Then he took my mother. The Pie-wie women are ugly but very devoted. Most of the men and women living in this savannah are my children. That is why they obey–for that reason and because I have the gun. My father lived to a great age. It is not twenty years since he died. He was a man of education. Can you read?'

'Yes, of course.'

'It is not everyone who is so fortunate. I cannot.'

Tony laughed apologetically. 'But I suppose you haven't much opportunity here.'

'Oh yes, that is just it. I have a *great* many books. I will show you when you are better. Until five years ago there was an Englishman–at least a black man, but he was well educated in Georgetown. He died. He used to read to me every day until he died. You shall read to me when you are better.'

'I shall be delighted to.'

'Yes, you shall read to me,' Mr Todd repeated, nodding over the calabash.

During the early days of his convalescence Tony had little conversation with his host. He lay in the hammock staring up at the thatched roof and thinking about Brenda. The days, exactly twelve hours each, passed without distinction. Mr Todd retired to sleep at sundown, leaving a little lamp burning–a handwoven wick drooping from a pot of beef fat–to keep away vampire bats.

The first time that Tony left the house Mr Todd took him for a little stroll around the farm.

'I will show you the black man's grave,' he said, leading him to a mound between the mango trees. 'He was very kind. Every afternoon until he died, for two hours, he used to read to me. I think I will put up a cross–to commemorate his death and your arrival–a pretty idea. Do you believe in God?'

'I suppose so. I've never really thought about it much.'

'I have thought about it a great deal and still I do not know . . . Dickens did.'

'I suppose so.'

'Oh yes, it is apparent in all his books. You will see.'

That afternoon Mr Todd began the construction of a headpiece for the negro's grave. He worked with a large spokeshave in a wood so hard that it grated and rang like metal.

At last when Tony had passed six or seven consecutive nights without fever, Mr Todd said, 'Now I think you are well enough to see the books.'

At one end of the hut there was a kind of loft formed by a rough platform erected in the eaves of the roof. Mr Todd propped a ladder against it and mounted. Tony followed, still unsteady after his illness. Mr Todd sat on the platform and Tony stood at the top of the ladder looking over. There was a heap of bundles there, tied up with rag, palm leaf and raw hide.

'It has been hard to keep out the worms and ants. Two are practically destroyed. But there is an oil the Indians make that is useful.'

He unwrapped the nearest parcel and handed down a calf bound book. It was an early American edition of *Bleak House*.

'It does not matter which we take first.'

'You are fond of Dickens?'

'Why, yes, of course. More than fond, far more. You see, they are the only books I have ever heard. My father used to read them and then later the black man . . . and now you. I have heard them all several times by now but I never get tired; there is always more to be learned and noticed, so many characters, so many changes of scene, so many words . . . I have all Dickens's books here except those that the ants devoured. It takes a long time to read them all–more than two years.'

'Well,' said Tony lightly, 'they will well last out my visit.'

'Oh, I hope not. It is delightful to start again. Each time I think I find more to enjoy and admire.'

They took down the first volume of *Bleak House* and that afternoon Tony had his first reading.

He had always rather enjoyed reading aloud and in the first year of marriage had shared several books in this way with Brenda, until one day, in a moment of frankness, she remarked that it was torture to her. He had read to John Andrew, late in the afternoon, in winter, while the child sat before the nursery fender eating his supper. But Mr Todd was a unique audience.

The old man sat astride his hammock opposite Tony, fixing him throughout with his eyes, and following the words, soundlessly, with his lips. Often when a new character was introduced he would say, 'Repeat the name, I have forgotten him,' or 'Yes, yes, I remember her well. She dies, poor woman.' He would frequently interrupt with questions; not as Tony would have imagined about the circumstances of the story–such things as the procedure of the Lord Chancellor's Court or the social conventions of the time, though they must have been unintelligible, did not concern him–but always about the characters. 'Now, why does she say that? Does she really mean it? Did she feel faint because of the heat of the fire or of something in that paper?' He laughed loudly at all the jokes and at some passages which did not seem humorous to Tony, asking him to repeat them two or three times, and later at the description of the sufferings of the outcasts in 'Tom-all-alone's' tears ran down his cheeks into his beard. His comments on the story were usually simple. 'I think that Dedlock is a very proud man,' or, 'Mrs Jellyby does not take enough care of her children.'

Tony enjoyed the readings almost as much as he did.

At the end of the first day the old man said, 'You read beautifully, with far better accent than the black man. And you explain better. It is almost as though my father were here again.' And always at the end of a session he thanked his guest courteously. 'I enjoyed that *very* much. It was an extremely distressing chapter. But, if I remember it rightly, it will all turn out well.'

By the time that they were in the second volume, however, the novelty of the old man's delight had begun to wane and Tony was feeling strong enough to be restless. He touched more than once on the subject of his departure, asking about canoes and rains and the possibility of finding guides. But Mr Todd seemed obtuse and paid no attention to these hints.

One day, running his thumb through the pages of *Bleak House* that remained to be read, Tony said, 'We still have a lot to get through. I hope I shall be able to finish it before I go.'

'Oh, yes,' said Mr Todd. 'Do not disturb yourself about that. You will have time to finish it, my friend.'

For the first time Tony noticed something slightly menacing in his host's manner. That evening at supper, a brief meal of farine and dried beef, eaten just before sundown, Tony renewed the subject.

'You know, Mr Todd, the time has come when I must be thinking about getting back to civilization. I have already imposed myself on your hospitality far too long.'

Mr Todd bent over the plate, crunching mouthfuls of farine, but made no reply.

'How soon do you think I shall be able to get a boat? . . . I said, how soon do you think I shall be able to get a boat? I appreciate all your kindness to me more than I can say, but . . .'

'My friend, any kindness I may have shown is amply repaid by your reading of Dickens. Do not let us mention the subject again.'

'Well, I'm very glad you have enjoyed it. I have, too. But I really must be thinking of getting back . . .'

'Yes,' said Mr Todd. 'The black man was like that. He thought of it all the time. But he died here . . .'

Twice during the next day Tony opened the subject, but his host was evasive. Finally, he said, 'Forgive me, Mr Todd, but I really must press the point. When can I get a boat?'

'There is no boat.'

'Well, the Indians can build one.'

'You must wait for the rains. There is not enough water in the river now.'

'How long will that be?'

'A month . . . two months . . .'

They had finished *Bleak House* and were nearing the end of *Dombey and Son* when the rain came.

'Now it is the time to make preparations to go.'

'Oh, that is impossible. The Indians will not make a boat during the rainy season–it is one of their superstitions . . .'

'You might have told me.'

'Did I not mention it? I forgot.'

Next morning Tony went out alone while his host was busy, and, looking as aimless as he could, strolled across the savannah to the group of Indian houses. There were four or five Pie-wies sitting in one of the doorways. They did not look up as he approached them. He addressed them in the few words of Macushi he had acquired during the journey but they made no sign whether they understood him or not. Then he drew a sketch of a canoe in the sand, he went through some vague motions of carpentry, pointed from them to him, then made motions of giving something to them and scratched out the outlines of a gun and a hat and a few other recognizable articles of trade. One of the women *giggled* but no one gave any sign of comprehension, and he went away unsatisfied.

At their mid-day meal Mr Todd said, 'Mr Last, the Indians tell me that you have been trying to speak with them. It is easier that you say anything you wish through me. You realize, do you not, that they would do nothing without my authority? They regard themselves, quite rightly in many cases, as my children.'

'Well, as a matter of fact, I was asking them about a canoe.'

'So they gave me to understand . . . and now if you have finished your meal perhaps we might have another chapter. I am quite absorbed in the book.'

They finished *Dombey and Son*; nearly a year had passed since Tony had left England, and his gloomy foreboding of permanent exile became suddenly acute when, between the pages of *Martin Chuzzlewit*, he found a document written in pencil in irregular characters.

Year 1919.

I James Todd of Brazil do swear to Barnabas Washington of Georgetown that if he finish this book in fact Martin Chuzzlewit I will let him go away back as soon as finished.

There followed a heavy pencil X and after it: *Mr Todd made this mark signed Barnabas Washington.*

'Mr Todd,' said Tony, 'I must speak frankly. You saved my life, and when I get back to civilization I will reward you to the best of my ability. I will give you anything within reason. But at present you are keeping me here against my will. I demand to be released.'

'But, my friend, what is keeping you? You are under no restraint. Go when you like.'

'You know very well that I can't get away without your help.'

'In that case you must humour an old man. Read me another chapter.'

'Mr Todd, I swear by anything you like that when I get to Manáos I will find someone to take my place. I will pay a man to read to you all day.'

'But I have no need of another man. You read so well.'

'I have read for the last time.'

'I hope not,' said Mr Todd politely.

That evening at supper only one plate of dried meat and farine was brought in and Mr Todd ate alone. Tony lay without speaking, staring at the thatch.

Next day at noon a single plate was put before Mr Todd but with it lay his gun, cocked, on his knee, as he ate. Tony resumed the reading of *Martin Chuzzlewit* where it had been interrupted.

Weeks passed hopelessly. They read *Nicholas Nickleby* and *Little Dorrit* and *Oliver Twist*. Then a stranger arrived in the savannah, a half-caste prospector, one of that lonely order of men who wander for a lifetime through the forests, tracing the little streams, sifting the gravel, and ounce by ounce, filling the little leather sack of gold dust, more often than not dying of exposure and starvation with five hundred dollars worth of gold hung round their necks. Mr Todd was vexed at his arrival, gave him farine and *tasso* and sent him on his journey within an hour of his arrival, but in that hour Tony had time to scribble his name on a slip of paper and put it into the man's hand.

From now on there was hope. The days followed their unvarying routine; coffee at sunrise, a morning of inaction while Mr Todd pottered about on the business of the farm, farine and *tasso* at noon, Dickens in the afternoon, farine and *tasso* and sometimes some fruit for supper, silence from sunset to dawn with the small wick glowing in the beef fat and the palm thatch overhead dimly discernible; but Tony lived in quiet confidence and expectation.

Sometime, this year or the next, the prospector would arrive at a Brazilian village with news of his discovery. The disasters of the Messinger expedition would not have passed unnoticed. Tony could imagine the headlines that must have appeared in the popular press; even now, probably, there were search parties working over the country he had crossed; any day English voices must sound over the savannah and a dozen friendly adventurers come crashing through the bush. Even as he was reading, while his lips mechanically followed the printed pages, his mind wandered away from his eager, crazy host opposite, and he began to narrate to himself incidents of his homecoming–the gradual re-encounters with civilization (he shaved and bought new clothes at Manáos, telegraphed for money, received wires of congratulation; he enjoyed the leisurely river journey to Belem, the big liner to Europe; savoured good claret and fresh meat and spring vegetables; he was shy at meeting Brenda and uncertain how to address her . . . '*Darling*, you've been much longer than you said. I quite thought you were lost . . .'

And then Mr Todd interrupted. 'May I trouble you to read that passage again? It is one I particularly enjoy.'

The weeks passed; there was no sign of rescue but Tony endured the day for hope of what might happen on the morrow; he even felt a slight stirring of cordiality towards his jailer and was therefore quite willing to join him when, one evening after a long conference with an Indian neighbour, he proposed a celebration.

'It is one of the local feast days,' he explained, 'and they have been making *pivari*. You may not like it but you should try some. We will go across to this man's home tonight.'

Accordingly after supper they joined a party of Indians that were assembled round the fire in one of the huts at the other side of the savannah. They were singing in an apathetic, monotonous manner and passing a large calabash of liquid from mouth to mouth. Separate bowls were brought for Tony and Mr Todd, and they were given hammocks to sit in.

'You must drink it all without lowering the cup. That is the etiquette.'

Tony gulped the dark liquid, trying not to taste it. But it was not unpleasant, hard and muddy on the palate like most of the beverages he had been offered in Brazil, but with a flavour of honey and brown bread. He leant back in the hammock feeling unusually contented. Perhaps at that very moment the search party was in camp a few hours' journey from them. Meanwhile he was warm and drowsy. The cadence of song rose and fell interminably, liturgically. Another calabash of *pivari* was offered him and he handed it back empty. He lay full length watching the play of shadows on the thatch as the Pie-wies began to dance. Then he shut his eyes and thought of England and Hetton and fell asleep.

He awoke, still in the Indian hut, with the impression that he had outslept his usual hour. By the position of the sun he knew it was late afternoon. No one else was about. He looked for his watch and found to his surprise that it was not on his wrist. He had left it in the house, he supposed, before coming to the party.

'I must have been tight last night,' he reflected. 'Treacherous drink that.' He had a headache and feared a recurrence of fever. He found when he set his feet to the ground that he stood with difficulty; his walk was unsteady and his mind confused as it had been during the first weeks of his convalescence. On the way across the savannah he was obliged to stop more than once, shutting his eyes and breathing deeply. When he reached the house he found Mr Todd sitting there.

'Ah, my friend, you are late for the reading this afternoon. There is scarcely another half hour of light. How do you feel?'

'Rotten. That drink doesn't seem to agree with me.'

'I will give you something to make you better. The forest has remedies for everything; to make you awake and to make you sleep.'

'You haven't seen my watch anywhere?'

'You have missed it?'

'Yes. I thought I was wearing it. I say, I've never slept so long.'

'Not since you were a baby. Do you know how long? Two days.'

'Nonsense. I can't have.'

'Yes, indeed. It is a long time. It is a pity because you missed our guests.'

'Guests?'

'Why, yes. I have been quite gay while you were asleep. Three men from outside. Englishmen. It is a pity you missed them. A pity for them, too, as they particularly wished to see you. But what could I do? You were so sound asleep. They had come all the way to find you, so–I thought you would not mind–as you could not greet them yourself, I gave them a little souvenir, your watch. They wanted something to take back to England where a reward is being offered for news of you. They were very pleased with it. And they took some photographs of the little cross I put up to commemorate your coming. They were pleased with that, too. They were very easily pleased. But I do not suppose they will visit us again, our life here is so retired . . . no pleasures except reading . . . I do not suppose we shall ever have visitors again . . . well, well, I will get you some medicine to make you feel better. Your head aches, does it not? . . . We will not have any Dickens today . . . but tomorrow, and the day after that, and the day after that. Let us read *Little Dorrit* again. There are passages in that book I can never hear without the temptation to weep.'

7

ENGLISH GOTHIC–III

A light breeze in the dewy orchards; brilliant, cool sunshine over meadows and copses; the elms were all in bud in the avenue; everything was early that year for it had been a mild winter.

High overhead among its gargoyles and crockets the clock chimed for the hour and solemnly struck fourteen. It was half-past eight. The clock had been irregular lately. It was one of the things that Richard Last intended to see to, when death duties were paid and silver foxes began to show a profit.

Molly Last bowled up the drive on her two-stroke motor-cycle; there was bran mash on her breeches and in her hair. She had been feeding the Angora rabbits.

On the gravel in front of the house the new memorial stood, shrouded in a flag. Molly propped the motor-cycle against the wall of the drawbridge and ran in to breakfast. Life at Hetton was busier but simpler since Richard Last's succession. Ambrose remained but there were no longer any footmen; he and a boy and four women servants did the work of the house. Richard Last called them his 'skeleton staff'. When things were easier he would extend the household; meanwhile the dining hall and the library were added to the state apartments which were kept locked and shuttered; the family lived in the morning-room, the smoking-room and what had been Tony's study. Most of the kitchen quarters, too, were out of use; an up-to-date and economical range had been installed in one of the pantries.

The family all appeared downstairs by half past eight, except Agnes, who took longer to dress and was usually some minutes late; Teddy and Molly had been out for an hour, she among the rabbits, he to the silver foxes. Teddy was twenty-two and lived at home. Peter was still at Oxford.

They breakfasted together in the morning-room. Mrs Last sat at one end of the table, her husband at the other; there was a constant traffic from hand to hand to and fro between them of cups, plates, honey jars and correspondence.

Mrs Last said, 'Molly, you have rabbit-feed on your head again.'

'Oh well, I shall have to tidy up anyway before the jamboree.'

Mr Last, said, '*Jamboree?* Is nothing sacred to you children?'

Teddy said, 'Another casualty at the stinkeries. That little vixen we bought from the people at Oakhampton got her brush bitten off during the night. Must have got it through the wire into the next cage. Tricky birds, foxes.'

Agnes came next; she was a neat, circumspect child of twelve, with large grave eyes behind her goggles. She kissed her father and mother and said, 'I'm sorry if I'm late.'

'*If* you're late . . .' said Mr Last tolerantly.

'How long will the show last?' asked Teddy. 'I've got to run over to Bayton and get some more rabbits for the foxes. Chivers says he's got about fifty waiting for me. We can't shoot enough here. Greedy little beggars.'

'It will be all over by half past eleven. Mr Tendril isn't going to preach a sermon. It's just as well really. He's got it into his head that cousin Tony died in Afghanistan.'

'There's a letter here from cousin Brenda. She's very sorry but she can't get down for the dedication.'

'Oh.'

There was a general silence.

'She says that Jock has a three-line whip for this afternoon.'

'Oh.'

'She could have come without him,' said Molly.

'She sends her love to us all and to Hetton.'

There was another pause.

'Well, I think it's a jolly good thing,' said Molly. '*She* couldn't show much widowy grief. It didn't take *her* long to get hitched up again.'

'*Molly!*'

'And you know you think the same.'

'I will not allow you to talk like that about Cousin Brenda, whatever we think. She had a perfect right to marry again and I hope she and Mr Grant-Menzies are very happy.'

'She was always jolly decent to us when she used to live here,' said Agnes.

'Well, I should hope so,' said Teddy. 'After all it's *our* place.'

The day was still fine at eleven o'clock, though the wind had got up, fluttering the papers on which the order of the service was printed and once threatening to unveil the memorial prematurely. Several relatives were present, Lady St Cloud, Aunt Frances, and the family of impoverished Lasts who had not profited by Tony's disappearance. All the household and estate servants were there, several tenants and most of the village; there were also a dozen or so neighbours, among them Colonel Inch–Richard Last and Teddy had hunted regularly that season with the Pigstanton. Mr Tendril conducted the brief service in resonant tones that were clearly audible above the blustering wind. When he pulled the cord the flag fell away from the memorial without mishap.

It was a plain monolith of local stone, inscribed:

ANTHONY LAST OF HETTON
EXPLORER
Born at Hetton, 1902
Died in Brazil, 1934

When the local visitors had left and the relatives had gone into the house to be shown the new labour-saving arrangements, Richard Last and Lady St Cloud remained for a short time on the gravel.

'I'm glad we put that up,' he said. 'You know, I should never have thought of it, if it had not been for a Mrs Beaver. She wrote to me as soon as the news of Tony's death was published. I didn't know her at the time. Of course we knew very few of Tony's friends.'

'It was her suggestion?'

'Yes, she said that as one of Tony's closest friends she knew he would wish to have some monument at Hetton. She was most considerate–even offering to arrange with the contractors for it. Her own plans were more ambitious. She proposed that we should have the Chapel redecorated as a chantry. But I think this is what he would have preferred. The stone comes from one of our own quarries and was cut by the estate workmen.'

'Yes, I think he would have preferred this,' said Lady St Cloud.

Teddy had chosen Galahad for his bedroom. He disengaged himself from the family and hurried up to change out of his dark clothes. Within ten minutes he was in his car driving to Chivers' farm. Before luncheon he was back with the rabbits. They were skinned and tied round the feet into bundles of four.

'Coming to the stinkeries?' he asked Agnes.

'No, I'm looking after cousin Frances. She got rather on mother's nerves through crabbing the new boiler.'

The silver-fox farm was behind the stables; a long double row of wire cages; they had wire floors covered with earth and cinders to prevent the animals digging their way out. They lived in pairs; some were moderately tame but it was unwise to rely upon them. Teddy and Ben Hacket–who helped with them–had been badly bitten more than once that winter.

They ran up to the doors when they saw Teddy come with the rabbits. The vixen who had lost her brush seemed little the worse for her accident.

Teddy surveyed his charges with pride and affection. It was by means of them that he hoped one day to restore Hetton to the glory that it had enjoyed in the days of his cousin Tony.

Scoop

EVELYN
WAUGH

SCOOP

A Novel about Journalists

For
Laura

PART I

THE STITCH SERVICE

1/i

While still a young man, John Courteney Boot had, as his publisher proclaimed, 'achieved an assured and enviable position in contemporary letters.' His novels sold 15,000 copies in their first year and were read by the people whose opinion John Boot respected. Between novels he kept his name sweet in intellectual circles with unprofitable but modish works on history and travel. His signed first editions sometimes changed hands at a shilling or two above their original price. He had published eight books–beginning with a life of Rimbaud written when he was eighteen, and concluding, at the moment, with *Waste of Time*, a studiously modest description of some harrowing months among the Patagonian Indians–of which most people who lunched with Lady Metroland could remember the names of three or four. He had many charming friends, of whom the most valued was the lovely Mrs Algernon Stitch.

Like all in her circle John Boot habitually brought his difficulties to her for solution. It was with this purpose, on a biting-cold mid-June morning, that he crossed the Park and called at her house (a superb creation by Nicholas Hawksmoor modestly concealed in a cul-de-sac near Saint James's Palace).

Algernon Stitch was standing in the hall; his bowler hat was on his head; his right hand, grasping a crimson, royally emblazoned dispatch case, emerged from the left sleeve of his overcoat; his other hand burrowed petulantly in the breast pocket. An umbrella under his left arm further inconvenienced him. He spoke indistinctly, for he was holding a folded copy of the morning paper between his teeth.

'Can't get it on,' he seemed to say.

The man who had opened the door came to his assistance, removed the umbrella and dispatch case and laid them on the marble table; removed the coat and held it behind his master. John took the newspaper.

'Thanks. Thanks very much. Much obliged. Come to see Julia, eh?'

From high overhead, down the majestic curves of the great staircase, came a small but preternaturally resonant voice.

'Try not to be late for dinner, Algy; the Kents are coming.'

'She's upstairs,' said Stitch. He had his coat on now and looked fully an English cabinet minister; long and thin, with a long, thin nose, and long, thin moustaches; the ideal model for continental caricaturists. 'You'll find her in bed,' he said.

'Your speech reads very well this morning.' John was always polite to Stitch; everybody was; Labour members loved him.

'Speech? Mine? Ah. Reads well, eh? Sounded terrible to me. Thanks all the same. Thanks very much. Much obliged.'

So Stitch went out to the Ministry of Imperial Defence and John went up to see Julia.

As her husband had told him, she was still in bed although it was past eleven o'clock. Her normally mobile face encased in clay was rigid and menacing as an Aztec mask. But she was not resting. Her secretary, Miss Holloway, sat at her side with account books, bills, and correspondence. With one hand Mrs Stitch was signing cheques; with the other she held the telephone to which, at the moment, she was dictating details of the costumes for a charity ballet. An elegant young man at the top of a step ladder was painting ruined castles on the ceiling. Josephine, the eight-year-old Stitch prodigy, sat on the foot of the bed construing her day's passage of Virgil. Mrs Stitch's maid, Brittling, was reading her the clues of the morning crossword. She had been hard at it since half past seven.

Josephine rose from her lesson to kick John as he entered. '*Boot*,' she said savagely, '*Boot*,' catching him first on one kneecap, then on the other. It was a joke of long standing.

Mrs Stitch turned her face of clay, in which only the eyes gave a suggestion of welcome, towards her visitor.

'Come in,' she said, 'I'm just going out. Why twenty pounds to Mrs Beaver?'

'That was for Lady Jean's wedding present,' said Miss Holloway.

'I must have been insane. About the lion's head for the centurion's breastplate; there's a beautiful one over the gate of a house near Salisbury, called Twisbury Manor; copy that as near as you can; ring up *Country Life* and ask for "back numbers"; there was a photograph of it about two years ago. You're putting too much ivy on the turret, Arthur; the owl won't show up unless you have him on the bare stone, and I'm particularly attached to the owl. *Munera*, darling, like tumtiddy; always a short a in neuter plurals. It sounds like an anagram: see if "Terracotta" fits. I'm *delighted* to see you, John. Where have you been? You can come and buy carpets with me; I've found a new shop in Bethnal Green, kept by a very interesting Jew who speaks no English; the most extraordinary things keep happening to his sister. Why should I go to Viola Chasm's Distressed Area; did she come to my Model Madhouse?'

'Oh, yes, Mrs Stitch.'

'Then I suppose it means two guineas. I absolutely loved *Waste of Time*. We read it aloud at Blakewell. The headless abbot is grand.'

'Headless abbot?'

'Not in Wasters. On Arthur's ceiling. I put it in the Prime Minister's room.'

'Did he read it?'

'Well, I don't think he *reads* much.'

'Terracotta is too long, madam, and there is no r.'

'Try hottentot. It's that kind of word. I can never do anagrams unless I can see them. No, *Twisbury*, you must have heard of it.'

'Floribus Austrum,' Josephine chanted, 'perditus et liquidis immisi fontibus apros; having been lost with flowers in the South and sent into the liquid fountain; apros is wild boars, but I couldn't quite make sense of that bit.'

'We'll do it tomorrow. I've got to go out now. Is "hottentot" any use?'

'No h, madam,' said Brittling with ineffable gloom.

'Oh, dear. I must look at it in my bath. I shall only be ten minutes. Stay and talk to Josephine.'

She was out of bed and out of the room. Brittling followed. Miss Holloway collected the cheques and papers. The young man on the ladder dabbed away industriously. Josephine rolled to the head of the bed and stared up at him.

'It's very banal, isn't it, Boot?'

'I like it very much.'

'Do you? I think all Arthur's work is banal. I read your book *Waste of Time*.'

'Ah.' John did not invite criticism.

'I thought it very banal.'

'You seem to find everything banal.'

'It is a new word whose correct use I have only lately learnt,' said Josephine with dignity. 'I find it applies to nearly everything; Virgil and Miss Brittling and my gymnasium.'

'How is the gymnasium going?'

'I am by far the best of my class, although there are several girls older than me and two middle-class boys.'

When Mrs Stitch said ten minutes, she meant ten minutes. Sharp on time she was back, dressed for the street; her lovely face, scraped clean of clay, was now alive with interest.

'Sweet Josephine, has Mr Boot been boring you?'

'It was all right really. I did most of the talking.'

'Show him your imitation of the Prime Minister.'

'No.'

'Sing him your Neapolitan song.'

'No.'

'Stand on your head. Just once for Mr Boot.'

'No.'

'Oh, dear. Well, we must go at once if we are to get to Bethnal Green and back before luncheon. The traffic's terrible.'

Algernon Stitch went to his office in a sombre and rather antiquated Daimler; Julia always drove herself, in the latest model of mass-produced baby car; brand-new twice a year, painted an invariable brilliant black, tiny and glossy as a midget's funeral hearse. She mounted the kerb and bowled rapidly along the pavement to the corner of St James's, where a policeman took her number and ordered her into the road.

'Third time this week,' said Mrs Stitch. 'I wish they wouldn't. It's such a nuisance for Algy.'

Once embedded in the traffic block, she stopped the engine and turned her attention to the crossword.

'It's "detonated",' she said, filling it in.

East wind swept the street, carrying with it the exhaust gas of a hundred motors and coarse particles of Regency stucco from a once decent Nash façade that was being demolished across the way. John shivered and rubbed some grit further into his eye. Eight minutes' close application was enough to finish the puzzle. Mrs Stitch folded the paper and tossed it over her shoulder into the back seat; looked about her resentfully at the stationary traffic.

'This is too much,' she said; started the engine, turned sharp again on to the kerb and proceeded to Piccadilly, driving before her at a brisk pace, until he took refuge on the step of Brooks's, a portly, bald young man; when he reached safety, he turned to remonstrate, recognized Mrs Stitch, and bowed profoundly to the tiny, black back as it shot the corner of Arlington Street. 'One of the things I like about these absurd cars,' she said, 'is that you can do things with them that you couldn't do in a real one.'

From Hyde Park Corner to Piccadilly Circus the line of traffic was continuous and motionless, still as a photograph, unbroken and undisturbed save at a few strategic corners where barricaded navvies, like desperate outposts of some proletarian defence, were rending the road with mechanical drills, mining for the wires and tubes that controlled the life of the city.

'I want to get away from London,' said John Boot.

'So it's come to that? All on account of your American girl?'

'Well, mostly.'

'I warned you, before you began. Is she being frightful?'

'My lips are sealed. But I've got to get far away or else go crazy.'

'To my certain knowledge she's driven three men into the bin. Where are you going?'

'That's just what I wanted to talk about.'

The line of cars jerked forwards for ten yards and again came to rest. The lunch-time edition of the evening papers was already on the streets; placards announcing

ISHMAELITE CRISIS

and

STRONG LEAGUE NOTE

were fluttering in the east wind.

'Ishmaelia seems to be the place. I was wondering if Algy would send me there as a spy.'

'Not a chance.'

'No?'

'Foregonners. Algy's been sacking ten spies a day for weeks. It's a grossly overcrowded profession. Why don't you go as a war correspondent?'

'Could you fix it?'

'I don't see why not. After all, you've been to Patagonia. I should think they would jump at you. You're sure you really want to go?'

'Quite sure.'

'Well, I'll see what I can do. I'm meeting Lord Copper at lunch today at Margot's. I'll try and bring the subject up.'

I/ii

When Lady Metroland said half past one she meant ten minutes to two. It was precisely at this time, simultaneously with her hostess, that Mrs Stitch arrived (having been obliged by press of traffic to leave her little car in a garage half-way to Bethnal Green, and return to Curzon Street by means of the Underground railway). Lord Copper, however, who normally lunched at one, was waiting with some impatience. Various men and women who appeared to know one another intimately and did not know Lord Copper, had been admitted from time to time and had disregarded him. His subordinates at the Megalopolitan Newspaper Corporation would have been at difficulties to recognize the uneasy figure which stood up each time the door was opened and sat down again unnoticed. He was a stranger in these parts; it was a thoughtless benefaction to one of Lady Metroland's charities that had exposed him, in the middle of a busy day, to this harrowing experience; he would readily, now, have doubled the sum to purchase his release. Thus when Mrs Stitch directed upon him some of her piercing shafts of charm she found him first numb, then dazzled, then extravagantly receptive.

From the moment of her entrance the luncheon party was transformed for Lord Copper; he had gotten a new angle on it. He knew of Mrs Stitch; from time to time he had seen her in the distance; now for the first time he found himself riddled through and through, mesmerized, inebriated. Those at the table, witnessing the familiar process, began to conjecture in tones which Lord Copper was too much entranced to overhear, what Julia could possibly want of him. 'It's her model madhouse,' said some; 'She wants the caricaturists to lay off Algy,' said others; 'Been losing money,' thought the second footman (at Lady Metroland's orders he was on diet and lunch-time always found him in a cynical mood); 'a job for someone or other,' came nearest the truth, but no one thought of John Courteney Boot until Mrs Stitch brought him into the conversation. Then they all played up loyally.

'You know,' she said, after coaxing Lord Copper into an uncompromising denunciation of the Prime Minister's public and private honesty, 'I expect he's all you say, but he's a man of far more taste than you'd suppose. He always sleeps with a Boot by his bed.'

'A boot?' asked Lord Copper, trustful but a little bewildered.

'One of John Boot's books.'

The luncheon party had got their cue.

'Dear John Boot,' said Lady Metroland, '*so* clever and amusing. I wish I could get him to come and see me more often.'

'Such a divine style,' said Lady Cockpurse.

The table buzzed with praise of John Boot. It was a new name to Lord Copper. He resolved to question his literary secretary on the subject. He had become Boot-conscious.

Mrs Stitch changed her ground and began to ask him in the most flattering way about the chances of peace in Ishmaelia. Lord Copper gave it as his opinion that civil war was inevitable. Mrs Stitch remarked how few of the famous war correspondents still survived.

'Isn't there one called Sir Something Hitchcock?' asked Lady Cockpurse. (This was a false step since the knight in question had lately left Lord Copper's service, after an acrimonious dispute about the date of the Battle of Hastings, and had transferred to the *Daily Brute* camp.)

'Who will you be sending to Ishmaelia?' asked Mrs Stitch.

'I am in consultation with my editors on the subject. We think it a very promising little war. A microcosm, as you might say, of world drama. We propose to give it fullest publicity. The workings of a great newspaper,' said Lord Copper, feeling at last thoroughly Rotarian, 'are of a complexity which the public seldom appreciates. The citizen little realizes the vast machinery put into motion for him in exchange for his morning penny.' ('O God,' said Lady Metroland, faintly but audibly.) 'We shall have our naval, military, and air experts, our squad of photographers, our colour reporters, covering the war from every angle and on every front.'

'Yes,' said Mrs Stitch. 'Yes, yes. I suppose you will . . . If I were you I should send someone like Boot. I don't suppose you could persuade *him* to go, but someone like him.'

'It has been my experience, dear Mrs Stitch, that the *Daily Beast* can command the talent of the world. Only last week the Poet Laureate wrote us an ode to the seasonal fluctuation of our net sales. We splashed it on the middle page. He admitted it was the most poetic and highly-paid work he had ever done.'

'Well, of course, if you *could* get him, Boot is your man. He's a brilliant writer, he's travelled everywhere and knows the whole Ishmaelite situation inside out.'

'Boot would be divine,' said Lady Cockpurse loyally.

Half an hour later Mrs Stitch rang up to say 'O.K., John. I think it's fixed. Don't take a penny less than fifty pounds a week.'

'God bless you, Julia. You've save my life.'

'It's just the Stitch Service,' said Mrs Stitch cheerfully.

I/iii

That evening, Mr Salter, foreign editor of *The Beast*, was summoned to dinner at his chief's country seat at East Finchley. It was a highly unwelcome invitation; Mr Salter normally worked at the office until nine o'clock. That evening he had planned a holiday at the opera; he and his wife had been looking forward to it with keen enjoyment for some weeks. As he drove out to Lord Copper's frightful mansion he thought sadly of those carefree days when he had edited the Woman's Page, or, better still, when he had chosen the jokes for one of Lord Copper's comic weeklies. It was the policy of the Megalopolitan to keep the staff alert by constant changes of occupation. Mr Salter's ultimate ambition was to take charge of the Competitions. Meanwhile he was Foreign

Editor and found it a dog's life.

The two men dined alone. They ate parsley soup, whiting, roast veal, cabinet pudding; they drank whisky and soda. Lord Copper explained Nazism, Fascism, and Communism; later, in his ghastly library, he outlined the situation in the Far East. '*The Beast* stands for strong mutually antagonistic governments everywhere,' he said. 'Self-sufficiency at home, self-assertion abroad.'

Mr. Salter's side of the conversation was limited to expressions of assent. When Lord Copper was right he said, 'Definitely, Lord Copper'; when he was wrong, 'Up to a point.'

'Let me see, what's the name of the place I mean? Capital of Japan? Yokohama, isn't it?'

'Up to a point, Lord Copper.'

'And Hong Kong belongs to us, doesn't it?'

'Definitely, Lord Copper.'

After a time: 'Then there's this civil war in Ishmaelia. I propose to feature it. Who did you think of sending?'

'Well, Lord Copper, the choice seems between sending a staff reporter who will get the news but whose name the public doesn't know, or to get someone from outside with a name as a military expert. You see, since we lost Hitchcock. . . .'

'Yes, yes. He was our only man with a European reputation. *I know*. Zinc will be sending him. *I know*. But he was wrong about the Battle of Hastings. It *was* 1066. I looked it up. I won't employ a man who isn't big enough to admit when he's wrong.'

'We might share one of the Americans?'

'No, I tell you who I want; Boot.'

'Boot?'

'Yes, Boot. He's a young man whose work I'm very much interested in. He has the most remarkable style and he's been in Patagonia and the Prime Minister keeps his books by his bed. Do *you* read him?'

'Up to a point, Lord Copper.'

'Well, get on to him tomorrow. Have him up to see you. Be cordial. Take him out to dinner. Get him at any price. Well, at any reasonable price,' he added, for there had lately been a painful occurrence when instructions of this kind, given in an expansive mood, had been too literally observed and a trick cyclist who had momentarily attracted Lord Copper's attention had been engaged to edit the Sports Page on a five years' contract at five thousand a year.

I / iv

Mr Salter went to work at midday. He found the Managing Editor cast in gloom.

'It's a terrible paper this morning,' he said. 'We paid Professor Jellaby thirty guineas for the feature article and there's not a word in it one can understand. Beaten by *The Brute* in every edition on the Zoo Mercy Slaying story. And *look at the Sports Page*.'

Together, in shame, the two men read the trick cyclist's Sports Page.

'Who's Boot?' asked Mr Salter at last.

'I know the name,' said the Managing Editor.

'The chief wants to send him to Ishmaelia. He's the Prime Minister's favourite writer.'

'Not the chap I was thinking of,' said the Managing Editor.

'Well, I've got to find him.' He listlessly turned the pages of the morning paper. 'Boot,' he said. 'Boot. Boot. Boot. Why! *Boot*–here he is. Why didn't the chief say he was a staff man?'

At the back of the paper, ignominiously sandwiched between Pip and Pop, the Bedtime Pets, and the recipe for a dish called 'Waffle Scramble', lay the bi-weekly half-column devoted to Nature:

LUSH PLACES, edited by William Boot, Countryman.

'Do you suppose that's the right one?'

'Sure of it. The Prime Minister is nuts on rural England.'

'He's supposed to have a particularly high-class style: "*Feather-footed through the plashy fen passes the questing vole*" . . . would that be it?'

'Yes,' said the Managing Editor. 'That must be good style. At least it doesn't sound like anything else to me. I know the name well now you mention it. Never seen the chap. I don't think he's ever been to London. Sends his stuff in by post. All written out in pen and ink.'

'I've got to ask him to dinner.'

'Give him cider.'

'Is that what countrymen like?'

'Yes, cider and tinned salmon are the staple diet of the agricultural classes.'

'I'll send him a telegram. Funny the chief wanting to send him to Ishmaelia.'

2/i

'Change and decay in all around I see,' sang Uncle Theodore, gazing out of the morning-room window.

Thus, with startling loudness, he was accustomed to relieve his infrequent fits of depression; but decay, rather than change, was characteristic of the immediate prospect.

The immense trees which encircled Boot Magna Hall, shaded its drives and rides, and stood (tastefully disposed at the whim of some forgotten, provincial predecessor of Repton), singly and in groups about the park, and suffered, some from ivy, some from lightning, some from the various malignant disorders that vegetation is heir to, but all principally from old age. Some were supported with trusses and crutches of iron, some were filled with cement; some, even now, in June, could show only a handful of green leaves at their extremities. Sap ran thin and slow; a gusty night always brought down a litter of dead timber.

The lake was moved by strange tides. Sometimes, as at the present moment, it sank to a single, opaque pool in a wilderness of mud and rushes; sometimes it rose and inundated five acres of pasture. There had once been an old man in one of the lodges who understood the workings of the water system; there were sluice gates hidden among the reeds, and manholes, dotted about in places known only to him, furnished with taps and cocks; that man had been able to control an ornamental cascade and draw a lofty jet of water from the mouth of the dolphin on the South terrace. But he had been in his grave fifteen years and the secret had died with him.

The house was large but by no means too large for the Boot family, which at this time numbered eight. There were in the direct line: William who owned the house and estate, William's sister Priscilla who claimed to own the horses, William's widowed mother who owned the contents of the house and exercised ill-defined rights over the flower garden, and William's widowed grandmother who was said to own 'the money'. No one knew how much she possessed; she had been bedridden as long as William's memory went back. It was from her that such large cheques issued as were from time to time necessary for balancing the estate accounts and paying for Uncle Theodore's occasional, disastrous visits to London. Uncle Theodore, the oldest of the male collaterals, was by far the gayest. Uncle Roderick was in many ways the least eccentric. He had managed the estates and household throughout William's minority and continued to do so with a small but regular deficit which was made up annually by one of grandmamma's cheques. The widowed Lady Trilby was William's Great-Aunt Anne, his father's elder sister; she owned the motor-car, a vehicle adapted to her own requirements; it had a horn which could be worked from the back seat; her weekly journey to church resounded through the village like the Coming of the Lord. Uncle Bernard devoted himself to a life of scholarship but had received little general recognition, for his researches, though profound, were narrow, being connected solely with his own pedigree. He had traced William's descent through three different lines from Ethelred the Unready and only lack of funds fortunately prevented him from prosecuting a claim to the abeyant barony of de Butte.

All the Boots, in one way or another, had about a hundred a year each as pocket money. It was therefore convenient for them to live together at Boot Magna where wages and household expenses were counted in with Uncle Roderick's annual deficit. The richest member of the household, in ready cash, was Nannie Bloggs, who had been bedridden for the last thirty years; she kept her savings in a red flannel bag under the bolster. Uncle Theodore made attempts on them from time to time, but she was a sharp old girl and, since she combined a long-standing aversion to Uncle Theodore with a preternatural aptitude for bringing off showy doubles during the flat racing season, her hoard continued to grow. The Bible and the Turf Guide were her only reading. She got great delight from telling each member of the family, severally and secretly, that he or she was her heir.

In other rooms about the house reposed: Nannie Price, ten years the junior of Nannie Bloggs, and bedridden from about the same age. She gave her wages to Chinese Missions and had little influence in the house; Sister Watts, old Mrs Boot's first nurse, and Sister Sampson, her second; Miss Scope, Aunt Anne's governess, veteran invalid, of some years seniority in bed to old Mrs Boot herself; and Bentinck the butler: James, the first footman, had been confined to his room for some time, but he was able on warm days to sit in an arm-chair at the window. Nurse Granger was still on her feet, but as her duties included the charge of all eight sick-rooms, it was thought she would not long survive. Ten servants waited upon the household and upon one another, but in a desultory fashion, for they could spare very little time from the five meat meals which tradition daily allowed them. In the circumstances the Boots did not entertain and were indulgently spoken of in the district as being 'poor as church mice'.

The fashionable John Courteney Boot was a remote cousin, or, as Uncle Bernard preferred, the member of a cadet branch. William had never met him; he had met very few people indeed. It was not true to say, as the Managing Editor of *The Beast* had said, that he had never been to London, but his visits had been infrequent enough for each to be distinct and perennially horrifying in his memory.

'Change and decay in all around I see,' sang Uncle Theodore. It was his habit to sing the same line over and over again. He was waiting for the morning papers. So were William and Uncle Roderick. They were brought by the butcher, often blotched with red, any time between eleven and midday, and then, if not intercepted, disappeared among the sick-rooms to return at tea-time hopelessly mutilated, for both Bentinck and old Mrs Boot kept scrap-books, and Sister Sampson had the habit of cutting out coupons and losing them in the bedclothes. This morning they were late. It was a matter of great anxiety to William.

He had never been to the Megalopolitan offices or met anyone connected with *The Beast*. His job as author of *Lush Places* had been passed on to him by the widow on the death of its previous holder, the Rector of Boot Magna. He had carefully modelled his style on the late Rector's, at first painfully, now almost without effort. The work was of the utmost importance to him: he was paid a guinea a time and it gave him the best possible excuse for remaining uninterruptedly in the country.

And now it was in danger. On the previous Thursday a very dreadful thing had happened. Drawing on the observations of a lifetime and after due cross-examination of the head keeper and half an hour with the encyclopedia, William had composed a lyrical but wholly accurate account of the habits of the badger; one of his more finished essays. Priscilla in a playful mood had found the manuscript and altered it, substituting for 'badger' throughout 'the crested grebe'. It was not until Saturday morning when, in this form, it appeared in *The Beast*, that William was aware of the outrage.

His mail had been prodigious; some correspondents were sceptical, others derisive; one lady wrote to ask whether she read him aright in thinking he condoned the practice of baiting these rare and beautiful birds with terriers and deliberately destroying their earthy homes; how could this be tolerated in the so-called twentieth century? A major in Wales challenged him categorically to produce a single authenticated case of a great crested grebe attacking young rabbits. It had been exceedingly painful. All through the week-end William had awaited his dismissal, but Monday and Tuesday passed without a word from *The Beast*. He composed and despatched a light dissertation on water voles and expected the worst. Perhaps the powers at *The Beast* were too much enraged even to send back his manuscript; when Wednesday's paper came he would find another tenant of *Lush Places*. It came. He hunted frantically for his half-column. It was there, a green oasis between Waffle Scramble and the Bed-time Pets. *'Feather-footed through the plashy fens passes the questing vole. . . .'* It was all right. By some miracle Saturday's shame had been covered.

His uncles peevishly claimed the paper; he surrendered it readily. He stood at the french window blinking at the summer landscape; the horses at grass beyond the ha-ha skipped and frolicked.

'Confound the thing,' said Uncle Roderick behind him. 'Can't find the cricket anywhere. Whole page seems to be given up to some damn-fool cycling championship at Cricklewood Stadium.'

William did not care. In the fullness of his gratitude he resolved to give rodents a miss that Saturday (though he was particularly attached to them) and write instead of wild flowers and birdsong. He might even risk something out of the poets.

'Nay not so much as out of bed?
When all the birds have Matins said,'

he sang, in his heart, to the recumbent figures above him. And then, wheezing heavily, with crumbs on his mouth, ponderously straddling across the morning-room, came Troutbeck, the aged boy, bearing a telegram. Curiosity and resentment contended for mastery in Troutbeck's demeanour; curiosity because telegrams were of rare occurrence at Boot Magna; resentment at the interruption of his 'elevenses'–a lavish and ruminative feast which occupied the servants' hall from ten-thirty until noon.

William's face quickly reassured him that he had not been called from the table on any frivolous pretext. 'Bad news,' he was able to report. 'Shocking bad news for Master William.'

'It couldn't hardly be a death,' said the third housemaid. 'All the family's here.'

'Whatever it was we shall soon know,' said Troutbeck. 'It struck Master William all of a heap. Might I thank you to pass the chutney.'

Bad news indeed! Oblivious to the sunshine and the grazing horses and the stertorous breathing of his Uncle Theodore, William re-read the frightful doom that had fallen on him.

REQUEST YOUR IMMEDIATE PRESENCE HERE URGENT LORD COPPERS PERSONAL DESIRE SALTER BEAST.

'Nothing serious, I hope!' said Uncle Theodore, to whom telegrams, in the past, had from time to time brought news as disquieting as to any man living.

'Yes,' said William, 'I have been called to London.'

'Have you, my boy? That's interesting. I was thinking of running up for a night myself . . .'

But Uncle Theodore was speaking to the air. William was already at work, setting into motion the elaborate household machinery which would, too soon, effect his departure.

2/ii

After an early luncheon, William went to say good-bye to his grandmother. She looked at him with doleful, mad eyes. 'Going to London, eh? Well, I hardly suppose I shall be alive when you return. Wrap up warm, dear.' It was eternal winter in Mrs Boot's sunny bedroom.

All the family who had the use of their legs attended on the steps to see William off; Priscilla bathed in tears of penitence. Nannie Bloggs sent him down three golden sovereigns. Aunt Anne's motor-car was there to take him away. At the last moment Uncle Theodore attempted to get in at the offside, but was detected and deterred, 'Just wanted to see a chap in Jermyn Street about some business,' he said wistfully.

It was always a solemn thing for a Boot to go to London; solemn as a funeral for William on this afternoon. Once or twice on the way to the station, once or twice as the train stopped on the route to Paddington, William was tempted to give up the expedition in despair. Why should he commit himself to this abominable city merely to be railed at and, for all he knew of Lord Copper's temperament, physically assaulted? But sterner counsels prevailed. He might bluff it out. Lord Copper was a townsman, a provincial townsman at that, and certainly did not know the difference between a badger and a great crested grebe. It was William's word against a few cantankerous correspondents, and people who wrote to the newspapers were proverbially unbalanced. By the time he reached Westbury he had sketched out a little scene for himself, in which he stood resolutely in the board-room defying the doctrinaire zoology of Fleet Street; every inch a Boot, thrice descended from Ethelred the Unready, rightful 15th Baron de Butte, haughty as a chieftain, honest as a peasant. 'Lord Copper,' he was saying, 'no man shall call me a liar unchastised. The great crested grebe *does* hibernate.'

He went to the dining-car and ordered some whisky. The steward said, 'We're serving teas. Whisky after Reading.' After Reading he tried again. 'We're serving dinners. I'll bring you one to your carriage.' When it came, William spilled it down his tie. He gave the steward one of Nannie Bloggs' sovereigns in mistake for a shilling. It was contemptuously refused and everyone in the carriage stared at him. A man in a bowler hat said, 'May I look? Don't often see one of them nowadays. Tell you what I'll do, I'll toss you for it. Call.'

William said, 'Heads.'

'Tails it is, said the man in the bowler hat, putting it in his waistcoat pocket. He then went on reading his paper and everyone stared harder at William. His spirits began to sink; the mood of defiance passed. It was always the way; the moment he left the confines of Boot Magna he found himself in a foreign and hostile world. There was a train back at ten o'clock that night. Wild horses would not keep him from it. He would see Lord Copper, explain the situation fully and frankly, throw himself upon his mercy, and, successful or defeated, catch the train at ten. By Reading he had worked out his new and humble policy. He would tell Lord Copper about Priscilla's tears; great men were proverbially vulnerable to appeals of that kind. The man opposite him looked over the top of his paper. 'Got any more quids?'

'No,' said William.

'Pity.'

At seven he reached Paddington and the atrocious city was all around him.

2/iii

The Megalopolitan building, numbers 700–853 Fleet Street, was disconcerting. At first William thought that the taxi-driver, spotting a bumpkin, had driven him to the wrong address.

His acquaintance with offices was very small. At the time of his coming of age he had spent several mornings with the family solicitor in King's Bench Walk. At home he knew the local Estate Agents and Auctioneers, the Bank and the Town Hall. He had once seen in Taunton a barely intelligible film about newspaper life in New York where neurotic men in shirt sleeves and eye-shades had rushed from telephone to tape machines, insulting and betraying one another in surroundings of unredeemed squalor. From these memories he had a confused expectation that was rudely shocked by the Byzantine vestibule and Sassanian lounge of Copper House. He thought at first that he must have arrived at some new and less exclusive rival of the R.A.C. Six lifts seemed to be in perpetual motion; with dazzling frequency their doors flew open to reveal now left, now right, now two or three at a time, like driven game, a series of girls in Caucasian uniform. 'Going up,' they cried in Punch-and-Judy accents and, before anyone could enter, snapped their doors and disappeared from view. A hundred or so men and women of all tanks and ages passed before William's eyes. The sole stationary objects were a chryselephantine effigy of Lord Copper in coronation robes, rising above the throng, on a polygonal malachite pedestal, and a concierge, also more than life size, who sat in a plate-glass enclosure, like a fish in an aquarium, and gazed at the agitated multitude with fishy, supercilious eyes. Under his immediate care were a dozen page boys in sky-blue uniforms, who between errands pinched one another furtively on a long bench. Medals of more battles than were ever fought by human arms or on earthly fields glittered on the porter's chest. William discovered a small vent in his tank and addressed him diffidently. 'Is his Lordship at home?'

'We have sixteen peers on the staff. Which was you referring to?'

'I wish to see Lord Copper.'

'Oh! Cyril, show this gentleman to a chair and give him a form.'

A minute blue figure led William to a desk and gave him a piece of paper. William filled it in. '*Mr Boot wishes to see Lord Copper. Subject: great crested grebes.*'

Cyril took the paper to the concierge, who read it, looked searchingly at William and mouthed, 'Fetch the gentleman.'

William was led forward.

'You wish to see Lord Copper?'

'Yes, please.'

'Oh! no you don't. Not about great crested grebes.'

'And badgers too,' said William. 'It is rather a long story.'

'I'll be bound it is. Tell you what, you go across the street and tell it to Lord Zinc at *The Daily Brute* office. That'll do just as well, now won't it?'

'I've got an appointment,' said William, and produced his telegram.

The concierge read it thoughtfully, held it up to the light, and said 'Ah!'; read it again and said: 'What you want to see is Mr Salter. Cyril, give the gentleman another form.'

Five minutes later William found himself in the office of the foreign editor.

It was an encounter of great embarrassment for both of them. For William it was the hour of retribution; he advanced, heavy with guilt, to meet whatever doom had been decreed for him. Mr Salter had the more active part. He was under orders to be cordial and spring Lord Copper's proposal on the poor hick when he had won his confidence by light conversation and heavy hospitality.

His knowledge of rural life was meagre. He had been born in West Kensington and educated at a large London day-school. When not engaged in one or other capacity in the vast Megalopolitan organization he led a life of blameless domesticity in Welwyn Garden City. His annual holiday was, more often than not, spent at home; once or twice when Mrs Salter complained of being run down, they had visited prosperous resorts on the East Coast. 'The country,' for him, meant what you saw in the train between Liverpool Street and Frinton. If a psychoanalyst, testing his associations, had suddenly said to Mr Salter the word 'farm,' the surprising response would have been 'Bang,' for he had once been blown up and buried while sheltering in a farm in Flanders. It was his single intimate association with the soil. It had left him with the obstinate though admittedly irrational belief that agriculture was something alien and highly dangerous. Normal life, as he saw it, consisted in regular journeys by electric train, monthly cheques, communal amusements and a cosy horizon of slates and chimneys; there was something unEnglish and not quite right about 'the country', with its solitude and self-sufficiency, its bloody recreations, its darkness and silence and sudden, inexplicable noises; the kind of place where you never knew from one minute to the next that you might not be tossed by a bull or pitch-forked by a yokel or rolled over and broken up by a pack of hounds.

He had been round the office canvassing opinions about the subjects of conversation proper to countrymen. 'Mangel-wurzels are a safe topic,' he had been told, 'only you mustn't call them that. It's a subject on which farmers are very touchy. Call them roots . . .'

He greeted William with cordiality. 'Ah, Boot, how are you? Don't think I've had the pleasure before. Know your work well of course. Sit down. Have a cigarette or'–had he made a floater?–'or do you prefer your churchwarden?'

William took a cigarette. He and Mr Salter sat opposite one another. Between them, on the desk, lay an open atlas in which Mr Salter had been vainly trying to find Reykjavik.

There was a pause, during which Mr Salter planned a frank and disarming opening. 'How are your roots, Boot?' It came out wrong.

'How are your boots, root?' he asked.

William, glumly awaiting some fulminating rebuke, started and said, 'I beg your pardon?'

'I mean brute,' said Mr Salter.

William gave it up. Mr Salter gave it up. They sat staring at one another, fascinated, hopeless. Then:

'How's hunting?' asked Mr Salter, trying a new line. 'Foxes pretty plentiful?'

'Well, we stop in the summer, you know.'

'Do you? Everyone away, I suppose?'

Another pause: 'Lot of foot and mouth, I expect,' said Mr Salter hopefully.

'None, I'm thankful to say.'

'Oh!'

Their eyes fell. They both looked at the atlas before them.

'You don't happen to know where Reykjavik is?'

'No.'

'Pity. I hoped you might. No one in the office does.'

'Was that what you wanted to see me about?'

'Oh, no, not at all! Quite the contrary.'

Another pause.

William saw what was up. This decent little man had been duped to sack him and could not get it out. He came to the rescue. 'I expect you want to talk about the great crested grebe.'

'Good God, no,' said Mr Salter, with instinctive horror, adding politely, 'At least not unless *you* do.'

'No, not at all,' said William, 'I thought *you* might want to.'

'Not at all,' said Mr Salter.

'That's all right, then.'

'Yes, that all right . . .' Desperately: 'I say, how about some zider?'

'Zider?'

'Yes. I expect you feel like a drop of zider about this time, don't you? We'll go out and have some.'

The journalists in the film had been addicted to straight rye. Silent but wondering, William followed the foreign editor. They shared the lift with a very extraordinary man, bald, young, fleshless as a mummy, dressed in brown and white checks, smoking a cheroot. 'He does the Sports Page now,' said Mr Salter apologetically, when he was out of hearing.

In the public house at the corner, where *The Beast* reporters congregated, the barmaid took their order with surprise. 'Cider? I'll see.' Then she produced two bottles of sweet and fizzy liquid. William and Mr Salter sipped suspiciously.

'Not quite what you're used to down on the farm, I'm afraid.'

'Well, to tell you the truth, I don't often drink it. We give it to the haymakers, of course, and I sometimes have some of theirs.' Then, fearing that this might sound snobbish, he added, 'My Uncle Bernard drinks it for his rheumatism.'

'You're sure you wouldn't sooner have something else?'

'No.'

'You mean you wouldn't?'

'I mean I would.'

'Really?'

'Really; much sooner.'

'Good for you, Garge,' said Mr Salter, and from that moment a new, more human note was apparent in their relationship; conversation was still far from easy, but they had this bond in common, that neither of them liked cider.

Mr Salter clung to it strenuously. 'Interesting you don't like cider,' he said. 'Neither do I.'

'No,' said William. 'I never have since I was sick as a small boy, in the hay field.'

'It upsets me inside.'

'Exactly.'

'Now whisky never did anyone any harm.'

'No.'

Interest seemed to flag. Mr Salter tried once more. 'Make much parsnip wine down your way?'

'Not much . . .' It was clearly his turn now. He sipped and thought and finally said: 'Pretty busy at the office, I expect?'

'Yes, very.'

'Tell me–I've often wondered–do you keep a machine of your own or send out to the printers?'

'We have machines of our own.'

'Do you? They must work jolly fast.'

'Yes.'

'I mean, you have to get it written and printed and corrected and everything all on the same day, otherwise the news would become stale. People would have heard it on the wireless, I mean.'

'Yes.'

'D'you do much of the printing yourself?'

'No. You see, I'm the foreign editor.'

'I suppose that's why you wanted to find Reykjavik?'

'Yes.'

'Jolly difficult knowing where all these places are.'

'Yes.'

'So many of them I mean.'

'Yes.'

'Never been abroad myself.'

This seemed too good an opening to be missed. 'Would you like to go to Ishmaelia?'

'No.'

'Not at all?'

'Not at all. For one thing I couldn't afford the fare.'

'Oh, we would pay the fare,' said Mr Salter, laughing indulgently.

So that was it. Transportation. The sense of persecution which had haunted William for the last three hours took palpable and grotesque shape before him. It was too much. Conscious of a just cause and a free soul he rose and defied the nightmare. 'Really,' he said, in ringing tones, 'I call that a bit thick. I admit I slipped up on the great crested grebe, slipped up badly. As it happened, it was not my fault. I came here prepared to explain, apologize and, if need be, make reparation. You refused to listen to me. "Good God, no", you said, when I offered to explain. And now you calmly propose to ship me out of the country because of a trifling and, in my opinion, justifiable error. Who does Lord Copper think he is? The mind boggles at the vanity of the man. If he chooses to forget my eighteen months' devoted and unremitting labour in his service, he is, I admit, entitled to dismiss me . . .'

'Boot, Boot, old man,' cried Mr Salter, 'you've got this all wrong. With the possible exception of the Prime Minister, you have no more ardent admirer than Lord Copper. He wants you to *work* for him in Ishmaelia.'

'Would he pay my fare back?'

'Yes, of course.'

'Oh, that's rather different . . . Even so it seems a silly sort of scheme. I mean, how will it look in *Lush Places* when I start writing about sandstorms and lions and whatever they have in Ishmaelia? Not *lush*, I mean.'

'Let me tell you about it at dinner.'

They took a taxicab down Fleet Street and the Strand to the grill room where *The Beast* staff always entertained when they were doing so at the paper's expense.

'Do you *really* want tinned salmon?'

'No.'

'Sure?'

'Quite sure.'

Mr Salter regarded his guest with renewed approval and handed him the menu.

The esteem William had won by his distaste for cider and tinned salmon survived the ordering of dinner. William did not, as had seemed only too likely, demand pickled walnuts and Cornish pasties; nor did he, like the Budapest correspondent whom Mr Salter had last entertained in his room, draw attention to himself by calling for exotic Magyar dishes, and, on finding no one qualified to make them, insist on preparing for himself, with chafing dish and spirit lamp, before a congregation of puzzled waiters, a nauseous sauce of sweet peppers, honey, and almonds. He ordered a mixed grill, and, while he was eating, Mr Salter attempted, artfully, to kindle his enthusiasm for the new project.

'See that man there, that's Pappenhacker.'

William looked, and saw.

'Yes?'

'The cleverest man in Fleet Street.'

William looked again. Pappenhacker was young and swarthy, with great horn goggles and a receding stubbly chin. He was having an altercation with some waiters.

'Yes?'

'He's going to Ishmaelia for the *Daily Twopence*.'

'He seems to be in a very bad temper.'

'Not really. He's always like that to waiters. You see, he's a communist. Most of the staff of the *Twopence* are–they're University men, you see. Pappenhacker says that every time you are polite to a proletarian you are helping bolster up the capitalist system. He's very clever, of course, but he gets rather unpopular.'

'He looks as if he were going to hit them.'

'Yes, he does sometimes. Quite a lot of restaurants won't have him in. You see, you'll meet a lot of interesting people when you go to Ishmaelia.'

'Mightn't it be rather dangerous?'

Mr Salter smiled; to him, it was as though an Arctic explorer had expressed a fear that the weather might turn cold. 'Nothing to what you are used to in the country,' he said. 'You'll be surprised to find how far the war correspondents keep from the fighting. Why Hitchcock reported the whole Abyssinia campaign from Asmara and gave us some of the most colourful, eye-witness stuff we ever printed. In any case your life will be insured by the paper for five thousand pounds. No, no, Boot, I don't think you need worry about risk.'

'And you'd go on paying me my wages?'

'Certainly.'

'*And* my fare there *and* back, *and* my expenses?'

'Yes.'

William thought the matter over carefully. At length he said: 'No.'

'No?'

'No. It's very kind of you, but I think I would sooner not go. I don't like the idea at all.' He looked at his watch. 'I must be going to Paddington soon to catch my train.'

'Listen,' said Mr Salter. 'I don't think you have fully understood the situation. Lord Copper is particularly interested in your work and, to be frank, he insists on you going. We are willing to pay a very fair salary. Fifty pounds a month was the sum suggested.'

'*Fifty pounds a month!*' said William, goggling.

'A week,' said Mr Salter hastily.

'Gosh,' said William.

'And think what you can make on your expenses,' urged Mr Salter. 'At least another twenty. I happened to see Hitchcock's expense sheet when he was working for us in Shanghai. He charged three hundred pounds for camels alone.'

'But I don't think I shall know what to do with a camel.'

Mr Salter saw he was not making his point clear. 'Take a single example,' he said. 'Supposing you want to have dinner. Well, you go to a restaurant and do yourself proud, best of everything. Bill perhaps may be two pounds. Well, you put down five pounds for entertainment on your expenses. You've had a slap-up dinner, you're three pounds to the good, and everyone is satisfied.'

'But you see I don't like restaurants and no one pays for dinner at home, anyway. The servants just bring it in.'

'Or supposing you want to send flowers to your girl. You just go to a shop, send a great spray of orchids and put them down as "Information".'

'But I haven't got a girl and there are heaps of flowers at home.' He looked at his watch again. 'Well, I'm afraid I must be going. You see, I have a day-return ticket. I tell you what I'll do. I'll consult my family and let you know in a week or two.'

'Lord Copper wants you to leave tomorrow.'

'Oh, I couldn't do that, anyway, you know. I haven't packed or anything. And I daresay I should need some new clothes. Oh, no, that's out of the question.'

'We might offer a larger salary.'

'Oh, no, thank you. It isn't that. It's just that I don't want to go.'

'Is there *nothing* you want?'

'D'you know, I don't believe there is. Except to keep my job in *Lush Places* and go on living at home.'

It was a familiar cry: during his fifteen years of service with the

Megalopolitan Company Mr Salter had heard it upon the lips of countless distressed colleagues; upon his own. In a moment of compassion he remembered the morning when he had been called from his desk in *Clean Fun*, never to return to it. The post had been his delight and pride; one for which he believed he had a particular aptitude . . . First he would open the morning mail and sort the jokes sent him by the private contributors (one man sent him thirty or forty a week) into those that were familiar, those that were indecent, and those that deserved the half-crown postal order payable upon publication. Then he would spend an hour or two with the bound *Punches* noting whatever seemed topical. Then the ingenious game began of fitting these legends to the funny illustrations previously chosen for him by the Art Editor. Serene and delicate sunrise on a day of tempest! From this task of ordered discrimination he had been thrown into the ruthless, cut-throat, rough-and-tumble of *The Beast* Woman's Page. From there, crushed and bedraggled, he had been tossed into the editorial chair of the Imperial and Foreign News . . . His heart bled for William, but he was true to the austere traditions of his service. He made the reply that had silenced so many resentful novices in the past.

'Oh, but Lord Copper expects his staff to work wherever the best interests of the paper call them. I don't think he would employ anyone of whose loyalty he was doubtful, *in any capacity*.'

'You mean if I don't go to Ishmaelia I get the sack?'

'Yes,' said Mr Salter. 'In so many words that is exactly what I–what Lord Copper means . . . Won't you have a glass of port before we return to the office?'

3/i

An oddly-placed, square window rising shoulder high from the low wainscot, fringed outside with ivy, brushed by the boughs of a giant monkey-puzzle; a stretch of faded wallpaper on which hung a water-colour of the village churchyard painted in her more active days by Miss Scope, a small shelf of ill-assorted books and a stuffed ferret, whose death from rat-poisoning had overshadowed the whole of one Easter holiday from his private school–these, according as he woke on his right or left side, greeted William daily at Boot Magna.

On the morning after his interview with Mr Salter, he opened his eyes, relieved from a night haunted by Lord Copper in a hundred frightful forms, to find himself in black darkness; his first thought was that there were still some hours to go before daylight; then, as he remembered the season of the year and the vast, semi-conscious periods through which he had passed, in the intervals of being pursued down badger runs in the showy plumage of the great crested grebe, he accepted the more harrowing alternative that he had been struck blind; then that he was mad, for a bell was ringing insistently a few inches, it seemed, from his ear. He sat up in bed and found that he was bare to the waist; totally bare, he learned by further researches. He stretched out his arm and found a telephone; as he lifted it, the ringing stopped; a voice said, 'Mr Salter on the line.' Then he remembered the awful occurrence of the previous evening.

'Good morning,' said Mr Salter. 'I thought I'd better get you early. I expect you've been up and about for hours, eh? Used to milking and cubbing and so on?'

'No,' said William.

'No? Well, I don't get to the office much before eleven or twelve. I wondered if everything was clear about your journey or are there one or two little things you'd like to go into first?'

'Yes.'

'Ah, I thought there might be. Well, come round to the office as soon as you're ready.'

Groping, William found one of the dozen or so switches which controlled the lighting of various parts of the bedroom. He found his watch and learned that it was ten o'clock. He found a row of bell-pushes and rang for valet and waiter.

The evening before he had been too much surfeited with new impressions to pay particular attention to the room to which eventually he had been led. It was two o'clock when Mr Salter left him; they had returned to the Megalopolitan office after dinner; William had been led from room to room; he had been introduced to the Managing Editor, the Assistant Managing Editor, the Art Editor (who had provided the camera), the Accounts Manager, the Foreign Contacts Adviser, and a multitude of men and women with visible means of support but no fixed occupation who had popped in from time to time on the various officials with whom William was talking. He had signed a contract, an application for Life Insurance, receipts for a camera, typewriter, a portfolio full of tickets, and a book of traveller's cheques to the value of £1,000. He had reached the hotel in a daze; the management had been told to expect him; they had led him to a lift, then, aloft, along a white, unnaturally silent passage and left him in his room with no desire except to sleep and awake from his nightmare in the familiar, shabby surroundings of Boot Magna.

The room was large and faultless. A psychologist, hired from Cambridge, had planned the decorations–magenta and gamboge; colours which–it had been demonstrated by experiments on poultry and mice–conduce to a mood of dignified gaiety. Every day carpet, curtains, and upholstery were inspected for signs of disrepair. A gentle whining note filled the apartment emanating from a plant which was thought to 'condition' the atmosphere. William's crumpled clothes lay on the magenta carpet; his typewriter and camera had been hidden from him by the night porter. The dressing table was fitted with a 'daylight' lamp so that women, before retiring to sleep, could paint their faces in a manner that would be becoming at dawn; but it was bare of brushes.

Presently a valet entered, drew back four or five layers of curtain and revealed the window–a model of ingenuity, devised to keep out the noise of traffic and admit the therapeutic elements of common daylight. He picked up William's clothes, inclined gracefully towards the bed in a High Anglican compromise between nod and genuflexion and disappeared from the room, leaving it bereft of any link with William's previous existence. Presently a waiter came with a bill of fare and William ordered breakfast.

'And I want a toothbrush.'

The waiter communicated this need to the hall porter and presently a page with a face of ageless evil brought it on a tray. 'It was five shillings,' he said. 'And two bob for the cab fare.'

'That's too much.'

'Oh, come on,' said the knowing midget. 'It isn't you that pays.'

William indicated some loose change on the table. The boy took it all. 'You want some pyjamas too,' he said. 'Shall I get you some?'

'No.'

'Please yourself,' said this vile boy leaving the room.

William ate his breakfast and rang for the valet.

'I want my clothes, please.'

'Here are your shoes and cuff-links, sir. I have sent the shirt and underclothes to the laundry. The suit is being cleaned. Your tie is being ironed by one of the ironing maids.'

'But I never told you to do that.'

'You gave no instructions to the contrary, sir. We naturally send *everything* away *always* unless we are specifically asked not to . . . Would that be all, sir?'

'I want something to wear, now.'

'No doubt the hall porter will be able to arrange something.'

Some time later the same abominable child brought him a series of parcels.

'Reach-me-downs,' he said. 'Not what I'd care to wear myself. But it's the best I could get. Twenty quid. Shall I have it put down?'

'Yes.'

'Nice job journalism. May take to it myself one day.'

'I'm sure you'd be very good at it.'

'Yes, I think I should. I didn't get you a razor. The barber is six floors down.'

3/ii

The bells of St Bride's were striking twelve when William reached Copper House. He found Mr Salter in a state of agitation. 'Oh dear, oh dear, you're late, Boot, and Lord Copper himself has asked for you twice. I must go and see if he is still accessible.'

William was left standing in the passage. Metal doors snapped in and out: 'Going up,' 'Going down,' cried the Caucasian lift girls; on all sides his colleagues in the great concern came and went, bustling past him–haggard men who had been up all night, elegant young ladies bearing trays of milk, oily figures in overalls bearing bits of machinery. William stood in a daze, fingered the stiff seams of his new suit. After a time he heard himself addressed: 'Hi, you,' said a voice, 'wake up.'

'If only I could,' said William.

'Eh?'

'Nothing.'

The man speaking to him was exactly the type William recognized as belonging to the film he had seen in Taunton; a short, shock-headed fellow in shirt sleeves, dicky, and eyeshade, waistcoat pocket full of pencils, first finger pointing accusingly.

'You. You're the new man, aren't you?'

'Yes, I suppose I am.'

'Well, here's a chance for you.' He pushed a typewritten slip into William's hand. 'Cut along there quick. Take a taxi. Don't bother about your hat. You're in a newspaper office now.'

William read the slip. *'Mrs Stitch. Gentlemen's Lavatory, Sloane Street.'*

'We've just had this phoned through from the policeman on duty. Find out what she is doing down there. Quick!'

A lift door flew open at their side. 'Going down,' cried a Caucasian.

'In there.'

The door snapped shut; the lift shot down; soon William was in a taxi making for Sloane Street.

There was a dense crowd round the public lavatory. William bobbed hopelessly on the fringe; he could see nothing about the heads except more heads, hats giving way to helmets at the hub. More spectators closed in behind him; suddenly he felt a shove more purposeful than the rest and a voice said, 'Way, please. Press. Make way for the Press.' A man with a camera was forging a way through. 'Press, please, Press. Make way for the Press.'

William joined in behind him and followed those narrow, irresistible shoulders on their progress towards the steps. At last they found themselves at the railings, among the policemen. The camera man nodded pleasantly to them and proceeded underground. William followed.

'Hi,' said a sergeant, 'where are *you* going?'

'Press,' said William. 'I'm on *The Beast*.'

'So am I,' said the sergeant. 'Go to it. She's down there. Can't think how she did it, not without hurting herself.'

At the foot of the steps, making, for the photographer, a happy contrast to the white tiles about it, stood a little black motor-car. Inside, her hands patiently folded in her lap, sat the most beautiful woman William had ever seen. She was chatting in a composed and friendly manner to the circle of reporters and plain-clothes men.

'I can't think what you're all making such a fuss about,' she said. 'It's simply a case of mistaken identity. There's a man I've been wanting to speak to for weeks and I thought I saw him popping in here. So I drove down after him. Well, it was someone quite different, but he behaved beautifully about it, and now I can't get out; I've been here nearly half an hour and I've a *great* deal to do. I do think some of you might help, instead of standing there asking questions.'

Six of them seized the little car and lifted it, effortlessly, on their shoulders. A cheer rose from the multitude as the jet black rose above the spikes of the railings. William followed, his hand resting lightly on the running board. They set Mrs Stitch back on the road; the police began to clear a passage for her. 'A very nice little story,' said one of William's colleagues. 'Just get in nicely for the evening edition.'

The throng began to disperse; the policemen pocketed their tips; the camera men scampered for their dark rooms. 'Boot, Boot,' cried an eager, slightly peevish voice. 'So there you are. Come back at once.' It was Mr Salter. 'I came to fetch you for Lord Copper and they told me you had gone out. It was only by sheer luck that I found where you had gone. It's been a terrible mistake. Someone will pay for this; I know they will. Oh dear, oh dear, get into the cab quickly.'

3/iii

Twenty minutes later William and Mr Salter passed the first of the great doors which divided Lord Copper's personal quarters from the general office. The carpets were thicker here, the lights softer, the expressions of the inhabitants more careworn. The typewriters were of a special kind; their keys made no more sound than the drumming of a bishop's fingertips on an upholstered priedieu; the telephone buzzers were muffled and purred like warm cats. The personal private secretaries padded through the ante-chambers and led them nearer and nearer to the presence. At last they came to massive double doors, encased in New Zealand rose-wood which by their weight, polish, and depravity of design, proclaimed unmistakably, 'Nothing but Us stands between you and Lord Copper.' Mr Salter paused, and pressed a little bell of synthetic ivory. 'It lights a lamp on Lord Copper's own desk,' he said reverently. 'I expect we shall have a long time to wait.'

But almost immediately a green light overhead flashed their permission to enter.

Lord Copper was at his desk. He dismissed some satellites and rose as William came towards him.

'Come in, Mr Boot. This is a great pleasure. I have wanted to meet you for a long time. It is not often that the Prime Minister and I agree, but we see eye to eye about your style. A very nice little style indeed . . . You may sit down too, Salter. Is Mr Boot all set for his trip?'

'Up to a point, Lord Copper.'

'Excellent. There are two invaluable rules for a special correspondent–Travel Light and Be Prepared. Have nothing which in a case of emergency you cannot carry in your own hands. But remember that the unexpected always happens. Little things we take for granted at home like . . .' he looked about him, seeking a happy example; the room, though spacious, was almost devoid of furniture; his eye rested on a bust of Lady Copper; that would not do; then, resourcefully, he said '. . . like a coil of rope or a sheet of tin, may save your life in the wilds. I should take some cleft sticks with you. I remember Hitchcock–Sir Jocelyn Hitchcock, a man who used to work for me once; smart enough fellow in his way, but *limited*, very little historical backing–I remember him saying that in Africa he always sent his dispatches in a cleft stick. It struck me as a very useful tip. Take plenty.

'With regard to Policy, I expect you already have your own views. I never hamper my correspondents in any way. What the British public wants first, last, and all the time is News. Remember that the Patriots are in the right and are going to win. *The Beast* stands by them four-square. But they must win quickly. The British public has no interest in a war which drags on indecisively. A few sharp victories, some conspicuous acts of personal bravery on the Patriot side and a colourful entry into the capital. That is *The Beast* Policy for the war.

'Let me see. You will get there in about three weeks. I should spend a day or two looking around and getting the background. Then a good, full-length dispatch which we can feature with your name. That's everything, I think, Salter?'

'Definitely, Lord Copper.' He and William rose.

It was not to be expected that Lord Copper would leave his chair twice in the morning, but he leant across the desk and extended his hand. 'Good-bye, Mr Boot, and the best of luck. We shall expect the first victory about the middle of July.'

When they had passed the final ante-room and were once more in the humbler, frequented by-ways of the great building, Mr Salter uttered a little sigh. 'It's an odd thing,' he said, 'that the more I see of Lord Copper, the less I feel I really know him.'

The affability with which William had been treated was without precedent in Mr Salter's experience. Almost with diffidence he suggested, 'It's one o'clock; if you are going to catch the afternoon aeroplane, you ought to be getting your kit, don't you think?'

'Yes.'

'I don't suppose that after what Lord Copper has said there is anything more you want to know.'

'Well, there is one thing. You see, I don't read the papers very much. Can you tell me who is fighting who in Ishmaelia?'

'I think it's the Patriots and the Traitors.'

'Yes, but which is which?'

'Oh, I don't know *that*. *That's* Policy, you see. It's nothing to do with me. You should have asked Lord Copper.'

'I gather it's between the Reds and the Blacks.'

'Yes, but it's not quite as easy as that. You see, they are all Negroes. And the Fascists won't be called black because of their racial pride, so they are called White after the White Russians. And the Bolshevists *want* to be called black because of *their* racial pride. So when you *say* black you mean red, and when you *mean* red you say white and when the party who call themselves blacks say traitors they mean what *we* call blacks, but what *we* mean when *we* say traitors I really couldn't tell you. But from your point of view it will be quite simple. Lord Copper only wants Patriot victories and both sides call themselves patriots, and of course both sides will claim all the victories. But, of course, it's really a war between Russia and Germany and Italy and Japan who are all against one another on the patriotic side. I hope I make myself plain?'

'Up to a point,' said William, falling easily into the habit.

3/iv

The Foreign Contacts Adviser of *The Beast* telephoned the emporium where William was to get his kit and warned them of his arrival; accordingly it was General Cruttwell, F.R.G.S., himself who was waiting at the top of the lift shaft. An imposing man: Cruttwell Glacier in Spitsbergen, Cruttwell Falls in Venezuela, Mount Cruttwell in the Pamirs, Cruttwell's Leap in Cumberland marked his travels; Cruttwell's Folly, a waterless and indefensible camp near Salonika, was notorious to all who had served with him in the war. The shop paid him six hundred a year and commission, out of which, by contract, he had to find his annual subscription to the R.G.S. and the electric treatment which maintained the leathery tan of his complexion.

Before either had spoken, the General sized William up; in any other department he would have been recognized as a sucker; here, amid the trappings of high adventure, he was, more gallantly, a greenhorn.

'Your first visit to Ishmaelia, eh? Then perhaps I can be of some help to you. As no doubt you know, I was there in '97 with poor "Sprat" Larkin . . .'

'I want some cleft sticks, please,' said William firmly.

The General's manner changed abruptly. His leg had been pulled before, often. Only last week there had been an idiotic young fellow dressed up as a missionary . . . 'What the devil for?' he asked tartly.

'Oh, just for my dispatches, you know.'

It was with exactly such an expression of simplicity that the joker had asked for a tiffin gun, a set of chota pegs and a chota mallet. 'Miss Barton will see to you,' he said, and turning on his heel he began to inspect a newly-arrived consignment of rhinoceros hide whips in a menacing way.

Miss Barton was easier to deal with. 'We can have some cloven for you,' she said brightly. 'If you will make your selection I will send them down to our cleaver.'

William, hesitating between polo sticks and hockey sticks, chose six of each; they were removed to the workshop. Then Miss Barton led him through the departments of the enormous store. By the time she had finished with him, William had acquired a well-, perhaps rather over-, furnished tent, three months' rations, a collapsible canoe, a jointed flagstaff and Union Jack, a hand-pump and sterilizing plant, an astrolabe, six suits of tropical linen and a sou'wester, a camp operating table and set of surgical instruments, a portable humidor, guaranteed to preserve cigars in condition in the Red Sea, and a Christmas hamper complete with Santa Claus costume and a tripod mistletoe stand, and a cane for whacking snakes. Only anxiety about time brought an end to his marketing. At the last moment he added a coil of rope and a sheet of tin; then he left under the baleful stare of General Cruttwell.

3/V

It had been arranged for him that William should fly to Paris and there catch the Blue Train to Marseilles. He was just in time. His luggage, which followed the taxi in a small pantechnicon, made him a prominent figure at the office of the Air Line.

'It will cost you one hundred and three pounds supplement on your ticket,' they said, after it had all been weighed.

'Not *me*,' said William cheerfully, producing his travellers' cheques.

They telephoned to Croydon and ordered an additional aeroplane.

Mr Pappenhacker of the *Twopence* was a fellow passenger. He travelled as a man of no importance; a typewriter and single 'featherweight' suitcase constituted his entire luggage; only the unobtrusive *Messageries Maritimes* labels distinguished him from the surrounding male and female commercial travellers. He read a little Arabic Grammar, holding it close to his nose, oblivious to all about him. William was the centre of interest in the motor omnibus, and in his heart he felt a rising, wholly pleasurable excitement. His new possessions creaked and rattled on the roof, canoe against astrolabe, humidor against ant-proof clothes box; the cleft sticks lay in a bundle on the opposite seat; the gardens of South London sped past. William sat in a happy stupor. He had never wanted to go to Ishmaelia, or, for that matter, to any foreign country, to earn £50 a week or to own a jointed flagstaff or a camp operating table; but when he told Mr Salter that he wanted nothing except to live at home and keep his job, he had hidden the remote and secret ambition of fifteen years or more. He did, very deeply, long to go up in an aeroplane. It was a wish so far from the probabilities of life at Boot Magna that William never spoke of it; very rarely consciously considered it. No one at home knew of it except Nannie Bloggs. She had promised him a flight if she won the Irish Sweepstake, but after several successive failures she had decided that the whole thing was a popish trick and refused to take further tickets, and with her decision William's chances seemed to fade beyond the ultimate horizon. But it still haunted his dreams and returned to him, more vividly, in the minutes of transition between sleep and wakefulness, on occasions of physical exhaustion and inner content, hacking home in the twilight after a good day's hunt, fuddled with port on the not infrequent birthdays of the Boot household. And now its imminent fulfilment loomed through the haze that enveloped him as the single real and significant feature. High over the chimneys and the giant monkey-puzzle, high among the clouds and rainbows and clear blue spaces, whose alternations figures so largely and poetically in *Lush Places*; high above the most ecstatic skylark, above earth-bound badger and great crested grebe, away from people and cities to a region of light and void and silence–that was where William was going in the Air Line omnibus; he sat mute, rapt, oblivious of the cleft sticks and the portable typewriter.

At Croydon he was received with obeisance; a special official had been detailed to attend to him. 'Good day, Mr Boot . . . This way, Mr Boot . . . The men will see to your baggage, Mr Boot.' On the concrete court in front of the station stood his aeroplane, her three engines tuning up, one screw swinging slow, one spinning faster, one totally invisible, roaring all-out. 'Good afternoon, Mr Boot,' said a man in overalls.

'Good afternoon, Mr Boot,' said a man in a peaked cap.

Pappenhacker and the commercial travellers were being herded into the service plane. William watched his crates being embarked. Men like gym instructors moved at the double behind rubber-tyred trolleys. 'All in, Mr Boot,' they said, touching their caps. William distributed silver.

'Excuse me, Mr Boot,' a little man in a seedy soft hat stood at William's elbow, 'I haven't yet had the pleasure of stamping your passport.'

4/i

'Oh dear, oh dear,' said Mr Salter. 'D'you know, I believe it would be as well to keep Lord Copper in ignorance of this incident. The *Twopence* will be a day ahead of us–perhaps more. Lord Copper would not like that. It might cause trouble for the Foreign Contacts Adviser or–or someone.'

William's luggage was piled in the Byzantine Hall; even there, under the lofty, gilded vaults, it seemed enormous. He and Mr Salter regarded it sadly. 'I'll have all this sent on to your hotel. It must not be seen by the Personal Staff. Here is your application form for an emergency passport. The Art Department will take your photograph and we have an Archdeacon in the Religious Department who will witness it. Then I think you had better keep away from the office until you start. I'm afraid that you've missed the Messageries ship, but there's a P. and O. next day to Aden. You can get across from there. And, officially, remember, you left this afternoon.'

It was a warm evening, heavy with the reek of petrol. William returned sadly to his hotel and re-engaged his room. The last edition of the evening papers was on the streets. '*Society Beauty in Public Convenience*' they said. '*Mrs Stitch Again.*'

William walked to Hyde Park. A black man, on a little rostrum, was explaining to a small audience why the Ishmaelite patriots were right and the traitors were wrong. William turned away. He noticed with surprise a tiny black car bowling across the grass; it sped on, dexterously swerving between the lovers; he raised his hat but the driver was intent on her business. Mrs Stitch had just learned that a baboon, escaped from the Zoo, was up a tree in Kensington Gardens and she was out to catch it.

'Who built the Pyramids?' cried the Ishmaelite orator. 'A Negro. Who invented the circulation of the blood? A Negro. Ladies and gentlemen, I ask you as impartial members of the great British public, who discovered America?'

And William went sadly on his way to a solitary dinner and an early bed.

4/ii

At the passport office next morning they told William that he would want a visa for Ishmaelia. 'In fact you may want two. Someone's just opened a rival legation. We haven't recognized it officially, of course, but you may find it convenient to visit them. Which part are you going to?'

'The patriotic part.'

'Ah, then you'd better get two visas,' said the official.

William drove to the address they gave him. It was in Maida Vale. He rang the bell and presently a tousled woman opened the door.

'Is this the Ishmaelite Legation?' he asked.

'No, it's Doctor Cohen's and he's out.'

'Oh . . . I wanted an Ishmaelite visa.'

'Well, you'd better call again. I daresay Doctor Cohen will have one, only he doesn't come here not often except sometimes to sleep.'

The lower half of another woman appeared on the landing overhead. William could see her bedroom slippers and a length of flannel dressing-gown.

'What is it, Effie?'

'Man at the door.'

'Tell him whatever it is we don't want it.'

'He says will the Doctor give him something or other.'

'Not without an appointment.'

The legs disappeared and door slammed.

'That's Mrs Cohen,' said Effie. 'You see how it is; they're Yids.'

'Oh dear,' said William. 'I was told to come here by the passport office.'

'Sure it isn't the nigger downstairs you want?'

'Perhaps it is.'

'Well, why didn't you say so? He's downstairs.'

William then noticed, for the first time, that a little flag was flying from the area railings. It bore a red hammer and sickle on a black ground. He descended to the basement where, over a door between two dustbins, a notice proclaimed:

REPUBLIC OF ISHMAELIA
LEGATION AND CONSULATE-GENERAL

If away leave letters with tobacconist at No. 162b

William knocked and the door was opened by the Negro whom he had seen the evening before in Hyde Park. The features, to William's undiscriminating eye, were not much different from those of any other Negro, but the clothes were unforgettable.

'Can I see the Ishmaelite consul-general, please?'

'Are you from the Press?'

'Yes, I suppose in a way I am.'

'Come in. I'm him. As you see, we are a little under-staffed at the moment.'

The consul-general led him into what had once been the servants' hall. Photographs of Negroes in uniform and ceremonial European dress hung on the walls. Samples of tropical produce were disposed on the table and along the bookshelves. There was a map of Ishmaelia, an eight-piece office suite and a radio. William sat down. The consul-general turned off the music and began to talk.

'The patriotic cause in Ishmaelia,' he said, 'is the cause of the coloured man and of the proletariat throughout the world. The Ishmaelite worker is threatened by a corrupt and foreign coalition of capitalistic exploiters, priests and imperialists. As that great Negro Karl Marx has so nobly written . . .' He talked for about twenty minutes. The black-backed, pink palmed, fin-like hands beneath the violet cuffs flapped and slapped. 'Who built the Pyramids?' he asked. 'Who invented the circulation of the blood . . . Africa for the African worker; Europe for the African worker; Asia, Oceania, America, Arctic, and Antarctic for the African worker.'

At length he paused and wiped the line of froth from his lips.

'I came about a visa,' said William diffidently.

'Oh,' said the consul-general, turning on the radio once more. 'There's fifty pounds deposit and a form to fill in.'

William declared that he had not been imprisoned, that he was not suffering from any contagious or outrageous disease, that he was not seeking employment in Ishmaelia or the overthrow of its political institutions; paid his deposit and was rewarded with a rubber stamp on the first page of his new passport.

'I hope you have a pleasant trip,' said the consul-general. 'I'm told it's a very interesting country.'

'But aren't you an Ishmaelite?'

'*Me?* Certainly not. I'm a graduate of the Baptist College of Antigua. But the cause of the Ishmaelite worker is the cause of the Negro worker of the world.'

'Yes,' said William. 'Yes. I suppose it is. Thank you very much.'

'Who discovered America?' demanded the consul-general to his retreating back, in tones that rang high above the sound of the wireless concert. 'Who won the Great War?'

4/iii

The rival legation had more spacious quarters in an hotel in South Kensington. A gold swastika on a white ground hung proudly from the window. The door of the suite was opened by a Negro clad in a white silk shirt, buckskin breeches and hunting boots who clicked his spurs and gave William a Roman salute.

'I've come for a visa.'

The pseudo-consul led him to the office. 'I shall have to delay you for a few minutes. You see the Legation is only just open and we have not yet got our full equipment. We are expecting the rubber stamp any minute now. In the meantime let me explain the Ishmaelite situation to you. There are many misconceptions. For instance, the Jews of Geneva, subsidized by Russian gold, have spread the story that we are a black race. Such is the ignorance, credulity, and prejudice of the tainted European states that the absurd story has been repeated in the press. I must ask you to deny it. As you will see for yourself, we are pure Aryans. In fact we were the first white colonizers of Central Africa. What Stanley and Livingstone did in the last century, our Ishmaelite ancestors did in the Stone Age. In the course of the years the tropical sun has given to some of us a healthy, in some cases almost a swarthy tan. But all responsible anthropologists . . .'

William fingered his passport and became anxious about luncheon. It was already past one.

'. . . The present so-called government bent on the destruction of our great heritage . . .' There was an interruption. The pseudo-consul went to the door. 'From the stationer's,' said a cockney voice. 'Four and eight to pay.'

'Thank you, that is all.'

'Four and eight to pay or else I takes it away again.'

There was a pause. The pseudo-consul returned.

'There is a fee of five shillings for the visa,' he said.

William paid. The pseudo-consul returned with the rubber stamp, jingling four pennies in his breeches pocket.

'You will see the monuments of our glorious past in Ishmaelia,' he said, taking the passport. 'I envy you very much.'

'But are you not an Ishmaelite?'

'Of course; by descent. My parents migrated some generations ago. I was brought up in Sierra Leone.'

Then he opened the passport.

4/iv

The bells of St Bride's were striking four when, after a heavy luncheon, William returned to the Megalopolitan Building.

'Boot. Oh dear, oh dear,' said Mr Salter. 'You ought to be at the aerodrome. What on earth has happened?'

'He burned my passport.'

'Who did?'

'The patriot consul.'

'Why?'

'It had a traitor visa on it.'

'I see. How very unfortunate. Lord Copper would be *most* upset if he came to hear of it. I think we had better go and ask the Foreign Contacts Adviser what to do.'

On the following afternoon, provided with two passports, William left Croydon aerodrome in his special plane.

4/v

He did not leave alone.

The propellers were thundering; the pilot threw away his cigarette and adjusted his helmet; the steward wrapped a rug round William's feet and tenderly laid in his lap a wad of cotton wool, a flask of smelling salts and an empty paper bag; the steps were being wheeled from the door. At that moment three figures hurried from the shelter of the office. One was heavily enveloped in a sand-coloured ulster; a check cap was pulled low on his eyes and his collar was fastened high against the blast of the engines. He was a small man in a hurry, yet, bustling and buttoned up as he was, a man of unmistakable importance, radiating something of the dignity of a prize Pekingese. This impression was accentuated by the extreme deference with which he was treated by his companions, one a soldierly giant carrying an attaché case, the other wearing the uniform of high rank in the company.

This official now approached William, and, above the engine, asked his permission to include a passenger and his servant. The name was lost in the roar of the propellers. 'Mr ... I needn't tell you who *he* is ... only plane available . . . request from a very high quarter . . . infinitely obliged if . . . as far as Le Bourget.'

William gave his assent and the two men bowed silently and took their places. The official withdrew. The little man delicately plugged his ears and sank deeper into his collar. The door was shut; the ground staff fell back. The machine moved forward, gathered speed, hurtled and bumped across the rough turf, ceased to bump, floated clear of the earth, mounted and wheeled above the smoke and traffic and very soon hung, it seemed motionless, above the Channel, where the track of a steamer, far below them, lay in the bright water like a line of smoke on a still morning. William's heart rose with it and gloried, lark-like, in the high places.

4/vi

All too soon they returned to earth. The little man and his servant slipped unobtrusively through the throng and William was bayed on all sides by foreigners. The parcels and packing cases seemed to fill the shed, and the customs officers, properly curious, settled down to a thorough examination.

'Tous sont des effets personnels–tous usés,' William said gallantly, but one by one, with hammers and levers, the crates were opened and their exotic contents spread over the counter.

It was one of those rare occasions when the humdrum life of the *douanier* is exalted from the tedious traffic in vegetable silks and subversive literature to realms of adventure; such an occasion as might have inspired the jungle scenes of Rousseau. Not since an Egyptian lady had been caught cosseting an artificial baby stuffed with hashish had the customs officials of Le Bourget had such a beano.

'Comment dit-on humidor?' William cried in his distress. 'C'est une chose pour garder les cigares dans la Mer Rouge–et dedans ceci sont les affaires de l'hospitale pour couper les bras et les jambes, vous comprenez–et ça c'est pour tuer les serpents et ceci est un bateau qui collapse et ces branches de mistletoe sont pour Noël, pour baiser dessous, vous savez . . .'

'Monsieur, il ne faut pas se moquer des douanes.'

The cleft sticks alone passed without question, with sympathy.

'Ils sont pour porter les dépêches.'

'C'est un Sport?'

'Oui, oui, certainement–le Sport.'

There and at the Gare de Lyon he spent vast sums; all the porters of Paris seemed to have served him, all the officials to need his signature on their sheaves of documents. At last he achieved his train, and, as they left Paris, made his way uncertainly towards the restaurant car.

4/vii

Opposite him at the table to which he was directed sat a middle-aged man, at the moment engaged in a homily to the waiter in fluent and apparently telling argot. His head was totally bald on the top and of unusual conical shape; at the sides and back the hair was closely cut and dyed a strong, purplish shade of auburn. He was neatly, rather stiffly dressed for the time of year, and heavily jewelled; a cabochon emerald, massive and dull, adorned his tie; rubies flashed on his fingers and cuff-links as his hands rose and spread configuring the swell and climax of his argument; pearls and platinum stretched from pocket to pocket of his waistcoat. William wondered what his nationality could be and thought perhaps Turkish. Then he spoke, in a voice that was not exactly American or Levantine or Eurasian or Latin or Teuton, but a blend of them all.

'The moment they recognize an Englishman they think they can make a monkey of him,' he said in this voice. 'That one was Swiss; they're the worst; tried to make me buy mineral water. The water in the carafes is excellent. I have drunk quantities of it in my time without ever being seriously affected–and I have a particularly delicate stomach. May I give you some?'

William said he preferred wine.

'You are interested in clarets? I have a little vineyard in Bordeaux–on the opposite slope of the hill to Château Mouton-Rothschild where in my opinion the soil is rather less delicate than mine. I like to have something to give my friends. They are kind enough to find it drinkable. It has never been in the market, of course. It is a little hobby of mine.'

He took two pills, one round and white, the other elliptical and black, from a rococo snuff-box and laid them on the tablecloth beside his plate. He drew a coroneted crêpe de Chine handkerchief from his pocket, carefully wiped his glass, half-filled it with murky liquid from the water bottle, swallowed his medicine and then said:

'You are surprised at my addressing you?'

'Not at all,' said William politely.

'But it *is* surprising. I make a point of never addressing my fellow travellers. Indeed I usually prefer to dine in the coupé. But this is not our first meeting. You were kind enough to give me a place in your aeroplane this afternoon. It was a service I greatly appreciate.'

'Not at all,' said William. 'Not at all. Very glad to have been any help.'

'It was the act of an Englishman–a fellow Englishman,' said the little man simply. 'I hope that one day I shall have the opportunity of requiting it . . . I probably shall,' he added rather sadly. 'It is one of the pleasant if quite onerous duties of a man of my position to requite the services he receives–usually on a disproportionately extravagant scale.'

'Please,' said William, 'do not give the matter another thought.'

'I never do. I try to let these things slip from my mind as one of the evanescent delights of travel. But it has been my experience that sooner or later

I am reminded of them by my benefactor . . . You are on your way to the Côte d'Azur?'

'No, only as far as Marseille.'

'I rejoice in the Côte d'Azur. I try to get there every year, but too often I am disappointed. I have so much on my hands–naturally–and in winter I am much occupied with sport. I have a little pack of hounds in the Midlands.'

'Oh? Which?'

'You might not have heard of us. We march with the Fernie. I suppose it is the best hunting country in England. It is a little hobby of mine, but at times, when there is a frost, I long for my little house at Antibes. My friends are kind enough to say I have made it comfortable. I expect you will one day honour me with a visit there.'

'It sounds delightful.'

'They tell me the bathing is good but that does not interest me. I have some plantations of flowering trees which horticulturists are generous enough to regard with interest, and the largest octopus in captivity. The chef too is, in his simple seaside way, one of the best I have. Those simple pleasures suffice for me . . . You are surely not making a long stay in Marseille?'

'No, I sail tomorrow for East Africa. For Ishmaelia,' William added with some swagger.

The effect on his companion was gratifying. He blinked twice and asked with subdued courtesy:

'Forgive me; I think I must have misheard you. Where are you going?'

'To Ishmaelia. You know, the place where they say there is a war.'

There was a pause. Finally: 'Yes, the name is in some way familiar. I must have seen it in the newspapers.' And, taking a volume of pre-Hitler German poetry from the rack above him, he proceeded to read, shaping the words with his lips like a woman in prayer, and slowly turning the leaves.

Undeviating as the train itself, the dinner followed its changeless course from consommé to bombe. William's companion ate little and said nothing. With his coffee he swallowed two crimson cachets. Then he closed his book of love poems and nodded across the restaurant car.

The soldierly valet who had been dining at the next table rose to go.

'Cuthbert.'

'Sir?'

He stood attentively at his master's side.

'Did you give my sheets to the *conducteur*?'

'Yes, sir.'

'See that he has made them up properly. Then you may go to bed. You know the time in the morning?'

'Yes, sir; thank you, sir; good night, sir.'

'Good night, Cuthbert . . .' Then he turned to William and said with peculiar emphasis: 'A very courageous man that. He served with me in the war. He never left my side, so I recommended him for the V.C. He never leaves me now. And he is adequately armed.'

William returned to his carriage to lie awake, doze fitfully and at last to raise the blinds upon a landscape of vines and olives and dusty aromatic scrub.

4/viii

At Marseille he observed, but was too much occupied to speculate upon the fact, that his companion of the evening before had also left the train. He saw the dapper, slightly rotund figure slip past the barrier a few paces ahead of the valet, but immediately the stupendous responsibilities of his registered baggage pressed all other concerns from his mind.

5/i

The ships which William had missed had been modern and commodious and swift; not so the *Francmaçon* in which he was eventually obliged to sail. She had been built at an earlier epoch in the history of steam navigation and finished in the style of the day, for service among the high waves and icy winds of the North Atlantic. Late June in the Gulf of Suez was not her proper place or season. There was no space on her decks for long chairs; her cabins, devoid of fans, were aired only by tiny portholes, built to resist the buffeting of an angrier sea. The passengers sprawled listlessly on the crimson plush settees of the lounge. Carved mahogany panels shut them in; a heraldic ceiling hung threateningly overhead; light came to them, dimly, from behind the imitation windows of stained, armorial glass, and, blinding white, from the open door, whence too came the sounds of the winch, the smell of cargo and hot iron, the patter of bare feet and the hoarse, scolding voice of the second officer.

William sat in a hot, soft chair, a map of Ishmaelia open upon his knees, his eyes shut, his head lolling forwards on his chest, fast asleep, dreaming about his private school, now, he noted without surprise, peopled by Negroes and governed by his grandmother. An appalling brass percussion crashed and sang an inch or two from his ear. A soft voice said, 'Lunce pliss.' The Javanese with the gong proceeded on his apocalyptic mission, leaving William hot and wet, without appetite, very sorry to be awake.

The French colonial administrator, who had been nursing his two children in the next arm-chair to William's, rose briskly. It was the first time that day they had met face to face, so they shook hands and commented on the heat. Every morning, William found, it was necessary to shake hands with all the passengers.

'And madame?'

'She suffers. You are still studying the map of Ishmaelia . . .' They turned together and descended the staircase towards the dining saloon; the functionary leading a tottering child by either hand. '. . . It is a country of no interest.'

'No.'

'It is not rich at all. If it were rich it would already belong to England.

Why do you wish to take it?'

'But I do not wish to.'

'There is no oil, there is no tin, no gold, no iron–positively none,' said the functionary, growing vexed at such unreasonable rapacity. 'What do you want with it?'

'I am going as a journalist.'

'Ah, well, to the journalist every country is rich.'

They were alone at their table. The functionary arranged his napkin about his open throat, tucked the lowest corner into his cummerbund and lifted a child on to either knee. It was always thus that he sat at meals, feeding them to repletion, to surfeit, alternately, from his own plate. He wiped his glass on the tablecloth, put ice into it, and filled it with the harsh, blue-red wine that was included free in the menu. The little girl took a deep draught. 'It is excellent for their stomachs,' he explained, refilling for his son.

There were three empty places at their table. The administrator's wife, the Captain's, and the Captain's wife's. The last two were on the bridge directing the discharge of cargo. The Captain led a life of somewhat blatant domesticity; half the boat deck was given up to his quarters, where a vast brass bedstead was visible through the portholes, and a variety of unseamanlike furniture. The Captain's wife had hedged off a little veranda for herself with pots of palm and strings of newly laundered underclothes. Here she passed the day stitching, ironing, flopping in and out of the deck-house in heelless slippers, armed with a feather brush, often emerging in a dense aura of Asiatic perfume to dine in the saloon; a tiny, hairless dog capered about her feet. But in port she was always at her husband's side, exchanging civilities with the company's agents and the quarantine inspectors, and arranging, in a small way, for the transfer of contraband.

'Even supposing there is oil in Ishmaelia,' said the administrator, resuming the conversation which had occupied him ever since, on the first night of the voyage, William had disclosed his destination, 'how are you going to get it out?'

'But I have no interest in commerce. I am going to report the war.'

'War is all commerce.'

William's command of French, just adequate, inaccurately, for the exchange of general information and the bare courtesies of daily intercourse, was not strong enough for sustained arguments, so now, as at every meal, he left the Frenchman victorious, saying '*Peut-être*,' with what he hoped was Gallic scepticism, and turning his attention to the dish beside him.

It was a great, white fish, cold and garnished; the children had rejected it with cries of distress; it lay on a charger of imitation silver; the two brown thumbs of the coloured steward lay just within the circle of mayonnaise; lozenges and roundels of coloured vegetable spread symmetrically about its glazed back. William looked sadly at this fish. 'It is very dangerous,' said the administrator. 'In the tropics one easily contracts disease of the skin . . .'

. . . Far away the trout were lying among the cool pebbles, nose upstream, meditative, hesitant, in the waters of his home; the barbed fly, unnaturally brilliant overhead; they were lying, blue-brown, scarred by the grill, with white-bead eyes, in chaste silver dishes. 'Fresh green of the river bank; faded terra-cotta of the dining-room wallpaper, colours of distant Canaan, of deserted Eden,' thought William–'are they still there? Shall I ever revisit those familiar places . . . ?'

. . . '*Il faut manger, il faut vivre*,' said the Frenchman, '*qu'est-ce qu'il y a comme viande?*'

And at that moment, suddenly, miasmically, in the fiery wilderness, there came an apparition.

A voice said in English, 'Anyone mind if I park myself here?' and a stranger stood at the table, as though conjured there by William's unexpressed wish; as though conjured, indeed, by a djinn who had imperfectly understood his instructions.

The new-comer was British but, at first sight, unprepossessing. His suit of striped flannel had always, as its tailor proudly remarked, fitted snugly at the waist. The sleeves had been modishly narrow. Now in the midday heat it had resolved into an alternation of wrinkles and damp adherent patches; steaming visibly. The double-breasted waistcoat was unbuttoned and revealed shirt and braces.

'Not dressed for this climate,' remarked the young man, superfluously. 'Left in a hurry.'

He sat down heavily in the chair next to William's and ran his napkin round the back of his collar. 'Phew. What does one drink on this boat?'

The Frenchman who had regarded him with resentment from the moment of his appearance, now leant forward and spoke, acidly.

The hot man smiled in an encouraging way and turned to William.

'What's old paterfamilias saying?'

William translated literally. 'He says that you have taken the chair of the Captain's lady.'

'Too bad. What's she like? Any good?'

'Bulky,' said William.

'There was a whopper upstairs with the captain. What I call the Continental Figure. Would that be her?'

'Yes.'

'Definitely no good, old boy. Not for Corker anyway.'

The Frenchman leaned towards William.

'This is the Captain's table. Your friend must not come here except by invitation.'

'I do not know him,' said William. 'It is his business.'

'The Captain should present him to us. This is a reserved place.'

'Hope I'm not butting in,' said the Englishman.

The steward offered him the fish; he examined its still unbroken ornaments and helped himself. 'If you ask me,' he said cheerfully, his mouth full, 'I'd say it was a spot off colour, but I never do care much for French cooking. Hi, you Alphonse, comprenez pint of bitter?'

The steward gaped at him, then at the fish, then at him again. 'No like?' he said at last.

'No like one little bit, but that's not the question under discussion. Me like a big tankard of Bass, Worthington, whatever you got. Look, comme ça'–he made the motions of drinking–'I say, what's the French for bitter?'

William tried to help.

The steward beamed and nodded.

'Whisky-soda?'

'All right, Alphonse, you win. Whisky-soda it shall be. Beaucoup whisky, beaucoup soda, tout-de-suite. The truth is,' he continued, turning to William, 'my French is a bit rusty. You're Boot of *The Beast*, aren't you? Thought I might run into you. I'm Corker of the U.N. Just got on board with an hour to spare. Think of it; I was in Fleet Street on Tuesday; got my marching orders at ten o'clock, caught the plane to Cairo, all night in a car and here I am, all present and, I hope, correct. God, I can't think how you fellows can eat this fish.'

'We can't,' said William.

'Found it a bit high?'

'Exactly.'

'That's what I thought,' said Corker, 'the moment I saw it. Here, Alphonse, mauvais poisson–parfume formidable–prenez–et portez vite le whisky, you black bum,'

The Frenchman continued to feed his children. It is difficult for a man nursing two children, aged five and two and clumsy eaters at that, to look supercilious, but the Frenchman tried and Corker noticed it.

'Does the little mother understand English?' he asked William.

'No,'

'That's lucky. Not a very matey bird?'

'No.'

'Fond of la belle France?'

'Well, I can't say I've ever been there–except to catch this ship.'

'Funny thing, neither have I. Never been out of England except once, when I went to Ostend to cover a chess congress. Ever play chess?'

'No.'

'Nor do I. God, that was a cold story.' The steward placed on the table a syphon and a bottle of whisky which carried the label '*Edouard VIII: Very old Genuine Scotch Whisky: André Bloc et Cie, Saigon*,' and the coloured picture of a Regency buck, gazing sceptically at the consumer through a quizzing glass.

'Alphonse,' said Corker. 'I'm surprised at you.'

'No like?'

'Bloody well no like.'

'Whisky-soda,' the man explained, patiently, almost tenderly, as though in the nursery. 'Nice.'

Corker filled his glass, tasted, grimaced, and then resumed the interrupted inquiry. 'Tell me honestly, had you ever heard of Ishmaelia before you were sent on this story?'

'Only very vaguely.'

'So had I. And the place I'd heard of was something quite different in the Suez Canal. You know, when I first started in journalism I used to think that foreign correspondents spoke every language under the sun and spent their lives studying international conditions. Brother, look at us! On Monday afternoon I was in East Sheen breaking the news to a widow of her husband's death leap with a champion girl cyclist–the wrong widow as it turned out; the husband came back from his business while I was there and cut up very nasty. Next day the Chief has me in and says, "Corker, you're off to Ishmaelia." "Out of town job?" I asked. "East Africa," he said, just like that, "pack your traps."

"What's the story?" I asked. "Well," he said, "a lot of niggers are having a war. I don't see anything in it myself, but the other agencies are sending feature men, so we've got to do something. We want spot news," he said, "and some colour stories. Go easy on the expenses." "What are they having a war about?" I asked. "That's for you to find out," he said, but I haven't found out yet. Have you?'

'No.'

'Well, I don't suppose it matters. Personally I can't see that foreign stories are ever news–not *real* news of the kind U.N. covers.'

'Forgive me,' said William. 'I'm afraid I know very little about journalism. What is U.N.?'

'No kidding?'

'No,' said William, 'no kidding.'

'Never heard of Universal News?'

'I'm afraid not.'

'Well, I won't say we're the biggest news agency in the country–some of the stuffier papers won't take us–but we certainly are the hottest.'

'And what, please,' asked William, 'is a news agency?'

Corker told him.

'You mean that everything that you write goes to *The Beast*?'

'Well, that's rather a sore point, brother. We've been having a row with you lately. Something about a libel action one of our boys let you in for. But you take the other agencies, of course, and I daresay you'll patch it up with us. They're featuring me as a special service.'

'Then why do they want to send me?'

'All the papers are sending specials.'

'And all the papers have reports from three or four agencies?'

'Yes.'

'But if we all send the same thing it seems a waste.'

'There would soon be a row if we did.'

'But isn't it very confusing if we all send different news?'

'It gives them a choice. They all have different policies, so of course, they have to give different news.'

They went up to the lounge and drank their coffee together.

The winches were silent; the hatches covered. The agents were making their ceremonious farewells to the Captain's wife. Corker sprawled back in his plush chair and lit a large cheroot.

'Given me by a native I bought some stuff off,' he explained. 'You're buying much stuff?'

'Stuff?'

'Oriental stuff–you know, curios.'

'No,' said William.

'I'm a collector–in a small way.' said Corker. 'That's one of the reasons why I was glad to be sent on this story. Ought to be able to pick up some pretty useful things out East. But it's going to be a tough assignment from all I hear. Cut-throat competition. That's where I envy you–working for a paper. You only have to worry about getting your story in time for the first edition. We have to race each other all day.'

'But the papers can't use your reports any earlier than ours.'

'No, but they use the one that comes in first.'

'But if it's exactly the same as the one that came in second and third and fourth and they are all in time for the same edition . . . ?'

Corker looked at him sadly. 'You know, you've got a lot to learn about journalism. Look at it this way. News is what a chap who doesn't care much about anything wants to read. And it's only news until he's read it. After that it's dead. We're paid to supply news. If someone else had sent a story before us, our story isn't news. Of course there's colour. Colour is just a lot of bull's-eyes about nothing. It's easy to write and easy to read, but it costs too much in cabling, so we have to go slow on that. See?'

'I think so.'

That afternoon Corker told William a great deal about the craft of journalism. The *Francmaçon* weighed anchor, swung about, and steamed into the ochre hills, through the straits and out into the open sea while Corker recounted the heroic legends of Fleet Street; he told of the classic scoops and hoaxes; of the confessions wrung from hysterical suspects; of the innuendo and intricate misrepresentations, the luscious, detailed inventions that composed contemporary history; of the positive, daring lies that got a chap a rise of screw; how Wenlock Jakes, highest paid journalist of the United States, scooped the world with an eye-witness story of the sinking of the *Lusitania* four hours before she was hit; how Hitchcock, the English Jakes, straddling over his desk in London, had chronicled day by day the horrors of the Messina earthquake; how Corker himself, not three months back, had had the rare good fortune to encounter a knight's widow trapped by the foot between lift and landing. 'It was through that story I got sent here,' said Corker. 'The boss promised me the first big chance that turned up. I little thought it would be this.'

Many of Corker's anecdotes dealt with the fabulous Wenlock Jakes. '. . . syndicated all over America. Gets a thousand dollars a week. When he turns up in a place you can bet your life that as long as he's there it'll be the news centre of the world.

'Why, once Jakes went out to cover a revolution in one of the Balkan capitals. He overslept in his carriage, woke up at the wrong station, didn't know any different, got out, went straight to an hotel, and cabled off a thousand-word story about barricades in the streets, flaming churches, machine-guns answering the rattle of his typewriter as he wrote, a dead child, like a broken doll, spreadeagled in the deserted roadway below his window–*you* know.

'Well, they were pretty surprised at his office, getting a story like that from the wrong country, but they trusted Jakes and splashed it in six national newspapers. That day every special in Europe got orders to rush to the new revolution. They arrived in shoals. Everything seemed quiet enough, but it was as much as their jobs were worth to say so, with Jakes filing a thousand words of blood and thunder a day. So they chimed in too. Government stocks dropped, financial panic, state of emergency declared, army mobilized, famine, mutiny and in less than a week there *was* an honest to God revolution under way, just as Jakes had said. There's the power of the press for you.

'They gave Jakes the Nobel Peace Prize for his harrowing descriptions of the carnage–but that was colour stuff.'

Towards the conclusion of this discourse–William took little part beyond an occasional expression of wonder–Corker began to wriggle his shoulders restlessly, to dive his hand into his bosom and scratch his chest, to roll up his sleeve and gaze fixedly at a forearm which was rapidly becoming mottled and inflamed.

It was the fish.

5/ii

For two days Corker's nettle-rash grew worse, then it began to subside.

William used often to see him at his open door; he sat bare to the waist, in his pyjama trousers, typing long, informative letters to his wife and dabbing himself with vinegar and water as prescribed by the ship's doctor; often his disfigured face would appear over the gallery of the dining saloon calling petulantly for Vichy water.

'He suffers,' remarked the functionary with great complacency.

Not until they were nearing Aden did the rash cool a little and allow of Corker coming down to dinner. When he did so William hastened to consult him about a radiogram which had arrived that morning and was causing him grave bewilderment. It read:

OPPOSITION SPLASHING FRONTWARD SPEEDILIEST STOP ADEN REPORTED PREPARED WAR-WISE FLASH FACTS BEAST.

'I can't understand it,' said William.

'No?'

'The only thing that makes any sense is Stop Aden.'

'Yes?' Corker's face, still brightly patterned, was, metaphorically, a blank.

'What d'you think I'd better do?'

'Just what they tell you, old boy.'

'Yes, I suppose I'd better.'

'Far better.'

But William was not happy about it. 'It doesn't make any sense, read it how you will. I wonder if the operator has made a muddle somewhere,' he said at last.

'I should ask him,' said Corker, scratching. 'And now if you don't mind I must get back to the vinegar bottle.'

There had been something distinctly unmatey about his manner, William thought. Perhaps it was the itch.

5/iii

Early next morning they arrived off Steamer Point. The stewards, in a frenzy of last-minute avarice, sought to atone for ten days' neglect with a multitude of unneeded services. The luggage was appearing on deck. The companion ladder was down, waiting the arrival of the official launch. William leant on the taffrail gazing at the bare heap of clinker half a mile distant. It did not seem an inviting place for a long visit. There seemed no frontward splashing to oppose. The sea was dead calm and the ship's refuse lay all round it–a bank-holiday litter of horrible scraps–motionless, undisturbed except for an Arab row-boat peddling elephants of synthetic ivory. At William's side Corker bargained raucously for the largest of these toys.

Presently the boy from the wireless room brought him a message. 'Something about you,' he said, and passed it on to William.

It said: CO-OPERATING BEAST AVOID DUPLICATION BOOT UNNATURAL.

'What does that mean?'

'It means our bosses have been getting together in London. You're taking our special service on this Ishmaelia story. So you and I can work together after all.'

'And what is unnatural?'

'That's our telegraphic name.' Corker completed his purchase, haggled over the exchange from francs to rupees, was handsomely cheated, and drew up his elephant on a string. Then he said casually, 'By the by, have you still got that cable you had last night?'

William showed it to him.

'Shall I tell you what this says? "Opposition splashing" means that the rival papers are giving a lot of space to this story. "Frontward speediliest"–go to the front as fast as you can–full stop–Aden is reported here to be prepared on a war-time footing–"Flash Facts"–send them the details of this preparation at once.'

'Good heavens!' said William. 'Thank you. What an extraordinary thing . . . It wouldn't have done at all if I'd stayed on at Aden, would it?'

'No, old boy, not at all.'

'But why didn't you tell me this last night?'

'Old boy, have some sense. last night we were competing. It was a great chance, leaving you behind. Then the *Beast* would have had to take U.N. Laugh? I should have bust my pants. However, they've fixed things up without that. Glad to have you with me on the trip, old boy. And while you're working with me, don't go showing service messages to anybody else, see?'

Happily nursing his bakelite elephant Corker sauntered back to his cabin.

Passport officers came on board and sat in judgement in the first-class smoking room. The passengers who were to disembark assembled to wait their turn. William and Corker passed without difficulty. They elbowed their way to the door, through the little knot of many-coloured, many-tongued people who had emerged from the depths of the ship. Among them was a plump, dapper figure redolent of hair-wash and shaving soap and expensive scent; there was a glint of jewellery in the shadows, a sparkle of reflected sunlight on the hairless, conical scalp; it was William's dining companion from the Blue Train. They greeted one another warmly.

'I never saw you on board,' said William.

'Nor I you. I wish I had known you were with us. I would have asked you to dine with me in my little suite. I always maintain a certain privacy on the sea. One so easily forms acquaintances which become tedious later.'

'This is a long way from Antibes. What's brought you here?'

'Warmth,' said the little man simply. 'The call of the sun.'

There was a pause and, apparently, some uncertainty at the official table behind them.

'How d'you suppose this bloke pronounces his name?' asked the first passport officer.

'Search me,' said the second.

'Where's the man with the Costa-Rican passport?' said the first passport officer, addressing the room loudly.

A Hindu who had no passport tried to claim it, was detected and held for further inquiry.

'Where's the Costa-Rican?' said the officer again.

'Forgive me,' said William's friend, 'I have a little business to transact with these gentlemen,' and, accompanied by his valet, he stepped towards the table.

'Who's the pansy?' asked Corker.

'Believe it or not,' William replied, 'I haven't the faintest idea.'

His business seemed to take a long time. He was not at the gangway when the passengers disembarked, but as they hugged slowly to shore in the crowded tender a speed-boat shot past them in a glitter of sunlit spray, bouncing on the face of the sea and swamping their bulwarks in its wash. In it sat Cuthbert the valet, and his enigmatic master.

5/iv

There were two nights to wait in Aden for the little ship which was to take them to Africa. William and Corker saw the stuffed mermaid and the wells of Solomon. Corker bought some Japanese shawls and a set of Benares trays; he had already acquired a number of cigarette boxes, an amber necklace, and a model of Tutankhamen's sarcophagus during his few hours in Cairo; his bedroom at the hotel was an emporium of Oriental Art. 'There's something about the East always gets me,' he said. 'The missus won't know the old home when I've finished with it.'

These were his recreations. In his serious hours he attempted to interview the Resident, and was rebuffed; tried the captain of a British sloop which was coaling for a cruise in the Persian Gulf; was again rebuffed; and finally spent two hours in conference with an Arab guide who for twenty rupees supplied material for a detailed cable about the defences of the settlement. 'No use our both covering it,' he said to William. 'Your story had better be British unpreparedness. If it suits them, they'll be able to work that up into something at the office. You know–"Aden the focal point of British security in the threatened area still sunk in bureaucratic lethargy"–that kind of thing.'

'Good heavens! how can I say that?'

'That's easy, old boy. Just cable ADEN UNWARWISE.'

On the third morning they sailed for the little Italian port from which the railway led into the mountains of independent Ishmaelia.

5/V

In London it was the night of the Duchess of Stayle's ball. John Boot went there because he was confident of finding Mrs Stitch. It was the kind of party she liked. For half an hour he hunted her among the columns and arches. On all sides stood dignified and vivacious groups of the older generation. Elderly princesses sat in little pools of deportment, while the younger generation loped between buffet and ballroom in subdued and selfconscious couples. Dancing was not an important part of the entertainment; the Duchess's daughters were all admirably married; at eleven o'clock the supper room was full of elderly, hearty eaters.

John Boot sought Mrs Stitch high and low; soon it would be too late, for she invariably went home at one; she was indeed just speaking of going when he finally ran her to earth in the Duke's dressing-room, sitting on a bed, eating *foie-gras* with an ivory shoe-horn. Three elderly admirers glared at him.

'John,' she said. 'how *very* peculiar to see you. I thought you were at the war.'

'Well, Julia, I'm afraid we must go,' said the three old boys.

'Wait for me downstairs,' said Mrs Stitch.

'You won't forget the Opera on Friday?' said one.

'I hope Josephine will like the jade horse,' said another.

'You *will* be at Alice's on Sunday?' said the third.

When they had gone, Mrs Stitch said: 'I must go too. Just tell me in three words what happened. The last thing I heard was from Lord Copper. He telephoned to say you had left.'

'Not a word from him. It's been very awkward.'

'The American girl?'

'Yes, exactly. We said good-bye a fortnight ago. She gave me a lucky pig to wear round my neck–it was made of bog-oak from Tipperary. We were both very genuinely affected. Since then I haven't dared go out or answer the telephone. I only came here because I knew she wouldn't be coming.'

'Poor John. I wonder what went wrong . . . I like the bit about the pig *very* much.'

PART II

STONES £20

1/i

Ishmaelia, that hitherto happy commonwealth, cannot conveniently be approached from any part of the world. It lies in the North-Easterly quarter of Africa, giving colour by its position and shape to the metaphor often used of it–'the Heart of the Dark Continent'. Desert, forest, and swamp, frequented by furious nomads, protect its approaches from those more favoured regions which the statesmen of Berlin and Geneva have put to school under European masters. An inhospitable race of squireens cultivate the highlands and pass their days in the perfect leisure which those peoples alone enjoy who are untroubled by the speculative or artistic itch.

Various courageous Europeans, in the seventies of the last century, came to Ishmaelia, or near it, furnished with suitable equipment of cuckoo clocks, phonographs, opera hats, draft-treaties and flags of the nations which they had been obliged to leave. They came as missionaries, ambassadors, tradesmen, prospectors, natural scientists. None returned. They were eaten, every one of them; some raw, others stewed and seasoned–according to local usage and the calendar (for the better sort of Ishmaelites have been Christian for many centuries and will not publicly eat human flesh, uncooked, in Lent, without special and costly dispensation from their bishop). Punitive expeditions suffered more harm than they inflicted, and in the nineties humane counsels prevailed. The European powers independently decided they they did not want that profitless piece of territory; that the one thing less desirable than seeing a neighbour established there was the trouble of taking it themselves. Accordingly, by general consent, it was ruled off the maps and its immunity guaranteed. As there was no form of government common to the peoples thus segregated, nor tie of language, history, habit, or belief, they were called a Republic. A committee of jurists, drawn from the Universities, composed a constitution, providing a bicameral legislature, proportional representation by means of the single transferable vote, an executive removable by the President on the recommendation of both houses, an independent judicature, religious liberty, secular education, *habeas corpus*, free trade, joint stock banking, chartered corporations, and numerous other agreeable features. A pious old darky named Mr Samuel Smiles Jackson from Alabama was put in as the first President; a choice whose wisdom seemed to be confirmed by history, for, forty years later, a Mr Rathbone Jackson held his grandfather's office in succession to his father Pankhurst, while the chief posts of the state were held by Messrs Garnett Jackson, Mander Jackson, Huxley Jackson, his uncle and brothers, and by Mrs Athol (*neé* Jackson) his aunt. So strong was the love which the Republic bore the family that General Elections were known as 'Jackson Ngomas' wherever and whenever they were held. These, by the constitution, should have been quinquennial, but since it was found in practice that difficulty of communication rendered it impossible for the constituencies to vote simultaneously, the custom had grown up for the receiving officer and the Jackson candidate to visit in turn such parts of the Republic as were open to travel, and entertain the neighbouring chiefs to a six days' banquet at their camp, after which the stupefied aborigines recorded their votes in the secret and solemn manner prescribed by the constitution.

It had been found expedient to merge the functions of national defence and inland revenue in an office then held in the capable hands of General Gollancz Jackson; his forces were in two main companies, the Ishmaelite Mule Taxgathering Force and the Rifle Excisemen with a small Artillery Death Duties Corps for use against the heirs of powerful noblemen; it was their job to raise the funds whose enlightened expenditure did so much to enhance President Jackson's prestige among the rare foreign visitors to his capital. Towards the end of each financial year the General's flying columns would lumber out into the surrounding country on the heels of the fugitive population and returned in time for budget day laden with the spoils of the less nimble; coffee and hides, silver coinage, slaves, livestock, and firearms would be assembled and assessed in the Government warehouses; salaries would be paid, and cover in kind deposited at the bank for the national overdraft, and donations made, in the presence of the diplomatic corps, to the Jackson Nonsectarian Co-educational Technical Schools and other humane institutions. On the foundation of the League of Nations, Ishmaelia became a member.

Under this liberal and progressive régime, the republic may be said, in some way, to have prospered. It is true that the capital city of Jacksonburg became unduly large, its alleys and cabins thronged with landless men of native and alien blood, while the country immediately surrounding it became depopulated, so that General Golancz Jackson was obliged to start earlier and march further in search of the taxes; but on the main street there were agencies for many leading American and European firms; there was, moreover, a railway to the Red Sea coast, bringing a steady stream of manufactured imports which relieved the Ishmaelites of the need to practise their few clumsy crafts, while the adverse trade balance was rectified by an elastic system of bankruptcy law. In the remote provinces, beyond the reach of General Gollancz, the Ishmaelites followed their traditional callings of bandit, slave, or gentleman of leisure, happily ignorant of their connexion with the town of which a few of them, perhaps, had vaguely and incredulously heard.

Occasional travelling politicians came to Jacksonburg, were entertained and conducted round the town, and returned with friendly reports. Big game hunters on safari from the neighbouring dominions sometimes strayed into the hinterland, and if they returned at all dined out for years to come on the experience. Until a few months before William Boot's departure no one in Europe knew of the deep currents that were flowing in Ishmaelite politics;

nor did many people know of them in Ishmaelia.

It began during Christmas week with a domestic row in the Jackson family. By Easter the city, so lately a model of internal amity, was threatened by civil war.

A Mr Smiles Soum was reputed to lead the Fascists. He was only one-quarter Jackson (being grandson in the female line of President Samuel Smiles Jackson), and three-quarters pure Ishmaelite. He was thus by right of cousinship admitted to the public pay-roll, but he ranked low in the family and had been given no more lucrative post than that of Assistant Director of Public Morals.

Quarrels among the ruling family were not unusual, particularly in the aftermath of weddings, funerals, and other occasions of corporate festivity, and were normally settled by a readjustment of public offices. It was common knowledge in the bazaars and drink-shops that Mr Smiles was not satisfied with his post at the Ministry of Public Morals, but it was a breach of precedent and, some thought, the portent of a new era in Ishmaelite politics, when he followed up his tiff by disappearing from Jacksonburg and issuing a manifesto, which, it was thought by those who knew him best, he could not conceivably have composed himself.

The White Shirt movement which he called into being had little in common with the best traditions of Ishmaelite politics. Briefly his thesis was that: the Jacksons were effete, tyrannical, and alien; the Ishmaelites were a white race who, led by Smiles, must purge themselves of the Negro taint; the Jacksons had kept Ishmaelia out of the Great War and thus deprived her of the fruits of victory; the Jacksons had committed Ishmaelia to the control of international Negro finance and secret subversive Negro Bolshevism, by joining the League of Nations; they were responsible for the various endemic and epidemic diseases that ravaged crops, livestock, and human beings; all Ishmaelites who were suffering the consequences of imprudence or ill-fortune in their financial or matrimonial affairs were the victims of international Jacksonism; Smiles was their Leader.

The Jacksons rose above it. Life in Ishmaelia went on as before and the Armenian merchant in Main Street who had laid in a big consignment of white cotton shirtings found himself with the stuff on his hands. In Moscow, Harlem, Bloomsbury, and Liberia, however, keener passions were aroused. In a hundred progressive weeklies and Left Study Circles the matter was taken up and the cause of the Jacksons restated in ideological form.

Smiles represented international finance, the subjugation of the worker, sacerdotalism; Ishmaelia was black, the Jacksons were black, collective security and democracy and the dictatorship of the proletariat were black. Most of this was unfamiliar stuff to the Jacksons, but tangible advantages followed. A subscription list was opened in London and received support in chapels and universities; wide publicity was given to the receipt in Ishmaelia of three unused penny stamps addressed to the President by 'A little worker's daughter in Bedford Square'.

In the chief cities of Europe a crop of 'patriot consulates' sprang up devoted to counter-propaganda.

Newspaper men flocked to Jacksonburg. It was the wet season when business was usually at a standstill; everything boomed this year. At the end of August the rains would stop. Then, everybody outside Ishmaelia agreed, there would be a war. But, with the happy disposition of their race, the Ishmaelites settled down to exploit and enjoy their temporary good fortune.

I/ii

The Hotel Liberty, Jacksonburg, was folded in the peace of Saturday afternoon, so to be broken by the arrival of the weekly train from the coast but, at the moment, at four o'clock, serene and all-embracing. The wireless station was shut and the fifteen journalists were at rest. Mrs Earl Russell Jackson padded in stockinged feet across the bare boards of the lounge looking for a sizeable cigar-end, found one, screwed it into her pipe, and settled down in the office rocking-chair to read her Bible. Outside–and, in one or two places, inside–the rain fell in torrents. It rang on the iron roof in a continuous, restful monotone; it swirled and gurgled in the channels it had cut in the terrace outside; it seeped under the front door in an opaque pool. Mrs Earl Russell Jackson puffed at her pipe, licked her thumb, and turned a page of the good book. It was very pleasant when all those noisy white men were shut away in their rooms; quite like old times; they brought in good money, these journalists–heavens, what she was charging them!–but they were a great deal of trouble; brought in a nasty kind of customer too–Hindus, Ishmaelites from up country, poor whites and near-whites from the town, police officers, the off-scourings of the commercial cafés and domino saloons, interpreters and informers and guides, not the kind of person Mrs Earl Russell Jackson liked to see about her hotel. What with washing and drinking and telephoning and driving about in the mud in taxi-cabs and developing films and cross-questioning her old and respectable patrons, there never seemed a moment's peace.

Even now they were not all idle; in their austere trade they had forfeited the arts of leisure.

Upstairs in his room, Mr Wenlock Jakes was spending the afternoon at work on his forthcoming book *Under the Ermine*. It was to be a survey of the undercurrents of English political and social life. '*I shall never forget*,' he typed, '*the evening of King Edward's abdication. I was dining at the Savoy Grill as the guest of Silas Shock of the* New York Guardian. *His guests were well chosen, six of the most influential men and woman in England; men and women such as only exists in England, who are seldom in the news but who control the strings of the national purse. On my left was Mrs Tiffin, the wife of the famous publisher; on the other side was Prudence Blank, who has been described to me as "the Mary Selena Wilmark of Britain"; opposite was John Titmuss whose desk at the* News Chronicle *holds more secrets of state than any ambassador's . . . big business was represented by John Nought, agent of the Credential Assurance Co. . . . I at once raised the question of the hour. Not one of that brilliant company expressed any opinion. There, in a nutshell, you have* England, *her greatness–and her littleness.*'

Jakes was to be paid an advance of 20,000 dollars for this book.

In the next room were four furious Frenchmen. They were dressed as though for the cinema camera in breeches, open shirts, and brand new chocolate-coloured riding boots cross-laced from top to bottom; each carried a bandolier of cartridges round his waist and a revolver-holster on his hip. Three were seated, the fourth strode before them, jingling his spurs as he turned and stamped on the bare boards. They were composing a memorandum of their wrongs.

We the undersigned members of the French Press in Ishmaelia, they had written, *protest categorically and in the most emphatic manner against the partiality shown against us by the Ishmaelite Press Bureau and at the discourteous lack of co-operation of our so-called colleagues . . .*

In the next room, round a little table, sat Shumble, Whelper, Pigge, and a gigantic, bemused Swede. Shumble and Whelper and Pigge were special correspondents; the Swede was resident correspondent to a syndicate of Scandinavian papers–and more; he was Swedish Vice-Consul, head surgeon at the Swedish Mission Hospital, and proprietor of the combined Tea, Bible, and Chemist shop which was the centre of European life in Jacksonburg; a pre-crisis resident of high standing. All the journalists tried to make friends with him; all succeeded; but they found him disappointing as a news source.

These four were playing cards.

'I will go four no hearts,' said Erik Olafsen.

'You can't do that.'

'Why cannot I do that? I have no hearts.'

'But we explained just now . . .'

'Will you please be so kind and explain another time?'

They explained; the cards were thrown in and the patient Swede collected them in his enormous hand. Shumble began to deal.

'Where's Hitchcock today?' he asked.

'He's on to something. I tried his door. It was locked.'

'His shutters have been up all day.'

'I looked through the keyhole,' said Shumble. 'You bet he's on to something.'

'D'you think he's found the Fascist headquarters?'

'Wouldn't put it past him. Whenever that man disappears you can be sure that a big story is going to break.'

'If you please, what is Hitchcock?' asked the Swede.

Mr Pappenhacker of *The Twopence* was playing with a toy train–a relic of College at Winchester, with which he invariably travelled. In his youth he had delighted to address it in Latin alcaics and to derive Greek names for each part of the mechanism. Now it acted as a sedative to his restless mind.

The Twopence did not encourage habits of expensive cabling. That day he had composed a long 'turnover' on Ishmaelite conditions and posted it in the confidence that, long before it arrived at London, conditions would be unrecognizable.

Six other journalists of six nationalities were spending their day of leisure in this hotel. Time lay heavily on them. The mail train was due some time that evening to relieve their tedium.

Fifty yards distant in the annexe, secluded from the main block of the hotel by a water-logged garden, lay Sir Jocelyn Hitchcock, fast asleep. The room was in half-darkness; door and windows were barred. On the table, before his typewriter, stood a primus stove. There was a small heap of tins and bottles in the corner. On the walls hung the official, wildly deceptive map of Ishmaelia; a little flag in the centre of Jacksonburg marked Hitchcock's present position. He slept gently; his lips under the fine, white moustache curved in a barely perceptible smile of satisfaction. For reasons of his own he was in retirement.

I / iii

And the granite sky wept.

In the rainy season it was impossible to say, within twelve hours or so, the time of the train's arrival. Today it had made a good journey. It was still light when the telephone rang in Mrs Jackson's office to tell her that it had left the last station and would soon be there. Instantly the Hotel Liberty came to life. The hall-boy donned his peaked cap and set out with Mrs Jackson to look for clients. Shumble, Whelper, and Pigge left their game and put on their mackintoshes; the Frenchmen struggled into Spahi capes. The six other journalists emerged from their rooms and began shouting for taxis. Paleologue, Jake's jackal, reported for duty and was dispatched to observe arrivals. The greater and more forbidding part of the population of Jacksonburg was assembled on the platform to greet William's arrival.

He and Corker had had a journey of constant annoyance. For three days they had been crawling up from the fierce heat of the coast into the bleak and sodden highlands. There were four first-class compartments on their train; one was reserved for a Swiss ticket collector. In the remaining three, in painful proximity, sat twenty-four Europeans, ten of whom were the advance party of the Excelsior Movie-Sound News of America. The others were journalists. They had lunched, dined, and slept at the rest houses on the line. During the first day, when they were crossing the fiery coastal plain, there had been no ice; on the second night, in the bush, no mosquito nets; on the third night, in the mountains, no blankets. Only the little Swiss official enjoyed tolerable comfort. At every halt fellow employees brought him refreshment–frosted beer, steaming coffee, baskets of fruit; at the restaurants there were special dishes for him and rocking-chairs in which to digest them; there were bedrooms with fine brass bedsteads and warm hip-baths. When Corker and his friends discovered that he was only the ticket collector they felt very badly about this.

Some time during the second day's journey the luggage van became detached from the rest of the train. Its loss was discovered that evening when the passengers wanted their mosquito nets.

'Here's where that little beaver can be useful,' said Corker.

He and William went to ask his help. He sat in his rocking-chair smoking a thin, mild cheroot, his hands folded over his firm little dome of stomach. They stood and told him of their troubles. He thanked them and said it was quite all right.

'Such things often happen. I always travel with all my possessions in the compartment with me.'

'I shall write to the Director of the Line about it,' said Corker.

'Yes, that is the best thing to do. It is always possible that the van will be traced.'

'I've got some very valuable curios in my luggage.'

'Unfortunate. I am afraid it is less likely to be recovered.'

'D'you know who we are?'

'Yes,' said the Swiss, with a little shudder. 'Yes, I know.'

By the end of the journey Corker had come to hate this man. And his nettle-rash was on him again. He reached Jacksonburg in a bad humour.

Shumble, Whelper, and Pigge knew Corker; they had loitered together of old on many a doorstep and forced an entry into many a stricken home. 'Thought you'd be on this train,' said Shumble. 'Your name's posted for collect facilities in the radio station. What sort of trip?'

'Lousy. How are things here?'

'Lousy. Who's with you?'

Corker told him, adding: 'Who's here already?'

Shumble told him.

'All the old bunch.'

'Yes, and there's a highbrow yid from *The Twopence*–but we don't count him.'

'No, no competition there.'

'*The Twopence* isn't what you would call a *newspaper*, is it? . . . Still, there's enough to make things busy and there's more coming. They seem to have gone crazy about this story at home. Jakes is urgenting eight hundred words a day.'

'*Jakes here?* Well, there must be something in it.'

'Who's the important little chap with the beard?'–they looked towards the customs shed through which the Swiss was being obsequiously conducted.

'You'd think he was an ambassador,' said Corker bitterly.

The black porter of the Hotel Liberty interrupted them. Corker began to describe in detail his lost elephant. Shumble disappeared in the crowd.

'Too bad, too bad,' said the porter. 'Very bad men on railway.'

'But it was registered through.'

'Maybe he'll turn up.'

'Do things often get lost on your damned awful line?'

'Most always.'

All round them the journalists were complaining about their losses. '. . . Five miles of film,' said the leader of the Excelsior Movie-Sound News. 'How am I going to get *that* through the expenses department?'

'Very bad men on railway. They like film plenty–him make good fire.'

William alone was reconciled to the disaster; his cleft sticks were behind him; it was as though, on a warm day, he had suddenly shed an enormous, fur-lined motoring-coat.

I/iv

So far as their profession allowed them time for such soft feelings, Corker and Pigge were friends.

'. . . It was large and very artistic,' said Corker, describing his elephant, 'just the kind of thing Madge likes.'

Pigge listened sympathetically. The bustle was over. William and Corker had secured a room together at the Liberty; their sparse hand-luggage was unpacked and Pigge had dropped in for a drink.

'What's the situation?' asked William, when Corker had exhausted his information–though not his resentment–about the shawls and cigarette boxes.

'Lousy,' said Pigge.

'I've been told to go to the front.'

'That's what we all want to do. But in the first place there isn't any front, and in the second place we couldn't get to it if there was. You can't move outside the town without a permit, and you can't get a permit.'

'Then what are you sending?' asked Corker.

'Colour stuff,' said Pigge, with great disgust. 'Preparations in the threatened capital, soldiers of fortune, mystery men, foreign influences, volunteers . . . there isn't any hard news. The Fascist headquarters are up-country somewhere in the mountains. No one knows where. They're going to attack when the rain stops in about ten days. You can't get a word out of the government. They won't admit there *is* a crisis.'

'What, not with Jakes and Hitchcock here?' said Corker in wonder. 'What's this President like, anyway?'

'Lousy.'

'Where is Hitchcock, by the way?'

'That's what we all want to know.'

I/v

'Where's Hitchcock?' asked Jakes.

Paleologue shook his head sadly. He was finding Jakes a hard master. For over a week he had been on his pay-roll. It seemed a lifetime. But the pay was fabulous and Paleologue was a good family man; he had two wives to support and countless queer-coloured children on whom he lavished his love. Until the arrival of the newspaper men–that decisive epoch in Ishmaelite social history–he had been dragoman and interpreter at the British Legation, on wages which–though supplemented from time to time by the sale to his master's colleague of any waste-paper he could find lying around the Chancery–barely sufficed for the necessaries of his household; occasionally he had been able to provide amusement for bachelor attachés; occasionally he sold objects of native art to the ladies of the compound. But it had been an exiguous living. Now he was getting fifty American dollars a week. It was a wage beyond the bounds of his wildest ambition . . . but Mr Jakes was very exacting and very peremptory.

'Who was on the train?'

'No one except the newspaper gentlemen and M. Giraud.'

'Who's he?'

'He is in the Railway. He went down to the coast with his wife last week, to see her off to Europe.'

'Yes, yes, I remember. That was the "panic-stricken refugees" story. No one else?'

'No, Mr Jakes.'

'Well, go find Hitchcock.'

'Yes, sir.'

Jakes turned his attention to his treatise. *The dominant member of the new cabinet,* he typed, *was colourful Kingsley Wood* . . .

I/vi

Nobody knew exactly at what time or through what channels word went round the Hotel Liberty that Shumble had got a story. William heard it from Corker who heard it from Pigge. Pigge had guessed it from something odd in Shumble's manner during dinner–something abstracted, something of high excitement painfully restrained. He confided in Whelper, 'He's been distinctly rummy ever since he came back from the station. Have you noticed it?'

'Yes,' said Whelper. 'It sticks out a mile. If you ask me, he's got something under his hat.'

'Just what I thought,' said Pigge gloomily.

And before bedtime everyone in the hotel knew it.

The French were furious. They went in a body to their Legation. 'It is too much,' they said. 'Shumble is receiving secret information from the Government. Hitchcock, of course, is pro-British, and now, at a moment like this, when as Chairman of the Foreign Press Association he should forward our protest officially to the proper quarter, he has disappeared.'

'Gentlemen,' said the Minister. 'Gentlemen, it is Saturday night. No Ishmaelite official will be available until noon on Monday.'

'The Press Bureau is draconic, arbitrary, and venal; it is in the hands of a clique; we appeal for justice.'

'Certainly, without fail, on Monday afternoon.' . . .

'We'll stay awake in shifts,' said Whelper, 'and listen. He may talk in his sleep.'

'I suppose you've searched his papers?'

'Useless. He never takes a note.'. . .

Paleologue threw up his hands hopelessly.

'Have his boy bring you his message on the way to the wireless station.'

'Mr Shumble always take it himself.'

'Well, go find out what it is. I'm busy.'. . .

Shumble sat in the lounge radiating importance. Throughout the evening everyone in turn sat by his side, offered him whisky and casually reminded him of past acts of generosity. He held his own counsel. Even the Swede got wind of what was going and left home to visit the hotel.

'Schombol,' he said, 'I think you have some good news, no?'

'Me?' said Shumble. 'Wish I had.'

'But forgive me, please, everyone say you have some good news. Now I have to telegraph to my newspapers in Scandinavia. Will you please tell me what your news is?'

'I don't know anything, Erik.'

'What a pity. It is so long since I sent my paper any good news.'

And he mounted his motor cycle and drove sadly away into the rain.

I/vii

At a banquest given in his honour. Sir Jocelyn Hitchcock once modestly attributed his great success in life to the habit of 'getting up earlier than the other fellow'. But this was partly metaphorical, partly false, and in any case wholly relative, for journalists are as a rule late risers. It was seldom that in England, in those night-refuges they called their homes, Shumble, Whelper, Pigge, or Corker reached the bathroom before ten o'clock. Nor did they in Jacksonburg, for there was no bath in the Hotel Liberty; but they and their fellows had all been awake since dawn.

This was due to many causes–the racing heart, nausea, dry mouth and smarting eyes, the false hangover produced by the vacuous mountain air, to the same symptoms of genuine hangover, for, with different emotions, they had been drinking deeply the evening before in the anxiety over Shumble's scoop; but more especially to the structural defects of the building. The rain came on sharp at sunrise, and every bedroom had a leak somewhere in its iron ceiling. And with the rain and the drips came the rattle of Wenlock Jakes's typewriter as he hammered away at another chapter of *Under The Ermine*. Soon the bleak passages resounded with cries of 'Boy!' 'Water!' 'Coffee!'

As early arrivals Shumble, Whelper, and Pigge might, like the Frenchmen, have had separate rooms, but they preferred to live at close quarters and watch one another's movements. The cinema men had had little choice. There were two rooms left; the Contacts and Relations Pioneer Co-ordinating Director occupied one; the rest of the outfit had the other.

'Boy!' cried Corker, standing barefoot in a dry spot at the top of the stairs. 'Boy!'

'Boy!' cried Whelper.

'Boy!' cried the Frenchmen. 'It is formidable. The types attend to no one except the Americans and the English.'

'They have been bribed. I saw Shumble giving money to one of the boys yesterday.'

'We must protest.'

'I have protested.'

'We must protest again. We must demonstrate.'

'Boy! Boy! Boy!' shouted everyone in that hotel, but nobody came.

In the annexe, Sir Jocelyn Hitchcock slipped a raincoat over his pyjamas and crept like a cat into the bushes.

I/viii

Presently Paleologue arrived to make his morning report to his master. He met Corker at the top of the stairs. 'You got to have boy for yourself in this country,' he said.

'Yes,' said Corker. 'It seems I ought.'

'I fix him. I find you very good boy from Adventist Mission, read, write, speak English, sing hymns, everything.'

'Sounds like hell to me.'

'Please?'

'Oh, all right, it doesn't matter. Send him along.'

In this way Paleologue was able to supply servants for all the new-comers. Later the passages were clustered with moon-faced mission-taught Ishmaelites. These boys had many responsibilities. They had to report their masters' doings, morning and evening, to the secret police; they had to steal copies of their masters' cables for Wenlock Jakes. The normal wage for domestic service was a dollar a week; the journalists paid five, but Paleologue pocketed the difference. In the meantime they formulated new and ingenious requests for cash in advance–for new clothes, funerals, weddings, fines, and entirely imaginary municipal taxes: whatever they exacted, Paleologue came to know about it and levied his share.

I/ix

Inside the bedroom it was sunless, draughty, and damp; all round there was rattling and shouting and tramping and the monotonous splash and patter and gurgle of rain. Corker's clothing lay scattered about the room. Corker sat on his bed stirring condensed milk into his tea. 'Time you were showing a leg, old boy,' he said.

'Yes.'

'If you ask me, we were all a bit tight last night.'

'Yes.'

'Feeling lousy?'

'Yes.'

'It'll soon pass off when you get on your feet. Are my things in your way?'

'Yes.'

Corker lit his pipe and a frightful stench filled the room. 'Don't think much of this tobacco,' he said. 'Home grown. I bought it off a nigger on the way up. Care to try some?'

'No thanks,' said William, and rose queasily from his bed.

While they dressed Corker spoke in a vein of unaccustomed pessimism. 'This isn't the kind of story I'm used to,' he said. 'We aren't getting anywhere. We've got to work out a routine, make contacts, dig up some news sources, jolly up the locals a bit. I don't feel settled.'

'Is that my toothbrush you're using?'

'Hope not. Has it got a white handle?'

'Yes.'

'Then I am. Silly mistake to make; mine's green . . . but, as I was saying, we've got to make friends in this town. Funny thing, I don't get that sense of popularity I expect.' He looked at himself searchingly in the single glass. 'Suffer much from dandruff?'

'Not particularly.'

'I do. They say it comes from acidity. It's a nuisance. Gets all over one's collar, and one has to look smart in our job. Good appearance is half the battle.'

'D'you mind if I have my brushes?'

'Not a bit, old boy, just finished with them . . . Between ourselves that's always been Shumble's trouble–bad appearance. But, of course, a journalist is welcome everywhere, even Shumble. That's what's so peculiar about this town. As a rule, there is one thing you can always count on in our job–popularity. There are plenty of disadvantages, I grant you, but you *are* liked and respected. Ring people up any hour of the day or night, butt into their homes uninvited, make them answer a string of damn fool questions when they want to do something else–they like it. Always a smile and the best of everything for the gentlemen of the Press. But I don't feel it here. I damn well feel the exact opposite. I ask myself, are we known, loved and trusted? and the answer comes back, "No Corker, you are not."'

There was a knock on the door, barely audible above the general hubbub, and Pigge entered.

'Morning, chaps. Cable for Corker. It came last night. Sorry it's been opened. They gave it to me and I didn't notice the address.'

'Oh, no?' said Corker.

'Well, there's nothing in it. Shumble had that query yesterday.'

Corker read: INTERNATIONAL GENDARMERIE PROPOSED PREVENT CLASH TEST REACTIONS UNNATURAL. 'Crumbs, they must be short of news in London. What's Gendarmerie?'

'A sissy word for cops,' said Pigge.

'Well, it's a routine job. I suppose I must do something about it. Come round with me . . . We may make some contacts,' he added, not very hopefully.

Mrs Earl Russell Jackson was in the lounge. 'Good morning, madam,' said Corker, 'and how are you today?'

'I aches,' said Mrs Jackson with simple dignity. 'I aches terrible all round the sit-upon. It's the damp.'

'The Press are anxious for your opinion upon a certain question, Mrs Jackson.'

'Aw, go ask somebody else. They be coming to mend that roof as quick as they can, and they can't come no quicker than that not for the Press, nor nobody.'

'See what I mean, old boy–not popular.' Then, turning again to Mrs Jackson with his most elaborate manner he said, 'Mrs Jackson, you misunderstand me. This is a matter of public importance. What do the women of Ishmaelia think of the proposal to introduce a force of international police?'

Mrs Jackson took the question badly. 'I will not stand for being called a woman in my own house,' she said. 'And I've never had the police here but once, and that was when I called them myself for to take out a customer that went lunatic and hanged himself.' And she swept wrathfully away to her office and her rocking-chair.

'Staunchly anti-interventionist,' said Corker. 'Doyen of Jacksonburg hostesses bans police project as unwarrantable interference with sanctity of Ishmaelite home . . . but it's not the way I'm used to being treated.'

They went to the front door to call a taxi. Half a dozen were waiting in the courtyard; their drivers, completely enveloped in sodden blankets, dozed on the front seats. The hotel guard prodded one of them with the muzzle of his gun. The bundle stirred; a black face appeared, then a brilliant smile. The car lurched forward through the mud.

'The morning round,' said Corker. 'Where to first?'

'Why not the station to ask about the luggage?'

'Why not? *Station*,' he roared at the chauffeur. 'Understand–station? Puff-puff.'

'All right,' said the chauffeur, and drove off at break-neck speed through the rain.

'I don't believe this is the way,' said William.

They were bowling up the main street of Jacksonburg. A strip of tarmac ran down the middle; on either side were rough tracks for mules, men, cattle, and camels; beyond these the irregular outline of the commercial quarter; a bank, in shoddy concrete, a Greek provisions store in timber and tin, the Café de La Bourse, the Carnegie Library, the Ciné-Parlant, and numerous gutted sites, relics of an epidemic of arson some years back when an Insurance Company had imprudently set up shop in the city.

'I'm damn well sure it's not,' said Corker. 'Hi, you! *Station*, you black booby!'

The coon turned round in his seat and smiled. 'All right,' he said.

The car swerved off the motor road and bounced perilously among the caravans. The chauffeur turned back, shouted opprobriously at a camel driver and regained the tarmac.

Armenian liquor, Goanese tailoring, French stationery, Italian hardware, Swiss plumbing, Indian haberdashery, the statue of the first President Jackson, the statue of the second President Jackson, the American Welfare Centre, the latest and most successful innovation in Ishmaelite life–Popotakis's Ping-Pong Parlour–sped past in the rain. The mule trains plodded by, laden with rock salt and cartridges and paraffin for the villages of the interior.

'Kidnapped,' said Corker cheerfully. 'That's what's happened to us. What a story.'

But at last they came to a stop.

'This isn't the station, you baboon.'

'Yes, all right.'

They were at the Swedish Consulate, Surgery, Bible and Tea Shop. Erik Olafsen came out to greet them.

'Good morning. Please to come in.'

'We told this ape to drive us to the station.'

'Yes, it is a custom here. When they have a white man they do not understand, they always drive him to me. Then I can explain. But please to come in. We are just about to start our Sunday hymn singing.'

'Sorry, old boy. Have to wait till next Sunday. We've got work to do.'

'They say Schombol has some news.'

'Not really?'

'No, not really. I asked him . . . but you can do no work here on Sunday. Everything is closed.'

So they found. They visited a dozen barred doors and returned disconsolately to luncheon. One native whom they questioned fled precipitately at the word 'police'. That was all they could learn about local reactions.

'We've got to give it up for the day,' said Corker. 'Reactions are easy, anyway. I'll just say that the government will co-operate with the democracies of the world in any measures calculated to promote peace and justice, but are confident in their ability to maintain order without foreign intervention. This is going to be a day of rest for Corker.'

Shumble kept his story under his hat and furtively filed a long message–having waited for a moment when the wireless station was empty of his colleagues.

So the rain fell and the afternoon and evening were succeeded by another night and another morning.

I/X

William and Corker went to the Press Bureau. Dr Benito, the director, was away, but his clerk entered their names in his ledger and gave them cards of identity. They were small orange documents, originally printed for the registration of prostitutes. The space for thumb-print was now filled with a passport photograph, and at the head the word 'journalist' substituted in neat Ishmaelite characters.

'What sort of bloke is this Benito?' Corker asked.

'Creepy,' said Pigge.

They visited their Consulate, five miles out of town in the Legation compound. Here, too, they had to register and, in addition, buy a guinea stamp. The Vice-Consul was a young man with untidy ginger hair. When he took William's passport he stared and said, 'By God, you're Beastly.'

William said, 'Moke.'

These two had known each other at their private school. Corker was nonplussed.

'What the hell are you doing here?' said the Vice-Consul.

'I'm supposed to be a journalist.'

'God, how funny. Come to dinner?'

'Yes.'

'Tonight?'

'Yes.'

'Grand.'

Outside the door Corker said, 'He might have asked me too. Just the kind of contact I can do with.'

I/xi

At lunch-time that day Shumble's story broke.

Telegrams in Jacksonburg were delivered irregularly and rather capriciously, for none of the messengers could read. The usual method was to wait until half a dozen had accumulated and then send a messenger to hawk them about the most probable places until they were claimed. On precisely such an errand a bowed old warrior arrived in the dining-room of the Liberty and offered William and Corker a handful of envelopes. 'Righto, old boy,' said Corker, 'I'll take charge of these.' He handed the man a tip, was kissed on the knee in return, and proceeded to glance through the bag. 'One for you, one for me, one for everyone in the bunch.'

William opened his. It read: BADLY LEFT DISGUISED SOVIET AMBASSADOR RUSH FOLLOW BEAST. 'Will you please translate?'

'Bad news, old boy. Look at mine. ECHO SPLASHING SECRET ARRIVAL RED AGENT FLASH INTERVIEW UNNATURAL. Let's see some more.'

He opened six before he was caught. All dealt with the same topic. *The Twopence* said: KINDLY INVESTIGATE AUTHENTICITY ALLEGED SPECIAL SOVIET DELEGATION STOP CABLE DEFERRED RATE. Jakes's was the fullest: LONDON ECHO REPORTS RUSSIAN ENVOY ORGANISER ARRIVED SATURDAY DISGUISED RAILWAY OFFICIAL STOP MOSCOW DENIES STOP DENY OR CONFIRM WITH DETAILS. Shumble's said: WORLD SCOOP CONGRATULATIONS CONTINUE ECHO.

'D'you see now?' said Corker.

'I think so.'

'It's that nasty bit of work with the beard. I knew he was going to give us trouble.'

'But he *is* a railway employee. I saw him in the ticket office today when I went to ask about my luggage.'

'Of course he is. But what good does that do us? Shumble's put the story across. Now we've got to find a red agent or boil.'

'Or explain the mistake.'

'Risky, old boy, and unprofessional. It's the kind of thing you can do once or twice in a real emergency, but it doesn't pay. They don't like printing details–naturally. Shakes public confidence in the Press. Besides, it looks as if we weren't doing our job properly. It would be too easy if every time a chap got a scoop the rest of the bunch denied it. And I will hand it to Shumble, it was a pretty idea . . . the beard helped, of course . . . might have thought of it myself if I hadn't been so angry.'

Other journalists were now crowding round claiming their radiograms. Corker surrendered them reluctantly. He had not had time to open Pigge's. 'Here you are, old boy,' he said. 'I've been guarding it for you. Some of these chaps might want to see inside.'

'You don't say,' said Pigge coldly. 'Well, they're welcome.'

It was like all the rest. BOLSHEVIST MISSION REPORTED OVERTAKEN CONTROL RUSH FACTS.

The hunt was up. No one had time for luncheon that day. They were combing the town for Russians.

Wenlock Jakes alone retained his composure. He ate in peace and then summoned Paleologue. 'We're killing this story,' he said. 'Go round to the Press Bureau and have Benito issue an official *démenti* before four o'clock. See it's posted in the hotel and in the wireless station. And put it about among the boys that the story's dead.

He spoke gravely, for he hated to kill a good story.

So the word went round.

A notice was posted in French and English at all the chief European centres of the capital.

> It is categorically denied that there is any Russian diplomatic representative accredited to the Republic of Ishmaelia. Nor is there any truth in the report, spread by subversive interests, that a Russian national of any description whatever arrived in Jacksonburg last Saturday. The train was occupied exclusively by representatives of the foreign press and an employee of the Railway.
>
> GABRIEL BENITO
>
> Minister of Foreign Affairs and Propaganda

The Press acted in unison and Shumble's scoop died at birth. William sent his first press message from Ishmaelia: ALL ROT ABOUT BOLSHEVIK HE IS ONLY TICKET COLLECTOR ASS CALLED SHUMBLE THOUGHT HIS BEARD FALSE BUT IT'S PERFECTLY ALL RIGHT REALLY WILL CABLE AGAIN IF THERE IS ANY NEWS VERY WET HERE YOURS WILLIAM BOOT–and went out to dinner with the British Vice-Consul.

I/xii

Jack Bannister, known at the age of ten as 'Moke', inhabited a little villa in the Legation compound. He and William dined alone at a candle-lit table. Two silent boys, in white gowns, waited on them. Bannister's pet–but far from tame–cheetah purred beside the log fire. There were snipe, lately bagged by the first secretary. They drank some sherry, and some Burgundy and some port, and, to celebrate William's arrival, a good deal more port. Then they settled themselves in easy chairs and drank brandy. They talked about school and the birds and beasts of Ishmaelia. Bannister showed his collection of skins and eggs.

They talked about Ishmaelia. 'No one knows if it's got any minerals because no one's been to see. The map's a complete joke,' Bannister explained. 'The country has never been surveyed at all; half of it's unexplored. Why, look here,' he took down a map from his shelves and opened it. 'See this place, Laku. It's marked as a town of some five thousand inhabitants, fifty miles north of Jacksonburg. Well, there never has been such a place. Laku is the Ishmaelite for "I don't know." When the boundary commission were trying to get through to the Sudan in 1898 they made a camp there and asked one of their boys the name of the hill, so as to record it in their log. He said "Laku," and they've copied it from map to map ever since. President Jackson likes the country to look important in the atlases, so when this edition was printed he had Laku marked good and large. The French once appointed a Consul to Laku when they were getting active in this part of the world.'

Finally they touched on politics.

'I can't think why all you people are coming out here,' said Bannister plaintively. 'You've no idea how it adds to my work. The Minister doesn't like it, either. The F.O. are worrying the life out of him.'

'But isn't there going to be a war?'

'Well, we usually have a bit of scrapping after the rains. There's a lot of bad men in the hills. Gollancz usually shoots up a few when he goes out after the taxes.'

'Is that all?'

'Wish we knew. There's something rather odd going on. Our information is simply that Smiles had a row with the Jacksons round about Christmas time and took to the hills. That's what everyone does out here when he gets in wrong with the Jacksons. We thought no more about it. The next thing we hear is from Europe that half a dozen bogus consulates have been set up and that Smiles has declared a Nationalist Government. Well, that doesn't make much sense. There never has been any Government in Ishmaelia outside Jacksonburg, and, as you see, everything is dead quiet here. But Smiles is certainly getting money from someone, and arms, too, I expect. What's more, we aren't very happy about the President. Six months ago he was eating out of our hand. Now he's getting quite standoffish. There's a concession to a British Company to build the new coast road. It was all settled but for the signing last November. Now the Ministry of Works is jibbing, and they say that the President is behind them. I can't say I like the look of things, and having all you journalists about doesn't make it any easier.'

'We've been busy all day with a lunatic report about a Russian agent who had come to take charge of the Government.'

'Oh!' said Bannister with sudden interest. 'They've got hold of that, have they? What was the story exactly?'

William told him.

'Yes, they've got it pretty mixed.'

'D'you mean to say there's any truth in it?'

Bannister looked diplomatic for a minute and then said, 'Well, I don't see any harm in your knowing. In fact, from what the Minister said to me today, I rather think he'd welcome a little publicity on the subject. There is a Russian here, name of Smerdyakev, a Jew straight from Moscow. He didn't come disguised as a ticket collector, of course. He's been here some time–in fact, he came up by the same train as Hitchcock and that American chap. But he's lying low, living with Benito. We don't quite know what he's up to; whatever it is, it doesn't suit H.M.G.'s book. If you want a really interesting story I should look into him.'

It was half an hour's drive, at this season, from the Legation quarter to the centre of the town. William sat in the taxi, lurching and jolting, in a state of high excitement. In the last few days he had caught something of the professional infection of Corker and his colleagues, had shared their consternation at Hitchcock's disappearance, had rejoiced quietly when Shumble's scoop was killed. Now *he* had something under his hat; a tip-off straight from headquarters, news of high international importance. His might be the agency which would avert or precipitate a world war; he saw his name figuring in future history books '. . . *the Ishmaelite crisis of that year whose true significance was only realized and exposed through the resources of an English journalist, William Boot . . .*' Slightly dizzy with this prospect, as with the wine he had drunk and the appalling rigours of the drive, he arrived at the Liberty to find the lights out in the lounge and all his colleagues in bed.

He woke Corker, with difficulty.

'For Christ's sake. You're tight. Go to bed, old boy.'

'Wake up, I've got a story.'

At that electric word Corker roused himself and sat up in bed.

William told him, fully and proudly, all that he had learned at dinner. When he had finished. Corker lay back again among the crumpled pillows. 'I might have known,' he said bitterly.

'But don't you see? This really is news. And we've got the Legation behind us. The Minister wants it written up.'

Corker turned over on his side.

'That story's dead,' he remarked.

'But Shumble had it all wrong. Now we've got the truth. It may make a serious difference in Europe.'

Corker spoke again with finality. 'Now go to bed, there's a good chap. No one's going to print your story after the way it's been denied. Russian agents are off the menu, old boy. It's a bad break for Shumble, I grant you. He got on to a good thing without knowing–and the false beard was a very pretty touch. His story was better than yours all round, and we killed it. Do turn out the light.'

I/xiii

In his room in the annexe Sir Jocelyn Hitchcock covered his key-hole with stamp-paper and, circumspectly, turned on a little shaded lamp. He boiled some water and made himself a cup of cocoa; drank it; then he went to the map on the wall and took out his flag, considered for a minute, hovering uncertainly over the unscaled peaks and uncharted rivers of that dark terrain, finally decided, and pinned it firmly in the spot marked as the city of Laku. Then he extinguished his light and went happily back to bed.

2/i

Tuesday morning; rain at six; Jakes's typewriter at a quarter past; the first cry of 'Boy' soon after.

'Boy,' shouted Corker. 'Where's *my* boy?'

'Your boy in plison,' said William's boy.

'Holy smoke, what's he been up to?'

'The police were angry with them,' said William's boy.

'Well, I want some tea.'

'All right. Just now.'

The Archbishop of Canterbury who, it is well known, is behind Imperial Chemicals . . . wrote Jakes.

Shumble, Whelper, and Pigge awoke and breakfasted and dressed, but they scarcely spoke. 'Going out?' said Whelper at last.

'What d'you think?' said Shumble.

'Not sore about anything, are you?' said Pigge.

'What d'you think?' said Shumble, leaving the room.

'He's sore,' said Pigge.

'About his story,' said Whelper.

'Who wouldn't be?' said Pigge.

Sir Jocelyn made himself some cocoa and opened a tin of tongue. He counted the remaining stores and found them adequate.

Presently William and Corker set out to look for news.

'Better try the station first,' said Corker, 'just in case the luggage has turned up.'

They got a taxi.

'Station,' said Corker.

'All right,' said the driver, making off through the rain down main street.

'Oh, Christ, he's going to the Swede again.'

Sure enough, that was where they stopped.

'Good morning,' said Erik Olafsen. 'I am very delighted to see you. I am very delighted to see all my colleagues. They come so often. Almost whenever they take a taxi. Come in, please. Have you heard the news?'

'No,' said Corker.

'They are saying in the town that there was a Russian in the train on Saturday.'

'Yes, we've heard that one.'

'But it is a mistake.'

'You don't say.'

'Yes, indeed, it is a mistake. The man was a Swiss ticket collector. I know him many years. But please to come in.'

William and Corker followed their host into his office. There was a stove in the corner, and on the stove a big coffee pot; the smell of coffee filled the room. Olafsen poured out three cupfuls.

'You are comfortable at the Liberty, yes, no?'

'No,' said William and Corker simultaneously.

'I suppose not,' said Olafsen. 'Mrs Jackson is a very religious woman. She comes every Sunday to our musical evening. But I suppose you are not comfortable. Do you know my friends Shumble and Whelper and Pigge?'

'Yes.'

'They are very nice gentlemen, and very clever. They say they are not comfortable, too.'

The thought of so much discomfort seemed to overwhelm the Swede. He gazed over the heads of his guests with huge, pale eyes that seemed to see illimitable, receding vistas of discomfort, and himself a blinded and shackled Samson with his bandages and bibles and hot, strong coffee scarcely able to shift a pebble from the vast mountain which oppressed humanity. He sighed.

The bell rang over the shop-door. Olafsen leapt to his feet. 'Excuse,' he said, 'the natives steal so terribly.'

But it was not a native. William and Corker could see the new-comer from where they sat in the office. She was a white woman; a girl. A straggle of damp gold hair clung to her cheek. She wore red gum boots, shiny and wet, spattered with the mud of the streets. Her mackintosh dripped on the linoleum and she carried a half open, dripping umbrella, held away from her side; it was short and old; when it was new it had been quite cheap. She spoke in German, bought something, and went out again into the rain.

'Who was the Garbo?' asked Corker when the Swede came back.

'She is a German lady. She has been here some time. She had a husband but I think she is alone now. He was to do some work outside the city but I do not think she knows where he is. I suppose he will not come back. She lives at the German pension with Frau Dressler. She came for some medicine.'

'Looks as though she needed it,' said Corker. 'Well, we must go to the station.'

'Yes. There is a special train this evening. Twenty more journalists are arriving.'

'Christ!'

'For me it is a great pleasure to meet so many distinguished confrères. It is a great honour to work with them.'

'Decent bloke that,' said Corker, when they again drove off. 'You know, I never feel Swedes are really foreign. More like you and me, if you see what I mean.'

2/ii

Three hours later Corker and William sat down to luncheon. The menu did not vary at the Liberty; sardine, beef, and chicken for luncheon; soup, beef, and chicken for dinner; hard, homogeneous cubes of beef, sometimes with Worcester Sauce, sometimes with tomato ketchup; fibrous spindles of chicken with grey-green dented peas.

'Don't seem to have any relish for my food,' said Corker. 'It must be the altitude.'

Everyone was in poor spirits; it had been an empty morning; the absence of Hitchcock lay heavy as thunder over the hotel, and there was a delay of fourteen hours in transmission at the wireless station, for Wenlock Jakes had been letting himself go on the local colour.

'The beef's beastly,' said Corker. 'Tell the manageress to come here . . .'

At a short distance Jakes was entertaining three blacks. Everyone watched that table suspiciously and listened when they could, but he seemed to be talking mostly about himself. After a time the boy brought them chicken.

'Where's that manageress?' asked Corker.

'No come.'

'What d'you mean "no come"?'

'Manageress say only journalist him go boil himself,' said the boy more explicitly.

'What did I tell you? No respect for the Press. *Savages.*'

They left the dining-room. In the lounge standing on one foot and leaning on his staff, was the aged warrior who delivered the telegrams. William's read:

PRESUME YOUR STEPTAKING INSURE SERVICE EVENT GENERAL UPBREAK.

'It's no good answering,' said Corker. 'They won't send till tomorrow morning. Come to think of it,' he added moodily, 'there's no point in answering anyway. Look at mine.'

CABLE FULLIER OFTENER PROMPTLIER STOP YOUR SERVICE BADLY BEATEN ALROUND LACKING HUMAN INTEREST COLOUR DRAMA PERSONALITY HUMOUR INFORMATION ROMANCE VITALITY.

'Can't say that's not frank, can you?' said Corker. 'God rot 'em.'

That afternoon he took Shumble's place at the card table. William slept.

2/iii

The special train got in at seven. William went to meet it; so did everyone else.

The Ishmaelite Foreign Minister was there with his suite. ('Expecting a nob,' said Corker.) The Minister wore a Derby hat and ample military cape. The station-master set a little gilt chair for him where he sat like a daguerrotype, stiffly posed, a Victorian worthy in negative, black face, white whiskers, black hands. When the camera men began to shoot, his Staff scrambled to get to the front of the picture, eclipsing their chief. It was all the same to the camera men, who were merely passing the time and had no serious hope that the portrait would be of any interest.

At length the little engine came whistling round the bend, wood sparks dancing over the funnel. It stopped and at once the second and third class passengers–natives and near-whites–tumbled on to the platform, greeting their relatives with tears and kisses. The station police got in among them, jostling the levantines and whacking the natives with swagger-canes. The first class passengers emerged more slowly; they had already acquired that expression of anxious resentment that was habitual to whites in Jacksonburg. They were all, every man-jack of them, journalists and photographers.

The distinguished visitor had not arrived. The Foreign Minister waited until the last cramped and cautious figure emerged from the first class coach; then he exchanged civilities with the station-master and took his leave. The station police made a passage of a kind, but it was only with a struggle that he regained his car.

The porters began to unload, and take the registered baggage to the customs shed. On the head of the foremost William recognized his bundle of cleft sticks; then more of his possessions–the collapsible canoe, the mistletoe, the ant proof wardrobes. There was a cry of delight from Corker, at his side. The missing van had arrived. Mysteriously it had become attached to the special train; had in fact been transposed. Somewhere, in a siding at one of the numerous stops down the line, lay the new-comers' luggage. Their distress deepened but Corker was jubilant and before dinner that evening introduced his elephant to a place of prominence in the bedroom. He also, in his good humour, introduced two photographers for whom he had an affection.

'Tight fit,' they said.

'Not at all,' said Corker. 'Delighted to have your company; aren't we, Boot?'

One of them took William's newly arrived camp bed; the other expressed a readiness to 'doss down' on the floor for the night. Everyone decided to doss down in the Liberty. Mrs Jackson recommended other lodgings available from friends of hers in the town. But, 'No,' they said. 'We've got to doss down with the bunch.'

The bunch now overflowed the hotel. There were close on fifty of them. All over the lounge and dining-room they sat and stood and leaned; some whispered to one another in what they took to be secrecy; others exchanged chaff and gin. It was their employers who paid for all this hospitality, but the conventions were decently observed–'My round, old boy,' 'No, no, my round' . . . 'Have this one on me.' 'Well, the next is mine'–except by Shumble who, from habit, drank heartily, and without return wherever it was offered.

'What are you all here for?' asked Corker petulantly of a new-comer. 'What's come over them at home? What's supposed to be going on, anyway?'

'It's ideological. And we're only half of it. There's twenty more at the coast who couldn't get on the train. Weren't they sick at seeing us go? It's lousy on the coast.'

'It's lousy here.'

'Yes, I see what you mean . . .'

There was not much sleep that night for anyone in William's room. The photographer who was dossing down found the floor wet and draughty and, as the hours passed, increasingly hard. He turned from side to side, lay flat on his back, then on his face. At each change of position he groaned as though in agony. Every now and then he turned on the light to collect more coverings. At dawn, when the rain began to drip near his head, he was dozing uneasily, fully dressed in overcoat and tweed cap, enveloped in every available textile, including the tablecloth, the curtains, and Corker's two oriental shawls. Nor did the other photographer do much better; the camp bed seemed less stable than William had supposed when it was sold to him; perhaps it was wrongly assembled; perhaps essential parts were still missing. Whatever the reason, it collapsed repeatedly and roused William's apprehensions of the efficacy of his canoe.

Early next morning he rang up Bannister and, on his advice, moved to Frau Dressler's pension. 'Bad policy, old boy,' said Corker, 'but since you're going I wonder if you'll take charge of my curios. I don't at all like the way Shumble's been looking at them.'

2/iv

The Pension Dressler stood in a side street and had, at first glance, the air rather of a farm than of an hotel. Frau Dressler's pig, tethered by one hind trotter to the jamb of the front door, roamed the yard and disputed the kitchen scraps with the poultry. He was a prodigious beast. Frau Dressler's guests prodded him appreciatively on their way to the dining-room, speculating on how soon he would be ripe for killing. The milch-goat was allowed a narrower radius; those who kept strictly to the causeway were safe, but she never reconciled herself to this limitation and, day in, day out, essayed a series of meteoric onslaughts on the passers-by, ending, at the end of her rope, with a jerk which would have been death to an animal of any other species. One day the rope would break; she knew it, and so did Frau Dressler's guests.

There was also a gander, the possession of the night watchman, and a three-legged dog, who barked furiously from the mouth of a barrel and was said to have belonged to the late Herr Dressler. Other pets came and went with Frau Dressler's guests–baboons, gorillas, cheetahs, all inhabited the yard in varying degrees of liberty and moved uneasily for fear of the milch-goat.

As a consequence perhaps of the vigour of the livestock, the garden had not prospered. A little bed, edged with inverted bottles, produced nothing except, annually, a crop of the rank, scarlet flowers which burst out everywhere in Jacksonburg at the end of the rains. Two sterile banana palms grew near the kitchens and between them a bush of Indian hemp which the cook tended and kept for his own indulgence. The night watchman, too, had a little shrub, to whose seed-pods he attributed medical properties of a barely credible order.

Architecturally, the Pension Dressler was a mess. There were three main buildings disposed irregularly in the acre of ground–single-storied, tin-roofed, constructed of timber and rubble, with wooden verandas; the two larger were divided into bedrooms; the smallest contained the dining-room, the parlour, and the mysterious, padlocked room where Frau Dressler slept. Everything of value or interest in the pension was kept in this room, and whatever was needed by anyone–money, provisions, linen, back numbers of European magazines–could be produced, on demand, from under Frau Dressler's bed. There was a hut called the bathroom, where, after due notice and the recruitment of extra labour, a tin tub could be filled with warm water and enjoyed in the half darkness among a colony of bats. There was the kitchen not far from the other buildings, a place of smoke and wrath, loud with Frau Dressler's scolding. And there were the servants' quarters–a cluster of thatched cabins, circular, windowless, emitting at all hours a cosy smell of woodsmoke and curry; the centre of a voluble round of hospitality which culminated often enough in the late evening with song and rhythmical clapping. The night watchman had his own lair where he lived morosely with two wrinkled wives. He was a tough old warrior who passed his brief waking hours in paring the soles of his feet with his dagger or buttering the bolt of his ancient rifle.

Frau Dressler's guests varied as a rule from three to a dozen in number. They were Europeans, mostly of modest means and good character. Frau Dressler had lived all her life in Africa and had a sharp nose for the unfortunate. She had drifted here from Tanganyika after the war, shedding Herr Dressler, none knew exactly where or how, on her way. There were a number of Germans in Jacksonburg employed in a humble way in the cosmopolitan commercial quarter. Frau Dressler was their centre. She allowed them to come in on Saturday evenings after the guests had dined, to play cards or chess and listen to the wireless. They drank a bottle of beer apiece; sometimes they only had coffee, but there was no place for the man who tried to get away without spending. At Christmas there was a decorated tree and a party which the German Minister attended and subsidized. The missionaries always recommended Frau Dressler to visitors in search of cheap and respectable lodgings.

She was a large shabby woman of unbounded energy. When William confronted her she was scolding a group of native peasants from the dining-room steps. The meaning of her words was hidden from William; from the peasants also; for she spoke Ishmaelite, and bad Ishmaelite at that, while they knew only a tribal patois; but the tone was unmistakable. The peasants did not mind. This was a daily occurrence. Always at dawn they appeared outside Frau Dressler's dining-room and exposed their wares–red peppers, green vegetables, eggs, poultry, and fresh local cheese. Every hour or so Frau Dressler asked them their prices and told them to be off. Always at half-past eleven, when it was time for her to begin cooking the midday dinner, she made her purchases at the price which all parties had long ago decided would be the just one.

'They are thieves and imposters,' she said to William. 'I have been fifteen years in Jacksonburg and they still think they can cheat. When I first came I paid the most wicked prices–two American dollars for a lamb; ten cents a dozen for eggs. Now I know better.'

William said that he wanted a room. She received him cordially and led him across the yard. The three-legged dog barked furiously from his barrel; the milch-goat shot out at him like a cork from a popgun and, like it, was brought up short at the end of her string; the night watchman's gander hissed and ruffled his plumage. Frau Dressler picked up a loose stone and caught him square in the chest. 'They are playful,' she explained, 'particularly the goat.'

They gained the veranda, sheltered from rain and livestock. Frau Dressler threw open a door. There was luggage in the bedroom, a pair of woman's stockings across the foot of the bed, a woman's shoes against the wall. 'We have a girl here at the moment. She shall move.'

'Oh, but please . . . I don't want to turn anyone out.'

'She shall move,' repeated Frau Dressler. 'It's my best room. There is everything you want here.'

William surveyed the meagre furniture; the meagre, but still painfully superfluous ornaments. 'Yes,' he said. 'Yes, I suppose there is.'

A train of porters carried William's luggage from the Hotel Liberty. When it was all assembled, it seemed to fill the room. The men stood on the veranda waiting to be paid. William's own boy had absented himself on the first signs of packing. Frau Dressler drove them off with a few copper coins and a torrent of abuse. 'You had better give me anything of value,' she said to William, 'the natives are all villains.'

He gave her Corker's objects of art; she carried them off to her room and stored them safely under the bed. William began to unpack. Presently there was a knock outside. The door opened. William had his back to it. He was kneeling over his ant-proof chest.

'Please,' said a woman's voice. William turned round. 'Please may I have my things?'

It was the girl he had seen the day before at the Swedish mission. She wore the same mackintosh, the same splashed gumboots. She seemed to be just as wet. William jumped to his feet.

'Yes, of course, please let me help.'

'Thank you. There's not very much. But this one is heavy. It has some of my husband's things.'

She took her stockings from the end of the bed, ran her hand into one and showed him two large holes, smiled, rolled them into a ball and put them in the pocket of her raincoat. 'This is the heavy one,' she said, pointing to a worn leather bag. William attempted to lift it. It might have been full of stone. The girl opened it. It *was* full of stone. 'They are my husband's specimens,' she said. 'He wants me to be very careful of them. They are very important. But I don't think anyone could steal them. They are so heavy.'

William succeeded in dragging the bag across the floor. 'Where to?'

'I have a little room by the kitchen. It is up a ladder. It will be difficult to carry the specimens. I wanted Frau Dressler to keep them in her room but she did not want to. She said they were of no value. You see, she is not an engineer.'

'Would you like to leave them here?'

Her face brightened. 'May I? It would be very kind. That is what I hoped, but I did not know what you would be like. They said you were a journalist.'

'So I am.'

'The town is full of journalists, but I should not have thought you were one.'

'I can't think why Frau Dressler has put me in this room,' said William. 'I should be perfectly happy anywhere else. Did you want to move?'

'I must move. You see this is Frau Dressler's best room. When I came here it was with my husband. Then she gave us the best room. But now he is at work, so I must move. I do not want a big room now I am alone. But it would be very kind if you would keep our specimens.'

There was a suitcase which belonged to her. She opened it and threw in the shoes and other woman's things that lay about the room. When it was full she looked from it to the immense pile of trunks and crates and smiled. 'It is all I have,' she said. 'Not like you.'

She went over to the pile of cleft sticks. 'How do you use these?'

'They are for sending messages.'

'You're teasing me.'

'No, indeed I'm not. Lord Copper said I was to send my messages with them.'

The girl laughed. 'How funny. Have all the journalists got sticks like this?'

'Well, no; to tell you the truth I don't believe they have.'

'How funny you are.' Her laugh became a cough. She sat on the bed and coughed until her eyes were full of tears. 'Oh, dear. It is so long since I laughed and now it hurts me . . . What is in this?'

'A canoe.'

'Now I know you are teasing me.'

'Honestly, it's a canoe. At least they said it was at the shop. Look, I'll show you.'

Together they prised up the lid of the case and filled the floor with packing. At last they found a neat roll of cane and proofed canvas.

'It is a tent,' she said.

'No, canoe. Look.'

They spread the canvas on the floor. With great difficulty they assembled the framework of jointed cane. Twice they had to stop when the girl's laughter turned to a paroxysm of coughing. At last it was finished and the little boat rose in a sea of shavings. 'It *is* a canoe,' she cried. 'Now I will believe you about those sticks. I will believe everything you tell me. Look, there are seats. Get in, quick, we must get in.'

They sat opposite one another in the boat, their knees touching. The girl laughed, clear and loud, and this time did not cough. 'But it's beautiful,' she said. 'And so *new*. I have not seen anything so new since I came to this city. Can you swim?'

'Yes.'

'So can I. I swim *very* well. So it will not matter if we are upset. Give me one of the message sticks and I will row you . . .'

'Do I intrude?' asked Corker. He was standing on the veranda outside the window, leaning into the room.

'Oh, dear,' said the girl.

She and William left the boat and stood among the shavings.

'We were just trying the canoe,' William explained.

'Yes,' said Corker. 'Whimsical. How about trying the mistletoe?'

'This is Mr Corker, a fellow journalist.'

'Yes, yes. I see he is. I must go away now.'

'Not Garbo,' said Corker. 'Bergner.'

'What does he mean'?

'He says you are like a film star.'

'Does he? Does he really say that?' Her face, clouded at Corker's interruption, beamed. 'That is how I should like to be. Now I must go. I will send a boy for the valise.'

She went, pulling the collar of her raincoat close round her throat.

'Not bad, old boy, not bad at all. I will say you're a quick worker. Sorry to barge in on the tender scene, but there's trouble afoot. Hitchcock's story has broken. He's at the Fascist headquarters scooping the world.'

'Where?'

'Town called Laku.'

'But he can't be. Bannister told me there was no such place.'

'Well, there is now, old boy. At this very moment it's bang across the front page of the *Daily Brute* and it's where we are all going or know the reason why.

A meeting of the Foreign Press Association has been called for six this evening at the Liberty. Feeling is running very high in the bunch.'

The German girl came back.

'Is the journalist gone?'

'Yes. I am sorry. I'm afraid he was rather rude.'

'Was he teasing, or did he really mean I was like a film star?'

'I'm sure he meant it.'

'Do you think so too?' She leaned on the dressing-table studying her face in the mirror. She pushed back a strand of hair that had fallen over her forehead; she turned her head on one side, smiled at herself, put out her tongue. 'Do you think so?'

'Yes, very like a film star.'

'I am glad.' She sat on the bed. 'What's your name?'

William told her.

'Mine is Kätchen,' she said. 'You must put away the boat. It is in the way and it makes us seem foolish.'

Together they dismembered the frame and rolled up the canvas. 'I have something to ask,' she said. 'What do you think is the value of my husband's specimens?'

'I'm afraid I have no idea.'

'He said they were very valuable.'

'I expect they are.'

'Ten English pounds?'

'I daresay.'

'More? Twenty?'

'Possibly.'

'Then I will sell them to you. It is because I like you. Will you give me twenty pounds for them?'

'Well, you know, I've got a great deal of luggage already. I don't know quite what I should do with them.'

'I know what you are thinking–that it is wrong for me to sell my husband's valuable specimens. But he has been away for six weeks now and he left me with only eight dollars. Frau Dressler is becoming most impolite. I am sure he would not want Frau Dressler to be impolite. So this is what we will do. You shall buy them and then, when my husband comes back and says they are worth more than twenty pounds, you will pay him the difference. There will be nothing wrong in that, will there? He could not be angry?'

'No, I don't think he could possibly be angry about that.'

'Good. Oh, you have made me glad that you came here. Please, will you give me the money now? Have you an account at the bank?'

'Yes.'

'Then write a cheque. I will take it to the bank myself. Then it will be no trouble to you.'

When she had gone, William took out his expense sheet and dutifully entered the single, enigmatic item: '*Stones . . . £20.*'

2/V

Every journalist in Jacksonburg except Wenlock Jakes, who had sent Paleologue to represent him, attended the meeting of the Foreign Press Association; all, in their various tongues, voluble with indignation. The hotel boys pattered amongst them with trays of whisky; the air was pungent and dark with tobacco smoke. Pappenhacker was in the chair, wearily calling for order. 'Order, gentlemen. Attention, je vous en prie. Order, *please*. Messieurs, gentlemen. . .'

'Order, order,' shouted Pigge, and Pappenhacker's voice was drowned in cries of silence.

'. . . secretary to read the minutes of the last meeting?'

The voice of the secretary could occasionally be heard above the chatter. '. . . held at the Hotel Liberty . . . Sir Jocelyn Hitchcock in the chair . . . resolution . . . unanimously passed . . . protest in the most emphatic manner against . . . Ishmaelite government . . . militates against professional activities. . .

'. . . objections to make or questions to ask about these minutes. . .'

The correspondents for *Paris-Soir* and *Havas* objected and after a time the minutes were signed. Pappenhacker was again on his feet. 'Gentlemen, in the absence of Sir Jocelyn Hitchcock. . .'

Loud laughter and cries of 'Shame.'

'Mr Chairman, I must protest that this whole question is being treated with highly undesirable levity.'

'Translate.'

'On traite toute la question avec une légèreté indésirable.'

'Thank you, Mr Porter . . .

'If you pliss to spik Sherman . . .

'Italiano . . . piacere . . .'

'. . . tutta domanda con levità spiacevole . . .'

'. . . Sherman . . .'

Gentlemen, gentlemen, Doctor Benito has consented to meet us here in a few minutes and it is essential that I know the will of the meeting, so that I can present our demands in proper form.'

At this stage one half of the audience–those nearest to William–were distracted from the proceedings by an altercation, unconnected with the business in hand, between two rival photographers.

'Did you call me a scab?'

'I did not, but I will.'

'You will?'

'Sure, you're a scab. Now what?'

'Call me a scab outside.'

'I call you a scab here.'

'Say that outside and see what you'll get.'

Cries of 'Shame' and 'Aw, pipe down.'

'... gravely affecting out professional status. We welcome fair and free competition ... obliged to enforce coercive measures ...'

'Go on, sock me one and see what you get.'

'I don't want to sock you one. *You* sock *me* first.'

'Aw, go sock him one.'

'Just you give me a poke in the nose and see what you'll get.'

'... Notre condition professionnelle. Nous souhaitons la bienvenue à toute la compétition égale et libre.'

'Nostra condizione professionale ...'

'*You* poke *me* in the nose.'

'Aw, why can't you boys sock each other and be friendly?'

'Resolution before the meeting ... protest against the breach of faith on the part of the Ishmaelite government and demand that all restrictions on their movements be instantly relaxed. I call for a show of hands on this resolution.'

'Mr Chairman, I object to the whole tone of this resolution.'

'May I propose the amendment that facilities be withheld from Sir Jocelyn Hitchcock until we have had time to get level with him?'

'... demand an enquiry into how and from whom he received his permission to travel and the punishment of the responsible official ...'

'I protest, Mr Chairman, that the whole tone is peremptory and discourteous.'

'... The motion as amended reads ...'

Then Doctor Benito arrived; he came from the main entrance and the journalists fell back to make way. It was William's first sight of him. He was short and brisk and self-possessed; soot-black in face, with piercing boot-button eyes; he wore a neat black suit; his linen and his teeth were brilliantly white, he carried a little black attaché case; in the lapel of his coat he wore the button of the Star of Ishmaelia, fourth class. As he passed through them the journalists were hushed; it was as though the head-mistress had suddenly appeared among an unruly class of schoolgirls. He reached the table, shook Pappenhacker by the hand and faced his audience with a flash of white teeth.

'Gentlemen,' he said, 'I will speak first in English' (the correspondents of *Havas* and *Paris-soir* began to protest) 'after that in French.'

'I have a communication to make on the part of the President. He wishes to state first that he reserves for himself absolutely the right to maintain or relax the regulations he has made for the comfort and safety of the Press, either generally or in individual cases. Secondly, that, so far, no relaxation of these regulations has been made in any case. If, as is apparently believed, a journalist has left Jacksonburg for the interior it is without the Government's consent or knowledge. Thirdly, that the roads to the interior are at the moment entirely unfit for travel, provisions are impossible to obtain and travellers would be in danger from disaffected elements of the population. Fourthly, that he has decided, in view of the wishes of the foreign Press, to relax the restrictions he has hitherto made. Those wishing to do so, may travel to the interior. They must first apply formally to my bureau where the necessary passes will be issued and steps taken for their protection. That is all, gentlemen.'

He then repeated his message in accurate French, bowed and left the meeting in deep silence. When he had, gone, Pappenhacker said, 'Well, gentlemen, I think that concludes our evening's business in a very satisfactory manner,' but it was with a dissatisfied air that the journalists left the hotel for the wireless station.

'A triumph for the power of the Press,' said Corker. 'They caved in at once.'

'Yes,' said William.

'You sound a bit doubtful, old boy.'

'Yes.'

'I know what you're thinking of–something in Benito's manner. I noticed it too. Nothing you could actually take hold of, but he seemed kind of superior to me.'

'Yes,' said William.

They sent off their service messages. William wrote: THEY HAVE GIVEN US PERMISSION TO GO TO LAKU AND EVERYONE IS GOING BUT THERE IS NO SUCH PLACE AM I TO GO TOO SORRY TO BE A BORE BOOT.

Corker, more succinctly: PERMISSION GRANTED LAKUWARD.

That night the wireless carried an urgent message in similar terms from every journalist in Jacksonburg.

William and Corker returned to the Liberty for a drink. All the journalists were having drinks. The two photographers were clinking glasses and slapping one another on the shoulder. Corker reverted to the topic that was vexing him. 'What's that blackamoor got to be superior about?' he asked moodily, 'Funny that you noticed it too.'

2/vi

Next day Corker brought William a cable: UNPROCEED LAKUWARD STOP AGENCIES COVERING PATRIOTIC FRONT STOP REMAIN CONTACTING CUMREDS STOP NEWS EXYOU UNRECEIVED STOP DAILY HARD NEWS ESSENTIALEST STOP REMEMBER RATES SERVICE CABLES ONE ETSIX PER WORD BEAST.

Kätchen stood at his elbow as he read it. 'What does it mean?' she asked.

'I'm to stay in Jacksonburg.'

'Oh, I am pleased.'

William answered the cable:

NO NEWS AT PRESENT THANKS WARNING ABOUT CABLING PRICES BUT IVE PLENTY MONEY LEFT AND ANYWAY WHEN I OFFERED TO PAY WIRELESS MAN SAID IT WAS ALL RIGHT PAID OTHER END RAINING HARD HOPE ALL WELL ENGLAND WILL CABLE AGAIN IF ANY NEWS.

Then he and Kätchen went to play ping-pong at Popotakis's.

2/vii

The journalists left.

For three days the town was in turmoil. Lorries were chartered and provisioned; guides engaged; cooks and guards and muleteers and caravan boys and hunters, cooks' boys, guards' boys, muleteers' boys, ravan-boys' boys and hunters' boys were recruited at unprecedented rates of pay; all over the city, in the offices and legations, resident Europeans found themselves deserted by their servants; seminarists left the missions, male-nurses the hospital, highly placed clerks their government departments to compete for the journalists' wages. The price of benzine was doubled overnight and rose steadily until the day of the exodus. Terrific deals were done in the bazaar in tinned foodstuffs; they were cornered by a Parsee and unloaded on a Banja, cornered again by an Arab, resold and rebought, before they reached the journalists' stores. Shumble bought William's rifle and sold a half share in it to Whelper. Everyone now emulated the costume of the Frenchmen; sombreros, dungarees, jodhpurs, sunproof shirts and bullet-proof waistcoats, holsters, bandoliers, Newmarket boots, cutlasses, filled the Liberty. The men of the Excelsior Movie-Sound News, sporting horsehair capes and silk shirts of native chieftains, made camp in the Liberty garden and photographed themselves at great length in attitudes of vigilance and repose. Paleologue made his pile.

There was an evening of wild indignation when it was falsely put around that Jakes had been lent a balloon by the Government for his journey. There was an evening of anxiety when, immediately before the day fixed for their departure, the journalists were informed that the passes for their journey had not yet received the stamp of the Ministry of the Interior. A meeting of the Press Association was hastily called; it passed a resolution of protest and dissolved in disorder. Late that evening Doctor Benito delivered the passes in person. They were handsome, unintelligible documents printed in Ishmaelite and liberally decorated with rubber stamps, initials, and patriotic emblems. Benito brought one to William at the Pension Dressler.

'I'm not going, after all,' William explained.

'Not going, Mr Boot? But your pass is here, made out in order.'

'Sorry if it has caused extra work, but my editor has told me to stay on here.'

An expression of extreme annoyance came over the affable, black face.

'But your colleagues have made every arrangement. It is very difficult for my bureau if the journalists do not keep together. You see, your pass to Laku automatically cancels your permission to remain in Jacksonburg. I'm afraid, Mr Boot, it will be necessary for you to go.'

'Oh, rot,' said William. 'For one thing there is no such place as Laku.'

'I see you are very well informed about my country, Mr Boot. I should not have thought it from the tone of your newspaper.'

William began to dislike Dr Benito.

'Well, I'm not going. Will you be good enough to cancel the pass and renew my permission for Jacksonburg?'

There was a pause; then the white teeth flashed in a smile.

'But of course, Mr Boot. It will be a great pleasure. I cannot hope to offer you anything of much interest during your visit. As you have seen, we are a very quiet little community. The Academic year opens at Jackson College. General Gollancz Jackson is celebrating his silver wedding. But I do not think any of these things are of great importance in Europe. I am sure your colleagues in the interior will find far more exciting matter for their dispatches. Are you sure nothing can make you alter your decision?'

'Quite sure.'

'Very well.' Dr Benito turned to go. Then he paused. 'By the way, have you communicated to any of your colleagues your uncertainty about the existence of the city of Laku?'

'Yes, but they wouldn't listen.'

'I suppose not. Perhaps they have more experience in their business. Good night.'

2/viii

Next morning, at dawn, the first lorry started. It was shared by Corker and Pigge. They sat in front with the driver. They had been drinking heavily and late the night before and, in the grey light, showed it. Behind, among the crates and camp furniture, lay six torpid servants.

William rose to see them off. They had kept the time of their departure a secret. Everyone, the evening before, had spoken casually of 'making a move at tennish', but when William arrived at the Liberty the whole place was astir. Others beside Pigge and Corker conceived that an advantage might come from a few hours' start; all the others. Corker and Pigge were away first, by a negligible margin. One after another their colleagues took the road behind them. Pappenhacker drove a little two-seater he had bought from the British Legation. Many of the cars flew flags of Ishmaelia and of their countries. One lorry was twice the size of any other; it rode gallantly on six wheels; its sides were armour-plated; it had been purchased, irregularly and at enormous expense, from the War Office, and bore in vast letters of still tacky paint the inscription:

EXCELSIOR MOVIE-SOUND EXPEDITIONARY UNIT
TO THE ISHMAELITE IDEOLOGICAL FRONT.

During these latter days the rains had notably declined, giving promise of spring. The clouds lay high over the town, revealing a wider horizon, and, as the cavalcade disappeared from view, the road to Laku lay momentarily bathed in sunshine. William waved them good-bye from the steps of the Jackson memorial and turned back towards the Pension Dressler, but as he went the sky darkened and the first drops began to fall.

He was at breakfast when his boy reported: 'All come back.'

'Who?'

'All newspaper fellows come back. Soldiers catch 'em one time and take 'em plison.'

William went out to investigate.

Sure enough the lorries were lined up outside the police station, and inside, each with an armed guard, sat the journalists. They had found the barricades of the town shut against them; the officer in charge had not been warned to expect them; he had been unable to read their passes and they were all under arrest.

At ten when Doctor Benito began his day's routine at the Press Bureau, he received them apologetically but blandly. 'It is a mistake,' he said. 'I regret it infinitely. I understood that you proposed to start at ten. If I had known that you intended to start earlier I would have made the necessary arrangements. The night-guard have orders to let no one through. You will now find the day-guard on duty. They will present arms as you pass. I have given special instructions to that effect. Good-bye, gentlemen, and a good journey.'

Once more the train of lorries set off; rain was now falling hard. Corker and Pigge still led; Wenlock Jakes came last in a smart touring car. William waved: the populace whistled appreciatively; at the gates of the city the guard slapped the butts of their carbines. William once more turned to the Pension Dressler; the dark clouds opened above him; the gutters and wet leaves sparkled in sunlight and a vast, iridescent fan of colour, arc beyond arc of splendour, spread across the heavens. The journalists had gone, and a great peace reigned in the city.

3/i

Kätchen was smoking in a long chair on the veranda. 'Lovely,' she said. 'Lovely. In a few days now the rains will be over.'

She had been early to the hairdresser and, in place of the dank wisps of yesterday, her golden head was a tuft of curls. She had a new dress; she wore scarlet sandals and her toe-nails were painted to match them. 'The dress came yesterday,' she said. 'There is an Austrian lady who sewed it for me. I wanted to put it on last night, when we went to play ping-pong, but I thought you would like it best when my hair was done. You *do* like it?'

'Immensely.'

'And I got this,' she said. 'It is French.' She showed him an enamelled vanity case. 'The hairdresser sold it to me . . . From Paris. Lipstick, powder, looking-glass, comb, cigarettes. Pretty?'

'Very pretty.'

'And now Frau Dressler is angry with me again, because of her bill. But I don't care. What business of hers is it if I sell my husband's specimens? I offered them to her and she said they were not valuable. I don't care, I don't care. Oh, William, I am so happy. Look at the rainbow. It gets bigger and bigger. Soon there will be no room in the sky for it. Do you know what I should like to do today? I should like us to take a motor-car and drive into the hills. We could get some wine and, if you ask her, Frau Dressler will make a hamper. Do not say it is for me. Let us get away from this city for a day . . .'

Frau Dressler packed a hamper; Doctor Benito stamped a pass; Paleologue arranged for the hire of a motor-car. At midday William and Kätchen drove off towards the hills.

'Kätchen, I love you. Darling, darling Kätchen, I love you . . .'

He meant it. He was in love. It was the first time in twenty-three years; he was suffused and inflated and tipsy with love. It was believed at Boot Magna, and jocularly commented upon from time to time, that an attachment existed between him and a neighbouring Miss Caldicote; it was not so. He was a stranger alike to the bucolic jaunts of the hayfield and the dark and costly expeditions of his Uncle Theodore. For twenty-three years he had remained celibate and heart-whole; land-bound. Now for the first time he was far from shore, submerged among deep waters, below wind and tide, where huge trees raised their spongy flowers and monstrous things without fur or feather, wing or foot, passed silently, in submarine twilight. A lush place.

3/ii

Sir Jocelyn Hitchcock threw open the shutters of his room and welcomed the sunshine. He thrust his head out of the window and called loudly for attention. They brought him a dozen steaming jugs and filled his tub. He bathed and shaved and rubbed his head with eau de quinine until his sparse hairs were crowned with foam and his scalp smarted and glowed. He dressed carefully, set his hat at an angle and sauntered to the wireless station.

CONSIDER ISHMAELITE STORY UP-CLEANED, he wrote, SUGGEST LEAVING AGENCIES COVER UP-FOLLOWS. Then he returned to the hotel and ate a late breakfast of five lightly boiled eggs.

He packed his luggage and waited for his reply. It came before sundown, for there was little traffic at the wireless station that day. PROCEED LUCERNE COVER ECONOMIC NON-INTERVENTION CONGRESS. There was a train to the coast that night. He paid his bill at the hotel and, with three hours to spare, took a walk in the town.

The promise of the morning had been barely fulfilled. At noon the rain had started again; throughout the afternoon had streamed monotonously, and now, at sundown, ceased; for a few minutes the shoddy roofs were ablaze with scarlet and gold.

With loping steps, Erik Olafsen came down the street towards Sir Jocelyn; his face was uplifted to the glory of the sunset and he would have walked blandly by. It was Sir Jocelyn's first impulse to let him; then, changing his mind, he stepped forward and greeted him.

'Sir Hitchcock, you are back so soon. It will disappoint our colleagues to find you not at Laku. You have had many interests in your journey, yes?'

'Yes,' said Sir Jocelyn briefly.

Across the street, deriding the splendour of the sky, there flashed the electric sign of Popotakis's Ping Pong Parlour while, from his door, an ancient French two-step, prodigiously amplified, heralded the day's end.

'Come across and have a drink,' said Sir Jocelyn.

'Not to drink, thank you so much, but to hear the interests of your journey.

I was told that Laku was no such place, no?'

'No,' said Sir Jocelyn.

Even as they crossed the street, the sky paled.

Popotakis had tried a cinema, a dance hall, baccarat, and miniature golf; now he had four ping-pong tables. He had made good money, for the smart set of Jacksonburg were always hard put to get through the rainy season; the polyglot professional class had made it their rendezvous; even attachés from the legations and younger members of the Jackson family had come there. Then for a few delirious days it had been overrun with journalists; prices had doubled, quarrels had raged, the correspondent of the *Methodist Monitor* had been trussed with a net and a photographer had lost a tooth. Popotakis's old clients melted away to other, more seemly resorts; the journalists had broken his furniture and insulted his servants and kept him awake till four in the morning, but they had drunk his home-made whisky at an American dollar a glass and poured his home-made champagne over the bar at ten dollars a bottle. Now they had all gone and the place was nearly empty. Only William and Kätchen sat at the bar. Popotakis had some genuine sixty per cent absinthe; that is what they were drinking. They were in a sombre mood, for the picnic had been a failure.

Olafsen greeted them with the keenest pleasure. 'So you have not gone with the others, Boot? And you are now friends with Kätchen? Good, good. Sir Hitchcock, to present my distinguished colleague Boot of the London *Beast*.'

Sir Jocelyn was always cordial to fellow journalists, however obscure. 'Drink up,' he said. 'And have another. Sending much?'

'Nothing,' said William, 'nothing seems to happen.'

'Why aren't you with the bunch? You're missing a grand trip. Mind you, I don't know they'll get much of a story at Laku. Shouldn't be surprised if they found the place empty already. But it's a grand trip. Scenery, you know, and wild life. What are you drinking, Eriksen?'

'Olafsen. Thank you, some grenadine. That absinthe is very dangerous. It was so I killed my grandfather.'

'You killed your grandfather, Erik?'

'Yes, did you not know? I thought it was well known. I was very young at the time and had taken a lot of sixty per cent. It was with a chopper.'

'May we know, sir,' asked Sir Jocelyn sceptically, 'how old you were when this thing happened?'

'Just seventeen. It was my birthday; that is why I had so much drunk. So I came to live in Jacksonburg, and now I drink this.' He raised, without relish, his glass of crimson syrup.

'Poor man,' said Kätchen.

'Which is poor man? Me or the grandfather?'

'I meant you.'

'Yes, I am poor man. When I was very young I used often to be drunk. Now it is very seldom. Once or two time in the year. But always I do something I am very sorry for. I think, perhaps, I shall get drunk tonight,' he suggested, brightening.

'No, Erik, not tonight.'

'No? Very well, not tonight. But it will be soon. It is very long since I was drunk.'

The confession shed a momentary gloom. All four sat in silence. Sir Jocelyn stirred himself and ordered some more absinthe.

'There were parrots, too,' he said with an effort. 'All along the road to Laku. I never saw such parrots–green and red and blue and–and every colour you can think of, talking like mad. And gorillas.'

'Sir Hitchcock,' said the Swede, 'I have lived in this country ever since I killed my grandfather and I never saw or heard of a gorilla.'

'I saw six,' said Sir Jocelyn stoutly, 'sitting in a row.'

The Swede rose abruptly from his stool. 'I do not understand,' he said. 'So I think I shall go.' He paid for his grenadine and left them at the bar.

'Odd chap that,' said Sir Jocelyn. 'Moody. Men get like that when they live in the tropics. I daresay it was all a delusion about his grandfather.'

There was food of a kind procurable at Popotakis's Ping Pong Parlour. 'Will you dine with me here,' asked Sir Jocelyn, 'as it's my last evening?'

'Your last evening?'

'Yes, I've been called away. Public interest in Ishmaelia is beginning to wane.'

'But nothing has happened yet.'

'Exactly. There was only one story for a special–my interview with the Fascist leader. Of course, it's different with the Americans–fellows like Jakes. They have a different sense of news from us–personal stuff, you know. The job of an English special is to spot the story he wants, get it–then clear out and leave the rest to the agencies. The war will be ordinary routine reporting. Fleet Street have spent a lot on this already. They'll have to find something to justify it and then they'll draw in their horns. You take it from me. As soon as they get anything that smells like front page, they'll start calling back their men. Personally I'm glad to have got my work over quick. I never did like the place.'

They dined at Popotakis's and went to the station to see Hitchcock off. He had secured the single sleeping car which was reserved for official visitors and left in great good humour. 'Good-bye, Boot, remember me to them at the *Beast*. I wonder how they are feeling now about having missed that Laku story?'

The train left, and William found himself the only special correspondent in Jacksonburg.

3/iii

He and Kätchen drove back. Kätchen said: 'Frau Dressler was very angry again this afternoon.'

'Beast.'

'William, you *do* like me.'

'I love you. I've told you so all day.'

'No, you must not say that. My husband would not allow it. I mean, as a friend.'

'No, not as a friend.'

'Oh, dear, you make me so sad.'

'You're crying.'

'No.'

'You are.'

'Yes. I am so sad you are not my friend. Now I cannot ask you what I wanted.'

'What?'

'No, I cannot ask you. You do not love me as a friend. I was so lonely, and when you came I thought everything was going to be happy. But now it is spoiled. It is so easy for you to think here is a foreign girl and her husband is away. No one will mind what happens to her . . . No, you are not to touch me. I hate you.'

William sat back silently in his corner.

'William.'

'Yes.'

'He is not going to the Pension Dressler. It is to the Swede again.'

'I don't care.'

'But I am so tired.'

'So am I.'

'Tell him to go to the Pension Dressler.'

'I told him. It's no good.'

'Very well, If you wish to be a beast . . .'

The Swede was still up, mending with patient, clumsy hands the torn backs of his hymn books. He put down the paste and scissors and came out to direct the taxi driver.

'It was not true what Sir Hitchock said. There are no gorillas in this country. He cannot have seen six. Why does he say that?' His broad forehead was lined and his eyes wide with distress and bewilderment. 'Why did he say that, Boot?'

'Perhaps he was joking.'

'Joking? I never thought of that. Of course, it was a joke. Ha, ha, ha. I am so glad. Now I understand. A joke.' He returned to his lighted study, laughing with relief and amusement. As he settled himself to work once more, he hummed a tune. One by one the tattered books were set in order, restored and fortified, and the Swede chuckled over Sir Jocelyn's joke.

William and Kätchen drove home in complete silence. The night-watchman flung open the gates and raised his spear in salute. While William was wrangling with the taxi driver, Kätchen slipped away to her own room. William undressed and lay among his heaps of luggage. His anger softened and turned to shame, then to a light melancholy; soon he fell asleep.

3/iv

There was one large table in the Pension dining-room. Kätchen was sitting at its head, alone; she had pushed the plate away and put her coffee in its place between her bare elbows; she crouched over it, holding the cup in both hands; the saucer was full and drops of coffee formed on the bottom of the cup and splashed like tears. She did not answer when William wished her good morning. He went to the door and called across to the kitchen for his breakfast. It was five minutes in coming, but still she did not speak or leave the table. Frau Dressler bustled through, on the way to her room, and returned laden with folded sheets. She spoke to Kätchen gruffly in German. Kätchen nodded. The cup dripped on the tablecloth. She put her hand down to hide the spot, but Frau Dressler saw it and spoke again. Kätchen began to cry; she did not raise her head and the tears fell, some in the cup, some in the saucer, some on the tablecloth.

William said, 'Kätchen . . . Kätchen, darling, what's the matter?'

'I have no handkerchief.'

He gave her his. 'What did Frau Dressler say?'

'She was angry because I have made the tablecloth dirty. She said why did I not help with the washing?' She dabbed her face and the tablecloth with William's handkerchief.

'I am afraid I was very disagreeable last night.'

'Yes, why were you like that? It had been so nice until then. Perhaps it was the Pernod. Why were you like that, William?'

'Because I love you.'

'I have told you you are not to say that. . . . My husband has been away for six weeks. When he left he said he would return in a month or at the most six weeks. It is six weeks this morning. I am very worried what may have become of him . . . I have been with him for two years now.'

'Kätchen, there's something I must ask you. Don't be angry. It's very important to me. Is he really your husband?'

'But of course he is. It is just that he has gone away for his work.'

'I mean, were you married to him properly in church?'

'No, not in church.'

'At a government office, then?'

'No. You see, it was not possible because of his other wife in Germany.'

'He has another wife, then?'

'Yes, in Germany, but he hates her. I am his *real* wife.'

'Does Frau Dressler know about the other wife?'

'Yes, that is why she treats me so impolitely. The German consul told her after my husband had gone away. There was a question of my papers. They would not register me at the German consulate.'

'But you are German?'

'My husband is German, so I am German, but there is a difficulty with my papers. My father is Russian and I was born in Budapest.'

'Is you mother German?'

'Polish.'

'Where is your father now?'

'I think he went to South America to look for my mother after she went away. But why do you ask me so many questions when I am unhappy? You are worse than Frau Dressler. It is not your tablecloth. You do not have to pay if it is dirty.'

She left William alone at the breakfast table.

3/V

Twelve miles out of town Corker and Pigge were also at breakfast.

'I never slept once,' said Corker. 'Not a wink, the whole night. Did you hear the lions?'

'Hyenas,' said Pigge.

'Hyenas laugh. These were lions or wolves. Almost in the tents.' They sat beside their lorry drinking soda water and eating sardines from a tin. The cook and the cook's boy, the driver and the driver's boy. Corker's boy and Pigge's boy, were all heavily asleep in the lorry under a pile of blankets and tarpaulin.

'Six black bloody servants and no breakfast,' said Corker bitterly.

'They were up all night making whoopee round the fire. Did you hear them?'

'Of course I heard them. Singing and clapping. I believe they'd got hold of our whisky. I shouted to them to shut up, and they said, "Must have fire. Many bad animals."'

'Yes, hyenas.'

'Lions.'

'We've got to get the lorry out of the mud, somehow. I suppose the rest of the bunch are half-way to Laku by now.'

'I didn't think it of them,' said Corker, bitterly. 'Going past us like that without a bloody word. Shumble I can understand, but Whelper and the Excelsior Movie-News bunch. . . . With that great lorry of theirs they could have towed us out in five minutes. What have *they* got to be competitive about? . . . and those two photographers I gave up half my room to at the hotel–just taking a couple of shots of us and then driving off. Two white men, alone, in a savage country . . . it makes one despair of human nature . . .'

The preceding day had been one of bitter experience.

Within a quarter of a mile of the city the metalled strip had come to an end and the road became a mud-track. For four hours the lorry had crawled along at walking pace, lurching, sticking, and skidding; they had forged through a swollen stream which washed the under-carriage; they had been thrown from side to side of the cab; the binding of the stores had broken and Pigge's typewriter had fallen into the mud behind them to be retrieved, hopelessly injured, by the grinning cook's boy. It had been an abominable journey.

Presently the track had lost all semblance of unity and split into a dozen diverging and converging camel paths, winding at the caprice of the beasts who had made them, among thorn and rock and anthills in a colourless, muddy plain. Here, without warning, the back wheels had sunk to their axles, and here the lorry had stayed while the caravan it had led disappeared from view. Tents had been pitched and the fire lighted. The cook, opening some tins at random, had made them a stew of apricots and curry powder and turtle soup and tunny fish, which in the final analysis had tasted predominantly of benzine.

In bitter cold they had sat at the tent door, while Pigge tried vainly to repair his typewriter, and Corker, struck with nostalgia, composed a letter to his wife;

at eight they had retired to their sleeping-bags and lain through the long night while their servants caroused outside.

Corker surveyed the barren landscape and the gathering storm clouds, the mud-bound lorry, the heap of crapulous black servants, the pasty and hopeless face of Pigge, the glass of soda-water and the jagged tin of fish. 'It makes one despair of human nature,' he said again.

3/vi

It was some days since William had seen Bannister, so he drove out that morning to the Consulate. There was the usual cluster of disconsolate Indians round the door. Bannister sent them away, locked the office and took William across the garden to his house for a drink.

'Looking for news?' he asked. 'Well, the Minister's got a tea-party on Thursday. D'you want to come?'

'Yes.'

'I'll get them to bung you a card. It's the worst day of the year for us. Everyone in the place comes who's got a clean collar. It's the public holiday in honour of the end of the rainy season and it always pours.'

'D'you think you could ask a German girl at my boarding-house? She's rather lonely.'

'Well, frankly, Lady G. isn't very keen on lonely German girls. But I'll see. Is that why you didn't go off on that wild goose chase to Laku? You're wise. I shouldn't be at all surprised if there weren't some rather sensational happenings here in a day or two.'

'The war?'

'No, there's nothing in that. But things are looking queer in the town. I can't tell you more, but if you want a hint look out for that Russian I told you about and watch your friend Doctor Benito. What's the girl's name?'

'Well, I'm not sure about her surname. There's some difficulty about her papers.'

'Doesn't sound at all Lady G.'s cup of tea. Is she pretty?'

'Lovely.'

'Then I think you can count her off the Legation list. Paleologue's been trying to interest me in a lovely German girl for weeks. I expect it's her. Bring her along to dinner here one evening.'

Kächen was delighted with the invitation. 'But we must buy a dress,' she said. 'There is an Armenian lady who has a very pretty one–bright green. She has never worn it because she bought it by mail and she has grown too fat. She asked fifty American dollars. I think if she were paid at once it would be cheaper.' She had become cheerful again. 'Wait,' she said, 'I have something to show you.'

She ran to her room and returned with a sodden square of bandana silk. 'Look, I *have* been doing some washing after all. It is your handkerchief. I do not need it now. I have stopped crying for today. We will go and play ping-pong and then see the Armenian lady's green dress.'

After luncheon Bannister telephoned. 'We've had a cable about you from London.'

'Good God, why?'

'*The Beast* have been worrying the F.O. Apparently they think you've been murdered. Why don't you send them some news?'

'I don't know any.'

'Well, for heaven's sake invent some. The Minister will go crazy if he has any more bother with the newspapers. We get about six telegrams a day from the coast. Apparently there's a bunch of journalists there trying to get up and the Ishmaelite frontier authorities won't let them through. Two of them are British, unfortunately. And now the Liberals are asking questions in the House of Commons and are worrying his life out as it is about some infernal nonsense of a concentration of Fascist troops at Laku.'

William returned to his room and sat for a long time before his typewriter. It was over a week now since he had communicated with his employers, and his failure weighed heavily on him. He surveyed the events of the day, of all the last days. What would Corker have done?

Finally, with one finger, he typed a message. PLEASE DONT WORRY QUITE SAFE AND WELL IN FACT RATHER ENJOYING THINGS WEATHER IMPROVING WILL CABLE AGAIN IF THERE IS ANY NEWS YOURS BOOT.

3/vii

It was late afternoon in London; at Copper House secretaries were carrying cups of tea to the more leisured departments; in Mr Salter's office there was tension and consternation.

'*Weather improving*,' said Mr Salter. '*Weather improving*. He's been in Jacksonburg ten days, and all he can tell us is that the weather is improving.'

'I've got to write a first leader on the Ishmaelite question,' said the first leader-writer. 'Lord Copper says so. I've got to wring the withers of the Government. What do I know about it? What have I got to go on? What are special correspondents for? Why don't you cable this Boot and wake him up?'

'How many times have we cabled Boot?' asked the foreign editor.

'Daily for the first three days, Mr Salter,' said his secretary. 'Then twice a day. Three times yesterday.'

'You see.'

'And in the last message we mentioned *Lord Copper's name*,' added the secretary.

'I never felt Boot was really suited to the job,' said Mr Salter mildly. 'I was very much surprised when he was chosen. But he's all we've got. It would take three weeks to get another man out there, and by that time anything may have happened.'

'Yes, the weather may have got still better,' said the first leader-writer, bitterly. He gazed out of the window; it opened on a tiled, resonant well; he gazed at a dozen drain pipes; he gazed straight into the office opposite where the Art Editor was having tea; he gazed up to the little patch of sky and down to the concrete depths where a mechanic was washing his neck at a cold tap: he gazed with eyes of despair.

'I have to denounce the vacillation of the government in the strongest terms,' he said. 'They fiddle while Ishmaelia burns. A spark is set to the corner-stone of civilization which will shake its roots like a chilling breath. That's what I've got to say, and all I know is that Boot is safe and well and that the weather is improving . . .'

3/viii

Kätchen and William dropped into the Liberty for an apéritif.

It was the first time he had been there since his change of residence.

'Do either of you happen to know a gentleman by the name of Boot?' asked Mrs Jackson.

'Yes, it's me.'

'Well, there's some cables for you somewhere.'

They were found and delivered. William opened them one by one. They all dealt with the same topic.

BADLY LEFT ALL PAPERS ALL STORIES.

IMPERATIVE RECEIVE FULL STORY TONIGHT SIX YOUR TIME WHY NO NEWS ARE YOU ILL FLASH REPLY.

YOUR CABLES UNARRIVED FEAR SUBVERSIVE INTERFERENCE SERVICE ACKNOWLEDGE RECEIPT OUTS IMMEDIATELY.

There were a dozen of them in all; the earliest of the series were modestly signed SALTER; as the tone strengthened his name gave place to MONTGOMERY MOWBRAY GENERAL EDITOR BEAST, then to ELSENGRATZ MANAGING DIRECTOR MEGALOPOLITAN NEWSPAPERS. The last, which had arrived that morning, read: CONFIDENTIAL AND URGENT STOP LORD COPPER HIMSELF GRAVELY DISSATISFIED STOP LORD COPPER PERSONALLY REQUIRES VICTORIES STOP ON RECEIPT OF THIS CABLE VICTORY STOP CONTINUE CABLING VICTORIES UNTIL FURTHER NOTICE STOP LORD COPPERS CONFIDENTIAL SECRETARY.

'What are they all about?' asked Kätchen.

'They don't seem very pleased with me in London. They seem to want more news.'

'How silly. Are you upset?'

'No . . . Well, yes, a little.'

'Poor William. I will get you some news. Listen. I have a plan. I have lived in this town for two months. I have many friends. That is to say, I *had* them before my husband went away. They will be my friends again now that they know you are helping me. It will be a good thing for both of us. Listen–all the journalists who were here had men in the town they paid to give them news. Mr Jakes the American pays Paleologue fifty dollars a week. You like me more than Mr Jakes likes Paleologue?'

'Much more.'

'Twice as much?'

'Yes.'

'Then you will pay me a hundred dollars a week and Frau Dressler will not be angry with me any more, so it will be a good thing for all of us. Will you think it very greedy if I ask for a hundred dollars now; you know how impolite Frau Dressler is–well, perhaps two hundred, because I shall work for you more than one week?'

'Very well,' said William.

'Look, I brought your cheque book for you from your room in case you might need it. What a good secretary I should be.'

'Do you really think you can get some news?'

'Why, yes, of course. For instance, I am very friendly with an Austrian man–it is his wife who made me this dress–and his sister is governess to the President's children, so they know everything that goes on. I will visit them tomorrow . . . only,' she added doubtfully, 'I don't think it would be polite to go to her house and not buy anything. You are paid expenses by your paper?'

'Yes.'

'For everything? The canoe and for this vermouth and all the things in your room?'

'Yes.'

'Then I will be paid expenses too . . . the Austrian has some nightgowns she made for a lady at the French legation, only the lady's husband did not like them, so they are *very* cheap. There are four of them in crêpe-de-Chine. She would sell them for sixty American dollars. Shall I get them?'

'You don't think she would give you news if you did not?'

'It would be impolite to ask.'

'Very well.'

'And the man who cut my hair–he shaves the Minister of the Interior. He would know a great deal. Only I cannot have my hair washed again so soon. Shall I buy some scent from him? And I should like a rug for my room; the floor is cold and has splinters; the Russian who sells fur is the lover of one of the Miss Jacksons. Oh, William, what fun we shall have working together.'

'But, Kätchen, you know, this isn't my money. You know that if I was rich, I should give you everything you wanted, but I can't go spending the paper's money . . .'

'Silly William, it is because it is the paper's money that I can take it. You know I could not take *yours*. My husband would not let me take money from a *man*, but from a *newspaper* . . . I think that Mr Gentakian knows a great deal of news, too–you know his shop opposite the Ping-Pong? . . . Oh, William, I feel so happy tonight. Let us not go back to dine at the Pension where Frau Dressler disapproves. Let us dine again at the Ping-Pong. We can buy some tinned caviare at Benakis, and Popotakis will make us some toast . . .'

After dinner Kätchen became grave. 'I was so happy just now,' she said. 'But now I am thinking, what is to become of me? A few weeks and you will go away. I have waited so long for my husband; perhaps he will not come.'

'Do you think you could bear to live in England?'

'I have lived in England. That is where I learned to speak. It was when I was sixteen, after my father went to South America; I worked in a dance hall.'

'Where?'

'I don't know. It was by the sea. I met my husband there; he was so pleased to find someone who would talk German with him. How he talked . . . Now you have made me think of him and I am ashamed to be drinking champagne when perhaps he is in trouble.'

'Kätchen, how long must you wait for him?'

'I don't know.' She unwrapped the speckled foil from the bottle of champagne. 'He is not a good husband to me,' she admitted, 'to go away for so long.' She held the foil to her face and carefully modelled it round her nose.

'Dear Kätchen, will you marry me?'

She held the false nose up to William's.

'Too long,' she said.

'Too long to wait?'

'Two long for your nose.'

'Damn!' said William.

'Now you are upset.'

'Won't you ever be serious?'

'Oh, I have been serious too much, too often.' Then she added hopefully, 'I might go with you now, and then when he comes back I will go with him. Will that do?'

'I want you to come to England with me. How long must I wait?'

'Do not spoil the evening with questions. We will play ping pong.'

That night when they reached the Pension Dressler they walked through the yard arm in arm; the livestock were asleep, and overhead the sky was clear and brilliant with stars.

'How long must I wait? How long?'

'Not long. Soon. When you like,' said Kätchen, and ran to her loft.

The three-legged dog awoke, and all over the town, in yards and refuse heaps, the pariahs took up his cries of protest

4/i

Next morning William awoke in a new world.

As he stood on the veranda calling for his boy, he slowly became aware of the transformation which had taken place overnight. The rains were over. The boards were warm under his feet; below the steps the dank weeds of Frau Dressler's garden had suddenly burst into crimson flower; a tropic sun blazed in the sky, low at present but with promise of a fiery noon, while beyond the tin roofs of the city, where before had hung a blank screen of slaty cloud, was now disclosed a vast landscape, mile upon mile of sunlit highland, rolling green pastures, dun and rosy terraces, villas and farms and hamlets, gardens and crops and tiny stockaded shrines; crest upon crest receding to the blue peaks of the remote horizon. William called for his boy and called in vain.

'He is gone,' said Frau Dressler, crossing the yard with a load of earthenware. 'All the boys have gone today. They are making holiday for the end of the rains. Some German friends have come to help me.'

And William's breakfast was eventually brought him by a destitute mechanic who owed Frau Dressler for his share of the last Christmas tree.

4/ii

It was an eventful day.

At nine Erik Olafsen came to say good-bye. There was an outbreak of plague down the line and he was off to organize a hospital. He went without enthusiasm.

'It is stupid work,' he said. 'I have been in a plague hospital before. How many do you think we cured?'

'I've no idea.'

'None at all. We could only catch the patients who were too ill to move. The others ran away to the villages, so more and more people got it. In the civilized colonies they send soldiers, not doctors. They make a ring all round the place where there is plague and shoot anyone who tries to get out. Then in a few days when everyone is dead they burn the huts. But here one can do nothing for the poor people. Well, the Government have asked me to go, so I leave now. Where is Kätchen?'

'She's out shopping.'

'Good. That is very good. She was sad with such old, dirty clothes. I am very glad she has become your friend. You will say good-bye to her?'

At ten she returned laden with packages. 'Darling,' she said, 'I have been so happy. Everyone is excited that the summer is come and they are all so kind and polite now they know I have a friend. Look at what I have brought.'

'Lovely. Did you get any news?'

'It was difficult. I had so much to say about the things I was buying that I did not talk politics. Except to the Austrian. The President's governess had tea with the Austrian yesterday, but I am afraid you will be disappointed. She has not seen the President for four days. You see, he is locked up.'

'Locked up?'

'Yes, they have shut him in his bedroom. They often do that when there are important papers for him to sign. But the governess is unhappy about it. You see, it is generally his family who lock him up and then it is only for a few hours. This time it is Doctor Benito and the Russian and the two black secretaries who came from America; they locked him up three days ago, and when his relatives try to see him they say he is drunk. They would not let him go to the opening of Jackson College. The governess says something is wrong.'

'Do you think I ought to report that to the *Beast*?'

'I wonder,' said Kätchen doubtfully. 'It is such a lovely morning. We ought to go out.'

'I believe Corker would make something of it . . . the editor seems very anxious for news.'

'Very well. Only be quick. I want to go for a drive.'

She left William to his work.

He sat at the table, stood up, sat down again, stared gloomily at the wall for some minutes, lit his pipe, and then, laboriously, with a single first finger and his heart heavy with misgiving, he typed the first news story of his meteoric career. No one observing that sluggish and hesitant composition could have guessed that this was a moment of history–of legend, to be handed down among the great traditions of his trade, told and retold over the milk-bars of Fleet Street, quoted in books of reminiscence, held up as a model to aspiring pupils of Correspondence Schools of Profitable Writing, perennially fresh in the jaded memories of a hundred editors; the moment when Boot began to make good.

PRESS COLLECT BEAST LONDON he wrote.

NOTHING MUCH HAS HAPPENED EXCEPT TO THE PRESIDENT WHO HAS BEEN IMPRISONED IN HIS OWN PALACE BY REVOLUTIONARY JUNTA HEADED BY SUPERIOR BLACK CALLED BENITO AND RUSSIAN JEW WHO BANNISTER SAYS IS UP TO NO GOOD THEY SAY HE IS DRUNK WHEN HIS CHILDREN TRY TO SEE HIM BUT GOVERNESS SAYS MOST UNUSUAL LOVELY SPRING WEATHER BUBONIC PLAGUE RAGING.

He got so far when he was interrupted.

Frau Dressler brought him a cable: YOUR CONTRACT TERMINATED STOP ACCEPT THIS STIPULATED MONTHS NOTICE AND ACKNOWLEDGE STOP BEAST.

William added to his message, SACK RECEIVED SAFELY THOUGHT I MIGHT AS WELL SEND THIS ALL THE SAME.

Kätchen's head appeared at the window.

'Finished?'

'Yes.'

He rolled the cable he had received into a ball and threw it into the corner of the room. The yard was bathed in sunshine. Kätchen wanted a drive. It was not a good time to tell her of his recall.

4/iii

Twelve miles out of the town the coming of summer brought no joy to Corker and Pigge.

'Look at the flowers,' said Pigge.

'Yes. Like a bloody cemetery,' said Corker.

The lorry stood where it had sunk, buried in mud to the axles. On all sides lay evidence of the unavailing efforts of yesterday–stones painfully collected from a neighbouring water-course and bedded round the back wheels; bruised and muddy boughs dragged in the rain from the sparse woods a mile or more distant; the great boulder which they had rolled, it seemed, from the horizon to make a base for the jack–vainly; the heaps thrown up behind as the wheels, like a dog in a rabbit-hole, spun and burrowed. Listlessly helped by their boys, Pigge and Corker had worked all day, their faces blackened by exhaust smoke, their hands cut, soaked with rain, weary of limb, uncontrollable in temper.

It was a morning of ethereal splendour–such a morning as Noah knew as he gazed from his pitchy bulwarks over limitless, sunlit waters while the dove circled and mounted and became lost in the shining heavens; such a morning as only the angels saw on the first day of that rash cosmic experiment that had resulted, at the moment, in landing Corker and Pigge here in the mud, stiff and unshaven and disconsolate.

The earth-bound journalists turned hopelessly to the four quarters of the land.

'You can see for miles,' said Pigge.

'Yes,' said Corker bitterly, 'and not a bloody human being in sight.'

Their boys were dancing to celebrate the new season, clapping and shuffling and shouting a low, rhythmical song of praise. 'What the hell have they got to be cheerful about?'

'They've been at the whisky again,' said Corker.

4/iv

That afternoon there was the party at the British legation. Kätchen had not got her card, so William went alone. It did not rain. Nothing marred the summer serenity of the afternoon. Guests of all colours and nationalities paraded the gravel walks, occasionally pausing behind the flowering shrubs to blow their noses–delicately between forefinger and thumb–as though trumpeting against the defeated devils of winter.

'The President usually comes,' said Bannister, 'but he doesn't seem to be here today. Odd thing, but there isn't a single Jackson in sight. I wonder what's become of them all.'

'I don't know about the others, but the President is locked in his bedroom.'

'Good Lord, is he? I say, you'd better talk to the old man about this. I'll try and get hold of him.'

The Minister was regarding the scene with an expression of alarm and despair; he stood on the top step of the terrace, half in, half out of the french windows, in a position dimly remembered from the hide-and-seek of his childhood as strategically advantageous; it afforded a general survey of the dispositions of the attacking forces and offered alternative lines of retreat, indoors or through the rose garden.

Bannister introduced William.

The Minister gave the Vice-Consul a glance of mild reproach and smiled bleakly, the wry smile of one heroically resisting an emotion of almost overwhelming repulsion.

'So glad you could come,' he said. 'Being looked after all right? Good, excellent.'

He peered over his shoulder into the shady refuge of his study. As he did so the door opened and three obese Indians waddled into the room; each wore a little gold skull cap, a long white shirt, and a short black coat, each carried a strawberry ice. 'How did they get in?' he asked petulantly. 'They've no business there at all. Get them out. Get them out.'

Bannister hurried to head them off and the Minister was left along with William.

'You are from the *Beast*?'

'Yes.'

'Can't say I read it myself. Don't like its politics. Don't like any politics . . . Finding Ishmaelia interesting?'

'Yes, very interesting.'

'Are you? Wish I was. But, then, you've got a more interesting job. Better paid, too, I expect. I wonder, how does one get a job like that? Pretty difficult, I suppose, stiff examination, eh?'

'No, no examination.'

'No examination? My word, that's interesting. I must tell my wife. Didn't know you could get any jobs nowadays without examinations. Wretched system, ruining all the services. I've got a boy in England now, lazy fellow, can't pass any examinations, don't know what to do with him. D'you suppose they'd give him a job on your paper?'

'I expect so. It seemed quite easy to me.'

'I say, that's splendid. Must tell my wife. Here she is. My dear, Mr Boot here says he will give Archie a job on his paper.'

'I'm afraid *I* can't be much help. I got the sack this morning.'

'Did you? Did you really? Pity. Then you can't be any help to Archie.'

'No, I'm afraid not.'

'My dear,' said the Minister's wife, 'I'm very sorry indeed, but I've got to introduce a new missionary you haven't met.'

She led him away and presented a blinking giant of a young man; the Minister nodded absently to William as he left him.

Doctor Benito was at the party, very near, very affable, very self-possessed, smiling wickedly on all sides. He approached William.

'Mr Boot,' he said, 'you must be very lonely without your colleagues.'

'No, I much prefer it.'

'And it is dull for you,' Doctor Benito insisted, in the level patient tones of a mesmerist, 'very dull, with so little happening in the town. So I have arranged a little divertissement for you.'

'It is very kind, but I am greatly diverted here.'

'You are too kind to our simple little city. But I think I can promise you something better. Now that the summer has come there will be no difficulty. You shall have a little tour of our country and see some of its beauties–the forest of Popo, for instance, and the great waterfall at Chip.'

'It's very kind of you . . . some other time, perhaps.'

'No, no, at once. It is all arranged. I have a motor car. I cannot, alas, go with you myself, but I will send a charming young man–very cultured, a university graduate–who will be able to explain everything as well as I can. You will find my country people very hospitable. I have arranged for you to spend tonight just outside the city at the villa of the postmaster-general. Then you will be able to start early in the morning for the mountains. You will see much more than any of your colleagues, who, I hear, are not being fortunate in their trip to Laku. Perhaps you will be able to do a little lion shooting.'

'Thank you very much indeed, Doctor Benito, but I don't want to leave Jacksonburg at the moment.'

'There will be room for any companion you care to take.'

'No, thank you.'

'And you will, of course, be the guest of the Government.'

'It's not that.'

'You will see most interesting native dances, curious customs,' he smiled more horribly than before, 'some of the tribes are most primitive and interesting.'

'I'm very sorry, I can't go.'

'But it is all arranged.'

'I'm very sorry. You should have consulted me before you took so much trouble.'

'My government would not like you to lose financially by their hospitality. I quite see that you would not be able to do your work fully during your absence, but any reasonable recompense . . .'

'Look here, Doctor Benito,' said William. 'You're being a bore. I'm not going.'

Doctor Benito suddenly stopped smiling. 'Everyone will be very disappointed,' he said.

William told Bannister what had been said.

'Yes, they want to get you out of the way. They don't want any journalists here when the fun starts. They even took the trouble to shift Olafsen. They told him there was cholera down the line.'

'Plague.'

'Some lie, anyway. I'm in communication with our agent there by telephone. Everyone's as fit as a flea.'

'Perhaps if he knew I'd got the sack he wouldn't bother so much.'

'He wouldn't believe it. He must have seen your cable; all the foreign cables go to his office before they're delivered. He thinks it a trick. That's the disadvantage of being clever in Benito's way.'

'You seem to know most things that go on in this town.'

'It's a hobby. Must do something. If I stuck to my job I should spend the day answering commercial questionnaires. Did you get anything interesting out of the Minister?'

'No.'

'He sticks to his job.'

4/V

As William drove back from the Legation he pondered over the question of when and in what terms he should break the news of his recall to Kätchen.

He need not have worried.

In the first place he found a cable awaiting him, CONGRATULATIONS STORY CONTRACT UNTERMINATED UPFOLLOW FULLEST SPEEDILIEST.

In the second place Kätchen was no longer at the Pension Dressler; a posse of soldiers had come for her that afternoon and taken her away in a closed motor car.

'I suppose it is because of her papers,' said Frau Dressler. 'She telephoned to the German Consulate, but they would not help her. She should not have been upset. When they put white people in prison here they are well looked after. She will be as comfortable,' she added with unprofessional candour, 'as she was here. There is one of the secret police waiting to see you. I would not let him into your room. He is in the dining-room.'

William found a natty young Negro smoking from a long cigarette holder. 'Good evening,' he said. 'I have come from Doctor Benito to take you for a little tour in the mountains.'

'I told Doctor Benito I could not go.'

'He hoped you would change your mind.'

'Why have you arrested Miss Kätchen?'

'It is a temporary measure, Mr Boot. She is being very well looked after. She is at the villa of the postmaster-general, just outside the town. She asked me to collect some luggage for her–a parcel of geological specimens that were left in your room.'

'They are my property.'

'So I understand. You paid a hundred American dollars for them, I think. Here is the money.'

William was by nature a man of mild temper; on the rare occasions when he gave way to rage the symptoms were abundantly evident. The Negro stood up, removed the cigarette end from its holder and added, 'Perhaps I should tell you that when I was at the Adventist University of Alabama I was welter-weight champion of my year . . . May I repeat my offer? Doctor Benito wishes very much to examine these specimens; they are the property of the Government, for they were collected by a foreigner who came here without the formality of obtaining a prospecting licence from the Ministry of Mines–a foreigner who unfortunately is at the moment protected by the capitulations–at the moment only. Arrangements are being made about him. Since you bought these specimens under a misapprehension the Government decided very generously to make an offer of reimbursement—'

'Get out! said William.

'Very well. You will hear of this matter again.'

He rose with dignity and swaggered into the yard.

The milch-goat looked up from her supper of waste paper; her perennial optimism quickened within her, and swelled to a great and mature confidence; all day she had shared the exhilaration of the season, her pelt had glowed under the newborn sun; deep in her heart she too had made holiday, had cast off the doubts of winter and exulted among the crimson flowers; all day she had dreamed gloriously; now in the limpid evening she gathered her strength, stood for a moment rigid, quivering from horn to tail; then charged, splendidly, irresistibly, triumphantly; the rope snapped and the welter-weight champion of the Adventist University of Alabama sprawled on his face amid the kitchen garbage.

4/vi

The events of that day were not yet ended.

As soon as the black had gone, limping and dishevelled, and the goat, sated and peaceably disposed to retrospection, recaptured and secured, William drove back to the British Consulate with his bag of minerals.

'The party's over,' said Bannister. 'We all want a rest.'

'I've brought some luggage for you to keep an eye on.'

He explained the circumstances.

'If you knew the amount of work you were causing,' said Bannister, 'you wouldn't do this. From tomorrow onwards for the next six years I shall get a daily pile of bumf from the Ministry of Mines and in the end the Mixed Court will decide against you–God damn all capitulations. What's in the sack, anyway?'

He opened it and examined the stones. 'Yes,' he said, 'just what I expected–gold ore. The mountains in the West are stiff with it. We knew it was bound to cause international trouble sooner or later. There have been two companies after a mineral concession–German and Russian. So far as the Jacksons have any political principles it has been to make the country unprofitable for foreign investment. The President kept his end up pretty well–played one company off against the other for months. Then the Smiles trouble started. We are pretty certain that the Germans were behind it. The Russians have been harder to follow–we only learned a day or two ago that they had bought Benito and the Young Ishmaelite party. It's between Smiles and Benito now and it looks to me as if Benito had won hands down. I'm sorry–the Jacksons were a pack of rogues, but they suited the country and they suited H.M.G. We stand to lose quite a lot if they start a Soviet state here . . . Now you've stopped being a journalist I can tell you these things.'

'As a matter of fact I've just become a journalist again. D'you mind if I cable this to the *Beast*?'

'Well, don't let on that you got it from me . . . as a matter of fact a newspaper campaign at the moment might just do the trick.'

'There's another thing. Can you help me get a girl friend out of jug?'

'Certainly not,' said Bannister. 'I'm a keen supporter of the local prison system; it's the one thing that keeps the British Protected Persons off my doorstep. Its only weakness is you can buy yourself out when you want to for a fiver.'

4/vii

When it was dinner-time in Jacksonburg, it was tea-time in London.

'Nothing more from Boot,' said Mr Salter.

'Well, make up the Irish edition with his morning cable–rewrite it and splash it. If the follow-up comes in before six in the morning, run a special.'

4/viii

William returned home with a mission; he was going to do down Benito. Dimly at first, then in vivid detail, he foresaw a spectacular, cinematographic consummation, when his country should rise chivalrously to arms; Bengal Lancers and kilted highlanders invested the heights of Jacksonburg; he at their head burst open the prison doors; with his own hands he grappled with Benito, shook him like a kitten and threw him choking out of his path; Kätchen fluttered towards him like a wounded bird and he bore her in triumph to Boot Magna . . . Love, patriotism, zeal for justice, and personal spite flamed within him as he sat at his typewriter and began his message. One finger was not enough; he used both hands. The keys rose together like bristles on a porcupine, jammed and were extricated; curious anagrams appeared on the paper before him; vulgar fractions and marks of punctuation mingled with the letters. Still he typed.

The wireless station closed at nine; at five minutes to William pushed his sheaf of papers over the counter.

'Sending tomorrow,' said the clerk.

'Must send tonight; urgent,' said William.

'No tonight. Summer holiday tonight.'

William added a handful of banknotes to the typewritten sheets. 'Sending tonight,' he said.

'All right.'

Then William went round to dinner alone at Popotakis's.

4/ix

'Two thousand words from Boot,' said Mr Salter.

'Any good?' asked the general editor.

'Look at it.'

The general editor looked. He saw '*Russian plot . . . coup d'état . . . overthrow constitutional government . . . red dictatorship . . . goat butts head of police . . . imprisoned blonde . . . vital British interest jeopardized.*' It was enough; it was news. 'It's news,' he said. 'Stop the machines at Manchester and Glasgow. Clear the line to Belfast and Paris. Scrap the whole front page. Kill the Ex-Beauty Queen's pauper funeral. Get in a photograph of Boot.'

'I don't suppose we've got a photograph of Boot in the office.'

'Ring up his relatives. Find his best girl. There must be a photograph of him somewhere in the world.'

'They took one for his passport,' said Mr Salter doubtfully, 'but I remember thinking at the time it was an extremely poor likeness.'

'I don't care if it looks like a baboon—'

'That's just how it does look.'

'Give it two columns' depth. This is the first front page foreign news we've had for a month.'

When the final edition had left the machines, carrying William's sensational message into two million apathetic homes, Mr Salter left the office.

His wife was still up when he got home.

'I've made your Ovaltine,' she said. 'Has it been a bad day?'

'Terrible.'

'You didn't have to dine with Lord Copper.'

'No, not as bad as that. But we had to remake the whole paper after it had gone to bed. That fellow Boot.'

'The one who upset you so all last week. I thought you were sacking him.'

'We did. Then we took him back. He's all right. Lord Copper knew best.'

Mr Salter took off his boots and Mrs Salter poured out the Ovaltine. When he had drunk it, he felt calmer.

'You know,' he said meditatively, 'it's a great experience to work for a man like Lord Copper. Again and again I've thought he was losing grip. But always it turns out he knew best. What made him spot Boot? It's a sixth sense . . . real genius.'

4/X

Popotakis's was empty and William was tired. He ate his dinner and strolled home. When he reached his room he found it filled with tobacco smoke; a cheroot, one of his cheroots, glowed in the darkness. A voice, with a strong German accent, said, 'Close the shutters, please, before you turn on the light.'

William did as he was asked. A man rose from the armchair, clicked his heels and made a guttural sound. He was a large blond man of military but somewhat dilapidated appearance. He wore khaki shorts and an open shirt, boots ragged and splashed with mud. His head, once shaven, was covered with stubble, uniform with his chin, like a clipped yew in a neglected garden.

'I beg your pardon?' said William.

The man clicked his heels again and made the same throaty sound, adding, 'That is my name.'

'Oh,' said William. Then he came to attention and said 'Boot.'

They shook hands.

'I must apologize for using your room. Once it was mine. I did not know until

I found your luggage here that there had been a change. I left some specimens of ore. Do you by any chance know what has become of them?'

'I have them safe.'

'Well, it is of no importance now . . . I left a wife, too. Have you seen her?'

'She is in prison.'

'Yes,' said the German, without surprise. 'I suppose she is. They will put me in prison too. I have just come from my Consulate. They say they cannot protect me. I cannot complain. They warned me before we started that if I failed they could not protect me . . . and I have failed . . . if you will excuse me, I will sit down. I am very tired.'

'Have you had any dinner?'

'Not for two days. I have just returned from the interior. We could not stop to sleep or to look for food. All the way back they were trying to kill me. They had paid the bandits. I am very tired and very hungry.'

William took a case from the pile of stores; it was corded and wired and lined and battened to resist all emergencies. He struggled for some time while the German sat in a kind of melancholy stupor; then he said, 'There's some food in here if you can get it open.'

'Food.' At the word the German came to his senses. With surprising dexterity he got the blade of his clasp knife under the lid of the box; it fell open revealing William's Christmas dinner.

They spread it on the table–turkey, plum pudding, crystallized plums, almonds, raisins, champagne and crackers. The German cried a little, nostalgically, teutonically. Then he began to gorge, at first in silence, later, with the dessert, loquaciously.

'. . . three times they shot at me on the road–but the bandits have very old rifles. Not like the rifles we gave to Smiles. We gave him everything, machine-guns, tanks, consulates; we bought him two Paris newspapers, a column a day week after week–you know what that costs. There were five thousand volunteers ready to sail. He could have been in Jacksonburg in a month. No one wants the Jacksons here. They are foolish people. For a year we have been trying to make business with them. They said first one thing, then another. We gave them money; we gave them all money; heavens, how many Jacksons there are! Still, they would not make business . . .'

'I ought to warn you that I am a journalist.'

'That is well. When you come to write of this affair say that it was not my fault that we failed. It was Smiles. We gave him money and he ran away to the Sudan. He wanted me to go with him.'

'Wouldn't that have been better?'

'I had left my wife in Jacksonburg . . . besides, it is not good for me to go to the Sudan. I was once in trouble in Khartoum. There are many countries where it is not good for me to go. I have often been very foolish.' At the thought of his wife and of his former indiscretions he seemed once more to be overcome with melancholy. He sat in silence. William began to fear he would fall asleep.

'Where are you going to now?' he asked. 'You can't stay here, you know, or they will come and arrest you.'

'No,' said the German. 'I can't stay here.' And immediately he fell asleep, mouth open, head back, a crumpled cracker in his right hand, breathing uproariously.

And still that day was not ended.

Hardly had the German's preliminary, convulsive snorts and gurgles given place to the gentler, automatic, continuous snoring of regular sleep than William was again disturbed.

The night watchman stood clucking in the doorway, pointing towards the gates, smiling and nodding unintelligibly. The German never stirred; his snores followed William across the yard.

At the gates a motor car was waiting. It's lights had been turned off. The yard and the lane outside it were in darkness. A voice, from inside the car, said, 'William, is it you?' Kätchen scrambled out and ran to him–as he had imagined it, like a wounded bird. 'Darling, darling,' he said.

They clung together. In the darkness he could discern over Kätchen's shoulder the figure of the night watchman, stork-like, on one leg, his spear behind his shoulders.

'Darling,' said Kätchen. 'Have you got any money with you?'

'Yes.'

'A lot?'

'Yes.'

'I promised the driver a hundred American dollars. Was it too much?'

'Who is he?'

'The postmaster-general's chauffeur. They have arrested the postmaster-general. He was a Jackson. All the Jacksons are being arrested. He got the key of the room when the soldiers were having supper. I said I would give him a hundred dollars if he brought me back.'

'Tell him to wait. I'll get the money from my room.'

The driver wrapped himself in his blanket and settled down over the wheel. Kätchen and William stood together in the yard.

'I must go away,' said Kätchen. '*We* must go away. I have thought about it in the motor car. You must marry me. Then I shall be British and they will not be able to hurt me. And we will leave Ishmaelia at once. No more journalism. We will go to Europe together. Will you do that?'

'Yes,' said William without hesitation.

'And will you marry me properly–in an office?'

'Yes.'

'It will be the first time I have been properly married.' The tremendous respirations echoed across the yard. 'What is that? William, there is something making a noise in your room.'

'Yes I had forgotten . . . you made me forget. Come and see who it is.'

They climbed the steps, hand in hand, crossed the veranda and reached the door of William's room.

Kätchen dropped his hand and ran forward with a little cry. She knelt at the German's side and held him, shook him. He stirred and grunted and opened his eyes. They spoke to one another in German; Kätchen nestled against him; he laid his cheek against her head and lapsed again into coma.

'How happy I am,' she said. 'I thought he would never come back, that he was dead or had left me. How he sleeps. Is he well? Is he hungry?'

'No,' said William. 'I don't think you need have any anxiety on that point. Within the last hour, to my certain knowledge, he has consumed an entire Christmas dinner designed for four children or six adults.'

'He must have been starving. Is he not thin?'

'No,' said William. 'Frankly I should not have called him thin.'

'Ah, you should have seen him before he went away . . . How he snores. That is a good sign. Whenever he is well he snores like this.' She brooded fondly over the unconscious figure. 'But he is dirty.'

'Yes,' said William, 'very dirty indeed.'

'William, you sound so cross suddenly. Are you not glad my husband has come back to me?'

'Come back *to you*?'

'William, you are not jealous. How I despise jealousy. You could not be jealous of my husband. I have been with him for two years, before ever you and I met. I knew he would not leave me. But what are we to do now? I must think . . .'

They both thought, not on the same lines.

'I have a plan,' said Kätchen at last.

'Yes?' said William gloomily.

'I think it will work nice. My husband is German, so the Ishmaelites will not be allowed to hurt him. It is harder for me because of my papers. So I will marry you. Then I shall be English and I and my husband can go away together. You will give us our tickets to Europe. It will not be expensive, we will travel in the second class. . . . How is that?'

'There are several serious objections; for one thing the German Legation are not going to protect your friend.'

'Oh, dear. I thought if one had papers one was always safe everywhere . . . I must think of another plan . . . If, after I marry you, I marry my husband, he would then be English, yes?'

'No.'

'Oh, dear.'

They had to speak with raised voices to make themselves heard above the German's snores. 'Would it be very unkind to wake my husband? He is always full of ideas. He has great experience of difficulties.'

She shook him into sensibility and they spoke together earnestly in German.

William began to collect the distasteful remains of the Christmas dinner; he put the crackers back in their box and arranged the empty tins and bottles outside his door beside his dirty shoes.

'Our only hope is the postmaster-general's chauffeur,' said Kätchen at last. 'The town guards know him. If they have not yet heard that the postmaster-general is in prison he can drive through the barricades without difficulty. But he could not get to the frontier. They would telegraph for him to be stopped. The railway is impossible.'

'There is the river,' said the German. 'It is high. We could strike it below the cataract fifteen miles from here. Then we could sail down to French territory–if we had a boat.'

'How much would a boat cost?' asked Kätchen.

'Once in the Matto Grosso I made a boat,' said the German dreamily. 'I burned out the centre of an ironwood tree. It took ten weeks to make, and it sank like a stone.'

'A boat,' said Kätchen. 'But you have a boat–*our* boat.'

4/xi

They drove through the streets of the sleeping city, the German in front with the postmaster-general's chauffeur, Kätchen and William at the back with the canoe. A few hyenas flashed red eyes at them from the rubbish heaps, then turned their mangy quarters and scuttled off into the night.

The guards at the barrier saluted and let them pass into the open country. They drove in silence.

'I will send you a postcard,' said Kätchen, at last, 'to tell you we are well.'

Day was breaking as they reached the river; they came upon it suddenly where it flowed black and swift between low banks. There they assembled the canoe; William and Kätchen did the work, as they had done before; it was familiar; there was no adventure now in fitting the sockets. The German sat on the running-board of the car, still stupefied with the lack of sleep; his eyes were open; his mouth also. When the boat was ready they called to him to join them.

'It is very small,' he said.

William stood knee deep among the reeds holding it with difficulty; the current tugged and sucked, Kätchen climbed in, balancing precariously, with a hand on William's arm; then the German; the boat sank almost to the gunwales.

'We shall not have room for the stores,' said Kätchen.

'My boat in Matto Grosso was twenty feet long,' said the German drowsily, 'it turned over and went straight to the bottom. Two of my boys were drowned. They had always said it would sink.'

'If we get safely to the French border,' said Kätchen, 'shall we leave the boat there for you? Will you want it again?'

'No.'

'We might sell it and send you the money.'

'Yes.'

'Or we could keep the money until we get to Europe–it will be easier to send.'

'It is an abstract speculation,' said the German, suddenly awake, and impatient. 'It is a question purely of academic interest. We shall not reach the French border. Let us start.'

'Good-bye,' said Kätchen.

The two figures sat opposite one another, knees touching, expectant, as though embarking upon the ornamental waters of a fair-ground; lovers for the day's outing, who had stood close in a queue, and now waited half reluctant to launch into the closer intimacy of the grottoes and transparencies.

William released the boat; it revolved once or twice, slowly, as it drifted into mid-stream; there it was caught in the full power of the flood, and, spinning dizzily, was swept out of sight into the dawn.

William returned to his empty room. The boy had put back the debris of the Christmas dinner, carefully ranged upon the writing-table. A cleft stick lay across the bed, bearing no message for William. He sat down at his table and with his eyes fixed on the label of the turkey tin, began to compose his dispatch.

'Take to wireless,' he ordered his boy. 'Sit on step till open. Then come back and sit on this step. Don't let anyone in. Want to sleep very much.'

But he did not sleep very much.

The boy shook him at half-past ten. 'No send,' he said, waving the typewritten message.

William painfully roused himself from his brief sleep. 'Why no send?'

'No Jacksons. No Government. No send.'

William dressed and went to the wireless bureau. A jaunty black face smiled at him through the guichet; starched collar, bow tie, long ivory cigarette-holder–the welter-weight.

'Good morning,' said William. 'I hope you are not feeling too sore after your meeting with the goat. Where is the wireless clerk?'

'He is on a little holiday. I have taken over from him.'

'My boy says that this cable has been refused.'

'That is so. We are very much occupied with government business. I think we shall be occupied all day, perhaps for several days. It would have been far better if you had gone for the tour we had planned for you. Meanwhile perhaps you would like to see the manifesto that we are issuing. I think you do not read Ishmaelite?'

'No.'

'A very barbarous language. I have never learned it. Soon we shall make Russian the official language of the country, I have a copy here in English.'

He handed William a sheet of crimson paper headed WORKERS OF ISHMAELIA UNITE and snapped down the trap of the guichet.

William stepped out into the sunlight. A black man on a ladder was painting out the name of Jackson Street. Someone had stencilled a sickle and hammer on the front of the post office, a red flag hung limp overhead. He read the manifesto.

. . . *development of mineral resources of the workers by the workers for the workers* . . . *Jacksons to be speedily brought to trial* . . . *arraigned for high treason to the Revolution* . . . *liquidated* . . . *New Calendar. Year One of the Soviet State of Ishmaelia* . . .

He crumpled the paper into a scarlet ball and tossed it to the goat; it went down like an oyster.

He stood on his veranda and looked across the yard to the beastly attic from which Kätchen used to greet him, at about this time in the morning, calling him to come out to Popotakis's Ping-Pong Parlour.

'Change and decay in all around I see,' he sang softly, almost unctuously. It was the favourite tune of his uncle Theodore.

He bowed his head.

'Oh, great crested grebe,' he prayed, 'maligned fowl, have I not expiated the wrong my sister did you; am I still to be an exile from the green places of my heart? Was there not even in the remorseless dooms of antiquity a god from the machine?'

He prayed without hope.

And then above the multitudinous noises of the Pension Dressler came a small sound, an insistent, swelling monotone. The servants in the yard looked up. The sound increased and high above them in the cloudless sky, rapidly approaching, there appeared an aeroplane. The sound ceased as the engine was cut off. The machine circled and dropped silently. It was immediately overhead when a black speck detached itself and fell towards them; white stuff streamed behind it, billowed and spread. The engine sang out again; the machine swooped up and away, out of sight and hearing. The little domed tent paused and gently sank, as though immersed in depths of limpid water.

'If he comes on to my roof,' said Frau Dressler. 'If he breaks anything . . .'

The parachutist came on the roof; he broke nothing. He landed delicately on the tips of his toes; the great sail crumpled and collapsed behind him; he deftly extricated himself from the bonds and stood clear. He took a comb from his pocket and settled the slightly disordered auburn hair about his temples, glancing at his watch, bowed to Frau Dressler and asked for a ladder, courteously in five or six languages. They brought him one. Rung by rung, on pointed, snake-skin toes he descended to the yard. The milch-goat reverently made way for him. He smiled politely at William; then recognized him.

'Why!' he exclaimed. 'It is my fellow traveller, the journalist. How agreeable to meet a fellow Britisher in this remote spot.'

5/i

The sun sank behind the gum trees and the first day of the Soviet of Ishmaelia ended in crimson splendour. The deserted bar-room of Popotakis's Ping-Pong Parlour glowed in the fiery sunset.

'I really do not know how to thank you,' said William.

'Please,' said his companion, laying a hand lightly on his, 'please do not embarrass me. The words you have just used seem to haunt me, wherever I go. Ever since that auspicious afternoon when you were kind enough to give me a place in your aeroplane, I have feared, sooner or later, to hear them on your lips. I suggested as much at the time, I think, if my memory does not deceive me.'

Mr Popotakis switched on the lights above the ping-pong table and asked. 'You want a game, Mr Baldwin?' for it was by this name that William's friend now preferred to be called.

('It is a convenient name,' he had explained. 'Non-committal, British and above all easily memorable. I am often obliged to pursue my business interests under an alias. My man Cuthbert chooses them for me. He has a keen sense of what is fitting, but he sometimes luxuriates a little. There have been times when his more fanciful inventions have entirely slipped my memory, at important moments. So now I am plain Mr Baldwin. I beg you to respect my confidence.')

Mr Baldwin resumed his little dissertation.

'In the rough and tumble of commercial life,' he said, 'I endeavour to requite the kindnesses I receive. The kindnesses have become more profuse and the rewards more substantial of recent years . . . however, I am sure that in you I met an entirely disinterested benefactor. I am glad to have prospered your professional career so inexpensively.

'Do you know, my first impression of you was not of a young man destined for great success in journalism? Quite the reverse. In fact, to be frank with you,

I was sceptical of your identity and, when you told me of your destination, I feared you might be coming here with some ulterior object. If I seemed evasive in the early days of our–I hope I may say–friendship, you must forgive me.

'And now Mr Popotakis is offering us a game of ping-pong. For my part, I think it might be refreshing.'

Mr Baldwin removed his coat and rolled the sleeves of his crêpe-de-Chine shirt. Then he took his bat and poised himself expectantly at the end of the table. William served. Love, fifteen; love, thirty; love, forty, game; fifteen, love; thirty, love; forty, love, game. The little man was ubiquitous, ambidextrous. He crouched and bounded and skipped, slamming and volleying; now spanning the net, now five yards back, now flicking the ball from below his knees, now rocketing high among the electric lights; keeping up all the while a bright, bantering conversation in demotic Greek with Mr Popotakis.

At the end of the love set he resumed his coat and said, 'Quarter past six. No doubt you are impatient to send your second message . . .'

For a private wireless transmitter was one of the amenities to which William had been introduced that day.

Since Mr Baldwin's arrival Jacksonburg–or Marxville as it had been called since early that morning–had proved a town of unsuspected convenience.

'I have a little *pied à terre* here,' Mr Baldwin had explained, when William suggested their lunching at the Pension Dressler. 'My man Cuthbert has been putting it in order. I have not seen it and I fear the worst, but he is a sensitive fellow and might be put out if I lunched away from home on the day of my arrival. Will you not share the adventure of lunching with me?'

They walked, for Mr Baldwin complained that his flight had brought on a slight stiffness of the legs. He took William's arm, guiding him through the less frequented by-ways of the town and questioning him earnestly about the events of the last twenty-four hours.

'And where are your colleagues? I anticipated being vexed by them.'

'They have all gone off into the interior to look for Smiles.'

'That is excellent. You will be the sole spectator at the last of our little drama.'

'It won't be much help. They've shut the wireless bureau.'

'It shall be opened soon. Meanwhile I have no doubt Cuthbert will be able to accommodate you. He and a Swiss associate of mine have fixed up a little makeshift which appears to work. I have been in correspondence with them daily.'

Even in the side streets there was evidence of the new régime; twice they were obliged to shelter as police lorries thundered past them laden with glaucous prisoners. The Café Wilberforce had changed its name to Café Lenin. There had been a distribution of red flags, which, ingeniously knotted or twisted, had already set a fashion in head-dresses among the women of the market.

'I ought to have come yesterday,' said Mr Baldwin peevishly. 'It would have saved a great deal of unnecessary reorganization. God bless my soul, there's a another of those police vans.' They skipped for a doorway. In the centre of a machine-gun squad, William recognized the dignified figure of Mr Earl Russell Jackson.

At length their way led them to the outskirts of the city, to the nondescript railway quarter, where sidings and goods yards and warehouses stood behind a stockade of blue guns and barbed wire. They passed an iron gate and approached a bungalow.

'It is M. Giraud's,' said Mr Baldwin. 'And this is M. Giraud, but I think that introductions are superflous.'

The bearded ticket collector greeted them deferentially from the veranda.

'M. Giraud has been in my service for some time,' said Mr Baldwin. 'He had, in fact, been in consultation with me when you had the pleasure of travelling with him from the coast. I followed his brief period of public prominence with interest and, to be quite frank, with anxiety. If I may criticize without offence the profession you practise–at this particular moment with almost unique success–I should say that you reporters missed a good story in M. Giraud's little trip. I read the newspapers with lively interest. It is seldom that they are absolutely, point-blank wrong. That is the popular belief, but those who are in the know can usually discern an embryo truth, a little grit of fact, like the core of a pearl, round which have been deposited the delicate layers of ornament. In the present case, for instance, there *was* a Russian agent arranging to take over the government; M. Giroud *was* an important intermediary. But he was not the Russian. The workings of commerce and politics are very, very simple, but not quite as simple as your colleagues represent them. My man Cuthbert was also on the train with you. He should have given you a clue, but no one recognized him. He drove the engine. It was due to his ignorance of local usage that the lost luggage van was eventually recovered.'

'And may I ask,' said William diffidently, 'since you are telling me so much–whose interests do *you* represent?'

'My own,' said the little man simply. 'I plough a lonely furrow . . . Let us see what they have been able to scrape up for luncheon.'

They had scraped up fresh river fish, and stewed them with white wine and aubergines; also a rare local bird which combined the tender flavour of partridge with the solid bulk of the turkey; they had roasted it and stuffed it with bananas, almonds, and red peppers; also a baby gazelle which they had seethed with truffles in its mother's milk; also a dish of feathery Arab pastry and a heap of unusual fruits. Mr Baldwin sighed wistfully. 'Well,' he said, 'I suppose it will not hurt us to rough it for once. We shall appreciate the pleasures of civilization all the more . . . but my descent in the parachute gave me quite an appetite. I had hoped for something a little more enterprising.'

He swallowed his digestive pills, praised the coffee, and then expressed a desire to sleep.

'Cuthbert will look after you,' he said. 'Give him anything you want sent to your paper.'

The wireless transmitter was in and beneath the garage; its mast rose high overhead, cleverly disguised as a eucalyptus tree. William watched the first words of his rejected dispatch sputter across the ether to Mr Salter; then he, too, decided to sleep.

At five o'clock, when Mr Baldwin reappeared, he was in a different, more conspicuous suit and the same mood of urbanity and benevolence.

'Let us visit the town,' he said, and, inevitably, they had gone to Popotakis's and they sat there at sunset in the empty bar-room.

'. . . No doubt you are impatient to send off your second message; I trust that the little mystery of the situation here is now perfectly clear to you.'

'Well . . . No . . . not exactly.'

'No? There are still gaps? Tut, tut, Mr Boot, the foreign correspondent of a great newspaper should be able to piece things together for himself. It is all very simple. There has been a competition for the mineral rights of Ishmaelia which, I may say as their owner, have been preposterously over-valued. In particular the German and the Russian Governments were willing to pay extravagantly–but in kind. Unhappily for them the commodities they had to offer–treasures from the Imperial palaces, timber, toys, and so forth–were not much in demand in Ishmaelia–in presidential circles at any rate. President Jackson had long wanted to make adequate provision for his retirement, and I was fortunately placed in being able to offer him gold for his gold concession, and my rivals found themselves faced by the alternative of abandoning their ambitions or upsetting President Jackson. They both preferred the latter, more romantic course. The Germans, with a minimum of discernment, chose to set up a native of low character named Smiles as prospective dictator. I never had any serious fears of him. The Russians, more astutely, purchased the Young Ishmaelite party and are, as you see, momentarily in the ascendant.

'That, I think, should give you your material for an article.'

'Yes,' said William. 'Thank you very much. I'm sure Mr Salter and Lord Copper will be very grateful.'

'Dear me, how little you seem to have mastered the correct procedure of your profession. You should ask me whether I have any message for the British public. I have. It is this: *Might must find a way*. Not "*Force*", remember; other nations use "force"; we Britons alone use "Might". Only one thing can set things right–sudden and extreme violence, or, better still, the effective threat of it. I am committed to very considerable sums in this little gamble and, alas, our countrymen are painfully tolerant, nowadays, of the losses of their financial superiors. One sighs for the days of Pam or Dizzy. I possess a little influence in political quarters, but it will strain it severely to provoke a war on my account. Some semblance of popular support, such as your paper can give, would be very valuable . . . But I dislike embarrassing my affairs with international issues. I should greatly prefer it, if the thing could be settled neatly and finally, here and now.'

As he spoke there arose from the vestibule a huge and confused tumult; the roar of an engine which, in the tranquil bar-room, sounded like a flight of heavy aeroplanes, a series of percussions like high explosive bombs, shrill, polyglot human voices inarticulate with alarm, and above them all a deep bass, trolling chant, half nautical, half ecclesiastical. The flimsy structure throbbed and shook from its shallow foundation to its asbestos roof; the metal-bound doors flew open revealing, first, the two black commissionaires backing into the bar and, next, driving them before him, a very large man astride a motor-cycle. He rode slowly between the ping-pong tables, then put his feet to the floor and released the handle-bars. The machine shot from under him, charged the bar, and lay on its side with its back wheel spinning in a cloud of exhaust-gas, while the rider, swaying ponderously from side to side like a performing bear, surveyed the room in a puzzled but friendly spirit.

It was the Swede; but a Swede transfigured, barely recognizable as the mild apostle of the coffee pot and the sticking plaster. The hair of his head stood like a tuft of ornamental, golden grass; a vinous flush lit the upper part of his face, the high cheek bones, the blank, calf-like eyes; on the broad concavities of his forehead the veins bulged varicosely. Still singing his nordic dirge he saluted the empty chairs and ambled towards the bar.

At the first alarm Mr Popotakis had fled the building. The Swede spanned the counter and fumbled on the shelf beyond. William and Mr Baldwin watched him fascinated as he raised bottle after bottle to his nose, sniffed and tossed them disconsolately behind him. Presently he found what he wanted–the sixty per cent. He knocked off the neck, none too neatly, and set the jagged edge to his lips; his Adam's apple rose and fell. Then, refreshed, he looked about him again. The motor-cycle at his feet, churning and stinking, attracted his notice and he silenced it with a single tremendous kick.

'Might,' said Mr Baldwin reverently.

The Swede's eyes travelled slowly about him, settled on William, goggled, squinted, and betrayed signs of recognition. He swayed across the room and took William's hand in a paralysing grip: he jabbed hospitably at his face with the broken bottle and addressed him warmly and at length in Swedish.

Mr Baldwin replied. The sound of his own tongue in a strange land affected Olafsen strongly. He sat down and cried while Mr Baldwin, still in Swedish, spoke to him comfortably.

'Sometimes it is necessary to dissemble one's nationality,' he explained to William. 'I have given our friend here to believe that I am a compatriot.'

The black mood passed. Olafsen gave a little whoop and lunged in a menacing manner with the absinthe bottle.

He introduced William to Mr Baldwin.

'This is my great friend, Boot,' he said, 'a famous journalist. He is my friend though I have been made a fool. I have been made a fool,' he cried louder and more angrily, 'by a lot of blacks. They sent me down the line to an epidemic and I was laughed at. But I am going to tell the President. He is a good old man and he will punish them. I will go to his residence, now, and explain everything.'

He rose from the table and bent over the disabled motor-cycle. Mr Popotakis peeped round the corner of the service door and, seeing the Swede still in possession, popped back out of sight.

'Tell me,' said Mr Baldwin. 'Your friend here–does he become more or less pugnacious with drink?'

'I believe, more.'

'Then let us endeavour to repay his hospitality.'

With his own hands Mr Baldwin fetched a second bottle of sixty per cent from the shelf. Tolerantly conforming to the habits of the place, he snapped off the neck and took a hearty swig; then he passed the bottle to the Swede. In a short time they were singing snatches of lugubrious Baltic music, Mr Baldwin matching the Swede's deep bass, in his ringing alto. Between their songs they drank, and between drinks Mr Baldwin explained concisely, but with many repetitions, the constitutional changes of the last twenty-four hours.

'Russians are bad people.'

'Very bad.'

'They say they are Princes and they borrow money!'

'Yes.'

'President Jackson is a good old man. He gave me a harmonium for my mission. Some of the Jacksons are silly fellows, but the President is my friend.'

'Exactly.'

'I think,' said the Swede, rising, 'we will go and see my friend Jackson.'

5/ii

The Presidential Residence, on this first, and, as it turned out, last, evening of the Soviet Union of Ishmaelia, was ceremoniously illuminated, not with the superb floods of concealed arc lamps dear to the more mature dictatorships, but, for want of better, with a multitude of 'fairy lights' with which the Jacksons were wont to festoon the veranda on their not infrequent official birthdays; all the windows of the façade, ten of them, were unshuttered and the bright lamps behind gave cosy glimpses of Nottingham lace, portières, and enlarged photographs. A red flag hung black against the night sky. Dr Benito, backed by a group of 'Young Ishmaelites', stood on the central balcony. A large crowd of Ishmaelites had assembled to see the lights.

'What is he saying?' asked William.

'He has proclaimed the abolition of Sunday and he is calling for volunteers for a ten-day, ten-hour week. I do not think he has chosen the occasion with tact.'

The Swede had left them, pushing forward on his errand of liberation. William and Mr Baldwin stood at the back of the crowd. The temper of the people was apathetic. They liked to see the place lit up. Oratory pleased them, whatever its subject; sermons, educational lectures, political programmes, panegyrics of the dead or living, appeals for charity–all had the same soporific effect. They liked the human voice in all its aspects, most particularly when it was exerted in sustained athletic effort. They had, from time to time, heard too many unfilled prophecies issue from that balcony to feel any particular apprehensions about the rigours of the new régime. Then, while Benito was well in his stride, a whisper of interest passed through them; necks were stretched. The Swede had appeared at the ground floor window. Benito, sensing the new alertness in his audience, raised his voice, rolled his eyes, and flashed his white teeth. The audience stood tip-toe with expectation. They could see what he could not–the Swede, in a lethargic but effective manner, liquidating the front parlour. He pulled the curtains down, he swept the fourteen ornamental vases off the chimney-piece, with a loud crash he threw a pot of fern through the window. The audience clapped enthusiastically. The 'Young Ishmaelites' behind Benito began to consult, but the speaker, oblivious to all except his own eloquence, continued to churn the night air with Marxian precepts.

To the spectators at the back of the crowd, out of earshot of the minor sounds, the sequence unfolded itself with the happy inconsequence of an early comedy film. The revolutionary committee left their leader's side and disappeared from view to return almost immediately in rout, backwards, retreating before the Swede who now came into the light of the upper drawing-room brandishing a small gilt chair over his head.

It was not ten feet drop from the balcony. The traditional, ineradicable awe of the white man combined with the obvious immediate peril of the whirling chair legs to decide the issue. With one accord they plunged over the rail on to the woolly pates below. Benito was the last to go, proclaiming class war with his last audible breath.

The Swede addressed the happy people in Ishmaelite.

'He says he is looking for his friend President Jackson,' explained Mr Baldwin.

A cheer greeted the announcement. 'Jackson' was one of the perennially exhilarating words in the Ishmaelite vocabulary; a name associated since childhood with every exciting event in Ishmaelite life. They had been agreeably surprised to learn that the Jacksons had that morning all been sent to prison; now, it would be a treat to see them all again. As long as something, good or ill, was happening to the Jacksons, the Ishmaelites felt an intelligent interest in politics. Soon they were all crying: 'Jackson. Jackson. Jackson.'

'Jackson. Jackson,' shouted Mr Baldwin, at William's side. 'I think we may be satisfied that the counter-revolution has triumphed.'

5/iii

An hour later William sat in his room at the Pension Dressler and began his dispatch to *The Beast*.

From the main street a short distance away could be heard sounds of rejoicing from the populace. President Jackson had been found, locked in the wood shed. Now, dazed and stiff, he was being carried shoulder high about the city; other processions had formed about other members of the liberated family. Now and then rival processions met and came to blows. Mr Popotakis had boarded up his café but several Indian drink shops had been raided and the town was settling down to a night of jollity.

PRESS COLLECT URGENT MAN CALLED MISTER BALDWIN HAS BOUGHT COUNTRY, William began.

'No,' said a gentle voice behind him. 'If you would not resent my co-operation, I think I can compose a dispatch more likely to please my good friend Copper.'

Mr Baldwin sat at William's table and drew the typewriter towards himself. He inserted a new sheet of paper, tucked up his cuffs and began to write with immense speed:

MYSTERY FINANCIER RECALLED EXPLOITS RHODES LAWRENCE TODAY SECURING VAST EAST AFRICAN CONCESSION BRITISH INTERESTS IN TEETH ARMED OPPOSITION BOLSHEVIST SPIES . . .

'It will make about five full columns,' he said, when it was finished. 'From my experience of newspapers I think I can safely say that they will print it in full. I am afraid we are too late for tomorrow's paper, but there is no competition to fear. Perhaps I shall have the felicity of finding you as my fellow traveller on the return journey.'

The sounds of rejoicing drew nearer and rose to a wild hubbub in the lane outside.

'Dear me,' said Mr Baldwin. 'How disconcerting. I believe they have found me out.'

But it was only General Gollancz Jackson being pulled about the town in his motor-car. The bare feet pattered away in the darkness. The cries of acclamation faded.

A knock on the door.

Cuthbert reported that, in view of the disturbed state of the town, he had taken the liberty of bringing his master's sheets to the Pension Dressler and making up a bed for him there.

'You did quite right, Cuthbert . . . And now, if you will forgive me, I will say good night. I have had an unusually active day.'

PART III

BANQUET

1/i

The bells of St Bride's chimed unheard in the customary afternoon din of the Megalopolitan Building. The country edition had gone to bed; below traffic-level, in grotto-blue light, leagues of paper ran noisily through the machines; overhead, where floor upon floor rose from the dusk of the streets to the clear air of day, ground-glass doors opened and shut; figures in frayed and perished braces popped in and out; on a hundred lines reporters talked at cross purposes; sub-editors busied themselves with their humdrum task of reducing to blank nonsense the sheaves of misinformation which whistling urchins piled before them; beside a hundred typewriters soggy biscuits lay in a hundred tepid saucers. At the hub and still centre of all this animation, Lord Copper sat alone in splendid tranquillity. His massive head, empty of thought, rested in sculptural fashion upon his left fist. He began to draw a little cow on his writing pad.

Four legs with cloven feet, a ropy tail, swelling udder and modestly diminished teats, a chest and head like an Elgin marble–all this was straightforward stuff. Then came the problem–which was the higher, horns or ears? He tried it one way, he tried it the other; both looked equally unconvincing; he tried different types of ear–tiny, feline triangles, asinine tufts of hair and gristle, even, in desperation, drooping flaps remembered from a guinea-pig in the backyard of his earliest home; he tried different types of horn–royals, the elegant antennae of the ibis, the vast armoury of moose and buffalo. Soon the paper before him was covered like the hall of a hunter with freakish heads. None looked right. He brooded over them and found no satisfaction.

It was thus that Mr Salter found him.

Mr Salter had not wanted to come and see Lord Copper. He had nothing particular to say. He had not been summoned. But he had the right of entry to his owner's presence, and it was only thus, he believed, by unremitting, wholly uncongenial self-assertion, that he could ever hope for a change of job.

'I wanted to consult you about Bucarest,' he said.

'Ah.'

'There's a long story from Jepson about a pogrom. Have we any policy in Bucarest?'

Lord Copper roused himself from his abstraction. 'Someone on this paper must know about cows,' he said petulantly.

'Cows, Lord Copper?'

'Don't we keep a man to write about the country?'

'Oh. That was Boot, Lord Copper.'

'Well, have him come and see me.'

'We sent him to Africa.'

'Well, have him come back. What's he doing there? Who sent him?'

'He is on his way back now. It was Boot who brought off the great story in Ishmaelia. When we scooped Hitchcock,' he added, for Lord Copper was frowning in a menacing way.

Slowly the noble face lightened.

'Ah, yes, smart fellow, Boot. He was the right man for that job.'

'It was you who discovered him, Lord Copper.'

'Of course, naturally . . . had my eye on him for some time. Glad he made good. There's always a chance for real talent on the *Beast*, eh, Salter?'

'Definitely, Lord Copper.'

'Preparations going ahead for Boot's reception?'

'Up to a point.'

'Let me see, what was it we decided to do for him?'

'I don't think, Lord Copper, that the question was ever actually raised.'

'Nonsense. It is a matter I have particularly at heart. Boot has done admirably. He is an example to everyone on the staff–*everyone*. I wish to show my appreciation in a marked manner. When do you say he gets back?'

'At the end of next week.'

'I will thank him personally . . . You never had any faith in that boy, Salter.'

'Well . . .'

'I remember it quite distinctly. You wished to have him recalled. But I knew he had the makings of a journalist in him. Was I right?'

'Oh, definitely, Lord Copper.'

'Well, then, let us have no more of these petty jealousies. The office is riddled with them. I shall make it my concern to see that Boot is substantially rewarded . . . What, I wonder, would meet the case? . . .' Lord Copper paused, undecided. His eye fell on the page of drawings and he covered it with his blotting paper. 'Suppose,' he said at length, 'we gave him another good foreign assignment. There is this all-women expedition to the South Pole–bound to be a story in that. Do you think that would meet the case?'

'Up to a point, Lord Copper.'

'Not too lavish?'

'Definitely not.'

'I imagine that the expenses of an expedition of that kind will be heavy. Have to charter his own ship–I understand they will have no man on board.' He paused dissatisfied. 'The trouble is that it is the kind of story that may not break for two years and then we shall have to put Boot's name before the public all over again. We ought to do something *now*, while the news is still hot. I gave that illiterate fellow Hitchcock a knighthood for less.' For the first time since the question of the cow had risen to perplex him, Lord Copper smiled. 'We certainly wiped Hitchcock's eye in Ishmaelia.' He paused, and his smile broadened as he recalled the triumph of ten days ago when the *Brute* had had to remake their front page at seven in the morning and fill a special late edition with a palpable fake.

'I don't want to cheapen official honours among the staff,' he said, 'but I have a very good mind to give a knighthood to Boot. How does that strike you, Salter?'

'You don't think, Lord Copper, that he is rather an inexperienced man . . . ?'

'No, I don't. And I deplore this grudging attitude in you, Salter. You should welcome the success of your subordinates. A knighthood is a very suitable recognition. It will not cost us a penny. As I say, honours of this kind must be distributed with discretion but, properly used, they give a proper air of authority to the paper.'

'It will mean an increase of salary.'

'He shall have it. And he shall have a banquet. Send my social secretary to me. I will make the arrangements at once.'

I/ii

No. 10 Downing Street was understaffed; the principal private secretary was in Scotland; the second secretary was on the Lido; Parliament was in vacation but there was no rest for the Prime Minister; he was obliged to muddle along, as best he could, with his third and fourth secretaries–unreliable young men related to his wife.

'Another name for the K.C.B.'s,' he said petulantly. 'Boot–gratis.'

'Yes, Uncle Mervyn. Are you–we giving any particular reason?'

'It's someone of Copper's. Call it "Services to Literature." It's some time since Copper asked for anything–I was getting nervous. I'll send him a personal note to tell him it is all right. You might drop a line to Boot.'

'O.K., Uncle.'

Later his secretary said to his less important colleague:

'More birthdays. Boot–writer. Do you know anything about him?'

'Yes, he's always lunching with Aunt Agnes. Smutty novels.'

'Well, write, and tell him he's fixed up, will you?'

Two days later, among his bills, John Courtenay Boot found forwarded to him a letter which said:

'I am instructed by the Prime Minister to inform you that your name has been forwarded to H.M. the King with the recommendation for your inclusion in the Order of Knights Commanders of the Bath.'

'Golly,' said Boot, 'It must be Julia.'

Mrs Stitch was staying in the same house. He went and sat on her bed while she had breakfast. Presently he said:

'By the way, what d'you think? They're making me a Knight.'

'Who are?'

'The King and the Prime Minister. You know . . . a real Knight . . . Sir John Boot, I mean.'

'*Well . . .*'

'Is it your doing?'

'*Well* . . . I hardly know what to say, John. Are you pleased about it?'

'It's hard to say yet . . . taken by surprise. But I *think* I am . . . In fact I know I am . . . Come to think of it, I'm very pleased indeed.'

'Good,' said Mrs Stitch. 'I'm very pleased too,' and added, 'I suppose I did have something to do with it.'

'It was angelic of you. But why?'

'Just the Stitch service. I felt you had been disappointed about that job on the newspaper.'

Later, when Algernon Stitch came back from a day with the partridges, she said:

'Algie. What's come over your Prime Minister? He's making John a Knight.'

'John Gassoway? Oh, well, he's had his tongue hanging out for something ever since we got it.'

'No, John Boot.'

It was not often that Algernon Stitch showed surprise. He did then.

'Boot,' he said. 'Good God!' and added after a long pause, 'Overwork. Breaking up. Pity.'

John Boot was not sure whether to make a joke of it. He extended his confidence to a Lady Greenidge and a Miss Montesquieu. By dinner time the house was buzzing with the news. There was no doubt in anyone else's mind whether it was a joke or not.

I / iii

'Anything to declare?'

'Nothing.'

'What, not with all this?'

'I bought it in London in June.'

'All of it?'

'More. There was a canoe . . .'

The customs officer laid hands on the nearest of the crates which lay conspicuously among the hand luggage of returning holiday-makers. Then he read the label and his manner changed.

'Forgive me asking, sir, but are you by any chance Mr Boot of the *Beast*?'

'Yes, I suppose I am.'

'Ah. Then I don't think I need trouble you, sir . . . the missus *will* be pleased to hear I've seen you. We've been reading a lot about you lately.'

Everyone seemed to have read about William. From the moment he touched the fringe of the English-speaking world in the train de luxe from Marseille, William had found himself the object of undisguised curiosity. On his way round Paris he had bought a copy of the *Beast*. The front page was mainly occupied with the preparations of the Ladies' Antarctic Expedition but, inset in the middle, was a framed notice:

BOOT IS BACK

The man who made journalistic history, Boot of the Beast, *will tomorrow tell in his own inimitable way the inner story of his meteoric leap to fame. How does it feel to tell the truth to two million registered readers? How does it feel to have risen in a single week to the highest pinnacle of fame? Boot will tell you.*

That had been the paper of the day before. At Dover William bought the current issue. There, above a facsimile of his signature and a composite picture of his passport photograph surcharged on an Ishmaelite landscape, in the size which the *Beast* reserved for its most expensive contributors, stood the promised article.

'Two months ago,' it said, *'when Lord Copper summoned me from my desk in the* Beast *office, to handle the biggest news story of the century, I had never been to Ishmaelia, I knew little of foreign politics. I was being pitted against the most brilliant brains, the experience, and the learning of the civilized world. I had nothing except my youth, my will to succeed, and what–for want of a better word–I must call my flair. In the two months' battle of wits . . .'*

William could read no more. Overcome with shame he turned towards the train. A telegraph boy was loafing about the platform uttering monotonous, monosyllabic, plaintive, gull-like cries which, in William's disturbed mind, sounded like 'Boot. Boot. Boot.' William turned guiltily towards him; he bore a cardboard notice, stuck, by a felicitous stroke of fancy, into a cleft stick, on which was inscribed in unmistakable characters, '*Boot.*'

'I'm afraid that must be for me,' said William.

'There's a whole lot of them.'

The train seemed likely to start. William took the telegrams and opened them in the carriage, under the curious eyes of his fellow travellers.

PERSONALLY GRATIFIED YOUR SAFE RETURN COPPER.

BEAST REPRESENTATIVE WILL MEET YOU VICTORIA STOP PLEASE REPORT HERE IMMEDIATELY YOU RETURN STOP TALK BUSINESS NO ONE SALTER.

WILL YOU ACCEPT FIVE YEAR CONTRACT FIVE THOUSAND YEAR ROVING CORRESPONDENT EDITOR BRUTE.

PLEASE WIRE AUTHORITY NEGOTIATE BOOK SERIAL CINEMA RIGHTS AUTOBIOGRAPHY PAULS LITERARY AGENCY.

There were others, similarly phrased. William released them, one by one as he read them, at the open window. The rush of air whirled them across the charred embankment to the fields of stubble and stacked corn beyond.

At Victoria it was, once again, William's luggage which betrayed him. As he stood among the crates and bundles waiting for a taxi, a very young man approached him and said, 'I say, please, are you William Boot?' He had a pimply, eager face.

'Yes.'

'I'm from the *Beast*. They sent me to meet you. Mr Salter did.'

'Very kind of him.'

'I expect you would like a drink after your journey.'

'No, thank you.'

'Mr Salter said I was to ask you.'

'Very kind of him.'

'I say, please have a drink. Mr Salter said I could put it down as expenses.'

The young man seemed very eager.

'All right,' said William.

'You wouldn't know me,' said the young man as they walked to the buffet. 'I'm Bateson. I've only been on the paper three weeks. This is the first time I've charged anything on expenses. In fact it is the first time I've drawn any money from the *Beast* at all. I'm "on space", you see.'

'Ah.'

They reached the buffet and Bateson bought some whisky. 'I say,' he said, 'would you think it awful cheek if I asked you to do something?'

'What?'

'It's your big story. I've got a first edition of it.' He drew a grubby newspaper from his pocket. 'Would you sign for me?'

William signed.

'I say, thanks awfully. I'll get it framed. I've been carrying it about ever since it appeared–studying it, you know. That's the way they told me in the Correspondence School. Did you ever take a Correspondence School?'

'No.'

Bateson looked disappointed. 'Oh, dear, aren't they a good thing? They're terribly expensive.'

'I expect they are a very good thing.'

'You do think so, don't you? I'm a graduate of the Aircastle School. I paid fifteen shillings a month and I got a specially recommended diploma. That's how I got taken on the *Beast*. It's a great chance, I know. I haven't had anything in the paper yet. But one has to start sometime. It's a great profession, isn't it?'

'Yes, I suppose in a way it is.'

'It must be wonderful to be like you,' said Bateson wistfully. 'At the top. It's been a great chance my meeting you like this. I could hardly believe it when Mr Salter picked me to come. "Go and greet Boot," he said. "Give him a drink. Get him here before he signs on with the *Brute*." You wouldn't want to sign on with the *Brute*, would you?'

'No.'

'You do think the *Beast* is the leading paper, don't you? I mean it's the greatest chance you can have working for the *Beast*?'

'Yes.'

'I *am* glad. You see it's rather depressing sometimes, day after day and none of one's stories getting printed. I'd like to be a foreign correspondent like you. I say, would you think it awful cheek if I showed you some of the stuff I write? In my spare time I do it. I imagine some bit piece of news and then I see how I should handle it. Last night in bed I imagined an actress with her throat cut. Shall I show it to you?'

'Please do,' said William, 'some time. But I think we ought to be going now.'

'Yes, I suppose we should. But you do think it's a good way of training oneself–inventing imaginary news?'

'None better,' said William.

They left the bar. The porter was keeping guard over the baggage. 'You'll need two cabs,' he said.

'Yes . . . Suppose you take the heavy stuff in one, Bateson, I'll follow with my own bags in the other.' He packed the young man in among the tropical equipment. 'Give them to Mr Salter and say I shan't need them any more.'

'But you're coming too?'

'I'm taking the cab behind,' said William.

They drove off down Victoria Street. When Bateson's cab was some distance ahead, William leant through the window and said, 'I've changed my mind. Go to Paddington instead.'

There was time before his train to telegraph to Boot Magna, '*Returning tonight William.*'

'Boot said he didn't want these any more.'

'No,' said Mr Salter, surveying with distaste the heap of travel-worn tropical equipment which encumbered his room. 'No, I suppose not. And where is Boot?'

'Just behind.'

'You ought to have stayed with him.'

'I'm sorry, Mr Salter.'

'There's no need for you to wait.'

'All right.'

'Well, what are you waiting for?'

'I was wondering, would you think it awful cheek if I asked for a souvenir.'

'Souvenir?'

'Of my meeting with Boot. Could you spare one of those sticks?'

'Take the lot.'

'I say, may I really. I say, thank you ever so much.'

'That boy, Bateson. Is he balmy or something?'

'I daresay.'

'What's he doing here?'

'He comes from the Aircastle Correspondence School. They guarantee a job to all their star pupils. They've a big advertising account with us, so we sometimes take one of their chaps "on space" for a bit.'

'Well, he's lost Boot. I suppose we can fire him now?'

'Surely.'

The harvest moon hung, brilliant and immense, over the elm trees. In the lanes around Boot Magna motor-cycles or decrepit cars travelled noisily home from the village whist drive; Mr Atwater, the bad character, packed his pockets for the night's sport; the smell of petrol hung about the hedges but inside the park everything was sweet and still. For a few feet ahead the lights of the car shed a feeble, yellow glow; beyond, the warm land lay white as frost, and, as they emerged from the black tunnel of evergreen around the gates into the open pasture, the drive with its sharply defined ruts and hollows might have been a strip of the moon itself, a volcanic field cold since the creation.

A few windows were alight; only Uncle Theodore was still up. He opened the door to William.

'Ah,' he said, 'train late?'

'I don't think so.'

'Ah,' he said. 'We got your telegram.'

'Yes.'

'Had a good time?'

'Yes, fairly.'

'You must tell us all about it tomorrow. Your grandmother will want to hear, I know. Had any dinner?'

'Yes, thank you, on the train.'

'Good. We thought you might. We didn't keep anything hot. Rather short-handed at the moment. James hasn't been at all well, getting too old for his work–but there are some biscuits in the dining-room.'

'Thanks very much,' said William. 'I don't think I want anything.'

'No. Well, I think I'll be going along. Glad you've had such a good time. Don't forget to tell us about it. Can't say I read your articles. They were always cut out by the time I got the paper. Nannie Price disapproved of them. I must get hold of them, want to read them very much. . . .' They were walking upstairs together; they reached the landing where their ways diverged. William carried his bag to his own room and laid it on the bed. Then he went to the window and, stooping, looked out across the moonlit park.

On such a night as this, not four weeks back, the tin roofs of Jacksonburg had laid open to the sky, a three-legged dog had awoken, started from his barrel in Frau Dressler's garden, and all over the town, in yards and refuse heaps, the pariahs had taken up his cries of protest.

I/iv

'Well,' said Mr Salter, 'I've heard from Boot.'

'Any good?'

'No. No good.'

He handed the News Editor the letter that had arrived that morning from William.

> Dear Mr Salter, *it ran*,
>
> Thank you very much for your letter and the invitation. It is very kind of Lord Copper, please thank him, but if you don't mind I think I won't come to the banquet. You see it is a long way and there is a great deal to do here and I can't make speeches. I have to every now and then for things in the village and they are bad enough–a banquet would be worse.
>
> I hope you got the tent and things. Sorry about the canoe. I gave it to a German, also the Xmas dinner. I still have some of your money left. Do you want it back? Will you tell the other editor that I shall be sending him Lush Places on Wednesday.
>
> Yours ever,
> William Boot
>
> P.S.–Sorry. They forgot to post this. Now it's Saturday, so you won't get it till Monday.

'You think he's talking turkey with the *Brute*.'

'If he's not already signed up.'

'Ours is a nasty trade, Salter. No gratitude.'

'No loyalty.'

'I've seen it again and again since I've been in Fleet Street. It's enough to make one cynical.'

'What does Lord Copper say?'

'He doesn't know. For the moment, fortunately, he seems to have forgotten the whole matter. But he may raise it again at any moment.'

He did, that morning.

'. . . ah, Salter, I was talking to the Prime Minister last night. The honours list will be out on Wednesday. How are the preparations going for the Boot banquet? It's on the Thursday, I think.'

'That *was* the date, Lord Copper.'

'Good. I shall propose the health of our guest of honour. By the way, did Boot ever come and see me?'

'No, Lord Copper.'

'But I asked for him.'

'Yes, Lord Copper.'

'Then, why was he not brought? Once and for all, Salter, I will not have a barrier erected between me and my staff. I am as accessible to the humblest' . . . Lord Copper paused for an emphatic example . . . 'the humblest book reviewer as I am to my immediate entourage. I will have no cliques in the *Beast*, you understand me?'

'Definitely.'

'Then bring Boot here.'

'Yes, Lord Copper.'

It was an in auspicious beginning to Mr Salter's working day; worse was to come.

That afternoon he was sitting disconsolately in the News Editor's room when they were interrupted by the entry of a young man whose face bore that puffy aspect, born of long hours in the golf-house, which marked most of the better paid members of the *Beast* staff on their return from their summer holidays. Destined by his trustees for a career in the Household Cavalry, this young man had lately reached the age of twenty-five and plunged into journalism with a zeal which Mr Salter found it difficult to understand. He talked to them cheerfully for some time on matters connected with his handicap. Then he said:

'By the way, I don't know if there's a story in it, but I was staying last week with my Aunt Trudie. John Boot was there among other people–you know, the novelist. He'd just got a letter from the King or someone like that, saying he was going to be knighted.' The look of startled concern on the two editors' faces checked him. 'I see you don't think much of it. Oh, well, I thought it might be worth mentioning. You know. "Youth's Opportunity in New Reign", that kind of thing.'

'*John* Boot–the novelist.'

'Yes. Rather good–at least I always read him. But it seemed a new line for the Prime Minister . . .'

'No,' said the Prime Minister with unusual finality.

'No?'

'No. It would be utterly impossible to change the list now. The man has been officially notified. And I could not consider knighting two men of the same name on the same day. Just the kind of thing the Opposition would jump on. Quite rightly. Smacks of jobbery, you know.'

'*Two Boots.*'

'Lord Copper must know.'

'Lord Copper must never know. . . . There's only one comfort. We haven't committed ourselves to which Boot we are welcoming on Thursday or where he's come from.' He pointed to the engraved card which had appeared, during the week-end, on the desks of all the four-figure men in the office.

VISCOUNT COPPER

and

the Directors of the Megalopolitan Newspaper Company request the honour of your company to dinner on Wednesday, September 16th, at the Braganza Hotel, to welcome the return of

BOOT of THE BEAST

7.45 for 8 o'clock.

'We had a row with the social secretary about that. He said it wasn't correct. Lucky how things turned out.'

'It makes things little better.'

'A little.'

'Salter, this is a case for personal contact. We've got to sign up this new Boot and any other Boot that may be going and one of them has got to be welcomed home on Thursday. There's only one thing for it, Salter, you must go down to the country and see Boot. I'll settle with the other.'

'To the country?'

'Yes, tonight.'

'Oh, but I couldn't go tonight.'

'Tomorrow, then.'

'You think it is really necessary?'

'Either that, or we must tell Lord Copper the truth.'

Mr Salter shuddered. 'But wouldn't it be better,' he said, 'if *you* went to the country?'

'No. I'll see this novelist and get him signed up.'

'And sent away.'

'Or welcomed home. And you will offer the other Boot any reasonable terms to lie low.'

'Any reasonable terms.'

'Salter, old man, what's come over you? You keep repeating things.'

'It's nothing. It's only . . . travelling . . . always upsets me.'

He had a cup of strong tea and later rang up the Foreign Contacts Adviser to find how he could best get to Boot Magna.

2/i

At the outbreak of the war of 1914 Uncle Roderick had declared for retrenchment. 'It's up to all of us who are over military age to do what we can. All unnecessary expenses must be cut down.'

'Why?' asked Great Aunt Anne.

'It is a question of national emergency and patriotism.'

'How will our being uncomfortable hurt the Germans? It's just what they want.'

'Everything is needed at the front,' explained William's mother.

Discussion had raged for some days; every suggested economy seemed to strike invidiously at individual members of the household. At last it was decided to give up the telephone. Aunt Anne sometimes spoke bitterly of the time when 'my nephew Roderick won the war by cutting me off from my few surviving friends,' but the service had never been renewed. The antiquated mahogany box still stood at the bottom of the stairs, dusty and silent, and telegrams which arrived in the village after tea were delivered next day with the morning post. Thus, William found Mr Salter's telegram waiting for him on the breakfast table.

His mother, Priscilla, and his three uncles sat round the table. They had finished eating and were sitting there, as they often sat for an hour or so, doing nothing at all. Priscilla alone was occupied, killing wasps in the honey on her plate.

'There's a telegram for you,' said his mother. 'We were wondering whether we ought to open it or send it up to you.'

It said: MUST SEE YOU IMMEDIATELY URGENT BUSINESS ARRIVING BOOT MAGNA HALT TOMORROW AFTERNOON 6.10 SALTER.

The message was passed from hand to hand around the table.

Mrs Boot said, 'Who is Mr Salter, and what urgent business can he possibly have here?'

Uncle Roderick said, 'He can't stay the night. Nowhere for him to sleep.'

Uncle Bernard said, 'You must telegraph and put him off.'

Uncle Theodore said, 'I knew a chap called Salter once, but I don't suppose it's the same one.'

Priscilla said, 'I believe he means to come today. It's dated yesterday.'

'He's the foreign editor of the *Beast*,' William explained 'The one I told you about who sent me abroad.'

'He must be a very pushful fellow, inviting himself here like this. Anyway, as Roderick says, we've no room for him.'

'We could send Priscilla to the Caldicotes for the night.'

'I like that,' said Priscilla, adding illogically, 'Why don't you send William, it's his friend.'

'Yes,' said Mrs Boot. 'Priscilla could go to the Caldicotes.'

'I'm cubbing tomorrow,' said Priscilla, 'right in the other direction. You can't expect Lady Caldicote to send me thirty miles at eight in the morning.'

For over an hour the details of Priscilla's hunt occupied the dining-room. Could she send her horse overnight to a farm near the meet; could she leave the Caldicotes at dawn, pick up her horse at Boot Magna, and ride on: sould she borrow Major Watkins's trailer and take her horse to the Caldicotes for the night, then as far as Major Watkins's in the morning and ride on from there; if she got the family car from Aunt Agnes and Major Watkins's trailer, would Lady Caldicote lend her a car to take it to Major Watkins's; would Aunt Anne allow the car to stay the night; would she discover it was taken without her permission? They discussed the question exhaustively, from every angle; Troutbeck twice glowered at them from the door and finally began to clear the table; Mr Salter and the object of his visit were not mentioned.

2/ii

That evening, some time after the advertised hour, Mr Salter alighted at Boot Magna Halt. An hour earlier, at Taunton, he had left the express, and changed into a train such as he did not know existed outside the imagination of his Balkan correspondents; a single tram-like, one-class coach, which had pottered in a desultory fashion through a system of narrow, under-populated valleys. It had stopped eight times, and at every station there had been a bustle of passengers succeeded by a long, silent pause, before it started again; men had entered who, instead of slinking and shuffling and wriggling themselves into corners and decently screening themselves behind newspapers, as civilized people should when they travelled by train, had sat down squarely quite close to Mr Salter, rested their hands on their knees, stared at him fixedly and uncritically and suddenly addressed him on the subject of the weather in barely intelligible accents; there had been very old, unhygienic men and women, such as you never saw in the Underground, who ought long ago to have been put away in some public institution; there had been women carrying a multitude of atrocious little baskets and parcels which they piled on the seats; one of them had put a hamper containing a live turkey under Mr Salter's feet. It had been a horrible journey.

At last, with relief, Mr Salter alighted. He lifted his suitcase from among the sinister bundles on the rack and carried it to the centre of the platform. There was no one else for Boot Magna. Mr Salter had hoped to find William waiting to meet him, but the little station was empty except for a single porter who was leaning against the cab of the engine engaged in a kind of mute, telepathic converse with the driver, and a cretinous native youth who stood on the further side of the paling, leant against it and picked at the dry paint-bubbles with a toe-like thumb nail. When Mr Salter looked at him, he glanced away and grinned wickedly at his boots.

The train observed its customary two minutes' silence and then steamed slowly away. The porter shuffled across the line and disappeared into a hut labelled 'Lamps'. Mr Salter turned towards the palings; the youth was still leaning there, gazing; his eyes dropped; he grinned. Three times, shuttlecock fashion, they alternately glanced up and down till Mr Salter, with urban impatience, tired of the flirtation and spoke up.

'I say.'

'Ur.'

'Do you happen to know whether Mr Boot has sent a car for me?'

'Ur.'

'He has?'

'Noa. She've a taken of the harse.'

'I am afraid you misunderstand me.' Mr Salter's voice sounded curiously flutey and querulous in contrast to the deep tones of the moron. 'I'm coming to visit Mr Boot. I wondered if he had sent a motor-car for me.'

'He've a sent me.'

'With the car?'

'Noa. Motor-car's over to Lady Caldicote's taking of the harse. The bay,' he explained, since Mr Salter seemed not to be satisfied with this answer. 'Had to be the bay for because the mare's sick . . . The old bay's not up yet,' he added as though to make everything perfectly clear.

'Well, how am I to get to the house?'

'Why, along of me and Bert Tyler.'

'Has this Mr Tyler got a car, then?'

'Noa. I tell e car's over to Lady Caldicote's along of Miss Priscilla and the bay . . . Had to be the bay,' he persisted, 'because for the mare's sick.'

'Yes, yes, I quite appreciate that.'

'And the old bay's still swole up with grass. So you'm to ride along of we.'

'Ride?' A hideous vision rose before Mr Salter.

'Ur. Along of me and Bert Tyler and the slag.'

'Slag?'

'Ur. Mr Roderick's getting in the slag now for to slag Westerheys. Takes a tidy bit.'

Mr Salter was suffused with relief. 'You mean that you have some kind of vehicle outside full of slag?'

'Ur. Cheaper now than what it will be when Mr Roderick wants it.'

Mr Salter descended the steps into the yard where, out of sight from the platform, an open lorry was standing; an old man next to the driving seat touched his cap; the truck was loaded high with sacks; bonnet and back bore battered learner plates. The youth took Mr Salter's suitcase and heaved it up among the slag. 'You'm to ride behind,' he said.

'If it's all the same to you,' said Mr Salter rather sharply, 'I should prefer to sit in front.'

'It's all the same to *me*, but I durstn't let you. The police would have I.'

'Good gracious, why?'

'Bert Tyler have to ride along of me, for because of the testers.'

'Testers?'

'Ur. Police don't allow for me to drive except along of Bert Tyler. Bert Tyler he've a had a licence twenty year. There wasn't no testers for Bert Tyler. But police they took and tested I over to Taunton.'

'And you failed?'

A great grin spread over the young man's face. 'I busted tester's leg for he,' he said proudly. 'Ran he bang into the wall, going a fair lick.'

'Oh, dear. Wouldn't it be better for your friend Tyler to drive us?'

'Noa. He can't see for to drive, Bert Tyler can't. Don't e be afeared. I can *see* all right. It be the corners do for I.'

'And are there many corners between here and the house?'

'Tidy few.'

Mr Salter, who had had his foot on the hub of the wheel preparatory to mounting, now drew back. His nerve, never strong, had been severely tried that afternoon; now it failed him.

'I'll walk,' he said. 'How far is it?'

'Well, it's all according as you know the way. We do call it three mile over the fields. It's a tidy step by the road.'

'Perhaps you'll be good enough to show me the field path.'

'Tain't exactly what you could call a path. E just keeps straight.'

'Well, I daresay I shall find it. If . . . if by any chance you get to the house before me, will you tell Mr Boot that I wanted a little exercise after the journey?'

The learner-driver looked at Mr Salter with undisguised contempt. 'I'll tell e as you was afeared to ride along of me and Bert Tyler,' he said.

Mr Salter stepped back into the station porch to avoid the dust as the lorry drove away. It was as well that he did so, for, as he mounted the incline, the driver mistakenly changed into reverse and the machine charged precipitately back in its tracks, and came noisily to rest against the wall where Mr Salter had been standing. The second attempt was more successful and it reached the lane with no worse damage than a mudguard crushed against the near gatepost.

Then with rapid, uncertain steps Mr Salter set out on his walk to the house.

2/iii

It was eight o'clock when Mr Salter arrived at the front door. He had covered a good six miles tacking from field to field under the setting sun; he had scrambled through fences and ditches; in one enormous pasture a herd of cattle had closed silently in on him and followed at his heels–the nearest not a yard away–with lowered heads and heavy breath; Mr Salter had broken into a run and they had trotted after him; when he gained the stile and turned to face them, they began gently grazing in his tracks; dogs had flown at him in three farmyards where he had stopped to ask the way, and to be misdirected; at last, when he felt he could go no further but must lie down and perish from exposure under the open sky, he had stumbled through an overgrown stile to find himself in the main road with the lodge gates straight ahead; the last mile up the drive had been the bitterest of all.

And now he stood under the porch, sweating, blistered, nettlestung, breathless, parched, dizzy, dead-beat and dishevelled, with his bowler hat in one hand and umbrella in the other, leaning against a stucco pillar waiting for someone to open the door. Nobody came. He pulled again at the bell; there was no answering ring, no echo in the hall beyond. No sound broke the peace of the evening save, in the elms that stood cumbrously on every side, the crying of the rooks, and, not unlike it but nearer at hand, directly it seemed over Mr Salter's head, a strong baritone decanting irregular snatches of sacred music.

'In Thy courts no more are needed, sun by day nor moon by night,' sang Uncle Theodore blithely, stepping into his evening trousers; he remembered it as a treble solo rising to the dim vaults of the school chapel, touching the toughest adolescent hearts; he remembered it imperfectly but with deep emotion.

Mr Salter listened, unmoved. In despair he began to pound the front door with his umbrella. The singing ceased and the voice in fruity, more prosaic tones demanded, 'What, ho, without there?'

Mr Salter hobbled down the steps, clear of the porch, and saw framed in the ivy of a first-floor window, a ruddy, Hanoverian face and plump, bare torso. 'Good-evening,' he said politely.

'Good-evening.' Uncle Theodore leaned out as far as he safely could and stared at Mr Salter through a monocle. 'From where you are standing,' he said, 'you might easily take me to be totally undraped. Let me hasten to assure you that such is not the case. Seemly black shrouds me from the waist down. No doubt you are the friend my nephew William is expecting?'

'Yes . . . I've been ringing the bell.'

'It sounded to me,' said Uncle Theodore severely, 'as though you were hammering the door with a stick.'

'Yes, I was. You see . . .'

'You'll be late for dinner, you know, if you stand out there kicking up a rumpus. And so shall I if I stay talking to you. We will meet again shortly in more conventional circumstances. For the moment–*a rivederci*.'

The head withdrew and once more the melody rose into the twilight, mounted to the encircling tree-tops and joined the chorus of the homing rooks.

Mr Salter tried the handle of the door. It opened easily. Never in his life had he made his own way into anyone else's house. Now he did so and found himself in a lobby cluttered with implements of sport, overcoats, rugs, a bicycle or two and a stuffed bear. Beyond it, glass doors led into the hall. He was dimly aware of a shadowy double staircase which rose and spread before him, of a large, carpetless chequer of black and white marble pavings, of islands of furniture and some potted palms. Quite near the glass doors stood a little arm-chair where no one ever sat; there Mr Salter sank and there he was found twenty minutes later by William's mother when she came down to dinner. His last action before he lapsed into coma had been to remove his shoes.

Mrs Boot surveyed the figure with some distaste and went on her way to the drawing-room. It was one of the days when James was on his feet; she could hear him next door rattling the silver on the dining-room table. 'James,' she called, through the double doors.

'Yes, madam.'

'Mr William's friend has arrived. I think perhaps he would like to wash.'

'Very good, madam.'

Mr Salter was not really asleep; he had been aware, remotely and impersonally, of Mrs Boot's scrutiny; he was aware, now, of James's slow passage across the hall.

'Dinner will be in directly, sir. May I take you to your room?'

For a moment Mr Salter thought he would be unable ever to move again; then, painfully, he rose to his feet. He observed his discarded shoes; so did James; neither of them felt disposed to stoop; each respected the other's feeling; Mr Salter padded upstairs beside the footman.

'I regret to say, sir, that your luggage is not yet available. Three of the outside men are delving for it at the moment.'

'Delving?'

'Assiduously, sir. It was inundated with slag at the time of the accident.'

'Accident?'

'Yes, sir, there has been a misadventure to the farm lorry that was conveying it from the station; we attribute it to the driver's inexperience. He overturned the vehicle in the back drive.'

'Was he hurt?'

'Oh yes, sir; gravely. Here is your room, sir.'

An oil lamp, surrounded by moths and autumnal beetles, burned on Priscilla's dressing-table, illuminating a homely, girlish room. Little had been done, beyond the removal of loofah and nightdress, to adapt it for male occupation. Twenty or thirty china animals stood on brackets and shelves, together with slots of deer, brushes of foxes, pads of otters, a horse's hoof, and other animal trophies; a low, bronchial growl came from under the bed.

'Miss Priscilla hoped you would not object to taking charge of Amabel for the night, sir. She's getting an old dog now and doesn't like to be moved. You'll find her perfectly quiet and good. If she barks in the night, it is best to feed her.'

James indicated two saucers of milk and minced meat which stood on the bed table that had already attracted Mr Salter's attention.

'Would that be all, sir?'

'Thank you,' said Mr Salter, weakly.

James left, gently closing the door which, owing to a long-standing defect in its catch, as gently swung open again behind him.

Mr Salter poured some warm water into the prettily flowered basin on the washhand stand.

James returned. 'I omitted to tell you, sir, the lavatory on this floor is out of order. The gentlemen use the one opening on the library.'

'Thank you.'

James repeated the pantomime of shutting the door.

Nurse Grainger was always first down in the drawing-room. Dinner was supposed to be at quarter past eight, and for fifteen years she had been on time. She was sitting there, stitching a wool mat of modernistic design, when Mrs Boot first entered. When Mrs Boot had given her order to James, she smiled at her and said, 'How is your patient tonight, nurse?' and Nurse Grainger answered as she had answered nightly for fifteen years, 'A little low-spirited.'

'Yes,' said Mrs Boot, 'she gets low-spirited in the evenings.'

The two women sat in silence, Nurse Grainger snipping and tugging at the magenta wool; Mrs Boot reading a gardening magazine to which she subscribed. It was not until Lady Trilby entered the room that she expressed her forebodings.

'The boys are late,' said Lady Trilby.

'Aunt Agnes,' said Mrs Boot gravely, 'William's friend has arrived in a *most peculiar condition.*'

'I know. I watched him come up the drive. Reeling all over the shop.'

'He let himself in and went straight off to sleep in the hall.'

'Best thing for him.'

'You mean . . . You don't think he could have been . . .?'

'The man was squiffy,' said Aunt Agnes. 'It was written all over him.'

Nurse Grainger uttered a knowing little cluck of disapproval.

'It's lucky Priscilla isn't here. What had we better do?'

'The boys will see to him.'

'Here is Theodore. I will ask him at once. Theodore, William's friend from London has arrived, and Aunt Agnes and I very much fear that he has taken too much.'

'Has he, by Jove,' said Uncle Theodore, rather enviously. 'Now you mention it, I shouldn't be at all surprised. I talked to the fellow out of my window. He was pounding the front door fit to knock it in.'

'What ought we to do?'

'Oh, he'll sober up,' said Uncle Theodore, from deep experience. Uncle Roderick joined them. 'I say, Rod, what d'you think? That journalist fellow of William's–he's sozzled.'

'We'd better keep an eye on him to see he doesn't get any more.'

'Yes. I'll tell James.'

Uncle Bernard joined the family circle. 'Good evening, good evening,' he said in his courtly fashion. 'I'm nearly the last, I see.'

'Bernard, we have something to tell you.'

'And I have something to tell *you*. I was sitting in the library not two minutes ago when a dirty little man came prowling in–without any shoes on.'

'Was he tipsy?'

'I dare say . . . now you mention it, I think he was.'

'That's William's friend.'

'Well, he should be taken care of. Where is William?'

William was playing dominoes with Nannie Bloggs. It was this custom of playing dominoes with her from six till seven every evening which had prevented him meeting Mr Slater at the station. On this particular evening the game had been prolonged far beyond its usual limit. Three times he had attempted to leave, but the old woman was inflexible. 'Just you stay where you sit,' she said. 'You always were a headstrong, selfish boy. Worse than your Uncle Theodore. Gallivanting about all over Africa with a lot of heathens, and now you *are* home you don't want to spend a few minutes with your old Nannie.'

'But, Nannie, I've got a guest arriving.'

'*Guest*. Time enough for him. It's not *you* he's after, I'll be bound. It's my pretty Priscilla. You leave them be . . . I'll make it half a sovereign this time.'

Not until the gong sounded for dinner would she let him go. 'Wash your hands,' she said, 'and brush your hair nicely. I don't know what your mother will say at you going down to dinner in your flannels. And mind you bring Priscilla's young man up afterwards and we'll have a nice game of cards. It's thirty-three shillings you owe me.'

Mr Salter had no opportunity of talking business at dinner. He sat between Mrs Boot and Lady Trilby; never an exuberant man, he now felt subdued almost to extinction and took his place glumly between the two formidable ladies; he might feel a little stronger, he hoped, after a glass of wine.

James moved heavily round the table with the decanters; claret for the ladies, William and Uncle Bernard, whisky and water for Uncle Theodore, medicated cider for Uncle Roderick. 'Water, sir?' said a voice in Mr Salter's ear.

'Well, I think perhaps I would sooner . . .' A clear and chilling cascade fell into his tumbler and James returned to the sideboard.

William, noticing a little shudder pass over his guest, leaned forward across the table. 'I say, Salter, haven't they given you anything to drink?'

'Well, as a matter of fact . . .'

Mrs Boot frowned at her son–a frown like a sudden spasm of pain. 'Mr Salter *prefers* water.'

'Nothing like it,' said Uncle Theodore. 'I respect him for it.'

'Well, as a matter of fact . . .'

Both ladies addressed him urgently and simultaneously; 'You're a great walker, Mr Salter,' in challenging tones from Lady Trilby; 'It is quite a treat for you to get away from your work into the country,' more gently from Mrs Boot. By the time that Mr Salter had dealt civilly with these two misstatements, the subject of wine was closed.

Dinner was protracted for nearly an hour, but not by reason of any great profusion or variety of food. It was rather a bad dinner; scarcely better than he would have got at Lord Copper's infamous table; greatly inferior to the daintily garnished little dishes which he enjoyed at home. In course of time each member of the Boot family had evolved an individual style of eating; before each plate was ranged a little store of seasonings and delicacies, all marked with their owner's initials–onion salt, Bombay duck, gherkins, garlic vinegar, Dijon mustard, pea-nut butter, icing sugar, varieties of biscuit from Bath and Tunbridge Wells, Parmesan cheese, and a dozen other jars and bottles and tins mingled incongruously with the heavy, Georgian silver; Uncle Theodore had a little spirit lamp and chafing dish with which he concocted a sauce. The dishes as sent in from the kitchen were rather the elementary materials of dinner than the dinner itself. Mr Salter found them correspondingly dull and unconscionably slow in coming. Conversation was general and intermittent.

Like foreign news bulletins, Boot family table talk took the form of antithetical statements rather than of free discussion.

'Priscilla took Amabel with her to the Caldicotes,' said Lady Trilby.

'She left her behind,' said Mrs Boot.

'A dirty old dog,' said Uncle Bernard.

'Too old to go visiting,' said Uncle Roderick.

'Too dirty.'

'Mr Salter is having Amabel to sleep with him,' said Mrs Boot.

'Mr Salter is very fond of her,' said Lady Trilby.

'He doesn't know her,' said Uncle Bernard.

'He's very fond of all dogs,' said Mrs Boot.

There was a pause in which James announced: 'If you please, madam, the men have sent up to say it is too dark to go on moving the slag.'

'Very awkward,' said Uncle Roderick. 'Blocks the back drive.'

'And Mr Salter will have no things for the night,' said Mrs Boot.

'William will lend him some.'

'Mr Salter will not mind. He will understand.'

'But he is sorry to have lost his things.'

Presently Mr Salter got the hang of it. 'It is a long way from the station,' he ventured.

'You stopped on the way.'

'Yes, to ask . . . I was lost.'

'You stopped several times.'

At last dinner came to an end.

'He got better towards the end of dinner,' said Lady Trilby in the drawing-room.

'He is practically himself again,' said Mrs Boot.

'Roderick will see that he does not get at the port.'

'You won't take port,' said Uncle Roderick.

'Well, as a matter of fact . . .'

'Push it round to Bernard, there's a good fellow.'

'You and William have business to discuss.'

'Yes,' said Mr Salter eagerly. 'Yes, it's most important.'

'You could go to the library.'

'Yes.'

William led his guest from the table and out of the room.

'Common little fellow,' said Uncle Roderick.

'It's a perfectly good name,' said Uncle Bernard. 'An early corruption of saltire, which no doubt he bears on his coat. But of course it may have been assumed irregularly.'

'Can't hold it,' said Uncle Theodore.

'I always understood that the true Salters became extinct in the fifteenth century . . .'

In the library William for the first time had the chance of apologizing for the neglect of his guest.

'Of course, of course. I quite understand that living where you do, you are naturally distracted . . . I would not have intruded on you for the world. But it was a matter of first-rate importance–of Lord Copper's personal wishes, you understand.

'There are two things. First, your contract with us . . . Boot,' said Mr Salter earnestly, 'you won't desert the ship.'

'Eh?'

'I mean it was the *Beast* that gave you your chance. You mustn't forget that!'

'No.'

'I suppose the *Brute* have made a very attractive offer. But believe me, Boot, I've known Fleet Street longer than you have. I've seen several men transfer from us to them. They thought they were going to be better off, but they weren't. It's no life for a man of individuality, working for the *Brute*. You'd be selling your soul, Boot . . . You haven't by the way, sold it?'

'No. They did send me a telegram. But to tell you the truth I was so glad to be home that I forgot to answer it.'

'Thank heaven. I've got a contract here, ready drawn up. Duplicate copies. They only need your signature. Luckily I did not pack them in my suitcase. A life contract for two thousand a year. Will you sign?'

William signed. He and Mr Salter each folded his copy and put it in his pocket; each with a feeling of deep satisfaction.

'And then there's the question of the banquet. There won't be any difficulty about that now. I quite understand that while the *Brute* offer was still in the air . . . Well, I'm delighted it's settled. You had better come up with me tomorrow morning. Lord Copper may want to see you beforehand.'

'No.'

'But, my dear Boot . . . You need have no worry about your speech. That is being written for you by Lord Copper's social secretary. It will be quite simple. Five minutes or so in praise of Lord Copper.'

'No.'

'The banquet will be widely reported. There may even be a film made of it.'

'No.'

'Really, Boot, I can't understand you at all.'

'Well,' said William with difficulty, 'I should feel an ass.'

'Yes,' said Mr Salter, 'I can understand that. But it's only for one evening.'

'I've felt an ass for weeks. Ever since I went to London. I've been treated like an ass.'

'Yes,' said Mr Salter sadly. 'That's what we are paid for.'

'It's one thing being an ass in Africa. But if I go to this banquet they may learn about it down here.'

'No doubt they would.'

'Nannie Bloggs and Nannie Price and everyone.'

Mr Salter was not in fighting form and he knew it. The strength was gone out of him. He was dirty and blistered and aching in every limb, cold sober and unsuitably dressed. He was in a strange sountry. These people were not his people nor their laws his. He felt like a Roman legionary, heavily armed, weighted with the steel and cast brass of civilization, tramping through forests beyond the Roman pale, harassed by silent, elusive savages, the vanguard of an advance that had pushed too far and lost touch with the base . . . or was he the abandoned rear-guard of a retreat; had the legions sailed?

'I think,' he said, 'I'd better ring up the office and ask their advice.'

'You can't do that,' said William cheerfully. 'The nearest office is three miles away; there's no car; and anyway it shuts at seven.'

Silence fell in the library. Once more Mr Salter rallied to the attack. He tried sarcasm.

'These ladies you mention; no doubt they are estimable people, but surely, my dear Boot, you will admit that Lord Copper is a little more important.'

'No,' said William gravely 'Not down here.'

They were still sitting in silence when Troutbeck came to them, ten minutes later.

'Miss Price says she is expecting you upstairs to play cards.'

'You don't mind?' William asked.

Mr Salter was past minding anything. He was led upstairs, down long lamp-lit corridors, through doors of faded baize to Nannie Price's room. Uncle Theodore was already there arranging the card table beside her bed. 'So this is him,' she said. 'Why hasn't he got any shoes?'

'It's a long story,' said William.

The beady old eyes studied Mr Salter's careworn face; she put on her spectacles and looked again. 'Too old,' she said.

Coming from whom it did, this criticism seemed a bit thick; even in his depressed condition, Mr Salter was roused to resentment. 'Too old for what?' he asked sharply.

Nannie Price, though hard as agate about matters of money and theology, had, in old age, a soft spot for a lover. 'There, there, dearie,' she said. 'I don't mean anything. There's many a young heart beats in an old body. Sit down.

Cut the cards, Mr Theodore. You've had a disappointment, I know, her being away. She always was a contrary girl. The harder the wooing the sweeter the winning, they say–two spades–and there's many a happy marriage between April and December–don't go peeping over my hand, Mr Theodore–and she's a good girl at heart, though she does forget her neck sometimes–three spades–comes out of the bath as black as she went in. I don't know what she does there . . .'

They played three rubbers and Mr Salter lost twenty-two shillings. As they rose to leave, Nannie Price, who had from long habit kept up a more or less continuous monologue during the course of the game, said, 'Don't give up, dearie. If it wasn't that your hair was thinning you mightn't be more than thirty-five. She doesn't know her own mind yet, and that's the truth.'

They left. William and Uncle Theodore accompanied Mr Salter to his room. William said 'Good night.' Uncle Theodore lingered.

'Pity you doubled our hearts,' he said.

'Yes.'

'Got you down badly.'

'Yes.'

A single candle stood on the table by the bed. In its light Mr Salter saw a suit of borrowed pyjamas laid out. Sleep was coming on him like a vast, pea-soup fog, rolling down Fleet Street from Ludgate Hill. He did not want to discuss their game of bridge.

'We had all the cards,' said Uncle Theodore magnanimously, sitting down on the bed.

'Yes.'

'I expect you keep pretty late hours in London.'

'Yes . . . no . . . that is to say, sometimes.'

'Hard to get used to country hours. I don't suppose you feel a bit sleepy?'

'Well, as a matter of fact . . .'

'When I lived in London,' began Uncle Theodore . . .

The candle burned low.

'Funny thing that . . .'

Mr Salter awoke with a start. He was sitting in Priscilla's chintz-covered arm-chair; Uncle Theodore was still on the bed, reclining now like a surfeited knight of the age of Heliogabalus . . .

'Of course you couldn't print it. But I've quite a number of stories you *could* print. Hundreds of 'em. I was wondering if it was the kind of thing your newspaper . . .'

'Quite outside my province, I'm afraid. You see, I'm the Foreign editor.'

'Half of them deal with Paris; *more* than half. For instance . . .'

'I should love to hear them, *all* of them, sometime, later, not now . . .'

'You pay very handsomely, I believe, on the *Beast*.'

'Yes.'

'Now suppose I was to write a series of articles . . .'

'Mr Boot,' said Mr Salter desperately, 'let us discuss it in the morning.'

'I'm never in my best form in the morning,' said Uncle Theodore doubtfully. 'Now after dinner I can talk quite happily until *any* time.'

'Come to London. See the features editor.'

'Yes,' said Uncle Theodore. 'I will. But I don't want to shock him; I should like your opinion first.'

The mists rose in Mr Salter's brain; a word or two loomed up and was lost again . . . 'Willis's rooms . . . "Pussy" Gresham . . . Romano's . . . believe it or not, fifteen *thousand* pounds . . .' Then all was silence.

When Mr Salter awoke he was cold and stiff and fully dressed except for his shoes; the candle was burned out. Autumnal dawn glimmered in the window, and Priscilla Boot, in riding habit, was ransacking the wardrobe for a lost tie.

2/iv

The managing editor of the *Beast* was not easily moved to pity. 'I say, Salter,' he said, almost reverently, 'you look terrible.'

'Yes,' said Mr Salter, lowering himself awkwardly into a chair, 'that's the only word for it.'

'These heavy drinking country squires, eh?'

'No. It wasn't *that*.'

'Have you got Boot?'

'Yes and no. Have you?'

'Yes and no. He signed all right.'

'So did mine. But he won't come to the banquet.'

'I've sent my Boot off to the Antarctic. He said he had to go abroad at once. Apparently some woman is pursuing him.'

'Mr Boot,' said Mr Salter, 'is afraid of losing the esteem of his old nurse.'

'*Women*,' said the managing editor.

One thought was in both men's minds. 'What are we going to say to Lord Copper?'

The social secretary, whom they went to consult, was far from helpful.

'Lord Copper is looking forward very much to his speech,' she said. 'He has been rehearsing it all the afternoon.'

'You could rewrite it a little,' said the managing editor. '"Even in the moment of triumph, duty called. Here today, gone tomorrow . . . honouring the empty chair . . . the high adventure of modern journalism . . ."' But even as he spoke, his voice faltered.

'No,' said the social secretary. 'That is not the kind of speech Lord Copper intends to make. You can hear him, in there, now.' A dull booming sound, like breakers on shingle, rose and fell beyond the veneered walnut doors. 'He's getting it by heart,' she added.

The two editors went sadly back to their own quarters.

'I've worked with the Megalopolitan, one way and another, for fifteen years,' said Mr Salter. 'I've got a wife to consider.'

'You at least might get other employment,' said the managing editor. 'You've been educated. There's nothing in the world I'm fit to do except edit the *Beast*.'

'It was your fault in the first place for engaging Boot at all. He wasn't a foreign page man.

'You sent him to Ishmaelia.'

'*I* wanted to sack him. You made him a hero. You made a monkey of him. It was you who thought of that article which upset him.'

'You encouraged Lord Copper to give him a knighthood.'

'You encouraged the banquet.'

'We were both at fault,' said the managing editor. 'But there's no point in our both suffering. Let's toss for who takes the blame.'

The coin spun in the air, fell and rolled away out of sight. Mr Salter was on his knees, searching, when the features editor looked in.

'Do either of you know anything about an old chap called Boot?' he asked. 'I can't get him out of my room. He's been sitting there telling me dirty stories since I got back from lunch. Says Salter sent him.'

3/i

Lord Copper quite often gave banquets; it would be an understatement to say that no one enjoyed them more than the host, for no one else enjoyed them at all, while Lord Copper positively exulted in every minute. For him they satisfied every requirement of a happy evening's entertainment; like everything that was to Lord Copper's taste, they were a little over life-size, unduly large and unduly long; they took place in restaurants which existed solely for such purposes, amid decorations which reminded Lord Copper of his execrable country seat at East Finchley; the provisions were copious, very bad and very expensive; the guests were assembled for no other reason than that Lord Copper had ordered it; they did not want to see each other; they had no reason to rejoice on the occasions which Lord Copper celebrated; they were there either because it was part of their job or because they were glad of a free dinner. Many were already on Lord Copper's pay roll and they thus found their working day prolonged by some three hours without recompense–with the forfeit, indeed, of the considerable expenses of dressing up, coming out at night, and missing the last train home; those who were normally the slaves of other masters were, Lord Copper felt, his for the evening. He had bought them and bound them, hand and foot, with consommé and cream of chicken, turbot and saddle, duck and pêche melba; and afterwards, when the cigars had been furtively pocketed and the brandy glasses filled with the horrible brown compound for which Lord Copper was paying two pounds a bottle, there came the golden hour when he rose to speak at whatever length he liked and on whatever subject, without fear of rivalry or interruption.

Often the occasion was purely contingent on Lord Copper's activities–some reshuffling of directorships, an amalgamation of subsidiary companies, or an issue of new stocks; sometimes some exhausted and resentful celebrity whom the *Beast* had adopted sat on Lord Copper's right hand as the guest of honour, and there, on this particular evening, at half-past eight, sat Mr Theodore Boot; he had tucked up his coat tails behind him, spread his napkin across his knees and, unlike any of Lord Copper's guests of honour before or since, was settling down to enjoy himself.

'Don't think I've ever been to this place before,' he began.

'No,' said Lord Copper. 'No, I suppose not. It is, I believe, the best place of its kind.'

'Since my time,' said Uncle Theodore tolerantly. 'New places always springing up. Other places closing down. The old order changeth, eh?'

'Yes,' said Lord Copper coldly.

It was not thus that he was accustomed to converse with junior reporters, however promising. There was a type, Lord Copper had learned, who became presumptuous under encouragement. Uncle Theodore, it was true, did not seem to belong to this type; it was hard to know exactly what type Uncle Theodore did belong to.

Lord Copper turned away rather petulantly and engaged his other neighbour–a forgotten and impoverished ex-Viceroy who for want of other invitations spent three or four evenings a week at dinners of this kind–but his mind was not in the conversation; it was disturbed. It had been disturbed all the evening, ever since, sharp on time, he had made his entrance to the inner reception room where the distinguished guests were segregated. Uncle Theodore had been standing there between Mr Slater and the managing editor. He wore a tail coat of obsolete cut, a black waistcoat, and a very tall collar; his purplish patrician fase had beamed on Lord Copper, but there had been no answering cordiality in Lord Copper's greeting. Boot was a surprise. Images were not easily formed or retained in Lord Copper's mind, but he had had quite a clear image of Boot, and Uncle Theodore did not conform to it. Was *this* Mrs Stitch's protégé? Was this the youngest K.G.B.? Had Lady Cockpurse commended *this* man's style? And–it gradually came back to him–was this the man he had himself met not two months back, and speeded on his trip to Ishmaelia? Lord Copper took another look and encountered a smile so urbane, so patronizing, so intolerably knowing, that he hastily turned away.

Someone had blundered.

Lord Copper turned to the secretary who stood, with the toast master, behind his chair.

'Wagstaff.'

'Yes, Lord Copper.'

'Take memo for tomorrow. "See Salter".'

'Very good, Lord Copper.'

The banquet must go on, thought Lord Copper.

The banquet went on.

The general hum of conversation was becoming louder. It was a note dearer to Lord Copper than the tongue of hounds in covert. He tried to close his mind to the enigmatic and, he was inclined to suspect, obnoxious presence on his right. He heard the unctuous voice rising and falling, breaking now and then into a throaty chuckle. Uncle Theodore, after touching infelicitously on a variety of topics, had found common ground with the distinguished guest on his right; they had both, in another age, known a man named Bertie Wodehouse-Bonner.

Uncle Theodore enjoyed his recollection and he enjoyed his champagne, but politeness at last compelled him reluctantly to address Lord Copper–a dull dog, but his host.

He leant nearer to him and spoke in a confidential manner.

'Tell me,' he asked, 'where does one go on to nowadays?'

'I beg your pardon.'

Uncle Theodore leered. 'You know. To round off the evening? . . .'

'Personally,' said Lord Copper, 'I intend to go to bed without any delay.'

'*Exactly*. Where's the place, nowadays?'

Lord Copper turned to his secretary.

'Wagstaff.'

'Yes, Lord Copper.'

'Memo for tomorrow. "Sack Salter".'

'Very good, Lord Copper.'

Only once did Uncle Theodore again tackle his host. He advised him to eat mustard with duck for the good of his liver. Lord Copper seemed not to hear. He sat back in his chair, surveying the room–for the evening, *his* room. The banquet must go on. At the four long tables which ran at right angles to his own the faces above the white shirt fronts were growing redder; the chorus of male conversation swelled in volume. Lord Copper began to see himself in a new light, as the deserted leader, shouldering alone the great burden of Duty. The thought comforted him. He had made a study of the lives of other great men; loneliness was the price they had all paid. None, he reflected, had enjoyed the devotion they deserved; there was Caesar and Brutus, Napoleon and Josephine, Shakespeare and–someone, he believed, had been disloyal to Shakespeare.

The time of his speech was drawing near. Lord Copper felt the familiar, infinitely agreeable sense of well-being which always preceded his after-dinner speeches; his was none of the nervous inspiration, the despair and exaltation of more ambitious orators; his was the profound, incommunicable contentment of monolocution. He felt himself suffused with a gentle warmth; he felt magnanimous.

'Wagstaff.'

'Lord Copper?'

'What was the last memo I gave you?'

'"Sack Salter", Lord Copper.'

'Nonsense. You must be more accurate. I said "Shift Salter".'

At last the great moment came. The toast master thundered on the floor with his staff and his tremendous message rang through the room.

'My Lords and Gentlemen. Pray silence for the Right Honourable the Viscount Copper.'

Lord Copper rose and breasted the applause. Even the waiters, he noticed with approval, were diligently clapping. He leant forwards on his fists, as it was his habit to stand on these happy occasions, and waited for silence. His secretary made a small, quite unnecessary adjustment to the microphone. His speech lay before him in a sheaf of typewritten papers. Uncle Theodore murmured a few words of encouragement. 'Cheer up,' he said. 'It won't last long.'

'Gentlemen,' he began, 'many duties fall to the lot of a man of my position, some onerous, some pleasant. It is a very pleasant duty to welcome tonight a colleague who though—' and Lord Copper saw the words 'young in years' looming up at him; he swerved–'young in his service to Megalopolitan Newspapers, has already added lustre to the great enterprise we have at heart–Boot of the *Beast*.' Uncle Theodore, who had joined the staff of the *Beast* less than six hours ago, smirked dissent and began to revise his opinion of Lord Copper; he was really an uncommonly civil fellow, thought Uncle Theodore.

At the name of Boot applause broke out thunderously, and Lord Copper, waiting for it to subside, glanced grimly through the pages ahead of him. For some time now his newspapers had been advocating a new form of driving test, by which the applicant for a licence sat in a stationary car while a cinema film unfolded before his eyes a nightmare drive down a road full of obstacles. Lord Copper had personally inspected a device of the kind and it was thus that his speech now appeared to him. The opportunities and achievements of youth had been the theme. Lord Copper looked from the glowing sentences to the guest of honour beside him (who at the moment had buried his nose in his brandy glass and was inhaling stertorously) and he rose above it. The banquet must go on.

The applause ended and Lord Copper resumed his speech. His hearers sank low in their chairs and beguiled the time in a variety of ways; by drawing little pictures on the menu, by playing noughts and crosses on the table-cloth, by having modest bets as to who could keep the ash longest on his cigar; and over them the tropic tide of oratory rose and broke in foaming surf, over the bowed, bald head of Uncle Theodore. It lasted thirty-eight minutes by Mr Salter's watch.

'Gentlemen,' said Lord Copper at last, 'in giving you the toast of Boot, I give you the toast of the Future . . .'

The Future . . . A calm and vinous optimism possessed the banquet . . .

A future for Lord Copper that was full to surfeit of things which no sane man seriously coveted–of long years of uninterrupted oratory at other banquets in other causes; of yearly, prodigious payments of super-tax crowned at their final end by death duties of unprecedented size; of a deferential opening and closing of doors, of muffled telephone bells and almost soundless typewriters.

A future for Uncle Theodore such as he had always at heart believed to be attainable. Two thousand a year, shady little gentlemen's chambers, the opportunity for endless reminiscence; sunlit morning saunterings down St James's Street between hatter and boot-maker and club; feline prowlings after dark; a buttonhole, a bowler hat with a curly brim, a clouded malacca cane, a kindly word to commissionaires and cab drivers.

A future for Mr Salter as art editor of *Home Knitting*; punctual domestic dinners; Sundays at home among the crazy pavements.

A future for Sir John Boot with the cropped amazons of the Antarctic.

A future for Mrs Stitch heaped with the spoils of every continent and every century, gadgets from New York and bronzes from the Aegean, new entrées and old friends.

A future for Corker and Pigge; they had travelled six hundred miles by now and were nearing the Sudanese frontier. Soon they will be kindly received by a District Commissioner, washed and revictualled and sent on their way home.

A future for Kätchen. She was sitting, at the moment, in the second class saloon of a ship bound for Madagascar, writing a letter:

Darling William,

We are going to Madagascar. My husband used to have a friend there and he says it is more comfortable than to come to Europe so will you please send us the money there. Not care of the consul because that would not be comfortable but poste restante. My husband says I should not have sold the specimens but I explained that you would pay what they are worth so now he does not mind. They are worth £50. It will be better if you will buy francs because he says you will get more than we should. We look forward very much to getting the money, so please send it by the quickest way. The boat was not worth very much money when we got to French territory. I am very well.

Ever your loving,
Kätchen

A future for William . . .

. . . *the waggons lumber in the lane under their golden glory of harvested sheaves*, he wrote; *maternal rodents pilot their furry brood through the stubble;* . . .

He laid down his pen. *Lush Places* need not be finished until tomorrow evening.

The rest of the family had already gone up. William took the last candle from the table and put out the lamps in the hall. Under the threadbare carpet the stair-boards creaked as he mounted to his room.

Before getting into bed he drew the curtain and threw open the window. Moonlight streamed into the room.

Outside the owls hunted maternal rodents and their furry brood.

Put Out More Flags

EVELYN WAUGH

PUT OUT MORE FLAGS

Author's Note

The military operation described in Chapter III is wholly imaginary. No existing unit of His Majesty's Forces is represented there, or anywhere, directly or indirectly. No character is derived from any living man or woman.

E.W.

'A man getting drunk at a farewell party should strike a musical tone, in order to strengthen his spirit . . . and a drunk military man should order gallons and put out more flags in order to increase his military splendour.'

Dedicatory Letter to
Major Randolph Churchill
Fourth Hussars, Member of Parliament

Dear Randolph,

I am afraid that these pages may not be altogether acceptable to your ardent and sanguine nature. They deal, mostly, with a race of ghosts, the survivors of the world we both knew ten years ago, which you have outflown in the empyrean of strenuous politics, but where my imagination still fondly lingers. I find more food for thought in the follies of Basil Seal and Ambrose Silk, than in the sagacity of the higher command. These characters are no longer contemporary in sympathy; they were forgotten even before the war; but they lived on delightfully in holes and corners and, like everyone else, they have been disturbed in their habits by the rough intrusion of current history. Here they are in that odd, dead period before the Churchillian renaissance, which people called at the time the Great Bore War.

So please accept them with the sincere regards of

Your affectionate friend,

THE AUTHOR

I

AUTUMN

I

In the week which preceded the outbreak of the Second World War–days of surmise and apprehension which cannot, without irony, be called the last days of peace–and on the Sunday morning when all doubts were finally resolved and misconceptions corrected, three rich women thought first and mainly of Basil Seal. They were his sister, his mother and his mistress.

Barbara Sothill was at Malfrey; in recent years she had thought of her brother as seldom as circumstances allowed her, but on that historic September morning, as she walked to the village, he predominated over a multitude of worries.

She and Freddy had just heard the Prime Minister's speech, broadcast by wireless. 'It is an evil thing we are fighting,' he had said and as Barbara turned her back on the house where, for the most part, the eight years of her marriage had been spent, she felt personally challenged and threatened, as though, already, the mild, autumnal sky were dark with circling enemy and their shadows were trespassing on the sunlit lawns.

There was something female and voluptuous in the beauty of Malfrey; other lovely houses maintained a virginal modesty or a manly defiance, but Malfrey had no secret from the heavens; it had been built more than two hundred years ago in days of victory and ostentation and lay, spread out, sumptuously at ease, splendid, defenceless and provocative; a Cleopatra among houses; across the sea, Barbara felt, a small and envious mind, a meanly ascetic mind, a creature of the conifers, was plotting the destruction of her home. It was for Malfrey that she loved her prosaic and slightly absurd husband; for Malfrey, too, that she had abandoned Basil and with him the part of herself which, in the atrophy endemic to all fruitful marriages, she had let waste and die.

It was half a mile to the village down the lime avenue. Barbara walked because, just as she was getting into the car, Freddy had stopped her saying, 'No petrol now for gadding about.'

Freddy was in uniform, acutely uncomfortable in ten-year-old trousers. He had been to report at the yeomanry headquarters the day before, and was home for two nights collecting his kit, which, in the two years since he was last at camp, had been misused in charades and picnics and dispersed about the house in a dozen improbable places. His pistol, in particular, had been a trouble. He had had the whole household hunting it, saying fretfully, 'It's all very well, but I can get court-martialled for this,' until, at length, the nurserymaid found it at the back of the toy cupboard. Barbara was now on her way to look for his binoculars which she remembered vaguely having lent to the scoutmaster.

The road under the limes led straight to the village; the park gates of elaborately wrought iron swung on rusticated stone piers, and the two lodges formed a side of the village green; opposite them stood the church, on either side two inns, the vicarage, the shop and a row of grey cottages; three massive chestnuts grew from the roughly rectangular grass plot in the centre. It was a Beauty spot, justly but reluctantly famous, too much frequented of late by walkers but still, through Freddy's local influence, free of charabancs; a bus stopped three times a day on weekdays, four times on Tuesdays when the market was held in the neighbouring town, and to accommodate passengers Freddy had that year placed an oak seat under the chestnuts.

It was here that Barbara's thoughts were brought up sharply by an unfamiliar spectacle; six dejected women sat in a row staring fixedly at the closed doors of the Sothill Arms. For a moment Barbara was puzzled; then she remembered. These were Birmingham women. Fifty families had arrived at Malfrey late on Friday evening, thirsty, hot, bewildered and resentful after a day in train and bus. Barbara had chosen the five saddest families for herself and dispersed the rest in the village and farms.

Punctually next day the head housemaid, a veteran of old Mrs Sothill's regime, had given notice of leaving. 'I don't know how we shall do without you,' said Barbara.

'It's my legs, madam. I'm not strong enough for the work. I could just manage as things were, but now with children all over the place . . .'

'You know we can't expect things to be easy in war time. We must expect to make sacrifices. This is our war work.'

But the woman was obdurate. 'There's my married sister at Bristol,' she said. 'Her husband was on the reserve. I ought to go and help her now he's called up.'

An hour later the remaining three housemaids had appeared with prim expressions of face.

'Edith and Olive and me have talked it over and we want to go and make aeroplanes. They say they are taking on girls at Brakemore's.'

'You'll find it terribly hard work, you know.'

'Oh, it's not the work, madam. It's the Birmingham women. The way they leave their rooms.'

'It's all very strange for them at first. We must do all we can to help. As soon as they settle down and get used to our ways . . .' but she saw it was hopeless while she spoke.

'They say they want girls at Brakemore's,' said the maids.

In the kitchen Mrs Elphinstone was loyal. 'But I can't answer for the girls,' she said. 'They seem to think war is an excuse for a lark.'

It was the kitchen-maids, anyway, and not Mrs Elphinstone, thought Barbara, who had to cope with the extra meals . . .

Benson was sound. The Birmingham women caused *him* no trouble. But James would be leaving for the Army within a few weeks. It's going to be a difficult winter, thought Barbara.

These women, huddled on the green, were not Barbara's guests, but she saw on their faces the same look of frustration and defiance. Dutifully, rather than prudently, she approached the group and asked if they were comfortable. She spoke to them in general and each felt shy of answering; they looked away from her sullenly towards the locked inn. Oh dear, thought Barbara, I suppose they wonder what business it is of mine.

'I live up there,' she said, indicating the gates. 'I've been arranging your billets.'

'Oh, have you?' said one of the mothers. 'Then perhaps you can tell us how long we've got to stop.'

'That's right,' said another.

'D'you know,' said Barbara, 'I don't believe anyone has troubled to think about that. They've all been too busy getting you away.'

'They got no right to do it,' said the first mother. 'You can't keep us here compulsory.'

'But surely you don't *want* to have your children bombed, do you?'

'We won't stay where we're not wanted.'

'That's right,' said the yes-woman.

'But of *course* you're wanted.'

'Yes, like the stomach-ache.'

'That's right.'

For some minutes Barbara reasoned with the fugitives until she felt that her only achievement had been to transfer to herself all the odium which more properly belonged to Hitler. Then she went on her way to the scoutmaster's, where, before she could retrieve the binoculars, she had to listen to the story of the Birmingham schoolmistress, billeted on him, who refused to help wash up.

As she crossed the green on her homeward journey, the mothers looked away from her.

'I hope the children are enjoying themselves a little,' she said, determined not to be cut in her own village.

'They're down at the school. Teacher's making them play games.'

'The park's always open, you know, if any one of you care to go inside.'

'We had a park where we came from. With a band Sundays.'

'Well, I'm afraid I can't offer a band. But it's thought rather pretty, particularly down by the lake. Do take the children in if you feel like it.'

When she had left the chief mother said: 'What's she? Some kind of inspector, I suppose, with her airs and graces. The idea of inviting us into the park. You'd think the place belonged to her the way she goes on.'

Presently the two inns opened their doors and the scandalized village watched a procession of mothers assemble from cottage, farm and mansion and make for the bar parlours.

Luncheon decided him; Freddy went upstairs immediately he left the dining-room and changed into civilian clothes. 'Think I'll get my maid to put me into something loose,' he said in the voice he used for making jokes. It was this kind of joke Barbara had learned to recognize during her happy eight years in his company.

Freddy was large, masculine, prematurely bald and superficially cheerful; at heart he was misanthropic and gifted with that sly, sharp instinct for self-preservation that passes for wisdom among the rich; his indolence was qualified with enough basic bad temper to ensure the respect of those about him. He took in most people, but not his wife or his wife's family.

Not only did he have a special expression of face for making jokes; he had one for use when discussing his brother-in-law Basil. It should have conveyed lofty disapproval tempered by respect for Barbara's loyalty; in fact it suggested sulkiness and guilt.

The Seal children, for no reason that was apparent to the rest of the world, had always held the rest of the world in scorn. Freddy did not like Tony; he found him supercilious and effeminate, but he was prepared to concede to him certain superiorities; no one doubted that there was a brilliant career ahead of him in diplomacy. The time would come when they would all be very proud of Tony. But Basil from his earliest days had been a source of embarrassment and reproach. On his own terms Freddy might have been willing to welcome a black sheep in the Seal family, someone who was 'never mentioned', to whom he might, every now and then, magnanimously unknown to anyone except Barbara, extend a helping hand; someone, even, in whom he might profess to see more good than the rest of the world. Such a kinsman might very considerably have redressed the balance of Freddy's self-esteem. But, as Freddy found as soon as he came to know the Seals intimately, Basil, so far from being never mentioned, formed the subject of nearly half their conversation. At that time they were ever ready to discuss with relish his latest outrage, ever hopeful of some splendid success for him in the immediate future, ever contemptuous of the disapproval of the rest of the world. And Basil himself regarded Freddy pitilessly, with eyes which, during his courtship and the first years of marriage, he had recognized in Barbara herself.

For there was a disconcerting resemblance between Basil and Barbara; she, too, was *farouche* in a softer and deadlier manner, and the charm which held him breathless, flashed in gross and acquisitive shape in Basil. Maternity and the tranquil splendour of Malfrey had wrought changes in her; it was very rarely, now, that the wild little animal in her came above ground; but it was there in its earth, and from time to time he was aware of it, peeping out after long absences; a pair of glowing eyes at the twist in the tunnel watching him as an enemy.

Barbara herself pretended to no illusions about Basil. Years of disappointment and betrayal had convinced her, in the reasoning part of her, that he was no good. They had played pirates together in the nursery and the game was over. Basil played pirates alone. She apostatized from her faith in him almost with formality, and yet, as a cult will survive centuries after its myths have been exposed and its sources of faith tainted, there was still deep in her that early piety, scarcely discernible now in a little residue of superstition, so that this morning when her world seemed rocking about her, she turned back to Basil. Thus, when earthquake strikes a modern city and the pavements gape, the sewers buckle up and the great buildings tremble and topple, men in bowler hats and natty, ready-made suitings, born of generations of literates and rationalists, will suddenly revert to the magic of the forest and cross their fingers to avert the avalanche of concrete.

Three times during luncheon Barbara had spoken of Basil and now, as she and Freddy walked arm in arm on the terrace, she said, 'I believe it's what he's been waiting for all these years.'

'Who, waiting for what?'

'Basil, for the war.'

'Oh . . . Well, I suppose in a way we all have really . . . the gardens are going to be a problem. I suppose we could get some of the men exemption on the grounds that they're engaged in agriculture, but it hardly seems playing the game.'

It was Freddy's last day at Malfrey and he did not want to spoil it by talking of Basil. It was true that the yeomanry were not ten miles away; it was true, also, that they were unlikely to move for a very long time; they had recently been mechanized, in the sense that they had had their horses removed; few of them had ever seen a tank; he would be back and forwards continually during the coming months; he meant to shoot the pheasants; but although this was no final leave taking he felt entitled to more sentiment than Barbara was showing.

'Freddy, don't be bloody.' She kicked him sharply on the ankle for she had found, early in married life, that Freddy liked her to swear and kick in private. 'You know exactly what I mean. Basil *needed* a war. He's not meant for peace.'

'That's true enough. The wonder is he's kept out of prison. If he'd been born in a different class he wouldn't have.'

Barbara suddenly chuckled. 'D'you remember how he took mother's emeralds, the time he went to Azania? But then you see that would never have happened if there'd been a war of our own for him to go to. He's always been mixed up in fighting.'

'If you call living in a gin palace in La Paz and seeing generals shoot one another . . .'

'And Spain.'

'Journalist and gun runner.'

'He's always been a soldier *manqué*.'

'Well, he hasn't done much about it. While he's been gadding about the rest of us have been training as territorials and yeomanry.'

'Darling, a fat lot of training you've done.'

'If there'd been more like us and fewer like Basil there'd never have been a war. You can't blame Ribbentrop for thinking us decadent when he saw people like Basil about. I don't suppose they'll have much use for him in the army. He's thirty-six. He might get some sort of job connected with censorship. He seems to know a lot of languages.'

'You see,' said Barbara. 'Basil will be covered with medals while your silly old yeomanry are still messing in a Trust House and waiting for your tanks.'

There were duck on the lake and she let Freddy talk about them. She led him down his favourite paths. There was a Gothic pavilion where by long habit Freddy often became amorous; he did become amorous. And all the time she thought of Basil. She thought of him in terms of the war books she had read. She saw him as Siegfried Sassoon, an infantry subaltern in a mud-bogged trench standing to at dawn, his eyes on his wrist watch, waiting for zero hour; she saw him as Compton Mackenzie, spider in a web of Balkan intrigue, undermining a monarchy among olive trees and sculptured marble; she saw him as T.E. Lawrence and Rupert Brooke.

Freddy, assuaged, reverted to sport. 'I won't ask any of the regiment over for the early shoots,' he said. 'But I don't see why we shouldn't let some of them have a bang at the cocks round about Christmas.'

II

Lady Seal was at her home in London. She had taken fewer precautions against air raids than most of her friends. Her most valuable possession, her small Carpaccio, had been sent to safe keeping at Malfrey; the miniatures and Limoges enamels were at the bank; the Sèvres was packed in crates and put below stairs. Otherwise there was no change in her drawing-room. The ponderous old curtains needed no unsightly strips of black paper to help them keep in the light.

The windows were open now on the balcony. Lady Seal sat in an elegant rosewood chair gazing out across the square. She had just heard the Prime Minister's speech. Her butler approached from the end of the room.

'Shall I remove the radio, my lady?'

'Yes, by all means. He spoke very well, very well indeed.'

'It's all very sad, my lady.'

'Very sad for the Germans, Anderson.'

It was quite true, thought Lady Seal; Neville Chamberlain had spoken surprisingly well. She had never liked him very much, neither him nor his brother–if anything she had preferred the brother, but they were uncomfortable, drab fellows both of them. However, he had spoken very creditably that morning, as though at last he were fully alive to his responsibilities. She would ask him to luncheon. But perhaps he would be busy; the most improbable people were busy in war time, she remembered.

Her mind went back to the other war, that until that morning had been The War. No one very near to her had fought. Christopher had been too old, Tony, just too young; her brother Edward had begun by commanding a brigade–they thought the world of him at the Staff College–but, inexplicably, his career had come to very little; he was still brigadier in 1918, at Dar-es-Salaam. But the war had been a sad time; so many friends in mourning and Christopher fretful about the coalition. It had been a bitter thing for them all, accepting Lloyd George, but Christopher had patriotically made the sacrifice with the rest of them; probably only she knew how much he had felt it. The worst time had been after the armistice, when peerages were sold like groceries and the peace terms were bungled. Christopher had always said they would have to pay for it in the long run.

The hideous, then unfamiliar shriek of the air-raid sirens sang out over London.

'That was the warning, my lady.'

'Yes, Anderson. I heard it.'

'Will you be coming downstairs?'

'No, not yet at any rate. Get all the servants down and see they are quiet.'

'Will you require your respirator, my lady?'

'I don't suppose so. From what Sir Joseph tells me the danger of gas is very slight. In any case I dare say this is only a practice. Leave it on the table.'

'Will that be all, my lady?'

'That's all. See that the maids don't get nervous.'

Lady Seal stepped on to the balcony and looked up into the clear sky. They'll get more than they bargain for if they try and attack *us*, she thought. High time that man was taught a lesson. He's made nothing but trouble for years. She returned to her chair thinking. Anyway *I* never made a fuss of that vulgar man von Ribbentrop. I wouldn't have him inside the house, even when that goose Emma Granchester was plaguing us all to be friendly to him. I hope she feels foolish this morning.

Lady Seal waited with composure for the bombardment to begin. She had told Anderson it was probably only a practice. That was what one told servants; otherwise they might panic–not Anderson but the maids. But in her heart Lady Seal was sure that the attack was coming; it would be just like the Germans, always blustering and showing off and pretending to be efficient. The history Lady Seal had learned in the schoolroom had been a simple tale of the maintenance of right against the superior forces of evil and the battle honours of her country rang musically in her ears–Crécy, Agincourt, Cadiz, Blenheim, Gibraltar, Inkerman, Ypres. England had fought many and various enemies with many and various allies, often on quite recondite pretexts, but always justly, chivalrously, and with ultimate success. Often, in Paris, Lady Seal had been proud that her people had never fallen to the habit of naming streets after their feats of arms; that was suitable enough for the short-lived and purely professional triumphs of the French, but to put those great manifestations of divine rectitude which were the victories of England to the use, for their postal addresses, of milliners and chiropodists, would have been a baseness to which even the radicals had not stooped. The steel engravings of her schoolroom lived before her eyes, like tableaux at a charity fête–Sydney at Zutphen, Wolfe at Quebec, Nelson at Trafalgar (Wellington, only, at Waterloo was excluded from the pageant by reason of the proximity of Blücher, pushing himself forward with typical Prussian effrontery to share the glory which the other had won) and to this tremendous assembly (not unlike in Lady Seal's mind those massed groups of wealth and respectability portrayed on the Squadron Lawn at Cowes and hung with their key plans in lobbies and billiard rooms) was added that morning a single new and rather improbable figure, Basil Seal.

The last war had cost her little; nothing, indeed, except a considerable holding of foreign investments and her brother Edward's reputation as a strategist. Now she had a son to offer her country. Tony had weak eyes and a career, Freddy was no blood of hers and was not cast in a heroic mould, but Basil, her wayward and graceless and grossly disappointing Basil, whose unaccountable taste for low company had led him into so many vexatious scrapes in the last ten years, whose wild oats refused to correspond with those of his Uncle Edward; Basil who had stolen her emeralds and made Mrs Lyne distressingly conspicuous; Basil, his peculiarities merged in the manhood of England, at last was entering on his inheritance. She must ask Jo about getting him a commission in a decent regiment.

At last, while she was still musing, the sirens sounded the All Clear.

Sir Joseph Mainwaring was lunching with Lady Seal that day. It was an arrangement made early in the preceding week before either of them knew that the day they were choosing was one which would be marked in the world's calendars until the end of history. He arrived punctually, as he always did; as he had done, times out of number, in the long years of their friendship.

Sir Joseph was not a church-going man except when he was staying at one of the very rare, very august houses where it was still the practice; on this Sunday morning, however, it would not have been fantastic to describe his spirit as inflamed by something nearly akin to religious awe. It *would* be fantastic to describe him as purged, and yet there had been something delicately purgative in the experiences of the morning and there was an unfamiliar buoyancy in his bearing as though he had been at somebody's Eno's. He felt ten years younger.

Lady Seal devoted to this old booby a deep, personal fondness which was rare among his numerous friends and a reliance which was incomprehensible but quite common.

'There's only ourselves, Jo,' she said as she greeted him. 'The Granchesters were coming but he had to go and see the King.'

'Nothing could have been more delightful. Yes, I think we shall all be busy again now. I don't know exactly what I shall be doing yet. I shall know better after I've been to Downing Street to-morrow morning. I imagine it will be some advisory capacity to the War Cabinet. It's nice to feel in the centre of things again, takes one back ten years. Stirring times, Cynthia, stirring times.'

'It's one of the things I wanted to see Emma Granchester about. There must be so many committees we ought to start. Last war it was Belgian refugees. I suppose it will be Poles this time. It's a great pity it isn't people who talk a language one knows.'

'No, no Belgians this time. It will be a different war in many ways. An economic war of attrition, that is how I see it. Of course we had to have all this A.R.P. and shelters and so on. The radicals were making copy out of it. But I think we can take it there won't be any air raids, not on London at any rate. Perhaps there may be an attempt on the sea-ports, but I was having a most interesting talk yesterday to Eddie Beste-Bingham at the Beefsteak; we've got a most valuable invention called R.D.F. That'll keep 'em off.'

'Dear Jo, you always know the most encouraging things. What is R.D.F.?'

'I'm not absolutely clear about that. It's very secret.'

'Poor Barbara has evacuees at Malfrey.'

'What a shocking business! Dear, dreaming Malfrey. Think of a Birmingham board school in that exquisite Grinling Gibbons saloon. It's all a lot of nonsense, Cynthia. You know I'm the last man to prophesy rashly, but I think we can take one thing as axiomatic. There will be no air attack on London. The Germans will never attempt the Maginot line. The French will hold on for ever, if needs be, and the German air-bases are too far away for them to be able to attack us. If they do, we'll R.D.F. them out of the skies.'

'Jo,' said Lady Seal, when they were alone with the coffee. 'I want to talk to you about Basil.'

How often in the last twenty years had Sir Joseph heard those heavy words, uttered with so many intonations in so wide a variety of moods, but always, without fail, the prelude, not, perhaps to boredom, but to a lowering of the interest and warmth of their converse! It was only in these maternal conferences that Cynthia Seal became less than the perfect companion, only then that, instead of giving, she demanded, as it were, a small sumptuary duty upon the riches of her friendship.

Had he been so minded Sir Joseph could have drawn a graph of the frequency and intensity of these discussions. There had been the steady rise from nursery through school to the university, when he had been called on to applaud each new phase of Basil's precocious development. In those days he had accepted Basil at his face value as an exceptionally brilliant and beautiful youth in danger of being spoiled. Then, towards the end of Basil's second year at Balliol, had come a series of small seismic disturbances, when Cynthia Seal was alternately mutely puzzled or eloquently distressed; then the first disaster, rapidly followed by Christopher's death. From then onwards for fifteen years the line had dipped and soared dizzily as Basil's iniquities rose on the crest or fell into the trough of notoriety, but with the passing years there had been a welcome decline in the mean level; it was at least six months since he had heard the boy's name.

'Ah,' he said. 'Basil, eh,' trying to divine from his hostess's manner whether he was required to be judicial, compassionate or congratulatory.

'You've so often been helpful in the past.'

'I've tried,' said Sir Joseph recalling momentarily his long record of failures on Basil's behalf. 'Plenty of good in the boy.'

'I feel so much happier about him since this morning, Jo. Sometimes, lately, I've begun to doubt whether we shall ever find the proper place for Basil. He's been a square peg in so many round holes. But this war seems to take the responsibility off our hands. There's room for everyone in war time, every *man*. It's always been Basil's *individuality* that's been wrong. You've said that often, Jo. In war time individuality doesn't matter any more. There are just *men*, aren't there?'

'Yes,' said Sir Joseph doubtfully. 'Yes. Basil's individuality has always been rather strong, you know. He must be thirty-five or thirty-six now. That's rather old for starting as a soldier.'

'Nonsense, Jo. Men of forty-five and fifty enlisted in the ranks in the last war and died as gallantly as anyone else. Now I want you to see the Lieutenant-Colonels of the foot guard regiments and see where he will fit in best . . .'

In her time Cynthia Seal had made many formidable demands on Basil's behalf. This, which she was now asking with such assumption of ease, seemed to Sir Joseph one of the most vexatious. But he was an old and loyal friend and a man of affairs, moreover, well practised, by a lifetime of public service, in the evasion of duty. 'Of course, my dear Cynthia, I can't promise any results. . . .'

III

Angela Lyne was returning by train from the South of France. It was the time when, normally, she went to Venice, but this year, with international politics tediously on every tongue, she had lingered at Cannes until and beyond the last moment. The French and Italians whom she met had said war was impossible; they said it with assurance before the Russian pact, with double assurance after it. The English said there would be war, but not immediately. Only the

Americans knew what was coming, and exactly when. Now she was travelling in unwonted discomfort through a nation moving to action under the dour precepts, '*il faut en finir*' and '*nous gagnerons parce que nous sommes les plus forts*'.

It was a weary journey; the train was already eight hours late; the restaurant car had disappeared during the night at Avignon. Angela was obliged to share a two-berth sleeper with her maid and counted herself lucky to have got one at all; several of her acquaintances had stayed behind, waiting for things to get better; at the moment no reservations were guaranteed and the French seemed to have put off their politeness and packed it in moth-ball for the duration of hostilities.

Angela had a glass of Vichy water on the table before her. She sipped, gazing out at the passing landscape every mile of which gave some evidence of the changing life of the country; hunger and the bad night she had spent raised her a hair's breadth above reality and her mind, usually so swift and orderly, fell into pace with the train, now rocking in haste, now barely moving, seeming to grope its way from point to point.

A stranger passing the open door of her compartment might well have speculated on her nationality and place in the world and supposed her to be American, the buyer perhaps for some important New York dress shop whose present abstraction was due to the worries of war-time transport for her 'collection'. She wore the livery of the highest fashion, but as one who dressed to inform rather than to attract: nothing which she wore, nothing it might be supposed in the pigskin jewel-case above her head, had been chosen by or for a man. Her smartness was individual; she was plainly not one of those who scrambled to buy the latest gadget in the few breathless weeks between its first appearance and the inundation of the cheap markets of the world with its imitations; her person was a record and criticism of succeeding fashions, written as it were, year after year, in one clear and characteristic fist. Had the curious fellow passenger stared longer–as he was free to do without offence, so absorbed was Angela in her own thoughts–he would have been checked in his hunt when he came to study his subject's face. All her properties–the luggage heaped above and around her, the set of her hair, her shoes, her finger-nails, the barely perceptible aura of scent that surrounded her, the Vichy water and the paper-bound volume of Balzac on the table before her–all these things spoke of what (had she been, as she seemed, American) she would have called her - personality'. But the face was mute. It might have been carved in jade, it was so smooth and cool and conventionally removed from the human. A stranger might have watched her for mile after mile, as a spy or a lover or a newspaper reporter will loiter in the street before a closed house, and see no chink of light, hear no whisper of movement behind the shuttered façade, and in direct proportion to his discernment, he would have gone on his way down the corridor baffled and disturbed. Had he been told the bare facts about this seemingly cosmopolitan, passionless, barren, civilised woman, he might have despaired of ever again forming his judgment of a fellow being; for Angela Lyne was Scottish, the only child of a Glasgow millionaire–a jovial, rascally millionaire who had started life in a street gang–she was the wife of a dilettante architect, the mother of a single robust and unattractive son, the dead spit, it was said, of his grandfather, and her life had so foundered on passion that this golden daughter of fortune was rarely spoken of by her friends without the qualifying epithet of 'poor' Angela Lyne.

Only in one respect would the casual observer have hit upon the truth. Angela's appearance was not designed for man. It is sometimes disputed–and opinions are canvassed in popular papers to decide the question–whether woman alone on a desert island would concern herself with clothes; Angela, as far as she herself was concerned, disposed of the question finally. For seven years she had been on a desert island; her appearance had become a hobby and distraction, a pursuit entirely self-regarding and self-rewarding; she watched herself moving in the mirrors of the civilized world as a prisoner will watch the antics of a rat, whom he has domesticated to the dungeon. (In the case of her husband, grottoes took the place of fashion. He had six of them now, bought in various parts of Europe, some from Naples, some from Southern Germany, and painfully transported, stone by stone, to Hampshire.)

For seven years, ever since she was twenty-five and two years married to her dandy-aesthete, 'poor' Angela Lyne had been in love with Basil Seal. It was one of those affairs which, beginning lightheartedly as an adventure and accepted lightheartedly by their friends as an amusing scandal, seemed somehow petrified by a Gorgon glance and endowed with an intolerable permanence; as though in a world of capricious and fleeting alliances, the ironic Fates had decided to set up a standing, frightful example of the natural qualities of man and woman, of their basic aptitude to fuse together; a label on the packing case 'These chemicals are dangerous'–an admonitory notice, like the shattered motor-cars erected sometimes at dangerous turns in the road, so that the least censorious were chilled by the spectacle and recoiled saying, 'Really, you know, there's something rather squalid about those two.'

It was a relationship which their friends usually described as 'morbid', by which they meant that sensuality played a small part in it, for Basil was attracted only to very silly girls and it was by quite other bonds that he and Angela were fettered together.

Cedric Lyne pottering disconsolately in his baroque solitudes and watching with dismay the progress of his blustering son used to tell himself, with the minimum of discernment, that a béguine like that could not possibly last. For Angela there seemed no hope of release. Nothing, she felt in despair, would ever part them but death. Even the flavour of the Vichy water brought thoughts of Basil as she remembered the countless nights in the last seven years when she had sat late with him, while he got drunk and talked more and more wildly, and she sipping her water waited her turn to strike, hard and fierce, at his conceit, until as he got more drunk he became superior to her attacks and talked her down and eventually came stupidly away.

She turned to the window as the train slackened to walking pace, passing truck after truck of soldiers. '*Il faut en finir*', '*Nous gagnerons parce que nous sommes les plus forts*'. A hard-boiled people, the French. Two nights ago at Cannes, an American had been talking about the mutinous regiments decimated in the last war. 'It's a pity they haven't got anyone like old Pétain to command them this time,' he had said.

The villa at Cannes was shut now and the key was with the gardener. Perhaps she would never go back. This year she remembered it only as the place where she had waited in vain for Basil. He had telegraphed: 'International situation forbids joy riding.' She had sent him the money for his journey but there had been no answer. The gardener would make a good thing out of the vegetables. A hard-boiled people, the French; Angela wondered why that was thought to be a good thing; she had always had a revulsion from hard-boiled eggs, even at picnics in the nursery; hard-boiled; over-cooked; over-praised for their cooking. When people professed a love of France, they meant love of eating; the ancients located the deeper emotions in the bowels. She had heard a commercial traveller in the Channel packet welcome Dover and English food. 'I can't stomach that French messed-up stuff.' A commonplace criticism, thought Angela, that applied to French culture for the last two generations–'messed-up stuff', stale ingredients from Spain and America and Russia and Germany, disguised in a sauce of white wine from Algeria. France died with her monarchy. You could not even eat well, now, except in the provinces. It all came back to eating. 'What's eating you?' . . . Basil claimed to have eaten a girl once in Africa; he had been eating Angela now for seven years. Like the Spartan boy and the fox . . . Spartans at Thermopylae, combing their hair before the battle; Angela had never understood that, because Alcibiades had cut off his hair in order to make himself acceptable. What did the Spartans think about hair really? Basil would have to cut his hair when he went into the army. Basil the Athenian would have to sit at the public tables of Sparta, clipped blue at the neck where before his dark hair had hung untidily to his collar. Basil in the pass at Thermopylae . . .

Angela's maid returned from gossiping with the conductor. 'He says he doesn't think the sleeping cars will go any farther than Dijon. We shall have to change into day coaches. Isn't it wicked, madam, when we've paid?'

'Well, we're at war now. I expect there'll be a lot to put up with.'

'Will Mr Seal be in the army?'

'I shouldn't be surprised.'

'He will look different, won't he, madam?'

'Very different.'

They were both silent, and in the silence Angela knew, by an intuition which defied any possible doubt, exactly what her maid was thinking. She was thinking: 'Supposing Mr Seal gets himself killed. Best thing really for all concerned.'

. . . Flaxman Greeks reclining in death among the rocks of Thermopylae; riddled scarecrows sprawling across the wire of no-man's land . . . Till death us do part . . . Through the haphazard trail of phrase and association, a single, unifying thought recurred, like the sentry posts at the side of the line, monotonously in Angela's mind. Death. 'Death the Friend' of the sixteenth-century woodcuts, who released the captive and bathed the wounds of the fallen; Death in frock coat and whiskers, the discreet undertaker, spreading his sable pall over all that was rotten and unsightly; Death the macabre paramour in whose embrace all earthly loves were forgotten; Death for Basil, that Angela might live again . . . that was what she was thinking as she sipped her Vichy water, but no one, seeing the calm and pensive mask of her face, could ever possibly have guessed.

IV

Rupert Brooke, Old Bill, the Unknown Soldier–thus three fond women saw him, but Basil breakfasting late in Poppet Green's studio fell short and wide of all these ideals. He was not at his best that morning, both by reason of his heavy drinking with Poppet's friends the night before and the loss of face he was now suffering with Poppet in his attempts to explain his assertion that there would be no war. He had told them this the night before, not as a speculation, but as a fact known only to himself and half a dozen leading Germans; the Prussian military clique, he had told them, were allowing the Nazis to gamble just as long as their bluff was not called; he had had this, he said, direct from von Fritsch. The army had broken the Nazi Party in the July purge of 1936; they had let Hitler and Goering and Goebbels and Ribbentrop remain as puppets just as long as they proved valuable. The army, like all armies, was intensely pacifist; as soon as it became clear that Hitler was heading for war, he would be shot. Basil had expounded this theme not once but many times, over the table of the Charlotte Street restaurant, and because Poppet's friends did not know Basil, and were unused to people who claimed acquaintance with the great, Poppet had basked in vicarious esteem. Basil was little used to being heard with respect and was correspondingly resentful at being reproached with his own words.

'Well,' Poppet was saying crossly, from the gas stove. 'When do the army step in and shoot Hitler?'

She was a remarkably silly girl, and, as such, had commanded Basil's immediate attention when they met, three weeks earlier, with Ambrose Silk. With her Basil had spent the time he had promised to Angela at Cannes; on her he had spent the twenty pounds Angela had sent him for the journey. Even now when her fatuous face pouted in derision, she found a soft place in Basil's heart.

Evidence of her silliness abounded in the canvases, finished and unfinished, which crowded the studio. Eighty years ago her subjects would have been knights in armour, ladies in wimples and distress; fifty years ago 'nocturnes'; twenty years ago pierrots and willow trees; now, in 1939, they were bodiless heads, green horses and violet grass, sea-weed, shells and fungi, neatly executed, conventionally arranged in the manner of Dali. Her work in progress on the easel was an overlarge, accurate but buttercup-coloured head of the Aphrodite of Melos, poised against a background of bull's-eyes and barley-sugar.

'My dear,' Ambrose had said, 'you can positively hear her imagination *creaking*, as she does them, like a pair of old, old *corsets*, my dear, on a *harridan*.'

'They'll destroy London. What shall I do?' asked Poppet plaintively. 'Where can I go? It's the end of my painting. I've a good mind to follow Parsnip and Pimpernell' (two great poets of her acquaintance who had recently fled to New York).

'You'll be in more danger crossing the Atlantic than staying in London,' said

Basil. 'There won't be any air raids on London.'

'For God's sake don't say that.' Even as she spoke the sirens wailed. Poppet stood paralysed with horror. 'Oh God,' she said. 'You've done it. They've come.'

'Faultless timing,' said Basil cheerfully. 'That's always been Hitler's strong point.'

Poppet began to dress in an ineffectual fever of reproach. 'You *said* there wouldn't be a war. You *said* the bombers would never come. Now we shall all be killed and you just sit there talking and talking.'

'You know I should have thought an air raid was just the thing for a surrealist; it ought to give you plenty of compositions–limbs and things lying about in odd places, you know.'

'I wish I'd never met you. I wish I'd been to church. I was brought up in a convent. I wanted to be a nun once. I wish I was a nun. I'm going to be killed. Oh, I wish I was a nun. Where's my gas-mask? I shall go mad if I don't find my gas-mask.'

Basil lay back on the divan and watched her with fascination. This was how he liked to see women behave in moments of alarm. He rejoiced, always, in the spectacle of women at a disadvantage: thus he would watch, in the asparagus season, a dribble of melted butter on a woman's chin, marring her beauty and making her ridiculous, while she would still talk and smile and turn her head, not knowing how she appeared to him.

'Now do make up your mind what you're frightened of,' he urged. 'If you're going to be bombed with high explosive, run down to the shelter; if you're going to be gassed, shut the skylight and stay up here. In any case I shouldn't bother about that respirator. If they use anything it'll be arsenical smoke and it's no use against that. You'll find arsenical smoke quite painless at first. You won't know you've been gassed for a couple of days; then it'll be too late. In fact for all we know we're being gassed at this moment. If they fly high enough and let the wind carry the stuff they may be twenty miles away. The symptoms, when they do appear, are rather revolting . . .'

But Poppet was gone, helter-skelter, downstairs, making little moaning noises as she went.

Basil dressed and, pausing only to paint in a ginger moustache across Poppet's head of Aphrodite, strolled out into the streets.

The normal emptiness of Sunday in South Kensington was made complete that morning by the air-raid scare. A man in a tin helmet shouted at Basil from the opposite pavement. 'Take cover, there. Yes, it's you I'm talking to.'

Basil crossed over to him and said in a low tone, 'M.I.13.'

'Eh?'

'M.I.13.'

'I don't quite twig.'

'But you *ought* to twig,' said Basil severely. 'Surely you realize that members of M.I.13 are free to go everywhere at all times?'

'Sorry, I'm sure,' said the warden. 'I was only took on yesterday. What a lark getting a raid second time on!' As he spoke the sirens sounded the All Clear. 'What a sell!' said the warden.

It seemed to Basil that this fellow was altogether too cheerful for a public servant in the first hours of war; the gas scare had been wasted on Poppet; in her panic she had barely listened; it was worthy of a more receptive audience. 'Cheer up,' he said. 'You may be breathing arsenical smoke at this moment. Watch your urine in a couple of days' time.'

'Coo. I say, what did you say you was?'

'M.I.13.'

'Is that to do with gas?'

'It's to do with almost everything. Good morning.'

He turned to walk on but the warden followed. 'Wouldn't we smell it or nothing?'

'No.'

'Or cough or anything?'

'No.'

'And you think they've dropped it, just in that minute and gone away leaving us all for dead?'

'My dear fellow, *I* don't think so. It's your job as a warden to find out.'

'Coo.'

That'll teach him to shout at me in the street, thought Basil.

After the All Clear various friends of Poppet's came together in her studio.

'I wasn't *the least* frightened. I was so surprised at my own courage I felt quite giddy.'

'I wasn't *frightened*, I just felt glum.'

'*I* felt postively glad. After all we've all said for years that the present order of things was doomed, haven't we? I mean it's always been the choice for *us* between a concentration camp and being blown up, hasn't it? I just sat thinking how much I preferred being blown up to being beaten with rubber truncheons.'

'*I* was frightened,' said Poppet.

'Dear Poppet, you always have the *healthiest* reactions. Erchman really did wonders for you.'

'Well, I'm not sure they *were* so healthy this time. D'you know, I found myself actually *praying*.'

'I say, did you? That's bad.'

'Better see Erchman again.'

'Unless he's in a concentration camp.'

'We shall all be in concentration camps.'

'If anyone so much as mentions concentration camps again,' said Ambrose Silk, 'I shall go frankly hay-wire.' ('He had an unhappy love affair in Munich,' one of Poppet's friends explained to another, 'then they found he was half Jewish and the Brown Shirt was shut away.') 'Let's look at Poppet's pictures and forget the war. Now *that*,' he said, pausing before the Aphrodite, '*that* I consider *good*. I consider it *good*, Poppet. The moustache . . . it shows you have crossed one of the artistic rubicons and feel strong enough to be facetious. Like those wonderfully dramatic old *chestnuts* in Parsnip's *Guernica Revisited*. You're growing up, Poppet, my dear.'

'I wonder if it's the effect of that old adventurer of hers.'

'Poor Basil, it's sad enough for him to be an *enfant terrible* at the age of thirty-six; but to be regarded by the younger generation as a kind of dilapidated Bulldog Drummond . . .'

Ambrose Silk was older than Poppet and her friends; he was, in fact, a contemporary of Basil's, with whom he had maintained a shadowy, mutually derisive acquaintance since they were undergraduates. In those days, the mid '20's at Oxford, when the last of the ex-service men had gone down and the first of the puritanical, politically minded had either not come up or, at any rate, had not made himself noticed, in those days of broad trousers and high-necked jumpers and cars parked nightly outside the Spread Eagle at Thame, there had been few sub-divisions; a certain spiritual extravagance in the quest for pleasure had been the sole common bond between friends who in subsequent years had drifted far apart, beyond hailing distance, on the wider seas. Ambrose, in those days, had ridden ridiculously and ignominiously in the Christ Church Grind, and Peter Pastmaster had gone to a Palais de Danse in Reading dressed as a woman. Alastair Digby-Vane-Trumpington, absorbed in immature experiments into the question of how far various lewd debutantes would go with him, still had time when tippling his port at Mickleham to hear, without disapproval, Ambrose's recitals of unrequited love for a rowing blue. Nowadays Ambrose saw few of his old friends except Basil. He fancied that he had been dropped and sometimes in moments of vainglory, to the right audience, represented himself as a martyr to Art; as one who made no concessions to Mammon. 'I can't come all the way with you,' he said once to Parsnip and Pimpernell when they explained that only by becoming proletarian (an expression to which they attached no pedantic suggestion of childbearing; they meant that he should employ himself in some ill-paid, unskilled labour of a mechanical kind) could he hope to be a valuable writer, 'I can't come all the way with you, dear Parsnip and Pimpernell. But at least you know I have never sold myself to the upper class.' In this mood he saw himself as a figure in a dream, walking down an endless fashionable street; every door stood open and the waiting footmen cried, 'Come in and join us; flatter our masters and we will feed you,' but Ambrose always marched straight ahead unheeding. 'I belong, hopelessly, to the age of the ivory tower,' he said.

It was his misfortune to be respected as a writer by almost everyone except those with whom he most consorted. Poppet and her friends looked on him as a survival from the Yellow Book. The more conscientiously he strove to put himself in the movement and to ally himself with the dour young proletarians of the new decade, the more antiquated did he seem to them. His very appearance, with the swagger and flash of the young Disraeli, made him a conspicuous figure among them. Basil with his natural shabbiness was less incongruous.

Ambrose knew this, and repeated the phrase 'old adventurer' with relish.

V

Alastair and Sonia Trumpington changed house, on an average, once a year, ostensibly for motives of economy, and were now in Chester Street. Wherever they went they carried with them their own inalienable, inimitable disorder. Ten years ago, without any effort or desire on their part, merely by pleasing themselves in their own way, they had lived in the full blaze of fashionable notoriety; to-day without regret, without in fact being aware of the change, they formed a forgotten cove, where the wreckage of the roaring twenties, long tossed on the high seas, lay beached, dry and battered, barely worth the attention of the most assiduous beachcomber. Sonia would sometimes remark how odd it was that the papers nowadays never seemed to mention anyone one had ever heard of; they had been such a bore once, never leaving one alone.

Basil, when he was in England, was a constant visitor. It was really, Alastair said, in order to keep him from coming to stay that they had to live in such painfully cramped quarters.

Wherever they lived Basil developed a homing instinct towards them, an aptitude which, in their swift moves from house to house, often caused consternation to subsequent tenants, who, before he had had time to form new patterns of behaviour, would quite often wake in the night to hear Basil swarming up the drain pipes and looming tipsily in the bedroom window or, in the morning, to find him recumbent and insensible in the area. Now, on this catastrophic morning, Basil found himself orientated to them as surely as though he were in wine, and he arrived on their new door-step without conscious thought of direction. He went upstairs immediately for, wherever they lived, it was always in Sonia's bedroom, as though it were the scene of an unending convalescence, that the heart of the household beat.

Basil had attended Sonia's levees (and there were three or four levees daily for, whenever she was at home, she was in bed) off and on for nearly ten years, since the days of her first, dazzling loveliness, when, almost alone among the chaste and daring brides of London, she had admitted mixed company to her bathroom. It was an innovation, or rather the revival of a more golden age, which, like everything Sonia did, was conceived without any desire for notoriety; she enjoyed company, she enjoyed her bath. There were usually three or four breathless and giddy young men, in those days, gulping Black Velvet in the steam, pretending to take their reception as a matter of common occurrence.

Basil saw little change in her beauty now and none in the rich confusion of letters, newspapers, half opened parcels and half empty bottles, puppies, flowers and fruit which surrounded the bed where she sat sewing (for it was one of the vagaries of her character to cover acres of silk, yearly, with exquisite embroidery).

'Darling Basil, have you come to be blown up with us? Where's your horrible girl friend?'

'She took fright.'

'She was a beast, darling, one of your very worst. Look at Peter. Isn't it all crazy?' Peter Pastmaster sat at the foot of her bed in uniform. Once, for reasons he had now forgotten, he had served, briefly, in the cavalry; the harvest of that early sowing had ripened, suddenly, overnight. 'Won't it be too ridiculous, starting all over again, lunching with young men on guard.'

'Not young, Sonia. You should see us. The average age of the subalterns is about forty, the colonel finished the last war as a brigadier, and our troopers are all either weather-beaten old commissionaires or fifteen-stone valets.'

Alastair came in from the bathroom. 'How's the art tart?' He opened bottles and began mixing stout and champagne in a deep jug. 'Blackers?' They had always drunk this sour and invigorating draught.

'Tell us all about the war,' said Sonia.

'Well–' Basil began.

'No, darling, I didn't mean that. Not *all*. Not about who's going to win or why we are fighting. Tell us what everyone is going to do about it. From what Margot tells me the last war was absolute heaven. Alastair wants to go for a soldier.'

'Conscription has rather taken the gilt off that particular gingerbread,' said Basil. 'Besides, this ain't going to be a soldier's war.'

'Poor Peter,' said Sonia, as though she was talking to one of the puppies. 'It isn't going to be your war, sweetheart.'

'Suits me,' said Peter.

'I expect Basil will have the most tremendous adventures. He always did in peace time. Goodness knows what he'll do in war.'

'There are too many people in on the racket,' said Basil.

'Poor sweet, I don't believe any of you are nearly as excited about it as I am.'

The name of the poet Parsnip, casually mentioned re-opened the great Parsnip-Pimpernell controversy which was torturing Poppet Green and her friends. It was a problem which, not unlike the Schleswig-Holstein question of the preceding century, seemed to admit of no logical solution, for, in simple terms, the postulates were self-contradictory. Parsnip and Pimpernell, as friends and collaborators, were inseparable; on that all agreed. But Parsnip's art flourished best in England, even an embattled England, while Pimpernell's needed the peaceful and fecund soil of the United States. The complementary qualities which, many believed, made them together equal to one poet now threatened the dissolution of partnership.

'I don't say that Pimpernell is the *better* poet,' said Ambrose. 'All I say is that I *personally* find him the more nutritious; so I *personally* think they are right to go.'

'But I've always felt that Parsnip is so much more dependent on environment.'

'I know what you mean, Poppet, but I don't agree . . . Aren't you thinking only of *Guernica Revisited* and forgetting the Christopher Sequence . . .'

Thus the aesthetic wrangle might have run its familiar course, but there was in the studio that morning a cross, red-headed girl in spectacles from the London School of Economics; she believed in a People's Total War; an uncompromising girl whom none of them liked; a suspect of Trotskyism.

'What I don't see,' she said (and what this girl did not see was usually a very conspicuous embarrassment to Poppet's friends)–'What I don't see is how these two can claim to be *Contemporary* if they run away from the biggest event in contemporary history. They were contemporary enough about Spain when no one threatened to come and bomb *them*.'

It was an awkward question; one that in military parlance was called 'a swift one'. At any moment, it was felt in the studio, this indecent girl would use the word 'escapism'; and, in the silence which followed her outburst, while everyone in turn meditated and rejected a possible retort, she did, in fact, produce the unforgivable charge. 'It's just sheer escapism,' she said.

The word startled the studio, like the cry of 'Cheat' in a card-room.

'That's a foul thing to say, Julia.'

'Well, what's the answer?' . . .

The answer, thought Ambrose, he knew an answer or two. There was plenty that he had learned from his new friends, that he could quote to them. He could say that the war in Spain was 'contemporary' because it was a class war; the present conflict, since Russia had declared herself neutral, was merely a phase in capitalist disintegration; that would have satisfied, or at least silenced, the red-headed girl. But that was not really the answer. He sought for comforting historical analogies, but every example which occurred to him was on the side of the red-head. She knew them too, he thought, and would quote them with all her post-graduate glibness–Socrates marching to the sea with Xenophon, Virgil sanctifying Roman military rule, Horace singing the sweetness of dying for one's country, the troubadours riding to war, Cervantes in the galleys at Lepanto, Milton working himself blind in the public service, even George IV, for whom Ambrose had a reverence which others devoted to Charles I, believed he had fought at Waterloo. All these, and a host of other courageous contemporary figures rose in Ambrose's mind. Cézanne had deserted in 1870, but Cézanne in the practical affairs of life was a singularly unattractive figure; moreover, he was a painter whom Ambrose found insufferably boring. There was no answer to be found on those lines.

'You're just sentimental,' said Poppet, 'like a spinster getting tearful at the sound of a military band.'

'Well, they have military bands in Russia, don't they? I expect plenty of spinsters get tearful in the Red Square when they march past Lenin's tomb.'

You can always stump them with Russia, thought Ambrose; they can always stump each other. It's the dead end of all discussion.

'The question is, would they write any better for being in danger,' said one.

'Would they help the People's Cause?' said another.

It was the old argument, gathering speed again after the rude girl's interruption. Ambrose gazed sadly at the jaundiced, mustachioed Aphrodite. What was he doing, he asked himself, in this galley?

Sonia was trying to telephone to Margot, to invite themselves all to luncheon.

'An odious man says that only official calls are being taken this morning.'

'Say you're M.I.13,' said Basil.

'I'm M.I.13. . . . What can that mean? Darling, I believe it's going to work . . . It *has* worked . . . Margot, this is Sonia . . . I'm dying to see you to . . .'

Aphrodite gazed back at him, blind, as though sculptured in butter; Parsnip and Pimpernell, Red Square and Brown House, thus the discussion raged. What was all this to do with him?

Art and Love had led him to this inhospitable room.

Love for a long succession of louts–rugger blues, all-in wrestlers, naval ratings; tender, hopeless love that had been rewarded at the best by an occasional episode of rough sensuality, followed, in sober light, with contempt, abuse and rapacity.

A pansy. An old queen. A habit of dress, a tone of voice, an elegant, humorous deportment that had been admired and imitated, a swift, epicene felicity of wit, the art of dazzling and confusing those he despised–these had been his, and now they were the current exchange of comedians; there were only a few restaurants, now, which he could frequent without fear of ridicule and there he was surrounded, as though by distorting mirrors, with gross reflections and caricatures of himself. Was it thus that the rich passions of Greece and Arabia and the Renaissance had worn themselves out? Did they simper when Leonardo passed and imitate with mincing grace the warriors of Sparta; was there a snigger across the sand outside the tents of Saladin? They burned the Knights Templar at the stake; their loves, at least, were monstrous and formidable, a thing to call down destruction from heaven, if man neglected his duty of cruelty and repression. Beddoes had died in solitude, by his own hand; Wilde had been driven into the shadows, tipsy and garrulous, but, to the end, a figure of tragedy looming big in his own twilight. But Ambrose, thought Ambrose, what of him? Born after his time, in age which made a type of him, a figure of farce; like mothers-in-law and kippers, the century's contribution to the national store of comic objects; akin with the chorus boys who tittered under the lamps of Shaftesbury Avenue. And Hans, who at last, after so long a pilgrimage, had seemed to promise rest, Hans so simple and affectionate, like a sturdy young terrier, Hans lay in the unknown horrors of a Nazi concentration camp.

The huge, yellow face with scrawled moustaches offered Ambrose no comfort.

There was a young man of military age in the studio; he was due to be called up in the near future. 'I don't know what to do about it,' he said. 'Of course, I could always plead conscientious objections, but I haven't got a conscience. It would be a denial of everything we've stood for if I said I had a conscience.'

'No, Tom,' they said to comfort him. 'We know you haven't a conscience.'

'But then,' said the perplexed young man, 'if I haven't got a conscience, why in God's name should I mind so much saying that I have?'

'. . . Peter's here and Basil. We're all feeling very gay and warlike. May we come to luncheon? Basil says there's bound to be an enormous air raid to-night so it may be the last time we shall ever see each other. . . . What's that? Yes, I told you I'm (What am I, Basil?) I'm M.I.13. There's a ridiculous woman on the line saying is this a private call?) . . . Well, Margot, then we'll all come round to you. That'll be heaven . . . hello, *hello*, I do believe that damned woman has cut us off.'

Nature I loved, and next to Nature, Art. Nature in the raw is seldom mild; red in tooth and claw; matelots in Toulon smelling of wine and garlic, with tough brown necks, cigarettes stuck to the lower lip, lapsing into unintelligible, contemptuous argot.

Art: this was where Art had brought him, to this studio, to these coarse and tedious youngsters, to that preposterous yellow face among the boiled sweets.

It had been a primrose path in the days of Diaghilev; at Eton he had collected Lovat Frazer rhyme sheets; at Oxford he had recited *In Memoriam* through a megaphone to an accompaniment hummed on combs and tissue paper; in Paris he had frequented Jean Cocteau and Gertrude Stein; he had written and published his first book there, a study of Montparnasse Negroes that had been banned in England by Sir William Joynson-Hicks. That way the primrose path led gently downhill to the world of fashionable photographers, stage sets for

Cochrane, Cedric Lyne and his Neapolitan grottoes.

He had made his decision then, turned aside from the primrose path, had deliberately chosen the austere and the heroic; it was the year of the American slump, a season of heroic decisions, when Paul had tried to enter a monastery and David had succeeded in throwing himself under a train. Ambrose had gone to Germany, lived in a workman's quarter, found Hans, begun a book, a grim, abstruse, interminable book, a penance for past frivolity; the unfinished manuscript lay somewhere in an old suitcase in Central Europe, and Hans was behind barbed wire; or worse, perhaps, had given in, as with his simple, easy-going acceptance of things was all too likely, was back among the Brown Shirts, a man with a mark against his name, never again to be trusted, but good enough for the firing line, good enough to be jostled into battle.

The red-headed girl was asking inconvenient questions again. 'But Tom,' she was saying. 'Surely if it was a good thing to share the life of the worker in a canned fruit factory, why isn't it a good thing to serve with him in the army?'

'Julia's just the type who used to go about distributing white feathers.'

'If it comes to that, why the hell not,' said Julia.

Ars longa, thought Ambrose, a short life but a grey one.

Alastair plugged his electric razor into the lamp on Sonia's writing table and shaved in the bedroom, so as not to miss what was going on. He had once in the past seen Peter in full-dress uniform at a Court Ball and had felt sorry for him because it meant that he could not come on afterwards to a night club; this was the first time he had seen him in khaki and he was jealous as a schoolboy. There was still a great deal of the schoolboy about Alastair; he enjoyed winter sports and sailing and squash racquets and the chaff round the bar at Bratts; he observed certain immature taboos of dress, such as wearing a bowler hat in London until after Goodwood week; he had a firm, personal sense of schoolboy honour. He felt these prejudices to be peculiar to himself; none of them made him at all censorious of anyone else; he accepted Basil's outrageous disregard for them without question. He kept his sense of honour as he might have kept an expensive and unusual pet; as, indeed, once, for a disastrous month, Sonia had kept a small kangaroo named Molly. He knew himself to be as eccentric, in his own way, as Ambrose Silk. For a year, at the age of twenty-one, he had been Margot Metroland's lover; it was an apprenticeship many of his friends had served; they had forgotten about it now, but at the time all their acquaintances knew about it; but never, even to Sonia, had Alastair alluded to the fact. Since marriage he had been unfaithful to Sonia for a week every year, during Bratts Club golf tournament at Le Touquet, usually with the wife of a fellow member. He did this without any scruple because he believed Bratts week to be in some way excluded from the normal life of loyalties and obligations; a Saturnalia when the laws did not run. At all other times he was a devoted husband.

Alastair had never come nearer to military service than in being senior private in the Corps at Eton; during the General Strike he had driven about the poorer quarters of London in a closed van to break up seditious meetings and had clubbed several unoffending citizens; that was his sole contribution to domestic politics, for he had lived, in spite of his many moves, in uncontested constituencies. But he had always held it as axiomatic that, should anything as preposterous and antiquated as a large-scale war occur, he would take a modest but vigorous part. He had no illusions about his abilities, but believed, justly, that he would make as good a target as anyone else for the King's enemies to shoot at. It came as a shock to him now to find his country at war and himself in pyjamas, spending his normal Sunday noon with a jug of Black Velvet and some chance visitors. Peter's uniform added to his uneasiness. It was as though he had been taken in adultery at Christmas or found in mid-June on the steps of Bratts in a soft hat.

He studied Peter, with the rapt attention of a small boy, taking in every detail of his uniform, the riding boots, Sam Browne belt, the enamelled stars of rank, and felt disappointed but, in a way, relieved, that there was no sword; he could not have borne it if Peter had had a sword.

'I know I look awful,' Peter said. 'The adjutant left me in no doubt on that subject.'

'You look sweet,' said Sonia.

'I heard they had stopped wearing cross straps on the Sam Browne,' said Alastair.

'Yes, but technically *we* still carry swords.'

Technically. Peter *had* a sword, technically.

'Darling, do you think that if we went past Buckingham Palace the sentries will salute?'

'It's quite possible. I don't think Belisha has quite succeeded in putting it down yet.'

'We'll go there at once. I'll dress. Can't wait to see them.'

So they walked from Chester Street to Buckingham Palace; Sonia and Peter in front, Alastair and Basil a pace or two behind. The sentries saluted and Sonia pinched Peter as he acknowledged it. Alastair said to Basil:

'I suppose we'll be doing that soon.'

'They don't want volunteers in this war, Alastair. They'll call people up when they want them without any recruiting marches or popular songs. They haven't the equipment for the men in training now.'

'Who do you mean by "they"?'

'Hore-Belisha.'

'Who cares what *he* wants?' said Alastair. For him there was no 'they'. England was at war; he, Alastair Trumpington, was at war. It was not the business of any politician to tell him when or how he should fight. But he could not put this into words; not into words, anyway, which Basil would not make ridiculous, so he walked on in silence behind Peter's martial figure until Sonia decided to take a cab.

'I know what I want,' said Basil. 'I want to be one of those people one heard about in 1919; the hard-faced men who did well out of the war.'

VI

Although it was common for Freddie Sothill, Sir Joseph Mainwaring and various others who from time to time were enlisted to help solve the recurrent problem of Basil's future, to speak of him in terms they normally reserved for the mining community of South Wales, as feckless and unemployable, the getting of jobs, of one kind and another, had, in fact, played a large part in his life, for it was the explanation and excuse of most of Basil's vagaries that he had never had any money of his own. Tony and Barbara by their father's will each enjoyed a reasonable fortune, but Sir Christopher Seal had died shortly after the first of Basil's major disgraces. If it were conceivable that one who held the office of Chief Whip for a quarter of a century could be shocked at any spectacle of human depravity, it might have been thought that shame hastened his end, so fast did one event follow upon the other. Be that as it may, it was on his deathbed that Sir Christopher, in true melodramatic style, disinherited his younger son, leaving his future entirely in his mother's hands.

Lady Seal's most devoted friend–and she had many–would not have credited her with more than human discretion, and some quite preternatural power would have been needed to deal with Basil's first steps in adult life. The system she decided on was, at the best, unimaginative and, like many such schemes, was suggested to her by Sir Joseph Mainwaring; it consisted, in his words, of 'giving the boy his bread and butter and letting him find the jam.' Removed from the realm of metaphor to plain English, this meant allowing Basil £400 a year, conditional on his good behaviour, and expecting him to supplement it by his own exertions if he wished for a more ample way of life.

The arrangement proved disastrous from the first. Four times in the last ten years Lady Seal had paid Basil's debts; once on condition of his living at home with her; once on condition of his living somewhere, anywhere, abroad; once on condition of his marrying; once on condition of refraining from his marriage. Twice he had been cut off with a penny; twice taken back to favour; once he had been set up in chambers in the Temple with an allowance of a thousand a year; several times a large lump sum of capital had been dangled before his eyes as the reward of his giving himself seriously to commerce; once he had been on the verge of becoming the recipient of a sisal farm in Kenya. Throughout all these changes of fortune Sir Joseph Mainwaring had acted the part of political agent to a recalcitrant stipendiary sultan, in a way which embittered every benevolence and minimized the value of every gift he brought. In the intervals of neglect and independence, Basil had fended for himself and had successively held all the jobs which were open to young men of his qualifications. He had never had much difficulty in getting jobs; the trouble had always been in keeping them, for he regarded a potential employer as his opponent in a game of skill. All Basil's resource and energy went into hoodwinking him into surrender; once he had received his confidence he lost interest. Thus English girls will put themselves to endless exertion to secure a husband and, once married, will think their labour at an end.

Basil had been leader writer on the *Daily Beast*, he had served in the personal entourage of Lord Monomark, he had sold champagne on commission, composed dialogue for the cinema and given the first of what was intended to be a series of talks for the B.B.C. Sinking lower in the social scale he had been press agent for a female contortionist and had once conducted a party of tourists to the Italian lakes (he dined out for some time on the story of that tour which had, after a crescendo of minor vexations, culminated in Basil making a bundle of all the tickets and all the passports and sinking them in Lake Garda. He had then travelled home alone by an early train, leaving fifty penniless Britons, none of whom spoke a word of any foreign language, to the care of whatever deity takes charge of forsaken strangers; for all Basil knew, they were still there).

From time to time he disappeared from the civilized area and returned with tales to which no one attached much credence–of having worked for the secret police in Bolivia and advised the Emperor of Azania on the modernization of his country. Basil was in the habit, as it were, of conducting his own campaigns, issuing his own ultimatums, disseminating his own propaganda, erecting about himself his own blackout; he was an obstreperous minority of one in a world of otiose civilians. He was used, in his own life, to a system of push, appeasement, agitation, and blackmail, which, except that it had no more distant aim than his own immediate amusement, ran parallel to Nazi diplomacy.

Like Nazi diplomacy it postulated for success a peace-loving, orderly and honourable world in which to operate. In the new, busy, secretive, chaotic world which developed during the first days of the war, Basil for the first time in his life felt himself at a disadvantage. It was like being in Latin America at a time of upheaval, and, instead of being an Englishman, being oneself a Latin American.

The end of September found Basil in a somewhat fretful mood. The air-raid scare seemed to be over for the time and those who had voluntarily fled from London were beginning to return, pretending that they had only been to the country to see that everything was all right there. The women and children of the poor, too, were flocking home to their evacuated streets. The newspapers said that the Poles were holding out; that their cavalry was penetrating deep into Germany; that the enemy was already short of motor oil; that Saarbrücken would fall to the French within a day or two; air-raid wardens roamed the remote hamlets of the kingdom, persecuting yokels who walked home from the inn with glowing pipes. Londoners who were slow to acquire the habit of the domestic hearth groped their way in darkness from one place of amusement to another, learning their destination by feeling the buttons on the commissionaires' uniforms; revolving, black glass doors gave access to a fairy land; it was as though, when children, they had been led blindfold into the room with the lighted Christmas tree. The casualty list of street accidents became formidable and there were terrifying tales of footpads who leaped on the shoulders of old gentlemen on the very steps of their clubs, or beat them to jelly on Hay Hill.

Everyone whom Basil met was busy getting a job. Some consciously or unconsciously had taken out an insurance policy against unemployment by joining some military unit in the past; there were those like Peter, who in early youth had gratified a parental whim by spending a few expensive years in the regular army, and those like Freddy who had gone into the yeomanry as they sat on the Bench and the county council as part of the normal obligations of rural life. These were now in uniform with their problems solved. In later months, as they sat idle in the Middle East, they were to think enviously of those who had made a more deliberate and judicious choice of service, but at the moment their minds were enviably at rest. The remainder were possessed with a passion to enrol in some form of public service, however uncongenial. Some formed ambulance parties and sat long hours at their posts waiting for air-raid victims; some became firemen, some minor civil servants. None of these honourable occupations made much appeal to Basil.

He was exactly the type of man who, if English life had run as it did in books of adventure, should at this turn in world affairs have been sent for. He should have been led to an obscure address in Maida Vale and there presented to a lean, scarred man with hard grey eyes; one of the men behind the scenes; one of the men whose names were unknown to the public and the newspapers, who passed unnoticed in the street, a name known only to the inner circle of the Cabinet and to the XXX heads of the secret police of the world . . . 'Sit down, Seal. We've followed your movements with interest ever since that affair in La Paz in '32. You're a rascal, but I'm inclined to think you're the kind of rascal the country needs at this moment. I take it you're game for anything?'

'I'm game.'

'That's what I expected you to say. These are your orders. You will go to Uxbridge aerodrome at 4.30 this afternoon where a man will meet you and give you your passport. You will travel under the name of Blenkinsop. You are a tobacco-grower from Latakia. A civil aeroplane will take you by various stages to Smyrna where you will register at the Miramar Hotel and await orders. Is that clear . . . ?'

It was clear, and Basil, whose life up to the present had been more like an adventure story than most people's, did half expect some such summons. None came. Instead he was invited to luncheon by Sir Joseph Mainwaring at the Travellers' Club.

Basil's luncheons at the Travellers' with Sir Joseph Mainwaring had for years formed a series of monuments in his downward path. There had been the luncheons of his four major debt settlements, the luncheon of his political candidature, the luncheons of his two respectable professions, the luncheon of the threatened divorce of Angela Lyne, the Luncheon of the Stolen Emeralds, the Luncheon of the Knuckledusters, the Luncheon of Freddy's Last Cheque–each would provide both theme and title for a work of popular fiction.

Hitherto these feasts had taken place *à deux* in a secluded corner. The Luncheon of the Commission in the Guards was altogether a more honourable affair and its purpose was to introduce Basil to the Lieutenant-Colonel of the Bombardiers–an officer whom Sir Joseph wrongly believed to have a liking for him.

The Lieutenant-Colonel did not know Sir Joseph well and was surprised and slightly alarmed by the invitation, for his distrust was based not, as might have been expected, on any just estimate of his capabilities, but, paradoxically, on the fear of him as a politician and man of affairs. All politicians were, to the Lieutenant-Colonel, not so much boobies as bogies. He saw them all, even Sir Joseph, as figures of Renaissance subtlety and intrigue. It was by being in with them that the great professional advances were achieved; but it was by falling foul of them that one fell into ignominy. For a simple soldier–and if ever anyone did, the Lieutenant-Colonel qualified for that honourable title–the only safe course was to avoid men like Sir Joseph. When met with, they should be treated with bluff and uncompromising reserve. Sir Joseph thus found himself, through his loyal friendship with Cynthia Seal, in the equivocal position of introducing, with a view of this advancement, a man for whom he had a deep-seated horror to a man who had something of the same emotion towards himself. It was not a concurrence which, on the face of it, seemed hopeful of good results.

Basil, like 'Lord Monmouth', 'never condescended to the artifice of the toilet', and the Lieutenant-Colonel studied him with distaste. Together the ill-assorted trio went to their table.

Soldier and statesman spread their napkins on their knees and in the interest of ordering their luncheon allowed a silence to fall between them into which Basil cheerfully plunged.

'We ought to do something about Liberia, Colonel,' he said.

The Colonel turned on him the outraged gaze with which a good regimental soldier always regards the discussion of war in its larger aspects.

'I expect those whose business it is have the question in hand,' he said.

'Don't you believe it,' said Basil. 'I don't expect they've given it a thought,' and for some twenty minutes he explained why and how Liberia should be immediately annexed.

The two elder men ate in silence. At length a chance reference to Russia gave Sir Joseph the chance to interpose an opinion.

'I always distrust prophecy in any form,' he said. 'But there is one thing of which I am certain. Russia will come in against us before the end of the year. That will put Italy and Japan on our side. Then it is simply a question of time before our blockade makes itself felt. All kinds of things that you and I have never heard of, like manganese and bauxite, will win the war for us.'

'And infantry.'

'*And* infantry.'

'Teach a man to march and shoot. Give him the right type of officer. Leave the rest to him.'

This seemed to Basil a suitable moment to introduce his own problems. 'What do you think is the right type of officer?'

'The officer-type.'

'It's an odd thing,' Basil began, 'that people always expect the upper class to be good leaders of men. That was all right in the old days when most of them were brought up with tenantry to look after. But now three-quarters of your officer-type live in towns. *I* haven't any tenantry.'

The Lieutenant-Colonel looked at Basil with detestation. 'No, no. I suppose not.'

'Well, have *you* any tenantry?'

'*I*? No. My brother sold the old place years ago.'

'Well, there you are.'

It was crystal-clear to Sir Joseph and faintly perceptible to Basil that the Lieutenant-Colonel did not take this well.

'Seal was for a time conservative candidate down in the West,' said Sir Joseph, anxious to remove one possible source of prejudice.

'Some pretty funny people have been calling themselves conservatives in the last year or two. Cause of half the trouble if you ask me.' Then, feeling he might have been impolite, he added graciously: 'No offence to you. Daresay you were all right. Don't know anything about you.'

Basil's political candidature was not an episode to be enlarged upon. Sir Joseph turned the conversation. 'Of course, the French will have to make some concessions to bring Italy in. Give up Jibuti or something like that.'

'Why the devil should they?' asked the Lieutenant-Colonel petulantly. 'Who wants Italy in?'

'To counterbalance Russia.'

'How? Why? Where? I don't see it at all.'

'Nor do I,' said Basil.

Threatened with support from so unwelcome a quarter, the Lieutenant-Colonel immediately abandoned his position. 'Oh, don't you?' he said. 'Well, I've no doubt Mainwaring knows best. His job to know these things.'

Warmed by these words Sir Joseph proceeded for the rest of luncheon to suggest some of the concessions which he thought France might reasonably make to Italy–Tunisia, French Somaliland, the Suez Canal. 'Corsica, Nice, Savoy?' asked Basil. Sir Joseph thought not.

Rather than ally himself with Basil the Lieutenant-Colonel listened to these proposals to dismember an ally in silence and fury. He had not wanted to come out to luncheon. It would be absurd to say that he was busy, but he was busier than he had ever been in his life before and he looked on the two hours or so which he allowed himself in the middle of the day as a time for general recuperation. He liked to spend them among people to whom he could relate all that he had done in the morning; to people who would appreciate the importance and rarity of such work; either that, or with a handsome woman. He left the Travellers' as early as he decently could and returned to his mess. His mind was painfully agitated by all he had heard and particularly by the presence of that seedy-looking young radical whose name he had not caught. That at least, he thought, he might have hoped to be spared at Sir Joseph's table.

'Well, Jo, is everything arranged?'

'Nothing is exactly *arranged* yet, Cynthia, but I've set the ball rolling.'

'I hope Basil made a good impression.'

'I hope he did, too. I'm afraid he said some rather unfortunate things.'

'Oh dear. Well, what is the next step?'

Sir Joseph would have liked to say that there was no next step in that direction; that the best Basil could hope for was oblivion; perhaps in a month or so, when the luncheon was forgotten . . . 'It's up to Basil now, Cynthia. I have introduced him. He must follow it up himself if he really wants to get into that regiment. But I have been wondering since you first mentioned the matter, do you really think it is quite suitable . . .'

'I'm told he could not do better,' said Lady Seal proudly.

'No, that is so. In one way he could not do better.'

'Then he shall follow up the introduction,' said that unimaginative mother.

The Lieutenant-Colonel was simmering quietly in his office; an officer–not a young officer but a mature reservist–had just been to see him without gloves, wearing suède shoes; the consequent outburst had been a great relief; the simmering was an expression of content, a kind of mental purr; it was a mood which his subordinates recognized as a good mood. He was feeling that as long as there was someone like himself at the head of the regiment, nothing much could go wrong with it (a feeling which, oddly enough, was shared by the delinquent officer). To the Lieutenant-Colonel, in this mood, it was announced that a civilian gentleman, Mr Seal, wanted to see him. The name was unfamiliar; so, for the moment, was Basil's appearance, for Angela had been at pains and expense to fit him up suitably for the interview. His hair was newly cut, he wore a stiff white collar, a bowler hat, a thin gold watch-chain and other marks of respectability, and he carried a new umbrella. Angela had also schooled him in the first words of his interview. 'I know you are very busy, Colonel, but I hoped you would spare me a few minutes to ask your advice . . .'

All this went fairly well. 'Want to go into the army?' said the Lieutenant-Colonel. 'Well, I suppose we must expect a lot of people coming in from outside nowadays. Lot of new battalions being formed, even in the Brigade. I presume you'll join the infantry. No point in going into the cavalry nowadays. All these machines. Might just as well be an engine driver and have done with it. There's a lot of damn fool talk about this being a mechanized war and an air war and a commercial war. All wars are infantry wars. Always have been.'

'Yes, it was infantry I was thinking of.'

'Quite right. I hear some of the line regiments are very short of officers. I don't imagine you want to go through the ranks, ha! ha! There's been a lot of nonsense about that lately. Not that it would do any harm to some of the young gentlemen I've seen about the place. But for a fellow of your age the thing to do is to join the Supplementary Reserve, put down the regiment you want to join–there are a number of line regiments who do very useful work in their way, and get the commanding officer to apply for you.'

'Exactly, sir, that's what I came to see you about. I was hoping that *you*–'

'That *I* . . . ?' Slowly to that slow mind there came the realization that Basil, this dissolute-looking young man who had so grossly upset his lunch interval the day before, this radical who had impugned the efficiency of the officer-type, was actually proposing to join the Bombardier Guards.

'I've always felt,' said Basil, 'that if I had to join the Foot Guards, I'd soonest join yours. You aren't as stuffy as the Grenadiers and you haven't got any of those bogus regional connections like the Scots and Irish and Welsh.'

Had there been no other cause of offence; had Basil come to him with the most prepossessing appearance, the most glittering sporting record, a manner in which deference to age was most perfectly allied with social equality, had he been lord of a thousand loyal tenants, had he been the nephew of the Colonel-in-Chief, the use by a civilian of such words as 'stuffy' and 'bogus' about the Brigade of Guards would have damned him utterly.

'So what I suggest,' Basil continued, 'is that I sign up for this Supplementary Reserve and put you down as my choice of regiment. Will that be O.K.?'

The Lieutenant-Colonel found his voice; it was not a voice of which he had full control; it might have been the voice of a man who had been suspended for a few seconds from a gibbet and then cut down. He fingered his collar as though, indeed, expecting to find the hangman's noose there. He said: 'That would *not* be O.K. We do not take our officers from the Supplementary Reserve.'

'Well, how *do* I join you?'

'I'm afraid I must have misled you in some way. I have no vacancy for you in the regiment. I'm looking for platoon commanders. As it is I've got six or seven ensigns of over thirty. Can you imagine yourself leading a platoon in action?'

'Well, as a matter of fact I can, but that's the last thing I want. In fact that's why I want to keep away from the line regiments. After all there is always a number of interesting staff jobs going for anyone in the Guards, isn't there? What I thought of doing was to sign up with you and then look round for something more interesting. I should be frightfully bored with regimental life, you know, but everyone tells me it's a great help to start in a decent regiment.'

The noose tightened about the Lieutenant-Colonel's throat. He could not speak. It was with a scarcely human croak and an eloquent gesture of the hand that he indicated that the interview was over.

In the office it quickly became known that he was in one of his bad moods again.

Basil went back to Angela.

'How did it go, darling?'

'Not well. Not well at all.'

'Oh dear, and you looked so particularly presentable.'

'Yes; it can't have been that. And I was tremendously polite. Said all the right things. I expect that old snake Jo Mainwaring has been making mischief again.'

VII

'When we say that Parsnip can't write in war-time Europe surely we mean that he can't write as he has written up till now? Mightn't it be better for him to stay here, even if it meant holding up production for a year or so, so that he can *develop*?'

'Oh, I don't think Parsnip and Pimpernell *can* develop. I mean an organ doesn't *develop*; it just goes on playing different pieces of music but remains the same. I feel Parsnip and Pimpernell have perfected themselves as an instrument.'

'Then suppose Parsnip were to develop and Pimpernell didn't. Or suppose they developed in different directions. What would happen then?'

'Yes, what would happen then?'

'Why does it take two to write a poem?' asked the red-headed girl.

'Now Julia, don't short-circuit the argument.'

'I should have thought poetry was a one-man job. Part-time work at that.'

'But Julia, you'll admit you don't know very much about poetry, dear.'

'That's exactly why I'm asking.'

'Don't pay any attention, Tom. She doesn't really want to know. She's only being tiresome.'

They were lunching at a restaurant in Charlotte Street; there were too many of them for the table; when you put out your hand for your glass and your neighbour at the same time put out his knife for the butter, he gave you a greasy cuff; too many for the menu; a single sheet of purple hand-writing that was passed from hand to hand with indifference and indecision; too many for the waiter, who forgot their various orders; there were only six of them but it was too many for Ambrose. The talk was a series of assertions and interjections. Ambrose lived in and for conversation; he rejoiced in the whole intricate art of it–the timing and striking the proper juxtaposition of narrative and comment, the bursts of spontaneous parody, the allusion one would recognize and one would not, the changes of alliance, the betrayals, the diplomatic revolutions, the waxing and waning of dictatorships that could happen in an hour's session about a table. But could it happen? Was that, too, most exquisite and exacting of the arts, part of the buried world of Diaghilev?

For months, now, he had seen no one except Poppet Green and her friends, and now, since Angela Lyne's return, Basil had dropped out of the group as abruptly as he had entered it, leaving Ambrose strangely forlorn.

Why, he wondered, do real intellectuals always prefer the company of rakes to that of their fellows? Basil is a philistine and a crook; on occasions he can be a monumental bore; on occasions a grave embarrassment; he is a man for whom there will be no place in the coming workers' state; and yet, thought Ambrose, I hunger for his company. It is a curious thing, he thought, that every creed promises a paradise which will be absolutely uninhabitable for anyone of civilized taste. Nanny told me of a Heaven that was full of angels playing harps; the communists tell me of an earth full of leisured and contented factory hands. I don't see Basil getting past the gate of either. Religion is acceptable in its destructive phase; the desert monks carving up that humbug Hypatia; the anarchist gangs roasting the monks in Spain. Hellfire sermons in the chapels; soap-box orators screaming their envy of the rich. Hell is all right. The human mind is inspired enough when it comes to inventing horrors; it is when it tries to invent a Heaven that it shows itself cloddish. But Limbo is the place. In Limbo one has natural happiness without the beatific vision; no harps; no communal order; but wine and conversation and imperfect, various humanity. Limbo for the unbaptized, for the pious heathen, the sincere sceptic. Am I baptized into this modern world? At least I haven't taken a new name. All the rest of the left-wing writers have adopted plebeian monosyllables. Ambrose is irredeemably bourgeois. Parsnip often said so. Damn Parsnip, damn Pimpernell. Do these atrocious young people never discuss anything else?

They were disputing the bill now, and forgetting what he or she had eaten; passing the menu from hand to hand to verify the prices.

'When you've decided what it is, tell me.'

'Ambrose's bill is always the largest,' said the red-headed girl.

'Dear Julia, please don't tell me that I could have fed a worker's family for a week. I still feel definitely *peckish*, my dear. I am sure workers eat ever so much more.'

'D'you *know* the index figure for a family of four?'

'No,' said Ambrose wistfully, 'no, I don't know the index figure. Please don't tell me. It wouldn't surprise me in the least. I like to think of it as dramatically small.' (Why do I talk like this, nodding and fluttering my eyelids, as though with a repressed giggle; why can I not speak like a man? Mine is the brazen voice of Apuleius's ass, turning its own words to ridicule.)

The party left the restaurant and stood in an untidy group on the pavement, unable to make up their minds who was going with whom, in what direction, for what purpose. Ambrose bade them good-bye and hurried away, with his absurd, light step and his heavy heart. Two soldiers outside a public-house made rude noises as he passed. 'I'll tell your sergeant-major of you,' he said gaily, almost gallantly, and flounced down the street. I should like to be one of them, he thought. I should like to go with them and drink beer and make rude noises at passing aesthetes. What does world revolution hold in store for *me*? Will it make me any nearer them? Shall I walk differently, speak differently, be less bored with Poppet Green and her friends? Here is the war, offering a new deal for everyone; I alone bear the weight of my singularity.

He crossed Tottenham Court Road and Gower Street, walking without any particular object except to take the air. It was not until he was under its shadow and saw the vast bulk of London University insulting the autumnal sky, that he remembered that here was the Ministry of Information and that his publisher, Mr Geoffrey Bentley, was working there at the head of some newly-formed department. Ambrose decided to pay him a call.

It was far from easy to gain admission; only once in his life, when he had had an appointment in a cinema studio in the outer suburbs, had Ambrose met such formidable obstruction. All the secrets of all the services might have been hidden in that gross mass of masonry. Not until Mr Bentley had been summoned to the gate to identify him was Ambrose allowed to pass.

'We have to be very careful,' said Mr Bentley.

'Why?'

'Far too many people get in as it is. You've no conception how many. It adds terribly to our work.'

'What is your work, Geoffrey?'

'Well, mostly it consists of sending people who want to see me on to someone they don't want to see. I've never liked authors–except of course,' he added, 'my personal friends. I'd no idea there were so many of them. I suppose, now I come to think of it, that explains why there are so many books. And I've never liked books–except, of course, books by personal friends.'

They rose in a lift and walked down a wide corridor, passing on the way Basil who was talking a foreign language which sounded like a series of expectorations to a sallow man in a tarboosh.

'That's *not* one of my personal friends,' said Mr Bentley bitterly.

'Does he work here?'

'I don't suppose so. No one works in the Near East department. They just lounge about talking.'

'The tradition of the bazaar.'

'The tradition of the Civil Service. This is my little room.'

They came to the door of what had once been a chemical laboratory, and entered. There was a white porcelain sink in the corner into which a tap dripped monotonously. In the centre of the oil-cloth floor stood a card table and two folding chairs. In his own office Mr Bentley sat under a ceiling painted by Angela Kauffmann, amid carefully chosen pieces of empire furniture. 'We have to rough it, you see,' he said. 'I brought those to make it look more human.'

'Those' were a pair of marble busts by Nollekens; they failed, in Ambrose's opinion, to add humanity to Mr Bentley's room.

'You don't like them? You remember them in Bedford Square.'

'I like them very much. I remember them well, but don't you think, dear Geoffrey, that here they are just a weeny bit macabre?'

'Yes,' said Mr Bentley sadly. 'Yes. I know what you mean. They're really here to annoy the civil servants.'

'Do they?'

'To a frenzy. Look at this.' He showed Ambrose a long typewritten memorandum which was headed *Furniture, Supplementary to Official Requirements, Undesirability of*. 'I sent back this.' He showed a still longer message headed *Art, Objets d', conducive to spiritual repose, Absence of in the* quarters of advisory staff. 'To-day I got this.' *Flowers, Framed Photographs and other minor ornaments, Massive marble and mahogany, Decorative features of, Distinction between.* 'Quite alliterative with rage, you see. There, for the moment, the matter rests, but as you see, it's uphill work to get anything done.'

'I suppose it would make no difference if you explained that Nollekens had inspired the greatest biography in the English language.'

'None, I should think.'

'What terrible people to work with. You are *brave*, Geoffrey. I couldn't do it.'

'But, bless my soul, Ambrose, isn't that what you came about?'

'No. I came to see you.'

'Yes, everyone comes to see me, but they all come hoping to be taken on in the Ministry. You'd better join now you're here.'

'No. No.'

'You might do worse, you know. We all abuse the old M. Of I., but there are a number of quite human people here already, and we are gradually pushing more in every day. You might do much worse.'

'I don't want to do *anything*. I think this whole war's crazy.'

'You might write a book for us then. I'm getting out a very nice little series on "What We are Fighting For". I've signed up a retired admiral, a Church of England curate, an unemployed docker, a Negro solicitor from the Gold Coast, and a nose and throat specialist from Harley Street. The original idea was to have a symposium in one volume, but I've had to enlarge the idea a little. All our authors had such very different ideas it might have been a little confusing. We could fit you in very nicely. "I used to think war crazy." It's a new line.'

'But I *do* think war crazy *still*.'

'Yes,' said Mr Bentley, his momentary enthusiasm waning. 'I know what you mean.'

The door opened and a drab, precise little man entered. 'I beg your pardon,' he said coldly. 'I didn't expect to find *you* working.'

'This is Ambrose Silk. I expect you know his work.'

'No.'

'No? He is considering doing a book in our "Why We Are at War" series. This is Sir Philip Hesketh-Smithers, our departmental assistant director.'

'If you'll excuse me a minute, I came about a memorandum RQ/1082/B4. The director is very worried.'

'Was that *Documents, Confidential, destruction by fire of*?'

'No. No. Marble decorative features.'

'Massive marble and mahogany?'

'Yes. Mahogany has no application to your sub-department. That has reference to a *prie-dieu* in the religious department. The Church of England advisor has been hearing confessions there and the director is very concerned. No, it's these effigies.'

'You refer to my Nollekenses.'

'These great statues. They won't do, Bentley, you know, they really won't do.'

'Won't do for what?' said Mr Bentley bellicosely.

'They won't do for the departmental director. He says, very properly, that portraits of sentimental association . . .'

'These are full of the tenderest association for me.'

'Of relatives . . .'

'These are family portraits.'

'Really, Bentley. Surely that is George III?'

'A distant kinsman,' said Mr Bentley blandly, 'on my mother's side.'

'And Mrs Siddons?'

'A slightly closer kinswoman, on my father's side.'

'Oh,' said Sir Philip Hesketh-Smithers. 'Ah. I didn't realize . . . I'll explain that to the director. But I'm sure,' he said suspiciously, 'that such a contingency was definitely excluded from the director's mind.'

'Flummoxed,' said Mr Bentley, as the door closed behind Sir Philip. 'Completely flummoxed. I'm glad you were there to see my little encounter. But you see what we have to contend with. And now to your affairs. I wonder where we can fit you in to our little household.'

'I don't want to be fitted in.'

'You would be a great asset. Perhaps the religious department. I don't think atheism is properly represented there.'

The head of Sir Philip Hesketh-Smithers appeared round the door. 'Could you tell me, please, *how* you are related to George III? Forgive my asking, but the director is bound to want to know.'

'The Duke of Clarence's natural daughter Henrietta married Gervase Wilbraham of Acton–at that time, I need not remind you, a rural district. His daughter Gertrude married my maternal grandfather who was, not that it matters, three times mayor of Chippenham. A man of substantial fortune, all, alas, now dissipated. . . . Flummoxed again, I think,' he added as the door closed.

'Was that true?'

'That my grandfather was mayor of Chippenham? Profoundly true.'

'About Henrietta?'

'It has always been believed in the family,' said Mr Bentley.

In another cell of that great hive Basil was explaining a plan for the annexation of Liberia. 'The German planters there outnumber the British by about fourteen to one. They're organized as a Nazi unit; they've been importing arms through Japan and they are simply waiting for the signal from Berlin to take over the government of the state. With Monrovia in enemy hands, with submarines based there, our West Coast trade route is cut. Then all the Germans have to do is to shut the Suez Canal, which they can do from Massawa whenever they like, and the Mediterranean is lost. Liberia is our one weak spot in West Africa. We've got to get in first. Don't you see?'

'Yes, yes, but I don't know why you come to me about it.'

'You'll have to handle all the preliminary propaganda there and the explanations in America afterwards.'

'But why *me*? This is the Near East Department. You ought to see Mr Pauling.'

'Mr Pauling sent me to you.'

'Did he? I wonder why. I'll ask him.' The unhappy official took up the telephone and after being successively connected with Films, the shadow cabinet of the Czecho-Slovaks and the A.R.P. section, said: 'Pauling. I have a man called Seal here. He says you sent him.'

'Yes.'

'Why?'

'Well, you sent me that frightful Turk this morning.'

'He was child's play to this.'

'Well, let it be a lesson to you not to send me any more Turks.'

'You wait and see what I send you . . . Yes,' turning to Basil, 'Pauling made a mistake. Your business is really his. It's a most interesting scheme. Wish I could do more for you. I'll tell you who, I think, would like to hear about it–Digby-Smith; he handles propaganda and subversive activities in enemy territory, and, as you say, Liberia is to all intents and purposes enemy territory.'

The door opened and there entered a beaming, bearded, hair-bunned figure in a long black robe; a gold cross swung from his neck; a brimless top-hat crowned his venerable head.

'I am the Archimandrite Antonios,' he said. 'I am coming in please?'

'Come in, Your Beatitude; please sit down.'

'I have been telling how I was expulsed from Sofia. They said I must be telling you.'

'You have been to our religious department?'

'I have been telling your office clergymen about my expulsing. The Bulgar peoples say it was for fornications, but it was for politics. They are not expulsing from Sofia for fornications unless there is politics too. So now I am the ally of the British peoples since the Bulgar peoples say it was for fornications.'

'Yes, yes, I quite understand, but that is not really the business of this department.'

'You are not dealing with the business of the Bulgar peoples?'

'Well, yes, but I think your case opens up a wider issue altogether. You must go and see Mr Pauling. I'll give you someone to show the way. He deals especially with cases like yours.'

'So? You have here a department of fornications?'

'Yes, you might call it that.'

'I find that good. In Sofia is not having any such department.'

His Beatitude was sent on his way. 'Now you want to see Digby-Smith, don't you?'

'Do I?'

'Yes, he'll be *most* interested in Liberia.'

Another messenger came; Basil was led away. In the corridor they were stopped by a small, scrubby man carrying a suitcase.

'Pardon me, can you put me right for the Near East?'

'There,' said Basil, 'in there. But you won't get much sense out of him.'

'Oh, he's bound to be interested in what I've got here. Everyone is. They're bombs. You could blow the roof off the whole of this building with what I got here,' said this lunatic. 'I've been carting 'em from room to room ever since the blinking war began and often I think it wouldn't be a bad plan if they did go off sudden.'

'Who sent you to the Near East?'

'Chap called Smith, Digby-Smith. Very interested in my bombs he was.'

'Have you been to Pauling, yet?'

'Pauling? Yes, I was with him yesterday. Very interested he was in my bombs. I tell you everyone is. It was him said I ought to show them to Digby-Smith.'

Mr Bentley talked at length about the difficulties and impossibilities of bureaucratic life. 'If it was not for the journalists and the civil servants,' he said, 'everything would be perfectly easy. They seem to think the whole Ministry exists for their convenience. Strictly, of course, I shouldn't have anything to do with the journalists–I deal with books here–but they always seem to shove them on to me when they get impatient. Not only journalists; there was a man here this morning with a suitcase full of bombs.'

'Geoffrey,' said Ambrose at length. 'Tell me, would you say I was pretty well known as a left wing writer?'

'Of course, my dear fellow, very well known.'

'As a *left* wing writer?'

'Of course, *very* left wing.'

'Well known, I mean, outside the left wing itself?'

'Yes, certainly. Why?'

'I was only wondering.'

They were now interrupted for some minutes by an American war correspondent who wanted Mr Bentley to verify the story of a Polish submarine which was said to have arrived at Scapa; to give him a pass to go there and see for himself; to provide him with a Polish interpreter; to explain why in hell that little runt Pappenhacker of the Hearst press had been told of this submarine and not himself.

'Oh dear,' said Mr Bentley. 'Why have they sent you to me?'

'It seems I'm registered with you and not with the press bureau.'

This proved to be true. As the author of *Nazi Destiny*, a work of popular history that had sold prodigiously on both sides of the Atlantic, this man had been entered as a 'man of letters' instead of as a journalist.

'You mustn't mind,' said Mr Bentley. 'In this country we think much more of men-of-letters than we do of journalists.'

'Does being a man of letters get me to Scapa?'

'Well, no.'

'Does it get me a Polish interpreter?'

'No.'

'To Hell with being a man-of-letters.'

'I'll get you transferred,' said Mr Bentley. 'The press bureau is the place for you.'

'There's a snooty young man at that bureau looks at me as if I was something the cat brought in,' complained the author of *Nazi Destiny*.

'He won't once you're registered with him. I wonder, since you're here, if you'd like to write a book for us.'

'No.'

'No? Well, I hope you get to Scapa all right . . . He won't, you know,' added Mr Bentley as the door closed. 'You may be absolutely confident that he'll never get there. Did you ever read his book? It was exceedingly silly. He said

Hitler was secretly married to a Jewess. I don't know what he'd say if we let him go to Scapa.'

'What do you think he'll say if you don't?'

'Something very offensive. I've no doubt. But we shan't be responsible. At least, I wonder, shall we?'

'Geoffrey, when you say well known as a left wing writer, do you suppose that if the fascists got into power here, I should be on their black list?'

'Yes, certainly, my dear fellow.'

'They did frightful things to the Left Wing Intellectuals in Spain.'

'Yes.'

'And in Poland, now.'

'So the press department tell me.'

'I see.'

The Archimandrite dropped in for a few moments. He expressed great willingness to write a book about Axis intrigues in Sofia.

'You think you can help bring Bulgaria in on our side?' asked Mr Bentley.

'I am spitting in the face of the Bulgar peoples,' said His Beatitude.

'I believe he'd write a very good autobiography,' said Mr Bentley, when the prelate left them. 'In the days of peace I should have signed him up for one.'

'Geoffrey, you were serious when you said that I should be on the black list of Left Wing Intellectuals?'

'Quite serious. You're right at the top. You and Parsnip and Pimpernell.'

Ambrose winced at the mention of these two familiar names. '*They're* all right,' he said. '*They're* in the United States.'

Basil and Ambrose met as they left the Ministry. Together they loitered for a minute to watch a brisk little scene between the author of *Nazi Destiny* and the policeman on the gate; it appeared that in a fit of nervous irritation the American had torn up the slip of paper which had admitted him to the building; now they would not let him leave.

'I'm sorry for him in a way,' said Ambrose. 'It's not a place I'd care to spend the rest of the war in.'

'They wanted me to take a job there,' said Basil, lying.

'They wanted *me* to,' said Ambrose.

They walked together through the sombre streets of Bloomsbury. 'How's Poppet?' said Basil at length.

'She's cheered up wonderfully since you left. Painting away like a mowing machine.'

'I must look her up again sometime. I've been busy lately. Angela's back. Where are we going to?'

'I don't know. I've nowhere to go.'

'*I've* nowhere to go.'

An evening chill was beginning to breathe down the street.

'I nearly joined the Bombardier Guards a week or two ago,' said Basil.

'I once had a *great* friend who was a corporal in the Bombardiers.'

'We'd better go and see Sonia and Alastair.'

'I haven't been near them for years.'

'Come on.' Basil wanted someone to pay for the cab.

But when they reached the little house in Chester Street they found Sonia alone and packing. 'Alastair's gone off,' she said. 'He's joined the army–in the ranks. They said he was too old for a commission.'

'My dear, how very 1914.'

'I'm just off to join him. He's near Brookwood.'

'You'll be beautifully near the Necropolis,' said Ambrose. 'It's the most enjoyable place. Three public houses, my dear, inside the cemetery, right among the graves. I asked the barmaid if the funeral parties got very tipsy and she said, "No. It's when they come back to visit the graves. They seem to need something then." And did you know the Corps of Commissionaires have a special burial place. Perhaps if Alastair is a very good soldier they might make him an honorary member . . .' Ambrose chattered on. Sonia packed. Basil looked about for bottles. 'Nothing to drink.'

'All packed, darling. I'm sorry. We might go out somewhere.'

They went out later, when the packing was done, into the blackout to a bar. Other friends came to join them.

'No one seems interested in my scheme to annex Liberia.'

'Beasts.'

'No imagination. They won't take suggestions from outsiders. You know, Sonia, this war is developing into a kind of club enclosure on a racecourse. If you aren't wearing the right badge they won't let you in.'

'I think that's rather what Alastair felt.'

'It's going to be a long war. There's plenty of time. I shall wait until there's something amusing to do.'

'I don't believe it's going to be that kind of war.'

This is all that anyone talks about, thought Ambrose; jobs and the kind of war it is going to be. War in the air, war of attrition, tank war, war of nerves, war of propaganda, war of defence in depth, war of movement, people's war, total war, indivisible war, war infinite, war incomprehensible, war of essence without accidents or attributes, metaphysical war, war in time-space, war eternal . . . all war is nonsense, thought Ambrose. I don't care about their war. It's got nothing on me. But if, thought Ambrose, I was one of these people, if I were not a cosmopolitan, Jewish pansy, if I were not all that the Nazis mean when they talk about 'degenerates', if I were not a single, sane individual, if I were part of a herd, one of these people, normal and responsible for the welfare of my herd, Gawd strike me pink, thought Ambrose, I wouldn't sit around discussing what kind of war it was going to be. I'd make it my kind of war. I'd set about killing and stampeding the other herd as fast and as hard as I could. Lord love a duck, thought Ambrose, there wouldn't be any animals nosing about for suitable jobs in *my* herd.

'Bertie's hoping to help control petrol in the Shetland Isles.'

'Algernon's off to Syria on the most secret kind of mission.'

'Poor John hasn't got anything yet.'

Cor chase my Aunt Fanny round a mulberry bush, thought Ambrose, what a herd.

So the leaves fell and the blackout grew earlier and earlier, and autumn became winter.

2

WINTER

I

Winter set in hard. Poland was defeated; east and west the prisoners rolled away to slavery. English infantry cut trees and dug trenches along the Belgian frontier. Parties of distinguished visitors went to the Maginot Line and returned, as though from a shrine, with souvenir-medals. Belisha was turned out; the radical papers began a clamour for his return and then suddenly shut up. Russia invaded Finland and the papers were full of tales of white-robed armies scouting through the forests. English soldiers on leave brought back reports of the skill and daring of Nazi patrols and of how much better the blackout was managed in Paris. A number of people were saying quietly and firmly that Chamberlain must go. The French said the English were not taking the war seriously, and the Ministry of Information said the French were taking it very seriously indeed. Sergeant instructors complained of the shortage of training stores. How could one teach the three rules of aiming without aiming discs?

The leaves fell in the avenue at Malfrey, and this year, where once there had been a dozen men to sweep them, there were now four and two boys. Freddy was engaged in what he called 'drawing in his horns a bit'. The Grinling Gibbons saloon and the drawing-rooms and galleries round it were shut up and shut off, carpets rolled, furniture sheeted, chandeliers bagged, windows shuttered and barred, hall and staircase stood empty and dark. Barbara lived in the little octagonal parlour which opened on the parterre; she moved the nursery over to the bedrooms next to hers; what had once been known as 'the bachelors' wing', in the Victorian days when bachelors were hardy fellows who could put up with collegiate and barrack simplicity, was given over to the evacuees. Freddy came over for the four good shoots which the estate provided; he made his guests stay out this year, one at the farm, three at the bailiff's house, two at the Sothill Arms. Now, at the end of the season, he had some of the regiment over to shoot off the cocks; bags were small and consisted mostly of hens.

When Freddy came on leave the central heating was lit; at other times an intense cold settled into the house; it was a system which had to be all or nothing; it would not warm Barbara's corner alone but had to circulate, ticking and guggling, through furlongs of piping, consuming cartloads of coke daily. 'Lucky we've got plenty of wood,' said Freddy; damp green logs were brought in from the park to smoke tepidly on the hearths. Barbara used to creep into the orangery to warm herself. 'Must keep the heat up there,' said Freddy. 'Got some very rare stuff in it. Man from Kew said some of the best in the country.' So Barbara had her writing table put there, and sat, absurdly, among tropical vegetation while outside, beyond the colonnade, the ground froze hard and the trees stood out white against the leaden sky.

Then, two days before Christmas, Freddy's regiment was moved to another part of the country. He had friends with a commodious house in the immediate neighbourhood, where he spent his week-ends, so the pipes were never heated and the chill in the house, instead of being a mere negation of warmth, became something positive and overwhelming. Soon after Christmas there was a great fall of snow and with the snow came Basil.

He came, as usual, unannounced. Barbara, embowered in palm and fern, looked up from her letter-writing to see him standing in the glass door. She ran to kiss him with a cry of delight. 'Darling, how very nice. Have you come to stay?'

'Yes, Mother said you were alone.'

'I don't know where we'll put you. Things are very odd here. You haven't brought anyone else, have you?' It was one of Freddy's chief complaints that Basil usually came not only uninvited but attended by undesirable friends.

'No, no one. There isn't anyone nowadays. I've come to write a book.'

'Oh, Basil. I am sorry. Is it as bad as that?'

There was much that needed no saying between brother and sister. For years now, whenever things were very bad with Basil, he had begun writing a book. It was as near surrender as he ever came and the fact that these books–two novels, a book of travel, a biography, a work of contemporary history–never got beyond the first ten thousand words was testimony to the resilience of his character.

'A book on strategy,' said Basil. 'I'm sick of trying to get ideas into the heads of the people in power. The only thing is to appeal over their heads to the thinking public. Chiefly, it is the case for the annexation of Liberia, but I shall touch on several other vital places as well. The difficulty will be to get it out in time to have any influence.'

'Mother said you were joining the Bombardier Guards.'

'Yes. Nothing came of it. They say they want younger men. It's a typical army paradox. They say we are too old now and that they will call us up in two years' time. I shall bring that out in my book. The only logical policy is to kill off the old first, while there's still some kick in them. I shan't deal only with strategy. I shall outline a general policy for the nation.'

'Well, it's very nice to see you, anyway. I've been lonely.'

'*I've* been lonely.'

'What's happened to everyone?'

'You mean Angela. She's gone home.'

'Home?'

'That house we used to call Cedric's Folly. It's hers really, of course. Cedric's gone back to the army. It's scarcely credible but apparently he was a dashing young subaltern once. So there was the house and the Lyne hooligan and the government moving in to make it a hospital, so Angela had to go back and see to things. It's full of beds and nurses and doctors waiting for air-raid victims and a woman in the village got appendicitis and she had to be taken forty miles to be operated on because she wasn't an air-raid victim and she died on the way. So Angela is carrying on a campaign about it and I should be surprised if she doesn't get something done. She seems to have made up her mind I ought to be killed. Mother's the same. It's funny. In the old days when from time to time there really were people gunning for me, no one cared a hoot. Now that I'm living in enforced safety and idleness, they seem to think it rather disgraceful.'

'No new girls?'

'There was one called Poppet Green. You wouldn't have liked her. I've been having a very dull time. Alastair is a private at Brookwood. I went down to see them. He and Sonia have got a horrible villa on a golf course where he goes whenever he's off duty. He says the worst thing about his training is the entertainments. They get detailed to go twice a week and the sergeant always picks on Alastair. He makes the same joke each time. "We'll send the playboy." Otherwise it's all very matey and soft, Alastair says. Peter has joined a very secret corps to go and fight in the Arctic. They had a long holiday doing winter sports in the Alps. I don't suppose you'd remember Ambrose Silk. He's starting a new magazine to keep culture alive.'

'Poor Basil. Well, I hope you don't have to write the book for long.' There was so much between brother and sister that did not need saying.

That evening Basil began his book; that is to say he lay on the rug before the column of smoke which rose from the grate of the octagonal parlour, and typed out a list of possible titles.

A Word to the Unwise.

Prolegomenon to Destruction.

Berlin or Cheltenham; the Choice for the General Staff.

Policy or Generalship; some questions put by a Civilian to vex the Professional Soldiers.

Policy or Professionalism.

The Gentle Art of Victory.

The Lost Art of Victory.

How to Win the War in Six Months; a simple lesson book for ambitious soldiers.

They all looked pretty good to him and looking at the list Basil was struck anew, as he had been constantly struck during the preceding four months, with surprise that anyone of his ability should be unemployed at a time like the present. It makes one despair of winning, he thought.

Barbara sat beside him reading. She heard him sigh and put out a sisterly hand to touch his hair. 'It's terribly cold,' she said. 'I wonder if it would be any good trying to black-out the orangery. Then we could sit there in the evenings.'

Suddenly there was a knock on the door and there entered a muffled, middle-aged woman; she wore fur gloves and carried an electric torch, dutifully dimmed with tissue paper; her nose was very red, her eyes were watering and she stamped snow off high rubber boots. It was Mrs Fremlin of the Hollies. Nothing but bad news would have brought her out on a night like this. 'I came straight in,' she said superfluously. 'Didn't want to stand waiting outside. Got some bad news. The Connollys are back.'

It was indeed bad news. In the few hours that he had been at Malfrey, Basil had heard a great deal about the Connollys.

'Oh God,' said Barbara. 'Where are they?'

'Here, outside in the lobby.'

Evacuation to Malfrey had followed much the same course as it had in other parts of the country and had not only kept Barbara, as billeting officer, constantly busy, but had transformed her, in four months, from one of the most popular women in the countryside into a figure of terror. When her car was seen approaching people fled through covered lines of retreat, through side doors and stable yards, into the snow, anywhere to avoid her persuasive, 'But surely you could manage *one* more. He's a boy this time and a very well-behaved little fellow,' for the urban authorities maintained a steady flow of refugees well in excess of the stream of returning malcontents. Few survived of the original party who had sat glumly on the village green on the first morning of war. Some had gone back immediately; others more reluctantly in response to ugly rumours of their husbands' goings on; one had turned out to be a fraud, who, herself childless, had kidnapped a baby from a waiting perambulator in order to secure her passage to safety, so impressed had she been by the propaganda of the local officials. It was mostly children now who assembled, less glumly, on the village green, and showed the agricultural community how another part of the world lived. They were tolerated now as one of the troubles of the time. Some had even endeared themselves to their hosts. But everyone, when evacuees were spoken of, implicitly excluded for all generalities the family of Connolly.

These had appeared as an act of God apparently without human agency; their names did not appear on any list; they carried no credentials; no one was responsible for them. They were found lurking under the seats of a carriage when the train was emptied on the evening of the first influx. They had been dragged out and stood on the platform where everyone denied knowledge of them, and since they could not be left there, they were included in the party that was being sent by bus to Malfrey village. From that moment they were on a list; they had been given official existence and their destiny was inextricably involved with that of Malfrey.

Nothing was ever discovered about the Connollys' parentage. When they could be threatened or cajoled into speaking of their antecedents they spoke, with distaste, of an 'Auntie'. To this woman, it seemed, the war had come as a God-sent release. She had taken her dependents to the railway station, propelled them into the crowd of milling adolescence, and hastily covered her tracks by decamping from home. Enquiry by the police in the street where the Connollys professed to have lived produced no other information than that the woman had been there and was not there any longer. She owed a little for milk; otherwise she had left no memorial on that rather unimpressionable district.

There was Doris, ripely pubescent, aged by her own varied accounts anything from ten years to eighteen. An early and ingenious attempt to have her certified as an adult was frustrated by an inspecting doctor who put her at about fifteen. Doris had dark, black bobbed hair, a large mouth and dark pig's eyes. There was something of the Eskimo about her head, but her colouring was ruddy and her manner more vivacious than is common among that respectable race. Her figure was stocky, her bust prodigious, and her gait, derived from the cinematograph, was designed to be alluring.

Micky, her junior by the length of a rather stiff sentence for house-breaking, was of lighter build; a scrawny, scowling little boy; a child of few words and those, for the most part, foul.

Marlene was presumed to be a year younger. But for Micky's violent denials she might have been taken for his twin. She was the offspring of unusually prolonged coincident periods of liberty in the lives of her parents which the sociologist must deplore, for Marlene was simple. An appeal to have her certified imbecile was disallowed by the same inspecting doctor, who expressed an opinion that country life might work wonders with the child.

There the three had stood, on the eve of the war, in Malfrey Parish Hall, one leering, one lowering, and one drooling, as unprepossessing a family as could be found in the kingdom. Barbara took one look at them, looked again to see that her weary eyes were not playing tricks with her, and consigned them to the Mudges of Upper Lamstock, a tough farming family on a remote homestead.

Within a week Mr Mudge was at the Park, with the three children in the back of his milk truck. 'It's not for myself, Mrs Sothill; I'm out and about all day and in the evenings I'm sleepy, and being with animals so much I don't take on so. But it's my old woman. She *do* take on and she won't stand for it. She've locked herself in upstairs and she won't come down till they've gone, and when she do say that she means of it, Mrs Sothill. We're willing to do anything in reason to help the war, but these brats aren't to be borne and that's flat.'

'Oh dear, Mr Mudge, which of them is giving trouble?'

'Why it's all of 'em, m'am. There's the boy was the best of 'em at first though you can't understand what he do say, speaking as they do where he come from. Nasty, unfriendly ways he had but he didn't do much you could call harm not till he'd seen me kill the goose. I took him out to watch to cheer him up like, and uncommon interested he was, and I thought I'll make a country lad of you yet. I gave him the head to play with and he seemed quite pleased. Then no sooner was I off down to the root field, then blessed if he didn't get hold of a knife and when I came back supper time there was six of my ducks dead and the old cat. Yes, mum, blessed if he hadn't had the head off of our old yellow cat. Then the little un, she's a dirty girl, begging your pardon, mum. It's not only her wetting the bed; she've wetted everywhere, chairs, floor and not only wetting, mum. Never seem to have been taught to be in a house where she comes from.'

'But doesn't the elder girl do anything to help?'

'If you ask me, mum, she's the worst of the lot. My old woman would stick it but for her, but it's that Doris makes her take on like she do. Soft about the men, she is, mum. Why she even comes making up to me and I'm getting on to be her grandfer. She won't leave our Willie alone not for a minute, and he's a bashful boy our Willie and he can't get on with the work, her always coming after him. So there it is, mum. I'm sorry not to oblige, but I've promised my old woman I won't come back with 'em and I dusn't go back on what I've said.'

Mr Mudge was the first of a succession of hosts. The longest that the Connollys stayed in any place was ten days; the shortest was an hour and a quarter. In six weeks they had become a legend far beyond the parish. When influential old men at the Turf in London put their heads together and said, 'The whole scheme has been a mistake. I was hearing last night some examples of the way some of the evacuees are behaving . . .' the chances were that the scandal originated with the Connollys. They were cited in the House of Commons; there were paragraphs about them in official reports.

Barbara tried separating them, but in their first night apart Doris climbed out of her window and was lost for two days, to be found in a barn eight miles away, stupefied with cider; she gave no coherent account of her adventure. On the same evening Micky bit the wife of the roadman on whom he was quartered, so that the district nurse had to be called in; while Marlene had a species of seizure which aroused unfulfilled hopes that she might be dead. Everyone agreed that the only place for the Connollys was 'an institution' and at last, just before Christmas, after formalities complicated by the obscurity of their origins, to an institution they were sent, and Malfrey settled back to entertain its guests with a Christmas tree and a conjurer, with an air of relief which could be sensed for miles around. It was as though the All Clear had sounded after a night of terror. And now the Connollys were back.

'What's happened, Mrs Fremlin? Surely the Home *can't* send them away.'

'It's been evacuated. All the children are being sent back to the places they came from. Malfrey was the only address they had for the Connollys, so here they are. The Welfare Woman brought them to the Parish Hall. I was there with the Guides so I said I'd bring them up to you.'

'They might have warned us.'

'I expect they thought that if we had time we should try and stop them coming.'

'How right they were. Have the Connollys been fed?'

'I think so. At any rate Marlene was terribly sick in the car.'

'I'm dying to see these Connollys,' said Basil.

'You shall,' said his sister grimly.

But they were not in the lobby where they had been left. Barbara rang the bell. 'Benson, you remember the Connolly children?'

'Vividly, madam.'

'They're back.'

'Here, madam?'

'Here. Somewhere in the house. You'd better institute a search.'

'Very good, madam. And when they are found, they will be going away immediately?'

'Not immediately. They'll have to stay here to-night. We'll find somewhere for them in the village to-morrow.'

Benson hesitated. 'It won't be easy, madam.'

'It won't be, Benson.'

He hesitated again; thought better of whatever he meant to say, and merely added: 'I will start the search, madam.'

'I know what that means,' said Barbara as the man left them. 'Benson is yellow.'

The Connollys were found at last and assembled. Doris had been in Barbara's bedroom trying out her make-up, Micky in the library tearing up a folio, Marlene grovelling under the pantry sink eating the remains of the dogs' dinners. When they were together again, in the lobby, Basil inspected them. Their appearance exceeded anything he had been led to expect. They were led away to the bachelors' wing and put together into a large bedroom.

'Shall we lock the door?'

'It would be no good. If they want to get out, they will.'

'Could I speak to you for a moment, madam?' said Benson.

When Barbara returned she said, 'Benson *is* yellow. He can't take it.'

'Wants to leave?'

'It's him or the Connollys, he says. I can't blame him. Freddy will never forgive me if I let him go.'

'Babs, you're blubbing.'

'Who wouldn't?' said Barbara, pulling out a handkerchief and weeping in earnest. 'I ask you, who wouldn't?'

'Don't be a chump,' said Basil, relapsing, as he often did with Barbara, into the language of the schoolroom. 'I'll fix it for you.'

'Swank. Chump yourself. Double chump.'

'Double chump with knobs on.'

'Darling Basil, it is nice to have you back. I do believe if anyone could fix it, you could.'

'Freddy couldn't, could he?'

'Freddy isn't here.'

'I'm cleverer than Freddy. Babs, say I'm cleverer than Freddy.'

'I'm cleverer than Freddy. Sucks to you.'

'Babs, say you love me more than Freddy.'

'You love me more than Freddy. Double sucks.'

'Say I, Barbara, love you, Basil, more than him, Freddy.'

'I won't. I don't . . . Beast, you're hurting.'

'Say it.'

'Basil, stop at once or I shall call Miss Penfold.'

They were back twenty years, in the schoolroom again. 'Miss Penfold, Miss Penfold, Basil's pulling my hair.'

They scuffled on the sofa. Suddenly a voice said, ''Ere, Mrs.' It was Doris. 'Mrs.'

Barbara stood up, panting and dishevelled. 'Well, Doris, what is it?'

'Marlene's queer again.'

'Oh dear. I'll come up. Run along.'

Doris looked languishingly at Basil. ''Aving a lark, eh?' she said. 'I like a lark.'

'Run along. Doris. You'll get cold.'

'I ain't cold. Pull my hair if you like, Mister.'

'I wouldn't dream of it,' said Basil.

'Dessay I shall. I dream a lot of funny things. Go on Mister, pull it. Hard. I don't mind.' She offered her bobbed head to Basil and then with a giggle ran out of the room.

'You see,' said Barbara. 'A problem child.'

When Marlene had been treated for her queerness, Barbara came back to say good night.

'I'll stay up a bit and work on this book.'

'All right, darling. Good night.' She bent over the back of the sofa and kissed the top of his head.

'Not blubbing any more?'

'No, not blubbing.'

He looked up at her and smiled. She smiled back; it was the same smile. They saw themselves, each in the other's eyes. There's no one like Basil, thought Barbara, seeing herself, no one like him, when he's nice.

II

Next morning Basil was called by Benson, who was the only manservant indoors since Freddy drew in his horns. (He had taken his valet with him to the yeomanry and supported him now, in a very much lower standard of comfort, at the King's expense.) Lying in bed and watching the man put out his clothes, Basil reflected that he still owed him a small sum of money from his last visit.

'Benson, what's this about your leaving?'

'I was cross last night, Mr Basil. I couldn't ever leave Malfrey and Mrs Sothill ought to know that. Not with the Captain away, too.'

'Mrs Sothill was very upset.'

'So was I, Mr Basil. You don't know what those Connollys are. They're not human.'

'We'll find a billet for them.'

'No one will take the Connollys in these parts. Not if they were given a hundred pounds.'

'I have an idea I owe you some money.'

'You do, Mr Basil. Twelve pound ten.'

'As much as that? Time I paid it back.'

'It is.'

'I will, Benson.'

'I hope so, sir, I'm sure.'

Basil went to his bath pondering. No one will take the Connollys in these parts. Not for a hundred pounds. Not for a hundred pounds.

Since the war began Barbara had taken to breakfasting downstairs in the mistaken belief that it caused less trouble. Instead of the wicker bed-table tray, a table had to be laid in the small dining-room, the fire had to be lit there two hours earlier, silver dishes had to be cleaned and the wicks trimmed under them. It was an innovation deplored by all.

Basil found her crouched over the fire with her cup of coffee; she turned her curly black head and smiled; both of them had the same devastating combination of dark hair and clear blue eyes. Narcissus greeted Narcissus from the watery depths as Basil kissed her.

'Spooney,' she said.

'I've squared Benson for you.'

'Darling, how clever of you.'

'I had to give the old boy a fiver.'

'Liar.'

'All right, don't believe me then.'

'I don't, knowing Benson and knowing you. I remember last time you stayed here I had to pay him over ten pounds that you'd borrowed.'

'You paid him?'

'Yes. I was afraid he'd ask Freddy.'

'The old double-crosser. Anyway he's staying.'

'Yes; thinking it over I knew he would. I don't know why I took it so hard last night. I think it was the shock of seeing the Connollys.'

'We must get them settled to-day.'

'It's hopeless. No one will take them.'

'You've got powers of coercion.'

'Yes, but I can't possibly use them.'

'*I* can,' said Basil. 'I shall enjoy it.'

After breakfast they moved from the little dining-room to the little parlour. The corridor, though it was one of the by-ways of the house, had a sumptuous cornice and a high, covered ceiling; the door cases were enriched with classic pediments in whose broken entablature stood busts of philosophers and composers. Other busts stood at regular intervals on marble pedestals. Everything in Malfrey was splendid and harmonious; everything except Doris who, that morning, lurked in their path rubbing herself on a pilaster like a cow on a stump.

'Hallo,' she said.

'Hallo, Doris. Where are Micky and Marlene?'

'Outside. They're all right. They've found the snow man the others made and they're mucking him up.'

'Run along and join them.'

'I want to stay here with you–and *him*.'

'I bet you do,' said Basil. 'No such luck. I'm going to find you a nice billet miles and miles away.'

'I want to stay with you.'

'You go and help muck up the snow man.'

'That's a kid's game. I'm not a kid. Mister, why wouldn't you pull my hair last night? Was it because you thought I had nits? I haven't any more. The nurse combed them all out at the institution and put oil on. That's why it's a bit greasy.'

'I don't pull girls' hair.'

'You do. I saw you. You pulled *hers* . . . he's your boy, isn't he?' she said, turning to Barbara.

'He's my brother, Doris.'

'Ah,' she said, her pig eyes dark with the wisdom of the slums, 'but you fancy him, don't you? I saw.'

'She really is an atrocious child,' said Barbara.

III

Basil set about the problem of finding a home for the Connollys with zeal and method. He settled himself at a table with an ordnance map, the local newspaper and the little red leather-covered address book which had been one of old Mrs Sothill's legacies to Barbara; in this book were registered all her more well-to-do neighbours for a radius of twenty miles, the majority of whom were marked with the initials G.P.O. which stood for Garden Party Only. Barbara had done her best to keep this invaluable work of reference up to date, and had from time to time crossed out those who had died or left the district and added the names of newcomers.

Presently Basil said, 'What about the Harknesses of Old Mill House, North Grappling?'

'Middle-aged people. He retired from some sort of job abroad. I think she's musical. Why?'

'They're advertising for boarders.' He pushed the paper across to her, where she read in the *Accommodation* column: *Paying Guests accepted in lovely modernized fifteenth-century mill. Ideal surroundings for elderly or artistic people wishing to avoid war worries. All home produce. Secluded old-world gardens. 6 gns weekly. Highest references given and expected. Harkness, Old Mill House, North Grappling.*

'How about that for the Connollys?'

'Basil, you can't.'

'Can't I just? I'll get to work on them at once. Do they allow you extra petrol for your billeting work?'

'Yes, but . . .'

'That's grand. I'll take the Connollys over there this morning. D'you know, this is the first piece of serious war work I've done so far?'

Normally, whenever the car left the garage there was a stampede of evacuees to the running boards crying, 'Give us a ride.' This morning, however, seeing the three forbidding Connollys in the back seat, the other children fell back silently. They were not allowed by their mothers to play with the Connollys.

'Mister, why can't I sit in front with you?'

'You've got to keep the other two in order.'

'They'll be good.'

'That's what you think.'

'They'll be good if I tell them, Mister.'

'Then why aren't they?'

''Cos I tell 'em to be bad. In fun you know. Where are we going?'

'I'm finding a new home for you, Doris.'

'Away from you?'

'Far away from me.'

'Mister, listen. Micky ain't bad really nor Marlene isn't silly. Are you, Marlene?'

'Not very silly,' said Marlene.

'She can be clean if she wants to be, if I tell her. See here, Mister, play fair. You let us stay with you and I'll see the kids behave themselves.'

'And what about you, Doris?'

'I don't have to behave. I'm not a kid. Is it on?'

'It is not.'

'You going to take us away?'

'You bet I am.'

'Then just you wait and see what we give them where we're going.'

'I shan't wait and see,' said Basil, 'but I've no doubt I shall hear about it in good time.'

North Grappling was ten miles distant, a stone-built village of uneven stone tile roofs none of which was less than a century old. It lay off the main road in a fold of the hills; a stream ran through it following the line of its single street and crossing it under two old stone bridges. At the upper end of the street stood the church, which declared by its size and rich decoration that in the centuries since it was built, while the rest of the world was growing, North Grappling had shrunk; at the lower end, below the second bridge, stood Old Mill House. It was just such a home of ancient peace as a man might dream of who was forced to earn his living under a fiercer sky. Mr Harkness had in fact dreamed of it, year in, year out, as he toiled in his office at Singapore, or reclined after work on the club veranda, surrounded by gross vegetation and rude colours. He bought it from his father's legacy while on leave, when he was still a young man, meaning to retire there when the time came, and his years of waiting had been haunted by only one fear; that he would return to find the place 'developed', new red roofs among the grey and a tarmac road down the uneven street. But modernity spared North Grappling; he returned to find the place just as he had first come upon it, on a walking tour, late in the evening with the stones still warm from the afternoon sun and the scent of the gillyflowers sweet and fresh on the breeze.

This morning, half lost in snow, the stones which in summer seemed grey were a golden brown, and the pleached limes, which in their leaf hid the low front, now revealed the mullions and dripstones, the sundial above the long, centre window, and the stone hood of the door carved in the shape of a scallop shell. Basil stopped the car by the bridge.

'Jesus,' said Doris. 'You aren't going to leave us here.'

'Sit tight,' said Basil. 'You'll know soon enough.'

He threw a rug over the radiator of the car, opened the little iron gate and walked up the flagged path, grimly, a figure of doom. The low, winter sun cast his shadow before him, ominously, against the door which Mr Harkness had had painted apple green. The gnarled trunk of a wistaria rose from beside the door-jamb and twisted its naked length between the lines of the windows. Basil glanced once over his shoulder to see that his young passengers were invisible and then put his hand to the iron bell. He heard it ring melodiously not far away, and presently the door was opened by a maid dressed in apple green, with an apron of sprigged muslin and a starched white cap that was in effect part Dutch, part conventual, and wholly ludicrous. This figure of fancy led Basil up a step, down a step and into a living room, where he was left long enough to observe the decorations. The floor was covered in coarse rush matting and in places by bright Balkan rugs. On the walls were Thornton's flower prints (with the exception of his masterpiece, *The Night-Flowering Cereus*), samplers and old maps. The most prominent objects of furniture were a grand piano and a harp. There were also some tables and chairs of raw-looking beech. From an open hearth peat smoke billowed periodically into the room, causing Basil's eyes to water. It was just such a room as Basil had imagined from the advertisement and Mr and Mrs Harkness were just such a couple. Mrs Harkness wore a hand-woven woollen garment, her eyes were large and poetic, her nose was long and red with the frost, her hair nondescript in colour and haphazard in arrangement. Her husband had done all that a man can to disguise the effects of twenty years of club and bungalow life in the Far East. He had grown a little pointed beard; he wore a homespun suit of knickerbockers in the style of the pioneers of bicycling; he wore a cameo ring round his loose silk tie; yet there was something in his bearing which still suggested the dapper figure in white ducks who had stood his round of pink gins, evening after evening, to other dapper white figures, and had dined twice a year at Government House.

They entered from the garden door. Basil half expected Mr Harkness to say 'take a pew', and clap his hands for the gin. Instead they stood looking at him with enquiry and some slight distaste.

'My name is Seal. I came about your advertisement in the *Courier*.'

'Our advertisement. Ah yes,' said Mr Harkness vaguely. 'It was just an idea we had. We felt a little ashamed here, with so much space and beauty; the place is a little large for our requirements these days. We did think that perhaps if we heard of a few people like ourselves–the same simple tastes–we might, er, join forces as it were during the present difficult times. As a matter of fact we have one newcomer with us already. I don't think we *really* want to take anyone else, do we, Agnes?'

'It was just an idle thought,' said Mrs Harkness. 'A green thought in a green place.'

'This is not a Guest House, you know. We take in paying guests. Quite a different thing.'

Basil understood their difficulties with a keenness of perception that was rare to him. 'It's not for myself that I was enquiring,' he said.

'Ah, that's different. I daresay we might take in one or two more if they were, if they were *really* . . .'

Mrs Harkness helped him out. 'If we were sure they were the kind of people who would be happy here.'

'Exactly. It is essentially a *happy* house.'

It was like his housemaster at school. 'We are essentially a keen House, Seal. We may not win many cups but at least we try.'

'I can see it is,' he said gallantly.

'I expect you'd like to look round. It looks quite a little place from the road, but is surprisingly large, really, when you come to count up the rooms.'

A hundred years ago the pastures round North Grappling had all been corn-growing land and the mill had served a wide area. Long before the Harknesses' time it had fallen into disuse and, in the 'eighties, had been turned into a dwelling house by a disciple of William Morris. The stream had been diverted, the old mill pool drained and levelled and made into a sunken garden. The rooms that had held the grindstones and machinery, and the long lofts where the grain had been stored, had been tactfully floored and plastered and partitioned. Mrs Harkness pointed out all the features with maternal pride.

'Are your friends who were thinking of coming here artistic people?'

'No, I don't think you could call them that.'

'They don't write?'

'No, I don't think so.'

'I've always thought this would be an ideal place for someone who wanted to write. May I ask, what *are* your friends?'

'Well, I suppose you might call them evacuees.'

Mr and Mrs Harkness laughed pleasantly at the little joke. 'Townsfolk in search of sanctuary, eh?'

'Exactly.'

'Well, they will find it here, eh, Agnes?'

They were back in the living room. Mrs. Harkness laid her hand on the gilded neck of the harp and looked out across the sunken garden with a dreamy look in her grey eyes. Thus she had looked out across the Malaya golf course, dreaming of home.

'I like to think of this beautiful old house still being of use in the world. After all it was built for *use*. Hundreds of years ago it gave bread to the people. Then with the change of the times it was left forlorn and derelict. Then it became a home, but it was still out of the world, shut off from the life of the people. And now at last it comes into its own again. Fulfilling a *need*. You may think me fanciful,' she said, remote and whimsical, 'but in the last few weeks I feel sometimes I can see the old house smiling to itself and hear the old timbers whispering, "They thought we were no use. They thought we were old stick-in-the-muds. But they can't get on without us, all these busy go-ahead people. They come back to us when they're in trouble."'

'Agnes was always a poet,' said Mr Harkness. 'I have had to be the practical housewife. You saw our terms in the advertisement?'

'Yes.'

'They may have seemed to you a little heavy, but you must understand that our guests live exactly as we do ourselves. We live simply but we like our comfort. Fires,' he said, backing slightly from the belch of aromatic smoke which issued into the room as he spoke, 'the garden,' he said, indicating the frozen and buried enclosure outside the windows. 'In the summer we take our meals under the old mulberry tree. Music. Every week we have chamber music. There are certain *imponderabilia* at the Old Mill which, to be crude, have their market value. I *don't* think,' he said coyly, 'I *don't* think that in the circumstances'–and the circumstances Basil felt sure were meant to include a good fat slice of Mrs Harkness' poetic imagination—'six guineas is too much to ask.'

The moment for which Basil had been waiting was come. This was the time for the grenade he had been nursing ever since he opened the little, wrought-iron gate and put his hand to the wrought-iron bell-pull. 'We pay eight shillings and sixpence a week,' he said. That was the safety pin; the lever flew up, the spring struck home; within the serrated metal shell the primer spat and, invisibly, flame crept up the finger's-length of fuse. Count seven slowly, then throw. One, two, three, four . . .

'Eight shillings and sixpence?' said Mr Harkness. 'I'm afraid there's been some misunderstanding.'

Five, six, *seven*. Here it comes. Bang! 'Perhaps I should have told you at once. I am the billeting officer. I've three children for you in the car outside.'

It was magnificent. It was war. Basil was something of a specialist in shocks. He could not recall a better.

After the first tremendous silence there were three stages of Harkness reaction; the indignant appeal to reason and justice, then the humble appeal to mercy, then the frigid and dignified acceptance of the inevitable.

First:

'I shall telephone to Mrs Sothill. . . . I shall go and see the County authorities. . . . I shall write to the Board of Education and the Lord

Lieutenant. This is perfectly ridiculous; there must be a hundred cottagers who would be *glad* to take these children in.'

'Not *these* children,' said Basil. 'Besides, you know, this is a war for democracy. It looks awfully bad if the rich seem to be shirking their responsibilities.'

'*Rich*. It's only because we find it so hard to make both ends meet that we take paying guests at all.'

'Besides this is a *most* unsuitable place for children. They might fall into the stream and be drowned. There's no school within four miles . . .'

Secondly:

'We're not as young as we were. After living so long in the East the English winter is very difficult. Any additional burden . . .'

'Mr Seal, you've seen for yourself this lovely old house and the kind of life we live here. Don't you *feel* that there is something *different* here, something precious that could so easily be killed.'

'It's just this kind of influence these children need,' said Basil cheerfully. 'They're rather short on culture at the moment.'

Thirdly:

A hostility as cold as the winter hillside above the village. Basil led the Connollys up the flagged path, through the apple-green door, into the passage which smelled of peat smoke and pot-pourri. 'I'm afraid they haven't any luggage,' he said. 'This is Doris, this is Micky, and that–that is little Marlene. I expect after a day or two you'll wonder how you ever got on without them. We meet that over and over again in our work; people who are a little shy of children to begin with, and soon want to adopt them permanently. Good-bye, kids, have a good time. Good-bye, Mrs Harkness. We shall drop in from time to time just to see that everything is all right.'

And Basil drove back through the naked lanes with a deep interior warmth which defied the gathering blizzard.

That night there was an enormous fall of snow, telephone wires were down, the lane to North Grappling became impassable, and for eight days the Old Mill was cut off physically, as for so long it had been cut in spirit, from all contact with the modern world.

IV

Barbara and Basil sat in the orangery after luncheon. The smoke from Basil's cigar hung on the humid air, a blue line of cloud, motionless, breast high between the paved floor and the exotic foliage overhead. He was reading aloud to his sister.

'So much for the supply services,' he said, laying down the last sheet of manuscript. The book had prospered during the past week.

Barbara awoke, so gently that she might never have been asleep. 'Very good,' she said. 'First class.'

'It ought to wake them up,' said Basil.

'It ought,' said Barbara, on whom the work had so different an effect. Then she added irrelevantly, 'I hear they've dug the way through to North

Grappling this morning.'

'There was providence in that fall of snow. It's let the Connollys and the Harknesses get properly to grips. Otherwise, I feel, one or other side might have despaired.'

'I dare say we shall hear something of the Harknesses shortly.'

And immediately, as though they were on the stage, Benson came to the door and announced that Mr Harkness was in the little parlour.

'I *must* see him,' said Barbara.

'Certainly not,' said Basil. 'This is my war effort,' and followed Benson into the house.

He had expected some change in Mr Harkness, but not so marked a change as he now saw. The man was barely recognizable. It was as though the crust of tropical respectability that had survived below the home-spun and tie-ring surface had been crushed to powder; the man was abject. The clothes were the same. It must be imagination which gave that trim beard a raffish look, imagination fired by the haunted look in the man's eyes.

Basil on his travels had once visited a prison in Transjordan where an ingenious system of punishment had been devised. The institution served the double purpose of penitentiary and lunatic asylum. One of the madmen was a tough old Arab of peculiar ferocity who could be subdued by one thing only–the steady gaze of the human eye. Bat an eyelid, and he was at you. Refractory convicts were taken to this man's cell and shut in with him for periods of anything up to forty-eight hours according to the gravity of their offences. Day and night the madman lurked in his corner with his eyes fixed, fascinated, on those of the delinquent. The heat of midday was his best opportunity; then even the wariest convict sometimes allowed his weary eyelids to droop and in that moment he was across the floor, tooth and nail, in a savage attack. Basil had seen a gigantic felon led out after a two days' session. There was something in Mr Harkness' eyes that brought the scene back vividly to him.

'I am afraid my sister's away,' said Basil.

Whatever hope had ever been in Mr Harkness' breast died when he saw his old enemy. 'You are Mrs Sothill's brother?'

'Yes; we are thought rather alike. I'm helping her here now that my brother-in-law's away. Is there anything I can do?'

'No,' he said brokenly. 'No. It doesn't matter. I'd hoped to see Mrs Sothill. When will she be back?'

'You can never tell,' said Basil. 'Most irresponsible in some ways. Goes off for months at a time. But this time she has me to watch out for her. Was it about your evacuees you wanted to see her? She was *very* glad to hear they had been happily settled. It meant she could go away with a clear conscience. That particular family had been something of an anxiety, if you understand me.'

Mr Harkness sat down uninvited. He sat on a gilt chair in that bright little room, like a figure of death. He seemed disposed neither to speak nor move.

'Mrs Harkness well?' said Basil affably.

'Prostrate.'

'And your paying guest?'

'She left this morning–as soon as the road was cleared. Our two maids went with her.'

'I hope Doris is making herself useful about the house.'

At the mention of that name Mr Harkness broke. He came clean. 'Mr Seal, I can't stand it. We neither of us can. We've come to the end. You must take those children away.'

'You surely wouldn't suggest sending them back to Birmingham to be bombed?'

This was an argument which Barbara often employed with good effect. As soon as Basil spoke he realized it was a false step. Suffering had purged Mr Harkness of all hypocrisy. For the first time something like a smile twisted his lips.

'There is nothing would delight me more,' he said.

'Tut, tut. You do yourself an injustice. Anyway it is against the law. I should like to help you. What can you suggest?'

'I thought of giving them weed-killer,' said Mr Harkness wistfully.

'Yes,' said Basil, 'that would be one way. Do you think Marlene could keep it down?'

'Or hanging.'

'Come, come, Mr Harkness, this is mere wishful thinking. We must be more practical.'

'Everything I've thought of has had Death in it; ours or theirs.'

'I'm sure there must be a way,' said Basil, and then, delicately, watching Mr Harkness while he spoke for any expression of distrust or resentment, he outlined a scheme which had come to him, vaguely, when he first saw the Connollys, and had grown more precise during the past week. 'The difficulty about billeting on the poor,' he said, 'is that the allowance barely covers what the children eat. Of course, where they are nice, affectionate children people are often glad enough to have them. But one wouldn't call the Connollys nice or affectionate'–Mr Harkness groaned. 'They are destructive, too. Well, I needn't tell you that. The fact is that it would be inflicting a very considerable hardship–a *financial* hardship–to put them in a cottage. Now if the meagre allowance paid by the Government were *supplemented*– do you follow me?'

'You mean I might *pay* someone to take them. Of course I will, anything–at least almost anything. How much shall I offer? How shall I set about it?'

'Leave it to me,' said Basil, suddenly dropping his urbane manner. 'What's it worth to you to have those children moved?'

Mr Harkness hesitated; with the quickening of hope came a stir of self-possession. One does not work in the East without acquiring a nose for a deal. 'I should think a pound a week would make all the difference to a poor family,' he said.

'How about a lump sum? People–poor people that is–will often be dazzled by the offer of a lump sum who wouldn't consider an allowance.'

'Twenty-five pounds.'

'Come, Mr Harkness, that's what you proposed paying over six months. The war is going to last longer than that.'

'Thirty. I can't go higher than thirty.'

He was not a rich man, Basil reflected; very likely thirty was all be could afford. 'I dare say I could find someone to take them for that,' he said. 'Of course, you realize that this is all highly irregular.'

'Oh, I realize that.' Did he? Basil wondered; perhaps he did. 'Will you fetch those children to-day?'

'To-day?'

'Without fail.' Mr Harkness seemed to be dictating terms now. 'The cheque will be waiting for you. I will make it out to bearer.'

'What a long time you've been,' said Barbara. 'Have you pacified him?'

'I've got to find a new home for the Connollys.'

'Basil, you've let him off!'

'He was so pathetic. I softened.'

'Basil, how very unlike you.'

'I must get to work with that address book again. We shall have to have the Connollys here for the night. I'll find them a new home in the morning.'

He drove over to North Grappling in the twilight. On either side of the lane the new-dug snow was heaped high, leaving a narrow, passable track. The three Connollys were standing outside the apple-green door waiting for him.

'The man with the beard said to give you this,' said Doris.

It was an envelope containing a cheque; nothing more. Neither Harkness appeared to see them off.

'Mister, am I glad to see you again?' said Doris.

'Jump in,' said Basil.

'May I come in front with you?'

'Yes, jump in.'

'Really? No kidding?'

'Come on, it's cold.' Doris got in beside Basil. 'You're here on sufferance.'

'What does that mean?'

'You can sit here as long as you behave yourself, and as long as Micky and Marlene do too. Understand?'

'Hear that, you brats?' said Doris with sudden authority. 'Behave, or I'll tan yer arses for yer. They'll be all right, Mister, if I tell 'em.'

They were all right.

'Doris, I think it's a very good game of yours making the kids be a nuisance, but we're going to play it my way in future. When you come to the house where I live you're to behave, always. See? I may take you to other houses from time to time. There you can usually be as bad as you like, but not until I give the word. See?'

'O.K. partner. Give us a cig.'

'I'm beginning to like you, Doris.'

'*I love you*,' said Doris with excruciating warmth, leaning back and blowing a cloud of smoke over the solemn children in the back. 'I love you more than anyone I ever seen.'

'Their week with the Harknesses seems to have had an extraordinary effect on the children,' said Barbara after dinner that night. 'I can't understand it.'

'Mr Harkness said there were *imponderabilia* at Mill House. Perhaps it's that.'

'Basil, you're up to something. I wish I knew what it was.'

Basil turned on her his innocent blue eyes, as blue as hers and as innocent; they held no hint of mischief. 'Just war work, Babs,' he said.

'Slimy snake.'

'I'm not.'

'Crawly spider.' They were back in the schoolroom, in the world where once they had played pirates. 'Artful monkey,' said Barbara, very fondly.

V

Companies paraded at a quarter past eight; immediately after inspection men were fallen out for the company commander's orderly room; that gave time to sift out the genuine requests from the spurious, deal with minor offences, have the charge sheets made out properly and the names entered in the guard report of serious defaulters for the C.O.

'Private Tatton charged with losing by neglect one respirator, anti-gas, value 18*s.* 6*d.*'

Private Tatton fell into a rambling account of having left his respirator in the NAAFI and going back for it ten minutes later, having found it gone.

'Case remanded for the commanding officer.' Captain Mayfield could not give a punishment involving loss of pay.

'Case remanded for the commanding officer. About turn. As you were. I didn't say anything about saluting. About turn. Quick march.'

Captain Mayfield turned to the IN basket on his table.

'O.C.T.U. candidates,' said the company sergeant-major.

'Who have we got? The adjutant doesn't take nil returns.'

'Well, sir, there's Brodie.'

Brodie was a weedy solicitor who had appeared with the last draft.

'Really, sergeant-major, I can't see Brodie making much of an officer.'

'He's not much good in the company, sir, and he's a man of very superior education.'

'Well, put him down for one. What about Sergeant Harris?'

'Not suitable, sir.'

'He's a man of excellent character, fine disciplinarian, knows his stuff backwards, the men will follow him anywhere.'

'Yessir.'

'Well, what have you got against him?'

'Nothing against him, sir. But we can't get on without Sergeant Harris in the company football.'

'No. Well, who do you suggest?'

'There's our baronet, sir.' The sergeant-major said this with a smile. Alastair's position in the ranks was a slight embarrassment to Captain Mayfield but it was a good joke to the sergeant-major.

'Trumpington? All right, I'll see him and Brodie right away.'

The orderly brought them. The sergeant-major marched them in singly. 'Quick march. Halt. Salute. Brodie, sir.'

'Brodie. They want the names of two men from this company as O.C.T.U. candidates. I'm putting your name in. Of course the C.O. makes the decision. I don't say you *will* go to an O.C.T.U. I take it you would have no objection if the C.O. approves.'

'None, sir, if you really think I should make a good officer.'

'I don't suppose you'll make a *good* officer. They're very rare. But I dare say you'll make an officer of some kind.'

'Thank you, sir.'

'And as long as you're in my company you won't come into my office with a fountain pen sticking out of your pocket.'

'Sorry, sir.'

'Not so much talk,' said the sergeant-major.

'All right, that's all, sergeant-major.'

'About turn. Quick march. As you were. Swing the right arm forward as you step out.'

'I believe we'll have to give him a couple of stripes before we can get rid of him. I'll see the adjutant about that.'

Alastair was marched in. He had changed little since he joined the army. Perhaps there was a slight shifting of bulk from waist line to chest, but it was barely perceptible under the loose battle-dress.

Captain Mayfield addressed him in precisely the same words as he had used to Brodie.

'Yes, sir.'

'You don't want to take a commission?'

'No, sir.'

'That's very unusual, Trumpington. Any particular reason?'

'I believe a lot of people felt like that in the last war.'

'So I've heard. And a very wasteful business it was. Well if you won't, I can't make you. Afraid of responsibility, eh?'

Alastair made no answer. Captain Mayfield nodded and the sergeant-major marched him out.

'What d'you make of that?' asked Captain Mayfield.

'I've known men who think it's *safer* to stay in the ranks.'

'Shouldn't think that's the case with Trumpington. He's a volunteer, over age to have been called up.'

'Very rum, sir.'

'Very rum, sergeant-major.'

Alastair took his time about returning to his platoon. At this time of the morning they were doing P.T. It was the one part of the routine he really hated. He lurked behind the cookhouse until his watch told him that they would have finished. When he reported back the platoon were putting on their jackets, panting and sticky. He fell in and marched with them to the dining hut, where it was stuffy and fairly warm, to hear a lecture on hygiene from the medical officer. It dealt with the danger of flies; the medical officer described with appalling detail the journey of the fly from the latrine to the sugar basin; how its hairy feet carried the germs of dysentery; how it softened its food with contaminated saliva before it ate; how it excreted while it fed. This lecture always went down well. 'Of course,' he added rather lamely, 'this may not seem very important at the moment,' snow lay heavy on every side of them, 'but if we go to the East . . .'

When the lecture was finished the company fell out for twenty minutes; they smoked and ate chocolate and exchanged gossip, qualifying every noun, verb or adjective with the single, unvarying obscenity which punctuated all their speech like a hiccup; they stamped their feet and chafed their hands.

'What did the — company commander want?'

'He wanted to send me to a — O.C.T.U.,' said Alastair.

'Well some — are — lucky. When are you off?'

'I'm staying here.'

'Don't you want to be a — officer?'

'Not — likely,' said Alastair.

When people asked Alastair, as they quite often did, why he did not put in for a commission, he sometimes said, 'Snobbery. I don't want to meet the officers on social terms'; sometimes he said, 'Laziness. They work too hard in wartime'; sometimes he said, 'The whole thing's so crazy one might as well go the whole hog.' To Sonia he said, 'We've had a pretty easy life up to now. It's probably quite good for one to have a change sometimes.' That was the nearest he ever came to expressing the nebulous satisfaction which lay at the back of his mind. Sonia understood it, but left it undefined. Once, much later, she said to Basil, 'I believe I know what Alastair felt all that first winter of the war. It sounds awfully unlike him, but he was a much odder character than anyone knew. You remember that man who used to dress as an Arab and then went into the air force as a private because he thought the British Government had let the Arabs down. I forget his name but there were lots of books about him. Well, I believe Alastair felt like that. You see he'd never done anything for the country and though we were always broke we had lots of money really and lots of fun. I believe he thought that perhaps if we hadn't had so much fun perhaps there wouldn't have been any war. Though how he could blame himself for Hitler I never quite saw. . . . At least I do now in a way,' she added. 'He went into the ranks as a kind of penance or whatever it's called that religious people are always supposed to do.'

It was a penance whose austerities, such as they were, admitted of relaxation. After the stand-easy they fell in for platoon training. Alastair's platoon commander was away that morning. He was sitting on a Court of Enquiry. For three hours he and two other officers heard evidence, and recorded it at length, on the loss of a swill tub from H.Q. lines. At length it was clear either that there was a conspiracy of perjury on the part of all the witnesses, or that the tub had disappeared by some supernatural means independent of human agency; the Court therefore entered a verdict that no negligence was attributable to anyone in the matter and recommended that the loss be made good out of public funds. The President said, 'I don't expect the C.O. will approve that verdict. He'll send the papers back for fresh evidence to be taken.'

Meanwhile the platoon, left in charge of the sergeant, split up into sections and practised immediate action on the Bren gun.

'Gun fires two rounds and stops again. What do you look at now, Trumpington?'

'Gas regulator' . . . Off with the magazine. Press, pull back, press. 'Number Two gun clear.'

'What's he forgotten?'

A chorus, 'Butt strap.'

One man said, 'Barrel locking nut.' He had said it once, one splendid day, when asked a question, and he had been right when everyone else was stumped, and he had been commended. So now he always said it, like a gambler obstinately backing the same colour against a long run of bad luck; it was bound to turn up again one day.

The corporal ignored him. 'Quite right, he's forgotten the butt strap. Down again, Trumpington.'

It was Saturday. Work ended at twelve o'clock; as the platoon commander was away, they knocked off ten minutes earlier and got all the gear stowed so that as soon as the call was sounded off on the bugle they could run straight for their quarters. Alastair had his leave pass for reveille on Monday. He had no need to fetch luggage. He kept everything he needed at home. Sonia was waiting in the car outside the guardroom; they did not go away for week-ends but spent them mostly in bed, in the furnished house which they had taken nearby.

'I was pretty good with the Bren this morning,' said Alastair. 'Only one mistake.'

'Darling, you are clever.'

'And I managed to shirk P.T.'

They had packed up ten minutes early too; altogether it had been a very satisfactory morning. And now he could look forward to a day and a half of privacy and leisure.

'I've been shopping in Woking,' said Sonia, 'and I've got all kinds of delicious food and all the weekly papers. There's a film there we might go and see.'

'We might,' said Alastair doubtfully. 'It will probably be full of a lot of — soldiers.'

'Darling, I've never before heard words like that spoken. I thought they only came in print, in novels.'

Alastair had a bath and changed into tweeds. (It was chiefly in order that he might wear civilian clothes that he stayed indoors during week-ends; for that and the cold outside and the ubiquitous military.) Then he took a whisky and soda and watched Sonia cooking; they had fried eggs, sausages, bacon and cold plum pudding; after luncheon he lit a large cigar; it was snowing again, piling up round the steel-framed windows, shutting out the view of the golf course; there was a huge fire and at tea-time they toasted crumpets.

'There's all this evening, and all to-morrow,' said Sonia. 'Isn't it lovely. You know, Alastair, you and I always seem to manage to have fun, don't we, wherever we are.'

This was February 1940, in that strangely cosy interlude between peace and war, when there was leave every week-end and plenty to eat and drink and plenty to smoke, when France stood firm on the Maginot Line and the Finns stood firm in Finland, and everyone said what a cruel winter they must be having in Germany. During one of these week-ends Sonia conceived a child.

VI

As Mr Bentley had foretold, it was not long before Ambrose found himself enrolled on the staff of the Ministry of Information. He was in fact one of the reforms introduced at the first of the many purges. Questions had been asked about the Ministry in the House of Commons; the Press, hampered in so much else, was free to exploit its own grievances. Redress was promised and after a week of intrigue the new appointments were made. Sir Philip Hesketh-Smithers went to the folk-dancing department; Mr Pauling went to woodcuts and weaving; Mr Digby-Smith was given the Arctic circle; Mr Bentley himself, after a dizzy period in which, for a day, he directed a film about postmen, for another day filed press-cuttings from Istanbul, and for the rest of the week supervised the staff catering, found himself at length back beside his busts in charge of the men of letters. Thirty or forty officials retired thankfully into competitive commercial life, and forty or fifty new men and women appeared to take their place; among them, he never quite knew how, Ambrose. The Press, though sceptical of good results, congratulated the public upon maintaining a system of government in which the will of the people was given such speedy effect. *The lesson of the muddle at the Ministry of Information–for muddle there undoubtedly was–is not that such things occur under a democracy, but that they are susceptible to remedy,* they wrote; *the wind of democratic criticism has blown, clear and fresh, through the departments of the Ministry; charges have been frankly made and frankly answered. Our enemies may ponder this portent.*

Ambrose's post as sole representative of Atheism in the religious department was not, at this stage of the war, one of great importance. He was in no position, had he wished it, to introduce statuary into his quarters. He had for his use a single table and a single chair. He shared a room and a secretary with a fanatical young Roman Catholic Layman who never tired of exposing discrepancies between *Mein Kampf* and the encyclical *Quadragesimo Anno*, a bland Noncomformist minister, and a Church of England clergyman who had been brought in to succeed the importer of the mahogany prie-dieu. 'We must re-orientate ourselves to Geneva,' this cleric said; 'the first false step was taken when the Lytton report was shelved.' He argued long and gently, the Roman Catholic argued long and fiercely, while the Nonconformist sat as a bemused umpire between them. Ambrose's task consisted in representing to British and colonial atheists that Nazism was at heart agnostic with a strong tinge of religious superstition; he envied the lot of his colleagues who had at their finger-tips long authentic summaries of suppressed Sunday Schools, persecuted monks, and pagan Nordic rites. His was uphill work; he served a small and critical public; but whenever he discovered in the pile of foreign newspapers which passed from desk to desk any reference to German church-going, he circulated it to the two or three magazines devoted to his cause. He counted up the number of times the word 'God' appeared in Hitler's speeches and found the sum impressive; he wrote a pointed little article to show that Jew-baiting was religious in origin. He did his best, but time lay heavy on his hands and, more and more, as the winter wore on, he found himself slipping away from his rancorous colleagues, to the more human companionship of Mr Bentley.

The great press of talent in search of occupation which had thronged the Ministry during its first weeks had now dropped to a mere handful; the door-keeper was schooled to detect and deter the job seekers. No one wanted another reorganization for some time to come. Mr Bentley's office became an enclave of culture in a barbaric world. It was here that the Ivory Tower was first discussed.

'Art for Art's sake, Geoffrey. Back to the lily and the lotus, away from these dusty young *immortelles*, these dandelions sprouting on the vacant lot.'

'A kind of new Yellow Book,' suggested Mr Bentley sympathetically.

Ambrose turned sharply from his contemplation of Mrs Siddons. '*Geoffrey*. How *can* you be so unkind?'

'My dear Ambrose . . .'

'That's just what they'll call it.'

'Who will?'

'Parsnip,' said Ambrose with venom, 'Pimpernell, Poppet and Tom. They'll say we're deserting the workers' cause.'

'I'm not aware that I ever joined it,' said Mr Bentley. 'I claim to be one of the very few living liberals.'

'We've allowed ourselves to be dominated by economists.'

'*I* haven't.'

'For years now we've allowed ourselves to think of nothing but concrete mixers and tractors.'

'*I* haven't,' said Mr Bentley crossly. 'I've thought a great deal about Nollekens.'

'Well,' said Ambrose, 'I've had enough. *Il faut en finir*,' and added, '*nous gagnerons parce que nous sommes les plus forts*.'

Later he said, 'I was never a party member.'

'Party?'

'Communist party. I was what they call in their horrible jargon a fellow traveller.'

'Ah.'

'Geoffrey, they do the most brutal things, don't they, to communists who try to leave the party?'

'So I've heard.'

'Geoffrey, you don't think they'd do that to fellow travellers, do you?'

'I don't expect so.'

'But they *might*?'

'Oh yes, they *might*.'

'Oh dear.'

Later he said, 'You know, Geoffrey, even in fascist countries they have underground organizations. Do you think the underground organizations would get hold of us?'

'Who?'

'The fellow travellers.'

'Really it's too ridiculous to talk like this of fellow travellers and the underground. It sounds like strap-hangers on the Bakerloo railway.'

'It's all very well for you to laugh. You were never one of them.'

'But my dear Ambrose, why should these political friends of yours mind so very much if you produce a purely artistic paper?'

'I heard of a 'cellist in America. He'd been a member of the party and he accepted an invitation to play at an anniversary breakfast of the Colonial Dames. It was during the Scottsboro' trials when feeling was running high. They tied him to a lamp-post and covered him with tar and set him on fire.'

'The Colonial Dames did?'

'No, no, the communists.'

After a long pause he said, 'But Russia's doing very badly in Finland.'

'Yes.'

'If only we knew what was going to happen.'

He returned pensively to the Religious Department.

'This is more in your line than mine,' said the Catholic representative, handing him a cutting from a Swiss paper.

It said that Storm Troopers had attended a requiem mass in Salzburg. Ambrose clipped it to a piece of paper and wrote 'Copies to *Free Thought*, the *Atheist Advertizer* and to *Godless Sunday at Home*'; then he placed it in his basket market OUT. Two yards distant the Nonconformist minister was checking statistics about the popularity of beer-gardens among Nazi officials. The Church of England clergyman was making the most of some rather scrappy Dutch information about cruelty to animals in Bremen. There was no foundation here for an ivory tower, thought Ambrose, no cloud to garland its summit, and his thoughts began to soar lark-like into a tempera, fourteenth-century sky; into a heaven of flat, blank, blue and white clouds cross-hatched with gold leaf on their sunward edges; a vast altitude painted with shaving soap on a panel of lapis lazuli; he stood on a high, sugary pinnacle, on a new Tower of Babel; like a muezzin calling his message to a world of domes and clouds; beneath him, between him and the absurd little figures bobbing and bending on their striped praying mats, lay fathoms of clear air where doves sported with the butterflies.

VII

Most of Mrs Sothill's Garden-Party-Only list were people of late middle age who, on retirement from work in the cities or abroad, had bought the smaller manor houses and the larger rectories; houses that once had been supported on the rent of a thousand acres and a dozen cottages now went with a paddock and a walled garden and their life subsisted on pensions and savings. To these modest landholders the rural character of the neighbourhood was a matter of particular jealousy; magnates like Freddy would eagerly sell off outlying farms for development. It was the G.P.O. list who suffered and protested. A narrow corner could not be widened or a tree lopped to clear the telegraph wires without its being noted and regretted in those sunny morning-rooms. These were benevolent, companionable people; their carefully limited families were 'out in the world' and came to them only for occasional visits. Their daughters had flats and jobs and lives of their own in London; their sons were self-supporting in the services and in business. The tribute of Empire flowed gently into the agricultural countryside, tithe barns were converted into village halls, the boy scouts had a new bell tent and the district nurse a motor-car; the old box pews were taken out of the churches, the galleries demolished, the Royal Arms and the Ten Commandments moved from behind the altar and replaced with screens of blue damask supported at the four corners with gilt Sarum angels; the lawns were close mown, fertilized and weeded, and from their splendid surface rose clumps of pampas grass and yucca; year in, year out, gloved hands grubbed in the rockeries, gloved hands snipped in the herbaceous border;

baskets of bass stood beside trays of visiting cards on the hall tables. Now in the dead depths of winter, when ice stood thick on the lily ponds, and the kitchen gardens at night were a litter of sacking, these good people fed the birds daily with the crumbs from the dining-room table and saw to it that no old person in the village went short of coal.

It was this unfamiliar world that Basil contemplated in the leather-bound pages of Mrs Sothill's address book. He contemplated it as a marauder might look down from the hills into the fat pastures below; as Hannibal's infantry had looked down from the snow-line as the first elephants tried the etched footholds which led to the Lombardy plains below them and went lurching and trumpeting over the edge.

After the successful engagement at North Grappling, Basil took Doris into the nearest town and fed her liberally on fried fish and chipped potatoes; afterwards he took her to the cinema, allowed her to hold his hand in a fierce and sticky grasp throughout the length of two deeply sentimental films and brought her back to Malfrey in a state of entranced docility.

'You don't like blondes, do you?' she asked anxiously in the car.

'Yes, very much.'

'More than brunettes?'

'I'm not particular.'

'They say like goes to like. *She's* dark.'

'Who?'

'Her you call your sister.'

'Doris, you must get this idea out of your head. Mrs Sothill *is* my sister.'

'You aren't sweet on her.'

'Certainly not.'

'Then you *do* like blondes,' said Doris sadly.

Next day she disappeared alone into the village, returned mysteriously with a small parcel, and remained hidden all the morning in the bachelors' wing. Just before luncheon she appeared in the orangery with her head in a towel.

'I wanted you to see,' she said, and uncovered a damp mop of hair which was in part pale yellow, in part its original black, and in part mottled in every intervening shade.

'Good heavens, child,' said Barbara. 'What have you done?'

Doris looked only at Basil. 'D'you like it? I'll give it another go this afternoon.'

'I wouldn't,' said Basil. 'I'd leave it just as it is.'

'You like it?'

'I think it's fine.'

'Not too streaky?'

'Not a bit too streaky.'

If anything had been needed to complete the horror of Doris's appearance, that morning's work had done it.

Basil studied the address book with care. 'Finding a new home for the Connollys,' he said.

'Basil, we must do something to that poor child's head before we pass her on.'

'Not a bit of it. It suits her. What d'you know of the Graces of the Old Rectory, Adderford?'

'It's a pretty little house. He's a painter.'

'Bohemian?'

'Not the least. Very refined. Portraits of children in watercolour and pastel.'

'Pastel? He sounds suitable.'

'She's rather delicate I believe.'

'Perfect.'

The Connollys stayed two days at the Old Rectory and earned twenty pounds.

VIII

London was full again. Those who had left in a hurry returned; those who had made arrangements to go after the first air raid remained. Margot Metroland shut her home and moved to the Ritz; opened her home and moved back; decided that after all she really preferred the Ritz and shut her home, this time, though she did not know it, for ever. No servant ever folded back the shutters from the long windows; they remained barred until late in the year when they were blown into Curzon Street; the furniture was still under dust sheets when it was splintered and burned.

Sir Joseph Mainwaring was appointed to a position of trust and dignity. He was often to be seen with Generals now and sometimes with an Admiral. 'Our first war aim,' he said, 'is to keep Italy out of the war until she is strong enough to come in on our side.' He summed up the situation at home saying, 'One takes one's gas-mask to one's office but *not* to one's club.'

Lady Seal had not troubled him again about Basil. 'He's at Malfrey, helping Barbara with her evacuees,' she said. 'The army is very full just at present. Things will be much easier when we have had some casualties.'

Sir Joseph nodded but at heart he was sceptical. There were not going to be many casualties. Why, he had been talking to a very interesting fellow at the Beefsteak who knew a German Professor of History; this Professor was now in England; they thought a great deal of him at the Foreign Office; he said there were fifty million Germans ready to declare peace tomorrow on our own terms. It was just a question of outing those fellows in the government. Sir Joseph had seen many governments outed. It was quite easy in war time–they had outed Asquith quite easily and he was a far better fellow than Lloyd George who succeeded him. Then they outed Lloyd George and then they outed Macdonald. Christopher Seal knew how to do it. He'd soon out Hitler if he were alive and a German.

Poppet Green was in London with her friends.

'Ambrose has turned fascist,' she said.

'Not really?'

'He's working for the Government in the Ministry of Information and they've bribed him to start a new paper.'

'Is it a fascist paper?'

'You bet it is.'

'I heard it was to be called the *Ivory Tower*.'

'That's fascist if you like.'

'Escapist.'

'Trotskyist.'

'Ambrose never had the proletarian outlook. I can't think why we put up with him as we did. Parsnip always said . . .'

Peter Pastmaster came into Bratts wearing battle-dress and, on his shoulder, the name of a regiment to which he had not formerly belonged.

'Hullo. Why on earth are you dressed like that?'

Peter smirked as only a soldier can when he knows a secret. 'Oh, no particular reason.'

'Have they thrown you out of the regiment?'

'I'm seconded, temporarily, for special duty.'

'You're the sixth chap I've seen in disguise this morning.'

'That's the idea–security, you know.'

'What's it all about?'

'You'll hear in time, I expect,' said Peter with boundless smugness.

They went to the bar.

'Good morning, my lord,' said MacDougal, the barman. 'I see you're off to Finland too. Quite a number of our gentlemen are going to-night.'

Angela Lyne was back in London; the affairs of the hospital were in order, her son was at his private school, transported at the outbreak of war from the East coast to the middle of Dartmoor. She sat at the place she called 'home' listening to wireless news from Germany.

This place was a service flat and as smart and non-committal as herself, a set of five large rooms high up in the mansard floor of a brand new block in Grosvenor Square. The decorators had been at work there while she was in France; the style was what passes for Empire in the fashionable world. Next year, had there been no war, she would have had it done over again during August.

That morning she had spent an hour with her brokers giving precise, prudent directions for the disposition of her fortune; she had lunched alone, listening to the radio from Europe, after luncheon she had gone alone to the cinema in Curzon Street. It was darkening when she left the cinema and quite dark now outside, beyond the heavy crimson draperies which hung in a dozen opulent loops and folds, girded with gold cord, fringed with gold at the hem, over the new black shutters. Soon she would go out to dine with Margot at the Ritz. Peter was off somewhere and Margot was trying to get a party together for him.

She mixed herself a large cocktail; the principal ingredients were vodka and calvados; the decorators had left an electric shaker on the Pompeian side table. It was their habit to litter the houses where they worked with expensive trifles of this sort, parsimonious clients sent them back; the vaguer sort believed them to be presents for which they had forgotten to thank anyone, used them, broke them and paid for them a year later when the bills came in. Angela liked gadgets. She switched on the electric shaker and, when her drink was mixed, took the glass with her to the bathroom and drank it slowly in her bath.

Angela never drank cocktails except in private; there was something about them which bore, so faintly as to be discernible to no one but herself, a suggestion of good fellowship and good cheer; an infinitely small invitation to familiarity, derived perhaps from the days of prohibition when gin had ceased to be Hogarthian and had become chic; an aura of naughtiness, of felony compounded; a memory of her father's friends who sometimes had raised their glasses to her, of a man in a ship who had said '*à tes beaux yeux*'. And so Angela who hated human contact on any but her own terms never drank cocktails except in solitude. Lately all her days seemed to be spent alone.

Steam from the bath formed in a mist, and later in great beads of water, on the side of the glass. She finished her cocktail and felt the fumes rise inside her. She lay for a long time in the water, scarcely thinking, scarcely feeling anything except the warm water round her and the spirit within her. She called for her maid, from next door, to bring her a cigarette, smoked it slowly to the end, called for an ash tray and then for a towel. Presently she was ready to face the darkness, and the intense cold, and Margot Metroland's dinner party. She noticed in the last intense scrutiny before her mirrors that her mouth was beginning to droop a little at the corners. It was not the disappointed pout that she knew in so many of her friends; it was as the droop you sometimes saw in death masks, when the jaw had been set and the face had stiffened in lines which told those waiting round the bed that the will to live was gone.

At dinner she drank Vichy water and talked like a man. She said that France was no good any more and Peter used a phrase that was just coming into vogue, accusing her of being 'fifth column'. They went on to a dance at the Suivi. She danced and drank her Vichy water and talked sharply and well like a very clever man. She was wearing a new pair of earrings–an arrow set with a ruby point, the shaft a thin bar of emerald that seemed to transfix the lobe; she had designed them for herself and had called for them that morning on her way home from seeing her man of business. The girls in the party noticed Angela's earrings; they noticed everything about her clothes; she was the best-dressed woman there, as she usually was wherever she went.

She stayed to the end of the party and then returned to Grosvenor Square alone. Since the war there was no liftman on duty after midnight. She shut herself in, pressed the button for the mansard floor and rose to the empty, uncommunicative flat. There were no ashes to stir in the grate; illuminated glass coals glowed eternally in an elegant steel basket; the temperature of the rooms never varied, winter or summer, day or night. She mixed herself a large whisky and water and turned on the radio.

Tirelessly, all over the world, voices were speaking in their own and in foreign tongues. She listened and fidgeted with the knob; sometimes she got a burst of music, once a prayer. Presently she fetched another whisky and water.

Her maid lived out and had been told not to wait up. When she came in the morning she found Mrs Lyne in bed but awake; the clothes she had worn the evening before had been carefully hung up, not broadcast about the carpet as they used sometimes to be. 'I shan't be getting up this morning, Grainger,' she said. 'Bring the radio here and the newspapers.'

Later she had her bath, returned to bed, took two tablets of Dial and slept, gently, until it was time to fit the black, ply-wood screens into the window frames and hide them behind the velvet draperies.

IX

'What about Mr and Mrs Prettyman-Partridge of the Malt House, Grantley Green?'

Basil was choosing his objectives from the extreme quarters of the Malfrey billeting area. He had struck East and North. Grantley Green lay South where the land of spur and valley fell away and flattened out into a plain of cider orchards and market gardens.

'They're very old, I think,' said Barbara. 'I hardly know them. Come to think of it, I heard something about Mr Prettyman-Partridge the other day. I can't remember what.'

'Pretty house? Nice things in it?'

'As far as I remember.'

'People of regular habits? Fond of quiet?'

'Yes, I suppose so.'

'They'll do.'

Basil bent over the map tracing the road to Grantley Green which he would take next day.

He found the Malt House without difficulty. It had been a brewhouse in the seventeenth century and later was converted to a private house. It had a large, regular front of dressed stone, facing the village green. The curtains and the china in the window proclaimed that it was in 'good hands'. Basil noted the china with approval–large, black Wedgwood urns–valuable and vulnerable and no doubt well loved. When the door opened it disclosed a view straight through the house to a white lawn and a cedar tree laden with snow.

The door was opened by a large and lovely girl. She had fair curly hair and a fair skin, huge, pale blue eyes, a large, shy mouth. She was dressed in a tweed suit and woollen jumper as though for country exercise, but the soft, fur-lined boots showed that she was spending the morning at home. Everything about this girl was large and soft and round and ample. A dress shop might not have chosen her as a mannequin but she was not a fat girl; a more civilized age would have found her admirably proportioned; Boucher would have painted her half clothed in a flutter of blue and pink draperies, a butterfly hovering over a breast of white and rose.

'Miss Prettyman-Partridge?'

'No. Please don't say you've come to sell something. It's terribly cold standing here and if I ask you in I shall have to buy it.'

'I want to see Mr and Mrs Prettyman-Partridge.'

'They're dead. At least one is; the other sold us the house last summer. Is that all, please; I don't want to be rude but I must shut the door or freeze.'

So that was what Barbara had heard about the Malt House. 'May I come in?'

'Oh dear,' said this splendid girl, leading him into the room with the Wedgwood urns. 'Is it something to buy or forms to fill in or just a subscription? If it's the first two I can't help because my husband's away with the yeomanry; if it's a subscription I've got some money upstairs. I've been told to give the same as Mrs Andrews, the doctor's wife. If you haven't been to her yet, come back when you find what she's good for.'

Everything in the room was new; that is to say the paint was new and the carpets and the curtains, and the furniture had been newly put in position. There was a very large settee in front of the fireplace whose cushions, upholstered in *toile-de-jouy*, still bore the impress of that fine young woman; she had been lying there when Basil rang the bell. He knew that if he put his hand in the round concavity where her hip had rested, it would still be warm; and that further cushions had been tucked under her arm. The book she had been reading was on the lambskin hearth-rug. Basil could reconstruct the position, exactly, where she had been sprawling with the langour of extreme youth.

The girl seemed to sense an impertinence in Basil's scrutiny. 'Anyway,' she said. 'Why aren't you in khaki?'

'Work of national importance,' said Basil. 'I am the district billeting officer. I'm looking for a suitable home for three evacuated children.'

'Well, I hope you don't call this suitable. I ask you. I can't even look after Bill's sheepdog. I can't even look after myself very well. What should I do with three children?'

'These are rather exceptional children.'

'They'd have to be. Anyway I'm not having any, thank you. There was a funny little woman called Harkness came to call here yesterday. I do think people might let up on calling in war time, don't you? She told me the most gruesome things about some children that were sent to her. They had to bribe the man, literally bribe him with money, to get the brutes moved.'

'These are the same children.'

'Well, for God's sake, why pick on me?'

Her great eyes held him dazzled, like a rabbit before the headlights of a car. It was a delicious sensation. 'Well, actually, I picked on the Prettyman-Partridges . . . I don't even know your name.'

'I don't know yours.'

'Basil Seal.'

'Basil Seal?' There was a sudden interest in her voice. 'How very funny.'

'Why funny?'

'Only that I used to hear a lot about you once. Weren't you a friend of a girl called Mary Nichols?'

'Was I?' Was he? Mary Nichols? Mary Nichols?

'Well, she used to talk a lot about you. She was much older than me. I used to think her wonderful when I was sixteen. You met her in a ship coming from Copenhagen.'

'I dare say. I've been to Copenhagen.'

The girl was looking at him now with a keen and not wholly flattering attention. 'So you're Basil Seal,' she said. 'Well, I never . . .'

Four years ago in South Kensington, at Mary Nichols's home, there was a little back sitting-room on the first floor which was Mary's room. Here Mary entertained her girl friends to tea. Here she had come, day after day, to sit before the gas fire and eat Fuller's walnut cake and hear the details of Mary's

Experience. 'But aren't you going to see him again?' she asked. 'No, it was something so beautiful, so complete in itself'–Mary had steeped herself in romantic literature since her Experience. 'I don't want to spoil it.' 'I don't think he sounds half good enough for you, darling.' 'He's absolutely *different*. You mustn't think of him as one of the young men one meets at dances . . .' The girl did not go to dances yet, and Mary knew it. Mary's tales of the young men she met at dances had been very moving, but not as moving as this tale of Basil Seal. The name had become graven on her mind.

And Basil, still standing, searched his memory. Mary Nichols? Copenhagen? No, it registered nothing. It was very consoling, he thought, the way in which an act of kindness, in the fullness of time, returns to bless the benefactor. One gives a jolly-up to a girl in a ship. She goes her way, he goes his. He forgets; he has so many benefactions of the kind to his credit. But she remembers and then one day, when it is least expected, Fate drops into his lap the ripe fruit of his reward, this luscious creature waiting for him, all unaware, in the Malt House, Grantley Green.

'Aren't you going to offer me a drink–on the strength of Mary Nichols?'

'I don't think there's anything in the house. Bill's away, you see. He's got some wine downstairs in the cellar, but the door's locked.'

'I expect we could open it.'

'Oh! I wouldn't do that. Bill would be furious.'

'Well, I don't suppose he'll be best pleased to come home on leave and find the Connolly family hacking up his home. By the way, you haven't seen them yet; they're outside in the car; I'll bring them in.'

'*Please* don't!' There was genuine distress and appeal in those blue cow-eyes.

'Well, take a look at them through the window.'

She went and looked. 'Good God,' said the girl. 'Mrs Harkness wasn't far wrong. I thought she was laying it on thick.'

'It cost her thirty pounds to get rid of them.'

'Oh, but I haven't got anything like that'–again the distress and appeal in her wide blue eyes. 'Bill makes me an allowance out of his pay. It comes in monthly. It's practically all I've got.'

'I'll take payment in kind,' said Basil.

'You mean the sherry?'

'I'd like a glass of sherry very much,' said Basil.

When they got to work with the crowbar on the cellar door, it was clear that this high-spirited girl thoroughly enjoyed herself. It was a pathetic little cellar; a poor man's treasury. Half a dozen bottles of hock, a bin of port, a dozen or two of claret. 'Mostly wedding presents,' explained the girl. Basil found some sherry and they took it up to the light.

'I've no maid now,' she explained. 'A woman comes in once a week.'

They found glasses in the pantry and a corkscrew in the dining-room.

'Is it any good?' she said anxiously, while Basil tasted the wine.

'Delicious.'

'I'm so glad. Bill knows about wine. I don't.'

So they began to talk about Bill, who was married in July to this lovely creature, who had a good job in an architect's office in the nearby town, had settled at Grantley Green in August, and in September had gone to join the yeomanry as a trooper. . . .

Two hours later Basil left the Malt House and returned to his car. It was evidence of the compelling property of love that the Connolly children were still in their seats.

'Gawd, Mister, you haven't half been a time,' said Doris. 'We're fair froze. Do we get out here?'

'No.'

'We aren't going to muck up this house?'

'No, Doris, not this time. You're coming back with me.'

Doris sighed blissfully. 'I don't care how froze we are if we can come back with you,' she said.

When they returned to Malfrey, and Barbara once more found the children back in the bachelors' wing, her face fell. 'Oh, Basil,' she said. 'You've failed me.'

'Well not exactly. The Prettyman-Partridges are dead.'

'I knew there was something about them. But you've been a long time.'

'I met a friend. At least a friend of a friend. A very nice girl. I think you ought to do something about her.'

'What's her name?'

'D'you know, I never discovered. But her husband's called Bill. He joined Freddy's regiment as a trooper.'

'Who's she a friend of?'

'Mary Nichols.'

'I've never heard of her.'

'Old friend of mine. Honestly, Babs, you'll like this girl.'

'Well, ask her to dinner.' Barbara was not enthusiastic; she had known too many of Basil's girls.

'I have. The trouble is she hasn't got a car. D'you mind if I go and fetch her?'

'Darling, we simply haven't the petrol.'

'We can use the special allowance.'

'Darling, I *can't*. This has nothing to do with billeting.'

'Believe it or not Babs, it has.'

X

The frost broke; the snow melted away; Colony Bog, Bagshot Heath, Chobham Common and all the little polygons of gorse and bush which lay between the high roads of Surrey, patches of rank land marked on the signposts W.D., marked on the maps as numbered training areas, reappeared from the brief period of comeliness.

'We can get on with the tactical training,' said the C.O.

For three weeks there were platoon schemes and company schemes. Captain Mayfield consumed his leisure devising ways of transforming into battlefields the few acres of close, soggy territory at his disposal. For the troops these schemes varied only according to the distance of the training area from camp, and the distance that had to be traversed before the cease-fire. Then for three days in succession the C.O. was seen to go out with the adjutant in the Humber Snipe, each carrying a map case. 'We're putting on a battalion exercise,' said

Captain Mayfield. It was all one to his troops. 'It's our first battalion exercise. It's absolutely essential that every man in the company shall be in the picture all the time.'

Alastair was gradually learning the new languages. There was the simple tongue, the unchanging reiteration of obscenity, spoken by his fellow soldiers. That took little learning. There was also the language spoken by his officers, which from time to time was addressed to him. The first time that Captain Mayfield had asked him, 'Are you in the picture, Trumpington?' he supposed him to mean, was he personally conspicuous. He crouched at the time waterlogged to the knees, in a ditch; he had, at the suggestion of Mr Smallwood–the platoon commander–ornamented his steel helmet with bracken. 'No, sir,' he had said, stoutly.

Captain Mayfield had seemed rather gratified than not by the confession. 'Put these men in the picture, Smallwood,' he said, and there had followed a tedious and barely credible narrative about the unprovoked aggression of Southland against Northland (who was not party to the Geneva gas protocol), about How support batteries, A.F.V.s and F.D.L.s.

Alastair learned, too, that all schemes ended in a 'shambles' which did not mean, as he feared, a slaughter, but a brief restoration of individual freedom of movement, when everyone wandered where he would, while Mr Smallwood blew his whistle and Captain Mayfield shouted, 'Mr Smallwood, will you kindly get your platoon to hell out of here and fall them in on the road.'

On the day of the battalion scheme they marched out of camp as a battalion. Alastair had been made mortar-man in Mr Smallwood's platoon. It was a gamble, the chances of which were hotly debated. At the moment there were no mortars and he was given instead a light and easily manageable counterfeit of wood which was slung on the back of his haversack, relieving him of a rifle. At present it was money for old rope, but a day would come, spoken of as 'when we get over 1098'; in that dire event he would be worse off than the riflemen. Two other men in the platoon had rashly put in to be anti-tank men; contrary to all expectations anti-tank rifles had suddenly arrived. One of these men had prudently gone sick on the eve of the exercise; the other went sick after it.

Water-bottles were filled, haversack rations were packed in mess-tins, and, on account of Northland's frank obduracy at Geneva, gas respirators frustrated the aim of the designers of the equipment to leave the man's chest unencumbered. Thus they marched out and after ten minutes at the command to march at ease, they began singing 'Roll out the Barrel', 'We'll hang out the Washing on the Siegfried Line', and 'The Quartermaster's Store'. Presently the order came back to march tactically. They knew all about that; it meant stumbling along in the ditch; singing stopped; the man with the anti-tank rifle swore monotonously. Then the order came back 'Gas'; they put on their respirators and the man with the anti-tank rifle suffered in silence.

'Gas clear. *Don't* put the respirators back in the haversacks. Leave them out a minute to dry.'

They marched eight miles or so and then turned off the main road into a lane and eventually halted. It was now eleven o'clock.

'This is the battalion assembly position,' announced Captain Mayfield. 'The C.O. has just gone forward with his recce group to make his recce.'

It was as though he were announcing to a crowd of pilgrims, 'This is the Vatican. The Pope has just gone into the Sistine Chapel.'

'It makes things much more interesting,' said Mr Smallwood rather apologetically, 'if you try and understand what is going on. Yes, carry on smoking.'

The company settled itself on the side of the road and began eating its haversack rations.

'I say, you know, said Mr Smallwood. 'There'll be a halt for dinner.'

They ate, mostly in silence.

'Soon the C.O. will send for his O group,' announced Captain Mayfield.

Presently a runner appeared, not running but walking rather slowly, and led Captain Mayfield away.

'The C.O. *has* sent for his O group,' said Mr Smallwood. 'Captain Brown is now in command.'

Captain Brown announced, 'The C.O. has given out his orders. He is now establishing advanced Battalion H.Q. The company commanders are now making their recces. Soon *they* will send for *their* O groups.'

'Can't think what they want *us* here for at all,' said the man with the anti-tank rifle.

Three-quarters of an hour passed and then an orderly arrived with a written message for Captain Brown. He said to the three platoon commanders, 'You're to meet the company commander at the third E in "Bee Garden". I'm bringing the Company on to the B in Bee.'

Mr Smallwood and his orderly and his batman left platoon headquarters and drifted off uncertainly into the scrub.

'Get the company fallen in, sergeant-major.'

Captain Brown was not quite happy about his position; they tacked along behind him across the common; several times they halted while Captain Brown worried over the map. At last he said, 'This is the company assembly position. The company commander is now giving out orders to his O group.'

At this moment, just as the men were beginning to settle down, Captain Mayfield appeared. 'Where the hell are those platoon commanders?' he asked. 'And what is the company doing here? I said the B in Bee, this is the E in Garden.'

A discussion followed, inaudible to Alastair except for an occasional phrase, 'ring contour', 'track junction' and again and again 'well, the map's wrong.' Captain Brown seemed to get the better of the argument; at any rate Captain Mayfield went away in search of his O group and left the company in possession.

Half an hour passed. Captain Brown felt impelled to explain the delay.

'The platoon commanders are making their recces,' he said.

Presently the C.O. arrived. 'Is this C Company?' he asked.

'Yes, sir.'

'Well, what's happening? You ought to be on the start line by now.' Then since it was clearly no use attacking Captain Brown about that, he said in a way Captain Brown had learned to dread, 'I must have missed your sentries coming along. Just put me in the picture, will you, of your local defence.'

'Well, sir, we've just halted here . . .'

The C.O. led Captain Brown away.

'He's getting a rocket,' said the anti-tank man. It was the first moment of satisfaction he had known that day.

Captain Brown came back looking shaken and began posting air look-outs and gas sentries with feverish activity. While he was in the middle of it the platoon orderlies came back to lead the platoons to assembly positions. Alastair advanced with the platoon another half mile. Then they halted. Mr Smallwood appeared and collected the section commanders round him. The C.O. was there too, listening to Mr Smallwood's orders. When they were finished he said, 'I don't think you mentioned the R.A.P., did you, Smallwood?'

'R.A.P. sir. No, sir, I'm afraid I don't know where it is.'

The C.O. led Mr Smallwood out of hearing of his platoon.

'Now *he's* getting a rocket,' said the anti-tank man with glee.

The section-commanders came back to their men. Mr Smallwood's orders had been full of detail; start line, zero hour, boundaries inclusive and exclusive, objectives, supporting fire. 'It's like this,' said Corporal Deacon. 'They're over there and we're here. So then we go for un.'

Another half-hour passed. Captain Mayfield appeared. 'For Christ's sake, Smallwood, you ought to be half-way up the ridge by this time.'

'Oh,' said Mr Smallwood. 'Sorry. Come on. Forward.'

The platoon collected its equipment and toiled into action up the opposing slope. Major Bush, the second-in-command, appeared before them. They fired their blanks at him with enthusiasm. 'Got him,' said the man next to Alastair.

'You're coming under heavy fire,' said the Major. 'Most of you are casualties.'

'He's a casualty himself.'

'Well, what are you going to do, Smallwood?'

'Get down, sir.'

'Well *get* down.'

'Get down,' ordered Mr Smallwood.

'What are you going to do now?'

Mr Smallwood looked round desperately for inspiration. 'Put down smoke, sir.'

'Well, *put* down smoke.'

'Put down smoke,' said Mr Smallwood to Alastair.

The Major went on his way to confuse the platoon on their flank.

'Come on,' said Mr Smallwood. 'We've got to get up this infernal hill sometime. We might as well do it now.'

It was shorter than it looked; they were up in twenty minutes and at the summit there was a prolonged shambles. Bit by bit the whole battalion appeared from different quarters. C Company was collected and fallen in; then they were fallen out to eat their dinners. No one had any dinner left, so they lay on their backs and smoked.

Marching home the C.O. said, 'Not so bad for a first attempt.'

'Not so bad, Colonel,' said Major Bush.

'Bit slow off the mark.'

'A bit sticky.'

'Smallwood didn't do too well.'

'He was very slow off the mark.'

'Well, I think we learned some lessons. The men were interested. You could see that.'

It was dark by the time the battalion reached camp. They marched to attention passing the guard-room, split into companies, and halted on the company parade grounds.

'All rifles to be pulled through before supper,' said Captain Mayfield. 'Platoon sergeants collect empties. Foot inspection by platoons.' Then he dismissed the company.

Alastair had time to slip away to the telephone box and summon Sonia before Mr Mayfield came round the hut examining feet with an electric torch. He pulled on a clean pair of socks, pushed his boots under his palliasse and put on a pair of shoes; then he was ready. Sonia was outside the guard-room, waiting for him in the car. 'Darling, you smell very sweaty,' she said. 'What have you been doing?'

'I put down smoke,' said Alastair proudly. 'The whole advance was held up until I put down smoke.'

'Darling, you *are* clever. I've got a tinned beefsteak and kidney pudding for dinner.'

After dinner Alastair settled in a chair. 'Don't let me go to sleep,' he said. 'I must be in by midnight.'

'I'll wake you.'

'I wonder if a real battle is much like that,' said Alastair just before he dropped off.

Peter Pastmaster's expedition never sailed. He resumed his former uniform and his former habits. His regiment was in barracks in London; his mother was still at the Ritz; most of his friends were still to be found round the bar at Bratts. With time on his hands and the prospect of action, for a few days imminent, now postponed, but always present as the basis of any future plans, Peter began to suffer from pangs of dynastic conscience. He was thirty-three years old. He might pop off any day. 'Mama,' he said, 'd'you think I ought to marry?'

'Who?'

'Anyone.'

'I don't see that you can say anyone *ought* to marry *anyone*.'

'Darling, don't confuse me. What I mean is, supposing I get killed.'

'I don't see a great deal in it for the poor girl,' said Margot.

'I mean I should like to have a son.'

'Well, then, you had better marry, darling. D'you know any girls?'

'I don't think I do.'

'I don't think I do either, come to think of it. I believe Emma Granchester's second girl is very pretty–try her. There are probably lots of others. I'll make enquiries.'

So Peter, little accustomed to their society, began, awkwardly at first, taking out a series of very young and very eligible girls; he quickly gained confidence; it was easy as falling off a log. Soon there were a dozen mothers who were old-fashioned enough to be pleasurably excited at the prospect of finding in their son-in-law all the Victorian excellences of an old title, a new fortune, and a shapely leg in blue overalls.

'Peter,' Margot said to him one day. 'D'you ever give yourself time from debutantes to see old friends? What's become of Angela? I never see her now.'

'I suppose she's gone back to the country.'

'Not with Basil?'

'No, not with Basil.'

But she was living still above the block of flats in Grosvenor Square. Below, layer upon layer of rich men and women came and went about their business, layer below layer down to street level; below that again, underground, the management were adapting the basement to serve as an air-raid shelter. Angela seldom went beyond her door, except once or twice a week to visit the cinema; she always went alone. She had taken to wearing spectacles of smoked glass; she wore them indoors, as well as out; she wore them in the subdued, concealed lighting of her drawing-room, as she sat hour after hour with the radio standing by the decanter and glass at her elbow; she wore them when she looked at herself in the mirror. Only Grainger, her maid, knew what was the matter with Mrs Lyne, and she only knew the shell of it. Grainger knew the number of bottles, empty and full, in the little pantry; she saw Mrs Lyne's face when the blackout was taken down in the morning. (She never had to wake Mrs Lyne nowadays; her eyes were always open when the maid came to call her; sometimes Mrs Lyne was up and sitting in her chair; sometimes she lay in bed, staring ahead, waiting to be called.) She knew the trays of food that came up from the restaurant and went back, as often as not, untasted. All this Grainger knew and, being a dull sensible girl, she kept her own counsel; but, being a dull and sensible girl, she was spared the knowledge of what went on in Mrs Lyne's mind.

So the snows vanished and the weeks of winter melted away with them; presently, oblivious of the hazards of war, the swallows returned to their ancestral building grounds.

3

SPRING

I

Two events decided Basil to return to London. First, the yeomanry moved back to the country under canvas. Freddy telephoned to Barbara:

'Good news,' he said, 'we're coming home.'

'Freddy, how splendid,' said Barbara, her spirits falling a little. 'When?'

'I arrive to-morrow. I'm bringing Jack Cathcart; he's our second-in-command now. We're going to lay out a camp. We'll stay at Malfrey while we're doing it.'

'Lovely,' said Barbara.

'We'll be bringing servants, so we'll be self-supporting as far as that goes. There'll be a couple of sergeants Benson can look after them. And I say, Barbara, what do you say to having the camp in the Park?'

'Oh, no, Freddy, for God's sake.'

'We could open up the saloon and have the mess there. I could live in. You'd have to have old Colonel Sproggin and probably Cathcart, too, but you wouldn't mind that, would you?'

'Please, Freddy, don't decide anything in a hurry.'

'Well, I have practically decided. See you to-morrow. I say, is Basil still with you?'

'Yes.'

'I can't see him getting on terribly well with Cathcart. Couldn't you give him a gentle hint?'

Barbara hung up sadly and went to make arrangements for Freddy's and Major Cathcart's reception.

Basil was at Grantley Green. He returned to Malfrey after dinner, to find Barbara still up.

'Darling, you've got to go away.'

'Yes, how did you know?'

'Freddy's coming home.'

'Oh, damn Freddy; who cares for him? *Bill's* coming home.'

'What does she say?'

'Believe it or not, she's as pleased as Punch.'

'Ungrateful beast,' said Barbara, and, after a pause, 'You never wrote that book either.'

'No, but we've had a lovely time, haven't we, Babs? Quite like the old days.'

'I suppose you'll want some money.'

'I could always do with some more, but as it happens I'm quite rich at the moment.'

'Basil, how?'

'One thing and another. I tell you what I will do before I go. I'll get the Connollys off your hands again. I'm afraid I've been neglecting them rather in the last few weeks.'

That led to the second deciding event.

On his way to and from Grantley Green, Basil had noticed a pretty stucco house standing in paddock and orchard, which seemed exactly suited to harbour the Connollys. He had asked Barbara about it, but she could tell him nothing. Basil was getting lax and, confident now in his methods, no longer bothered himself with much research before choosing his victims. The stucco house was marked down and next day he packed the Connollys into the car and drove over to do his business.

It was ten in the morning but he found the proprietor at breakfast. He did not appear to be quite the type that Basil was used to deal with. He was younger than the G.P.O. list. A game leg, stuck awkwardly askew, explained why he was not in uniform. He had got this injury in a motor race, he explained later to Basil. He had ginger hair and a ginger moustache and malevolent pinkish eyes. His name was Mr Todhunter.

He was eating kidneys and eggs and sausages and bacon and an overcooked chop; his teapot stood on the hob. He looked like a drawing by Leach for a book by Surtees.

'Well,' he said, cautious but affable. 'I know about you. You're Mrs Sothill's brother at Malfrey. I don't know Mrs Sothill but I know all about her. I don't know Captain Sothill but I know about him. What can I do for you?'

'I'm the billeting officer for this district,' said Basil.

'*Indeed.* I'm interested to meet you. Go on. You don't mind my eating, I'm sure.'

Feeling a little less confident than usual, Basil went through his now stereotyped preface. '. . . Getting harder to find billets, particularly since the anti-aircraft battery had come to South Grappling and put their men in the cottages there . . . important to stop the backwash to the towns . . . bad impression if the bigger houses seemed not to be doing their share . . . natural reluctance to employ compulsory powers but these powers *were* there, if necessary . . . three children who had caused some difficulty elsewhere . . .'

Mr Todhunter finished his breakfast, stood with his back to the fire and began to fill his pipe. 'And what if I don't want these hard cases of yours,' he said. 'What if I'd sooner pay the fine?'

Basil embarked on the second part of his recitation. '. . . official allowance barely covered cost of food . . . serious hardship to poor families . . . poor people valued their household gods even more than the rich . . . possible to find a cottage where a few pounds would make all the difference between dead loss and a small and welcome profit . . .'

Mr Todhunter heard him in silence. At last he said, 'So *that's* how you do it. Thank you. That was most instructive, very instructive indeed. I liked the bit about household gods.'

Basil began to realize that he was dealing with a fellow of broad and rather dangerous sympathies; someone like himself. 'In more cultured circles I say Lares et Penates.'

'Household gods is good enough. Household gods is very good indeed. What d'you generally count on raising?'

'Five pounds is the worst, thirty-five the best I've had so far.'

'So far? Do you hope to carry on long with this trade?'

'I don't see why not.'

'Don't you? Well I'll tell you something. D'you know who's billeting officer in this district? I am. Mrs Sothill's district ends at the main road. You're muscling in on my territory when you come past the crossing. Now what have you got to say for yourself?'

'D'you mean to say that Grantley Green is yours?'

'Certainly.'

'How damned funny.'

'Why funny?'

'I can't tell you, said Basil. 'But it *is*—exquisitely funny.'

'So I'll ask you to keep to your own side of the road in future. Not that I'm ungrateful for your visit. It's given me some interesting ideas. I always felt there was money in this racket somehow, but I could never quite see my way to get it. Now I know. I'll remember about the household gods.'

'Wait a minute,' said Basil. 'It isn't quite as easy as all that, you know. It isn't just a matter of having the idea; you have to have the Connollys too. You don't understand it, and I don't understand it, but the fact remains that quite a number of otherwise sane human beings are perfectly ready to take children in; they like them; it makes them feel virtuous; they like the little pattering feet about the house—I know it sounds screwy but it's the truth. I've seen it again and again.'

'So have I,' said Mr Todhunter. 'There's no sense in it, but it's a fact–they make household gods of them.'

'Now the Connollys are something quite special; no one could make a household god of them. Come and have a look.'

He and Mr Todhunter went out into the circle of gravel in front of the porch where Basil had left the car.

'Doris,' he said. 'Come out and meet Mr Todhunter. Bring Micky and Marlene too.'

The three frightful children stood in a line to be inspected.

'Take that scarf off your head, Doris. Show him your hair.'

In spite of himself Mr Todhunter could not disguise the fact that he was profoundly moved. 'Yes,' he said, 'I give you that. They *are* special. If it's not a rude question, what did you pay for them?'

'I got them free. But I've put a lot of money into them since–fried fish and cinemas.'

'How did you get the girl's hair that way?'

'She did it herself,' said Basil, 'for love.'

'They certainly are special,' repeated Mr Todhunter with awe.

'You haven't seen anything yet. You should see them in action.'

'I can imagine it,' said Mr Todhunter. 'Well, what d'you want for them?'

'Five pounds a leg and that's cheap, because I'm thinking of closing down the business anyhow.'

Mr Todhunter was not a man to haggle when he was on a good thing. 'Done,' he said.

Basil addressed the Connollys. 'Well, children, this is your new headquarters.'

'Are we to muck 'em about?' asked Doris.

'That's up to Mr Todhunter. I'm handing you over to him now. You'll be working for him in future.'

'Ain't we never going to be with you again?' asked Doris.

'Never again, Doris. But you'll find you like Mr Todhunter just as much. He's very handsome, isn't he?'

'Not as handsome as you.'

'No, perhaps not, but he's got a fine little red moustache, hasn't he?'

'Yes, it's a lovely moustache,' Doris conceded; she looked from her old to her new master critically. 'But he's shorter than you.'

'Dammit, girl,' said Basil impatiently. 'Don't you realize there's a war on. We've all got to make sacrifices. There's many a little girl would be very grateful for Mr Todhunter. Look at his fine red nob.'

'Yes, it *is* red.'

Mr Todhunter tired of the comparison and stumped indoors to fetch his cheque book.

'Can't we muck his house up, just a bit?' said Micky wistfully.

'Yes, I don't see why not, just a bit.'

'Mister,' said Doris, near tears. 'Kiss me once before you go.'

'No. Mr Todhunter wouldn't like it. He's terribly jealous.'

'Is he?' she said lightening. 'I love jealous men.'

When Basil left her, her fervent, volatile affections were already plainly engaged with her new host. Marlene remained passive throughout the interview; she had few gifts, poor child, and those she was allowed to employ only on rare occasions. 'Mayn't I be sick here Doris? Just once?'

'Not here, ducky. Wait till the gentleman billets you.'

'Will that be long?'

'No,' said Mr Todhunter decisively, 'not long.'

So the scourge of the Malfrey area moved South into the apple-growing country, and the market gardens; and all over the park at Malfrey, dispersed irregularly under the great elms, tents sprang up; and the yeomanry officers set up their mess in the Grinling Gibbons saloon; and Barbara had Colonel Sproggin and Major Cathcart to live in the house; and Freddy made an agreeable sum of money out of the arrangement; and Bill spent many blissful uxorious hours in the Malt House, Grantley Green (he was quite satisfied with the explanation he was given about the cellar door). And Basil returned to London.

II

He decided to pay one of his rare, and usually rather brief, visits to his mother. He found her busy and optimistic, serving on half a dozen benevolent committees connected with comforts for the troops, seeing her friends regularly. The defeat of Finland had shocked her, but she found it a compensation that Russia was at last disclosed in its true light. She welcomed Basil to the house, heard his news of Barbara and gave him news of Tony. 'I want to have a little talk with you some time,' she said, after half an hour's gossip.

Basil, had he not been inured to his mother's euphemisms, might have supposed that a little talk was precisely what she had just had; but he knew what a little talk meant; it meant a discussion of his 'future'.

'Have you arranged anything for to-night?'

'No, mother, not yet.'

'Then we will dine in, Just the two of us.'

And that night after dinner she said, 'Basil, I never thought I should have to say this to you. I've been pleased, of course, that you were able to be of help to Barbara with her evacuees, but now that you have returned to London, I must tell you that I do not think it is *man's* work. At a time like this you ought to be *fighting*.'

'But mother, as far as I know, no one's fighting much at the moment.'

'Don't quibble, dear, you know what I mean.'

'Well, I went to see that colonel when you asked me to.'

'Yes. Sir Joseph explained that to me. They only want very young officers in the Guards. But he says that there are a number of other excellent regiments that offer a far better career. General Gordon was a Sapper, and I believe quite a number of the generals in this war were originally only gunners. I don't want you just lounging about London in uniform like your friend Peter Pastmaster. He seems to spend his whole time with girls. That goose Emma Granchester is seriously thinking of him for Molly. So is Etty Flintshire and so is poor Mrs Van Antrobus for *their* daughters. I don't know what they're thinking of. I knew his poor father. Margot led him a terrible dance. That was long before she married Metroland of course–before he was called Metroland, in fact. No,' said Lady Seal, abruptly checking herself in the flow of reminiscence. 'I want to see you doing something *important*. Now Sir Joseph has got me one of the forms you fill in to become an officer. It is called the Supplementary Reserve. Before you go to bed I want you to sign it. Then we'll see about getting it sent to the proper quarter. I'm sure that everything will be much easier now that that disgraceful Mr Belisha has been outed.'

'But you know, mother, I don't really fancy myself much as a subaltern.'

'No, dear,' said Lady Seal decisively, 'and if you had gone into the army when you left Oxford you would be a major by now. Promotion is very quick in war time because so many people get killed. I'm sure once you're in, they'll find great use for you. But you must begin somewhere. I remember Lord Kitchener told me that even he was once a subaltern.'

Thus it was that Basil found himself again in danger of being started on a career. 'Don't worry,' said Peter. 'No one ever gets taken off the Supplementary Reserve.' But Basil did worry. He had a rooted distrust of official forms. He felt that at any moment a telegram might summon him to present himself at some remote barracks, where he would spend the war, like Alastair's Mr Smallwood, teaching fieldcraft to thirty militiamen. It was not thus that he had welcomed the war as the ne'er-do-well's opportunity. He fretted about it for three days and then decided to pay a visit to the War Office.

He went there without any particular object in view, impelled by the belief that somewhere in that large organization was a goose who would lay eggs for him. In the first days of the war when he was seeking to interest the authorities in the annexation of Liberia, he had more than once sought an entrance. Perhaps, he felt now, he had pitched a little too high. The Chief of the Imperial General Staff was a busy man. This time he would advance humbly.

The maelstrom, which in early September had eddied round the vestibule of the buildings, seemed to have subsided very little. There was a similar–perhaps, he reflected sadly, an identical–crowd of officers of all ranks attempting to gain admission. Among them he saw a single civilian figure whom he recognized from his visits to the Ministry of Information.

'Hullo,' he said. 'Still hawking bombs?'

The little lunatic with the suitcase greeted him with great friendliness. 'They won't pay any attention. It's a most unsatisfactory office,' he said. 'They won't let me in. I was sent on here from the Admiralty.'

'Have you tried the Air Ministry?'

'Why, bless you, it was them sent me to the Ministry of Information. I've tried them all. I will say for the Ministry of Information they were uncommon civil. Not at all like they are here. At the M. of I. they were never too busy to see one. The only thing was, I felt I wasn't getting anywhere.'

'Come along,' said Basil. 'We'll get in.'

Veterans of the Ashanti and the Zulu campaigns guarded the entrance. Basil watched them stop a full general. 'If you'll fill in a form, sir, please, one of the boys will take you up to the department.' They were a match for anyone in uniform, but Basil and the bagman were a more uncertain quantity; a full general was just a full general, but a civilian might be anyone.

'Your passes, gentlemen, please.'

'That's all right, sergeant,' said Basil. 'I'll vouch for this man.'

'Yes, sir, but who are you, sir?'

'You ought to know by this time. M.I.13. We don't carry passes or give our names in my department.'

'Very good, sir; beg parden, sir. D'you know the way or shall I send a boy up with you?'

'Of course I know my way,' said Basil sharply, 'and you might take a look at this man. He won't give his name or show a pass, but I expect you'll see him here often.'

'Very good, sir.'

The two civilians passed through the seething military into the calm of the corridors beyond.

'I'm sure I'm very obliged,' said the man with the suitcase; 'where shall I go now?'

'The whole place lies open to you,' said Basil. 'Take your time. Go where you like. I think if I were you I should start with the Chaplain General.'

'Where's he?'

'Up there,' said Basil vaguely. 'Up there and straight on.'

The little man thanked him gravely, trotted off down the corridor with the irregular, ill co-ordinated steps of the insane, and was lost to view up the bend in the staircase. Not wishing to compromise himself further by his act of charity, Basil took the opposing turning. A fine vista lay before him of twenty or more closed doors, any one of which might open upon prosperity and adventure. He strolled down the passage in a leisurely but purposeful manner; thus, he thought, an important agent might go to keep an appointment; thus, in fact, Soapy Sponge might have walked in the gallery of Jawleyford Court.

It was a vista full of potentiality but lacking, at the moment, in ornament–a vista of linoleum and sombre dado; the light came solely from the far end, so that a figure approaching appeared in silhouette, and in somewhat indistinct silhouette; a figure now approached and it was not until she was within a few yards of Basil that he realized that here was the enrichment which the austere architectural scheme demanded: a girl dressed in uniform with a lance-corporal's stripe on her arm–with a face of transparent, aethereal silliness which struck deep into Basil's heart. The classical image might have been sober fact, so swift and silent and piercing was the dart of pleasure. He turned in his tracks and followed the lance-corporal down the lane of linoleum which seemed, momentarily, as buoyant as the carpet of a cinema or theatre.

The lance-corporal led him a long way; she stopped from time to time to exchange greetings with passers-by, showing to all ranks from full general to second-class scout the same cheerful affection; she was clearly a popular girl in these parts. At length she turned into a door marked ADDIS; Basil followed her in. There was another lance-corporal–male–in the room.

This lance-corporal sat behind a typewriter; he had a white, pimply face, large spectacles and a cigarette in the corner of his mouth. He did not look up. The female lance-corporal smiled and said, 'So now you know where I live. Drop in any time you're passing.'

'What is ADDIS?' asked Basil.

'It's Colonel Plum.'

'What's Colonel Plum?'

'He's a perfect lamb. Go and take a peer at him if you like. He's in there.' She nodded towards a glass door marked KEEP OUT.

'Assistant Deputy Director Internal Security,' said the male lance-corporal without looking up from his typing.

'I think I'd like to come and work in this office,' said Basil.

'Yes, everyone says that. It was the same when I was in pensions.'

'I might take *his* job.'

'You're welcome,' said the male lance-corporal sourly. 'Suspects, suspects, suspects all day long, all with foreign names, none of them ever shot.'

A loud voice from beyond the glass door broke into the conversation. 'Susie, you slut, come here.'

'That's him, the angel. Just take a peer while the door's open. He's got the sweetest little moustache.'

Basil peered round the corner and caught a glimpse of a lean, military face and, as Susie had said, the sweetest little moustache. The colonel caught a glimpse of Basil.

'Who the devil's that?'

'I don't know,' said Susie lightly. 'He just followed me in.'

'Come here you,' said the Colonel. 'Who are you and what d'you want in my office?'

'Well,' said Basil, 'what the lance-corporal says is strictly true. I just followed her in. But since I'm here I can give you some valuable information.'

'If you can you're unique in this outfit. What is it?'

Until now the word 'Colonel' for Basil had connoted an elderly rock-gardener on Barbara's G.P.O. list. This formidable man of his own age was another kettle of fish. Here was a second Todhunter. What could he possibly tell him which would pass for valuable information?

'Can I speak freely before the lance-corporal?' he asked, playing for time.

'Yes, of course. She doesn't understand a word of any language.'

Inspiration came. 'There's a lunatic loose in the War Office,' Basil said.

'Of course there is. There are some hundreds of them. Is that all you came to tell me?'

'He's got a suitcase full of bombs.'

'Well I hope he finds his way to the Intelligence Branch. I don't suppose you know his name? No, well make out a card for him, Susie, with a serial number and index him under suspects. If his bombs go off we shall know where he is; if they don't it doesn't matter. These fellows usually do more harm to themselves than to anyone else. Run along, Susie, and shut the door. I want to talk to Mr Seal.'

Basil was shaken. When the door shut he said, 'Have we met before?'

'You bet we have. Jibuti 1936, St Jean de Luz 1937, Prague 1938. You wouldn't remember me. I wasn't dressed up like this then.'

'Were you a journalist?'

Vaguely at the back of Basil's mind was the recollection of an unobtrusive, discreet face among a hundred unobtrusive, discreet faces, that had passed in and out of his ken from time to time. During the past ten years he had usually managed to find himself, on one pretext or another, on the outer fringe of contemporary history; in that half-world there were numerous slightly sinister figures whose orbits crossed and recrossed, ubiquitous men and women camp-followers of diplomacy and the Press; among those shades he dimly remembered seeing Colonel Plum.

'Sometimes. We got drunk together once at the Bar Basque, the night you fought the United Press correspondent.'

'As far as I remember he won.'

'You bet he did. I took you back to your hotel. What are you doing now besides making passes at Susie?'

'I thought of doing counter-espionage.'

'Yes,' said Colonel Plum. 'Most people who come here seem to have thought of that. Hullo —' he added as a dull detonation shook the room slightly, 'that sounds as if your man has had a success with his bombs' That was a straight tip, anyway. I dare say you'd be no worse in the job than anyone else.'

Here it was at last, the scene that Basil had so often rehearsed, the scene, very slightly adapted by a later hand, in order to bring it up to date, from the adventure stories of his youth. Here was the lean, masterful man who had followed Basil's career saying, 'One day his country will have a use for him . . .'

'What are your contacts?'

What were his contacts? Alastair Digby-Vane-Trumpington, Angela Lyne, Margot Metroland, Peter Pastmaster, Barbara, the bride of Grantley Green, Mr Todhunter, Poppet Green–*Poppet Green*; there was his chicken.

'I know some very dangerous communists,' said Basil.

'I wonder if they're on our files. We'll look in a minute. We aren't doing much about communists at the moment. The politicians are shy of them for some reason. But we keep an eye on them, on the side, of course. I can't pay you much for communists.'

'As it happens,' said Basil with dignity, 'I came here to serve my country. I don't particularly want money.'

'The devil you don't? What *do* you want, then? You can't have Susie. I had the hell of a fight to get her away from the old brute in charge of pensions.'

'We can fight that out later. What I really want most at the moment is a uniform.'

'Good God! Why?'

'My mother is threatening to make me a platoon commander.'

Colonel Plum accepted this somewhat surprising statement with apparent understanding. 'Yes,' he said. 'There's a lot to be said for a uniform. For one thing you'll have to call me "sir" and if there's any funny stuff with the female staff I can take disciplinary action. For another thing it's the best possible disguise for a man of intelligence. No one ever suspects a soldier of taking a serious interest in the war. I think I can fix that.'

'What'll my rank be?'

'Second-Lieutenant, Crosse and Blackwell's regiment.'

'Crosse and Blackwell?'

'General Service List.'

'I say, can't you do anything better than that?'

'Not for watching communists. Catch a fascist for me and I'll think about making you a Captain of Marines.' At this moment the telephone bell rang. 'Yes, ADDIS speaking . . . oh, yes, the bomb . . . yes, we know all about that . . . the Chaplain General? I say that's bad . . . oh, only the Deputy Assistant Chaplain General and you think he'll recover. Well, what's all the fuss about? . . . Yes, we know all about the man in this branch. We've had him indexed a long time. He's nuts–yes, N for nuts, U for uncle, nuts, you've got it. No I don't want to see him. Lock him up. There must be plenty of padded cells in this building, I should imagine.'

News of the attempt to assassinate the Chaplain General reached the Religious Department of the Ministry of Information late in the afternoon, just when they were preparing to pack up for the day. It threw them into a fever of activity.

'Really,' said Ambrose pettishly. 'You fellows get all the fun. I shall be *most* embarrassed when I have to explain this to the editor of *The Godless Sunday at Home*.'

Lady Seal was greatly shocked.

'Poor man,' she said, 'I understand that his eyebrows have completely gone. It must have been Russians.'

III

For the third time since his return to London, Basil tried to put a call through to Angela Lyne. He listened to the repeated buzz, five, six, seven times, then hung up the receiver. Still away, he thought. I should have liked to show her my uniform.

Angela counted the rings, five, six, seven; then there was silence in the flat; silence except for the radio which said, '. . . dastardly attempt which has shocked the conscience of the civilized world. Messages of sympathy continue to pour into the Chaplain General's office from the religious leaders of four continents . . .'

She switched over to Germany where a rasping, contemptuous voice spoke of 'Churchill's attempt to make a second *Athenia* by bombing the military bishop.'

She switched on to France where a man of letters gave his impressions of a visit to the Maginot Line. Angela filled her glass from the bottle at her elbow. Her distrust of France was becoming an obsession with her now. It kept her awake at night and haunted her dreams by day; long, tedious dreams born of barbituric, dreams which had no element of fantasy or surprise, utterly real, drab dreams which, like waking life, held no promise of delight. She often spoke aloud to herself nowadays, living, as she did, so much alone; it was thus that lonely old women spoke, passing in the street with bags of rubbish in their hands, squatting, telling their rubbish. Angela was like an old woman squatting in a doorway picking over her day's gleaning of rubbish, talking to herself while she sorted the scraps of garbage. She had seen and heard old women like that, often, at the end of the day, in the side streets near the theatres.

Now she said to herself as loudly as though to someone sitting opposite on the white Empire day-bed, 'Maginot Line–Angela Lyne–both lines of least resistance' and laughed at her joke until the tears came and suddenly she found herself weeping in earnest.

Then she took a pull at herself. This wouldn't do at all. She had better go out to the cinema.

Peter Pastmaster was taking a girl out that evening. He looked very elegant and old-fashioned in his blue patrol jacket and tight overall trousers. He and the girl dined at a new restaurant in Jermyn Street.

She was Lady Mary Meadowes, Lord Granchester's second daughter. In his quest for a wife Peter had narrowed the field to three–Molly Meadowes; Sarah, Lord Flintshire's daughter; and Betty, daughter of the Duchess of Stayle. Since he was marrying for old-fashioned, dynastic reasons he proposed to make an old-fashioned, dynastic choice from among the survivors of the Whig oligarchy. He really could see very little difference between the three girls; in fact he sometimes caused offence by addressing them absent-mindedly by the wrong names. None of them carried a pound of superfluous flesh; they all had an enthusiasm for the works of Mr Ernest Hemingway; all had pet dogs of rather similar peculiarities. They had all found that the way to keep Peter amused was to get him to brag about his past iniquities.

During dinner he told Molly about the time when Basil Seal had stood for Parliament and he and Sonia and Alastair had done him dirt in his constituency. She laughed dutifully at the incident of Sonia throwing a potato at the mayor.

'Some of the papers got it wrong and said it was a bun,' he explained.

'What a lovely time you all seem to have had,' said Lady Mary wistfully.

'All past and done with,' said Peter primly.

'Is it? I *do* hope not.'

Peter looked at her with a new interest. Sarah and Betty had taken this tale as though it were one of highwaymen; something infinitely old-fashioned and picturesque.

Afterwards they walked to the cinema next door.

The vestibule was in darkness except for a faint blue light in the box office. Out of the darkness the voice of the commissionaire announced. 'No three and sixes. Plenty of room up in the five and nines. Five and nines this way. Don't block up the gangway please.'

There was some kind of disturbance going on at the guichet. A woman was peering stupidly at the blue light and saying, 'I don't want five and nines. I want one three and sixpenny.'

'No three and sixes. Only five and nines.'

'But you don't understand. It isn't the price. The five and nines are too far away. I want to be *near*, in the three and sixpennies.'

'No three and sixes. Five and nines,' said the girl in the blue light.

'Come on, lady, make up your mind,' said a soldier, waiting.

'She's got a look of Mrs Cedric Lyne,' said Molly.

'Why,' said Peter, 'it *is* Angela. What on earth's the matter with her?'

She had now bought her ticket and moved away from the window, trying to read what was on it in the half-light and saying peevishly, 'I *told* them it was too far away. I can't see if I'm far away. I *said* three and sixpence.'

She held the ticket close up to her eyes, trying to read it; she did not notice the step, stumbled and sat down. Peter hurried forward.

'Angela, are you all right? Have you hurt yourself?'

'Perfectly all right,' said Angela, sitting quietly in the twilight. 'Not hurt at all, thank you.'

'Well for God's sake get up.'

Angela squinnied up at him from the step.

'*Peter*,' she said, 'I didn't recognize you. Too far away to recognize anyone in the five and ninepennies. *How* are you?'

'Angela, do get up.'

He held out his hand to help her up. She took it cordially. 'How's Margot?' she said affably. 'Haven't seen her lately. I've been so busy. Well, that's not quite true. As a matter of fact I've not been altogether well.'

A crowd was beginning to assemble in the twilight. From the darkness beyond came the voice of the commissionaire, policemanlike, saying, 'What's going on here?'

'Pick her up, you coot,' said Molly Meadowes.

Peter got behind Angela, put his arms round her and picked her up. She was not heavy.

'Ups-a-daisy,' said Angela, making to sit down again.

Peter held her firm; he was glad of the darkness; this was no position for an officer of the Household Cavalry in uniform.

'A lady has fainted,' said Molly in a clear, authoritative voice. 'Please don't crowd round her,' and to the commissionaire, 'Call a cab.'

Angela was silent in the taxi.

'I say,' said Peter, 'I can't apologize enough for letting you in for this.'

'My dear man,' said Molly, 'don't be ridiculous. I'm thoroughly enjoying it.'

'I can't think what's the matter with her,' he said.

'Can't you?'

When they reached Grosvenor Square, Angela got out of the taxi and looked about her, puzzled. 'I thought we were going to the cinema,' she said. 'Wasn't it good?'

'It was full.'

'I remember,' said Angela, nodding vigorously. 'Five and nines.' Then she sat down again on the pavement.

'Look here,' said Peter to Lady Mary Meadowes. 'You take the taxi back to the cinema. Leave my ticket at the box-office. I'll join you in half an hour. I think I'd better see Angela home and get hold of a doctor.'

'Bumbles,' said Molly. 'I'm coming up too.'

Outside her door Angela suddenly rallied, found her key, opened the flat and walked steadily in. Grainger was still up.

'You need not have stayed in,' said Angela. 'I told you I shouldn't want you.'

'I was worried. You shouldn't have gone out like that,' and then seeing Peter, 'Oh, good evening, my lord.'

Angela turned and saw Peter, as though for the first time. 'Hullo, Peter,' she said. 'Come in.' She fixed Molly with eyes that seemed to focus with difficulty. 'You know,' she said, 'I'm sure I know you quite well, but I can't remember your name.'

'Molly Meadowes,' said Peter. 'We just came to see you home. We must be going along now. Grainger, Mrs Lyne isn't at all well. I think you ought to get her doctor.'

'Molly Meadowes. My dear, I used to stay at Granchester when you were in the nursery. How old that sounds. You're very pretty, Molly, and you're wearing a lovely dress. Come in, both of you.'

Peter frowned at Molly, but she went into the flat.

'Help yourself to something to drink, Peter,' said Angela. She sat down in her armchair by the radio. 'My dear,' she said to Molly, 'I don't think you've seen my flat. I had it done up by David Lennox just before the war. David Lennox. People say unkind things about David Lennox . . . well, you can't blame them . . .' her mind was becoming confused again. She made a resolute attempt to regain control of herself. 'That's a portrait of me by John. Ten years ago; nearly done when I was married. Those are my books . . . my dear, I'm afraid I'm rather distraite this evening. You must forgive me,' and, so saying, she fell into a heavy sleep.

Peter looked about him helplessly. Molly said to Grainger, 'Had we better get her to bed?'

'When she wakes up, I shall be here. I can manage.'

'Sure?'

'Quite sure.'

'Well then, Peter, we'd better get back to our film.'

'Yes,' said Peter. 'I'm awfully sorry for bringing you here.'

'I wouldn't have missed it for anything,' said Molly.

Peter was still puzzled by the whole business.

'Grainger,' he said. 'Had Mrs Lyne been out this evening? To a party or anything?'

'Oh, no, my lord. She's been in all day.'

'Alone?'

'Quite alone, my lord.'

'Extraordinary thing. Well come on, Molly. Good night, Grainger. Take care of Mrs Lyne. I think she ought to see a doctor.'

'I'll take care of her,' said Grainger.

They went down in the lift together, in silence, each full of thought. When they reached the hall Peter said, 'Well, that was rum.'

'Very rum.'

'You know,' said Peter, 'if it had been anyone else but Angela, I should have thought she was tight.'

'Darling, she was plastered.'

'Are you sure?'

'My dear, stinko paralytico.'

'Well, I don't know what to think. It certainly looked like it. But *Angela* . . . besides her maid said she hadn't been out all the evening. I mean to say people don't get tight alone.'

Suddenly Molly put her arms round Peter's neck and kissed him warmly. 'Bless you,' she said. 'Now we'll go to that cinema.'

It was the first time anyone had ever kissed Peter like that. He was so surprised that in the taxi he made no attempt to follow it up; so surprised that he thought about nothing else all through the film. 'God Save the King' brought him back to a reality with a jolt. He was still pensive while he led Molly to supper. It was hysteria, he decided; the girl was naturally upset at the scene they had been through. She's probably frightfully embarrassed about it now; best not to refer to it.

But Molly was not prepared to let the matter drop.

'Oysters,' she said. 'Only a dozen. Nothing else,' and then, though the waiter was still beside her, 'Were you surprised when I kissed you just now?'

'No,' said Peter hastily, 'certainly not. Not at all.'

'Not at all? You mean to say you *expected* me to?'

'No, no. Of course not. You know what I mean.'

'I certainly don't. I think it's very conceited of you not to be surprised. Do you always have this effect on girls, or is it just the uniform?'

'Molly, don't be a beast. If you must know, I *was* surprised.'

'And shocked?'

'No, just surprised.'

'Yes,' said Molly, seeing it was not kind to tease him any more. 'I was surprised, too. I've been wondering about it in the cinema.'

'So have I,' said Peter.

'*That's* how I like you,' said Molly, as though she were a photographer catching a happy expression. She saw the likeness herself and added, 'Hold it.'

'Really, Molly, I don't understand you a bit to-night.'

'Oh but you must, really you must, Peter. I'm sure you were a fascinating little boy.'

'Come to think of it, I believe I was.'

'You mustn't ever try playing the old rip again, Peter. Not with me, at any rate. Now don't pretend you don't understand that. I like you puzzled, Peter, but not *absolutely cretinous*. You know, I nearly despaired of you to-night. You would go on bucking about what a gay dog you'd been. I thought I could never go through with it.'

'Through with what?'

'Marrying you. Mother's terribly keen I should, though I can't think why. I should have thought from her point of view you were about the end. But no, nothing else would do but that I must marry you. So I've tried to be good and I've let you bound away about the good old days till I thought I should have to pour something on your head. Thought I couldn't bear it any more and I'd decided to tell mother it was off. Then we met Mrs Lyne and everything was all right.'

'It seemed awfully awkward to me.'

'Of course it did. You looked like a little boy at his private school when his father has come to the sports in the wrong kind of hat. An adorable little boy.'

'Well,' said Peter, 'I suppose as long as you're satisfied . . .'

'Yes, I think "satisfied" is the word. You'll do. And Sarah and Betty'll be as sick as cats.'

'How did you decide?' asked Margot, when Peter told her of his engagement.

'Well, as a matter of fact, I don't think I did. Molly decided.'

'Yes, that's usually the way. Now I suppose I shall have to do something friendly about that ass Emma Granchester.'

'I really know Lady Metroland very little,' said Lady Granchester. 'But I suppose now I must invite her to luncheon. I'm afraid she's far too smart for us.' And by 'smart' Lady Granchester meant nothing at all complimentary.

But the mothers met and decided on an immediate marriage.

IV

The news of Peter's engagement was not unexpected and, even had it come as a surprise, would have been eclipsed in interest by the story of Angela Lyne's uncharacteristic behaviour at the cinema. Peter and Molly, before parting that night, had resolved to tell no one of the incident; a renunciation from which each made certain implicit reservations. Peter told Margot because he thought she ought to do something about it, Basil because he was still dubious about the true explanation of the mystery and thought that Basil, if anyone could, would throw light on it, and three members of Bratts because he happened to run into them at the bar next morning when his mind was still full of the matter. Molly told her two sisters and Lady Sarah from long habit, because whenever she promised secrecy in any matter she meant, even at the time, to tell these three. These initiates in their turn told their cronies until it was widely known that the temperate, cynical, aloof, impeccably dressed, sharply dignified Mrs Lyne; Mrs Lyne who never 'went out' in a general sense but lived in a rarefied and enviable coterie; Mrs Lyne whose conversation was that of a highly intelligent man, who always cleverly kept out of the gossip columns and picture papers, who for fifteen years had set a high and wholly individual standard of all that Americans meant by 'poise'; this almost proverbial lady had been picked up by Peter in the gutter where she had been thrown struggling by two bouncers from the cinema where she had created a drunken disturbance.

It could scarcely have been more surprising had it been Mrs Stitch herself. It was indeed barely credible and many refused to believe it. Drugs possibly, they conceded, but Drink was out of the question. What Parsnip and Pimpernell were to the intelligentsia, Mrs Lyne and the bottle became to the fashionable world; topic number one.

It was still topic number one three months later at Peter's wedding. Basil persuaded Angela to come to the little party with which Lady Granchester honoured the occasion.

He had gone round to see her when Peter told him the news; not immediately, but within twenty-four hours of hearing it. He found her up and dressed, but indefinably raffish in appearance; her make-up was haphazard and rather garish, like a later Utrillo.

'Angela you look awful.'

'Yes, darling, I feel awful. You're in the army.'

'No, the War Office.'

She began talking intensely and rather wildly about the French. Presently she said, 'I must leave you for a minute,' and went into her bedroom. She came back half a minute later with an abstracted little smile; the inwardly happy smile of a tired old nun–almost. There was a difference.

'Angela,' said Basil, 'if you want a drink you might drink fair with a chap.'

'I don't know what you mean,' she said.

Basil was shocked. There had never been any humbug about Angela before, none where he was concerned anyway.

'Oh, come off it,' he said.

Angela came off it. She began to weep.

'Oh, for Christ's sake,' said Basil.

He went into her bedroom and helped himself to whisky from the bottle by the bed.

'Peter was here the other evening with some girl. I suppose they've told everyone.'

'He told *me*. Why don't you switch to rum? It's much better for you.'

'Is it? I don't think I've ever tasted it. Should I like it?'

'I'll send you some round. When did you start on this bat?'

There was no humbug about Angela now. 'Oh, weeks ago.'

'It's not a bit like you.'

'Isn't it, Basil? Isn't it?'

'You were always bloody to me when I had a bat.'

'Yes, I suppose I was. I'm sorry. But then you see I was in love with you.'

'Was?'

'Oh, I don't know. Fill up the glasses, Basil.'

'That's the girl.'

'"Was" is wrong. I do love you, Basil.'

'Of course you do. Is that how you take it?' he asked, respectfully.

'That's how I take it.'

'Good and strong.'

'Good and strong.'

'But I think we'd be better suited to rum.'

'Doesn't it smell rather?'

'I don't see it matters.'

'Don't want to smell.'

'Whisky smells.'

'Well, I suppose it doesn't matter. It's nice drinking with you, Basil.'

'Of course it's nice. I think it's pretty mean of you to drink without me as you've been doing.'

'I'm not mean.'

'You usen't to be. But you have been lately, haven't you? Drinking by yourself.'

'Yes, that was mean.'

'Now listen, next time you want to go on a bat, let me know. Just ring me up and I'll come round. Then we can drink together.'

'But I want to so often, Basil.'

'Well, I'll come round often. Promise me.'

'I promise.'

'That's the girl.'

The rum was a failure, but in general the new arrangement worked well. Angela drank a good deal less and Basil a good deal more than they had done for the last few weeks and both were happier as a result.

Margot tackled Basil on the matter. 'What's the matter with her?' she asked.

'She doesn't like the war.'

'Well, no one does.'

'Don't they? I can't think why not. Anyway, why shouldn't the girl have a drink?'

'You don't think we ought to get her into a home?'

'Good God, no.'

'But she sees nobody.'

'She sees me.'

'Yes, but. . .'

'Honestly, Margot, Angela's fine. A little break like this is what she's been needing all these years. I'll make her come to the wedding if you like and you can see for yourself.'

So Angela came to the wedding. She and Basil did not make the church but they came to the little party at Lady Granchester's house afterwards, and stole the scene. Molly had had her moment of prominence; she had had her double line of troopers and her arch of cavalry sabres; she had had her veil of old lace. In spite of the war it was a pretty wedding. But at her mother's house all eyes were on Mrs Lyne. Even Lady Anchorage and the Duchess of Stayle could not dissemble their interest.

'My dear, *there she is.*'

There she was, incomparably dressed, standing by Basil, talking gravely to Sonia; she wore dark glasses; otherwise there was nothing unusual about her. A footman brought a tray of champagne. 'Is there such a thing as a cup of tea,' she said, 'without cream or sugar?'

Molly and Peter stood at one end of the long drawing-room, Angela at the other. As the guests filed past the bride and bridegroom and came into the straight, you could see them come to the alert at the sight of Angela and draw one another's attention to her. Her own coterie formed round her and she talked like a highly intelligent man. When the last of the guests had shaken hands with them–they were comparatively few–Molly and Peter joined the group at the far end.

'Molly, you are the prettiest girl I've ever seen,' said Angela. 'I'm afraid I was a bore the other night.'

A silly girl would have been embarrassed and said, 'No, not at all.' Molly said, 'Not a *bore*. You were rather odd.'

'Yes,' said Angela. '"Odd" is the word. I'm not always like that, you know.'

'May Peter and I come and see you again? He's only got a week, you know, and then we shall be in London.'

'That's an unusually good girl Peter's picked for himself,' said Angela to Basil when they were alone after the party at her flat. 'You ought to marry someone like that.'

'I could never marry anyone, except, I suppose, you.'

'No, I don't believe you could, Basil.'

When their glasses were filled she said, 'I seem to be getting to the age when I enjoy weddings. I liked that girl this afternoon. D'you know who was here this morning? Cedric.'

'How very odd.'

'It was rather touching really. He came to say good-bye. He's off to-morrow. He couldn't say where, but I guess it's Norway. I never thought of him as a soldier, somehow, but he used to be one till he married me–a very bad one I believe. Poor Cedric, he's had a raw deal.'

'He's not done so badly. He's enjoyed himself messing about with grottoes. And he's had Nigel.'

'He brought Nigel this morning. They gave him a day away from school to say good-bye. You never knew Cedric when I married him. He was most romantic–genuinely. I'd never met anyone like him. Father's friends were all hard-boiled and rich–men like Metroland and Copper. They were the only people I ever saw. And then I met Cedric who was poor and very, very soft-boiled and tall and willowy and very unhappy in a boring smart regiment because he only cared about Russian ballet and baroque architecture. He had the most charming manner and he was always laughing up his sleeve about people like my father and his officers in the regiment. Poor Cedric, it used to be such fun finding things to give him. I bought him an octopus once and we had a case made for its tank, carved with dolphins and covered with silver leaf.'

'It wouldn't have lasted, even if I hadn't come along.'

'No, it wouldn't have lasted. I'm afraid the visit this morning was rather a disappointment to him. He'd planned it all in an attitude of high tragedy, and, my dear, I had such a hangover I had to keep my eyes shut nearly all the time he was here. He's worried about what will happen to the house if he gets killed.'

'Why should he get killed?'

'Why, indeed? Except that he was always such a bad soldier. You know, when the war started I quite made up my mind you were for it.'

'So did my mother. But I'm taking care of that. Which reminds me I ought to go and see Colonel Plum again. He'll be getting restive. I'll go along now.'

'Will he be there?'

'He never leaves. A very conscientious officer.'

Susie was there, too, waiting till the Colonel was free to take her out to dinner. At the sight of the office, some of Basil's elation began to fade away. Basil's job at the War Office looked like going the way of all the others; once secured, it had few attractions for him. Susie was proving a disappointment; in spite of continued remonstrance, she still seemed to prefer Colonel Plum.

'Good evening, handsome,' she said. 'Plummy has been asking for you.'

Basil went through the door marked KEEP OUT.

'Good evening, Colonel.'

'You can call me "sir".'

'None of the best regiments call their commanding officers "sir".'

'You're not in one of the best regiments. You're General Service. What have you been doing all day?'

'You don't think it will improve the tone of the department if I called you "Colonel", sir?'

'I do not. Where have you been and what have you been doing?'

'You think I've been drinking, don't you?'

'I bloody well know you have.'

'But you don't know the reason. You wouldn't understand if I told you. I've been drinking out of chivalry. That doesn't make any sense to you, does it?'

'No.'

'I thought it wouldn't. Coarse grained, sir. If they put on my grave, "He drank out of chivalry", it would simply be the sober truth. But you wouldn't understand. What's more you think I've been idle, don't you?'

'I do.'

'Well, sir, that's where you're wrong. I have been following up a very interesting trail. I hope to have some valuable information very soon.'

'What have you got up to date?'

'You wouldn't sooner wait until I can give you the whole case cut and dried?'

'No.'

'Well, I'm on to a very dangerous woman who calls herself Green. Among her intimates she's known as "Poppet". She pretends to be a painter, but you have only to look at her work to realize it is a cloak for other activities. Her studio is the meeting place for a communist cell. She has an agent in the United States named Parsnip; he has the alias of Pimpernell; he puts it about that he is a poet, two poets in fact, but there again, the work betrays him. Would you like me to quote some Parsnip to you?'

'No.'

'I have reason to believe that Green is the head of an underground organization by which young men of military age are smuggled out of the country. Those are the lines I have been working on. What d'you think of them?'

'Rotten.'

'I was afraid you might say that. It's your own fault. Give me time and I would have had a better story.'

'Now you can do some work. Here's a list of thirty-three addresses of suspected fascists. Check them up.'

'Now?'

'Now.'

'Shan't I keep track of the woman Green?'

'Not in office hours.'

'I can't think what you see in your Plum,' said Basil when he regained the outer office. 'It must simply be snobbery.'

'It's not: it's love. The officer in the pensions office was a full Colonel, so there.'

'I expect you'll be reduced to subalterns, yet. And by the way, lance-corporal, you can call me "sir".'

Susie giggled. 'I believe you're drunk,' she said.

'Drunk with chivalry,' said Basil.

That evening Cedric Lyne left to rejoin his regiment. The forty-eight hours' embarkation leave was over and although he had chosen to start an hour earlier rather than travel by the special train, it was only with difficulty that he found a carriage free from brother officers who had made the same choice. They were going to the North to embark at dawn next day and sail straight into action.

The first-class carriage was quite full, four a side, and the racks were piled high with baggage. Black funnel-shaped shields cast the light on to the passengers' laps; their faces in the surrounding darkness were indistinguishable; a naval paymaster-commander slept peacefully in one corner; two civilians strained their eyes over the evening papers; the other four were soldiers. Cedric sat between two soldiers, stared at the shadowy luggage above the civilians' heads, and ruminated, chewing the last, bitter essence from the events of the last two days.

Because he was thirty-five years of age, and spoke French and was built rather for grace than smartness, they had made Cedric battalion intelligence officer. He kept the war diary, and on wet days was often borrowed by the company commanders to lecture on map reading, security, and the order of battle of a German infantry division. These were Cedric's three lectures. When they were exhausted he was sent on a gas-course and after that on a course of interpretation of air photographs. On exercise he stuck pins in a map and kept a file of field messages.

'There really isn't very much you can do until we get into action,' said his commanding officer. 'You might ring up the photographers in Aldershot about taking that regimental group.'

They put him in charge of the Officers' Mess and made his visits there hideous with complaints.

'We're out of Kümmel again, Cedric.'

'Surely there's some perfectly simple way of keeping the soup hot, Lyne.'

'If officers *will* take the papers to their quarters, the only answer is to order more papers.'

'The Stilton has been allowed to go dry again.'

That had been his life; but Nigel did not know this. For Nigel, at eight years of age, his father was a man-at-arms and a hero. When they were given embarkation leave, Cedric telephoned to Nigel's headmaster and the child met him at their station in the country. Pride in his father and pleasure at an unforeseen holiday made their night at home an enthralling experience for Nigel. The home was given over to empty wards and an idle hospital staff. Cedric and his son stayed in the farm where, before she left, Angela had fitted up a few rooms with furniture from the house. Nigel was full of questions; why Cedric's buttons were differently arranged from the fathers' and brothers' buttons of most of the fellows; what was the difference between a Bren and a Vickers; how much faster were our fighters than the Germans'; whether Hitler had fits, as one fellow said, and, if so, did he froth at the mouth and roll his eyes as the girl at the lodge had once done.

That evening, Cedric took a long farewell of his water garden. It was for the water principally that he and Angela had chosen the place, ten years ago, when they were first engaged. It rose in a clear and copious spring in the hillside above the house and fell in a series of natural cascades to join the considerable stream which flowed more solemnly through the park. He and Angela had eaten a picnic lunch by this spring and looked down on the symmetrical, rectangular building below.

'It'll do,' said Angela. 'I'll offer them fifteen thousand.'

It never embarrassed Cedric to be married to a rich woman. He had not married for money in any gross sense, but he loved the rare and beautiful things which money could buy, and Angela's great fortune made her trebly rare and beautiful in his eyes.

It was surprising that they should have met at all. Cedric had been for years in his regiment, kept there by his father who gave him an allowance, which he could ill spare, on that condition alone. It was that or an office for Cedric and, despite the tedious company, there was just enough pageantry about peace-time soldiering to keep his imagination engaged. Cedric was accomplished; he beautiful horseman but hated the rigours of fox-hunting; he was a very fine shot, and because that formed a single tenuous bond with his brother officers and because it was agreeable to do anything pre-eminently well, he accepted invitations to pheasant-shooting in houses where, when they were not at the coverts, he felt lost and lonely. Angela's father had a celebrated shoot in Norfolk; he had also, Cedric was told, a collection of French impressionists. Thither that autumn ten years ago Cedric had gone and found the pictures too obvious and the birds too tame and the party tedious beyond description, except for Angela, past her debutante days, aloof now and living in a cool and mysterious solitude of her own creation. She had resisted at first every attempt on the the defences she had built up against a noisy world and then, quite suddenly, she had accepted Cedric as being like herself a stranger in these parts, as being, unlike herself, full of understanding of another, more splendid, attainable world outside. Angela's father thought Cedric a poor fellow, settled vast sums on them, and let them go their own way.

And this was the way they had gone. Cedric stood by the spring, enshrined, now, in a little temple. The architrave was covered with stalactites, the dome was set with real shells and the clear water bubbled out from the feet of a Triton. Cedric and Angela had bought this temple on their honeymoon at a deserted villa in the hills behind Naples.

Below in the hillside lay the cave which Cedric had bought the summer that Angela had refused to come with him to Salzburg; the summer when she met Basil. The lonely and humiliating years after that summer each had its monument.

'Daddy, what are you waiting for?'

'I'm just looking at the grottoes.'

'But you've seen them thousands of times. They're always the same.'

Always the same; joys for ever; not like men and women with their loves and hates.

'Daddy, there's an aeroplane. Is it a Hurricane?'

'No, Nigel, a Spitfire.'

'How d'you tell the difference?'

Then, on an impulse, he had said, 'Nigel, shall we go to London and see mummy?'

'We might see "The Lion has Wings" too. The fellows say it's awfully decent.'

'All right, Nigel, we'll see both.'

So the two of them went to London by the early morning train. 'Let's surprise her,' said Nigel, but Cedric telephoned first, wryly remembering the story of the pedantic adulterer–'My dear, it is *I* who am *surprised; you* are *astounded*.'

'I am coming round to see Mrs Lyne.'

'She isn't very well this morning.'

'I'm sorry to hear that. Is she able to see people?'

'Yes, I think so, sir. I'll ask . . . yes, madam will be very pleased to see you and Master Nigel.'

They had not met for three years, since they discussed the question of divorce. Cedric understood exactly what Angela had felt about that; it was curious, he reflected, how some people were shy of divorce because of their love of society; they did not want there to be any occasion when their presence might be an embarrassment, they wanted to keep their tickets for the Ascot enclosure. With Angela reluctance came from precisely the opposite motives; she could not brook any intrusion on her privacy; she did not want to answer questions in court or allow the daily paper a single item of information about herself. 'It's not as though you wanted to marry anyone else, Cedric.'

'You don't think the present arrangement makes me look rather foolish?'

'Cedric, what's come over you? You used not to talk like that.'

So he had given way and that year had spanned the stream with a bridge in the Chinese Taste, taken direct from Batty Langley.

In the five minutes of waiting before Grainger took him into Angela's bedroom, he studied David Lennox's grisailles with distaste.

'Are they old, Daddy?'

'No, Nigel, they're not old.'

'They're awfully feeble.'

'They are.' Regency: this was the age of Waterloo and highwaymen and duelling and slavery and revivalist preaching and Nelson having his arm off with no anaesthetic but rum, and Botany Bay–and *this* is what they make of it.

'Well, I prefer the pictures at home, even if they are old. Is that mummy?'

'Yes.'

'Is that old?'

'Older than you, Nigel.'

Cedric turned from the portrait of Angela. What a nuisance John had been about the sittings. It was her father who had insisted on their going to him.

'Is it finished?'

'Yes. It was very hard to make the man finish it, though.'

'It hardly looks finished now, does it Daddy? It's all sploshy.'

Then Grainger opened the door. 'Come in, Cedric,' Angela called from her bed.

Angela was wearing dark glasses. Her make-up things lay on the quilt before her, with which she had been hastily doing her face. Nigel might have asked if it was finished; it was sploshy, like the John portrait.

'I had no idea you were ill,' said Cedric stiffly.

'I'm not really. Nigel, haven't you got a kiss for mummy?'

'Why are you wearing those glasses?'

'My eyes are tired, darling.'

'Tired of what?'

'Cedric,' said Angela petulantly, 'for God's sake don't let him be a bore. Go with Miss Grainger into the next room, darling.'

'Oh, all right,' said Nigel. 'Don't be long, Daddy.'

'You and he seem to be buddies these days.'

'Yes, it's the uniform.'

'Funny your being in the army again.'

'I'm off to-night, abroad.'

'France?'

'I don't think so. I mustn't tell about it. That's why I came to see you.'

'About not talking about not going to France?' said Angela in something of her old teasing way.

Cedric began to talk about the house; he hoped Angela would keep on to it, even if anything happened to him; he thought he saw some glimmerings of taste in the boy; he might grow to appreciate it later. Angela was inattentive and answered absently.

'I'm afraid I'm tiring you.'

'Well, I'm not feeling terribly well to-day. Did you want to see me about anything special?'

'No, I don't think so. Just to say good-bye.'

'Daddy,' came a voice from the next room. 'Aren't you coming?'

'Oh, dear, I wish I could do something about it. I feel there's something I ought to do. It's quite an occasion really, isn't it? I'm not being beastly, Cedric, I really mean it. I think it's sweet of you to come. I only wish I felt up to doing something about it.'

'Daddy, come on. We want to get to Bassett-Lowke's before lunch.'

'Take care of yourself,' said Angela.

'Why?'

'Oh, I don't know. Why will you all ask questions?'

And that had been the end of the visit. At Bassett-Lowke's, Nigel had chosen a model of a Blenheim bomber. 'The fellows *will* be jealous,' he said.

After luncheon they went to see 'The Lion has Wings', and then it was time to put Nigel into the train back to school. 'It's been absolutely ripping, Daddy,' he said.

'Has it really?'

'The rippingest two days I ever spent.'

So after these ripping days Cedric sat in the half-dark, with the pool of light falling on the unread book on his knees, returning to duty.

Basil went to the Café Royal to keep his watch on 'the woman Green'. He found her sitting among her cronies and was greeted with tepid affection.

'So you're in the army now,' she said.

'No, the great uniformed bureaucracy. How are all the Reds?'

'Very well thank you, watching your imperialists making a mess of your war.'

'Been to many communist meetings lately?'

'Why?'

'Just wondering.'

'You sound like a police spy.'

'That's the very last impression I want to make,' and, changing the subject hastily, added 'Seen Ambrose lately?'

'He's over there now, the lousy fascist.'

Basil looked where she indicated and saw Ambrose at a table by the rail of the opposing gallery, sitting with a little, middle-aged man of nondescript appearance.

'Did you say "fascist"?'

'Didn't you know? He's gone to the Ministry of Information and he's bringing out a fascist paper next month.'

'This is very interesting,' said Basil. 'Tell me some more.'

Ambrose sat, upright and poised, with one hand on the stem of his glass and one resting stylishly on the balustrade. There was no particular feature of his clothes which could be mentioned as conspicuous; he wore a dark, smooth suit that fitted perhaps a little closely at waist and wrists, a shirt of plain, cream-coloured silk; a dark, white spotted bow tie; his sleek black hair was not unduly long (he went to the same barber as Alastair and Peter); his pale Semitic face gave no hint of special care and yet it always embarrassed Mr Bentley somewhat to be seen with him in public. Sitting there, gesticulating very slightly as he talked, wagging his head very slightly, raising his voice occasionally in a suddenly stressed uncommon epithet or in a fragment of slang embedded in his precise and literary diction, giggling between words now and then as something which he had intended to say changed shape and became unexpectedly comic in the telling–Ambrose like this caused time to slip back to an earlier age than his own youth or Mr Bentley's, when amid a more splendid décor of red plush and gilt caryatides *fin-de-siècle* young worshippers crowded to the tables of Oscar and Aubrey.

Mr Bentley smoothed his sparse grey hairs and fidgeted with his tie and looked about anxiously for fear he was observed.

The Café Royal, perhaps because of its distant associations with Oscar and Aubrey, was one of the places where Ambrose preened himself, spread his feathers and felt free to take wing. He had left his persecution mania downstairs with his hat and umbrella. He defied the universe.

'The decline of England, my dear Geoffrey,' he said, 'dates from the day we abandoned coal fuel. No, I'm not talking about distressed areas, but about distressed *souls*, my dear. We used to live in a fog, the splendid, luminous, tawny fogs of our early childhood. The golden aura of the Golden Age. Think of it, Geoffrey, there are children now coming to manhood who never saw a London fog. We designed a city which was meant to be seen in a fog. We had a foggy habit of life and a rich, obscure, choking literature. The great catch in the throat of English lyric poetry is just *fog*, my dear, on the vocal chords. And out of the fog we could rule the world; we were a Voice, like the Voice of Sinai smiling through the clouds. Primitive peoples always choose a God who speaks from a cloud. *Then*, my dear Geoffrey,' said Ambrose, wagging an accusing finger and fixing Mr Bentley with a black accusing eye, as though the poor publisher were personally responsible for the whole thing, '*then*, some busybody invents electricity or oil fuel or whatever it is they use nowadays. The fog lifts, the world sees us as we are, and worse still we see ourselves as we are. It was a carnival ball, my dear, which when the guests unmasked at midnight, was found to be composed entirely of imposters. Such a *rumpus*, my dear.'

Ambrose drained his glass with a swagger, surveyed the café haughtily and saw Basil, who was making his way towards them.

'We are talking of fogs,' said Mr Bentley.

'They're eaten hollow with communism,' said Basil, introducing himself in the part of *agent provocateur*. 'You can't stop a rot that's been going on twenty years by imprisoning a handful of deputies. Half the thinking men in France have begun looking to Germany as their real ally.'

'*Please* Basil, don't start politics. Anyway, we were talking of Fogs, not Frogs.'

'Oh, Fogs.' Basil attempted to tell of a foggy adventure of his own, sailing a yawl round Bear Island, but Ambrose was elated to-night and in no mood for these loose leaves of Conrad drifting in the high wind of his talk. 'We must return to the Present,' he said prophetically.

'Oh dear,' said Mr Bentley. 'Why?'

'Everyone is either looking back or forward. Those with reverence and good taste, like you, my dear Geoffrey, look back to an Augustan age; those with generous hearts and healthy lives and the taste of the devil, like Poppet Green over there, look forward to a Marxian Jerusalem. *We* must accept the Present.'

'You would say, wouldn't you,' said Basil, persevering, 'that Hitler was a figure of the present?'

'I regard him as a page for *Punch*,' said Ambrose. 'To the Chinese scholar the military hero was the lowest of human types, the subject for ribaldry. We must return to Chinese scholarship.'

'It's a terribly difficult language, I believe,' said Mr Bentley.

'I knew a Chink in Valparaiso . . .' began Basil; but Ambrose was now in full gallop.

'European scholarship has never lost its monastic character,' he said. 'Chinese scholarship deals with taste and wisdom, not with the memorizing of facts. In China the man whom we make a don sat for the Imperial examinations and became a bureaucrat. Their scholars were lonely men of few books and fewer pupils, content with a single concubine, a pine tree and the prospect of a stream. European culture has become conventional; we must make it cenobitic.'

'I knew a hermit in the Ogaden desert once . . .'

'Invasions swept over China; the Empire split up into warring kingdoms. The scholars lived their frugal and idyllic lives undisturbed, occasionally making exquisite private jokes which they wrote on leaves and floated downstream.'

'I read a lot of Chinese poetry once,' said Mr Bentley, 'in the translation, of course. I became fascinated by it. I would read of a sage who, as you say, lived frugally and idyllically. He had a cottage and a garden and a view. Each flower had its proper mood and phase of the climate; he would smell the jasmine after recovering from the toothache and the lotus when drinking tea with a monk. There was a little clearing where the full moon cast no shadow, where his concubine would sit and sing to him when he got drunk. Every aspect of this little garden corresponded to some personal mood of the most tender and refined sort. It was quite intoxicating to read.'

'It is.'

'This sage had no tame dog, but he had a cat and a mother. Every morning he greeted his mother on his knees and every evening, in winter, he put charcoal under her mattress and himself drew the bed-curtains. It sounded the most exquisite existence.'

'It was.'

'And then,' said Mr Bentley, 'I found a copy of the *Daily Mirror* in a railway carriage and I read an article there by Godfrey Winn about his cottage and his flowers and his moods, and for the life of me, Ambrose, I couldn't see the difference between that young gentleman and Yuan Ts'e-tsung.'

It was cruel of Mr Bentley to say this, but it may be argued for him that he had listened to Ambrose for three hours and now that Basil had joined their table he wanted to go home to bed.

The interruption deflated Ambrose and allowed Basil to say, 'These scholars of yours, Ambrose–they didn't care if their empire was invaded?'

'Not a hoot, my dear, not a *tinker's* hoot.'

'And you're starting a paper to encourage this sort of scholarship.'

Basil sat back and ordered a drink, as an advocate in a film will relax, saying in triumph, 'Mr District Attorney, *your* witness.'

There were four hours of darkness to go when Cedric arrived at the port of embarkation. There was a glimmer of light in some of the offices along the quayside, but the quay itself and the ship were in complete darkness; the top-hamper was just discernible as a darker mass against the dark sky. An E.S.O. told Cedric to leave his gear on the quay. The advanced working party were handling that. He left his valise and carried his suitcase up the gangway; at the head an invisible figure directed him to the first-class quarters forward. He found his C.O. in the saloon.

'Hullo, Lyne. You're back already. Lucky. Billy Allgood broke his collar-bone on leave and isn't coming with us. You'd better take charge of the embarkation. There's a hell of a lot to do. Some blasted Highlanders have come to the wrong ship and are all over our troop decks. Had any dinner?'

'I got some oysters in London before starting.'

'Very wise. I tried to get something kept hot. Told them we should all be coming on board hungry, but they're still working peace-time routine here. This is all I could raise.'

He pointed to a large, silvery tray where, disposed on a napkin, lay a dozen lozenges of toast covered with sardines, slivers of cheese and little glazed pieces of tongue. This was the tray that was always brought to the first-class saloon at ten o'clock at night.

'Come back when you've found your cabin.'

Cedric found his cabin, perfectly in order, complete with three towels of different sizes and the photograph of a mustachioed man putting on his life-jacket in the correct manner. He left his suitcase and returned to the C.O.

'Our men will be coming on board in an hour and a half. I don't know what the devil these Highlanders are doing. Find out and clear them off.'

'Very good, Colonel.'

Cedric plunged down again into the darkness and found the E.S.O. They studied the embarkation orders with the aid of a dimmed torch. There was no doubt about it; the Highlanders were in the wrong ship. This was the *Duchess of Cumberland;* they should be in the *Duchess of Clarence*. 'But the *Clarence* isn't here,' said the E.S.O. 'I dare say they were told to go to the *Cumberland* by someone.'

'By whom?'

'Not by me, old man,' said the E.S.O.

Cedric went on board and looked for the C.O. of the Highlanders and found him at length in his cabin asleep in his battledress.

'These are my orders,' said the Highland Colonel, taking a sheaf of typewritten sheets from the pocket on his thigh. They were already tattered and smeared by constant reference. '*Duchess of Cumberland*. Embark 23·00 hrs with full 1097 stores. That's plain enough.'

'But our men come on board in an hour.'

'Can't help you, I'm afraid. These are my orders.'

He was not going to discuss the matter with a subaltern. Cedric fetched his

C.O. Colonel to Colonel they talked the thing out and decided to clear the after troop decks. Cedric was sent to wake the Highland duty officer. He found the duty sergeant. Together they went aft to the troop decks.

There were dim lights along the ceiling–electric bulbs recently daubed with blue paint, not yet scratched clear by the troops. Equipment and kit-bags lay about the deck in heaps; there were Bren gun boxes and ammunition and the huge coffin-shaped chests of the anti-tank rifles.

'Oughtn't that to be stored in the armoury?' asked Cedric.

'Not unless you want to get it pinched.'

Amid the heaps of stores half a battalion lay huddled in blankets. Very few of them, on this first night, had slung hammocks. These lay, with the other gear, adding to the piles.

'We'll never get them moved to-night.'

'We've got to try,' said Cedric.

Very slowly the inert mass was got into movement. They began collecting their own gear and swearing monotonously. Working parties began man-handling the stores. They had to go up the ladders on to the main deck, forward through the darkness and down the forward hatches.

Presently a voice from the top of the ladder said, 'Is Lyne down there?'

'Yes.'

'I've been told to bring my company to this troop deck.'

'They'll have to wait.'

'They're coming on board now.'

'Well for God's sake stop them.'

'But isn't this D deck?'

'Yes.'

'Then this is where we are to come to. Who the hell are all these men?'

Cedric went up the ladder and to the head of the gangway. A stream of heavily-laden men of his regiment were toiling up. 'Go back,' ordered Cedric.

'Who the hell's that?' asked a voice from the darkness.

'Lyne. Take your men back to the quay. They can't come on board yet.'

'Oh, but they've got to. D'you realize half of them've had nothing to eat since midday?'

'There's nothing to eat here till breakfast.'

'Oh but, I say, what rot. The R.T.O. at Euston said he'd telegraph through and have a hot meal ready on arrival. Where's the Colonel?'

The line of soldiers on the gangway turned about and began a slow descent. When the last of them was on the quay, invisible in the darkness, their officer came on board.

'You seem to have made a pretty good muck-up,' he said.

The deck was full of the other regiment carrying stores.

'There's a man there smoking,' shouted a ship's officer from above. 'Put that cigarette out.'

Matches began to spurt up on the quay. 'Put those cigarettes out, down there.'

'—y well travelling all the —ing day. No —ing supper. —ed about on the —ing quay. Now a — won't let me have a —ing smoke. I'm —ing —ed with being —ed about by these —ers.'

A dark figure passed Cedric muttering desperately. 'Nominal rolls in triplicate. Nominal rolls in triplicate. Why the devil can't they tell us beforehand they want nominal rolls in triplicate?'

Another dark figure whom Cedric recognized as the E.S.O.

'I say, the men are supposed to strip down their equipment and pack it in green sea bags before embarking.'

'Oh,' said Cedric.

'They don't seem to have done it.'

'Oh.'

'It upsets all the storage arrangements if they don't.'

'Oh.'

An orderly came up. 'Mr Lyne, sir, will you go and see the C.O.?'

Cedric went.

'Look here Lyne, aren't those infernal Scotsmen out of our troop decks yet? I ordered that deck to be clear two hours ago. I thought you were looking after that.'

'I'm sorry, Colonel. They're getting a move on now.'

'I should bloody well hope so. And look here, half our men have had nothing to eat all day. Go up to the purser and see what you can rout out for them. And find out on the bridge exactly what the sailing orders are. When the troops come on board see that everyone knows where everything is. We don't want anything lost. We may be in action before the end of the week. I hear these Highlanders lost a lot of kit on the way up. We don't want them making up deficiencies at our expense.'

'Very good, sir.'

As he went out on deck the ghostly figure brushed past him in the darkness muttering in tones that seemed to echo from another and even worse world. 'Nominal rolls in triplicate. Nominal rolls in triplicate.'

At seven o'clock the Colonel said, 'For God's sake someone take over from Lyne. He seems to have lain down on the job.'

Cedric went to his cabin; he was unspeakably tired; all the events and emotions of the last forty-eight hours were lost in the single longing for sleep; he took off his belt and his shoes and lay on his bunk. Within a quarter of a minute he was unconscious; within five minutes he was woken by the steward placing a tray by his side; it contained tea, an apple, a thin slice of brown bread and butter. That was how the day always began on this ship, whether she was cruising to the midnight sun or West Indies. An hour later another steward passed by striking a musical gong with a little hammer. That was the second stage of the day in this ship. He passed, tinkling prettily, through the first-class quarters, threading his path delicately between valises and kitbags. Unshaven, ill-tempered officers who had not been asleep all night scowled at him as he passed. Nine months ago the ship had been in the Mediterranean and a hundred cultured spinsters had welcomed his music. It was all one to him.

After breakfast the Colonel saw all his officers in the smoking-room. 'We've got to get everything out of the ship,' he said. 'It's got to be loaded tactically. We shan't be sailing until to-night anyway. I've just seen the Captain and he says he isn't fuelled yet. Also we're overloaded and he insists on our putting two hundred men ashore. Also, there's a field hospital coming on board this morning, that we've got to find room for. There is also Field Security Police, Field Force Institute, N.A.A.F.I., two Pay Corps officers, four chaplains, a veterinary surgeon, a Press photographer, a naval beach party, some Marine anti-aircraft gunners, an air support liaison unit–whatever that is–and a detachment of Sappers to be accommodated. All ranks are confined to the ship. There will be no communication of any kind with the shore. Duty company will find sentries for the post and telephone boxes on the quay. That's all, gentlemen.'

Everyone said, 'Lyne made nonsense of the embarkation.'

V

When Mr Bentley, in the first flush of patriotic zeal, left publishing and took service with the Ministry of Information, it was agreed between him and the senior partner that his room should be kept for his use and that he should come in whenever he could to keep an eye on his interests. Mr Rampole, the senior partner, would see to the routine of the office.

Rampole and Bentley was not a large or a very prosperous firm; it owed its continued existence largely to the fact that both partners had a reasonable income derived from other sources. Mr Bentley was a publisher because ever since he was a boy he had had a liking for books; he thought them a Good Thing; the more of them the merrier. Wider acquaintance had not increased his liking for authors, whom he found as a class avaricious, egotistical, jealous, and ungrateful, but he had always the hope that one day one of these disagreeable people would turn out to be a messiah of genius. And he liked the books themselves; he liked to see in the window of the office the dozen bright covers which were that season's new titles; he liked the sense of vicarious authorship which this spectacle gave him. Not so old Rampole. Mr Bentley often wondered why his senior partner had ever taken to publishing and why, once disillusioned, he persisted in it. Old Rampole deplored the propagation of books. 'It won't do,' he always said whenever Mr Bentley produced a new author, 'no one ever reads first novels.'

Once or twice a year old Rampole himself introduced an author, always with well-justified forecasts of its failure. 'Terrible thing,' he would say. 'Met old So-and-so at the club. Got button-holed. Fellow's just retired from Malay States. Written his reminiscences. We shall have to do them for him. No getting out of it now. One comfort he won't ever write another book.'

That was one superiority he had over Mr Bentley which he was fond of airing. His authors never came back for more, like Mr Bentley's young friends.

The idea of the *Ivory Tower* was naturally repugnant to old Rampole. 'I've never known a literary review succeed yet,' he said.

He had a certain grudging regard for Ambrose because he was one of the few writers on their list who were incontestably profitable. Other writers always involved an argument, Mr Bentley having an ingenious way of explaining over advances and overhead charges and stock in hand in such a way that he seemed to prove that obvious failures had indeed succeeded. But Ambrose's books sold fifteen thousand copies. He didn't like the fellow, but he had to concede him a certain knack of writing. It shocked him that Ambrose should be so blind to his own interests as to propose such a scheme.

'Has the fellow got money?' he asked Mr Bentley privately.

'Very little, I think.'

'Then what is he thinking of? What's he *after*?'

To Ambrose he said, 'But a literary review, now of all times!'

'Now *is* the time of all times,' said Ambrose. 'Don't you *see*?'

'No, I don't. Costs are up and going higher. Can't get paper. Who'll want to read this magazine anyway? It isn't a woman's paper. It isn't, as I see it, a man's. It isn't even topical. Who's going to advertise in it?'

'I wasn't thinking of having advertisements. I thought of making it something like the old Yellow Book.'

'Well that was a failure,' said old Rampole triumphantly, 'in the end.'

But presently he gave his consent. He always gave his consent in the end to all Mr Bentley's suggestions. That was the secret of their long partnership. He had registered his protest. No one could blame him. It was all Bentley's doing. Often he had opposed Mr Bentley's projects out of habit, on the widest grounds that publication of any kind was undesirable. In the case of the *Ivory Tower* he stood on firm ground and knew it. It gave him positive satisfaction to detect his partner in such indefensible folly. So Mr Bentley's room, which was the most ornamental in the fine old building which they used as their offices, became the editorial room of Ambrose's paper.

There was not, at this stage, much editorial work to be done.

'There's one criticism I foresee,' said Mr Bentley, studying the proof sheets, 'the entire issue seems to be composed by yourself.'

'No one's to guess that,' said Ambrose. 'If you like we'll put some pseudonyms in.' Ambrose had always rather specialized in manifestoes. He had written one at school; he had written a dozen at the University; once, in the late twenties, he and his friends Hat and Malpractice had even issued the invitation to a party in the form of a manifesto. It was one of his many reasons for shunning communism that its manifesto had been written for it, once and for all, by somebody else. Surrounded, as he believed himself to be, by enemies of all kinds, Ambrose found it exhilarating from time to time to trumpet his defiance. The first number of the *Ivory Tower* somewhat belied the serenity and seclusion which it claimed, for Ambrose had a blow for every possible windmill.

The Minstrel Boys or Ivory Tower v. *Manhattan Skyscraper* defined once and for all Ambrose's attitude in the great Parsnip-Pimpernell controversy. *Hermit or Choirmaster* was an expansion of Ambrose's theme at the Café Royal. 'Culture must be cenobitic not conventual.' He struck ferocious unprovoked blows at those who held that literature was of value to the community. Mr J. B. Priestley came in for much personal abuse in these pages. There followed *The Bakelite Tower*, an onslaught on David Lennox and the decorative school of fashionable artists. *Majors and Mandarins* followed, where was defined the proper degree of contempt and abhorrence due to the military, and among the military Ambrose included by name all statesmen of an energetic and war-like disposition.

'It's all very controversial,' said Mr Bentley sadly. 'When you first told me about it, I thought you meant it to be a purely artistic paper.'

'We must show people where we stand,' said Ambrose. 'Art will follow–anyway there's *Monument to a Spartan*.'

'Yes,' said Mr Bentley. 'There's that.'

'It covers fifty pages, my dear. All pure Art.'

He said this with a facetious, shop assistant's intonation as though he was saying, 'All Pure Silk'; he said it as though it were a joke, but in his heart he believed–and he knew Mr Bentley understood him in this sense–he was speaking the simple truth. It *was* all pure art.

He had written it two years ago on his return from Munich after his parting with Hans. It was the story of Hans. Now, after the passage of two years, he could not read it without tears. To publish it was a symbolic action of the laying down of an emotional burden he had carried too long.

Monument to a Spartan described Hans, as Ambrose had loved him, in every mood; Hans immature, the provincial *petit-bourgeois* youth floundering and groping in the gloom of Teutonic adolescence, unsuccessful in his examinations, world-weary, brooding about suicide among the conifers, uncritical of direct authority, unreconciled to the order of the universe; Hans affectionate, sentimental, roughly sensual, guilty; above all, Hans guilty, haunted by the taboos of the forest; Hans credulous, giving his simple and generous acceptance to all the nonsense of Nazi leaders; Hans reverent to those absurd instructors who harangued the youth camps, resentful at the injustices of man to man, at the plots of the Jews and the encirclement of his country, at the blockade and disarmament; Hans loving his comrades, finding in a deep tribal emotion an escape from the guilt of personal love; Hans singing with his Hitler Youth comrades, cutting trees with them, making roads, still loving his old friend, puzzled that he could not fit the old love into the scheme of the new; Hans growing a little older, joining the Brown Shirts, lapped in a kind of benighted chivalry, bemused in a twilight where the demagogues and party hacks loomed and glittered like Wagnerian heroes; Hans faithful to his old friend, like a woodcutter's boy in a fairy-tale who sees the whole forest peopled with the great ones of another world and, rubbing his eyes, returns at evening to his hut and his fireside. The Wagnerians shone in Ambrose's story as they did in Hans's eyes. He austerely denied himself any hint of satire. The blustering, cranky, bone-headed party men were all heroes and philosophers. All this Ambrose had recorded with great delicacy and precision at a time when his heart was consumed by the final tragedy. Hans's Storm Troop comrades discover that his friend is a Jew; they have resented this friend before because in their gross minds they knew him to represent something personal and private in a world where only the mob and the hunting-pack had the right to live. So the mob and the hunting-pack fall on Hans's friendship. With a mercy they are far from feeling they save Hans from facing the implications of his discovery. For him, alone, it would have been the great climacteric of his retarded adolescence; the discovery that his own, personal conviction conflicted with the factitious convictions drummed into him by the crooks and humbugs he took for his guides. But the hunting-pack and the mob left Hans no time to devise his own, intense punishment; that at least was spared him in the swift and savage onslaught; that was left to Ambrose returning by train to England.

It was a story which a popular writer would have spun out to 150,000 words; Ambrose missed nothing; it was all there, delicately and precisely, in fifty pages of the *Ivory Tower*.

'Quite frankly, Geoffrey, I regard this as a major work of Art.'

'Yes, Ambrose, I know you do. So do I. I only wish we were publishing it without all the controversial stuff.'

'Not controversial, Geoffrey. We invite acceptance, not argument. We are showing our credentials and *laissez-passer*. That's all.'

'Old Rampole won't like it,' said Mr Bentley.

'We won't let old Rampole see it,' said Ambrose.

'I'm on to a very good thing, Colonel.'

'Will you kindly address me as "sir" in this office?'

'You wouldn't prefer to be called "chief"?'

'You'll call me "sir" or get out of that uniform.'

'It's funny,' said Basil. 'I should much sooner be called "chief". In fact that's what Susie does call me. However, sir, may I tell you about my discovery?'

When Basil had told him, Colonel Plum said, 'That's all right as far as it goes. We can't take any action, of course. This fellow Silk is a well-known writer, working in the Ministry of Information.'

'He's a most dangerous type. I know him well. He was living in Munich before the war–never out of the Brown House.'

'That's as may be, but this isn't Spain. We can't go arresting people for what they say in a private conversation in a café. I've no doubt we shall come to that eventually, but at the present stage of our struggle for freedom, it just can't be done.'

'But this paper he's starting.'

'Yes, that's another matter. But Rampole and Bentley are a perfectly respectable little firm. I can't apply for a search warrant until I've got something to go on. We've got pretty wide powers, but we have to be careful how we use them. We'll keep an eye on this paper and if it seems dangerous we'll stop it. Meanwhile, get to work. Here's an anonymous denunciation of a retired admiral in South Kensington. There won't be anything in it. See what the police know about him.'

'Don't we ever investigate night clubs? I'm sure they're bursting with enemy agents.'

Susie said, 'I do. You don't.'

A quiet day at the Ministry of Information. The more energetic neutral correspondents had mostly left the country by now, finding Axis sources a happier hunting-ground for front-page news. The Ministry could get on with its work undisturbed. That afternoon a film was showing in the Ministry theatre; it dealt with otter-hunting and was designed to impress neutral countries with the pastoral beauty of English life. The religious department were all keen filmgoers. Basil found the room empty. On Ambrose's table lay two sets of galley-proofs of the new magazine. Basil pocketed one of them. There was also a passport; Basil took it up with interest. He had never seen an Irish one before. It was made out for a Father Flanagan, S.J., Professor of Dublin University. The photograph showed a cadaverous face of indeterminate age. Father Flanagan was in his leisure from higher education the correspondent of an Irish newspaper. He wanted to visit the Maginot Line during his vacation and after numerous disappointments had found his way to the religious department of the Ministry of Information, where the Roman

Catholic director had promised to try and get him a visa. Basil took this too; an additional passport often came in useful. Then he sauntered away.

He took the proofs home and read until dinner, marking a passage here and there as material to his brief. The style throughout was homogeneous but the author's names were multiform. Ambrose rather let himself go on names. 'Hucklebury Squib', 'Bartholomew Grass', 'Tom Barebones-Abraham'. Only *Monument to a Spartan* bore Ambrose's own name. Later that evening Basil sought Ambrose where he was sure to find him, at the Café Royal.

'I've been reading your magazine,' he said.

'So it *was* you. I thought one of those nasty Jesuits had stolen it. They're always flapping in and out the department like jackdaws. Geoffrey Bentley was in a great stew about it. He doesn't want old Rampole to see a copy until the thing's out.'

'Why should the Jesuits want to show your magazine to old Rampole?'

'They're up to any mischief. What d'you think of it?'

'Well,' said Basil, 'I think you might have made it a bit stronger. You know what you want to do is to shock people a bit. That's the way to put a new magazine across. You can't shock people nowadays with sex, of course; I don't mean that. But suppose you had a little poem in praise of Himmler–something like that?'

'I don't believe that would be a good idea; besides, as far as I know no one has written a poem like that.'

'I dare say I could rake one up for you.'

'No,' said Ambrose. 'What did you think of *Monument to a Spartan*?'

'All the first part is first rate. I suppose they made you put on that ending?'

'Who?'

'The Ministry of Information.'

'They've had nothing to do with it.'

'Haven't they? Well, of course, you know best. I can only say how it reads to an outsider. What I felt was–here is a first-class work of art; something no one but you could have written. And then, suddenly, it degenerates into mere propaganda. Jolly good propaganda, of course; I wish half the stuff your Ministry turns out was as good–but propaganda. An atrocity story–the sort of stuff American journalists turn out by the ream. It glares a bit, you know, Ambrose. Still, of course, we all have to make sacrifices in war time. Don't think I don't respect you for it. But artistically, Ambrose, it's shocking.'

'Is it?' said Ambrose, dismayed. 'Is that how it reads?'

'Leaps to the eye, old boy. Still it ought to give you a leg up in the department.'

'Basil,' said Ambrose solemnly, 'if I thought that was how people would take it, I'd scrap the whole thing.'

'Oh, I shouldn't do that. The first forty-five pages are grand. Why don't you leave it like that, with Hans still full of his illusions, marching into Poland?'

'I might.'

'And you could bring Himmler in, just at the end, in a kind of apotheosis of Nazism.'

'No.'

'Well, Himmler isn't necessary. Just leave Hans in the first exhilaration of victory.'

'I'll think about it. . . . D'you really mean that intelligent readers would think

I was writing propaganda?'

'They couldn't think anything else, old boy, could they?'

A week later by the simple process of going to Rampole and Bentley's office and asking for one, Basil obtained an advance copy of the new magazine. He turned eagerly to the last page and found that *Monument to a Spartan* now ended as he had suggested; he read it again with relish; to anyone ignorant of Ambrose's private history it bore one plain character–the triumphant paean of Hitler Youth; Doctor Ley himself might have been the author. Basil took the magazine with him to the War Office; before approaching Colonel Plum he marked with red chalk the *Monument to a Spartan* and passages in the preceding articles which cast particular ridicule upon the army and the War Cabinet and which urged on the artist the duty of non-resistance to violence. Then he laid it on Colonel Plum's desk.

'I think sir, you promised to make me a Captain of Marines if I caught a fascist.'

'It was a figurative expression.'

'Meaning what?'

'That you might have done something to excuse your presence in my office. What have you got there?'

'Documentary evidence. A fifth column nest.'

'Well, put it down. I'll have a look at it when I've time.'

It was not Colonel Plum's habit to show enthusiasm before subordinates, but as soon as Basil was gone he began reading the marked passages with close attention. Presently he called for Basil.

'I believe you're on to something here,' he said. 'I'm taking this round to Scotland Yard. Who are these men Squib, Grass and Barebones-Abraham?'

'Don't you think they sound like pseudonyms?'

'Nonsense. When a man chooses an alias he called himself Smith or Brown.'

'Have it your own way, sir. I shall be interested to see them in the dock.'

'There won't be any dock. We shall get this bunch under a special warrant.'

'Shall I come round to Scotland Yard with you?'

'No.'

'Just for that I won't introduce him to Barebones-Abraham,' said Basil when the Colonel was gone.

'Have we really caught some fifth column at last?' asked Susie.

'I don't know about "we"; *I* have.'

'Will they be shot?'

'Not all of them, I should think.'

'Seems a shame really,' said Susie. 'I expect they're only a bit touched.'

In the pleasure of setting his trap, Basil had not looked forward to its consequences. When Colonel Plum returned to his office two hours later, things seemed to have gone far beyond Basil's control. 'They're pleased as Punch at Scotland Yard,' he said. 'Handing out some very handsome bouquets. The whole thing is buttoned up. We've taken out a special warrant for authors, publishers and printers, but I don't think we need worry the printers much. To-morrow morning the man Silk will be arrested at the Ministry of Information; simultaneously Rampole and Bentley's will be surrounded and entered, all copies of the paper and all correspondence seized. All the office staff will be held pending investigation. What we need now is a description of the men Grass, Squib and Barebones-Abraham. You might get on to that. I'm going round to see the Home-Secretary now.'

There was, at first hearing, a lot about this speech which displeased Basil, and more still when he began to turn the thing over in his mind. In the first place Colonel Plum seemed to be getting all the credit and all the fun. It was he himself, Basil felt, who should be going to see the Home Secretary; *he* should have been to Scotland Yard to make arrangements for the morrow's raid; *he* should have had the handsome bouquets of which Colonel Plum had spoken. It was not for this that he had planned the betrayal of an old friend. Colonel Plum was putting on altogether too much dog.

In the second place the sensation of being on the side of the law was novel to Basil and not the least agreeable. Police raids, for Basil, had in the past always meant escaping over the tiles or through the area; it made him ashamed to hear these things spoken of with tolerance and familiarity.

In the third place he was not absolutely happy in his mind about what Ambrose might say. Even though he was to be deprived of the right of public trial, there would presumably be some kind of investigation at which he would be allowed to give an account of himself. Basil's share in editing *Monument to a Spartan* was, he felt, better kept as a good story to tell in the right company at the right time; not to be made the subject of official and semi-legal enquiry.

And in the fourth place Basil had from long association an appreciable softness of disposition towards Ambrose. Other things being equal, he wished him well rather than ill.

These considerations, in that order of importance, worked in Basil's mind.

Ambrose's flat lay in the neighbourhood of the Ministry of Information; it was the top floor of a large Bloomsbury mansion, where the marble stairs changed to deal. Ambrose ascended into what had once been the servants' bedrooms; it was an attic and, so called, satisfied the ascetic promptings which had affected Ambrose in the year of the great slump. There was, however, little else about the flat to suggest hardship. He had the flair of his race for comfort and for enviable possessions. There were expensive continental editions of works on architecture, there were deep armchairs, an object like an ostrich egg sculptured by Brancusi, a gramophone with a prodigious horn and a library of records–these and countless other features made the living-room dear to him. It is true that the bath was served only by a gas-burning apparatus which at the best gave a niggardly trickle of warm water and, at the worst, exploded in a cloud of poisonous vapours, but apparatus of this kind is the hall mark of the higher intellectuals all the world over. Ambrose's bedroom compensated for the dangers and discomforts of the bathroom. In this flat he was served by a motherly old Cockney who teased him at intervals for not marrying.

To this flat Basil came very late that night. He had delayed his arrival on purely artistic grounds. Colonel Plum might deny him the excitements of Scotland Yard and the Home Office, but there should be every circumstance of melodrama here. Basil knocked and rang for some time before he made himself heard. Then Ambrose came to the door in a dressing-gown.

'Oh God,' he said. 'I suppose you're drunk,' for no friend of Basil's who maintained a fixed abode in London could ever consider himself immune from his occasional nocturnal visits.

'Let me in. We haven't a moment to spare.' Basil spoke in a whisper. 'The police will be here at any moment.'

Slightly dazed with sleep, Ambrose admitted him. There are those for whom the word 'police' holds no terror. Ambrose was not of them. All his life he had been an outlaw and the days in Munich were still fresh in his memory when friends disappeared suddenly in the night, leaving no address.

'I've brought you this,' said Basil, 'and this and this.' He gave Ambrose a clerical collar, a black clerical vest ornamented with a double line of jet buttons and an Irish passport. 'You are Father Flanagan returning to Dublin University. Once in Ireland you'll be safe.'

'But surely there's no train at this time.'

'There's one at eight. You mustn't be found here. You can sit in the waiting-room at Euston till it comes in. Have you got a breviary?'

'Of course not.'

'Then read a racing paper. I suppose you've got a dark suit.'

It was significant both of Basil's fine urgency of manner, and of Ambrose's constitutionally guilty disposition, that he was already clothed as a clergyman before he said, 'But what have I done? Why are they after me?'

'Your magazine. It's being suppressed. They're rounding up everyone connected with it.'

Ambrose asked no more. He accepted the fact as a pauper accepts the condition of being perpetually 'moved on'. It was something inalienable from his state; the artist's birthright.

'How did you hear about it?'

'In the War Office.'

'What am I to do about all this?' asked Ambrose helplessly. 'The flat, and the furniture and my books and Mrs Carver.'

'I tell you what. If you like I'll move in and take care of it for you until it's safe to come back.'

'Would you really, Basil?' said Ambrose, touched. 'You're being very kind.'

For some time now Basil had felt himself unfairly handicapped in his pursuit of Susie by the fact of his living with his mother. He had not thought of this solution. It had come providentially, with rapid and exemplary justice all too rare in life; goodness was being rewarded quite beyond his expectations, if not beyond his deserts.

'I'm afraid the geyser is rather a bore,' said Ambrose apologetically.

They were not far from Euston Station. Packing was the work of a quarter of an hour.

'But, Basil, I *must* have *some* clothes.'

'You are an Irish priest. What d'you think the Customs are going to say when they open a trunk full of Charvet ties and crêpe-de-Chine pyjamas?'

Ambrose was allowed one suitcase.

'I'll look after this for you,' said Basil, surveying the oriental profusion of expensive underclothes which filled the many drawers and presses of the bedroom. 'You'll have to walk to the station, you know.'

'Why, for God's sake?'

'Taxi might be traced. Can't take any chances.'

The suitcase had seemed small enough when Basil first selected it as the most priestly of the rather too smart receptacles in Ambrose's box-room; it seemed enormous as they trudged northward through the dark streets of Bloomsbury. At last they reached the classic columns of the railway terminus. It is not a cheerful place at the best of times, striking a chill in the heart of the gayest holiday-maker. Now in war time, before dawn on a cold Spring morning, it seemed the entrance to a sepulchre.

'I'll leave you here,' said Basil. 'Keep out of sight until the train is in. If anyone speaks to you, tell your beads.'

'I haven't any beads.'

'Then contemplate. Go into an ecstasy. But don't open your mouth or you're done.'

'I'll write to you when I get to Ireland.'

'Better not,' said Basil, cheerfully.

He turned away and was immediately lost in the darkness. Ambrose entered the station. A few soldiers slept on benches, surrounded by their kit and equipment. Ambrose found a corner darker, even, than the general gloom. Here, on a packing-case that seemed by its smell to contain fish of a sort, he sat waiting for dawn; black hat perched over his eyes, black overcoat wrapped close about his knees, mournful and black eyes open, staring into the blackness. From the fishy freight below him water oozed slowly on to the pavement making a little pool, as though of tears.

Mr Rampole was not, as many of his club acquaintances supposed, a bachelor, but a widower of long standing. He lived in a small but substantial house at Hampstead and there maintained in servitude a spinster daughter. On this fateful morning his daughter saw him off from the front gate as had been her habit years without number, at precisely 8.45. Mr Rampole paused in the flagged path to comment on the buds which were breaking everywhere in the little garden.

Look well at those buds, old Rampole; you will not see the full leaf.

'I'll be back at six,' he said.

Presumptuous Rampole, who shall tell what the day will bring forth? Not his daughter, who returned, unmoved by the separation, to eat a second slice of toast in the dining-room; not old Rampole, who strode at a good pace towards the Hampstead Underground.

He showed his season ticket to the man at the lift.

'I shall have to get it renewed the day after to-morrow,' he said affably, and tied a knot in the corner of his large white handkerchief to remind him of the fact.

There is no need for that knot, old Rampole; you will never again travel in the Hampstead Underground.

He opened his morning paper as he had done, five days a week, years without number. He turned first to the Deaths, then to the correspondence, then, reluctantly, to the news of the day.

Never again, old Rampole, never again.

The police raid on the Ministry of Information, like so many similar enterprises, fell flat. First the plain clothes men had the utmost difficulty in getting past the gatekeeper.

'Is Mr Silk expecting you?'

'We hope not.'

'Then you can't see him.'

When finally they were identified and allowed to pass, there was a confused episode in the religious department where they found only the Nonconformist minister, whom, too zealously, they proceeded to handcuff. It was explained that Ambrose was unaccountably absent from duty that morning. Two constables were left to await his arrival. All through the day they sat there, casting a gloom over the religious department. The plain clothes men proceeded to Mr Bentley's room where they were received with great frankness and charm.

Mr Bentley answered all their questions in a manner befitting an honest citizen. Yes, he knew Ambrose Silk both as a colleague at the Ministry and, formerly, as one of their authors at Rampole's. No, he had almost nothing to do with publishing these days; he was too busy with all this (an explanatory gesture which embraced the dripping sink, the Nollekens busts and the page of arabesques beside the telephone). Mr Rampole was in entire charge of the publishing firm. Yes, he thought he had heard of some magazine which Silk was starting, the *Ivory Tower*? Was that the name? Very likely. No, he had no copy. Was it already out? Mr Bentley had formed the impression that it was not yet ready for publication. The contributors? Hucklebury Squib, Bartholomew Grass, Tom Barebones-Abraham? Mr Bentley thought he had heard the names; he might have met them in literary circles in the old days. He had the idea that Barebones-Abraham was rather below normal height, corpulent, bald–yes, Mr Bentley was quite sure he was bald as an egg; he spoke with a stammer and dragged his left leg as he walked. Hucklebury Squib was a very tall young man; easily recognizable for he had lost the lobe of his left ear in extraordinary circumstances when sailing before the mast; he had a front tooth missing and wore gold earrings.

The plain clothes men recorded these details in shorthand. This was the sort of witness they liked, circumstantial, precise, unhesitating.

When it came to Bartholomew Grass, Mr Bentley's invention flagged. He had never seen the man. He rather thought it might be the pseudonym for a woman.

'Thank you, Mr Bentley,' said the chief of the plain clothes men. 'I don't think we need trouble you any more. If we want you I suppose we can always find you here.'

'Always,' said Mr Bentley sweetly. 'I often, whimsically, refer to this little table as my grindstone. I keep my nose to it. We live in arduous times, Inspector.'

A posse of police went to Ambrose's flat, where all they got was a piece of his housekeeper's mind.

'Our man's got away,' they reported when they returned to their superiors.

Colonel Plum, the Inspector of Police, and Basil were summoned late that afternoon to the office of the Director of Internal Security.

'I can't congratulate you,' he said, 'on the way this case has been handled. I'm not blaming you, Inspector, or you, Seal,' and he fixed Colonel Plum with a look of detestation. 'We were clearly on to a very dangerous set of men and you let four out of five slip through your fingers. I've no doubt that at this moment they are sitting in a German submarine, laughing at us.'

'We've got Rampole, sir,' said Colonel Plum. 'I'm inclined to think he's the ringleader.'

'I'm inclined to think he's an old booby.'

'He has behaved in the most hostile and defiant manner throughout. He refuses to give any particulars about any of his accomplices.'

'He threw a telephone directory at one of our men,' said the Inspector, 'and used the following expressions about them: "nincompoops", "jacks-in-office" . . .'

'Yes, yes, I have the report. Rampole is obviously a violent and thoroughly unreasonable type. It won't do him any harm to cool his heels for the rest of the war. But he's not the ringleader. This fellow Barebones-Abraham is the man I want and you haven't been able to find a trace of him.'

'We've got his description.'

'A fat lot of good that is when he's half-way back to Germany. No, the whole thing has been grossly mismanaged. The Home Secretary takes a very poor view of it. *Somebody talked* and I mean to find out who.'

When the interview, painfully protracted, came to an end, the Director told Basil to remain behind.

'Seal,' he said. 'I understand you were the first man to get on to this gang. Have you any idea how they were warned?'

'You put me in a very difficult position, sir.'

'Come, come, my boy, this is no time for petty loyalties when your country's future is at stake.'

'Well, sir, I've felt for some time that there's been too much feminine influence in our department. Have you seen Colonel Plum's secretary?'

'Hokey-pokey, eh?'

'You could call it that, sir.'

'Enemy agent, eh?'

'On, no, sir. Have a look at her.'

The Director sent for Susie. When she had gone he said, 'No, not an enemy agent.'

'Certainly not, sir, but a frivolous, talkative girl. Colonel Plum's intimacy. . . .'

'Yes, I quite understand. You did perfectly right to tell me.'

'What did he want, sending for me like that and just staring?' asked Susie.

'I think I've arranged promotion for you.'

'Ooh, you are sweet.'

'I'm just moving into a new flat.'

'Lucky you,' said Susie.

'I wish you'd come and advise me about the decorations. I'm no good at that kind of thing.'

'Oh no?' said Susie in a voice she had learned at the cinema. 'And what would Colonel Plum say?'

'Colonel Plum won't have anything to say. You're rising far above ADDIS.'

'Ooh.'

Next morning Susie received an official intimation that she was to move to the Director's office.

'Lucky you,' said Basil.

She had admired all Ambrose's decorations except the Brancusi sculpture. That had been put away, out of sight, in the box room.

At Brixton Gaol Mr Rampole enjoyed many privileges that were not accorded to common criminals. There was a table in his cell and a tolerably comfortable chair. He was allowed, at his own expense, some additions to prison fare. He might smoke. *The Times* was delivered to him every morning and for the first time in his life he accumulated a small library. Mr Bentley from time to time brought him papers for which his signature was required. In every way his life was much easier than it would have been in similar circumstances in any country.

But Mr Rampole was not content. There was an obnoxious young man next to him who, when they met at exercise, said 'Heil Mosley,' and at night attempted to tap out messages of encouragement in Morse. Moreover Mr Rampole missed his club and his home at Hampstead. In spite of a multitude of indulgences he faced the summer without enthusiasm.

In a soft, green valley where a stream ran through close-cropped, spongy pasture and the grass grew down below the stream's edge and merged there with the water-weeds; where a road ran between grass verges and tumbled walls, and the grass merged into moss which spread upwards and over the tumbled stones of the walls, outwards over the pocked metalling and deep ruts of the road; where the ruins of a police barracks, built to command the road through the valley, burnt in the troubles, had once been white, then black, and now were one green with the grass and the moss and the water-weed; where the smoke of burned turf drifted down from the cabin chimneys and joined the mist that rose from the damp, green earth; where the prints of ass and pig, goose and calf and horse mingled indifferently with those of barefoot children; where the soft, resentful voices rose and fell in the smoky cabins merging with the music of the stream and the treading and shifting and munching of the beasts at pasture; where mist and smoke never lifted and the sun never fell direct, and evening came slowly in infinite gradations of shadow; where the priest came seldom because of the rough road and the long climb home to the head of the valley, and no one except the priest ever came from one month's end to another, there stood an inn which was frequented in by-gone days by fishermen. Here in the summer nights when their sport was over they had sat long over their whisky and their pipes–professional gentlemen from Dublin and retired military men from England. No one fished the stream now and the few trout that remained were taken by ingenious and illicit means without respect for season or ownership. No one came to stay; sometimes a couple on a walking tour, once or twice a party of motorists, paused for supper, hesitated, discussed the matter and then regretfully pushed on to the next village. Here Ambrose came, perched on an outside-car, from the railway station over the hill six miles distant.

He had discarded his clerical disguise, but there was something about his melancholy air and his precision of speech which made the landlord, who had never had contact before with an intellectual Jew, put him down as a 'spoilt priest'. He had heard about this inn from a garrulous fellow in the packet-boat;

it was kept by a distant connexion of this man's wife, and though he had not himself visited the place, he never lost an opportunity of putting in a good word for it.

Here Ambrose settled, in the only bedroom whose windows were unbroken. Here he intended to write a book, to take up again the broken fragments of his artistic life. He spread foolscap paper on the dining-room table and the soft, moist air settled on it and permeated it so that when, on the third day, he sat down to make a start, the ink spread and the lines ran together, leaving what might have been a brush stroke of indigo paint where there should have been a sentence of prose. Ambrose laid down the pen and because the floor sloped where the house had settled, it rolled down the table, and down the floor-boards and under the mahogany sideboard, and lay there among napkin rings and small coins and corks and the sweepings of half a century. And Ambrose wandered out into the mist and the twilight, stepping soundlessly on the soft, green turf.

In London Basil set Susie to work. She wanted to be taken out in the evenings too often and in too expensive a style. He set her to work with needle and silk and embroidery scissors, unpicking the A's from the monograms on Ambrose's crêpe-de-Chine underclothes and substituting on their place a B.

VI

Like horses in a riding school, line ahead to the leading mark, changing the rein, circling to the leading mark on the opposite wall, changing rein again, line ahead again, orderly and regular and graceful, the aeroplanes manoeuvred in the sharp sunlight. The engines sang in the morning sky, the little black bombs tumbled out, turning over in the air, drifting behind the machines, breaking in silent upheavals of rock and dust which were already subsiding when the sound of the explosions shook the hillside where Cedric Lyne sat with his binoculars, trying to mark their fall.

There was no sign of Spring in this country. Everywhere the land lay frozen and dead, deep snow in the hills, thin ice in the valleys; the buds on the thorn were hard and small and black.

'I think they've found A Company, Colonel,' said Cedric.

Battalion headquarters were in a cave in the side of the hill; a shallow cave made by a single great rock which held up the accumulations of smaller stone which in years had slid down from above and settled round it. The Colonel and the adjutant and Cedric had room to sit here; they had arrived by night and had watched dawn break over the hills. Immediately below them the road led farther inland, climbing the opposing heights in a series of bends and tunnels. At their feet, between them and the opposite escarpment, the land lay frozen and level. The reserve company was concealed there. The headquarter troops formed a small protective perimeter round the cave. Twenty yards away under another rock two signallers lay with a portable wireless set.

'Ack, Beer, Charley, Don . . . Hullo Lulu, Koko calling; acknowledge my signal; Lulu to Koko–over.'

They had marched forward all the preceding night. When they arrived at the cave Cedric had first been hot and sweaty, then, after they halted in the chill of dawn, cold and sweaty. Now with the sun streaming down on them he was warm and dry and a little sleepy.

The enemy were somewhere beyond the farther hills. They were expected to appear late that afternoon.

'That's what they'll do,' said the Colonel. 'Make their assault in the last hour of daylight so as to avoid a counter-attack. Well, we can hold them for ever on this front. I wish I felt sure of our left flank.'

'The Loamshires are falling back there. They ought to be in position now,' said the adjutant.

'I know. But where are they? They ought to have sent over.'

'All this air activity in front means they'll come this way,' said the adjutant.

'I hope so.'

The high school finished its exercise, took up formation in arrow shape and disappeared droning over the hills. Presently a reconnaissance plane appeared and flew backwards and forwards overhead searching the ground like an old woman after a lost coin.

'Tell those bloody fools to keep their faces down,' said the Colonel.

When the aeroplane had passed he lit his pipe and stood in the mouth of the cave looking anxiously to his left.

'Can you see anything that looks like the Loamshires?'

'Nothing, Colonel.'

'The enemy may have cut in across them yesterday evening. That's what I'm afraid of. Can't you get Brigade?' he said to the signalling corporal.

'No answer from Brigade, sir. We keep trying. Hullo Lulu, Koko calling, acknowledge my signal, acknowledge my signal; Koko to Lulu–over. . .'

'I've a good mind to push D Company over on that flank.'

'It's outside our boundary.'

'Damn the boundary.'

'We'd be left without a reserve if they come straight down the road.'

'I know, that's what's worrying me.'

An orderly came up with a message. The Colonel read it and passed it to Cedric to file. 'C Company's in position. That's all our forward companies reported. We'll go round and have a look at them.'

Cedric and the Colonel went forward, leaving the adjutant in the cave. They visited the company headquarters and asked a few routine questions. It was a simple defensive scheme, three companies up, one in reserve in the rear. It was suitable ground for defence. Unless the enemy had infantry tanks–and all the reports said he had not–the road could be held as long as ammunition and rations lasted.

'Made a water recce?'

'Yes, Colonel, there's a good spring on the other side of those rocks. We're refilling the bottles by relays now.'

'That's right.'

A Company had been bombed, but without casualties, except for a few cuts from splintered rock. They were unshaken by the experience, rapidly digging dummy trenches at a distance from their positions to draw the fire when the aeroplanes returned. The Colonel returned from his rounds in a cheerful mood; the regiment was doing all right. If the flanks held they were sitting pretty.

'We're through to Lulu, sir,' said the signalling corporal.

The Colonel reported to brigade headquarters that he was in position; air activity; no casualties; no sign of enemy troops. 'I've no contact on the left flank . . . yes, I know it's beyond the brigade boundary. I know the Loamshires ought to be there. But *are* they? Our . . . Yes, but that flank's completely in the air, if they don't turn up . . .'

It was now midday. Battalion headquarters ate some luncheon–biscuits and chocolate; the adjutant had a flask of whisky. No one was hungry but they drank their bottles empty and sent the orderlies to refill them at the spring B Company had found. When the men came back the Colonel said, 'I'm not happy about the left flank. Lyne, go across and see where those bloody Loamshires are.'

It was two miles along a side track to the mouth of the next pass, where the Loamshires should be in defence. Cedric left his servant behind at battalion headquarters. It was against the rules, but he was weary of the weight of dependent soldiery which throughout the operations encumbered him and depressed his spirits. As he walked alone he was exhilarated with the sense of being one man, one pair of legs, one pair of eyes, one brain, sent on a single intelligible task; one man alone could go freely anywhere on the earth's surface; multiply him, put him in a drove and by each addition of his fellows you subtract something that is of value, make him so much less a man; this was the crazy mathematics of war. A reconnaissance plane came overhead. Cedric moved off the path but did not take cover, did not lie on his face or gaze into the earth and wonder if there was a rear gunner, as he would have done if he had been with headquarters. The great weapons of modern war did not count in single lives; it took a whole section to make a target worth a burst of machine-gun fire; a platoon or a motor lorry to be worth a bomb. No one had anything against the individual; as long as he was alone he was free and safe; there's danger in numbers; divided we stand, united we fall, thought Cedric, striding happily towards the enemy, shaking from his boots all the frustration of corporate life. He did not know it, but he was thinking exactly what Ambrose had thought when he announced that culture must cease to be conventual and become cenobitic.

He came to the place where the Loamshires should have been. There was no sign of them. There was no sign of any life, only rock and ice and beyond, in the hills, snow. The valley ran clear into the hills, parallel with the main road he had left. They may be holding it, higher up, he thought, where it narrows, and he set off up the stony track towards the mountains.

And there he found them; twenty of them under the command of a subaltern. They had mounted their guns to cover the track at its narrowest point and were lying, waiting for what the evening would bring. It was a ragged and weary party.

'I'm sorry I didn't send across to you,' said the subaltern. 'We were all in. I didn't know where you were exactly and I hadn't a man to spare.'

'What happened?'

'It was all rather a nonsense,' said the subaltern, in the classic phraseology of his trade which comprehends all human tragedy. 'They bombed us all day yesterday and we had to go to ground. We made a mile or two between raids but it was sticky going. Then at just before sunset they came clean through us in armoured cars. I managed to get this party away. There may be a few others wandering about, but I rather doubt it. Luckily the Jerries decided to call it a day and settled down for a night's rest. We marched all night and all to-day. We only arrived an hour ago.'

'Can you stop them here?'

'What d'you think?'

'No.'

'No, we can't stop them. We may hold them up half an hour. They may think we're the forward party of a battalion and decide to wait till to-morrow before they attack. It all depends what time they arrive. Is there any chance of your being able to relieve us?'

'Yes. I'll get back right away.'

'We could do with a break,' said the subaltern.

Cedric ran most of the way to the cave. The Colonel heard his story now removed. I never prophesy, but I am confident that before the year is out they will have made a separate and permanent peace with us. The Germans have wasted their strength. They cannot possibly repair their losses. They have squandered the flower of their army. They have enlarged their boundaries beyond all reason and given themselves an area larger than they can possibly hold down. The war has entered into a new and more glorious phase.'
break up and deploy.

'We're too late,' said the Colonel. 'Here come the armoured cars.'

They had overrun the party of Loamshires and were spreading fanwise across the low plain. Cedric counted twenty of them; behind them an endless stream of lorries full of troops. At the first shot the lorries stopped and under cover of the armoured cars the infantry fell in on the ground, broke into open order and began their advance with parade-ground deliberation. With the cars came a squadron of bombers, flying low along the line of the track. Soon the whole battalion area was full of bursting bombs.

The Colonel was giving orders for the immediate withdrawal of the forward companies.

Cedric stood in the cave. It was curious, he thought, that he should have devoted so much of his life to caves.

'Lyne,' said the Colonel. 'Go up to A Company and explain what's happening. If they come in now from the rear the cars may jink round and give the other companies a chance to get out.'

Cedric set out across the little battlefield. All seemed quite unreal to him still.

The bombers were not aiming at any particular target; they were plastering the ground in front of their cars, between battalion headquarters and the mouth of the valley where A Company were dug in. The noise was incessant and shattering. Still it did not seem real to Cedric. It was part of a crazy world where he was an interloper. It was nothing to do with him. A bomb came whistling down, it seemed from directly over his head. He fell on his face and it burst fifty yards away, bruising him with a shower of small stones.

'Thought they'd got him,' said the Colonel. 'He's up again.'

'He's doing all right,' said the adjutant.

The armoured cars were shooting it out with D Company. The infantry spread out in a long line from hillside to hillside and were moving steadily up. They were not firing yet; just tramping along behind the armoured cars, abreast, an arm's length apart. Behind them another wave was forming up. Cedric had to go across this front. The enemy were still out of effective rifle range from him, but spent bullets were singing round him among the rocks.

'He'll never make it,' said the Colonel.

I suppose, thought Cedric, I'm being rather brave. How very peculiar. I'm not the least brave, really; it's simply that the whole thing is so damned silly.

A Company were on the move now. As soon as they heard the firing, without waiting for orders, they were doing what the Colonel intended, edging up the opposing hillside among the boulders, getting into position where they could outflank the out-flanking party. It did not matter now whether Cedric reached them. He never did; a bullet got him, killing him instantly while he was a quarter of a mile away.

Epilogue

SUMMER

Summer came and with it the swift sequence of historic events which left all the world dismayed and hardly credulous; all, that is to say, except Sir Joseph Mainwaring, whose courtly and ponderous form concealed a peppercorn lightness of soul, a deep unimpressionable frivolity, which left him bobbing serenely on the great waves of history which splintered more solid natures to matchwood. Under the new administration he found himself translated to a sphere of public life where he could do no serious harm to anyone, and he accepted the change as a well-earned promotion. In the dark hours of German victory he always had some light anecdote; he believed and repeated everything he heard; he told how, he had it on the highest authority, the German infantry was composed of youths in their teens, who were intoxicated before the battle with dangerous drugs; 'those who are not mown down by machine guns die within a week,' he said. He told, as vividly as if he had been there and seen it himself, of Dutch skies black with descending nuns, of market women who picked off British officers, sniping over their stalls with sub-machine guns, of waiters who were caught on hotel roofs marking the rooms of generals with crosses as though on a holiday post card. He believed, long after hope had been abandoned in more responsible quarters, that the French line was intact. 'There is a little bulge,' he explained. 'All we have to do is to pinch it out,' and he illustrated the action with his finger and thumb. He daily maintained that the enemy had outrun his supplies and was being lured on to destruction. Finally when it was plain, even to Sir Joseph, that in the space of a few days England had lost both the entire stores and equipment of her regular army and her only ally; that the enemy were less than twenty-five miles from her shores; that there were only a few battalions of fully armed, fully trained troops in the country; that she was committed to a war in the Mediterranean with a numerically superior enemy; that her cities lay open to air attack from fields closer to home than the extremities of her own islands; that her sea-routes were threatened from a dozen new bases, Sir Joseph said, 'Seen in the proper perspective I regard this as a great and tangible success. Germany set out to destroy our army and failed; we have demonstrated our invincibility to the world. Moreover, with the French off the stage, the last obstacle to our proper understanding with Italy is now removed. I never prophesy, but I am confident that before the year is out they will have made a separate and permanent peace with us. The Germans have wasted their strength. They cannot possibly repair their losses. They have squandered the flower of their army. They have enlarged their boundaries beyond all reason and given themselves an area larger than they can possibly hold down. The war has entered into a new and more glorious phase.'

And in this last statement, perhaps for the first time in his long and loquacious life, Sir Joseph approximated to reality; he had said a mouthful.

A new and more glorious phase: Alastair's battalion found itself overnight converted from a unit in the early stages of training into first-line troops. Their 1098 stores arrived; a vast profusion of ironmongery which, to his pride, included Alastair's mortar. It was a source of pride not free from compensating disadvantages. Now, when the platoon marched, Alastair's pouches were filled with bombs and his back was harnessed to the unnaturally heavy length of steel piping; the riflemen thought they had the laugh of him.

Parachute landings were looked for hourly. The duty company slept in their boots and stood to at dawn and dusk. Men going out of camp carried charged rifles, steel helmets, anti-gas capes. Week-end leave ceased abruptly. Captain Mayfield began to take a censorious interest in the swill tubs; if there was any waste of food, he said, rations would be reduced. The C.O. said, 'There is no such thing nowadays as working hours' and to show what he meant he ordered a series of parades after tea. A training memorandum was issued which had the most formidable effect upon Mr Smallwood; now, when the platoon returned exhausted from field exercises, Mr Smallwood gave them twenty minutes' arms drill before they dismissed; this was the 'little bit extra' for which the memorandum called. The platoon referred to it as '—ing us about'.

Then with great suddenness the battalion got orders to move to an unknown destination. Everyone believed this meant foreign service, and a great breath of exhilaration inflated the camp. Alastair met Sonia outside the guardroom.

'Can't come out to-night. We're moving. I don't know where. I think we're going into action.'

He gave her instructions about where she should go and what she should do while he was away. They now knew that she was to have a child.

There was a special order that no one was to come to the station to see the battalion off; no one in fact was supposed to know they were moving. To make secrecy absolute they entrained by night, disturbing the whole district with the tramp of feet and the roar of lorries going backwards and forwards between camp and station, moving their stores.

Troops in the train manage to achieve an aspect of peculiar raffishness; they leave camp in a state of ceremonial smartness; they parade on the platform as though on the barrack square; they are detailed to their coaches and there a process of transformation and decay sets in; coats are removed, horrible packages of food appear, dense clouds of smoke obscure the windows, in a few minutes the floor is deep in cigarette ends, lumps of bread and meat, waste paper; in repose the bodies assume attitudes of extreme abandon; some look like corpses that have been left too long unburied; others like the survivors of some saturnalian debauch. Alastair stood in the corridor most of the night, feeling that for the first time he had cut away from the old life.

Before dawn it was well known, in that strange jungle process by which news travels in the ranks, that they were not going into action but to 'coastal —ing defence'.

The train travelled, as troop trains do, in a series of impetuous rushes between long delays. At length in the middle of the forenoon they arrived at their destination and marched through a little seaside town of round-fronted stucco early Victorian boarding-houses, an Edwardian bandstand, and a modern, concrete bathing pool, three foot deep, blue at the bottom, designed to keep children from the adventure and romance of the beach. (Here there were no shells or starfish, no jelly-fish to be melted, no smooth pebbles of glass to be found, no bottles that might contain messages from shipwrecked sailors, no waves which, bigger than the rest, suddenly knocked you off your feet. The nurses might sit round this pool in absolute peace of mind.) Two miles out, through a suburb of bungalows and converted railway carriages, there was a camp prepared for them in the park of what, in recent years, had been an unsuccessful holiday club.

That night Alastair summoned Sonia by telephone and she came next day, taking rooms in the hotel. It was a simple and snug hotel and Alastair came there in the evenings when he was off duty. They tried to recapture the atmosphere of the winter and spring, of the days in Surrey when Alastair's life as a soldier had been a novel and eccentric interruption of their domestic routine; but things were changed. The war had entered on a new and more glorious phase. The night in the train when he thought he was going into action stood between Alastair and the old days.

The battalion was charged with the defence of seven miles of inviting coastline, and they entered with relish into the work of destroying local amenities. They lined the sands with barbed wire and demolished the steps leading from esplanade to beach; they dug weapon pits in the corporation's gardens, sandbagged the bow-windows of private houses and with the co-operation of some neighbouring sappers blocked the roads with dragons'-teeth and pill boxes; they stopped and searched all cars passing through this area and harassed the inhabitants with demands to examine their identity cards. Mr Smallwood sat up on the golf course every night for a week, with a loaded revolver, to investigate a light which was said to have been seen flashing there. Captain Mayfield discovered that telegraph posts are numbered with brass-headed nails and believed it to be the work of the fifth column; when mist came rolling in from the sea one evening, the corporal in command of Alastair's section reported an enemy smoke screen, and for miles round word of invasion was passed from post to post.

'I don't believe you're enjoying the army any more,' said Sonia after three weeks of coastal defence.

'It isn't that. I feel I could be doing something more useful.'

'But darling, you told me your mortar was one of the key points of the defence.'

'So it is,' said Alastair loyally.

'So what?' Then Alastair said, 'Sonia, would you think it bloody of me if I volunteered for special service?'

'Dangerous?'

'I don't suppose so really. But very exciting. They're getting up special parties for raiding. They go across to France and creep up behind Germans and cut their throats in the dark.' He was excited, turning a page in his life, as, more than twenty years ago lying on his stomach before the fire, with a bound volume of *Chums*, he used to turn over to the next instalment of the serial.

'It doesn't seem much of a time to leave a girl,' said Sonia, 'but I can see you want to.'

'They have special knives and tommy-guns and knuckle-dusters; they wear rope-soled shoes.'

'Bless you,' said Sonia.

'I heard about it from Peter Pastmaster. A man in his regiment is raising one. Peter's got a troop in it. He says I can be one of his section commanders; they can fix me up with a commission apparently. They carry rope ladders round their waists and files sewn in the seams of their coats to escape with. D'you mind very much if I accept?'

'No, darling. I couldn't keep you from the rope ladder. Not from the rope ladder I couldn't. I see that.'

Angela had never considered the possibility of Cedric's death. She received the news in an official telegram and for some days would speak to no one, not even to Basil, about the subject. When she mentioned it, she spoke from the middle rather than from the beginning or the end of her progression of thought.

'I knew we needed a death,' she said. 'I never thought it was his.'

Basil said, 'Do you want to marry me?'

'Yes, I think so. Neither of us could ever marry anyone else, you know.'

'That's true.'

'You'd like to be rich, wouldn't you?'

'Will anyone be rich after this war?'

'If anyone is, I shall be. If no one is, I don't suppose it matters so much being poor.'

'I don't know that I want to be rich,' said Basil, after a pause. 'I'm not acquisitive, you know. I only enjoy the funnier side of getting money–not having it.'

'Anyway it's not an important point. The thing is that we aren't separable any more.'

'Let nothing unite us but death. You always thought *I* was going to die, didn't you?'

'Yes.'

'The dog it was that died . . . Anyway, this is no time to be thinking of marrying. Look at Peter. He's not been married six weeks and there he is joining a gang of desperadoes. What's the sense of marrying with things as they are? I don't see what there is to marriage, if it isn't looking forward to a comfortable old age.'

'The only thing in war-time is not to think ahead. It's like walking in the blackout with a shaded torch. You can just see as far as the step you're taking.'

'I shall be a terrible husband.'

'Yes, darling, don't I know it? But you see one can't expect anything to be perfect now. In the old days if there was one thing wrong it spoiled everything; from now on for all our lives, if there's one thing right the day is made.'

'That sounds like poor Ambrose in his Chinese mood.'

Poor Ambrose had moved west. Only the wide, infested Atlantic lay between him and Parsnip. He had taken rooms in a little fishing town and the great waves pounded on the rocks below his windows. The days passed and he did absolutely nothing. The fall of France had no audible echo on that remote shore.

This is the country of Swift, Burke, Sheridan, Wellington, Wilde, T.E. Lawrence, he thought; this is the people who once lent fire to an imperial race, whose genius flashed through two stupendous centuries of culture and success, who are now quietly receding into their own mists, turning their backs on the world of effort and action. Fortunate islanders, thought Ambrose, happy, drab escapists, who have seen the gold lace and the candlelight and left the banquet before dawn revealed stained table linen and a tipsy buffoon!

But he knew it was not for him; the dark, nomadic strain in his blood, the long heritage of wandering and speculation allowed him no rest. Instead of Atlantic breakers he saw the camels swaying their heads resentfully against the lightening sky, as the caravan woke to another day's stage in the pilgrimage.

Old Rampole sat in his comfortable cell and turned his book to catch the last, fading light of evening. He was absorbed and enchanted. At an age when most men are rather concerned to preserve familiar joys than to seek for new, at, to be exact, the age of sixty-two, he had suddenly discovered the delights of light literature.

There was an author on the list of his firm of whom Mr Bentley was slightly ashamed. She wrote under the name of Ruth Mountdragon, a pseudonym which hid the identity of a Mrs Parker. Every year for seventeen years Mrs Parker had written a novel dealing with the domestic adventures of a different family; radically different that is to say in name, exhibiting minor differences of composition and circumstance, but spiritually as indistinguishable as larches; they all had the quality of 'charm'; once it was a colonel's family of three girls in reduced circumstances on a chicken farm, once it was an affluent family on a cruise in the Adriatic, once a newly-married doctor in Hampstead; all the permutations and combinations of upper middle-class life had been methodically exploited for seventeen years; but the charm was constant. Mrs Parker's public was not vast, but it was substantial; it lay, in literary appreciation, midway between the people who liked some books and disliked others, and the people who merely liked reading, inclining rather to the latter group. Mr Rampole knew her name as one of the authors who were not positively deleterious to his pocket, and consequently when his new manner of life and the speculative tendencies which it fostered caused him to take up novel reading he began on her. He was transported into a strange world of wholly delightful, estimable people whom he had rightly supposed not to exist. With each page a deeper contentment settled on the old publisher. He had already read ten books and looked forward eagerly to re-reading them when he came to the end of the seventeenth. Mr Bentley was even engaged to bring Mrs Parker to visit him at a future, unspecified date. The prison chaplain was also an admirer of Mrs Parker's. Old Rampole gained great face from disclosing her real name. He half-promised to allow the chaplain to meet her. He was happier than he could remember ever having been.

Peter Pastmaster and the absurdly youthful colonel of the new force were drawing up a list of suitable officers in Bratts Club.

'Most of war seems to consist of hanging about,' he said. 'Let's at least hang about with our own friends.'

'I've a letter from a man who says he's a friend of yours. Basil Seal.'

'Does he want to join?'

'Yes. Is he all right?'

'Perfect,' said Peter. 'A tough nut.'

'Right. I'll put him down with Alastair Trumpington as your other subaltern.'

'No. For God's sake don't do that. But make him liaison officer.'

'You see, I know everything about you,' said Angela.

'There's one thing you don't know,' said Basil. 'If you really want to be a widow again, we'd better marry quick. I don't think I told you. I'm joining a new racket.'

'Basil, what?'

'Very secret.'

'But why?'

'Well, you know, things haven't been quite the same at the War House lately. I don't know why it is, but Colonel Plum doesn't seem to love me as he did. I think he's a bit jealous about the way I pulled off the *Ivory Tower* business. We've never really been matey since. Besides, you know, that racket was all very well in the winter, when there wasn't any real war. It won't do now. There's only one serious occupation for a chap now, that's killing Germans. I have an idea I shall rather enjoy it.'

'Basil's left the War Office,' said Lady Seal.

'Yes,' said Sir Joseph, with sinking heart. Here it was again; the old business. The news from all over the world might be highly encouraging–and, poor booby, he believed it was–; we might have a great new secret weapon–and, poor booby, he thought we had; he might himself enjoy a position of great trust and dignity–poor booby, he was going, that afternoon, to address a drawing-room meeting on the subject of hobbies for the A.T.S.–but in spite of all this, Basil was always with him, a grim *memento mori* staring him out of countenance. 'Yes,' he said, 'I suppose he has.'

'He has joined a special corps d'élite that is being organized. They are going to do great things.'

'He has actually joined?'

'Oh, yes.'

'There's nothing I can do to help him?'

'Dear Jo, always so kind. No. Basil has arranged it all himself. I expect that his excellent record at the War Office helped. It isn't every boy who would settle to a life of official drudgery when everyone else was going out for excitement–like Emma's silly girl in the fire brigade. No, he did his duty where he found it. And now he is getting his reward. I am not quite sure what they are going to do, but I know it is very dashing and may well have a decisive effect on the war.'

The grey moment was passed; Sir Joseph, who had not ceased smiling, now smiled with sincere happiness.

'There's a new spirit abroad,' he said. 'I see it on every side.'

And, poor booby, he was bang right.

Brideshead Revisited

EVELYN WAUGH

BRIDESHEAD REVISITED

The sacred and profane memories
of Captain Charles Ryder

To Laura

Author's Note
I am not I: thou art not he or she:
they are not they

E.W.

PREFACE

This novel, which is here re-issued with many small additions and some substantial cuts, lost me such esteem as I once enjoyed among my contemporaries and led me into an unfamiliar world of fan-mail and press photographers. Its theme–the operation of divine grace on a group of diverse but closely connected characters–was perhaps presumptuously large, but I make no apology for it. I am less happy about its form, whose more glaring defects may be blamed on the circumstances in which it was written.

In December 1943 I had the good fortune when parachuting to incur a minor injury which afforded me a rest from military service. This was extended by a sympathetic commanding officer, who let me remain unemployed until June 1944 when the book was finished. I wrote with a zest that was quite strange to me and also with impatience to get back to the war. It was a bleak period of present privation and threatening disaster–the period of soya beans and Basic English–and in consequence the book is infused with a kind of gluttony, for food and wine, for the splendours of the recent past, and for rhetorical and ornamental language, which now with a full stomach I find distasteful. I have modified the grosser passages but have not obliterated them because they are an essential part of the book.

I have been in two minds as to the treatment of Julia's outburst about mortal sin and Lord Marchmain's dying soliloquy. These passages were never, of course, intended to report words actually spoken. They belong to a different way of writing from, say, the early scenes between Charles and his father. I would not now introduce them into a novel which elsewhere aims at verisimilitude. But I have retained them here in something near their original form because, like the Burgundy (misprinted in many editions) and the moonlight they were essentially of the mood of writing; also because many readers liked them, though that it not a consideration of first importance.

It was impossible to foresee, in the spring of 1944, the present cult of the English country house. It seemed then that the ancestral seats which were our chief national artistic achievement were doomed to decay and spoliation like the monasteries in the sixteenth century. So I piled it on rather, with passionate sincerity. Brideshead today would be open to trippers, its treasures rearranged by expert hands and the fabric better maintained than it was by Lord Marchmain. And the English aristocracy has maintained its identity to a degree that then seemed impossible. The advance of Hooper has been held up at several points. Much of this book therefore is a panegyric preached over an empty coffin. But it would be impossible to bring it up to date without totally destroying it. It is offered to a younger generation of readers as a souvenir of the Second War rather than of the twenties or of the thirties, with which it ostensibly deals.

E.W.

Combe Florey 1959

PROLOGUE

BRIDESHEAD REVISITED

When I reached 'C' Company lines, which were at the top of the hill, I paused and looked back at the camp, just coming into full view below me through the grey mist of early morning. We were leaving that day. When we marched in, three months before, the place was under snow; now the first leaves of spring were unfolding. I had reflected then that, whatever scenes of desolation lay ahead of us, I never feared one more brutal than this, and I reflected now that it had no single happy memory for me.

Here love had died between me and the army.

Here the tram lines ended, so that men returning fuddled from Glasgow could doze in their seats until roused by their journey's end. There was some way to go from the tram-stop to the camp gates; quarter of a mile in which they could button their blouses and straighten their caps before passing the guard-room, quarter of a mile in which concrete gave place to grass at the road's edge. This was the extreme limit of the city. Here the close, homogeneous territory of housing estates and cinemas ended and the hinterland began.

The camp stood where, until quite lately, had been pasture and ploughland; the farmhouse still stood in a fold of the hill and had served us for battalion offices; ivy still supported part of what had once been the walls of a fruit garden; half an acre of mutilated old trees behind the wash-houses survived of an orchard. The place had been marked for destruction before the army came to it. Had there been another year of peace, there would have been no farmhouse, no wall, no apple trees. Already half a mile of concrete road lay between bare clay banks, and on either side a chequer of open ditches showed where the municipal contractors had designed a system of drainage. Another year of peace would have made the place part of the neighbouring suburb. Now the huts where we had wintered waited their turn for destruction.

Over the way, the subject of much ironical comment, half hidden even in winter by its embosoming trees, lay the municipal lunatic asylum, whose cast-iron railings and noble gates put our rough wire to shame. We could watch the madmen, on clement days, sauntering and skipping among the trim gravel walks and pleasantly planted lawns; happy collaborationists who had given up the unequal struggle, all doubts resolved, all duty done, the undisputed heirs-at-law of a century of progress, enjoying the heritage at their ease. As we marched past, the men used to shout greetings to them through the railings–'Keep a bed warm for me, chum. I shan't be long'–but Hooper, my newest-joined platoon-commander, grudged them their life of privilege; 'Hitler would put them in a gas chamber,' he said; 'I reckon we can learn a thing or two from him.'

Here, when we marched in at mid-winter, I brought a company of strong and hopeful men; word had gone round among them, as we moved from the moors to this dockland area, that we were at last in transit for the Middle East. As the days passed and we began clearing the snow and levelling a parade ground, I saw their disappointment change to resignation. They snuffed the smell of the fried-fish shops and cocked their ears to familiar, peace-time sounds of the works' siren and the dance-hall band. On off-days they slouched now at street corners and sidled away at the approach of an officer for fear that, by saluting, they would lose face with their new mistresses. In the company office there was a crop of minor charges and requests for compassionate leave; while it was still half-light, day began with the whine of the malingerer and the glum face and fixed eye of the man with a grievance.

And I, who by every precept should have put heart into them–how could I help them, who could so little help myself? Here the colonel under whom we had formed, was promoted out of our sight and succeeded by a younger and less lovable man, cross-posted from another regiment. There were few left in the mess now of the batch of volunteers who trained together at the outbreak of war; one way and another they were nearly all gone–some had been invalided out, some promoted to other battalions, some posted to staff jobs, some had volunteered for special service, one had got himself killed on the field firing range, one had been court-martialled–and their places were taken by conscripts; the wireless played incessantly in the ante-room nowadays, and much beer was drunk before dinner; it was not as it had been.

Here at the age of thirty-nine I began to be old. I felt stiff and weary in the evenings and reluctant to go out of camp; I developed proprietary claims to certain chairs and newspapers; I regularly drank three glasses of gin before dinner, never more or less, and went to bed immediately after the nine o'clock news. I was always awake and fretful an hour before reveille.

Here my last love died. There was nothing remarkable in the manner of its death. One day, not long before this last day in camp, as I lay awake before reveille, in the Nissen hut, gazing into the complete blackness, amid the deep breathing and muttering of the four other occupants, turning over in my mind what I had to do that day–had I put in the names of two corporals for the weapon-training course? Should I again have the largest number of men overstaying their leave in the batch due back that day? Could I trust Hooper to take the candidates class out map-reading?–as I lay in that dark hour, I was aghast to realize that something within me, long sickening, had quietly died, and felt as a husband might feel, who, in the fourth year of his marriage, suddenly knew that he had no longer any desire, or tenderness, or esteem, for a once-beloved wife; no pleasure in her company, no wish to please, no curiosity about anything she might ever do or say or think; no hope of setting things right, no self-reproach for the disaster. I knew it all, the whole drab compass of marital disillusion; we had been through it together, the Army and I, from the first importunate courtship until now, when nothing remained to us except the chill bonds of law and dury and custom. I had played every scene in the domestic tragedy, had found the early tiffs become more frequent, the tears less affecting, the reconciliations less sweet, till they engendered a mood of aloofness and cool criticism, and the growing conviction that it was not myself but the loved one who was at fault. I caught the false notes in her voice and learned to listen for them apprehensively; I recognized the blank, resentful stare of incomprehension in her eyes, and the selfish, hard set of the corners of her mouth. I learned her, as one must learn a woman one has kept house with, day in, day out, for three and a half years; I learned her slatternly ways, the routine and mechanism of her charm, her jealousy and self-seeking, and her nervous trick with the fingers when she was lying. She was stripped of all enchantment now and I knew her for an uncongenial stranger to whom I had bound myself indissolubly in a moment of folly.

So, on this morning of our move, I was entirely indifferent as to our destination. I would go on with my job, but I could bring to it nothing more than acquiescence. Our orders were to entrain at 0915 hours at a nearby siding, taking in the haversack the unexpired portion of the day's ration; that was all I needed to know. The company second-in-command had gone on with a small advance party. Company stores had been packed the day before. Hooper had been detailed to inspect the lines. The company was parading at 0730 hours with their kit-bags piled before the huts. There had been many such moves since the wildly exhilarating morning in 1940 when we had erroneously believed ourselves destined for the defence of Calais. Three or four times a year since then we had changed our location; this time our new commanding officer was making an unusual display of 'security' and had even put us to the trouble of removing all distinguishing badges from our uniforms and transport. It was 'valuable training in active service conditions', he said. 'If I find any of these female camp followers waiting for us the other end, I'll know there's been a leakage.'

The smoke from the cook-houses drifted away in the mist and the camp lay revealed as a planless maze of short-cuts, superimposed on the unfinished housing-scheme, as though disinterred at a much later date by a party of archaeologists.

'*The Pollock diggings provide a valuable link between the citizen-slave communities of the twentieth century and the tribal anarchy which succeeded them. Here you see a people of advanced culture, capable of an elaborate draining system and the construction of permanent highways, over-run by a race of the lowest type.*'

Thus, I thought, the pundits of the future might write; and, turning away, I greeted the company sergeant-major: 'Has Mr Hooper been round?'

'Haven't seen him at all this morning, sir.'

We went to the dismantled company office, where I found a window newly broken since the barrack-damages book was completed. 'Wind-in-the-night, sir,' said the sergeant-major.

(All breakages were thus attributable or to 'Sappers'-demonstration, sir.')

Hooper appeared; he was a sallow youth with hair combed back, without parting, from his forehead, and a flat, Midland accent; he had been in the company two months.

The troops did not like Hooper because he knew too little about his work and would sometimes address them individually as 'George' at stand-easies, but I had a feeling which almost amounted to affection for him, largely by reason of an incident on his first evening in mess.

The new colonel had been with us less than a week at the time and we had not yet taken his measure. He had been standing rounds of gin in the ante-room and was slightly boisterous when he first took notice of Hooper.

'That young officer is one of yours, isn't he, Ryder?' he said to me. 'His hair wants cutting.'

'It does, sir,' I said. It did. 'I'll see that it's done.'

The colonel drank more gin and began to stare at Hooper, saying audibly, 'My God, the officers they send us now!'

Hooper seemed to obsess the colonel that evening. After dinner he suddenly said very loudly: 'In my late regiment if a young officer turned up like that, the other subalterns would bloody well have cut his hair for him.'

No one showed any enthusiasm for this sport, and our lack of response seemed to inflame the colonel, 'You,' he said, turning to a decent boy in 'A' Company, 'go and get a pair of scissors and cut that young officer's hair for him.'

'Is that an order, sir?'

'It's your commanding officer's wish and that's the best kind of order I know.'

'Very good, sir.'

And so, in an atmosphere of chilly embarrassment, Hooper sat in a chair while a few snips were made at the back of his head. At the beginning of the operation I left the ante-room, and later apologized to Hooper for his reception. 'It's not the sort of thing that usually happens in this regiment,' I said.

'Oh, no hard feelings,' said Hooper. 'I can take a bit of sport.'

Hooper had no illusions about the Army–or rather no special illusions distinguishable from the general, enveloping fog from which he observed the universe. He had come it it reluctantly, under compulsion, after he had made every feeble effort in his power to obtain deferment. He accepted it, he said, 'like the measles'. Hooper was no romantic. He had not as a child ridden with Rupert's horse or sat among the camp fires at Xanthus-side; at the age when my eyes were dry to all save poetry–that stoic, red-skin interlude which our schools introduce between the fast-flowing tears of the child and the man–Hooper had wept often, but never for Henry's speech on St Crispin's day, nor for the epitaph at Thermopylae. The history they taught him had had few battles in it but, instead, a profusion of detail about humane legislation and recent industrial change. Gallipoli, Balaclava, Quebec, Lepanto, Bannockburn, Roncevales, and Marathon–these, and the Battle in the West where Arthur fell, and a hundred such names whose trumpet-notes, even now in my sere and lawless state, called to me irresistibly across the intervening years with all the clarity and strength of boyhood, sounded in vain to Hooper.

He seldom complained. Though himself a man to whom one could not confidently entrust the simplest duty, he had an over-mastering regard for efficiency and, drawing on his modest commercial experience, he would sometimes say of the ways of the Army in pay and supply and the use of 'man-hours': 'They couldn't get away with that in business.'

He slept sound while I lay awake fretting.

In the weeks that we were together Hooper became a symbol to me of Young England, so that whenever I read some public utterance proclaiming what Youth demanded in the Future and what the world owed to Youth, I would test these general statements by substituting 'Hooper' and seeing if they still seemed as plausible. Thus in the dark hour before reveille I sometimes pondered: 'Hooper Rallies', 'Hooper Hostels', International Hooper Cooperation', and 'the Religion of Hooper'. He was the acid test of all these alloys.

So far as he had changed at all, he was less soldierly now than when he arrived from his OCTU. This morning, laden with full equipment, he looked scarcely human. He came to attention with a kind of shuffling dance-step and spread a wool-gloved palm across his forehead.

'I want to speak to Mr Hooper, sergeant-major . . . well, where the devil have you been? I told you to inspect the lines.'

''M I late? Sorry. Had a rush getting my gear together.'

'That's what you have a servant for.'

'Well, I suppose it is, strictly speaking. But you know how it is. He had his own stuff to do. If you get on the wrong side of these fellows they take it out of you other ways.'

'Well, go and inspect the lines now.'

'Rightyoh.'

'And for Christ's sake don't say "rightyoh".'

'Sorry. I do try to remember. It just slips out.'

When Hooper left the sergeant-major returned.

'C.O. just coming up the path, sir,' he said.

I went out to meet him.

There were beads of moisture on the hog-bristles of his little red moustache.

'Well, everything squared up here?'

'Yes, I think so, sir.'

'*Think so?* You ought to know.'

His eyes fell on the broken window. 'Has that been entered in the barrack damages?'

Not yet, sir.'

'*Not yet?* I wonder when it would have been, if I hadn't seen it.'

He was not at ease with me, and much of his bluster rose from timidity, but I thought none the better of it for that.

He led me behind the huts to a wire fence which divided my area from the carrier-platoon's, skipped briskly over, and made for an overgrown ditch and bank which had once been a field boundary on the farm. Here he began grubbing with his walking-stick like a truffling pig and presently gave a cry of triumph. He had disclosed one of those deposits of rubbish, which are dear to the private soldier's sense of order: the head of a broom, the lid of a stove, a bucket rusted through, a sock, a loaf of bread, lay under the dock and nettle among cigarette packets and empty tins.

'Look at that,' said the commanding officer. 'Fine impression that gives to the regiment taking over from us.'

'That's bad,' I said.

'It's a disgrace. See everything there is burned before you leave camp.'

'Very good, sir. Sergeant-major, send over to the carrier-platoon and tell Captain Brown that the C.O. wants this ditch cleared up.'

I wondered whether the colonel would take this rebuff; so did he. He stood a moment irresolutely prodding the muck in the ditch, then he turned on his heel and strode away.

'You shouldn't do it, sir,' said the sergeant-major, who had been my guide and prop since I joined the company. 'You shouldn't really.'

'That wasn't our rubbish.'

'Maybe not, sir, but you know how it is. If you get on the wrong side of senior officers they take it out of you other ways.'

As we marched past the madhouse, two or three elderly inmates gibbered and mouthed politely behind the railings.

'Cheeroh, chum, we'll be seeing you'; 'We shan't be long now'; 'Keep smiling till we meet again', the men called to them.

I was marching with Hooper at the head of the leading platoon.

'I say, any idea where we're off to?'

'None.'

'D'you think it's the real thing?'

'No.'

'Just a flap?'

'Yes.'

'Everyone's been saying we're for it. I don't know what to think really. Seems so silly somehow, all this drill and training if we never go into action.'

'I shouldn't worry. There'll be plenty for everyone in time.'

'Oh, I don't want *much* you know. Just enough to say I've been in it.'

A train of antiquated coaches was waiting for us at the siding; an R.T.O. was in charge; a fatigue party was loading the last of the kit-bags from the trucks to the luggage vans. In half an hour we were ready to start and in an hour we started.

My three platoon commanders and myself had a carriage to ourselves. They ate sandwiches and chocolate, smoked and slept. None of them had a book. For the first three or four hours they noted the names of the towns and leaned out of the windows when, as often happened, we stopped between stations. Later they lost interest. At midday and again at dark some tepid cocoa was ladled from a container into our mugs. The train moved slowly south through flat, drab main-line scenery.

The chief incident in the day was the C.O.'s 'order group'. We assembled in his carriage, at the summons of an orderly, and found him and the adjutant wearing their steel helmets and equipment. The first thing he said was: 'This is an Order Group. I expect you to attend properly dressed. The fact that we happen to be in a train is immaterial.' I thought he was going to send us back but, after glaring at us, he said, 'Sit down.'

'The camp was left in a disgraceful condition. Wherever I went I found evidence that officers are not doing their duty. The state in which a camp is left is the best possible test of the efficiency of regimental officers. It is on such matters that the reputation of a battalion and its commander rests. And'–did he in fact say this or am I finding words for the resentment in his voice and eye? I think he left it unsaid–'I do not intend to have my professional reputation compromised by the slackness of a few temporary officers.'

We sat with our note-books and pencils waiting to take down the details of our next jobs. A more sensitive man would have seen that he had failed to be impressive; perhaps he saw, for he added in a petulant schoolmasterish way: 'All I ask is loyal cooperation.'

Then he referred to his notes and read:

'Orders.

'Information. The battalion is now in transit between location A and location B. This is a major L of C and is liable to bombing and gas attack from the enemy.

'Intention. I intend to arrive at location B.

'Method. Train will arrive at destination at approximately 2315 hours . . .' and so on.

The sting came at the end under the heading, 'Administration'. 'C' Company, less one platoon, was to unload the train on arrival at the siding where three three-tonners would be available for moving all stores to a battalion dump in the new camp; work to continue until completed; the remaining platoon was to find a guard on the dump and perimeter sentries for the camp area.

'Any questions?'

'Can we have an issue of cocoa for the working party?'

'No. Any more questions?'

When I told the sergeant-major of these orders he said: 'Poor old "C" Company struck unlucky again,; and I knew this to be a reproach for my having antagonized the commanding officer.

I told the platoon commanders.

'I say,' said Hooper, 'it makes it awfully awkward with the chaps. They'll be fairly browned off. He always seems to pick on us for the dirty work.'

'You'll do guard.'

'Okeydoke. But I say, how am I to find the perimeter in the dark?'

Shortly after blackout we were disturbed by an orderly making his way lugubriously down the length of the train with a rattle. One of the more sophisticated sergeants called out '*Deuxième service*.'

'We are being sprayed with liquid mustard-gas,' I said. 'See that the windows are shut.' I then wrote a neat little situation-report to say that there were no casualties and nothing had been contaminated; that men had been detailed to decontaminate the outside of the coach before detraining. This seemed to satisfy the commanding officer, for we heard no more from him. After dark we all slept.

At last, very late, we came to our siding. It was part of our training in security and active service conditions that we should eschew stations and platforms. The drop from the running board to the cinder track made for disorder and breakages in the darkness.

'Fall in on the road below the embankment. "C" Company seem to be taking their time as usual, Captain Ryder.'

'Yes, sir. We're having a little difficulty with the bleach.'

'Bleach?'

'For decontaminating the outside of the coaches, sir.'

'Oh, very conscientious, I'm sure. Skip it and get a move on.'

By now my half-awake and sulky men were clattering into shape on the road. Soon Hooper's platoon had marched off into the darkness; I found the lorries, organized lines of men to pass the stores from hand to hand down the steep bank, and, presently, as they found themselves doing something with an apparent purpose in it, they got more cheerful. I handled stores with them for the first half hour; then broke off to meet the company second-in-command who came down with the first returning truck.

'It's not a bad camp,' he reported; 'big private house with two or three lakes. Looks as if we might get some duck if we're lucky. Village with one pub and a post office. No town within miles. I've managed to get a hut between the two of us.'

By four in the morning the work was done. I drove in the last lorry, through tortuous lanes where the overhanging boughs whipped the windscreen; somewhere we left the lane and turned into a drive; somewhere we reached an open space where two drives converged and a ring of storm lanterns marked the heap of stores. Here we unloaded the truck and, at long last, followed the guides to our quarters, under a starless sky, with a fine drizzle of rain beginning now to fall.

I slept until my servant called me, rose wearily, dressed and shaved in silence. It was not till I reached the door that I asked the second-in-command, 'What's this place called?'

He told me and, on the instant, it was as though someone had switched off the wireless, and a voice that had been bawling in my ears, incessantly, fatuously, for days beyond number, had been suddenly cut short; an immense silence followed, empty at first, but gradually, as my outraged sense regained authority, full of a multitude of sweet and natural and long forgotten sounds: for he had spoken a name that was so familiar to me, a conjuror's name of such ancient power, that, at its mere sound, the phantoms of those haunted late years began to take flight.

Outside the hut I stood bemused. The rain had ceased but the clouds hung low and heavy overhead. It was a still morning and the smoke from the cookhouse rose straight to the leaden sky. A cart-track, once metalled, then overgrown, now rutted and churned to mud, followed the contour of the hillside and dipped out of sight below a knoll, and on either side of it lay the haphazard litter of corrugated iron, from which rose the rattle and chatter and whistling and catcalls, all the zoo-noises of the battalion beginning a new day. Beyond and about us, more familiar still, lay an exquisite man-made landscape. It was a sequestered place, enclosed and embraced in a single, winding valley. Our camp lay along one gentle slope; opposite us the ground led, still unravished, to the neighbourly horizon, and between us flowed a stream–it was named the Bride and rose not two miles away at a farm called Bridesprings, where we used sometimes to walk to tea; it became a considerable river lower down before it joined the Avon–which had been dammed here to form three lakes, one no more than a wet slate among the reeds, but the others more spacious, reflecting the clouds and the mighty beeches at their margin. The woods were all of oak and beech, the oak grey and bare, the beech faintly dusted with green by the breaking buds; they made a simple, carefully designed pattern with the green glades and the wide green spaces–Did the fallow deer graze here still?–and, lest the eye wander aimlessly, a Doric temple stood by the water's edge, and an ivy-grown arch spanned the lowest of the connecting weirs. All this had been planned and planted a century and a half ago so that, at about this date, it might be seen in its maturity. From where I stood the house was hidden by a green spur, but I knew well how and where it lay, couched among the lime trees like a hind in the bracken.

Hooper came sidling up and greeted me with his much imitated but inimitable salute. His face was grey from his night's vigil and he had not yet shaved.

'"B" Company relieved us. I've sent the chaps off to get cleaned up.'

'Good.'

'The house is up there, round the corner.'

'Yes,' I said.

'Brigade Headquarters are coming there next week. Great barrack of a place. I've just had a snoop round. Very ornate, I'd call it. And a queer thing, there's a sort of R.C. Church attached. I looked in and there was a kind of service going on–just a padre and one old man. I felt very awkward. More in your line than mine.' Perhaps I seemed not to hear; in a final effort to excite my interest he said: 'There's a frightful great fountain, too, in front of the steps, all rocks and sort of carved animals. You never saw such a thing.'

'Yes, Hooper, I did. I've been here before.'

The words seemed to ring back to me enriched from the vaults of my dungeon.

'Oh well, you know all about it. I'll go and get cleaned up.'

I had been there before; I knew all about it.

PART I

ET IN ARCADIA EGO

I

'I have been here before,' I said; I had been there before; first with Sebastian more than twenty years ago on a cloudless day in June, when the ditches were creamy with meadowsweet and the air heavy with all the scents of summer; it was a day of peculiar splendour, and though I had been there so often, in so many moods, it was to that first visit that my heart returned on this, my latest.

That day, too, I had come not knowing my destination. It was Eights Week. Oxford–submerged now and obliterated, irrecoverable as Lyonnesse, so quickly have the waters come flooding in–Oxford, in those days, was still a city of aquatint. In her spacious and quiet streets men walked and spoke as they had done in Newman's day; her autumnal mists, her grey springtime, and the rare glory of her summer days–such as that day–when the chestnut was in flower and the bells rang out high and clear over her gables and cupolas, exhaled the soft airs of centuries of youth. It was this cloistral hush which gave our laughter its resonance, and carried it still, joyously, over the intervening clamour. Here, discordantly, in Eights Week, came a rabble of womankind, some hundreds strong, twittering and fluttering over the cobbles and up the steps, sight-seeing and pleasure-seeking, drinking claret cup, eating cucumber sandwiches; pushed in punts about the river, herded in droves to the college barges; greeted in the *Isis* and in the Union by a sudden display of peculiar, facetious, wholly distressing Gilbert-and-Sullivan badinage, and by peculiar choral effects in the College chapels. Echoes of the intruders penetrated every corner, and in my own College was no echo, but an original fount of the grossest disturbance. We were giving a ball. The front quad, where I lived, was floored and tented; palms and azaleas were banked round the porter's lodge; worst of all, the don who lived above me, a mouse of a man connected with the Natural Sciences, had lent his rooms for a Ladies' Cloakroom, and a printed notice proclaiming this outrage hung not six inches from my oak.

No one felt more strongly about it than my scout.

'Gentlemen who haven't got ladies are asked as far as possible to take their meals out in the next few days,' he announced despondently. 'Will you be lunching in?'

'No, Lunt.'

'So as to give the servants a chance, they say. What a chance! I've got to buy a *pin-cushion* for the Ladies' Cloakroom. What do they want with dancing? I don't see the reason in it. There never was dancing before in Eights Week. Commem. now is another matter being in the vacation, but not in Eights Week, as if teas and the river wasn't enough. If you ask me, sir, it's all on account of the war. It couldn't have happened but for that.' For this was 1923 and for Lunt, as for thousands of others, things could never be the same as they had been in 1914. 'Now wine in the evening,' he continued, as was his habit half in and half out of the door, 'or one or two gentlemen to luncheon, there's reason in. But not dancing. It all came in with the men back from the war. They were too old and they didn't know and they wouldn't learn. That's the truth. And there's some even goes dancing with the town at the Masonic–but the proctors will get *them*, you see . . . Well, here's Lord Sebastian. I mustn't stand here talking when there's pin-cushions to get.'

Sebastian entered–dove-grey flannel, white *crêpe de Chine*, a Charvet tie, my tie as it happened, a pattern of postage stamps–'Charles–what in the world's happening at your college? Is there a circus? I've seen everything except elephants. I must say the whole of Oxford has become *most* peculiar suddenly. Last night it was pullulating with women. You're to come away at once, out of danger. I've got a motor-car and a basket of strawberries and a bottle of Château Peyraguey–which isn't a wine you've ever tasted, so don't pretend. It's heaven with strawberries.'

'Where are we going?'

'To see a friend.'

'Who?'

'Name of Hawkins. Bring some money in case we see anything we want to buy. The motor-car is the property of a man called Hardcastle. Return the bits to him if I kill myself; I'm not very good at driving.'

Beyond the gate, beyond the winter garden that was once the lodge, stood an open, two-seater Morris-Cowley. Sebastian's teddy bear sat at the wheel. We put him between us–'Take care he's not sick'–and drove off. The bells of St Mary's were chiming nine; we escaped collision with a clergyman, black-straw-hatted, white-bearded, pedalling quietly down the wrong side of the High Street, crossed Carfax, passed the station, and were soon in open country on the Botley Road; open country was easily reached in those days.

'Isn't it early?' said Sebastian. 'The women are still doing whatever women do to themselves before they come downstairs. Sloth has undone them. We're away. God bless Hardcastle.'

'Whoever he may be.'

'He thought he was coming with us. Sloth undid him too. Well, I did tell him *ten*. He's a very gloomy man in my college. He leads a double life. At least I assume he does. He couldn't go on being Hardcastle, day and night, always, could he?–or he'd die of it. He says he knows my father, which is impossible.'

'Why?'

'No one knows papa. He's a social leper. Hadn't you heard?'

'It's a pity neither of us can sing,' I said.

At Swindon we turned off the main road and, as the sun mounted high, we were among dry-stone walls and ashlar houses. It was about eleven when Sebastian, without warning, turned the car into a cart track and stopped. It was hot enough now to make us seek the shade. On a sheep-cropped knoll under a clump of elms we ate the strawberries and drank the wine–as Sebastian promised, they were delicious together–and we lit fat, Turkish cigarettes and lay on our backs, Sebastian's eyes on the leaves above him, mine on his profile, while the blue-grey smoke rose, untroubled by any wind, to the blue-green shadows of foliage, and the sweet scent of the tobacco merged with the sweet summer scents around us and the fumes of the sweet, golden wine seemed to lift us a finger's breadth above the turf and hold us suspended.

'Just the place to bury a crock of gold,' said Sebastian. 'I should like to bury something precious in every place where I've been happy and then, when I was old and ugly and miserable, I could come back and dig it up and remember.'

This was my third term since matriculation, but I date my Oxford life from my first meeting with Sebastian, which had happened, by chance, in the middle of the term before. We were in different colleges and came from different schools; I might well have spent my three or four years in the University and never have met him, but for the chance of his getting drunk one evening in my college and of my having ground-floor rooms in the front quadrangle.

I had been warned against the dangers of these rooms by my cousin Jasper, who alone, when I first came up, thought me a suitable subject for detailed guidance. My father offered me none. Then, as always, he eschewed serious conversation with me. It was not until I was within a fortnight of going up that he mentioned the subject at all; then he said, shyly and rather slyly: 'I've been talking about you. I met your future Warden at the Athenaeum. I wanted to talk about Etruscan notions of immortality; he wanted to talk about extension lectures for the working-class; so we compromised and talked about you. I asked him what your allowance should be. He said, "Three hundred a year; on no account give him more; that's all most men have." I thought that a deplorable answer. *I* had more than most men when *I* was up, and my recollection is that nowhere else in the world and at no other time, do a few hundred pounds, one way or the other, make so much difference to one's importance and popularity. I toyed with the idea of giving you six hundred,' said my father, snuffling a little, as he did when he was amused, 'but I reflected that, should the Warden come to hear of it, it might sound deliberately impolite. So I shall give you five hundred and fifty.'

I thanked him.

'Yes, it's indulgent of me, but it all comes out of capital, you know. . . . I suppose this is the time I should give you advice. I never had any myself except once from your cousin Alfred. Do you know, in the summer before I was going up, your cousin Alfred rode over to Boughton especially to give me a piece of advice? And do you know what that advice was? "Ned," he said, "there's one thing I must beg of you. *Always* wear a tall hat on Sundays during term. It is by that, more than anything, that a man is judged." And do you know,' continued my father, snuffling deeply, 'I *always did*? Some men did, some didn't. I never saw any difference between them or heard it commented on, but I *always wore mine*. It only shows what effect judicious advice can have, properly delivered at the right moment. I wish I had some for you, but I haven't.'

My cousin Jasper made good the loss; he was the son of my father's elder brother, to whom he referred more than once, only half facetiously, as 'the Head of the Family'; he was in his fourth year and, the term before, had come within appreciable distance of getting his rowing blue; he was secretary of the

Canning and president of the J.C.R.; a considerable person in college. He called on me formally during my first week and stayed to tea; he ate a very heavy meal of honey-buns, anchovy toast, and Fuller's walnut cake, then he lit his pipe and, lying back in the basket-chair, laid down the rules of conduct which I should follow; he covered most subjects; even today I could repeat much of what he said, word for word. '... You're reading History? A perfectly respectable school. The very worst is English literature and the next worst is Modern Greats. You want either a first or a fourth. There is no value in anything between. Time spent on a good second is time thrown away. You should go to the best lectures–Arkwright on Demosthenes for instance–irrespective of whether they are in your school or not ... Clothes. Dress as you do in a country house. Never wear a tweed coat and flannel trousers–always a suit. And go to a London tailor; you get better cut and longer credit. ... Clubs. Join the Carlton now and the Grid at the beginning of your second year. If you want to run for the Union–and it's not a bad thing to do–make your reputation *outside* first, at the Canning or the Chatham, and begin by speaking on the paper. ... Keep clear of Boar's Hill. ...' The sky over the opposing gables glowed and then darkened; I put more coal on the fire and turned on the light, revealing in their respectability his London-made plus-fours and his Leander tie. ... 'Don't treat dons like schoolmasters; treat them as you would the vicar at home. ... You'll find you spend half your second year shaking off the undesirable friends you made in your first. ... Beware of the Anglo-Catholics–they're all sodomites with unpleasant accents. In fact, steer clear of all the religious groups; they do nothing but harm. ...'

Finally, just as he was going, he said, 'One last point. Change your rooms.'–They were large, with deeply recessed windows and painted, eighteenth-century panelling; I was lucky as a freshman to get them. 'I've seen many a man ruined through having ground-floor rooms in the front quad,' said my cousin with deep gravity. 'People start dropping in. They leave their gowns here and come and collect them before hall; you start giving them sherry. Before you know where you are, you've opened a free bar for all the undesirables of the college.'

I do not know that I ever, consciously, followed any of this advice. I certainly never changed my rooms; there were gillyflowers growing below the windows which on summer evenings filled them with fragrance.

It is easy, retrospectively, to endow one's youth with a false precocity or a false innocence; to tamper with the dates marking one's stature on the edge of the door. I should like to think–indeed I sometimes do think–that I decorated those rooms with Morris stuffs and Arundel prints and that my shelves were filled with seventeenth-century folios and French novels of the second empire in Russia-leather and watered silk. But this was not the truth. On my first afternoon I proudly hung a reproduction of Van Gogh's *Sunflowers* over the fire and set up a screen, painted by Roger Fry with a Provençal landscape, which I had bought inexpensively when the Omega workshops were sold up. I displayed also a poster by McKnight Kauffer and Rhyme Sheets from the Poetry Bookshop, and, most painful to recall, a porcelain figure of Polly Peachum which stood between black tapers on the chimney-piece. My books were meagre and commonplace–Roger Fry's *Vision and Design*, the Medici Press edition of *A Shropshire Lad*, *Eminent Victorians*, some volumes of

Georgian Poetry, *Sinister Street* and *South Wind*–and my earliest friends fitted well into this background; they were Collins, a Wykehamist, an embryo don, a man of solid reading and childlike humour, and a small circle of college intellectuals, who maintained a middle course of culture between the flamboyant 'aesthetes' and the proletarian scholars who scrambled fiercely for facts in the lodging houses of the Iffley Road and Wellington Square. It was by this circle that I found myself adopted during my first term; they provided the kind of company I had enjoyed in the sixth form at school, for which the sixth form had prepared me; but even in the earliest days, when the whole business of living at Oxford, with rooms of my own and my own cheque book, was a source of excitement, I felt at heart that this was not all which Oxford had to offer.

At Sebastian's approach these grey figures seemed quietly to fade into the landscape and vanish, like highland sheep in the misty heather. Collins had exposed the fallacy of modern aesthetics to me: '. . . the whole argument from Significant Form stands or falls by *volume*. If you allow Cézanne to represent a third dimension on his two-dimensional canvas, then you must allow Landseer his gleam of loyalty in the spaniel's eye' . . . but it was not until Sebastian, idly turning the page of Clive Bell's *Art*, read: '"Does anyone feel the same kind of emotion for a butterfly or a flower that he feels for a cathedral or a picture?" Yes. *I* do,' that my eyes were opened.

I knew Sebastian by sight long before I met him. That was unavoidable for, from his first week, he was the most conspicuous man of his year by reason of his beauty, which was arresting, and his eccentricities of behaviour, which seemed to know no bounds. My first sight of him was in the door of Germer's, and, on that occasion, I was struck less by his looks than by the fact that he was carrying a large teddy-bear.

'That,' said the barber, as I took his chair, 'was Lord Sebastian Flyte. A *most* amusing young gentleman.'

'Apparently,' I said coldly.

'The Marquis of Marchmain's second boy. His brother the Earl of Brideshead, went down last term. Now he was *very* different, a very quiet gentleman, quite like an old man. What do you suppose Lord Sebastian wanted? A hair brush for his teddy-bear; it had to have very stiff bristles, *not*, Lord Sebastian said, to brush him with, but to threaten him with a spanking when he was sulky. He bought a very nice one with an ivory back and he's having "Aloysius" engraved on it–that's the bear's name.' The man, who, in his time, had had ample chance to tire of undergraduate fantasy, was plainly captivated. I, however, remained censorious, and subsequent glimpses of him, driving in a hansom cab and dining at the George in false whiskers, did not soften me, although Collins, who was reading Freud, had a number of technical terms to cover everything.

Nor, when at last we met, were the circumstances propitious. It was shortly before midnight in early March; I had been entertaining the college intellectuals to mulled claret; the fire was roaring, the air of my room heavy with smoke and spice, and my mind weary with metaphysics. I threw open my windows and from the quad outside came the not uncommon sounds of bibulous laughter and unsteady steps. A voice said: 'Hold up'; another, 'Come on'; another, 'Plenty of time . . . House . . . till Tom stops ringing'; and another, clearer than the rest, 'D'you know I feel most unaccountably unwell. I must leave you a minute,' and there appeared at my window the face I knew to be Sebastian's, but not, as I had formerly seen it, alive and alight with gaiety; he looked at me for a moment with unfocused eyes and then, leaning forward well into the room, he was sick.

It was not unusual for dinner parties to end in that way; there was in fact a recognized tariff for the scout on such occasions; we were all learning, by trial and error, to carry our wine. There was also a kind of insane and endearing orderliness about Sebastian's choice, in his extremity, of an open window. But, when all is said, it remained an unpropitious meeting.

His friends bore him to the gate and, in a few minutes, his host, an amiable Etonian of my year, returned to apologize. He, too, was tipsy and his explanations were repetitive and, towards the end, tearful. 'The wines were too various,' he said: 'it was neither the quality nor the quantity that was at fault. It was the mixture. Grasp that and you have the root of the matter. To understand all is to forgive all.'

'Yes,' I said, but it was with a sense of grievance that I faced Lunt's reproaches next morning.

'A couple of jugs of mulled claret between the five of you,' Lunt said, 'and *this* had to happen. Couldn't even get to the window. Those that can't keep it down are better without it.'

'It wasn't one of my party. It was someone from out of college.'

'Well, it's just as nasty clearing it up, whoever it was.'

'There's five shillings on the sideboard.'

'So I saw and thank you, but I'd rather not have the money and not have the mess, *any* morning.'

I took my gown and left him to his task. I still frequented the lecture-room in those days, and it was after eleven when I returned to college. I found my room full of flowers; what looked like, and, in fact, was, the entire day's stock of a market-stall stood in every conceivable vessel in every part of the room. Lunt was secreting the last of them in brown paper preparatory to taking them home.

'Lunt, *what* is all this?'

'The gentleman from last night, sir, he left a note for you.'

The note was written in *conté* crayon on a whole sheet of my choice Whatman H.P. drawing paper:

> I am very contrite. Aloysius won't speak to me until he sees I am forgiven, so please come to luncheon today.
>
> Sebastian Flyte

It was typical of him, I reflected, to assume I knew where he lived; but, then, I *did* know.

'A most amusing gentleman, I'm sure it's quite a pleasure to clean up after him. I take it you're lunching out, sir. I told Mr Collins and Mr Partridge so–they wanted to have their commons in here with you.'

'Yes, Lunt, lunching out.'

That luncheon party–for party it proved to be–was the beginning of a new epoch in my life.

I went there uncertainly, for it was foreign ground and there was a tiny, priggish, warning voice in my ear which in the tones of Collins told me it was seemly to hold back. But I was in search of love in those days, and I went full of curiosity and the faint, unrecognized apprehension that here, at last, I should find that low door in the wall, which others, I knew, had found before me, which opened on an enclosed and enchanted garden, which was somewhere, not overlooked by any window, in the heart of that grey city.

Sebastian lived at Christ Church, high in Meadow Buildings. He was alone when I came, peeling a plover's egg taken from the large nest of moss in the centre of his table.

'I've just counted them,' he said. 'There were five each and two over, so I'm having the two. I'm unaccountably hungry today. I put myself unreservedly in the hands of Dolbear and Goodall, and fell so drugged that I've begun to believe that the whole of yesterday evening was a dream. Please don't wake me up.'

He was entrancing, with the epicene beauty which in extreme youth sings aloud for love and withers at the first cold wind.

His room was filled with a strange jumble of objects–a harmonium in a gothic case, an elephant's-foot waste-paper basket, a dome of wax fruit, two disproportionately large Sèvres vases, framed drawings by Daumier–made all the more incongruous by the austere college furniture and the large luncheon table. His chimney-piece was covered in cards of invitation from London hostesses.

'That beast Hobson has put Aloysius next door,' he said. 'Perhaps it's as well, as there wouldn't have been any plovers' eggs for him. D'you know, Hobson hates Aloysius. I wish I had a scout like yours. He was sweet to me this morning where some people might have been quite strict.'

The party assembled. There were three Etonian freshmen, mild, elegant, detached young men who had all been to a dance in London the night before, and spoke of it as though it had been the funeral of a near but unloved kinsman. Each as he came into the room made first for the plovers' eggs, then noticed Sebastian and then myself with a polite lack of curiosity which seemed to say: 'We should not dream of being so offensive as to suggest that you never met us before.'

'The first this year,' they said. 'Where do you get them?'

'Mummy sends them from Brideshead. They always lay early for her.'

When the eggs were gone and we were eating the lobster Newburg, the last guest arrived.

'My dear,' he said, 'I couldn't get away before. I was lunching with my p-p-preposterous tutor. He thought it very odd my leaving when I did. I told him that I had to change for *F-f-footer*.'

He was tall, slim, rather swarthy, with large saucy eyes. The rest of us wore rough tweeds and brogues. He had on a smooth chocolate-brown suit with loud white stripes, suède shoes, a large bow-tie and he drew off yellow, wash-leather gloves as he came into the room; part Gallic, part Yankee, part, perhaps, Jew; wholly exotic.

This, I did not need telling, was Anthony Blanche, the 'aesthete' *par excellence*, a byword of iniquity from Cherwell Edge to Somerville. He had been pointed out to me often in the streets, as he pranced along with his high peacock tread; I had heard his voice in the George challenging the conventions;

and now meeting him, under the spell of Sebastian, I found myself enjoying him voraciously.

After luncheon he stood on the balcony with a megaphone which had appeared surprisingly among the bric-à-brac of Sebastian's room, and in languishing tones recited passages from *The Waste Land* to the sweatered and muffled throng that was on its way to the river.

'*I, Tiresias, have foresuffered all*,' he sobbed to them from the Venetian arches;

> '*Enacted on this same d-divan or b-bed,*
> *I who sat by Thebes below the wall*
> *And walked among the l-l-lowest of the dead . . .*'

And then, stepping lightly into the room, 'How I have surprised them! All b-boatmen are Grace Darlings to me.'

We sat on sipping Cointreau while the mildest and most detached of the Etonians sang: 'Home they brought her warrior dead' to his own accompaniment on the harmonium.

It was four o'clock before we broke up.

Anthony Blanche was the first to go. He took formal and complimentary leave for each of us in turn. To Sebastian he said: 'My dear, I should like to stick you full of barbed arrows like a p-p-pin-cushion,' and to me: 'I think it's perfectly brilliant of Sebastian to have discovered you. Where do you lurk? I shall come down your burrow and ch-chivvy you out like an old st-t-toat.'

The others left soon after him. I rose to go with them, but Sebastian said: 'Have some more Cointreau,' so I stayed and later he said, 'I must go to the Botanical Gardens.'

'Why?'

'To see the ivy.'

It seemed a good enough reason and I went with him. He took my arm as we walked under the walls of Merton.

'I've never been to the Botanical Gardens,' I said.

'Oh, Charles, what a lot you have to learn! There's a beautiful arch there and more different kinds of ivy than I knew existed. I don't know where I should be without the Botanical Gardens.'

When at length I returned to my rooms and found them exactly as I had left them that morning, I detected a jejune air that had not irked me before. What was wrong? Nothing except the golden daffodils seemed to be real. Was it the screen? I turned it face to the wall. That was better.

It was the end of the screen. Lunt never liked it, and after a few days he took it away, to an obscure refuge he had under the stairs, full of mops and buckets.

That day was the beginning of my friendship with Sebastian, and thus it came about, that morning in June, that I was lying beside him in the shade of the high elms watching the smoke from his lips drift up into the branches.

Presently we drove on and in another hour were hungry. We stopped at an inn, which was half farm also, and ate eggs and bacon, pickled walnuts and cheese, and drank our beer in a sunless parlour where an old clock ticked in the shadows and a cat slept by the empty grate.

We drove on and in the early afternoon came to our destination: wrought-iron gates and twin, classical lodges on a village green, an avenue, more gates, open park-land, a turn in the drive; and suddenly a new and secret landscape opened before us. We were at the head of a valley and below us, half a mile distant, grey and gold amid a screen of boskage, shone the dome and columns of an old house.

'Well?' said Sebastian, stopping the car. Beyond the dome lay receding steps of water and round it, guarding and hiding it, stood the soft hills.

'Well?'

'What a place to live in!' I said.

'You must see the garden front and the fountain.' He leaned forward and put the car into gear. 'It's where my family live'; and even then, rapt in the vision, I felt, momentarily, an ominous chill at the words he used–not, 'that is my house', but 'it's where my family live'.

'Don't worry,' he continued, 'they're all away. You won't have to meet them.'

'But I should like to.'

'Well, you can't. They're in London.'

We drove round the front into a side court–'Everything's shut up. We'd better go in this way'–and entered through the fortress-like, stone-flagged, stone-vaulted passages of the servants' quarters–'I want you to meet Nanny Hawkins. That's what we've come for'–and climbed uncarpeted, scrubbed elm stairs, followed more passages of wide boards covered in the centre by a thin strip of drugget, through passages covered by linoleum, passing the wells of many minor staircases and many rows of crimson and gold fire buckets, up a final staircase, gated at the head. The dome was false, designed to be seen from below like the cupolas of Chambord. Its drum was merely an additional storey full of segmental rooms. Here were the nurseries.

Sebastian's nanny was seated at the open window; the fountain lay before her, the lakes, the temple, and, far away on the last spur, a glittering obelisk; her hands lay open in her lap and, loosely between them, a rosary; she was fast asleep. Long hours of work in her youth, authority in middle life, repose and security in her age, had set their stamp on her lined and serene face.

'Well,' she said, waking; 'this *is* a surprise.'

Sebastian kissed her.

'Who's this?' she said, looking at me. 'I don't think I know him.'

Sebastian introduced us.

'You've come just the right time. Julia's here for the day. Such a time they're all having. It's dull without them. Just Mrs Chandler and two of the girls and old Bert. And then they're all going on holidays and the boiler's being done out in August and you going to see his Lordship in Italy, and the rest on visits, it'll be October before we're settled down again. Still, I suppose Julia must have her enjoyment the same as other young ladies, though what they always want to go to London for in the best of the summer and the gardens all out, I never have understood. Father Phipps was here on Thursday and I said exactly the same to him,' she added as though she had thus acquired sacerdotal authority for her opinion.

'D'you say Julia's here?'

'Yes, dear, you must have just missed her. It's the Conservative Women. Her

Ladyship was to have done them, but she's poorly. Julia won't be long; she's leaving immediately after her speech, before the tea.'

'I'm afraid we may miss her again.'

'Don't do that, dear, it'll be such a surprise to her seeing you, though she ought to wait for the tea, I told her, it's what the Conservative Women come for. Now what's the news? Are you studying hard at your books?'

'Not very, I'm afraid, nanny.'

'Ah, cricketing all day long I expect, like your brother. He found time to study, too, though. He's not been here since Christmas, but he'll be here for the Agricultural, I expect. Did you see this piece about Julia in the paper? She brought it down for me. Not that it's nearly good enough of her, but what it says is *very* nice. "The lovely daughter whom Lady Marchmain is bringing out this season . . . witty as well as ornamental . . . the most popular débutante", well that's no more than the truth, though it was a shame to cut her hair; such a lovely head of hair she had, just like her Ladyship's. I said to Father Phipps it's not natural. He said: "Nuns do it," and I said, "Well, surely, father, you aren't going to make a nun out of Lady Julia? The very idea!"'

Sebastian and the old woman talked on. It was a charming room, oddly shaped to conform with the curve of the dome. The walls were papered in a pattern of ribbon and roses. There was a rocking horse in the corner and an oleograph of the Sacred Heart over the mantelpiece; the empty grate was hidden by a bunch of pampas grass and bulrushes; laid out on the top of the chest of drawers and carefully dusted, were the collection of small presents which had been brought home to her at various times by her children, carved shell and lava, stamped leather, painted wood, china, bog-oak, damascened silver, blue-john, alabaster, coral, the souvenirs of many holidays.

Presently nanny said: 'Ring the bell, dear, and we'll have some tea. I usually go down to Mrs Chandler, but we'll have it up here today. My usual girl has gone to London with the others. The new one is just up from the village. She didn't know anything at first, but she's coming along nicely. Ring the bell.'

But Sebastian said we had to go.

'And miss Julia? She *will* be upset when she hears. It would have been *such* a surprise for her.'

'Poor nanny,' said Sebastian when we left the nursery. 'She does have such a dull life. I've a good mind to bring her to Oxford to live with me, only she'd always be trying to send me to church. We must go quickly before my sister gets back.'

'Which are you ashamed of, her or me?'

'I'm ashamed of myself,' said Sebastian gravely. 'I'm not going to have you get mixed up with my family. They're so madly charming. All my life they've been taking things away from me. If they once got hold of you with their charm, they'd make you *their* friend not mine, and I won't let them.'

'All right,' I said. 'I'm perfectly content. But am I not going to be allowed to see any more of the house?'

'It's all shut up. We came to see nanny. On Queen Alexandra's day it's all open for a shilling. Well, come and look if you want to. . . .'

He led me through a baize door into a dark corridor; I could dimly see a gilt cornice and vaulted plaster above; then, opening a heavy, smooth-swinging, mahogany door, he led me into a darkened hall. Light streamed through the cracks in the shutters. Sebastian unbarred one, and folded it back; the mellow afternoon sun flooded in, over the bare floor, the vast, twin fireplaces of sculptured marble, the coved ceiling frescoed with classic deities and heroes, the gilt mirrors and *scagliola* pilasters, the islands of sheeted furniture. It was a glimpse only, such as might be had from the top of an omnibus into a lighted ballroom; then Sebastian quickly shut out the sun. 'You see,' he said; 'it's like this.'

His mood had changed since we had drunk our wine under the elm trees, since we had turned the corner of the drive and he had said: 'Well?'

'You see, there's nothing to see. A few pretty things I'd like to show you one day–not now. But there's the chapel. You must see that. It's a monument of *art nouveau*.'

The last architect to work at Brideshead had added a colonnade and flanking pavilions. One of these was the chapel. We entered it by the public porch (another door led direct to the house); Sebastian dipped his fingers in the water stoup, crossed himself, and genuflected; I copied him. 'Why do you do that?' he asked crossly.

'Just good manners.'

'Well, you needn't on my account. You wanted to do sight-seeing; how about this?'

The whole interior had been gutted, elaborately refurnished and redecorated in the arts-and-crafts style of the last decade of the nineteenth century. Angels in printed cotton smocks, rambler-roses, flower-spangled meadows, frisking lambs, texts in Celtic script, saints in armour, covered the walls in an intricate pattern of clear, bright colours. There was a triptych of pale oak, carved so as to give it the peculiar property of seeming to have been moulded in Plasticine. The sanctuary lamp and all the metal furniture were of bronze, hand-beaten to the patina of a pock-marked skin; the altar steps had a carpet of grass-green, strewn with white and gold daisies.

'Golly,' I said.

'It was papa's wedding present to mama. Now, if you've seen enough, we'll go.'

On the drive we passed a closed Rolls-Royce driven by a chauffeur; in the back was a vague, girlish figure who looked round at us through the window.

'Julia,' said Sebastian. 'We only just got away in time.'

We stopped to speak to a man with a bicycle–'That was old Bat,' said Sebastian–and then were away, past the wrought-iron gates, past the lodges, and out on the road heading back to Oxford.

'I'm sorry,' said Sebastian after a time. 'I'm afraid I wasn't very nice this afternoon. Brideshead often has that effect on me. But I had to take you to see nanny.'

Why? I wondered; but said nothing–Sebastian's life was governed by a code of such imperatives. 'I *must* have pillar-box red pyjamas,' 'I *have* to stay in bed until the sun works round to the windows,' 'I've absolutely *got* to drink champagne tonight!'–except, 'It had quite the reverse effect on me.'

After a long pause he said petulantly, 'I don't keep asking you questions about *your* family.'

'Neither do I about yours.'

'But you look inquisitive.'

'Well, you're so mysterious about them.'

'I hoped I was mysterious about everything.'

'Perhaps I am rather curious about people's families–you see, it's not a thing I know about. There is only my father and myself. An aunt kept an eye on me for a time but my father drove her abroad. My mother was killed in the war.'

'Oh . . . how very unusual.'

'She went to Serbia with the Red Cross. My father has been rather odd in the head ever since. He just lives alone in London with no friends and footles about collecting things.'

Sebastian said, 'You don't know what you've been saved. There are lots of us. Look them up in Debrett.'

His mood was lightening now. The further we drove from Brideshead, the more he seemed to cast off his uneasiness–the almost furtive restlessness and irritability that had possessed him. The sun was behind us as we drove, so that we seemed to be in pursuit of our own shadows.

'It's half past five. We'll get to Godstow in time for dinner, drink at the Trout, leave Hardcastle's motor-car, and walk back by the river. Wouldn't that be best?'

That is the full account of my first brief visit to Brideshead; could I have known then that it would one day be remembered with tears by a middle-aged captain of infantry?

2

Towards the end of that summer term I received the last visit and Grand Remonstrance of my cousin Jasper. I was just free of the schools, having taken the last paper of History Previous on the afternoon before; Jasper's subfusc suit and white tie proclaimed him still in the thick of it; he had, too, the exhausted but resentful air of one who fears he has failed to do himself full justice on the subject of Pindar's Orphism. Duty alone had brought him to my rooms that afternoon at great inconvenience to himself and, as it happened, to me, who, when he caught me in the door, was on my way to make final arrangements about a dinner I was giving that evening. It was one of several parties designed to comfort Hardcastle–one of the tasks that had lately fallen to Sebastian and me since, by leaving his car out, we had got him into grave trouble with the proctors.

Jasper would not sit down; this was to be no cosy chat; he stood with his back to the fireplace and, in his own phrase, talked to me 'like an uncle'.

'. . . I've tried to get in touch with you several times in the last week or two. In fact, I have the impression you are avoiding me. If that is so, Charles, I can't say I'm surprised.

'You may think it none of my business, but I feel a sense of responsibility. You know as well as I do that since your–well, since the war, your father has not been really in touch with things–lives in his own world. I don't want to sit back and see you making mistakes which a word in season might save you from.

'I expected you to make mistakes your first year. We all do. I got in with some thoroughly objectionable O.S.C.U. men who ran a mission to hop-pickers during the long vac. But you, my dear Charles, whether you realize it or not, have gone straight, hook line and sinker, into the *very worst set in the University*. You may think that, living in digs, I don't know what goes on in college; but I hear things. In fact, I hear all too much. I find that I've become a figure of mockery on your account at the Dining Club. There's that chap Sebastian Flyte you seem inseparable from. He may be all right, I don't know. His brother Brideshead was a very sound fellow. But this friend of yours looks odd to me and he gets himself talked about. Of course, they're an odd family. The Marchmains have lived apart since the war, you know. An extraordinary thing; everyone thought they were a devoted couple. Then he went off to France with his Yeomanry and just never came back. It was as if he'd been killed. She's a Roman Catholic, so she can't get a divorce–or *won't*, I expect. You can do anything at Rome with money, and they're enormously rich. Flyte *may* be all right, but *Anthony Blanche*–now there's a man there's absolutely no excuse for.'

'I don't particularly like him myself,' I said.

'Well, he's always hanging round here, and the stiffer element in college don't like it. They can't stand him at the House. He was in Mercury again last night. None of these people you go about with pull any weight in their own colleges, and that's the real test. They think because they've got a lot of money to throw about, they can do anything.

'And that's another thing. I don't know what allowance my uncle makes you, but I don't mind betting you're spending double. All *this*,' he said, including in a wide sweep of his hand the evidence of profligacy about him. It was true; my room had cast its austere winter garments, and, by not very slow stages, assumed a richer wardrobe. 'Is *that* paid for?' (the box of a hundred cabinet Partagas on the sideboard) 'or *those*?' (a dozen frivolous, new books on the table) 'or those?' (a Lalique decanter and glasses) 'or *that* peculiarly noisome object?' (a human skull lately purchased from the School of Medicine, which, resting in a bowl of roses, formed, at the moment, the chief decoration of my table. It bore the motto '*Et in Arcadia ego*' inscribed on its forehead.)

'Yes,' I said, glad to be clear of one charge. 'I had to pay cash for the skull.'

'You can't be doing any work. Not that that matters, particularly if you're making something of your career elsewhere–but are you? Have you spoken at the Union or at any of the clubs? Are you connected with any of the magazines? Are you even making a position in the O.U.D.S.? And *your clothes*!' continued my cousin. 'When you came up I remember advising you to dress as you would in a country house. Your present get-up seems an unhappy compromise between the correct wear for a theatrical party at Maidenhead and a glee-singing competition in a garden suburb.

'And drink–no one minds a man getting tight once or twice a term. In fact, he ought to, on certain occasions. But I hear you're constantly seen drunk in the middle of the afternoon.'

He paused, his duty discharged. Already the perplexities of the examination school were beginning to reassert themselves in his mind.

'I'm sorry, Jasper,' I said. 'I know it must be embarrassing for you, but I happen to *like* this bad set. I *like* getting drunk at luncheon, and though I haven't yet spent quite double my allowance, I undoubtedly shall before the end of term. I usually have a glass of champagne about this time. Will you join me?'

So my cousin Jasper despaired and, I learned later, wrote to his father on the subject of my excesses who, in his turn, wrote to *my* father, who took no action or particular thought in the matter, partly because he had disliked my uncle for nearly sixty years and partly because, as Jasper had said, he lived in his own world now, since my mother's death.

Thus, in broad outline, Jasper sketched the more prominent features of my first year; some detail may be added on the same scale.

I had committed myself earlier to spend the Easter vacation with Collins and, though I would have broken my word without compunction, and left my former friend friendless, had Sebastian made a sign, no sign was made; accordingly Collins and I spent several economical and instructive weeks together in Ravenna. A bleak wind blew from the Adriatic among those mighty tombs. In an hotel bedroom designed for a warmer season, I wrote long letters to Sebastian and called daily at the post office for his answers. There were two, each from a different address, neither giving any plain news of himself, for he wrote in a style of remote fantasy–

> . . . Mummy and two attendant poets have three bad colds in the head, so I have come here. It is the feast of S. Nichodemus of Thyatira, who was martyred by having goatskin nailed to his pate, and is accordingly the patron of bald heads. Tell Collins, who I am sure will be bald before us. There are too many people here, but one, praise heaven! has an ear-trumpet, and that keeps me in good humour. And now I must try to catch a fish. It is too far to send it to you so I will keep the backbone . . .

–which left me fretful. Collins made notes for a little thesis pointing out the inferiority of the original mosaics to their photographs. Here was planted the seed of what became his life's harvest. When, many years later, there appeared the first massive volume of his still unfinished work on Byzantine Art, I was touched to find among two pages of polite, preliminary acknowledgements of debt, my own name: '. . . *to Charles Ryder, with the aid of whose all-seeing eyes I first saw the Mausoleum of Galla Placidia and San Vitale* . . .'

I sometimes wonder whether, had it not been for Sebastian, I might have trodden the same path as Collins round the cultural water-wheel. My father in his youth sat for All Souls and, in a year of hot competition, failed; other successes and honours came his way later, but that early failure impressed itself on him, and through him on me, so that I came up with an ill-considered sense that there lay the proper and natural goal of the life of reason. I, too, should doubtless have failed, but, having failed, I might perhaps have slipped into a less august academic life elsewhere. It is conceivable, but not, I believe, likely, for the hot spring of anarchy rose from depths where was no solid earth, and burst into the sunlight–a rainbow in its cooling vapours–with a power the rocks could not repress.

In the event, that Easter vacation formed a short stretch of level road in the precipitous descent of which Jasper warned me. Descent or ascent? It seems to me that I grew younger daily with each adult habit that I acquired. I had lived a lonely childhood and a boyhood straitened by war and overshadowed by bereavement; to the hard bachelordom of English adoloscence, the premature dignity and authority of the school system, I had added a sad and grim strain of my own. Now, that summer term with Sebastian, it seemed as though I was being given a brief spell of what I had never known, a happy childhood, and though its toys were silk shirts and liqueurs and cigars and its naughtiness high in the catalogue of grave sins, there was something of nursery freshness about us that fell little short of the joy of innocence. At the end of the term I took my first schools; it was necessary to pass, if I was to remain at Oxford, and pass I did, after a week in which I forbade Sebastian my rooms and sat up to a late hour, with iced black coffee and charcoal biscuits, cramming myself with the neglected texts. I remember no syllable of them now, but the other, more ancient lore which I acquired that term will be with me in one shape or another to my last hour.

'I like this bad set and I like getting drunk at luncheon'; that was enough then. Is more needed now?

Looking back, now, after twenty years, there is little I would have left undone or done otherwise. I could match my cousin Jasper's game-cock maturity with a sturdier fowl. I could tell him that all the wickedness of that time was like the spirit they mix with the pure grape of the Douro, heady stuff full of dark ingredients; it at once enriched and retarded the whole process of adolescence as the spirit checks the fermentation of the wine, renders it undrinkable, so that it must lie in the dark, year in, year out, until it is brought up at last fit for the table.

I could tell him, too, that to know and love one other human being is the root of all wisdom. But I felt no need for these sophistries as I sat before my cousin, saw him, freed from his inconclusive struggle with Pindar, in his dark grey suit, his white tie, his scholar's gown; heard his grave tones and, all the time, savoured the gillyflowers in full bloom under my windows. I had my secret and sure defence, like a talisman worn in the bosom, felt for in the moment of danger, found and firmly grasped. So I told him what was not in fact the truth, that I usually had a glass of champagne about that time, and asked him to join me.

On the day after Jasper's Grand Remonstrance I received another, in different terms and from an unexpected source.

All the term I had been seeing rather more of Anthony Blanche than my liking for him warranted. I lived now among his friends, but our frequent meetings were more of his choosing than mine, for I held him in considerable awe.

In years, he was barely my senior, but he seemed then to be burdened with the experience of the Wandering Jew. He was indeed a nomad of no nationality.

An attempt had been made in his childhood to make an Englishman of him; he was two years at Eton; then in the middle of the war he had defied the submarines, rejoined his mother in the Argentine, and a clever and audacious schoolboy was added to the valet, the maid, the two chauffeurs, the pekinese, and the second husband. Criss-cross about the world he travelled with them, waxing in wickedness like the Hogarthian page boy. When peace came they returned to Europe, to hotels and furnished villas, spas, casinos, and bathing beaches. At the age of fifteen, for a wager, he was disguised as a girl and taken to play at the big table in the Jockey Club at Buenos Aires; he dined with Proust and Gide and was on closer terms with Cocteau and Diaghilev; Firbank sent him his novels with fervent inscriptions; he had aroused three irreconcilable feuds in Capri; by his own account he had practised black art in Cefalù and had been cured of drug-taking in California and of an Oedipus complex in Vienna.

At times we all seemed children beside him–at most times, but not always, for there was a bluster and zest in Anthony which the rest of us had shed somewhere in our more leisured adolescence, on the playing field or in the school-room; his vices flourished less in the pursuit of pleasure than in the wish to shock, and in the midst of his polished exhibitions I was often reminded of an urchin I had once seen in Naples, capering derisively, with obscene, unambiguous gestures, before a party of English tourists; as he told the tale of his evening at the gaming table, one could see in the roll of his eye just how he had glanced, covertly, over the dwindling pile of chips at his step-father's party; while we had been rolling one another in the mud at football and gorging ourselves with crumpets, Anthony had helped oil-fading beauties on sub-tropical sands and had sipped his apéritif in smart little bars, so that the savage we had tamed was still rampant in him. He was cruel, too, in the wanton, insect-maiming manner of the very young, and fearless like a little boy, charging, head down, small fists whirling, at the school prefects.

He asked me to dinner, and I was a little disconcerted to find that we were to dine alone. 'We are going to Thame,' he said. 'There is a delightful hotel there, which luckily doesn't appeal to the Bullingdon. We will drink Rhine wine and imagine ourselves . . . where? Not on a j-j-jaunt with J-J-Jorrocks, anyway. But first we will have our apéritif.'

At the George bar he ordered 'Four Alexandra cocktails, please,' ranged them before him with a loud 'Yum-yum' which drew every eye, outraged, upon him. 'I expect you would prefer sherry, but, my dear Charles, you are not going to *have* sherry. Isn't this a delicious concoction? You don't like it? Then I will drink it for you. One, two, three, four, down the red lane they go. *How* the students stare!' And he led me out to the waiting motor-car.

'I hope we shall find no undergraduates there. I am a little out of sympathy with them for the moment. You heard about their treatment of me on Thursday? It was too naughty. Luckily I was wearing my *oldest* pyjamas and it was an evening of oppressive heat, or I might have been seriously cross.' Anthony had a habit of putting his face near one when he spoke; the sweet and creamy cocktail had tainted his breath. I leaned away from him in the corner of the hired car.

'Picture me, my dear, alone and studious. I had just bought a rather forbidding book called *Antic Hay*, which I knew I must read before going to Garsington on Sunday, because everyone was bound to talk about it, and it's so banal saying you have not read the book of the moment, if you haven't. The solution I suppose is not to go to Garsington, but that didn't occur to me until this moment. *So*, my dear, I had an omelet and a peach and a bottle of Vichy water and put on my pyjamas and settled down to read. I must say my thoughts wandered, but I kept turning the pages and watching the light fade, which in Peckwater, my dear, is quite an experience–as darkness falls the stone seems positively to decay under one's eyes. I was reminded of some of those leprous façades in the *vieux port* at Marseille, until suddenly I was disturbed by such a bawling and caterwauling as you never heard, and there, down in the little piazza, I saw a mob of about twenty terrible young men, and do you know what they were chanting? "*We want Blanche. We want Blanche*," in a kind of litany. Such a *public* declaration! Well, I saw it was all up with Mr Huxley for the evening, and I must say I had reached a point of tedium when any interruption was welcome. I was stirred by the bellows, but, do you know, the louder they shouted, the shyer they seemed? They kept saying "Where's Boy?" "He's Boy Mulcaster's friend," "Boy must bring him down." Of course you've met Boy? He's always popping in and out of dear Sebastian's rooms. He's everything we dagos expect of an English lord. A great *parti* I can assure you. All the young ladies in London are after him. He's very hoity-toity with them, I'm told. My dear, he's scared stiff. A great oaf–that's Mulcaster–and what's more, my dear, a *cad*. He came to Le Touquet at Easter and, in some extraordinary way, I seemed to have asked him to stay. He lost some infinitesimal sum at cards, and as a result expected me to pay for all his treats–well, Mulcaster was in this party; I could see his ungainly form shuffling about below and hear him saying: "It's no good. He's out. Let's go back and have a drink?" So then I put my head out of the window and called to him; "Good evening, Mulcaster, old sponge and toady, are you lurking among the hobbledehoys? Have you come to repay me the three hundred francs I lent you for the poor drab you picked up in the Casino? It was a niggardly sum for her trouble, and *what* a trouble, Mulcaster. Come up and pay me, poor hooligan!"

'That, my dear, seemed to put a little life into them, and up the stairs they came, clattering. About six of them came into my room, the rest stood mouthing outside. My dear, they looked *too* extraordinary. They had been having one of their ridiculous club dinners, and they were all wearing coloured tail-coats–a sort of livery. "My dears," I said to them, "you look like a lot of most disorderly footmen." Then one of them, rather a juicy little piece, accused me of unnatural vices. "My dear," I said, "I may be inverted but I am not insatiable. Come back when you are *alone*." Then they began to blaspheme in a very shocking manner, and suddenly I, too, began to be annoyed. "Really," I thought, "when I think of all the hullabaloo there was when I was seventeen, and the Duc de Vincennes (old Armand, of course, not Philippe) challenged me to a duel for an affair of the heart, and very much *more* than the heart, I assure you, with the duchess (Stefanie, of course, not old Poppy)–now, to submit to impertinence from these pimply, tipsy virgins . . ." Well, I gave up the light, bantering tone and let myself be just a *little* offensive.

'Then they began saying, "Get hold of him. Put him in Mercury." Now as you know I have two sculptures by Brancusi and several pretty things and I did not want them to start getting rough, so I said, pacifically, "Dear sweet clodhoppers, if you knew anything of sexual psychology you would know that nothing could give me keener pleasure than to be manhandled by you meaty boys. It would be an ecstacy of the very naughtiest kind. So if any of you wishes to be my partner in joy come and seize me. If, on the other hand, you simply wish to satisfy some obscure and less easily classified libido and see me bathe, come with me quietly, dear louts, to the fountain."

'Do you know, they all looked a little foolish at that? I walked down with them and no one came within a yard of me. Then I got into the fountain and, you know, it was really most refreshing, so I sported there a little and struck some attitudes, until they turned about and walked sulkily home, and I heard Boy Mulcaster saying, "Anyway, we *did* put him in Mercury." You know, Charles, that is just what they'll be saying in thirty years' time. When they're all married to scraggy little women like hens and have cretinous porcine sons like themselves getting drunk at the same club dinner in the same coloured coats, they'll still say, when my name is mentioned, "We put him in Mercury one night," and their barnyard daughters will snigger and think their father was quite a dog in his day, and what a pity he's grown so dull. Oh, *la fatigue du Nord!*'

It was not, I knew, the first time Anthony had been ducked, but the incident seemed much on his mind, for he reverted to it again at dinner.

'Now you can't imagine an *unpleasantness* like that happening to Sebastian, can you?'

'No,' I said; I could not.

'No, Sebastian has charm'; he held up his glass of hock to the candle-light and repeated, '*such* charm. Do you know, I went round to call on Sebastian next day? I thought the tale of my evening's adventures might amuse him. And what do you think I found–besides, of course, his *amusing* toy bear? Mulcaster and two of his cronies of the night before. *They* looked *very* foolish and Sebastian, as composed as Mrs P-p-ponsonby-de-Tomkyns in *P-p-punch*, said "You know Lord Mulcaster, of course," and the oafs said, "Oh, we just came to see how Aloysius was," for they find the toy bear just as amusing as we do–or, shall I hint, just a *teeny* bit more? So off they went. And I said, "S-s-sebastian, do you realize that those s-sycophantic s-slugs insulted me last night, and but for the warmth of the weather might have given me a s-s-severe cold," and he said, "Poor things. I expect they were drunk." He has a kind word for everyone, you see; he has such charm.

'I can see he has completely captivated you, my dear Charles. Well, I'm not surprised. Of course, you haven't known him as long as I have. I was at school with him. You wouldn't believe it, but in those days people used to say he was a little *bitch*; just a few unkind boys who knew him well. Everyone in pop liked him, of course, and all the masters. I expect it was really that they were jealous of him. He never seemed to get into trouble. The rest of us were constantly being beaten in the most savage way, on the most frivolous pretexts, but never Sebastian. He was the only boy in my house who was never beaten at all. I can see him now, at the age of fifteen. He never had spots you know; all the other boys were spotty. Boy Mulcaster was positively scrofulous. But not Sebastian. Or did he have one, rather a stubborn one at the back of his neck? I think, now, that he did. Narcissus, with one pustule. He and I were both Catholics, so we used to go to mass together. He used to spend *such* a time in the confessional, I used to wonder what he had to say, because he never did anything wrong; never *quite*; at least, he never got punished. Perhaps he was just being charming through the grille. I left under what is called a cloud, you know–I can't think why it is called that; it seemed to me a glare of unwelcome light; the process involved a series of harrowing interviews with m' tutor. It was disconcerting to find how observant that mild old man proved to be. The *things* he knew about me, which I thought no one–except possibly Sebastian–knew. It was a lesson never to trust mild old men–or charming school boys, which?

'Shall we have another bottle of this wine, or of something different?

Something different, some bloody, old Burgundy, eh? You see, Charles, I understand *all* your tastes. You must come to France with me and drink the wine. We will go at the vintage. I will take you to stay at the Vincennes. It is all made up with them now, and he has the finest wine in France; he and the Prince de Portallon–I will take you there, too. I think they would amuse you, and of course they would *love* you. I want to introduce you to a lot of my friends. I have told Cocteau about you. He is all agog. You see, my dear Charles, you are that very rare thing, An Artist. Oh yes, you must not look bashful. Behind that cold, English, phlegmatic exterior you are An Artist. I have seen those little drawings you keep hidden away in your room. They are *exquisite*. And you, dear Charles, if you will understand me, are *not* exquisite; but not at all. Artists are not exquisite. I am; Sebastian, in a kind of way, is exquisite, but the artist is an eternal type, solid, purposeful, observant–and, beneath it all, p-p-passionate, eh, Charles?

'But who recognizes you? The other day I was speaking to Sebastian about you, and I said, "But you know Charles is *an artist*. He draws like a young Ingres," and do you know what Sebastian said?–"Yes, Aloysius draws very prettily, too, of course he's rather more modern." *So* charming; *so* amusing.

'Of course those that have charm don't really need brains. Stefanie de Vincennes really tickled me four years ago. My dear, I even used the same coloured varnish for my toe-nails. I used her words and lit my cigarette in the same way and spoke with her tone on the telephone so that the duke used to carry on long and intimate conversations with me, thinking that I was her. It was largely that which put his mind on pistol and sabres in such an old-fashioned manner. My step-father thought it an excellent education for me. He thought it would make me grow out of what he calls my "English habits". Poor man, he is very South American. . . . I never heard anyone speak an ill word of Stefanie, except the Duke: and *she*, my dear, is positively cretinous.'

Anthony had lost his stammer in the deep waters of his old romance. It came floating back to him, momentarily, with the coffee and liqueuers. 'Real G-g-green Chartreuse, made before the expulsion of the monks. There are five distinct tastes as it trickles over the tongue. It is like swallowing a sp-spectrum. Do you wish Sebastian was with us? Of course you do. Do I? I wonder. How our thoughts do run on that little bundle of charm to be sure. I think you must be mesmerizing me, Charles. I bring you here, at very considerable expense, my dear, simply to talk about myself, and I find I talk of no one except Sebastian. It's odd because there's really no mystery about him except how he came to be born of such a *very sinister* family.

'I forget if you know his family. I don't suppose he'll ever let you meet them. He's far too clever. They're quite, quite *gruesome*. Do you ever feel there is something a *teeny* bit gruesome about Sebastian? No? Perhaps I imagine it; it's simply that he *looks* so like the rest of them, sometimes.

'There's Brideshead who's something archaic, out of a cave that's been sealed for centuries. He has the face as though an Aztec sculptor had attempted a portrait of Sebastian; he's a learned bigot, a ceremonious barbarian, a snow-bound lama. . . . Well, anything you like. And Julia, you know what *she* looks like. Who could help it? Her photograph appears as regularly in the illustrated papers as the advertisements for Beecham's Pills. A face of flawless Florentine *quattrocento* beauty; almost anyone else with those looks would have been tempted to become artistic; not Lady Julia; she's as smart as–well, as smart as Stefanie. Nothing greenery-yallery about her. So gay, so correct, so unaffected. I wonder if she's incestuous. I doubt it; all she wants is power. There ought to be an Inquisition especially set up to burn her. There's another sister, too, I believe, in the schoolroom. Nothing is known of her *yet* except that her governess went mad and drowned herself not long ago. I'm sure she's abominable. So you see there was really very little left for poor Sebastian to do except be sweet and charming.

'It's when one gets to the parents that a bottomless pit opens. My dear, *such* a pair. *How does Lady Marchmain manage it?* It is one of the questions of the age. You have seen her? Very, very beautiful; no artifice, her hair just turning grey in elegant silvery streaks, no rouge, very pale, huge-eyed–it is extraordinary how large those eyes look and how the lids are veined blue where anyone else would have touched them with a finger-tip of paint; pearls and a few great starlike jewels, heirlooms, in ancient settings, a voice as quiet as a prayer, and as powerful. And Lord Marchmain, well, a little fleshy perhaps, but *very* handsome, a magnifico, a voluptuary, Byronic, bored, infectiously slothful, not at all the sort of man you would expect to see easily put down. And that Reinhardt nun, my dear, has destroyed him–but utterly. He daren't show his great purple face anywhere. He is the last, historic, authentic case of someone being hounded out of society. Brideshead won't see him, the girls mayn't, Sebastian does, of course, because he's so charming. No one else goes near him. Why, last September Lady Marchmain was in Venice staying at the Palazzo Fogliere. To tell you the truth she was just a teeny bit ridiculous in Venice. She never went near the Lido, of course, but she was always drifting about the canals in a gondola with Sir Adrian Porson–such attitudes, my dear, like Madame Récamier; once I passed them and I caught the eye of the Fogliere gondolier, whom, of course, I knew, and, my dear, he gave me *such* a wink. She came to all the parties in a sort of cocoon of gossamer, my dear, as though she were part of some Celtic play or a heroine from Maeterlinck; and she *would* go to church. Well, as you know, Venice is the *one* town in Italy where *no one* ever *has* gone to church. Anyway, she was rather a figure of fun that year, and then who should turn up in the Maltons' yacht, but poor Lord Marchmain. He'd taken a little palace there, but was he allowed in? Lord Malton put him and his valet into a dinghy, my dear, and transhipped him there and then into the steamer for Trieste. He hadn't even his mistress with him. It was her yearly holiday. No one ever knew how they heard Lady Marchmain was there. And, do you know, for a week Lord Malton slunk about as if *he* was in disgrace? And he *was* in disgrace. The Principessa Fogliere gave a ball and Lord Malton was not asked nor anyone from his yacht–even the de Pañoses. *How does Lady Marchmain do it?* She has convinced the world that Lord Marchmain is a monster. And what is the truth? They were married for fifteen years or so and then Lord Marchmain went to the war; he never came back but formed a connexion with a highly talented dancer. There are a thousand such cases. She refuses to divorce him because she is so pious. Well, there have been cases of that before. Usually, it arouses sympathy for the adulterer; not for Lord Marchmain though. You would think that the old reprobate had tortured her, stolen her patrimony, flung her out of doors, roasted, stuffed, and eaten his children, and gone frolicking about wreathed in all the flowers of Sodom and

Gomorrah; instead of what? Begetting four splendid children by her, handing over to her Brideshead and Marchmain House in St James's and all the money she can possibly want to spend, while he sits with a snowy shirt front at Larue's with a personable, middle-aged lady of the theatre, in most conventional Edwardian style. And she meanwhile keeps a small gang of enslaved and emaciated prisoners for her exclusive enjoyment. *She sucks their blood.* You can see the tooth marks all over Adrian Porson's shoulders when he is bathing. And he, my dear, was the greatest, the *only*, poet of our time. He's bled dry; there's nothing left of him. There are five or six others of all ages and sexes, like wraiths following her around. They never escape once she's had her teeth into them. It is witchcraft. There's no other explanation.

'So you see we mustn't blame Sebastian if at times he seems a little insipid–but then you don't blame him, do you, Charles? With that very murky background, what could he do except set up as being simple and charming, particularly as he isn't very well endowed in the Top Storey. We couldn't claim *that* for him, could we, much as we love him?

'Tell me candidly, have you ever heard Sebastian say *anything* you have remembered for five minutes? You know, when I hear him talk, I am reminded of that in some ways nauseating picture of "*Bubbles*". Conversation should be like juggling; up go the balls and the plates, up and over, in and out, good solid objects that glitter in the footlights and fall with a bang if you miss them. But when dear Sebastian speaks it is like a little sphere of soapsud drifting off the end of an old clay pipe, anywhere, full of rainbow light for a second and then–phut! vanished, with nothing left at all, nothing.'

And then Anthony spoke of the proper experiences of an artist, of the appreciation and criticism and stimulus he should expect from his friends, of the hazards he should take in the pursuit of emotion, of one thing and another while I fell drowsy and let my mind wander a little. So we drove home, but his words, as we swung over Magdalen Bridge, recalled the central theme of our dinner. 'Well, my dear, I've no doubt that first thing tomorrow you'll trot round to Sebastian and tell him *everything* I've said about him. And I will tell you two things; one, that it will not make the slightest difference to Sebastian's feeling for me and secondly, my dear–and I beg you to remember this though I have plainly bored you into a condition of coma–that he will immediately start talking about that amusing bear of his. Good night. Sleep innocently.'

But I slept ill. Within an hour of tumbling drowsily to bed I was awake again, thirsty, restless, hot and cold by turns, and unnaturally excited. I had drunk a lot, but neither the mixture, nor the Chartreuse, nor the Mavrodaphne Trifle, nor even the fact that I had sat immobile and almost silent throughout the evening instead of clearing the fumes, as we normally did, in puppyish romps and tumbles, explains the distress of that hag-ridden night. No dream distorted the images of the evening into horrific shapes. I lay awake and clear-headed. I repeated to myself Anthony's words, catching his accent, soundlessly, and the stress and cadence of his speech, while under my closed lids I saw his pale, candle-lit face as it had fronted me across the dinner table. Once during the hours of darkness I brought to light the drawings in my sitting-room and sat at the open window, turning them over. Everything was black and dead-still in the quadrangle; only at the quarter-hours the bells awoke and sang over the gables. I drank soda-water and smoked and fretted, until light began to break and the rustle of a rising breeze turned me back to my bed.

When I awoke Lunt was at the open door. 'I let you lie,' he said. 'I didn't think you'd be going to the Corporate Communion.'

'You were quite right.'

'Most of the freshmen went and quite a few second and third year men. It's all on account of the new chaplain. There was never Corporate Communion before–just Holy Communion for those that wanted it and Chapel and Evening Chapel.'

It was the last Sunday of term; the last of the year. As I went to my bath, the quad filled with gowned and surpliced undergraduates drifting from chapel to hall. As I came back they were standing in groups, smoking; Jasper had bicycled in from his digs to be among them.

I walked down the empty Broad to breakfast, as I often did on Sundays, at a tea-shop opposite Balliol. The air was full of bells from the surrounding spires and the sun, casting long shadows across the open spaces, dispelled the fears of night. The tea-shop was hushed as a library; a few solitary men in bedroom slippers from Balliol and Trinity looked up as I entered, then turned back to their Sunday newspapers. I ate my scrambled eggs and bitter marmalade with the zest which in youth follows a restless night. I lit a cigarette and sat on, while one by one the Balliol and Trinity men paid their bills and shuffled away, slip-slop, across the street to their colleges. It was nearly eleven when I left, and during my walk I heard the change-ringing cease and, all over the town, give place to the single chime which warned the city that service was about to start.

None but church-goers seemed abroad that morning; undergraduates and graduates and wives and trades-people, walking with that unmistakable English church-going pace which eschewed equally both haste and idle sauntering; holding, bound in black lamb-skin and white celluloid, the liturgies of half a dozen conflicting sects; on their way to St Barnabas, St Columba, St Aloysius, St Mary's, Pusey House, Blackfriars, and heaven knows where besides; to restored Norman and revived Gothic, to travesties of Venice and Athens; all in the summer sunshine going to the temples of their race. Four proud infidels alone proclaimed their dissent; four Indians from the gates of Balliol, in freshly-laundered white flannels and neatly pressed blazers, with snow-white turbans on their heads, and in their plump, brown hands bright cushions, a picnic basket and the *Plays Unpleasant* of Bernard Shaw, making for the river.

In the Cornmarket a party of tourists stood on the steps of the Clarendon Hotel discussing a road map with their chauffeur, while opposite, through the venerable arch of the Golden Cross, I greeted a group of undergraduates from my college who had breakfasted there and now lingered with their pipes in the creeper-hung courtyard. A troop of boy scouts, church-bound, too, bright with coloured ribbons and badges, loped past in unmilitary array, and at Carfax I met the Mayor and corporation, in scarlet gowns and gold chains, preceded by wand-bearers and followed by no curious glances, in procession to the preaching at the City Church. In St Aldates I passed a crocodile of choir boys, in starched collars and peculiar caps, on their way to Tom Gate and the Cathedral. So through a world of piety I made my way to Sebastian.

He was out. I read the letters, none of them very revealing, that littered his writing table and scrutinized the invitation cards on his chimney-piece–there were no new additions. Then I read *Lady into Fox* until he returned.

'I've been to mass at the Old Palace,' he said. 'I haven't been all this term, and Monsignor Bell asked me to dinner twice last week, and I know what that means. Mummy's been writing to him. So I sat bang in front where he couldn't help seeing me and absolutely shouted the Hail Marys at the end; so that's over. How was dinner with Antoine? What did you talk about?'

'Well, he did most of the talking. Tell me, did you know him at Eton?'

'He was sacked my first half. I remember seeing him about. He always has been a noticeable figure.'

'Did he go to church with you?'

'I don't think so, why?'

'Has he met any of your family?'

'Charles, how very peculiar you're being today. No. I don't suppose so.'

'Not your mother at Venice?'

'I believe she did say something about it. I forget what. I think she was staying with some Italian cousins of ours, the Foglieres, and Anthony turned up with his family at the hotel, and there was some party the Foglieres gave that they weren't asked to. I know Mummy said something about it when I told her he was a friend of mine. I can't think why he should want to go to a party at the Foglieres–the princess is so proud of her English blood that she talks of nothing else. Anyway, no one objected to Antoine–*much*, I gather. It was his mother they thought difficult.'

'And who is the Duchesse of Vincennes?'

'Poppy?'

'Stefanie.'

'You must ask Antoine that. He claims to have had an affair with her.'

'Did he?'

'I dare say. I think it's more or less compulsory at Cannes. Why all this interest?'

'I just wanted to find out how much truth there was in what Anthony said last night.'

'I shouldn't think a word. That's his great charm.'

'You may think it charming. I think it's devilish. Do you know he spent the whole of yesterday evening trying to turn me against you, and almost succeeded?'

'Did he? How silly. Aloysius wouldn't approve of that at all, would you, you pompous old bear?'

And then Boy Mulcaster came into the room.

3

I returned home for the Long Vacation without plans and without money. To cover end-of-term expenses I had sold my Omega screen to Collins for ten pounds, of which I now kept four; my last cheque overdrew my account by a few shillings, and I had been told that, without my father's authority, I must draw no more. My next allowance was not due until October. I was thus faced with a bleak prospect and, turning the matter over in my mind, I felt something not far off remorse for the prodigality of the preceding weeks.

I had started the term with my battels paid and over a hundred pounds in hand. All that had gone, and not a penny paid out where I could get credit. There had been no reason for it, no great pleasure unattainable else; it had gone in ducks and drakes. Sebastian used to tease me–'You spend money like a bookie'–but all of it went on and with him. His own finances were perpetually, vaguely distressed. 'It's all done by lawyers,' he said helplessly, 'and I suppose they embezzle a lot. Anyway, I never seem to get much. Of course, mummy would give me anything I asked for.'

'Then why don't you ask her for a proper allowance?'

'Oh, mummy likes everything to be a present. She's so sweet,' he said, adding one more line to the picture I was forming of her.

Now Sebastian had disappeared into that other life of his where I was not asked to follow, and I was left, instead, forlorn and regretful.

How ungenerously in later life we disclaim the virtuous moods of our youth, living in retrospect long, summer days of unreflecting dissipation. There is no candour in a story of early manhood which leaves out of account the home-sickness for nursery morality, the regrets and resolutions of amendment, the black hours which, like zero on the roulette table, turn up with roughly calculable regularity.

Thus I spent the first afternoon at home, wandering from room to room, looking from the plate-glass windows in turn on the garden and the street, in a mood of vehement self-reproach.

My father, I knew, was in the house, but his library was inviolable, and it was not until just before dinner that he appeared to greet me. He was then in his late fifties, but it was his idiosyncrasy to seem much older than his years; to see him one might have put him at seventy, to hear him speak at nearly eighty. He came to me now, with the shuffling, mandarin-tread which he affected, and a shy smile of welcome. When he dined at home–and he seldom dined elsewhere–he wore a frogged velvet smoking suit of the kind which had been fashionable many years before and was to be so again, but, at that time, was a deliberate archaism.

'My dear boy, they never told me you were here. Did you have a very exhausting journey? They gave you tea? You are well? I have just made a somewhat audacious purchase from Sonerscheins–a terra-cotta bull of the fifth century. I was examining it and forgot your arrival. Was the carriage *very* full? You had a corner seat?' (He travelled so rarely himself that to hear of others doing so always excited his solicitude.) 'Hayter brought you the evening paper? There is no news, of course–such a lot of nonsense.'

Dinner was announced. My father from long habit took a book with him to the table and then, remembering my presence, furtively dropped it under his chair. 'What do you like to drink? Hayter, what have we for Mr Charles to drink?'

'There's some whisky.'

'There's whisky. Perhaps you like something else? What else have we?'

'There isn't anything else in the house, sir.'

'There's nothing else. You must tell Hayter what you would like and he will get it in. I never keep any wine now. I am forbidden it and no one comes to see me. But while you are here, you must have what you like. You are here for long?'

'I'm not quite sure, father.'

'It's a *very* long vacation,' he said wistfully. 'In my day we used to go on what were called reading parties, always in mountainous areas. Why? Why', he repeated petulantly, 'should alpine scenery be thought conducive to study?'

'I thought of putting in some time at an art school–in the life class.'

'My dear boy, you'll find them all shut. The students go to Barbizon or such places and paint in the open air. There was an institution in my day called a "sketching club"–mixed sexes' (snuffle), 'bicycles' (snuffle), 'pepper-and-salt knickerbockers, holland umbrellas, and, it was popularly thought, free love' (snuffle), '*such* a lot of nonsense. I expect they still go on. You might try that.'

'One of the problems of the vacation is money, father.'

'Oh, I shouldn't worry about a thing like that at your age.'

'You see, I've run rather short.'

'Yes?' said my father without any sound of interest.

'In fact I don't quite know how I'm going to get through the next two months.'

'Well, I'm the worst person to come to for advice. I've never been "short" as you so painfully call it. And yet what else could you say? Hard up? Penurious? Distressed? Embarrassed? Stony-broke?' (snuffle). 'On the rocks? In Queer Street? Let us say you are in Queer Street and leave it at that. Your grandfather once said to me, "Live within your means, but if you do get into difficulties, come to me. Don't go to the Jews." Such a lot of nonsense. You try. Go to those gentlemen in Jermyn Street who offer advances on note of hand only. My dear boy, they won't give you a sovereign.'

'Then what do you suggest my doing?'

'Your cousin Melchior was imprudent with his investments and got into a very queer street. *He* went to Australia.'

I had not seen my father so gleeful since he found two pages of second-century papyrus between the leaves of Lombardic breviary.

'Hayter, I've dropped my book.'

It was recovered for him from under his feet and propped against the *épergne*. For the rest of dinner he was silent save for an occasional snuffle of merriment which could not, I thought, be provoked by the work he read.

Presently we left the table and sat in the garden-room; and there, plainly, he put me out of his mind; his thoughts, I knew, were far away, in those distant ages where he moved at ease, where time passed in centuries and all the figures were defaced and the names of his companions were corrupt readings of words of quite other meaning. He sat in an attitude which to anyone else would have been one of extreme discomfort, askew in his upright armchair, with his book held high and obliquely to the light. Now and then he took a gold pencil-case from his watch-chain and made an entry in the margin. The windows were open to the summer night; the ticking of the clocks, the distant murmur of traffic on the Bayswater Road, and my father's regular turning of the pages were the only sounds. I had thought it impolitic to smoke a cigar while pleading poverty; now in desperation I went to my room and fetched one. My father did not look up. I pierced it, lit it, and with renewed confidence said, 'Father, you surely don't want me to spend the whole vacation here with you?'

'Eh?'

'Won't you find it rather a bore having me at home for so long?'

'I trust I should not betray such an emotion even if I felt it,' said my father mildly and turned back to his book.

The evening passed. Eventually all over the room clocks of diverse pattern musically chimed eleven. My father closed his book and removed his spectacles. 'You are very welcome, my dear boy,' he said. 'Stay as long as you find it convenient.' At the door he paused and turned back. 'Your cousin Melchoir worked his passage to Australia *before the mast*.' (Snuffle.) 'What, I wonder, is "before the mast"?'

During the sultry week that followed, my relations with my father deteriorated sharply. I saw little of him during the day; he spent hours on end in the library; now and then he emerged and I would hear him calling over the banisters: 'Hayter, get me a cab.' Then he would be away, sometimes for half an hour or less, sometimes for a whole day; his errands were never explained. Often I saw trays going up to him at odd hours, laden with meagre nursery snacks–rusks, glasses of milk, bananas, and so forth. If we met in a passage or on the stairs he would look at me vacantly and say 'Ah-ha,' or 'Very warm,' or 'Splendid, splendid,' but in the evening, when he came to the garden-room in his velvet smoking suit, he always greeted me formally.

The dinner table was our battlefield.

On the second evening I took my book with me to the dining-room. His mild and wandering eye fastened on it with sudden attention, and as we passed through the hall he surreptitiously left his own on a side table. When we sat down, he said plaintively: 'I do think, Charles, you might talk to me. I've had a very exhausting day. I was looking forward to a little conversation.'

'Of course, father. What shall we talk about?'

'Cheer me up. Take me out of myself,' petulantly, 'tell me all about the new plays.'

'But I haven't been to any.'

'You should, you know, you really should. It's not natural in a young man to spend all his evenings at home.'

'Well, father, as I told you, I haven't much money to spare for theatre-going.'

'My dear boy, you must not let money become your master in this way. Why, at your age, your cousin Melchior was part-owner of a musical piece. It was one of his few happy ventures. You should go to the play as part of your education. If you read the lives of eminent men you will find that quite half of them made their first acquaintance with drama from the gallery. I am told there is no pleasure like it. It is there that you find the real critics and devotees. It is called "sitting with the gods". The expense is nugatory, and even while you wait for admission in the street you are diverted by "buskers". We will sit with the gods together one night. How do you find Mrs Abel's cooking?'

'Unchanged.'

'It was inspired by your Aunt Philippa. She gave Mrs Abel ten menus, and they have never been varied. When I am alone I do not notice what I eat, but now that you are here, we must have a change. What would you like? What is in season? Are you fond of lobsters? Hayter, tell Mrs Abel to give us lobsters tomorrow night.'

Dinner that evening consisted of a white, tasteless soup, over-fried fillets of sole with a pink sauce, lamb cutlets propped against a cone of mashed potato, stewed pears in jelly standing on a kind of sponge cake.

'It is purely out of respect for your Aunt Philippa that I dine at this length. She laid it down that a three-course dinner was middle-class. "If you once let the servants get their way," she said, "you will find yourself dining nightly off a single chop." There is nothing I should like more. In fact, that is exactly what I do when I go to my club on Mrs Abel's evening out. But your aunt ordained that at home I must have soup and three courses; some nights it is fish, meat, and savoury, on others it is meat, sweet, savoury–there are a number of possible permutations.

'It is remarkable how some people are able to put their opinions in lapidary form; your aunt had that gift.

'It is odd to think that she and I once dined together nightly–just as you and I do, my boy. Now *she* made unremitting efforts to take me out of myself. She used to tell me about her reading. It was in *her* mind to make a home with me, you know. She thought I should get into funny ways if I was left on my own. Perhaps I *have* got into funny ways. Have I? But it didn't do. I got her out in the end.'

There was an unmistakable note of menace in his voice as he said this.

It was largely by reason of my Aunt Philippa that I now found myself so much a stranger in my father's house. After my mother's death she came to live with my father and me, no doubt, as he said, with the idea of making her home with us. I knew nothing, then, of the nightly agonies at the dinner table. My aunt made herself my companion, and I accepted her without question. That was for a year. The first change was that she reopened her house in Surrey which she had meant to sell, and lived there during my school terms, coming to London only for a few days' shopping and entertainment. In the summer we went to lodgings together at the seaside. Then in my last year at school she left England. '*I got her out in the end*,' he said with derision and triumph of that kindly lady, and he knew that I heard in the words a challenge to myself.

As we left the dining-room my father said, 'Hayter, have you yet said anything to Mrs Abel about the lobsters I ordered for tomorrow?'

'No, sir.'

'Do not do so.'

'Very good, sir.'

And when we reached our chairs in the garden-room he said:

'I wonder whether Hayter had any intention of mentioning lobsters. I rather think not. Do you know, I believe he thought I was *joking*?'

Next day, by chance, a weapon came to hand. I met an old acquaintance of school-days, a contemporary of mine named Jorkins. I never had much liking for Jorkins. Once, in my Aunt Philippa's day, he had come to tea, and she had condemned him as being probably charming at heart, but unattractive at first sight. Now I greeted him with enthusiasm and asked him to dinner. He came and showed little alteration. My father must have been warned by Hayter that there was a guest, for instead of his velvet suit he wore a tail coat; this, with a black waistcoat, very high collar, and very narrow white tie, was his evening dress; he wore it with an air of melancholy as though it were court mourning, which he had assumed in early youth and, finding the style sympathetic, had retained. He never possessed a dinner jacket.

'Good evening, good evening. So nice of you to come all this way.'

'Oh, it wasn't far,' said Jorkins, who lived in Sussex Square.

'Science annihilates distance,' said my father disconcertingly. 'You are over here on business?'

'Well, I'm *in* business, if that's what you mean.'

'I had a cousin who was in business–you wouldn't know him; it was before your time. I was telling Charles about him only the other night. He has been much in my mind. He came', my father paused to give full weight to the bizarre word–'a *cropper*.'

Jorkins giggled nervously. My father fixed him with a look of reproach.

'You find his misfortune the subject of mirth? Or perhaps the word I used was unfamiliar; *you* no doubt would say that he "folded up".'

My father was master of the situation. He had made a little fantasy for himself, that Jorkins should be an American, and throughout the evening he played a delicate, one-sided parlour-game with him, explaining any peculiarly English terms that occurred in the conversation, translating pounds into dollars, and courteously deferring to him with such phrases as 'Of course, by *your* standards . . .'; 'All this must seem very parochial to Mr Jorkins'; 'In the vast spaces to which *you* are accustomed . . .' so that my guest was left with the vague sense that there was a misconception somewhere as to his identity, which he never got the chance of explaining. Again and again during dinner he sought my father's eye, thinking to read there the simple statement that this form of address was an elaborate joke, but met instead a look of such mild benignity that he was left baffled.

Once I thought my father had gone too far, when he said: 'I am afraid that, living in London, you must sadly miss your national game.'

'My national game?' asked Jorkins, slow in the uptake, but scenting that here, at last, was the opportunity for clearing the matter up.

My father glanced from him to me and his expression changed from kindness to malice; then back to kindness again as he turned once more to Jorkins. It was the look of a gambler who lays down fours against a full house. 'Your national game,' he said gently, '*cricket*,' and he snuffled uncontrollably, shaking all over and wiping his eyes with his napkin. 'Surely, working in the City, you find your time on the cricket-field greatly curtailed?'

At the door of the dining-room he left us. 'Good night, Mr Jorkins,' he said. 'I hope you will pay us another visit when you next "cross the herring pond".'

'I say, what did your governor mean by that? He seemed almost to think I was American.'

'He's rather odd at times.'

'I mean all that about advising me to visit Westminster Abbey. It seemed rum.'

'Yes. I can't quite explain.'

'I almost thought he was pulling my leg,' said Jorkins in puzzled tones.

My father's counter-attack was delivered a few days later. He sought me out and said, 'Mr Jorkins is still here?'

'No, father, of course not. He only came to dinner.'

'Oh, I hoped he was staying with us. Such a *versatile* young man. But you will be dining in?'

'Yes.'

'I am giving a little dinner party to diversify the rather monotonous series of your evenings at home. You think Mrs Abel is up to it? No. But our guests are not exacting. Sir Cuthbert and Lady Orme-Herrick are what might be called the nucleus. I hope for a little music afterwards. I have included in the invitations some young people for you.'

My presentiments of my father's plan were surpassed by the actuality. As the guests assembled in the room which my father, without self-consciousness, called 'the Gallery', it was plain to me that they had been carefully chosen for my discomfort. The 'young people' were Miss Gloria Orme-Herrick, a student of the cello; her fiancé, a bald young man from the British Museum; and a monoglot Munich publisher. I saw my father snuffling at me from behind a case of ceramics as he stood with them. That evening he wore, like a chivalric badge of battle, a small red rose in his button-hole.

Dinner was long and chosen, like the guests, in a spirit of careful mockery. It was not of Aunt Philippa's choosing, but had been reconstructed from a much earlier period, long before he was of an age to dine downstairs. The dishes were ornamental in appearance and regularly alternated in colour between red and white. They and the wine were equally tasteless. After dinner my father led the German publisher to the piano and then, while he played, left the drawing-room to show Sir Cuthbert Orme-Herrick the Etruscan bull in the gallery.

It was a gruesome evening, and I was astonished to find, when at last the party broke up, that it was only a few minutes after eleven. My father helped himself to a glass of barley-water and said: 'What very dull friends I have! You know, without the spur of your presence I should never have roused myself to invite them. I have been very negligent about entertaining lately. Now that you are paying me such a long visit, I will have many such evenings. You liked Miss Gloria Orme-Herrick?'

'No.'

'No? Was it her little moustache you objected to or her very large feet? Do you think she enjoyed herself?'

'No.'

'That was my impression also. I doubt if any of our guests will count this as one of their happiest evenings. That young foreigner played atrociously, I thought. Where can I have met him? And Miss Constantia Smethwick–where can I have met *her*? But the obligations of hospitality must be observed. As long as you are here, you shall not be dull.'

Strife was internecine during the next fortnight, but I suffered the more, for my father had greater reserves to draw on and a wider territory for manoeuvre, while I was pinned to my bridgehead between the uplands and the sea. He never declared his war aims, and I do not to this day know whether they were purely punitive–whether he had really at the back of his mind some geopolitical idea of getting me out of the country, as my Aunt Philippa had been driven to Bordighera and cousin Melchior to Darwin, or whether, as seems most likely, he fought for the sheer love of a battle in which indeed he shone.

I received one letter from Sebastian, a conspicuous object which was brought to me in my father's presence one day when he was lunching at home; I saw him look curiously at it and bore it away to read in solitude. It was written on, and enveloped in, heavy late-Victorian mourning paper, black-coroneted and black-bordered. I read it eagerly:

Brideshead Castle,
Wiltshire.
I wonder what the date is

Dearest Charles,

I found a box of this paper at the back of a bureau so I must write to you as I am mourning for my lost innocence. It never looked like living. The doctors despaired of it from the start.

Soon I am off to Venice to stay with my papa in his palace of sin. I wish you were coming. I wish you were here.

I am never quite alone. Members of my family keep turning up and collecting luggage and going away again but the white raspberries are ripe.

I have a good mind not to take Aloysius to Venice. I don't want him to meet a lot of horrid Italian bears and pick up bad habits.

Love or what you will. S.

I knew his letters of old; I had had them at Ravenna; I should not have been disappointed; but that day, as I tore the stiff sheet across and let it fall into the basket, and gazed resentfully across the grimy gardens and irregular backs of Bayswater, at the jumble of soil-pipes and fire-escapes and protuberant little conservatories, I saw, in my mind's eye, the pale face of Anthony Blanche, peering through the straggling leaves as it had peered through the candle flames at Thame, and heard, above the murmur of traffic, his clear tones . . . 'You mustn't blame Sebastian if at times he seems a little insipid. . . . When I hear him talk I am reminded of that in some ways nauseating picture of "*Bubbles*".'

For days after that I thought I hated Sebastian; then one Sunday afternoon a telegram came from him, which dispelled that shadow, adding a new and darker one of its own.

My father was out and returned to find me in a condition of feverish anxiety. He stood in the hall with his panama hat still on his head and beamed at me.

'You'll never guess how I have spent the day; I have been to the Zoo. It was most agreeable; the animals seem to enjoy the sunshine so much.'

'Father, I've got to leave at once.'

'Yes?'

'A great friend of mine–he's had a terrible accident. I must go to him at once. Hayter's packing for me, now. There's a train in half an hour.'

I showed him the telegram, which read simply: GRAVELY INJURED COME AT ONCE SEBASTIAN.

'Well,' said my father. 'I'm sorry you are upset. Reading this message I should not say that the accident was as serious as you seem to think–otherwise it would hardly be signed by the victim himself. Still, of course, he may well be fully conscious but blind or paralysed with a broken back. Why exactly is your presence so necessary? You have no medical knowledge. You are not in holy orders. Do you hope for a legacy?'

'I told you, he is a great friend.'

'Well, Orme-Herrick is a great friend of mine, but I should not go tearing off to his deathbed on a warm Sunday afternoon. I should doubt whether Lady Orme-Herrick would welcome me. However, I see you have no such doubts. I shall miss you, my dear boy, but do not hurry back on my account.'

Paddington Station on that August Sunday evening, with the sun streaming through the obscure panes of its roof, the bookstalls shut, and the few passengers strolling unhurried beside their porters, would have soothed a mind less agitated than mine. The train was nearly empty. I had my suitcase put in the corner of a third-class carriage and took a seat in the dining-car. 'First dinner after Reading, sir; about seven o'clock. Can I get you anything now?' I ordered gin and vermouth; it was brought to me as we pulled out of the station. The knives and forks set up their regular jingle; the bright landscape rolled past the windows. But I had no mind for these smooth things; instead, fear worked like yeast in my thoughts, and the fermentation brought to the surface, in great gobs of scum, the images of disaster; a loaded gun held carelessly at a stile, a horse rearing and rolling over, a shaded pool with a submerged stake, an elm bough falling suddenly on a still morning, a car at a blind corner; all the catalogue of threats to civilized life rose and haunted me; I even pictured a homicidal maniac mouthing in the shadows, swinging a length of lead pipe. The cornfields and heavy woodland sped past, deep in the golden evening, and the throb of the wheels repeated monotonously in my ears, 'You've come too late. You've come too late. He's dead. He's dead. He's dead.'

I dined and changed trains to the local line, and in twilight came to Melstead Carbury, which was my destination.

'Brideshead, sir? Yes, Lady Julia's in the yard.'

She was sitting at the wheel of an open car. I recognized her at once; I could not have failed to do so.

'You're Mr Ryder? Jump in.' Her voice was Sebastian's and his her way of speaking.

'How is he?'

'Sebastian? Oh, he's fine. Have you had dinner? Well, I expect it was beastly. There's some more at home. Sebastian and I are alone, so we thought we'd wait for you.'

'What's happened to him?'

'Didn't he say? I expect he thought you wouldn't come if you knew. He's cracked a bone in his ankle so small that it hasn't a name. But they X-rayed it yesterday, and told him to keep it up for a month. It's a great bore to him, putting out all his plans; he's been making the most enormous fuss. . . . Everyone else has gone. He tried to make me stay back with him. Well, I expect you know how maddeningly pathetic he can be. I almost gave in, and then I said: "Surely there must be *someone* you can get hold of," and he said everybody was away or busy and, anyway, no one else would do. But at last he agreed to try you, and I promised I'd stay if you failed him, so you can imagine how popular you are with me. I must say it's noble of you to come all this way at a moment's notice.' But as she said it, I heard, or thought I heard, a tiny note of contempt in her voice that I should be so readily available.

'How did he do it?'

'Believe it or not, playing croquet. He lost his temper and tripped over a hoop. *Not* a very honourable scar.'

She so much resembled Sebastian that, sitting beside her in the gathering dusk, I was confused by the double illusion of familiarity and strangeness. Thus, looking through strong lenses, one may watch a man approaching from afar, study every detail of his face and clothes, believe one has only to put out a hand to touch him, marvel that he does not hear one and look up as one moves, and then, seeing him with the naked eye, suddenly remember that one is to him a distant speck, doubtfully human. I knew her and she did not know me. Her dark hair was scarcely longer than Sebastian's, and it blew back from her forehead as his did; her eyes on the darkling road were his, but larger; her painted mouth was less friendly to the world. She wore a bangle of charms on her wrist and in her ears little gold rings. Her light coat revealed an inch or two of flowered silk; skirts were short in those days, and her legs, stretched forward to the controls of the car, were spindly, as was also the fashion. Because her sex was the palpable difference between the familiar and the strange, it seemed to fill the space between us, so that I felt her to be especially female, as I had felt of no woman before.

'I'm terrified of driving at this time of the evening,' she said. 'There doesn't seem anyone left at home who can drive a car. Sebastian and I are practically camping out here. I hope you haven't come expecting a pompous party.' She leaned forward to the locker for a box of cigarettes.

'No thanks.'

'Light one for me, will you?'

It was the first time in my life that anyone had asked this of me, and as I took the cigarette from my lips, and put it in hers, I caught a thin bat's squeak of sexuality, inaudible to any but me.

'Thanks. You've been here before. Nanny reported it. We both thought it very odd of you not to stay to tea with me.'

'That was Sebastian.'

'You seem to let him boss you about a good deal. You shouldn't. It's very bad for him.'

We had turned the corner of the drive now; the colour had died in the woods and sky, and the house seemed painted in *grisaille*, save for the central golden square at the open doors. A man was waiting to take my luggage.

'Here we are.'

She led me up the steps and into the hall, flung her coat on a marble table, and stooped to fondle a dog which came to greet her. 'I wouldn't put it past Sebastian to have started dinner.'

At that moment he appeared between the pillars at the further end, propelling himself in a wheel-chair. He was in pyjamas and dressing-gown, with one foot heavily bandaged.

'Well, darling, I've collected your chum,' she said, again with a barely perceptible note of contempt.

'I thought you were dying,' I said, conscious then, as I had been ever since I arrived, of the predominating emotion of vexation, rather than of relief, that I had been bilked of my expectations of a grand tragedy.

'I thought I was, too. The pain was excruciating. Julia, do you think, if *you* asked him, Wilcox would give us champagne tonight?'

'I hate champagne and Mr Ryder has had dinner.'

'*Mister* Ryder? *Mister* Ryder? Charles drinks champagne at all hours. Do you know, seeing this great swaddled foot of mine, I can't get it out of my mind that I have gout, and that gives me a craving for champagne.'

We dined in a room they called 'the Painted Parlour'. It was a spacious octagon, later in design than the rest of the house; its walls were adorned with wreathed medallions, and across its dome prim Pompeian figures stood in pastoral groups. They and the satin-wood and ormolu furniture, the carpet, the hanging bronze candelabrum, the mirrors and sconces, were all a single composition, the design of one illustrious hand. 'We usually eat here when we're alone' said Sebastian, 'it's so cosy.'

While they dined I ate a peach and told them of the war with my father.

'He sounds a perfect poppet,' said Julia. 'And now I'm going to leave you boys.'

'Where are you off to?' 'The nursery. I promised nanny a last game of halma.' She kissed the top of Sebastian's head. I opened the door for her. 'Good night, Mr Ryder, and good-bye. I don't suppose we'll meet tomorrow. I'm leaving early. I can't tell you how grateful I am to you for relieving me at the sick-bed.'

'My sister's very pompous tonight,' said Sebastian, when she was gone.

'I don't think she cares for me,' I said.

'I don't think she cares for anyone much. I love her. She's so like me.'

'*Do you? Is she?*'

'In looks I mean and the way she talks. I wouldn't love anyone with a character like mine.'

When we had drunk our port, I walked beside Sebastian's chair through the pillared hall to the library, where we sat that night and nearly every night of the ensuing month. It lay on the side of the house that overlooked the lakes; the windows were open to the stars and the scented air, to the indigo and silver, moonlit landscape of the valley and the sound of water falling in the fountain.

'We'll have a heavenly time alone,' said Sebastian, and when next morning, while I was shaving, I saw from my bathroom window Julia, with luggage at her back, drive from the forecourt and disappear at the hill's crest, without a backward glance, I felt a sense of liberation and peace such as I was to know years later when, after a night of unrest, the sirens sounded the 'All Clear'.

4

The languor of Youth–how unique and quintessential it is! How quickly, how irrecoverably, lost! The zest, the generous affections, the illusions, the despair, all the traditional attributes of Youth–all save this–come and go with us through life. These things are a part of life itself; but languor–the relaxation of yet unwearied sinews, the mind sequestered and self-regarding–that belongs to Youth alone and dies with it. Perhaps in the mansions of Limbo the heroes enjoy some such compensation for their loss of the Beatific Vision; perhaps the Beatific Vision itself has some remote kinship with this lowly experience; I, at any rate, believed myself very near heaven, during those languid days at Brideshead.

'Why is this house called a "Castle"?'

'It used to be one until they moved it.'

'What can you mean?'

'Just that. We had a castle a mile away, down by the village. Then we took a fancy to the valley and pulled the castle down, carted the stones up here, and built a new house. I'm glad they did, aren't you?'

'If it was mine I'd never live anywhere else.'

'But you see, Charles, it isn't mine. Just at the moment it is, but usually it's full of ravening beasts. If it could only be like this always–always summer, always alone, the fruit always ripe, and Aloysius in a good temper. . . .'

It is thus I like to remember Sebastian, as he was that summer, when we wandered alone together through that enchanted palace; Sebastian in his wheel chair spinning down the box-edged walks of the kitchen gardens in search of alpine strawberries and warm figs, propelling himself through the succession of hot-houses, from scent to scent and climate to climate, to cut the muscat grapes and choose orchids for our button-holes; Sebastian hobbling with a pantomime of difficulty to the old nurseries, sitting beside me on the threadbare, flowered carpet with the toy-cupboard empty about us and Nanny Hawkins stitching complacently in the corner, saying. 'You're one as bad as the other; a pair of children the two of you. Is that what they teach you at College?' Sebastian supine on the sunny seat in the colonnade, as he was now, and I in a hard chair beside him, trying to draw the fountain.

'Is the dome by Inigo Jones, too? It looks later.'

'Oh, Charles, don't be such a tourist. What does it matter when it was built, if it's pretty?'

'It's the sort of thing I like to know.'

'Oh dear, I thought I'd cured you of all that–the terrible Mr Collins.'

It was an aesthetic education to live within those walls, to wander from room to room, from the Soanesque library to the Chinese drawing-room, adazzle with gilt pagodas and nodding mandarins, painted paper and Chippendale fretwork, from the Pompeian parlour to the great tapestry-hung hall which stood unchanged, as it had been designed two hundred and fifty years before; to sit, hour after hour, in the shade looking out on the terrace.

This terrace was the final consummation of the house's plan; it stood on massive stone ramparts above the lakes, so that from the hall steps it seemed to overhang them, as though, standing by the balustrade, one could have dropped a pebble into the first of them immediately below one's feet. It was embraced by the two arms of the colonnade; beyond the pavilions groves of lime led to the wooded hillsides. Part of the terrace was paved, part planted with flower-beds and arabesques of dwarf box; taller box grew in a dense hedge, making a wide oval, cut into niches and interspersed with statuary, and, in the centre, dominating the whole splendid space rose the fountain; such a fountain as one might expect to find in a piazza of southern Italy; such a fountain as was, indeed, found there a century ago by one of Sebastian's ancestors; found, purchased, imported, and re-erected in an alien but welcoming climate.

Sebastian set me to draw it. It was an ambitious subject for an amateur–an oval basin with an island of sculptured rocks at its centre; on the rocks grew, in stone, formal tropical vegetation and wild English fern in its natural fronds; through them ran a dozen streams that counterfeited springs and round them sported fantastic tropical animals, camels and camelopards and an ebullient lion, all vomiting water; on the rocks, to the height of the pediment, stood an Egyptian obelisk of red sandstone–but, by some odd chance, for the thing was far beyond me, I brought it off and, by judicious omissions and some stylish tricks, produced a very passable echo of Piranesi. 'Shall I give it to your mother?' I asked.

'Why? You don't know her.'

'It seems polite. I'm staying in her house.'

'Give it to nanny,' said Sebastian.

I did so, and she put it among the collection on the top of her chest of drawers, remarking that it had quite a look of the thing, which she had often heard admired but could never see the beauty of, herself.

For me the beauty was new-found.

Since the days when, as a schoolboy, I used to bicycle round the neighbouring parishes, rubbing brasses and photographing fonts, I had nursed a love of architecture, but, though in opinion I had made that easy leap, characteristic of my generation, from the puritanism of Ruskin to the puritanism of Roger Fry, my sentiments at heart were insular and medieval.

This was my conversion to the Baroque. Here under that high and insolent dome, under those coffered ceilings; here as I passed through those arches and broken pediments to the pillared shade beyond and sat, hour by hour, before the fountain, probing its shadows, tracing its lingering echoes, rejoicing in all its clustered feats of daring and invention, I felt a whole new system of nerves alive within me, as though the water that spurted and bubbled among its stones, was indeed a life-giving spring.

One day in a cupboard we found a large japanned-tin box of oil-paints still in workable condition.

'Mummy bought them a year or two ago. Someone told her that you could only appreciate the beauty of the world by trying to paint it. We laughed at her a great deal about it. She couldn't draw at all, and however bright the colours were in the tubes, by the time mummy had mixed them up, they came out a kind of khaki.' Various dry, muddy smears on the palette confirmed this statement. 'Cordelia was always made to wash the brushes. In the end we all protested and made mummy stop.'

The paints gave us the idea of decorating the office; this was a small room opening on the colonnade; it had once been used for estate business, but was now derelict, holding only some garden games and a tub of dead aloes; it had plainly been designed for a softer use, perhaps as a tea-room or study, for the plaster walls were decorated with delicate Rococo panels and the roof was prettily groined. Here, in one of the smaller oval frames, I sketched a romantic landscape, and in the days that followed filled it out in colour, and, by luck and the happy mood of the moment, made a success of it. The brush seemed somehow to do what was wanted of it. It was a landscape without figures, a summer scene of white cloud and blue distances, with an ivy-clad ruin in the foreground, rocks and a waterfall affording a rugged introduction to the receding parkland behind. I knew little of oil-painting and learned its ways as I worked. When, in a week, it was finished, Sebastian was eager for me to start on one of the larger panels. I made some sketches. He called for a *fête champêtre* with a ribboned swing and a Negro page and a shepherd playing the pipes, but the thing languished. I knew it was good chance that had made my landscape, and that this elaborate pastiche was too much for me.

One day we went down to the cellars with Wilcox and saw the empty bays which had once held a vast store of wine; one transept only was used now; there the bins were well stocked, some of them with vintages fifty years old.

'There's been nothing added since his Lordship went abroad,' said Wilcox. 'A lot of the old wine wants drinking up. We ought to have laid down the eighteens and twenties. I've had several letters about it from the wine merchants, but her Ladyship says to ask Lord Brideshead, and he says to ask his Lordship, and his Lordship says to ask the lawyers. That's how we get low. There's enough here for ten years at the rate it's going, but how shall we be then?'

Wilcox welcomed our interest; we had bottles brought up from every bin, and it was during those tranquil evenings with Sebastian that I first made a serious acquaintance with wine and sowed the seed of that rich harvest which was to be my stay in many barren years. We would sit, he and I, in the Painted Parlour with three bottles open on the table and three glasses before each of us; Sebastian had found a book on wine-tasting, and we followed its instructions in detail. We warmed the glass slightly at a candle, filled it a third high, swirled the wine round, nursed it in our hands, held it to the light, breathed it, sipped it, filled our mouths with it, and rolled it over the tongue, ringing it on the palate like a coin on a counter, tilted our heads back and let it trickle down the throat. Then we talked of it and nibbled Bath Oliver biscuits, and passed on to another wine; then back to the first, then on to another, until all three were in circulation and the order of glasses got confused, and we fell out over which was which, and we passed the glasses to and fro between us until there were six glasses, some of them with mixed wines in them which we had filled from the wrong bottle, till we were obliged to start again with three clean glasses each, and the bottles were empty and our praise of them wilder and more exotic.

'. . . It is a little, shy wine like a gazelle.'

'Like a leprechaun.'

'Dappled, in a tapestry meadow.'

'Like a flute by still water.'

'. . . And this is a wise old wine.'

'A prophet in a cave.'

'. . . And this is a necklace of pearls on a white neck.'

'Like a swan.'

'Like the last unicorn.'

And we would leave the golden candlelight of the dining-room for the starlight outside and sit on the edge of the fountain, cooling our hands in the water and listening drunkenly to its splash and gurgle over the rocks.

'Ought we to be drunk *every* night?' Sebastian asked one morning.

'Yes, I think so.'

'I think so too.'

We saw few strangers. There was the agent, a lean and pouchy colonel, who crossed our path occasionally and once came to tea. Usually we managed to hide from him. On Sundays a monk was fetched from a neighbouring monastery to say mass and breakfast with us. He was the first priest I ever met; I noticed how unlike he was to a parson, but Brideshead was a place of such enchantment to me that I expected everything and everyone to be unique; Father Phipps was in fact a bland, bun-faced man with an interest in county cricket which he obstinately believed us to share.

'You know, father, Charles and I simply don't *know* about cricket.'

'I wish I'd seen Tennyson make that fifty-eight last Thursday. That must have been an innings. The account in *The Times* was excellent. Did you see him against the South Africans?'

'I've never seen him.'

'Neither have I. I haven't seen a first-class match for years–not since Father Graves took me when we were passing through Leeds, after we'd been to the induction of the Abbot at Ampleforth. Father Graves managed to look up a train which gave us three hours to wait on the afternoon of the match against Lancashire. That *was* an afternoon. I remember every ball of it. Since then I've had to go by the papers. You seldom go to see cricket?'

'Never,' I said, and he looked at me with the expression I have seen since in the religious, of innocent wonder that those who expose themselves to the dangers of the world should avail themselves so little of its varied solace.

Sebastian always heard his mass, which was ill-attended. Brideshead was not an old-established centre of Catholicism. Lady Marchmain had introduced a few Catholic servants, but the majority of them, and all the cottagers, prayed, if anywhere, among the Flyte tombs in the little grey church at the gates.

Sebastian's faith was an enigma to me at that time, but not one which I felt particularly concerned to solve. I had no religion. I was taken to church weekly as a child, and at school attended chapel daily, but, as though in compensation, from the time I went to my public school I was excused church in the holidays. The masters who taught me Divinity told me that biblical texts were highly untrustworthy. They never suggested I should try to pray. My father did not go to church except on family occasions and then with derision. My mother, I think, was devout. It once seemed odd to me that she should have thought it her duty to leave my father and me and go off with an ambulance, to Serbia, to die of exhaustion in the snow in Bosnia. But later I recognized some such spirit in myself. Later, too, I have come to accept claims which then, in 1923, I never troubled to examine, and to accept the supernatural as the real. I was aware of no such needs that summer at Brideshead.

Often, almost daily, since I had known Sebastian, some chance word in his conversation had reminded me that he was a Catholic, but I took it as a foible, like his teddy-bear. We never discussed the matter until on the second Sunday at Brideshead, when Father Phipps had left us and we sat in the colonnade with the papers, he surprised me by saying: 'Oh dear, it's very difficult being a Catholic.'

'Does it make much difference to you?'

'Of course. All the time.'

'Well, I can't say I've noticed it. Are you struggling against temptation? You don't seem much more virtuous than me.'

'I'm very, very much wickeder,' said Sebastian indignantly.

'Well then?'

'Who was it used to pray, "O God, make me good, but not yet"?'

'I don't know. You, I should think.'

'Why, yes, *I* do, every day. But it isn't that.' He turned back to the pages of the *News of the World* and said, 'Another naughty scout-master.'

'I suppose they try and make you believe an awful lot of nonsense?'

'Is it nonsense? I wish it were. It sometimes sounds terribly sensible to me,'

'But my dear Sebastian, you can't seriously *believe* it all.'

'Can't I?'

'I mean about Christmas and the star and the three kings and the ox and the ass.'

'Oh yes, I believe that. It's a lovely idea.'

'But you can't *believe* things because they're a lovely idea.'

'But I *do*. That's how I believe.'

'And in prayers? Do you think you can kneel down in front of a statue and say a few words, not even out loud, just in your mind, and change the weather; or that some saints are more influential than others, and you must get hold of the right one to help you on the right problem?'

'Oh yes. Don't you remember last term when I took Aloysius and left him behind I didn't know where. I prayed like mad to St Anthony of Padua that morning, and immediately after lunch there was Mr Nichols at Canterbury Gate with Aloysius in his arms, saying I'd left him in his cab.'

'Well,' I said, 'if you can believe all that and you don't want to be good, where's the difficulty about your religion?'

'If you can't see, you can't.'

'Well, where?'

'Oh, don't be a *bore*, Charles. I want to read about a woman in Hull who's been using an instrument.'

'You started the subject. I was just getting interested.'

'I'll never mention it again . . . thirty-eight other cases were taken into consideration in sentencing her to six months–golly!'

But he did mention it again, some ten days later, as we were lying on the roof of the house, sunbathing and watching through a telescope the Agricultural Show which was in progress in the park below us. It was a modest two-day show serving the neighbouring parishes, and surviving more as a fair and social gathering than as a centre of serious competition. A ring was marked out in flags, and round it had been pitched half a dozen tents of varying size; there was a judges' box and some pens for livestock; the largest marquee was for refreshments, and there the farmers congregated in numbers. Preparations had been going on for a week. 'We shall have to hide,' said Sebastian as the day approached. 'My brother will be here. He's a big part of the Agricultural Show.' So we lay on the roof under the balustrade.

Brideshead came down by train in the morning and lunched with Colonel Fender, the agent. I met him for five minutes on his arrival. Anthony Blanche's description was peculiarly apt; he had the Flyte face, carved by an Aztec. We could see him now, through the telescope, moving awkwardly among the tenants, stopping to greet the judges in their box, leaning over a pen gazing seriously at the cattle.

'Queer fellow, my brother,' said Sebastian.

'He looks normal enough.'

'Oh, but he's not. If you only knew, he's much the craziest of us, only it doesn't come out at all. He's all twisted inside. He wanted to be a priest, you know.'

'I didn't.'

'I think he still does. He nearly became a Jesuit, straight from Stonyhurst. It was awful for mummy. She couldn't exactly try to stop him, but of course it was the last thing she wanted. Think what people would have said–the eldest son; it's not as if it had been me. And poor papa. The church has been enough trouble to him without that happening. There was a frightful to-do–monks and monsignori running round the house like mice, and Brideshead just sitting glum and talking about the will of God. He was the most upset, you see, when papa went abroad–much more than mummy really. Finally they persuaded him to go to Oxford and think it over for three years. Now he's trying to make up his mind. He talks of going into the Guards and into the House of Commons and of marrying. He doesn't know what he wants. I wonder if I should have been like that, if I'd gone to Stonyhurst. I should have gone, only papa went abroad before I was old enough, and the first thing he insisted on was my going to Eton.'

'Has your father given up religion?'

'Well, he's had to in a way; he only took to it when he married mummy. When he went off, he left that behind with the rest of us. You must meet him. He's a very nice man.'

Sebastian had never spoken seriously of his father before.

I said: 'It must have upset you all when your father went away.'

'All but Cordelia. She was too young. It upset *me* at the time. Mummy tried to explain it to the three eldest of us so that we wouldn't hate papa. I was the only one who didn't. I believe she wishes I did. I was always his favourite. I should be staying with him now, if it wasn't for this foot. I'm the only one who goes. Why don't you come too? You'd like him.'

A man with a megaphone was shouting the results of the last event in the field below; his voice came faintly to us.

'So you see we're a mixed family religiously. Brideshead and Cordelia are both fervent Catholics; he's miserable, she's bird-happy; Julia and I are half-heathen; I am happy, I rather think Julia isn't; mummy is popularly believed to be a saint and papa is excommunicated–and I wouldn't know which of them was happy. Anyway, however you look at it, happiness doesn't seem to have much to do with it, and that's all I want. . . . I wish I liked Catholics more.'

'They seem just like other people.'

'My dear Charles, that's exactly what they're not–particularly in this country, where they're so few. It's not just that they're a clique–as a matter of fact, they're at least four cliques all blackguarding each other half the time–but they've got an entirely different outlook on life; everything they think important is different from other people. They try and hide it as much as they can, but it comes out all the time. It's quite natural, really, that they should. But you see it's difficult for semi-heathens like Julia and me.'

We were interrupted in this unusually grave conversation by loud, childish cries from beyond the chimney-stacks, 'Sebastian, Sebastian.'

'Good heavens!' said Sebastian, reaching for a blanket. 'That sounds like my sister Cordelia. Cover yourself up.'

'Where are you?'

There came into view a robust child of ten or eleven; she had the unmistakable family characteristics, but had them ill-arranged in a frank and chubby plainness; two thick old-fashioned pigtails hung down her back.

'Go away, Cordelia. We've got no clothes on.'

'Why? You're quite decent. I guessed you were here. You didn't know I was about, did you? I came down with Bridey and stopped to see Francis Xavier.' (To me) 'He's my pig. Then we had lunch with Colonel Fender and then the show. Francis Xavier got a special mention. That beast Randal got first with a mangy animal. *Darling* Sebastian, I am pleased to see you again. How's your poor foot?'

'Say how-d'you-do to Mr Ryder.'

'Oh, sorry. How d'you do?' All the family charm was in her smile. 'They're all getting pretty boozy down there, so I came away. I say, who's been painting the office? I went in to look for a shooting-stick and saw it.'

'Be careful what you say. It's Mr Ryder.'

'But it's *lovely*. I say, did you really? You *are* clever. Why don't you both dress and come down? There's no one about.'

'Bridey's sure to bring the judges in.'

'But he won't. I heard him making plans not to. He's very sour today. He didn't want me to have dinner with you, but I fixed that. Come on. I'll be in the nursery when you're fit to be seen.'

We were a sombre little party that evening. Only Cordelia was perfectly at ease, rejoicing in the food, the lateness of the hour, and her brothers' company. Brideshead was three years older than Sebastian and I, but he seemed of another generation. He had the physical tricks of his family, and his smile, when it rarely came, was as lovely as theirs; he spoke, in their voice, with a gravity and restraint which in my cousin Jasper would have sounded pompous and false, but in him was plainly unassumed and unconscious.

'I am so sorry to miss so much of your visit,' he said to me. 'You are being looked after properly? I hope Sebastian is seeing to the wine. Wilcox is apt to be rather grudging when he is on his own.'

'He's treated us very liberally.'

'I am delighted to hear it. You are fond of wine?'

'Very.'

'I wish I were. It is such a bond with other men. At Magdalen I tried to get drunk more than once, but I did not enjoy it. Beer and whisky I find even less appetizing. Events like this afternoon's are a torment to me in consequence.'

'I like wine,' said Cordelia.

'My sister Cordelia's last report said that she was not only the worst girl in the school, but the worst there had ever been in the memory of the oldest nun.'

'That's because I refused to be an Enfant de Marie. Reverend Mother said that if I didn't keep my room tidier I couldn't be one, so I said, well, I won't be one, and I don't believe our Blessed Lady cares two hoots whether I put my gym shoes on the left or the right of my dancing shoes. Reverend Mother was livid.'

'Our Lady cares about obedience.'

'Bridey, you mustn't be pious,' said Sebastian. 'We've got an atheist with us.'

'Agnostic,' I said.

'Really? Is there much of that at your college? There was a certain amount at Magdalen.'

'I really don't know. I was one long before I went to Oxford.'

'It's everywhere,' said Brideshead.

Religion seemed an inevitable topic that day. For some time we talked about the Agricultural Show. Then Brideshead said, 'I saw the Bishop in London last week. You know, he wants to close our chapel.'

'Oh, he couldn't,' said Cordelia.

'I don't think mummy will let him,' said Sebastian.

'It's too far away,' said Brideshead. 'There are a dozen families round Melstead who can't get here. He wants to open a mass centre there.'

'But what about us?' said Sebastian. 'Do we have to drive out on winter mornings?'

'We must have the Blessed Sacrament here,' said Cordelia. 'I like popping in at odd times; so does mummy.'

'So do I,' said Brideshead, 'but there are so few of us. It's not as though we were old Catholics with everyone on the estate coming to mass. It'll have to go sooner or later, perhaps after mummy's time. The point is whether it wouldn't be better to let it go now. You are an artist, Ryder, what do you think of it aesthetically?'

'I think it's *beautiful*,' said Cordelia with tears in her eyes.

'Is it Good Art?'

'Well, I don't quite know what you mean,' I said warily. 'I think it's a remarkable example of its period. Probably in eighty years it will be greatly admired.'

'But surely it can't be good twenty years ago and good in eighty years, and not good now?'

'Well, it may be *good* now. All I mean is that I don't happen to like it much.'

'But is there a difference between liking a thing and thinking it good?'

'Bridey, don't be so Jesuitical,' said Sebastian, but I knew that this disagreement was not a matter of words only, but expressed a deep and impassable division between us; neither had any understanding of the other, nor ever could.

'Isn't that just the distinction you made about wine?'

'No. I like and think good the end to which wine is sometimes the means–the promotion of sympathy between man and man. But in my own case it does not achieve that end, so I neither like it nor think it good for me.'

'Bridey, do stop.'

'I'm sorry,' he said, 'I thought it rather an interesting point.'

'Thank God I went to Eton,' said Sebastian.

After dinner Brideshead said: 'I'm afraid I must take Sebastian away for half an hour. I shall be busy all day tomorrow, and I'm off immediately after the show. I've a lot of papers for father to sign. Sebastian must take them out and explain them to him. It's time you were in bed, Cordelia.'

'Must digest first,' she said. 'I'm not used to gorging like this at night. I'll talk to Charles.'

'"*Charles*"?' said Sebastian. '"*Charles*"? "Mr Ryder" to you, child.'

'Come on, Charles.'

When we were alone she said: 'Are you really an agnostic?'

'Does your family always talk about religion all the time?'

'Not all the time. It's a subject that just comes up naturally, doesn't it?'

'Does it? It never has with me before.'

'Then perhaps you *are* an agnostic. I'll pray for you.'

'That's very kind of you.'

'I can't spare you a whole rosary you know. Just a decade. I've got such a long list of people. I take them in order and they get a decade about once a week.'

'I'm sure it's more than I deserve.'

'Oh, I've got some harder cases than you. Lloyd George and the Kaiser and Olive Banks.'

'Who is she?'

'She was bunked from the convent last term. I don't quite know what for. Reverend Mother found something she'd been writing. D'you know, if you weren't an agnostic, I should ask you for five shillings to buy a black goddaughter.'

'Nothing will surprise me about your religion.'

'It's a new thing a missionary priest started last term. You send five bob to some nuns in Africa and they christen a baby and name her after you. I've got six black Cordelias already. Isn't it lovely?'

When Brideshead and Sebastian returned, Cordelia was sent to bed. Brideshead began again on our discussion.

'Of course, you are right really,' he said. 'You take art as a means not as an end. That is strict theology, but it's unusual to find an agnostic believing it.'

'Cordelia has promised to pray for me,' I said.

'She made a novena for her pig,' said Sebastian.

'You know all this is very puzzling to me,' I said.

'I think we're causing scandal,' said Brideshead.

That night I began to realize how little I really knew of Sebastian, and to understand why he had always sought to keep me apart from the rest of his life. He was like a friend made on board ship, on the high seas; now we had come to his home port.

Brideshead and Cordelia went away; the tents were struck on the show ground, the flags uprooted; the trampled grass began to regain its colour; the month that had started in leisurely fashion came swiftly to its end. Sebastian walked without a stick now and had forgotten his injury.

'I think you'd better come with me to Venice,' he said.

'No money.'

'I thought of that. We live on papa when we get there. The lawyers pay my fare–first class and sleeper. We can both travel third for that.'

And so we went; first by the long, cheap sea-crossing to Dunkirk, sitting all night on deck under a clear sky, watching the grey dawn break over the sand dunes; then to Paris, on wooden seats, where we drove to the Lotti, had baths and shaved, lunched at Foyot's, which was hot and half-empty, loitered sleepily among the shops, and sat long in a café waiting till the time of our train; then in the warm, dusty evening to the Gare de Lyon, to the slow train south, again the wooden seats, a carriage full of the poor, visiting their families–travelling, as the poor do in Northern countries, with a multitude of small bundles and an air of patient submission to authority–and sailors returning from leave. We slept fitfully, jolting and stopping, changed once in the night, slept again and awoke in an empty carriage, with pine woods passing the windows and the distant view of mountain peaks. New uniforms at the frontier, coffee and bread at the station buffet, people round us of Southern grace and gaiety; on again into the plains, conifers changing to vine and olive, a change of trains at Milan; garlic sausage, bread, and a flask of Orvieto bought from a trolley (we had spent all our money save for a few francs, in Paris); the sun mounted high and the country glowed with heat; the carriage filled with peasants, ebbing and flowing at each station, the smell of garlic was overwhelming in the hot carriage. At last in the evening we arrive at Venice.

A sombre figure was there to meet us. 'Papa's valet, Plender.'

'I met the express,' said Plender. 'His Lordship thought you must have looked up the train wrong. This seemed only to come from Milan.'

'We travelled third.'

Plender tittered politely. 'I have the gondola here. I shall follow with the luggage in the *vaporetto*. His Lordship had gone to the Lido. He was not sure he would be home before you–that was when we expected you on the Express. He should be there by now.'

He led us to the waiting boat. The gondoliers wore green and white livery and silver plaques on their chests; they smiled and bowed.

'*Palazzo. Pronto.*'

'*Sì, signore Plender.*'

And we floated away.

'You've been here before?'

'No.'

'I came once before–from the sea. This is the way to arrive.'

'*Ecco ci siamo, signori.*'

The palace was a little less than it sounded, a narrow Palladian façade, mossy steps, a dark archway of rusticated stone. One boatman leapt ashore, made fast to the post, rang the bell; the other stood on the prow keeping the craft in to the steps. The doors opened; a man in rather raffish summer livery of striped linen led us up the stairs from shadow into light; the *piano nobile* was in full sunshine, ablaze with frescoes of the school of Tintoretto.

Our rooms were on the floor above, reached by a precipitous marble staircase; they were shuttered against the afternoon sun; the butler threw them open and we looked out on the grand canal; the beds had mosquito nets.

'*Mostica* not now.'

There was a little bulbous press in each room, a misty, gilt-framed mirror, and no other furniture. The floor was of bare marble slabs.

'A bit bleak?' asked Sebastian.

'Bleak? Look at that.' I led him again to the window and the incomparable pageant below and about us.

'No, you couldn't call it bleak.'

A tremendous explosion drew us next door. We found a bathroom which seemed to have been built in a chimney. There was no ceiling; instead the walls ran straight through the floor above to the open sky. The butler was almost invisible in the steam of an antiquated geyser. There was an overpowering smell of gas and a tiny trickle of cold water.

'No good.'

'*Sì, Sì, subito, signori.*'

The butler ran to the top of the staircase and began to shout down it; a female voice, more strident than his, answered. Sebastian and I returned to the spectacle below our windows. Presently the argument came to an end and a woman and child appeared, who smiled at us, scowled at the butler, and put on Sebastian's press a silver basin and ewer of boiling water. The butler meanwhile unpacked and folded our clothes and, lapsing into Italian, told us of the unrecognized merits of the geyser, until suddenly cocking his head sideways he became alert, said '*Il marchese*,' and darted downstairs.

'We'd better look respectable before meeting papa,' said Sebastian. 'We needn't dress. I gather he's alone at the moment.'

I was full of curiosity to meet Lord Marchmain. When I did so I was first struck by his normality, which, as I saw more of him, I found to be studied. It was as though he were conscious of a Byronic aura, which he considered to be in bad taste and was at pains to suppress. He was standing on the balcony of the saloon and, as he turned to greet us, his face was in deep shadow. I was aware only of a tall and upright figure.

'Darling papa,' said Sebastian, 'how young you are looking!'

He kissed Lord Marchmain on the cheek and I, who had not kissed my father since I left the nursery, stood shyly behind him.

'This is Charles. Don't you think my father very handsome, Charles?'

Lord Marchmain shook my hand.

'Whoever looked up your train,' he said–and his voice also was Sebastian's–'made a *bêtise*. There's no such one.'

'We came on it.'

'You can't have. There was only a slow train from Milan at that time. I was at the Lido. I have taken to playing tennis there with the professional in the early evening. It is the only time of day when it is not too hot. I hope you boys will be fairly comfortable upstairs. This house seems to have been designed for the comfort of only one person, and I am that one. I have a room the size of this and a very decent dressing-room. Cara has taken possession of the other sizeable room.'

I was fascinated to hear him speak of his mistress so simply and casually; later I suspected that it was done for effect, for me.

'How is she?'

'Cara? Well, I hope. She will be back with us tomorrow. She is visiting some American friends at a villa on the Brenta canal. Where shall we dine? We might go to the Luna, but it is filling up with English now. Would you be too dull at home? Cara is sure to want to go out tomorrow, and the cook here is really quite excellent.'

He had moved away from the window and now stood in the full evening sunlight, with the red damask of the walls behind him. It was a noble face, a controlled one, just, it seemed, as he planned it to be; slightly weary, slightly sardonic, slightly voluptuous. He seemed in the prime of life; it was odd to think that he was only a few years younger than my father.

We dined at a marble table in the windows; everything was either of marble, or velvet, or dull, gilt *gesso*, in this house. Lord Marchmain said, 'And how do you plan your time here? Bathing or sight-seeing?'

'*Some* sight-seeing, anyway,' I said.

'Cara will like that–she, as Sebastian will have told you, is your hostess here. You can't do both, you know. Once you go to the Lido there is no escaping–you play backgammon, you get caught at the bar, you get stupefied by the sun. Stick to the churches.'

'Charles is very keen on painting,' said Sebastian.

'Yes?' I noticed the hint of deep boredom which I knew so well in my own father. 'Yes? Any particular Venetian painter?'

'Bellini,' I answered rather wildly.

'Yes? Which?'

'I'm afraid I didn't know there were two of them.'

'Three to be precise. You will find that in the great ages painting was very much a family business. How did you leave England?'

'It has been lovely,' said Sebastian.

'Was it? *Was* it? It has been my tragedy that I abominate the English countryside. I suppose it is a disgraceful thing to inherit great responsibilities and to be entirely indifferent to them. I am all the socialists would have me be, and a great stumbling-block to my own party. Well, my elder son will change all that, I've no doubt, if they leave him anything to inherit. . . . Why, I wonder, are Italian sweets always thought to be so good? There was always an Italian pastry-cook at Brideshead until my father's day. He had an Austrian, so much better. And now I suppose there is some British matron with beefy forearms.'

After dinner we left the palace by the street door and walked through a maze of bridges and squares and alleys, to Florian's for coffee, and watched the grave crowds crossing and recrossing under the campanile. 'There is nothing quite like a Venetian crowd,' said Lord Marchmain. 'The city is crawling with Anarchists, but an American woman tried to sit here the other night with bare shoulders and they drove her away by coming to stare at her, quite silently; they were like circling gulls coming back and back to her, until she left. Our countrymen are much less dignified when they attempt to express moral disapproval.'

An English party had just then come from the water-front, made for a table near us, and then suddenly moved to the other side, where they looked askance at us and talked with their heads close together. 'That is a man and his wife I used to know when I was in politics. A prominent member of your church, Sebastian.'

As we went up to bed that night Sebastian said: 'He's rather a poppet, isn't he?'

Lord Marchmain's mistress arrived next day. I was nineteen years old and completely ignorant of women. I could not with any certainty recognize a prostitute in the streets. I was therefore not indifferent to the fact of living under the roof of an adulterous couple, but I was old enough to hide my interest. Lord Marchmain's mistress, therefore, found me with a multitude of conflicting expectations about her, all of which were, for the moment, disappointed by her appearance. She was not a voluptuous Toulouse-Lautrec odalisque; she was not a 'little bit of fluff'; she was a middle-aged, well-preserved, well-dressed, well-mannered woman such as I had seen in countless public places and occasionally met. Nor did she seem marked by any social stigma. On the day of her arrival we lunched at the Lido, where she was greeted at almost every table.

'Vittoria Corombona has asked us all to her ball on Saturday.'

'It is very kind of her. You know I do not dance,' said Lord Marchmain.

'But for the boys? It is a thing to be seen–the Corombona palace lit up for the ball. One does not know how many such balls there will be in the future.'

'The boys can do as they like. We must refuse.'

'And I have asked Mrs Hacking Brunner to luncheon. She has a charming daughter. Sebastian and his friend will like her.'

'Sebastian and his friend are more interested in Bellini than heiresses.'

'But that is what I have always wished,' said Cara, changing her point of attack adroitly. 'I have been here more times than I can count and Alex had not once let me inside San Marco even. We will become *tourists*, yes?'

We became tourists; Cara enlisted as guide a midget Venetian nobleman to whom all doors were open, and with him at her side and a guide book in her hand, she came with us, flagging sometimes but never giving up, a neat, prosaic figure amid the immense splendours of the place.

The fortnight at Venice passed quickly and sweetly–perhaps too sweetly; I was drowning in honey, stingless. On some days life kept pace with the gondola, as we nosed through the side-canals and the boatman uttered his plaintive musical bird-cry of warning; on other days with the speed-boat bouncing over the lagoon in a stream of sun-lit foam; it left a confused memory of fierce sunlight on the sands and cool, marble interiors; of water everywhere, lapping on smooth stone, reflected in a dapple of light on painted ceilings; of a night at the Corombona palace such as Byron might have known, and another Byronic night fishing for scampi in the shallows of Chioggia, the phosphorescent wake of the little ship, the lantern swinging in the prow, and the net coming up full of weed and sand and floundering fishes; of melon and *prosciutto* on the balcony in the cool of the morning; of hot cheese sandwiches and champagne cocktails at Harry's bar.

I remember Sebastian looking up at the Colleoni statue and saying, 'It's rather sad to think that whatever happens you and I can never possibly get involved in a war.'

I remember most particularly one conversation towards the end of my visit.

Sebastian had gone to play tennis with his father and Cara at last admitted to fatigue. We sat in the late afternoon at the windows overlooking the Grand Canal, she on the sofa with a piece of needlework, I in an armchair, idle. It was the first time we had been alone together.

'I think you are very fond of Sebastian,' she said.

'Why certainly.'

'I know of these romantic friendships of the English and the Germans. They are not Latin. I think they are very good if they do not go on too long.'

She was so composed and matter-of-fact that I could not take her amiss, but I failed to find an answer. She seemed not to expect one but continued stitching, pausing sometimes to match the silk from a work-bag at her side.

'It is a kind of love that comes to children before they know its meaning. In England it comes when you are almost men; I think I like that. It is better to have that kind of love for another boy than for a girl. Alex you see had it for a girl, for his wife. Do you think he loves *me?*'

'Really, Cara, you ask the most embarrassing questions. How should I know? I assume . . .'

'He does not. But not the littlest piece. Then why does he stay with me? I will tell you; because I protect him from Lady Marchmain. He hates her; but you can have no conception how he hates her. You would think him so calm and English–the milord, rather blasé, all passion dead, wishing to be comfortable and not to be worried, following the sun, with me to look after that one thing that no man can do for himself. My friend, he is a volcano of hate. He cannot breathe the same air as she. He will not set foot in England because it is her home; he can scarcely be happy with Sebastian because he is her son. But Sebastian hates her too.'

'I'm sure you're wrong there.'

'He may not admit it to you. He may not admit it to himself; they are full of hate–hate of themselves. Alex and his family. . . . Why do you think he will never go into society?'

'I always thought people had turned against him.'

'My dear boy, you are very young. People turn against a handsome, clever, wealthy man like Alex? Never in your life. It is he who has driven them away. Even now they come back again and again to be snubbed and laughed at. And all for Lady Marchmain. He will not touch a hand which may have touched hers. When we have guests I see him thinking, "Have they perhaps just come from Brideshead? Are they on their way to Marchmain House? Will they speak of me to my wife? Are they a link between me and her whom I hate?" But, seriously, with my heart, that is how he thinks. He is mad. And how has she deserved all this hate? She has done nothing except to be loved by someone who was not grown up. I have never met Lady Marchmain; I have seen her once only; but if you live with a man you come to know the other woman he has loved. I know Lady Marchmain very well. She is a good and simple woman who has been loved in the wrong way.

'When people hate with all that energy, it is something in themselves they are hating. Alex is hating all the illusions of boyhood–innocence, God, hope. Poor Lady Marchmain has to bear all that. A woman has not all these ways of loving.

'Now Alex is very fond of me and I protect him from his own innocence. We are comfortable.

'Sebastian is in love with his own childhood. That will make him very unhappy. His teddy-bear, his nanny . . . and he is nineteen years old. . . .'

She stirred on her sofa, shifting her weight so that she could look down at the passing boats, and said in fond, mocking tones: 'How good it is to sit in the shade and talk of love,' and then added with a sudden swoop to earth, 'Sebastian drinks too much.'

'I suppose we both do.'

'With you it does not matter. I have watched you together. With Sebastian it is different. He will be a drunkard if someone does not come to stop him. I have known so many. Alex was nearly a drunkard when he met me; it is in the blood. I see it in the *way* Sebastian drinks. It is not your way.'

We arrived in London on the day before term began. On the way from Charing Cross I dropped Sebastian in the forecourt of his mother's house; 'Here is "Marchers",' he said with a sigh which meant the end of a holiday. 'I won't ask you in, the place is probably full of my family. We'll meet at Oxford'; I drove across the park to my home.

My father greeted me with his usual air of mild regret.

'Here today,' he said; 'gone tomorrow. I seem to see very little of you. Perhaps it is dull for you here. How could it be otherwise? You have enjoyed yourself?'

'Very much. I went to Venice.'

'Yes. Yes. I suppose so. The weather was fine?'

When he went to bed after an evening of silent study, he paused to ask: 'The friend you were so much concerned about, did he die?'

'No.'

'I am very thankful. You should have written to tell me. I worried about him so much.'

5

'It is typical of Oxford,' I said, 'to start the new year in autumn.'

Everywhere, on cobble and gravel and lawn, the leaves were falling and in the college gardens the smoke of the bonfires joined the wet river mist, drifting across the grey walls; the flags were oily underfoot and as, one by one, the lamps were lit in the windows round the quad, the golden lights were diffuse and remote, new figures in new gowns wandered through the twilight under the arches and the familiar bells now spoke of a year's memories.

The autumnal mood possessed us both as though the riotous exuberance of June had died with the gillyflowers, whose scent at my windows now yielded to the damp leaves, smouldering in a corner of the quad.

It was the first Sunday evening of term.

'I feel precisely one hundred years old,' said Sebastian.

He had come up the night before, a day earlier than I, and this was our first meeting since we parted in the taxi.

'I've had a talking-to from Mgr Bell this afternoon. That makes the fourth since I came up–my tutor, the junior dean, Mr Samgrass of All Souls, and now Mgr Bell.'

'Who is Mr Samgrass of All Souls?'

'Just someone of mummy's. They all say that I made a very bad start last year, that I have been *noticed*, and that if I don't mend my ways I shall get sent down. How does one mend one's ways? I suppose one joins the League of Nations Union, and reads the *Isis* every week, and drinks coffee in the morning at the Cadena café, and smokes a great pipe and plays hockey and goes out to tea on Boar's Hill and to lectures at Keble, and rides a bicycle with a little tray full of notebooks and drinks cocoa in the evening and discusses sex seriously. Oh, Charles, what has happened since last term? I feel so old.'

'I feel middle-aged. That is infinitely worse. I believe we have had all the fun we can expect here.'

We sat silent in the firelight as darkness fell.

'Anthony Blanche has gone down.'

'Why?'

'He wrote to me. Apparently he's taken a flat in Munich–he has formed an attachment to a policeman there.'

'I shall miss him.'

'I suppose I shall, too, in a way.'

We fell silent again and sat so still in the firelight that a man who came in to see me, stood for a moment in the door and then went away thinking the room empty.

'This is no way to start a new year,' said Sebastian; but this sombre October evening seemed to breathe its chill, moist air over the succeeding weeks. All that term and all that year Sebastian and I lived more and more in the shadows and, like a fetish, hidden first from the missionary and at length forgotten, the toy bear, Aloysius, sat unregarded on the chest-of-drawers in Sebastian's bedroom.

There was a change in both of us. We had lost the sense of discovery which had infused the anarchy of our first year. I began to settle down.

Unexpectedly, I missed my cousin Jasper, who had got his first in Greats and was now cumbrously setting about a life of public mischief in London; I needed him to shock; without that massive presence the college seemed to lack solidity; it no longer provoked and gave point to outrage as it had done in the summer. Moreover, I had come back glutted and a little chastened; with the resolve to go slow. Never again would I expose myself to my father's humour; his whimsical persecution had convinced me, as no rebuke could have done, of the folly of living beyond my means. I had had no talking-to this term; my success in History Previous and a beta minus in one of my Collections papers had put me on easy terms with my tutor which I managed to maintain without undue effort.

I kept a tenuous connexion with the History School, wrote my two essays a week, and attended an occasional lecture. Besides this I started my second year by joining the Ruskin School of Art; two or three mornings a week we met, about a dozen of us–half, at least, the daughters of north Oxford–among the casts from the antique at the Ashmolean Museum; twice a week we drew from the nude in a small room over a teashop; some pains were taken by the authorities to exclude any hint of lubricity on these evenings, and the young woman who sat to us was brought from London for the day and not allowed to reside in the University city; one flank, that nearer the oil stove, I remember, was always rosy and the other mottled and puckered as though it had been plucked. There, in the smell of the oil lamp, we sat astride the donkey stools and evoked a barely visible wraith of Trilby. My drawings were worthless; in my own rooms I designed elaborate little pastiches, some of which, preserved by friends of the period, come to light occasionally to embarrass me.

We were instructed by a man of about my age, who treated us with defensive hostility; he wore very dark blue shirts, a lemon-yellow tie, and horn-rimmed glasses, and it was largely by reason of this warning that I modified my own style of dress until it approximated to what my cousin Jasper would have thought suitable for country-house visiting. Thus soberly dressed and happily employed I became a fairly respectable member of my college.

With Sebastian it was different. His year of anarchy had filled a deep, interior need of his, the escape from reality, and as he found himself increasingly hemmed in, where he once felt himself free, he became at times listless and morose, even with me.

We kept very much to our own company that term, each so much bound up in the other that we did not look elsewhere for friends. My cousin Jasper had told me that it was normal to spend one's second year shaking off the friends of one's first, and it happened as he said. Most of my friends were those I had made through Sebastian; together we shed them and made no others. There was no renunciation. At first we seemed to see them as often as ever; we went to parties but gave few of our own. I was not concerned to impress the new freshmen who, like their London sisters, were here being launched in Society; there were strange faces now at every party and I, who a few months back had been voracious of new acquaintances, now felt surfeited; even our small circle of intimates, so lively in the summer sunshine, seemed dimmed and muted now in the pervading fog, the river-borne twilight that softened and obscured all that year for me. Anthony Blanche had taken something away with him when he went; he had locked a door and hung the key on his chain; and all his friends, among whom he had always been a stranger, needed him now.

The Charity matinée was over, I felt; the impresario had buttoned his astrakhan coat and taken his fee and the disconsolate ladies of the company were without a leader. Without him they forgot their cues and garbled their lines; they needed him to ring the curtain up at the right moment; they needed him to direct the lime-lights; they needed his whisper in the wings, and his imperious eye on the leader of the band; without him there were no photographers from the weekly press, no prearranged goodwill and expectation of pleasure. No stronger bond held them together than common service; now the gold lace and velvet were packed away and returned to the costumier and the drab uniform of the day put on in its stead. For a few happy hours of rehearsal, for a few ecstatic minutes of performance, they had played splendid parts, their own great ancestors, the famous paintings they were thought to resemble; now it was over and in the bleak light of day they must go back to their homes; to the husband who came to London too often, to the lover who lost at cards, and to the child who grew too fast.

Anthony Blanche's set broke up and became a bare dozen lethargic, adolescent Englishmen. Sometimes in later life they would say: 'Do you remember that extraordinary fellow we used all to know at Oxford–Anthony Blanche? I wonder what became of him.' They lumbered back into the herd from which they had been so capriciously chosen and grew less and less individually recognizable. The change was not so apparent to them as to us, and they still congregated on occasions in our rooms; but we gave up seeking them. Instead we formed the taste for lower company and spent our evenings, as often as not, in Hogarthian little inns in St Ebb's and St Clement's and the streets between the old market and the canal, where we managed to be gay and were, I believe, well liked by the company. The Gardener's Arms and the Nag's Head, the Druid's Head near the theatre, and the Turf in Hell Passage knew us well; but in the last of these we were liable to meet other undergraduates–pub-crawling hearties from BNC–and Sebastian became possessed by a kind of phobia, like that which sometimes comes over men in uniform against their own service, so that many an evening was spoilt by their intrusion, and he would leave his glass half empty and turn sulkily back to college.

It was thus that Lady Marchmain found us when, early in that Michaelmas term, she came for a week to Oxford. She found Sebastian subdued, with all his host of friends reduced to one, myself. She accepted me as Sebastian's friend and sought to make me hers also, and in doing so, unwittingly struck at the roots of our friendship. That is the single reproach I have to set against her abundant kindness to me.

Her business in Oxford was with Mr Samgrass of All Souls, who now began to play an increasingly large part in our lives. Lady Marchmain was engaged in making a memorial book for circulation among her friends, about her brother, Ned, the eldest of three legendary heroes all killed between Mons and Passchendaele; he had left a quantity of papers–poems, letters, speeches, articles; to edit them, even for a restricted circle, needed tact and countless decisions in which the judgement of an adoring sister was liable to err. Acknowledging this, she had sought outside advice, and Mr Samgrass had been found to help her.

He was a young history don, a short, plump man, dapper in dress, with sparse hair brushed flat on an over-large head, neat hands, small feet, and the general appearance of being too often bathed. His manner was genial and his speech idiosyncratic. We came to know him well.

It was Mr Samgrass's particular aptitude to help others with their work, but he was himself the author of several stylish little books. He was a great delver in muniment-rooms and had a sharp nose for the picturesque. Sebastian spoke less than the truth when he described him as 'someone of mummy's'; he was someone of almost everyone's who possessed anything to attract him.

Mr Samgrass was a genealogist and a legitimist; he loved dispossessed royalty and knew the exact validity of the rival claims of the pretenders to many thrones; he was not a man of religious habit, but he knew more than most Catholics about their Church; he had friends in the Vatican and could talk at length of policy and appointments, saying which contemporary ecclesiastics were in good favour, which in bad, what recent theological hypothesis was suspect, and how this or that Jesuit or Dominican had skated on thin ice or sailed near the wind in his Lenten discourses; he had everything except the Faith, and later liked to attend benediction in the chapel of Brideshead and see the ladies of the family with their necks arched in devotion under their black lace mantillas; he loved forgotten scandals in high life and was an expert in putative parentage; he claimed to love the past, but I always felt that he thought all the splendid company, living or dead, with whom he associated slightly absurd; it was Mr Samgrass who was real, the rest were an insubstantial pageant. He was the Victorian tourist, solid and patronizing, for whose amusement these foreign things were paraded. And there was something a little too brisk about his literary manners; I suspected the existence of a dictaphone somewhere in his panelled rooms.

He was with Lady Marchmain when I first met them, and I thought then that she could not have found a greater contrast to herself than this intellectual-on-the-make, nor a better foil to her own charm. It was not her way to make a conspicuous entry into anyone's life, but towards the end of that week Sebastian said rather sourly: 'You and mummy seem very thick,' and I realized that in fact I was being drawn into intimacy by swift, imperceptible stages, for she was impatient of any human relationship that fell short of it. By the time that she left I had promised to spend all next vacation, except Christmas itself, at Brideshead.

One Monday morning a week or two later I was in Sebastian's room waiting for him to return from a tutorial, when Julia walked in, followed by a large man whom she introduced as 'Mr Mottram' and addressed as 'Rex'. They were motoring up from a house where they had spent the week-end, they explained. Rex Mottram was warm and confident in a check ulster; Julia cold and rather shy in furs; she made straight for the fire and crouched over it shivering.

'We hoped Sebastian might give us luncheon,' she said. 'Failing him we can always try Boy Mulcaster, but I somehow thought we should eat better with Sebastian, and we're very hungry. We've been literally starved all the week-end at the Chasms.'

'He and Sebastian are both lunching with me. Come too.'

So, without demur, they joined the party in my rooms, one of the last of the old kind that I gave. Rex Mottram exerted himself to make an impression. He was a handsome fellow with dark hair growing low on his forehead and heavy black eyebrows. He spoke with an engaging Canadian accent. One quickly learned all that he wished one to know about him, that he was a lucky man with money, a member of parliament, a gambler, a good fellow; that he played golf regularly with the Prince of Wales and was on easy terms with 'Max' and 'F.E.' and 'Gertie' Lawrence and Augustus John and Carpentier–with anyone, it seemed, who happened to be mentioned. Of the University he said: 'No, I was never here. It just means you start life three years behind the other fellow.'

His life, so far as he made it known, began in the war, where he had got a good M.C. serving with the Canadians and had ended as A.D.C. to a popular general.

He cannot have been more than thirty at the time we met him, but he seemed very old to us in Oxford. Julia treated him, as she seemed to treat all the world, with mild disdain, but with an air of possession. During luncheon she sent him to the car for her cigarettes, and once or twice when he was talking very big, she apologized for him, saying: 'Remember he's colonial,' to which he replied with boisterous laughter.

When he had gone I asked who he was.

'Oh, just someone of Julia's,' said Sebastian.

We were slightly surprised a week later to get a telegram from him asking us and Boy Mulcaster to dinner in London on the following night for 'a party of Julia's'.

'I don't think he knows anyone young,' said Sebastian; 'all his friends are leathery old sharks in the City and the House of Commons. Shall we go?'

We discussed it, and because our life at Oxford was now so much in the shadows, we decided that we would.

'Why does he want Boy?'

'Julia and I have known him all our lives. I suppose, finding him at lunch with you, he thought he was a chum.'

We had no great liking for Mulcaster, but the three of us were in high spirits when, having got leave for the night from our colleges, we drove off on the London road in Hardcastle's car.

We were to spend the night at Marchmain House. We went there to dress and, while we dressed, drank a bottle of champagne, going in and out of one another's rooms which were together three floors up and rather shabby compared with the splendours below. As we came downstairs Julia passed us going up to her room still in her day clothes.

'I'm going to be late,' she said; 'you boys had better go on to Rex's. It's heavenly of you to come.'

'What is this party?'

'A ghastly charity ball I'm involved with. Rex insisted on giving a dinner party for it. See you there.'

Rex Mottram lived within walking distance of Marchmain House.

'Julia's going to be late,' we said, 'she's only just gone up to dress.'

'That means an hour. We'd better have some wine.'

A woman who was introduced as 'Mrs Champion' said: 'I'm sure she'd sooner we started, Rex.'

'Well, let's have some wine first anyway.'

'Why a Jeroboam, Rex?' she said peevishly. 'You always want to have everything too big.'

'Won't be too big for us,' he said, taking the bottle in his own hands and easing the cork.

There were two girls there, contemporaries of Julia's; they all seemed involved in the management of the ball. Mulcaster knew them of old and they, without much relish I thought, knew him. Mrs Champion talked to Rex. Sebastian and I found ourselves drinking alone together as we always did.

At length Julia arrived, unhurried, exquisite, unrepentant. 'You shouldn't have let him wait,' she said. 'It's his Canadian courtesy.'

Rex Mottram was a liberal host, and by the end of dinner the three of us who had come from Oxford were rather drunk. While we were standing in the hall waiting for the girls to come down and Rex and Mrs Champion had drawn away from us, talking, acrimoniously, in low voices, Mulcaster said, 'I say, let's slip away from this ghastly dance and go to Ma Mayfield's.'

'Who is Ma Mayfield?'

'You know Ma Mayfield. Everyone knows Ma Mayfield of the Old Hundredth. I've got a regular there–a sweet little thing called Effie. There'd be the devil to pay if Effie heard I'd been to London and hadn't been in to see her. Come and meet Effie at Ma Mayfield's.'

'All right,' said Sebastian, 'let's meet Effie at Ma Mayfield's.'

'We'll take another bottle of pop off the good Mottram and then leave the bloody dance and go to the Old Hundredth. How about that?'

It was not a difficult matter to leave the ball; the girls whom Rex Mottram had collected had many friends there and, after we had danced together once or twice, our table began to fill up; Rex Mottram ordered more and more wine; presently the three of us were together on the pavement.

'D'you know where this place is?'

'Of course I do. A hundred Sink Street.'

'Where's that?'

'Just off Leicester Square. Better take the car.'

'Why?'

'Always better to have one's own car on an occasion like this.'

We did not question this reasoning, and there lay our mistake. The car was in the forecourt of Marchmain House within a hundred yards of the hotel where we had been dancing. Mulcaster drove and, after some wandering, brought us safely to Sink Street. A commissionaire at one side of a dark doorway and a middle-aged man in evening dress on the other side of it, standing with his face to the wall cooling his forehead on the bricks, indicated our destination.

'Keep out, you'll be poisoned,' said the middle-aged man.

'Members?' said the commissionaire.

'The name is Mulcaster,' said Mulcaster. 'Viscount Mulcaster.'

'Well, try inside,' said the commissionaire.

'You'll be robbed, poisoned and infected and robbed,' said the middle-aged man.

Inside the dark doorway was a bright hatch.

'Members?' asked a stout woman, in evening dress.

'I like that,' said Mulcaster. 'You ought to know me by now.'

'Yes, dearie,' said the woman without interest. 'Ten bob each.'

'Oh, look here, I've never paid before.'

'Daresay not, dearie. We're full up tonight so it's ten bob. Anyone who comes after you will have to pay a quid. You're lucky.'

'Let me speak to Mrs Mayfield.'

'I'm Mrs Mayfield. Ten bob each.'

'Why, Ma, I didn't recognize you in your finery. You know me, don't you? Boy Mulcaster.'

'Yes, duckie. Ten bob each.'

We paid, and the man who had been standing between us and the inner door now made way for us. Inside it was hot and crowded, for the Old Hundredth was then at the height of its success. We found a table and ordered a bottle; the waiter took payment before he opened it.

'Where's Effie tonight?' asked Mulcaster.

'Effie 'oo?'

'Effie, one of the girls who's always here. The pretty dark one.'

'There's lots of girls works here. Some of them's dark and some of them's fair. You might call some of them pretty. I haven't the time to know them by name.'

'I'll go and look for her,' said Mulcaster.

While he was away two girls stopped near our table and looked at us curiously. 'Come on,' said one to the other, 'we're wasting our time. They're only fairies.'

Presently Mulcaster returned in triumph with Effie to whom, without its being ordered, the waiter immediately brought a plate of eggs and bacon.

'First bite I've had all the evening,' she said. 'Only thing that's any good here is the breakfast; makes you fair peckish hanging about.'

'That's another six bob,' said the waiter.

When her hunger was appeased, Effie dabbed her mouth and looked at us.

'I've seen you here before, often, haven't I?' she said to me.

'I'm afraid not.'

'But I've seen *you*?' to Mulcaster.

'Well, I should rather hope so. You haven't forgotten our little evening in September?'

'No, darling, of course not. You were the boy in the Guards who cut your toe, weren't you?'

'Now, Effie, don't be a tease.'

'No, that was another night, wasn't it? I know–you were with Bunty the time the police were in and we all hid in the place they keep the dust-bins.'

'Effie loves pulling my leg, don't you, Effie? She's annoyed with me for staying away so long, aren't you?'

'Whatever you say, I know I *have* seen you before somewhere.'

'Stop teasing.'

'I wasn't meaning to tease. Honest. Want to dance?'

'Not at the minute.'

'Thank the Lord. My shoes pinch something terrible tonight.'

Soon she and Mulcaster were deep in conversation. Sebastian leaned back and said to me: 'I'm going to ask that pair to join us.'

The two unattached women who had considered us earlier, were again circling towards us. Sebastian smiled and rose to greet them: soon they, too, were eating heartily. One had the face of a skull, the other of a sickly child. The Death's Head seemed destined for me. 'How about a little party,' she said, 'just the six of us over at my place?'

'Certainly,' said Sebastian.

'We thought you were fairies when you came in.'

'That was our extreme youth.'

Death's Head giggled. 'You're a good sport,' she said.

'You're very sweet really,' said the Sickly Child. 'I must just tell Mrs Mayfield we're going out.'

It was still early, not long after midnight, when we regained the street. The commissionaire tried to persuade us to take a taxi. 'I'll look after your car, sir, I wouldn't drive yourself, sir, really I wouldn't.'

But Sebastian took the wheel and the two women sat one on the other beside him, to show him the way. Effie and Mulcaster and I sat in the back. I think we cheered a little as we drove off.

We did not drive far. We turned into Shaftesbury Avenue and were making for Piccadilly when we narrowly escaped a head-on collision with a taxi-cab.

'For Christ's sake,' said Effie, 'look where you're going. D'you want to murder us all?'

'Careless fellow that,' said Sebastian.

'It isn't safe the way you're driving,' said Death's Head. 'Besides, we ought to be on the other side of the road.'

'So we should,' said Sebastian, swinging abruptly across.

'Here, stop. I'd sooner walk.'

'Stop? Certainly.'

He put on the brakes and we came abruptly to a halt broadside across the road. Two policemen quickened their stride and approached us.

'Let me out of this,' said Effie, and made her escape with a leap and a scamper.

The rest of us were caught.

'I'm sorry if I am impeding the traffic, officer,' said Sebastian with care, 'but the lady insisted on my stopping for her to get out. She would take no denial. As you will have observed, she was pressed for time. A matter of nerves you know.'

'Let me talk to him,' said Death's Head. 'Be a sport, handsome; no one's seen anything but you. The boys don't mean any harm. I'll get them into a taxi and see them home quiet.'

The policemen looked us over, deliberately, forming their own judgement. Even then everything might have been well had not Mulcaster joined in. 'Look here, my good man,' he said. 'There's no need for you to notice anything. We've just come from Ma Mayfield's. I reckon she pays you a nice retainer to keep your eyes shut. Well, you can keep 'em shut on us too, and you won't be the losers by it.'

That resolved any doubts which the policemen may have felt. In a short time we were in the cells.

I remember little of the journey there or the process of admission. Mulcaster, I think, protested vigorously and, when we were made to empty our pockets, accused his gaolers of theft. Then we were locked in, and my first clear memory is of tiled walls with a lamp set high up under thick glass, a bunk, and a door which had no handle on my side. Somewhere to the left of me Sebastian and Mulcaster were raising Cain. Sebastian had been steady on his legs and fairly composed on the way to the station; now, shut in, he seemed in a frenzy and was pounding the door, and shouting: 'Damn you, I'm not drunk. Open this door. I insist on seeing the doctor. I tell you I'm not drunk,' while Mulcaster, beyond, cried: 'My God, you'll pay for this! You're making a great mistake, I can tell you. Telephone the Home Secretary. Send for my solicitors. I will have *habeas corpus*.'

Groans of protest rose from the other cells where various tramps and pickpockets were trying to get some sleep: 'Aw, pipe down!' 'Give a man some peace, can't yer?' . . . 'Is this a blinking lock-up or a looney-house?'–and the sergeant, going his rounds, admonished them through the grille. 'You'll be here all night if you don't sober up.'

I sat on the bunk in low spirits and dozed a little. Presently the racket subsided and Sebastian called: 'I say, Charles, are you there?'

'Here I am.'

'This is the hell of a business.'

'Can't we get bail or something?'

Mulcaster seemed to have fallen asleep.

'I tell you the man–Rex Mottram. He'd be in his element here.'

We had some difficulty in getting in touch with him; it was half an hour before the policeman in charge answered my bell. At last he consented, rather sceptically, to send a telephone message to the hotel where the ball was being held. There was another long delay and then our prison doors were opened.

Seeping through the squalid air of the police station, the sour smell of dirt and disinfectant, came the sweet, rich smoke of a Havana cigar–of two Havana cigars, for the sergeant in charge was smoking also.

Rex stood in the charge-room looking the embodiment–indeed, the burlesque–of power and prosperity; he wore a fur-lined overcoat with broad astrakhan lapels and a silk hat. The police were deferential and eager to help.

'We had to do our duty,' they said. 'Took the young gentlemen into custody for their own protection.'

Mulcaster looked crapulous and began a confused complaint that he had been denied legal representation and civil rights. Rex said: 'Better leave all the talking to me.'

I was clear-headed now and watched and listened with fascination while Rex settled our business. He examined the charge sheets, spoke affably to the men who had made the arrest; with the slightest perceptible nuance he opened the way for bribery and quickly covered it when he saw that things had now lasted too long and the knowledge had been too widely shared; he undertook to deliver us at the magistrate's court at ten next morning, and then led us away. His car was outside.

'It's no use discussing things tonight. Where are you sleeping?'

'Marchers,' said Sebastian.

'You'd better come to me. I can fix you up for tonight. Leave everything to me.'

It was plain that he rejoiced in his efficiency.

Next morning the display was even more impressive. I awoke with the startled and puzzled sense of being in a strange room, and in the first seconds of consciousness the memory of the evening before returned, first as though of a nightmare, then of reality. Rex's valet was unpacking a suitcase. On seeing me move he went to the wash-hand stand and poured something from a bottle. 'I think I have everything from Marchmain House,' he said. 'Mr Mottram sent round to Heppell's for this.'

I took the draught and felt better.

A man was there from Trumper's to shave us.

Rex joined us at breakfast. 'It's important to make a good appearance at the court,' he said. 'Luckily none of you look much the worse for wear.'

After breakfast the barrister arrived and Rex delivered a summary of the case.

'Sebastian's in a jam,' he said. 'He's liable to anything up to six months' imprisonment for being drunk in charge of a car. You'll come up before Grigg unfortunately. He takes rather a grim view of cases of this sort. All that will happen this morning is that we shall ask to have Sebastian held over for a week to prepare the defence. You two will plead guilty, say you're sorry, and pay your five bob fine. I'll see what can be done about squaring the evening papers. The *Star* may be difficult.

'Remember, the important thing is to keep out all mention of the Old Hundredth. Luckily the tarts were sober and aren't being charged, but their names have been taken as witnesses. If we try and break down the police evidence, they'll be called. We've got to avoid that at all costs, so we shall have to swallow the police story whole and appeal to the magistrate's good nature not to wreck a young man's career for a single boyish indiscretion. It'll work all right. We shall need a don to give evidence of good character. Julia tells me you have a tame one called Samgrass. He'll do. Meanwhile *your* story is simply that you came up from Oxford for a perfectly respectable dance, weren't used to wine, had too much, and lost the way driving home.

'After that we shall have to see about fixing things with your authorities at Oxford.'

'I told them to call my solicitors,' said Mulcaster, 'and they refused. They've put themselves hopelessly in the wrong, and I don't see why they should get away with it.'

'For heaven's sake don't start any kind of argument. Just plead guilty and pay up. Understand?'

Mulcaster grumbled but submitted.

Everything happened at court as Rex had predicted. At half past ten we stood in Bow Street, Mulcaster and I free men, Sebastian bound over to appear in a week's time. Mulcaster had kept silent about his grievance; he and I were admonished and fined five shillings each and fifteen shillings costs. Mulcaster was becoming rather irksome to us, and it was with relief that we heard his plea of other business in London. The barrister bustled off and Sebastian and I were left alone and disconsolate.

'I suppose mummy's got to hear about it,' he said. 'Damn, damn, damn! It's cold. I won't go home. I've nowhere to go. Let's just slip back to Oxford and wait for *them* to bother *us*.'

The raffish habitués of the police court came and went, up and down the steps; still we stood on the windy corner, undecided.

'Why not get hold of Julia?'

'I might go abroad.'

'My dear Sebastian, you'll only be given a talking-to and fined a few pounds.'

'Yes, but it's all the *bother*–mummy and Bridey and all the family and the dons. I'd sooner go to prison. If I just slip away abroad they can't get me back, can they? That's what people do when the police are after them. I know mummy will make it seem she has to bear the whole brunt of the business.'

'Let's telephone Julia and get her to meet us somewhere and talk it over.'

We met at Gunter's in Berkeley Square. Julia, like most women then, wore a green hat pulled down to her eyes with a diamond arrow in it; she had a small dog under her arm, three-quarters buried in the fur of her coat. She greeted us with an unusual show of interest.

'Well, you are a pair of pickles; I must say you look remarkably well on it. The only time I got tight I was paralysed all the next day. I do think you might have taken me with you. The ball was positively lethal, and I've always longed to go to the Old Hundredth. No one will ever take me. Is it heaven?'

'So you know all about that, too?'

'Rex telephoned me this morning and told me everything. What were your girl friends like?'

'Don't be prurient,' said Sebastian.

'Mine was like a skull.'

'Mine was like a consumptive.'

'*Goodness*.' It had clearly raised us in Julia's estimation that we had been out with women; to her they were the point of interest.

'Does mummy know?'

'Not about your skulls and consumptives. She knows you were in the clink. I told her. She was divine about it, of course. You know anything Uncle Ned did was always perfect, and he got locked up once for taking a bear into one of Lloyd George's meetings, so she really feels quite human about the whole thing. She wants you both to lunch with her.'

'Oh God!'

'The only trouble is the papers and the family. Have you got an awful family, Charles?'

'Only a father. He'll never hear about it.'

'Ours are awful. Poor mummy is in for a ghastly time with them. They'll be writing letters and paying visits of sympathy, and all the time at the back of their minds one half will be saying, "That's what comes of bringing the boy up a Catholic," and the other half will say, "That's what comes of sending him to Eton instead of Stonyhurst." Poor mummy can't get it right.'

We lunched with Lady Marchmain. She accepted the whole thing with humorous resignation. Her only reproach was: 'I can't think why you went off and stayed with Mr Mottram. You might have come and told me about it first.'

'How am I going to explain it to all the family?' she asked. 'They will be so shocked to find that they're more upset about it than I am. Do you know my sister-in-law, Fanny Rosscommon? She has always thought I brought the children up badly. Now I am beginning to think she must be right.'

When we left I said: 'She couldn't have been more charming. What were you so worried about?'

'I can't explain,' said Sebastian miserably.

A week later when Sebastian came up for trial he was fined ten pounds. The newspapers reported it with painful prominence, one of them under the ironic headline: '*Marquis's son unused to wine*.' The magistrate said that it was only through the prompt action of the police that he was not up on a grave charge . . . 'It is purely by good fortune that you do not bear the responsibility of a serious accident . . .' Mr Samgrass gave evidence that Sebastian bore an irreproachable character and that a brilliant future at the University was in jeopardy. The papers took hold of this too–'*Model Student's Career at Stake*.' But for Mr Samgrass's evidence, said the magistrate, he would have been disposed to give an exemplary sentence; the law was the same for an Oxford undergraduate as for any young hooligan; indeed the better the home the more shameful the offence. . . .

It was not only at Bow Street that Mr Samgrass was of value. At Oxford he showed all the zeal and acumen which were Rex Mottram's in London. He interviewed the college authorities, the proctors, the Vice-Chancellor; he induced Mgr Bell to call on the Dean of Christ Church; he arranged for Lady Marchmain to talk to the Chancellor himself; and, as a result of all this, the three of us were gated for the rest of the term. Hardcastle, for no very clear reason, was again deprived of the use of his car, and the affair blew over. The most lasting penalty we suffered was our intimacy with Rex Mottram and Mr Samgrass, but since Rex's life was in London in a world of politics and high finance and Mr Samgrass's nearer to our own at Oxford, it was from him we suffered the more.

For the rest of that term he haunted us. Now that we were 'gated' we could not spend our evenings together, and from nine o'clock onwards were alone and at Mr Samgrass's mercy. Hardly an evening seemed to pass but he called on one or the other of us. He spoke of 'our little escapade' as though he, too, had been in the cells, and had that bond with us. . . . Once I climbed out of college and Mr Samgrass found me in Sebastian's rooms after the gate was shut and that, too, he made into a bond. It did not surprise me, therefore, when I arrived at Brideshead, after Christmas, to find Mr Samgrass, as though in wait for me, sitting alone before the fire in the room they called the 'Tapestry Hall'.

'You find me in solitary possession,' he said, and indeed he seemed to possess the hall and the sombre scenes of venery that hung round it, to possess the caryatids on either side of the fireplace, to possess me, as he rose to take my hand and greet me like a host: 'This morning,' he continued, 'we had a lawn meet of the Marchmain Hounds–a deliciously archaic spectacle–and all our young friends are fox-hunting, even Sebastian who, you will not be surprised to hear, looked remarkably elegant in his pink coat. Brideshead was impressive rather than elegant; he is Joint-master with a local figure of fun named Sir Walter Strickland-Venables. I wish the two of them could be included in these rather humdrum tapestries–they would give a note of fantasy.

'Our hostess remained at home; also a convalescent Dominican who has read too much Maritain and too little Hegel; Sir Adrian Porson, of course, and two rather forbidding Magyar cousins–I have tried them in German and in French, but in neither tongue are they diverting. All these have now driven off to visit a neighbour. I have been spending a cosy afternoon before the fire with the incomparable Charlus. Your arrival emboldens me to ring for some tea. How can I prepare you for the party? Alas, it breaks up tomorrow. Lady Julia departs to celebrate the New Year elsewhere, and takes the *beau-monde* with her. I shall miss the pretty creatures about the house–particularly one Celia; she is the sister of our old companion in adversity, Boy Mulcaster, and wonderfully unlike him. She has a bird-like style of conversation, pecking away at the subject in a way I find most engaging, and a school-monitor style of dress which I can only call "saucy". I shall miss her, for I do not go tomorrow. Tomorrow I start work in earnest on our hostess's book–which, believe me, is a treasure-house of period gems; pure authentic 1914.'

Tea was brought and, soon after it, Sebastian returned; he had lost the hunt early, he said, and hacked home; the others were not long after him, having been fetched by car at the end of the day; Brideshead was absent; he had business at the kennels and Cordelia had gone with him. The rest filled the hall and were soon eating scrambled eggs and crumpets; and Mr Samgrass, who had lunched at home and dozed all the afternoon before the fire, ate eggs and crumpets with them. Presently Lady Marchmain's party returned, and when, before we went upstairs to dress for dinner, she said 'Who's coming to chapel for the Rosary?' and Sebastian and Julia said they must have their baths at once, Mr Samgrass went with her and the friar.

'I wish Mr Samgrass would go,' said Sebastian, in his bath; 'I'm sick of being grateful to him.'

In the course of the next fortnight distaste for Mr Samgrass came to be a little unspoken secret throughout the house; in his presence Sir Adrian Porson's fine old eyes seemed to search a distant horizon and his lips set in classic pessimism. Only the Hungarian cousins who, mistaking the status of tutor, took him for an unusually privileged upper servant, were unaffected by his presence.

Mr Samgrass, Sir Adrian Porson, the Hungarians, the friar, Brideshead, Sebastian, Cordelia were all who remained of the Christmas party.

Religion predominated in the house; not only in its practices–the daily mass and Rosary, morning and evening in the chapel–but in all its intercourse. 'We must make a Catholic of Charles,' Lady Marchmain said, and we had many little talks together during my visits when she delicately steered the subject into a holy quarter. After the first of these Sebastian said: 'Has mummy been having one of her "little talks" with you? She's always doing it. I wish to hell she wouldn't.'

One was never summoned for a little talk, or consciously led to it; it merely happened, when she wished to speak intimately, that one found oneself alone with her, if it was summer, in a secluded walk by the lakes or in a corner of the walled rose-gardens; if it was winter, in her sitting-room on the first floor.

This room was all her own; she had taken it for herself and changed it so that, entering, one seemed to be in another house. She had lowered the ceiling and the elaborate cornice which, in one form or another, graced every room was lost to view; the walls, one panelled in brocade, were stripped and washed blue and spotted with innumerable little water-colours of fond association; the air was sweet with the fresh scent of flowers and musty potpourri; her library in soft leather covers, well-read works of poetry and piety, filled a small rosewood bookcase; the chimneypiece was covered with small personal treasures–an ivory Madonna, a plaster St Joseph, posthumous miniatures of her three soldier brothers. When Sebastian and I lived alone at Brideshead during that brilliant August we had kept out of his mother's room.

Scraps of conversation came back to me with the memory of her room. I remember her saying: 'When I was a girl we were comparatively poor, but still much richer than most of the world, and when I married I became very rich. It used to worry me, and I thought it wrong to have so many beautiful things when others had nothing. Now I realize that it is possible for the rich to sin by coveting the privileges of the poor. The poor have always been the favourites of God and his saints, but I believe that it is one of the special achievements of Grace to sanctify the whole of life, riches included. Wealth in pagan Rome was necessarily something cruel; it's not any more.'

I said something about a camel and the eye of a needle and she rose happily to the point.

'But of *course*,' she said, 'it's very unexpected for a camel to go through the eye of a needle, but the gospel is simply a catalogue of unexpected things. It's not to be *expected* that an ox and an ass should worship at the crib. Animals are always doing the oddest things in the lives of the saints. It's all part of the poetry, the Alice-in-Wonderland side, of religion.'

But I was as untouched by her faith as I was by her charm: or, rather, I was touched by both alike. I had no mind then for anything except Sebastian, and I saw him already as being threatened, though I did not yet know how black was the threat. His constant, despairing prayer was to be let alone. By the blue waters and rustling palms of his own mind he was happy and harmless as a Polynesian; only when the big ship dropped anchor beyond the coral reef, and the cutter beached in the lagoon, and, up the slope that had never known the print of a boot, there trod the grim invasion of trader, administrator, missionary, and tourist–only then was it time to disinter the archaic weapons of the tribe and sound the drums in the hills; or, more easily, to turn from the sunlit door and lie alone in the darkness, where the impotent, painted deities paraded the walls in vain, and cough his heart out among the rum bottles.

And since Sebastian counted among the intruders his own conscience and all claims of human affection, his days in Arcadia were numbered. For in this, to me, tranquil time Sebastian took fright. I knew him well in that mood of alertness and suspicion, like a deer suddenly lifting his head at the far notes of the hunt; I had seen him grow wary at the thought of his family or his religion, now I found I, too, was suspect. He did not fail in love, but he lost his joy of it, for I was no longer part of his solitude. As my intimacy with his family grew, I became part of the world which he sought to escape; I became one of the bonds which held him. That was the part for which his mother, in all our little talks, was seeking to fit me. Everything was left unsaid. It was only dimly and at rare moments that I suspected what was afoot.

Outwardly Mr Samgrass was the only enemy. For a fortnight Sebastian and I remained at Brideshead, leading our own life. His brother was engaged in sport and estate management; Mr Samgrass was at work in the library on Lady Marchmain's book; Sir Adrian Porson demanded most of Lady Marchmain's time. We saw little of them except in the evenings; there was room under that wide roof for a wide variety of independent lives.

After a fortnight Sebastian said: 'I can't stand Mr Samgrass any more. Let's go to London,' so he came to stay with me and now began to use my home in preference to 'Marchers'. My father liked him. 'I think your friend very amusing,' he said. 'Ask him *often*.'

Then, back at Oxford, we took up again the life that seemed to be shrinking in the cold air. The sadness that had been strong in Sebastian the term before gave place to a kind of sullenness even towards me. He was sick at heart somewhere, I did not know how, and I grieved for him, unable to help.

When he was gay now it was usually because he was drunk, and when drunk he developed an obsession of 'mocking Mr Samgrass'. He composed a ditty of which the refrain was, 'Green arse, Samgrass–Samgrass green arse', sung to the tune of St Mary's chime, and he would thus serenade him, perhaps once a week, under his windows. Mr Samgrass was distinguished as being the first don to have a private telephone installed in his rooms. Sebastian in his cups used to ring him up and sing him this simple song. And all this Mr Samgrass took in good part, as it is called, smiling obsequiously when we met, but with growing confidence, as though each outrage in some way strengthened his hold on Sebastian.

It was during this term that I began to realize that Sebastian was a drunkard in quite a different sense to myself. I got drunk often, but through an excess of high spirits, in the love of the moment, and the wish to prolong and enhance it; Sebastian drank to escape. As we together grew older and more serious I drank less, he more. I found that sometimes after I had gone back to my college, he sat up late and alone, soaking. A succession of disasters came on him so swiftly and with such unexpected violence that it is hard to say when exactly I recognized that my friend was in deep trouble. I knew it well enough in the Easter vacation.

Julia used to say, 'Poor Sebastian. It's something chemical in him.'

That was the cant phrase of the time, derived from heaven knows what misconception of popular science. 'There's something chemical between them' was used to explain the over-mastering hate or love of any two people. It was the old concept of determinism in a new form. I do not believe there was anything chemical in my friend.

The Easter party at Brideshead was a bitter time, culminating in a small but unforgettably painful incident. Sebastian got very drunk before dinner in his mother's house, and thus marked the beginning of a new epoch in his melancholy record, another stride in the flight from his family which brought him to ruin.

It was at the end of the day when the large Easter party left Brideshead. It was called the Easter party, though in fact it began on the Tuesday of Easter Week, for the Flytes all went into retreat at the guest-house of a monastery from Maundy Thursday until Easter. This year Sebastian had said he would not go, but at the last moment had yielded, and came home in a state of acute depression from which I totally failed to raise him.

He had been drinking very hard for a week–only I knew how hard–and drinking in a nervous, surreptitious way, totally unlike his old habit. During the party there was always a grog tray in the library, and Sebastian took to slipping in there at odd moments during the day without saying anything even to me. The house was largely deserted during the day. I was at work painting another panel in the little garden-room in the colonnade. Sebastian complained of a cold, stayed in, and during all that time was never quite sober; he escaped attention by being silent. Now and then I noticed him attract curious glances, but most of the party knew him too slightly to see the change in him, while his own family were occupied, each with their particular guests.

When I remonstrated he said, 'I can't stand all these people about,' but it was when they finally left and he had to face his family at close quarters that he broke down.

The normal practice was for a cocktail tray to be brought into the drawing-room at six; we mixed our own drinks and the bottles were removed when we went to dress; later, just before dinner, cocktails appeared again, this time handed round by the footmen.

Sebastian disappeared after tea; the light had gone and I spent the next hour playing mah-jongg with Cordelia. At six I was alone in the drawing-room, when he returned; he was frowning in a way I knew all too well, and when he spoke I recognized the drunken thickening in his voice.

'Haven't they brought the cocktails yet?' He pulled clumsily on the bell-rope.

I said, 'Where have you been?'

'Up with nanny.'

'I don't believe it. You've been drinking somewhere.'

'I've been reading in my room. My cold's worse today'.

When the tray arrived he slopped gin and vermouth into a tumbler and carried it out of the room with him. I followed him upstairs, where he shut his bedroom door in my face and turned the key.

I returned to the drawing-room full of dismay and foreboding.

The family assembled. Lady Marchmain said: 'What's become of Sebastian?'

'He's gone to lie down. His cold is worse.'

'Oh dear, I hope he isn't getting flu. I thought he had a feverish look once or twice lately. Is there anything he wants?'

'No, he particularly asked not to be disturbed.'

I wondered whether I ought to speak to Brideshead, but that grim, rock-crystal mask forbade all confidence. Instead, on the way upstairs to dress, I told Julia.

'Sebastian's drunk.'

'He can't be. He didn't even come for a cocktail.'

'He's been drinking in his room all the afternoon.'

'How very peculiar! What a bore he is! Will he be all right for dinner?'

'No.'

'Well, *you* must deal with him. It's no business of mine. Does he often do this?'

'He has lately.'

'How very boring.'

I tried Sebastian's door, found it locked, and hoped he was sleeping, but, when I came back from my bath, I found him sitting in the chair before my fire; he was dressed for dinner, all but his shoes, but his tie was awry and his hair on end; he was very red in the face and squinting slightly. He spoke indistinctly.

'Charles, what you said was quite true. Not with nanny. Been drinking whisky up here. None in the library now party's gone. Now party's gone and only mummy. Feeling rather drunk. Think I'd better have something-on-a-tray up here. Not dinner with mummy.'

'Go to bed,' I told him. 'I'll say your cold's worse.'

'Much worse.'

I took him to his room which was next to mine and tried to get him to bed, but he sat in front of his dressing-table squinnying at himself in the glass, trying to remake his bow-tie. On the writing-table by the fire was a half-empty decanter of whisky. I took it up, thinking he would not see, but he spun round from the mirror and said: 'You put that down.'

'Don't be an ass, Sebastian. You've had enough.'

'What the devil's it got to do with you? You're only a guest here–*my* guest. I drink what I want to in my own house.'

He would have fought me for it at that moment.

'Very well,' I said, putting the decanter back, 'only for God's sake keep out of sight.'

'Oh, mind your own business. You came here as my friend; now you're spying on me for my mother, I know. Well, you can get out, and tell her from me that I'll choose my friends and she her spies in future.'

So I left him and went down to dinner.

'I've been in to Sebastian,' I said. 'His cold has come on rather badly. He's gone to bed and says he doesn't want anything.'

'Poor Sebastian,' said Lady Marchmain. 'He'd better have a glass of hot whisky. I'll go and have a look at him.'

'Don't mummy, I'll go,' said Julia rising.

'*I'll* go,' said Cordelia, who was dining down that night, for a treat to celebrate the departure of the guests. She was at the door and through it before anyone could stop her.

Julia caught my eye and gave a tiny, sad shrug.

In a few minutes Cordelia was back, looking grave. 'No, he doesn't seem to want anything,' she said.

'How was he?'

'Well, I don't *know*, but I *think* he's very drunk,' she said.

'*Cordelia.*'

Suddenly the child began to giggle. '"Marquis's Son Unused to Wine",' she quoted. '"Model Student's Career Threatened".'

'Charles, is this true?' asked Lady Marchmain.

'Yes.'

Then dinner was announced, and we went to the dining-room where the subject was not mentioned.

When Brideshead and I were left alone he said: 'Did you say Sebastian was drunk?'

'Yes.'

'Extraordinary time to choose. Couldn't you stop him?'

'No.'

'No,' said Brideshead, 'I don't suppose you could. I once saw my father drunk, in this room. I wasn't more than about ten at the time. You can't stop people if they want to get drunk. My mother couldn't stop my father, you know.'

He spoke in his odd, impersonal way. The more I saw of this family, I reflected, the more singular I found them. 'I shall ask my mother to read to us tonight.'

It was the custom, I learned later, always to ask Lady Marchmain to read aloud on evenings of family tension. She had a beautiful voice and great humour of expression. That night she read part of *The Wisdom of Father Brown*. Julia sat with a stool covered with manicure things and carefully revarnished her nails; Cordelia nursed Julia's Pekinese; Brideshead played patience; I sat unoccupied studying the pretty group they made, and mourning my friend upstairs.

But the horrors of that evening were not yet over.

It was sometimes Lady Marchmain's practice, when the family were alone, to visit the chapel before going to bed. She had just closed her book and proposed going there when the door opened and Sebastian appeared. He was dressed as I had last seen him, but now instead of being flushed he was deathly pale.

'Come to apologize,' he said.

'Sebastian, dear, do go back to your room,' said Lady Marchmain. 'We can talk about it in the morning.'

'Not to you. Come to apologize to Charles. I was bloody to him and he's my guest. He's my guest and my only friend and I was bloody to him.'

A chill spread over us. I led him back to his room; his family went to their prayers. I noticed when we got upstairs that the decanter was now empty. 'It's time you were in bed,' I said.

Sebastian began to weep. 'Why do you take their side against me? I knew you would if I let you meet them. Why do you spy on me?'

He said more than I can bear to remember, even at twenty years' distance. At last I got him to sleep and very sadly went to bed myself.

Next morning, he came to my room very early, while the house still slept; he drew the curtains and the sound of it woke me, to find him there fully dressed, smoking, with his back to me, looking out of the windows to where the long dawn-shadows lay across the dew and the first birds were chattering in the budding tree-tops. When I spoke he turned a face which showed no ravages of the evening before, but was fresh and sullen as a disappointed child's.

'Well,' I said. 'How do you feel?'

'Rather odd. I think perhaps I'm still a little drunk. I've just been down to the stables trying to get a car but everything was locked. We're off.'

He drank from the water-bottle by my pillow, threw his cigarette from the window, and lit another with hands which trembled like an old man's.

'Where are you going?'

'I don't know. London, I suppose. Can I come and stay with you?'

'Of course.'

'Well, get dressed. They can send our luggage on by train.'

'We can't just go like this.'

'We can't stay.'

He sat on the window seat looking away from me, out of the window. Presently he said: 'There's smoke coming from some of the chimneys. They must have opened the stables now. Come on.'

'I can't go,' I said. 'I must say good-bye to your mother.'

'Sweet bulldog.'

'Well, I don't happen to like running away.'

'And I couldn't care less. And I shall go on running away, as far and as fast as I can. You can hatch up any plot you like with my mother; I shan't come back.'

'That's how you talked last night.'

'I know. I'm sorry, Charles. I told you I was still drunk. If it's any comfort to you, I absolutely detest myself.'

'It's no comfort at all.'

'It must be a little, I should have thought. Well, if you won't come, give my love to nanny.'

'You're really going?'

'Of course.'

'Shall I see you in London?'

'Yes, I'm coming to stay with you.'

He left me but I did not sleep again; nearly two hours later a footman came with tea and bread and butter and set my clothes out for a new day.

Later that morning I sought Lady Marchmain; the wind had freshened and we stayed indoors; I sat near her before the fire in her room, while she bent over her needlework and the budding creeper rattled on the window panes.

'I wish I had not *seen* him,' she said. 'That was cruel. I do not mind the *idea* of his being drunk. It is a thing all men do when they are young. I am used to the *idea* of it. My brothers were wild at his age. What hurt last night was that there was nothing *happy* about him.'

'I know,' I said. 'I've never seen him like that before.'

'And last night of all nights . . . when everyone had gone and there were only ourselves here–you see, Charles, I look on you very much as one of ourselves. Sebastian loves you–when there was no need for him to make an effort to be gay. And he wasn't gay. I slept very little last night, and all the time I kept coming back to that one thing; he was so unhappy.'

It was impossible for me to explain to her what I only half understood myself; even then I felt, 'She will learn it soon enough. Perhaps she knows it now.'

'It was horrible,' I said. 'But please don't think that's his usual way.'

'Mr Samgrass told me he was drinking too much all last term.'

'Yes, but not like that–never before.'

'Then why now? here? with us? All night I have been thinking and praying and wondering what I was to say to him, and now, this morning, he isn't here at all. That was cruel of him, leaving without a word. I don't want him to be ashamed–it's being ashamed that makes it all so wrong of him.'

'He's ashamed of being unhappy,' I said.

'Mr Samgrass says he is noisy and high-spirited. I believe,' she said, with a faint light of humour streaking the clouds, 'I believe you and he tease Mr Samgrass rather. It's naughty of you. I'm very fond of Mr Samgrass, and you should be too, after all he's done for you. But I think perhaps if I were your age and a man, I might be just a little inclined to tease Mr Samgrass myself. No, I don't mind that, but last night and this morning are something quite different. You see, *it's all happened before*.'

'I can only say I've seen him drunk often and I've been drunk with him often, but last night was quite new to me.'

'Oh, I don't mean with Sebastian. I mean years ago. I've been through it all before with someone else whom I loved. Well, you must know what I mean–with his father. He used to be drunk in just that way. Someone told me he is not like that now. I pray God it's true and thank God for it with all my heart, if it is. But the *running away–he* ran away, too, you know. It was as you said just now, he was ashamed of being unhappy. Both of them unhappy, ashamed, and running away. It's too pitiful. The men I grew up with'–and her great eyes moved from the embroidery to the three miniatures in the folding leather case on the chimney-piece–'were not like that. I simply don't understand it. Do you, Charles?'

'Only very little.'

'And yet Sebastian is fonder of you than of any of us, you know. You've got to help him. I can't.'

I have here compressed into a few sentences what, there, required many. Lady Marchmain was not diffuse, but she took hold of her subject in a feminine, flirtatious way, circling, approaching, retreating, feinting; she hovered over it like a butterfly; she played 'grandmother's steps' with it, getting nearer the real point imperceptibly while one's back was turned, standing rooted when she was observed. The unhappiness, the running away–these made up her sorrow, and in her own way she exposed the whole of it, before she was done. It was an hour before she had said all she meant to say. Then, as I rose to leave her, she added as though in an afterthought: 'I wonder have you seen my brothers' book? It has just come out.'

I told her I had looked through it in Sebastian's rooms.

'I should like you to have a copy. May I give you one? They were three splendid men; Ned was the best of them. He was the last to be killed, and when the telegram came, as I knew it would come, I thought: "Now it's my son's turn to do what Ned can never do now." I was alone then. He was just going to Eton. If you read Ned's book you'll understand.'

She had a copy lying ready on her bureau. I thought at the time, 'She planned this parting before ever I came in. Had she rehearsed all the interview? If things had gone differently would she have put the book back in the drawer?'

She wrote her name and mine on the fly leaf, the date and place.

'I prayed for you, too, in the night,' she said.

I closed the door behind me, shutting out the *bondieu-serie*, the low ceiling, the chintz, the lambskin bindings, the views of Florence, the bowls of hyacinth and potpourri, the *petit-point*, the intimate feminine, modern world, and was back under the coved and coffered roof, the columns and entablature of the central hall, in the august, masculine atmosphere of a better age.

I was no fool; I was old enough to know that an attempt had been made to suborn me and young enough to have found the experience agreeable.

I did not see Julia that morning, but just as I was leaving Cordelia ran to the door of the car and said: 'Will you be seeing Sebastian? Please give him my special love. Will you remember–my *special* love?'

In the train to London I read the book Lady Marchmain had given me. The frontispiece reproduced the photograph of a young man in Grenadier uniform, and I saw plainly revealed there the origin of that grim mask which, in Brideshead, overlaid the gracious features of his father's family; this was a man of the woods and caves, a hunter, a judge of the tribal council, the repository of the harsh traditions of a people at war with their environment. There were other illustrations in the book, snapshots of the three brothers on holiday, and in each I traced the same archaic lines; and remembering Lady Marchmain, starry and delicate, I could find no likeness to her in these sombre men.

She appeared seldom in the book; she was older than the eldest of them by nine years and had married and left home while they were schoolboys; between her and them stood two other sisters; after the birth of the third daughter there had been pilgrimages and pious benefactions in request for a son, for theirs was a wide property and an ancient name; male heirs had come late and, when they came, in a profusion which at the time seemed to promise continuity to the line which, in the tragic event, ended abruptly with them.

The family history was typical of the Catholic squires of England; from Elizabeth's reign till Victoria's they lived sequestered lives, among their tenantry and kinsmen, sending their sons to school abroad, often marrying there, inter-marrying, if not, with a score of families like themselves, debarred from all preferment, and learning, in those lost generations, lessons which could still be read in the lives of the last three men of the house.

Mr Samgrass's deft editorship had assembled and arranged a curiously homogeneous little body of writing–poetry, letters, scraps of a journal, an unpublished essay or two, which all exhaled the same high-spirited, serious, chivalrous, other-worldly air and the letters from their contemporaries, written after their deaths, all in varying degrees of articulateness, told the same tale of men who were, in all the full flood of academic and athletic success, of popularity and the promise of great rewards ahead, seen somehow as set apart from their fellows, garlanded victims, devoted to the sacrifice. These men must die to make a world for Hooper; they were the aborigines, vermin by right of law, to be shot off at leisure so that things might be safe for the travelling salesman, with his polygonal pince-nez, his fat wet hand-shake, his grinning dentures. I wondered, as the train carried me farther and farther from Lady Marchmain, whether perhaps there was not on her, too, the same blaze, marking her and hers for destruction by other ways than war. Did she see a sign in the red centre of her cosy grate and hear it in the rattle of creeper on the window-pane, this whisper of doom?

Then I reached Paddington and, returning home, found Sebastian there, and the sense of tragedy vanished, for he was gay and free as when I first met him.

'Cordelia sent you her special love.'

'Did you have a "little talk" with mummy?'

'Yes.'

'Have you gone over to her side?'

The day before I would have said: 'There aren't two sides'; that day I said, 'No, I'm with you, "Sebastian *contra mundum*".'

And that was all the conversation we had on the subject, then or ever.

But the shadows were closing round Sebastian. We returned to Oxford and once again the gillyflowers bloomed under my windows and the chestnut lit the streets and the warm stones strewed their flakes upon the cobble; but it was not as it had been; there was mid-winter in Sebastian's heart.

The weeks went by; we looked for lodgings for the coming term and found them in Merton Street, a secluded, expensive little house near the tennis court.

Meeting Mr Samgrass, whom we had seen less often of late, I told him of our choice. He was standing at the table in Blackwell's where recent German books were displayed, setting aside a little heap of purchases.

'You're sharing digs with Sebastian?' he said. 'So he *is* coming up next term?'

'I suppose so. Why shouldn't he be?'

'I don't know why; I somehow thought perhaps he wasn't. I'm always wrong about things like that. I like Merton Street.'

He showed me the books he was buying, which, since I knew no German, were not of interest to me. As I left him he said: 'Don't think me interfering, you know, but I shouldn't make any *definite* arrangement in Merton Street until you're sure.'

I told Sebastian of this conversation and he said: 'Yes, there's a plot on. Mummy wants me to go and live with Mgr Bell.'

'Why didn't you tell me about it?'

'Because I'm *not* going to live with Mgr Bell.'

'I still think you might have told me. When did it start?'

'Oh, it's been going on. Mummy's very clever, you know. She saw she'd failed with you. I expect it was the letter you wrote after reading Uncle Ned's book.'

'I hardly said anything.'

'That was it. If you were going to be any help to her, you would have said a lot. Uncle Ned is the test, you know.'

But it seemed she had not quite despaired, for a few days later I got a note from her which said:

> I shall be passing through Oxford on Tuesday and hope to see you and Sebastian. I would like to see you alone for five minutes before I see him. Is that too much to ask? I will come to your rooms at about twelve.

She came; she admired my rooms. . . . 'My brothers Simon and Ned were here, you know. Ned had rooms on the garden front. I wanted Sebastian to come here, too, but my husband was at Christ Church and, as you know, he took charge of Sebastian's education'; she admired my drawings . . .'*everyone* loves your paintings in the garden-room. We shall never forgive you if you don't finish them.' Finally, she came to her point.

'I expect you've guessed already what I have come to ask. Quite simply, is

Sebastian drinking too much this term?'

I had guessed; I answered: 'If he were, I shouldn't answer. As it is, I can say, "No".'

She said: 'I believe you. Thank God!' and we went together to luncheon at Christ Church.

That night Sebastian had his third disaster and was found by the junior dean at one o'clock, wandering round Tom Quad hopelessly drunk.

I had left him morose but completely sober at a few minutes before twelve. In the succeeding hour he had drunk half a bottle of whisky alone. He did not remember much about it when he came to tell me next morning.

'Have you been doing that a lot,' I asked, 'drinking by yourself after I've gone?'

'About twice; perhaps four times. It's only when they start bothering me. I'd be all right if they'd only leave me alone.'

'They won't now,' I said.

'I know.'

We both knew that this was a crisis. I had no love for Sebastian that morning; he needed it, but I had none to give.

'Really,' I said, 'if you are going to embark on a solitary bout of drinking every time you see a member of your family, it's perfectly hopeless.'

'Oh, yes,' said Sebastian with great sadness. 'I *know*. It's hopeless.'

But my pride was stung because I had been made to look a liar and I could not respond to his need.

'Well, what do you propose to do?'

'I shan't do anything. They'll do it all.'

And I let him go without comfort.

Then the machinery began to move again, and I saw it all repeated as it had happened in December; Mr Samgrass and Mgr Bell saw the Dean of Christ Church; Brideshead came up for a night; the heavy wheels stirred and the small wheels spun. Everyone was exceedingly sorry for Lady Marchmain, whose brothers' names stood in letters in gold on the war memorial, whose brothers' memory was fresh in many breasts.

She came to see me and, again, I must reduce to a few words a conversation which took us from Holywell to the Parks, through Mesopotamia, and over the ferry to north Oxford, where she was staying the night with a houseful of nuns who were in some way under her protection.

'You *must* believe', I said, 'that when I told you Sebastian was not drinking, I was telling you the truth, as I knew it.'

'I know you wish to be a good friend to him.'

'That is not what I mean. I believed what I told you. I still believe it to some extent. I believe he has been drunk two or three times before, not more.'

'It's no good, Charles,' she said. 'All you can mean is that you have not as much influence or knowledge of him as I thought. It is no good either of us trying to believe him. I've known drunkards before. One of the most terrible things about them is their deceit. Love of truth is the first thing that goes.

'After that happy luncheon together. When you left he was so sweet to me, just as he used to be as a little boy, and I agreed to all he wanted. You know I had been doubtful about his sharing rooms with you. I know you'll understand me when I say that. You know that we are all fond of you apart from your being

Sebastian's friend. We should miss you so much if you ever stopped coming to stay with us. But I want Sebastian to have all sorts of friends, not just one. Mgr Bell tells me he never mixes with the other Catholics, never goes to the Newman, very rarely goes to mass even. Heaven forbid that he should only know Catholics, but he must know *some*. It needs a very strong faith to stand entirely alone and Sebastian's isn't strong.

'But I was so happy at luncheon on Tuesday that I gave up all my objections; I went round with him and saw the rooms you had chosen. They are charming. And we decided on some furniture you could have from London to make them nicer. And then, on the very night after I had seen him!–No Charles, it is not in the Logic of the Thing.'

As she said it I thought, 'That's a phrase she's picked up from one of her intellectual hangers-on'.

'Well,' I said, 'have you a remedy?'

'The college are being extraordinarily kind. They say they will not send him down provided he goes to live with Mgr Bell. It's not a thing I could have suggested myself, but it was the Monsignor's own idea. He specially sent a message to you to say how welcome you would always be. There's not room for you actually in the Old Palace, but I daresay you wouldn't want that yourself.'

'Lady Marchmain, if you want to make him a drunkard that's the way to do it. Don't you see that any idea of his being *watched* would be fatal?'

'Oh, dear, it's no good trying to explain. Protestants always think Catholic priests are spies.'

'I don't mean that.' I tried to explain but made a poor business of it. 'He must feel free.'

'But he's been free, always, up till now, and look at the result.'

We had reached the ferry; we had reached a deadlock. With scarcely another word I saw her to the convent, then took the bus back to Carfax.

Sebastian was in my rooms waiting for me. 'I'm going to cable to papa,' he said. 'He won't let them force me into this priest's house.'

'But if they make it a condition of your coming up?'

'I shan't come up. Can you imagine me–serving mass twice a week, helping at tea parties for shy Catholic freshmen, dining with the visiting lecturer at the Newman, drinking a glass of port when we have guests, with Mgr Bell's eye on me to see I don't get too much, being explained, when I was out of the room, as the rather embarrassing local inebriate who's being taken in because his mother is so charming?'

'I told her it wouldn't do,' I said.

'Shall we get really drunk tonight?'

'It's the one time it could do no conceivable harm,' I said.

'*Contra mundum?*'

'*Contra mundum.*'

'Bless you, Charles. There aren't many evenings left to us.'

And that night, the first time for many weeks, we got deliriously drunk together; I saw him to the gate as all the bells were striking midnight, and reeled back to my rooms under a starry heaven which swam dizzily among the towers, and fell asleep in my clothes as I had not done for a year.

Next day Lady Marchmain left Oxford, taking Sebastian with her. Brideshead and I went to his rooms to sort out what he would have sent on and what leave behind.

Brideshead was as grave and impersonal as ever. 'It's a pity Sebastian doesn't know Mgr Bell better,' he said. 'He'd find him a charming man to live with. I was there my last year. My mother believes Sebastian is a confirmed drunkard. Is he?'

'He's in danger of becoming one.'

'I believe God prefers drunkards to a lot of respectable people.'

'For God's sake,' I said, for I was near to tears that morning, 'why bring God into everything?'

'I'm sorry. I forgot. But you know that's an extremely funny question.'

'Is it?'

'To me. Not to you.'

'No, not to me. It seems to me that without your religion Sebastian would have the chance to be a happy and healthy man.'

'It's arguable,' said Brideshead. 'Do you think he will need this elephant's foot again?'

That evening I went across the quad to visit Collins. He was alone with his texts, working by the failing light at his open window. 'Hullo,' he said. 'Come in. I haven't seen you all the term. I'm afraid I've nothing to offer you. Why have you deserted the smart set?'

'I'm the loneliest man in Oxford,' I said. 'Sebastian Flyte's been sent down.'

Presently I asked him what he was doing in the long vacation. He told me; it sounded excruciatingly dull. Then I asked him if he had got digs for next term. Yes, he told me, rather far out but very comfortable. He was sharing with Tyngate, the secretary of the college Essay Society.

'There's one room we haven't filled yet. Barker was coming, but he feels, now he's standing for president of the Union, he ought to be nearer in.'

It was in both our minds that perhaps I might take that room.

'Where are you going?'

'I *was* going to Merton Street with Sebastian Flyte. That's no use now.'

Still neither of us made the suggestion and the moment passed. When I left he said: 'I hope you find someone for Merton Street,' and I said, 'I hope you find someone for the Iffley Road,' and I never spoke to him again.

There was only ten days of term to go; I got through them somehow and returned to London as I had done in such different circumstances the year before, with no plans made.

'That very good-looking friend of yours,' asked my father. 'Is he not with you?'

'No.'

'I quite thought he had taken this over as his home. I'm sorry, I liked him.'

'Father, do you particularly want me to take my degree?'

'*I* want you to? Good gracious, why should *I* want such a thing? No use to me. Not much use to you either, as far as I've seen.'

'That's exactly what I've been thinking. I thought perhaps it was rather a waste of time going back to Oxford.'

Until then my father had taken only a limited interest in what I was saying: now he put down his book, took off his spectacles, and looked at me hard. 'You've been sent down,' he said. 'My brother warned me of this.'

'No, I've not.'

'Well, then, what's all the talk about?' he asked testily, resuming his spectacles, searching for his place on the page. 'Everyone stays up at least three years. I knew one man who took seven to get a pass degree in theology.'

'I only thought that if I was not going to take up one of the professions where a degree is necessary, it might be best to start now on what I intend doing. I intend to be a painter.'

But to this my father made no answer at the time.

The idea, however, seemed to take root in his mind; by the time we spoke of the matter again it was firmly established.

'When you're a painter,' he said at Sunday luncheon, 'you'll need a studio.'

'Yes.'

'Well, there isn't a studio here. There isn't even a room you could use decently as a studio. I'm not going to have you painting in the gallery.'

'No. I never meant to.'

'Nor will I have undraped models all over the house, nor critics with their horrible jargon. And I don't like the smell of turpentine. I presume you intend to do the thing thoroughly and use oil paint?' My father belonged to a generation which divided painters into the serious and the amateur, according as they used oil or water.

'I don't suppose I should do much painting the first year. Anyway, I should be working at a school.'

'Abroad?' asked my father hopefully. 'There are some excellent schools abroad, I believe.'

It was all happening rather faster than I intended.

'Abroad or here. I should have to look round first.'

'Look round abroad,' he said.

'Then you agree to my leaving Oxford?'

'Agree? Agree? My dear boy, you're twenty-two.'

'Twenty,' I said, 'twenty-one in October.'

'Is that all? It seems *much* longer.'

A letter from Lady Marchmain completes this episode.

My dear Charles, *she wrote*,

Sebastian left me this morning to join his father abroad. Before he went I asked him if he had written to you. He said no, so I must write, tho' I can hardly hope to say in a letter what I could not say on our last walk. But you must not be left in silence.

The college has sent Sebastian down for a term only, and will take him back after Christmas on condition he goes to live with Mgr Bell. It is for him to decide. Meanwhile Mr Samgrass has very kindly consented to take charge of him. As soon as his visit to his father is over Mr Samgrass will pick him up and they will go together to the Levant, where Mr Samgrass has long been anxious to investigate a number of orthodox monasteries. He hopes this may be a new interest for Sebastian.

Sebastian's stay here has not been happy.

When they come home at Christmas I know Sebastian will want to see you, and so shall we all. I hope your arrangements for next term have not been too much upset and that everything will go well with you.

Yours sincerely,
Teresa Marchmain

I went to the garden-room this morning and was so very sorry.

PART II

BRIDESHEAD DESERTED

I

'And when we reached the top of the pass,' said Mr Samgrass, 'we heard the galloping horses behind, and two soldiers rode up to the head of the caravan and turned us back. The General had sent them, and they reached us only just in time. There was a Band, not a mile ahead.'

He paused, and his small audience sat silent, conscious that he had sought to impress them but in doubt as to how they could politely show their interest.

'*A Band?*' said Julia. '*Goodness!*'

Still he seemed to expect more. At last Lady Marchmain said, 'I suppose the sort of folk-music you get in those parts *is* very monotonous.'

'Dear Lady Marchmain, a Band of *Brigands*.' Cordelia, beside me on the sofa, began to giggle noiselessly. 'The mountains are full of them. Stragglers from Kemal's army; Greeks who got cut off in the retreat. Very desperate fellows, I assure you.'

'Do pinch me,' whispered Cordelia.

I pinched her and the agitation of the sofa-springs ceased. 'Thanks,' she said, wiping her eyes with the back of her hand.

'So you never got to wherever-it-was,' said Julia. 'Weren't you terribly disappointed, Sebastian?'

'Me?' said Sebastian from the shadows beyond the lamplight, beyond the warmth of the burning logs, beyond the family circle, and the photographs spread out on the card-table. 'Me? Oh, I don't think I was there that day, was I, Sammy?'

'That was the day you were ill.'

'I was ill,' he repeated like an echo, 'so I never should have got to wherever-it-was should I, Sammy?

'Now *this*, Lady Marchmain, is the caravan at Aleppo in the courtyard of the inn. That's our Armenian cook, Begedbian; that's me on the pony; that's the tent folded up; that's a rather tiresome Kurd who would follow us about at the time. . . . Here I am in Pontus, Ephesus, Trebizond, Krak-des-chevaliers, Samothrace, Batum–of course, I haven't got them in chronological order yet.'

'All guides and ruins and mules,' said Cordelia. 'Where's Sebastian?'

'He,' said Mr Samgrass, with a hint of triumph in his voice, as though he had expected the question and prepared the answer, 'he held the camera. He became quite an expert as soon as he learned not to put his hand over the lens, didn't you, Sebastian?'

There was no answer from the shadows. Mr Samgrass delved again into his pigskin satchel.

'Here', he said, 'is a group taken by a street photographer on the terrace of the St George Hotel at Beirut. There's Sebastian.'

'Why,' I said, 'there's Anthony Blanche, surely?'

'Yes, we saw quite a lot of him; met him by chance at Constantinople. A delightful companion. I can't think how I missed knowing him. He came with us all the way to Beirut.'

Tea had been cleared away and the curtains drawn. It was two days after Christmas, the first evening of my visit; the first, too, of Sebastian's and Mr Samgrass's, whom to my surprise I had found on the platform when I arrived.

Lady Marchmain had written three weeks before:

> I have just heard from Mr Samgrass that he and Sebastian will be home for Christmas as we hoped. I had not heard from them for so long that I was afraid they were lost and did not want to make any arrangements until I knew. Sebastian will be longing to see you. Do come to us for Christmas if you can manage it, or as soon after as you can.

Christmas with my uncle was an engagement I could not break, so I travelled across country and joined the local train midway, expecting to find Sebastian already established; there he was, however, in the next carriage to mine, and when I asked him what he was doing, Mr Samgrass replied with such glibness and at such length, telling me of mislaid luggage and of Cook's being shut over the holidays, that I was at once aware of some other explanation which was being withheld.

Mr Samgrass was not at ease; he maintained all the physical habits of self-confidence, but guilt hung about him like stale cigar smoke, and in Lady Marchmain's greeting of him I caught a note of anticipation. He kept up a lively account of his tour during tea, and then Lady Marchmain drew him away with her, upstairs, for a 'little talk'. I watched him go with something near compassion; it was plain to anyone with a poker sense that Mr Samgrass held a very imperfect hand and, as I watched him at tea, I began to suspect that he was not only bluffing but cheating. There was something he must say, did not want to say, and did not quite know how to say to Lady Marchmain about his doings over Christmas, but, more than that, I guessed, there was a great deal he ought to say and had no intention at all of saying, about the whole Levantine tour.

'Come and see nanny,' said Sebastian.

'Please, can I come, too?' said Cordelia.

'Come on.'

We climbed to the nursery in the dome. On the way Cordelia said: 'Aren't you at all pleased to be home?'

'Of course I'm pleased,' said Sebastian.

'Well, you might show it a bit. I've been looking forward to it so much.'

Nanny did not particularly wish to be talked to; she liked visitors best when they paid no attention to her and let her knit away, and watch their faces and think of them as she had known them as small children; their present goings-on did not signify much beside those early illnesses and crimes.

'Well,' she said, 'you *are* looking peaky. I expect it's all that foreign food doesn't agree with you. You must fatten up now you're back. Looks as though you'd been having some late nights, too, by the look of your eyes–dancing, I suppose.' (It was ever Nanny Hawkins's belief that the upper classes spent most of their leisure evenings in the ballroom.) 'And that shirt wants darning. Bring it to me before it goes to the wash.'

Sebastian certainly did look ill; five months had wrought the change of years in him. He was paler, thinner, pouchy under the eyes, drooping in the corners of his mouth, and he showed the scars of a boil on the side of his chin; his voice seemed flatter and his movements alternately listless and jumpy; he looked down-at-heel, too, with clothes and hair, which formerly had been happily negligent, now unkempt; worst of all, there was a wariness in his eye which I had surprised there at Easter, and which now seemed habitual to him.

Restrained by this wariness I asked him nothing of himself, but told him instead about my autumn and winter. I told him about my rooms in the Île Saint-Louis and the art school, and how good the old teachers were and how bad the students.

'They never go near the Louvre,' I said, 'or, if they do, it's only because one of their absurd reviews has suddenly "discovered" a master who fits in with that month's aesthetic theory. Half of them are out to make a popular splash like Picabia; the other half quite simply want to earn their living doing advertisements for *Vogue* and decorating night clubs. And the teachers still go on trying to make them paint like Delacroix.'

'Charles,' said Cordelia, 'Modern Art is all bosh, isn't it?'

'Great bosh.'

'Oh, I'm so glad. I had an argument with one of our nuns and she said we shouldn't try and criticize what we didn't understand. Now I shall tell her I have had it straight from a real artist, and snubs to her.'

Presently it was time for Cordelia to go to her supper, and for Sebastian and me to go down to the drawing-room for our cocktails. Brideshead was there alone, but Wilcox followed on our heels to say to him: 'Her Ladyship would like to speak to you upstairs, my Lord.'

'That's unlike mummy, sending for anyone. She usually lures them up herself.'

There was no sign of the cocktail tray. After a few minutes Sebastian rang the bell. A footman answered. 'Mr Wilcox is upstairs with her Ladyship.'

'Well, never mind, bring in the cocktail things.'

'Mr Wilcox has the keys, my Lord.'

'Oh . . . well, send him in with them when he comes down.'

We talked a little about Anthony Blanche–'He had a beard in Istanbul, but I made him take it off'–and after ten minutes Sebastian said: 'Well, I don't want a cocktail, anyway; I'm off to my bath,' and left the room.

It was half past seven; I supposed the others had gone to dress, but, as I was going to follow them, I met Brideshead coming down.

'Just a moment, Charles, there's something I've got to explain. My mother has given orders that no drinks are to be left in any of the rooms. You'll understand why. If you want anything, ring and ask Wilcox–only better wait until you're alone. I'm sorry, but there it is.'

'Is that necessary?'

'I gather very necessary. You may or may not have heard, Sebastian had another outbreak as soon as he got back to England. He was lost over Christmas. Mr Samgrass only found him yesterday evening.'

'I guessed something of the kind had happened. Are you sure this is the best way of dealing with it?'

'It's my mother's way. Will you have a cocktail, now that he's gone upstairs?'

'It would choke me.'

I was always given the room I had on my first visit; it was next to Sebastian's, and we shared what had once been a dressing-room and had been changed to a bathroom twenty years back by the substitution for the bed of a deep, copper, mahogany-framed bath, that was filled by pulling a brass lever heavy as a piece of marine engineering; the rest of the room remained unchanged; a coal fire always burned there in winter. I often think of that bathroom–the water colours dimmed by steam and the huge towel warming on the back of the chintz armchair–and contrast it with the uniform, clinical, little chambers, glittering with chromium-plate and looking-glass, which pass for luxury in the modern world.

I lay in the bath and then dried slowly by the fire, thinking all the time of my friend's black home-coming. Then I put on my dressing gown and went to Sebastian's room, entering, as I always did, without knocking. He was sitting by his fire half-dressed, and he started angrily when he heard me and put down a tooth glass.

'Oh, it's you. You gave me a fright.'

'So you got a drink,' I said.

'I don't know what you mean.'

'For Christ's sake,' I said, 'you don't have to pretend with me! You might offer me some.'

'It's just something I had in my flask. I've finished it now.'

'What's going on?'

'Nothing. A lot. I'll tell you some time.'

I dressed and called in for Sebastian, but found him still sitting as I had left him, half-dressed over his fire.

Julia was alone in the drawing-room.

'Well,' I asked, 'what's going on?'

'Oh, just another boring family *potin*. Sebastian got tight again, so we've all got to keep an eye on him. It's too tedious.'

'It's pretty boring for him, too.'

'Well, it's his fault. Why can't he behave like anyone else? Talking of keeping an eye on people, what about Mr Samgrass? Charles, do you notice anything at all fishy about that man?'

'Very fishy. Do you think your mother saw it?'

'Mummy only sees what suits her. She can't have the whole household under surveillance. *I'm* causing anxiety, too, you know.'

'I didn't know,' I said, adding humbly, 'I've only just come from Paris,' so as to avoid giving the impression that any trouble she might be in was not widely notorious.

It was an evening of peculiar gloom. We dined in the Painted Parlour. Sebastian was late, and so painfully excited were we that I think it was in all our minds that he would make some sort of low-comedy entrance, reeling and hiccuping. When he came it was, of course, with perfect propriety; he apologized, sat in the empty place, and allowed Mr Samgrass to resume his monologue, uninterrupted and, it seemed, unheard. Druses, patriarchs, icons, bed-bugs, Romanesque remains, curious dishes of goat and sheeps' eyes, French and Turkish officials–all the catalogue of Near Eastern travel was provided for our amusement.

I watched the champagne go round the table. When it came to Sebastian he said: 'I'll have whisky, please,' and I saw Wilcox glance over his head to Lady Marchmain and saw her give a tiny, hardly perceptible nod. At Brideshead they used small individual spirit decanters which held about a quarter of a bottle, and were always placed, full, before anyone who asked for it; the decanter which Wilcox put before Sebastian was half-empty. Sebastian raised it very deliberately, tilted it, looked at it, and then in silence poured the liquor into his glass, where it covered two fingers. We all began talking at once, all except Sebastian, so that for a moment Mr Samgrass found himself talking to no one, telling the candlesticks about the Maronites; but soon we fell silent again, and he had the table until Lady Marchmain and Julia left the room.

'Don't be long, Bridey,' she said, at the door, as she always said, and that evening we had no inclination to delay. Our glasses were filled with port and the decanter was at once taken from the room. We drank quickly and went to the drawing-room, where Brideshead asked his mother to read, and she read *The Diary of a Nobody* with great spirit until ten o'clock, when she closed the book and said she was unaccountably tired, so tired that she would not visit the chapel that night.

'Who's hunting tomorrow?' she asked.

'Cordelia,' said Brideshead. 'I'm taking that young horse of Julia's, just to show him the hounds; I shan't keep him out more than a couple of hours.'

'Rex is arriving some time,' said Julia. 'I'd better stay in to greet him.'

'Where's the meet?' said Sebastian suddenly.

'Just here at Flyte St Mary.'

'Then I'd like to hunt, please, if there's anything for me.'

'Of course. That's delightful. I'd have asked you, only you always used to complain so of being made to go out. You can have Tinkerbell. She's been going very nicely this season.'

Everyone was suddenly pleased that Sebastian wanted to hunt; It seemed to undo some of the mischief of the evening. Brideshead rang the bell for whisky.

'Anyone else want any?'

'Bring me some, too,' said Sebastian, and, though it was a footman this time and not Wilcox, I saw the same exchange of glance and nod between the servant and Lady Marchmain. Everyone had been warned. The two drinks were brought in, poured out already in the glasses, like 'doubles' at a bar, and all our eyes followed the tray, as though we were dogs in a dining-room smelling game.

The good humour engendered by Sebastian's wish to hunt persisted, however; Brideshead wrote out a note for the stables, and we all went to bed quite cheerfully.

Sebastian got straight to bed; I sat by his fire and smoked a pipe. I said: 'I rather wish I was coming out with you tomorrow.' 'Well,' he said, 'you wouldn't see much sport. I can tell you exactly what I'm going to do. I shall leave Bridey at the first covert, hack over to the nearest good pub, and spend the entire day quietly soaking in the bar parlour. If they treat me like a dipsomaniac, they can bloody well have a dipsomaniac. I hate hunting, anyway.'

'Well, I can't stop you.'

'You can, as a matter of fact–by not giving me any money. They stopped my banking account, you know, in the summer. It's been one of my chief difficulties. I pawned my watch and cigarette case to ensure a happy Christmas, so I shall have to come to you tomorrow for my day's expenses.'

'I won't. You know perfectly well I can't.'

'Won't you, Charles? Well, I daresay I shall manage on my own somehow. I've got rather clever at that lately–managing on my own. I've had to.'

'Sebastian, what *have* you and Mr Samgrass been up to?'

'He told you at dinner–ruins and guides and mules, that's what Sammy's been up to. We decided to go our own ways, that's all. Poor Sammy's really behaved rather well so far. I hoped he would keep it up, but he seems to have been very indiscreet about my happy Christmas. I suppose he thought if he gave too good an account of me, he might lose his job as keeper.

'He makes quite a good thing out of it, you know. I don't mean that he steals. I should think he's fairly honest about money. He certainly keeps an embarrassing little note-book in which he puts down all the travellers' cheques he cashes and what he spends it on, for mummy and the lawyer to see. But he wanted to go to all these places, and it's very convenient for him to have me to take him in comfort, instead of going as dons usually do. The only disadvantage was having to put up with my company, and we soon solved that for him.

'We began very much on a Grand Tour, you know, with letters to all the chief people everywhere, and stayed with the Military Governor at Rhodes and the Ambassador at Constantinople. That was what Sammy had signed on for in the first place. Of course, he had his work cut out keeping his eye on me, but he warned all our hosts beforehand that I was not responsible.'

'Sebastian.'

'Not *quite* responsible–and as I had no money to spend I couldn't get away very much. He even did the tipping for me, put the note into the man's hand and jotted the amount down then and there in his note-book. My lucky time was at Constantinople. I managed to make some money at cards one evening when Sammy wasn't looking. Next day I gave him the slip and was having a very happy hour in the bar at the Tokatlian when who should come in but Anthony Blanche with a beard and a Jew boy. Anthony lent me a tenner just before Sammy came panting in and recaptured me. After that I didn't get a minute out of sight; the Embassy staff put us in the boat to Piraeus and watched us sail away. But in Athens it was easy. I simply walked out of the Legation one day after lunch, changed my money at Cook's, and asked about sailings to Alexandria just to fox Sammy, then went down to the port in a bus, found a sailor who spoke American, lay up with him till his ship sailed, and popped back to Constantinople, and that was that.

'Anthony and the Jew boy shared a very nice, tumble-down house near the bazaars. I stayed there till it got too cold, then Anthony and I drifted south till we met Sammy by appointment in Syria three weeks ago.'

'Didn't Sammy mind?'

'Oh, I think he quite enjoyed himself in his own ghastly way–only of course there was no more high life for him. I think he was a bit anxious at first. I didn't want him to get the whole Mediterranean Fleet out, so I cabled him from Constantinople that I was quite well and would he send money to the Ottoman Bank. He came hopping over as soon as he got my cable. Of course he was in a difficult position, because I'm of age and not certified yet, so he couldn't have me arrested. He couldn't leave me to starve while he was living on my money, and he couldn't tell mummy without looking pretty silly. I had him all ways, poor Sammy. My original idea had been to leave him flat, but Anthony was very helpful about that, and said it was far better to arrange things amicably; and he *did* arrange things very amicably. So here I am.'

'After Christmas.'

'Yes, I was determined to have a happy Christmas.'

'Did you?'

'I think so. I don't remember it much, and that's always a good sign, isn't it?'

Next morning at breakfast Brideshead wore scarlet; Cordelia, very smart herself, with her chin held high over her white stock, wailed when Sebastian appeared in a tweed coat: '*Oh, Sebastian*, you can't come out like that. Do go and change. You look so lovely in hunting clothes.'

'Locked away somewhere. Gibbs couldn't find them.'

'That's a fib. I helped get them out myself before you were called.'

'Half the things are missing.'

'It just encourages the Strickland-Venableses. They're behaving rottenly. They've even taken their grooms out of top hats.'

It was a quarter to eleven before the horses were brought round, but no one else appeared downstairs; it was as though they were in hiding, listening for Sebastian's retreating hooves before showing themselves.

Just as he was about to start, when the others were already mounted, Sebastian beckoned me into the hall. On the table beside his hat, gloves, whip, and sandwiches, lay the flask he had put out to be filled. He picked it up and shook it; it was empty.

'You see,' he said, 'I can't even be trusted that far. It's they who are mad, not me. Now you can't refuse me money.'

I gave him a pound.

'More,' he said.

I gave him another and watched him mount and trot after his brother and sister.

Then, as though it were his cue on the stage, Mr Samgrass came to my elbow, put an arm in mine, and led me back to the fire. He warmed his neat little hands and then turned to warm his seat.

'So Sebastian is in pursuit of the fox,' he said, 'and our little problem is shelved for an hour or two?'

I was not going to stand this from Mr Samgrass.

'I heard all about your Grand Tour, last night,' I said.

'Ah, I rather supposed you might have.' Mr Samgrass was undismayed, relieved, it seemed, to have someone else in the know. 'I did not harrow our hostess with all that. After all, it turned out far better than one had any right to expect. I did feel, however, that some explanation was due to her of Sebastian's Christmas festivities. You may have observed last night that there were certain precautions.'

'I did.'

'You thought them excessive? I am with you, particularly as they tend to compromise the comfort of our own little visit. I have seen Lady Marchmain this morning. You must not suppose I am just out of bed. I have had a little talk upstairs with our hostess. I think we may hope for some relaxation tonight. Yesterday was *not* an evening that any of us would wish to have repeated. I earned less gratitude than I deserved, I think, for my efforts to distract you.'

It was repugnant to me to talk about Sebastian to Mr Samgrass, but I was compelled to say: 'I'm not sure that tonight would be the best time to start the relaxation.'

'But surely? Why not tonight, after a day in the field under Brideshead's inquisitorial eye? Could one choose better?'

'Oh, I suppose it's none of my business really.'

'Nor mine strictly, now that he is safely home. Lady Marchmain did me the honour of consulting me. But it is less Sebastian's welfare than our own I have at heart at the moment. I need my third glass of port; I need that hospitable tray in the library. And yet you specifically advise against it *tonight*. I wonder why. Sebastian can come to no mischief today. For one thing, he has no money. I happen to know. I saw to it. I even have his watch and cigarette case upstairs. He will be quite harmless . . . as long as no one is so wicked as to give him any. . . . Ah, Lady Julia, good morning to you, good morning. And how is the peke this hunting morning?'

'Oh, the peke's all right. Listen. I've got Rex Mottram coming here today. We simply can't have another evening like last night. Someone must speak to mummy.'

'Someone *has*. I spoke. I think it will be all right.'

'Thank God for that. Are you painting today, Charles?'

It had been the custom that on every visit to Brideshead I painted a medallion on the walls of the garden-room. The custom suited me well, for it gave me a good reason to detach myself from the rest of the party; when the house was full, the garden-room became a rival to the nursery, where from time to time people took refuge to complain about the others; thus without effort I kept in touch with the gossip of the place. There were three finished medallions now, each rather pretty in its way, but unhappily each in a different way, for my tastes had changed and I had become more dexterous in the eighteen months since the series was begun. As a decorative scheme, they were a failure. That morning was typical of the many mornings when I had found the garden-room a sanctuary. There I went and was soon at work. Julia came with me to see me started and we talked, inevitably, of Sebastian.

'Don't you get bored with the subject?' she asked. 'Why must everyone make such a Thing about it?'

'Just because we're fond of him.'

'Well. I'm fond of him too, in a way, I suppose, only I wish he'd behave like anybody else. I've grown up with one family skeleton, you know–papa. Not to be talked of before the servants, not to be talked of before us when we were children. If mummy is going to start making a skeleton out of Sebastian, it's *too* much. If he wants to be always tight, why doesn't he go to Kenya or somewhere where it doesn't matter?'

'Why does it matter less being unhappy in Kenya than anywhere else?'

'Don't pretend to be stupid, Charles. You understand perfectly.'

'You mean there won't be so many embarrassing situations for you? Well, all I was trying to say was that I'm afraid there may be an embarrassing situation tonight if Sebastian gets the chance. He's in a bad mood.'

'Oh, a day's hunting will put that all right.'

It was touching to see the faith which everybody put in the value of a day's hunting. Lady Marchmain, who looked in on me during the morning, mocked herself for it with that delicate irony for which she was famous.

'I've always detested hunting,' she said, 'because it seems to produce a particularly gross kind of caddishness in the nicest people. I don't know what it is, but the moment they dress up and get on a horse they become like a lot of Prussians. And so boastful after it. The evenings I've sat at dinner appalled at seeing the men and women I know, transformed into half-awake, self-opinionated, mono-maniac louts! . . . and yet, you know–it must be something derived from centuries ago–my heart is quite light today to think of Sebastian out with them. "There's nothing wrong with him really," I say, "he's gone hunting"–as though it were an answer to prayer.'

She asked me about my life in Paris. I told her of my rooms with their view of the river and the towers of Notre Dame. 'I'm hoping Sebastian will come and stay with me when I go back.'

'It would have been lovely,' said Lady Marchmain, sighing as though for the unattainable.

'I hope he's coming to stay with me in London.'

'Charles, you know it isn't possible. London's the worst place. Even Mr Samgrass couldn't hold him there. We have no secrets in this house. He was *lost*, you know, all through Christmas. Mr Samgrass only found him because he couldn't pay his bill in the place where he was, so they telephoned our house. It's too horrible. No, London is impossible; if he can't behave himself here, with us . . . We must keep him happy and healthy here for a bit, hunting, and then send him abroad again with Mr Samgrass. . . . You see, I've been through all this before.'

The retort was there, unspoken, well-understood by both of us–'You couldn't keep *him*; *he* ran away. So will Sebastian. Because they both hate you.'

A horn and the huntsman's cry sounded in the valley below us.

'There they go now, drawing the home woods. I hope he's having a good day.'

Thus with Julia and Lady Marchmain I reached deadlock, not because we failed to understand one another, but because we understood too well. With Brideshead, who came home to luncheon and talked to me on the subject–for the subject was everywhere in the house like a fire deep in the hold of a ship, below the water-line, black and red in the darkness, coming to light in acrid wisps of smoke that oozed under hatches and billowed suddenly from the scuttles and air pipes–with Brideshead, I was in a strange world, a dead world to me, in a moon-landscape of barren lava, a high place of toiling lungs.

He said: 'I hope it is dipsomania. That is simply a great misfortune that we must all help him bear. What I used to fear was that he just got drunk deliberately when he liked and because he liked.'

'That's exactly what he did–what we both did. It's what he does with me now. I can keep him to that, if only your mother would trust me. If you worry him with keepers and cures he'll be a physical wreck in a few years.'

'There's nothing *wrong* in being a physical wreck, you know. There's no moral obligation to be Postmaster-General or Master of Foxhounds or to live to walk ten miles at eighty.'

'*Wrong*,' I said. '*Moral obligation*–now you're back on religion again.'

'I never left it,' said Brideshead.

'D'you know, Bridey, if I ever felt for a moment like becoming a Catholic, I should only have to talk to you for five minutes to be cured. You manage to reduce what seem quite sensible propositions to stark nonsense.'

'It's odd you should say that. I've heard it before from other people. It's one of the many reasons why I don't think I should make a good priest. It's something in the way my mind works, I suppose.'

At luncheon Julia had no thoughts except for her guest who was coming that day. She drove to the station to meet him and brought him home to tea.

'Mummy, do look at Rex's Christmas present.'

It was a small tortoise with Julia's initials set in diamonds in the living shell, and this slightly obscene object, now slipping impotently on the polished boards, now striding across the card-table, now lumbering over a rug, now withdrawn at a touch, now stretching its neck and swaying its withered, antediluvian head, became a memorable part of the evening, one of those needle-hooks of experience which catch the attention when larger matters are at stake.

'Dear me,' said Lady Marchmain. 'I wonder if it eats the same sort of things as an ordinary tortoise.'

'What will you do when it's dead?' asked Mr Samgrass. 'Can you have another tortoise fitted into the shell?'

Rex had been told about the problem of Sebastian–he could scarcely have endured in that atmosphere without–and had a solution pat. He propounded it cheerfully and openly at tea, and after a day of whispering it was a relief to hear the thing discussed. 'Send him to Borethus at Zürich. Borethus is the man. He works miracles every day at that sanatorium of his. You know how Charlie Kilcartney used to drink.'

'No,' said Lady Marchmain, with that sweet irony of hers. 'No, I'm afraid I don't know how Charlie Kilcartney drank.'

Julia, hearing her lover mocked, frowned at the tortoise, but Rex Mottram was impervious to such delicate mischief.

'Two wives despaired of him,' he said. 'When he got engaged to Sylvia, she made it a condition that he should take the cure at Zürich. And it worked. He came back in three months a different man. And he hasn't touched a drop since, even though Sylvia walked out on him.'

'Why did she do that?'

'Well, poor Charlie got rather a bore when he stopped drinking. But that's not really the point of the story.'

'No, I suppose not. In fact, I suppose, really, it's meant to be an encouraging story.'

Julia scowled at her jewelled tortoise.

'He takes sex cases, too, you know.'

'Oh dear, what very peculiar friends poor Sebastian will make in Zürich.'

'He's booked up for months ahead, but I think he'd find room if I asked him.

I could telephone him from here tonight.'

(In his kindest moments Rex displayed a kind of hectoring zeal as if he were thrusting a vacuum cleaner on an unwilling housewife.)

'We'll think about it.'

And we were thinking about it when Cordelia returned from hunting.

'Oh, Julia, *what*'s that? How *beastly*.'

'It's Rex's Christmas present.'

'Oh, sorry. I'm always putting my foot in it. But how cruel! It must have hurt frightfully.'

'They can't feel.'

'How d'you know? Bet they can.'

She kissed her mother, whom she had not seen that day, shook hands with Rex, and rang for eggs.

'I had one tea at Mrs Barney's, where I telephoned for the car, but I'm still hungry. It was a spiffing day. Jean Strickland-Venables fell in the mud. We ran from Bengers to Upper Eastrey without a check. I reckon that's five miles, don't you, Bridey?'

'Three.'

'Not as he ran. . . .' Between mouthfuls of scrambled egg she told us about the hunt. '. . . You should have seen Jean when she came out of the mud.'

'Where's Sebastian?'

'He's in disgrace.' The words, in that clear, child's voice had the ring of a bell tolling, but she went on: 'Coming out in that beastly rat-catcher coat and mean little tie like something from Captain Morvin's Riding Academy. I just didn't recognize him at the meet, and I hope nobody else did. Isn't he back? I expect he got lost.'

When Wilcox came to clear the tea, Lady Marchmain asked: 'No sign of Lord Sebastian?'

'No, my Lady.'

'He must have stopped for tea with someone. How every unlike him.'

Half an hour later, when Wilcox brought in the cocktail tray, he said: 'Lord Sebastian has just rung up to be fetched from South Twining.'

'South Twining? Who lives there?'

'He was speaking from the hotel, my Lady.'

'South Twining?' said Cordelia. 'Goodness, he *did* get lost!'

When he arrived he was flushed and his eyes were feverishly bright; I saw that he was two-thirds drunk.

'Dear boy,' said Lady Marchmain. 'How nice to see you looking so well again. Your day in the open has done you good. The drinks are on the table; do help yourself.'

There was nothing unusual in her speech but the fact of her saying it. Six months ago it would not have been said.

'Thanks,' said Sebastian. 'I will.'

A blow, expected, repeated, falling on a bruise, with no smart or shock of surprise, only a dull and sickening pain and the doubt whether another like it could be borne–that was how it felt, sitting opposite Sebastian at dinner that night, seeing his clouded eye and groping movements, hearing his thickened voice breaking in, ineptly, after long brutish silences. When at length Lady

Marchmain and Julia and the servants left us, Brideshead said: 'You'd best go to bed, Sebastian.'

'Have some port first.'

'Yes, have some port if you want it. But don't come into the drawing-room.'

'Too bloody drunk,' said Sebastian nodding heavily. 'Like olden times. Gentlemen always too drunk join ladies in olden times.'

('And yet, you know, it *wasn't*,' said Mr Samgrass, trying to be chatty with me about it afterwards, 'it wasn't at all like olden times. I wonder where the difference lies. The lack of good humour? The lack of companionship? You know I think he must have been drinking by himself today. Where did he get the money?')

'Sebastian's gone up,' said Brideshead when we reached the drawing-room.

'Yes? Shall I read?'

Julia and Rex played bezique; the tortoise, teased by the pekinese, withdrew into his shell; Lady Marchmain read *The Diary of a Nobody* aloud until, quite early, she said it was time for bed.

'Can't I stay up and play a little longer, mummy? Just three games?'

'Very well, darling. Come in and see me before you go to bed. I shan't be asleep.'

It was plain to Mr Samgrass and me that Julia and Rex wanted to be left alone, so we went, too; it was not plain to Brideshead, who settled down to read *The Times*, which he had not yet seen that day. Then, going to our side of the house, Mr Samgrass said: 'It wasn't at all like olden times.'

Next morning I said to Sebastian: 'Tell me honestly, do you want me to stay on here?'

'No, Charles, I don't believe I do.'

'I'm no help?'

'No help.'

So I went to make excuses to his mother.

'There's something I must ask you, Charles. Did you give Sebastian money yesterday?'

'Yes.'

'Knowing how he was likely to spend it?'

'Yes.'

'I don't understand it,' she said. 'I simply don't understand how anyone can be so callously wicked.'

She paused, but I do not think she expected any answer; there was nothing I could say unless I were to start all over again on that familiar, endless argument.

'I'm not going to reproach you,' she said. 'God knows it's not for me to reproach anyone. Any failure in my children is my failure. But I don't understand it. I don't understand how you can have been so nice in so many ways, and then do something so wantonly cruel. I don't understand how we all liked you so much. Did you hate us all the time? I don't understand how we deserved it.'

I was unmoved; there was no part of me remotely touched by her distress. It was as I had often imagined being expelled from school. I almost expected to hear her say: 'I have already written to inform your unhappy father.' But as I drove away and turned back in the car to take what promised to be my last view of the house, I felt that I was leaving part of myself behind, and that wherever I went afterwards I should feel the lack of it, and search for it hopelessly, as ghosts are said to do, frequenting the spots where they buried material treasures without which they cannot pay their way to the nether world.

'I shall never go back,' I said to myself.

A door had shut, the low door in the wall I had sought and found in Oxford; open it now and I should find no enchanted garden.

I had come to the surface, into the light of common day and the fresh sea-air, after long captivity in the sunless coral palaces and waving forests of the ocean bed.

I had left behind me–what? Youth? Adolescence? Romance? The conjuring stuff of these things, 'the Young Magician's Compendium', that neat cabinet where the ebony wand had its place beside the delusive billiard balls, the penny that folded double, and the feather flowers that could be drawn into a hollow candle.

'I have left behind illusion,' I said to myself. 'Henceforth I live in a world of three dimensions–with the aid of my five senses.'

I have since learned that there is no such world, but then, as the car turned out of sight of the house, I thought it took no finding, but lay all about me at the end of the avenue.

Thus I returned to Paris, and to the friends I had found there and the habits I had formed. I thought I should hear no more of Brideshead, but life has few separations as sharp as that. It was not three weeks before I received a letter in Cordelia's Frenchified convent hand:

> Darling Charles, *she said,*
>
> I was so very miserable when you went. You might have come and said good-bye!
>
> I heard all about your disgrace, and I am writing to say that I am in disgrace, too. I sneaked Wilcox's keys and got whisky for Sebastian and got caught. He did seem to want it so. And there was (and is) an awful row.
>
> Mr Samgrass had gone (good!), and I think he is a bit in disgrace, too, but I don't know why.
>
> Mr Mottram is very popular with Julia (bad!) and is taking Sebastian away (bad! bad!) to a German doctor.
>
> Julia's tortoise disappeared. We think it buried itself, as they do, so there goes a packet (expression of Mr Mottram's).
>
> I am very well.
>
> With love from
>
> Cordelia

It must have been about a week after receiving this letter that I returned to my rooms one afternoon to find Rex waiting for me.

It was about four, for the light began to fail early in the studio at that time of year. I could see by the expression on the concierge's face, when she told me I had a visitor waiting, that there was something impressive upstairs; she had a vivid gift of expressing differences of age or attraction; this was the expression which meant someone of the first consequence, and Rex indeed seemed to justify it, as I found him in his big travelling coat, filling the window that looked over the river.

'Well,' I said. 'Well.'

'I came this morning. They told me where you usually lunched but I couldn't see you there. Have you got him?'

I did not need to ask whom. 'So he's given you the slip, too?'

'We got here last night and were going on to Zürich today. I left him at the Lotti after dinner, as he said he was tired, and went round to the Travellers' for a game.'

I noticed how, even with me, he was making excuses, as though rehearsing his story for retelling elsewhere. 'As he said he was tired' was good. I could not well imagine Rex letting a half-tipsy boy interfere with his cards.

'So you came back and found him gone?'

'Not at all. I wish I had. I found him sitting up for me. I had a run of luck at the Travellers' and cleaned up a packet. Sebastian pinched the lot while I was asleep. All he left me was two first-class tickets to Zürich stuck in the edge of the looking-glass. I had nearly three hundred quid, blast him!'

'And now he may be almost anywhere.'

'Anywhere. You're *not* hiding him by any chance?'

'No. My dealings with that family are over.'

'I think mine are just beginning,' said Rex. 'I say, I've got a lot to talk about, and I promised a chap at the Travellers' I'd give him his revenge this afternoon. Won't you dine with me?'

'Yes. Where?'

'I usually go to Ciro's.'

'Why not Paillard's?'

'Never heard of it. I'm paying you know.'

'I know you are. Let me order dinner.'

'Well, all right. What's the place again?' I wrote it down for him. 'Is it the sort of place you see native life?'

'Yes, you might call it that.'

'Well, it'll be an experience. Order something good.'

'That's my intention.'

I was there twenty minutes before Rex. If I had to spend an evening with him, it should, at any rate, be in my own way. I remember the dinner well–soup of *oseille*, a sole quite simply cooked in a white-wine sauce, a *caneton à la presse*, a lemon soufflé. At the last minute, fearing that the whole thing was too simple for Rex, I added *caviar aux blinis*. And for wine I let him give me a bottle of 1906 Montrachet, then at its prime, and, with the duck, a Clos de Bèze of 1904.

Living was easy in France then; with the exchange as it was, my allowance went a long way and I did not live frugally. It was very seldom, however, that I had a dinner like this, and I felt well disposed to Rex, when at last he arrived and gave up his hat and coat with the air of not expecting to see them again. He looked round the sombre little place with suspicion as though hoping to see apaches or a drinking party of students. All he saw was four senators with napkins tucked under their beards eating in absolute silence. I could imagine him telling his commercial friends later: '. . . interesting fellow I know; an art student living in Paris. Took me to a funny little restaurant–sort of place you'd pass without looking at–where there was some of the best food I ever ate. There were half a dozen senators there, too, which shows you it was the right place. Wasn't at all cheap either.'

'Any sign of Sebastian?' he asked.

'There won't be,' I said, 'until he needs money.'

'It's a bit thick, going off like that. I was rather hoping that if I made a good job of him, it might do me a bit of good in another direction.'

He plainly wished to talk of his own affairs; they could wait, I thought, for the hour of tolerance and repletion, for the cognac; they could wait until the attention was blunted and one could listen with half the mind only; now in the keen moment when the *maître d'hôtel* was turning the blinis over in the pan, and, in the background, two humbler men were preparing the press, we would talk of myself.

'Did you stay long at Brideshead? Was my name mentioned after I left?'

'Was it mentioned? I got sick of the sound of it, old boy. The Marchioness got what she called a "bad conscience" about you. She piled it on pretty thick, I gather, at your last meeting.'

'"Callously wicked", "wantonly cruel".'

'Hard words.'

'"It doesn't matter what people call you unless they call you pigeon pie and eat you up."'

'Eh?'

'A saying.'

'Ah.' The cream and hot butter mingled and overflowed, separating each glaucous bead of caviar from its fellows, capping it in white and gold.

'I like a bit of chopped onion with mine,' said Rex. 'Chap-who-knew told me it brought out the flavour.'

'Try it without first,' I said. 'And tell me more news of myself.'

'Well, of course, Greenacre, or whatever he was called–the snooty don–he came a cropper. That was well received by all. He was the blue-eyed boy for a day or two after you left. Shouldn't wonder if he hadn't put the old girl up to pitching you out. He was always being pushed down our throats, so in the end Julia couldn't bear it any more and gave him away.'

'*Julia* did?'

'Well, he'd begun to stick his nose into *our* affairs, you see. Julia spotted he was a fake, and one afternoon when Sebastian was tight–he was tight most of the time–she got the whole story of the Grand Tour out of him. And that was the end of Mr Samgrass. After that the Marchioness began to think she might have been a bit rough with you.'

'And what about the row with Cordelia?'

'That eclipsed everything. That kid's a walking marvel–she'd been feeding Sebastian whisky right under our noses for a week. We couldn't think where he was getting it. That's when the Marchioness finally crumbled.'

The soup was delicious after the rich blinis–hot, thin, bitter, frothy.

'I'll tell you a thing, Charles, that Ma Marchmain hasn't let on to anyone. She's a very sick woman. Might peg out any minute. George Anstruther saw her in the autumn and put it at two years.'

'How on earth do you know?'

'It's the kind of thing I hear. With the way her family are going on at the moment, I wouldn't give her a year. I know just the man for her in Vienna. He put Sonia Bamfshire on her feet when everyone including Anstruther had despaired of her. But Ma Marchmain won't do anything about it. I suppose it's something to do with her crack-brain religion, not to take care of the body.'

The sole was so simple and unobtrusive that Rex failed to notice it. We ate to the music of the press–the crunch of the bones, the drip of blood and marrow, the tap of the spoon basting the thin slices of breast. There was a pause here of a quarter of an hour, while I drank the first glass of the Clos de Bèze and Rex smoked his first cigarette. He leaned back, blew a cloud of smoke across the table, and remarked, 'You know, the food here isn't half bad; someone ought to take this place up and make something of it.'

Presently he began again on the Marchmains:

'I'll tell you another thing, too–they'll get a jolt financially soon if they don't look out.'

'I thought they were enormously rich.'

'Well, they are rich in the way people are who just let their money sit quiet. Everyone of that sort is poorer than they were in 1914, and the Flytes don't seem to realize it. I reckon those lawyers who manage their affairs find it convenient to give them all the cash they want and no questions asked. Look at the way they live–Brideshead and Marchmain House both going full blast, pack of foxhounds, no rents raised, nobody sacked, dozens of old servants doing damn all, being waited on by other servants, and then besides all that there's the old boy setting up a separate establishment–and setting it up on no humble scale either. D'you know how much they're overdrawn?'

'Of course I don't.'

'Jolly near a hundred thousand in London. I don't know what they owe elsewhere. Well, that's quite a packet, you know, for people who aren't *using* their money. Ninety-eight thousand last November. It's the kind of thing I hear.'

Those were the kind of things he heard, mortal illness and debt, I thought.

I rejoiced in the Burgundy. It seemed a reminder that the world was an older and better place than Rex knew, that mankind in its long passion had learned another wisdom than his. By chance I met this same wine again, lunching with my wine merchant in St James's Street, in the first autumn of the war; it had softened and faded in the intervening years, but it still spoke in the pure, authentic accent of its prime, the same words of hope.

'I don't mean that they'll be paupers; the old boy will always be good for an odd thirty thousand a year, but there'll be a shake-up coming soon, and when the upper-classes get the wind up, their first idea is usually to cut down on the girls. I'd like to get the little matter of a marriage settlement through, before it comes.'

We had by no means reached the cognac, but here we were on the subject of himself. In twenty minutes I should have been ready for all he had to tell. I closed my mind to him as best I could and gave myself to the food before me, but sentences came breaking in on my happiness, recalling me to the harsh, acquisitive world which Rex inhabited. He wanted a woman; he wanted the best on the market, and he wanted her at his own price; that was what it amounted to.

'. . . Ma Marchmain doesn't like me. Well, I'm not asking her to. It's not her I want to marry. She hasn't the guts to say openly: "You're not a gentleman. You're an adventurer from the Colonies." She says we live in different atmospheres. That's all right, but Julia happens to fancy my atmosphere. . . . Then she brings up religion. I've nothing against her Church; we don't take much account of Catholics in Canada, but that's different; in Europe you've got some very post Catholics. All right, Julia can go to church whenever she wants to. I shan't try and stop her. It doesn't mean two pins to her, as a matter of fact, but I like a girl to have religion. What's more, she can bring the children up Catholic. I'll make all the "promises" they want. . . . Then there's my past. "We know so little about you." She knows a sight too much. You may know I've been tied up with someone else for a year or two.'

I knew; everyone who had ever met Rex knew of his affair with Brenda Champion; knew also that it was from this affair that he derived everything which distinguished him from every other stock-jobber; his golf with the Prince of Wales, his membership of Bratt's, even his smoking-room comradeship at the House of Commons, for, when he first appeared there, his party chiefs did not say of him, 'Look, there is the promising young member for north Gridley who spoke so well on Rent Restrictions.' They said: 'There's Brenda Champion's latest'; it had done him a great deal of good with men; women he could usually charm.

'Well, that's all washed up. Ma Marchmain was too delicate to mention the subject; all she said was that I had "notoriety". Well, what does she expect as a son-in-law–a sort of half-baked monk like Brideshead? Julia knows all about the other thing; if she doesn't care, I don't see it's anyone else's business.'

After the duck came a salad of watercress and chicory in a faint mist of chives. I tried to think only of the salad. I succeeded for a time in thinking only of the soufflé. Then came the cognac and the proper hour for these confidences. '. . . Julia's just rising twenty. I don't want to wait till she's of age. Anyway, I don't want to marry without doing the thing properly . . . nothing hole-in-corner. . . . I have to see she isn't jockeyed out of her proper settlement. So as the Marchioness won't play ball I'm off to see the old man and square him. I gather he's likely to agree to anything he knows will upset her. He's at Monte Carlo at the moment. I'd planned to go there after dropping Sebastian off at Zürich. That's why it's such a bloody bore having lost him.'

The cognac was not to Rex's taste. It was clear and pale and it came to us in a bottle free from grime and Napoleonic cyphers. It was only a year or two older than Rex and lately bottled. They gave it to us in very thin tulip-shaped glasses of modest size.

'Brandy's one of the things I do know a bit about,' said Rex. 'This is a bad colour. What's more, I can't taste it in this thimble.'

They brought him a balloon the size of his head. He made them warm it over the spirit lamp. Then he rolled the splendid spirit round, buried his face in the fumes, and pronounced it the sort of stuff he put soda in at home.

So, shamefacedly, they wheeled out of its hiding place the vast and mouldy bottle they kept for people of Rex's sort.

'That's the stuff,' he said, tilting the treacly concoction till it left dark rings round the sides of his glass. 'They've always got some tucked away, but they won't bring it out unless you make a fuss. Have some.'

'I'm quite happy with this.'

'Well, it's a crime to drink it, if you don't really appreciate it.'

He lit his cigar and sat back at peace with the world; I, too, was at peace in another world than his. We both were happy. He talked of Julia and I heard his voice, unintelligible at a great distance, like a dog's barking miles away on a still night.

At the beginning of May the engagement was announced. I saw the notice in the *Continental Daily Mail* and assumed that Rex had 'squared the old man'. But things did not go as were expected. The next news I had of them was in the middle of June, when I read that they had been married very quietly at the Savoy Chapel. No royalty was present; nor was the Prime Minister; nor were any of Julia's family. It sounded like a 'hole-in-the-corner' affair, but it was not for several years that I heard the full story.

2

It is time to speak of Julia, who till now has played an intermittent and somewhat enigmatic part in Sebastian's drama. It was thus she appeared to me at the time, and I to her. We pursued separate aims which brought us near to one another, but we remained strangers. She told me later that she had made a kind of note of me in her mind, as, scanning the shelf for a particular book, one will sometimes have one's attention caught by another, take it down, glance at the title page and, saying 'I must read that, too, when I've the time,' replace it, and continue the search. On my side the interest was keener, for there was always the physical likeness between brother and sister, which, caught repeatedly in different poses, under different lights, each time pierced me anew; and, as Sebastian in his sharp decline seemed daily to fade and crumble, so much the more did Julia stand out clear and firm.

She was thin in those days, flat-chested, leggy; she seemed all limbs and neck, bodiless, spidery; thus far she conformed to the fashion, but the hair-cut and the hats of the period, and the blank stare and gape of the period, and the clownish dabs of rouge high on the cheekbones, could not reduce her to type.

When I first met her, when she met me in the station yard and drove me home through the twilight, that high summer of 1923, she was just eighteen and fresh from her first London season.

Some said it was the most brilliant season since the war, that things were getting into their stride again. Julia was at the centre of it. There were then remaining perhaps half a dozen London houses which could be called 'historic'; Marchmain House in St James's was one of them, and the ball given for Julia, in spite of the ignoble costume of the time, was by all accounts a splendid spectacle. Sebastian went down for it and half-heartedly suggested my coming with him; I refused and came to regret my refusal, for it was the last ball of its kind given there; the last of a splendid series.

How could I have known? There seemed time for everything in those days; the world was open to be explored at leisure. I was so full of Oxford that summer; London could wait, I thought.

The other great houses belonged to kinsmen or to childhood friends of Julia's, and besides them there were countless substantial houses in the squares of Mayfair and Belgravia, alight and thronged, one or other of them, night after night. Foreigners returning on post from their own waste lands wrote home that here they seemed to catch a glimpse of the world they had believed lost for ever among the mud and mire, and through those halcyon weeks Julia darted and shone, part of the sunshine between the trees, part of the candle-light in the mirror's spectrum, so that elderly men and women, sitting aside with their memories, saw her as herself the blue-bird. '"Bridey" Marchmain's eldest girl,' they said. 'Pity he can't see her tonight.'

That night and the night after and the night after, wherever she went, always in her own little circle of intimates, she brought a moment of joy, such as strikes deep to the heart on the river's bank when the kingfisher suddenly flares across the water.

This was the creature, neither child nor woman, that drove me through the dusk that summer evening, untroubled by love, taken aback by the power of her own beauty, hesitating on the cool edge of life; one who had suddenly found herself armed, unawares; the heroine of a fairy story turning over in her hands the magic ring; she had only to stroke it with her fingertips and whisper the charmed word, for the earth to open at her feet and belch forth her titanic servant, the fawning monster who would bring her whatever she asked, but bring it, perhaps, in unwelcome shape.

She had no interest in me that evening; the jinn rumbled below us uncalled; she lived apart in a little world, within a little world, the innermost of a system of concentric spheres, like the ivory balls laboriously carved in China; a little problem troubling her mind–little, as she saw it, in abstract terms and symbols. She was wondering, dispassionately and leagues distant from reality, whom she should marry. Thus strategists hesitate over the map, the few pins and lines of coloured chalk, contemplating a change in the pins and lines, a matter of inches, which outside the room, out of sight of the studious officers, may engulf past, present, and future in ruin or life. She was a symbol to herself then, lacking the life of both child and woman; victory and defeat were changes of pin and line; she knew nothing of war.

'If only one lived abroad,' she thought, 'where these things are arranged between parents and lawyers.'

To be married, soon and splendidly, was the aim of all her friends. If she looked further than the wedding, it was to see marriage as the beginning of individual existence; the skirmish where one gained one's spurs, from which one set out on the true quests of life.

She outshone by far all the girls of her age, but she knew that, in that little world within a world which she inhabited, there were certain grave disabilities from which she suffered. On the sofas against the wall where the old people counted up the points, there were things against her. There was the scandal of her father; that slight, inherited stain upon her brightness that seemed deepened by something in her own way of life–waywardness and wilfulness, a less disciplined habit than most of her contemporaries'; but for that, who knows? . . .

One subject eclipsed all others in importance for the ladies along the wall; who would the young princes marry? They could not hope for purer lineage or a more gracious presence than Julia's; but there was this faint shadow on her that unfitted her for the highest honours; there was also her religion.

Nothing could have been further from Julia's ambitions than a royal marriage. She knew, or thought she knew, what she wanted and it was not that. But wherever she turned, it seemed, her religion stood as a barrier between her and her natural goal.

As it seemed to her, the thing was a dead loss. If she apostatized now, having been brought up in the Church, she would go to hell, while the Protestant girls of her acquaintance, schooled in happy ignorance, could marry eldest sons, live at peace with their world, and get to heaven before her. There could be no eldest son for her, and younger sons were indelicate things, necessary, but not to be much spoken of. Younger sons had none of the privileges of obscurity; it was their plain duty to remain hidden until some disaster perchance promoted them to their brothers' places, and, since this was their function, it was desirable that they should keep themselves wholly suitable for succession. Perhaps in a family of three or four boys, a Catholic might get the youngest without opposition. There were of course the Catholics themselves, but these came seldom into the little world Julia had made for herself; those who did were her mother's kinsmen, who, to her, seemed grim and eccentric. Of the dozen or so rich and noble Catholic families, none at that time had an heir of the right age. Foreigners–there were many among her mother's family–were tricky about money, odd in their ways, and a sure mark of failure in the English girl who wed them. What was there left?

This was Julia's problem after her weeks of triumph in London. She knew it was not insurmountable. There must, she thought, be a number of people outside her own world who were well qualified to be drawn into it; the shame was that she must seek them. Not for her the cruel, delicate luxury of choice, the indolent, cat-and-mouse pastimes of the hearth-rug. No Penelope she; she must hunt in the forest.

She had made a preposterous little picture of the kind of man who would do: he was an English diplomat of great but not very virile beauty, now abroad, with a house smaller than Brideshead, nearer to London; he was old, thirty-two or -three, and had been recently and tragically widowed; Julia thought she would prefer a man a little subdued by earlier grief. He had a great career before him but had grown listless in his loneliness; she was not sure he was not in danger of falling into the hands of an unscrupulous foreign adventuress; he needed a new infusion of young life to carry him to the Embassy at Paris. While professing a mild agnosticism herself, he had a liking for the shows of religion and was perfectly agreeable to having his children brought up Catholic; he believed, however, in the prudent restriction of his family to two boys and a girl, comfortably spaced over twelve years, and did not demand, as a Catholic husband might, yearly pregnancies. He had twelve thousand a year above his pay, and no near relations. Someone like that would do, Julia thought, and she was in search of him when she met me at the railway station. I was not her man. She told me as much, without a word, when she took the cigarette from my lips.

All this I learned about Julia, bit by bit, as one does learn the former–as it seems at the time, the preparatory–life of a woman one loves, so that one thinks of oneself as having been part of it, directing it by devious ways, towards oneself.

Julia left Sebastian and me at Brideshead and went to stay with an aunt, Lady Rosscommon, in her villa at Cap Ferrat. All the way she pondered her problem. She had given a name to her widower-diplomat; she called him 'Eustace', and from that moment he became a figure of fun to her, a little interior, incommunicable joke, so that when at last such a man did cross her path–though he was not a diplomat but a wistful major in the Life Guards–and fall in love with her and offer her just those gifts she had chosen, she sent him away moodier and more wistful than ever; for by that time she had met Rex Mottram.

Rex's age was greatly in his favour, for among Julia's friends there was a kind of gerontophilic snobbery; young men were held to be gauche and pimply; it was thought very much more chic to be seen lunching alone at the Ritz–a thing, in any case, allowed to few girls of that day, to the tiny circle of Julia's intimates; a thing looked at askance by the elders who kept the score, chatting pleasantly against the walls of the ballrooms–at the table on the left as you came in, with a starched and wrinkled old roué whom your mother had been warned of as a girl, than in the centre of the room with a party of exuberant young bloods. Rex, indeed, was neither starched nor wrinkled; his seniors thought him a pushful young cad, but Julia recognized the unmistakable chic–the flavour of 'Max' and 'F.E.' and the Prince of Wales, of the big table in the Sporting Club, the second magnum, and the fourth cigar, of the chauffeur kept waiting hour after hour without compunction–which her friends would envy. His social position was unique; it had an air of mystery, even of crime, about it; people said Rex went about armed. Julia and her friends had a fascinated abhorrence of what they called 'Pont Street'; they collected phrases that damned their user, and among themselves–and often, disconcertingly, in public–talked a language made up of them. It was 'Pont Street' to wear a signet ring and to give chocolates at the theatre; it was 'Pont Street' at a dance to say, 'Can I forage for you?' Whatever Rex might be, he was definitely not 'Pont Street'. He had stepped straight from the underworld into the world of Brenda Champion who was herself the innermost of a number of concentric ivory spheres. Perhaps Julia recognized in Brenda Champion an intimation of what she and her friends might be in twelve years' time; there was an antagonism between the girl and the woman that was hard to explain otherwise. Certainly the fact of his being Brenda Champion's property sharpened Julia's appetite for Rex.

Rex and Brenda Champion were staying at the next villa on Cap Ferrat, taken that year by a newspaper magnate and frequented by politicians. They would not normally have come within Lady Rosscommon's ambit, but, living so close, the parties mingled and at once Rex began warily to pay his court.

All that summer he had been feeling restless. Mrs Champion had proved a dead end; it had all been intensely exciting at first, but now the bonds had begun to chafe. Mrs Champion lived as, he found, the English seemed apt to do, in a little world within a little world; Rex demanded a wider horizon. He wanted to consolidate his gains; to strike the black ensign, go ashore, hang the cutlass up over the chimney, and think about the crops. It was time he married; he, too, was in search of a 'Eustace', but, living as he did, he met few girls. He knew of Julia; she was by all accounts top débutante, a suitable prize.

With Mrs Champion's cold eyes watching behind her sun-glasses, there was little Rex could do at Cap Ferrat except establish a friendliness which could be widened later. He was never entirely alone with Julia, but he saw to it that she was included in most things they did; he taught her chemin-de-fer, he arranged that it was always in his car that they drove to Monte Carlo or Nice; he did enough to make Lady Rosscommon write to Lady Marchmain, and Mrs

Champion move him, sooner than they had planned, to Antibes.

Julia went to Salzburg to join her mother.

'Aunt Fanny tells me you made great friends with Mr Mottram. I'm sure he can't be very nice.'

'I don't think he is,' said Julia. 'I don't know that I like nice people.'

There is proverbially a mystery among most men of new wealth, how they made their first ten thousand; it is the qualities they showed then, before they became bullies, when every man was someone to be placated, when only hope sustained them and they could count on nothing from the world but what could be charmed from it, that make them, if they survive their triumph, successful with women. Rex, in the comparative freedom of London, became abject to Julia; he planned his life about hers, going where he would meet her, ingratiating himself with those who could report well of him to her; he sat on a number of charitable committees in order to be near Lady Marchmain; he offered his services to Brideshead in getting him a seat in Parliament (but was there rebuffed); he expressed a keen interest in the Catholic Church until he found that this was no way to Julia's heart. He was always ready to drive her in his Hispano wherever she wanted to go; he took her and parties of her friends to ring-side seats at prize-fights and introduced them afterwards to the pugilists; and all the time he never once made love to her. From being agreeable, he became indispensable to her; from having been proud of him in public she became a little ashamed, but by that time, between Christmas and Easter, he had become indispensable. And then, without in the least expecting it, she suddenly found herself in love.

It came to her, this disturbing and unsought revelation, one evening in May, when Rex had told her he would be busy at the House, and, driving by chance down Charles Street, she saw him leaving what she knew to be Brenda Champion's house. She was so hurt and angry that she could barely keep up appearances through dinner; as soon as she could, she went home and cried bitterly for ten minutes; then she felt hungry, wished she had eaten more at dinner, ordered some bread-and-milk, and went to bed saying: 'When Mr Mottram telephones in the morning, whatever time it is, say I am not to be disturbed.'

Next day she breakfasted in bed as usual, read the papers, telephoned to her friends. Finally she asked: 'Did Mr Mottram ring up by any chance?'

'Oh yes, my lady, four times. Shall I put him through when he rings again?'

'Yes. No. Say I've gone out.'

When she came downstairs there was a message for her on the hall table. *Mr Mottram expects Lady Julia at the Ritz at 1.30*. 'I shall lunch at home today,' she said.

That afternoon she went shopping with her mother; they had tea with an aunt and returned at six.

'Mr Mottram is waiting, my Lady. I've shown him into the library.'

'Oh, mummy, I can't be bothered with him. Do tell him to go home.'

'That's not at all kind, Julia. I've often said he's not my favourite among your friends, but I have grown quite used to him, almost to like him. You really mustn't take people up and drop them like this–particularly people like Mr Mottram.'

'Oh, mummy, *must* I see him? There'll be a scene if I do.'

'Nonsense, Julia, you twist that poor man round your finger.'

So Julia went into the library and came out an hour later engaged to be married.

'Oh, mummy, I warned you this would happen if I went in there.'

'You did nothing of the kind. You merely said there would be a scene. I never conceived of a scene of *this* kind.'

'Anyway, you do like him, mummy. You said so.'

'He has been very kind in a number of ways. I regard him as entirely unsuitable as your husband. So will everyone.'

'Damn everybody.'

'We know nothing about him. He may have black blood–in fact he is suspiciously dark. Darling, the whole thing's impossible. I can't see how you can have been so foolish.'

'Well, what right have I got otherwise to be angry with him if he goes with that horrible old woman? You make a great thing about rescuing fallen women. Well, I'm rescuing a fallen man for a change. I'm saving Rex from mortal sin.'

'Don't be irreverent, Julia.'

'Well, isn't it mortal sin to sleep with Brenda Champion?'

'Or indecent.'

'He's promised never to see her again. I couldn't ask him to do that unless I admitted I was in love with him could I?'

'Mrs Champion's morals, thank God, are not my business. Your happiness is. If you must know, I think Mr Mottram a kind and useful friend, but I wouldn't trust him an inch, and I'm sure he'll have very unpleasant children. They always revert. I've no doubt you'll regret the whole thing in a few days. Meanwhile *nothing is to be done*. No one must be told anything or allowed to suspect. You must stop lunching with him. You may see him here, of course, but nowhere in public. You had better send him to me and I will have a little talk to him about it.'

Thus began a year's secret engagement for Julia; a time of great stress, for Rex made love to her that afternoon for the first time; not, as had happened to her once or twice before with sentimental and uncertain boys, but with a passion that disclosed the corner of something like it in her. Their passion frightened her, and she came back from the confessional one day determined to put an end to it.

'Otherwise I must stop seeing you,' she said.

Rex was humble at once, just as he had been in the winter, day after day, when he used to wait for her in the cold in his big car.

'If only we could be married immediately,' she said.

For six weeks they remained at arm's length, kissing when they met and parted, sitting meantime at a distance, talking of what they would do and where they would live and of Rex's chances of an under-secretaryship. Julia was content, deep in love, living in the future. Then, just before the end of the session, she learned that Rex had been staying the week-end with a stockbroker at Sunningdale, when he said he was at his constituency, and that Mrs Champion had been there, too.

On the evening she heard of this, when Rex came as usual to Marchmain House, they re-enacted the scene of two months before.

'What do you expect?' he said. 'What right have you to ask so much, when you give so little?'

She took her problem to Farm Street and propounded it in general terms, not in the confessional, but in a dark little parlour kept for such interviews.

'Surely, Father, it can't be wrong to commit a small sin myself in order to keep him from a much worse one?'

But the gentle old Jesuit was unyielding. She barely listened to him; he was refusing her what she wanted, that was all she needed to know.

When he had finished he said, 'Now you had better make your confession.'

'No, thank you,' she said, as though refusing the offer of something in a shop. 'I don't think I want to today,' and walked angrily home.

From that moment she shut her mind against her religion.

And Lady Marchmain saw this and added it to her new grief for Sebastian and her old grief for her husband and to the deadly sickness in her body, and took all these sorrows with her daily to church; it seemed her heart was transfixed with the swords of her dolours, a living heart to match the plaster and paint; what comfort she took home with her, God knows.

So the year wore on and the secret of the engagement spread from Julia's confidantes to their confidantes, until, like ripples at last breaking on the mud-verge, there were hints of it in the Press, and Lady Rosscommon as Lady-in-Waiting was closely questioned about it, and something had to be done. Then, after Julia had refused to make her Christmas communion and Lady Marchmain had found herself betrayed first by me, then by Mr Samgrass, then by Cordelia, in the first grey days of 1925, she decided to act. She forbade all talk of an engagement; she forbade Julia and Rex ever to meet; she made plans for shutting Marchmain House for six months and taking Julia on a tour of visits to their foreign kinsmen. It was characteristic of an old, atavistic callousness that went with her delicacy that, even at this crisis, she did not think it unreasonable to put Sebastian in Rex's charge on the journey to Dr Borethus, and Rex, having failed her in that matter, went on to Monte Carlo, where he completed her rout. Lord Marchmain did not concern himself with the finer points of Rex's character; those, he believed, were his daughter's business. Rex seemed a rough, healthy, prosperous fellow whose name was already familiar to him from reading the political reports; he gambled in an open-handed but sensible manner; he seemed to keep reasonably good company; he had a future; Lady Marchmain disliked him. Lord Marchmain was, on the whole, relieved that Julia should have chosen so well, and gave his consent to an immediate marriage.

Rex gave himself to the preparations with gusto. He bought her a ring, not, as she expected, from a tray at Cartier's, but in a back room in Hatton Garden from a man who brought stones out of a safe in little bags and displayed them for her on a writing-desk; then another man in another back room made designs for the setting with a stub of pencil on a sheet of notepaper, and the result excited the admiration of all her friends.

'How d'you know about these things, Rex?' she asked.

She was daily surprised by the things he knew and the things he did not know; both, at the time, added to his attraction.

His present house in Hertford Street was large enough for them both, and had lately been furnished and decorated by the most expensive firm. Julia said she did not want a house in the country yet; they could always take places furnished when they wanted to go away.

There was trouble about the marriage settlement with which Julia refused to interest herself. The lawyers were in despair. Rex absolutely refused to settle any capital. 'What do I want with trustee stock?' he asked.

'I don't know, darling.'

'I make money work for me,' he said. 'I expect fifteen, twenty per cent and I get it. It's pure waste tying up capital at three and a half.'

'I'm sure it is, darling.'

'These fellows talk as though I were trying to rob you. It's *they* who are doing the robbing. They want to rob you of two-thirds of the income I can make you.'

'Does it matter, Rex? We've got heaps, haven't we?'

Rex hoped to have the whole of Julia's dowry in his hands, to make it work for him. The lawyers insisted on tying it up, but they could not get, as they asked, a like sum from him. Finally, grudgingly, he agreed to insure his life, after explaining at length to the lawyers that this was merely a device for putting part of his legitimate profits into other people's pockets; but he had some connexion with an insurance office which made the arrangement slightly less painful to him, by which he took for himself the agent's commission which the lawyers were themselves expecting.

Last and least came the question of Rex's religion. He had once attended a royal wedding in Madrid, and he wanted something of the kind for himself.

'That's one thing your Church can do,' he said, 'put on a good show. You never saw anything to equal the cardinals. How many do you have in England?'

'Only one, darling.'

'Only *one*? Can we hire some others from abroad?'

It was then explained to him that a mixed marriage was a very unostentatious affair.

'How d'you mean "mixed"? I'm not a nigger or anything.'

'No, darling between a Catholic and a Protestant.'

'Oh, *that*? Well, if that's all, it's soon unmixed. I'll become a Catholic. What does one have to do?'

Lady Marchmain was dismayed and perplexed by this new development; it was no good her telling herself that in charity she must assume his good faith; it brought back memories of another courtship and another conversion.

'Rex,' she said. 'I sometimes wonder if you realize how big a thing you are taking on in the Faith. It would be very wicked to take a step like this without believing sincerely.'

He was masterly in his treatment of her.

'I don't pretend to be a very devout man,' he said, 'nor much of a theologian, but I know it's a bad plan to have two religions in one house. A man needs a religion. If your Church is good enough for Julia, it's good enough for me.'

'Very well,' she said, 'I will see about having you instructed.'

'Look, Lady Marchmain, I haven't the time. Instruction will be wasted on me. Just you give me the form and I'll sign on the dotted line.'

'It usually takes some months–often a lifetime.'

'Well, I'm a quick learner. Try me.'

So Rex was sent to Farm Street to Father Mowbray, a priest renowned for his triumphs with obdurate catechumens. After the third interview he came to tea with Lady Marchmain.

'Well, how do you find my future son-in-law?'

'He's the most difficult convert I have ever met.'

'Oh dear, I thought he was going to make it so easy.'

'That's exactly it. I can't get anywhere near him. He doesn't seem to have the least intellectual curiosity or natural piety.

'The first day I wanted to find out what sort of religious life he had till now, so I asked him what he meant by prayer. He said: "*I* don't mean anything. *You* tell *me*." I tried to, in a few words, and he said: "Right. So much for prayer. What's the next thing?" I gave him the catechism to take away. Yesterday I asked him whether Our Lord had more than one nature. He said: "Just as many as you say, Father."

'Then again I asked him: "Supposing the Pope looked up and saw a cloud and said 'It's going to rain', would that be bound to happen?" "Oh, yes, Father." "But supposing it didn't?" He thought a moment and said, "I suppose it would be sort of raining spiritually, only we were too sinful to see it."

'Lady Marchmain, he doesn't correspond to any degree of paganism known to the missionaries.'

'Julia,' said Lady Marchmain, when the priest had gone, 'are you sure that Rex isn't doing this thing purely with the idea of pleasing us?'

'I don't think it enters his head,' said Julia.

'He's really sincere in his conversion?'

'He's absolutely determined to become a Catholic, mummy,' and to herself she said: 'In her long history the Church must have had some pretty queer converts. I don't suppose all Clovis's army were exactly Catholic-minded. One more won't hurt.'

Next week the Jesuit came to tea again. It was the Easter holidays and Cordelia was there, too,

'Lady Marchmain,' he said. 'You should have chosen one of the younger fathers for this task. I shall be dead long before Rex is a Catholic.'

'Oh dear, I thought it was going so well.'

'It was, in a sense. He was exceptionally docile, said he accepted everything I told him, remembered bits of it, asked no questions. I wasn't happy about him. He seemed to have no sense of reality, but I knew he was coming under a steady Catholic influence, so I was willing to receive him. One has to take a chance sometimes–with semi-imbeciles, for instance. You never know quite how much they have understood. As long as you know there's someone to keep an eye on them, you *do* take the chance.'

'How I wish Rex could hear this!' said Cordelia.

'But yesterday I got a regular eye-opener. The trouble with modern education is you never know how ignorant people are. With anyone over fifty you can be fairly confident what's been taught and what's been left out. But these young people have such an intelligent, knowledgeable surface, and then the crust suddenly breaks and you look down into the depths of confusion you didn't know existed. Take yesterday. He seemed to be doing very well. He learned large bits of the catechism by heart, and the Lord's Prayer, and the Hail Mary. Then I asked him as usual if there was anything troubling him, and he looked at me in a crafty way and said, "Look, Father, I don't think you're being straight with me. I want to join your Church and I'm going to join your

Church, but you're holding too much back." I asked what he meant, and he said: "I've had a long talk with a Catholic–a very pious, well-educated one, and I've learned a thing or two. For instance, that you have to sleep with your feet pointing East because that's the direction of heaven, and if you die in the night you can walk there. Now I'll sleep with my feet pointing any way that suits Julia, but d'you expect a grown man to believe about walking to heaven? And what about the Pope who made one of his horses a Cardinal? And what about the box you keep in the church porch, and if you put in a pound note with someone's name on it, they get sent to hell. I don't say there mayn't be a good reason for all this," he said, "but you ought to tell me about it and not let me find out for myself."'

'What *can* the poor man have meant?' said Lady Marchmain.

'You see he's a long way from the Church yet,' said Father Mowbray.

'But who can he have been talking to? Did he dream it all? Cordelia, what's the matter?'

'What a chump! Oh, mummy, what a glorious chump!'

'Cordelia, it was *you*.'

'Oh, mummy, who could have dreamed he'd swallow it? I told him such a lot besides. About the sacred monkeys in the Vatican–all kinds of things.'

'Well, you've very considerably increased *my* work,' said Father Mowbray.

'Poor Rex,' said Lady Marchmain. 'You know, I think it makes him rather lovable. You must treat him like an idiot child, Father Mowbray.'

So the instruction was continued, and Father Mowbray at length consented to receive Rex a week before his wedding.

'You'd think they'd be all over themselves to have me in,' Rex complained. 'I can be a lot of help to them one way and another; instead they're like the chaps who issue cards for a casino. What's more,' he added, 'Cordelia's got me so muddled I don't know what's in the catechism and what she's invented.'

Thus things stood three weeks before the wedding; the cards had gone out, presents were coming in fast, the bridesmaids were delighted with their dresses. Then came what Julia called 'Bridey's bombshell'.

With characteristic ruthlessness he tossed his load of explosive without warning into what, till then, had been a happy family party. The library at Marchmain House was being devoted to wedding presents; Lady Marchmain, Julia, Cordelia, and Rex were busy unpacking and listing them. Brideshead came in and watched them for a moment.

'Chinky vases from Aunt Betty,' said Cordelia. 'Old stuff. I remember them on the stairs at Buckborne.'

'What's all this?' asked Brideshead.

'Mr, Mrs, *and* Miss Pendle-Garthwaite, one early morning tea set. Goode's, thirty shillings, jolly mean.'

'You'd better pack all that stuff up again.'

'Bridey, what *do* you mean?'

'Only that the wedding's off.'

'*Bridey*.'

'I thought I'd better make some inquiries about my prospective brother-in-law, as no one else seemed interested,' said Brideshead. 'I got the final answer tonight. He was married in Montreal in 1915 to a Miss Sarah Evangeline Cutler, who is still living there.'

'Rex, is this true?'

Rex stood with a jade dragon in his hand looking at it critically; then he set it carefully on its ebony stand and smiled openly and innocently at them all.

'Sure it's true,' he said. 'What about it? What are you all looking so het up about? She isn't a thing to me. She never meant any good. I was only a kid, anyhow. The sort of mistake anyone might make. I got my divorce back in 1919. I didn't even know where she was living till Bridey here told me. What's all the rumpus?'

'You might have told me,' said Julia.

'You never asked. Honest, I've not given her a thought in years.'

His sincerity was so plain that they had to sit down and talk about it calmly.

'Don't you realize, you poor sweet oaf,' said Julia, 'that you can't get married as a Catholic when you've another wife alive?'

'But I *haven't*. Didn't I just tell you we were divorced six years ago.'

'But you *can't* be divorced as a Catholic.'

'I wasn't a Catholic and I was divorced. I've got the papers somewhere.'

'But didn't Father Mowbray explain to you about marriage?'

'He said I wasn't to be divorced from you. Well, I don't want to be. I can't remember all he told me–sacred monkeys, plenary indulgences, four last things–if I remembered all he told me I shouldn't have time for anything else. Anyhow, what about your Italian cousin, Francesca?–she married twice.'

'She had an annulment.'

'All right then, I'll get an annulment. What does it cost? Who do I get it from? Has Father Mowbray got one? I only want to do what's right. Nobody told me.'

It was a long time before Rex could be convinced of the existence of a serious impediment to his marriage. The discussion took them to dinner, lay dormant in the presence of the servants, started again as soon as they were alone, and lasted long after midnight. Up, down, and round the argument circled and swooped like a gull, now out to sea, out of sight, cloud-bound, among irrelevances and repetitions, now right on the patch where the offal floated.

'What d'you want me to do? Who should I see?' Rex kept asking. 'Don't tell me there isn't someone who can fix this.'

'There's nothing to do, Rex,' said Brideshead. 'It simply means your marriage can't take place. I'm sorry from everyone's point of view that it's come so suddenly. You ought to have told us yourself.'

'Look,' said Rex. 'Maybe what you say is right; maybe strictly by law I shouldn't get married in your cathedral. But the cathedral is booked; no one there is asking any questions; the Cardinal knows nothing about it; Father Mowbray knows nothing about it. Nobody except us knows a thing. So why make a lot of trouble? Just stay mum and let the thing go through, as if nothing had happened. Who loses anything by that? Maybe I risk going to hell. Well, I'll risk it. What's it got to do with anyone else?'

'Why not?' said Julia. 'I don't believe these priests know everything. I don't believe in hell for things like that. I don't know that I believe in it for anything. Anyway, that's our look-out. We're not asking you to risk your souls. Just keep away.'

'Julia, I hate you,' said Cordelia, and left the room.

'We're all tired,' said Lady Marchmain. 'If there was anything to say,

I'd suggest our discussing it in the morning.'

'But there's nothing to discuss,' said Brideshead, 'except what is the least offensive way we can close the whole incident. Mother and I will decide that. We must put a notice in *The Times* and the *Morning Post*; the presents will have to go back. I don't know what is usual about the bridesmaids' dresses.'

'Just a moment,' said Rex. 'Just a moment. Maybe you can stop us marrying in your cathedral. All right, to hell, we'll be married in a Protestant church.'

'I can stop that, too,' said Lady Marchmain.

'But I don't think you will, mummy,' said Julia. 'You see, I've been Rex's mistress for some time now, and I shall go on being, married or not.'

'Rex, is this true?'

'No damn it, it's not,' said Rex. 'I wish it were.'

'I see we *shall* have to discuss it all again in the morning.' said Lady Marchmain faintly. 'I can't go on any more now.'

And she needed her son's help up the stairs.

'What on earth made you tell your mother that?' I asked, when, years later, Julia described the scene to me.

'That's exactly what Rex wanted to know. I suppose because I thought it was true. Not literally–though you must remember I was only twenty, and no one really knows the "facts of life" by being told them–but, of course, I didn't mean it was true literally. I didn't know how else to express it. I meant I was much too deep with Rex just to be able to say "the marriage arranged will not now take place", and leave it at that. I wanted to be made an honest woman. I've been wanting it ever since–come to think of it.'

'And then?'

'And then the talks went on and on. Poor mummy. And priests came into it and aunts came into it. There were all kinds of suggestions–that Rex should go to Canada, that Father Mowbray should go to Rome and see if there were any possible grounds for an annulment; that I should go abroad for a year. In the middle of it Rex just telegraphed to papa: "Julia and I prefer wedding ceremony take place by Protestant rites. Have you any objection?" He answered, "Delighted", and that settled the matter as far as mummy stopping us legally went. There was a lot of personal appeal after that. I was sent to talk to priests and nuns and aunts. Rex just went on quietly–or fairly quietly–with the plans.

'Oh, Charles, what a squalid wedding! The Savoy Chapel was the place where divorced couples got married in those days–a poky little place not at all what Rex had intended. I wanted just to slip into a registry office one morning and get the thing over with a couple of char-women as witnesses, but nothing else would do but Rex had to have bridesmaids and orange blossom and the Wedding March. It was gruesome.

'Poor mummy behaved like a martyr and insisted on my having her lace in spite of everything. Well, she more or less had to–the dress had been planned round it. My own friends came, of course, and the curious accomplices Rex called *his* friends; the rest of the party were very oddly assorted. None of mummy's family came, of course; one or two of papa's. All the stuffy people stayed away–you know, the Anchorages and Chasms and Vanbrughs–and I thought, "Thank God for that, they always look down their noses at me, anyhow,'' but Rex was furious, because it was just them he wanted apparently.

'I hoped at one moment there'd be no party at all. Mummy said we couldn't use Marchers, and Rex wanted to telegraph papa and invade the place with an army of caterers headed by the family solicitor. In the end it was decided to have a party the evening before at home to see the presents–apparently that was all right according to Father Mowbray. Well, no one can ever resist going to see her own present, so that was quite a success, but the reception Rex gave next day at the Savoy for the wedding guests was very squalid.

'There was great awkwardness about the tenants. In the end Bridey went down and gave them a dinner and bonfire there which wasn't at all what they expected in return for their silver soup tureen.

'Poor Cordelia took it hardest. She had looked forward so much to being my bridesmaid–it was a thing we used to talk about long before I came out–and of course she was a very pious child, too. At first she wouldn't speak to me. Then on the morning of the wedding–I'd moved to Aunt Fanny Rosscommon's the evening before; it was thought more suitable–she came bursting in before I was up, straight from Farm Street, in floods of tears, begged me not to marry, then hugged me, gave me a dear little brooch she'd bought, and said she prayed I'd always be happy. *Always happy*, Charles!

'It was an awfully unpopular wedding, you know. Everyone took mummy's side, as everyone always did–not that she got any benefit from it. All through her life mummy had all the sympathy of everyone except those she loved. They all said I'd behaved abominably to her. In fact, poor Rex found he'd married an outcast, which was exactly the opposite of all he'd wanted.

'So you see things never looked like going right. There was a hoodoo on us from the start. But I was still nuts about Rex.

'Funny to think of, isn't it?

'You know Father Mowbray hit on the truth about Rex at once, that it took me a year of marriage to see. He simply wasn't all there. He wasn't a complete human being at all. He was a tiny bit of one, unnaturally developed; something in a bottle, an organ kept alive in a laboratory. I thought he was a sort of primitive savage, but he was something absolutely modern and up-to-date that only this ghastly age could produce. A tiny bit of a man pretending he was the whole.

'Well, it's all over now.'

It was ten years later that she said this to me in a storm in the Atlantic.

3

I returned to London in the spring of 1926 for the General Strike.

It was the topic of Paris. The French, exultant as always at the discomfiture of their former friends, and transposing into their own precise terms our mistier notions from across the Channel, foretold revolution and civil war. Every evening the kiosks displayed texts of doom, and, in the cafés, acquaintances greeted one half-derisively with: 'Ha, my friend, you are better off here than at home, are you not?' until I and several friends in circumstances like my own came seriously to believe that our country was in danger and that our duty lay there. We were joined by a Belgian Futurist, who lived under the, I think, assumed name of Jean de Brissac la Motte, and claimed the right to bear arms in any battle anywhere against the lower classes.

We crossed together, in a high-spirited, male party, expecting to find unfolding before us at Dover the history so often repeated of late, with so few variations, from all parts of Europe, that I, at any rate, had formed in my mind a clear, composite picture of 'Revolution'–the red flag on the post office, the overturned tram, the drunken N.C.O.s, the gaol open and gangs of released criminals prowling the streets, the train from the capital that did not arrive. One had read it in the papers, seen it in the films, heard it at café tables again and again for six or seven years now, till it had become part of one's experience, at second hand, like the mud of Flanders and the flies of Mesopotamia.

Then we landed and met the old routine of the customs-sheds, the punctual boat-train, the porters lining the platform at Victoria and converging on the first-class carriages; the long line of waiting taxis.

'We'll separate,' we said, 'and see what's happening. We'll meet and compare notes at dinner,' but we knew already in our hearts that nothing was happening; nothing, at any rate, which needed our presence.

'Oh dear,' said my father, meeting me by chance on the stairs, 'how delightful to see you again so soon.' (I had been abroad fifteen months.) 'You've come at a very awkward time, you know. They're having another of those strikes in two days–such a lot of nonsense–and I don't know when you'll be able to get away.'

I thought of the evening I was forgoing, with the lights coming out along the banks of the Seine, and the company I should have had there–for I was at the time concerned with two emancipated American girls who shared a *garçonnière* in Auteuil–and wished I had not come.

We dined that night at the Café Royal. There things were a little more warlike, for the Café was full of undergraduates who had come down for 'National Service'. One group, from Cambridge, had that afternoon signed on to run messages for Transport House, and their table backed on another group's, who were enrolled as special constables. Now and then one or other party would shout provocatively over the shoulder, but it is hard to come into serious conflict back to back, and the affair ended with their giving each other tall glasses of lager beer.

'You should have been in Budapest when Horthy marched in,' said Jean. '*That* was politics.'

A party was being given that night in Regent's Park for the 'Black Birds' who had newly arrived in England. One of us had been asked and thither we all went.

To us, who frequented Bricktop's and the Bal Nègre in the Rue Blomet, there was nothing particularly remarkable in the spectacle; I was scarcely inside the door when I heard an unmistakable voice, an echo from what now seemed a distant past.

'*No*,' it said, 'they are not animals in a *zoo*, Mulcaster, to be *goggled at*. They are *artists*, my dear, very great artists, to be *revered*.'

Anthony Blanche and Boy Mulcaster were at the table where the wine stood.

'Thank God here's someone I know,' said Mulcaster, as I joined them. 'Girl brought me. Can't see her anywhere.'

'She's given you the *slip*, my dear, and do you know why? Because you look ridiculously *out of place*, Mulcaster. It isn't your kind of party at all; you ought not to be here; you ought to go away, you know, to the Old Hundredth or some lugubrious dance in Belgrave Square.'

'Just come from one,' said Mulcaster. 'Too early for the Old Hundredth. I'll stay on a bit. Things may cheer up.'

'I spit on you,' said Anthony. 'Let me talk to *you*, Charles.'

We took a bottle and our glasses and found a corner in another room. At our feet five members of the 'Black Birds' orchestra squatted on their heels and threw dice.

'*That* one,' said Anthony, 'the rather *pale* one, my dear, conked Mrs Arnold Frickheimer the other morning on the *nut*, my dear, with a bottle of milk.'

Almost immediately, inevitably, we began to talk of Sebastian.

'My dear, he's such a *sot*. He came to live with me in Marseille last year when you threw him over, and really it was as much as I could stand. Sip, sip, sip like a dowager all day long. And so *sly*. I was always missing little things, my dear, things I rather liked; once I lost two suits that had arrived from Lesley and Roberts that morning. Of course, I didn't *know* it was Sebastian–there were some rather queer fish, my dear, in and out of my little apartment. Who knows better than you my taste for queer fish? Well, eventually, my dear, we found the pawnshop where Sebastian was p-p-popping them and *then* he hadn't got the tickets; there was a market for them, too, at the bistro.

'I can see that puritanical, disapproving look in your eye, dear Charles, as though you thought I had led the boy on. It's one of Sebastian's less lovable qualities that he always gives the impression of being l-l-led on–like a little horse at a circus. But I assure you I did everything. I said to him again and again, "Why drink? If you want to be intoxicated there are so many much more delicious things." I took him to quite the best man; well, you know him as well as I do, Nada Alopov and Jean Luxmore and *everyone we know* has been to him for years–he's always in the Regina Bar–and then we had trouble over that because Sebastian gave him a bad cheque–a *s-s-stumer*, my dear–and a whole lot of very menacing men came round to the flat–*thugs*, my dear–and Sebastian was making no sense at the time and it was all most unpleasant.'

Boy Mulcaster wandered towards us and sat down, without encouragement, by my side.

'Drink running short in there,' he said, helping himself from our bottle and emptying it. 'Not a soul in the place I ever set eyes on before–all black fellows.'

Anthony ignored him and continued: 'So then we left Marseille and went to Tangier, and *there*, my dear, Sebastian took up with his *new* friend. How can I describe him? He is like the footman in *Warning Shadows*–a great clod of a German who'd been in the Foreign Legion. He got out by shooting off his great toe. It hadn't healed yet. Sebastian found him, starving as tout to one of the houses in the Kasbah, and brought him to stay with us. It was *too* macabre. So back I came, my dear, to good old England–*Good old England*,' he repeated, embracing with a flourish of his hand the Negroes gambling at our feet, Mulcaster staring blankly before him, and our hostess who, in pyjamas, now introduced herself to us.

'Never seen you before,' she said. 'Never asked you. Who are all this white trash, anyway? Seems to me I must be in the wrong house.'

'A time of national emergency,' said Mulcaster. 'Anything may happen.'

'Is the party going well?' she asked anxiously. 'D'you think Florence Mills would sing? We've met before,' she added to Anthony.

'Often, my dear, but you never asked me tonight.'

'Oh dear, perhaps I don't like you. I thought I liked everyone.'

'Do you think,' asked Mulcaster, when our hostess had left us, 'that it might be witty to give the fire alarm?'

'Yes, Boy, run away and ring it.'

'Might cheer things up, I mean.'

'Exactly.'

So Mulcaster left us in search of the telephone.

'I think Sebastian and his lame chum went to French Morocco,' continued Anthony. 'They were in trouble with the Tangier police when I left them. The Marchioness has been a positive pest ever since I came to London, trying to make me get into touch with them. What a time that poor woman's having! It only shows there's some justice in life.'

Presently Miss Mills began to sing and everyone, except the crap players, crowded to the next room.

'That's my girl,' said Mulcaster. 'Over there with that black fellow. That's the girl who brought me.'

'She seems to have forgotten you now.'

'Yes. I wish I hadn't come. Let's go somewhere.'

Two fire engines drove up as we left and a host of helmeted figures joined the throng upstairs.

'That chap, Blanche,' said Mulcaster, '*not* a good fellow. I put him in Mercury once.'

We went to a number of night clubs. In two years Mulcaster seemed to have attained his simple ambition of being known and liked in such places. At the last of them he and I were kindled by a great flame of patriotism.

'You and I,' he said, 'were too young to fight in the war. Other chaps fought, millions of them dead. Not us. We'll show them. We'll show the dead chaps we can fight, too.'

'That's why I'm here,' I said. 'Come from overseas, rallying to old country in hour of need.'

'Like Australians.'

'Like the poor dead Australians.'

'What you in?'

'Nothing yet. War not ready.'

'Only one thing to join–Bill Meadows' show–Defence Corps. All good chaps. Being fixed in Bratt's.'

'I'll join.'

'You remember Bratt's?'

'No. I'll join that, too.'

'That's right. All good chaps like the dead chaps.'

So I joined Bill Meadows' show, which was a flying squad, protecting food deliveries in the poorest parts of London. First I was enrolled in the Defence Corps, took an oath of loyalty, and was given a helmet and truncheon; then I was put up for Bratt's Club and, with a number of other recruits, elected at a committee meeting specially called for the occasion. For a week we sat under orders in Bratt's, and thrice a day we drove out in a lorry at the head of a convoy of milk vans. We were jeered at and sometimes pelted with muck, but only once did we go into action.

We were sitting round after luncheon that day when Bill Meadows came back from the telephone in high spirits.

'Come on,' he said. 'There's a perfectly good battle in the Commercial Road.'

We drove at great speed and arrived to find a steel hawser stretched between lamp posts, an overturned truck and a policeman, alone on the pavement, being kicked by half a dozen youths. On either side of this centre of disturbance, and at a little distance from it, two opposing parties had formed. Near us, as we disembarked, a second policeman was sitting on the pavement, dazed, with his head in his hands and blood running through his fingers; two or three sympathizers were standing over him; on the other side of the hawser was a hostile knot of young dockers. We charged in cheerfully, relieved the policeman, and were just falling upon the main body of the enemy when we came into collision with a party of local clergy and town councillors who arrived simultaneously by another route to try persuasion. They were our only victims, for just as they went down there was a cry of 'Look out. The coppers,' and a lorry-load of police drew up in our rear.

The crowd broke and disappeared. We picked up the peacemakers (only one of whom was seriously hurt), patrolled some of the side streets looking for trouble and finding none, and at length returned to Bratt's. Next day the General Strike was called off and the country everywhere, except in the coal fields, returned to normal. It was as though a beast long fabled for its ferocity had emerged for an hour, scented danger, and slunk back to its lair. It had not been worth leaving Paris.

Jean, who joined another company, had a pot of ferns dropped on his head by an elderly widow in Camden Town and was in hospital for a week.

It was through my membership of Bill Meadows' squad that Julia learned I was in England. She telephoned to say her mother was anxious to see me.

'You'll find her terribly ill,' she said.

I went to Marchmain House on the first morning of peace. Sir Adrian Porson passed me in the hall, leaving, as I arrived; he held a bandanna handkerchief to his face and felt blindly for his hat and stick; he was in tears.

I was shown in the library and in less than a minute Julia joined me. She shook hands with a gentleness and gravity that were unfamiliar; in the gloom of that room she seemed a ghost.

'It's sweet of you to come. Mummy has kept asking for you, but I don't know if she'll be able to see you now, after all. She's just said "good-bye" to Adrian Porson and it's tired her.'

'Good-bye?'

'Yes. She's dying. She may live a week or two or she may go at any minute. She's so weak. I'll go and ask nurse.'

The stillness of death seemed in the house already. No one ever sat in the library at Marchmain House. It was the one ugly room in either of their houses.

The bookcases of Victorian oak held volumes of Hansard and obsolete encyclopedias that were never opened; the bare mahogany table seemed set for the meeting of a committee; the place had the air of being both public and unfrequented; outside lay the forecourt, the railings, the quiet cul-de-sac.

Presently Julia returned.

'No, I'm afraid you can't see her. She's asleep. She may lie like that for hours; I can tell you what she wanted. Let's go somewhere else. I hate this room.'

We went across the hall to the small drawing-room where luncheon parties used to assemble, and sat on either side of the fireplace. Julia seemed to reflect the crimson and gold of the walls and lose some of her warmness.

'First, I know, mummy wanted to say how sorry she is she was so beastly to you last time you met. She's spoken of it often. She knows now she was wrong about you. I'm quite sure you understood and put it out of your mind immediately, but it's the kind of thing mummy can never forgive *herself*–it's the kind of thing she so seldom did.'

'Do tell her I understood completely.'

'The other thing, of course, you have guessed–Sebastian. She wants him. I don't know if that's possible. Is it?'

'I hear he's in a very bad way.'

'We heard that, too. We cabled to the last address we had, but there was no answer. There still may be time for him to see her. I thought of you as the only hope, as soon as I heard you were in England. Will you try and get him? It's an awful lot to ask, but I think Sebastian would want it, too, if he realized.'

'I'll try.'

'There's no one else we can ask. Rex is so busy.'

'Yes. I heard reports of all he's been doing organizing the gas works.'

'Oh yes,' Julia said with a touch of her old dryness. 'He's made a lot of kudos out of the strike.'

Then we talked for a few minutes about the Bratt's squad. She told me Brideshead had refused to take any public service because he was not satisfied with the justice of the cause; Cordelia was in London, in bed now, as she had been watching by her mother all night. I told her I had taken up architectural painting and that I enjoyed it. All this talk was nothing; we had said all we had to say in the first two minutes; I stayed for tea and then left her.

Air France ran a service of a kind to Casablanca; there I took the bus to Fez, starting at dawn and arriving in the new town at evening. I telephoned from the hotel to the British Consul and dined with him that evening, in his charming house by the walls of the old town. He was a kind, serious man.

'I'm delighted someone has come to look after young Flyte at last,' he said. 'He's been something of a thorn in our sides here. This is no place for a remittance man. The French don't understand him at all. They think everyone who's not engaged in trade is a spy. It's not as though he lived like a Milord. Things aren't easy here. There's war going on not thirty miles from this house, though you might not think it. We had some young fools on bicycles only last week who'd come to volunteer for Abdul Krim's army.

'Then the Moors are a tricky lot; they don't hold with drink and our young friend, as you may know, spends most of his day drinking. What does he want to come here for? There's plenty of room for him at Rabat or Tangier, where they cater for tourists. He's taken a house in the native town, you know. I tried to stop him, but he got it from a Frenchman in the Department of Arts. I don't say there's any harm in him, but he's an anxiety. There's an awful fellow sponging on him–a German out of the Foreign Legion. A thoroughly bad hat by all accounts. There's bound to be trouble.

'Mind you, I *like* Flyte. I don't see much of him. He used to come here for baths until he got fixed up at his house. He was always perfectly charming, and my wife took a great fancy to him. What he needs is occupation.'

I explained my errand.

'You'll probably find him at home now. Goodness knows there's nowhere to go in the evenings in the old town. If you like I'll send the porter to show you the way.'

So I set out after dinner, with the consular porter going ahead lantern in hand. Morocco was a new and strange country to me. Driving that day, mile after mile, up the smooth, strategic road, past the vineyards and military posts and the new, white settlements and the early crops already standing high in the vast, open fields, and the hoardings advertising the staples of France–Dubonnet, Michelin, Magasin du Louvre–I had thought it all very suburban and up-to-date; now, under the stars, in the walled city, whose streets were gentle, dusty stairways, and whose walls rose windowless on either side, closed overhead, then opened again to the stars; where the dust lay thick among the smooth paving stones and figures passed silently, robed in white, on soft slippers or hard, bare soles; where the air was scented with cloves and incense and wood smoke–now I knew what had drawn Sebastian here and held him so long.

The consular porter strode arrogantly ahead with his light swinging and his tall cane banging; sometimes an open doorway revealed a silent group seated in golden lamplight round a brazier.

'Very dirty peoples,' the porter said scornfully, over his shoulder. 'No education. French leave them dirty. Not like British peoples. My peoples,' he said, 'always very British peoples.'

For he was from the Sudan Police, and regarded this ancient centre of his culture as a New Zealander might regard Rome.

At length we came to the last of many studded doors, and the porter beat on it with his stick.

'British Lord's house,' he said.

Lamplight and a dark face appeared at the grating. The consular porter spoke peremptorily; bolts were withdrawn and we entered a small courtyard with a well in its centre and a vine trained overhead.

'I wait here,' said the porter. 'You go with this native fellow.'

I entered the house, down a step and into the living-room I found a gramophone, an oil-stove and, between them, a young man. Later, when I looked about me, I noticed other, more agreeable things–the rugs on the floor, the embroidered silk on the walls, the carved and painted beams of the ceiling, the heavy, pierced lamp that hung from a chain and cast soft shadows of its own tracery about the room. But on first entering these three things, the gramophone for its noise–it was playing a French record of a jazz band–the stove for its smell, and the young man for his wolfish look, struck my senses. He was lolling in a basket chair, with a bandaged foot stuck forward on a box; he was dressed in a kind of thin, mid-European imitation tweed with a tennis shirt open at the neck; the unwounded foot wore a brown canvas shoe. There was a brass tray by his side on wooden legs, and on it were two beer bottles, a dirty plate, and a saucer full of cigarette ends; he held a glass of beer in his hand and a cigarette lay on his lower lip and stuck there when he spoke. He had long fair hair combed back without a parting and a face that was unnaturally lined for a man of his obvious youth; one of his front teeth was missing, so that his sibilants came sometimes with a lisp, sometimes with a disconcerting whistle, which he covered with a giggle; the teeth he had were stained with tobacco and set far apart.

This was plainly the 'thoroughly bad hat' of the consul's description, the film footman of Anthony's.

'I'm looking for Sebastian Flyte. This is his house, is it not?' I spoke loudly to make myself heard above the dance music, but he answered softly in English fluent enough to suggest that it was now habitual to him.

'Yeth. But he isn't here. There's no one but me.'

'I've come from England to see him on important business. Can you tell me where I can find him?'

The record came to its end. The German turned it over, wound up the machine, and started it playing again before answering.

'Sebastian's sick. The brothers took him away to the Infirmary. Maybe they'll let you thee him, maybe not. I got to go there myself one day thoon to have my foot dressed. I'll ask them then. When he's better they'll let you thee him, maybe.'

There was another chair and I sat down on it. Seeing that I meant to stay, the German offered me some beer.

'You're not Thebastian's brother?' he said. 'Cousin maybe? Maybe you married hith thister?'

'I'm only a friend. We were at the university together.'

'I had a friend at the university. We studied History. My friend was cleverer than me; a little weak fellow–I used to pick him up and shake him when I was angry–but *tho* clever. Then one day we said: "What the hell? There is no work in Germany. Germany is down the drain," so we said good-bye to our professors, and they said: "Yes, Germany is down the drain. There is nothing for a student to do here now," and we went away and walked and walked and at last we came here. Then we said, "There is no army in Germany now, but we must be tholdiers," so we joined the Legion. My friend died of dysentry last year, campaigning in the Atlas. When he was dead, I said, "What the hell?" so I shot my foot. It is now full of pus, though I have done it one year.'

'Yes,' I said. 'That's very interesting. But my immediate concern is with Sebastian. Perhaps you would tell me about him.'

'He is a very good fellow, Sebastian. He is all right for me. Tangier was a stinking place. He brought me here–nice house, nice food, nice servant–everything is all right for me here, I reckon. I like it all right.'

'His mother is very ill,' I said. 'I have come to tell him.'

'She rich?'

'Yes.'

'Why don't she give him more money? Then we could live at Casablanca, maybe, in a nice flat. You know her well? You could make her give him more money?'

'What's the matter with him?'

'I don't know. I reckon maybe he drink too much. The brothers will look after him. It's all right for him there. The brothers are good fellows. Very cheap there.'

He clapped his hands and ordered more beer.

'You thee? A nice thervant to look after me. It is all right.'

When I had got the name of the hospital I left.

'Tell Thebastian I am still here and all right. I reckon he's worrying about me, maybe.'

The hospital, where I went next morning, was a collection of bungalows between the old and the new towns. It was kept by Franciscans. I made my way through a crowd of diseased Moors to the doctor's room. He was a layman, clean shaven, dressed in white, starched overalls. We spoke in French, and he told me Sebastian was in no danger, but quite unfit to travel. He had had the grippe, with one lung slightly affected; he was very weak; he lacked resistance; what could one expect? He was an alcoholic. The doctor spoke dispassionately, almost brutally, with the relish men of science sometimes have for limiting themselves to inessentials, for pruning back their work to the point of sterility; but the bearded, barefooted brother in whose charge he put me, the man of no scientific pretensions who did the dirty jobs of the ward, had a different story.

'He's so patient. Not like a young man at all. He lies there and never complains–and there is much to complain of. We have no facilities. The Government give us what they can spare from the soldiers. And he is so kind. there is a poor German boy with a foot that will not heal and secondary syphilis, who comes here for treatment. Lord Flyte found him starving in Tangier and took him in and gave him a home. A real Samaritan.'

'Poor simple monk,' I thought, 'poor booby.' God forgive me!

Sebastian was in the wing kept for Europeans, where the beds were divided by low partitions into cubicles with some air of privacy. He was lying with his hands on the quilt staring at the wall, where the only ornament was a religious oleograph.

'Your friend,' said the brother.

He looked round slowly.

'Oh, I thought he meant Kurt. What are *you* doing here, Charles?'

He was more than ever emaciated; drink, which made others fat and red, seemed to wither Sebastian. The brother left us, and I sat by his bed and talked about his illness.

'I was out of my mind for a day or two,' he said. 'I kept thinking I was back in Oxford. You went to my house? Did you like it? Is Kurt still there? I won't ask you if you liked Kurt; no one does. It's funny–I couldn't get on without him, you know.'

Then I told him about his mother. He said nothing for some time, but lay gazing at the oleograph of the Seven Dolours. Then:

'Poor mummy. She really was a *femme fatale*, wasn't she? She killed at a touch.'

I telegraphed to Julia that Sebastian was unable to travel, and stayed a week at Fez, visiting the hospital daily until he was well enough to move. His first sign of returning strength, on the second day of my visit, was to ask for brandy.

By next day he had got some, somehow, and kept it under the bedclothes.

The doctor said: 'You friend is drinking again. It is forbidden here. What can I do? This is not a reformatory school. I cannot police the wards. I am here to cure people, not to protect them from vicious habits, or teach them self-control. Cognac will not hurt him now. It will make him weaker for the next time he is ill, and then one day some little trouble will carry him off, pouff. This is not a home for inebriates. He must go at the end of the week.'

The lay-brother said: 'Your friend is so much happier today, it is like one transfigured.'

'Poor simple monk,' I thought, 'poor booby'; but he added, 'You know why? He has a bottle of cognac in bed with him. It is the second I have found. No sooner do I take one away than he gets another. He is so naughty. It is the Arab boys who fetch it for him. But it is good to see him happy again when he has been so sad.'

On my last afternoon I said, 'Sebastian, now your mother's dead'–for the news had reached us that morning–'do you think of going back to England?'

'It *would* be lovely, in some ways,' he said, 'but do you think Kurt would like it?'

'For God's sake,' I said, 'you don't mean to spend your life with Kurt, do you?'

'I don't know. He seems to mean to spend it with me. "It'th all right for him, I reckon, maybe,"' he said, mimicking Kurt's accent, and then he added what, if I had paid more attention, should have given me the key I lacked; at the time I heard and remembered it, without taking notice. 'You know, Charles,' he said, 'it's rather a pleasant change when all your life you've had people looking after you, to have someone to look after yourself. Only of course it has to be someone pretty hopeless to need looking after by *me*.'

I was able to straighten his money affairs before I left. He had lived till then by getting into difficulties and then telegraphing for odd sums to his lawyers. I saw the branch manager of the bank and arranged for him, if funds were forthcoming from London, to receive Sebastian's quarterly allowance and pay him a weekly sum of pocket money with a reserve to be drawn in emergencies. This sum was only to be given to Sebastian personally, and only when the manager was satisfied that he had a proper use for it. Sebastian agreed readily to all this.

'Otherwise,' he said, 'Kurt will get me to sign a cheque for the whole lot when I'm tight and then he'll go off and get into all kinds of trouble.'

I saw Sebastian home from the hospital. He seemed weaker in his basket chair than he had been in bed. The two sick men, he and Kurt, sat opposite one another with the gramophone between them.

'It was time you came back,' said Kurt. 'I need you.'

'Do you, Kurt?'

'I reckon so. It's not so good being alone when you're sick. That boy's a lazy fellow–always slipping off when I want him. Once he stayed out all night and there was no one to make my coffee when I woke up. It's no good having a foot full of pus. Times I can't sleep good. Maybe another time I shall slip off, too, and go where I can be looked after.' He clapped his hands but no servant came. 'You see? he said.

'What d'you want?'

'Cigarettes. I got some in the bag under my bed.'

Sebastian began painfully to rise from his chair.

'I'll get them,' I said. 'Where's his bed?'

'No, that's my job,' said Sebastian.

'Yeth,' said Kurt, 'I reckon that's Sebastian's job.'

So I left him with his friend in the little enclosed house at the end of the alley. There was nothing more I could do for Sebastian.

I had meant to return direct to Paris, but this business of Sebastian's allowance meant that I must go to London and see Brideshead. I travelled by sea, taking the P. & O. from Tangier, and was home in early June.

'Do you consider,' asked Brideshead, 'that there is anything vicious in my brother's connexion with this German?'

'No. I'm sure not. It's simply a case of two waifs coming together.'

'You say he is a criminal?'

'I said "a criminal type". He's been in the military prison and was dishonourably discharged.'

'And the doctor says Sebastian is killing himself with drink?'

'Weakening himself. He hasn't D.T.s or cirrhosis.'

'He's not insane?'

'Certainly not. He's found a companion he happens to like and a place where he happens to like living.'

'Then he must have his allowance as you suggest. The thing is quite clear.'

In some ways Brideshead was an easy man to deal with. He had a kind of mad certainty about everything which made his decisions swift and easy.

'Would you like to paint this house?' he asked suddenly. 'A picture of the front, another of the back on the park, another of the staircase, another of the big drawing-room? Four small oils; that is what my father wants done for a record, to keep at Brideshead. I don't know any painters. Julia said you specialized in architecture.'

'Yes,' I said. 'I should like to very much.'

'You know it's being pulled down? My father's selling it. They are going to put up a block of flats here. They're keeping the name–we can't stop them apparently.'

'What a sad thing.'

'Well, I'm sorry of course. But you think it good architecturally?'

'One of the most beautiful houses I know.'

'Can't see it. I've always thought it rather ugly. Perhaps your pictures will make me see it differently.'

This was my first commission; I had to work against time, for the contractors were only waiting for the final signature to start their work of destruction. In spite, or perhaps, because, of that–for it is my vice to spend too long on a canvas, never content to leave well alone–those four paintings are particular favourites of mine, and it was their success, both with myself and others, that confirmed me in what has since been my career.

I began in the long drawing-room, for they were anxious to shift the furniture, which had stood there since it was built. It was a long, elaborate, symmetrical Adam room, with two bays of windows opening into Green Park. The light, streaming in from the west on the afternoon when I began to paint there, was fresh green from the young trees outside.

I had the perspective set out in pencil and the detail carefully placed. I held back from painting, like a diver on the water's edge; once in I found myself buoyed and exhilarated. I was normally a slow and deliberate painter; that afternoon and all next day, and the day after, I worked fast. I could do nothing wrong. At the end of each passage I paused, tense, afraid to start the next, fearing, like a gambler, that luck must turn and the pile be lost. Bit by bit, minute by minute, the thing came into being. There were no difficulties; the intricate multiplicity of light and colour became a whole; the right colour was where I wanted it on the palette; each brush stroke, as soon as it was complete, seemed to have been there always.

Presently on the last afternoon I heard a voice behind me say: 'May I stay here and watch?'

I turned and found Cordelia.

'Yes,' I said, 'if you don't talk,' and I worked on, oblivious of her, until the failing sun made me put up my brushes.

'It must be lovely to be able to do that.'

I had forgotten she was there.

'It is.'

I could not even now leave my picture, although the sun was down and the room fading to monochrome. I took it from the easel and held it up to the windows, put it back and lightened a shadow. Then, suddenly weary in head and eyes and back and arm, I gave it up for the evening and turned to Cordelia.

She was now fifteen and had grown tall, nearly to her full height, in the last eighteen months. She had not the promise of Julia's full *quattrocento* loveliness; there was a touch of Brideshead already in her length of nose and high cheekbone; she was in black, mourning for her mother.

'I'm tired,' I said.

'I bet you are. Is it finished?'

'Practically. I must go over it again tomorrow.'

'D'you know it's long past dinner time? There's no one here to cook anything now. I only came up today, and didn't realize how far the decay had gone. You wouldn't like to take me out to dinner, would you?'

We left by the garden door, into the park, and walked in the twilight to the Ritz Grill.

'You've seen Sebastian? He won't come home, even now?'

I did not realize till then that she had understood so much. I said so.

'Well, I love him more than anyone,' she said. 'It's sad about Marchers, isn't it? Do you know they're going to build a block of flats, and that Rex wanted to take what he called a "penthouse" at the top. Isn't it like him? Poor Julia. That was too much for her. He couldn't understand at all; he thought she would like to keep up with her old home. Things have all come to an end very quickly, haven't they? Apparently papa has been terribly in debt for a long time. Selling Marchers has put him straight again and saved I don't know how much a year in rates. But it seems a shame to pull it down. Julia says she'd sooner that than to have someone else live there.'

'What's going to happen to you?'

'What, indeed? there are all kinds of suggestions. Aunt Fanny Rosscommon wants me to live with her. Then Rex and Julia talk of taking over half

Brideshead and living there. Papa won't come back. We thought he might, but no.

'They've closed the chapel at Brideshead, Bridey and the Bishop; mummy's Requiem was the last mass said there. After she was buried the priest came in–I was there alone. I don't think he saw me–and took out the altar stone and put it in his bag; then he burned the wads of wool with the holy oil on them and threw the ash outside; he emptied the holy-water stoop and blew out the lamp in the sanctuary, and left the tabernacle open and empty, as though from now on it was always to be Good Friday. I suppose none of this makes any sense to you, Charles, poor agnostic. I stayed there till he was gone, and then, suddenly, there wasn't any chapel there any more, just an oddly decorated room. I can't tell you what it felt like. You've never been to Tenebrae, I suppose?'

'Never.'

'Well, if you had you'd know what the Jews felt about their temple. *Quomodo sedet sola civitas* . . . it's a beautiful chant. You ought to go once, just to hear it.'

'Still trying to convert me, Cordelia?'

'Oh, no. That's all over, too. D'you know what papa said when he became a Catholic? Mummy told me once. He said to her: "You have brought back my family to the faith of their ancestors." Pompous, you know. It takes people different ways. Anyhow, the family haven't been very constant, have they? There's him gone and Sebastian gone and Julia gone. But God won't let them go for long, you know. I wonder if you remember the story mummy read us the evening Sebastian first got drunk–I mean the *bad* evening. "Father Brown" said something like "I caught him" (the thief) "with an unseen hook and an invisible line which is long enough to let him wander to the ends of the world and still to bring him back with a twitch upon the thread."'

We scarcely mentioned her mother. All the time we talked, she ate voraciously. Once she said:

'Did you see Sir Adrian Porson's poem in *The Times?* It's funny: he knew her best of anyone–he loved her all his life, you know–and yet it doesn't seem to have anything to do with her at all.

'I got on best with her of any of us, but I don't believe I ever really loved her. Not as she wanted or deserved. It's odd I didn't, because I'm full of natural affections.'

'I never really knew your Mother,' I said.

'You didn't like her. I sometimes think when people wanted to hate God they hated mummy.'

'What do you mean by that, Cordelia?'

'Well, you see, she was saintly but she wasn't a saint. No one could really hate a saint, could they? They can't really hate God either. When they want to hate him and his saints they have to find something like themselves and pretend it's God and hate that. I suppose you think that's all bosh.'

'I heard almost the same thing once before–from someone very different.'

'Oh, I'm quite serious. I've thought about it a lot. It seems to explain poor mummy.'

Then this odd child tucked into her dinner with renewed relish. 'First time I've ever been taken out to dinner alone at a restaurant,' she said.

Later: 'When Julia heard they were selling Marchers she said: "Poor Cordelia. She won't have her coming-out ball there after all." It's a thing we used to talk about–like my being her bridesmaid. That didn't come off either. When Julia had her ball I was allowed down for an hour, to sit in the corner with Aunt Fanny, and she said, "In six years' time you'll have all this." . . . I hope I've got a vocation.'

'I don't know what that means.'

'It means you can be a nun. If you haven't a vocation it's no good however much you want to be; and if you have a vocation, you can't get away from it, however much you hate it. Bridey thinks he has a vocation and hasn't. I used to think Sebastian had and hated it–but I don't know now. Everything has changed so much suddenly.'

But I had no patience with this convent chatter. I had felt the brush take life in my hand that afternoon; I had had my finger in the great, succulent pie of creation. I was a man of the Renaissance that evening–of Browning's renaissance. I, who had walked the streets of Rome in Genoa velvet and had seen the stars through Galileo's tube, spurned the friars, with their dusty tomes and their sunken, jealous eyes and their crabbed hair-splitting speech.

'You'll fall in love,' I said.

'Oh, pray not. I say, do you think I could have another of those scrumptious meringues?'

PART III

A TWITCH UPON THE THREAD

I

My theme is memory, that winged host that soared about me one grey morning of war-time.

These memories, which are my life–for we possess nothing certainly except the past–were always with me. Like the pigeons of St Mark's, they were everywhere, under my feet, singly, in pairs, in little honey-voiced congregations, nodding, strutting, winking, rolling the tender feathers of their necks, perching sometimes, if I stood still, on my shoulder; until, suddenly, the noon gun boomed and in a moment, with a flutter and sweep of wings, the pavement was bare and the whole sky above dark with a tumult of fowl. Thus it was that morning of war-time.

For nearly ten dead years after that evening with Cordelia I was borne along a road outwardly full of change and incident, but never during that time, except sometimes in my painting–and that at longer and longer intervals–did I come alive as I had been during the time of my friendship with Sebastian. I took it to be youth, not life, that I was losing. My work upheld me, for I had chosen to do what I could do well, did better daily, and liked doing; incidentally it was something which no one else at that time was attempting to do. I became an architectural painter.

More even than the work of the great architects, I loved buildings that grew silently with the centuries, catching and keeping the best of each generation, while time curbed the artist's pride and the Philistine's vulgarity, and repaired the clumsiness of the dull workman. In such buildings England abounded, and, in the last decade of their grandeur, Englishmen seemed for the first time to become conscious of what before was taken for granted, and to salute their achievement at the moment of extinction. Hence my prosperity, far beyond my merits; my work had nothing to recommend it except my growing technical skill, enthusiasm for my subject, and independence of popular notions.

The financial slump of the period, which left many painters without employment, served to enhance my success, which was, indeed, itself a symptom of the decline. When the water-holes were dry people sought to drink at the mirage. After my first exhibition I was called to all parts of the country to make portraits of houses that were soon to be deserted or debased; indeed, my arrival seemed often to be only a few paces ahead of the auctioneer's, a presage of doom.

I published three splendid folios–*Ryder's Country Seats*, *Ryder's English Homes*, and *Ryder's Village and Provincial Architecture*, which each sold its thousand copies at five guineas apiece. I seldom failed to please, for there was no conflict between myself and my patrons; we both wanted the same thing. But, as the years passed, I began to mourn the loss of something I had known in the drawing-room of Marchmain House and once or twice since, the intensity and singleness and the belief that it was not all done by hand–in a word, the inspiration.

In quest of this fading light I went abroad, in the augustan manner, laden with the apparatus of my trade, for two years' refreshment among alien styles. I did not go to Europe; her treasures were safe, too safe, swaddled in expert care, obscured by reverence. Europe could wait. There would be a time for Europe, I thought; all too soon the days would come when I should need a man at my side to put up my easel and carry my paints; when I could not venture more than an hour's journey from a good hotel; when I should need soft breezes and mellow sunshine all day long; then I would take my old eyes to Germany and Italy. Now while I had the strength I would go to the wild lands where man had deserted his post and the jungle was creeping back to its old strongholds.

According, by slow but not easy stages, I travelled through Mexico and Central America in a world which had all I needed, and the change from parkland and hall should have quickened me and set me right with myself. I sought inspiration among gutted palaces and cloisters embowered in weed, derelict churches where the vampire-bats hung in the dome like dry seed-pods and only the ants were ceaselessly astir tunnelling in the rich stalls; cities where no road led, and mausoleums where a single, agued family of Indians sheltered from the rains. There in great labour, sickness, and occasionally in some danger, I made the first drawings for *Ryder's Latin America*. Every few weeks I came to rest, finding myself once more in the zone of trade or tourism, recuperated, set up my studio, transcribed my sketches, anxiously packed the complete canvases, dispatched them to my New York agent, and then set out again, with my small retinue, into the wastes.

I was in no great pains to keep in touch with England. I followed local advice for my itinerary and had no settled route, so that much of my mail never reached me, and the rest accumulated until there was more than could be read at a sitting. I used to stuff a bundle of letters into my bag and read them when I felt inclined, which was in circumstances so incongruous–swinging in my hammock, under the net, by the light of a storm-lantern; drifting down river, amidships in the canoe, with the boys astern of me lazily keeping our nose out of the bank, with the dark water keeping pace with us, in the green shade, with the great trees towering above us and the monkeys screeching in the sunlight, high overhead among the flowers on the roof of the forest; on the veranda of a hospitable ranch, where the ice and the dice clicked, and a tiger cat played with its chain on the mown grass–that they seemed voices so distant as to be meaningless; their matter passed clean through the mind, and out, leaving no mark, like the facts about themselves which fellow travellers distribute so freely in American railway trains.

But despite this isolation and this long sojourn in a strange world, I remained unchanged, still a small part of myself pretending to be whole. I discarded the experiences of those two years with my tropical kit and returned to New York as I had set out. I had a fine haul–eleven paintings and fifty odd drawings–and when eventually I exhibited them in London, the art critics, many of whom hitherto had been patronizing in tone, as my success invited, acclaimed a new and richer note in my work. *Mr Ryder*, the most respected of them wrote, *rises like a fresh young trout to the hypodermic injection of a new culture and discloses a powerful facet in the vista of his potentialities ... By focusing the frankly traditional battery of his elegance and erudition on the maelstrom of Barbarism, Mr Ryder has at last found himself.*

Grateful words, but, alas, not true by a long chalk. My wife, who crossed to New York to meet and saw the fruits of our separation displayed in my agent's office, summed the thing up better by saying: 'Of course, I can see they're perfectly brilliant and really rather beautiful in a sinister way, but somehow I don't feel they are quite *you*.'

In Europe my wife was sometimes taken for an American because of her dapper and jaunty way of dressing, and the curiously hygienic quality of her prettiness; in America she assumed an English softness and reticence. She arrived a day or two before me, and was on the pier when my ship docked.

'It has been a long time,' she said fondly when we met.

She had not joined the expedition; she explained to our friends that the country was unsuitable and she had her son at home. There was also a daughter now, she remarked, and it came back to me that there had been talk of this before I started, as an additional reason for her staying behind. There had been some mention of it, too, in her letters.

'I don't believe you read my letters,' she said that night, when at last, late, after a dinner party and some hours at a cabaret, we found ourselves alone in our hotel bedroom.

'Some went astray. I remember distinctly you telling me that the daffodils in the orchard were a dream, that the nursery-maid was a jewel, that the Regency four-poster was a find, but frankly I do not remember hearing that your new baby was called Caroline. Why did you call it that?'

'After Charles, of course.'

'Ah!'

'I made Bertha Van Halt godmother. I thought she was safe for a good present. What do you think she gave?'

'Bertha Van Halt is a well-known trap. What?'

'A fifteen shilling book-token. Now that Johnjohn has a companion—'

'Who?'

'Your son, darling. You haven't forgotten him, too?'

'For Christ's sake,' I said, 'why do you call him that?'

'It's the name he invented for himself. Don't you think it sweet? Now that Johnjohn has a companion I think we'd better not have any more for some time, don't you?'

'Just as you please.'

'Johnjohn talks of you such a lot. He prays every night for your safe return.'

She talked in this way while she undressed, with an effort to appear at ease; then she sat at the dressing table, ran a comb through her hair, and with her bare back towards me, looking at herself in the glass, said: 'Shall I put my face to bed?'

It was a familiar phrase, one that I did not like; she meant, should she remove her make-up, cover herself with grease and put her hair in a net.

'No.' I said, 'not at once.'

Then she knew what was wanted. She had neat, hygienic ways for that too, but there were both relief and triumph in her smile of welcome; later we parted and lay in our twin beds a yard or two distant, smoking. I looked at my watch; it was four o'clock, but neither of us was ready to sleep, for in that city there is neurosis in the air which the inhabitants mistake for energy.

'I don't believe you've changed at all, Charles.'

'No, I'm afraid not.'

'D'you want to change?'

'It's the only evidence of life.'

'But you might change so that you didn't love me any more.'

'There is that risk.'

'Charles, you haven't stopped loving me?'

'You said yourself I hadn't changed.'

'Well, I'm beginning to think you have. I haven't.'

'No,' I said, 'no; I can see that.'

'Were you at all frightened at meeting me today?'

'Not the least.'

'You didn't wonder if I should have fallen in love with someone else in the meantime?'

'No. Have you?'

'You know I haven't. Have you?'

'No, I'm not in love.'

My wife seemed content with this answer. She had married me six years ago at the time of my first exhibition, and had done much since then to push our interests. People said she had 'made' me, but she herself took credit only for supplying me with a congenial background; she had firm faith in my genius and in the 'artistic temperament', and in the principle that things done on the sly are not really done at all.

Presently she said: 'Looking forward to getting home?' (My father gave me as a wedding present the price of a house, and I bought an old rectory in my wife's part of the country.) 'I've got a surprise for you.'

'Yes?'

'I've turned the old barn into a studio for you, so that you needn't be disturbed by the children or when we have people to stay. I got Emden to do it. Everyone thinks it a great success. There was an article on it in *Country Life*; I bought it for you to see.'

She showed me the article: '. . . *happy example of architectural good manners. . . . Sir Joseph Emden's tactful adaptation of traditional material to modern needs* . . .'; there were some photographs; wide oak boards now covered the earthen floor; a high, stone-mullioned bay-window had been built in the north wall, and the great timbered roof, which before had been lost in shadow, now stood out stark, well lit, with clean white plaster between the beams; it looked like a village hall. I remembered the smell of the place, which would now be lost.

'I rather liked that barn,' I said.

'But you'll be able to work there, won't you?'

'After squatting in a cloud of sting-fly,' I said, 'under a sun which scorched the paper off the block as I drew, I could work on the top of an omnibus. I expect the vicar would like to borrow the place for whist drives.'

'There's a lot of work waiting for you. I promised Lady Anchorage you would do Anchorage House as soon as you got back. That's coming down, too, you know–shops underneath and two-roomed flats above. You don't think, do you, Charles, that all this exotic work you've been doing, is going to spoil you for that sort of thing?'

'Why should it?'

'Well, it's so different. Don't be cross.'

'It's just another jungle closing in.'

'I know just how you feel, darling. The Georgian Society made such a fuss, but we couldn't do anything. . . . Did you ever get my letter about Boy?'

'Did I? What did it say?'

('Boy' Mulcaster was her brother.)

'About his engagement. It doesn't matter now because it's all off, but father and mother were terribly upset. She was an awful girl. They had to give her money in the end.'

'No, I heard nothing of Boy.'

'He and Johnjohn are tremendous friends, now. It's so sweet to see them together. Whenever he comes the first thing he does is to drive straight to the Old Rectory. He just walks into the house, pays no attention to anyone else, and hollers out: "Where's my chum Johnjohn?" and Johnjohn comes tumbling downstairs and off they go into the spinney together and play for hours. You'd think, to hear them talk to each other, they were the same age. It was really Johnjohn who made him see reason about that girl; seriously, you know, he's frightfully sharp. He must have heard mother and me talking because next time Boy came he said: "Uncle Boy shan't marry horrid girl and leave Johnjohn," and that was the very day he settled for two thousand pounds out of court. Johnjohn admires Boy so tremendously and imitates him in everything. It's so good for them both.'

I crossed the room and tried once more, ineffectively, to moderate the heat of the radiators; I drank some iced water and opened the window, but, besides the sharp night air, music was borne in from the next room where they were playing the wireless. I shut it and turned back towards my wife.

At length she began talking again, more drowsily. . . . 'The garden's come on a lot. . . . The box hedges you planted grew five inches last year. . . . I had some men down from London to put the tennis court right . . . first-class cook at the moment . . .'

As the city below us began to wake, we both fell asleep, but not for long; the telephone rang and a voice of hermaphroditic gaiety said: 'Savoy-Carlton-Hotel-goodmorning. It is now a quarter of eight.'

'I didn't ask to be called, you know.'

'Pardon me?'

'Oh, it doesn't matter.'

'You're welcome.'

As I was shaving, my wife from the bath said: 'Just like old times. I'm not worrying any more, Charles.'

'Good.'

'I was so terribly afraid that two years might have made a difference. Now I know we can start again exactly where we left off.'

'When?' I asked. 'What? When we left off what?'

'When you went away, of course.'

'You are not thinking of something else, a little time before?'

'Oh, Charles, that's old history. That was nothing. It was never anything. It's all over and forgotten.'

'I just wanted to know,' I said. 'We're back as we were the day I went abroad, is that it?'

So we started that day exactly where we left off two years before, with my wife in tears.

My wife's softness and English reticence, her very white, small regular teeth, her neat rosy finger-nails, her schoolgirl air of innocent mischief and her schoolgirl dress, her modern jewellery, which was made at great expense to give the impression, at a distance, of having been mass produced, her ready, rewarding smile, her deference to me and her zeal in my interests, her motherly heart which made her cable daily to the nanny at home–in short, her peculiar charm–made her popular among the Americans, and our cabin on the day of departure was full of cellophane packages–flowers, fruit, sweets, books, toys for the children–from friends she had known for a week. Stewards, like sisters in a nursing home, used to judge their passengers' importance by the number and value of these trophies; we therefore started the voyage in high esteem.

My wife's first thought on coming aboard was of the passenger list.

'Such a lot of friends,' she said. 'It's going to be a lovely trip. Let's have a cocktail party this evening.'

The companion-ways were no sooner cast off than she was busy with the telephone.

'Julia. This is Celia–Celia Ryder. It's lovely to find you on board. What have you been up to? Come and have a cocktail this evening and tell me all about it.'

'Julia who?'

'Mottram. I haven't seen her for years.'

Nor had I; not, in fact, since my wedding day, not to speak to for any time, since the private view of my exhibition where the four canvases of Marchmain House, lent by Brideshead, had hung together attracting much attention. Those pictures were my last contact with the Flytes; our lives, so close for a year or two, had drawn apart. Sebastian, I knew, was still abroad; Rex and Julia, I sometimes heard said, were unhappy together. Rex was not prospering quite as well as had been predicted; he remained on the fringe of the Government, prominent but vaguely suspect. He lived among the very rich, and in his speeches seemed to incline to revolutionary policies, flirting, with Communists and Fascists. I heard the Mottrams' names in conversation; I saw their faces now and again peeping from the *Tatler*, as I turned the pages impatiently waiting for someone to come, but they and I had fallen apart, as one could in England and only there, into separate worlds, little spinning planets of personal relationship; there is probably a perfect metaphor for the process to be found in physics, from the way in which, I dimly apprehended, particles of energy group and regroup themselves in separate magnetic systems; a metaphor ready to hand for the man who can speak of these things with assurance; not for me, who can only say that England abounded in these small companies of intimate friends, so that, as in this case of Julia and myself, we could live in the same street in London, see at times, a few miles distant, the rural horizon, could have a liking one for the other, a mild curiosity about the other's fortunes, a regret, even, that we should be separated, and the knowledge that either of us had only to pick up the telephone and speak by the other's pillow, enjoy the intimacies of the levee, coming in, as it were, with the morning orange juice and the sun, yet be restrained from doing so by the centripetal force of our own worlds, and the cold, interstellar space between them.

My wife, perched on the back of the sofa in a litter of cellophane and silk ribbons, continued telephoning, working brightly through the passenger list . . . 'Yes, do of course bring him, I'm told he's sweet. . . . Yes, I've got Charles back from the wilds at last; isn't it lovely. . . . What a treat seeing your name in the list! It's made my trip . . . darling, we were at the Savoy-Carlton, too; how can we have missed you?' . . . Sometimes she turned to me and said: 'I have to make sure you're still really there. I haven't got used to it yet.'

I went up and out as we steamed slowly down the river to one of the great glass cases where the passengers stood to watch the land slip by. 'Such a lot of friends,' my wife had said. They looked a strange crowd to me; the emotions of leave-taking were just beginning to subside; some of them, who had been drinking till the last moment with those who were seeing them off, were still boisterous; others were planning where they would have their deck chairs; the band played unnoticed – all were as restless as ants.

I turned into some of the halls of the ship, which were huge without any splendour, as though they had been designed for a railway coach and preposterously magnified. I passed through vast bronze gates on which paper-thin Assyrian animals cavorted; I trod carpets the colour of blotting paper, too–kindergarten work in flat, drab colours–and between the walls were yards and yards of biscuit-coloured wood which no carpenter's tool had ever touched, wood that had been bent round corners, invisibly joined strip to strip, steamed and squeezed and polished; all over the blotting-paper carpet were strewn tables designed perhaps by a sanitary engineer, square blocks of stuffing, with square holes for sitting in, and upholstered, it seemed, in blotting paper also; the light of the hall was suffused from scores of hollows, giving an even glow, casting no shadows–the whole place hummed from its hundred ventilators and vibrated with the turn of the great engines below.

'Here I am,' I thought, 'back from the jungle, back from the ruins. Here, where wealth is no longer gorgeous and power has no dignity. *Quomodo sedet sola civitas*' (for I had heard that great lament, which Cordelia once quoted to me in the drawing-room of Marchmain House, sung by a half-caste choir in Guatemala, nearly a year ago).

A steward came up to me.

'Can I get you anything, sir?'

'A whisky and soda, not iced.'

'I'm sorry, sir, *all* the soda is iced.'

'Is the water iced, too?'

'Oh yes, sir.'

'Well, it doesn't matter.'

He trotted off, puzzled, soundless in the pervading hum.

'Charles.'

I looked behind me. Julia was sitting in a cube of blotting paper, her hands folded in her lap, so still that I had passed by without noticing her.

'I heard you were here. Celia telephoned to me. It's delightful.'

'What are you doing?'

She opened the empty hands in her lap with a little eloquent gesture. 'Waiting. My maid's unpacking; she's been so disagreeable ever since we left England. She's complaining now about my cabin. I can't think why. It seems a lap to me.'

The steward returned with whisky and two jugs, one of iced water, the other of boiling water; I mixed them to the right temperature. He watched and said: 'I'll remember that's how you take it, sir.'

Most passengers had fads; he was paid to fortify their self-esteem. Julia asked for a cup of hot chocolate. I sat by her in the next cube.

'I never see you now,' she said. 'I never seem to see anyone I like. I don't know why.'

But she spoke as though it were a matter of weeks rather than of years; as though, too, before our parting we had been firm friends. It was dead contrary to the common experience of such encounters, when time is found to have built its own defensive lines, camouflaged vulnerable points, and laid a field of mines across all but a few well-trodden paths, so that, more often than not, we can only signal to one another from either side of the tangle of wire. Here she and I, who were never friends before, met on terms of long and unbroken intimacy.

'What have you been doing in America?'

She looked up slowly from her chocolate and, her splendid, serious eyes in mine, said: 'Don't you know? I'll tell you about it sometime. I've been a mug. I thought I was in love with someone, but it didn't turn out that way.' And my mind went back ten years to the evening at Brideshead, when that lovely, spidery child of nineteen, as though brought in for an hour from the nursery and nettled by lack of attention from the grown-ups, had said: '*I'm* causing anxiety, too, you know,' and I had thought at the time, though scarcely, it now seemed to me, in long trousers myself, 'How important these girls make themselves with their love affairs.'

Now it was different; there was nothing but humility and friendly candour in the way she spoke.

I wished I could respond to her confidence, give some token of acceptance, but there was nothing in my last, flat, eventful years that I could share with her. I began instead to talk of my time in the jungle, of the comic characters I had met and the lost places I had visited, but in this mood of old friendship the tale faltered and came to an end abruptly.

'I long to see the paintings,' she said.

'Celia wanted me to unpack some and stick them round the cabin for her cocktail party. I couldn't do that.'

'No . . . is Celia as pretty as ever? I always thought she had the most delicious looks of any girl of my year.'

'She hasn't changed.'

'You have, Charles. So lean and grim; not at all the pretty boy Sebastian brought home with him. Harder, too.'

'And you're softer.'

'Yes, I think so . . . and very patient now.'

She was not yet thirty, but was approaching the zenith of her loveliness, all her rich promise abundantly fulfilled. She had lost that fashionable, spidery look; the head that I used to think *quattrocento*, which had sat a little oddly on her, was now part of herself and not at all Florentine; not connected in any way with painting or the arts or with anything except herself, so that it would be idle to itemize and dissect her beauty, which was her own essence, and could only be known in her and by her authority and in the love I was soon to have for her.

Time had wrought another change, too; not for her the sly, complacent smile of la Gioconda; the years had been more than 'the sound of lyres and flutes', and had saddened her. She seemed to say: 'Look at me. I have done my share. I am beautiful. It is something quite out of the ordinary, this beauty of mine. I am made for delight. But what do *I* get out of it? Where is *my* reward?'

That was the change in her from ten years ago; that, indeed, was her reward, this haunting, magical sadness which spoke straight to the heart and struck silence; it was the completion of her beauty.

'Sadder, too,' I said.

'Oh yes, much sadder.'

My wife was in exuberant spirits when, two hours later, I returned to the cabin.

'I've had to do everything. How does it look?'

We had been given, without paying more for it, a large suite of rooms, one so large, in fact, that it was seldom booked except by directors of the line, and on most voyages, the chief purser admitted, was given to those he wished to honour. (My wife was adept in achieving such small advantages, first impressing the impressionable with her chic and my celebrity and, superiority once firmly established, changing quickly to a pose of almost flirtatious affability.) In token of her appreciation the chief purser had been asked to our party and he, in token of his appreciation, had sent before him the life-size effigy of a swan, moulded in ice and filled with caviar. This chilly piece of magnificence now dominated the room, standing on a table in the centre, thawing gently, dripping at the beak into its silver dish. The flowers of the morning delivery hid as much as possible of the panelling (for this room was a miniature of the monstrous hall above).

'You must get dressed at once. Where have you been all this time?'

'Talking to Julia Mottram.'

'D'you know her? Oh, of course, you were a friend of the dipso brother. Goodness, her glamour!'

'She greatly admires your looks, too.'

'She used to be a girl friend of Boy's.'

'Surely not?'

'He always said so.'

'Have you considered,' I asked, 'how your guests are going to eat this caviar?'

'I have. It's insoluble. But there's all this'–she revealed some trays of glassy titbits–'and anyway, people always find ways of eating things at parties. D'you remember we once ate potted shrimps with a paper knife?'

'Did we?'

'Darling, it was the night you popped the question.'

'As I remember, you popped.'

'Well, the night we got engaged. But you haven't said how you like the arrangements.'

The arrangements, apart from the swan and the flowers, consisted of a steward already inextricably trapped in the corner behind an improvised bar, and another steward, tray in hand, in comparative freedom.

'A cinema actor's dream,' I said.

'Cinema actors,' said my wife; 'that's what I want to talk about.'

She came with me to my dressing-room and talked while I changed. It had occurred to her that, with my interest in architecture, my true *métier* was designing scenery for the films, and she had asked two Hollywood magnates to the party with whom she wished to ingratiate me.

We returned to the sitting-room.

'Darling, I believe you've taken against my bird. Don't be beastly about it in front of the purser. It was sweet of him to think of it. Besides, you know, if you had read about it in the description of a sixteenth-century banquet in Venice, you would have said those were the days to live.'

'In sixteenth-century Venice it would have been a somewhat different shape.'

'Here *is* Father Christmas. We were just in raptures over your swan.'

The chief purser came into the room and shook hands, powerfully.

'Dear Lady Celia,' he said, 'if you'll put on your warmest clothes and come on an expedition into the cold storage with me tomorrow, I can show you a whole Noah's Ark of such objects. The toast will be along in a minute. They're keeping it hot.'

'Toast!' said my wife, as though this was something beyond the dreams of gluttony. 'Do you hear that, Charles? *Toast.*'

Soon the guests began to arrive; there was nothing to delay them. 'Celia,' they said, 'what a grand cabin and what a beautiful swan!' and, for all that it was one of the largest in the ship, our room was soon painfully crowded; they began to put out their cigarettes in the little pool of ice-water which now surrounded the swan.

The purser made a sensation, as sailors like to do, by predicting a storm. 'How can you be so beastly?' asked my wife, conveying the flattering suggestion that not only the cabin and the caviar, but the waves, too, were at his command. 'Anyway, storms don't affect a ship like this, do they?'

'Might hold us back a bit.'

'But it wouldn't make us sick?'

'Depends if you're a good sailor. I'm always sick in storms, ever since I was a boy.'

'I don't believe it. He's just being sadistic. Come over here, there's something I want to show you.'

It was the latest photograph of her children. 'Charles hasn't even seen Caroline yet. Isn't it thrilling for him?'

There were no friends of mine there, but I knew about a third of the party, and talked away civilly enough. An elderly woman said to me, 'So you're Charles. I feel I know you through and through, Celia's talked so much about you.'

'Through and through,' I thought. 'Through and through is a long way, madam. Can you indeed see into those dark places where my own eyes seek in vain to guide me? Can you tell me, dear Mrs Stuyvesant Oglander–if I am correct in thinking that is how I heard my wife speak of you–why it is that at this moment, while I talk to you, here, about my forthcoming exhibition, I am thinking all the time only of when Julia will come? Why can I talk like this to you, but not to her? Why have I already set her apart from humankind, and myself with her? What is going on in those secret places of my spirit with which you make so free? What is cooking, Mrs Stuyvesant Oglander?'

Still Julia did not come, and the noise of twenty people in that tiny room, which was so large that no one hired it, was the noise of a multitude.

Then I saw a curious thing. There was a little red-headed man whom no one seemed to know, a dowdy fellow quite unlike the general run of my wife's guests; he had been standing by the caviar for twenty minutes eating as fast as a rabbit. Now he wiped his mouth with his handkerchief and, on the impulse apparently, leaned forward and dabbed the beak of the swan, removing the drop of water that had been swelling there and would soon have fallen. Then he looked round furtively to see if he had been observed, caught my eye, and giggled nervously.

'Been wanting to do that for a long time,' he said. 'Bet you don't know how many drops to the minute. I do, I counted.'

'I've no idea.'

'Guess. Tanner if you're wrong; half a dollar if you're right. That's fair.'

'Three,' I said.

'Coo, you're a sharp one. Been counting 'em yourself.' But he showed no inclination to pay this debt. Instead he said: 'How d'you figure this out. I'm an Englishman born and bred, but this is my first time on the Atlantic.'

'You flew out perhaps?'

'No, nor over it.'

'Then I presume you went round the world and came across the Pacific.'

'You *are* a sharp one and no mistake. I've made quite a bit getting into arguments over that one.'

'What was your route?' I asked, wishing to be agreeable.

'Ah, that'd be telling. Well, I must skedaddle. So long.'

'Charles,' said my wife, 'this is Mr Kramm, of Interastral Films.'

'So you are Mr Charles Ryder,' said Mr Kramm.

'Yes.'

'Well, well, well,' he paused. I waited. 'The purser here says we're heading for dirty weather. What d'you know about that?'

'Far less than the purser.'

'Pardon me, Mr Ryder, I don't quite get you.'

'I mean I know less than the purser.'

'Is that so? Well, well, well. I've enjoyed our talk very much. I hope that it will be the first of many.'

An Englishwoman said: 'Oh, that swan! Six weeks in America has given me an absolute phobia of ice. Do tell me, how did it feel meeting Celia again after two years? I know I should feel indecently bridal. But Celia's never quite got the orange blossom out of her hair, has she?'

Another woman said: 'Isn't it heaven saying good-bye and knowing we shall meet again in half an hour and go on meeting every half-hour for days?'

Our guests began to go, and each on leaving informed me of something my wife had promised to bring me to in the near future; it was the theme of the evening that we should all be seeing a lot of each other, that we had formed one of those molecular systems that physicists can illustrate. At last the swan was wheeled out, too, and I said to my wife, 'Julia never came.'

'No, she telephoned. I couldn't hear what she said, there was such a noise going on–something about a dress. Quite lucky really, there wasn't room for a cat. It was a lovely party, wasn't it? Did you hate it very much? You behaved beautifully and looked so distinguished. Who was your red-haired chum?'

'No chum of mine.'

'How *very* peculiar! Did you say anything to Mr Kramm about working in Hollywood?'

'Of course not.'

'Oh, Charles, you are a worry to me. It's not enough just to stand about looking distinguished and a martyr for Art. Let's go to dinner. We're at the Captain's table. I don't suppose he'll dine down tonight, but it's polite to be fairly punctual.'

By the time that we reached the table the rest of the party had arranged themselves. On either side of the Captain's empty chair sat Julia and Mrs Stuyvesant Oglander; besides them there was an English diplomat and his wife, Senator Stuyvesant Oglander, and an American clergyman at present totally isolated between two pairs of empty chairs. This clergyman later described himself–redundantly it seemed–as an Episcopalian Bishop. Husbands and wives sat together here. My wife was confronted with a quick decision, and although the steward attempted to direct us otherwise, sat so that she had the senator and I the Bishop. Julia gave us both a little dismal signal of sympathy.

'I'm miserable about the party,' she said, 'my beastly maid totally disappeared with every dress I have. She only turned up half an hour ago. She'd been playing ping-pong.'

'I've been telling the Senator what he missed,' said Mrs Stuyvesant Oglander. 'Wherever Celia is, you'll find she knows all the significant people.'

'On my right,' said the Bishop, 'a significant couple are expected. They take all their meals in their cabin except when they have been informed in advance that the Captain will be present.'

We were a gruesome circle; even my wife's high social spirit faltered. At moments I heard bits of her conversation.

'. . . an extraordinary little red-haired man. Captain Foulenough in person.'

'But I understood you to say, Lady Celia, that you were unacquainted with him.'

'I meant he was *like* Captain Foulenough.'

'I begin to comprehend. He impersonated this friend of yours in order to come to your party.'

'No, no. Captain Foulenough is simply a comic character.'

'There seems to have been nothing very amusing about this other man. Your friend is a comedian?'

'No, no. Captain Foulenough is an imaginary character in an English paper. You know, like your "Popeye".'

The senator laid down knife and fork. 'To recapitulate: an imposter came to your party and you admitted him because of a fancied resemblance to a fictitious character in a cartoon.'

'Yes, I suppose that was it really.'

The senator looked at his wife as much as to say: 'Significant people, huh!'

I heard Julia across the table trying to trace, for the benefit of the diplomat, the marriage-connexions of her Hungarian and Italian cousins. The diamonds flashed in her hair and on her fingers, but her hands were nervously rolling little balls of crumb, and her starry head drooped in despair.

The Bishop told me of the goodwill mission on which he was travelling to Barcelona . . . 'a very, very valuable work of clearance has been performed, Mr Ryder. The time has now come to rebuild on broader foundations. I have made it my aim to reconcile the so-called Anarchists and the so-called Communists, and with that in view I and my committee have digested all the available documentation of the subject. Our conclusion, Mr Ryder, is unanimous. There is *no* fundamental diversity between the two ideologies. It is a matter of personalities, Mr Ryder, and what personalities have put asunder personalities can unite. . . .'

On the other side I heard: 'And may I make so bold as to ask what institutions sponsored your husband's expedition?'

The diplomat's wife bravely engaged the Bishop across the gulf that separated them.

'And what language will you speak when you get to Barcelona?'

'The language of Reason and Brotherhood, madam,' and, turning back to me, 'The speech of the coming century is in thoughts not in words. Do you not agree, Mr Ryder?'

'Yes,' I said. 'Yes.'

'What are words?' said the Bishop.

'What indeed?'

'Mere conventional symbols, Mr Ryder, and this is an age rightly sceptical of conventional symbols.'

My mind reeled; after the parrot-house fever of my wife's party, and unplumbed emotions of the afternoon, after all the exertions of my wife's pleasures in New York, after the months of solitude in the steaming, green shadows of the jungle, this was too much. I felt like Lear on the heath, like the Duchess of Malfi bayed by madmen. I summoned cataracts and hurricanoes, and as if by conjury the call was immediately answered.

For some time now, though whether it was a mere trick of the nerves I did not then know, I had felt a recurrent and persistently growing motion–a heave and shudder of the large dining-room as of the breast of a man in deep sleep. Now my wife turned to me and said: 'Either I am a little drunk or it's getting rough,' and, even as she spoke we found ourselves leaning sideways in our chairs; there was a crash and tinkle of falling cutlery by the wall, and on our table the wine glasses all together toppled and rolled over, while each of us steadied the plate and forks and looked at the other with expressions that varied between frank horror in the diplomat's wife and relief in Julia.

The gale which, unheard, unseen, unfelt, in our enclosed and insulated world had, for an hour, been mounting over us, had now veered and fallen full on our bows.

Silence followed the crash, then a high, nervous babble of laughter. Stewards laid napkins on the pools of spilt wine. We tried to resume the conversation, but all were waiting, as the little ginger man had watched the drop swell and fall from the swan's beak, for the next great blow; it came, heavier than the last.

'This is where I say good night to you all,' said the diplomat's wife, rising.

Her husband led her to their cabin. The dining-room was emptying fast. Soon only Julia, my wife, and I were left at the table, and, telepathically, Julia said, 'Like King Lear.'

'Only each of us is all three of them.'

'What can you mean?' asked my wife.

'Lear, Kent, Fool.'

'Oh, dear, it's like that agonizing Foulenough conversation over again. Don't try and explain.'

'I doubt if I could,' I said.

Another climb, another vast drop. The stewards were at work making things fast, shutting things up, hustling away unstable ornaments.

'Well, we've finished dinner and set a fine example of British phlegm,' said my wife. 'Let's go and see what's on.'

Once, on our way to the lounge, we had all three to cling to a pillar; when we got there we found it almost deserted; the band played but no one danced; the tables were set for tombola but no one bought a card, and the ship's officer, who made a speciality of calling the numbers with all the patter of the lower deck–'sweet sixteen and never been kissed–key of the door, twenty-one–clickety-click, sixty-six'–was idly talking to his colleagues; there were a score of scattered novel readers, a few games of bridge, some brandy drinking in the smoking-room, but all our guests of two hours before had disappeared.

The three of us sat for a little by the empty dance floor; my wife was full of schemes by which, without impoliteness, we could move to another table in the dining-room. 'It's crazy to go to the restaurant,' she said, 'and pay extra for exactly the same dinner. Only film people go there, anyway. I don't see why we should be made to.'

Presently she said: 'It's making my head ache and I'm tired, anyway. I'm going to bed.'

Julia went with her. I walked round the ship, on one of the covered decks where the wind howled and the spray leaped up from the darkness and smashed white and brown against the glass screen; men were posted to keep the passengers off the open decks. Then I, too, went below.

In my dressing-room everything breakable had been stowed away, the door to the cabin was hooked open, and my wife called plaintively from within.

'I feel terrible. I didn't know a ship of this size could pitch like this,' she said, and her eyes were full of consternation and resentment, like those of a woman who, at the end of her time, at length realizes that however luxurious the nursing home, and however well paid the doctor, her labour is inevitable; and the lift and fall of the ship came regularly as the pains of childbirth.

I slept next door; or, rather, I lay there between dreaming and waking. In a narrow bunk, on a hard mattress, there might have been rest, but here the beds were broad and buoyant; I collected what cushions I could find and tried to wedge myself firm, but through the night I turned with each swing and twist of the ship–she was rolling now as well as pitching–and my head rang with the creak and thud.

Once, an hour before dawn, my wife appeared like a ghost in the doorway, supporting herself with either hand on the jambs, saying: 'Are you awake? Can't you do something? Can't you get something from the doctor?'

I rang for the night steward, who had a draught ready prepared, which comforted her a little.

And all night between dreaming and waking I thought of Julia; in my brief dreams she took a hundred fantastic and terrible and obscene forms, but in my waking thoughts she returned with her sad, starry head just as I had seen her at dinner.

After first light I slept for an hour or two, then awoke clear-headed, with a joyous sense of anticipation.

The wind had dropped a little, the steward told me, but was still blowing hard and there was a very heavy swell; 'which there's nothing worse than a heavy swell', he said, 'for the enjoyment of the passengers. There's not many breakfasts wanted this morning.'

I looked in at my wife, found her sleeping, and closed the door between us; then I ate salmon kedgeree and cold Bradenham ham and telephoned for a barber to come and shave me.

'There's a lot of stuff in the sitting-room for the lady,' said the steward; 'shall I leave it for the time?'

I went to see. There was a second delivery of cellophane parcels from the shops on board, some ordered by radio from friends in New York whose secretaries had failed to remind them of our departure in time, some by our guests as they left the cocktail party. It was no day for flower vases; I told him to leave them on the floor and then, struck by the thought, removed the card from Mr Kramm's roses and sent them with my love to Julia.

She telephoned while I was being shaved.

'What a deplorable thing to do, Charles! How unlike you!'

'Don't you like them?'

'What can I do with roses on a day like this?'

'Smell them.'

There was a pause and a rustle of unpacking. 'They've absolutely no smell at all.'

'What have you had for breakfast?'

'Muscat grapes and cantaloup.'

'When shall I see you?'

'Before lunch. I'm busy till then with a masseuse.'

'A masseuse?'

'Yes, isn't it peculiar? I've never had one before, except once when I hurt my shoulder hunting. What is it about being on a boat that makes everyone behave like a film star?'

'I don't.'

'How about these very embarrassing roses?'

The barber did his work with extraordinary dexterity–indeed, with agility, for he stood like a swordsman in a ballet sometimes on the point of one foot, sometimes on the other, lightly flicking the lather off his blade, and swooping back to my chin as the ship righted herself; I should not have dared use a safety razor on myself.

The telephone rang again.

It was my wife.

'How are you, Charles?'

'Tired.'

'Aren't you coming to see me?'

'I came once. I'll be in again.'

I brought her the flowers from the sitting-room; they completed the atmosphere of a maternity ward which she had managed to create in the cabin; the stewardess had the air of a midwife, standing by the bed, a pillar of starched linen and composure. My wife turned her head on the pillow and smiled wanly; she stretched out a bare arm and caressed with the tips of her fingers the cellophane and silk ribbons of the largest bouquet. 'How sweet people are,' she said faintly, as though the gale were a private misfortune of her own for which the world in its love was condoling with her.

'I take it you're not getting up.'

'Oh no, Mrs Clark is being so sweet'; she was always quick to get servants' names. 'Don't bother. Come in sometimes and tell me what's going on.'

'Now, now, dear,' said the stewardess, 'the less we are disturbed today the better.'

My wife seemed to make a sacred, female rite even of seasickness.

Julia's cabin, I knew, was somewhere below ours. I waited for her by the lift on the main deck; when she came we walked once round the promenade; I held the rail; she took my other arm. It was hard going; through the streaming glass we saw a distorted world of grey sky and black water. When the ship rolled heavily I swung her round so that she could hold the rail with her other hand; the howl of the wind was subdued, but the whole ship creaked with strain. We made the circuit once, then Julia said: 'It's no good. That woman beat hell out of me, and I feel limp, anyway. Let's sit down.'

The great bronze doors of the lounge had torn away from their hooks and were swinging free with the roll of the ship; regularly and, it seemed, irresistibly, first one, then the other, opened and shut; they paused at the completion of each half circle, began to move slowly and finished fast with a resounding clash. There was no real risk in passing them, except of slipping and being caught by that swift, final blow; there was ample time to walk through unhurried but there was something forbidding in the sight of that great weight of uncontrolled metal, flapping to and fro, which might have made a timid man flinch or skip through too quickly; I rejoiced to feel Julia's hand perfectly steady on my arm and know, as I walked beside her, that she was wholly undismayed.

'Bravo,' said a man sitting nearby. 'I confess I went round the other way. I didn't like the look of those doors somehow. They've been trying to fix them all the morning.'

There were few people about that day, and that few seemed bound together by a camaraderie of reciprocal esteem; they did nothing except sit rather glumly in their armchairs, drink occasionally, and exchange congratulations on not being seasick.

'You're the first lady I've seen,' said the man.

'I'm very lucky.'

'*We* are very lucky,' he said, with a movement which began as a bow and ended as a lurch forward to his knees, as the blotting-paper floor dipped steeply between us. The roll carried us away from him, clinging together but still on our feet, and we quickly sat where our dance led us, on the further side, in isolation; a web of life-lines had been stretched across the lounge, and we seemed like boxers, roped into the ring.

The steward approached. 'Your usual, sir? Whisky and tepid water, I think. And for the lady? Might I suggest a nip of champagne?'

'D'you know, the awful thing is I *would* like champagne very much,' said Julia. 'What a life of pleasure–roses, half an hour with a female pugilist, and now champagne!'

'I wish you wouldn't go on about the roses. It wasn't my idea in the first place. Someone sent them to Celia.'

'Oh, that's quite different. It lets you out completely. But it makes my massage worse.'

'I was shaved in bed.'

'I'm glad about the roses,' said Julia. 'Frankly, they were a shock. They made me think we were starting the day on the wrong foot.'

I knew what she meant, and in that moment felt as though I had shaken off some of the dust and grit of ten dry years; then and always, however she spoke to me, in half sentences, single words, stock phrases of contemporary jargon, in scarcely perceptible movements of eyes or lips or hands, however inexpressible her thought, however quick and far it had glanced from the matter in hand, however deep it had plunged, as it often did, straight from the surface to the depths, I knew; even that day when I still stood on the extreme verge of love, I knew what she meant.

We drank our wine and soon our new friend came lurching towards us down the life-line.

'Mind if I join you? Nothing like a bit of rough weather for bringing people together. This is my tenth crossing, and I've never seen anything like it. I can see you are an experienced sailor, young lady.'

'No. As a matter of fact, I've never been at sea before except coming to New York and, of course, crossing the Channel. I don't feel sick, thank God, but I feel tired. I thought at first it was only the massage, but I'm coming to the conclusion it's the ship.'

'My wife's in a terrible way. She's an experienced sailor. Only shows, doesn't it?'

He joined us at luncheon, and I did not mind his being there; he had clearly taken a fancy to Julia, and he thought we were man and wife; this misconception and his gallantry seemed in some way to bring her and me closer together. 'Saw you two last night at the Captain's table,' he said, 'with all the nobs.'

'Very dull nobs.'

'If you ask me, nobs always are. When you get a storm like this you find out what people are really made of.'

'You have a predilection for good sailors?'

'Well, put like that I don't know that I do–what I mean is, it makes for getting together.'

'Yes.'

'Take us for example. But for this we might never have met. I've had some very romantic encounters at sea in my time. If the lady will excuse me, I'd like to tell you about a little adventure I had in the Gulf of Lions when I was younger than I am now.'

We were both weary; lack of sleep, the incessant din, and the strain every movement required, wore us down. We spent that afternoon apart in our cabins. I slept and when I awoke the sea was as high as ever, inky clouds swept over us, and the glass streamed still with water, but I had grown used to the storm in my sleep, had made its rhythm mine, had become part of it, so that I arose strongly and confidently and found Julia already up and in the same temper.

'What d'you think?' she said. 'That man's giving a little "get-together party" tonight in the smoking-room for all the good sailors. He asked me to bring my husband.'

'Are we going?'

'Of course. . . . I wonder if I ought to feel like the lady our friend met on the way to Barcelona. I don't, Charles not a bit.'

There were eighteen people at the 'get-together party'; we had nothing in common except immunity from seasickness. We drank champagne, and presently our host said: 'Tell you what, I've got a roulette wheel. Trouble is we can't go to my cabin on account of the wife, and we aren't allowed to play in public.'

So the party adjourned to my sitting-room and we played for low stakes until late into the night, when Julia left and our host had drunk too much wine to be surprised that she and I were not in the same quarters. When all but he had gone, he fell asleep in his chair, and I left him there. It was the last I saw of him, for later–so the steward told me when he came from returning the roulette things to the man's cabin–he broke his thigh, falling in the corridor, and was taken to the ship's hospital.

All next day Julia and I spent together without interruption; talking, scarcely moving, held in our chairs by the swell of the sea. After luncheon the last hardy passengers went to rest and we were alone as though the place had been cleared for us, as though tact on a titanic scale had sent everyone tip-toeing out to leave us to one another.

The bronze doors of the lounge had been fixed, but not before two seamen had been badly injured. They had tried various devices, lashing with ropes and, later, when these failed, with steel hawsers, but there was nothing to which they could be made fast; finally, they drove wooden wedges under them, catching them in the brief moment of repose when they were full open, and these held firm.

When, before dinner, she went to her cabin to get ready (no one dressed that night) and I came with her, uninvited, unopposed, expected, and behind closed doors took her in my arms and first kissed her, there was no alteration from the mood of the afternoon. Later, turning it over in my mind, as I turned in my bed with the rise and fall of the ship, through the long, lonely, drowsy night, I recalled the courtships of the past, dead, ten years; how, knotting my tie before setting out, putting the gardenia in my buttonhole, I would plan my evening and think at such and such a time, at such and such an opportunity, I shall cross the start-line and open my attack for better or worse; 'this phase of the battle has gone on long enough', I would think; 'a decision must be reached.' With Julia there were no phases, no start-line, no tactics at all.

But later that night when she went to bed and I followed her to her door, she stopped me.

'No, Charles, not yet. Perhaps never. I don't know. I don't know if I want love.'

Then something, some surviving ghost from those dead ten years–for one cannot die, even for a little, without some loss–made me say, 'Love? I'm not asking for love.'

'Oh yes, Charles, you are,' she said, and putting up her hand gently stroked my cheek; then shut her door.

And I reeled back, first on one wall, then on the other, of the long, softly lighted, empty corridor; for the storm, it appeared, had the form of a ring; all day we had been sailing through its still centre; now we were once more in the full fury of the wind–and that night was to be rougher than the one before.

Ten hours of talking: what had we to say? Plain fact mostly, the record of our two lives, so long widely separate, now being knit to one. Through all that storm-tossed night I rehearsed what she had told me; she was no longer the alternate succubus and starry vision of the night before; she had given all that was transferable of her past into my keeping. She told me, as I have already retold, of her courtship and marriage; she told me, as though fondly turning the pages of an old nursery-book, of her childhood, and I lived long, sunny days with her in the meadows, with Nanny Hawkins on her camp stool and Cordelia asleep in the pram, slept quiet nights under the dome with the religious pictures fading round the cot as the nightlight burned low and the embers settled in the grate. She told me of her life with Rex and of the secret, vicious, disastrous escapade that had taken her to New York. She, too, had had her dead years. She told me of her long struggle with Rex as to whether she should have a child; at first she wanted one, but learned after a year that an operation was needed to make it possible; by that time Rex and she were out of love, but he still wanted his child, and when at last she consented, it was born dead.

'Rex has never been unkind to me intentionally,' she said. 'It's just that he isn't a real person at all; he's just a few faculties of a man highly developed; the rest simply isn't there. He couldn't imagine why it hurt me to find two months after we came back to London from our honeymoon, that he was still keeping up with Brenda Champion.'

'I was glad when I found Celia was unfaithful,' I said. 'I felt it was all right for me to dislike her.'

'Is she? Do you? I'm glad. I don't like her either. Why did you marry her?'

'Physical attraction. Ambition. Everyone agrees she's the ideal wife for a painter. Loneliness, missing Sebastian.'

'You loved him, didn't you?'

'Oh yes. He was the forerunner.'

Julia understood.

The ship creaked and shuddered, rose and fell. My wife called to me from the next room: 'Charles, are you there?'

'Yes.'

'I've been asleep such a long while. What time is it?'

'Half past three.'

'It's no better, is it?'

'Worse.'

'I feel a little better, though. D'you think they'd bring me some tea or something if I rang the bell?'

I got her some tea and biscuits from the night steward.

'Did you have an amusing evening?'

'Everyone's seasick.'

'Poor Charles. It was going to have been such a lovely trip, too. It may be better tomorrow.'

I turned out the light and shut the door between us.

Waking and dreaming, through the strain and creak and heave of the long night, firm on my back with my arms and legs spread wide to check the roll, and my eyes open to the darkness, I lay thinking of Julia.

'. . . We thought papa might come back to England after mummy died, or that he might marry again, but he lives just as he did. Rex and I often go to see him now. I've grown fond of him. . . . Sebastian's disappeared completely . . . Cordelia's in Spain with an ambulance . . . Bridey leads his own extraordinary life. He wanted to shut Brideshead after mummy died, but papa wouldn't have it for some reason, so Rex and I live there now, and Bridey has two rooms up in the dome, next to Nanny Hawkins, part of the old nurseries. He's like a character from Chekhov. One meets him sometimes coming out of the library or on the stairs–I never know when he's at home–and now and then he suddenly comes in to dinner like a ghost quite unexpectedly.

'. . . Oh, Rex's parties! Politics and money. They can't do anything except for money; if they walk round the lake they have to make bets about how many swans they see . . . sitting up till two, amusing Rex's girls, hearing them gossip, rattling away endlessly on the backgammon board while the men play cards and smoke cigars. The cigar smoke. I can smell it in my hair when I wake up in the morning; it's in my clothes when I dress at night. Do I smell of it now? D'you think that woman who rubbed me, felt it in my skin?

'. . . At first I used to stay away with Rex in his friends' houses. He doesn't make me any more. He was ashamed of me when he found I didn't cut the kind of figure he wanted, ashamed of himself for having been taken in. I wasn't at all the article he'd bargained for. He can't see the point of me, but whenever he's made up his mind there isn't a point and he's begun to feel comfortable, he gets a surprise–some man, or even woman, he respects, takes a fancy to me and he suddenly sees that there is a whole world of things we understand and he doesn't . . . he was upset when I went away. He'll be delighted to have me back. I was faithful to him until this last thing came along. There's nothing like a good upbringing. Do you know last year, when I thought I was going to have a child, I'd decided to have it brought up a Catholic? I hadn't thought about religion before; I haven't since; but just at that time, when I was waiting for the birth, I thought, "That's one thing I can give her. It doesn't seem to have done me much good, but my child shall have it." It was odd, wanting to give something one had lost oneself. Then, in the end, I couldn't even give that: I couldn't even give her life. I never saw her; I was too ill to know what was going on, and afterwards, for a long time, until now, I didn't want to speak about her–she was a daughter, so Rex didn't so much mind her being dead.

'I've been punished a little for marrying Rex. You see, I can't get all that sort of thing out of my mind, quite–Death, Judgement, Heaven, Hell, Nanny

Hawkins, and the catechism. It becomes part of oneself, if they give it one early enough. And yet I wanted my child to have it . . . now I suppose I shall be punished for what I've just done. Perhaps that is why you and I are here together like this . . . part of a plan.'

That was almost the last thing she said to me–'part of a plan'–before we went below and I left her at the cabin door.

Next day the wind had again dropped, and again we were wallowing in the swell. The talk was less of seasickness now than of broken bones; people had been thrown about in the night, and there had been many nasty accidents on bathroom floors.

That day, because we had talked so much the day before and because what we had to say needed few words, we spoke little. We had books; Julia found a game she liked. When after long silences we spoke, our thoughts, we found, had kept pace together side by side.

Once I said, 'You are standing guard over your sadness.'

'It's all I have earned. You said yesterday. My wages.'

'An I.O.U. from life. A promise to pay on demand.'

Rain ceased at midday; at evening the clouds dispersed and the sun, astern of us, suddenly broke into the lounge where we sat, putting all the lights to shame.

'Sunset,' said Julia, 'the end of our day.'

She rose and, though the roll and pitch of the ship seemed unabated, led me up to the boat-deck. She put her arm through mine and her hand into mine, in my great-coat pocket. The deck was dry and empty, swept only by the wind of the ship's speed. As we made our halting, laborious way forward, away from the flying smuts of the smoke stack, we were alternately jostled together, then strained, nearly sundered, arms and fingers interlocked as I held the rail and Julia clung to me, thrust together again, drawn apart; then, in a plunge deeper than the rest, I found myself flung across her, pressing her against the rail, warding myself off her with the arms that held her prisoner on either side, and as the ship paused at the end of its drop as though gathering strength for the ascent, we stood thus embraced, in the open, cheek against cheek, her hair blowing across my eyes; the dark horizon of tumbling water, flashing now with gold, stood still above us, then came sweeping down till I was staring through Julia's dark hair into a wide and golden sky, and she was thrown forward on my heart, held up by my hands on the rail, her face still pressed to mine.

In that minute, with her lips to my ear and her breath warm in the salt wind, Julia said, though I had not spoken, 'Yes, now,' and as the ship righted herself and for the moment ran into calmer waters, Julia led me below.

It was no time for the sweets of luxury; they would come, in their season, with the swallow and the lime flowers. Now on the rough water there was a formality to be observed, no more. It was as though a deed of conveyance of her narrow loins had been drawn and sealed. I was making my first entry as the freeholder of a property I would enjoy and develop at leisure.

We dined that night high up in the ship, in the restaurant, and saw through the bow windows the stars come out and sweep across the sky as once, I remembered, I had seen them sweep above the towers and gables of Oxford. The stewards promised that tomorrow night the band would play again and the place be full. We had better book now, they said, if we wanted a good table.

'Oh dear,' said Julia, 'where can we hide in fair weather, we orphans of the storm?'

I could not leave her that night, but early next morning, as once again I made my way back along the corridor, I found I could walk without difficulty; the ship rode easily on a smooth sea, and I knew that our solitude was broken.

My wife called joyously from her cabin: 'Charles, Charles, I feel so well. What do you think I am having for breakfast?'

I went to see. She was eating a beef steak.

'I've fixed up for a visit to the hairdresser–do you know they couldn't take me till four o'clock this afternoon, they're so busy suddenly? So I shan't appear till the evening, but lots of people are coming in to see us this morning, and I've asked Miles and Janet to lunch with us in our sitting-room. I'm afraid I've been a worthless wife to you the last two days. What have you been up to?'

'One gay evening', I said, 'we played roulette till two o'clock, next door in the sitting-room, and our host passed out.'

'Goodness. It sounds very disreputable. Have you been behaving, Charles? You haven't been picking up sirens?'

'There was scarcely a woman about. I spent most of the time with Julia.'

'Oh, good. I always wanted to bring you together. She's one of my friends I knew you'd like. I expect you were a godsend to her. She's had rather a gloomy time lately. I don't expect she mentioned it, but . . .' my wife proceeded to relate a current version of Julia's journey to New York. 'I'll ask her to cocktails this morning,' she concluded.

Julia came among the others, and it was happiness enough, now merely to be near her.

'I hear you've been looking after my husband for me,' my wife said.

'Yes, we've become very matey. He and I and a man whose name we don't know.'

'Mr Kramm, what have you done to your arm?'

'It was the bathroom floor,' said Mr Kramm, and explained at length how he had fallen.

That night the captain dined at his table and the circle was complete, for claimants came to the chairs on the Bishop's right, two Japanese who expressed deep interest in his projects for world-brotherhood. The captain was full of chaff at Julia's endurance in the storm, offering to engage her as a seaman; years of sea-going had given him jokes for every occasion. My wife, fresh from the beauty parlour, was unmarked by her three days of distress, and in the eyes of many seemed to outshine Julia, whose sadness had gone and been replaced by an incommunicable content and tranquillity; incommunicable save to me; she and I, separated by the crowd, sat alone together close enwrapped, as we had lain in each other's arms the night before.

There was a gala spirit in the ship that night. Though it meant rising at dawn to pack, everyone was determined that for this one night he would enjoy the luxury the storm had denied him. There was no solitude. Every corner of the ship was thronged; dance music and high, excited chatter, stewards darting everywhere with trays of glasses, the voice of the officer in charge of tombola–'Kelly's eye–number one; legs, eleven; and we'll Shake the Bag'–Mrs Stuyvesant Oglander in a paper cap, Mr Kramm and his bandages, the two Japanese decorously throwing paper streamers and hissing like geese.

I did not speak to Julia, alone, all that evening.

We met for a minute next day on the starboard side of the ship while everyone else crowded to port to see the officials come aboard and to gaze at the green coastline of Devon.

'What are your plans?'

'London for a bit,' she said.

'Celia's going straight home. She wants to see the children.'

'You, too?'

'No.'

'In London then.'

'Charles, the little red-haired man–Foulenough. Did you see? Two plain clothes police have taken him off.'

'I missed it. There was such a crowd on that side of the ship.'

'I found out the trains and sent a telegram. We shall be home by dinner. The children will be asleep. Perhaps we might wake Johnjohn up, just for once.'

'You go down,' I said. 'I shall have to stay in London.'

'Oh, but Charles, you *must* come. You haven't seen Caroline.'

'Will she change much in a week or two?'

'Darling, she changes every day.'

'Then what's the point of seeing her now? I'm sorry, my dear, but I must get the pictures unpacked and see how they've travelled. I must fix up for the exhibition right away.'

'Must you?' she said, but I knew that her resistance ended when I appealed to the mysteries of my trade. 'It's very disappointing. Besides, I don't know if Andrew and Cynthia will be out of the flat. They took it till the end of the month.'

'I can go to an hotel.'

'But that's so grim. I can't bear you to be alone your first night home. I'll stay and go down tomorrow.'

'You mustn't disappoint the children.'

'No.' Her children, my art, the two mysteries of our trades.

'Will you come for the week-end?'

'If I can.'

'All British passports to the smoking-room, please,' said a steward.

'I've arranged with that sweet Foreign Office man at our table to get us off early with him,' said my wife.

2

It was my wife's idea to hold the private view on Friday.

'We are out to catch the critics this time,' she said. 'It's high time they began to take you seriously, and they know it. This is their chance. If you open on Monday, they'll most of them have just come up from the country, and they'll dash off a few paragraphs before dinner–I'm only worrying about the weeklies of course. If we give them the week-end to think about it, we shall have them in an urbane Sunday-in-the-country mood. They'll settle down after a good luncheon, tuck up their cuffs, and turn out a nice, leisurely full-length essay, which they'll reprint later in a nice little book. Nothing less will do this time.'

She was up and down from the Old Rectory several times during the month of preparation, revising the list of invitations and helping with the hanging.

On the morning of the private view I telephoned to Julia and said: 'I'm sick of the pictures already and never want to see them again, but I suppose I shall have to put in an appearance.'

'D'you want me to come?'

'I'd much rather you didn't.'

'Celia sent a card with "Bring everyone" written across it in green ink. When do we meet?'

'In the train. You might pick up my luggage.'

'If you'll have it packed soon I'll pick you up, too, and drop you at the gallery. I've got a fitting next door at twelve.'

When I reached the gallery my wife was standing looking through the window to the street. Behind her half a dozen unknown picture-lovers were moving from canvas to canvas, catalogue in hand; they were people who had once bought a wood-cut and were consequently on the gallery's list of patrons.

'No one has come yet,' said my wife. 'I've been here since ten and it's been very dull. Whose car was that you came in?'

'Julia's.'

'Julia's? Why didn't you bring her in? Oddly enough, I've just been talking about Brideshead to a funny little man who seemed to know us very well. He said he was called Mr Samgrass. Apparently he's one of Lord Copper's middle-aged young men on the *Daily Beast*. I tried to feed him some paragraphs, but he seemed to know more about you than I do. He said he'd met me years ago at Brideshead. I wish Julia had come in; then we could have asked her about him.'

'I remember him well. He's a crook.'

'Yes, that stuck out a mile. He's been talking all about what he calls the "Brideshead set". Apparently Rex Mottram has made the place a nest of party mutiny. Did you know? What would Teresa Marchmain have thought?'

'I'm going there tonight.'

'Not tonight, Charles; you can't go there *tonight*. You're expected at home. You promised, as soon as the exhibition was ready, you'd come home. Johnjohn and Nanny have made a banner with "Welcome" on it. And you haven't seen Caroline yet.'

'I'm sorry, it's all settled.'

'Besides, Daddy will think it so odd. And Boy is home for Sunday. And you haven't seen the new studio. You can't go tonight. Did they ask me?'

'Of course; but I knew you wouldn't be able to come.'

'I can't now. I could have, if you'd let me know earlier. I should adore to see the "Brideshead set" at home. I do think you're perfectly beastly, but this is no time for a family rumpus. The Clarences promised to come in before luncheon; they may be here any minute.'

We were interrupted, however, not by royalty, but by a woman reporter from one of the dailies, whom the manager of the gallery now led up to us. She had not come to see the pictures but to get a "human story" of the dangers of my journey. I left her to my wife, and next day read in her paper: '*Charles "Stately Homes" Ryder steps off the map. That the snakes and vampires of the jungle have nothing on Mayfair is the opinion of socialite artist Ryder, who has abandoned the houses of the great for the ruins of equatorial Africa. . . .*'

The rooms began to fill and I was soon busy being civil. My wife was everywhere, greeting people, introducing people, deftly transforming the crowd into a party. I saw her lead friends forward one after another to the subscription list that had been opened for the book of *Ryder's Latin America*; I heard her say: 'No, darling, I'm not at all surprised, but you wouldn't expect *me* to be, would you? You see Charles lives for one thing–Beauty. I think he got bored with finding it ready-made in England; he had to go and create it for himself. He wanted new worlds to conquer. After all, he has said the last word about country houses, hasn't he? Not, I mean, that he's given that up altogether. I'm sure he'll always do one or two more for *friends*.'

A photographer brought us together, flashed a lamp in our faces, and let us part.

Presently there was the slight hush and edging away which follows the entry of a royal party. I saw my wife curtsey and heard her say: 'Oh, sir, you are sweet'; then I was led into the clearing and the Duke of Clarence said: 'Pretty hot out there I should think.'

'It was, sir.'

'Awfully clever the way you've hit off the impression of heat. Makes me feel quite uncomfortable in my great-coat.'

'Ha, ha.'

When they had gone my wife said: 'Goodness, we're late for lunch. Margot's giving a party in your honour,' and in the taxi she said: 'I've just thought of something. Why don't you write and ask the Duchess of Clarence's permission to dedicate *Latin America* to her?'

'Why should I?'

'She'd love it so.'

'I wasn't thinking of dedicating it to anyone.'

'There you are; that's typical of you, Charles. Why miss an opportunity to give pleasure?'

There were a dozen at luncheon, and though it pleased my hostess and my wife to say that they were there in my honour, it was plain to me that half of them did not know of my exhibition and had come because they had been invited and had no other engagement. Throughout luncheon they talked, without stopping, of Mrs Simpson, but they all, or nearly all, came back with us to the gallery.

The hour after luncheon was the busiest time. There were representatives of the Tate Gallery and the National Art Collections Fund, who all promised to return shortly with colleagues and, in the meantime, reserved certain pictures for further consideration. The most influential critic, who in the past had dismissed me with a few wounding commendations, peered out at me from between his slouch hat and woollen muffler, gripped my arm, and said: 'I knew you had it. I saw it there. I've been waiting for it.'

From fashionable and unfashionable lips alike I heard fragments of praise. 'If you'd asked me to guess,' I overheard, 'Ryder's is the last name would have occurred to me. They're so virile, so passionate.'

They all thought they had found something new. It had not been thus at my last exhibition in these same rooms, shortly before my going abroad. Then there had been an unmistakable note of weariness. Then the talk had been less of me than of the houses, anecdotes of their owners. That same woman, it came back to me, who now applauded my virility and passion, had stood quite near me, before a painfully laboured canvas, and said, 'So facile'.

I remembered the exhibition, too, for another reason; it was the week I detected my wife in adultery. Then, as now, she was a tireless hostess, and I heard her say: 'Whenever I see anything lovely nowadays–a building or a piece of scenery–I think to myself, "that's by Charles". I see everything through his eyes. He *is* England to me.'

I heard her say that; it was the sort of thing she had the habit of saying. Throughout our married life, again and again, I had felt my bowels shrivel within me at the things she said. But that day, in this gallery, I heard her unmoved, and suddenly realized that she was powerless to hurt me any more; I was a free man; she had given me my manumission in that brief, sly lapse of hers; my cuckold's horns made me lord of the forest.

At the end of the day my wife said: 'Darling, I must go. It's been a terrific success, hasn't it? I'll think of something to tell them at home, but I wish it hadn't got to happen quite this way.'

'So she knows,' I thought. 'She's a sharp one. She's had her nose down since luncheon and picked up the scent.'

I let her get clear of the place and was about to follow–the rooms were nearly empty–when I heard a voice at the turnstile I had not heard for many years, an unforgettable self-taught stammer, a sharp cadence of remonstration.

'No. I have *not* brought a card of invitation. I do not even know whether I received one. I have not come to a social function; I do not seek to scrape acquaintance with Lady Celia; I do not want my photograph in the *Tatler*; I have not come to exhibit myself. I have come to see the *pictures*. Perhaps you are unaware that there are any pictures here. I happen to have a personal interest in the *artist*–if that word has any meaning for you.'

'Antoine,' I said, 'come in.'

'My dear, there is a g-g-gorgon here who thinks I am g-g-gate-crashing. I only arrived in London yesterday, and heard quite by chance at luncheon that you were having an exhibition, so of course I dashed impetuously to the shrine to pay homage. Have I changed? Would you recognize me? Where are the pictures? Let me explain them to you.'

Anthony Blanche had not changed from when I last saw him; not, indeed, from when I first saw him. He swept lightly across the room to the most prominent canvas–a jungle landscape–paused a moment, his head cocked like a knowing terrier, and asked: 'Where, my dear Charles, did you find this sumptuous greenery? The corner of a hothouse at T-t-trent or T-t-tring? What gorgeous usurer nurtured these fronds for your pleasure?'

Then he made a tour of the two rooms; once or twice he sighed deeply, otherwise he kept silence. When he came to the end he sighed once more, more deeply than ever, and said: 'But they tell me, my dear, you are happy in love. That is everything, is it not, or nearly everything?'

'Are they as bad as that?'

Anthony dropped his voice to a piercing whisper: 'My dear, let us not expose your little imposture before these good, plain people'–he gave a conspiratorial glance to the last remnants of the crowd–'let us not spoil their innocent pleasure. We know, you and I, that this is all t-t-terrible t-t-tripe. Let us go, before we offend the connoisseurs. I know of a *louche* little bar quite near here. Let us go there and talk of your other c-c-conquests.'

It needed this voice from the past to recall me; the indiscriminate chatter of praise all that crowded day had worked on me like a succession of advertisement hoardings on a long road, kilometre after kilometre between the poplars, commanding one to stay at some new hotel, so that when at the end of the drive, stiff and dusty, one arrives at the destination, it seems inevitable to turn into the yard under the name that had first bored, then angered one, and finally become an inseparable part of one's fatigue.

Anthony led me from the gallery and down a side street to a door between a disreputable newsagent and a disreputable chemist, painted with the words 'Blue Grotto Club. Members only.'

'Not quite your milieu, my dear, but mine, I assure you. After all, you have been in your milieu all day.'

He led me downstairs, from a smell of cats to a smell of gin and cigarette-ends and the sound of a wireless.

'I was given the address by a dirty old man in the Bœuf sur le Toit. I am most grateful to him. I have been out of England so long, and really sympathetic little joints like this change so fast. I presented myself here for the first time yesterday evening, and already I feel *quite* at home. Good evening, Cyril.'

''Lo, Toni, back again?' said the youth behind the bar.

'We will take our drinks and sit in a corner. You must remember, my dear, that *here* you are just as conspicuous and, may I say, abnormal, my dear, as I should be in B-b-bratt's.'

The place was painted cobalt; there was cobalt linoleum on the floor. Fishes of silver and gold paper had been pasted haphazard on ceilings and walls. Half a dozen youths were drinking and playing with the slot-machines; an older, natty, crapulous-looking man seemed to be in control; there was some sniggering round the fruit-gum machine; then one of the youths came up to us and said, 'Would your friend care to rhumba?'

'No, Tom, he would *not*, and I'm not going to give you a drink; not yet, anyway. That's a very impudent boy, a regular little gold-digger, my dear.'

'Well,' I said, affecting an ease I was far from feeling in that den, 'what have you been up to all these years?'

'My dear, it is what *you* have been up to that we are here to talk about. I've been watching you, my dear. I'm a faithful old body and I've kept my eye on you.' As he spoke the bar and the bar-tender, the blue wicker furniture, the gambling-machines, the gramophone, the couple of youths dancing on the oil-cloth, the youths sniggering round the slots, the purple-veined, stiffly-dressed elderly man drinking in the corner opposite us, the whole drab and furtive joint seemed to fade, and I was back in Oxford looking out over Christ Church meadow through a window of Ruskin-Gothic. 'I went to your first exhibition,' said Anthony; 'I found it–charming. There was an interior of Marchmain House, very English, very correct, but quite delicious. "Charles has done something," I said; "not all he will do, not all he can do, but something."

'Even then, my dear, I wondered a little. It seemed to me that there was something a little *gentlemanly* about your painting. You must remember I am not English; I cannot understand this keen zest to be well-bred. English snobbery is more macabre to me even than English morals. However, I said. "Charles has done something delicious. What will he do next?"

'That next thing I saw was your very handsome volume–"Village and Provincial Architecture", was it called? Quite a tome, my dear, and what did I find? Charm again. "Not quite my cup of tea," I thought; "this is too English." I have the fancy for rather spicy things, you know, not for the shade of the cedar tree, the cucumber sandwich, the silver cream-jug, the English girl dressed in whatever English girls do wear for tennis–not that, not Jane Austen, *not* M-m-miss M-m-mitford. Then, to be frank, dear Charles, I despaired of you. "I am a degenerate old d-d-dago," I said "and Charles–I speak of your art, my dear–is a dean's daughter in flowered muslin."

'Imagine then my excitement at luncheon today. Everyone was talking about you. My hostess was a friend of my mother's, a Mrs Stuyvesant Oglander; a friend of yours, too, my dear. Such a frump! Not at all the society I imagined you to keep. However, they had all been to your exhibition, but it was *you* they talked of, how you had broken away, my dear, gone to the tropics, become a Gauguin, a Rimbaud. You can imagine how my old heart leaped.

'"Poor Celia," they said, "after all she's done for him." "He owes everything to her. It's too bad." "And with Julia," they said, "after the way she behaved in America." "Just as she was going back to Rex."

'"But the pictures," I said; "Tell me about *them*."

'"Oh, the pictures," they said; "they're most peculiar." "Not at all what he usually does." "Very forceful." "Quite barbaric." "I call them downright unhealthy," said Mrs Stuyvesant Oglander.

'My dear, I could hardly keep still in my chair. I wanted to dash out of the house and leap in a taxi and say, "Take me to Charles's unhealthy pictures." Well, I went, but the gallery after luncheon was so full of absurd women in the sort of hats they should be made to *eat*, that I rested a little–I rested here with Cyril and Tom and these saucy boys. Then I came back at the unfashionable time of five o'clock, all agog, my dear; and what did I find? I found, my dear, a very naughty and very successful practical joke. It reminded me of dear Sebastian when he liked so much to dress up in false whiskers. It was charm again, my dear, simple, creamy English charm, playing tigers.'

'You're quite right,' I said.

'My dear, of course I'm right. I was right years ago–more years, I am happy to say, than either of us shows–when I *warned* you. I took you out to dinner to warn you of charm. I warned you expressly and in great detail of the Flyte family. Charm is the great English blight. It does not exist outside these damp islands. It spots and kills anything it touches. It kills love; it kills art; I greatly fear, my dear Charles, it has killed *you*.'

The youth called Tom approached us again. 'Don't be a tease, Toni; buy me a drink.' I remembered my train and left Anthony with him.

As I stood on the platform by the restaurant-car I saw my luggage and Julia's go past with Julia's sour-faced maid strutting beside the porter. They had begun shutting the carriage doors when Julia arrived, unhurried, and took her place in front of me. I had a table for two. This was a very convenient train;

there was half an hour before dinner and half an hour after it; then, instead of changing to the branch line, as had been the rule in Lady Marchmain's day, we were met at the junction. It was night as we drew out of Paddington, and the glow of the town gave place first to the scattered lights of the suburbs, then to the darkness of the fields.

'It seems days since I saw you,' I said.

'Six hours; and we were together all yesterday. You look worn out.'

'It's been a day of nightmare–crowds, critics, the Clarences, a luncheon party at Margot's, ending up with half an hour's well-reasoned abuse of my pictures in a pansy bar. . . . I think Celia knows about us.'

'Well, she had to know some time.'

'Everyone seems to know. My pansy friend had not been in London twenty-four hours before he'd heard.'

'Damn everybody.'

'What about Rex?'

'Rex isn't anybody at all,' said Julia; 'he just doesn't exist.'

The knives and forks jingled on the tables as we sped through the darkness; the little circle of gin and vermouth in the glasses lengthened to oval, contracted again, with the sway of the carriage, touched the lip, lapped back again, never spilt; I was leaving the day behind me. Julia pulled off her hat and tossed it into the rack above her, and shook her night-dark hair with a little sigh of ease–a sigh fit for the pillow, the sinking firelight, and a bedroom window open to the stars and the whisper of bare trees.

'It's great to have you back, Charles; like the old days.'

'Like the old days?' I thought.

Rex, in his early forties, had grown heavy and ruddy; he had lost his Canadian accent and acquired instead the hoarse, loud tone that was common to all his friends, as though their voices were perpetually strained to make themselves heard above a crowd, as though, with youth forsaking them, there was no time to wait the opportunity to speak, no time to listen, no time to reply; time for a laugh–a throaty mirthless laugh, the base currency of goodwill.

There were half a dozen of these friends in the Tapestry Hall: politicians; 'young Conservatives' in the early forties, with sparse hair and high blood-pressure; a Socialist from the coal-mines who had already caught their clear accents, whose cigars came to pieces on his lips, whose hand shook when he poured himself out a drink; a financier older than the rest, and, one might guess from the way they treated him, richer; a love-sick columnist, who alone was silent, gloating sombrely on the only woman of the party; a woman they called 'Grizel', a knowing rake whom, in their hearts, they all feared a little.

They all feared Julia, too, Grizel included. She greeted them and apologized for not being there to welcome them, with a formality which hushed them for a minute; then she came and sat with me near the fire, and the storm of talk arose once more and whirled about our ears.

'Of course, he can marry her and make her queen tomorrow.'

'We had our chance in October. Why didn't we send the Italian fleet to the bottom of Mare Nostrum? Why didn't we blow Spezia to blazes? Why didn't we land on Pantelleria?'

'Franco's simply a German agent. They tried to put him in to prepare air bases to bomb France. That bluff has been called, anyway.'

'It would make the monarchy stronger than it's been since Tudor times. The people are with him.'

'The Press are with him.'

'I'm with him.'

'Who cares about divorce now except a few old maids who aren't married, anyway?'

'If he has a show-down with the old gang, they'll just disappear like, like . . .'

'Why didn't we close the canal? Why didn't we bomb Rome?'

'It wouldn't have been necessary. One firm note . . .'

'One firm speech.'

'One show-down.'

'Anyway, Franco will soon be skipping back to Morocco. Chap I saw today just come from Barcelona. . . .'

'. . . Chap just come from Fort Belvedere. . . .'

'. . . Chap just come from the Palazzo Venezia. . . .'

'All we want is a show-down.'

'A show-down with Baldwin.'

'A show-down with Hitler.'

'A show-down with the Old Gang.'

'. . . That I should live to see my country, the land of Clive and Nelson. . . .'

'. . . *My* country of Hawkins and Drake.'

'. . . *My* country of Palmerston. . . .'

'Would you very much mind not doing that?' said Grizel to the columnist, who had been attempting in a maudlin manner to twist her wrist; 'I don't happen to enjoy it.'

'I wonder which is the more horrible,' I said, 'Celia's Art and Fashion or Rex's Politics and Money.'

'Why worry about them?'

'Oh, my darling, why is it that love makes me hate the world? It's supposed to have quite the opposite effect. I feel as though all mankind, and God, too, were in a conspiracy against us.'

'They are, they are.'

'But we've got our happiness in spite of them; here and now, we've taken possession of it. They can't hurt us, can they?'

'Not tonight; not now.'

'Not for how many nights?'

3

'Do you remember,' said Julia, in the tranquil, lime-scented evening, 'do you remember the storm?'

'The bronze doors banging.'

'The roses in cellophane.'

'The man who gave the "get-together" party and was never seen again.'

'Do you remember how the sun came out on our last evening just as it has done today?'

It had been an afternoon of low cloud and summer squalls, so overcast that at times I had stopped work and roused Julia from the light trance in which she sat–she had sat so often; I never tired of painting her, forever finding in her new wealth and delicacy–until at length we had gone early to our baths and, on coming down, dressed for dinner, in the last half-hour of the day, we found the world transformed; the sun had emerged; the wind had fallen to a soft breeze which gently stirred the blossom in the limes and carried its fragrance, fresh from the late rains, to merge with the sweet breath of box and the drying stone. The shadow of the obelisk spanned the terrace.

I had carried two garden cushions from the shelter of the colonnade and put them on the rim of the fountain. There Julia sat, in a tight little gold tunic and a white gown, one hand in the water idly turning an emerald ring to catch the fire of the sunset; the carved animals mounted over her dark head in a cumulus of green moss and glowing stone and dense shadow, and the waters round them flashed and bubbled and broke into scattered flames.

'. . . So much to remember,' she said. 'How many days have there been since then, when we haven't seen each other; a hundred, do you think?'

'Not so many.'

'Two Christmases'–those bleak, annual excursions into propriety. Boughton, home of my family, home of my cousin Jasper, with what glum memories of childhood I revisited its pitch-pine corridors and dripping walls! How querulously my father and I, seated side by side in my uncle's Humber, approached the avenue of Wellingtonias knowing that at the end of the drive we should find my uncle, my aunt, my Aunt Phillippa, my cousin Jasper, and, of recent years, Jasper's wife and children; and besides them, perhaps already arrived, perhaps every moment expected, my wife and my children. This annual sacrifice united us; here among the holly and mistletoe and the cut spruce, the parlour games ritually performed, the brandy-butter and the Carlsbad plums, the village choir in the pitch-pine minstrels' gallery, gold twine and sprigged wrapping-paper, she and I were accepted, whatever ugly rumours had been afloat in the past year, as man and wife. 'We must keep it up, whatever it costs us, for the sake of the children,' my wife said.

'Yes, two Christmases. . . . And the three days of good taste before I followed you to Capri.'

'Our first summer.'

'Do you remember how I hung about Naples, then followed, how we met by arrangement on the hill path and how flat it fell?'

'I went back to the villa and said, "Papa, who do you think has arrived at the hotel?" and he said, "Charles Ryder, I suppose." I said, "Why did you think of him?" and papa replied, "Cara came back from Paris with the news that you and he were inseparable. He seems to have a penchant for my children. However, bring him here; I think we have the room."'

'There was the time you had jaundice and wouldn't let me see you.'

'And when I had flu and you were afraid to come.'

'Countless visits to Rex's constituency.'

'And Coronation Week, when you ran away from London. Your goodwill mission to your father-in-law. The time you went to Oxford to paint the picture they didn't like. Oh, yes, quite a hundred days.'

'A hundred days wasted out of two years and a bit . . . not a day's coldness or mistrust or disappointment.'

'Never that.'

We fell silent; only the birds spoke in a multitude of small, clear voices in the lime-trees; only the waters spoke among their carved stones.

Julia took the handkerchief from my breast pocket and dried her hand; then lit a cigarette. I feared to break the spell of memories, but for once our thoughts had not kept pace together, for when at length Julia spoke, she said sadly: 'How many more? Another hundred?'

'A lifetime.'

'I want to marry you, Charles.'

'One day; why now?'

'War,' she said, 'this year, next year, sometime soon. I want a day or two with you of real peace.'

'Isn't this peace?'

The sun had sunk now to the line of woodland beyond the valley; all the opposing slope was already in twilight, but the lakes below us were aflame; the light grew in strength and splendour as it neared death, drawing long shadows across the pasture, falling full on the rich stone spaces of the house, firing the panes in the windows, glowing on cornices and colonnade and dome, spreading out all the stacked merchandise of colour and scent from earth and stone and leaf, glorifying the head and golden shoulders of the woman beside me.

'What do you mean by "peace", if not this?'

'So much more'; and then in a chill, matter-of-fact tone she continued: 'Marriage isn't a thing we can take when the impulse moves us. There must be a divorce–two divorces. We must make plans.'

'Plans, divorce, war–on an evening like this.'

'Sometimes,' said Julia, 'I feel the past and the future pressing so hard on either side that there's no room for the present at all.'

Then Wilcox came down the steps into the sunset to tell us that dinner was ready.

Shutters were up, curtains drawn, candles lit, in the Painted Parlour.

'Hullo, it's laid for three.'

'Lord Brideshead arrived half an hour ago, my lady. He sent a message would you please not wait dinner for him as he may be a little late.'

'It seems months since he was here last,' said Julia. 'What *does* he do in London?'

It was often a matter for speculation between us–giving birth to many fantasies, for Bridey was a mystery; a creature from underground; a hard-snouted, burrowing, hibernating animal who shunned the light. He had been completely without action in all his years of adult life; the talk of his going into the army and into parliament and into a monastery, had all come to nothing. All that he was known with certainty to have done–and this because in a season of scant news it had formed the subject of a newspaper article entitled '*Peer's Unusual Hobby*'–was to form a collection of match-boxes; he kept them mounted on boards, card-indexed, yearly occupying a larger and larger space in his small house in Westminster. At first he was bashful about the notoriety which the newspaper caused, but later greatly pleased, for he found it the means of his getting into touch with other collectors in all parts of the world with whom he now corresponded and swapped duplicates. Other than this he was not known to have any interests. He remained Joint-Master of the Marchmain and hunted with then dutifully on their two days a week when he was at home; he never hunted with the neighbouring pack, who had the better country. He had no real zest for sport, and had not been out a dozen times that season; he had few friends; he visited his aunts; he went to public dinners held in the Catholic interest. At Brideshead he performed all unavoidable local duties, bringing with him to platform and fête and committee room his own thin mist of clumsiness and aloofness.

'There was a girl found strangled with a piece of barbed wire at Wandsworth last week,' I said, reviving an old fantasy.

'That must be Bridey. He is naughty.'

When we had been a quarter of an hour at the table, he joined us, coming ponderously into the room in the bottle-green velvet smoking suit which he kept at Brideshead and always wore when he was there. At thirty-eight he had grown heavy and bald, and might have been taken for forty-five.

'Well,' he said, 'well, only you two; I hoped to find Rex here.'

I often wondered what he made of me and of my continual presence; he seemed to accept me, without curiosity, as one of the household. Twice in the past two years he had surprised me by what seemed to be acts of friendship; that Christmas he had sent me a photograph of himself in the robes of a Knight of Malta, and shortly afterwards asked me to go with him to a dining club. Both acts had an explanation: he had had more copies of his portrait printed than he knew what to do with; he was proud of his club. It was a surprising association of men quite eminent in their professions who met once a month for an evening of ceremonious buffoonery; each had his sobriquet – Bridey was called 'Brother Grandee'–and a specially designed jewel worn like an order of chivalry, symbolizing it; they had club buttons for their waistcoats and an elaborate ritual for the introduction of guests; after dinner a paper was read and facetious speeches were made. There was plainly some competition to bring guests of distinction, and since Bridey had few friends, and since I was tolerably well known, I was invited. Even on that convivial evening I could feel my host emanating little magnetic waves of social uneasiness, creating, rather, a pool of general embarrassment about himself in which he floated with log-like calm.

He sat down opposite me and bowed his sparse, pink head over his plate.

'Well, Bridey. What's the news?'

'As a matter of fact,' he said, 'I have some news. But it can wait.'

'Tell us now.'

He made a grimace which I took to mean 'not in front of the servants', and said, 'How is the painting, Charles?'

'Which painting?'

'Whatever you have on the stocks.'

'I began a sketch of Julia, but the light was tricky all today.'

'Julia? I thought you'd done her before. I suppose it's a change from architecture, and much more difficult.'

His conversation abounded in long pauses during which his mind seemed to remain motionless; he always brought one back with a start to the exact point where he had stopped. Now after more than a minute he said: 'The world is full of different subjects.'

'Very true, Bridey.'

'If I were a painter,' he said, 'I should choose an entirely different subject every time; subjects with plenty of action in them like . . .' Another pause. What, I wondered was coming? The Flying Scotsman? The Charge of the Light Brigade? Henley Regatta? Then surprisingly he said: '. . . like Macbeth.' There was something supremely preposterous in the idea of Bridey as a painter of action pictures; he was usually preposterous yet somehow achieved a certain dignity by his remoteness and agelessness; he was still half-child, already half-veteran; there seemed no spark of contemporary life in him; he had a kind of massive rectitude and impermeability, an indifference to the world, which compelled respect. Though we often laughed at him, he was never wholly ridiculous; at times he was even formidable.

We talked of the news from central Europe until, suddenly cutting across this barren topic, Bridey asked: 'Where are mummy's jewels?'

'This was hers,' said Julia, 'and this. Cordelia and I had all her own things. The family jewels went to the bank.'

'It's so long since I've seen them–I don't know that I ever saw them all. What is there? Aren't there some rather famous rubies, someone was telling me?'

'Yes, a necklace. Mummy used often to wear it, don't you remember? And there are the pearls–she always had those out. But most of it stayed in the bank year after year. There are some hideous diamond fenders, I remember, and a Victorian diamond collar no one could wear now. There's a mass of good stones. Why?'

'I'd like to have a look at them some day.'

'I say, papa isn't going to pop them, is he? He hasn't got into debt again?'

'No, no, nothing like that.'

Bridey was a slow and copious eater. Julia and I watched him between the candles. Presently he said: 'If I was Rex'–his mind seemed full of such suppositions: 'If I was Archbishop of Westminster', 'If I was head of the Great Western Railway', 'If I was an actress', as though it were a mere trick of fate that he was none of these things, and he might awake any morning to find the matter adjusted–'if I was Rex I should want to live in my constituency.'

'Rex says it saves four days' work a week not to.'

'I'm sorry he's not here. I have a little announcement to make.'

'Bridey, don't be so mysterious. Out with it.'

He made the grimace which seemed to mean 'not before the servants'.

Later when port was on the table and we three were alone Julia said: 'I'm not going till I hear the announcement.'

'Well,' said Bridey, sitting back in his chair and gazing fixedly at his glass. 'You have only to wait until Monday to see it in black and white in the newspapers. I am engaged to be married. I hope you are pleased.'

'Bridey. How . . . how very exciting! Who to?'

'Oh, no one you know.'

'Is she pretty?'

'I don't think you would exactly call her pretty; "Comely" is the word I think of in her connexion. She is a big woman.'

'Fat?'

'No, big. She is called Mrs Muspratt; her Christian name is Beryl. I have known her for a long time, but until last year she had a husband; now she is a widow. Why do you laugh?'

'I'm sorry. It isn't the least funny. It's just so unexpected. Is she . . . is she about your own age?'

'Just about, I believe. She has three children, the eldest boy has just gone to Ampleforth. She is not at all well off.'

'But Bridey, where did you find her?'

'Her late husband, Admiral Muspratt, collected match-boxes,' he said with complete gravity.

Julia trembled on the verge of laughter, recovered her self-possession, and asked: 'You're not marrying her for her match-boxes?'

'No, no; the whole collection was left to the Falmouth Town Library. I have a great affection for her. In spite of all her difficulties she is a very cheerful woman, very fond of acting. She is connected with the Catholic Players' Guild.'

'Does papa know?'

'I had a letter from him this morning giving me his approval. He has been urging me to marry for some time.'

It occurred both to Julia and myself simultaneously that we were allowing curiosity and surprise to predominate; now we congratulated him in gentler tones from which mockery was almost excluded.

'Thank you,' he said, 'thank you. I think I am very fortunate.'

'But when are we going to meet her? I do think you might have brought her down with you.'

He said nothing, sipped and gazed.

'Bridey,' said Julia. 'You sly, smug old brute, why haven't you brought her here?'

'Oh, I couldn't do that, you know.'

'Why couldn't you? I'm dying to meet her. Let's ring her up now and invite her. She'll think us most peculiar leaving her alone at a time like this.'

'She has the children,' said Brideshead. 'Besides, you *are* peculiar, aren't you?'

'What can you mean?'

Brideshead raised his head and looked solemnly at his sister, and continued in the same simple way, as though he were saying nothing particularly different from what had gone before, 'I couldn't ask her here, as things are. It wouldn't be suitable. After all, I am a lodger here. This is Rex's house at the moment, so far as it's anybody's. What goes on here is his business. But I couldn't bring Beryl here.'

'I simply don't understand,' said Julia rather sharply. I looked at her. All the gentle mockery had gone; she was alert, almost scared, it seemed. 'Of course, Rex and I want her to come.'

'Oh, yes, I don't doubt that. The difficulty is quite otherwise.' He finished his port, refilled his glass, and pushed the decanter towards me. 'You must understand that Beryl is a woman of strict Catholic principle fortified by the prejudices of the middle class. I couldn't possibly bring her here. It is a matter of indifference whether you choose to live in sin with Rex or Charles or both–I have always avoided inquiry into the details of your *ménage*–but in no case would Beryl consent to be your guest.'

Julia rose. 'Why, you pompous ass . . .' she said, stopped, and turned towards the door.

At first I thought she was overcome by laughter; then, as I opened the door to her, I saw with consternation that she was in tears. I hesitated. She slipped past me without a glance.

'I may have given the impression that this was a marriage of convenience,' Brideshead continued placidly. 'I cannot speak for Beryl; no doubt the security of my position has some influence on her. Indeed, she has said as much. But for myself, let me emphasize, I am ardently attracted.'

'Bridey, what a bloody offensive thing to say to Julia!'

'There was nothing she should object to. I was merely stating a fact well known to her.'

She was not in the library; I mounted to her room, but she was not there. I paused by her laden dressing table wondering if she would come. Then through the open window, as the light streamed out across the terrace into the dusk, to the fountain which in that house seemed always to draw us to itself for comfort and refreshment, I caught the glimpse of a white skirt against the stones. It was nearly night. I found her in the darkest refuge, on a wooden seat, in a bay of the clipped box which encircled the basin. I took her in my arms and she pressed her face to my heart.

'Aren't you cold out here?'

She did not answer, only clung closer to me, and shook with sobs.

'My darling, what is it? Why do you mind? What does it matter what that old booby says?'

'I don't; it doesn't. It's just the shock. Don't laugh at me.'

In the two years of our love, which seemed a lifetime, I had not seen her so moved or felt so powerless to help.

'How dare he speak to you like that?' I said. 'The cold-blooded old humbug . . .' But I was failing her in sympathy.

'No,' she said, 'it's not that. He's quite right. They know all about it, Bridey and his widow; they've got it in black and white; they bought it for a penny at the church door. You can get anything there for a penny, in black and white, and nobody to see that you pay; only an old woman with a broom at the other end, rattling round the confessionals, and a young woman lighting a candle at the Seven Dolours. Put a penny in the box, or not, just as you like; take your tract. There you've got it, in black and white.

'All in one word, too, one little, flat, deadly word that covers a lifetime.

'"Living in sin"; not just doing wrong, as I did when I went to America; doing wrong, knowing it is wrong, stopping doing it, forgetting. That's not what they mean. That's not Bridey's pennyworth. He means just what it says in black and white.

'*Living in sin*, with sin, always the same, like an idiot child carefully nursed, guarded from the world. "Poor Julia," they say, "she can't go out. She's got to take care of her sin. A pity it ever lived," they say, "but it's so strong. Children like that always are. Julia's so good to her little, mad sin."'

'An hour ago,' I thought, 'under the sunset, she sat turning her ring in the water and counting the days of happiness; now under the first stars and the last grey whisper of day, all this mysterious tumult of sorrow! What had happened to us in the Painted Parlour? What shadow had fallen in the candlelight? Two rough sentences and a trite phrase.' She was beside herself; her voice, now muffled in my breast, now clear and anguished, came to me in single words and broken sentences.

'Past and future; the years when I was trying to be a good wife, in the cigar smoke, while the counters clicked on the backgammon board, and the man who was "dummy" at the men's table filled the glasses; when I was trying to bear his child, torn in pieces by something already dead; putting him away, forgetting him, finding you, the past two years with you, all the future with you, all the future with or without you, war coming, world ending–sin.

'A word from so long ago, from Nanny Hawkins stitching by the hearth and the nightlight burning before the Sacred Heart. Cordelia and me with the catechism, in mummy's room, before luncheon on Sundays. Mummy carrying my sin with her to church, bowed under it and the black lace veil, in the chapel; slipping out with it in London before the fires were lit; taking it with her through the empty streets, where the milkman's ponies stood with their forefeet on the pavement; mummy dying with my sin eating at her, more cruelly than her own deadly illness.

'Mummy dying with it; Christ dying with it, nailed hand and foot; hanging over the bed in the night-nursery; hanging year after year in the dark little study at Farm Street with the shining oilcloth; hanging in the dark church where only the old charwoman raises the dust and one candle burns; hanging at noon, high among the crowds and the soldiers; no comfort except a sponge of vinegar and the kind words of a thief; hanging for ever; never the cool sepulchre and the grave clothes spread on the stone slab, never the oil and spices in the dark cave; always the midday sun and the dice clicking for the seamless coat.

'No way back; the gates barred; all the saints and angels posted along the walls. Thrown away, scrapped, rotting down; the old man with lupus and the forked stick who limps out at nightfall to turn the rubbish, hoping for something to put in his sack, something marketable, turns away with disgust.

'Nameless and dead, like the baby they wrapped up and took away before I had seen her.'

Between her tears she talked herself into silence. I could do nothing; I was adrift in a strange sea; my hands on the metal-spun threads of her tunic were cold and stiff, my eyes dry; I was as far from her in spirit, as she clung to me in the darkness, as when years ago I had lit her cigarette on the way from the station; as far as when she was out of mind, in the dry, empty years at the Old Rectory, and in the jungle.

Tears spring from speech; presently in her silence her weeping stopped. She sat up, away from me, took my handkerchief, shivered, rose to her feet.

'Well,' she said, in a voice much like normal. 'Bridey is one for bombshells, isn't he?'

I followed her into the house and to her room; she sat at her looking-glass. 'Considering that I've just recovered from a fit of hysteria,' she said, 'I don't call that at all bad.' Her eyes seemed unnaturally large and bright, her cheeks pale with two spots of high colour, where, as a girl, she used to put a dab of rouge. 'Most hysterical women look as if they had a bad cold. You'd better change your shirt before going down; it's all tears and lipstick.'

'Are we going down?'

'Of course, we mustn't leave poor Bridey on his engagement night.'

When I went back to her she said: 'I'm sorry for that appalling scene, Charles. I can't explain.'

Brideshead was in the library, smoking his pipe, placidly reading a detective story.

'Was it nice out? If I'd known you were going I'd have come, too.'

'Rather cold.'

'I hope it's not going to be inconvenient for Rex moving out of here. You see, Barton Street is much too small for us and the three children. Besides, Beryl likes the country. In his letter papa proposed making over the whole estate right away.'

I remembered how Rex had greeted me on my first arrival at Brideshead as Julia's guest. 'A very happy arrangement,' he had said. 'Suits me down to the ground. The old boy keeps the place up; Bridey does all the feudal stuff with the tenants; I have the run of the house rent free. All it costs me is the food and the wages of the indoor servants. Couldn't ask fairer than that, could you?'

'I should think he'll be sorry to go,' I said.

'Oh, he'll find another bargain somewhere,' said Julia; 'trust him.'

'Beryl's got some furniture of her own she's very attached to. I don't know if it would go very well here. You know, oak dressers and coffin stools and things. I thought she could put it in mummy's old room.'

'Yes, that would be the place.'

So brother and sister sat and talked about the arrangement of the house until bed-time. 'An hour ago,' I thought, 'in the black refuge in the box hedge, she wept her heart out for the death of her God; now she is discussing whether Beryl's children shall take the old smoking-room or the school-room for their own.' I was all at sea.

'Julia,' I said later, when Brideshead had gone upstairs, 'have you ever seen a picture of Holman Hunt's called "The Awakened Conscience"?'

'No.'

I had seen a copy of *Pre-Raphaelitism* in the library some days before; I found it again and read her Ruskin's description. She laughed quite happily.

'You're perfectly right. That's exactly what I did feel.'

'But, darling, I won't believe that great spout of tears came just from a few words of Bridey's. You must have been thinking about it before.'

'Hardly at all; now and then; more, lately, with the Last Trump so near.'

'Of course it's a thing psychologists could explain; a preconditioning from childhood; feelings of guilt from the nonsense you were taught in the nursery. You do know at heart that it's all bosh, don't you?'

'How I wish it was!'

'Sebastian once said almost the same thing to me.'

'He's gone back to the Church, you know. Of course, he never left it as definitely as I did. I've gone too far; there's no turning back now; I know that, if that's what you mean by thinking it all bosh. All I can hope to do is to put my life in some sort of order in a human way, before all human order comes to an end. That's why I want to marry you. I should like to have a child. That's one thing I can do. . . . Let's go out again. The moon should be up by now.'

The moon was full and high. We walked round the house; under the limes Julia paused and idly snapped off one of the long shoots, last year's growth, that fringed their boles, and stripped it as she walked, making a switch, as children do, but with petulant movements that were not a child's, snatching nervously at the leaves and crumbling them between her fingers; she began peeling the bark, scratching it with her nails.

Once more we stood by the fountain.

'It's like the setting of a comedy,' I said. 'Scene: a Baroque fountain in a nobleman's grounds. Act one, sunset; act two, dusk; act three, moonlight. The characters keep assembling at the fountain for no very clear reason.'

'Comedy?'

'Drama. Tragedy. Farce. What you will. This is the reconciliation scene.'

'Was there a quarrel?'

'Estrangement and misunderstanding in act two.'

'Oh, don't talk in that damned bounderish way. Why must you see everything second-hand? Why must this be a play? Why must my conscience be a pre-Raphaelite picture?'

'It's a way I have.'

'I hate it.'

Her anger was as unexpected as every change on this evening of swift veering moods. Suddenly she cut me across the face with her switch, a vicious, stinging little blow as hard as she could strike.

'Now do you see how I hate it?'

She hit me again.

'All right,' I said, 'go on.'

Then, though her hand was raised, she stopped and threw the half-peeled wand into the water, where it floated white and black in the moonlight.

'Did that hurt?'

'Yes.'

'Did it? . . . Did I?'

In the instant her rage was gone; her tears, newly flowing, were on my cheek. I held her at arm's length and she put down her head, stroking my hand on her shoulder with her face, cat-like, but, unlike a cat, leaving a tear there.

'Cat on the roof-top,' I said.

'Beast!'

She bit at my hand, but when I did not move it and her teeth touched me, she changed the bite to a kiss, the kiss to a lick of her tongue.

'Cat in the moonlight.'

This was the mood I knew. We turned towards the house. When we came to the lighted hall she said: 'Your poor face,' touching the weals with her fingers. 'Will there be a mark tomorrow?'

'I expect so.'

'Charles, am I going crazy? What's happened tonight? I'm so tired.'

She yawned; a fit of yawning took her. She sat at her dressing table, head bowed, hair over her face, yawning helplessly, when she looked up I saw over her shoulder in the glass a face that was dazed with weariness like a retreating soldier's, and beside it my own, streaked with two crimson lines.

'So tired,' she repeated, taking off her gold tunic and letting it fall to the floor, 'tired and crazy and good for nothing.'

I saw her to bed; the blue lids fells over her eyes; her pale lips moved on the pillow, but whether to wish me good night or to murmur a prayer–a jingle of the nursery that came to her now in the twilight world between sorrow and sleep: some ancient pious rhyme that had come down to Nanny Hawkins from centuries of bedtime whispering, through all the changes of language, from the days of pack-horses on the Pilgrim's Way–I did not know.

Next night Rex and his political associates were with us.

'They won't fight.'

'They can't fight. They haven't the money; they haven't the oil.'

'They haven't the wolfram; they haven't the men.'

'They haven't the guts.'

'They're afraid.'

'Scared of the French; scared of the Czechs; scared of the Slovaks; scared of us.'

'It's a bluff.'

'Of course it's a bluff. Where's their tungsten? Where's their manganese?'

'Where's their chrome?'

'I'll tell you a thing . . .'

'Listen to this; it'll be good; Rex will tell you a thing.'

'. . . Friend of mine motoring in the Black Forest, only the other day, just came back and told me about it while we played a round of golf. Well, this friend driving along, turned down a lane into the high road. What should he find but a military convoy? Couldn't stop, drove right into it, smack into a tank, broadside on. Gave himself up for dead. . . . Hold on, this is the funny part.'

'This is the funny part.'

'Drove clean through it, didn't scratch his paint. What do you think? It was made of canvas–a bamboo frame and painted canvas.'

'They haven't the steel.'

'They haven't the tools. They haven't the labour. They're half starving. They haven't the fats. The children have rickets.'

'The women are barren.'

'The men are impotent.'

'They haven't the doctors.'

'The doctors were Jewish.'

'Now they've got consumption.'

'Now they've got syphilis.'

'Goering told a friend of mine . . .'

'Goebbels told a friend of mine . . .'

'Ribbentrop told me that the army just kept Hitler in power so long as he was able to get things for nothing. The moment anyone stands up to him, he's finished. The army will shoot him.'

'The Liberals will hang him.'

'The Communists will tear him limb from limb.'

'He'll scupper himself.'

'He'd do it now if it wasn't for Chamberlain.'

'If it wasn't for Halifax.'

'If it wasn't for Sir Samuel Hoare.'

'And the 1922 Committee.'

'Peace Pledge.'

'Foreign Office.'

'New York Banks.'

'All that's wanted is a good strong line.'

'A line from Rex.'

'And a line from me.'

'We'll give Europe a good strong line. Europe is waiting for a speech from Rex.'

'And a speech from me.'

'And a speech from me. Rally the freedom-loving peoples of the world. Germany will rise; Austria will rise. The Czechs and the Slovaks are bound to rise.'

'To a speech from Rex and a speech from me.'

'What about a rubber? How about a whisky? Which of you chaps will have a big cigar? Hullo, you two going out?'

'Yes, Rex,' said Julia. 'Charles and I are going into the moonlight.'

We shut the windows behind us and the voices ceased; the moonlight lay like hoar-frost on the terrace and the music of the fountain crept in our ears; the stone balustrade of the terrace might have been the Trojan walls, and in the silent park might have stood the Grecian tents where Cressid lay that night.

'A few days, a few months.'

'No time to be lost.'

'A lifetime between the rising of the moon and its setting. Then the dark.'

4

'And of course Celia will have custody of the children.'

'Of course.'

'Then what about the Old Rectory? I don't imagine you'll want to settle down with Julia bang at our gates. The children look on it as their home, you know. Robin's got no place of his own till his uncle dies. After all, you never used the studio, did you? Robin was saying only the other day what a good play-room it would make–big enough for Badminton.'

'Robin can have the Old Rectory.'

'Now with regard to money, Celia and Robin naturally don't want to accept anything for themselves, but there's the question of the children's education.'

'That will be all right. I'll see the lawyers about it.'

'Well, I think that's everything,' said Mulcaster. 'You know, I've seen a few divorces in my time, and I've never known one work out so happily for all concerned. Almost always, however matey people are at the start, bad blood crops up when they get down to detail. Mind you, I don't mind saying there have been times in the last two years when I thought you were treating Celia a bit rough. It's hard to tell with one's own sister, but I've always thought her a jolly attractive girl, the sort of girl any chap would be glad to have–artistic, too, just down your street. But I must admit you're a good picker. I've always had a soft spot for Julia. Anyway, as things have turned out everyone seems satisfied. Robin's been mad about Celia for a year or more. D'you know him?'

'Vaguely. A half-baked, pimply youth as I remember him.'

'Oh, I wouldn't quite say that. He's rather young, of course, but the great thing is that Johnjohn and Caroline adore him. You've got two grand kids there, Charles. Remember me to Julia; wish her all the best for old times' sake.'

'So you're being divorced,' said my father. 'Isn't that rather unnecessary, after you've been happy together all these years?'

'We weren't particularly happy, you know.'

'Weren't you? Were you not? I distinctly remember last Christmas seeing you together and thinking how happy you looked, and wondering why. You'll find it very disturbing, you know, starting off again. How old are you–thirty-four? That's no age to be starting. You ought to be settling down. Have you made any plans?'

'Yes. I'm marrying again as soon as the divorce is through.'

'Well, I do call that a lot of nonsense. I can understand a man wishing he hadn't married and trying to get out of it–though I never felt anything of the kind myself–but to get rid of one wife and take up with another immediately, is beyond all reason. Celia was always perfectly civil to me. I had quite a liking for her, in a way. If you couldn't be happy with her, why on earth should you expect to be happy with anyone else? Take my advice, my dear boy, and give up the whole idea.'

'Why bring Julia and me into this?' asked Rex. 'If Celia wants to marry again, well and good; let her. That's your business and hers. But I should have thought Julia and I were quite happy as we are. You can't say I've been difficult. Lots of chaps would have cut up nasty. I hope I'm a man of the world. I've had my own fish to fry, too. But a divorce is a different thing altogether; I've never known a divorce do anyone any good.'

'That's your affair and Julia's.'

'Oh, Julia's set on it. What I hoped was, you might be able to talk her round. I've tried to keep out of the way as much as I could; if I've been around too much, just tell me; I shan't mind. But there's too much going on altogether at the moment, what with Bridey wanting me to clear out of the house; it's disturbing, and I've got a lot on my mind.'

Rex's public life was approaching a climacteric. Things had not gone as smoothly with him as he had planned. I knew nothing of finance, but I heard it said that his dealings were badly looked on by orthodox Conservatives; even his good qualities of geniality and impetuosity counted against him, for his parties at Brideshead got talked about. There was always too much about him in the papers; he was one with the Press lords and their sad-eyed, smiling hangers-on; in his speeches he said the sort of thing which 'made a story' in Fleet Street, and that did him no good with his party chiefs; only war could put Rex's fortunes right and carry him into power. A divorce would do him no great harm; it was rather that with a big bank running he could not look up from the table.

'If Julia insists on a divorce, I suppose she must have it,' he said. 'But she couldn't have chosen a worse time. Tell her to hang on a bit, Charles, there's a good fellow.'

'Bridey's widow said: "So you're divorcing one divorced man and marrying another. It sounds rather complicated, but my dear"–she called me "my dear" about twenty times–"I've usually found every Catholic family has one lapsed member, and it's often the nicest."'

Julia had just returned from a luncheon party given by Lady Rosscommon in honour of Brideshead's engagement.

'What's she like?'

'Majestic amd voluptuous; common, of course; husky voice, big mouth, small eyes, dyed hair–I'll tell you one thing, she's lied to Bridey about her age. She's a good forty-five. I don't see her providing an heir. Bridey can't take his eyes off her. He was gloating on her in the most revolting way all through luncheon.'

'Friendly?'

'Goodness, yes, in a condescending way. You see, I imagine she's been used to bossing things rather in naval circles, with flag-lieutenants trotting round and young officers on-the-make sucking up to her. Well, she clearly couldn't do a great deal of bossing at Aunt Fanny's, so it put her rather at ease to have me there as the black sheep. She concentrated on me in fact, asked my advice about shops and things, said, rather pointedly, she hoped to see me often *in London*. I think Bridey's scruples only extend to her sleeping under the same roof with me. Apparently I can do her no serious harm in a hat-shop or hairdresser's or lunching at the Ritz. The scruples are all on Bridey's part, anyway; the widow is madly tough.'

'Does she boss him?'

'Not yet, much. He's in an amorous stupor, poor beast, and doesn't quite know where he is. She's just a good-hearted woman who wants a good home for her children and isn't going to let anything get in her way. She's playing up the religious stuff at the moment for all it's worth. I daresay she'll go easier when she's settled.'

The divorces were much talked of among our friends; even in that summer of general alarm there were still corners where private affairs commanded first attention. My wife was able to make it understood that the business was at the same time a matter of congratulation for her and reproach for me; that she had behaved wonderfully, had stood it longer than anyone but she would have done. Robin was seven years younger and a little immature for his age, they whispered in their private corners, but he was absolutely devoted to poor Celia, and really she deserved it after all she had been through. As for Julia and me, that was an old story. 'To put it crudely,' said my cousin Jasper, as though he had ever in his life put anything otherwise: 'I don't see why you bother to marry.'

Summer passed; delirious crowds cheered Neville Chamberlain's return from Munich; Rex made a rabid speech in the House of Commons which sealed his fate one way or the other; sealed it, as is sometimes done with naval orders, to be opened later at sea. Julia's family lawyers, whose black, tin boxes, painted 'Marquis of Marchmain', seemed to fill a room, began the slow process of her divorce; my own, brisker firm, two doors down, were weeks ahead with my affairs. It was necessary for Rex and Julia to separate formally, and since, for the time being, Brideshead was still her home, she remained there and Rex removed his trunks and valet to their house in London. Evidence was taken against Julia and me in my flat. A date was fixed for Brideshead's wedding, early in the Christmas holidays, so that his future step-children might take part.

One afternoon in November Julia and I stood at a window in the drawing-room watching the wind at work stripping the lime trees, sweeping down the yellow leaves, sweeping them up and round and along the terrace and lawns, trailing them through puddles and over the wet grass, pasting them on walls and window-panes, leaving them at length in sodden piles against the stonework.

'We shan't see them in spring,' said Julia; 'perhaps never again.'

'Once before,' I said, 'I went away, thinking I should never return.'

'Perhaps years later, to what's left of it, with what's left of us . . .'

A door opened and shut in the darkling room behind us. Wilcox approached through the firelight into the dusk about the long windows.

'A telephone message, my Lady, from Lady Cordelia.'

'Lady Cordelia! Where was she?'

'In London, my Lady.'

'Wilcox, how lovely! Is she coming home?'

'She was just starting for the station. She will be here after dinner.'

'I haven't seen her for twelve years,' I said–not since the evening when we dined together and she spoke of being a nun; the evening when I painted the drawing-room at Marchmain House. 'She was an enchanting child.'

'She's had an odd life. First, the convent; then, when that was no good, the war in Spain. I've not seen her since then. The other girls who went with the ambulance came back when the war was over; she stayed on, getting people back to their homes, helping in the prison-camps. An odd girl. She's grown up quite plain, you know.'

'Does she know about us?'

'Yes, she wrote me a sweet letter.'

It hurt to think of Cordelia growing up 'quite plain'; to think of all that burning love spending itself on serum-injections and de-lousing powder. When she arrived, tired from her journey, rather shabby, moving in the manner of one who has no interest in pleasing, I thought her an ugly woman. It was odd, I thought, how the same ingredients, differently dispensed, could produce Brideshead, Sebastian, Julia, and her. She was unmistakably their sister, without any of Julia's or Sebastian's grace, without Brideshead's gravity. She seemed brisk and matter-of-fact, steeped in the atmosphere of camp and dressing-station so accustomed to gross suffering as to lose the finer shades of pleasure. She looked more than her twenty-six years; hard living had roughened her; constant intercourse in a foreign tongue had worn away the nuances of speech; she straddled a little as she sat by the fire, and when she said, 'It's wonderful to be home,' it sounded to my ears like the grunt of an animal returning to its basket.

Those were the impressions of the first half hour, sharpened by the contrast with Julia's white skin and silk and jewelled hair and with my memories of her as a child.

'My job's over in Spain,' she said; 'the authorities were very polite, thanked me for all I'd done, gave me a medal, and sent me packing. It looks as though there'll be plenty of the same sort of work over here soon.'

Then she said: 'Is it too late to see nanny?'

'No, she sits up to all hours with her wireless.'

We went up, all three together, to the old nursery. Julia and I always spent part of our day there. Nanny Hawkins and my father were two people who seemed impervious to change, neither an hour older than when I first knew them. A wireless set had now been added to Nanny Hawkins' small assembly of pleasures–the rosary, the Peerage with its neat brown-paper wrapping protecting the red and gold covers, the photographs, and holiday souvenirs–on her table. When we broke it to her that Julia and I were to be married, she said: 'Well, dear, I hope it's all for the best,' for it was not part of her religion to question the propriety of Julia's actions.

Brideshead had never been a favourite with her; she greeted the news of his engagement with: 'He's certainly taken long enough to make up his mind,' and, when the search through Debrett afforded no information about Mrs Muspratt's connexions: 'She's caught him, I daresay.'

We found her, as always in the evening, at the fireside with her teapot, and the wool rug she was making.

'I knew you'd be up,' she said. 'Mr Wilcox sent to tell me you were coming.'

'I brought you some lace.'

'Well, dear, that is nice. Just like her poor Ladyship used to wear at mass. Though why they made it black I never did understand, seeing lace is white naturally. That is very welcome, I'm sure.'

'May I turn off the wireless, nanny?'

'Why, of course; I didn't notice it was on, in the pleasure of seeing you. What have you done to your hair?'

'I know it's terrible. I must get all that put right now I'm back. Darling nanny.'

As we sat there talking, and I saw Cordelia's fond eyes on all of us, I began to realize that she, too, had a beauty of her own.

'I saw Sebastian last month.'

'What a time he's been gone! Was he quite well?'

'Not very. That's why I went. It's quite near you know from Spain to Tunis. He's with the monks there.'

'I hope they look after him properly. I expect they find him a regular handful. He always sends to me at Christmas, but it's not the same as having him home. Why you must all always be going abroad I never did understand. Just like his Lordship. When there was that talk about going to war with Munich, I said to myself, "There's Cordelia and Sebastian and his Lordship all abroad; that'll be very awkward for them."'

'I wanted him to come home with me, but he wouldn't. He's got a beard now, you know, and he's very religious.'

'That I won't believe, not even if I see it. He was always a little heathen. Brideshead was one for church, not Sebastian. And a beard, only fancy; such a nice fair skin as he had; always looked clean though he'd not been near water all day, while Brideshead there was no doing anything with, scrub as you might.'

'It's frightening,' Julia once said, 'to think how completely you have forgotten Sebastian.'

'He was the forerunner.'

'That's what you said in the storm. I've thought since, perhaps I am only a forerunner, too.'

'Perhaps,' I thought, while her words still hung in the air between us like a wisp of tobacco smoke–a thought to fade and vanish like smoke without a trace–'perhaps all our loves are merely hints and symbols; vagabond-language scrawled on gate-posts and paving-stones along the weary road that others have tramped before us; perhaps you and I are types and this sadness which sometimes falls between us springs from disappointment in our search, each straining through and beyond the other, snatching a glimpse now and then of the shadow which turns the corner always a pace or two ahead of us.'

I had not forgotten Sebastian. He was with me daily in Julia; or rather it was Julia I had known in him, in those distant Arcadian days.

'That's cold comfort for a girl,' she said when I tried to explain. 'How do I know I shan't suddenly turn out to be somebody else? It's an easy way to chuck.'

I had not forgotten Sebastian; every stone of the house had a memory of him, and hearing him spoken of by Cordelia as someone she had seen a month ago, my lost friend filled my thoughts. When we left the nursery, I said, 'I want to hear all about Sebastian.'

'Tomorrow. It's a long story.'

And next day, walking through the wind-swept park, she told me:

'I heard he was dying,' she said. 'A journalist in Burgos told me, who'd just arrived from North Africa. A down-and-out called Flyte, who people said was an English lord, whom the fathers had found starving and taken in at a monastery near Carthage. That was how the story reached me. I knew it couldn't be quite true–however little we did for Sebastian, he at least got his money sent him–but I started off at once.

'It was all quite easy. I went to the consulate first and they knew all about him; he was in the infirmary of the head house of some missionary fathers. The consul's story was that Sebastian had turned up in Tunis one day in a motor bus from Algiers, and had applied to be taken on as a missionary lay-brother. The Fathers took one look at him and turned him down. Then he started drinking. He lived in a little hotel on the edge of the Arab quarter. I went to see the place later; it was a bar with a few rooms over it, kept by a Greek, smelling of hot oil and garlic and stale wine and old clothes, a place where the small Greek traders came and played draughts and listened to the wireless. He stayed there a month drinking Greek absinthe, occasionally wandering out, they didn't know where, coming back and drinking again. They were afraid he would come to harm and followed him sometimes, but he only went to the church or took a car to the monastery outside the town. They loved him there. He's still loved, you see, wherever he goes, whatever condition he's in. It's a thing about him he'll never lose. You should have heard the proprietor and his family talk of him, tears running down their cheeks; they'd clearly robbed him right and left, but they'd looked after him and tried to make him eat his food. That was the thing that shocked them about him; that he wouldn't eat; there he was with all that money, so thin. Some of the clients of the place came in while we were talking in very peculiar French; they all had the same story; such a *good* man, they said, it made them unhappy to see him so low. They thought very ill of his family for leaving him like that; it couldn't happen with their people, they said, and I daresay they're right.

'Anyway, that was later; after the consulate I went straight to the monastery and saw the Superior. He was a grim old Dutchman who had spent fifty years in Central Africa. He told me his part of the story; how Sebastian had turned up, just as the consul said, with his beard and a suitcase, and asked to be admitted as a lay-brother. "He was very earnest," the Superior said'–Cordelia imitated his guttural tones; she had an aptitude for mimicry, I remembered, in the schoolroom–"Please do not think there is any doubt of that–he is quite sane and quite in earnest." He wanted to go to the bush, as far away as he could get, among the simplest people, to the cannibals. The Superior said: "We have no cannibals in our missions." He said, well, pygmies would do, or just a primitive village somewhere on a river, or lepers, lepers would do best of anything. The Superior said: "We have plenty of lepers, but they live in our settlements with doctors and nuns. It is all very orderly." He thought again, and said perhaps lepers were not what he wanted, was there not some small church by a river–he always wanted a river you see–which he could look after when the priest was away. The Superior said: "Yes, there are such churches. Now tell me about yourself." "Oh, I'm nothing," he said. "We see some queer fish,"' Cordelia lapsed again into mimicry; '"he was a queer fish but he was very earnest." The Superior told him about the novitiate and the training and said: "You are not a young man. You do not seem strong to me." He said: "No, I don't want to be trained. I don't want to do things that need training." The Superior said: "My friend, you need a missionary for yourself," and he said: "Yes, of course." Then he sent him away.

'Next day he came back again. He had been drinking. He said he had decided to become a novice and be trained. "Well," said the Superior, "there are certain things that are impossible for a man in the bush. One of them is drinking. It is not the worst thing, but it is nevertheless quite fatal. I sent him away." Then he kept coming two or three times a week, always drunk, until the Superior gave orders that the porter was to keep him out. I said, "Oh dear, I'm afraid he was a terrible nuisance to you," but of course that's a thing they don't understand in a place like that. The Superior simply said, "I did not think there was anything I could do to help him except pray." He was a very holy man and recognized it in others.'

'Holiness?'

'Oh yes, Charles, that's what you've got to understand about Sebastian.

'Well, finally one day they found Sebastian lying outside the main gate unconscious, he had walked out–usually he took a car–and fallen down and lain there all night. At first they thought he was merely drunk again; then they realized he was very ill, so they put him in the infirmary, where he'd been ever since.

'I stayed a fortnight with him till he was over the worst of his illness. He looked terrible, any age, rather bald with a straggling beard, but he had his old sweet manner. They'd given him a room to himself; it was barely more than a monk's cell with a bed and a crucifix and white walls. At first he couldn't talk much and was not at all surprised to see me; then he was surprised and wouldn't talk much, until just before I was going, when he told me all that had been happening to him. It was mostly about Kurt, his German friend. Well, you met him, so you know all about that. He sounds gruesome, but as long as Sebastian had him to look after, he was happy. He told me he'd practically given up drinking at one time while he and Kurt lived together. Kurt was ill and had a wound that wouldn't heal. Sebastian saw him through that. Then they went to Greece when Kurt got well. You know how Germans sometimes seem to discover a sense of decency when they get to a classical country. It seems to have worked with Kurt. Sebastian says he became quite human in Athens. Then he got sent to prison; I couldn't quite make out why; apparently it wasn't particularly his fault–some brawl with an official. Once he was locked up the German authorities got at him. It was the time when they were rounding up all their nationals from all parts of the world to make them into Nazis. Kurt didn't want to leave Greece, but the Greeks didn't want him, and he was marched straight from prison with a lot of other toughs into a German boat and shipped home.

'Sebastian went after him, and for a year could find no trace. Then in the end he ran him to earth dressed as a storm-trooper in a provincial town. At first he wouldn't have anything to do with Sebastian; spouted all the official jargon about the rebirth of his country, and his belonging to his country, and finding self-realization in the life of the race. But it was only skin deep with him. Six years of Sebastian had taught him more than a year of Hitler; eventually he chucked it, admitted he hated Germany, and wanted to get out. I don't know how much it was simply the call of the easy life, sponging on Sebastian, bathing in the Mediterranean, sitting about in cafés, having his shoes polished. Sebastian says it wasn't entirely that; Kurt had just begun to grow up in Athens. It may be he's right. Anyway, he decided to try and get out. But it didn't work. He always got into trouble whatever he did, Sebastian said. They caught him and put him in a concentration camp. Sebastian couldn't get near him or hear a word of him; he couldn't even find what camp he was in; he hung about for nearly a year in Germany, drinking again, until one day in his cups he took up with a man who was just out of the camp where Kurt had been, and learned that he had hanged himself in his hut the first week.

'So that was the end of Europe for Sebastian. He went back to Morocco, where he had been happy, and gradually drifted down the coast, from place to place, until one day when he had sobered up–his drinking goes in pretty regular bouts now–he conceived the idea of escaping to the savages. And there he was.

'I didn't suggest his coming home. I knew he wouldn't, and he was too weak still to argue it out. He seemed quite happy by the time I left. He'll never be able to go into the bush, of course, or join the order, but the Father Superior is going to take charge of him, They had the idea of making him a sort of under-porter; there are usually a few odd hangers-on in a religious house, you know; people who can't quite fit in either to the world or the monastic rule. I suppose I'm something of the sort myself. But as I don't happen to drink, I'm more employable.'

We had reached the turn in our walk, the stone bridge at the foot of the last and smallest lake, under which the swollen waters fell in a cataract to the stream below; beyond, the path doubled back towards the house. We paused at the parapet looking down into the dark water.

'I once had a governess who jumped off this bridge and drowned herself.'

'Yes, I know.'

'How could you know?'

'It was the first thing I ever heard about you–before I ever met you.'

'How very odd. . . .'

'Have you told Julia this about Sebastian?'

'The substance of it; not quite as I told you. She never loved him, you know, as we do.'

'*Do*.' The word reproached me; there was no past tense in Cordelia's verb, 'to love'.

'Poor Sebastian!' I said. 'It's too pitiful. How will it end?'

'I think I can tell you exactly, Charles. I've seen others like him, and I believe they are very near and dear to God. He'll live on, half in, half out of, the community, a familiar figure pottering round with his broom and his bunch of keys. He'll be a great favourite with the old fathers, something of a joke to the novices. Everyone will know about his drinking; he'll disappear for two or three days every month or so, and they'll all nod and smile and say in their various accents, "Old Sebastian's on the spree again," and then he'll come back dishevelled and shamefaced and be more devout for a day or two in the chapel. He'll probably have little hiding places about the garden where he keeps a bottle and takes a swig now and then on the sly. They'll bring him forward to act as guide, whenever they have an English-speaking visitor, and he will be completely charming so that before they go, they'll ask about him and perhaps be given a hint that he has high connexions at home. If he lives long enough, generations of missionaries in all kinds of remote places will think of him as a queer old character who was somehow part of the Home of their student days, and remember him in their masses. He'll develop little eccentricities of devotion, intense personal cults of his own; he'll be found in the chapel at odd times and missed when he's expected. Then one morning, after one of his drinking bouts, he'll be picked up at the gate dying, and show by a mere flicker of the eyelid that he is conscious when they give him the last sacraments. It's not such a bad way of getting through one's life.'

I thought of the youth with the teddy-bear under the flowering chestnuts. 'It's not what one would have foretold,' I said. 'I suppose he doesn't suffer?'

'Oh, yes, I think he does. One can have no idea what the suffering may be, to be maimed as he is–no dignity, no power of will. No one is ever holy without suffering. It's taken that form with him. . . . I've seen so much suffering in the last few years; there's so much coming for everybody soon. It's the spring of love . . .' and then in condescension to my paganism, she added: 'He's in a very beautiful place, you know, by the sea–white cloisters, a bell tower, rows of green vegetables, and a monk watering them when the sun is low.'

I laughed. 'You knew I wouldn't understand?'

'You and Julia . . .' she said. And then, as we moved on towards the house, 'When you met me last night did you think, "Poor Cordelia, such an engaging child, grown up a plain and pious spinster, full of good works"? Did you think "thwarted"?'

It was no time for prevarication. 'Yes,' I said, 'I did; I don't now, so much.'

'It's funny,' she said, 'that's exactly the word I thought of for you and Julia. When we were up in the nursery with nanny. "Thwarted passion," I thought.'

She spoke with that gentle, infinitesimal inflexion of mockery which descended to her from her mother, but later that evening the words came back to me poignantly.

Julia wore the embroidered Chinese robe which she often used when we were dining alone at Brideshead; it was a robe whose weight and stiff folds stressed her repose; her neck rose exquisitely from the plain gold circle at her throat; her hands lay still among the dragons in her lap. It was thus that I had rejoiced to see her nights without number, and that night, watching her as she sat between the firelight and the shaded lamp, unable to look away for love of her beauty, I suddenly thought, 'When else have I seen her like this? Why am I reminded of another moment of vision?' And it came back to me that this was how she had sat in the liner, before the storm; this was how she had looked, and I realized that she had regained what I thought she had lost for ever, the magical sadness which had drawn me to her, the thwarted look that had seemed to say, 'Surely I was made for some other purpose than this?'

That night I woke in the darkness and lay awake turning over in my mind the conversation with Cordelia. How I had said, 'You knew I would not understand.' How often, it seemed to me, I was brought up short, like a horse in full stride suddenly refusing an obstacle, backing against the spurs, too shy even to put his nose at it and look at the thing.

And another image came to me, of an arctic hut and a trapper alone with his furs and oil lamp and log fire; everything dry and ship-shape and warm inside, and outside the last blizzard of winter raging and the snow piling up against the door. Quite silently a great weight forming against the timber; the bolt straining in its socket; minute by minute in the darkness outside the white heap sealing the door, until quite soon when the wind dropped and the sun came out on the ice slopes and the thaw set in a block would move, slide, and tumble, high above, gather weight, till the whole hillside seemed to be falling, and the little lighted place would open and splinter and disappear, rolling with the avalanche into the ravine.

5

My divorce case, or rather my wife's, was due to be heard at about the same time as Brideshead was to be married. Julia's would not come up till the following term; meanwhile the game of General Post–moving my property from the Old Rectory to my flat, my wife's from my flat to the Old Rectory, Julia's from Rex's house and from Brideshead to my flat, Rex's from Brideshead to his house and Mrs Muspratt's from Falmouth to Brideshead–was in full swing and we were all, in varying degrees, homeless, when a halt was called and Lord Marchmain, with a taste for the dramatically inopportune which was plainly the prototype of his elder son's, declared his intention, in view of the international situation, of returning to England and passing his declining years in his old home.

The only member of the family to whom this change promised any benefit was Cordelia, who had been sadly abandoned in the turmoil. Brideshead, indeed, had made a formal request to her to consider his house her home for as long as it suited her, but when she learned that her sister-in-law proposed to install her children there for the holidays immediately after the wedding, in the charge of a sister of hers and the sister's friend, Cordelia had decided to move, too, and was talking of setting up alone in London. She now found herself, Cinderella-like, promoted *châtelaine*, while her brother and his wife who had till that moment expected to find themselves, within a matter of days, in absolute command, were without a roof; the deeds of conveyance, engrossed and ready for signing, were rolled up, tied, and put away in one of the black tin boxes in Lincoln's Inn. It was bitter for Mrs Muspratt; she was not an ambitious woman; something very much less grand than Brideshead would have contented her heartily, but she did aspire to find some shelter for her children over Christmas. The house at Falmouth was stripped and up for sale; moreover, Mrs Muspratt had taken leave of the place with some justifiably rather large talk of her new establishment; they could not return there. She was obliged in a hurry to move her furniture from Lady Marchmain's room to a disused coach-house and to take a furnished villa at Torquay. She was not, as I have said a woman of high ambition, but, having had her expectations so much raised, it was disconcerting to be brought so low so suddenly. In the village the working party who had been preparing the decorations for the bridal entry, began unpicking the Bs on the bunting and substituting Ms, obliterating the Earl's points and stencilling balls and strawberry leaves on the painted coronets, in preparation for Lord Marchmain's return.

News of his intentions came first to the solicitors, then to Cordelia, then to Julia and me, in a rapid succession of contradictory cables. Lord Marchmain would arrive in time for the wedding; he would arrive after the wedding, having seen Lord and Lady Brideshead on their way through Paris; he would see them in Rome. He was not well enough to travel at all; he was just starting; he had unhappy memories of winter at Brideshead and would not come until spring was well advanced and the heating apparatus overhauled; he was coming alone; he was bringing his Italian household; he wished his return to be unannounced and to lead a life of complete seclusion; he would give a ball. At last a date in January was chosen which proved to be the correct one.

Plender preceded him by some days; there was a difficulty here. Plender was not an original member of the Brideshead household; he had been Lord Marchmain's servant in the yeomanry, and had only once met Wilcox on the painful occasion of the removal of his master's luggage when it was decided not to return from the war; then Plender had been valet, as, officially, he still was, but he had in the past years introduced a kind of suffragan, a Swiss body-servant, to attend to the wardrobe and also, when occasion arose, lend a hand with less dignified tasks about the house, and had in effect become major-domo of that fluctuating and mobile household; sometimes he even referred to himself on the telephone as 'the secretary'. There was an acre of thin ice between him and Wilcox.

Fortunately the two men took a liking to one another, and the thing was solved in a series of three-cornered discussions with Cordelia. Plender and Wilcox became joint grooms of the chambers, like 'Blues' and Life Guards with equal precedence, Plender having as his particular province his Lordship's own apartments and Wilcox a sphere of influence in the public rooms; the senior footman was given a black coat and promoted butler, the nondescript Swiss, on arrival, was to have plain clothes and full valet's status; there was a general increase in wages to meet the new dignities, and all were content.

Julia and I, who had left Brideshead a month before, thinking we should not return, moved back for the reception. When the day came, Cordelia went to the station and we remained to greet him at home. It was a bleak and gusty day. Cottages and lodges were decorated; plans for a bonfire that night and for the village silver band to play on the terrace, were put down, but the house flag, that had not flown for twenty-five years, was hoisted over the pediment, and flapped sharply against the leaden sky. Whatever harsh voices might be bawling into the microphones of central Europe, and whatever lathes spinning in the armament factories, the return of Lord Marchmain was a matter of first importance in his own neighbourhood.

He was due at three o'clock. Julia and I waited in the drawing-room until Wilcox, who had arranged with the stationmaster to be kept informed, announced 'the train is signalled', and a minute later, 'the train is in; his Lordship is on the way.' Then we went to the front portico and waited there with the upper servants. Soon the Rolls appeared at the turn in the drive, followed at some distance by the two vans. It drew up; first Cordelia got out, then Cara; there was a pause, a rug was handed to the chauffeur, a stick to the footman; then a leg was cautiously thrust forward. Plender was by now at the car door; another servant–the Swiss valet–had emerged from a van; together they lifted Lord Marchmain out and set him on his feet; he felt for his stick, grasped it, and stood for a minute collecting his strength for the few low steps which led to the front door.

Julia gave a little sigh of surprise and touched my hand. We had seen him nine months ago at Monte Carlo, when he had been an upright and stately figure, little changed from when I first met him in Venice. Now he was an old man. Plender had told us his master had been unwell lately: he had not prepared us for this.

Lord Marchmain stood bowed and shrunken, weighed down by his greatcoat, a white muffler fluttering untidily at his throat, a cloth cap pulled low on his forehead, his face white and lined, his nose coloured by the cold; the tears which gathered in his eyes came not from emotion but from the east wind; he breathed heavily. Cara tucked in the end of his muffler and whispered something to him. He raised a gloved hand–a schoolboy's glove of grey wool–and made a small, weary gesture of greeting to the group at the door; then, very slowly, with his eyes on the ground before him, he made his way into the house.

They took off his coat and cap and muffler and the kind of leather jerkin which he wore under them; thus stripped he seemed more than ever wasted but more elegant; he had cast the shabbiness of extreme fatigue. Cara straightened his tie; he wiped his eyes with a bandanna handkerchief and shuffled with his stick to the hall fire.

There was a little heraldic chair by the chimney-piece, one of a set which stood against the walls, a little, inhospitable, flat-seated thing, a mere excuse for the elaborate armorial painting on its back, on which, perhaps, no one, not even a weary footman, had ever sat since it was made; there Lord Marchmain sat and wiped his eyes.

'It's the cold,' he said. 'I'd forgotten how cold it is in England. Quite bowled me over.'

'Can I get you anything, my Lord?'

'Nothing, thank you. Cara, where are those confounded pills?'

'Alex, the doctor said not more than three times a day.'

'Damn the doctor. I feel quite bowled over.'

Cara produced a blue bottle from her bag and Lord Marchmain took a pill. Whatever was in it, seemed to revive him. He remained seated, his long legs stuck out before him, his cane between them, his chin on its ivory handle, but he began to take notice of us all, to greet us and to give orders.

'I'm afraid I'm not at all the thing today; the journey's taken it out of me. Ought to have waited a night at Dover. Wilcox, what rooms have you prepared for me?'

'Your old ones, my Lord.'

'Won't do; not till I'm fit again. Too many stairs; must be on the ground floor. Plender, get a bed made up for me downstairs.'

Plender and Wilcox exchanged an anxious glance.

'Very good, my Lord. Which room shall we put it in?'

Lord Marchmain thought for a moment. 'The Chinese drawing-room; and, Wilcox, the "Queen's bed".'

'The Chinese drawing-room, my Lord, the "Queen's bed"?'

'Yes, yes. I may be spending some time there in the next few weeks.'

The Chinese drawing-room was one I had never seen used; in fact one could not normally go further into it than a small roped area round the door, where sight-seers were corralled on the days the house was open to the public; it was a splendid, uninhabitable museum of Chippendale carving and porcelain and lacquer and painted hangings; the Queen's bed, too, was an exhibition piece, a vast velvet tent like the *baldachino* at St Peter's. Had Lord Marchmain planned this lying-in-state for himself, I wondered, before he left the sunshine of Italy? Had he thought of it during the scudding rain of his long, fretful journey? Had it come to him at that moment, an awakened memory of childhood, a dream in the nursery–'When I'm grown up I'll sleep in the Queen's bed in the Chinese drawing-room'–the apotheosis of adult grandeur?

Few things, certainly, could have caused more stir in the house. What had been foreseen as a day of formality became one of fierce exertion; housemaids began making a fire, removing covers, unfolding linen; men in aprons, never normally seen, shifted furniture; the estate carpenters were collected to dismantle the bed. It came down the main staircase in pieces, at intervals during the afternoon; huge sections of Rococo, velvet-covered cornice; the twisted, gilt and velvet columns which formed its posts; beams of unpolished wood, made not to be seen, which performed invisible, structural functions below the draperies; plumes of dyed feathers, which sprang from gold-mounted ostrich eggs and crowned the canopy; finally, the mattresses with four toiling men to each. Lord Marchmain seemed to derive comfort from the consequences of his whim; he sat by the fire watching the bustle, while we stood in a half circle–Cara, Cordelia, Julia, and I–and talked to him.

Colour came back to his cheeks and light to his eyes. 'Brideshead and his wife dined with me in Rome,' he said. 'Since we are all members of the family'–and his eye moved ironically from Cara to me–'I can speak without reserve. I found her deplorable. Her former consort, I understand, was a seafaring man and, presumably, the less exacting, but how my son, at the ripe age of thirty-eight, with, unless things have changed very much, a very free choice among the women of England, can have settled on–I suppose I must call her so–*Beryl*. . . .' He left the sentence eloquently unfinished.

Lord Marchmain showed no inclination to move, so presently we drew up chairs–the little, heraldic chairs, for everything else in the hall was ponderous–and sat round him.

'I daresay I shall not be really fit again until summer comes,' he said. 'I look to you four to amuse me.'

There seemed little we could do at the moment to lighten the rather sombre mood; he, indeed, was the most cheerful of us. 'Tell me,' he said, 'the circumstances of Brideshead's courtship.'

We told him what we knew.

'Match-boxes,' he said. 'Match-boxes. I think she's past child-bearing.'

Tea was brought us at the hall fireplace.

'In Italy,' he said, 'no one believes there will be a war. They think it will all be "arranged". I suppose, Julia, you no longer have access to political information? Cara, here, is fortunately a British subject by marriage. It is not a thing she customarily mentions, but it may prove valuable. She is legally Mrs Hicks, are you not, my dear? We know little of Hicks, but we shall be grateful to him, none the less, if it comes to war. And you,' he said, turning the attack to me, 'you will no doubt become an official artist?'

'No. As a matter of fact I am negotiating now for a commission in the Special Reserve.'

'Oh, but you should be an artist. I had one with my squadron during the last war, for weeks–until we went up to the line.'

This waspishness was new. I had always been aware of a frame of malevolence under his urbanity; now it protruded like his own sharp bones through the sunken skin.

It was dark before the bed was finished; we went to see it, Lord Marchmain stepping quite briskly now through the intervening rooms.

'I congratulate you. It really looks remarkably well. Wilcox, I seem to remember a silver basin and ewer–they stood in a room we called "the Cardinal's dressing-room", I think–suppose we had them here on the console. Then if you will send Plender and Gaston to me, the luggage can wait till tomorrow–simply the dressing case and what I need for the night. Plender will know. If you will leave me with Plender and Gaston, I will go to bed. We will meet later; you will dine here and keep me amused.'

We turned to go; as I was at the door he called me back.

'It looks very well, does it not?'

'Very well.'

'You might paint it, eh–and call it the *Death Bed*?'

'Yes,' said Cara, 'he has come home to die.'

'But when he first arrived he was talking so confidently of recovery.'

'That was because he was so ill. When he is himself, he knows he is dying and accepts it. His sickness is up and down; one day, sometimes for several days on end, he is strong and lively and then he is ready for death, then he is down and afraid. I do not know how it will be when he is more and more down. That must come in good time. The doctors in Rome gave him less than a year. There is someone coming from London, I think tomorrow, who will tell us more.'

'What is it?'

'His heart; some long word at the heart. He is dying of a long word.'

That evening Lord Marchmain was in good spirits; the room had a Hogarthian aspect, with the dinner-table set for the four of us by the grotesque, *chinoiserie* chimney-piece, and the old man propped among his pillows, sipping champagne, tasting, praising, and failing to eat, the succession of dishes which had been prepared for his home-coming. Wilcox had brought out for the occasion the gold plate, which I had not before seen in use; that, the gilt mirrors, and the lacquer and the drapery of the great bed and Julia's mandarin coat gave the scene an air of pantomime, of Aladdin's cave.

Just at the end, when the time came for us to go, his spirits flagged.

'I shall not sleep,' he said. 'Who is going to sit with me? Cara, *carissima*, you are fatigued. Cordelia, will you watch for an hour in this Gethsemane?'

Next morning I asked her how the night had passed.

'He went to sleep almost at once. I came in to see him at two to make up the fire; the lights were on, but he was asleep again. He must have woken up and turned them on; he had to get out of bed to do that. I think perhaps he is afraid of the dark.'

It was natural, with her hospital experience, that Cordelia should take charge of her father. When the doctors came that day they gave their instructions to her, instinctively.

'Until he gets worse,' she said, 'I and the valet can look after him. We don't want nurses in the house before they are needed.'

At this stage the doctors had nothing to recommend except to keep him comfortable and administer certain drugs when his attacks came on.

'How long will it be?'

'Lady Cordelia, there are men walking about in hearty old age whom their doctors gave a week to live. I have learned one thing in medicine; never prophesy.'

These two man had made a long journey to tell her this; the local doctor was there to accept the same advice in technical phrases.

That night Lord Marchmain reverted to the topic of his new daughter-in-law; it had never been long out of his mind, finding expression in various sly hints throughout the day; now he lay back in his pillows and talked of her at length.

'I have never been much moved by family piety until now,' he said, 'but I am frankly appalled at the prospect of–of Beryl taking what was once my mother's place in this house. Why should that uncouth pair sit here childless while the place crumbles about their ears? I will not disguise from you that I have taken a dislike to Beryl.

'Perhaps it was unfortunate that we met in Rome. Anywhere else might have been more sympathetic. And yet, if one comes to consider it, where could I have met her without repugnance? We dined at Ranieri's; it is a quiet little restaurant I have frequented for years–no doubt you know it. Beryl seemed to fill the place. I, of course, was host, though to hear Beryl press my son with food, you might have thought otherwise. Brideshead was always a greedy boy; a wife who has his best interests at heart should seek to restrain him. However, that is a matter of small importance.

'She had no doubt heard of me as a man of irregular life. I can only describe her manner to me as roguish. A naughty old man, that's what she thought I was. I suppose she had met naughty old admirals and knew how they sould be humoured . . . I could not attempt to reproduce her conversation. I will give you one example.

'They had been to an audience at the Vatican that morning; a blessing for their marriage–I did not follow attentively–something of the kind had happened before, I gathered, some previous husband, some previous Pope. She described, rather vivaciously, how on this earlier occasion she had gone with a whole body of newly married couples, mostly Italians of all ranks, some of the simpler girls in their wedding dresses, and how each had appraised the other, the bridegrooms looking the brides over, comparing their own with one another's, and so forth. Then she said, "This time, of course, we were in private, but do you know, Lord Marchmain, I felt as though it was I who was leading in the bride."

'It was said with great indelicacy. I have not yet quite fathomed her meaning. Was she making a play on my son's name, or was she, do you think, referring to his undoubted virginity? I fancy the latter. Anyway, it was with pleasantries of that kind that we passed the evening.

'I don't think she would be quite in her proper element here, do you? Who shall I leave it to? The entail ended with me, you know. Sebastian, alas, is out of the question. Who wants it? *Quis?* Would you like it, Cara? No, of course you would not. Cordelia? I think I shall leave it to Julia and Charles.'

'Of course not, papa, it's Bridey's.'

'And . . . Beryl's? I will have Gregson down one day soon and go over the matter. It is time I brought my will up to date; it is full of anomalies and anachronisms. . . . I have rather a fancy for the idea of installing Julia here; so beautiful this evening, my dear; so beautiful always; much, much more suitable.'

Shortly after this he sent to London for his solicitor, but, on the day he came, Lord Marchmain was suffering from an attack and would not see him. 'Plenty of time,' he said, between painful gasps for breath, 'another day, when I am stronger,' but the choice of his heir was constantly in his mind, and he referred often to the time when Julia and I should be married and in possession.

'Do you think he really means to leave it to us?' I asked Julia.

'Yes, I think he does.'

'But it's monstrous for Bridey.'

'Is it? I don't think he cares much for the place. I do, you know. He and Beryl would be much more content in some little house somewhere.'

'You mean to accept it?'

'Certainly. It's papa's to leave as he likes. I think you and I could be very happy here.'

It opened a prospect; the prospect one gained at the turn of the avenue, as I had first seen it with Sebastian, of the secluded valley, the lakes falling away one below the other, the old house in the foreground, the rest of the world abandoned and forgotten; a world of its own of peace and love and beauty; a soldier's dream in a foreign bivouac; such a prospect perhaps as a high pinnacle of the temple afforded after the hungry days in the desert and the jackal-haunted nights. Need I reproach myself if sometimes I was taken by the vision?

The weeks of illness wore on and the life of the house kept pace with the faltering strength of the sick man. There were days when Lord Marchmain was dressed, when he stood at the window or moved on his valet's arm from fire to fire through the rooms of the ground floor, when visitors came and went–neighbours and people from the estate, men of business from London–parcels of new books were opened and discussed, a piano was moved into the Chinese drawing-room; once at the end of February, on a single, unexpected day of brilliant sunshine, he called for a car and got as far as the hall, had on his fur coat, and reached the front door. Then suddenly he lost interest in the drive, said 'Not now. Later. One day in the summer,' took his man's arm again and was led back to his chair. Once he had the humour of changing his room and gave detailed orders for a move to the Painted Parlour; the *chinoiserie*, he said, disturbed his rest–he kept the lights full on at night–but again lost heart, countermanded everything, and kept his room.

On other days the house was hushed as he sat high in bed, propped by his pillows, with labouring breath; even then he wanted to have us round him; night or day he could not bear to be alone; when he could not speak his eyes followed us, and if anyone left the room he would look distressed, and Cara, sitting often for hours at a time by his side against the pillows with an arm in his, would say, 'It's all right, Alex, she's coming back.'

Brideshead and his wife returned from their honeymoon and stayed a few nights; it was one of the bad times, and Lord Marchmain refused to have them near him. It was Beryl's first visit, and she would have been unnatural if she had shown no curiosity about what had nearly been, and now again promised soon to be, her home. Beryl was natural enough, and surveyed the place fairly thoroughly in the days she was there. In the strange disorder caused by Lord Marchmain's illness, it must have seemed capable of much improvement; she referred once or twice to the way in which establishments of similar size had been managed at various Government Houses she had visited. Brideshead took her visiting among the tenants by day, and in the evenings, she talked to me of painting, or to Cordelia of hospitals, or to Julia of clothes, with cheerful assurance. The shadow of betrayal, the knowledge of how precarious were their just expectations, was all one-sided. I was not easy with them; but that was no new thing to Brideshead; in the little circle of shyness in which he was used to move, my guilt passed unseen.

Eventually it became clear that Lord Marchmain did not intend to see more of them. Brideshead was admitted alone for a minute's leave-taking; then they left.

'There's nothing we can do here,' said Brideshead, 'and it's very distressing for Beryl. We'll come back if things get worse.'

The bad spells became longer and more frequent; a nurse was engaged. 'I never saw such a room,' she said, 'nothing like it anywhere; no conveniences of any sort.' She tried to have her patient moved upstairs, where there was running water, a dressing-room for herself, a 'sensible' narrow bed she could 'get round'–what she was used to–but Lord Marchmain would not budge. Soon, as days and nights became indistinguishable to him, a second nurse was installed; the specialists came again from London; they recommended a new and rather daring treatment, but his body seemed weary of all drugs and did not respond. Presently there were no good spells, merely brief fluctuations in the speed of his decline.

Brideshead was called. It was the Easter holidays and Beryl was busy with her children. He came alone, and having stood silently for some minutes beside his father, who sat silently looking at him, he left the room and, joining the rest of us, who were in the library, said, 'Papa must see a priest.'

It was not the first time the topic had come up. In the early days, when Lord Marchmain first arrived, the parish priest–since the chapel was shut there was a new church and presbytery in Melstead–had come to call as a matter of politeness. Cordelia had put him off with apologies and excuses, but when he was gone she said: 'Not yet. Papa doesn't want him yet.'

Julia, Cara, and I were there at the time; we each had something to say, began to speak, and thought better of it. It was never mentioned between the four of us, but Julia, alone with me, said, 'Charles, I see great Church trouble ahead.'

'Can't they even let him die in peace?'

'They mean something so different by "peace".'

'It would be an outrage. No one could have made it clearer, all his life, what he thought of religion. They'll come now, when his mind's wandering and he hasn't the strength to resist, and claim him as a death-bed penitent. I've had a certain respect for their Church up till now. If they do a thing like that I shall know that everything stupid people say about them is quite true–that it's all superstition and trickery.' Julia said nothing. 'Don't you agree?' Still Julia said nothing. 'Don't you agree?'

'I don't know, Charles. I simply don't know.'

And, though none of us spoke of it, I felt the question ever present, growing through all the weeks of Lord Marchmain's illness; I saw it when Cordelia drove off early in the mornings to mass; I saw it as Cara took to going with her; this little cloud, the size of a man's hand, that was going to swell into a storm among us.

Now Brideshead, in his heavy, ruthless way, planted the problem down before us.

'Oh, Bridey, do you think he would?' asked Cordelia.

'I shall see that he does,' said Brideshead. 'I shall take Father Mackay in to him tomorrow.'

Still the clouds gathered and did not break; none of us spoke. Cara and Cordelia went back to the sick-room; Brideshead looked for a book, found one, and left us.

'Julia,' I said, 'how can we stop this tomfoolery?'

She did not answer for some time; then: 'Why should we?'

'You know as well as I do. It's just–just an unseemly incident.'

'Who am I to object to unseemly incidents?' she asked sadly. 'Anyway, what harm can it do? Let's ask the doctor.'

We asked the doctor, who said: 'It's hard to say. It might alarm him of course; on the other hand, I have known cases where it has had a wonderfully soothing effect on a patient; I've even known it act as a positive stimulant. It certainly is usually a great comfort to the relations. Really I think it's a thing for Lord Brideshead to decide. Mind you, there is no need for immediate anxiety. Lord Marchmain is very weak today; tomorrow he may be quite strong again.

Is it not usual to wait a little?'

'Well, he wasn't much help,' I said to Julia, when we left him.

'Help? I really can't quite see why you've taken it so much to heart that my father shall not have the last sacraments.'

'It's such a lot of witchcraft and hypocrisy.'

'Is it? Anyway, it's been going on for nearly two thousand years. I don't know why you should suddenly get in a rage now.' Her voice rose; she was swift to anger of late months. 'For Christ's sake, write to *The Times*; get up and make a speech in Hyde Park; start a "No Popery" riot, but don't bore me about it. What's it got to do with you or me whether my father sees his parish priest?'

I knew these fierce moods of Julia's, such as had overtaken her at the fountain in moonlight, and dimly surmised their origin; I knew they could not be assuaged by words. Nor could I have spoken, for the answer to her question was still unformed; the sense that the fate of more souls than one was at issue; that the snow was beginning to shift on the high slopes.

Brideshead and I breakfasted together next morning with the night-nurse, who had just come off duty.

'He's much brighter today,' she said. 'He slept very nicely for nearly three hours. When Gaston came to shave him he was quite chatty.'

'Good,' said Brideshead. 'Cordelia went to mass. She's driving Father Mackay back here to breakfast.'

I had met Father Mackay several times; he was a stocky, middle-aged, genial Glasgow-Irishman who, when we met, was apt to ask me such questions as, 'Would you say now, Mr Ryder, that the painter Titian was more truly artistic than the painter Raphael?' and, more disconcertingly still, to remember my answers: 'To revert, Mr Ryder, to what you said when last I had the pleasure to meet you, would it be right now to say that the painter Titian . . .' usually ending with some such reflection as: 'Ah, it's a grand resource for a man to have the talent you have, Mr Ryder, and the time to indulge it.' Cordelia could imitate him.

This morning he made a hearty breakfast, glanced at the headlines of the paper, and then said with professional briskness: 'And now, Lord Brideshead, would the poor soul be ready to see me, do you think?'

Brideshead led him out; Cordelia followed, and I was left alone among the breakfast things. In less than a minute I heard the voices of all three outside the door.

'. . . can only apologize.'

'. . . poor soul. Mark you, it was seeing a strange face; depend upon it, it was that–an unexpected stranger. I well understand it.'

'. . . Father, I am sorry . . . bringing you all this way . . .'

'Don't think about it at all, Lady Cordelia. Why, I've had bottles thrown at me in the Gorbals. . . . Give him time. I've known worse cases make beautiful deaths. Pray for him . . . I'll come again . . . and now if you'll excuse me I'll just pay a little visit to Mrs Hawkins. Yes, indeed, I know the way well.'

Then Cordelia and Brideshead came into the room.

'I gather the visit was not a success.'

'It was not. Cordelia, will you drive Father Mackay home when he comes down from nanny? I'm going to telephone to Beryl and see when she needs me home.'

'Bridey, it was horrible. What are we to do?'

'We've done everything we can at the moment.' He left the room.

Cordelia's face was grave; she took a piece of bacon from the dish, dipped it in mustard and ate it. 'Damn Bridey,' she said. 'I knew it wouldn't work.'

'What happened?'

'Would you like to know? We walked in there in a line; Cara was reading the paper aloud to papa. Bridey said, "I've brought Father Mackay to see you"; papa said, "Father Mackay, I am afraid you have been brought here under a misapprehension. I am not *in extremis*, and I have not been a practising member of your Church for twenty-five years. Brideshead, show Father Mackay the way out." Then we all turned about and walked away, and I heard Cara start reading the paper again, and that, Charles, was that.'

I carried the news to Julia, who lay with her bed-table amid a litter of newspapers and envelopes. 'Mumbo-jumbo is off,' I said. 'The witch-doctor has gone.'

'Poor papa.'

'It's great sucks to Bridey.'

I felt triumphant. I had been right, everyone else had been wrong, truth had prevailed; the threat that I had felt hanging over Julia and me ever since that evening at the fountain, had been averted, perhaps dispelled for ever; and there was also–I can now confess it–another unexpressed, inexpressible, indecent little victory that I was furtively celebrating. I guessed that that morning's business had put Brideshead some considerable way further from his rightful inheritance.

In that I was correct; a man was sent for from the solicitors in London; in a day or two he came and it was known throughout the house that Lord Marchmain had made a new will. But I was wrong in thinking that the religious controversy was quashed; it flamed up again after dinner on Brideshead's last evening.

'. . . What papa said was, "I am not *in extremis*, I have not been a practising member of the Church for twenty-five years."'

'Not "*the* Church", "your Church".'

'I don't see the difference.'

'There's every difference.'

'Bridey, it's quite plain what he meant.'

'I presume he meant what he said. He meant that he had not been accustomed regularly to receive the sacraments, and since he was not at the moment dying, he did not mean to change his ways–*yet*.'

'That's simply a quibble.'

'Why do people always think that one is quibbling when one tries to be precise? His plain meaning was that he did not want to see a priest that day, but that he would when he was "*in extremis*".'

'I wish someone would explain to me,' I said, 'quite what the significance of these sacraments is. Do you mean that if he dies alone he goes to hell, and that if a priest puts oil on him—'

'Oh, it's not the oil,' said Cordelia, 'that's to heal him.'

'Odder still–well, whatever it is the priest does–that he then goes to heaven.

Is that what you believe?'

Cara then interposed: 'I think my nurse told me, someone did anyway, that if the priest got there before the body was cold it was all right. That's so, isn't it?'

The others turned on her.

'No, Cara, it's not.'

'Of course not.'

'You've got it all wrong, Cara.'

'Well, I remember when Alphonse de Grenet died, Madame de Grenet had a priest hidden outside the door–he couldn't bear the sight of a priest–and brought him in *before the body was cold*; she told me herself, and they had a full Requiem for him, and I went to it.'

'Having a Requiem doesn't mean you go to heaven necessarily.'

'Madame de Grenet thought it did.'

'Well, she was wrong.'

'Do any of you Catholics know what good you think this priest can do?' I asked. 'Do you simply want to arrange it so that your father can have Christian burial? Do you want to keep him out of hell? I only want to be told.'

Brideshead told me at some length, and when he had finished Cara slightly marred the unity of the Catholic front by saying in simple wonder, 'I never heard that before.'

'Let's get this clear,' I said; 'he has to make an act of will; he has to be contrite and wish to be reconciled; is that right? But only God knows whether he has really made an act of will; the priest can't tell; and if there isn't a priest there, and he makes the act of will alone, that's as good as if there were a priest. And it's quite possible that the will may still be working when a man is too weak to make any outward sign of it; is that right? He may be lying, as though for dead, and willing all the time, and being reconciled, and God understands that; is that right?'

'More or less,' said Brideshead.

'Well, for heaven's sake,' I said, 'what is the priest for?'

There was a pause in which Julia sighed and Brideshead drew breath as though to start further subdividing the propositions. In the silence Cara said, 'All I know is that *I* shall take very good care to have a priest.'

'Bless you,' said Cordelia, 'I believe that's the best answer.'

And we let the argument drop, each for different reasons, thinking it had been inconclusive.

Later Julia said: 'I wish you wouldn't start these religious arguments.'

'I didn't start it.'

'You don't convince anyone else and you don't really convince yourself.'

'I only want to know what these people believe. They say it's all based on logic.'

'If you'd let Bridey finish, he would have made it all quite logical.'

'There were four of you,' I said. 'Cara didn't know the first thing it was about, and may or may not have believed it; you knew a bit and didn't believe a word; Cordelia knew about as much and believed it madly; only poor Bridey knew and believed, and I thought he made a pretty poor show when it came to explaining. And people go round saying, "At least Catholics know what they believe." We had a fair cross-section tonight—'

'Oh, Charles, don't rant. I shall begin to think you're getting doubts yourself.'

The weeks passed and still Lord Marchmain lived on. In June my divorce was made absolute and my former wife married for the second time. Julia would be free in September. The nearer our marriage got, the more wistfully, I noticed, Julia spoke of it; war was growing nearer, too–we neither of us doubted that–but Julia's tender, remote, it sometimes seemed, desperate longing did not come from any uncertainty outside herself; it suddenly darkened, too, into brief accesses of hate when she seemed to throw herself against the restraints of her love for me like a caged animal against the bars.

I was summoned to the War Office, interviewed, and put on a list in case of emergency; Cordelia also, on another list; lists were becoming part of our lives once more, as they had been at school. Everything was being got ready for the coming 'Emergency'. No one in that dark office spoke the word 'war'; it was taboo; we should be called for if there was 'an emergency'–not in case of strife, an act of human will; nothing so clear and simple as wrath or retribution; an emergency; something coming out of the waters, a monster with sightless face and thrashing tail thrown up from the depths.

Lord Marchmain took little interest in events outside his own room; we took him the papers daily and made the attempt to read to him, but he turned his head on the pillows and with his eyes followed the intricate patterns about him. 'Shall I go on?' 'Please do if it's not boring you.' But he was not listening; occasionally at a familiar name he would whisper: 'Irwin . . . I knew him–a mediocre fellow'; occasionally some remote comment: 'Czechs make good coachmen; nothing else'; but his mind was far from world affairs; it was there, on the spot, turned in on himself; he had no strength for any other war than his own solitary struggle to keep alive.

I said to the doctor, who was with us daily: 'He's got a wonderful will to live, hasn't he?'

'Would you put it like that? I should say a great fear of death.'

'Is there a difference?'

'Oh dear, yes. He doesn't derive any strength from his fear, you know. It's wearing him out.'

Next to death, perhaps because they are like death, he feared darkness and loneliness. He liked to have us in his room and the lights burnt all night among the gilt figures; he did not wish us to speak much, but he talked himself, so quietly that we often could not hear him; he talked, I think, because his was the only voice he could trust, when it assured him that he was still alive; what he said was not for us, nor for any ears but his own.

'Better today. Better today. I can see now, in the corner of the fireplace, where the mandarin is holding his gold bell and the crooked tree is in flower below his feet, where yesterday I was confused and took the little tower for another man. Soon I shall see the bridge and the three storks and know where the path leads over the hill.

'Better tomorrow. We live long in our family and marry late. Seventy-three is no great age. Aunt Julia, my father's aunt, lived to be eighty-eight, born and died here, never married, saw the fire on beacon hill for the battle of Trafalgar, always called it "the New House"; that was the name they had for it in the nursery and in the fields when unlettered men had long memories. You can see where the old house stood near the village church; they call the field "Castle Hill", Horlick's field where the ground's uneven and half of it is waste, nettle, and brier in hollows too deep for ploughing. They dug to the foundations to carry the stone for the new house; the house that was a century old when Aunt Julia was born. Those were our roots in the waste hollows of Castle Hill, in the brier and nettle; among the tombs in the old church and the chantry where no clerk sings.

'Aunt Julia knew the tombs, cross-legged knight and doubleted earl, marquis like a Roman senator, limestone, alabaster, and Italian marble; tapped the escutcheons with her ebony cane, made the casque ring over old Sir Roger. We were knights then, barons since Agincourt, the larger honours came with the Georges. They came the last and they'll go the first; the barony goes on. When all of you are dead Julia's son will be called by the name his fathers bore before the fat days; the days of wool shearing and the wide corn lands, the days of growth and building, when the marshes were drained and the waste land brought under the plough, when one built the house, his son added the dome, his son spread the wings and dammed the river. Aunt Julia watched them build the fountain; it was old before it came here, weathered two hundred years by the suns of Naples, brought by man-o'-war in the days of Nelson. Soon the fountain will be dry till the rain fills it, setting the fallen leaves afloat in the basin; and over the lakes the reeds will spread and close. Better today.

'Better today. I have lived carefully, sheltered myself from the cold winds, eaten moderately of what was in season, drunk fine claret, slept in my own sheets; I shall live long. I was fifty when they dismounted us and sent us into the line; old men stay at the base, the orders said, but Walter Venables, my commanding officer, my nearest neighbour, said: "You're as fit as the youngest of them, Alex." So I was; so I am now, if I could only breathe.

'No air; no wind stirring under the velvet canopy. When the summer comes,' said Lord Marchmain, oblivious of the deep corn and swelling fruit and the surfeited bees who slowly sought their hives in the heavy afternoon sunlight outside his windows, 'when the summer comes, I shall leave my bed and sit in the open air and breathe more easily.

'Who would have thought that all these little gold men, gentlemen in their own country, could live so long without breathing? Like toads in the coal, down a deep mine, untroubled. God take it, why have they dug a hole for me? Must a man stifle to death in his own cellars? Plender, Gaston, open the windows.'

'The windows are all wide open, my Lord.'

A cylinder of oxygen was placed beside his bed, with a long tube, a face-piece, and a little stop-cock he could work himself. Often he said: 'It's empty; look nurse, there's nothing comes out.'

'No, Lord Marchmain, it's quite full; the bubble here in the glass bulb shows that; it's at full pressure; listen, don't you hear it hiss? Try and breathe slowly, Lord Marchmain; quite gently, then you get the benefit.'

'Free as air; that's what they say—"free as air". Now they bring me my air in an iron barrel.'

Once he said: 'Cordelia, what became of the chapel?'

'They locked it up, papa, when mummy died.'

'It was hers, I gave it to her. We've always been builders in our family. I built it for her; in the shade of the pavilion; rebuilt with the old stones behind the old walls; it was the last of the new house to come, the first to go. There used to be a chaplain until the war. Do you remember him?'

'I was too young.'

'Then I went away–left her in the chapel praying. It was hers. It was the place for her. I never came back to disturb her prayers. They said we were fighting for freedom; I had my own victory. Was it a crime?'

'I think it was, papa.'

'Crying to heaven for vengeance? Is that why they've locked me in this cave, do you think, with a black tube of air and the little yellow men along the walls, who live without breathing? Do you think that, child? But the wind will come soon, tomorrow perhaps, and we'll breathe again. The ill wind that will blow me good. Better tomorrow.'

Thus, till mid-July, Lord Marchmain lay dying, wearing himself down in the struggle to live. Then, since there was no reason to expect an immediate change, Cordelia went to London to see her women's organization about the coming 'emergency'. That day Lord Marchmain became suddenly worse. He lay silent and quite still, breathing laboriously; only his open eyes, which sometimes moved about the room, gave any sign of consciousness.

'Is this the end?' Julia asked.

'It is impossible to say,' the doctor answered; 'when he does die it will probably be like this. He may recover from the present attack. The only thing is not to disturb him. The least shock will be fatal.'

'I'm going for Father Mackay,' she said.

I was not surprised. I had seen it in her mind all the summer. When she had gone I said to the doctor, 'We must stop this nonsense.'

He said: 'My business is with the body. It's not my business to argue whether people are better alive or dead, or what happens to them after death. I only try to keep them alive.'

'And you said just now any shock would kill him. What could be worse for a man who fears death, as he does, than to have a priest brought to him–a priest he turned out when he had the strength?'

'I think it may kill him.'

'Then will you forbid it?'

'I've no authority to forbid anything. I can only give my opinion.'

'Cara, what do you think?'

'I don't want him made unhappy. That is all there is to hope for now; that he'll die without knowing it. But I should like the priest there, all the same.'

'Will you try and persuade Julia to keep him away–until the end? After that he can do no harm.'

'I will ask her to leave Alex happy, yes.'

In half an hour Julia was back with Father Mackay. We all met in the library.

'I've telegraphed for Bridey and Cordelia,' I said. 'I hope you agree that nothing must be done till they arrive.'

'I wish they were here,' said Julia.

'You can't take the responsibility alone,' I said; 'everyone else is against you. Doctor Grant, tell her what you said to me just now.'

'I said that the shock of seeing a priest might well kill him; without that he may survive this attack. As his medical man I must protest against anything being done to disturb him.'

'Cara?'

'Julia, dear, I know you are thinking for the best, but, you know, Alex was not a religious man. He scoffed always. We mustn't take advantage of him, now he's weak, to comfort our own consciences. If Father Mackay comes to him, when he is unconscious, then he can be buried in the proper way, can he not, Father?'

'I'll go and see how he is,' said the doctor, leaving us.

'Father Mackay,' I said. 'You know how Lord Marchmain greeted you last time you came; do you think it possible he can have changed now?'

'Thank God, by his grace it is possible.'

'Perhaps,' said Cara, 'you could slip in while he is sleeping, say the words of absolution over him; he would never know.'

'I have seen so many men and women die,' said the priest: 'I never knew them sorry to have me there at the end.'

'But they were Catholics; Lord Marchmain has never been one except in name–at any rate, not for years. He was a scoffer, Cara said so.'

'Christ came to call, not the righteous, but sinners to repentance.'

The doctor returned. 'There's no change,' he said.

'Now doctor,' said the priest, 'how would I be a shock to anyone?' He turned his bland, innocent, matter-of-fact face first on the doctor, then upon the rest of us. 'Do you know what I want to do? It is something so small, no show about it. I don't wear special clothes, you know. I go just as I am. He knows the look of me now. There's nothing alarming. I just want to ask him if he is sorry for his sins. I want him to make some little sign of assent; I want him, anyway, not to refuse me; then I want to give him God's pardon. Then, though that's not essential, I want to anoint him. It is nothing, a touch of the fingers, just some oil from this little box, look it is nothing to hurt him.'

'Oh, Julia,' said Cara, 'what are we to say? Let me speak to him.'

She went to the Chinese drawing-room; we waited in silence; there was a wall of fire between Julia and me. Presently Cara returned.

'I don't think he heard,' she said. 'I thought I knew how to put it to him. I said: "Alex, you remember the priest from Melstead. You were very naughty when he came to see you. You hurt his feelings very much. Now he's here again. I want you to see him just for my sake, to make friends." But he didn't answer. If he's unconscious, it couldn't make him unhappy to see the priest, could it, doctor?'

Julia, who had been standing still and silent, suddenly moved.

'Thank you for your advice, doctor,' she said. 'I take full responsibility for whatever happens. Father Mackay, will you please come and see my father now,' and without looking at me, led him to the door.

We all followed. Lord Marchmain was lying as I had seen him that morning, but his eyes were now shut; his hands lay, palm upwards, above the bed-clothes; the nurse had her fingers on the pulse of one of them. 'Come in,' she said brightly, 'you won't disturb him now.'

'D'you mean . . .?'

'No, no, but he's past noticing anything.'

She held the oxygen apparatus to his face and the hiss of escaping gas was the only sound at the bedside.

The priest bent over Lord Marchmain and blessed him. Julia and Clara knelt at the foot of the bed. The doctor, the nurse, and I stood behind them.

'Now,' said the priest, 'I know you are sorry for all the sins of your life, aren't you? Make a sign, if you can. You're sorry, aren't you?' But there was no sign. 'Try and remember your sins; tell God you are sorry. I am going to give you absolution. While I am giving it, tell God you are sorry you have offended him.' He began to speak in Latin. I recognized the words '*ego te absolvo in nomine Patris* . . .' and saw the priest make the sign of the cross. Then I knelt, too, and prayed: 'O God, if there is a God, forgive him his sins, if there is such a thing as sin,' and the man on the bed opened his eyes and gave a sigh, the sort of sigh I had imagined people made at the moment of death, but his eyes moved so that we knew there was still life in him.

I suddenly felt the longing for a sign, if only of courtesy, if only for the sake of the woman I loved, who knelt in front of me, praying, I knew, for a sign. It seemed so small a thing that was asked, the bare acknowledgement of a present, a nod in the crowd. I prayed more simply; 'God forgive him his sins' and 'Please God, make him accept your forgiveness.'

So small a thing to ask.

The priest took the little silver box from his pocket and spoke again in Latin, touching the dying man with an oily wad; he finished what he had to do, put away the box and gave the final blessing. Suddenly Lord Marchmain moved his hand to his forehead; I thought he had felt the touch of the chrism and was wiping it away. 'O God,' I prayed, 'don't let him do that.' But there was no need for fear; the hand moved slowly down his breast, then to his shoulder, and Lord Marchmain made the sign of the cross. Then I knew that the sign I had asked for was not a little thing, not a passing nod of recognition, and a phrase came back to me from my childhood of the veil of the temple being rent from top to bottom.

It was over; we stood up; the nurse went back to the oxygen cylinder; the doctor bent over his patient. Julia whispered to me: 'Will you see Father Mackay out? I'm staying here for a little.'

Outside the door Father Mackay became the simple, genial man I had known before. 'Well, now, and that was a beautiful thing to see. I've known it happen that way again and again. The devil resists to the last moment and then the Grace of God is too much for him. You're not a Catholic I think, Mr Ryder, but at least you'll be glad for the ladies to have the comfort of it.'

As we were waiting for the chauffeur, it occurred to me that Father Mackay should be paid for his services. I asked him awkwardly. 'Why, don't think about it, Mr Ryder. It was a pleasure,' he said, 'but anything you care to give is useful in a parish like mine.' I found I had three pounds in my note-case and gave them to him. 'Why, indeed, that's more than generous. God bless you, Mr Ryder. I'll call again, but I don't think the poor soul has long for this world.'

Julia remained in the Chinese drawing-room until, at five o'clock that evening, her father died, proving both sides right in the dispute, priest and doctor.

Thus I come to the broken sentences which were the last words spoken between Julia and me, the last memories.

When her father died Julia remained some minutes with his body; the nurse came to the next room to announce the news and I had a glimpse of her through the open door, kneeling at the foot of the bed, and of Cara sitting by her. Presently the two women came out together, and Julia said to me: 'Not now; I'm just taking Cara up to her room; later.'

While she was still upstairs Brideshead and Cordelia arrived from London; when at last we met alone it was by stealth, like young lovers.

Julia said: 'Here in the shadow, in the corner of the stair–a minute to say good-bye.'

'So long to say so little.'

'You knew?'

'Since this morning; since before this morning; all this year.'

'I didn't know till today. Oh, my dear, if you could only understand. Then I could bear to part, or bear it better. I should say my heart was breaking, if I believed in broken hearts. I can't marry you, Charles; I can't be with you ever again.'

'I know.'

'How can you know.'

'What will you do?'

'Just go on–alone. How can I tell what I shall do? You know the whole of me. You know I'm not one for a life of mourning. I've always been bad. Probably I shall be bad again, punished again. But the worse I am, the more I need God. I can't shut myself out from his mercy. That is what it would mean; starting a life with you, without him. One can only hope to see one step ahead. But I saw today there was one thing unforgivable–like things in the school-room, so bad they were unpunishable, that only mummy could deal with–the bad thing I was on the point of doing, that I'm not quite bad enough to do; to set up a rival good to God's. Why should I be allowed to understand that, and not you, Charles? It may be because of mummy, nanny, Cordelia, Sebastian–perhaps Bridey and Mrs Muspratt–keeping my name in their prayers; or it may be a private bargain between me and God, that if I give up this one thing I want so much, however bad I am, he won't quite despair of me in the end.

'Now we shall both be alone, and I shall have no way of making you understand.'

'I don't want to make it easier for you,' I said; 'I hope your heart may break; but I do understand.'

The avalanche was down, the hillside swept bare behind it; the last echoes died on the white slopes; the new mound glittered and lay still in the silent valley.

EPILOGUE

BRIDESHEAD REVISITED

'The worst place we've struck yet,' said the commanding officer; 'no facilities, no amenities, and Brigade sitting right on top of us. There's one pub in Flyte St Mary with capacity for about twenty–that, of course, will be out of bounds for officers; there's a Naafi in the camp area. I hope to run transport once a week to Melstead Carbury. Marchmain is ten miles away and damn-all when you get there. It will therefore be the first concern of company officers to organize recreation for their men. M.O., I want you to take a look at the lakes to see if they're fit for bathing.'

'Very good, sir.'

'Brigade expects us to clean up the house for them. I should have thought some of those half-shaven scrimshankers I see lounging round Headquarters might have saved us the trouble; however . . . Ryder, you will find a fatigue party of fifty and report to the Quartering Commandant at the house at 1045 hours; he'll show you what we're taking over.'

'Very good, sir.'

'Our predecessors do not seem to have been very enterprising. The valley has great potentialities for an assault course and a mortar range. Weapon-training officer, make a recce this morning and get something laid on before Brigade arrives.'

'Very good, sir.'

'I'm going out myself with the adjutant to recce training areas. Anyone happen to know this district?'

I said nothing.

'That's all then, get cracking.'

'Wonderful old place in its way,' said the Quartering Commandant; 'pity to knock it about too much.'

He was an old, retired, re-appointed lieutenant-colonel from some miles away. We met in the space before the main doors, where I had my half-company fallen-in, waiting for orders. 'Come in. I'll soon show you over. It's a great warren of a place, but we've only requisitioned the ground floor and half a dozen bedrooms. Everything else upstairs is still private property, mostly cram-full of furniture; you never saw such stuff, priceless some of it.

'There's a caretaker and a couple of old servants live at the top–they won't be any trouble to you–and a blitzed R.C. padre whom Lady Julia gave a home to–jittery old bird, but no trouble. He's opened the chapel; that's in bounds for the troops; surprising lot use it, too.

'The place belongs to Lady Julia Flyte, as she calls herself now. She was married to Mottram, the Minister of whatever-it-is. She's abroad in some woman's service, and I try to keep an eye on things for her. Queer thing the old marquis leaving everything to her–rough on the boys.

'Now this is where the last lot put the clerks; plenty of room, anyway. I've had the walls and fireplaces boarded up you see–valuable old work underneath. Hullo, someone seems to have been making a beast of himself here; destructive beggars, soldiers are! Lucky we spotted it, or it would have been charged to you chaps.

'This is another good-sized room, used to be full of tapestry. I'd advise you to use this for conferences.'

'I'm only here to clean up, sir. Someone from Brigade will allot the rooms.'

'Oh, well, you've got an easy job. Very decent fellows the last lot. They shouldn't have done that to the fireplace though. How did they manage it? Looks solid enough. I wonder if it can be mended?

'I expect the brigadier will take this for his office; the last did. It's got a lot of painting that can't be moved, done on the walls. As you see, I've covered it up as best I can, but soldiers get through anything–as the brigadier's done in the corner. There was another painted room, outside under pillars–modern work but, if you ask me, the prettiest in the place; it was the signal office and they made absolute hay of it; rather a shame.

'This eyesore is what they used as the mess; that's why I didn't cover it up; not that it would matter much if it did get damaged; always reminds me of one of the costlier knocking-shops, you know–"*Maison Japonaise*" . . . and this was the ante-room . . .'

It did not take us long to make our tour of the echoing rooms. Then we went outside on the terrace.

'Those are the other ranks' latrines and wash-house; can't think why they built them just there; it was done before I took the job over. All this used to be cut off from the front. We laid the road through the trees joining it up with the main drive; unsightly but very practical; awful lot of transport comes in and out; cuts the place up, too. Look where one careless devil went smack through the box-hedge and carried away all that balustrade; did it with a three-ton lorry, too; you'd think he had a Churchill tank at least.

'That fountain is rather a tender spot with our landlady; the young officers used to lark about in it on guest nights and it was looking a bit the worse for wear, so I wired it in and turned the water off. Looks a bit untidy now; all the drivers throw their cigarette-ends and the remains of the sandwiches there, and you can't get to it to clean it up, since I put the wire round it. Florid great thing, isn't it? . . .

'Well, if you've seen everything I'll push off. Good day to you.'

His driver threw a cigarette into the dry basin of the fountain; saluted and opened the door of the car. I saluted and the Quartering Commandant drove away through the new, metalled gap in the lime trees.

'Hooper,' I said, when I had seen my men started, 'do you think I can safely leave you in charge of the work-party for half an hour?'

'I was just wondering where we could scrounge some tea.'

'For Christ's sake,' I said, 'they've only just begun work.'

'They're awfully browned off.'

'Keep them at it.'

'Rightyoh.'

I did not spend long in the desolate ground-floor rooms, but went upstairs and wandered down the familiar corridors, trying doors that were locked, opening doors into rooms piled to the ceiling with furniture. At length I met an old housemaid carrying a cup of tea. 'Why,' she said, isn't it Mr Ryder?'

'It is. I was wondering when I should meet someone I know.'

'Mrs Hawkins is up in her old room. I was just taking her some tea.'

'I'll take it for you,' I said, and passed through the baize doors, up the uncarpeted stairs, to the nursery.

Nanny Hawkins did not recognize me until I spoke, and my arrival threw her into some confusion; it was not until I had been sitting some time by her fireside that she recovered her old calm. She, who had changed so little in all the years I knew her, had lately become greatly aged. The changes of the last years had come too late in her life to be accepted and understood; her sight was failing, she told me, and she could see only the coarsest needlework. Her speech, sharpened by years of gentle conversation, had reverted now to the soft, peasant tones of its origin.

'. . . only myself here and the two girls and poor Father Membling who was blown up, not a roof to his head nor a stick of furniture till Julia took him in with the kind heart she's got, and his nerves something shocking. . . . Lady Brideshead, too, Marchmain it is now, who I ought by rights to call her Ladyship now, but it doesn't come natural, it was the same with her. First, when Julia and Cordelia left to the war, she came here with the two boys and then the military turned them out, so they went to London, nor they hadn't been in their house not a month, and Bridey away with the yeomanry the same as his poor Lordship, when they were blown up too, everything gone, all the furniture she brought here and kept in the coach-house. Then she had another house outside London, and the military took that, too, and there she is now, when I last heard, in a hotel at the seaside, which isn't the same as your own home, is it? It doesn't seem right.

'. . . Did you listen to Mr Mottram last night? Very nasty he was about Hitler. I said to the girl Effie who does for me: "If Hitler was listening, and if he understands English, which I doubt, he must feel very small." Who would have thought of Mr Mottram doing so well? And so many of his friends, too, that used to stay here? I said to Mr Wilcox, who comes to see me regular on the bus from Melstead twice a month, which is very good of him and I appreciate it, I said: "We were entertaining angels unawares," because Mr Wilcox never liked Mr Mottram's friends, which I never saw, but used to hear about from all of you, nor Julia didn't like them, but they've done very well, haven't they?'

At last I asked her: 'Have you heard from Julia?'

'From Cordelia, only last week, and they're together still as they have been all the time, and Julia sent me love at the bottom of the page. They're both very well, though they couldn't say where, but Father Membling said, reading between the lines, it was Palestine, which is where Bridey's yeomanry is, so that's very nice for them all. Cordelia said they were looking forward to coming home after the war, which I am sure we all are, though whether I live to see it, is another story.'

I stayed with her for half an hour, and left promising to return often. When I reached the hall I found no sign of work and Hooper looking guilty.

'They had to go off to draw the bed-straw. I didn't know till Sergeant Block told me. I don't know whether they're coming back.'

'Don't know? What orders did you give?'

'Well, I told Sergeant Block to bring them back if he thought it was worthwhile; I mean if there was time before dinner.'

It was nearly twelve. 'You've been hotted again, Hooper. That straw was to be drawn any time before six tonight.'

'Oh Lor; sorry, Ryder. Sergeant Block—'

'It's my own fault for going away. . . . Fall in the same party immediately after dinner, bring them back here and keep them here till the job's done.'

'Rightyoh. I say, did you say you knew this place before?'

'Yes, very well. It belongs to friends of mine,' and as I said the words they sounded as odd in my ears as Sebastian's had done, when, instead of saying, 'It is my home,' he said, 'It is where my family live.'

'It doesn't seem to make any sense–one family in a place this size. What's the use of it?'

'Well, I suppose Brigade are finding it useful.'

'But that's not what it was built for, is it?'

'No,' I said, 'not what it was built for. Perhaps that's one of the pleasures of building, like having a son, wondering how he'll grow up. I don't know; I never built anything, and I forfeited the right to watch my son grow up. I'm homeless, childless, middle-aged, loveless, Hooper.' He looked to see if I was being funny, decided that I was, and laughed. 'Now go back to camp, keep out of the C.O.'s way, if he's back from his recce, and don't let on to anyone that we've made a nonsense of the morning.'

'Okay, Ryder.'

There was one part of the house I had not yet visited, and I went there now. The chapel showed no ill-effects of its long neglect; the *art-nouveau* paint was as fresh and bright as ever; the *art-nouveau* lamp burned once more before the altar. I said a prayer, an ancient, newly-learned form of words, and left, turning towards the camp; and as I walked back, and the cook-house bugle sounded ahead of me, I thought:

'The builders did not know the uses to which their work would descend; they made a new house with the stones of the old castle; year by year, generation after generation, they enriched and extended it; year by year the great harvest of timber in the park grew to ripeness; until, in sudden frost, came the age of Hooper; the place was desolate and the work all brought to nothing; *Quomodo sedet sola civitas*. Vanity of vanities, all is vanity.

'And yet,' I thought, stepping out more briskly towards the camp, where the bugles after a pause had taken up the second call and were sounding 'Pick-em-up, pick-em-up, hot potatoes', 'and yet that is not the last word; it is not even an apt word; it is a dead word from ten years back.

'Something quite remote from anything the builders intended, has come out of their work, and out of the fierce little human tragedy in which I played; something none of us thought about at the time; a small red flame–a beaten-copper lamp of deplorable design relit before the beaten-copper doors of a tabernacle; the flame which the old knights saw from their tombs, which they saw put out; that flame burns again for other soldiers, far from home, farther, in heart, than Acre or Jerusalem. It could not have been lit but for the builders and the tragedians, and there I found it this morning, burning anew among the old stones.'

I quickened my pace and reached the hut which served us for our ante-room.

'You're looking unusually cheerful today,' said the second-in-command.

AUGH EVELYN WAU

N WAUGH EVELYN W

AUGH EVELYN WAU

N WAUGH EVELYN W

AUGH EVELYN WAUG

N WAUGH EVELYN W

AUGH EVELYN WAUG

N WAUGH EVELYN W

AUGH EVELYN WAUG

N WAUGH EVELYN W

AUGH EVELYN WAUG